We Are Here

Michael Marshall

W F HOWES LTD

This large print edition published in 2013 by
W F Howes Ltd
Unit 4, Rearsby Business Park, Gaddesby Lane,
Rearsby, Leicester LE7 4YH

1 3 5 7 9 10 8 6 4 2

First published in the United Kingdom in 2013
by Orion Books.

A CIP catalogue record for this book is available
from the British Library

ISBN 978 1 47123 975 5

Typeset by Palimpsest Book Production Limited,
Falkirk, Stirlingshire
Printed and bound by
CPI Group (UK) Ltd, Croydon, CR0 4YY

In the realm of the emotions, the real is no different to the imaginary.

André Gide

PROLOGUE

He drove. There were times when he stopped for gas or to empty his bladder or buy cups of poor coffee out of machines, selecting isolated and windswept gas stations where no one was doing anything except filling up and staring vacantly at their cold hand on the pump as they waited, wanting to be back in their warm car and on the road to wherever it was they had to be. Nobody was looking or watching or caring about anyone who might happen to be doing the same thing. Nobody saw anything except another guy in bulky clothing getting into a big car and pulling back out onto the highway.

Sometimes it was raining. Sometimes there was sleet. Sometimes merely the wind coming across the great flatness. He did not listen to the radio. He did not consult a map. He didn't know where he was going and so he did not care where he was.

He just drove.

He had barely slept beyond nodding out for short stretches in the driver's seat, the car stashed behind abandoned farmhouses or in the parking lots of small-town businesses that would not open for several hours after he was back on the road. Other than bags of potato chips or dusty gas station trail mix, he hadn't eaten since he left what used to be his home. He already knew he wasn't going back there. He was light-headed with hunger but he could not eat. He was exhausted but he could not sleep. He was a single thought in a mind no longer capable of maintaining order. A thought needs somewhere to go, but flight does not provide a destination. Flight merely shrieks that you have to be somewhere other than where you are.

He had to stop. He had to keep going, too, but first he had to stop.

A little after four o'clock on the third day he passed a sign for a motel farther up the road. As is common practice in parts of the country where you can drive mile after mile without seeing anything of consequence, the business had given travelers plenty of warning to think about it and check their watches and decide yes, maybe it was time to call it a day. He had driven past several such signs without registering them. This one looked like it had been there forty years or more, from when drives cross-country were everybody's best hope of a vacation. It showed a basic-looking mom-and-pop motel with a foreign-sounding name. It was still thirty miles ahead at that point.

He shook his head and looked back at the road, but he already knew he was going to stop. He'd said no to a lot of things in his life, especially in the last month.

He'd gone ahead and done them anyway.

Half an hour later he pulled up outside a single-story L-shaped building down a short road off the highway. There were no cars outside the guest rooms, but a dim light showed in the office. When he went in, an old man came from the room out back. The old man looked him up and down and saw the kind of person who arrives alone at out-of-the-way motels in the back end of nowhere; he had never been a curious person and had stopped giving a shit about anything at all when his wife died three years before. The man paid him in cash for one night and got a key in return. A metal key, not one of those credit card swipers found everywhere else these days. A real key, one that opened a particular door and no other. The man looked at it, becalmed, trying to remember if he'd locked the door to his house when he left. He wasn't sure. It was too late to do anything about it. He asked the owner for the nearest place to get something to eat. The old man pointed up the road. The driver took a handful of matchbooks from the counter and went back out and got in his car.

Fifteen miles away he found a small store attached to a two-pump gas station that had nothing he wanted to eat but did sell things he could drink and smoke. He drove back to the motel and parked in front of Number 9. The rest of the lot remained empty. It was full dark now.

In the room he found a frigid rectangular space with two double beds and an ancient television. He locked and bolted the door. He shoved the closest bed over until it blocked entry. Years ago the bed had been retrofitted with a vibrating function – no longer working – and was extremely heavy. It took him ten minutes and used up the last of his strength. He turned the rusty heater on. It made a lot of noise but gradually started to make inroads on the cold.

In the meantime he lay on the other bed. He did not take off his coat. He stared up at the ceiling. He opened the bottle he'd bought. He smoked cigarette after cigarette as he drank, lighting them with matches from matchbooks. His face was wet.

He wept with exhaustion. He wept because his head hurt. He wept with the self-disgust that permeated every cell of his body, like the imaginary mites that plague habitual users of crystal meth, nerve misfirings that feel so much like burrowing insects that sufferers will scratch and scratch and scratch at them until their arms and faces are a mass of bloody scabs, writing their affliction for all to see.

His affliction was not thus written, however. His was a text only he could read, for now. He still appeared normal. To anyone else he would have looked like a chubby man in his early thirties, lying on a motel bed, very drunk now, sniveling by himself.

In his mind, however, he wept. There was majesty to it. A hero, lost and alone.

Sometime later he started from a dream that had not been a dream. He'd been getting a lot of these since he left home, waking possessed by shadows he wished were dreams but that he knew very well to be memory. The wall in the back of his head was breaking down, wearing out like something rubbed with sweaty fingers too hard for too long. His mind wasn't trying to mediate through dramatization any longer. It was feeding up the things it had seen through his eyes or felt through his fingertips. His mind was thinking about what had happened even when he was not.

He didn't lie to himself. He knew he wasn't innocent, and could never be again. He knew what he'd done. He wouldn't have done it alone, maybe, but that didn't mean it hadn't been done. By him.

The other man had suggested things, but he had done them. That was how it had always been.

He'd waited and watched down alleys and outside bars and in the late-night parking lots of the town he'd called home. He'd made the muscles in his face perform movements that looked like smiles. He'd selected forms of words that sounded helpful and charming. The other man planned the sentences, but it was he who'd spoken them aloud. The other had researched what would work best, but he'd been the one who slipped the ground-up pill into the wine he'd made available, offered casually, as if it was no big deal, and oh, what a coincidence – it just happens to be your favorite kind.

The other man invented the games he and his guest had played until she suddenly got scared, despite how drunk and confused she had become. Who had then raised his hand for the first blow? Impossible to tell. It didn't matter, when so many others had followed.

All he'd ever done was follow, but he'd wound up at the destination anyhow, and of course it's true that when you submit to someone's will then it's you who gives them power. You follow from in front. You can follow a long way like that. You can follow too far.

You can follow all the way to hell.

He rubbed his eyes against the last shards of the memory and sat up to see the other man was sitting in the armchair. He looked smart and trim and presentable as always. He looked strong. He was holding one of the motel matchbooks, turning it over in his fingers.

'I don't want to do it again,' the man on the bed said.

'You do,' the other man said. 'You just don't like that you do. That's why you've got me. We're a team.'

'Not anymore. You're not my friend.'

'Why don't you have another drink? It'll make you feel better.'

Despite himself, the man on the bed groped blearily for the vodka and raised it to his lips. He'd almost always done what the other man said. He saw two necks to the bottle. The alcohol had caught up with him while he dozed, and he was far drunker than he'd realized. Might as well keep drinking, then.

'You left a trail,' the other man said. 'Deliberately?'

'Of course not.' He wasn't sure if this was true.

'They'll be turning the house upside down tomorrow, or by the next day at the latest.'

'I cleaned up.'

'They'll find something. Then they'll come looking. Eventually they'll find you. Wherever you run.' The man's face turned cold. 'You fucked up, Edward. Again. Always. Always with the fucking up.'

The man on the bed felt dreadful fear and vertiginous guilt mingled with relief. If he was caught then he could not do it again. He would not find himself returning to the same Chinese restaurant night after night, hoping for a glimpse of one of the other customers, a young single woman who worked in the bank across the street and sometimes came to grab a cheap bite at the end of the workday, though with infuriating unpredictability. He would not gradually come to know where she lived – alone – and where she went to the gym, where and when she shopped for groceries, or that

7

her basket always included at least one bottle of wine.

The man on the bed shrugged, trying to feel glad that something like this could not happen again, though he knew every single moment of it had held a terrible excitement and that there could be other such women in other towns, if he chose to keep driving down this road. 'They catch me, they catch you.'

'I know that,' the man in the chair said. He opened the matchbook. With effort he managed to get one of the matches out. After a couple of pulls along the strip, he got it lit.

The man on the bed noticed, too late, that he'd piled all the other matchbooks on the bedspread of the bed that now blocked the door. The bedspread was old, not to code, flammable. Very flammable, it turned out.

'I'm not going to jail,' the other man said as he stood up from the chair. 'I'd rather die right here.'

He dropped the burning matchbook on the pile.

It didn't happen fast. The man on the bed, whose name was Edward Lake, had a little time to escape. He was far too drunk now to move the heavy bed from the door, however. He was too drunk to understand that the dead tone from the phone by the bed was because the other man had unplugged it while Edward crashed out.

By the time he got around to trying, he could not get past the flames to the window. He was too scared, and the truth is that the only real and meaningful thing Edward had done in his entire life was kill a woman, and there's no good way forward from that. So it's also possible that, deep inside, he did actually just want to die.

As his former friend burned alive, the other man watched from the parking lot. He knew the moment when Edward died, and was surprised and awestruck by what happened next.

The death of the girl back home had felt powerful. But this . . . this was completely other. This was something else.

He felt altered, very different indeed, and knew in that moment that he was finished with following, even if by the end he and Edward had been traveling side by side and hand in hand.

People who walk alone travel faster. It was time for new horizons and bigger goals.

Everything would be better now.

To mark the occasion, he glanced up at the motel sign – lit by flames as the remaining rooms of the structure caught alight and the owner choked to death in his bed – and renamed himself. Then he turned from the blaze and walked away up the road into the darkness, savoring with every step the solid feel of the earth beneath his feet.

Even with the immense degree of will at his disposal, it was a long and very tiring walk. The dawn found him sitting exhausted by the side of the road. A passing salesman, who'd risen early after a bad night's sleep and was running early and of a kindly disposition, stopped and gave the man a ride. The man realized what it meant to have been seen by a stranger, and he got in the back of the car with a faint smile on his face.

After fifty miles the salesman glanced in the rearview mirror to see that his passenger had fallen asleep. In this rare moment of defenselessness, the man looked pale and worn through.

But this all happened five years ago.

He is much stronger now.

PART I

The number of people here who think alone, sing alone, and eat and talk alone in the streets is mind-boggling. And yet they don't add up.

Jean Baudrillard
America

CHAPTER 1

It should have been a wonderful day – a day to photograph and frame, to Facebook and Tweet, an afternoon to cut out and save in that album of updates and keepsakes you return to in daydream and memory; the pressed flowers of our lives that we'll hold up to God or his gatekeeper when our moment comes, to prove we are worthy of entrance and have not merely been marking time.

It should have been one of those days.

And until the very end, it was.

They arrived at Penn Station just after ten, on the kind of fall morning when it's warm in the sun but chill in the shadows of the skyscraping monoliths; when the city feels pert and alert and struts with head high, marching to work with tightly specified coffees and a bounce in its step as if someone loosened everyone's bolts in the night. David was in town not as some sightseer or nostalgia seeker, either, but for a meeting followed by lunch – the Lunch of Legend that people conjure in their minds to keep them strong through the months and years spent doing lone, heroic (or merely stoic) battle against the Blank Page of Infinity and the Blinking Cursor of Doom.

Suddenly, David was going to be published.

No, seriously.

He'd assumed they'd take a cab uptown, but the streets were so traffic-tangled – not to mention they were *very* early, Dawn having selected a departure time that allowed for everything from minor delays to a full-scale terrorist attack on the line – that they strolled the twenty-some blocks instead. David was struck by how unfamiliar it all seemed. It wasn't merely that everywhere was much cleaner than ten years ago, or that he felt less likely to get attacked on any given street corner (though both were true). During his long-ago five months living in the city he'd simply been very unadventurous, he realized, sticking to the same haunts in a way that struck his older self as appallingly cautious. But when you look nostalgically back from thirty it's easy to forget how much of your twenties were spent feeling awkward and lonely, weaving a cloak of famil-iarity around you like the armor it eventually becomes.

They spent the last half hour in a Starbucks on Madison, perched at the window counter with-standing bland jazz and fiddling with stirring sticks. Dawn kept quiet. David didn't chatter in the face of anxiety, she knew, but gathered troops behind invisible walls. She people-watched

14

instead, wondering as always who everyone was and where they were going.

At a quarter to, she escorted David the final block, kissed him, and wished him luck – and told him he didn't need it. She waved as she left on a lightning strike up to Bloomingdale's, a wide, proud smile on her face.

For a moment, as he watched his wife disappear into the crowds, David felt nervous for her. He told himself it was merely his own anxiety.

At 11:55 he took a deep breath and strode into reception. He told the guy behind the desk who the hell he was and who the dickens he'd come to meet, speaking more loudly than usual. The receptionist made few bones about not giving a crap, but a few minutes later someone young and enthusiastic bounced out of an elevator, shaking hand already outstretched.

David was whisked upward many floors and finally got to meet his editor, Hazel, a gaunt fifty-something New Yorker who proved fractionally less intimidating in person than via e-mail, though still pretty scary. He was given a tour of untidy offices and book-infested cubicles while a selection of affable strangers told him that his book was great, that *he* was great, that everyone was unbelievably excited and that it was all going to be just . . . *great*. A lot of hand-shaking and smiling took place, and people stood around with notepads clasped to their chests as if ready to

15

jot down anything significant the moment it occurred, though evidently nothing of the sort happened, because nobody did.

Then suddenly they dispersed like birds startled by a rifle shot, and Hazel took his elbow and steered him firmly toward the elevator. 'Lunch,' she muttered darkly, as if warning him not to put up a fight.

Dawn had just arrived back outside, and stood hurriedly. David's agent, Ralph – another character he was meeting in person for the first time – was already in position at the restaurant two blocks away, an old-school grill and steak house that prided itself on serving cow by the slab in an environment of white linen, low lighting, and disconcertingly formal service.

David realized how nervous Dawn really was only when he saw her beaming glassily at the waiter, unable to comprehend a query concerning her desired genre of mineral water (fizzy or not). David squeezed her hand under the table, realized he was smiling at Ralph in exactly the same way, and tried to relax.

He'd told himself he wasn't going to drink wine with lunch, but when it became clear that his editor sure as hell was, he relented, combating the effects with so much water that he had to visit the bathroom three times. Meanwhile, he and Dawn watched as the professionals gossiped about people they'd never heard of – feeling like a pair of venturesome kids, a Hardy boy and Nancy

Drew on joint reconnaissance, ears pricked for intel about the curious new world they'd been told they would become a part of – if the capricious gods of market forces, key bloggers, and the zeitgeist willed it so.

Eventually the stupendous check was paid with reference to some protocol David didn't understand but knew wouldn't involve him. Everyone reemerged blinking into the sunlight, to part on excellent terms. Graphic artists were at work on a jacket design. Cover copy would soon be e-mailed for David's approval. David had never 'approved' anything before and was looking forward to the experience. He thought he might wear a special shirt for it. Everything was going perfectly, he was assured, perhaps even a little better than that.

'It's all good,' Hazel kept telling him sternly, as if he were well-known for championing an opposing school of thought. 'David, it's *all good*.'

By then he was in no mood to disagree.

They wandered down Park Avenue until David had an idea and cut across to Bryant Park. Back in the seventies it had by all accounts been a place where, should you wish to score drugs, get laid on a commercial basis, or have the living daylights mugged out of you, the locals would have lined up around the block to oblige. By the time David spent his few months in New York, it had turned around to become one of the most amenable spaces in Manhattan – and he'd spent hours sitting

17

in it with a notebook and dreams of a future that were only now coming true. The intervening decade had kicked it up further still. Not so much a park as a grassed plaza lined on all sides with trees, now there were coffee stands and walkways lined with planters, an upscale grill and bar to the rear of the reassuring bulk of the New York Public Library, and the only mugging going on involved the prices demanded for crab cakes and sauvignon blanc.

They took glasses of the latter to a table on the terrace and spent an hour excitedly going back over lunch. A voice in David's head seemed intent on convincing him it was a mirage, that there were twenty other authors having the exact same experience this afternoon and all would be back to working their day jobs (and bitterly grateful for them) in eighteen months' time. He even glanced around the park, a little drunk now, in case he could spot any of his fellow hopefuls.

He couldn't, and this wasn't an afternoon for doubt. It was for listening to the babble of conversation and to the warmth in Dawn's voice as she told him how wonderful everything was going to be, and finally the muttering voice retreated to the cave in the back of David's soul where it had lived for as long as he could remember.

Eventually it was time to leave, and that's when it happened.

They were leaving the park and David maybe

18

wasn't looking where he was going – wrapped up as he was in the day and with yet another glass of wine inside him. The sidewalks were a lot more crowded now, too, as the end of the workday approached and people set off for home.

It wasn't a hard knock. Just an accidental collision of shoulders, an urban commonplace, barely enough to jolt David off course and provoke a half turn that had him glancing back to see another man doing the same.

'Sorry,' David said. He wasn't sure he'd been at fault, but he was the kind to whom apology came easily.

The other man said nothing, but continued on his way, quickly becoming lost in the crowds.

Penn Station was a total zoo, epicenter of a three-way smackdown between baffled tourists, gimlet-eyed commuters, and circling members of the feral classes that make transit depots their hunting grounds. Twenty minutes before departure Dawn elected to visit the restrooms, leaving David to hold a defensive position near a pillar. He felt exhausted, eyes owlish from unaccustomed alcohol, feet sore. He experienced the passing throng as smeared colors and echoing sounds and nothing more.

Until he saw someone looking at him.

A man wearing jeans and a crumpled white shirt. He had dark hair, strong features, and he was looking right at David.

David blinked, and the man wasn't there anymore. Or he'd moved on, presumably. He'd barely been visible for a second, but David felt he'd been watching him – and also that he'd seen the man before.

'What's up?' Dawn returned, looking mildly shaken by the restroom experience. David shook his head.

They made their way toward the platform via which they'd arrived at the station that morning. This turned out *not* to be where the train was departing from, however, and all at once they were in a hurry and lost and oh-my-god-we're-screwed. David figured out where they were supposed to be and pointed at Dawn to lead the way. She forged ahead with the boisterous élan of someone having a fine old time in the city, emboldened by a bucketful of wine, clattering down the steps to the platform and starting to trot when she saw their train in preparation for departure.

As David hurried after her, someone appeared out of the crowd and banged into him – hard, knocking David back on his feet and getting right in his face.

Untucked white shirt and hard blue eyes.

The same man again.

'Hello, David,' he said. Then something else, before stepping around the corner and out of sight.

Winded and a little scared, David tried to see where the man had gone, but Dawn was calling him urgently now, and someone blew a whistle.

He hurried along to where his wife stood flushed and grinning.

'We made it,' she said, as they clambered onto the train. 'See? The gods are on our side now.'

Dawn started to crash within fifteen minutes, head on David's shoulder, hair tickling his neck. David sat bolt upright, trying to be distracted by the view as the carriages trundled over the river and out through urban sprawl. It wasn't working.

So he'd banged into some guy.

And so that man had evidently then followed them to the train station, watched David from across the concourse, and tracked them through the crowds to bang into him again.

Why would someone do that?

Because he was crazy, that's why. New Yorkers were famous for taking a hard-line approach. Even the well adjusted and affluent appeared to conduct human interaction as a contact sport. Insane people all the more so, presumably.

That's all it was. Big deal.

And yet . . .

As Dawn slipped into a doze and the train began to pick up speed into the hour-long journey to Rockbridge and home, there was one thing that David couldn't get out of his mind. It was what the stranger had said before he melted back into the crowd. Not the fact that he'd known David's name – he'd realized the man could have overheard Dawn using it, maybe.

It was the other thing. Just two words. Words that are usually framed as a question but this time sounded like a command. Or a threat.

'Remember me,' he'd said.

CHAPTER 2

When I stopped by the apartment to drop off the groceries, Kristina was still in bed. It had been a late night – they generally are, five nights out of seven at least – but I like to begin my days early, with a long walk. Kristina prefers to deal with them sprawled under the sheets like a pale, lanky spider that has been dropped from a very great height.

I finished wedging things into the tiny fridge (all we had room for, in a kitchen that's basically a specialized corner of the living room) and strode into the bedroom, an epic journey of three yards. The top of the window was open, proving Kristina must have groped her way out of bed at some point. It's shut at night or we'd never get to sleep on account of the racket from drunken good times in the streets below. The heater was ominously silent. The unit had been ailing for weeks, wheezing like an old smoker. Though the fall had so far been mild, finding someone to take it up a level from my own feeble attempts at repair (glaring at the machine, once in a while giving it an impotent kick) was high on my list of things to do today.

I put the massive Americano by the side of the bed. 'Beverage delivery. You have to sign for it.'

Her voice was muffled. 'Fuck off.'

'Right back atcha. It's a beautiful morning in the neighborhood, case you're interested.'

'Christ.'

'By the way. This woman later, Catherine. She gets that I'm just some guy, right?'

Kristina laboriously turned her head and blew long strands of black hair off her crumpled face. 'Don't worry,' she mumbled. 'I made a point of saying you were nothing special. Matter of fact, I went so far as to imply you were something of an asshole.'

'Seriously.'

She smiled, eyes still closed. 'Seriously. No biggie. And thank you for doing it. And for the coffee.'

'So I'll see you there. Three o'clock?'

'If I don't see you first.'

I looked down at her and thought it was disquieting how much you could come to like someone in only six months. Shouldn't our hearts be more cautious? A child or puppy learns after straying too close to a candle to hold back next time. It seems that emotional calluses are not as thick or permanent as they appear, however.

I bent down and kissed Kristina on the forehead.

She opened her eyes. 'What was that for?'

'Because I like you.'

'You're weird.'

'It's been said.'

'That's okay. Weird is good.' She stretched like a cat, all limbs pointed in the same direction. 'And you'll think about the other thing?'

'I will.'

'Good. Now scram. I need more sleep.'

'It's ten thirty.'

Her eyes closed. 'It's always ten thirty somewhere.'

'Very deep.'

'Really, John, I mean it. Don't make me get up out of here and kick your ass.'

I left her to it, jogged back down the five flights of stairs to street level, and stepped out into the big, strange city that lived – in all its train-wreck glory – right outside our door.

The rest of the morning was spent covering Paulo's shift at the restaurant's sidewalk window, hawking pizza and bottles of Poland Spring to passersby. This task is usually reserved for someone barely able to stand unassisted on their hind legs (currently Paulo, fresh-off-the-boat nephew of someone or other and an earthling so basic it's a miracle he can work out which way to face the street), but I didn't mind. Paulo's a sweet kid, eager to please, and was off trying to find somewhere to improve his English. Also, I kind of enjoy the job. There are only two styles of slice available – plain or pepperoni – and one drink. Each costs a dollar. It's hard to screw that up, and it's pleasant to lean on the counter exchanging banter with locals and making strangers' days better in straightforward ways. When your life has been overly complicated, simplicity can taste like a mouthful of clear, cool water. Available, this lunch hour, from me, near the corner of Second Avenue and 4th. Price – one dollar.

When my stint was over, I chatted with the owner, Mario, and his sister Maria – evidently the children of parents with either a sense of humor or a dearth of imagination – over a coffee at one of the sidewalk tables. The Adriatico has been holding down its patch – snug between a venerable Jewish bakery and a thrift store with pretensions of funkiness, a few minutes' walk from the dives of St Mark's Place and side street legends like McSorley's – for forty years, largely due to the family's willingness to embrace change, however bad-temperedly. In the time Kristina and I had been on staff (me waiting tables, Kristina running the popular late-night basement bar), the owners had replaced the awning, repainted the picket fence around the sidewalk tables a (much) brighter color, and tried adding the word 'organic' to everything on the menu: briefly offering an organic ragu with organic pasta and organic béchamel, oven-baked in the traditional organic manner – aka lasagna. I'd eventually convinced Mario not to pursue this (it made announcing the specials tiresome, and was moreover absolutely untrue), but I had to admire the ambition. It was certainly easier to understand why this restaurant was still in business than the last place I'd worked, on the other side of the country, on the Oregon coast.

I left with the customary mild buzz. The Adriatico's coffee is celebrated for its strength, to the point where there's a water-damaged poster in the restrooms (badly) hand-drawn by some long-ago college wit, suggesting it should be cited in strategic-arms-limitation treaties. Nobody can remember why the standard cup has three shots in it, but I'd come to learn that's how New York works. Someone does something one day for reasons outside their control and beyond anyone's recollection – and then winds up doing it for the next fifty years. The tangle of these traditions floats through the streets like mist and hangs like cobwebs among the trees and fire escapes. Tourist or resident – and it wasn't yet clear which I was – you're forever in the presence of these local heroes and ghosts.

I did my errands, including visiting the heater place. They promised they'd get to ours real soon. As both engineers were regulars at the bar I had reason to believe it.

With an hour still to kill, I took a long stroll down through the Village. There's always something to see in our part of town, and I liked watching it and walking it, and for the first time in some years I liked my life, too. It was simple, contained, and easy.

But I got the sense that was about to change.

★   ★   ★

27

What Kristina wanted me to consider was the idea of a new apartment. There was much about the East Village that we enjoyed. The remnants of the old immigrant population, their pockets of otherness. The leafy side streets and crumbling pre-war walkups, the area's determination to resist gentrification and order, forever tending toward chaos like some huge silverware drawer. The fact that if you came shambling out of a bar late at night waving your iPhone around then you were likely to only get robbed, with brisk efficiency, rather than killed.

At times, though – with roving hordes from NYU and Cooper Union, plus all the young tourists who wanted to show how cool and not just about Banana Republic and the Apple Store they were – it could feel like being shacked up in the low-rent end of a college town. There had been a spate of odd muggings recently, too – people having their bank cards stolen and their accounts immediately emptied at ATMs with mysterious ease.

I never got a chance to do the student thing – having spent those years and more in the army – and I was open to a second adolescence. Kristina was wearying of the locale, however, perhaps because she spent her evenings at the sharper end of the Asshole Service Industry. I'm thirty-seven, old enough for sketchy to have a retro charm. She's twenty-nine, sufficiently young for the idea of being a grown-up to remain appealing. She'd started talking about moving to SoHo or the West

Village, for the love of God. I kept reminding her that she ran bar and I served circular food in a fiercely down-market restaurant. She'd counter with the observation that I had money from the sale of my house in Washington State after the split from my ex-wife. Feeling old and dull, I'd observe that we weren't bringing in much *new* money, and nobody tied themselves to loft rentals under those circumstances, though I'd be willing to consider subletting somewhere tiny, as an experiment, if we committed to not eating for the foreseeable future – and anyway, it took less than half an hour to walk from our front door to the streets she was talking about, so what was the big deal?

And so on and so forth. The subject would eventually fade into abeyance, like a car drifting out of range of a local evangelical radio station, and I'd be left feeling like the patriarch who'd decreed that instead of eating in the lovely seafood restaurant with an ocean view, the family was going to make do with sandwiches in the parking lot. Again.

An hour later it would be like it never happened, however. Kristina did not study on things. She hit you between the eyes with the full payload, all at once. When that was spent, the storm was over – at least for now.

Two days ago she'd asked if I'd do her a favor, though, and I'd agreed because I felt I was letting her down in other ways. That meant a change was coming. If you're with a strong woman (and they're *all* strong, whatever they may have been told to the contrary; women have backbone men can only dream of), then once you've given ground you'll never be off the back foot again.

I was on the way to do that favor now.

CHAPTER 3

The café was on Greenwich Avenue. I deliberately walked the last forty yards on the opposite side of the street, and when I spotted them at one of the rickety tables outside I slowed down to take a look.

Kristina was wearing a skirt and jacket I hadn't seen before. It was probably only the second or third time in our entire acquaintance, in fact, that I'd seen her in anything except head-to-toe black. Opposite her sat a trim woman in her mid-thirties, attractive in the way that owes less to bone structure than to upkeep and confidence. Her hair was sleek and blond and impregnable, cut in a style that announces that the wearer will have valuable intelligence on the relative merits of local schools. I couldn't tell much else from a distance save that, judging from her clothes and bearing, the woman could probably afford an apartment more or less wherever she wanted.

I crossed the street. I was introduced to Catherine Warren and shook hands. We chatted about the weather and reprised background I already knew, like how the two women had met at a weekly

31

reading group held at Swift's, an independent bookstore in what we're supposed to call Nolita these days but is just a boutique wedge between SoHo and Little Italy. We agreed that Swift's was a swell little store and deserved our fervent support, and I elected not to mention my impression that the staff there always watched me as if they suspected I was about steal one of their hand-made gift cards, holocaust memoirs, or chunky anthologies of short stories about growing up poor but wise in Brooklyn.

When these subjects ran out of steam – and the wizened old gay couple from the next table had shuffled away up the street, bickering all the while – I put my cigarettes on the table. Now that you can barely smoke anywhere in the city, this is an effective shorthand for 'I'm not going to be here forever, so let's get to it.'

'Kristina said there was something you might want advice about.'

The woman nodded, looking diffident.

'And she explained to you I'm not a cop, right? Or private detective?'

Kristina rolled her eyes. 'She did,' Catherine said. 'She said you're a waiter.'

'That's true,' I agreed affably. 'So, what's up?'

She looked at the table for a while, then raised her eyes like someone being forced to make a confession.

'I think,' she said, 'that I'm being stalked.'

*   *   *

I'm not sure what I'd been expecting. Problems with a neighbor. Vague suspicions about her husband. A younger sister with an unsuitable boyfriend.

'That's not good. How long has it being going on?'

'On and off, nearly ten years.'

'Whoa,' Kristina said. 'Have you *reported* this? Haven't the police—'

'I've never told anyone,' Catherine said quickly. 'Apart from Mark. My husband,' she added. 'It hasn't been happening *all* that time or I would have. That's what's strange about it. Part of what's strange.'

'Tell me,' I said. 'From the start.'

'Well, I can't remember the day, not like, the actual date. It was around the time I met Mark, or a month or two before. We've been married nine years.'

'What does your husband do?'

'He's with Dunbar & Scott?' She delivered this as though I should have heard of the company and been impressed. I had not, though I doubted her husband was familiar with the Adriatico either.

'So how come you don't remember when it started? I would have thought that would be some-what memorable.'

Kristina shot me a warning look across the table.

'Of course. But . . .' Catherine raised her shoulders in a pantomime shrug. 'Where do you draw the line? If you walk the city at night – or even during the day – once in a while you're going

33

to get spooked. There's all these people around you all the time and you don't have a clue who any of them are, right? People at bus stops. In parks. In delis or diners or outside bars or reading magazines between the stacks at Barnes & Noble. Runaways. People *hanging around* . . . or heading down the same street as you are. Sometimes you wonder if they're genuinely on their way some-where, or if they're walking with you in mind. Or women do, anyway. Maybe you're not aware of it.'

I could have observed that the vast majority of random street violence happens to men, but I let it lie. 'I know what you're talking about.'

'So. There'd been *that* kind of stuff, but I put it down to urban living. But then I'd been out for a drink with girlfriends this one time, and afterward I took the subway home. Back then I had an apartment on Perry, on loan from my aunt.'

'Good deal,' I said. Perry is a leafy enclave of brownstones in the heart of the West Village, and somewhere I have no expectation of living in this lifetime. This time Kristina gave me a covert kick under the table. I moved my leg out of reach. 'And so?'

'I got out at 14th and Eighth and walked. After a while I realized I could hear footsteps. But when I stopped, I couldn't anymore. I know once you start listening to things they sound strange even if they're really not, but there was just . . . there was something weird about it.'

'What did you do?'

'Got home. That's the idea, right? Get inside, lock the doors, and if you can't see a psycho on the sidewalk holding a machete, you forget about it. Which I did.'

'But it happened again?'

'Not for two, three weeks. Then one night I was walking back after dark, taking the same route from the same subway, and . . . yes, it happened again.'

'What, exactly? I'm cloudy on what was actually taking place here.'

'I knew I was being followed. Isn't that enough?'

'Of course,' I said. 'But in terms of—'

'I turned to look a couple of times, didn't see anyone, but I had this *really* strong sense that someone I knew well was close by, watching me, trying to get closer. At one point I even thought I heard someone softly say my name. Then, as I was turning into my street, I caught a glimpse of someone on the corner of Bleecker.'

'What did he look like?'

'Average height, slim build. He was only there for a second, and it was dark. I couldn't see his face.'

'Any idea who he might have been?'

It seemed to me that she hesitated. 'No.'

'No guy across the hall who was always there to say good morning? No one at work who could have misunderstood the colleague/potential boyfriend boundary?'

'I don't think so. Though I suppose you never know the effect you have on other people.'

'And this has been going on for *ten years*?'

She glanced at me irritably. 'Of course not. I met Mark soon after, and we just clicked, and within a month I was effectively living at his place in Murray Hill. The feeling of being followed stopped when I moved there. And I forgot about it. I got married. Our daughters were born; they're six and four now. We moved to Chelsea five years ago. Everything was great. *Is* great.'

'Until?'

She exhaled in one short, sharp breath. 'We live on 18th. It's nice, quiet, close to the school, and you got all the restaurants and stuff on Eighth Avenue – though it's not exactly knee-deep in culture, right? Hence I've been going to the reading group at Swift's, which is how I met . . .' She gestured across the table.

'Kristina,' I said.

'Exactly. Until a few weeks ago I was taking a cab home. Now it's warmer, so I walk. I go via the market on Seventh – Mark's addicted to their shrimp salad, so there's domestic brownie points to be earned right there. But the last two, three times I've turned onto my street . . . someone's been back at the corner.'

'Eighth is busy, especially in the evening.'

She spoke sharply. 'Right. Which means people tend to *keep moving*. Going where they're headed. Not standing on the corner, looking down my street.'

'You've never got a good look at his face?'

36

'No.'

'So what makes you believe it's the same person?'

'I just *feel* it is. You . . . wouldn't understand.'

'Maybe not.' There are women who believe they have recourse to intuitive powers beyond the understanding of male kind, and what they 'feel' supersedes information available to the more conventional senses. This can be irritating, especially if you happen to be one of the dullard male robots who apparently can't see past the end of his own unspeakable genitals. In my own woman's case, I had reason to know such a belief could be justified, however, and so I didn't call Catherine on it. 'And it's never been more than that? This impression of being followed?'

'No. Though two weeks ago I was drawing the curtains in the girls' room and I saw someone on the sidewalk below. I *know* he was looking up at the window. But Ella started fussing and I had to deal with her and the next time I got a chance to look . . . he'd gone.'

She trailed off, looking at me defiantly. I didn't know what to say, and so I didn't say anything, which is generally my policy.

'I *knew* this was going to sound ridiculous,' she muttered. 'I'm sorry to have wasted your time.'

'You said you'd mentioned this to your husband?'

'I get the impression he thinks the same as you.'

'Which is?'

'I'm a woman, being silly.'

37

I was taken aback. 'I don't think that, Catherine. The question is what you can do about—'

'Assuming any of it is actually *happening*, right? That it's not an attack of the vapors or some other charmingly feminine malaise?'

'I'm just trying to be practical.'

'Absolutely. Men are good at that.' She pushed her chair back decisively. 'My friend's looking after Ella and Isabella. She's going to need to leave soon.'

'So, John – what should she do?' Kristina's voice was clipped. She was pissed at me, and not hiding it.

I shrugged. I'd been intending to follow that up with something more helpful, but wasn't given the chance.

'Thank you for your time, John,' Catherine said.

After telling the waitress to put the drinks on her account, she gave Kristina a peck on the cheek.

'See you tomorrow night,' she said. 'Nice to meet you,' she added to me. I've heard more convincing lies.

As the two of them headed out to the sidewalk together, I got out my wallet and covertly put a five-dollar bill on the table.

CHAPTER 4

When Catherine had disappeared up the street, Kristina turned to me. She had a look in her eye that I've seen her use on men in the bar, optimistic drunkards who've mistaken professional courtesy for a ticket to bed. The look works. The guys always elect to buy their next drink someplace else. Often in a different city altogether.

'What?' I asked, though I knew.

She kept glowering at me.

'I just don't get it,' I said. 'All she has is a vague impression of *maybe* being followed. So she got spooked walking home on a few occasions a very long time apart – there's not a woman in the city who couldn't say the same. And a few guys.'

'That doesn't mean she's—'

'I'd be more convinced without the big gap, to be honest. I don't know much about stalkers, but my impression is they tend to stick to the job at hand – not get distracted for a couple of presidential terms. What'd he do, set an alarm to remind himself to act crazy again after a decade-long vacation in normality?'

'You were being snippy before she even got to that part.'

'Possibly,' I admitted. 'She's not my type. You can't dismiss every disagreement with a male as institutionalized sexism. And who has an account at a coffee shop, for Christ's sake?'

'Lots of people.'

'Really?'

'Around here, yes.'

'Christ. Either way, you tip the waitress. Plus . . . her daughters' names rhyme.'

Kris cocked her head and stared at me ominously. 'What?'

I wasn't sure what I was trying to say and didn't want to keep trying to say it. 'Let's walk.'

For a moment it seemed like she wasn't going to follow, but eventually she did.

After fifteen minutes of silence we wound up in the streets on the other side of Bleecker. Close, in fact, to where Catherine had been living in the late 1990s and where she claimed to have first sensed someone following her. I didn't try to get Kris talking. I used to have two young sons. Still do have one, though I've seen him only once in the last three years, for reasons that are not entirely under my control. One of the few skills I'd started to develop before my marriage and family fell apart was the diffusion of unproductive conversations. Kids have far more focus and persistence than adults give them credit for, and may get a buzz out of the attention that conflict gains. Back them into a corner and they'll go at you toe-to-toe, and so the trick is to stop banging that drum and try something else instead. It works with grown-ups too. I use the technique on myself, when the conversations in my head threaten to become repetitive or obsessed with events that I cannot go back and change.

So rather than returning to Catherine Warren's problem – about which I wasn't sure more could be said – I wondered aloud how much the apartment she'd mentioned would cost to rent these days. After a *very* slow start, this led to discussing the area semi-seriously from a residential point of view, and back toward life in general, and finally to the fact that it was approaching time for us to get ready for work.

'You'll be changing your clothes, I take it.'

Kristina's skin is very pale, and when she flushes you notice it. 'There's no law that says I have to wear black jeans and a rock chick shirt all the time.'

'I know that.' I didn't mention I'd noticed she'd been drinking tea at the café, which she never does at home. She would reasonably have said there was no law against her drinking tea, either. 'I just thought maybe I could help. With the changing process.'

She was surprised into a reluctant laugh. 'I'm not sure you deserve that honor.'

'Perhaps. It's just I've heard that skirts can be

41

challenging. For those unaccustomed to their ways.'

'Is that right?'

'I'm just saying. If you need a hand when we get home, I'm there for you.' I left a beat. 'Of course, if we were living *here*, we'd be home already.'

She smiled and looked away. 'It's not so far,' she said. 'I'll race you.'

We got slammed that evening, the restaurant packed out the entire night. This wasn't enough to distract me from feeling like an ass over the discussion with Catherine Warren. So she'd rubbed me up the wrong way. It couldn't have been easy to talk about her concerns, and I hadn't provided a considerate audience.

When I took a cigarette break mid-evening I called an old friend on the other side of the country. Bill Raines answered promptly.

'Well, hey,' he said. 'How's tricks, pizza boy? Still keeping it thin and crispy?'

'Always,' I said, leaning back against the wall to watch people ambling the sidewalk, looking for the cheapest way to feel like shit tomorrow. 'How about you? Still lying through your teeth in pursuit of clients' claims, however mercenary and indeed fictitious they may be?'

'It's how I roll. S'up in your so-called life?'

'Wanted to pick your brain.'

'Shoot.'

I gave him the bones of Catherine's story. He listened without interrupting until I was done.

'I don't see you selling the movie rights,' he said. 'As jeopardy goes, it's kind of blah, right? Plus, what does she think *you* can do about it?'

'I'm not sure,' I said, realizing that the more I thought about it, the less I understood why the meeting had even taken place. 'Just hoping for some advice, I guess. I didn't have any. So I'm trying you.'

'I'm sure you haven't forgotten everything you knew about the law, John. The cops need probable cause. The sense you're being followed isn't enough, and an attorney's going to need a lot more for a restraining order – like knowing who the alleged perp *is*. You can't get those things filed "To Whom It May Concern."'

'The cops won't help in the meantime?'

'I'm not saying that. These days they take this stuff pretty seriously. Thousands of people every year believe they're receiving unwelcome attention, and most women who get murdered by ex-partners are stalked by them first. Your friend's not going to get a 'Hush, girlie; run along,' but you'll require actual evidence before they can do more than advise buying some Mace. Doesn't sound like she has any.'

'Nothing like.'

'Sensing you're not her biggest fan, either.'

'Christ. Is it that obvious?'

'You've always been a heart-on-the-sleeve kind

43

of guy, John. Least, I assumed it was your heart, though it was kind of shriveled. Could have been an unusually large raisin.'

I asked if he was intending to be in the city any day soon. 'If I am,' he said. 'I'll warn you. Give you plenty time to get out of town. We done here?'

'Always a pleasure, Bill.'

'Liar.'

As I slipped the phone back into my pocket I felt someone plucking at my sleeve. I turned to see Lydia looking up at me with anxious eyes.

'Have you seen Frankie?'

''Fraid not,' I said. 'But I'll keep an eye out.'

The old woman smiled, sending a car crash of deep lines across her face. 'Would you, dear? I'm *sure* I saw him earlier. Just by here. I *know* it was him.'

Within hours of starting work at the Adriatico I'd been told about Lydia. A long time ago she'd been an actress/singer/dancer in shows on (or within a cab ride of) Broadway, by all accounts talented and beautiful. Then one night thirty years ago someone close to her – her brother, lover, or just a friend, accounts varied – was murdered outside a bar on First Avenue.

That's what the police told her, anyway, though she refused to believe it – refused adamantly, no quarter given. She remained convinced that this guy, whatever he'd been to her, was still alive; that she saw her Frankie sometimes; that she called

44

out to him, but he never heard or never stopped. She had a brusque way with outreach volunteers who tried to boss her around, because she knew she was not crazy. She still turned heads on the streets, though nowadays that was because of her multilayered outfit of castoffs. She slept in Tompkins Square Park, holding her corner and snarling at runaways. Her hair was white, and decades of cigarettes had filled her throat with glass. When she hollered a show tune, which happened occasionally, it did not sound good.

'Need to get back to work, Lyds,' I said, slipping a few bucks into her hand. She would not accept money proffered in plain sight. 'Take care tonight.'

'I will. You're a good boy.'

I wasn't sure about that. But most of the time, I try.

After service ended, I went downstairs and propped up the bar until one thirty, lending a hand as required. Afterward, as often on lively nights, we went on to prop up a corner of someone else's bar in the company of cooks, waiters, and allied miscreants from other local dives. By the time we were walking home, things felt good between us again.

'She didn't say anything, did she?' I said.

'Huh?'

'Catherine. You guessed there was a problem. You talked *her* into speaking to me. She never asked.'

'You're smarter than you look,' Kristina said. 'I mean, you'd have to be.'

'And you've got an eye for bad things.'

'Does this mean you're taking her more seriously?'

'There's *something* up in her life. That I believe. It's also obvious you care about her, which means that I should too. So when you see her tomorrow at the book club, tell her that your boyfriend can be a dickhead but if she wants him to help, he'll try.'

'My boyfriend?'

'That would be me.'

'I see. 'Course, if we moved to the Village, you might rate being upgraded to "partner." I should add that comes with additional benefits.'

'Which are?'

'Oh no. My mother may have been a lunatic bitch, but she at least taught me not to toss away the farm.'

'You don't give up easy, do you?'

'I don't give up *at all*. You should know that about me by now.'

I put my arm around her shoulders and she looped hers around my waist and we walked the rest of the way listening to the sound of distant others shouting and laughing, a solar system of two spinning quietly home through the universe.

I was standing peaceably in the kitchen pouring glasses of water to take to bed when I heard Kristina padding quickly back out of the bedroom.

'I missed a call.'

'And?'

She jabbed a couple of buttons. 'Listen.'

Catherine Warren's voice came out of the speaker, tinny and hesitant.

'Kristina, it's me,' she said. 'I'm so sorry to call, but I don't know who else to talk to.'

There was a pause, and when she spoke again her voice was cracked. 'Someone's been in my house.'

CHAPTER 5

The man got to Bryant Park at eleven o'clock, the time the informal morning gathering started. There weren't many friends present – more made the effort to attend the gathering on Friday, and Union Square had become more fashionable recently – and nobody he wanted to talk to. He kept on the move. It wasn't long before people started to drift back out to the streets. He knew she would appear eventually, traditionally arriving from the Sixth Avenue side. He sat halfway up the steps that looked down over the central grassy area and waited.

He had no idea what her reaction was going to be. In general she preached acceptance, making the best of their situation. Might she feel differently about this?

He didn't know.

Three days he'd waited. Three days and three long nights of trying to live normally while a thought drummed in his head like a migraine. As a Fingerman he couldn't just up and leave. He had obligations. Some were arranged on a schedule –

his services could be booked – but it was also his time on call. He was required to make himself available in known locations (including this very park) for set periods, ready for requests relayed to him by local Cornermen or friends presenting in person. He did not consider abandoning his post. The rotation had been in place for many years, legacy of Lonely Clive and others. His skills put him in a privileged position, and responsibility came with it. If *they* couldn't man up and do the right thing by each other, then they could hardly criticize others for failing to do so. Thus the Gathered had said, and on this – if not everything else – he agreed. And after all, if he hadn't happened to be holding his post in Bryant Park at the right moment on the right day, this chance to reconnect would never have been born. (Though hadn't he also felt a peculiar pull to the park that afternoon? And hadn't he lingered for more than an hour after his slot had finished? Yes, he had.)

Either way, though the language of the fates is often garbled and obscure, when they speak it pays to listen. He didn't buy the 'everything happens for a reason' mantra so beloved of the girl he was waiting for, but when life drops a boon in your lap, you pay the fee.

So he'd waited, stoically, growing more and more tense, finding sometimes that his fists were bunching without him realizing it, knowing however that the important thing was that he was now in possession of information that could change his life.

'Hey,' said a voice.

He turned to see the girl, up on the top step. 'You came in the other way?'

'I like to remain mysterious.'

In silhouette she looked even more ethereal than usual. The sun hung behind her as a halo of gold against long, dark hair. As usual, she was wearing dark red under a black coat. If you glimpsed her flicking through old LPs in a thrift store you'd assume she was merely a tall and unusually fine-featured Goth. 'What's up?'

'How do you know something's up?'

She smiled. 'I know everything, remember?'

He told her everything as they walked around the park together. It had always been that way with them, since they first met in a stinking, moldy room above a boarded-up porno theater soon after he'd come to the city. When he'd finished – it didn't take long – her face was unreadable.

'How wonderful,' she said. 'Lucky you.'

'What do you think I should do?'

'What you're going to do.'

'I should . . . do whatever's in my heart?'

She laughed. 'No, but bless you for making the effort to speak in my language. I just mean you should do it. You're *going* to, regardless, and as it happens I think it's the right choice.'

'Really?' He studied her face. All he found was

what he always saw. Pale, open features that were symmetric and strong and yet delicate, and bloodred lips. 'Why?'

She shrugged her narrow shoulders. 'You could have done something without talking to me. You didn't. What's important to you is important to me. You've waited a long time for something like this. We all have. So do it.'

'Thank you, Lizzie.'

'*De nada.*' She looked as though she was about to say something else, but stopped.

He turned to see a figure approaching across the grass. Stocky, balding, pugnacious even from a distance. Coming up behind were three other people he recognized – two guys, one woman. Very tall, very thin. 'Christ.'

'Looks like someone's heading your way.'

'It won't take long to say no to whatever it is he wants. Will you wait?'

'Can't. Got things to do and wonders to perform,' Lizzie said, taking his hand and squeezing it briefly between her long, pale fingers. 'Will you have a phone number?'

He reeled it off to her.

'Be careful, Maj,' she said, before drifting away across the grass. 'And don't hurt anyone.'

As usual, Golzen was wearing a suit styled in the mode of the 1930s – double-breasted, with wide chalk-colored stripes and extravagant lapels. Maj had no idea why he did this. He didn't care.

'I'm in a hurry,' he said when the man reached him. The other three stayed well back, thirty feet away, in a huddle in the middle of the grass.

Golzen smiled, a thin, straight line that looked as if it had been drawn on his face and then just as quickly erased. 'I'm sure. Interesting business?'

'Not to you.'

'I have a proposal.'

'Same as usual?'

'Pretty much.'

'Guess my answer will be the same, too.'

'And I'll ask again, why?'

'Because he's a thief.'

'We're all thieves.'

'He's different.'

'Just more organized, which means better returns – for us. I don't see the difference between him and the lamer you're associating with. Except for the lameness, obviously.'

'Jeffers doesn't take anything.'

'Everybody takes something, Maj. Some do it more subtly, that's all. Sometimes just by looking.'

'What's that supposed to mean?'

'You'll work it out. My point is that with Reinhart the terms are clear and the rewards material.'

'You're wrong about him. You'll realize that sooner or later.'

Golzen seemed to swell, turning up prophet mode. 'No, *you'll* realize a change is coming. Perfect is calling, and it is nearly time to heed its voice.'

'You know I don't believe in that bullshit.'

'That's immaterial. Perfect believes in you. The question is whether you want to be on the winning side.'

'Since when were there sides?'

'Are you kidding? *Everything* has at least two sides. Even a single individual. You know that.'

'May be true for you. It doesn't have to be that way among the friends.'

'Jesus.' Golzen stared at him with open contempt. 'You spend far too much time with that hippy chick.'

'Like I said, I'm in a hurry. This all you got?'

'Just don't be gone too long. I'd hate for you to miss the excitement.'

Maj stared at him. Golzen smiled. 'There may be one more chance to change your mind,' he said. 'We're saving a place. We'll need friends like you, with skills, character, strength of mind. Assuming you can finally see where your best interests lie.' He walked away.

Maj watched him go. How could Golzen know he was planning on leaving town? Only by talking to the sole person Maj had discussed the matter with: a Journeyman he'd gone to for advice. Even so, it could only be guesswork, as Maj had been careful to appear to be conducting his inquiry out of hypothetical interest, and the Journeyman would never have talked.

So it was pure luck, that was all. It showed how widely Golzen's influence spread, however, and how determined he was. Maj had already suspected these things. For the time being, it didn't matter.

But consider it logged.

He stopped by the churchyard and tried to talk to Lonely Clive. Though he was able to get a few words out of him, he had to take his former mentor's blessing on trust, or decide to take it implicitly. He left unclear as to which it had been, but it didn't matter.

He was going to do it anyway.

CHAPTER 6

At a little after eight on Monday evening I was in SoHo. I'd been in the area for two hours already and I was cold and bored. I'd watched Catherine and Kristina arrive at Swift's ten minutes apart, and then I'd walked the neighboring blocks in a grid pattern. After I tired of this, I took a covert pass through the store and then wandered back out and eventually into the grounds of Old St Patrick's Church. An eight-foot-high brick wall surrounds most of a small block, augmented on one side by the tall, white side of another building. Inside the wall stands an unassuming sand-colored church, well-tended grass, and a clean graveyard arranged in orderly lines. It is a calm place and a good spot to stand for a while even if you do not believe in God. But also . . . very cold.

I emerged in time to observe as the reading group wrapped up and to see the two women buying coffees from the bookstore café before bringing them out to the concrete bench outside. This being, as I knew, their custom. They didn't hurry over their drinks.

I stood across the way, in the shadow of the wall around the church, and waited some more.

It had already been established that someone had *not* entered Catherine Warren's house the evening before – nobody who wasn't supposed to have, anyway.

Kristina tried calling right back, but it went to voice mail. Catherine's message had been left at eight thirty and it was after three a.m. by the time we found it. Kristina was awake and on her feet before me the next morning, for once. Catherine called early, to be fair, and was apologetic and amusing at her own expense. She'd called after noticing things had been moved in the office nook of their house. This had subsequently been explained. Her husband – who'd stopped by en route to a business dinner – had been told to drop everything and attend a meeting at the London office the next day, taking the oh-my-god-that's-early flight out of JFK. (This is something you don't have to put up with if you work in a pizza restaurant.) He'd been searching for his passport – neatly filed by Catherine somewhere else entirely – and hadn't tidied after himself. Some people wouldn't even have noticed, but Catherine evidently ran a tight ship, and so she did.

Panic over.

After the call, Kristina seemed embarrassed on her friend's behalf. Perversely, though I had to refrain from wondering aloud whether Catherine couldn't have made a second call to Kristina's phone to let her know everything was okay, the incident made me take her more seriously. My ex-wife, Carol, had been prone to anxiety even before the truly bad things happened to us, notably the death of our older son, Scott. I know from experience that anxiety is a very powerful force, as close to malign possession as makes no difference. It may not sound like much – so someone gets worked up over little things? Big deal. They should try coping with *real* problems, right?

Wrong. Real problems are easy. They have real solutions. Anxiety turns the world into an intangible and insoluble crisis and transforms every doubt into a rat intent on devouring its own tail. It is like being caught in a trap in the dark forest when you can hear big, hungry animals closing in on every side.

The confident, sleek woman I'd met outside the coffeehouse on Greenwich Avenue hadn't presented like someone so close to the edge, but that could mean she was hiding some problem a little too well, or else that there *was* something going on – something sufficient to have her putting two and two together to make twenty-five. I wouldn't have cared much either way except that the woman I loved evidently wanted to regard this person as a friend – and friends were something Kristina was generally willing to do without. I'm far from gregarious, but she can make me look positively needy. Catherine's presence at the reading group had kept her attending. If the other woman flipped out, it would stop.

That's why I was there, getting cold. Having made a bad job of being someone's man in the past, I was open to the idea of working harder at it this time around.

Eventually they finished their coffees and went separate ways. Kristina did not glance in the direction of the church because she didn't know I was there. I hadn't wanted her to convey inadvertent signals to Catherine. I was probably doing nothing more than wasting my evening off work (the Adriatico is closed on Mondays, to everyone's relief), but in that case I wanted to make doubly sure I got something out of it. If I followed Catherine home and saw nothing, I would have demonstrated that – on a night when her movements were predictable, and therefore an alleged stalker's ideal opportunity – there had been no one on her tail. I could choose whether or not to convey this to Kristina when I got home.

I stayed back as I followed Catherine up into the Village. I had a good idea of what route she'd take and so gave her plenty of space. She walked confidently, with the brisk stride of someone who knew the area and had lived in the city a long time. She lingered in front of a couple of stores but never came to a halt. From Bleecker she skirted Washington Square Park and took the predictable left onto Greenwich Avenue. From here she'd likely head up past the Westside Market. With her husband across the ocean, it was possible she'd give this a miss. I doubted it, though. If she'd fallen into the practice of going to the deli for his shrimp salad, chances were she'd do it tonight and find a reason while she was there. Humans are creatures of habit.

I kept an eye on other pedestrians. The young, the old, professionals and the half-dead homeless, the weird-looking and the painfully vanilla. New York is a place where you'd have to hail from the planet Zog and sport three heads to really stand out, though if you kept those heads down and didn't smoke in a public place you'd still have a chance of passing without notice. Of course, if Catherine *did* have a stalker he'd be going to some trouble not to attract attention. But by the time we were crossing 14th I was confident this was a bust.

Fine by me. I'd left a note for Kris saying I'd gone for a walk and would be home by nine bearing food. I'd shadow Catherine to her door in Chelsea – ten minutes from where we were now – then double back via Chong's.

Catherine slowed as she came up toward the Westside Market. She hesitated, then headed in.

I swore wearily. I was tiring of the game and wishing I were back at the apartment already, but I gave it a moment and then followed her inside.

★   ★   ★

I'd been there before and knew what to expect. Beautiful food at belligerent prices, a store that was large for the neighborhood but kept intimate by the height of the stacks and a layout dotted with islands of especial fabulousness. Increased proximity to places like this was one of Kristina's expressed reasons for wanting to move, and here I had no disagreement.

I realized I was reaching the limits of my competence. As I'd wanted to be sure that Catherine understood, I've never been an undercover cop or a detective. My years in the army were spent at the grunt end, where you generally want to ensure that people *do* know you're around, in the hope this will stop bad things breaking out in the first place. Skulking is therefore not one of my core skills. I caught a break as I entered the market, however. Catherine was heading toward the produce section. This meant I could head right, the problem being this would obscure her from view. Doing the opposite would make it more likely she'd spot me. Belatedly I realized what would have made much more sense was staying outside and waiting around the corner to pick her up again as she left. Duh.

I was about to act on this when I caught another glimpse of Catherine, in front of a cooler of prepared foods. The famous shrimp salad, of course. Her husband was going to get his treat after all.

Then I noticed someone.

60

I couldn't see his face or head, as it was obscured by hanging goods, but he stood a little over average height, slim build, wearing a long, dark coat and standing near the end of the aisle behind Catherine.

She moved away from the cabinet, and I stepped back into my aisle to keep out of view. I gave it a beat and leaned forward, catching a momentary glimpse of the other figure as he walked off down the distant aisle.

I hadn't seen him clearly and there were maybe fifteen, twenty other people in the store. But none of them had made me feel the need to see them a second time.

Catherine was heading for the checkout counter.

I skirted around the back. There was no sign of the other person. I returned to my original position and waited, glancing across to check on Catherine's progress. She was nearly done at the register, tucking a frequent-buyer card back in her purse.

I decided on an abrupt change of tactics and headed down the far aisle and out the side door instead.

Back outside, I walked a few yards down the street. The deli was on the corner, at the intersection. If I hung here and waited for Catherine to emerge, I'd be in a perfect position to see anyone following her.

Three minutes later Catherine emerged with an environmentally friendly hemp bag over her shoulder. The lights were in her favor and she strode straight across 15th. I held my position, watching for the figure in the coat. No sign. Maybe he was still inside. Maybe he'd already left. Very likely he'd never been more than some random guy come to score coffee and cat food.

I crossed the street and followed Catherine up the avenue, keeping close to the buildings. There were lots of people around, and Catherine looked relaxed. At the next intersection she did something I hadn't anticipated, however, unexpectedly cutting across the road.

I got caught behind a gaggle of French tourists who were laughing and shouting and clearly very lost but having a whale of a time. One of them picked at my sleeve, but I shrugged him off. Catherine was nearly at the other side of the avenue by then, heading toward 16th.

A figure in a dark coat was standing in a doorway on the other side.

It was too far for me to be sure it was the same guy, but he sure as hell looked similar. I still couldn't see his face, as he was turned away from the street and the collar of his coat was turned up.

He remained motionless as Catherine reached the west side of the avenue – and then moved to follow, entering the side street only about twenty yards behind her.

The lights had changed and it seemed like every car in the city had business that took it past my face, fast. I tried to weave my way through them, realized some asshole was going to run me down if I kept it up, and was forced to step back onto the sidewalk.

Catherine meanwhile had disappeared from sight, along with the figure that was either following her or just happened to be walking in the same direction.

I finally saw a gap in traffic and darted across the road. I got to the other side accompanied by loud honks and abuse in at least three languages, but kept going into the side street, where I slowed to a fast walk. It was quiet, residential, dotted with trees, and very still.

Catherine was fifty yards ahead. She was striding quickly now – faster than before. It could be that the cold had gotten to her or she'd realized she was going to be late for the sitter, but I didn't think so.

She glanced behind. She didn't see anyone.

How do I know? Because there was no one there.

I stopped dead in my tracks, confused, stared up and down the street. I'd seen the figure turning onto this street. He hadn't come back out before I got here – I would have seen him – but . . . he wasn't here now.

I saw houses. I saw a brick church with ornamental staircases leading up to a wooden door on either side. I saw cars and trees. I didn't see any people at all.

Catherine was moving even faster. Once she reached the corner she'd be two short blocks from her own street. It seemed like she wanted to cover the distance quickly. It looked as if she felt someone was after her.

But she was wrong.

There was no one there.

I followed her the rest of the way home. I even waited for half an hour at the end of the street, standing in shadow. Eventually I walked back to my own home, picking up food on the way.

I told Kristina what I'd done – I had to, I was so late – and got a big, tight hug for it. I didn't mention that I thought I'd seen a nondescript individual in Catherine's orbit in the Westside Market, or that he'd followed her afterward. I said I hadn't seen anyone, because as far as I could tell, that was true.

As I lay in bed later, however, listening to Kristina's breathing and waiting for sleep, I knew that when she glanced back, I'd seen genuine fear in Catherine's face.

I realized also that, for the first time, I was not convinced she was wrong to feel that way.

CHAPTER 7

The next morning I was up early. Kristina remained in bed, refining her impersonation of someone who'd passed away in the night. An idea struck me as I stood in the kitchen, provoked by the sight of her phone on the counter. I picked it up and went to her incoming log. Catherine's number was there. I made a note of it and went into the shower to think about the idea.

When I walked out onto the street half an hour later, I made the call.

We met at the café on Greenwich Avenue. Catherine looked warily up at me when I entered. All I'd said on the phone was that it would be a good idea if we talked alone.

'Here's the thing,' I said, sitting opposite her. 'I followed you last night.'

'You did *what*?'

'I walked the blocks around the bookstore during the reading group and shadowed when you left for home.'

'Kristina didn't say—'

'She had no idea it was happening.'

'Why did you do it?'

'You left a message on her phone the night before. A message that freaked her out. Kristina is not easy to freak out.'

'I called and explained all that.'

'The following morning.'

She looked impatient. 'I didn't know what time you went to bed. I didn't want to wake anyone.'

'Do you recall Kristina's occupation?'

'Of course I do. And I don't like your attitude.'

'It's never been popular. So – what does Kris do?'

Catherine looked flustered. 'She . . . She works in a restaurant. Like you.'

'She runs a late-night bar.'

'That's right. So . . . Okay, so probably you would have been awake. I get it. I'm sorry. But once I'd worked out no one had been in the house I wanted to forget about it. I didn't realize it would be a big deal.'

I didn't say anything.

'I'm sorry,' she said again, eventually.

'I didn't see anyone last night until you went into the Westside Market,' I said. 'I'm not sure I saw anything there either. One person caught my eye, though.'

Catherine's eyes were watchful. 'And?'

'I saw him a few minutes later, hanging around the entrance to 16th. When you went up it, he followed.'

'I knew it,' she said dully. 'Did you . . . Did you get a good look at him?'

'No, but it means I'm inclined to take your fears more seriously, which in turn means I have to ask you the obvious question. Again.'

'What question?'

'Who is it?'

'I don't *know*. Like I told you last time.'

'I remember. I still find it hard to believe. If you think this is the same guy from a decade ago, then it's not random and you must be able to come up with a name or two if you think hard enough.'

'I really don't—'

'Bullshit,' I said calmly. 'In a past life I spent a lot of time in small rooms with people who were not telling the truth. I believe I'm sitting opposite one again now. You've got two minutes to alter that impression or I'm out of there and that's the end of it.'

For a moment she looked furious, or as if she was going to cry. Then she started to talk.

I told Kristina about the meeting as soon as I got back to the apartment. I could tell from her body language that this was several hours too late.

'So who is he?'

'Ex-boyfriend. They went out for six months way back. She decided it wasn't working and let him down gently. She's now saying he could be the guy, maybe. Their relationship ended right before

67

the first night she thought she was being followed. She 'feels' it could be the same person now.'

Kristina looked out of the window onto the rooftops. 'Drop the quote marks, John. People feel stuff. And it's women who do, more often, and sometimes they're right.'

'I know,' I said.

'So why didn't she mention him before?'

'Didn't believe him capable, she says. Or didn't want to, anyway.'

'So what are you going to do?'

'What makes you think I'm going to do anything?'

'The fact that you're you.'

I had to smile, and after a moment, she smiled back. It looked underpowered. 'I'm sorry,' I said. 'I should have told you about arranging to meet her.'

'Yeah, you should have. You should have told me last night you thought you saw someone following her, too.'

'What's my punishment?'

'Don't know yet. But it's going to be severe. In the meantime, what's the plan?'

'This Clark guy lives in the back end of Williamsburg. Works there, at least.'

'Am I allowed to come?'

'Of course,' I said. 'I'm hoping you will.'

I'd been back and forth on this, in fact. I did want Kristina to come. Partly because she had skills when it came to assessing people – far better than I, and drawing on deeper wells – and also because it would make a nicer trip of it. Assuming the guy didn't become violent when confronted. In that case I'd prefer it to be just me and him.

'Well, I can't,' she said. 'The heater guys are coming, finally.' She looked cranky, but she often does, and I knew I'd said the right thing.

'So?'

'So be careful. And I want to know what happens. And not just the non-executive summary this time.'

I don't enjoy the subway. I know I should, that it's part of the fabric and texture of the city, and come, let us behold urban kind in its glorious variety, but I prefer to get that kind of experience above-ground, where you can walk away from it when you want. On the L line urban kind is like a too-tight, unwashed coat, and by the time I emerged in Brooklyn I was low on temper and pretty convinced that this was my second dumb idea of the day.

I'd traced Clark via Facebook. I'm not on it, but the restaurant is, courtesy of some nephew who thought it might shift more pizza. You can go like the Adriatico online if you want. I cannot imagine how that would help anything. It sure as hell will not get you a free pizza.

There were plenty of people listed under some variation of 'Thomas Clark' but only one who lived in the area Catherine had suggested and who showed other likely characteristics. When they'd dated, Clark had been a decorative fine artist with a high opinion of himself. It was evident from his page that he now co-ran a small gallery instead. The gallery had a website with its street address all over it. As a job of hiding, it sucked.

Assuming he had reason to hide, of course.

The gallery was at the far end of the hipster pocket and I arrived just after two o'clock. The entire width of the store front was glass, a single large, square painting on an easel in windows on either side of a central door. I have no idea what they were paintings of. Apparently that's not the point. In the back of the white-walled space beyond stood a minimalist white desk. A man sat behind it, slender in build. There was no long black coat with a high collar hanging on the wall. Life doesn't hand things up that neatly tied.

When I pushed the door open, a discreet bell chimed three times. The man looked up and smiled generically. He had longish but tidy dark hair and a pair of neat round spectacles. 'Good afternoon.'

I looked around the walls. Further large, square paintings – or canvases with paint on them, at any rate.

'Can I help you, or are we just browsing?'

I kept silent long enough for him to register something wasn't right with this encounter. Then I turned to look at him. 'Are you Thomas Clark?'

'Yes.'

'Catherine says hi.'

He looked confused. 'I'm embarrassed to admit this, but I don't think the name sounds familiar . . .'

'Back then you were going to make it as an artist yourself. Fancy handmade pots, she said.'

He blinked as the penny dropped. 'You mean . . . Catherine *Warren*?'

'I do.'

'But . . . I haven't seen her in years.'

'Really?'

'Ask her.'

'I talked with Catherine three hours ago. She gave me your name.'

'Why? Who *are* you?'

'My name is John Henderson. Someone's been following Catherine. At night. She thinks it could be you.'

'*What*? Why would I do that?'

'I have no idea,' I said. 'And your question doesn't answer mine.'

His eyes flicked to the side. A smart-looking middle-aged couple were drifting to a halt outside. I could not see the painting that had caught their attention, only their eyes and a desire to acquire.

I walked over and flipped the OPEN sign to CLOSED. The guy outside stared at me. I stared back. They went away.

Clark meanwhile remained at his desk. 'I haven't seen Catherine since I moved out of Manhattan,' he said. 'We split up and I called her a couple times afterward, I'll admit, but—'

'Why did you call her? Were you uncertain why she was ending the relationship?'

He laughed. 'Uncertain? Oh no. At first it was all, 'It's not you, it's me,' but it became clear she was leaving me for this guy she'd met. The marvelous Mark.'

That struck an off note, but I kept drilling. 'You remember his name?'

'Of course I do. I was *in love with her*. Then one night over the phone it's bam – she's with this other guy instead. My services are no longer required; could I please let myself out of her life.'

'Why did you try to contact her afterward?'

'She'd always said we'd be friends forever. It had been this big thing of hers. She didn't mean it, though. Once you stop being useful to Catherine you're cut out of the script for good. I called a few times. I sent her a letter . . . and two cards. I sent . . .'

He trailed off, memory dulling his face. 'I sent her a bunch of irises. They were her favorite. That was something I'd known about her back when we'd been friends, before we started dating. It was supposed to signal, you know, that we could go back to that, if she wanted. There was no response. I gave up.'

'When did you move out of Manhattan?'

'Eight years ago.'

'Do you go back?'

'Of course. I used to have an agent there, but he let me go about the same time I realized people

72

were using the pots I'd slaved long hours over . . . to keep flowers in. I visit an exhibition once in a while, see friends, and, well, yes – obviously I'm there sometimes. But my real life is here now.'

'Where were you last night?'

He gestured around. 'Hanging these. If you need witnesses you'll have to find someone who happened to walk by. It's a busy street at night and I'm sure there were some, but I don't know their names.'

'I don't need witnesses. I'm not a cop.'

He cocked his head. 'Then what right do you have to be asking all this?'

'None. I apologize if I've been intrusive.'

'So what happened? Did Catherine dump Mark? Is she with you now?'

'No. They're married. They have two kids.'

'Huh. Guess at least I can tell myself that I lost to the winning team.'

'If that helps. You got any message for her?'

'Seriously?'

'If you do, I'll pass it on.'

He thought about it. 'Sure,' he said, looking down at the papers on this desk. 'You can tell her to go fuck herself.'

CHAPTER 8

It was twenty-four hours before Golzen had a chance to speak to Reinhart. The man's movements were wholly unpredictable, and his presence could not be guaranteed even at the club he owned on Orchard, in the ratty, crumbling backstreets of the Lower East Side, south of the Village and east of anywhere good, above which Golzen and others laid their heads at night in exchange for services rendered.

He slipped in through the street door. It was ajar, as often in the mornings, in a vain attempt to clear the stale, secondhand air inside, a stealthy, underhand odor that seeped up from the crumbling building's foundation. The area beyond was empty, cavernous, and dark, a wide central space with black-painted walls shading off into low-ceilinged, shadowy little corridors and booths where the small hours would find the bar's racier patrons taking drugs and advantage of one another.

Golzen walked across this, past the bar along the right-hand wall, and into the office in the back. Reinhart was sitting behind his desk. The space was otherwise empty. No filing cabinets, no computer, no pictures on the wall. No second chair, even. Just a boxy old 1970s-style phone, positioned to line up neatly with the corners of the desk. As always, Reinhart was wearing a coat, as if he'd recently arrived or would be leaving almost immediately. He was watching the door as Golzen entered, as though waiting for him.

He didn't wait for Golzen to speak. If you needed that kind of fluff, you did business with someone else – the problem being, so far as Golzen knew (and his contacts were indeed good, and situated far and wide), there was no one else working this game in the entire city. It was Reinhart or nobody.

'Did you talk to him?'

'I tried.'

'The fuck is up with that guy?'

Golzen considered his response. Idealists who cleave to different ideals seldom mix well. His view was that Maj was unpredictable, full of himself, and basically an asshole. Moreover, a dangerously volatile asshole. He'd expressed this opinion more than once. Reinhart evidently saw something else in the guy, however, and wouldn't let the matter drop. 'He learned at Lonely Clive's knee.'

Reinhart grunted, irritable and dismissive combined. Golzen knew the man got what he'd meant – some of it, at least. Reinhart had taken the trouble to understand the world inhabited by the people he now did business with. He knew Golzen meant that when Maj arrived in the city he'd been taken under the wing of a member of the old guard – the ones sometimes called the Gathered, before the term became loosely applied to all of them. Originally it had referred to a cabal of friends who'd started introducing structures and systems into their lives. The Jesuits declared that if you gave them a boy, they'd give you the man. It had been the same with the Gathered, or the few that were left. The Scattered would be a better name now. They'd done good in the way back, for sure, dominating the scene for fifty years or more – but had been fading in authority even before Reinhart arrived. It had happened much faster since, and good riddance to them. They'd never listened to Golzen's ideas either.

'Keep on it,' Reinhart said. His hair was cropped short and the single bulb above caught the top of his hard, square head. 'Get your buddies to stick to him, too. Like glue. Any sign of an angle, tell them to work it. Hard.'

'Okay.'

Reinhart smiled. It was pitch perfect as a coordinated movement of muscles, but once you got to know the guy, his ability to do this only made him even more unnerving. 'Don't worry – you'll always be my number one. I'd simply prefer to have that guy inside the tent pissing out, instead of the other way around. Get it?'

Golzen shrugged. Talk of Maj bored him. 'Sure.'

'Good. Because we're getting close, my friend.'

No longer remotely bored, Golzen looked up. 'For real?'

'The time for change is upon us.'

Golzen felt his stomach flip. 'How soon?'

Reinhart closed his eyes, as if listening to something beyond the hearing of normal men, perhaps simply the dark workings of his own mind. 'I don't know. But *soon*. Maybe even within the week.'

He opened his eyes. 'Put out a broadcast to the chosen. Encourage readiness.'

'Saying . . . ?'

'I'll leave that to you. Just hold the date. There *is* no date yet, but . . . hold it anyway.'

Golzen grinned. 'You got it.'

'And bring me fresh blood. I'm going to lose some of my best stealers on this. We need replacements in training before I can open the door to Perfect and let us walk the road to our brave new world.'

'I'm on it.'

'Not while you're standing here.'

Golzen walked quickly out through the bar and onto the street. He already had ideas for friends to turn, clueless wanderers to bring into the fold: people who could learn to do what he and the others had been doing for Reinhart, while the chosen left on a mission Golzen had been preparing (and advocating and prophesying) for years. He had no problem with performing this task for Reinhart. Relished the prospect, in fact. He'd tell his buddies to sniff harder around Maj, too, if that's what Reinhart wanted. Why not? It wouldn't be much longer that he had to work with the man.

Golzen was built to hold impulses in check, most of the time. He'd been very patient, working every opportunity to bind the other eleven of the chosen to him through the treats and advantages he'd gained for them. The relationship between him and Reinhart had been very useful in this, symbiotic.

But such relationships end.

CHAPTER 9

As he entered Roast Me, David confirmed – with a sinking feeling – that Talia was working the counter. He considered turning around, but not seriously.

'Hey, Norman,' she hollered, as she cranked through the orders of those ahead of him in line.

He sighed. Yesterday it had been 'Ernest.' Couple days before that, 'F. Scott.' The previous week they'd been more contemporary – Richard, Don, and Jonathan (two or three guys she could have been shooting for with that last, the handle of choice for today's nascent Great American Novelist). She evidently believed she'd found a rich seam of comedy and was determined to mine it out.

And that was okay. He'd always liked Talia, a big, cheerful woman in her fifties who cussed freely and had been holding down the Gaggia in the town's only coffee shop since it opened. Very occasionally they let Dylan have a turn for light relief, but basically if you wanted a latte in Rockbridge, Talia was the go-to gal. She was fiercely resistant to the term 'barista' and happy to remain – as she was prone to tell their rare, easily intimidated tourists – just 'the fat chick who makes the fucking coffee.'

When David had been working in an office up the street he'd often passed the time of day with Talia, content that in Rockbridge everyone knew everybody else along with a fair portion of their business. He was aware that Talia lived with nine cats in a trailer on the other side of town near the creek, was long-term single but had once been the lover of a man called Ed who'd died under tragic circumstances, and that she possessed a strong creative urge, manifest in prolific journaling and collage-making and a vast novel of epic fantasy upon which she'd been working for at least five years.

And therein lay the problem.

While he'd been holding down a day job David had been happy to shoot the breeze with Talia. They'd been hobbyists, engaged in the same struggle. Since he got his deal, things had changed. Talia seemed to believe David had breached a citadel – like one of the characters in her forever-in-progress novel, perhaps, a book David really, *really* did not want to read – therein defeating the dragon who had guarded the How To Get Published Spell. Instead of something they could enjoy gossiping about, it had become a matter on which Talia wanted *clues*. She wanted to be sold the magic potion that put you onto the best-seller lists forever and stopped people from seeing you as just that big, noisy woman who had way too many cats.

David would have given her the secret if he knew. He was not a selfish man. The problem was he didn't have a clue what it was, and on mornings like this he almost wished he were back where he had been six months ago.

'So!' Talia bellowed, hands already in motion toward his customary drink. Her tone was partly due to the coffee machine doing something hectic, but mainly because she habitually addressed people as if across a field and against a heavy wind. 'How many of those bastards you caught in your net today?'

David shrugged mysteriously. He knew Talia would interpret this as coyness over how many words he'd nonchalantly hammered out that morning, instead of realizing it meant *None. No words at all.*

She laughed raucously. 'You dog.'

They chatted, Talia filling him on some 'consultant' she'd met on an Internet forum and passing on the advice he'd granted her, which – as far as David could tell – was total nonsense. When she told him, in hushed tones and all seriousness, that the guy had revealed it was best not to sign submission letters on the grounds publishers employed teams of graphologists to divine the worth of your manuscript from tells in your signature, he had to cough to cover a laugh – a desire that quickly faded when it became clear this asshole had gotten Talia to PayPal him a hundred bucks before he handed up this and other pearls of wisdom.

'You know what, Tal?' he said. 'I'm not sure about that. Can't see them doing that when it'd be simpler to get an intern to flip through the manuscript.'

Talia looked at him. 'Could be.'

David wasn't sure she meant it. It seemed to him she might actually be saying, *Yeah, and what do you care, big shot? You've already got it made.*

But the moment passed, and David realized that envy was something he might have to get used to. In time, that seemed possible. The problem was going to be convincing himself he deserved it.

He'd been intending to take the drink home to consume virtuously at his desk, but as he turned from the counter he realized he couldn't face it and headed to a table instead. He'd carried a notebook all the time since he was thirteen years old. He could sit and think and jot *bon mots*. Be that kind of writer. Live the lifestyle.

Right. Except it turned out the lifestyle . . . kind of sucked. He didn't mind spending every day by himself. He'd always been a solitary person (or, as his father had once put it – to his face and in public – 'a total loner geek'). Since giving up his job, however, he'd written fifteen pages all told. When he'd been writing at the end of eight hours of wage slavery that had seemed okay. As the product of fifty full days' labor, it was not.

There was another problem, too.

What he'd written *wasn't any good*.

His first novel had been about someone rather like David. An everyman forging a life in a small town, blessed with big dreams and a bigger heart. The raw material had come easy, but it had taken two years and seven drafts to make it feel like he'd written it. The characters were well drawn and mildly interesting things happened to them and there was a crisis that got semi-resolved and some people lived happily ever after while others did not. Nobody was expecting it to storm the bestseller lists when it came out in six months' time, but it was the kind of book that genteel reading groups might take to and David's editor was confident it would get good word of mouth. It had a chance, in other words.

It had also, unfortunately, said just about all David had to say about what it was like to be David.

The publishers wanted another. David wasn't sure he had one, and the last month had done nothing to convince him otherwise. He'd started and scrapped three storylines already. It seemed possible that he could keep coming up with ideas and pushing them around the screen before abandoning them . . . *for the rest of his life.*

Which was why he was here, in the coffeehouse, trying to do something else. It wasn't working. Like their increasingly quiet and desperate attempts to get pregnant, there seemed to be some kind of block. Something invisible but real. Something they couldn't get past. Something *in the way*.

He turned from his notebook – to which he hadn't added a word – and looked out the window, summoning up the energy to go home.

Outside, people wandered up and down. Some seemed like they had pressing goals, others like leaves being blown nowhere in particular. It seemed for a moment like there was someone on the opposite side of the street, looking at the coffeehouse, but then he or she was gone.

'How's it going? Really?'

Talia had appeared on the other side of his table. She seemed diminished when not behind the counter.

'Not great.'

She sat, plunking her big elbows down and supporting her chubby face in her hands. 'Must be tough, huh?'

David couldn't tell how much irony this carried. 'What do you mean?'

'Dreaming dreams is easy. Living them, not so much. That's why they're called "dreams" instead of "lives."'

'Nice. I may write that down.'

'Check the copyright position. Think I heard it in a country-and-western song, which is how the eternal truths are most often revealed.' She smiled. 'You'll get there, David. You done it once, you can do it again.'

'Got proof?'

'I feel it in my bones. And I got heavy bones.'

There was a loud clattering, and they turned to see the door to the coffee shop had swung open by itself. They stared at it together, and laughed.

'Huh,' David said, getting up to close the door. 'Doesn't even look that windy out there.'

Talia looked enthused. 'That reminds me! You know George Lofland, right?'

'Works at Bedloe's? Not really. By sight.'

'Well, he was in here at the crack of dawn, like always – that guy actually drinks *too much* coffee – but he looked a little whacked, so I asked if he was okay.'

'And?'

'*And* so early yesterday evening he's driving back from his mother's on the other side of Libertyville – she's rocking Alzheimer's big-time – and he's coming home through the woods and he sees this guy by the road. It's cold and windy with a pissy little drizzle on top and George decides to take pity on the asshole. He pulls over, asks where he's going. The guy says Rockbridge and George tells him to hop in, but the passenger seat is full of work files so he should get in the back if he doesn't mind. George drives on and they talk about this and that, though not much – George ain't no great talker when he's not selling something, never has been – but then he pulls over on the street here to let the guy out . . . and guess what?'

'I have no idea.'

Talia leaned forward. 'He wasn't there.'

David laughed. '*What*?'

'For real, and like, O-M-fucking-G. George says, 'Okay, here we are' – there's no reply. He looks around and . . . dum dum DUM: the backseat's *empty*, dude. He jumps out of the car and goes around to check. But there's *no one there*.' She sat back and folded her arms. 'Freaky, no?'

'But . . . you realize that's a classic FOAF story, right?'

'FOAF? WTF?'

'Stands for "friend of a friend." As in "This weird thing happened to me, well, not to *me*, actually, but to a friend . . . In fact, it wasn't even a friend. It happened to the *friend* of a friend of mine. But it's totally true and . . ." and so on. It's a way of making a story seem real without taking responsibility for it.'

'Gotcha,' Talia said. 'Though, like I said, this actually happened to George, or so he says.'

'But I don't know George,' David said, 'so . . . he's a friend of a friend, to me.'

Talia worked this through in her head, and smiled – a dazzler that took off thirty years. 'I see what you done there, smart boy. Guess that's why you get paid the big bucks.'

David spread his hands in mock self-appreciation. 'When genius strikes.'

'Uh-huh. So why don't you take those smarts and go home and do some actual work?'

David laughed. 'Good advice, as always.'

'Right. It's on account of me being so fucking wise. Now push off. It's easier for me to steal cake if there's only Dylan around.'

Just before he opened the door, David turned back. 'Talia,' he said. He hesitated. 'Your novel?'

'You want to help me set fire to it? I got matches.'

'It's not like I know much, but if you wanted me to take a look . . . I'd be glad to. For what it's worth.'

Talia blinked. Never mind losing thirty years; suddenly she looked about fifteen. 'Oh, David, that would be so cool. I'll e-mail it to you tonight, soon as I get home. I know there's a lot of work to do on it, but . . . It would mean a lot to me, really.'

'Can't guarantee how quickly I can get back to you, is the only thing.'

'Oh, I understand, totally. And I won't bug you about it. I promise. David, that's so kind. Thank you.'

He nodded, feeling shy. 'What are friends for?'

He walked home knowing he was going to regret the gesture but telling himself you had to pay it forward or sideways or whatever the hell it was. He owed Talia for picking up his mood, not least because the old chestnut of the phantom hitchhiker was working at him, becoming an itch in the hard-to-define area in the back of his brain from which the ideas came (when and if they did).

He went straight up to the bedroom that had been designated his study. As he settled at his desk, the phone rang. He grabbed the handset while reaching for the keyboard. Once something started working at him he had to start typing it *right now*, or it would fly away.

'Yes?'

Nobody said anything. 'Miller house,' David said irritably. There was silence; then he heard a noise down the line. It was quiet, as if coming from a long way away. 'Can you hear me?'

Silence, then a distant, muttered sound that might have been words, but was impossible to make out. There was something about the tone that did not sound friendly.

David put the phone down. If it was important they'd call back or try his cell, and either way he didn't care.

He started typing, slowly at first, and then faster, and the next few hours disappeared to wherever they go when the page opens up like a six-lane highway, for once.

CHAPTER 10

I have never been good at walking away from things. This is not a boast, a declaration that I'm the kind of guy who will by God get things done and rah-rah for me in particular and testosterone in general. Quite the opposite. There have been times when I've manifestly failed to do the right thing, when I've hidden from problems and let my life degrade and rust. I suspect the truth is when I do try to leave a situation I'll run, not walk – but in a circle. I believe I'm escaping from the problem but spin around it instead, maintaining orbit until a gravitational change plunges me back into the center. This is what happened after the death of my son. There was a period in the wilderness of alcohol and then a spell of affectless calm working at a restaurant in Oregon. But after that came a return to a small town in Washington State, where it turned out I had unfinished business. People died during the resolution of this business. I might have thought I was walking away from something, but it wasn't so. I'd merely been killing time before pulling the pin out of the grenade.

89

Put more simply, Catherine's stalker was beginning to annoy the hell out of me.

Rather than take the subway, I'd elected to walk back from Clark's gallery, which was doubtless good for my heart but took a very long time. I didn't like the fact that I'd spent the whole way back thinking about Catherine's stalker. I didn't like that I was mad at myself for losing the guy when I'd tracked Catherine – and for undertaking that without telling Kristina. Something that was supposed to have been a quick favor had gotten under my skin, and I wanted the situation gone.

By the time I arrived weary-footed back at our apartment, Kristina had left for work. I turned straight around and went to join her. As we walked home hours later, I filled her in on the discussion with Clark. I could see her wishing she'd been there to take her own reading.

'You really don't think he's the guy?'

'No.'

'So . . . ?'

'So I don't know. I guess I should call Catherine, tell her that he's probably not the man. Probably she should talk to the cops. Log her suspicions, so if the situation ramps up it's a matter of record.'

'But you said Bill felt they probably wouldn't do much.'

I shrugged. I had said that, and he had said that, and I didn't know what more there was to add.

As we turned onto a side street that we customarily used on our journey home, there was a noise from up ahead that sent a chill down my back. It was a sound that said someone was in pain, or needed help, and badly. Half the lights in the street were out and it was impossible to see what might be happening.

We trotted up until we could tell the noise was coming from someone standing in the middle of the street. It was a woman, not young. She was shrieking, apparently at a brick wall on the other side of the street.

It was Lydia. Her body was rigid, arms held down hard and straight, as if in face-to-face confrontation with someone. I'd never seen her like this.

I covered the last yards cautiously, walking in an arc so I came around the front and she got a good chance to realize someone was approaching, and who it was.

'Lydia?'

She stopped screaming as if someone had punched a mute button, but maintained the same position, every stringy tendon and underfed muscle taut.

'Lyds? It's John.'

She turned her head and slowly seemed to recognize me. 'Is that you?'

'Yes. It's John. From the restaurant.'

'For real?'

'Yes.' I held my hands up in a way that was supposed to be reassuring. 'Was somebody giving you trouble?'

'It was Frankie,' she said. Her voice was even more of a rasp than usual. 'And he was *close.*'

She grabbed me with hands that were bony and surprisingly strong. 'I tried to catch up to him. But . . . he ran away from me. He saw it was me, and *he ran*. He didn't want to see me.'

She started to cry, irrevocably, the tears of a child, the worst kind of all: the tears of someone who feels all the hope in the world disappear at once.

Kristina waited a few yards down the street, sadness in her face. 'Lydia,' I said, but I didn't know where to go afterward. The things it made sense to say – that the person hadn't really been there, or was some random stoner or thief taking a back route home and who ran because he'd been startled by being chased by an elderly street person – were not explanations she was going to accept.

Instead I put my arms around her shoulders. She did not smell good and I knew there would be a significant community of small, unwelcome insect life about her clothing, so I made the hug tight but quick.

'It's been a while,' I said, stepping back. 'Maybe he was just surprised to see you. Or maybe he feels shy or embarrassed that it's been so long.'

She gave this some thought. 'You think?'

'I don't know. But it could be. Right?'

She looked up at me hopefully, as if I'd told her that the pet we'd just buried together was absolutely *definitely* going to heaven. 'Maybe you're right.'

'You going to be okay?'

'Of course,' she said, old again. She stomped to the sidewalk to retrieve her bags. 'Why wouldn't I be?'

We watched as she headed off into the darkness that nests in the shadows of tall buildings in the night.

The next morning I called Catherine. I outlined my conversation with Clark but didn't pass on his interpretation of her behavior, or his final message. I suggested she talk to the cops. She uttered a sound that made it seem unlikely she would follow this advice – and perhaps it was this kind of thing that caused her to rub me the wrong way. She considered her options and made selections rather than drifting along highways of least resistance. Yes, she'd dropped Thomas Clark after she'd met Mark (I hadn't failed to notice that, in her version of events, it had happened that way around), but that made sense too. It's a cute idea that you can remain buddies with ex-lovers, but woefully adolescent. Love is not a charm that pops into the world from a better place to bless two individuals before flitting back home, leaving the couple broken back in two parts and forlorn but fundamentally unchanged. Love is a fire that burns in the soul, sometimes for good, sometimes just for now, sometimes hot enough to scorch and sometimes with a low and sustainable glow. Either way, it leaves the original constituents permanently altered. After the fact everything is different – not just the relationship, but the people involved. I didn't blame Catherine for what she'd done, but I was glad it wasn't me who'd fallen in love with her.

'Thank you,' she said.

'No problem,' I said. 'You've got our numbers. You get the sense something's up, then call, okay?'

I was about to add something designed to sound upbeat, but the line went dead. I realized that was something else that pissed me off about her. Always having to be the one in control.

Whatever. I was done. I made a cup of coffee and took it over to the rear window of the main room. I opened it and climbed out onto the ten-foot-square patch of roof outside, which I had colonized as my personal smoking domain. There's not much competition, to be honest, what with it being inaccessible from any other building and half submerged under bits of wind-blown debris and discarded material from long-ago roof maintenance. A few birds perch there once in a while, but even they don't seem to like it much. Soon after we moved into the apartment – disinclined to trudge down a billion stairs every time I wanted to fuck up my lungs – I semi-civilized the area with a battered chair I'd found on the street and a heavy glass ashtray from a thrift store. It's the little piece of New York that I can call my own.

I sat and looked out across the rooftops and listened to the street noise from below, sipped my coffee, and smoked a cigarette, and I told myself the Catherine Warren story was over.

I tell myself a lot of things.

CHAPTER 11

Meanwhile, Bob stands on the corner. He is on this corner every day except weekends. He stands there between the hours of ten in the morning and four in the afternoon, and he waits. There's always someone here. Most corners are covered only a few hours a day, to a schedule written by a Fingerman in chalk on the sidewalk or low on a wall nearby, someplace you wouldn't notice unless you were looking for it. If by chance they caught your eye, you might assume they related to a scheme of public works. They don't. A circle means daylight. The figure to the left indicates the start time, the one on the right, the number of hours it will run. A crescent works the same, but for night, obviously. At these corners you have to get there within the correct time frame or no one's going to be around and you're neither going to be able to leave a message, nor pick one up.

Bob's corner is in business twenty-four-seven and three-sixty-five. There are only five like it in the whole of Manhattan, and this one at the southern point of Union Square is the oldest of all. It's said that someone has been manning the spot for over sixty years. It could be longer, no one's sure, but word of mouth (the testimony of trusted friends among the Gathered, be they ever so hollow now) puts it back to the late 1940s without a doubt. Before that it gets cloudy, but if you come now, someone will always be there.

These are the Cornermen, and Bob is proud to be one of them.

The first qualification is the ability to keep in movement – the right *kind* of movement. Most people don't see past their own eyes, but there's always someone who does, or might. Children, animals – cats especially – plus the old and the slightly crazy. You have to keep in flux or a dog might start barking or madman try to strike up a conversation. Bob's corner is set up for movement, which might account for its longevity. There's a lot of foot traffic. Four days a week there's the greenmarket, plus the Strand Book Store and the B&N and Whole Foods. Even without those banner destinations it'd constitute the major cross-roads at this point in town. The most noticeable features in a river are the rocks that stand their ground. And so you move.

The second requirement is a good memory. Nothing gets written down. Most couldn't, anyway – anybody with that kind of skill would be promoted to Fingerman, which even Bob acknowledges is the premium role. Many of the

97

messages are straightforward instructions or pieces of information. Others are more personal. When a message is given to a Cornerman, he or she will hold it in confidence until it's passed, after which they'll forget it. Bob doesn't make moral judgments. It is not his place nor in his nature. Make the job any more complicated than it already is and the system would break down fast.

You need a memory for faces, too. Some will have made an arrangement ahead of time, but with many the message will be left merely in the hope the intended recipient will happen to pass. With those it's Bob's job to keep an eye out for the friend in question. When he sees them coming, he will move into their path and tell them what he's been asked to tell, before moving on, glancing back to make sure the message got across.

Then Bob forgets the message, to free up space for the next. At any given time he has maybe forty in his head. Twenty percent are broadcasts – 'Mention to everyone you see that . . .' Seventy percent are personal, one-to-one 'asks' – as in: 'Ask Diana to meet me at the corner of x and y at eight o'clock this Friday night.'

The remaining one in ten are the messages Bob doesn't like. They're the ones that never got where they were supposed to go. Once recently he happened to walk past old St Patrick's and saw someone against the interior wall of the boneyard there. Bob had been holding a message for this guy for over six months, but when he saw him slumped against the wall in twilight he knew it was too late. He went in and passed the message anyway, whispering it into the friend's ear. The Hollow slowly raised his head. There was no recognition in his eyes (though Bob had passed him perhaps a hundred messages down the years) and no suggestion that he'd understood.

Now and then you'd hear someone had gone for good – getting the Bloom and burning out, or much more rarely flicking off the light by themselves. Bob wasn't a romantic person and his expectations of life were low, but holding that last message in his head, for a person who'd passed on, was a way of giving them longer in the world, prolonging a life that had likely been full of neglect. He'd heard it was a tradition among retiring Cornermen to get a Fingerman to write down these orphaned messages, a representative word or two of them at least – on a wall or under a bridge – so they never died.

Bob didn't know if that was true, but that's what *he* was going to do. He'd ask Maj, probably. Maj had skills and was friendly, most of the time.

Everybody deserves to be remembered. Without that you're nothing.

It was almost three, only an hour before he would be relieved of his post and could go somewhere warmer, when Bob saw someone heading purposefully toward him.

He immediately felt tense. This friend often had messages. Recently they had been getting more frequent. They'd stopped making sense, too, and Bob was smart enough to know that implied they were in code. Since when did friends need code? Code said there were messages that were for some ears and not others. Bob didn't like the feel of that. They were supposed to be pulling together. That's what his job was about and why the Gathered had always stressed its importance – doing something for the greater good. Messages for the greater good do not need to be obscured, surely?

'Hey, Fictitious,' Golzen said. He looked even more self-important than usual. 'Got a broadcast.'

They always were, with Golzen. He didn't speak – he proclaimed.

'I'm listening.'

The two men kept walking, not looking at each other, in slow circular movement, like an eddy of wind.

'Broadcast runs: "For the twelve. Be ready. Follow signs until Jedburgh appears." Message ends.'

'That it?'

'That's all it needs,' Golzen said. 'You got it?'

''Course I got it.'

Golzen walked away. Bob ran the message through one time to lock it in his mind, and got ready to tell it to everyone he saw. That was his

100

job, and he was going to do it the best he could, as always.

He had no way of knowing how many people would die.

CHAPTER 12

David happened to be passing through the hall when Dawn got home. He felt guilty when he heard her key in the lock, as if he should be at his desk typing instead of self-indulgently larking about voiding his bladder.

'Just been to the john,' he said.

'Thanks for the status update.' She kissed him on the cheek. 'I'll be sure to like and retweet.'

Then she turned him around and felt up his ass. 'Well, hi,' he said, surprised.

She kept exploring his right buttock. 'You keep it here, don't you?'

'Actually, it's around the front,' he said, deadpan. 'I've been meaning to talk to you about that.'

She swatted his chest. 'Funny. Your loose change, I *meant*. You keep it in your back right pocket.'

'Well, yes. Though there's none at the moment.'

'Right. It's here.' She held up her other hand. Cupped in the palm was a couple of dollars' worth of quarters. David made like a question mark.

'It was lying on the step outside,' she said. 'I assumed you had a hole in your pocket and it fell out.'

102

'No. I put it in the pot like normal.'

'And there *is* no hole in your pocket. Which is what I was establishing, for the avoidance of doubt.'

As she plunked her bag on the chair and took off her coat, she peered into the pot on the table. The pot was squareish and unevenly glazed in unfashionable colors, the product of some long-ago creative urge or spasm of suburban boredom on the part of David's mother, and one of the few mementoes he had of her. It held small change leavened with buttons, paper clips, and a couple of dollar bills. 'So what was this doing outside?'

'No idea. Where was it, exactly?'

'Top step. Right in the middle.'

As Dawn headed kitchenward to begin assessing her charges' entanglements with the mysteries of basic math, David looked back at the three steps that led down from their door to the path and then out at the street.

There was nothing to see except a cloudy, darkening sky and the branches of trees that were starting to shiver from the top down.

David read a little more of Talia's book while putting together a pasta/salad dinner. The novel was . . . surprisingly okay, in fact. He'd already lost track of who the characters were, who they were in conflict with and why, but he decided to let it wash over him on the assumption that it would probably become clear. In the meantime it was easy to read and occasionally pretty funny or moving and in general starting to freak David out, through demonstrating he wasn't special after all and clearly *anyone* could write – and look, Talia wrote a *lot* more than he did, every day and all the time, without making such a big song and dance about it.

When supper was on the table, they ate in companionable silence, listening to the world outside. The wind was now buffeting the house with serious intent. Local news said it was going to be a big storm.

'That was nice,' Dawn said, setting her fork aside. There were a couple of mouthfuls left, but David had come to believe this was not a negative review but an ingrained nod toward keeping an eye on her weight.

'We aim to please.'

'You didn't come by the school today, did you?'

'No. Why?'

'Angela thought she saw a man standing outside the gates, mid-afternoon. When she went to see what he wanted he'd gone. She said it could have been you.'

'I've been here all day.'

'Working hard.'

'Right. And why would I come to the school anyway?'

'That's what I said. I also reminded her of the existence of cell phones. I like Angela, but I'm amazed she can find her way out of the house every morning.'

'Maybe she leaves a paper trail. Of unmarked art assignments.'

Dawn didn't reply. Normally the good-hearted dissing of her coworkers was something she enjoyed. She was not the kind of person to ever be rude to their faces, and didn't really *mean* most of it, but it was her low-key way of letting go of daily frustrations.

Not tonight, evidently. David tilted his head. 'You okay?'

'Yes, why?'

'Seem a little preoccupied, is all.'

'I'm fine.'

But she wasn't, quite. 'So . . . everything's okay?'

'Yes, worry-guts. Apart from the dumb-ass questions, anyway. And the weather. *Listen* to it out there.'

The wind got a lot louder and more violent, peaking in occasional mournful howls. As they watched a final chunk of random television, there was a banging sound out in the yard. They looked at each other, eyebrows raised, and David got up and went to the back window.

'Wow,' he said. 'It's the end times.'

Rain was lashing down from what appeared to be all directions. A newspaper appeared, in several installments, blown over the fence. It spun chaotically around the yard before reversing direction and rocketing toward the bench that stood in the middle. An austere wrought-iron two-seater, this had been a moving-gift of Dawn's parents. It stood in the middle of the yard because that's where Dawn's father liked to sit when he came to visit. David found the thing uncomfortable.

'What's happening? Is anything down?'

David was distracted by the newspaper. It looked like it was stuck on something. It could only have been the strange flicker light caused by branches moving back and forth in front of the moon, but it seemed almost as if the paper had become plastered around a shape on the bench, as if someone was sitting there.

Two seconds later it was yanked back up into the sky. The bench was empty. Of course.

'Nothing,' David said. 'Just the wind.'

Dawn was out long before he was. Sleep was Dawn's buddy and welcomed her with a warm smile and open arms. Sleep got a little goddamned fresh with Dawn, as a matter of fact. It was different for David. Sleep was the soul sister to his muse, and treated him much the same way. Sometimes she would be all friendly and hey-how's-it-going. At others she looked at him sideways, and with disdain, as if he'd suggested playing Twister, just the two of them.

After lying patiently on his right side and then his left, as was his practice, he wound up on his back listening to the wind. He tried to empty his mind, but after a while he made the decision to think about work instead. He could feel it stirring tendrils of panic but he kept focused on this for as long as he could, though he knew it was generally a one-way train to insomniaville.

Pretty soon he found himself running over the very thing he'd been attempting to avoid, however. The money Dawn had found on the top step.

It bugged him. He didn't understand why it bugged him quite so much. Sure, it was odd, but there could be mundane explanations. He'd already come up with several. Each had checked out for credibility, but then been dismissed. Why was that? Why did he think there was something more, something that he should know, and be taking seriously?

He couldn't remember, and that made him uncomfortable.

A while later it seemed like he'd managed to fall asleep after all, or at least be on the verge. He was distantly aware of the sound of the wind outside, sprays of rain thrown like gravel over the roof and windows, and the sound of some small metallic object cartwheeling down the road outside. Probably a stray soda can.

Then someone knocked on the door.

David lay rigid, listening so hard that the blood in his ears sounded like footsteps in the attic space above. He didn't hear anything else for a while. But then . . .

Yes, there it was again.

Someone was knocking on the front door of the house.

He got up and pulled on his robe, quietly left the room, and went downstairs. The noise had stopped. Now that he was up and about, David felt he'd better check, in case . . . in case . . . *what*? He wasn't sure. For whatever reason, you checked these things. He'd thought he'd heard a knocking and that could mean a neighbor was outside, desperate after an accident or a branch had come crashing through their roof. Either way, you checked out a noise. That was what grown-ups did, grown-up men in particular. It was the law.

As he unlocked the door, David realized how unconvinced he was that he *was* a grown-up after all.

Buffeted by the wind, the door flew open so hard that he had to use both hands to stop it swinging around to crash against the wall. Once he got it stable, he stepped forward to take a better look.

There was no one outside.

The lamp that hung above the doorway cast a light unequal to the conditions. It did enough, however, to show that on the top step, where Dawn had found the small change, something small and flat and square now lay.

David picked it up, squinting against the rain being driven into his face. It was a matchbook.

Plain white on the outside, with the name of

a bar – Kendricks – in red, and an address on the back.

It *could* have been dropped out on the road and blown across the yard to here.

David opened the matchbook. At first he thought the inside of the flap was plain too, and unmarked. As he moved it against the light he saw something. He held it up and looked more closely.

It was hard to tell if the marks had been made with a pen whose ink had run dry, or a fingernail, or toothpick. There were just three characters.

5pM

David thought it likely that the time and the name on the outside of the matchbook were supposed to be a message. The message could be a reminder for whoever had dropped the matchbook, in theory, the hypothetical person for whose existence he had no proof, only hope.

He didn't think so, though.

He slipped the matchbook into the pocket of his robe and went back inside and up to the bedroom.

He lay on his back, hands down by his sides, until an overcast morning finally arrived.

CHAPTER 13

This time it wasn't so cold, but it was raining, a persistent drizzle that reminded me of summer in Oregon. The upside was this empowered me to wear a workman's jacket with turned-up collar, which I borrowed from the thrift store near the restaurant. As I was likely to be in close proximity to Catherine for at least some of the afternoon, this could help keep me from being spotted too quickly – by her or anybody else. Wearing the coat made me feel ridiculous, but no more than being there in the first place. At least I wasn't alone this time.

The 'walking away' approach hadn't worked out. I didn't know whether this was down to the unhappiness I'd heard in Catherine's voice before she put down the phone or if I was an asshole who couldn't let things lie, but Kristina and I wound up talking about it and it became clear I was looking for ways of refining the investigation rather than ending it. Kristina hadn't helped by pointing out that (probably) removing Thomas Clark from the picture had made the situation *worse*, rather than better, for Catherine. What's more unsettling than being followed by someone you know? Being followed by someone you *don't* know. The threat level of a stranger is much harder to gauge. The only thing you can be sure of is their intentions are unlikely to be good.

Mario had been annoyed when I'd told him I wouldn't be able to cover for Jimmy that afternoon. Not as far as I was concerned – there are squirrels who can do my job – but because of Kristina and the bar. I reassured him we'd be back in plenty of time for evening service, and he was mollified, but gave me a lingering look as I left. It made me realize this was becoming too much of a hobby. We'd spent a lot of the last week talking about it – so much that it had even taken the idea of moving to the Village out of the picture. I wasn't sure what our joint obsession said about us or our lives. Perhaps, though I'd thought I was content to be a waiter living in a tiny apartment, the reality was I'd allowed myself to float downstream into a pleasant backwater that part of me knew was insufficient. I also had the feeling I was pandering to some unwholesome impulse – and not just to my own.

As we reached the sidewalk after leaving the apartment, I stopped and looked meaningfully at Kristina. 'This is it,' I told her. 'If nothing comes of this afternoon, I'm done. So are you.'

She cocked her head, but saw my face and

nodded. She knew we were getting fixated too. 'You're the boss.'

'Yeah, right.'

The idea – Kristina's – was to observe Catherine picking her daughters up from school, on the grounds that this was another predictable routine in her life. Once again, Catherine would be unaware we were watching. The Gower School is small and boutique and stands on the north side of 15th between Ninth and Tenth, sandwiched between town houses on a quiet and leafy Chelsea street. It had a cute hand-painted sign declaring that it specialized in the methods of Montessori or Steiner or some other educational haute cuisine. That made sense. Catherine Warren wasn't going to just go ahead and trust the New York school system. She'd have spent time researching the alternatives and debating the issue with husband and friends and selecting first the ideology and then its outpost, yet another existential choice in her life. I envied her this level of constant self-determination while knowing that I simply didn't have the energy.

We got to the street at 2:40. School got out at three o'clock. Early birds were spread along the sidewalk, chatting or consulting smart-phones, some huddled under umbrellas, others braving the drizzle without.

'How are we going to do this?'

'We take opposite ends of the block,' I said.

'I'll call you when I get down there, and we keep the line open. Holding the phones will give us cover, too.'

Kristina nodded. 'Nice.'

'When one of us sees Catherine, we say so, and stay put. The person at the *opposite* end drifts toward the school on the other side of the street. The other holds their position on the assumption Catherine will leave the street the same way she came in. When she comes back past with the kids, that person follows at a distance. The other walks parallel a block away, taking the third man role. This is assuming that—'

I noticed Kristina was grinning. 'What?'

'Can I buy you one of those slouch hats to go with that coat?'

'That won't be necessary.'

'Oh, go on. Once we solve this case, can we set up a private detective agency?'

'Ain't going to happen. And it's not a "case." And remember what I said about this being the end of it.'

She pouted and walked over to stand on the corner.

I walked briskly down the street and past the school. Weaving through the scattering of women near the school gate, I was confident they were all mothers. Mothers are the backbone of reality and the ether feels different around them. They broadcast a signal, even the ones that are convinced they're doing a lousy job. There was one male

113

present, but he had a very tidy beard and was chatting earnestly with two women who might as well have had the word 'parent' tattooed on their foreheads, so I was content to assume he was someone's telecommuting/creative/unemployed dad. When I got to Tenth, I looked back along the street and got out my phone.

Kristina answered quickly. 'Nothing?'

'Nothing,' I said.

'So now?'

'We wait.'

'That's all we *can* do now . . . wait,' Kristina intoned solemnly, and giggled.

'I hope you're taking this seriously.'

'Absolutely.'

'Good.'

'By the way, I've never been more attracted to you than I am right now.'

'Could be because we're eighty yards apart.'

'You know, I think that might be it.'

'Great. Now shh. Concentrate. If you want to diss me you can do it later, at leisure, in the comfort of our own ratty little home.'

And so we waited, in silence. Meanwhile the clouds got darker and the tips of my fingers started to go white.

'I'm hungry,' Kristina muttered. 'And cold.'

'Shh.'

At five minutes to the hour the street got a lot busier – many mothers evidently operating a just-in-time policy. They came toward the school from both ends like hordes of exceptionally well-groomed zombies. I panned my gaze across the throng, phone still up to my ear, walking in a circle as if in conversation. I didn't see anybody odd. Just mothers. En masse.

'Got her,' Kristina said. 'Brown coat. Walking fast, north side of the street.'

I started to head back along the sidewalk opposite the school. When I was fifty yards away, I slowed and stepped out into the street, skirting around the back of the main knot of people but keeping close enough to the fringes to remain part of the crowd.

Seconds later I spotted Catherine cutting through the gathered with the air of a woman who was by God going to be at the gates by 3:00:00. She got there with moments to spare and exchanged a businesslike nod with the teacher in black pantsuit who was manning the gate, clipboard in hand.

'Catherine's at the gate,' I said, cutting through the women to aim toward the sidewalk on the school side of the street, a decent distance from Catherine, so I could covertly look back through the crowd in the hope of spotting anyone taking an interest in her.

'And the condor flies tonight,' Kris intoned.

'Shut up.'

Before I even got to the sidewalk I noticed someone back in the mix, obscured behind the bearded man and two women. A knot of umbrellas

115

prevented me from seeing the newcomer's face, but I saw enough.

Tall, slim, in a long black coat.

'Got him,' I muttered into the phone.

'You sure?'

'Same guy. Even the same coat. Hold your position – I'm going to try to get around back.'

I started moving away, attempting to keep a line of people between me and the man. This was hard to do without banging into people, and there was a certain amount of maternal muttering.

'What's he doing now?'

'I don't know,' I said.

'What do you mean?'

The truth was, I'd lost sight of him. I started trying to arc through the crowd toward the back, near to where I'd seen him last. Over at the gate Catherine was waving at two little girls running across the small playground on the other side of the fence.

I looked back across the press of women focused on the school gate. I caught a glimpse of the dark coat through a gap. He seemed to be heading away. To leave? Or to get in position so he was ready to follow?

Catherine was leading her daughters away, but coming in my direction. I hurriedly turned my back.

'Change of plan,' I muttered. I gave Catherine twenty seconds and set off after her, trying to remain discreet. 'She's coming this way.'

'So now what do I do?'

'Head up Ninth. No, actually . . . come up this way too.'

Catherine was near the corner of Tenth now. The man in the coat was still following her, about forty yards back. I got a clear enough view of him from behind to confirm that the coat was very long, almost floor length, and he had thick, dark hair.

I had to turn away for a moment after banging into a mother with three apparently identical boys, but looked back in time to see one of Catherine's daughters disappearing around the corner holding her mother's hand.

But now I couldn't see the man in the coat. Kristina arrived at my shoulder, breathing hard. 'What's he doing now?'

'I've lost him again. Catherine just left the street. Come on.'

I started to trot. When we turned onto Tenth, I fanned wide to the edge of the sidewalk and saw Catherine hurrying her children up the block. 'I still don't see . . .'

'Is that him?'

Kristina was pointing across the avenue. 'It can't be,' I said, peering at a figure up at the next intersection on the other side. 'There's no way he could have . . . But yes, that's him.'

'What are we going to do?'

'Follow Catherine. I'm going over there.'

The traffic along the avenue was heavy but slow, snarled by the rain. I threaded across the street between cars and yellow cabs, glancing back to see Kristina heading up the other side after Catherine, and doing it right, not closing the gap too much.

By the time I got to the other side, the figure had crossed 15th and was heading up the next block. I hurried after, trying to work out how to play the next few minutes. The chances now looked high that the guy was going to track Catherine to 18th Street and her house. She'd told me she'd thought she'd seen someone on her corner, so he evidently knew where she lived. The question was if he'd go further today – and follow her right to her door – or if he'd hang back as usual. I had to make a judgment call and I didn't want to get it wrong, because something told me we were seeing a ramping up.

Following a woman on her own is one thing. Doing it when she's got kids with her is far more serious.

We were closing in on 18th. I saw Kristina slowing so as not to be too obvious. The person in the coat was a block ahead of me now, walking fast with his head down, but showed no signs of crossing the road – and so I signaled to Kris to abandon Catherine and come to my side instead, waving to indicate she should go on half a block before she crossed so the guy in the coat would be stuck between us.

She got it, taking a diagonal course across the road, jogging up between the two lanes of traffic.

I started walking faster too, closing the distance with the man ahead. When Kris reached the sidewalk, she was sixty yards in front. She caught sight of the guy in the coat, glanced back for instructions.

I pointed at him and mouthed the word 'Now.'

We started to run toward each other, matching pace so he would be trapped between us. It struck me that we hadn't established a plan for what would happen at that point. I hadn't really believed it would arise.

'Hey,' I said loudly when I was down to ten feet. 'I want to talk to you.'

The figure stopped dead and turned.

It was a woman.

Slim and tall with thick, dark hair and strong features, eyes the gray end of blue.

She stared at me like a cornered animal, body tensed for flight. Kristina faltered ten feet away on the other side, seeing the same as me and not knowing what to do.

Disbarred from throwing myself at the person and tackling her to the ground, I hesitated.

It was enough. The woman darted away from us and across the street with disconcerting speed.

I lunged across the street just as the lights went green. Kristina got stuck, so I left her to it and ran. On the other side of the avenue I slipped on the wet curb and went careering across the side-walk. By the time I got my balance, the woman was half a block down the avenue, headed back the way we'd just come, looking like she was going to take the turn onto 16th street.

I ran after her. She'd gotten a head start, but I'm pretty fit and was gathering speed fast. I hurtled around the corner and onto 16th, confident that somewhere along its hundred-yard stretch I'd be able to catch her.

I got twenty yards down the street before realizing I couldn't see her anymore. I kept moving, looking both ways, at passing doorways, even up at first-floor windows, convinced I was somehow just being dumb.

By halfway along I knew it wasn't so. The street was deserted but for a man at the bottom of one of the redbrick staircases I'd noticed a couple of nights before. He was middle-aged and dressed in a brown corduroy suit and watching me with an amused expression.

When I got closer I realized that he was wearing a priest's collar. I stopped running.

'Is everything okay?' His voice was calm and friendly.

I tried to catch my breath, looking back and forth up the street. 'Did you just see somebody?'

He raised one eyebrow eloquently.

'A woman,' I said. 'Long coat. Must have come past here about a minute before I did.'

'I'm sorry,' he said. 'I've just this moment come out. Is something wrong?'

'No,' I said. 'Everything's fine.'

I saw a winded-looking Kristina turning onto the street, and walked irritably away from the priest.

Kris was panting. 'Any sign?'

'No,' I said. 'She vanished.'

'But it *was* a woman, right?'

'Yes.'

'That changes things, doesn't it?'

'Yes.'

'So now what?'

'I don't know.'

CHAPTER 14

When David walked into Kendricks at a quarter of five, he realized how long it had been since he'd gone to a bar outside Rockbridge's downtown area. Bars downtown make an effort. There are napkins with logos, the staff were perky, and high chairs are available. They downplay the alcohol side of things and pitch themselves as no big deal, a place you can go as part of a perfectly sane existence and enjoy an afternoon from which you will not emerge on all fours or married to someone deplorable.

Bars outside the city limits are different. Plenty are decent businesses who chose their position on the basis of zoning, convenience to the highway, or any number of reasonable criteria – including the one that says this is where the bar's always been and who knows why or cares, and look, do you want a beer or not, pal. Their clientele will be more varied, however, and many of these people (and bars) aren't going to a lot of trouble to hide the bottom line: they're here because they don't need to be anyplace else and because liquor is served and they want a big old glass of it, right now, with a peace-and-quiet chaser.

Situated just outside Rockbridge by Route 74, Kendricks was firmly in the latter camp. It had been in business forty years and had an unusually large metal sign over it that once sported an apostrophe before the 'S,' but it blew down long ago and nobody had given enough of a crap to do anything about it, including Ryan Kendrick himself. The rusted punctuation mark was believed to still be around someplace, possibly in the overgrown creek that ran along the back of the parking lot. Once in a while the more intrepid sort of drunkard might amuse himself by having a look for it before lurching home. Kendrick died in 2008, following a short, bare-knuckle fight with lung cancer, and after a couple of years during which the bar seemed to change hands almost nightly, it had found its level once more, settling back into bleary, boozy equilibrium. Battered furniture, a pair of battered pool tables, a battered wooden bar, and some pretty battered regulars – these last in low numbers and staking out the corners with their backs to the door. Music played in the background, not too loud. Some guy earnestly advertised something or other on the TV screen above the bar, pointlessly, the sound off.

David tried to remember the last time he'd been in the place. It had to be five or six years, soon after he started seeing Dawn. Kendrick himself had still been alive, though a shell of the hulking bad-ass he'd once been. It had been a sketchy bar then. It was a sketchy bar now.

David got a beer from a barman who looked like he'd just received bad news about his dog. He took it to a table in the darkest corner and sat with his back to the door. It was unlikely he'd see anyone he knew, but the drinking-in-the-afternoon look was one he'd prefer to avoid. He hadn't wanted alcohol at all, but the barman didn't look like he'd respond positively to a request for a low-fat latte, extra shot or not.

David took a cautious sip of the beer and looked at a poster for a long-ago gig on the wall. Why was he even here? After a long night without sleep, he wasn't sure. However hard he'd tried to work, his mind kept returning to the change left on their top step. For some reason that was working at him even more than the matchbook. It reminded him of something, but he didn't know what. He kept trying to push it out of his head. It kept coming back. Each time it returned it felt as if someone was gripping his guts a little tighter in their fist.

He'd decided that he would come here and sit for half an hour. Dawn had a staff meeting and wouldn't be back until nine, so that was covered. He had the matchbook in his pocket and intended to leave it on the table when he went, along with any notion that there was something he was failing to remember.

If you spend your life trying to make things mean something, it can be hard to stop when you get up from your desk at the end of the workday. That was all this was. Some unexplained change. A few scratch marks. Big deal.

In twenty-five minutes he was walking away.

'Hello, David.'

David looked up, heart thumping. A man was standing over the table. He was lean and wearing jeans and a white shirt under a dark coat. His skin was tan, chin stubbled, and he had sharp blue eyes.

It was the man David had seen in Penn Station. The man who'd followed him. Seeing him again was like hearing a phone ring in the dead of night.

'Who . . .'

'Is this chair free?'

David stared dumbly up at him. The man grinned back, a little too wide. 'But then – are *any* of us truly free?'

'What?'

'You used to say that. It was funny.'

'I have no idea what you're talking about.'

The man sat in the chair opposite. 'It'll come.'

'What are you doing here?'

'I came to see you, of course.'

David put the matchbook on the table. 'I bumped into you in New York. It was an accident. I saw you again at the train station. That's all I know.'

'No. That's all you *remember*.'

'Look, is this some kind of scam? Because—'

The man held a finger up to his lips. 'Don't talk

so much. You'll learn more that way. And it'll look less weird while you remember how things are done.'

Despite himself, David lowered his voice. 'What are you talking about? What things?'

The man picked up David's beer and took an unhurried sip, before placing the glass back exactly where it had been on the table.

David stared at him. 'Are you *kidding* me?'

The man settled back and folded his hands behind his head. 'Look around, friend.'

David did so. The barman was watching an advert for a barbecue set. The other drinkers were staring into their glasses or space or, in the case of one throwback, reading a paperback novel.

'I didn't choose five o'clock by accident,' the man said. 'Afternoon shift's wandered home or too drunk to care. The evening crowd isn't here yet. In the meantime, everyone's giving each other plenty of space.'

'So?'

'Nobody saw what I did. So it didn't happen. Nobody sees, nobody knows, right? Does *that* ring a bell?'

David swallowed. It did, though he didn't know why. 'How did you find out where I live?'

'I saw the train you left the city on. 'Course that wouldn't have led me to this bump in the road, except I also overheard your wife mention some-where called Rockbridge. It wasn't hard and I'm not dumb. I usually get what I want. You should remember that.'

David felt the hand tighten around his guts – this time far worse than before, as if long fingernails were digging in. 'I'm going to leave now.'

'Don't. We've got a chance here, David. We can be friends again. That almost never happens.'

David tried to sound calm and firm. 'Look, I don't have much money. I don't have *anything* you might want.'

'You're so wrong,' the man said, leaning forward earnestly. 'Just being here like this, seeing Dawn . . . you have no idea of how much that means. And she's wonderful. You did well, my friend. Congratulations.'

David stared, chilled by the way the man had casually dropped his wife's name. 'This is going to stop,' he said. '*Now*. Or I'm walking out of here and going straight to the—'

There was a rasping noise.

The man swore and pulled a cheap cell phone out of his jacket, the disposable type that comes with pre-paid credit and no contract. The kind, David gathered from watching cop shows, that are called 'burners' and are favored by the criminal fraternity because they're easy to come by and dispose of. Was that what this guy was? Part of a group who'd singled him out for a complex shakedown – some real-world version of an e-mail phishing scam?

'I have to take this,' the man said. He looked torn. The phone vibrated again. 'You'll stay?'

His tone made David realize this encounter was more inexplicable than he'd realized. There was no threat in it, rather a kind of entreaty.

The phone rasped once more and the man got up and walked away, gesturing for David to stay where he was.

When he heard the door to the bar open and shut, David let out a shuddering breath. His hands were shaking. What should he do? There was only one way out of the place and if the guy was in the lot he'd be bound to see him. If David walked, would he follow? If so, what then? The man hadn't done anything overtly threatening. If anything, his mood had been one of off-kilter good cheer – albeit the kind of dark cheer that sometimes escalates into pulling out a concealed weapon.

David wanted to put distance between them. Leaving the bar was the only way. Walking out – and then talking to the cops. He'd seen too many movies where the hero kept quiet about some whacked-out situation for too long. He wasn't going to be that guy – especially now that he remembered Dawn saying Angela had thought she'd seen David outside the school gates.

She hadn't seen David, but perhaps she had seen *someone*. A man who'd just dropped Dawn's name into the conversation as if he knew her.

Or as if he had been watching her.

There was a coughing sound. David quickly turned, convinced the man had somehow slipped back in without him hearing. It was a man in his mid-fifties, however, heavy in the gut, with a broad, fleshy face. He stood a few yards behind David's chair, beer in hand.

David realized it was George, the guy who worked at Bedloe's Insurance up the street from his old office at It's Media.

'Hey,' the man said.

David nodded cautiously. 'George, right?'

'You're the writer guy. Friend of Talia's.'

'Yes.' One out of two, at least. It was the first time someone had referred to him as 'the' or even 'a' writer. It didn't feel a close fit. Meanwhile, the other man kept looking oddly at him.

'You okay, George?'

'It's been a strange week,' the man muttered.

David got the sense that George was a couple beers down already. Also that what he probably meant was the story he'd told Talia, about the hitchhiker who disappeared. David didn't know whether he was supposed to know about that. He was only a friend of a friend, after all.

'Huh,' he said, in the hope this would cover it.

'You here alone?'

'Yes,' David said, fighting the impulse to glance toward the door. Right now that was the truth. It occurred to him this might even be some kind of come-on, but if so he had no idea of how to respond.

'Really?'

'You see anyone?'

'No. Thought I did, though. Couple minutes ago. Sitting opposite you.'

The back of David's neck twitched.

'Didn't see him leave,' George went on thought-fully, as if to himself. 'Did you?'

'I'm not here with anyone,' David repeated.

George looked at the chair opposite a moment longer. 'Yeah, well, okay. Sorry to have bothered you.'

He wandered back toward the far corner. David waited until George settled at a table there, and then he got up and left the bar, taking care not to catch anyone's eye.

Outside it was dark with storm clouds and the wind was picking up. Cars and trucks stood at discreet distances from one another, like people awaiting the results of blood tests that would not reflect well on their lifestyles.

Down at the far end of the building David saw a shadow beneath the dim corner light. After a moment he heard a voice, too. It sounded like someone on the phone.

He marched toward it. The man must have heard him approaching, because he slipped around the corner into deeper shadow, presumably to protect his privacy. This was the final straw for David, who felt that *his* privacy had been plenty invaded.

'I don't know what you want,' he said loudly as he rounded the corner to confront the man. 'But if I see you again, I'm going straight to the—'

There was nobody there. The side of the bar was a graveyard for broken wooden crates. There were a few battered and rusting gas canisters and some old sacking too, tangled in the long grass like brown ghosts.

Nothing – and nobody – else.

The man must have slipped along the side.

David picked his way through the debris and grass toward the back, where the lot shaded into the edges of the creek that ran past the rear wall of the bar. Holding on to the wall to stop himself from sliding into muddy water, he looked along it.

No one there. David stared at absence, his guts now screwed so tight that it felt like he was going to vomit, then made his way back to the parking lot.

He noticed a shape drawn in the dusty gravel, a rectangle that tapered toward the bottom. It didn't mean anything to him.

He dragged his feet through it nonetheless, until the shape was completely gone.

CHAPTER 15

'Because I'm an idiot,' David said.

'Roger that, but you're always an idiot. This doesn't explain the specific omission today.'

They were in the kitchen and the discussion concerned supper. He always looked after what they ate. It was his job. Hunter-gather words, and also food. Today he'd forgotten. That was because of going to Kendricks, of course, which wasn't something he wanted to discuss. When he got back, he'd gone to his study to work but wound up reading more of Talia's book instead. It was easier than working on his own. Easier than thinking, too, and easier and better than trying to work out whether to go to the cops. Doing this had been Plan A for the entire walk home, but it ran out of steam when he got indoors. What could he tell them? That a stranger was bugging him in a way that seemed too genial and unobtrusive to count as stalking? That there was an excessive familiarity in his manner that made David feel not attacked but guilty, as if the situation was his responsibility? That David believed this stranger

132

had subsequently vanished out of a parking lot (yes, Officer, I had been drinking, just a little bit)?

No. Talking to the cops wasn't going to work, at least not yet, and the real reason was that David couldn't seem to think clearly about what had happened. The encounter felt intangible. Or like a day-dream. Something he'd made up. Nothing real.

But not unreal, either.

Eventually lack of sleep and an unaccustomed afternoon beer caught up with him, and he'd nodded off at his desk, waking at the sound of Dawn getting back to the house after her meeting. He felt bleary and caught out even though she wasn't giving him a hard time.

She laughed at the look on his face. 'No biggie, little boy lost. We can rustle up something from the cupboards, I'm sure. How did the day go otherwise?'

He was momentarily wary. 'In what way?'

'The *writing*, darling. Remember that?'

'I'm not a writer, babe. I just sit up there to keep the computer company.'

She smiled, but it looked a little forced. 'Actually it's going a lot better,' he said. Apart from that afternoon, this was broadly true. Although he hadn't written many actual *words*, the phantom hitchhiker thing still felt like it might pay off. 'Got a new idea.'

'That's great,' she said, much more warmly. 'Don't suppose you'll tell me what it is?'

He shook his head, as she'd known he would.

'I'm very proud of you, you know,' she said.

Taken aback by her seriousness, he struggled for a response. 'Well, let's see how the first one—'

'No,' she said. 'I'm *not* going to wait and see how it sells. You wrote it, and it's great, and it's going to be published. Everything else is out of your hands. I'm proud of what *you* do, not for what fate throws your way.'

'You probably won't be so proud of the fact I fell asleep at my desk this afternoon.'

'Oh, I already knew that.'

'You did?'

'You looked like the lurching dead when you came downstairs. No big deal. You didn't sleep well.'

'How do you know?'

'You were tossing and turning all night. It's okay. I'm proud of you anyway. Just don't make a habit of it.'

'Copy that. Look, I'm going to grab a shower, wake up properly, okay?'

'Please do. You smell *viiiile*,' she drawled, an old joke between them, as she bent to start looking in the cupboards. Then, as he headed out into the hallway, she straightened up again. 'Oh, and by the way.'

He turned. 'What?'

'I'm pregnant.'

At first he didn't believe it. He didn't think she'd be lying or joking, but after the last couple of years

134

it was like being casually informed that black was, in fact, white – look, here's a picture to prove it. When he sat for five whole minutes, gripping the printed-out results in his hands and staring at them, he finally got it. And it blew everything else away.

'This is it,' he said, folding her in his arms. She was crying, and felt both bulky and fragile, though there was no difference from the woman he'd hugged that morning before she left for work. 'This is the one. I can feel it. You've done it.'

'*We've* done it.'

'No,' he said, burying his head in the smell of her skin and hair. '*You* did.'

They foraged supper out of the cupboards, snacks at the counter as they talked and talked. 'There's still a long way to go,' she said. 'Nothing's ever sure. We've got to take it one day at a time.'

He couldn't. David knew this time it was going to work, and the prospect filled his head. It didn't matter how much you assumed you'd gotten a handle on human reproduction nor how steely-eyed and unromantic about the process you'd become after hours spent in doctors' waiting rooms glumly listening to the money meter ticking away, it was still a *total mind-fuck*. Somewhere deep in a hidden crucible in Dawn's body, magic had occurred. Things invisible to the naked eye had conjoined and as a result something real was growing inside her. An entirely separate being. It had Dawn within it – and David too – but wasn't merely their product or the sum or averaging of their souls. This wasn't two plus two making four. It was two plus two making lilac. It was different. It was other. It was – or would be – purely itself.

For the time being it might be attached to her by blood and tissue, but one day it would sit opposite David and call him dad, hopefully with a smile on his or her face rather than a snarl (though both would doubtless happen at one time or another), a being with words and emotions all of its own. And one day it would announce it was getting married. And then – assuming it took matters in the traditional order – announce a grandchild was on the way, yet *another* being, a further step along the road to infinity. Every act of creation only ever apes the *real* one: the creation of a new being that one day will walk away from you out into the world to do its thing, forever linked to you by history but the center and sole inhabitant of its own universe. Who cared about the imaginary, when reality could be so magical?

When they went to bed – earlier than usual, with much joking about how Dawn had to sleep for two now – she drifted off quickly, crashing out on her side. David lay next to her in the dark, for once happy to be awake, savoring the experience, in fact – though the sluggish shadows around his internal eye told him that tonight his sleep siren was going to come across for once, and soon.

He turned cautiously, slipped his hand under Dawn's arm, and placed it gently on her stomach. The shadows gathered, deep and warm, and soon he was asleep.

CHAPTER 16

It was Kristina's idea to call Catherine. It came to her after we'd been sitting in a bar in the Village for a couple of hours, which tells its own story. I could tell from what I overheard that Catherine wasn't wild about the idea of us dropping in, but she agreed if we'd wait a couple hours so she could get to the other side of the dinner/bath/bed routine. Kristina seemed impatient about this, but she'd never had her own kids to debrief and shut down, and didn't realize how badly the unscheduled arrival of strangers could derail the process. So we waited in the bar some more, during which Kristina called Mario at the restaurant and promised she'd be at work by nine, cross her heart and hope to die. Mario has no defenses against her and said, 'Okay, that's fine, Miss Kristina. See you later.'

Eventually we stepped out into the dark and made our way to Catherine's house. She opened the door looking well dressed and grown-up. I trooped in behind Kristina feeling like a teenager being let in by someone else's mom. It was one of those very vertical town houses with black-painted railings and cream detailing around the windows, like the dwellings you'd see in a child's illustrated tale about life in a big city. There were books everywhere and posters for recent exhibitions and well-framed black-and-white photos of family and relatives and everything looked like it had been tidied recently by a professional. At one point I thought I saw a mote of dust lurking under a chair but then realized it was just a trick of the light. I didn't have to watch Kristina's face to judge her take on the house, or see her thinking how jolly nice it must be to live there.

Catherine led us into a kitchen with eating space that took up half of the raised first story. It was bright and airy and the kids' art on the fridge was better than anything I could have done. A door at the end led onto a sitting room with stripped brick walls, a fireplace on one side and a television of judicious size on the other.

'The girls are in bed,' Catherine said brightly, as if briefing a new au pair. 'But Mark's due back from the airport in about an hour, so . . .'

Kris glanced at me, but I didn't say anything. I wasn't sure we should be here and had said so. So as far as I was concerned, this was her gig.

'We followed you this afternoon,' she said.

Catherine blinked, and I was reminded of an incident from childhood. I must have been about twelve, wandering around town with a couple of buddies, and we'd climbed up the big tree at the back of the library, as we sometimes did. Once there, we realized an older girl we kinda knew – she worked Saturdays in the general store, a regular stop on our wanders-around-town – was studying at the desk in the window, about ten feet away. So we hooted and waved and eventually she looked up and saw us.

I guess we'd been expecting . . . I'm not sure *what* we'd been expecting . . . that she'd be pleased or flattered or at least amused to see us. She evidently did not feel this way. She responded in a fashion that in retrospect made absolute sense. She reacted like a girl realizing she was being spied upon by a bunch of younger boys to whom she was polite in the store but whom she possibly somewhat dreaded seeing; boys who (and she was old enough to get this, even if we were not) would one day, and maybe soon, become even *more* interested in her.

Her face showed shock at first and then anger. We didn't wait to see what happened next. We scooted down the tree and walked away talking loudly about other things. We felt dumb and embarrassed and as if we'd had something revealed to us about ourselves that we hadn't previously understood. There'd been no harm in what we'd done. None intended, anyway. But we cut the store out of our Saturday routine for the rest of that summer.

When Catherine looked at us, I felt the same way.

Kristina didn't seem to notice. 'We've been

worried about you,' she said. 'And then it looked like Thomas wasn't the guy after all . . .'

'Yes,' Catherine said. Her voice was clipped. 'So?'

'Well, we thought we'd take another look today, see if we could see anyone.'

'When were you doing this?'

'After you picked up Ella and Isabella.'

'You waited outside the school? Hiding?'

'Well, not exactly hiding, but . . . yes.'

Catherine stared at her. 'Excellent,' she said. I was baffled Kris wasn't picking up on the atmosphere. She's preternaturally sharp. Right now she was failing to read Catherine on even the most basic level.

'I'm sorry if that was inappropriate,' I said. 'My fault. I felt bad after I spoke to you yesterday. I wanted to give it one more try. Macho pride, I guess.'

Catherine seemed to soften. 'Sorry,' she said. 'I've been tense all day and Isa did not go down easy. Do you want coffee?'

We said we did, and she got to work with an expensive-looking machine on the counter, and it seemed like all was going to be okay.

Though in fact it got worse, and pretty fast.

Kris and I didn't speak all evening at the restaurant. I understood why I was pissed at her, though not why she was pissed at me, but I guess that's the bottom line in most disagreements and she probably felt the exact same way. Wrong though she was.

The idea of her follower being a woman evidently hadn't occurred to Catherine. She asked what she'd looked like. We told her. She frowned, trying to make something of this, but gave up, looking a little scared.

'Was she pretty?'

'Yes,' I said.

Catherine stood nodding, eyes turned inward. Kristina apparently didn't have anything to say, so I asked Catherine the obvious question. 'Are you going to talk to your husband about this?'

Two minutes later Kristina and I were back out on the street. Catherine had abruptly realized there were a *lot* of very important things she simply had to get on with and while she was *very* grateful for our efforts she needed us to go, right now. She'd be in touch with Kris.

Real soon.

As the door closed firmly behind us, Kristina hissed at me and stomped down the steps. I followed, not understanding what the hell her problem was. She apprised me of it soon enough. She ranted at me all the way back to the East Village, in fact.

'What kind of an *asshole* question was that?'

'About talking to her husband?'

'Yes. I mean, Jesus, John. What the *fuck*?'

'A young woman stalking an older married one – do you have a better explanation?'

'Of *course* he's not having an affair. Christ, John, you can't go around making assumptions like that.

I know you don't like Catherine, but I *do* and I've spent a *lot* more time talking to her.'

'Yeah, so?'

'So I know her marriage is solid and that Mark's a good guy. For God's sake – you saw that house.'

'Kris, that's the most naive thing I've ever *heard*. Yes, it's a lovely house. So what? Having expensive taste and an efficient maid doesn't mean everything's immaculate underneath the water line.'

'Don't judge people by your own mistakes. Just because you fucked up a marriage doesn't mean everyone else is busy doing the same dumb thing.'

There was enough truth in this – after Carol and I fell apart I entered a liaison with Bill Raine's wife, which he knew about, and we'd worked through, but it remained the most damaging thing I'd ever done in my life – to make me as angry as Kristina.

This led me to snap that she was not experienced enough in long-term relationships to know what the hell she was talking about. She shouted back that she had more experience than I knew and furthermore was tired of me treating her like a kid all the time, which was so out of the blue I'd had *no* idea it was coming, and I didn't handle it well, and after that . . .

Well, CNN didn't actually cover the rest of our stomp back to the restaurant, or give us our own logo, but it was *loud*.

★   ★   ★

In the end I got tired of sitting at the bar being ignored by Kristina while she was bright-eyed and charming to everyone else. I left, reasoning that she knew where we lived and also, well, fuck, whatever.

As I stomped out onto the street I saw Lydia at the end of the block. She was facing traffic and, to be honest, I tried to slip past without her seeing me.

'Don't worry,' she said, however, without turning. 'I ain't seen him.'

'Okay,' I muttered. 'That's good.'

'See a lot of others, though,' she added thoughtfully. '*Lot* of people on the streets tonight.'

I looked around, confirming what I already knew – if anything, it looked quiet for the small hours of a Thursday night. 'Okay,' I said again.

She looked at me, a wistful smile on her face. For a moment her eyes were clear and I got the sense that, were it not for the lines and layers of grime, I'd be seeing in her what a man might have forty years before.

Then they went dead. 'Frankie was a dad bitch whore.'

'What?'

'What? What? What?' She took a fast step toward me, raising her bony fist to wave it in my face. 'Fuckers everywhere, that's what,' she snarled. 'You ain't going to steal from me, motherfuckers. I'll cut you bad.'

'Whatever you say, Lyds.'

'Fuck you, asshole. I'll fuck you up too.'

'Okay then. See you tomorrow.'

I walked away, simply not in the mood for New York tonight.

Kristina got home at two thirty. We talked. We did not kiss and make up – neither of us regard sexual intercourse as an effective means of arbitration in matters of serious dispute – but we did start to laugh at ourselves, and she eventually fell asleep in my arms. I lay waiting to follow her. The city below seemed quiet, far away, as though we were in a tiny room at the top of a stone tower in some other world. The wind was strong. We're always aware of it here up in the garret, but this was rowdier than usual. It sounded as though someone was bouncing little objects across the roof.

I don't like arguments. They always feel like a failure, which I presume must be mine. Pretty soon my head began to feel crowded, and it felt like a fight not to open my eyes.

Then I heard a real noise, from out in the main room. I carefully lifted Kris's arm off my chest and slipped out of bed.

The source of the sound was obvious and mundane. Kristina's cell phone lay on the counter, as usual, and the screen was glowing. A little red number on an icon in the dock said she had e-mail. At this time of night it would only be spam and so I put her phone facedown on the cushion on the sofa instead, where further vibrations wouldn't make the thing rattle so audibly.

I stood aimlessly for a moment before deciding to enact the only ritual that's ever helped me to sleep – a weak coffee and a cigarette. I know two stimulants taken together should do the opposite, but . . . they don't.

I made the drink on autopilot, trying not to worry about the problem of Catherine's follower. There was now only one credible explanation and it was down to Catherine to chase it down. I still found it hard not to keep thinking about, though. It was this that had been keeping me awake, along with dregs of the adrenaline occasioned by arguing violently with a woman whom I knew, increasingly, that I loved pretty hard.

The image that kept coming into my mind was the face of the girl in the coat when we'd cornered her. So much of our experience is mediated and cushioned. Car crash-style interactions are unnerving, cracking the paper-thin shell around our lives. Who *was* this woman? What did she want? Was she basically a good person, or a certifiable whack-job? What did she think would come from stalking Catherine, even if there *was* something going on between her and Mark? Was being confronted on the street going to make her back off, cause her to be more stealthy, or possibly escalate her behavior? Where was she now?

Abruptly I shook my head.

Whatever. I was done. For real this time.

I took the tea and a cigarette over to the window. It was the middle of the night and so I wasn't going to actually climb out onto the goddamned roof, but I'd at least open the windowpane and blow the smoke out.

As I started to pull up the sill, something happened outside. I don't know what it was, but it was fast and large and dark. It was as if a huge crow had been roosting on the roof area and took sudden, chaotic flight. In the fraction of a second in which I saw it, it seemed to split into two, maybe even three shapes – twisting shadows that disappeared or dispersed like a storm cloud ripped apart by the wind.

I heard noises, too – more of the pattering sounds I'd heard while in bed, the sounds I'd put down to the wind clattering objects over the roof.

My chest beating hard, I pushed the window up the rest of the way. I stuck my head cautiously out and saw the scrap of flat roof. The wooden chair. My heavy glass ashtray. The chair had been knocked over. It was windy, but nowhere near enough to have done that, nor for the ashtray to have somehow been upturned or broken in half.

'What's happening?'

Kristina's voice nearly gave me a heart attack. I whirled around to see her yawning in the doorway to the bedroom. 'What are you doing up?'

'Heard a noise,' she mumbled, turning on a table lamp. 'You opening the window for a crafty smoke, it seems. Couldn't have done it a *little* more quietly?'

'Sorry,' I said, pulling the window back down again. 'But . . . something weird just happened.'

I was about to say more but realized she was no longer looking at me, but at the window.

'What the hell is that?'

I looked where she was pointing and saw there were marks on the glass, revealed by the light now on in the room. I leaned closer and ran my fingers over the pane. The marks were on the other side of the glass, spidery tracks through layers of dust and airborne dirt that neither we nor the last ten sets of tenants had made any effort to clean.

Kristina was standing beside me now. I think we realized at the same time that the marks on the window, though faint and jagged, were letters, and that they spelled out three words.

They said:

LEAVE US ALONE

CHAPTER 17

David never saw how they began. He watched for the beginnings like some Midwest stormchaser, but they were invisible to him. He was learning with most things that you could observe cause before effect. Careless elbows knocked cups off tables. Mouthing off to teachers got you exiled to stand in the corner, head lowered, the shame of punishment evenly balanced by the welcome change it made from sitting at your boring desk. Shouting at Mom got you smacked – and in this case effect came lightning fast on the heels of cause, and hurt a *lot*. Cause and effect often came so close together there, in fact, that from time to time the order seemed reversed.

The fights between his parents stood outside this process, however. They just happened. There was no beginning and so, presumably, no end.

He tried to see it this way, at least, but couldn't ignore the fact that most of the time his mom and dad seemed happy together. So happy that they didn't need him, in fact. They would laugh and drink their special drinks from the cabinet, their conversations conducted in looks and implications that excluded him. If he was naughty or lazy, they'd gang up on him, two against one, and after he'd retreated – or been sent – to bed, he'd hear them on the deck, their voices calm and relaxed once again, now that he wasn't around to cause trouble.

Then some afternoon – for no apparent reason – he would hear the distant sound of the whistle coming out of the woods on the other side of town, and he'd know the train was on its way. He understood it wasn't a *real* train. He knew what he was hearing wasn't even a real *sound*, but an itch inside his head. A sign that, sometime soon, there was going to be a fight.

But why? There was no track leading to their house. So how did the train always know how to find the way? The child had come to believe that the reason he could not see the cause was that he *was* the cause. He was the nail on which they snagged themselves. He was the station the dark train was trying to find.

It was his fault. It had to be.

And sooner or later, the train reached town.

This time it happened during dinner. It took place at the big old wooden kitchen table, one of the few things the family had wound up with after the death of his mother's father. There hadn't been much to pass on, which had been something of a surprise to all concerned. When they'd visited Grandpa in the old days, Mom always put on something smart and Dad grumbled in the car and seemed smaller all the time they were in the big old Victorian house on the better side of town. Then Grandpa died and it turned out there wasn't much money in the house after all (in fact, there was *minus* money, though that didn't make sense). The child remembered his father's slow smile at this discovery. His face had radiated a warm, uncomplicated pleasure that the boy would have given anything to have caused.

After it had all been sorted out and bills paid and the big, grand house hurriedly sold, Grandma went to live with Mom's sister in North Carolina and they got two small, ugly paintings and some silverware they never used, and the vast table in the kitchen. It was too large for the room – even the child could see that – but that's where it went. He didn't mind the table at all – it was great for spreading art things out on and made an ideal fort, especially when the big white tablecloth was in place, as it reached down almost to the floor on all sides – but his father did. He complained about it a lot.

In fact . . . Yes, that's how the fight had started this time. It had been the trigger, at least.

The child had been finishing the last of his pasta with red sauce – his default fuel at the time – and in a vague world of his own, making up a story, as he so often did. Slowly he began to realize the weather system in the room had changed. He raised his head to listen.

No, his father declared, he was not prepared to work at this table. It was a big, dumb table and would not be convenient. The study was his domain and was going to stay that way. The subject was closed.

The child glanced at his mother and saw the subject was *not* closed. He was familiar with his father's study, a tiny room on the upper floor. His dad had a typewriter set up there on a little desk and sometimes spent a while sitting at it. There was a pile of paper on the left side of the desk, sheets on which his father had typed words. They lay facedown. The pile didn't ever seem to get bigger. That wasn't surprising, as there would be weeks and months in which his dad didn't go into the room. This appeared to be his mother's point. The room would be better deployed as a closet, she believed, rather indulging his father's futile 'hobby.' The child wasn't sure what a hobby was, but gathered it was a Bad Thing.

He swiveled his gaze from his mother's face, saw the way his father looked, and turned hurriedly back to his cooling pasta. He loved his father, but sometimes his face changed. His jaw clenched and his eyes went flat. Usually this was a fleeting condition, but sometimes it would settle in, and it made the child feel scared. His father was looking at his mother that way, and that could only mean one thing.

The train was pulling into the station.

Right now.

Things were said. Many things, with increasing volume. The child tried not to hear.

His father stood, banging the table with his thighs. He shouted, his face red, the fighting vein standing out on his forehead. His mother jumped up too, shouting back. His father stormed out into the hallway. His mother followed. Even though they were farther away, the noise got louder as they spiraled up into the thundercloud.

The child slid off his seat and slipped underneath the table. It always seemed safer under there, the big white tablecloth forming a barrier to the outside world – though the shouting remained perfectly audible. He heard his parents storming back into the kitchen, shouting over each other. He learned, or was reminded, of some facts:

His father was a loser who never completed any task. His mother was a bitch who complained all the time. His father was an asshole who looked at other women, which is not allowed. His mother was a bitch who thought she was better than everyone because of Grandpa, who it turned out wasn't the man everyone thought. His father was a liar and drank too much. His mother was a bitch, and was also a pot calling the kettle black.

The child closed his eyes and put his fingers in his ears. It wasn't enough. The shouting went on and on and on. His mother was better at coming up with different rude words to call his father. But his father . . .

Yes, there it was.

The sound of the first slap.

His father was better at that part, though Mom was pretty good at throwing things. If it hadn't been his parents doing this to each other, it might have been interesting to watch these evenly matched players hacking and sawing at each other's weak points. But they *were* his parents, and the boy loved them, and so it made him want to push pencils into his ears until he could not hear. It made him want to disappear, forever.

His mother's feet hurried past one end of the table as she moved to put the piece of furniture between her and the man at whom she was screaming obscenities. And . . .

Yes, there was the sound of something smashing on the wall. A plate or bowl. Possibly the child's bowl. It wouldn't be the first time his things had been used as ammunition. It would be replaced tomorrow, with hungover but heartfelt apologies. The apologies made the child feel angry and numb.

He screwed his eyes up tighter and pressed his hands harder over his ears. It helped, but not much. He tried to fill his head with light in the way that sometimes also helped, a white light of non-thought and non-hearing and non-seeing. He tried to find a place inside that was calm and the opposite of the dark woods from which the first sounds of the train whistle came.

Meanwhile the fight above him raged on, like arcs of red lightning. Did the opposing troops, these mythic armies, have any idea he was under there? Would they care? The child had never been sure whether he was his mother's fault or his father's – he'd heard arguments for both sides – but he was *someone's* fault, that was for sure. Best to keep out of the way, then. To lie low. To fade into the background, or further still.

Better to not be there at all.

But then . . .

Gradually the boy became aware of a prickling sensation on the back of his neck. It was a bit like the feeling he got when he heard the first echo of the faraway train, but it couldn't be that – the train had already arrived.

He opened his eyes, but the feeling didn't go away. He moved his hands from his ears – causing the sound of the fight to leap in volume – and lowered them to his lap, frowning. What worried him most was the idea that this might be some new kind of sign, a yet more ominous version of the train whistle: a warning that the fight was going to get more than usually out of hand, and that someone – his mother, probably, though that couldn't be for certain – was in danger of getting seriously hurt this time.

The feeling expanded, seeping downward from his neck until it felt like gentle pressure was being applied to his upper back, along his shoulders, and down the spine.

He turned and saw that a boy was sitting under the table behind him. The boy was sitting neatly, legs crossed, hands in his lap.

The child blinked, unable to speak, at first incapable even of working out what question he might ask.

The boy smiled – a bright, sunny smile that said he knew the boy and liked him very much, and wanted nothing more than to hang out and have fun together when the silly fuss raging around them had blown over, which at some point it would, as it always did, and so in the end everything would be okay.

'Hello, David,' he said.

'Who . . . who are you?' David whispered.

The boy's smile got broader, shining up into his sharp blue eyes.

'I'm your friend.'

David woke, rigid in the dead of night with his pregnant wife beside him, and finally knew where he'd first seen the man in the blue jeans and white shirt.

He remembered his name, too.

Maj.

PART II

I believe that the human imagination
never invented anything that was not true,
in this world or any other.

Gérard de Nerval
Aurélia

CHAPTER 18

My name is Billy, and in the mornings I wake up. The first adventure of the day is finding out where I am. It may be on a bench in a park. I may be propped against the wall in a backstreet or sitting in the bakery section in a grocery store. I may be on someone's floor.

I try to make it happen somewhere different every day, but sometimes when I open my eyes I realize I have woken there before. You'd think in a city as big as New York that would be impossible, but when it's time to turn in I'm so worn out these days that sometimes I end up doing what I've done before without realizing. Everybody's the same, I suppose. You get up, you go to work, you come home, you eat food that's very similar to what you had yesterday or last week, you sit in front of the shows you always watch, and finally you go to the same old bed. If you could retreat up into the sky like some alien or god and watch any given person, day after day, you'd see that however complex and variable their days might seem to them, they follow tracks. Once in a while this angers or saddens them and they make a big

159

deal of changing something. They leave their job, they move house, they screw somebody slightly different from their partner, and they get divorced.

Then, before too long, they find themselves rolling along a new set of near-identical tracks.

I have tracks of my own. They run to different destinations: sites of memory or places that have proven useful for killing time. There are some of us, Journeymen and Angels and Cornermen, who have found methods of spending their days that do not seem like a waste. I tried to find something too. Once I started to get the picture, however, I felt something break.

There was a period before all that when I used to be delighted with the whole deal, I'll admit. The Dozeno Phase, as the Gathered call it, otherwise known as dumb ignorance. There was an incredible sense of freedom. Nothing I had to do. Nowhere I had to be. An endless Friday night, one long freshman year or an endless spell in your early twenties, when it feels like infinity is there to play for, that no doors will ever close, and the only way life will change is by getting even better.

I didn't notice when it started to change, only that one day I didn't feel the same. I went through a period of feeling listless, depressed. Eventually one of the others took me to one side and explained the score.

Was it a surprise? Well, yes. Though . . . maybe I'd had some inkling. I'd known there was something missing, some point to life I hadn't been

160

able to find. But everyone feels like that, don't they, from time to time?

Everything was basically fine. Everything was sort of okay, though I couldn't seem to find the place I was meant to be. I knew people, counted some as friends, but they didn't feel as if they were the ones I'd been waiting for. I did things, and I had a life, of a kind. It just didn't feel like what I'd had in mind.

Time passed, years went by, but I never got the sense that I was getting closer to anything that I recognized from the dreams of the future that I'd once cherished. Assuming they were dreams and not memories.

Now I know what I am, but I cannot get it to sit right. I cannot accept this is all there is, all I can ever be. I was loved once – can it *never* be that way again? Can't things go back to the way they were, when we meant more to each other than anything in the world?

I guess not. It's never happened before that anyone knows of. That doesn't stop some from trying, of course. Rapping on windows. Living in their friend's house. Hiding their keys. Constantly on their shoulder, always a few steps behind. I heard recently that one of us has made real contact with his friend, even spoken to him. The guy's called Maj, and I counted him as a friend before I stopped caring much about that kind of thing. I still see him around. Maj is a very forceful person, though, one of the most accomplished Fingermen. He's got solidity and heft. If he can't pull the thing off, I doubt any of us can. Certainly not me. My heft was never strong, and I can feel it deserting me. Every morning I look at my hands. Each day they look less substantial.

Sometimes I can smell the odor of hospitals and hear the whisper of people shuffling down corridors in thin, papery gowns they will never take off.

I'm not sure I've got it in me to fight.

At night I stand in the street outside the house where I think I'm supposed to live. I recognize everything about it – the shape of the front and the color of the bricks, the arrangement of the lintels and the roof, the positions of the trees outside on the street. I know how it looks inside, too, though the glimpses I sometimes get through the windows suggest either that I'm not remembering it correctly or parts of it have changed – different color curtains, different color walls.

Several times it's gotten to be too much and I've walked up the steps to the door, four stone steps I remember running down so many times as a child – or think I do – and try to knock or ring the bell. Nobody ever comes, and the door never opens. I can touch things, but I can move almost nothing, so perhaps that's the problem. Maybe they just don't hear. I hope that's the answer. It's better than thinking that they hear but choose not to open the door, choose not to allow me to come home.

That's why I try to find somewhere different to spend each night. In the hope that when I wake in the morning, everything will be different, that I might even find myself in a bed in that house, in a life that makes sense. Lately I have begun to dream of that less, however, and find it harder to believe.

Lately I have also found myself looking at graveyards and thinking of cellars. There's one I know, under the control of a man who doesn't understand the world as well as he thinks. A number of us already nod there. I've started to wonder if perhaps it would be comfortable to go down there and sit with my own back to the wall.

To go in there and never come back out.

CHAPTER 19

David stepped off the train at the exact time he and Dawn had arrived the previous Friday. He'd climbed on the first available service from Libertyville – the nearest town to home with a train station – and hadn't even realized it was the same one until he saw the clock at Penn Station. This made him feel very guilty, even guiltier than he'd felt throughout the journey and in the shower and ever since the idea had first dropped into his head as the two of them sat eating cereal together.

But that was dumb, right? He was a grown-up. He was allowed to leave the house, and the town.

He set off for the escalator – still feeling guilty, and confused, and more than a little scared.

He'd waited until Dawn had left for school and then written a note explaining that the novel idea he'd been nurturing had given unexpected birth in the night, presenting him with a litter of sub-ideas and plotlings that he needed to bottle feed with fact. One of these storylines was going to unfold in New York. He needed to check out some locations, and sure, he could fire up Google Maps and get Street View on it, but he thought it might be cool to go check in person, soaking up the atmosphere and letting the city do some of the work. He hoped that was okay.

This last sentence, seeking permission, disappeared in the second draft. He didn't need her to say it was okay. This was the kind of thing writers did.

It went back for the third draft. It made him feel better. As he stood in the kitchen giving the note a final read, marveling at the unusual neatness of his handwriting, he was relieved to see the contents came across as credible and plausible and not-at-all-crazy.

Even if they weren't. He wasn't going to New York to research. He was going because . . . He didn't know why he was going. He was just going. And if he was going then he might as well go, instead of standing in the kitchen dicking around redrafting an excuse that wouldn't be found until after he was gone, or perhaps even back home.

He left the note in the center of the kitchen table – the one that, long ago, had graced the big kitchen in Grandpa's house, one of the handful of possessions he'd shipped to Rockbridge when he'd moved. It was a big, sturdy piece of furniture and (propped against a bowl full of wholesome red apples, and with a smiley at the bottom) the note looked like the most reasonable thing in the world.

He was careful not to look under the table, however.

It was colder than the last time. Overcast and windy, too, far more like he remembered it from his period living in the city, a time that included the tail end of winter and during which he'd been colder than ever before or since. The weather – and being by himself – made the streets feel more familiar, like a stranger in the street turning to resolve into an old acquaintance. New York was a place he associated with being alone.

He went into the first Starbucks he came across. While in line he texted Dawn, deciding to let her know he'd come to the city right away rather than waiting for her to find the note. The text was upbeat.

There was no immediate reply, which didn't surprise him – she'd be in class, knowing she now carried inside her the genesis of one of the little beings that sat around her. Remembering this gave David the same pang of bewildered hope and fear, and more than anything else he believed this was why he was here. There was something that needed to be put right, even if he was not sure what it was. There was unfinished business.

When he got to the counter, the barista did not know what he wanted before he asked for it and betrayed no obvious sign of caring about his day. David missed Talia for a moment, and realized he was actually looking forward to getting back to reading her book.

For want of any other plan, he walked the coffee up to Bryant Park, where he sat on a bench and stared across toward the library and the terrace where he and Dawn had taken celebratory glasses of wine. He recalled that for the second half of the nineteenth century, this site held the Croton Distributing Reservoir, a block-sized behemoth with fifty-foot walls for storing water transported down from Westchester County by aqueduct in an attempt to stop the citizens dying of cholera and yellow fever quite so enthusiastically. It was now impossible to imagine. But it was hard to remember being twenty, too, to imagine himself in the head and life of that former person, to recall who he'd been when he'd sat in this park then. Do we grow older by dint of additions and remodeling, or through knocking ourselves down to the foundations and rebuilding from the ground up? David supposed it was meant to be the former, but the latter had more of a ring of truth.

He left the park and headed east along 42nd. Two minutes later a text came in, Dawn bubbling with enthusiasm and telling him to take his time and she'd look forward to hearing about his adventures when he got home.

He kept walking east for a further few blocks and then turned to head downtown. The sky grew gray as he trudged, the wind more persistent. He tried – for whose benefit he wasn't sure – to maintain the pretence that he was here for research, peering meaningfully at the buildings and people he passed.

He walked for hours, crisscrossing back and forth as if searching for something he couldn't recall. Until eventually he arrived at the top of Union Square – and found himself slowing down.

Union Square runs from 17th down to 14th between Park and Broadway – the only major street that ignores the grid and carves on the diagonal, turning the park into a wedge. It's a block wide, the top four-fifths arranged in areas of grass and trees with a kids' playground way at the top right, half hidden behind high bushes. Tree-shaded paths paved with hexagonal bricks wander through all this, the grassy areas easily accessible on the other side of low metal fences. The bottom of the square is a major downtown pedestrian thoroughfare.

David wandered down the central path. It was almost three o'clock by then. People perched on benches, talking on the phone, meditatively working through late sandwiches. He remembered the park well. He must have crossed it a hundred times on the way to the Strand Book Store, where he'd picked up most of his secondhand reading when he'd lived there, selling the books frugally back again afterward. This afternoon something about the place felt off. Had they changed it? Altered the layout? He wasn't sure. It *looked* the same, but his memory had started to feel like a jigsaw where he had all the pieces around the outside and nothing in the middle at all.

Traffic coursed noisily back and forth across 14th. A pair of Japanese women wandered by, cheerfully consulting a city guide. A handful of business types strode past, deep in conversation, pant legs flapping in the wind.

David slowly got the feeling he was being watched, or at least observed. He turned to see a man standing in the center of the area. He looked about forty, with ginger hair, wearing the upper and lower halves of two quite different gray suits. The shades did not match and neither did the styles. The pants were too loose, the jacket too tight. He was watching David with an odd expression. Part cautious. Part curious.

David looked away, and then back. The man was still watching him. Everybody else was in transit, a mutating, rotating backdrop of watercolor hues. They were the only two people who were motionless.

Finally the man strolled over to David.

'What's your name, then?'

He spoke in a low tone. His accent was distinctive, with a strong hint of London Cockney. Too surprised to come up with an evasive response, David told him.

'Nice.' The man nodded. 'David. Good name. A *proper* name.' He winked. 'But then it would be, wouldn't it?'

'What . . . what do you mean?'

'I know what you are, David.'

The back of David's neck felt hot. 'You do?'

'I do. And . . . welcome, *welcome*. You want to be back up there in the trees though, really.'

'Why?'

'Well, who are you here for?'

'Here . . . for?'

'His *name*, David. I'm assuming it's a "he," anyway. Usually is with guys. Not always, though. *Could* be a "she." Could be a kangaroo, for all I know, right?'

David stared at him.

'So. *Is* it a he?' The man had an unusual odor, like the memory of cotton candy on a fall afternoon. He was leaning forward expectantly, conspiratorially, eager to help. David felt as if he'd wandered into some dark club and been greeted as a regular by a doorman he'd never seen before.

'I . . . don't know what you're talking about.'

The man winked. 'Fair enough, mate. Understood. I'll bugger off and leave you to it. Good luck, eh?'

He held up both hands, fingers crossed, and walked away, glancing around as if already on some other mission entirely. He curved around a group of Europeans wearing bright anoraks and seemed to fail to come back out the other side – presumably having crossed the road.

David felt scared now. Plain, downright scared, deep in his guts, seized with the certainty that whatever impulse had brought him to this place was faulty, and this wasn't somewhere that he should be. It was as if he'd come to a park and found himself standing up to his neck in a reservoir of dark water instead.

It was only then that he realized that the park, if seen from above, probably looked rather like a shape he had seen etched out in the gravel of the parking lot of Kendricks. That realization made being there feel wronger still. As if he had followed instructions that he hadn't even realized he'd been given.

It was half past three. If he was intending to walk back to the station, he ought to be setting off. Or maybe he should get a cab. But . . . he thought he should be leaving, either way. Leaving felt like a good plan. Getting on a train. He could be home in time for dinner.

Just . . . *be home.*

He was halfway back up the central path when he heard an intake of breath and glanced to the right to see a homeless man sitting on a bench. His skin was nicotine brown, thin black hair plastered across a mottled scalp, tatters of an old suit swaddled around a skeletal frame. He was glaring past David into one of the grassy areas. He screwed up his face and flapped his hands spastically, as if to ward something away from his face.

'No, not again. Fuck off, fuck off, fuck *off.*'

David turned to see what he was looking at and realized the park was full of people now.

Many seemed to be on their way somewhere,

striding along the paths. They flowed on either side of David, eyes ahead, as though he were a rock in a fast-moving stream.

Others were gathered in knots on the grassy areas, apparently in conference, but even these were not static. Each person within these groups was constantly on the move, walking in small circles, or in slow, weaving patterns among one another that left the basic shape of the groups intact. They were dressed in just about any outfit you could imagine, from a teenage girl in a gray hoodie to a plump woman of about fifty wearing a strapless ball gown in dark blue. There must have been two, maybe three hundred of them. There were animals, too. A few large dogs, a bright orange cat, and . . . for a bizarre moment, David even thought he saw a bear. Then they weren't there anymore.

None of them. The park was empty again.

David turned to the man on the bench. He smiled, revealing a mouth with hardly any teeth in it.

'You saw them?'

'I saw *something*,' David whispered, looking around, skin crawling. Everything was as it had been two minutes before. The paths and grassy spaces were empty but for fallen leaves. He spotted the two Japanese women he'd noticed earlier, sitting together on one of the benches now, consulting their guidebook and laughing.

'Where . . . where *did they all go*?'

'Nowhere,' the man on the bench said. 'I don't ever see them anywhere but here.' He stood, gathering his plastic bags. 'But *I'm* leaving. You should too. They don't like it if you can see them. I got bitten once.'

He walked away up the path.

David stood his ground, knowing now what he'd been feeling ever since he'd first come into the park. There was a disparity between the way it looked and the way it really was. It was . . . too *full*.

On impulse, he stretched both arms out to the side. The women on the bench looked at him strangely, but that wasn't the only effect. Something backed off a little, as if he'd become a bigger rock in a hidden stream.

He put his arms back down and hurried up toward the children's playground. At the heart of this was a castle-like construction with wooden walkways and turquoise turrets, planks and rope bridges connecting the different sections. Only the under-tens were allowed on this, a sign clearly stated, but there were adults on it now. Perhaps thirty of them. In pairs and threes and fours. Most of them dressed in black or rich colors, drapey, goth-style clothing that looked cobbled together from remnants. They were all moving, constantly. Back and forth, around and about. David got glimpses of pale faces in conversation, but most of the time it was as if you could see them only from behind.

If they were here, then . . .

He turned and trotted back to the center of the park. Yes – they were back here, too.

David ran toward the largest grassy area, off center in the park, sixty feet around with a fountain off to one side. He could barely see it now for the mass of people. There were no children – and only a handful under eighteen – but otherwise every age group was represented. Old, middle-aged, with a big peak in early to mid-twenties. Black, white, Asian. Most in casual clothes, a few in suits. Again, the thing that looked like a bear but surely had to be a man in a costume.

And then – they were gone again.

Except . . . they weren't. David couldn't see them, but he could *feel* them. There were people here in the park, people he couldn't see. There was no doubting that.

Unless I'm losing my mind.

The two Japanese women had gone back to giggling over what had to be the funniest NYC guidebook ever. A muscular guy walked past with a pair of very tiny dogs. Two men sat on a bench, both on the phone, presumably not to each other. All of these people seemed too far apart, like a scattered handful of books on a shelf.

'Hello, David,' said a voice.

He turned to see a man in battered jeans and untucked shirt, the one he'd last seen in Kendricks. The man was grinning, and this time it seemed more sincere and less threatening. Behind him

174

stood a slim woman in a long black coat. She was smiling too.

The man took a step forward and put out his hand. 'Welcome back,' he said.

CHAPTER 20

'This what you had in mind?'

I looked up from a sidewalk table outside the Adriatico. Kristina stood outside the fence dressed more or less as I'd suggested: raggedy black jeans and sweater under a cheap coat, hair pulled back in a ponytail, the whole outfit topped with a pair of sunglasses nondescript enough not to look like obfuscation.

'Perfect,' I said.

'For what?'

'Thinking of entering you in this "Hottest New York Bag Lady" pageant everyone's talking about.'

'Careful,' she said. 'We may not be back at the openly-mocking-each-other stage just yet.'

'Yeah, we are,' I said, coming around to kiss her on the cheek. 'It was a dumb argument and I've said I'm sorry. That's the end of it.'

'I see, master. So – what's the plan?'

Something had been nagging at me since I'd gotten up that morning. It nagged as I walked to work. It nagged when I took a break to go thank the heater guys for fixing our unit, watching their faces while I did so and seeing nothing untoward.

It nagged as I stood chain-drinking strong coffees and pushing pizza to passersby, and even while being patient with Mario's sister, who'd picked up on the coldness between Kristina and me the night before and was taking an excessively maternal interest.

The nagging didn't amount to much more than the idea that there was something I was missing, dots I was not joining up. Which was no help. But finally, halfway through selling someone two slices of pepperoni, I'd realized what the connecting line might be.

'We're going for a walk,' I said.

The message on our window could have been put there at any time in the last however many years, some previous tenant's thigh-slapping attempt to freak out a roommate that we'd never noticed simply because the lighting conditions hadn't been right and it hadn't ever occurred to us to clean the windows. I didn't believe that, though. Neither did Kristina. Together with the overturned chair and the broken ashtray out on the apartment roof, it didn't ring true – never mind the sensation I'd experienced when I opened the window, of someone (or perhaps more than one person) in sudden movement.

The message had been put there recently. It had to have been sometime after the last time I'd been out in my rooftop aerie to smoke, which was only the night before and so kept the timeframe tight.

177

'Face it,' Kristina said. Her pupils looked big and pale, green edging out the gray for once. 'You know this just happened. *Tonight.*'

Against Kristina's wishes I reopened the window (after taking a picture of the message on my phone) and climbed out. It was dark and the wind was strong and it felt like being on the battlements of a tottering castle tower. I confirmed what I'd suspected. If you were light and nimble – not to mention insanely reckless – you could probably access the scrap of flat roof from over the rooftops. By leaning against the nearest of these and standing on tiptoe, I got a glimpse over to the next building. Presumably if you kept going then somewhere there'd be a means of dropping into a gap and ultimately down to ground level. The tiles were wet and mossy and I wasn't going to get any more intrepid about the investigation than that, certainly not in the dark.

I climbed back in. 'There's another possibility,' Kris said.

'Yeah, I know. Our window wasn't locked. They could have got out there from our apartment. But that raises too many questions. Like how they'd have gotten in *here*.'

'Heater guys were here day before yesterday. They took forever and I had to leave for work, so I gave them a key to lock up. They shoved it back under the door, but I guess they could have made a copy and—'

'Nope. If Dack or Jez had tried to scrabble away

over that roof, we'd be listening to the sound of ambulances right now and there'd be blood-drenched dents in the sidewalk the size of two small cows.'

'They could have done it while they were here. We wouldn't have noticed until now.'

'But why? We pay them money and they drink in your bar and neither of them has a sense of humor that I've ever noticed.'

'So who did it?'

'You know who it's got to be. What I don't understand is why it says "us."'

Kristina and I live a small, contained life. We hadn't made any enemies in the city – one tries not to – or many acquaintances outside the restaurant and staff from others nearby. We'd barely seen the other people in our building. They had normal jobs and lived different hours. 'Maybe it *was* a guy you saw the other night after all,' Kristina mused. 'In the market, and afterward. Maybe there's more than one person following Catherine.'

'That would help, sure. But in that case, who are we dealing with?'

'You got me. The question is whether *Catherine* knows.'

I thought about it. 'I don't think so. If you're a woman being followed, you'll assume it's a man. She looked genuinely surprised when we told her we'd seen a girl. And I'm sure that was the same person as the one I saw the other night. The height and clothing were exactly the same. I just didn't see a face then and so I made the same wrong assumption that Catherine had.'

Kristina nodded. 'Okay. But here's the thing. A person or persons unknown evidently not only realizes we've been tracking them, but also knows *where we live*. Either someone followed you back the other night . . .'

'. . . or he/she/they were outside Catherine's tonight and followed us back to the restaurant.'

'Which would not have been hard. Raised voices were involved.'

'I recall. But what – then they kicked their heels for a few hours before following one of us back here?'

'This is a *stalker*, John. That shit's what they do.'

She had a point. I thought back over my solo walk home. I hadn't been aware of anyone following me, but I'd been an irritable frame of mind and the incident with Lydia had deflected my attention too. Nonetheless, I believed I would have noticed someone trailing me. That meant if they'd done it tonight they must have waited and followed Kristina as she walked home later. It wasn't far, and I knew Kris was capable of looking after herself – otherwise I'd never have considered letting her walk it alone, regardless of how bad a fight we'd had.

But still.

I locked the window and we went back to bed. I don't know who went to sleep first, but we were both awake, listening for sounds on the roof, for quite some time.

★　★　★

We walked quickly over to Chelsea, retracing in reverse our steps from Catherine's the night before. It was a nicer walk this time – except for being cold and cloudy – but there was no denying we were tense.

'I realized something,' I explained as we hurried west along 14th. 'The two occasions on which I or we saw someone started in totally different locations – the Westside Market and outside the girls' school – and at different times on different days of the week. It may have been the same person, it may not. But there's a constant I should have noticed right away.'

'The way they were dressed?'

'Yeah, well, that too – but that's not notable if it's the same individual both times. I'm talking about the fact that I lost her/him/them in the same place. Somewhere along 16th.'

Kristina frowned. 'That's not much.'

'It's all we've got,' I said. 'And this is now our problem, not Catherine's. Someone was outside our window last night. I want something done about that.'

We arrived on 16th Street without a plan. We walked along the north side and back on the south. Houses. Cars. The church. Trees. All in mid-afternoon mode with no one around. We stood halfway along the street for ten minutes. A car holding a woman and a child drove down the road and out the other end. Kristina was getting cold and cranky.

181

'If I pass out with all the excitement, leave me where I fall.'

'You were the one talking about setting up a detective agency. When I was a lawyer I dealt with private investigators, and this is how their lives are. You go somewhere and wait. For hours.'

'So their life sucks. But this is a nice street, John. We loiter here, someone's going to call the cops.'

'You got a better idea?'

'Going home. Going for a beer. Going to Hawaii. Pretty much any sentence showcasing verbs of movement in a non-metaphoric sense.'

I heard the sound of a door opening and turned, looking as bland as possible in case it was an eagle-eyed local making sure we weren't casing out their house. Thirty yards up the other side of the street, the door on the right-hand side of the church was now open. The man I'd seen the previous afternoon stood in it, talking to someone inside.

'It's the priest,' I said. Kristina was frank about not finding this an arresting development.

After a moment the man closed the door and trotted down the stairs. He let himself out the gate and closed it before setting off at a brisk pace.

I gestured to Kristina.

'What – we're going to *follow* the guy?'

'No,' I said. 'You are.'

'Say again?'

'I spoke to him yesterday. He'll recognize me. You're going let me know where he goes.'

'John, he's a fucking *priest*.'

'He was here when we lost that girl.'

She started walking reluctantly. 'What are *you* going to do?'

'I'm not sure yet.'

She rolled her eyes but got on it, scooting up the street after the priest's disappearing back.

I walked back to take a look at the church. The central portion was three stories high, the width of two of the houses that lined the rest of the street. The ground level held a row of small windows with darkness beyond, suggesting that they fronted office space or storage. The two stories above had bigger glass, though they still looked to have been designed with little more than a protractor and ruler and as if to withstand impact rather than to inspire spiritual fervor. On either side stood a staircase leading up to a wooden door at the left and right extremes of the second level. All of it looked dusty and city-grimed and weightily functional.

I let myself in through the gate and walked up the steps on the right. I knocked on the door, which was heavy and large and made of wood. Nothing happened, so I knocked again, this time using the brass knocker.

After a minute I turned the handle and pushed. The door swung open to reveal a short, tidy corridor with a wooden floor and white walls and an area on the left designed to hold coats. At the far end was another door.

'Hello?'

I stepped inside. I called hello once more, then opened the second door. I wandered into a big room that tapered upward toward a pointed roof with exposed beams. The walls were paneled too, somber paintings dotted here and there. It was dark and gloomy and gothic without anything in the way of richness, the domain of a faith that didn't pander to its audience by adding unnecessary pizzazz. Rows of battered chairs sat facing a single one, which faced back the other way. Behind this was a plain altar, surmounted by a simple metal cross. An unloved-looking upright piano stood to the side.

Turning, I was confronted with the street-side wall. There was a notice board with sheets of paper thumbtacked to it. Three big Palladian windows and five smaller ones above. The glass in each was a different shade of muted – blue, green, pale red, pale purple. Each had been protected from street-side vandalism by close-fitting sheets of chicken wire. As a spectacle of light it would not make you want to glorify anybody's name unless you'd already been of a mind to do so.

My phone rang. It was Kris. 'Where are you?'

'Heading back along 15th. He went into a deli. Came out with a bottle of water. Do you think that's significant? Should I get a picture with my spycam?'

'Kris . . .'

'Okay, okay.'

She hung up. I wandered out into the middle of the room along the aisle between the two groups of chairs. I noticed a plain, narrow door at the end, behind the altar and painted the same color as the wall. It seemed likely that it led to the lower level. I considered finding out but decided that would be taking this too far, especially as there was presumably somebody still in the building. Also . . . I have no strong views for or against organized religions, but their structures possess a certain psychic weight. If you're alone in a church they can make you feel you shouldn't be. Church doors are often left open, but that's for the faithful to come in and do their thing. I was not faithful and I wasn't here in the hope of finding God or even myself. I'd seen – or thought I'd seen – the priest stopping to exchange words with someone on his way out. That person must still be here. If they appeared and asked my business, I didn't have an answer.

As I was bringing my phone up to call Kris off the chase, it rang again in my hand. 'Okay,' I said. 'You're right. This is a waste of—'

'Get over here,' Kris said. 'Union Square.'

'Why?'

It sounded like she was running. 'Just come, John. *Now*.'

CHAPTER 21

Kris hadn't given me anywhere specific to head for and so I dropped south a couple blocks to hit Union Square at the most obvious entry point, the paved area at 14th.

There was no sign of her when I ran across the street. I called her phone. She picked up right away but didn't give me a chance to speak. 'Where are you?'

'The bottom,' I said, out of breath. 'Where are you? You okay?'

'Look around.'

I turned in a slow, winded circle. 'I don't see the priest, if that's what you mean. Or you.'

'Okay. Wait there.'

A minute later Kristina came walking quickly toward me along the central path. 'You scared me,' I said.

She smiled distractedly. 'I'm fine. Just . . . come with me.'

She led me up the path into the heart of the park. When we got to where the two main cross-ways intersected, she stopped. 'Stand here,' she said. 'And be still.'

She glanced around and then back up at me. 'Are you getting it?'

A father and small child, toddling past, in no hurry and going nowhere in particular. In the distance, a small group of what looked like students in a loose huddle, talking and laughing. Over on a bench, a couple of men in business suits. There was more than this, however. It reminded me of what I'd just experienced in the church. A sense of residue, of spaces not being voids. Two Japanese women ambled in our direction consulting a guidebook. A jogger appeared from nowhere and flashed past, leaving a waft of hot skin and self-satisfaction that seemed to linger longer than it should. I was aware of the sound of traffic and the rustle of distant chatter, but it sounded far away, as if there was something between me and it.

'I'm getting *something*. I have no idea what.'

'I lost the priest on the other side of Broadway,' Kristina said. 'I came to check just in case, and . . .'

I nodded, not wanting to dispel the atmosphere.

'Try over here,' she said, gesturing up the path. 'That's where I felt it first.'

I followed, knowing there was a conflict between what my senses were telling me, but not knowing which to trust.

'Look,' Kristina hissed suddenly. She was pointing at one of the grassy areas, a forty-yard stretch near Park Avenue.

The priest was close to one end. He was standing talking to a woman – a woman who looked a *lot*

187

like the one we'd lost after following Catherine home from school.

'That's *her*,' Kristina whispered. 'Christ – you were right. That's the woman, isn't it?'

'Could be. Try to get closer.'

She walked quickly up the path. I tried to keep myself out of the priest's line of sight while drifting in the same direction.

A moment later Kristina slipped her hand out of her coat pocket and made a fist with her thumb sticking up, down by her side, which I took to mean that it was indeed the same woman. What did that mean? And why was she here now, talking to a priest in a park?

When Kristina got to the next junction she slowed, waiting for me to catch up. 'It's definitely her,' she said. I took a good look at the woman and saw she was tall, with dark hair. A pitch-black coat with a high collar, edged at the sleeves and hem with black lace. In good light it looked a little threadbare. Underneath it she was wearing a dress made of muted red velvet, trimmed with cream around the neckline.

Two other people were standing just beyond. One was standing, at least – a nondescript man of about thirty, with brown hair. He was in conversation with another who was wearing jeans and a white shirt, and who was moving around in a kind of slow circle. Despite the fact that the second man was the taller and better-looking of the two, there was something more *present* about the first guy.

188

I glanced toward the priest and realized the same was true there. He was a man in early middle age, blandly decent-looking. The woman talking to him was slim and very attractive. Yet your eye tended to settle on *him* and stay there. I tried to look at the girl, and it happened again – my gaze slipped back toward the priest.

Then they were no longer talking, but walking rapidly in opposite directions.

'Shit,' Kristina said. 'Now what?'

'Follow her.'

She peeled off and strode up the central path. I was about to head after the priest but realized I knew where he'd be going, or at least where he could be found. So I stopped and looked back up through the park.

I saw nothing but trees and grass.

I was still there when my phone rang.

'I lost her.'

'Already?'

'Right away. I'm sorry, John. Either I'm crap at this or that girl really knows how to lose people.'

'You think she knew you were on her tail?'

'I don't see how. You still on the priest?'

'No. I'm in the park.'

'Why?'

'I don't know.'

We met where the two main paths crossed and sat on a bench. We waited half an hour but didn't see anything, and soon I stopped expecting to. It just felt like a park once more, and a cold and increasingly dark one at that.

'We'd better head back,' Kristina said. 'I need to be at work in an hour. So do you.'

'Yeah,' I said, though I'd already started to think that I'd be spending some of the favors I'd earned through handling Paulo's pizza shifts, and taking the evening off, in order to try to talk to someone.

Just before we crossed 14th to head down toward the East Village and the evening's work, we turned together and looked back at Union Square.

We still saw nothing.

CHAPTER 22

When David tried to think back over what happened in Union Square he got only fragments. He remembered turning to see Maj. He remembered a beautiful girl in a black coat standing to one side and taking a friendly interest before returning to an intense conversation with another man, who was wearing a brown suit.

'It's *not* Reinhart,' she said to him. 'It's somebody else.'

'Just consider staying at the church,' Brown Suit was saying. 'For a couple of days, that's all.'

She smiled, but it was obvious that meant 'no.'

There were others, too, including a listless man called Billy, all taking part in some kind of informal gathering or catch-up. Maj appeared torn between wanting to talk to David and having business with the girl and the man in the brown suit – and David overheard enough to gather that it was this that had sent Maj hurrying to the phone in Kendricks and brought him back to the city after that. They were talking fast and urgently. Billy stood off to one side throughout this. He looked ill.

191

In the back of David's mind a voice kept telling him he ought to be getting to the train station. That voice, the voice that always told him *not* to do things, to be careful, to stay safe, was taking up perhaps ten percent of his mental bandwidth. Thirty percent was insidiously suggesting the opposite.

All the rest was a cloud.

Sometimes he thought he could hear a hubbub of conversation, but it sounded like a combination of traffic around the square and the distant roar of a jet passing high overhead, and so it was possible that's all it was. If you blinked, everything came into focus. A New York park on a cold afternoon. If you let your attention wander . . . it became something else. David hadn't spent much time stoned – experiencing his parents out on the deck staring owlishly at him before breaking into high-pitched laughter had been enough to put him off the idea – but it's hard to grow up in semi-rural America and avoid drugs altogether. From his single experience with MDMA he remembered this sensation of being untethered, watching reality peeling off to stand to the side and of being unsure of whether it was you who'd taken this step, or the world – and what it would take to marry you again.

He observed groups of the circulating people, in conversation – some serious, some joking. Individuals and twos and threes walking up and down the thoroughfares. A very large dog came and stood and looked up at him as if waiting for him to say something. The dog appeared to be on his own, without an owner, and after a few moments trotted off. All of this was silent, as if seen through thick and grubby glass – but once in a while there'd be a bubble of noise, like opening the door to a room that held a party to which you hadn't been invited. Similarly, David stood there as if invisible most of the time, but once in a while someone would turn their head to look at him curiously, before turning away again.

Then he was down at the bottom end of the square once more, his head clear, as if jolted out of a daydream. Two women were walking toward him from the pedestrian crossing. He felt a panicky urge to step out of their way. They seemed too big. Not tall, or fat, just too *present*. One glared at him as they passed, as if to forestall him bothering them. He heard the other sniff, and saw rings of red around her nostrils.

Two normal women, one with a cold, but he felt disconcerted and frightened. Was *that* all this was? Some kind of panic attack? Was he seeing normal people, but just responding to them in the wrong way?

He realized belatedly that someone else was looking at him. About forty feet away, on the other side of Broadway, a man wearing a fedora and a dark suit with wide lapels. He was standing with his hands in his pants pockets, staring at David.

His face was hard and unfriendly.

*　　*　　*

193

'Let's go,' said a voice from behind.

It was Maj, alone now. The other man and the girl had disappeared. David glanced back toward where he'd seen the man in the hat, but he was no longer there either, and all the other people in the park had gone.

'*What just happened?* Who were all those people?'

'Come with me.'

'Why . . . would I do that?'

'You came to the city for answers, yes? You're not going to get any standing by yourself in a park.'

Maj started walking. David followed. The other man crossed 14th, striding along busy patches of sidewalk, avoiding oncoming pedestrians without ever dropping pace. After ten minutes he finally slowed, somewhere south of the Village, but kept switching in and out of backstreets before popping out opposite a high wall made of stained red brick. To the left was a metal fence, and beyond it David saw a church. It took a moment for his memory to serve up the name – old St Patrick's Church.

Maj stopped outside. 'I want to introduce you to some friends,' he said. 'But something happened while I was out of town. We've got outsiders taking too much interest. I need to try to talk to someone, get his advice. You can't come with me. He won't talk if you're there. He probably won't anyhow.'

'Why?'

'I won't be long. Half an hour. I'll meet you at Bid's. You remember that, at least?'

David didn't, or at least hadn't thought of the place in years, but then there it was – back in his head. A basement bar not far from where they now stood.

'Get a table in back if you can. In the meantime, there's something you should do.'

'What?'

'Call your wife,' Maj said, and walked away.

It took David ten minutes to get an approach straight in his head. Then he stood on a corner and called her.

'Plus amazingly I ran into someone,' he said, low-key, after he'd told her everything he'd done – up to but *not* including whatever he'd just experienced in Union Square. 'From when I lived here.'

'Would this be a man someone . . . or a lady someone?'

'Man, of course,' David said quickly.

'I'm joking,' Dawn said, though she sounded a little relieved. 'So who is he? I don't remember you mentioning anybody in particular from back then.'

'His name . . . he's called Maj.'

'Weird name.'

'He's . . . kind of a weird guy.'

'Do you want to stay there tonight and hang out?'

'Would that be okay?'

'Of course, silly. If you're going to set a book

there, this has to be a good thing, right? He should be able to help. With current stuff, atmosphere, what it's like living there now. It's been a while since you were in the city properly, after all.'

'Exactly,' David said.

'Where would you stay?'

'I don't know. Maybe with him. Crash on a couch or something.' There was silence down the line. 'What?'

'I wasn't going to tell you,' she said, in a bubbling rush. 'I wanted you to find it when you got home. But there's a letter for you from Ralph's office. Plus . . . I checked our account. Your advance came through.'

David felt exhausted. 'Oh, thank God.'

'So if you wanted to stay in a hotel or something, it's okay. Nowhere too fancy, though – save that for when we're there together.'

'I will,' he said, laughing, feeling relief wash over him – mingling with guilt he felt for not being honest with her. 'What will you do?'

'I'll muddle through somehow. I'm . . .' She hesitated. 'Maybe it's wrong. But I thought I might start sorting through the spare room.'

For a moment David didn't get what she meant – he couldn't imagine what would impel her to tackle the room on the second floor where all the homeless junk in their lives got thrown – but then he did.

'Go for it,' he said, momentarily nowhere else in the world except on this phone call, with this woman.

'You don't think it's too early?'

196

'I think it's a great idea.'

'And it won't . . . you know.'

He knew what she meant. That starting to prepare the room for a nursery would anger the gods, causing them to reach down to stir darkness back into their lives.

'No,' he said firmly. 'We walked a long way down Superstition Road the other times and it didn't help at all. Good things need welcoming too, and that's what we're going to do this time.'

'I love you,' she said.

'I love you too.'

'So go hang out. But get home early tomorrow. Remember what we're doing.'

'What?'

'The scan,' she said. 'I told you.'

'I knew that.'

'Hmm.'

'Be careful, okay? Don't move anything big. Wait until I get back.'

'I'll be fine. I'm only a bit pregnant.'

'That's like being a bit unique.'

'Pedant. Buzz off and have fun. But not too much.'

David lowered the phone from his ear, feeling a pang of regret for not being home, for not being able to hug his wife at the moment they'd discovered he'd been paid. He resolved that nothing like this should ever happen again, making it all the more important that he got to the bottom of what was happening right now, and end it.

* * *

It took him another five minutes to get to Bid's, down a side street not far from Bleecker. His feet remembered the way even if he didn't. He hesitated on the sidewalk. The door at the bottom of the steps was open and you could smell decades of stale beer from where he stood. He hadn't yet discounted the idea that this was a complicated con and/or set-up – and if so, that getting further into it was a very dumb idea. Right now, a voice was telling him, he could just split. There was no one here to stop him. He could get the hell out and just go home.

That was his rational mind, however.

Another part knew, though it didn't understand, that something else was going on, that even if he didn't remember Maj, he somehow knew him – and that things do not go away simply because you turn your back or run away, and that at least this was a public place.

It was this part that took him down the stairs and into the past.

CHAPTER 23

The bar was low-ceilinged and narrow and would have felt cramped even if there hadn't been a lot of people already filling it, drinking hard. When David reached the bottom of the stairs he was hit with a wave of recollection. He'd stood on this spot a number of times, looking out for someone – usually one of the aspiring artists/writers/whatevers he'd struck up acquaintance with while he lived there, and had never heard from since. The sensation wasn't one of simple nostalgia, however: he also knew that on some of those occasions he'd been feeling much as he was now – trepidation, a sense of duty he didn't want to fulfill. He took faltering steps into the mass of people milling around, propping up the bar, lurking at the few tables at the edges. Bid's made even less effort to be welcoming than Kendricks – took a typically New York pride in this, in fact – and evidently remained the lair of hard-core locals and hipsters.

Finally he saw someone he recognized, a face at the far end of the room. It wasn't Maj, however. It was the man in the ill-fitting suit who'd spoken to David when he first reached Union Square Park.

The man rolled his eyes as if glad to have finally gotten his attention, and beckoned with a small upward nod. When David didn't respond immediately, he gestured him to come over, more urgently. Not knowing what else to do, David started to shoulder his way through the drinkers.

When he got to the other side he saw the man was standing diffidently beside a small table with three stools around it. 'Sit down,' he said.

'Why?'

'Just do it, mate, eh? Quickly.'

His manner was deferential but insistent. David sat. The man immediately followed suit, selecting the stool on the opposite side of the table, so that David was facing the wall when he looked at him.

'Why did you wait for me to sit down?'

'Don't move your mouth so much when you talk, eh?'

'Why?'

'Because you'll look like a knob.'

'I don't . . . know you, do I?'

'Nah. Didn't know Maj back then, did I? The name's Bob. Fictitious Bob, if you want to be formal.'

'What can I get you?'

David looked up to see a straggle-haired girl standing over him with the air of a person for whom this encounter had gotten old and too dull for words before she'd even opened her mouth. 'Huh?'

'To *drink*.'

David ordered the first beer that came into his head and watched, baffled, as the girl barged off through the crowd. Bid's had been celebrated for the bad-temperedness of its staff, he remembered. He turned to Bob.

'Why didn't she ask you what *you* wanted?'

Bob shook his head as if every question David asked wrote the word 'buffoon' in bigger letters on his forehead.

At that moment Maj appeared out of the crowd and sat straight down at the remaining place. He glanced around as if taking the measure of the room, and moved the stool to be closer to Bob. He looked preoccupied.

'Got your work cut out here, Maj,' Bob said, nodding toward David. 'Makes your average Dozeno sound like Lonely Clive.'

'Being here didn't help? You still don't remember anything?' Maj asked David, exasperated. 'I was hoping the fact that you'd come to the city meant something. And we used to meet here often. Before you stopped.'

'I . . . had a dream last night.' David hesitated, looking at Bob.

'He's a friend,' Maj said. 'And a Cornerman. You don't get any more discreet than that.'

Bob nodded with what appeared to be pride.

'What's a Cornerman?'

Bob glanced at Maj as if warning him not to respond, but Maj overrode him. 'The closest we've got to newspapers, cell phones, and e-mail. What was the dream about, David? Quickly. It's too crowded here tonight. You won't be able to hold this table long.'

'Why?'

'David, seriously. The dream.'

'I was in my parents' house,' David said, feeling like a kid at school being railroaded into something by older boys who seemed to understand everything he did not. 'I couldn't stand their fighting, but I couldn't get away. So I went under the kitchen table.'

David had Maj's full attention now, and he realized how familiar the man's face seemed. Not as it was, but as it had been in an earlier incarnation. He'd known this man well. 'There was another boy under there.'

Maj didn't say anything.

'That was you, wasn't it? And it wasn't a dream. It was a memory.'

The man smiled – beautifully, looking in that instant so like the boy from David's dream that he didn't even have to answer the question. Something twisted in David's heart, forgotten joy cut with regret and loss.

'But . . . *how*?' David said.

The waitress reappeared, slapped a glass on the table, and barked a number at David. After paying for the beer he took a swallow. A familiar taste flooded his mouth, and he pulled the glass away and stared at it. 'This is Brooklyn Lager,' he said.

'What you ordered,' Bob said. 'Good choice. May I?'

'It's crowded, Bob,' Maj said.

'Oh, go on. It's been ages.'

Maj rolled his eyes. 'David, stand up a second.'

David did as he'd been told. Nearby drinkers glanced at the table, one couple even taking a meaningful step toward it. Realizing he had to send some kind of signal to hold them off, David hitched up his trousers, as if he'd stood for that purpose.

Meanwhile Maj and Bob ducked their heads toward the table. Bob took a big slurp from the top of the beer. Maj then tilted the depleted glass toward his own face without lifting it from the table and did the same before returning it to the upright position. They leaned back together. The whole thing took three seconds.

'Nice.' Bob ran his tongue around his lips appreciatively. 'Can't beat your local lagers.'

'Sit down,' Maj said to David.

David sat, and the seat vultures went back to their conversations, for now. Nobody seemed to have noticed what had happened at the table in the meantime, and David looked curiously at Maj.

'You get good at playing the angles,' Maj said. 'And misdirection, of course.'

'Maj is the best,' Bob said. 'Famous for it.'

'Maybe,' Maj said. 'But it doesn't pay to get overconfident.'

'You get anything out of St Pat's?' Bob asked, still eyeing David's beer. 'Talk to Clive?'

Maj shook his head. 'He's not there. Apparently he took himself to the basement two days ago. So . . . that's the end of him.'

'Sorry, mate.'

Maj shrugged, but it didn't look convincing.

'Worth checking any of the others?'

'They're even worse.'

'Doesn't *have* to be a problem though, does it?'

'No. It happens all the time. But Lizzie said these people seem very nosy and one might have sharper sight than normal – which is why I came back to the city in a hurry. Not to mention there are a few friends who'd like to capitalize on any outside threat right now.'

A shadow passed over Bob's face. 'Speak of the devil.'

Maj turned. At first David couldn't work out who they were talking about. Then a chill ran down his neck.

Four people were standing next to the bar in a line, their backs up against the wall. David realized with a start that he'd seen one of them before – the short, stocky one was the man who'd been glaring at him in Union Square Park, near the end. The others were thinner and taller, *weirdly* tall, dressed in clothing so dark it was hard to make out details of individual garments. Two men, one with long, gray straggly hair, the other cropped short over a skull that looked like it had

204

been shaped with blows from a shovel. Between them stood a painfully thin woman whose hair was dirty red. All had pale skin stretched over large and bony facial features, and they looked so similar they had to be related.

They were very still – or so David thought at first. Everyone around them was in movement, leaning toward one another, gesturing at bar staff, laughing, talking, looking around for seats. The four up against the wall appeared motionless . . . except if you looked at them long enough you realized they were vibrating slightly, enough to make their edges look a little blurry.

'Christ,' Maj said.

'How does he do it?' Bob asked, with what sounded like awe. 'Just *appear* like that – as if he knows someone's been talking about him?'

'Nothing magical about it,' Maj said irritably. 'Golzen's been sniffing around me for weeks, and his three spooks have been hard on my tail since I got back to the city. Golzen probably told them to follow me. That's all.'

Bob didn't look convinced.

'Who *is* that guy?' David asked. 'The shorter one? I've seen him before.'

'When?'

'In Union Square. He was staring at me.'

This seemed to confirm whatever concerns Bob had about the man. 'I'm not liking this, Maj,' he muttered. 'I don't want to get on Golzen's bad side.'

'Fuck him. He's just like the rest of us.'

'I'm not so sure. I hear a lot of things, remember. People are taking him seriously these days, more and more. There's chatter going back and forth.'

'Like what?'

'You know I can't tell you, Maj.'

'I meant in general.'

'They want to know what he's saying, that's all. And he left a broadcast with me a couple days ago. Sounded like he was telling people to get ready for something. But not everyone. Just them who knew some code.'

'What was the broadcast?'

'It was "For the twelve. Be ready. Follow signs until Jedburgh appears."'

'What?' Maj laughed. 'It's bullshit. He sends out random nonsense to make his acolytes think he knows something. He's crazy. All four of them are.'

'So you say. But I'd already been hearing rumors about twelve chosen ones, Golzen and eleven others. What if he's finally found out where Perfect is? I don't want to get left behind, do I?'

'Bob, it's a *myth*.'

'I dunno. I'm hearing things. Every day. They say getting to Perfect will be like the Bloom – but it lasts forever. And you get *strong*.'

'There's *no such place*. It's Chinese whispers and wishful thinking and the demagogue fantasies of a guy who's not right in the head. The Bloom is the Bloom and then it's done. End of story.'

'I'm *hearing* things, Maj,' Bob repeated stubbornly.

As the two men argued, David noticed there were a couple of small wet patches on the floor by their stools, as if a splash of water had dropped from the ceiling in front of each of them. When he glanced upward to see where it might have come from, he discovered his view was obscured. Two guys in T-shirts were standing over the table, very close. *Too* close. They had hard faces and the boxy, geometric shoulders of men who paid daily homage to their self-image with repetitive exercise.

'Waiting for someone?' the nearest one asked.

'No.'

The other smirked. 'You sure?'

For a moment David couldn't work out what this was supposed to mean, then realized the men were looking at him in a way that was predatory and unkind. 'Look . . .'

'No, *you* look. The place is slammed. Either drift or we're going to join you.'

'What are you talking about? There's no space left.'

'Are you being funny?'

David looked anxiously at Maj and Bob for backup. They weren't there. The stools on the other side of the table were empty.

The first guy squatted down so his face was close to David's. His eyes were very sharp and blue, but there was no depth to them at all.

'So what's the story, princess? You want to make some nice new friends?'

David got up hurriedly. He made his way into the crowd without looking back, but heard the two men laughing together all the same. In the last half hour the room had gotten so packed that he had to shove his way through the crowds. How had Maj and Bob managed to get away so quickly?

When he got to the door he glanced back, but couldn't see any sign of either of them. The other people remained at the end of the bar, however, in a line, their backs against the wall. They turned their heads as one to watch David as he left. The girl smiled at him.

It was not a good smile.

CHAPTER 24

Maj was waiting on the sidewalk in the twilight, looking distracted. Bob had gone.

'This isn't going how I hoped,' Maj muttered.

David stormed up to him. 'Look, just tell me *what the hell is happening*. Who *are* you?'

'I'm your friend.'

David felt hysterical with everything he didn't understand. 'Yes, you *keep saying that*, but how *can* you be if *I don't even know who you are?*'

'There's someone else,' Maj said. 'He's one of you, not one of us. He's wrong about a lot of things, but he might be able to explain the situation in a way you'll find easier to understand. The most important thing is the opportunity we've got now. This almost never happens, David. I don't know *anyone* who it happened to. Or where it happened and took. It's like . . .' He thought for a moment. 'Do you remember third grade science class?'

'*What*? Of course not.'

'Yeah, you were never keen on the science bits. I liked it, though. It's like magnets with opposite

209

charges. They *attract*, right? Magnets with opposite charges attract and stick together – and if the charge is strong, they stick *hard*. Pull them apart and they'll try to move back together, to be as one. That's how it was with us for a long time. But then . . .'

Maj stopped talking and started to walk away. David saw no option but to follow, and keep prompting him, in the hope that sooner or later he'd say something that made sense. 'Then what?'

'Something happens,' Maj said. 'The charge in one magnet starts to reverse. The magnet like you. *Always* the one like you.' He sounded bitter. 'After a while they won't stick anymore. They repel, in fact, so strongly that everything gets forgotten – by you, again, not by us. Cornermen like Bob may have the very best memories, but we're all pretty good at that shit. It's in our nature to look back. To act as custodians of what was.'

'But this reversal . . .'

'It can take place over weeks or months or years. It can happen early or it can happen late. You and I were unusually late, but then it fell apart *fast*.'

'You're saying we were friends,' David insisted doggedly.

'*Yes*. For God's sake.'

'But where?'

'From that moment under the table. Here, too, almost the whole time you lived in the city.'

'So how come I don't remember you?'

'You grew up. Kids are born without all the made-up rules, but then the world spends the first twenty years of everybody's life drumming the magic out. Training them to draw a line around each individual to separate them from the rest of the universe, turning them into "I" instead of being part of a cloud of interaction that stretches in all directions. Once the line's been inked around you, the shutters come down. That's what Lonely Clive used to say, anyway, and I figure he was right.'

David stuck with it. 'Who *was* this Clive?'

'He took me under his wing after you left the city, and he's the only one of us who ever got this close to a reconnect. It didn't work out, and that was the beginning of the end for him. He's hollow now.'

'I've tried,' David said. 'I really have. But I don't understand *a single thing you've said.*'

'You just don't *want* to remember,' Maj snapped. 'Which proves some part of you remembers *something.*'

'Yo, Maj!'

A teenage girl wearing a gray hoodie over a strange array of other garments came up the sidewalk toward them. David recognized her from the park, the girl who'd been near the woman in the ball gown. She looked like a runaway, about seventeen, and as if she'd selected her wardrobe in a concerted effort to piss off or perplex anyone over the age of twenty-three.

Maj smiled back. 'S'up, girl?'

'It's all epic.' She grinned. 'All the time. We're headed to a party down in 'packing. It's going to be awesome. Wanna come?'

'Love to,' Maj said. 'But I'm busy right now.'

She pouted. 'You've *always* got shit to do.'

'Shit don't get done by itself, right?'

The girl laughed and went off down the street. She seemed to turn her head a couple of times, as if to talk to someone beside her.

'Okay,' Maj said to David, starting to walk in the other direction. 'Come meet a guy.'

CHAPTER 25

I'm so loving my life right now. It's amazing.
I'm just chilling, doing my thing. I've got some
great new girlfriends, and every morning we
wake up and it's like, 'What are we going to do
today?' and we walk out of wherever we crashed
without looking back and then we'll hang in a park
or go look in stores or whatever. It's all so totally
laid-back and at night we'll find somewhere new
to sleep and there're always new people to meet,
too, and always a party somewhere. Lately I've
been meeting a load of these super-cool friends
called Angels, who are dressed in black the whole
time, and I never thought that look would be for
me, but I'm starting to kind of like it, especially
as it's not like total goth or anything because they'll
wear these bright clothes underneath, like a dress
or shirt or whatever. I'm not even sure why they're
so friendly to me because I don't really know them
and they didn't go to the school or come from the
neighborhood, but basically they're these super-
nice people and they go around doing epic things
and helping people out. Sometimes some of them
steal stuff, but not often and only from really big

corporations and so it's not a big deal. There're some other people who take a lot more stuff and they steal from normal people. They have, like, this leader or whatever, but they're not like the Angels. They're kind of heavy and scary instead and they don't do good things for other people and they have this idea of a place and it's like their heaven or something. There's twelve of them and I don't really get it, but I don't hang with them anyway because I think maybe it's okay if you just steal something every now and then, but if you're totally doing it the whole time that's so not cool. That's what Lizzie says, and she even says any stealing at all is not good and she doesn't do it anymore. She's one of the key Angels and I agree with her. She's like a big sister to me, and she said if I ever start to feel confused I should go talk to her and she'll explain things. I think maybe I might get into that whole Angel thing at some point, but not yet, because it's too much fun hanging out and partying with my friends even though sometimes it's complicated because they can't remember their names, and I can't either, so it's hard to make arrangements. But it always seems to work out and it's not a big deal.

The only thing that's a bummer is I don't see much of Jessica anymore. I go watch her every now and then, and sometimes if I can get in the house I sleep on the floor under her bed, but she's, like, doing this thing right now where she pretends not to see me the whole time, or even hear me, and she doesn't hang in the places we used to go. If I see her in the evenings, she's out with all these other people she knows from high school and I realize, how freaking long *is* it since we really hung together? And I think, huh, if she's in high school then it's got to be like a year or two or maybe four, but I'm sure it's all fine and she's just super-busy or something. We are so best friends forever and that never dies. It's not like she was with Cynthia Markham, a total bitch she was tight with in the sixth grade but who screwed her over and was like suddenly I'm not your friend anymore, end of story, and I stuck with Jessica through that time even though she wasn't friendly to me at all. That's what best friends are for, right? Okay so she's got like a boyfriend now, and if it's really five or six years since we spoke, then I've been living in the city a lot longer than I realized, but that's not going to change anything because when you're best friends nothing in the world can change that, *ever*. There was a while when I'd throw things around in the house and try to scare her, but it didn't work and I gave up and it was dumb anyway. She's just going through, like, a phase or something, but it's all good and it'll be okay in the end because true friendship never dies.

It never dies.

CHAPTER 26

As I walked across 16th I heard the sound of the piano. Once again it sounded like it was coming from one of the upper windows of the town house next to the church. The piece was familiar, measured and sane and beautiful. Bach, in other words. I drew to a halt beneath a streetlight. The player fumbled, stopped, repeated a section with the stress on different hands, then returned patiently to the beginning. Though he or she was not destined for Carnegie Hall they were better than competent, partly because the playing had the freedom of someone who is rehearsing for their own benefit and does not realize they are overheard. There are people for whom an audience is essential, who raise their game and feel more real when observed. The rest of us do much of what we do in an attempt to fill ourselves up, and that is more easily done in private.

I let myself in through the low iron gate and walked up the right staircase to the door of the church. I knocked. As before, there was no response. I tried the handle, but now it was locked.

I was about to knock again but noticed a

tarnished buzzer on the side. I pressed it. It didn't sound like anything happened. I hadn't banked on being stymied so quickly and was about to press it again, largely out of frustration, when I heard the sound of a window opening.

I stepped back and looked up to see a head and shoulders sticking out of the window on the second floor of the town house. It was the priest.

He waved. 'Just a moment,' he said, and disappeared.

I walked down to wait for him out on the sidewalk. He appeared out of the house a few minutes later and trotted down the steps, not looking at all put out.

'Had the bell rewired over to my quarters,' he said cheerfully. 'If I'm in the church, the door's always open. If I'm not, what's the point of the bell ringing in an empty room?'

'I'm sorry to interrupt your practice.'

'Oh, it's not important.'

'Bach?'

'Indeed. *The Well-Tempered Clavier*, Prelude Five.'

'You're pretty good.'

He made a face that was polite but dismissive, the expression you use when someone praises you for something they don't really understand.

'Seriously. Good separation, not too clinical or fast but you don't lean into the bends either. Difficult to guess whether you'd prefer the Barenboim or Angela Hewitt. Certainly not the early Gould.'

He raised an eyebrow. 'You play?'

'I used to, a little. Back in the day.'

'No longer?'

'I lost my audience.'

He nodded affably. 'I've never wanted one. It's something I do for myself. A kind of meditation, perhaps. It doesn't matter whether anyone hears.'

'That's what I used to tell myself. But it matters.'

He smiled in a way that remained friendly but was also final, which said I was wandering into territory he knew better than me, and which he had no wish to discuss.

He stuck out his hand. 'Father Robert,' he said. 'Or Robert Jeffers, if you'd prefer.'

'John Henderson.'

'How can I help you, Mr Henderson?'

'I was here earlier today,' I said. 'The door to the church was open then.'

'Of course. I was inside.'

'I'd just seen you walk off down the road.'

I assume priests get a lot of practice in developing a facial expression that says they're listening without judging. 'Of course,' Jeffers said. His eyes were tired, and his shave that morning, though close, had not been perfect. 'I received a call mid-afternoon, someone who wished to see me urgently. And you're correct – when I got back I realized I'd forgotten to lock up. Luckily nobody entered while I was away.'

'Actually, they did. Me.'

'Well, you seem like a person of good intent.'

'It comes and goes. The funny thing is, I thought I saw you exchange words with someone inside as you left.'

'Well, of course.'

'I didn't see anyone while I was in there.'

He smiled. 'I'm sorry. It's a conceit of mine. I meant the Lord. I always exchange a few words with him on entering or leaving the building.'

'Does he reply?'

'Naturally. You should try it sometime.'

'I will. If I ever think of something to ask.'

The priest smiled tolerantly, and it struck me how wearying it must be to work in a profession where people either ask too much of you or else don't believe a word you say. 'I've seen you before, haven't I?'

'Yes. Yesterday afternoon.'

'Of course. The running man. Did you find the person you were looking for?'

'No. She disappeared. Funny thing is – sorry to use the expression again, but it *is* kind of strange – I think the same woman disappeared in this same street a couple of nights before.'

'Are you a policeman?'

'No.'

'Then what is your interest?'

'She's been following a friend of mine.'

'Following?'

'Tracking her home from social engagements. Waiting when she picks her daughters up from school. Maybe even standing out in the street at night looking up at her windows. *That* kind of following. The not-good kind.'

'How unsettling.'

I didn't say anything. The best way of getting someone to volunteer information is to leave them hanging. People feel the need to fill awkward space, and while they won't give up what you want straightaway, often they'll show you the beginning of the path.

Jeffers had more self-possession than this, however – or else genuinely had no idea what I was talking about. He merely stood there, looking composed.

'A tall woman,' I said. 'Young, dark hair, long dark coat, red dress.'

'Doesn't sound like one of my flock, I'm afraid.'

'You guys really still say "flock"?'

'I do. I can't speak for others.'

'The *other* funny thing – and this really is the last time, I promise – is I'm pretty sure I saw the woman again after I left your church. In Union Square.' His face was blank now. 'Was she the person you left the church in such a hurry to see?'

'No. That was an elderly gentleman in quite the other direction,' Jeffers said. 'So I'm afraid you must have been mistaken.'

I took out one of the Adriatico's cards and wrote my number on the back. When I offered it to the priest, he looked at it and then at me as if my meaning was unclear. I kept holding it out until he took it.

'Is there anything else?' he asked.

I thanked him for his time and remained where I was while he headed back up the stairs and into his house. He walked more heavily this time, without the personable trot he'd arrived with, but he did not look back.

As I set off down the street I heard him start the second Prelude. It was good – nearly flawless, in fact, at least the portion I caught before I got out of range and the music became buried beneath the sound of traffic. That prelude is a compact little pocket of baroque fury, tight under the hands, and no one's idea of easy. A risky choice to switch from the fifth to that, unless perhaps you knew someone was still likely to be in earshot and might know enough to be impressed.

I thought the priest was kidding himself, just a little. He wanted to be heard.

He was also deluding himself if he believed he'd convinced me. Kristina had followed him to Union Square. I'd seen him there too. Had I learned anything by talking to him tonight? Only that he was willing to lie to me – but from this followed other things. First, there was some connection between him and the woman who'd been following Catherine. Them being together in the park said this, and that maybe she *had* come down this road the day before and he knew where she'd disappeared to.

Second, he was an amateur at misleading people. If someone puts you on the spot, you either avoid saying anything of consequence or tell the truth and dare the motherfucker to make something of it. This made me wonder how he'd gotten himself into a position where he was covering up for someone else.

What makes a priest lie?

I walked to the end of the street and left a message on Kristina's cell. She'd be busy in the bar but get it soon enough. I bought a lousy coffee from the nearest deli and wandered back to the corner.

I'd taken the night off and I didn't have anything else to do. I figured I'd wait a while.

CHAPTER 27

Half an hour later someone turned onto the street, a nondescript-looking man walking quickly. His movements were a little unusual, and at first I took him for one of those people who endlessly circulate the city's streets, alone, like bugs on a solo trek around a vast windowpane. He turned his head to the side once in a while, as if exercising a crick in his neck. After he'd come twenty yards toward me I caught the sound of conversation, however, and belatedly realized he wasn't alone. I'm not sure how I could have missed the other guy given he was actually in front, and it became clear that the man I'd noticed first was trying to keep up.

Luckily, they were coming up the other side of the street to where I'd been standing, getting cold. I took a step back into the shadows. As they drew level opposite I saw the man in front was wearing jeans and an untucked shirt and realized: these were the guys I'd observed near the priest in Union Square that afternoon.

The one in jeans led the other through the gates

of the church. They trotted up the stairs, and the leading man pressed the doorbell.

I turned my head to watch the priest's house. He'd stopped practicing soon after our conversation and it had been quiet from there since, though a light had come on once the night came in.

After a moment the upper window opened and Jeffers stuck his head out. He looked across to the church, then pulled his head back and shut the window.

Two minutes later he appeared out of the front door and walked quickly down the stairs.

'What do you want?' he asked when he reached the men. His tone was polite but less generically friendly than when he'd spoken to me.

I didn't hear what the taller man said, but a moment later the other said 'David.'

The priest took the other man aside and there was a short conversation. The guy called David stayed where he was. From forty feet away I could tell he wasn't happy to be there, but he waited anyway. At one point he glanced across the street, but I didn't move. Unless you're confident someone's already spotted you, moving is merely the best method of making sure that they will.

The priest eventually got keys out of his pocket and unlocked the church. He stood back to let the other men in, then followed. The door closed behind them with a solid clunk.

I stepped out of the shadows. I don't know much about the lives of priests. I can imagine that tending to the spiritual needs of others is not a nine-to-five job, and requests for guidance may arise at almost any time. I suspect it's still unusual for two guys to turn up together at eight thirty in the evening, however. They didn't look like they'd been in doubt that they would be received, either. The taller of the two had presented as though he felt he had a call upon the priest, or a high level of familiarity at least.

They could just be members of the flock, or perhaps the priest ran some kind of outreach program and these people were cautiously scaling the foothills of recovery.

It was none of my business, of course.

But I kept watching.

Fifteen minutes later someone else turned onto the street, but straightaway I knew there was something different about him. It was partly the way he dressed – a dark suit under an expensive-looking long coat – but mainly in the walk. There's a style of locomotion you see only in a city, the stride of a man – and it's always a man; women have their walks of power, but this is not one of them – who believes himself the dominant animal in his habitat. You never see this walk in the country or in small towns, which are insufficiently similar to the wild. You have to be in a city.

This is my track through this place, and yes, I do own the fucking road.

As he came up the street, heels making tapping

225

sounds on the sidewalk, I was taken aback to realize I'd made the same mistake *again*. Something about the arrangement of the streetlights and shadows clearly made it hard to pick people out. This man was also not walking alone, or at least hadn't been the only person to enter the street at more or less the same time.

Following behind him was a small group of people. One was a short, bulky man in a retro suit who looked like he was trying to walk the other man's walk and not carrying it off. The other three were much taller and thinner, and loped along with heads lowered.

The guy in the coat walked straight up to the church gate and let himself in. The others hung back. I watched the man walk up the stairs, and then glanced back at the second group to see that they'd disappeared.

The man in the coat opened the church door without knocking or ringing the bell. He didn't close it behind him either. It could be that I'd simply spent too long watching strangers do not very interesting things, but I thought that was kind of weird.

It was quiet for five minutes. Then I heard the sound of shouting, and something being broken.

It was still none of my business, but that's never really stopped me.

I stepped off the sidewalk and jogged across the street.

★   ★   ★

226

When I got to the church door I could see straight into the hall at the end of the corridor. The man in the long coat was walking up and down, hands on hips and coat flared out behind, like a ham actor delivering a key speech. I couldn't see anyone else and so I kept going.

The priest was in the middle of the hall surrounded by chairs – some of which had been overturned, a couple broken. The second of the two guys I'd seen earlier was behind him, looking totally out of his depth. There was no sign of the other, the man in the untucked shirt, though the door at the other end of the room was ajar.

The man in the coat turned to me. He looked about forty. His hair was cropped and his face broad but the features even. I could feel the power of his presence from where I stood. 'Who the fuck are you?'

His accent was flat. Not New York.

'One of the faithful,' I said. 'I need to talk with the father about something that's been troubling me.'

'You shitting me?'

'No. Why do you ask?'

'The father's *busy*,' he said. 'I suggest you come back another time.' He turned to face the priest.

'That's not convenient.'

The man was motionless for a moment. When he turned to face me again there was a smile on his face. It was quite like one, anyway. 'Say again?'

'You know how it is with spiritual matters. They crave instant solution. I assume that's why you're here too. Maybe we should go somewhere, compare notes.'

He laughed, and turned back to the priest. He liked his body movements, this guy. He was all about owning the space. 'Seriously, Jeffers – who the fuck is this person? He a friend of yours?'

The priest said nothing. The man behind him kept glancing at the door, and appeared to be trying to work out his chances of being able to run at it without being intercepted. It looked as though he had nowhere near enough experience of making that kind of calculation to be confident about it, and was aware of the fact.

The man in the coat grew thoughtful. 'Wait a minute,' he said to me. 'I know you.'

I hadn't been expecting this. I said nothing.

'Yeah.' He nodded to himself. 'I don't know where, but I've seen you.'

'Could be,' I said. 'I don't hide.'

He came and stood about a yard from me. 'Sometimes hiding is a good move, my friend. Running never works. But hiding? Sometimes it's the clever thing to do.'

Up close he smelled of cologne and self-confidence. He wasn't scared of me but he wasn't dumb, either. Something random had come into his orbit and he was too smart to do the obvious and throw a punch or pull out a gun – something I was by now pretty sure that he'd have about his person – and I realized maybe I should have sent Kris a message before I came barging in here.

There was a flurry of movement, the clatter of a chair knocked over, and receding footsteps. The scared-looking guy had chosen his moment, and run.

I kept my eyes straight ahead, on coat man's face. He looked at me a moment longer, then stepped back and laughed quietly to himself. The father remained where he was, hands by his side, looking pinched but composed.

'This guy's right,' the man in the coat said to him. 'I came here for a talk too. But you're busy tonight, it seems. You got all these people coming to you for help at once. Some other time.'

He gave me a nod and walked toward the door. Just before he left, he turned back.

'There *will* be another time,' he said, but not to me. I'd already been dismissed. 'We will talk.'

He seemed to be directing the remark toward the door at the other end of the hall. Then he was gone.

Jeffers let out a sharp, hard breath, and ran his hands quickly over his face. 'Thank you,' he said.

'Who's down there? Through the door?'

'Nobody.'

'You mind if I take a look?'

'Yes, I do,' he said. 'This is a church. But even if I let you, you wouldn't find anyone.'

Curiously, I didn't get the sense that he was lying. 'I don't know what you've got going,' I said, 'or who the hell that man was.'

'His name's Reinhart.'

'Whatever. I've met people like him before. You don't want them in your life.'

229

'Thank you for the advice,' he said. 'I'll be sure to bear it in mind.'

When I got back onto the street I looked for the man in the coat, but there was no sign. I did catch a glimpse of the guy who'd bolted, however. He was right up at the corner of Ninth, head down and hands stuffed in his pockets, walking fast.

As he turned the corner, I thought I saw something else – three tall figures, thirty feet behind him, also hurrying, as if following. The image didn't resolve, however, and I guess it must have been more of the street's strange shadow patterns.

I turned for home.

CHAPTER 28

After Henderson left, the priest stood for five minutes. He sent up a prayer for guidance, but ran out of steam after the initial formalities. Sometimes it went that way. You picked up the phone and got a dead tone. A lot of people gave up at this point. Jeffers knew some days the plea went to voice mail and that's that. He's a busy guy. Give Him a chance. Jeffers believed this, at least, on good days.

In the meantime he turned to dealing with the chairs that had been knocked over. He picked each up carefully, inspected it for damage, and returned it to its place in the rows facing toward the end of the hall. There were twelve of these, divided by an aisle in the middle. On both sides each held seven chairs. The days of the week, multiplied by two, multiplied again by the number of Christ's disciples, another of the private conceits he entertained in an effort to introduce meaning into his days. With faith, so much of what's important takes place behind the scenes. Not including the single chair at the head, which faced the other way and on which he sat while delivering his informal sermons, the church provided a hundred and forty-four places for the faithful to sit, less the three that had now been broken.

Too many chairs.

He gathered up the pieces and carried them to the side. One was damaged beyond repair – the chair that had been on the receiving end of Reinhart's kick. The other two were collateral casualities and had received only superficial damage – legs or spindles dislodged from sockets. Jeffers supposed that they would be relatively easy to repair if you knew what you were doing with a hammer or glue. The world of physical objects had never been his domain. Even as a child he'd been prone to playing with ideas rather than things, and had never made much of a distinction. He'd ask Dave to have a look at the chairs. Dave was an ex-alcoholic who'd been coming to the church for years (his conversion an early success of Jeffers's predecessor, Father Ronson) and transitioned more easily than some to the new priest. He functioned as an occasional unpaid cleaner, but from time to time he'd shown himself to be a halfway competent handyman too. Nothing ever quite worked as it should when he'd had his hands on it (the oil heater, for example, which was now discreetly stowed in the basement, along with its fuel, so as not to hurt the man's feelings), but fixing a few chairs would be within his capabilities . . . pointless though it would be. Jeffers was lucky to see twenty people in the church at any

232

one time. The other chairs were merely there to make up the numbers, and as a statement of intent.

One lived in hope, and worked in hope, and that was the way it should be. Hope is how the idea of faith operates in the world.

Hope is how you make faith do real things.

When Father Jeffers turned from the pile he saw Maj on the other side of the room. Maj didn't look happy.

'Who was the other guy?' Maj asked.

'The one I've told you about.'

'The guy who's been tracking Lizzie?'

Jeffers nodded.

'He looks like trouble.'

'Your friend ran away.'

'He's always had a tendency toward flight.'

'You're not going after him?'

'He'll be halfway to Penn Station by now. I know where he lives. Right now I'm more concerned about Reinhart turning up here.'

Jeffers sensed this wasn't entirely true and that the man was doing his best to cover intense disappointment. He also knew that Maj, like many of his kind, strongly resisted being told what to feel. Their emotions and memories were all they had.

'How do you think that happened?'

'Golzen must have led him here. He's building up to something. Fictitious Bob told me earlier that he's been sending out broadcasts designed to hide something. I had an encounter with Golzen myself before I left town, and he and the three ghouls turned up in a bar earlier.'

'Were the messages about Perfect?'

'Not self-evidently. But who knows?'

'If he's preparing to leave on his quest, why would he bring Reinhart here?'

'Could be it wasn't his idea. You met the guy. Does Reinhart seem like someone who lets people do what they choose?'

'I'd like a meeting tomorrow,' Jeffers said. 'You, Lizzie, Bob, and as many of the others as you can gather.'

Maj shrugged. 'Lizzie's being kind of . . . I think she's gotten spooked by these people following her. There's something on her mind. I don't know what it is.'

'I'd like it if you could try. Especially with her.'

When Maj had gone, the priest took a walk around the room, checking that everything else was in place. When he was satisfied, he went to the far end and closed the door there. He locked the church and went around to the house. He paused before going inside and looked up and down the street, half expecting to see someone in the shadows. There was nothing to see, but that didn't mean there was no one there. Reinhart would be back, too. He was sure of that. Though until tonight he'd known the man only by reputation, a confrontation had been inevitable. Black and white, right and wrong, good and evil. They rub along together most of the time, but a battle always comes.

So be it.

Upstairs he stood becalmed in his sitting room. Usually he spent this period preparing for the next day. Planning a schedule of visits for those unable to visit the church in person, which boiled down to reassuring the very old that no, they didn't look so bad and yes, God would be there waiting for them. There was nothing of the sort booked for the next day, however, which left working out what to say to the drop-in group at four and starting to gather his thoughts for the weekend's sermon. He was ahead of himself on the first task, and drawing a blank on the second except for reiterating the bottom line:

God is basically on your side, so if life seems to suck it's probably part of some big plan. In the meantime, pray. And keep coming to church, for Pete's sake. I'm not doing this for the fun of it.

He sat in the chair by the window. It was the single decent piece of furniture in a room that was otherwise Spartan. It didn't have to be that way. Nobody ever came up here. He could buy what he wanted, within reason and the constraints of his salary. He could pimp it out like a gangsta bordello, if he chose, or install a revolving bed with black satin sheets. He'd arrived owning little, however, and remained that way. Everything of substance in the room, excluding the piano, had belonged to Father Ronson. As a child of wealthy parents, Jeffers been brought up in the world of ownership and had found it wanting. Or . . . was choosing not to acquire merely an easy cop-out, a way of sidestepping the trials and risks of self-definition while appearing to live a virtuous life?

He didn't know. He'd been back and forth on the subject, sitting in this very chair, staring out at the simple beauty of the trees and the street-lights, which he saw as the real decorations of the room.

The results of three years of patient effort stood in the balance. Maj was right. Reinhart could only have been led here by Golzen. Perhaps he should have tried harder to reach out to Golzen. Their messages weren't so different. They preached parallel paradigms, up to a point: the only distinction being that Jeffers's was right, and Golzen's wrong. There were souls to be saved. Souls in danger, lives that had been lived in shadows and untruth but could now be steered toward the light. There was a limit to what Jeffers could do for the regular folks, those who attended because they were old and knew no different or middle-aged and felt they should, as if it was some kind of Book Club with Benefits.

He could make a difference with this other kind. Many were younger. Most lived outside the law, and almost all on the streets. He could bring them home. Through doing this he might also prove to the memory of Father Ronson that he was worthy of his post. Jeffers wasn't sure this would make a difference. That wasn't the point. In the realm of the spiritual, you do things because they're the right thing to do. That is all.

What happened this evening was a sign it was time to step up the campaign. To gather the ones he had influence with and forestall any ideas they might have of allowing themselves to slip into Reinhart's clutches – as so many had done – or following the road to the promised land, for which Golzen claimed to hold the key.

Tomorrow always holds the potential to be the very best of days.

Content to have reached this conclusion, the priest sat in the chair, his mind tending toward a comfortable blank. He started on hearing the sound of a distant thud.

He'd heard the sound more and more recently. He knew the city was loud enough at night that neighbors in the street would either not have heard the noise, or would dismiss it as one of those things, the sigh of a bending branch in the jungle night.

He knew also that when he went into the church tomorrow morning, however, the narrow door at the end of the hall would be hanging open.

CHAPTER 29

Kris woke earlier than usual. When she trudged yawning into the sort-of-kitchen she found a note on the counter next to an empty coffee mug. It was from John. It said he was going for a walk. There were two arrows underneath, drawn in his confident and surprisingly artistic hand. One pointed to the cup. The other pointed in the direction of the coffee machine, which was loaded and ready to go. She picked up the note and frowned at it.

It was considerate, of course. But that wasn't what struck her. He *always* went for a walk first thing. John went for a walk in the morning in the same way that the sun rose. John going for a walk was not news.

So why the note? The fight after the debacle at Catherine's had blown over. It had been, as John had said, a dumb fight – though possibly not as dumb as he'd made out. It was dumb because fighting never achieved anything, true that, but when two people who love each other bang heads that hard then *something* needs talking about. Kristina was damned if she knew what that was, which was making her twitchy. She suspected John would have even less idea, not least because he wouldn't have a clue that they were at . . .

The Six Month Suckfest.

It wasn't always literally six months when she bailed – that would be stupid and weird and she could have put a note in her diary in advance saying, 'Don't screw things up this week' – but it had fallen close enough on enough occasions that it had become the Six Month Suckfest in her head. She and John had already been together longer than that, in point of fact. More to the point – his stubbornness about moving aside – she was happier than she'd been in her entire life.

And yet . . . still there was this itch in the back of her mind, an unsettled feeling in her stomach: and a small, shriveled hand starting to reach out for the Bail Switch. She'd never been able to work out whose hand this was. A remnant of her mother, trying to keep her single? Some personification of insecurities she simply didn't feel (consciously, at least)? Pure perversity? She didn't know. In the meantime, the hand kept moving insidiously out of the darkness, its twisted fingers groping toward some agenda Kris didn't understand and wanted no part of.

She shoved it back into the shadows and reached for the switch on the coffee machine instead.

A couple of errands took her up into Midtown, a nice change. The big buildings and overshadowed streets there reminded her of the mountains and forests of Washington State. If you'd been raised accustomed to deep woods, a city was an easier transition than a town (and she should know, having bailed spectacularly from several of those in the past). In mountains and cities you are small in the face of geography and environment. Nobody knows your name, or cares, and that was generally fine with her.

Now it seemed as though some of these strangers were getting too close for comfort, however. More than twenty-four hours after the fact they still had no idea who'd been on their roof and left the message on the window. She wasn't easily unnerved and John sure as hell wasn't either. It was pretty strange, however, as the period yesterday afternoon in Union Square had also been. As John had pointed out, serious people who meant you real harm tended to get on and do it rather than leaving clues – but a warning was still a warning.

He'd said this with a distant look in his eye, as if considering ways of dealing with the situation that might not involve her – steps like taking the last night off from the restaurant and going to talk to the priest, a plan he hadn't told her about ahead of time. Yes, he told her what had happened when he came into the bar later, but he should have told her he was going, like he should have told her about meeting Catherine that time. It probably wasn't personal. Despite what society does in attempting to turn men into team players, they all think theirs is the only name above the title of the movie. She'd met John as a man who'd returned to his previous home in Black Ridge, Washington, to seek an explanation for the death of his older son, who'd perished there in what had appeared to be a freak accident. She'd watched John go at that situation like a bull at a gate, declining assistance until he'd already been shot by people he'd come to believe were implicated in his son's death, and the situation looked to be getting even worse. In the end it had been resolved, albeit messily. So why did it bug her so much that he kept doing these things? Was it because it felt just a little like he was treating her like some young girl?

And had he left the note this morning because he sort of knew he was doing it, too?

The next thing she noticed, she was in Little Brazil, a short stretch of 46th near Times Square, narrow and shadowed and unexceptional, a cut-through between Fifth and Sixth Avenues. Presumably there'd been reason for self-exiled denizens of a South American country to congregate in this corner of the grimy heart of Midtown, but all that remained of their passing – amid a smear of dusty buildings being knocked down or repurposed or ignored and a battered Irish bar – were a couple of small restaurants still flying the green and yellow flag and touting *feijoada* and *caipirinhas* – memories of a community now gone. Near the end of the block, she cut up an alley and onto 47th, the old diamond district, another historic enclave. The street still featured discount jewelry shops and stout men in homburgs but wasn't the separate universe it would once have been. The future homogenizes.

Kristina found herself slowing in front of one of the store windows, in front of tightly filled ranks of metal and shiny stones, arranged to catch the eye of commercial buyers rather than passing individuals. She'd been gazing vaguely at a tray in the center for a few minutes before she realized something.

Was she really looking at *rings*? Was *that* what this was about? It couldn't be. She'd never, in *any* relationship, started thinking along those lines. She sure as hell wasn't going to start now. Even though there was a ring on the left that . . .

No.

As she jerked her head away from the sun-bleached velvet cushions and their rows of expensive I-dos, she saw something reflected in the glass.

She hesitated, unsure what had caught her eye. Then she moved her gaze back down so she'd appear to be looking through the wares in the window again. She kept this up for fifteen slow seconds before allowing her eyes to drift up once more, pulling focus at the same time, so she was looking at the reflections in the glass rather than what lay beyond.

Yes. There, on the other side of the street, someone was standing in front of a boarded-up store.

Kristina held her position, moving now and then to make it look like she was still browsing – meanwhile drifting along the window and watching.

He or she kept in movement. Slow, but constant. Passersby kept coming between them, and it was hard to be sure, but it looked as though the figure was watching Kristina. The figure was tall and slim. The figure wore a dark coat. The figure looked a hell of a lot like . . .

'I give you good price.'

The voice made Kristina jump. A man had come out of the shop. He had the cheap charisma of the kind of person that will always be selling something, and offering discounts regardless of whether they've been sought.

'No,' Kristina said firmly, heart beating hard.

He reversed back into his store. Kristina took a chance and glanced directly across the street. There was nobody there now except for buyers and sellers of jewelry and a trio of tourists with bright anoraks and a big map.

Had there ever been? Or had she been confused by the shadows of passersby reflected in a dirty store window?

She started up the street and after twenty yards took a right into a narrow alley. It was filled with steam and the complex odors of old garbage. She slowed as she entered, to give anyone behind her a chance to see where she'd gone, and then headed along the alley, casting a quick look back after ten feet.

It was hard to be sure, but it *looked* like someone was now in position on the other side of the street she'd just left, opposite the alleyway, watching her.

It was morning and she was bang in the heart of Midtown. If this person was planning anything, they'd chosen the wrong time and place.

Unless, of course, they crossed the road and followed her up this alley, where there was no one to see anything at all.

She pulled out her phone as if to check incoming, to broadcast to anyone watching that she was plugged into the world and could summon assistance *right now*.

A glance to the left made her heart jump, a heavy double-thump. *Someone was at the other end, in silhouette against the light.*

It could be they were merely pausing on the street, but Kristina didn't think so.

'I'm not afraid of you,' she said in a quiet, low voice.

'Huh?' someone said, and she whirled to see a pudgy oriental man in the filthiest chef's whites she'd ever seen, sitting smoking in an open back doorway.

She shook her head, making a mental note to check the name of the restaurant and make sure she never, ever ate there. She walked the rest of the alleyway, not too fast . . . but not slowly either.

Sixth Avenue was reassuringly crowded, people striding up and down and across and back as if fired from a battery of cannons positioned at right angles. She didn't want to stand in a public place and call John, however. It wasn't only that it would make her feel like a damsel in distress, which would suck. She knew that if she pulled John up here, he'd arrive with a strong following wind and scare off her shadow, taking them back to square one.

So instead she walked down the avenue, dawdling at each street crossing, and bought an Americano from the kiosk at the corner of Bryant Park. She kept her eye on the smeary plastic window between her and the server as she waited for her change – just as she'd kept glancing in the windows of stores and banks for the last four blocks – but saw nothing behind her except solid citizens going about theirs and other people's business.

She took the drink down one of the plaza's side paths, under the trees. She found one of the small, rickety metal tables and sat down at it.

She waited and she watched.

And began to feel foolish. Nobody came into the park that looked like the figure she'd glimpsed. Just office workers with deli boxes, tourists, and some middle-aged guy ten feet away, sitting holding a Kindle that didn't seem to be commanding his full attention. Otherwise it was just a park, and not very warm.

Eventually she pulled out her phone and discovered there was a message on it – left forty minutes before, when she'd been hurrying out of the alley.

It was from John, asking where she was and if she wanted to have lunch. She was about to call back when she realized something had changed in her environment.

Someone had sat on the opposite side of the table.

A young woman, tall, with dark hair, wearing a dark coat with a red dress underneath. She had high cheekbones and a strong nose, red lips, and big, dark eyes.

'You can see me, can't you?' the woman said.

Her voice was soft, a little fuzzy around the edges, as if made up of facets of background noise.

Kristina stared at her. The girl seemed curious, but also wary, as if it was Kristina who'd been following *her*. 'You can, can't you?' she insisted, still quietly.

'Yes. Of course.'

'But . . . you're real.'

'Well, yeah,' Kristina said, with no idea what she was agreeing to. 'Who . . . are you?'

The girl made a puzzled face, as if unwilling to let the first matter go. 'I'm called Lizzie.'

'I'm Kristina.'

'I know.'

'How . . . how do you know?'

The girl looked sheepish. 'I heard your boyfriend call you that. He is your boyfriend, yes? John?'

'Yes. But *when* did you hear this?'

The girl seemed more nervous, glancing over Kristina's shoulder, and didn't answer.

246

'When?' Kristina pressed her. 'Were you on our roof? Why are you following Catherine?'

The girl stood up. 'I've got to go.'

She walked quickly away without looking back.

Kristina jumped to her feet to follow but realized someone else was now standing by the table. It was the man she'd noticed earlier, reading a Kindle.

'Hey,' he said.

Kristina glared at him. 'Yes, what?'

He smiled. 'Saw you sitting by yourself, wondered if you might like a little company.'

'No,' Kristina said.

'You sure?'

Kristina took a couple of steps past, trying to see where the girl had gone. She thought she got a glimpse of a dark coat at the top of the steps at the back of the library, but it could have been the shadow of the trees. The man was still standing by the table hopefully.

'What do you mean "by yourself"?'

'Hey, it's fine,' he said. 'I do it all the time. A bit of peace is good for the soul, right? Just, sometimes it means people might want to hook—'

Kristina threw a look that made him take a hurried step backward, and walked away dialing her phone.

'Hey,' John said, when he picked up. 'Fancy some—'

'They just made contact,' she said.

CHAPTER 30

David and Dawn held hands in the middle of the couch. Dr Chew sat on the other side of the desk, peering over his glasses at a scattering of papers across his desk. There was silence. David was reminded of the judges on reality television shows and the insufferable way they milk the moments of truth in which (according to pre-arranged and carefully constructed narratives) one hapless individual is eliminated from the competition, removing them forever from the hungry gaze and fickle affection of millions of box-watching morons. David *thought* they'd been given the news during the ultrasound itself, but now he wasn't sure. He could feel Dawn's fingers gripping his, and forced himself to breathe.

He didn't need this.

Not this morning. Not ever. They'd sat on this couch in exactly this position eight months before and been told that the woman wielding the ultrasound probe had misread the grainy black-and-white images on her screen – whoops! – and the little blob she'd cheerfully pointed out as showing clear indications of life had in fact been manifesting signs of being rather dead.

Did Chew remember that meeting? Presumably in a technical sense – it must be there in his notes – but did he recall it emotionally, the impact it'd had on this particular couple among the hundreds he saw? No. That style of remembrance wasn't the physician's job. For Chew, news was a subset of uninflected information. Somewhere in his mind there would probably be a formalized distinction between 'good' and 'bad' types of news – so he could differentiate when events occurred to someone within his own family or tribe – but he evidently didn't allow this to unbalance a dispassionate attention to whatever facts happened to obtain at any given moment. This doubtless made him an excellent physician.

It made him a mighty crappy news bearer, however.

Eventually he raised his head and smiled.

Even this wasn't enough to break the tension or give a clear indication of the direction in which the sheet of glass between their ignorance and his knowledge was going to break. The smile could equally have been one of affirmation of good, or soberness before the delivery of yet more bad. It could betoken nothing more than a fleeting happy recollection of the fact that he was due to get steak for dinner.

David believed he'd give the man maybe three, four more seconds, and then he was going to let

249

go of Dawn's hand, leap over the desk, and beat the guy senseless with his angle-poise lamp.

'Everything's fine,' Chew said.

Dawn remained rigid. David let out an explosive breath, and this time when Dawn gripped his hand it was to give rather than seek reassurance.

Having delivered his showstopper, Chew dispensed with the suspense and got on with it. 'As I indicated during the ultrasound, it all looks good and there's nothing in the numbers to make me think, ah, otherwise. It's going to be hard for you, I know, with your history, but right now you should feel happy that things are going well. Really. Happiness and calm are very positive during pregnancy. I believe that.'

Dawn started thanking him profusely. Chew waved this off as if it was a common but regrettable misunderstanding of his power, and shuffled the papers into a neater pile. 'Have you started thinking about a name?'

Silenced, Dawn shook her head, blinking rapidly. 'Well, no,' David said for her, and with some surprise. 'Not after what happened the last couple of times.'

'Of course,' Chew said. 'Very understandable. And it's early days. Always wise to remain poised in the face of fate. Actually, the question was my clumsy way of telling you something. The ultrasound was unclear, so the technician didn't mention it until I'd had a chance to examine the still images properly. But it's clear to me.'

He paused, frowning down at the pieces of paper in front of him, the very picture of someone witnessing a lack of clarity.

Then he looked up and smiled more broadly. 'You're going to have twins.'

They walked out of the hospital in a dream, still holding hands. After delivering the end-of-episode kicker, Chew had waxed cautious, warning that the passage of twins into the world was more arduous and uncertain and noting that – speculative though it could only be at this stage – though both showed a strong heartbeat, one of the fetuses appeared more developed, a common situation that would hopefully right itself.

This Columbo-style zinger had caused a familiar sinking feeling in David's stomach (nothing was *ever* simple, was it) but he'd decided to take Chew's businesslike delivery of this caveat as a good sign.

'I'm so glad you came home last night,' Dawn said, as they drew to a halt at the car.

'Me too.' And he was, though he felt bad about positioning this as a desire to make sure he was on time for the consultation. 'I still can't believe it.'

'Believe it, Daddio,' said Dawn. 'I guess I'll get back to school. Shall I drop you home?'

'Think I'll stop by and get a coffee first. Not sure I'll get much done for an hour or two anyway.'

Dawn started nodding, eyes brimming. David nodded back, equally senselessly, thinking how much harder it was to respond to good news. When they'd walked out of this hospital after the second miscarriage, it had been easy. They'd cried and held each other and said this wasn't the end, that they deserved a child and it would happen somehow. With bad news the bad thing has already happened. Hearing something good, or its promise, leaves you out on a limb, even *more* at the mercy of fate. It would be that the Bad Thing is still out there waiting to happen, enjoying its own shitty piece of showboating, waiting for maximum impact before revealing that, I'm so sorry, Dawn and David are out of the reproduction competition for good, but please give them a big hand.

Then David reached out for her, and they held each other and cried. News is news, and our bodies and minds respond much the same whether it's good or bad.

Dawn dropped him off on Main and then cruised off in the direction of the school, driving at about half her usual speed. David didn't think this was conscious caution, more likely that she hadn't stopped running the consultation over in her mind. He watched her to the end of the street and saw her indicate properly and was reassured she'd get to school without sailing serenely off the road into a house.

He hit the late-morning rush at Roast Me, and only as he waited in line did he realize he was going to have to say something to Talia about her book. He found it hard to remember much about it today, except that he'd been enjoying it. Hopefully that would do – along with something he recalled thinking during his last stretch of reading, after meeting Maj in Kendricks, which was that she could rein back on the fantasy elements and present it as something rather more edgy and urban, if she chose. Not that she'd be likely to, but saying this would at least prove that he'd been thinking about it.

When he'd arrived home at eleven the night before, Dawn was still awake. He'd warned her by text that he'd changed his mind and wasn't staying in the city after all, and she evidently felt this constituted a sufficient reversal to require debriefing. She sat up in bed as he told her that he and his friend had had a great conversation and would keep in touch, but he'd decided it was more important to ensure he was there for the scan rather than taking a risk with a tight train schedule the next morning. She nodded thoughtfully, as if hoping he'd gotten enough out of the trip, but he could tell she was pleased.

His sleep was deep and dreamless. After breakfast, Dawn led him up to the third bedroom and showed him what she'd achieved. Just about everything in the room had been thrown away, put downstairs ready for transportation to Goodwill, or otherwise made to vanish. The only stuff remaining was a small pile of boxes holding things that David had never unpacked since he moved to Rockbridge. He'd agreed to perform triage on this as soon as possible – hoping that he wouldn't be coming back to the house later in the day knowing it wouldn't be necessary.

Now, he guessed, it really was.

'Hey, big-shot,' Talia said, when he got to the head of the line. 'S'up? Finished your book yet?'

'Not so much. I'm enjoying yours, though.'

'Really?'

David wouldn't have believed that Talia could look vulnerable. 'Really. It's very good. I mean, I don't know the genre, but heck, I'm loving it, so that's probably an even better sign, right?'

Talia tried to look like she didn't give a crap but couldn't pull it off. 'Where are you up to? No, don't tell me. Dumb question. It's a big book, I know.'

'Dawn's pregnant,' he said.

He'd had no idea he was going to say this. He wasn't sure he'd have called Talia a friend, and certainly wouldn't have pegged her as the first person with whom he'd share this news. As soon as he'd said it, though, and seen the look on her face, he realized that yes, she was.

'Fuck me sideways,' Talia said quietly.

'Yeah.'

'No way.'

'Way. It's early days, but . . .'

She carefully put his cup to one side and then lunged across the counter to grab him around the shoulders with both arms. She was strong and heavy and her grip so fierce that she managed to lift both his feet clear off the floor. 'Holy crap,' she whispered in his ear. 'Chalk one up for the good guys, huh?'

Then she dropped him again, got businesslike with taking his money, and told off the guy in line behind David for grinning at them, though she didn't manage to stop smiling during any of this.

As David turned from the counter and looked for somewhere to sit, he realized he was grinning too.

He chose a table by the window and flicked through the local alternative newspaper, remaining untouched by its demands for his attention and empathy. Usually he didn't care about what the town's handful of hippies felt, but right now he wouldn't have minded a distraction.

He couldn't ignore what had happened the day before, though it felt far less tangible now that he was back in Rockbridge. He remembered being in Union Square and in Dib's. He remembered what happened in the church later, too. He'd barely been introduced to the priest before the guy in the coat had arrived and started shouting. When a *second* unpredictable-looking stranger breezed in, David decided he'd had quite enough weirdness for one day. Waiting for the right moment and then scooting out of the place and all the way to the station was, he believed, the most actualized thing he'd done in his entire life.

And yet none of it seemed real.

In his mind's eye it felt like something he could have made up, a daydream or speculative plot line for which he had no idea of what-happens-next. And he was okay with that. Plot lines, he knew all too well, could be jettisoned. You could decide they led nowhere good and elect to strike them from the story.

That's what he was going to do. He had no need to go back to New York. Maj knew where he lived, sure, but he evidently had other problems – not least the scary guy in the coat. David could simply decide not to re-engage.

They were, as Maj had put it, two magnets permanently set to repel.

While he got these thoughts in order, David watched people out on the street. He wasn't really seeing his environment – more concerned with tidying his thoughts, re-experiencing delight at the memory of Dawn's face after the consultation, and trying to drag his mind back to the idea of doing some *work*.

He did not notice the three tall figures around the table in the back corner. He didn't see the way the red-haired woman looked thoughtfully from David to Talia, as if drawing a line between them, or how other visitors to the coffeehouse chose to sit at other tables even if they were less well positioned or needed the leavings of previous customers to be removed first.

Five minutes later, without apparent signal, the three people all stood together.

Then they were at the door.

Then they were outside, looking back into the coffee shop through the window, standing right over David and smiling down at him. He didn't see them.

Then they were gone.

The sky was gray and cold.

CHAPTER 31

Sure, I'm a Journeyman. You ask me, it's the only way to live. What – you want to hang around your hometown your entire life, moping over what's not there anymore and ain't never going to be? No thanks. Ain't going to go live in some town, neither. Not a city kind of guy. Never have been, never will be. Too dark, too noisy, everything too close together. It's not the way I was raised.

When we were young we roamed the wild plains. If you don't remember, well, I do. We were heroes of the great outdoors, you and me. We lived in forts and trees and dried river beds. We were free. I can be free by myself if I have to. Do I go back? Hell no.

What would be the point?

It's not a job; it's a way of life. Wouldn't suit everyone, that's for sure. Seen a few try and pretty soon they go hurrying back to the city or whatever place they come from. They want predictable. They want routine. There's a few of us who don't, though. No idea how many – never see us all in the same place. That's kind of the point. It comes down to constitution. I don't need to buddy up. I'm good by myself. Those other friends . . . well, they want company. It's what they miss after the change, and that makes a kind of sense.

Company's what got taken away.

Every little town's going to have people of our general kind. Problem is . . . depends whether you happen to like those people or not. In the city – and I can see the point of this part, I suppose – you got a lot more choice. You can pick and choose. Find somebody you like, a whole group of them if you're lucky. Lot of the friends need that, too – they need enough people around to remind them who they are and keep them strong inside. They got those different things they do there, too. Hobbies, lifestyles, whatnot. Jobs, some of them. I was talking with a Fingerman just the other day, matter of fact, last time I was in New York City for the night. He wanted my advice on traveling on the trains and I told him some of what I know. Don't know why he was thinking of hitting the road, and I didn't ask. Far as I'm concerned, a friend's business is his own, and he – or she – should do what the hell they feel like. Ain't no other damned thing to do anyhow.

This particular friend, Maj was his name, I could see him making this lifestyle work, maybe. He's got substance. Most Fingermen do. Some of the others, well, that's part of why they gather in the cities, I guess. Need a network to make them feel alive.

I see other Journeymen on the trains sometimes. Once in a while we'll sit and talk. Not for long, though. It's not a matter of being unfriendly. It's just – and I don't think some of the city friends realize this – the more of you there are together, the easier it is for other folk to see you and start to wonder what's going on. So if I see a fellow traveler, generally I'll just nod. That's enough to say, 'I see you. I know what you are and respect you for it. Travel well, and may your road be ever long.'

Some Journeymen walk. Some hitchhike, though that can be a risky business. It's okay if you can slip into a car when the driver's not looking and get out the same way, but sometimes a more inexperienced person will wind up having to absent themselves in a way that's not so subtle, which can look weird to the person who gave them the ride. I would not advise you to take the hitch-hiking route unless you know what you're doing, bottom line.

Then there's some of us that head to the coast, walk onto boats or ocean liners, spend their time sailing back and forth. Others go to airports, get on planes, ride the air. Wouldn't neither of those suit me. I like the idea that I can get off at any time, change my mind and go some other way. Freedom. That's what we've got, if nothing else, and if you don't make the most of that then I don't know why you'd stick around.

Any kind of journeying amounts to the same

thing. You know that old saying – it's better to travel than to arrive? Well, that's the truth right there, my friend. Traveling is what it is. It's got its own point.

'Specially if there ain't no particular place to go, and ain't never going to be.

I told a white lie earlier, though. I *do* go back, once in a while. You go back to the beginning in your memories often enough – I don't see a problem in going back in body sometimes too. See the places where you used to walk or used to play. I returned only once to the actual house, though, about five years ago. I stood in the street outside and looked at the place. It's been fancied up some since the family left, got extra rooms in back and a swimming pool now, if you can believe that. He would have loved a swimming pool back then. Had to make do with getting our feet wet in the creek. That suited us well enough. Weren't no cowboys in swimming pools, right? And that's what we were, most days. Soldiers sometimes, commandos; then there was a ninja phase, though I never really got behind that. But mainly we was cowboys, every day and every night.

Until some asshole bought him a computer, and that was the end of all that. You don't need a friend to stare at a screen with you, and if you want company I guess there's all those shadow people out there on the Internet. The change came on pretty fast. It does for many of us. Was a time when I used to have a place set for me at the dinner table. Then six months later he couldn't have remembered my name.

Which means neither can I.

Guess the truth is that maybe I *was* a buddy person, way back. I had myself a buddy, but those days are gone and they ain't coming back. I know what I am, and I'm okay with it.

There's a lot of roads left to roam.

CHAPTER 32

Kristina was pissed when she got home. She was angry throughout her shower – and not just because it kept randomly going hot and cold in the infuriating way it always did. She was annoyed when she stomped out of the bathroom, shivering, and she was furious as she stood toweling her hair in the living area.

When she called John after her encounter with the girl in Bryant Park, she'd expected him to be pleased or excited. Instead he'd given her a hard time about not getting in touch with him *immediately* after she realized she was being followed. He hadn't backed off on this over their subsequent lunch, either.

She knew that he hadn't meant to piss her off. She understood his response came from love, rather than a desire to make her feel inadequate – and yes, when de beast come out of de forest it traditionally be de man's job to stand in harm's way, but John knew she was capable of looking after herself. Reminding him of this had been the last thing she did before stomping away from the sushi bar, leaving him to pay.

He'd texted twice since, and left two voice mail messages. She hadn't replied to any of them.

Slowly she stopped toweling. She was spending a lot of time being grouchy these days. Too much. The story was getting old even to her.

It was time to perk up, to go spend another night in the company of strangers, people she'd either never see again or who were wearily familiar components of her half life, two-dimensional regulars with one-dimensional needs. As she buttoned her shirt, she realized she was sick to death of her job. Sure, you could forge a life in the food and beverage industries, be the best damned barkeep the East Village had ever known, but she couldn't see down that road and she didn't want to. It had stopped feeling real. It didn't make her feel real.

She needed something bigger and wider. She needed to feel her feet on the earth and know that ground was either hers or she had a damned long lease on it. John was good at making mental connections – even when he didn't realize he'd made them – and perhaps he'd started to sense this, had put together that they didn't need a new apartment, but a new life.

They needed a conversation about this stuff, and soon. And she'd start one. When she was good and ready . . . and done with being pissed at him.

She grabbed her keys off the counter and looked around for her phone. She'd thrown it somewhere when she stormed into the apartment, to make it harder to hear the sound of John's texts. That this already struck her as *outrageously* childish proved she was calming down. She swept her gaze over the obvious surfaces before . . .

Aha: there it was, on the couch.

As she picked it up and turned to go, she let out a little scream.

She froze, staring at the window. From this angle all you could see through it was a glancing view of the gable and a patch of gray sky. If you pulled your focus closer, there was the glass of the window itself. The message from the other night was gone. John had rubbed it off the next morning. He'd done it in a hurry, however, leaving smears and blotches and redistributing years of grime rather than removing it.

There was something else written in it now.

Kristina took a cautious step closer, angling her head. As before, the marks on the window could almost have been made by raindrops, or the scrabbling claws of a pigeon blown into it by a high wind. Almost.

The marks were too close together to be random, however, and gathered right in the center of the pane. There was consistency in their weight, too, as if they'd been scrawled out by the same finger.

Were they supposed to be letters, or a drawing? It was hard to tell. The first mark was kind of like a capital J, though the second upright was shorter than the first, making it look reversed. The third symbol looked a *lot* like a 6. The curves in both were what made it impossible to believe them to be water tracks – there wasn't enough wind to have reversed gravity.

The thing in the middle was harder to make out. It could have been an angular O, or a zero, though she couldn't work out why you'd try to create one of those from a combination of lines rather than one long stroke.

So . . . it must be a square, presumably.

Reverse J, square, 6.

Kristina stared at it for five long minutes, and then finally got it.

By the time she ran breathless into the bottom of the park – at twenty minutes after six – she'd started to lose confidence in her guess, that the square might mean a square, the reversed J a malformed U, and the U short for 'Union' . . . and the numeral a time.

If someone wanted to leave a message, why wouldn't they have written the damned thing properly? She was well aware that she was behaving contrary to common sense because of how irritated John had made her earlier – and that this wasn't anywhere close to being a good reason.

But still, she was here. The park was emptying out, a handful of people crossing the lower section on their way home or toward an early dinner.

Kristina passed them, walking deeper, and felt like she was going the wrong way. During the day, parks are a destination. Come the evening, they get downgraded to cut-through and that-dark-patch-over-the-fence. A chunk of nature in the city turns unsettling after dark. They become home to the homeless, unwelcome reminders that having a place to rest your head is not a given. Even when surrounded by busy streets, parks remind us why we went to the trouble of inventing houses and artificial light. The humans that lurk there become a part of the wilderness, infiltrated by it – shards of the unknown come to nudge us out of comfort. Walking on the other side of the street seems wiser, lest we become infected too.

Nonetheless, Kristina headed up the path. There was no one at the benches or on the grassed areas. The leaves whispered but without any great intent. It took a strong wind to reach down here out of the canyons of buildings.

Kristina drew to a halt, unsure what to do, and whether to stay or go.

'You okay, ma'am?'

A cop stood ten feet away. 'Sure,' she said. 'Just taking a walk.'

The cop nodded, and it seemed to her like he took a beat too long over this, as if he was questioning her motives or her right to be there.

She stood her ground. 'Which is allowed, right?'

He walked away. Seemed like male kind was

determined to present its officious side today. And maybe it was different if you were born and bred in New York City, but it also felt like there was always someone determined to make you feel like a second-class citizen in it, to show how much they belonged here and you did not.

Either that or she was feeling dumb for being here and looking for someone to blame it on.

Yeah, she guessed, it could be that.

So . . . screw this, Kris. Go to the restaurant, make nice with John. Do the sensible thing for once in your bad-tempered and contrary life, huh?

Abruptly deciding she'd misinterpreted the marks on the window or added two and two together and made a billion, she turned toward the main pathway.

She faltered, however. There was something different now. She could feel it, though at first she couldn't work out why. Then something else changed.

There were three people standing in front of her.

Two girls, one guy. All were dressed in tattered black, with highlights of rich colors – blue, purple, emerald green. They stood in an arc, very still, looking at her.

She looked behind.

Two people were behind her, too. Both men, also dressed in black, the clothes so very dark that you couldn't make out what the layers were. There was nothing overtly threatening in the way they stood, except for the fact they were in a circle and were pale and hollowed-eyed and looking intently at her.

Which . . . was pretty threatening.

Kristina took a moment to wish she'd listened to what John had said, and that he was here, but knew she was going to have to deal with this herself. 'You going to get out of my way?'

Silence. Nobody moved.

'Who the hell are you?'

Nobody spoke. They were so very motionless that it was as if they were images layered on top of the park. A gust of wind finally made it down out of the trees, moving branches. Though the people in front of her were dressed in rags and tatters of layers and coats, none of these stirred.

'Kristina,' said a voice.

Another figure had joined the circle. It was Catherine's follower, the girl Kris had met in Bryant Park that afternoon. She didn't look harmless now, though. She looked like the leader of a small brigade of unknown allegiance and unpredictable behavior and power.

'Lizzie? Who are these people?'

The girl cocked her head to one side, birdlike. 'You can see them, too?'

'Two girls, three guys,' Kristina said. 'Dressed like you. They're freaking me out. I say again: *who are these people?*'

Lizzie looked thoughtful. Kristina was aware of the others glancing at one another now. One of the girls – plump in figure, dressed goth style with dyed white hair – whispered to the man next to her. It sounded like car tires two streets away in the night, or like the door to the bedroom closet falling open an inch in the dark.

'We're Angels,' Lizzie said. 'Would you like to walk with us?'

CHAPTER 33

With that, the girl started walking, going from stationary to moving fast with no step in between.

Kristina hesitated, but followed. 'What do you mean, you're . . .'

There was no point – the girl was already too far ahead. Kristina had a hundred questions she wanted to ask, but she had to catch up with the woman first. Meanwhile, Lizzie kept glancing back at Kristina curiously. The other people walked in loose formation around her, and were doing the same, casting glances at Kris and half smiles at one another, as if there were something odd and notable about her, rather than them.

'Why do they keep looking at me like that?' Kristina panted, finally managing to get alongside Lizzie as she crossed 14th and headed toward the Village.

'I'd like to walk with you,' Lizzie said, as if she hadn't heard the question. Her voice was clear, with none of the soft edges from when they'd met in Bryant Park. 'But we need rules.'

'What do you mean?'

The girl strode across Bleecker without appearing to care whether traffic was coming. Kristina almost got taken out by a cyclist and had to jump back onto the curb. Lizzie waited on the other side until Kris reached her, then immediately set off again.

'Look straight ahead,' she said. 'Instead of saying "yes" or "no," nod or shake your head. If you *do* speak, keep your head down and don't be loud. Okay?'

Kristina started to say yes, then nodded instead.

'Excellent!' Lizzie said, delighted, clapping her hands together like a girl who'd laid out the ground rules for a skipping game and received unexpectedly ready assent. 'I worked all that out last night.'

'Why are you walking so *fast*?'

'I'm not.'

They'd reached the fringes of the Village, heading toward SoHo, and the sidewalks were getting crowded. Kristina noticed the other people with them had spread out, one ahead and two behind, and that one couple had transferred to the other side of the street. They were holding hands, the plump girl and a rail-thin boy who'd dyed his hair pure white too. They were still glancing at her, though, with those odd smiles. It was like . . .

It was how Kristina imagined celebrities must feel. Strangers continually slipping glances your way, drinking you in, clocking and logging you as if it were a big deal to be sharing the same space. Why would they be doing that to her, of all people? She couldn't imagine, but it had the effect of making them seem less threatening, as if she had status in some invisible hierarchy.

Lizzie meanwhile kept surging onward, and Kristina found it increasingly hard to keep up. The girl carved down the street as though on a priority track. Sometimes she overtook other pedestrians, not leaving enough space for Kristina to follow. At others she dodged gracefully out of the way of oncoming walkers at the last second, leaving Kristina to clumsily attempt to do the same.

After glancing collisions with two sets of tourists more interested in gawking in store windows than watching where they were going, Kristina gave up.

'Look, slow *down*, will you? If you want to talk, then—'

Lizzie stopped in her tracks and turned to look at her. Someone banged hard into Kristina's back.

'For Christ's sake,' the man snarled. 'You have a fucking stroke, or what?'

Still fuming at the idiocy of someone who might pause on a sidewalk, for crying out loud, the man stormed off down the road of his angry little life.

Lizzie remained motionless.

'What?' The girl's eyes stayed on her, blank and dead. Kristina lowered her head and muttered, taking care not to move her lips much, 'Okay, I get it,' she said. 'But slow *down*, okay?'

The others had gathered and were clustered around her and Lizzie. A little too close, in fact, looking at her with their unnervingly steady gaze,

273

as if waiting for her to say something else, or do something.

Lizzie glanced around. 'Too crowded,' she conceded. 'Good for us, difficult for you.'

She considered, then pointed diagonally across the street. On the other side was a doorway next to a café that was shut for the evening. The doorway was dark, recessed, and partially obscured by trees on either side. 'Shoo, friends.'

With that, Kristina and Lizzie were alone.

Kristina assumed the girl would lead her into the building – and was weighing up just how dumb an idea it would be to follow – when she realized the doorway itself was their destination. When they were within its shadow Lizzie turned back and indicated for Kristina to stand at a certain angle, her back up against one side of the recess, facing away from the street.

'This should be okay. For a while.'

Kristina realized the woman had positioned her so she could speak normally without being seen by anyone passing by. 'Where did the others go?'

Lizzie shrugged, but not in a way that said she didn't know. 'I'm glad you got the message.'

'Was it you who put the other one there? About leaving you alone?'

'Not me. But one of us.'

'Why?'

'You were following me. You and John.'

'We weren't. We didn't even know who you are.

We were just trying to find out who was stalking a friend of mine. Catherine Warren.'

The girl's eyes clouded, and she looked away. Kris pressed it. 'Why *are* you following her?'

'I don't want to talk about that.'

'So . . . what *do* you want to talk about?'

'I'm not used to this,' the girl said, sounding defensive. 'I'm so out of practice. I don't know what to say to someone like you anymore.'

'What do you mean – someone like me?'

'Someone with things.'

'When I asked you what you were, you said—'

'Angels, yes,' Lizzie said. 'It's just a name. Like Journeyman or Dozeno or Fingerman.'

'Okay . . . so what's a Fingerman?'

Lizzie held her hand up and placed index and thumb tips together. 'Someone who can do this.'

'Well . . . *you* can do it.'

'Of course. Most Angels have some fingerskills, but we don't have the precision of someone like Maj.'

'Who's Maj?'

Lizzie smiled coyly. 'A friend.'

'Special friend, by the look of it.'

Lizzie wasn't saying. 'Did you tell John you were coming out to the park?'

'No.'

'Did . . . you mind me asking that?'

Kristina shook her head, but the girl was sharp: answering the question had made her feel awkward, disloyal. She didn't talk about John. Ever. When

Catherine nattered about Mark – even a corporate merger as successful as theirs experienced occasional interdepartmental gripes – Kristina listened without giving back. Her relationship with John was private, reality's core, not a subject for status updates.

'Is everything okay with him?'

Kristina was about to tell the girl to mind her own business, but realized that, strangely, she didn't want her to. The conversation felt appropriate. The usual barriers of embarrassment and caution didn't feel present. It was like being coaxed into overdue utterance by some friend you'd had back in school, before life got complicated, when it was possible to know *everything* about someone, every fact of their short life, to the bottom of their soul.

'We're . . . going through an odd patch,' she admitted.

The girl laughed, but not in a way that diminished what Kris had said. 'Even if two people stand in the ocean next to each other, the waves hit you at different angles.' She put a hand on Kristina's arm. 'But it will be okay.'

'You think?'

'Definitely.'

Kristina realized two of the other people were back, and standing beside her – the couple who'd been walking together. They seemed pleased with themselves.

'For you,' the man said.

Kristina couldn't work out what he was talking about. The girl glanced ostentatiously down. Kristina looked too and saw the guy had something cupped in his hand, held low, as if to prevent passersby from seeing.

'Quickly,' the girl said. 'He can't hold it for long.'

Kristina took the object. She kept her hands down low and saw she was holding a silver necklace, modern-looking. And expensive. 'What . . . what's this?'

'It's for you,' the girl said.

'Where did it come from?'

The man pointed across the street. Kristina saw a jewelry store among the boutiques. Women in expensive clothing stood in front of cabinets, heads reverentially bowed. It looked like the kind of place Catherine might head to pick out what Mark might want to give her for an anniversary.

She glanced at Lizzie. The girl smiled, but it looked guarded, or sad. She seemed resigned rather than disapproving. Turning back to the couple in front of her, Kris saw they now appeared worried.

'Don't you like it?' the girl asked. 'We could find something else.'

'No, it's lovely. But – did you steal it?'

They nodded like a pair of little dogs. 'I can't accept this,' Kristina said. 'It's sweet of you, but—'

But they were gone. Lizzie too.

Kristina was standing alone in the doorway. She shoved the necklace into her jeans pocket, panicked.

There was a man standing on the other side of the street, looking at her. Two men, in fact – one still, the other wandering up and down among the shoppers, hands in the pockets of an old-fashioned suit. The first was staring directly at her. His face was full of flat planes and he wore an ostentatious coat.

Cops?

Kristina had worked thirty bars and never dipped her fingers in the till, held jobs in stores all over the country and not once exercised a five-finger discount either. Now she was in possession of a piece of jewelry that had to be worth several thousand dollars. It wouldn't matter that she hadn't taken it. Having it stuffed into her jeans didn't make it look like she'd been on the verge of returning it to its rightful owner.

Meanwhile the men watched. One moving, the other motionless. The longer she stayed where she was, the more guilty she would look. But if she started to leave, would they come for her? Would they grab her right there, or wait until she hurried up a side street?

What if they weren't even cops?

Would you really dress like that if you were a policeman? A policeman whose job was trying to bust people for stealing from stores?

'Don't turn around.'

Not screaming took all the self-possession Kristina possessed. The voice was quiet, female. Lizzie.

Kristina stared at her feet and hissed: 'What the *hell* is going on?'

'Just walk away. They're not looking for you.'

'Then why are they staring *at* me?'

'It's us they want, not you. Walk away like there's nothing wrong. But tell me your number.'

Kristina muttered her phone number. There was silence. After a moment she glanced behind.

There was no one there.

She stepped out onto the sidewalk. The shorter of the two men had already disappeared. The man in the coat turned on his heel and strode off down the road without looking back.

Kristina willed herself to keep calm, to walk slowly. She strolled with the early-evening shoppers, doing her best to look like she was in the market for a handbag or an iPod. She allowed herself to look back only when she reached the next street corner. She saw no one.

She kept walking until the other side of SoHo.

And *then* she ran.

CHAPTER 34

Kris was over an hour late getting to the restaurant, and by the time she arrived I was tired of fielding the management's increasingly irritable inquiries as to her whereabouts, not least because *I didn't know*. I'd sent her a few texts, but she hadn't replied, and there wasn't much more I could do – except be concerned on her behalf and know how pissed she'd be if I let her see it. That's all I'd done at lunch, and it hadn't gone well. I was dealing with a table of Midwesterners who hadn't been expecting little bits of basil all over their pizzas and were extremely perturbed about them, and so when I saw Kris finally hurry into the restaurant I merely rolled my eyes and nodded in the direction of Mario, and then winked – as complex a non-verbal communication as I'm capable of without straining a muscle.

Kristina sent a smile back, a quick but heartfelt one that said she probably wasn't as annoyed at me as she had been earlier – and carrying something else that I couldn't determine – and went to placate the owners' wrath. Not for the first time it struck me that after six months of being model employees we'd begun to make a habit of not being where we were supposed to be, and that Mario and his sister hadn't lasted so many years in the restaurant business by tolerating flakiness for long.

I didn't see Kristina again until table service was done and I went downstairs to the bar. It was busy at first but gradually settled down to regulars. I perched at the corner of the bar and waited, drinking a line of beers – sent in my direction without need for interaction – until Kristina saw a gap in business and headed my way.

'I saw her again,' she said without preamble.

'Who?'

She told me about the message on the window of our apartment, working out what it might mean, and going to Union Square. 'And do *not* give me grief about this.'

'What do I care?' I said. 'I mean, it displeases me as a patriarchal asshole who mistrusts any woman's ability to handle any situation, but otherwise, why would I give a shit?'

She opened her mouth, then closed it. 'Sorry.'

'So what happened?'

She told me about walking with the girl – Lizzie – into SoHo, and the beginnings of a conversation that had been derailed first by a gift and then by . . . well, she wasn't too clear about what had happened after that.

'You think they were cops?'

'They didn't look it, but what do I know about fashion trends in undercover police?'

She was trying to make light, but I could tell she was unsettled. I put my hand on top of hers. She looked at it. 'Is this a public display of affection?'

'No. My hand was cold.'

'I hate it when we fight.'

'Me too. So let's not do it. Show me the thing.'

She pulled it out of her pocket, keeping it hidden in her hand until it had been dropped into mine. An attractive piece of modern jewelry. It didn't look cheap, either. 'And they handed this to you, even though they'd met you only an hour before?'

She nodded, then had to go serve someone. I clocked that the person sitting two stools along from me was paying a little too much attention – underground bars in the East Village are exactly the kind of place you'd go to buy something not legally come by – and so I dropped my hands into my lap.

By the time Kristina came back I thought I'd worked out what was going on. 'The guys. Describe them again.'

She did, and I nodded, feeling excited. 'That fits. The man who kept still – he sounds like the one I saw at the church, who had some beef with the priest – Reinhart. He's not a cop. He's a criminal.'

'How do you know?'

'Trust me. These people you met in the park, Lizzie and her friends: evidently they're skilled at fading into the background – we've already seen how good *she* is at that. And Lizzie didn't seem surprised that two of her friends had stolen something, right?'

'No. She looked disapproving, but she wasn't surprised.'

'So that's what they do. They're an urban tribe, whatever, living between the cracks – and they survive by stealing. So they're going to need someone more plugged into the world than they are, with connections for selling stolen goods. I'm thinking that's Reinhart.'

Kristina thought about it, nodded. 'Maybe. Though . . . they didn't seem like thieves.'

'Not archetypal assholes who take stuff because they're too lazy or dumb to do anything else, no. But you know what this city's like. There's the normal citizens but then all the other layers. Street people, thousands of them. Others living in the tunnels near Penn Station or crashing under a different bridge every night. What if some of these people got organized?'

'Lizzie mentioned people called 'Fingermen,' and others I don't remember,' Kristina said thoughtfully.

'Fingermen has to be a name for the ones who steal stuff, right? They have some people who are good at remaining unnoticed, slipping into places, and taking things, and specialize at it. The money they get goes into food and clothes and burner phones and whatever else they need. That's why Reinhart was taking an interest. He could have worried that *you* were a cop, or a competitor. If he's got a lucrative arrangement with these people, he's not going to want others muscling in. Could be that's why he was threatening the priest, too.'

'Why?'

'Maybe Jeffers is trying to lead them in a different direction. Stop being bad; walk toward the light. You said Lizzie didn't look happy about the stealing. The guy in the white shirt I saw going into the church – he was with her and the priest in Union Square, right? And he'd taken the scared-looking guy to the church, presumably to introduce him to Jeffers, maybe to start the process of getting him out of the criminal life. When Reinhart turned up the guy bolted – perhaps because he knew Reinhart was going to be pissed at him being there.'

'Maybe. But that's a lot of maybes. And . . .' She shook her head.

'What am I missing?'

'I don't know. There's something *about* these people. They didn't seem like runaways or homeless people. They had more to them than that.'

It seemed to me that one of the things they might have, in Kris's eyes, was a life that didn't involve living in a tiny apartment and serving beers underground, an existence that seemed edgier and

284

desirably off the grid of mundanity. I shrugged. 'It's the best I've got.'

'And I'm not saying it sucks. But then what's the deal with Lizzie and Catherine?'

'Didn't you ask?'

'Yes. She didn't want to talk about it. I got the sense . . . I don't know, that maybe Catherine did something to her, or something. Let her down.'

I had another idea. 'Maybe they case people's houses too. Stalk normal citizens, map their schedules and routines and work out when would be a good time to stage a burglary.'

'No way,' Kris said. 'I don't believe she'd be a party to something like that.'

'Kris, you only just met her.'

'Yeah, and tell me you don't make character assessments just as fast. You pegged this Reinhart guy as a villain in two seconds flat.'

'I trust your judgment. But people on the edge will countenance doing things that—'

Kris shook her head firmly and wouldn't talk about it anymore.

When we got back to the apartment the message on the window was gone. That meant someone had been out on our roof again, and while Kris seemed to be becoming comfortable with our window turning into some kind of low-tech Facebook, I was not.

As we lay in bed I asked Kristina if she'd at least talk to me before meeting with Lizzie or any of her friends again. She said she would. I wasn't sure that I believed her, however, and I wasn't sure I understood what this said about the way things stood between us.

CHAPTER 35

At two in the morning Maj rose from the floorboards where he'd been lying. Sometimes there were others here too, sometimes not. This night, he had lain alone. Sleep had never come easy, but he always made the effort. The Gathered used to say it was as important to them, and their minds, as to anyone else. So he tried. Recently he'd found it harder, however. And tonight, though he'd gone through the motions of returning to the upper floor of a boarded-up ex-digital goods store in Midtown (a recent casualty of online retail dominance; though the upstairs room was messy and pigeons had already made it in through a broken window to start spreading shit and feathers, the roof was in place and at least it wasn't damp) it had not come at all.

He'd suspected it might be that way after meeting with Lizzie earlier. She'd told him about her near encounter with Reinhart in SoHo. She'd done so even though she knew he'd disapprove of what she'd been doing – hanging out with a tourist from the other side. She was open about what she did

287

and thought and had told the truth. What she'd done wasn't what was bothering him, though he'd told her to be careful, both of Reinhart and her new acquaintance.

What was bothering him was the increasing suspicion that . . . *something was going on.*

None of the Angels worked for Reinhart. Several used to in the past, like Flaxon, but all had stopped after coming under Lizzie's influence. So why had Reinhart been watching them tonight? And why had he turned up at the church? The two events so close together had to be connected. So far, the world views of Jeffers and Reinhart had coexisted without contact. Both men knew of each other and the competing pulls they represented, but there had been dead space between them.

Last night Reinhart had crossed it.

He was making it personal, and once he'd started down that road it seemed unlikely he'd retreat. It had not been lost on Maj that Reinhart's parting comments had been delivered at him. Why? Golzen kept recycling his pitch that Maj should come and work for Reinhart – a transparent attempt to bind him into Golzen's messianic nonsense about Perfect – but last night was the first time they'd been in the same room.

So why had Reinhart spoken to him directly? As if he felt he had some kind of call on him?

Maj didn't know. He didn't like not knowing.

He slipped out of the building via the broken

window, walked across the next roof, and then dropped down into a backstreet.

Though he'd never been to the building on Orchard, it was easy to find. He'd heard tell of its general location, and had to walk the streets for only half an hour – keeping an eye out for surreptitious-looking friends, shadows slipping around street corners – before homing in on a walk-down with a black door at the bottom. A sketchy club, now empty for the night. The door was thick but lighter than it looked, and unlocked.

Maj walked into the large, empty space. There was no one there but for a slight figure sitting slumped at the bar. With a start, Maj realized who it was.

It was the teenager he'd last run into when he'd been walking with David, the girl in the gray hoodie who'd invited him to a party in the Meatpacking District. The change in twenty-four hours was disturbing. Gone was the it's-all-good teen he'd gotten used to bumping into on the streets. Her face was pale now. She'd been crying, and her eyes were ringed with smudged black makeup.

'Are you okay?'

She didn't say anything. She looked like a Missing Person poster, and when someone emerged from the shadows to the side of the bar, Maj put two and two together.

'You asshole,' Maj said. 'What did you do to her?'

'Provided enlightenment,' Golzen said. 'My business has always been to help people get where they're going.'

Maj turned to the girl. 'What did he tell you?'

She looked away. 'What I am.'

'What – friendly? Fun?'

'No. What I *really* am.'

'Then why are you here?'

'He said there was a man who could help me.'

'He lied,' Maj said. 'Reinhart will make you cheat and steal. Ask yourself what Lizzie would say about those things. You like Lizzie, right?'

'She's wonderful.'

'Right. And she thinks Reinhart is scum.'

'Hey, hey,' said a voice. Reinhart came striding toward him from a doorway at the end of the room. 'Good to see you, Maj. Glad you made it to the nest at last.'

'Leave Jeffers alone,' Maj said.

Reinhart grimaced, looked sad, held his hands out, palms up. Play-acting. '*That's* why you're here?'

'He helps people. You don't.'

'Wrong, my friend. That is my whole point. That is why I've been trying to get Golzen to put us together for a talk. Which he's apparently now done, for which I'm grateful.'

'He's a good dog, right?'

'There's a place in this world for people who do what they're told, Maj. Good things come to them.'

'Charity. Exactly the bullshit we've had enough of.'

290

'I agree. I agree. No more handouts. I can help with that, Maj. I can help all of you. Time is running out for the old-school. You need to step up, come enjoy a new way to be. I can get you there.'

Meanwhile the girl had slipped down off her stool and was approaching along a curved line, like a cat. She crept closer to Reinhart, looking up at his face.

'Are you Reinhart?'

He frowned at her. 'Who are you?'

'Are you going to like me?'

'Get away from me, you freak,' Reinhart said, turning to Golzen. 'Who the fuck is this?'

'A Dozeno. Just turned her,' Golzen said with pride. 'She's wide open. Dumb as a sack of rocks, but we could get her eavesdropping PIN numbers or something, once she's got her ditzy head around what she is.'

The girl kept staring up at Reinhart's face. 'Are you going to be my friend?'

He laughed. '*Friend*? If you were real, you'd be strapped facedown to a bed right now, getting broken in. As it is you're good to me for only one thing and I will get into that later, but right now I'm *busy*, so fuck off.'

'I don't understand.'

Reinhart sent a backhand blow at the girl's face. It went straight through her head, but she flinched and fell back. He looked at her thoughtfully.

'Actually,' he said to Golzen, 'there's substance

there. She might be able to do basic fingerwork, with training. Make a note.'

The girl straightened slowly, hand against her face. 'You know?' she said to Maj. 'I think you're right. He doesn't seem like a very nice man.'

'He's not,' Maj said. 'Go find Lizzie. Talk to her. She'll help. I can help too.'

'Maybe,' the girl said. 'But the thing is . . . I don't really know you either. Or Lizzie. Or anybody else.'

She turned from him, from everyone, and wandered away into the darkness in the corner of the big, empty basement, crying once more. Reinhart watched her go, as if finding the sight interesting. Or amusing.

Or . . . something.

'You're everything we don't need,' Maj said to him. 'Stay the hell out of our world.'

He walked out and didn't look back.

And that, Golzen felt, was hopefully that. Reinhart turned to him, however.

'I don't see your buddies,' he said irritably. 'I asked you to stick them to that guy. I think I said "like glue." I didn't see any glue. I don't see your guys. Were they outside, waiting? Tell me they're outside.'

Golzen shook his head. 'It's not hard to keep track of what Maj's up to. I had another idea. I sent them after Maj's friend.'

'Sent them? Where?'

'I don't know. Wherever the guy lives. They followed him after you confronted Jeffers in the church last night. They'll watch Maj's friend and return and tell me if there's any leverage we might be able to use on Maj, something from his friend's life. Assuming you think it's worth it, of course, after his attitude tonight.'

'Good work,' Reinhart said thoughtfully. 'I like what you've done there. Let me know.'

He nodded, then wandered off into the shadows in the direction the girl had gone, dismissing Golzen as if he'd vanished, or had never been there at all.

Just until we leave for Perfect, Golzen thought as he watched him go. *Then you'll have to find a new dog.*

In a way, he almost hoped it *would* be Maj.

He had a feeling Maj might bite.

CHAPTER 36

The first thing Talia did when she got home, as always, was take a bath. When you're living in a trailer of significant age and lackluster specifications this is not a quick or simple procedure, but it's hot working behind a coffee machine, and she'd always been a girl who liked to be clean. She supposed there weren't many people in town who thought of Talia Willocks as a girl these days. But she'd been one once. She still was. Mother fucking Teresa herself must have stopped to gawk at the clouds or check out a cute butt once in a while, even after she looked like she'd been exhumed.

When she was done bathing – she never rushed that part, having always believed in marking out her day into sections, like chapters maybe – she wandered back into her home's main area, clad in a pink terry-cloth bathrobe (she needed to replace it soon; it was starting to fray on the sleeves and okay, there was no one to see, but you had to keep on top of that stuff). Her living space was tidy. Keeping a place (or a life) in good order merely meant putting things where they were supposed to go, and if you lived in a trailer and didn't pick up that habit then you were going to be wallowing in a pigsty real fast.

The place gave her everything she needed. She had her sitting area, a pair of two-seater couches in an L shape, the second of which demarked the space from the kitchenette and the table where she ate and did administrative chores . . . and everything else. The real parts of her life. At present, approximately seven square feet of the horizontal surfaces – a portion of one of the couches, two patches of kitchen, a spot right in the middle of the table, and two apparently random positions on the floor – were home to the sides, paws, or posteriors of cats. Six were currently indoors, the others outside, who knows where, doing stuff, who knows what. A long time ago a man whom Talia had loved used to deliver a stock response to being asked whether he'd had enough pizza yet.

'Is there any left?' he'd say.

'Yes.'

'Well, no, then,' he'd answer, baffled.

Talia felt the same about cats. She knew people who believed nine was too many. For her the words 'too many' didn't compute with cats. Sure, you could be some batty old lady who let the place fill up with fur and uncleaned litter trays, but Talia was not that woman and wasn't ever going to be.

She wandered around, spending time with each of her friends. They craned their heads up into her hand, or rolled over, or sat focused on some interior thought. Once she'd said hello to each she felt like she was really home, and it was time to get on.

She changed into stretch pants and sweatshirt and put the robe back on over it all, then fixed herself a little food. She didn't eat much in the evening. She didn't eat much at *any* time, despite her running gag about stealing the cakes at Roast Me. Either she was falling foul of hidden calories somewhere or her body wanted to be this shape, and she was done pretending she gave a shit. She fixed a vegetable stir-fry with some of the smoked tofu she'd become mildly addicted to, flicking the pan in the way she'd seen that guy do it on television (and that, after some practice, she could replicate without shunting half the contents over the stove). When it was cooked, she reached to the magnetized strip on the left where her cooking implements hung.

Her fingers failed to find what they expected. Her spatula wasn't there.

She frowned, looked around – and spotted it on the magnetic strip on the other side. Well, that wasn't where it was supposed to be. That was for the knives. Huh. How had that happened? Nobody else would have moved it. She couldn't remember the last time someone had been in her home. A long time back it had been a popular destination for those in the county who enjoyed a beer and a smoke while one or more of them played Neil

Young songs to varying degrees of recognizability on battered guitars. The younger (and much slimmer) version of Talia Willocks could lay a harmony line on top and, moreover, kept a dependable stock of cold beer in the fridge and made fine brownies too, albeit of the kind that had you staring at the stars and talking all kinds of happy crap by the time you'd finished your second.

Those days were gone, and most of those people had drifted on or gone corporate – George Lofland was the only one she still passed the time of day with. The trailer parties had stopped the day Ed died. The heart had gone out of the town for a few months after the crash in which he was killed along with five other well-liked locals. It was a simple accident, nobody's fault, just one of those things, which somehow made it worse.

The heart had never quite gone out of Talia's life, though for a long time its beating had been quiet indeed, and there had been nights in the first months where she'd worried it might slow to nothing. Then one night, sitting in a chair by herself in front of the trailer and pretty deep in the bag, she'd happened to see a shooting star, cheap and easy though that might seem when the story's told. She'd been seeing them all her life and it wasn't any big deal, but that was the point.

Not everything is somebody's fault.

Magic happens, and shit happens, and neither lasts forever. You have to let the instances burn themselves out, arcing over the time horizon, and then get the fuck back on your feet and reengage the fight.

Ed's dead.

Get over it.

The next day she'd woken up with a vicious hangover but had hauled herself into town and bought a big notebook. That had been the start. She'd written something – and usually a lot – every day since. At first just a diary (which she still kept up, in ordered ranks of identical notebooks on the shelf behind the TV), then the more creative journaling, and finally . . . the novel. Ta-da.

She looked at the spatula hanging on the rail and decided she must have put it there herself.

Hey, girl, still got some wild in you. You put the spatula on a different rail for once.

Rock and fucking roll.

She fished the food out of the pan and onto a plate and took it to the table. Four of the cats came and watched while she did this, but in a companionable way, as they knew there was nothing on the plate for cats. Talia chatted with them about her day while she ate, and why not? There was nobody to hear.

Three hours later she sat back from the computer and blew strands of hair off her face. Writing always made her hot – though not that kind of hot, ha-ha. It just fired her up. She sympathized with David for the trouble he was having, but it never got her that way. Whether she was updating her diary or plowing into the sequel to *The Quest of Alegoria* (she knew she shouldn't until she'd heard from David what he thought about the first, but the characters had started doing their song and dance in her head and she couldn't stop herself from hooking up and seeing where they wanted to go next), words had always come easily. She was a relaxed kind of person, didn't care much what people thought, and maybe that helped. David was a nice guy and she still hadn't gotten over how touched she'd been by his offer to read her book (she got the sense that he thought fantasy was beneath him, and that was okay; a lot of people did), but he was kind of . . . *uptight*. Actually, that wasn't the word.

Talia put her elbows on the table and concentrated. Words were like cats (if you thought hard enough about it, pretty much everything was like cats, or unlike them, or whatever). Chase after cats or words and they'll outrun you every time. Sit still, act like you don't care, and they'll be all over you (another lesson that David could benefit from learning).

It wasn't *uptight*, it was . . .

Guarded. Yeah, that was closer. He was friendly and all, and obviously loved Dawn to death, but it was like his eyes were turned in – as if what happened inside his skull was the realest thing in his world. Talia loved to write, but she knew the difference between inside and out and which was important. She wasn't sure David *did* know this, and she'd been nearly blown out of her panties when he'd blurted out his news about the baby. It was touching as hell but out of character, as if he'd decided that it was worth interacting with real people for once. Of course, with what had happened to his parents, maybe it wasn't so surprising that he took a cautious approach. Maybe that was simply good sense, and one of these days he'd see his own shooting star – or hopefully something less obvious, as Talia believed David might think wake-up calls delivered via shooting star a little beneath him, too – and relax a little.

Clichéd though the star had been, it had worked. You didn't need fancy, not with things that counted. Ed used to say you could play half the songs in the world (and pretty much all of the good ones) with just three chords.

God, she hoped David liked her book.

If he did, surely that was a good sign. In her heart of hearts she knew she wrote for herself, but shit, a little money would come in handy and it would be kind of cool to go into libraries and see her book there, women waiting patiently for their chance to take it out and spend a little time in Talia's world of wonders.

We'll see. No point waiting on it. Not when there's so many more words out there to write.

She had her hands raised to go back to typing when she noticed something was up with the cats. During the time she'd been working, the cast of feline companions had been in flux. Some went out via the flap in the door; others came in. It was getting late now, though, after eleven, and . . . she counted, and confirmed what she'd already known (if you love cats, you know if they're around without having to check) – everybody was inside. All present and accounted for. Five spread over the couches. Two underneath them. And two . . .

It was the two on the table she noticed first. Sandy and Pickles. They'd been curled up at the far end (they were siblings and usually slept together) and then both raised their heads at the same time and stood up.

Talia heard a rustling, looked around, and saw most of the cats on the couches had done the same.

She wasn't fussed by this – they did it all the time, feline senses picking up on small creatures of the night unwisely straying too close outside. A mouse, vole, rat, whatever. At this time of night most of the cats would muse on it for a minute and then settle back down, reasoning that there'd be plenty of opportunity for terrorizing wildlife the following day, and it was late, and really it was pretty comfortable and warm inside.

Only Tilly – who Talia saw was now jumping down from the couch, tail up – would generally elect to make something of it. Though the smallest and one of the oldest of her cat friends, Tilly operated a Zero Tolerance and Nuke From Orbit approach to anything that strayed near her territory, and could be guaranteed to go and chase the living crap out of whatever was outside, sometimes returning with the remains in her mouth as an offering to the big human she lived with.

Now, however, she saw that Tilly had hesitated about halfway to the trailer door. She sat down abruptly. Looked back the way she'd come. Trying to pinpoint the noise from outside, presumably, which Talia hadn't even heard. Pickles and Sandy seemed to be doing the same, and none of the other cats had settled down yet either.

Kind of odd, but cats got ideas into their heads once in a while and just as quickly forgot them. Whatever. It was getting late and she had at least another blank line break in her before it was time for—

Someone knocked on the door.

Talia froze, hands still poised. There was no doubt that's what it had been. There were trees near the trailer, but none of them came close enough for a branch to have made the sound. It had come from the door, too, not the roof – a straightforward *rap rap rap*. Not loud. Like you'd do if you were half expected. But people didn't come visiting Talia, not down this road, and certainly not this late.

'Who's there?'

Her voice was strong. Talia Willocks had never taken any shit, and if some happy asshole had gotten themselves lost then they needed to know right away who they'd be dealing with when and if she opened her trailer door.

The cats were all looking in the same direction. Talia hit the key combination to save her work, strode over to the door, and opened it.

'Who is it?'

There was nobody outside. She looked both ways and plodded down the little metal stairs. From here you could see from her lot (somewhat over-grown; she didn't care much about the outside) down the twenty-foot path to the road. There was no one there either.

A hundred yards up the way was the graveyard. Its proximity had never bothered her. It was where you put dead people, right? Dead people wouldn't do you any harm. Ed lay up there, along with the other people who shared his death day, and hundreds of others who'd passed over the years. The thought had never yielded any comfort but on the other hand, neither did she mind.

She looked in the other direction. The road came to an end forty yards down the way, replaced by the foot-worn path of those who wanted to head down to the high-sided and rocky creek that had given the town its name, generally to make out. Talia's best bet was that some young couple, likely a few brews down, had rapped on her door as a joke – before tearing off down the path.

They'd've had to be quick, though. And it was kind of cold tonight. Colder than most people would find appealing for al fresco activities of the hot and heavy kind. There was a frisky wind, too. Talia couldn't see a fallen twig or anything obvious lying on the ground, but that didn't mean there wasn't one.

There was a soft feeling against her leg, and she jumped before realizing it was just Tilly cat, come to see. Talia bent down and scratched her head. The cat tolerated this for a moment and then wandered off.

Show's over, I guess.

Talia yawned massively. Maybe she didn't have those extra few paragraphs in her tonight after all. Could be the little fictional people were going to have to stay frozen in place for tonight.

Someone called her name.

She whipped her head around, heart stopping in her throat. She heard the wind moving the branches of the trees behind the trailer and along the road.

Meanwhile, Tilly nosed around in the long grass, not looking like a cat who'd detected any disturbance in the ether. She pounced on something – real or imaginary – and then trotted back up the steps and indoors.

The wind kept blowing, then died a little. Either way, the wind hadn't been what Talia had heard. It couldn't be, because it didn't make sense, but it had sounded like someone had called her name.

A man's voice. Soft, somewhere up the road, between here and the church. And yes . . . there it was again.

It hadn't called out 'Talia,' though. It had sounded like Tally-Anne. Her real name, the one

304

she'd been given at birth, which no one ever used now. No one had called her by it much even in the old days. Her mother and father, when they were still alive . . . and a man long dead, whom she'd once loved.

Talia stayed on the steps, pulling her robe tight but getting colder and colder, for ten more minutes.

She didn't hear anything else.

CHAPTER 37

Kristina wasn't alarmed when she realized someone was following her – only surprised it had taken so long. Truth be told, she'd been wandering around in the hope it might happen. She would prefer not to be called upon to tell that truth, though. She'd rather stick with what she'd told John, that she was heading over to Swift's to collect the book for next week's reading group. Which she dutifully did before taking a long walk uptown and back, including both Bryant and Union Square Parks and getting nothing for her trouble but feet that were sore enough to be a real pain when it came to working that evening.

She'd been convinced that somewhere along the way she'd have company. Lizzie, hopefully, but if not then one of her friends, who could presumably lead her to Lizzie. Eventually she got bored and headed for home. Well, maybe bored wasn't quite right. It was . . .

Disappointed.

And more than that.

Back when she was sixteen there'd been this

party in Black Ridge. She hadn't really known the girls throwing it – they'd been Ginny's pals – but she'd run into them a couple of times on the street and on nights when Kristina and Ginny and Henna had managed to slip into bars (not an impossible feat in the mountain backwoods of Washington State, if the three of you are tall for your age and, let's face it, somewhat cute). They hung out all the time, at one another's houses, at the Yakima mall when they could get a ride. They did everything as a group back in the days when it was essential to feel people had your back and were walking side by side with you into the strange rooms of adulthood. Henna and Ginny lived up the road, two houses apart, and the unspoken arrangement was they'd come walking down toward town, pick Kristina up, and head together into what passed for the bright lights of Black Ridge, there to behave as badly as possible within the limited options available.

Anyway, this party had been set up and the word was it was going to be *major*. It was even *themed* – everybody had to turn up dressed in black, white, and red. This presented a challenge for Kristina. Her mother was not one of those maternal souls who relished guiding her daughter toward adulthood. She had other things she wanted to inculcate in her, but not that. Kristina was forced to pick up the basics by herself, which frequently left her feeling that she hadn't got stuff quite right. She didn't have many clothes, certainly nothing that would look sufficiently kick-ass at a party that – Kristina was sure – was going to be life-changingly grown-up. Word was a bunch of *boys* were going to be there – new boys, different boys, not the ones who always hung around or who you saw at school.

Kris gathered together what she could. She had a black skirt that she thought she looked kind of okay in. She found some red stockings cheap in town. She had a white blouse. The last wasn't in any way cool and in fact made the whole ensemble look a bit odd, like some waitress who'd got dressed in the dark, but it was the best she could do and if the deal was it had to be black, white, and red, then that's what you had to do.

She showered. She put on makeup – somewhat inexpertly, as she didn't have any good stuff and her mother had never shown any interest in giving her tips. She looked at herself in the mirror and wondered how changed she would be, how many things she would have learned and done, by the end of the night. She dressed in her black, white, and red clothes. She looked in the mirror one more time and wished herself luck.

She went downstairs cautiously. Her mother was in position on the sofa, watching TV. Permission had been granted for Kristina to go to the party. Kristina's mother believed, entirely correctly, that her own reputation within the town would stop anybody from getting fresh with her daughter. That, at any rate, would be a charitable interpretation for her not minding her daughter going out: Kristina knew that not giving a shit also played a part. Ginny's and Henna's parents had been told artfully constructed mistruths about the event – excitement over which was by now causing Kristina to hyperventilate – and believed their daughters were going to a study session at another girl's house, a session that could go on very, very late. The tactical advantages of drinking vodka, assuming it was available (on the grounds that it didn't leave a smell on your breath) had been discussed and agreed upon by all three girls.

Kristina's mother ran her eyes up and down her daughter and grunted. 'What *do* you look like?'

She went back to watching her show. Kristina's father would have said something nicer, but he was dead, and he wouldn't have wanted her to go out. Kristina decided she didn't want to wait downstairs. She grabbed an apple from the kitchen – she knew she ought to put *something* in her stomach before all the vodka – and returned to her room. She could wait there. She could see the street corner from her window. As soon as the girls came into sight – and they'd probably be along soon; it was coming up for seven and the party was due to start at eight – she'd race downstairs and leave the house.

She sat on her window seat, gnawing at the apple, forcing herself to eat almost half of it despite the butterflies in her stomach. She waited. And she waited.

And they didn't come.

On Monday the school was full of stories about the party. The shadows cast by stories, anyhow. The people who'd attended only really talked to other people who'd been there. There was a lot of sniggering and implication and innuendo. Ginny had an outrageous hickey on her neck that came close to getting her sent home from school. There was talk of things that had been drunk and whispers of other, even more glittering deeds.

When Kristina diffidently asked Henna what happened, why they hadn't come to pick her up, her friend shrugged.

'You didn't call to make plans,' she said.

'But you always pick me up on the way into town,' Kristina said falteringly. 'I just assumed.'

'Yeah, well, maybe you assume too much.'

Basically it transpired that, though nothing had ever been said, the other two girls felt Kristina took them for granted. Nothing could have been further from the truth, but that was that.

Kristina didn't stop seeing them. They were her friends until she left town at eighteen and spent the next decade spiraling around the country and the world. They hung out and had some good times.

But sitting by yourself in a window and waiting, watching as the light turns and the night comes in, trying to work out what could have delayed things, whether you should call or if that made you look desperate or uncool, whether it had gotten too late or if it was still possible she would hear the doorbell – as it was now too dark to see them coming down the street . . . Kristina thought she'd always remember how that felt, and most of all how it had been to finally give up (she lasted until half past nine) and take the dumb fucking clothes off and go downstairs to get something proper to eat. Her mother had still been in her chair, the television off, staring into space.

She looked at Kristina. She didn't say anything, but she smiled. It was a bitter little thing.

If you'd have asked Kris, she would have said that evening was far behind her. But maybe evenings like that never get behind us. When you're young you're very raw, and if the world smacks you it really stings.

And when friends betray and forget you, it *scars*.

When Kristina realized what was going on in her head she laughed at herself, sent up a prayer that Henna had put on even *more* weight than the last time Kris had seen her, and headed home.

Just before she turned onto their street she remembered they were out of milk. And . . . well, pretty much everything else. She stopped by the Not Very Good Deli and gathered up some organic two percent and random cookies. It was as she was zoning out in front of the dried pasta – a clear

311

indication of having run out of inspiration: if there's one food people who work in an Italian restaurant tend not to crave on nights off, it's pasta – that she felt something. If you asked a scientist about it, he or she would put it down to a glimpse or a reflection, but it wasn't. Kris knew humans aren't confined by their bodies or skulls. They seep. With some strong souls, they can even stretch, sometimes for long distances.

She didn't turn to look.

She walked to the register as if nothing was happening, paid for her purchases, and stepped outside. She dawdled up the street, trying to figure out what to do. Should she head somewhere more private – or find a way to signal John that another meeting could be about to happen, to see if he could get in on it as well?

'Hey,' said a voice, suddenly very close.

It wasn't a woman's voice. It was a man's.

Kris turned. It was the man in the coat. The man who'd been watching her in SoHo the night before. 'You talking to me?'

'I think so,' he said, smiling. He gestured up and down the street. 'I don't see anybody else, do you?'

Kristina realized he was right. Something twisted in her stomach. Meanwhile the man took a couple of steps closer to her.

She faced him down. 'I don't know you, do I?'

'No. I don't know you either. But I saw you last night with some people I *do* know.'

'Yeah, I saw you too. What's your point?'

'What were you doing with them?'

'Look, Mr . . .'

'My name is Reinhart.'

'I need to get home. My boyfriend's expecting me.'

She hated falling back on the my-boyfriend's-waiting ploy, but something about the man in front of her said this was a situation she needed to exit as quickly and decisively as possible.

'Of course. Someone like you, there will always be a man waiting. But by the time this boyfriend starts thinking "I wonder where dear Kristina's got to?" it would be too late, you see.'

'Look. I don't know who you are—'

'Yes, you do. I told you. Reinhart. I can spell it for you, if you wish. And here's the thing. The people you were talking to last night, they're not important to me. They got their own life; we don't do business. Especially because the girl you were talking to, Lizzie, she doesn't like these guys to steal. That's okay. I respect that. But there are *other* people, friends of theirs, who *do* steal . . . and with them, I *do* have business. It's important to me. Understand?'

Kristina considered running, but dismissed the idea. Something about the heavy poise of the man said he would be able to move hard and fast if the need arose.

'I watch your face,' he said, 'and I think yes, she understands. This is good. The job of a businessman is taking care of business, right? I got people already trying to make things difficult for me. I don't need more. Your face also tells me you'd like to go now, and that's okay. I have other things I need to attend to. I hope I'll never see you again – especially not near anyone who works for me. You think we can agree to that?'

Kristina nodded.

'That's excellent. Because otherwise I will have to do something about it. And if *that* happens, your boyfriend can look for you all over the city, all over the state, but he's not going to find anything. Which would be a shame, yes? It's an ugly world we live in. It's always sad when something beautiful is destroyed.'

He reached up with disconcerting speed and stroked a finger along her left cheekbone. Then he walked away.

Kristina ran along the street and around the corner, and when she saw John at the top of the steps outside their apartment, she called out to him and ran faster still.

CHAPTER 38

David was thinking about magnets.

He was supposed to be thinking about work, of course, but he wasn't. Of all the things Maj had said, the one that stuck most clearly had been the stuff about magnets. Today David and his desk were behaving like two of the world's strongest, set to repel.

He wanted to work. He *needed* to. Yet there was some portion of his mind – one that held the keys to major muscle groups – that clearly desired otherwise. It was like having two people inhabiting the same body, Siamese twin souls determined to run in opposite directions.

And this morning, not-working David was wiping the floor with the opposition.

Taking a break from the screen and going across the hall into the spare bedroom hadn't helped either. He'd hoped having something to do with his hands might free his mind. It did not. Dawn had done almost everything already. The only job remaining was sorting the boxes David had shipped once he realized he was going to stay in Rockbridge. They held bits from his childhood, mainly books, and mementos of his parents.

David's parents had died in a car accident while he was living in New York City, a flashback he very seldom referred to in his personal narrative. He'd told Talia about it one afternoon because it was similar to what had happened to the guy she used to go out with. Dawn knew about it, of course. Otherwise, if the subject came up – around an inquiry as to whether he was seeing family at Thanksgiving, for example – he'd explain the situation and weather the inevitable sympathy, not volunteering the information that both his parents had been shit-faced drunk at the time, his father moreover high, and they'd been lucky not to take out an innocent family who'd happened to be driving late along the same highway.

His parents' car had gone off the road and smacked into a tree, and that was that. After their death he'd gone home from New York, sold the house and almost everything in it. He'd wandered the country for two years before settling on Rockbridge after meeting and falling in love with Dawn. He'd opened one of the storage boxes when they'd moved into this house – hence his mother's pottery piece downstairs – and then resealed it and never thought about it or the other two again. Reopening them now did not help his mood. He missed his parents, of course. He had loved them. His father's battered typewriter didn't bring him back, however, nor the brooch his mother had been wearing the night of the crash. A pair of their cocktail glasses did, sort of, but not in a good way.

His impulse was to seal the boxes back up again and either heft them up into the attic or take them down to the dump. He knew the former wouldn't play with Dawn, however – she was not someone who tolerated things merely being stowed; it was a miracle they'd lasted this long in the spare room – and the latter didn't seem right.

You can't throw the past away. You have to integrate it into your life or else it sits there just beyond the edge of your vision, dust-gathering, rotting.

The fact that you can't see something doesn't mean it's gone.

After forty minutes he'd given up and left the house, but walking wasn't helping either. His mind was still full of magnets. He knew Maj and the man's relationship to David's life was something he needed to work out – or at least *remember*. He couldn't do that and it scared him.

He knew he ought to talk to Dawn about it, too. He didn't want to sound crazy, however, especially with the news they'd had. The second reason was . . . harder to put his finger on. The situation made him feel vulnerable and exposed. It felt like a sleeping dog that should be let lie forever. Maybe even fed a little doctored steak, just to make sure.

He slowed as he came in view of Roast Me,

considering an afternoon coffee. He couldn't face talking to Talia about her book, however. What you create is like a person, as is the process itself. Talking to someone who's succeeding in writing when you're not is like hearing them describe just how much great and experimental sex they're having with your partner.

He could lie, maybe, saying he'd got to the end of the book and it was great – but then she'd ask him about the climax or something else he'd be supposed to know, and the lie would be exposed.

He got caught out. Talia wasn't inside, for once, but stomping around clearing cups off the benches built into the window. Without running across the road, he couldn't avoid her.

'Hey,' she said. Her smile was brief and her voice quiet. She did not ask him about his word count. In fact, that single word of greeting appeared to be all.

'I haven't had a chance to read any more of your book,' David said, disconcerted. 'Been busy.'

'No problemo.'

Concerned she might be pissed at him, he checked her face. It was blank. Uncharacteristically so. Usually Talia's weather was right there for everyone to read.

'I'm still loving it. I definitely think you've got something.'

She straightened, several cups in each large hand, and blew a strand of hair off her hot face. 'That's great, David. Thank you.'

'Are you . . . okay?'

'Sure. Why?'

'I don't know. You just seem . . .'

Every time he'd seen Talia she'd been extremely Talia-like. Today she wasn't. She seemed older. Old, in fact.

She glanced down the street. When she looked back, it was if something had changed, as if – as when he'd first offered to read her manuscript – many years and an accretion of events had been sanded off her face. 'Where do people go, do you think?'

'Go?'

'When they die.'

David shrugged. 'No idea. Why?'

'I just figured you might have a take. Because of, you know.'

David knew she meant his parents, but had never given the matter any thought. He said so.

'I always assumed they went up to heaven,' she said. 'Or maybe . . . maybe if there *was* no heaven, then they just stopped, bang, that's the end of it. Or if there *was* anything left, some kernel that doesn't die or fade away because the body starts to rot, then maybe that part was locked away in what's left, under the earth. In the bones and stuff.'

David wasn't sure what he could say. He didn't know what she might be hoping for.

'But maybe that's *not* it, huh? Maybe they *do* go somewhere, just not heaven. Or hell, I guess. Maybe it's such a big *thing*, death, that you can wind up out of sync with where you used to be. Like getting thrown clean out through the windshield of a car. But bigger than that. Getting thrown so hard that you wind up miles and miles away.' She glanced at him. 'You think?'

'Could be,' David said. It felt weak, but she didn't seem to be listening to his contribution anyway.

'Saw George this morning,' she went on, blindsiding him. 'He's having a hard time. He's still sure he saw someone on the road through the forest, and he gave the guy a lift into town and that he vanished when they got here. Weird, huh? Like bringing a ghost home.'

David opened his mouth – this *was* something he could contribute to, even if it'd just be the same gentle dismissal he'd given before – but he hesitated, as he finally put two and two together.

The hitchhiker was Maj, of course – Maj on his way to visit him. It must have been.

Talia mistook his silence. 'But that's just friend-of-a-friend bullshit, right?' she said, and laughed – looking like herself again. 'Anyway, stop bugging me, asshole. There's people waiting inside. I must repair to the counter, my wonders to perform.'

She kicked the door and strode back into the coffee shop, bellowing to the people in line that she was coming already; stop your fucking whining for the love of God.

David walked away quickly.

★   ★   ★

Meanwhile, fresh back from school and sitting in the kitchen, Dawn decided she simply could not face marking any more homework. She was finding it hard to focus. Could be hormones, she supposed. Could also be . . .

She looked up.

Directly above the kitchen was the spare room – the soon-to-be-nursery. She'd done everything she could, everything possible without David going through his boxes. Until he'd dispersed their contents she couldn't put dust sheets down properly, and that meant she couldn't repaint the room. She knew he was only being slow because he was trying to concentrate on the new book, and understood that meant he had to look inward and found it hard to maintain hooks into the real world. His 'Eddie Moscone' phase, she called it, after one of the kids in her class. That was fine, and understandable.

But she wanted *to get on*.

It occurred to her that perhaps she could go up and take a look through his boxes. Make easy calls on what he'd want to keep and what he would not. He'd likely want most of it – he had few enough mementoes of his childhood. Weirdly little, in her view, but she was a constitutional hoarder who occasionally took herself in hand. David was the opposite. He seemed to have left his past behind like yesterday's rain.

Going through the boxes would take only fifteen minutes. If she couldn't help, she couldn't help.

But if she could pre-sort them into little piles for him, it might finally get the thing done.

Plus . . . it would be a good excuse not to sit getting frustrated about how tough some kids found it to work out what you had left if you took a nickel and six cents away from a quarter, for the love of God.

She made herself a cup of herbal tea and cheerfully took it upstairs.

CHAPTER 39

It wasn't hard to find Reinhart. Something that might give patrons of the world's restaurants pause for thought, did they but know, is that the staff in the places they drop so much cash in are often one step from the criminal fraternity. Not through character – there are plenty of cooks, waiters, and bar staff whose moral fiber would stand favorable comparison with normal citizens, and walk all over that of the average banker or CEO. There's a degree of recreational drug use, however, and some of the people washing pans and dishes are doing so because their record makes it hard for them to do much else. A lot of the restaurant business happens at night, too, and that's always tended to be when the bad guys ply their ancient trades, or spend time propping up the kind of bars where kitchen workers may also go after work.

Bottom line is, I asked some questions and this led me on to other people in other bars, where I asked more questions, and pretty soon I knew where to go.

It wasn't hard to find him, and I probably should

have given that more thought at the time, but I did not.

It was in what you're supposed to call Clinton these days but will always be Hell's Kitchen to anyone but realtors. You don't have to look hard to find vestiges of the pre-gentrified voice of the area – you can't just line a couple blocks with bistros and expect everything else to disappear. The restaurant was called'. Yes, apostrophe. According to their website, this reflected the executive chef's belief that something was missing from contemporary American cuisine. Personally, I suspected it meant something was missing from the chef's brain, but he certainly didn't lack patrons. From the sidewalk you could see the place was full even on a Wednesday at lunchtime. Everybody looked very nice, and they sat in a space that was light and airy and dotted with round tables accented with linen and single white blooms in delicate little vases in the center. Staff buzzed around in gray slacks and lilac shirts and none of them looked like they'd been within shouting distance of illegal in their life. One of the guys in the kitchen had, though, and he'd told me to look for a table in the middle.

Reinhart sat with two other men. You could tell it was a business meeting and that the other guys were legit. Both wore charcoal suits, though one had removed his jacket to reveal a pale blue shirt. Reinhart was talking in a sober, considered fashion.

He looked tamped down, certainly compared to the man I'd seen in the church a couple of nights before.

He finished his presentation. The men nodded, looked at one another, lips pouted, as if whatever proposal had just been made was very hard to argue with.

Reinhart sat back, wiping his mouth with his napkin. Then he looked up and saw me. I took this as my cue to walk in off the street. A woman in a smart pantsuit tried to intercept me, but she was not hard to avoid.

I stood over the table. 'Good food?'

Reinhart looked up. 'Very good,' he said. 'The vongole is superb. I take lunch here almost every day. But . . . I suppose you knew that.'

'Correct,' I said, keeping my voice low so as not to impact on the eating pleasure of other diners, or cause anyone to call the cops just yet. Pantsuit had retreated to her podium but was keeping an eye on me. 'A creature of habit. That means either you're dumb or very confident. Unless you got someone at a table somewhere in the room? If so, they're kind of slow to their feet.'

I made a show of looking around, though of course I'd done so before I walked in. I'm not a total fool. There had been no male one-tops nor pairs of serious-looking guys casting casual glances across the room. 'I guess not. Which means either you *are* dumb, or you don't believe someone would have the balls.'

'You still look familiar,' Reinhart said, as if I were background music. 'Just can't work out where from.'

I tried not to clench my fists. 'I'm going to become *very* familiar if you don't listen. Last night you had a conversation on the street with a friend of mine.'

Reinhart glanced apologetically at his lunch companions. 'Are you the boyfriend? That makes sense. Two people popping up in my business, turns out they're together. A pair of problems. I should have figured that out. Maybe I am dumb after all.'

'Nah,' I said. 'Don't think so. What do *you* think?' I asked his companions. 'He seem stupid to you?'

One looked away. The other stared at the remains of his veal parmigiana as if wondering whether he should have ordered something else.

'Me neither,' I said. 'So here's the thing, Reinhart. Come near her again and I'll hurt you. *Threaten* her and that will be the end of you. Understand?'

He looked at me with vague interest, as if trying to work out what language I was speaking in.

'Whatever your business with this man, I'd walk away,' I told the guy with the veal. 'But finish your food first. Someone worked hard on that.'

The encounter did not leave me feeling good. I hadn't understood how angry I was until confronted with Reinhart, and I'd done nothing but embarrass both him and me. People do not like being embarrassed, most of all men like him. Or me – especially when I've done it to myself.

I hailed a cab with no destination in mind, but after a few blocks told the driver to take me down to Chelsea. I got out on 16th, but instead of going to the church went straight to the house next door and rang the buzzer.

'Who is it?'

'John Henderson.'

There was a pause. 'And?'

'I'd like to talk to you.'

'I'm afraid I'm busy right now.'

'Then I apologize for the inconvenience. But I just lit a fire under a man and I need you to explain to me what I've done.'

'What are you talking about?'

'Reinhart,' I said.

There was a pause, and then a click.

The hallway beyond was small and dark. After a moment I heard footsteps coming down the stairs. They stopped before I could see anyone.

'Come upstairs, won't you? It's the only part of the house that ever seems to get any light.'

The footsteps went back up again.

I trotted up past a first story with a landing and two closed doors, and onward to the top. Jeffers stood aside to let me into a room at the front of the house. It held a desk, two chairs that looked like they'd been borrowed from the church, and an upright piano. The only personal touch was an armchair, formerly luxurious but now threadbare, by the window. He saw me looking at it.

'My predecessor's. He lived here for thirty years.'

'Feel some days like he still is?'

My comment was intended as throwaway empathy, but he looked at me sharply. 'What happened with Reinhart?'

'He followed my partner yesterday and threatened her. I'm just back from talking to him.'

'You're in better shape than I would have expected.'

'I made sure it happened in a public place.'

Jeffers shook his head.

'What's that supposed to mean?'

'How did he know who your partner was? Why did even care? Because you were here the other night. Which shows he already *knows* where you live, and that means—'

'He didn't know about her because of me.'

'What do you mean?'

'Until I confronted him over lunch, he didn't know there was a connection between us.'

I realized with a sinking heart that I'd helped Reinhart draw a line between two people he had reason to have a problem with, and that sometimes men who don't hide are not merely excessively confident. They may also believe that they're well connected enough not to need to care. Sometimes they're right.

'I don't understand.'

'Kristina found a cryptic message a couple of days ago,' I said, sitting on one of the wooden chairs. 'It was written in the dirt on our window.'

'An unusual means of communication.'

'Right. Especially as we live on the fifth floor. She worked out the message and went to Union Square Park. She met some people there, including the woman I later saw you talking to in Union Square. You know the one. We've been through this. Her name's Lizzie.'

The priest listened with an expression I couldn't place at first.

'A couple stole jewelry and presented it to her. Then everyone ran off – leaving her stuck in a doorway still holding the goods . . . at which point she noticed two men watching. One was Reinhart. Yesterday he accosted her in a backstreet and was not subtle about warning her to stay out of his business.'

Jeffers's face had become composed again. I knew now what I'd seen in his face, however. It was the look of a man who has been found out over something personal: a matter that has been on his mind a great deal but not allowed out on show; a load he has been carrying by himself, which at times has felt very heavy indeed.

'Talk to me,' I said. 'Explain what I've gotten myself into. I may even be able to help.'

'No,' he said, sitting on the other chair. 'You won't. But I'll tell you what you need to know.'

★　★　★

He told me he'd been the priest there for three years. When he'd arrived he'd found a community in decline. His predecessor had been in place a long time and was much loved and just about managed to hold the place steady, acting as a bridge between the era when people believed by default and a new one in which they did not. Partly, Jeffers said, this change lay at the hands of science. While he had no personal issue with the objective assessment of verifiable facts, the reductionist agenda could lead in only one direction when it came to the worship of things unseen. Even more important, he believed, was that people just didn't have time for it. In the old days life was simple. You worked and slept and you attempted to reproduce. If you had time in between then what you craved was a sense of wonder, something to keep you reconciled to the drudgery of the day-to-day – and a sense of community, too. For hundreds of years the church was the go-to for both, but the Internet killed that. E-mail and Facebook took interaction and threw it somewhere non-concrete: up in the cloud, yes, but not one where angels sat jamming on golden harps. You didn't need to catch up outside the church gates on Sunday morning – you were constantly aware of your friends' and neighbors' every deed and thought and meal. If you wanted a glimpse of the lords of your manor, Twitter provided it in a parallel stream: endless updates on how vewwy, vewwy much your hallowed movie star loves the

330

husband who in reality she's enthusiastically cheating on with her personal trainer, amongst others. Instead of thinking about the nature of the universe, and your life, and wondering what kind of being or circumstance could have given rise to it, you thought 'Cool! Ashton Kutcher has tweeted again, just for me!'

After six months Jeffers had started to make do, settling for the status quo like the last Roman living in a far-flung European back-water after the empire had pulled the plug. It wasn't a bad life and there were still a few old people who cared. As a way of serving the Lord and filling in the years until he could take a meeting with Him in person, it would do.

'Then I met Lizzie,' the priest said, looking up at me. 'And Maj, and some others, and things changed.'

'Where did you first meet them?'

'I don't know.'

'You can't remember?'

'I can't recall where I first became aware of them.'

'I'm not sure I understand the distinction.'

'They're not easy to pin down.'

'Who are they?'

'People who've been forgotten by the rest of us and have no place in our society. That's a hard life to live. Unlike most, they're doing something about it.'

'Stealing, you mean.'

He shook his head. 'Very few. For most there's no point, or wasn't until Reinhart came along. They're organized, after a fashion. They have places they live and hide; there are roles and ways of being; there's even a kind of hierarchical society. There *was*, anyway. Then a few of the older ones, the people who'd put a lot of this in place, left the picture at the same time.'

'Died, you mean?'

I could see him choosing his words. 'It would be more accurate to say they stopped exerting an influence. Unfortunately Reinhart arrived during the same period, and he realized he could make criminal use of some of the skills the remaining had acquired.'

'Like?'

'Avoiding detection. Very successfully.'

'And stealing things.'

'Regretfully, yes.'

'How does it work?'

'Sometimes simply taking things out of stores – small, expensive goods that are handed on to Reinhart for sale. The thing is, there are very few of them who are skilled at that, and so he's always coming up with new ideas. He has them spying at ATMs, observing PIN numbers. Once the victim is around the corner, Reinhart's other accomplices intercept him or her and detain them until they've had a chance to use the number and the bank card to remove large sums of money.'

'Uh-huh,' I said, remembering the spate of

similar crimes in our neighborhood over the last months. 'And what do they get out of it?'

'Shelter. And attention.'

'If they want attention, why do they spend their lives in hiding?'

'It's . . . difficult to explain. I'd become aware of some of these people in the neighborhood. I befriended a few. It's not easy. When I realized how they were being used by Reinhart, I started a program. I tried to help them to see my church as a safe and supportive place. Tried to move them away from criminal acts, too. Partly on moral grounds. Mainly because sooner or later it'd mean exposure for them. Some have responded well.'

'Which Reinhart doesn't like. Hence him being here the other night, and also threatening Kristina.'

'Yes.'

'So why hasn't he just whacked you?'

The priest looked confused. 'Whacked?'

'Had you killed. These people tend to think in very straight lines.'

'You think someone would kill a priest over something like this? Are you serious?'

I looked into his sober, calm eyes, and tried to figure out how to break the news that people died every day for incomparably less. Then I realized from the corners of his mouth that he knew this fact very well.

'You're a smart man,' I said, standing. 'And probably a good one. But I'd think seriously about letting these people look after themselves.'

'That would not be the Lord's way. Or mine.'

'Maybe. But the Lord doesn't live by himself in a house that would be easy to break into. These people exist outside society for a reason. They know the score. They don't get anything out of our world, sure, but that means they also won't feel they have to give in return.'

He smiled, and I realized it was like talking to a great big bear, one who found the spectacle of the human in front of him mildly interesting, especially the noises he was making with his mouth, but who would not be altering his behavior on the basis of anything I said.

'Seriously,' I tried. 'If it comes down to it, these are not people you can trust to get your back.'

'They are lost,' he said. 'It's my job to bring them home.'

CHAPTER 40

Kristina's phone started being weird halfway through the afternoon. It rang, showing a number she didn't recognize – but there was no one there. The first time she didn't think anything of it. It was a Sprint phone and the service sucked. Attempts to discuss this with the company had achieved nothing but rage and the desire to hunt down and kill everyone who worked for them, which apparently you're not allowed to do. Forty minutes later it happened again. She stuffed the phone back in her pocket afterward, prey to the churning in the guts that comes when our inexplicable new tech starts misbehaving. In days of yore you prayed to God to keep the magic working. Now we navigate ritualistic menus, sit in prayer on hold, and pay homage to customer service representatives of indifferent competence and temper. It's a matter of debate which yields the more tangible results.

Then it happened *again*.

This time she didn't even bother to look. John had texted ten minutes before, and she'd replied. The only other person she could think of was

Catherine Warren, but her name would have shown on the screen.

Then she pulled the phone back out, prey to a thought. She navigated to the incoming log and confirmed the failed calls had all come from the same number and that the last time had left a message. Maybe it was Catherine after all – calling from another number after a phone fault or loss, perhaps to say she wouldn't be coming to the book club that evening. They hadn't spoken since the fabulously awkward meeting at her house.

Kristina thought she'd better check. Annoyingly, the message had also failed. A ten-second stretch of silence – or the strange, tidal version of it that dead telecommunication equipment sings – and it cut off.

She walked on, more slowly now, keeping the phone in her hand. Five minutes later, it rang again. 'Yes?' she said, getting it up to her ear fast. 'Who is it?' Silence. 'Don't hang up,' she said, hurrying into a side street. 'I can't hear you.'

The line went dead.

Swearing, she flicked back to voice mail. As she waited for the previous message to read back, she wandered down the street, cupping the earpiece with her other hand to cut out extraneous noise – and trying not to remember that it was a street pretty much like this where she'd been cornered and threatened the day before.

She listened to the tidal noise again, the silence that wasn't silence. Except . . . maybe it wasn't silence. Maybe she could hear . . . something. Something very faint.

She listened to the sound one more time, hunched next to a stairwell, a finger in her other ear, closing her eyes to hand everything over to a single sense.

It *could* just have been her mind trying to usher random sounds toward meaning, like those recordings people made in houses that were supposed to be haunted, in fact just meaningless white noise.

She didn't think so, however.

brprr, sssnn

That's what it sounded like – someone whispering in your ear before you were awake. The first part sounded a *little* like 'Bryant Park,' though. Perhaps only because it was in her mind as the first place she'd met Lizzie, but once she'd heard the sounds that way, she couldn't unhear the words. The second part sounded like it meant something, too. In fact, she heard that part first. It sounded like someone saying 'Seven.'

Bryant Park, seven.

She listened to the recording one more time and couldn't make herself hear it differently. Why it should sound so very faint and strange, she had no idea. Maybe a problem with her phone, or voice mail, or the movement of the spheres. She wasn't tangling with Sprint's asshole version of customer service to find out.

She could think of only one person who might be trying to leave a message – especially one that short, suggesting a meeting in a park. Lizzie had taken her number. If the whole thing wasn't Kristina's imagination, this had to be from her. And if it was an invitation to meet up, Kris wanted to take her up on it.

But what about Reinhart? She'd been *really* scared last night, and scaring Kris wasn't a job for the faint of heart. She'd gone running to John and he'd hugged her and made sure she was all right – and not done what she knew he wanted to, which was run off and try to find the guy. He hadn't said anything about him since, either, which must have taken herculean reserves of self-denial. And if what he'd since told her about his conversation with the priest that afternoon was true, and some of Lizzie's broader circle of friends were working for Reinhart, he wouldn't want that deal messed up by people like Kristina.

He'd warned her, and made the message good and clear.

A stray thought dropped into her head. It struck her that John had been vague about how he'd spent his morning. Just walking, he'd said, winding up in Chelsea with Jeffers more or less by chance. It occurred to her to wonder whether he'd been making inquiries about Reinhart instead, and if so, what he'd found. Not much, presumably, or he would have said.

Presumably.

It was six o'clock. She was a twenty-minute walk from the park. Said park was a ten- or fifteen-minute cab ride back down to Nolita. The reading group didn't start until seven thirty and it wasn't like you got shot for being five minutes late. Eyebrows might be raised – and God knows the raising of educated eyebrows could make you feel small as hell – but no one would actually stand up and point at her.

The park was nowhere near the part of town where Reinhart had caught her. There was no reason to expect him to be in this neighborhood. She wasn't expected at the restaurant for a few hours, but John *would* be working – which gave her a rare window of free will.

If it came right down to it, she didn't need a reason.

She wanted to go.

The park was almost empty. A couple of tourists sat huddled over one of the little tables at the top of the steps at the library end, looking cold and daunted. A few office workers cut down the side paths, heads down, focused on getting to the subway or a working dinner or somewhere to grab a couple of private drinks before getting into the next phase of their existence. If there was anything that working a bar taught you it was that there was a whole lot of parallel living going on – people who presented one way for ninety-five percent of the time but lived somewhere more private in the remaining sliver. Kristina had occasionally wondered what proportion of the city's inhabitants spent the hours between five thirty and eight either drinking or covertly holding the hand of a co-worker, but had decided it wasn't a question that led anywhere happy.

She walked to the middle of the grass and looked around. She watched the couple at the top of the steps get up and head wearily to their hotel to shower and re-group for an evening's fun in a foreign city and to try to ignore the fact that if they were honest, simply fabulous though it all was, just for tonight they'd prefer to be back at home watching TV and wearing sweatpants.

She checked her watch. Did she wait a little longer, or get a cab? That's what made sense, of course. Heading down to Swift's, meeting with Catherine and patching things up, an hour's chat about the gentle – and slim – novel they'd enjoyed (or, in Kristina's case, tolerated with growing irritation). Then get to the bar and her job and lover and life. Run along that track. *Her* track.

She didn't want to. Not tonight. She wanted something else. She wanted something *new*.

When she looked up she saw there were now people at all four points of the park. Dark figures, their faces unclear, alone or in pairs.

'Hey,' she said. Either it wasn't loud enough, or they chose not to respond. She said it again.

'Hello.'

The response came from much closer than she was expecting, and from behind. Kris turned and found Lizzie there. Her heart hit a heavy beat. 'Hey.'

'You got the message.'

'Just about. Why didn't you talk to me?'

'I can't.'

'Why? And why did it sound so weak?'

'It's too boring to explain,' Lizzie said. 'I'm glad you came.'

Kristina found herself tongue-tied, and nodded.

The figures from the corner of the park had moved while she wasn't looking, and congregated at the Sixth Avenue end. Kristina recognized several from the previous meeting, including the plump girl. They were all watching her, as if waiting for something.

Lizzie took Kristina's hand. 'Let's have some fun.'

CHAPTER 41

Kristina followed the Angels out of the park and into the streets as lights started to come on, and the mood of the streets shifted from afternoon to evening in a city that prides itself on never sleeping. She crossed the avenue, into a knot of streets lined with restaurants and bars on the other side, feeling – knowing – this was a gang that didn't let outsiders in very often, if at all. Sometimes they walked together, chattering to Kristina, asking her questions about her life. Then they'd be spread out across the street and both sidewalks, as if they had no connection to one another.

She let herself be led, following in their slipstream – sensing that it was kind of a buzz for them, leading someone like her. Sometimes they'd cut through side streets; at others they'd walk down the middle of the road, weaving between the cars with enough grace and timing that they never got honked (though Kris did, more than once), as if they were cold, hard streams of mountain water cutting through forest soil. She found herself being led into a bar. It was noisy and crowded and dark and it seemed to Kristina that her new friends relaxed when they were inside. Lizzie certainly did. When on the street she always seemed watchful. Here in the hectic gloom there was greater freedom in her movement.

Kristina was confused. Was this a stop off for a drink? No one seemed to be heading toward the bar, but if they weren't here for that, then what could it be? Or were they expecting *her* to step up? The idea didn't bother her – it was clear these people wouldn't have money for Midtown prices – but wasn't anyone going to say anything, or even look hopefully at her? It'd been a long time since Kristina felt gauche (except in Catherine Warren's company), but she didn't understand the rules or what was supposed to happen next. It reminded her of being an adolescent, or even younger – of being young enough to long to fit in, desperate to have a friend who'd show you the way and always have your back.

She noticed the plump girl was standing at the corner of the bar, behind a pair of women in business suits perched on stools with big glasses of wine. One was talking hard and fast. The other was listening intently.

The girl was watching them with the focus of a cat waiting for the mouse to stay still . . .

Then her hand whipped out like a frog tongue smacking on a fly. She grabbed the glass of the nearest woman, took a sip, and had it back on the counter within three seconds.

Kristina blinked.

Her male friend then did the same thing, to the other glass. He was even faster. Both only took sips.

The girl looked at Kris and grinned, then nodded her head toward the drink. *Dare ya.*

Kristina glanced at Lizzie, a pocket of calm in the crowd. 'I wouldn't,' Lizzie said. 'It's not a game everyone can play.'

The plump girl's head was still cocked with the same expression on her face, however.

Knowing it was dumb and risky, Kristina grabbed the drink, took a sip, and had it back on the counter before its owner looked back. The girl and her boyfriend laughed delightedly, clapping their hands.

A moment later the woman on the stool grabbed a mouthful of her wine, still listening to her companion, no idea of what had just happened – and apparently not noticing the girl standing next to her even though she was clapping and cheering.

Kristina realized the other Angels were grinning at her, too, delighted, as if she'd passed some kind of test. Even Lizzie smiled, though she rolled her eyes.

Then they all seemed to be leaving, slipping through the crowds toward the door like fish swimming against the current. Kristina followed, having a much harder time of it.

At the door she glanced back at the woman still perched on her stool at the bar, drinking her depleted wine. She realized that if you could do something that simple – if you could learn to always be standing where people weren't looking, and pick your moments so they didn't notice you – then there were a lot of gaps between people, and holes, in the city.

There was a whole world to explore, and to live, in the spaces in between.

Another bar, then a couple of restaurants, grabbing a sip here and a gulp there, even a mouthful of someone's neglected tapas. They passed a few stores and Kristina noticed some of the Angels looking in with a professional eye, as if with a mission in mind . . . but nobody did anything except for one time when an Angel slipped into a second-hand record place. Kristina saw the way he moved between the customers flicking through cases of retro vinyl, how he clocked shopping bags left on the floor and handbags hanging open off people's shoulders. The Angel did nothing but look, however, before floating back out toward the street. As far as Kris could tell, no one had noticed that he had been in the store at all.

By then it was full dark and something had begun to change about the quality of the streetlights or the relationship between the Angels and the normal citizens they moved among. It was like tipping over from being drunk to *very* drunk, or the point where recreational drugs that had so far been supporting an evening of good cheer abruptly gained the upper hand and started leading *you* rather than the other way around.

Quite a few covert mouthfuls of wine had been consumed by that time, but that wasn't it. Kristina felt *less* clumsy, rather than more so, and she stopped finding it hard to follow the Angels along the streets. It felt as if she'd started to hit the same rhythm they were following, as if she'd got the knack of stepping away at the correct time and being where people were not looking, breathing out when everyone else on the street – all the normal people, she caught herself thinking – were breathing in. The adaptation didn't happen all at once. It was more as if the tracks they'd been following started to wend closer and closer. She'd lose the knack for a moment and bash into someone, but then be right back in the groove.

Then the Angels all started running.

At first Kris thought they must be must be running *away* from someone, that they'd been spotted stealing drinks in the last bar. Then she realized this was merely her own sense of guilt, and that the Angels were instead running with a kind of joy, or glee.

They ran out of the road and down Eighth Avenue, and it seemed for a time that there were more of them than there had been before, many more. The newcomers weren't dressed in black and rich colors, however, so it was hard to be sure . . . but there seemed to be other people

346

running alongside them, or walking fast, or waving as they went by. People on street corners and at bus stops. People walking by. People whom you'd never look at twice when you passed. Background people, who for once had turned to look in your direction, revealing themselves not just to be a texture but living things after all.

Animals, too, dogs and cats and a weirdly large fox, and a little girl whose head seemed far too small . . .

Then it was back to the group in black again, and Kristina – slowing rapidly, by now out of breath – limped after Lizzie as she ducked off the avenue and onto a residential street. The Angels stopped too, laughing and high-fiving one another, as Kris bent over, leaning against the fence until she'd gotten her breath back and lost most of the spots before her eyes. None of the others seemed at all out of breath. Either they were a *lot* fitter than she was, or . . .

'Oh, look,' one of them said quietly – a short, squat guy who'd been on the periphery of the group until now. He was pointing across the street. 'Looky there.'

Everyone turned. The road was lined with houses. On one of these, three buildings along from where they stood, the front door hung open. Halfway down the street a man was struggling along with a huge and saggy cardboard box in his arms, toward a car.

'Easy as pie,' the plump girl said.

'Um, friends,' Lizzie said – but the group was already in movement across the street, heading toward the house. Kristina was carried along with them. Part of this was being drawn in their wake. A larger part was not wanting to be left behind.

The Angels ran up the steps in front of the house, but hesitated on the threshold. Though Lizzie had seemed doubtful, when they ceded control to her, she took it.

She glanced across at the man still trudging up the street with his box. Then smiled mischievously.

'Quickly, then,' she said, and they all went inside.

CHAPTER 42

They swarmed into the hallway. The floor was uncarpeted, bare boards. A similarly unclad staircase led up the left side of the hall to the upper floor. The man who'd cased out the record store went loping straight up it.

A corridor led off to a rear area where a small television played quietly, presumably a kitchen. On the right was a door, and Kristina followed Lizzie and the others through it, scarcely able to believe what was happening, knowing what they should be doing – what *she* should be doing, most of all – was getting the hell out before the guy came back and found them there.

What on earth would they say? Yes, of course there were more of them than there were of him, and maybe they could push past him and run away, but that didn't make it okay. This was . . . *a very bad thing to do*.

That awareness didn't stop her from following Lizzie into the middle of the room. The plump girl's boyfriend went to the window and checked back along the street, presumably acting as lookout – though by the time he saw the guy coming they'd have no chance of leaving without being seen. So what *was* the plan – would they just run straight past him, trusting on speed and the fact that the guy would be so freaked out that he wouldn't give chase? *Was* there even a plan? *Would* they retreat, or was she part of some kind of fucked-up home invasion?

A big shabby rug covered most of the floor. On the other side facing the door (and the battered TV next to it) squatted a lumpy sofa. An armchair lurked at one end. Dotted around the walls were unframed posters from gigs and exhibitions of yesteryear, low-rent versions of the artfully positioned look-what-we-do statements regimented over the walls of the homes of people like Catherine Warren thirty blocks downtown. Box-carrying guy evidently didn't spend too much time worrying about house-cleaning. You could see the dust on the empty portions of the shelves from halfway across the room, and the whole place looked like it could do with a wipe and then repainting.

Half of the wall under a back window was taken up with a wooden table. This was strewn with books, pens, and the insides of a laptop computer.

And on the floor underneath it was a child's toy.

Kristina stared at it, thinking: *Oh Christ.*

Then there was a noise out in the hallway. Her heart stopped. Someone was coming.

Kristina whirled around, desperately trying to see a way of escape. There was none. She was in the middle of a room with only one exit. Footsteps were coming along the hallway toward the door – and there was absolutely *no hope* of getting through it without being seen. She had to hide in this room, somewhere, some*how*.

She waited a second too long. A woman walked past the doorway carrying a baby over one shoulder.

Kristina froze, knowing she was caught.

But the woman walked past and to the front door instead, where she shouted something down the street – to the hapless guy with the big cardboard box, presumably. The guy who, it turned out, *didn't live alone.*

Knowing these extra seconds were all she had, Kristina took four giant steps toward the only thing she could see that might possibly help – the couch – trying to cover the ground as quickly as possible without making a sound. Halfway through the final lunging step her self-possession deserted her and she dived.

She landed with a thump just around the back of the sofa and yanked her long legs up to her chest. She felt indescribable relief to be behind something, but this was nowhere near as loud as the panicky, yammering part of her mind that knew it was a pathetically insufficient hiding place and the only question was whether she was discovered within minutes or seconds.

This dreadful attempt at hiding would only make things worse. If she'd been discovered standing in the room she could have made an attempt to appear demented, some confused lunatic wandered in off the street. No, she didn't think she could have pulled it off, but to be found hiding behind the sofa was a straight-down-the-line and no-excuses-possible nightmare.

I'm screwed. I'm screwed.

She heard footsteps and this time they didn't recede back down the corridor but came right into the room.

I'm totally . . . screwed.

'Lazy asshole,' said a voice – the woman. 'Tell him what, five or six *hundred* times before he does the thing, and then tell him one more time how to do it right? Yes?'

There was a chirrup from the baby, responding to the affectionate tone with no understanding of the content. Her mother sat down on the sofa. She landed heavily, in the middle – bang in front of where Kristina lay, eyes wide. Kris felt the air pushed out of the cushions.

The woman sighed – the heavy, brooding exhale of someone who's exhausted, tired of sleepless nights and having to tell someone what to do the whole time and just the whole damned unfairness of it all.

Kristina tried not to breathe.

A minute later she heard feet coming up the steps outside the house and the front door closing.

'Yeah, so it fits, okay?' A man's voice.

'My hero. You rock.'

'Why are you being so pissy?' His voice was louder as he walked into the room. How many more steps before he got the angle to see someone was behind the sofa? Two? One?

'I *told* you it would fit,' the woman sniped. 'I told you when I asked you to do it *three months ago.*'

'Karen, I'm busy, you know?'

'Too busy to pack up a box of your ex-girlfriend's old shit after *two years* and drive it to the crazy bitch's lair? And busy doing *what*? Oh yeah, that's right – all those YouTube videos don't watch themselves.'

'I work, remember? I have to leave the house every day and go do shit. To earn money. To *pay for stuff.*'

'I forgot. Because it's not like you go on about it the whole time. And baby girl here looks after herself. Me, I'm just sitting on the couch watching TV and jerking off.'

It was the man's turn to sigh.

Trying to ensure she made not a sound, Kristina wriggled a bit closer to the back of the sofa. Doing this altered the angle of her head. She'd been so focused on saving herself that she hadn't even given a thought as to what had happened to the others.

She saw that Lizzie was under the table down at the end. She sat Indian style and looked insanely relaxed. The short guy who'd suggested they come in here in the first place was next to her, arms around his knees, also apparently at ease.

Kristina titled her head down, looked past her

own fetal shape, and saw the plump girl's friend was still down at the window overlooking the street, standing behind the curtain. She remembered the friend who'd gone straight upstairs, and was presumably still up there.

So they were all hiding. Sort of. Except . . .

The plump girl hadn't moved at all. She was leaning against the wall, arms folded, watching the man and woman and child as if they were a television show.

How can that be? Okay, the man was facing away, in fact had his back to her – and the woman was focused on giving him a hard time.

But there was no *way* they would fail to notice a stranger *standing right there in the middle of the room.*

'Okay, well, it's gone now,' the man said weakly.

His partner was smartly back in the game. 'Not so much. Next time I get in the car it'll be right . . .'

'By which I meant *tomorrow afternoon.* I'll dump it around her place.'

'And have a nice cup of coffee, no doubt. Talk about old times. It's only polite, right?'

'Karen, the old times were crap. You know that. They ended and thank God. This is a box of old random shit she probably doesn't even remember she's missing. You want, I'll go dump it somewhere and be done with it.'

'You can't do that. It's her stuff.'

'*Right,*' he said exasperatedly. 'So you *said.* So

I'll drop it on the way home from work and we can get back to enjoying our so-called lives. Okay?'

'Yeah, yeah.'

Kristina had settled into a horrified holding pattern – keeping herself rigid, half listening to what was being said, wondering how long it could be before they noticed the girl standing and watching them or before the man happened to glance over the sofa to see Kristina lying there. She was jolted out of this by a sound and looked up. The baby was staring right at her.

Ignored while her parents thrashed over the same old ground, the baby had pulled itself higher on her mother's shoulder – enough to see over the back of the sofa. She was now staring down at what she'd found on the other side.

She blinked. Somewhere, deep in her tiny, unformed mind, a flag had gone up. The baby knew the woman who was holding her. It knew the man. But who was this other person? Who was this tall, skinny person behind the thing her mother was sitting on? The baby didn't know, but she sensed from the deep reaches of its instinct that unknown big people in the cave was not a good thing.

Her face scrunched up. She started to cry. Kristina stared at her, aghast, not knowing whether to smile or try to turn her face away or what.

'Great,' the woman said. 'Now she's off again.'

'Here, let me,' the man said.

The woman stood. 'Don't bother.'

'Climb off the fucking ledge, okay? Give her to me.'

'Okay, be my guest.'

Please don't turn around, Kristina prayed. *Please . . . just don't turn around.*

After a moment the baby's cries started to wind down. 'There you go,' the man said to his child, quiet love in his voice. 'It's all okay. There you go.'

'How do you even *do* that?' the woman muttered with grudging admiration.

'She senses a masterful male.'

'What – through the walls, in some other house?'

'Ha-ha.'

There was silence, then the sound of a kiss. A sigh, and the woman spoke again, more softly. 'At least you're not an asshole all the time.'

'Whereas you are a twenty-four-seven bitch.'

There was the sound of a man being swatted hard, but not without affection, on the behind. 'I'm sorry,' he said. 'I know Diana's stuff pisses you off and I should have done it long ago. My bad.'

'You bad, me bad too.'

'Bad as each other.'

'No, I wouldn't go that far.'

They laughed together, quietly.

'Don't you spend *any* time jerking off? *I* sure as hell would.'

'No. I save it up,' the woman said. 'You get princess here down to sleep, I may even show you.'

'Deal. I'll go upstairs and give it a try. You open some wine. Don't start without me.'

'Drinking, or the other thing?'

'Either.'

And then, praise God, Kristina heard them walk together out of the room.

She jerked her head to stare at Lizzie and the other friend under the table. Lizzie was looking right at her, already holding up a finger.

The message was clear – be quiet and ready to move.

Lizzie waited a beat, then quickly came out from under the table. Kristina jumped to her feet, her joints crackling like rifle shots, and the person behind the curtain slipped out at the same time.

'Yeah, so I guess now would be a good time,' the plump girl sniggered, making no effort to be quiet. 'Though I kinda want to stick around to catch part two of tonight's special presentation.'

The others ignored her. Kris followed Lizzie out into the hallway and to the front door.

'Open it,' Lizzie whispered. Kristina flipped the latch as gently as possible and the friends flooded past and out onto the steps. She followed, pulling the door closed as quietly as she'd opened it.

By the time that was done the others were on the sidewalk. She ran down to join them as they hurried off down the road . . . all starting to laugh.

'What the *fuck*?' Kristina shouted, stomping after them. 'Are you out of your *minds*? Do you have any *idea* how close we were to being caught?'

'Not very,' the plump girl said.

'What about the guy who went upstairs?'

'He'll be fine,' Lizzie said. 'But that's enough for one night. Let's go find somewhere quiet.'

'Screw this,' Kristina shouted, all the fear she'd felt spilling over into fury. 'I'm *done* here. That was *insane*. I don't understand why I'm not being arrested right now, and how the *hell* did those people not see someone who was standing right in front of them?'

Lizzie put a hand on her arm.

Kris shook it off. 'No. Tell me. *Why didn't they see her?*'

Lizzie hesitated, then appeared to make a decision.

CHAPTER 43

I had an encounter with Lydia on the way to work. Generally she didn't wind up near the restaurant until mid-evening, following the inexplicable tracks you run along when you have neither job nor house nor friends but for a shifting cast of unpredictable individuals whom life has pushed into the same position. There are a lot of these trails in cities. People like you and me may not know where they run, but they're there all the same, two species sharing the same environment, the only competition for resources coming in the shape of a hand held out and a voice asking diffidently for spare change.

As I came in view of the Adriatico on the way to evening service, however, Lydia was there at the corner.

'S'up, Lyds?'

It was obvious something was different. I don't know what it is about people who stand to the side of what's considered sane, but their energy is wrong – something hectic about their eyes or vague in their movements, a sense of the person being trapped in an invisible corner and struggling to gain voice.

Lydia didn't look so much that way this evening. She simply looked old, and lost, and as if she was sick to death of too many things to start making a list.

She shrugged. 'Aw, okay.'

'Really?'

'I guess.' She looked across the street, biting her lip. 'I'll tell you what it is. I ain't seen him.'

'Seen who?'

'Frankie, of course.'

'Since when?'

'Couple days. Since I saw you that night.'

'Does that happen? Gaps?'

She shook her head uncertainly. 'Don't see him every day. He hasn't ever been that way. Even way back, when he was . . . around more. But this seems long.'

'Why do you think that is?'

She lifted her shoulders sadly. I realized how bony they were. She'd always been birdlike under the layers of trash can cast-offs, but it looked like she'd lost weight. 'Wonder if I finally chased him off.'

I waited, to give her a chance to go on, but she didn't. I hadn't missed the reference to a time when Frankie had been 'around more.' I'd never her heard her say anything that danced around acknowledging there was something significantly different about her ex-lover's relationship to the world now.

'Is there anything you can do?' I asked.

'Do?'

'Something more likely to make him come around.'

She stared at me as if I were the most dumb-ass fool it'd been her misfortune to encounter. 'If there was, you think I wouldn't be doing it the whole damned time?'

I laughed. 'Yeah okay. Sorry.'

'He's alive, you know. I know everybody thinks I'm crazy. That he got kilt in that bar. But it didn't happen. There was some guys after him, that's true. He pissed them off bad. It's why he disappeared. Duh. But he ain't dead. You believe that?'

'You tell me he isn't, Lydia, then he isn't.'

'Hmm. I'll tell you something else. He's the last man I did it with. And I used to *like* doing it. Was real good at it, too. You believe *that*?'

I did my best to suggest that I did believe her, and also that it wasn't one of the most wildly uncomfortable questions I'd ever been asked.

'You think I'd have waited if he wasn't still alive?'

'No,' I said, 'I don't believe that.'

She nodded vigorously, and I saw that she was crying. 'Damn straight.'

I reached in my pocket and got out a scrap of paper. I scribbled a note on one side and an address on the other. 'You ever go to church?'

'Hell no,' she said. 'God's a cunt.'

'Okay, but I met a guy recently. He's a priest, but he seems like a good man.'

'So?'

'Sometimes it's good to have someone to talk to. A person who isn't going to hassle you about getting into a shelter and when was the last time you had a bath or took your meds, blah blah blah.'

Lydia squinted at the paper. 'Chelsea? I lived there, long time ago. Well, crashed in a guy's apartment. Was a lot less boring in that neighborhood back then, I'll tell you. The stuff I saw! It's different now.'

'You walked that road once; you can do it again.'

'And he ain't going to try to get me down on my knees praising God?'

'He might. But I reckon you'd be a match for him, don't you?'

She smiled. 'What the fuck you doing here talking to me, anyway? Ain't you got a job?'

Before I went into the restaurant I looked back. I saw Lydia stuff the piece of the paper into one of her pockets. Months ago I'd given her my cell phone number, and she'd done the same then. She'd never called, of course, and I felt sure the paper I'd just given her would be there in two or five or ten years, the day or night when some city employee had the distasteful job of checking for possessions among the clothes of the deceased.

But I was wrong about that.

I went in the back and changed into the black pants and white shirt that Mario insists upon, and got straight out onto the floor. The restaurant was already crowded – like the homeless, tourists and hungry locals have chaotic schedules and routines and it's impossible to predict how busy any given night is going to be, though that hasn't stopped Maria (who believes she harbors some kind of clairvoyant ability) from trying. She's dogged about it, too – making her prediction at precisely noon every day, and scoring herself at the end of every night. She's been doing it for fifteen years, which is a long time, though evidently not enough to read what her meticulous records are telling her, which is the cat who hangs around the bins at the back of the restaurant would make a better job of it.

By eight thirty she'd thrown up her hands and admitted she'd missed the signs (as usual). We were packed to the point of having an actual freaking line on the sidewalk. I knew Kristina wouldn't turn up at the usual time because it was book club night and she had a standing dispensation to arrive two hours late, and I didn't have the time to give her much thought because tonight, of all nights, Mario had decided to give Paulo a trial on the floor.

It wasn't working out. The restaurant has a strange internal shape due to the position of the pizza oven and the fact that it was carved out of two separate buildings god knows how long ago. There's a big main area covered by two waitresses, and two arms out – one along the window on the right (my domain, alongside Jimmy, a guy in his mid-fifties who has been on the job longer than he's been alive and can out-waiter any other living being), the other on the opposite side, in the back. The latter is the Adriatico's equivalent of Siberia and gets filled up last, which is why Paulo had been assigned there. Once the area started to fill up, however, it became clear that he wasn't cutting it. Something needed to be done, and fast.

Mario gave me the nod and I ceded control of the front area (and its higher tips) to Jimmy, who was man enough to pick up the slack. I intercepted Paulo where he was quaking by the kitchen pickup, and let him know I was on the case. His relief was so palpable you could have sat it in a chair and given it a glass of wine. I got him to fill me in on which tables' service was most obviously falling apart and settled to placating people and shouting at the kitchen to expedite the orders of those dying of hunger (none of them, of course, but customers can be assholes, especially when they scent weakness in a server). For fifteen minutes I was so focused on all this that I didn't even notice the table in the far corner, whose meal was proceeding in an orderly fashion and thus not on anybody's radar.

I was picking up from a table eight feet away when someone spoke. 'See. I was right. I knew that I knew you.'

Reinhart was sitting by himself. He'd turned so that his face was visible to me now, and was smiling, knife and fork in his hands over a plate of food.

'I know. I know,' he said, shrugging affably. 'Two restaurants in one day, right? But I get a lot of exercise. You only get so many meals in your life. You should make the most of them. And I do. I like my food. *Love* it, in fact. I savor all physical things.'

'Good for you.'

'I've been here before. A few months back. That's where I saw you. You don't remember me from then. Just another customer, right? Busy busy.'

'I'm busy now.'

'So I see. You got people to serve. That's a waiter's job. I just need to tell you something.'

People were watching now. That didn't matter. I could still have done the sensible thing, which was head back to the kitchen with the plates. But I did not.

With a be-there-in-a-minute nod to a four-top who were still waiting for appetizers, I walked over to Reinhart's table. 'This needs to be quick.'

'It will be.'

'So what did you want to say?'

He took one more bite of his steak and put his knife and fork down. 'People only embarrass me once.'

I spent years in the armed forces and other institutions of violence. I've had training, keep fit, and I've got game. But it wasn't even the plates I

365

was holding that handicapped me. Reinhart was just far too fast.

He was out of his seat like a jump cut, and I didn't have time to step back before the first punch hit me in the face like a cinder block. After that I barely knew what was happening. I was aware of fists crunching into my ribs and stomach with very regular frequency and intensity – fractionally aware, too, that while I was trying to avoid customers and their tables Reinhart was showing no such compunction. I fought back as best I could, but I was starting from way behind.

I staggered, and then fell back another step, managing to keep upright for maybe ten seconds and trying to throw blows back that dead-ended in the punches coming my way. Then I was on the ground, dimly conscious of people shouting and glasses shattering as kicks hammered into my stomach and chest and head so hard it felt like there was no flesh between my bones and his toe, or his heel when he started stomping down on me with that.

Then it stopped.

It was noisy around me but in the way the waves are when you're right in among them – alien, tidal, a cacophony with nothing to help differentiate meaning. I tried to push up off the ground but could not.

A patch of white light moved in front of my

right eye, getting bigger. I heard a smeary voice above me.

'Call Kristina,' it said, and only then did I realize Kris hadn't turned up yet and it must be late.

Then nothing.

CHAPTER 44

Kristina was sitting on a bench in a small empty park overlooking the Hudson River. It was cold and dark, silent but for the sound of traffic on the road behind and distant lapping in the water below. The other friends had shaded away on the walk over – either saying goodbye and smiling shyly, or simply reaching a point of not being there anymore – except for the plump girl and her boy, who were sitting on the grass thirty feet away.

'He's half right,' Lizzie said.

Once Kristina had calmed down a little and consented to go to the park, Lizzie had asked about John, if things had improved since they'd last met. Kristina surprised herself by answering, slowly starting to talk about their lives in a way she'd never done with Catherine. She even admitted that – despite his tendency to be *incredibly* annoying – she loved John. This was a word she'd never found easy to use. It felt okay, though, and she was glad she'd said it. Like weddings, and funerals, there are times when life needs a witness to feel real.

From this she'd gone on to telling Lizzie about John's theory about Reinhart's role in their world, and this was what Lizzie had responded to, after a long pause. 'Which half is right, and which is wrong?'

'Reinhart does have an arrangement,' Lizzie confirmed. 'He deals with one of us called Golzen. It's his group – they've taken to calling themselves the twelve – who are working most closely with Reinhart. It's not a forced arrangement. They do it freely.'

'Why?'

'They receive things in return. Which increases Golzen's status and ego . . . It's complicated. We've never had a situation like this. I hoped it would sort itself out. But I'm not so sure. I've been trying to get people to stop taking things. This is bringing them back to it.'

'But why would you steal in the first place?'

'It made us . . . popular. It's hard to describe. But the other part is that it's the most active behavior that most of us are capable of. It . . . makes you feel alive.'

Kristina guessed she understood. Though she'd never stolen as an adult, like most kids she and girlfriends had lifted things from stores as a dare. Both times she'd thrown away the trinket the same day. Though she had felt bad and compromised, she remembered the anticipation and thrill. Presumably that's what Lizzie was talking about.

She sensed the other woman was not comfortable, however, and turned the conversation to more personal areas. 'Do *you* have anybody? I mean, like a boyfriend?'

'There's someone who's more important to me than anyone else.'

'The guy you mentioned last time? Maj?'

Lizzie nodded.

'What's he like?'

'He's good-looking and he's smart and I'm happier when I'm with him than when I'm not. But he spends a lot of his time with his mind on other things.'

'So, he's a man, then. What the hell is that *about*?'

They laughed quietly together. It'd been a long time since Kris sat talking to anyone about their boyfriends – but for small talk to pass a slow evening with some other bartender, conversations that ran aground after it became obvious the only advice was *dump the asshole, change the locks, and do it now*. With Lizzie it felt different. Lizzie asked questions effortlessly. She was a good listener, too. Kris wasn't sure she knew how to do this kind of thing anymore. It had been too long since she'd had this kind of friend. If a friend was what Lizzie was, or could become. The funny thing was, it felt like she always had been.

'Where is he this evening?'

'Maj comes and he goes. Some of us like to stay in the same place. He's not so much like that. Plus he's got a job. I think he's on call tonight.'

'What kind of job?'

'He's a Fingerman.'

'You used that word before. What is it?'

'Someone who's good at using their hands.'

'Like a craftsman? He makes things?'

'No. We can't make anything, dead or alive. He touches things, when people need him to. Opens them, presses them, you know.'

Kristina nodded, though she was not sure what this was supposed to mean. 'Do you love him?'

Lizzie laughed. 'That's a big question.'

'You asked me. I answered it.'

'True. Well . . . yes, I suppose I do.'

'A lot?'

'As much as I can, given who I am and what he is. That's quite a lot.'

Kristina realized that's what she'd meant, too, and that she wasn't even sure what loving someone meant anymore. Yes, attraction of course, and wanting to be with; but it wasn't really about that kind of thing now, was it? It wasn't raised heartbeats and smoldering glances. It was feeling comfortable and secure and valued; it was less about how you felt right now and more about how you might in the future, about the things you might want until the day you died.

'Do you want children someday?'

Lizzie sat looking at her hands, and Kristina realized she had no idea how old the other woman was. Sometimes she seemed older than her – late thirties, maybe even forty. Most of the time, she seemed about the same age. Right now, she looked about thirteen.

'Kristina,' she said. 'I'm not real.'

'I hear you,' Kris replied, with feeling. 'But everybody feels like that from time to time, right? Doesn't mean you wouldn't make a good parent.'

'No,' Lizzie said patiently. 'I'm *not real*.'

Kristina stared at her, unsure whether to laugh. 'Okay. Right. So what are you?'

Lizzie looked distant and ashamed. 'I'm imaginary.'

'This is . . . some kind of metaphor thing, right?'

'No.'

'But . . . *what*?'

'We don't know how it works. There was one of us who had a theory. Every generation there's a few who think harder about things. Lonely Clive was one of those. I knew him, and Maj did too, very well. But Clive's hollow now. Even the strongest lose faith.'

'You mean . . . he's dead?'

'No. He's barely there. His idea was that we hollow when we become wholly forgotten by our real friend – when their mind heals over and loses any memory of us even in dreams. And he may have been right, but it can happen in other ways. I've known a few who've deliberately chosen that road. Who elected not to exist anymore. The irony is that you have to be strong to make that choice. The rest of us just fade . . . until the day our friend dies.'

Kristina had decided to let Lizzie keep talking until it started making sense. 'What . . . happens then?'

'The Bloom. A few hours, sometimes as much as a day, when you're stronger than you've ever been. And then . . .'

She held her hands in a loose ball, as if containing a soul, some energy, an idea; then she gently opened them out, to suggest nothing at all.

'Lizzie, if you guys choose to believe you're not real, if it's some big existential . . . whatever, then that's fine. But . . . *it's not true.*'

'Kris – you saw Flaxon in the house.'

'Who's Flaxon?'

Lizzie gestured toward the plump girl on the grass. 'She was a Dozeno until six months ago. That's what we call those who don't understand what they are. Some stay like that forever, which is sad. Most get it sooner or later. When Flaxon realized, she kicked *hard*. Took against real people in the worst way. She did some really bad stuff – and worked for Reinhart for a while, until we managed to get her to walk with us instead. She's a lot calmer now, but once in a while she still . . . well, you asked how she could stand there in front of that couple in the house. They didn't see her, did they?'

No, they had not. And Kristina knew that the people in the house should really have been able to see Lizzie and the other guy under the table, too.

'But *I* can see you.'

373

'Yes, you can. John too, evidently. Some people have always been able to see things out of the corner of their eye. And children sometimes, and animals, cats especially. With others it happens when we get drawn to their attention – if something gets knocked over, or someone points us out. Once you've seen one it's easier to see others, apparently. You call these people 'mediums.' Luckily, almost all of them are fake.'

'We saw you because we were trying to find out who was following Catherine Warren.'

Lizzie nodded.

'And why were you?'

'You can't work it out?' Lizzie's voice was almost too quiet to hear. 'I'm her imaginary friend. Or, I was.'

'What, like . . . the things that *kids* have?'

Lizzie smiled stiffly. 'Yes. Those things that kids have. And then forget. That's what happens. People grow up and forget. Doesn't mean we just *stop*.'

She turned to Kristina, looking old and miserable. 'You ever have a dream, something you thought you'd do one day, that you fantasized about for hour after hour, and planned to the last degree, and truly believed you'd make part of your future come what may . . . But then life changed, or you did, and you slowly forgot about it?'

'I guess.'

'We're like that. Like the guitars that sit in the corner of living rooms, never played. Like plans for the year in Paris that never happens. Like

374

months of unrequited longing that never ends in a kiss. Once that much energy has been poured into something it never completely goes away. It's a part of that person's life forever, something that didn't happen. Negatives shape people too, like white space on a page. A dream doesn't die just because it doesn't come true. And . . . neither do we.'

'Do you—'

But then Lizzie was standing, and a second later the plump girl leapt to her feet and was running, fast – the boyfriend not far behind. Lizzie set after them.

Kristina did her best to follow. She saw a woman weaving on the side of the street, fifty yards away, holding the hand of a child – a girl about four or five years old. Traffic was coursing up and down the street – not thickly, but fast.

The little girl seemed to be more aware of this fact than her mother, who was determined to cross the street and to do it right there and now. Flaxon was headed straight toward them. She was fast – eerily fast.

The little girl's mother kept making attempts to cross the road. The girl looked unsure, but this was her mother, and she had a tight grip on her hand. The little girl was not in control. She was going to have to trust that her mother knew what she was doing.

Flaxon got to within twenty feet and decelerated, so abruptly that Kristina had to pull her head back to see her again. She was catching up to Lizzie now but neither of them were going to make it there before whatever was about to happen took place.

The mother finally lost patience with the traffic. You could tell this from the set of her shoulders, from something that communicated itself through the air. She'd decided now was good enough and she was done waiting for the assholes to let her cross.

Her girl had become distracted and was no longer looking at the cars, but frowning . . . turning to look around her, as if aware something was coming her way.

Flaxon strode right past behind them, grabbing the mother's shoulder just as she started to step out into the road. She pulled it hard – a quick, sharp movement – before carrying on past.

The girl looked up, as if knowing something had passed behind them. Her mother was pulled off balance. With one foot raised to step out into the road, there was no way of keeping herself upright.

She toppled backward awkwardly, kept from crashing outright by her daughter's hold on her, just as a motorcycle came from out of nowhere.

It came so fast and so close that you could smell the leather the driver was wearing and hear the smeared residue of his snarl to get the fuck out of the way.

The woman landed flat on her back on the sidewalk, mouth open, eyes horribly wide. She knew damned well what had just happened and how it would have gone if chance hadn't caused her to slip and fall backward.

'Oh holy Jesus,' she said. 'Oh Jesus, Jesus.'

Her little girl stood blinking down at her. 'Mom, are you okay? What happened?'

'I'm okay,' the woman said, getting back to her feet. She looked around and saw a pedestrian crossing a hundred feet up the street. She seemed shaken, pulled back out of whatever mental or chemical fugue had brought her so close to being a small, sad item somewhere low down on page seven of tomorrow's newspaper. 'Let's use the cross-walk. We should *always* do that, right?'

'Right.' The girl reached up and took her mother's hand again.

Her mother gripped it tight and looked down at her, face trembling. 'Okay, honey.'

They waited at the light until it was safe to cross, and then did so slowly and very carefully. Kristina watched. Behind her she was aware of Lizzie going over to Flaxon and kissing her softly on the cheek.

'Get off,' Flaxon muttered. 'Weirdo.'

But she looked pleased.

As they got to the other side, the little girl looked back at where Kris stood with Lizzie and Flaxon and her guy. Kristina saw the girl looking right at her, didn't want to be a scary adult, and smiled.

The girl registered this, but it hadn't been Kris she was looking for.

★   ★   ★

Kristina became aware that her phone was ringing. It was the restaurant. For a while she'd forgotten she had a job and that she was now very late for it. Right now, in the midst of this evening and what had just (nearly) happened, she didn't give a crap about serving people more cheap wine than they needed. But she hit the button and prepared to use her charm on Mario one more time.

'I'm sorry,' she said. 'I got—'

It wasn't Mario, but his sister. She sounded freaked out. 'You have to hurry. You have to go there now.'

'What? Why?'

'It's John. He's in the hospital.'

CHAPTER 45

Talia sat at her table. Her laptop was in front of her but it was closed. That was okay. A growl in her stomach reminded her she hadn't eaten anything. That was okay too. The hunger was hypothetical. The words . . . well, she'd written nothing for two days. Nothing in the novel, nothing even into the diary where she'd written at least *something* every day since the shooting star. The conversation with George had planted a seed in her mind, a seed that had grown, sucking up whatever nutrients the words used to thrive on.

At work it was easier to ignore. There was always stuff going on, somebody to greet and serve, something to clean or refill. Except for her exchange with David – which she'd come out of feeling like a bit of an ass, though she doubted he'd have noticed anything – work just rolled on, lots of business as usual.

But at home . . .

Of course it was absurd, because not one thing had *changed*, but her home felt different. It was still tidy. It remained pretty full of cats. Everything, as far as she could tell, was in its place.

Her spatula was where it was supposed to be.

In the time since, she'd wondered about that. She'd wondered if maybe it *hadn't* been a case of her breaking the habit of many years by hanging the damned thing up on the other side, but if someone else had been in here, if they'd taken the spatula down to look at it and then put it back up in the wrong place.

Why would somebody do that? No reason.

Unless they'd recognized the spatula, perhaps. It was old and battered. Talia had owned it a very long time – had used it to lever some of those own-brand brownies out of the baking tray back in the mists of yesteryear. *Maybe* someone who'd been around back then might have thought to take a nostalgic look at it.

Maybe.

She'd looked around the trailer, looked *hard*, and hadn't been able to find much else out of place. Everything was shipshape and socked away, as Ed used to say. She'd noticed something about her diaries, though. These were kept in neat rows on the shelves behind the little TV, which she hardly ever watched. Every one was the same, inexpensive red exercise books of the type that didn't cost much at any time of year but you could get even cheaper during back-to-school promotions – which is what she'd always done, buying ten at once and stashing until needed. They stood in orderly ranks, the spines getting more faded as they went back in time, aged by the light that came through the window in the afternoons. She kept them in order. This wasn't some anal-retentive thing or the result of any effort. You finished a book, you put it next to the previous one and did the same the next time and the next. Much like events in the real world, chronology looked after itself.

Except . . . last night she'd found a couple out of order. Way back – from the early days, on the far left of the top shelf. It could be that she'd put them back in the wrong order; once in a while she'd pull a volume down to remind herself of things that had happened and to convince herself that keeping a diary wasn't a wholly pointless exercise. She made sure to put the book back in its right place, though, which was easy given each was numbered on the spine with the dates it covered and also a sequential number. It'd be hard to imagine messing that up, even if she'd had a beer or two, which (though she'd never again toyed with the too-many-is-not-enough approach from the months after Ed's death) was not unknown. Could also be a cat-related event. Some of the younger ones liked to go nuts mid-evening, galloping around the place and knocking things down. A couple of times they'd knocked books off those shelves. She might have been in a hurry to clean up the mess and shoved them back up there without worrying too much about the order.

Did she remember that happening? No.

But then, presumably she wouldn't.

She didn't lock the trailer when she went into

town. She took her laptop with her, always. There was nothing else worth stealing.

So somebody *could* have come in here, taken down a volume or two, and looked through. The town's younger element were likely too consistently stoned for a mission of that complexity, though, and lacked the imagination. Anyone who was enough of an asshole to do it would have probably messed the place up, too, and left a turd in the middle of the floor for good measure.

A little mystery, huh. Maybe she should tell David about it, see if he could use it to break through his writer's block. But she doubted she would. She'd seen the way he'd looked when she'd told him about George's hitchhiker. She'd given him enough.

After a while she tired of running the problem around and got up to feed the cats. It was nearly ten already. She should have done it hours before. The entire crew was in attendance, and most stood up with her, knowing it was well past time.

As she squatted down to shell the gunk out of tins into their bowls, Talia found herself noticing the bottom of the kitchen cabinets. Nicks. Little scrapes and rust spots. Her home felt small tonight. And make-do, and old. It'd never felt like that before. It was Talia Willocks's firm, comfortable exterior, the side she showed to the world – or would have, if anyone ever came to see. Now it felt like a bubble had burst, releasing whatever had made it a home and leaving a thin, empty skin.

She straightened. Looked around. A fifty-five-year-old woman living by herself in a trailer with a bunch of cats. Is this what the younger Tally-Anne thought was coming down the road? No. That hot little number had foreseen a few more years of fun and games and then a marriage day – be it ever so simple and small, catered by friends and served on the finest paper plates Dollar Tree had to offer. A handful of kids. A little house. School concerts. Yard sales. Stuff like that. She didn't miss most of it. By her age she'd be out the other side of those things, probably be cussing about how much free babysitting Grandma was getting hit up for.

But she'd have someone to complain to, someone who'd know she didn't really mean it, a man who'd be by her side for all the stuff coming down the pike, as he'd been there for everything before.

That's what was missing.

The cats snaffled and chomped around their bowls. Talia watched them with love.

And then the knocking came on the door.

As she stood outside the trailer, the wind rose. It had been that way the previous night, too, when the knocking had come a second time – though then she hadn't opened the door, but stayed inside, huddled on the couch. She felt that when someone who wasn't there came knocking, this was the best approach.

Tonight she'd decided differently. That was why, though she'd taken her bath as usual, she wasn't wearing stretch pants and the pink toweling robe. She wore a dress in beige and cream that she'd had a few years, and sure it was very tight around the hips and upper arms and everywhere else and she probably looked like a tank in desert camouflage, but it was the best she had.

There'd been no one there when she opened the door, but Talia had decided you didn't hear knocking on your house three nights running if there was truly nobody outside.

She heard a rustling sound and glanced down to see Tilly by her feet, looking up at her. Probably wondering why the big human was outside the mothership at this time of night.

'Mama's just waiting,' she told her, and bent to scratch her ears. 'Be back inside in a little while.'

Maybe the cat understood, maybe she didn't, but after a few more sniffs of the air she turned and went back in the trailer.

Talia stayed where she was. She wasn't waiting, not really. What could she be waiting for?

But she stayed.

Ten minutes later she heard someone call. It was faint, as it had been on the first night. Very weak, as if the caller had traveled some distance and was weary and that low cry was the best he could muster for now.

This time the sound did not come from up the direction of the graveyard, however. It came from the other direction, past the end of the road, from somewhere along the track that led toward the steep sides of the creek. It was about the same distance away, though, and she could hear what it said at least as clearly as before.

'Tally-Anne.'

So faint. As if the moment of death had thrown the person so far away, and into such blackness, that it had taken him twenty years to haul his way back home again. Traveling on foot, for the most part, even on hands and knees, except maybe for that helping hand over the last part, a ride into Rockbridge in the back of George Lofland's battered Toyota SUV – a ride from someone the deceased had known and drunk with, back in the day.

'I'm coming,' she said.

She closed the door of the trailer and walked down the road. Skirted the chain at the end and set up along the trail through the long grasses.

It took a few minutes to get to where the track veered left, following the ridge above the rocky sides down to the river. This started off passable but soon became choked with low bushes and tangling brambles. Talia stayed high for the time being, however – until the trees started to gather it'd be easier than finding a way to scramble down the ten-foot slope. It should be easier to spot him from up here, too, whoever he might be.

Who was she kidding? She knew who it was, or who she wanted it to be. Why else would she be out here at night, in her best dress, as the wind gathered above and it started to rain? She walked fast, shoving bushes out of her way. She could feel something, knew there was something up ahead.

'Tally-Anne.'

She started moving faster still. About a minute later she heard another sound, however, mixed in with the wind but seeming to come from the same direction.

It was a laugh, she thought. But if so, it had sounded high-pitched, almost like a woman's.

Talia hesitated. What if it *wasn't* Ed's voice she was hearing? What if some dumb-ass kids with evil intent had come in her home when she was at work, flicked through old diaries, and found the name she used to go by set down in some maudlin recollection of how much fuller her life had once been?

What if this was someone's cruel idea of a game?

But then she heard her name again. She started to trot, elbowing branches aside as the ridge started to get into the edges of the forest. She couldn't tell whether the voice was coming from up along the ridge or down from the narrow, jagged path by the creek. It was along here some-where, though, and she was getting closer, too.

'Tally-Anne. I'm over here.'

She started to run in earnest. Her feet caught in the brambles and she nearly tripped, but she kept running faster through the undergrowth, deeper into the trees. She thought maybe he was down there in the cutting, looking for her, too tired to make it all the way back into her arms and trusting her to get to him. She was worthy of that trust.

Then she saw him.

Thirty yards away, down in the dip. A tall man with long hair. She called out his name, again and again, running even faster, telling him she was coming, waiting for a break in the bushes before she could start to make her way down the slope to him.

But then someone stepped out from behind a tree right in front of her. It was a woman. Tall, painfully thin, with terribly red hair.

She started to smile, some dry, stretched movement of her lips away from dark teeth, and then she disappeared.

Talia screamed and lost her footing and started to slip, and when one leg got caught behind the remnants of an old tree stump, she lost her balance altogether and there was nothing to do except fall.

She fell nothing like a star.

PART III

Dreams are real as long as they last. Can we say more of life?

Havelock Ellis

CHAPTER 46

'I'm fine,' I said.

'John, you are so *not* fine.'

I repeated that I was fine. I was aware I was saying it for something like the fourth or fifth time, and groggily, and that neither was helping my case. Being able to make this simple opinion understood seemed very important, however.

'John . . . oh Jesus. *Look* at you.'

'I'm fine,' I said. Then I passed out.

When I opened my eyes again Kristina was still sitting by the bed. A nurse – the same one who'd been there all along, I believed, though the room was pretty dark and I wasn't entirely sure – was standing to one side.

'And . . . he's back,' the nurse said cheerfully, checking her watch. 'Barely five minutes that time. Your boy ain't one to take shit lying down, huh?'

'Hey,' I said thickly.

'Tell me one more time that you're fine,' Kris said in a low, sincere tone, 'and I'll punch you myself.'

'Okay,' I said. 'To be honest, it kind of hurts.'

'What does?' asked the nurse.

'Pretty much everything.'

'That's good.'

She gave me a looking over and got me to follow her finger while she moved it across various planes in front of my eyes and then marched out into the corridor to go about her business, evidently satisfied I was no closer to death than I deserved.

The last thing I remembered before waking up in the hospital was seeing – from my floor-level perspective – Reinhart leaving the restaurant. He had not stabbed a warning finger in my face or delivered gritty parting shots. The guys who do that learned their violence from television and their threats are like muscles acquired from the gym – they look good but lack the steel that comes from being tempered by real life. I was now ruefully convinced Reinhart had served his apprenticeship at the knee of people who were not interested in how things looked, but concerned rather with putting their enemies on the ground hard and fast. On it, or underneath. I knew he would have relented only because that kind of man has the sense to stop short of committing actual murder in front of fifty civilian witnesses – and that he would want very much to finish what he'd started, in private.

Mario's sister hadn't waited for an ambulance but drove me the twenty blocks up to Bellevue herself, once Jimmy and Paulo had dragged me out through tables of fascinated diners and laid me across the backseat of her car. She told me this when I woke, briefly, the first time. She also said she'd called Kris and that the nurse believed I wasn't going to die, probably, so she had to get back to work; it was a busy night and now they were down a waiter, for God's sake, and when it came to paying the hospital bills I was on my own, of course.

Kris was there when next I surfaced. And, thankfully, still here this third time.

I pushed myself up in bed. 'Where were you?'

'I'll tell you later,' she said. 'There's . . . there's a guy who wants to talk to you.'

From my newly elevated position I could see a man in the doorway. I thought for a moment there was someone else out in the dimly lit corridor beyond, but I didn't get a good look.

'Who are you?' I asked.

The man came and stood at the end of the bed. He pulled out a wallet and showed NYPD ID that said his name was Detective Raul Brooke.

'Okay,' I said. 'So what do you want?'

'For you to tell me what happened.'

'I got beat up.'

'That'd be obvious from about thirty feet away, sir. I was hoping for more in the way of detail.'

'I don't have any.'

'Uh-huh. A witness gave us a name, so I don't need you to volunteer that. I'd simply like you to explain the nature of your encounter with Mr Reinhart.'

'Personal.'

'Uh-huh,' he said again. 'Your assailant is known to us, Mr Henderson. You are not the first person to undergo an entanglement with him, though actually you came out of it better than some.'

'I got in his face over something. He came to the place where I work and got the jump on me. That's all.'

'If you know his name,' Kristina said, 'why can't you just arrest him?'

'Experience has shown that casual witnesses have a pattern of losing their memory when it comes to this man,' Brooke said. 'I'm wondering whether your boyfriend might be made of stronger stuff.'

'It was a private disagreement,' I said.

The cop smiled tightly and put his notebook away. 'Right,' he said. 'That's similar to what the other three said, the people we know had 'private disagreements' with him. One has disappeared. The other is in a wheelchair. He lives in a facility in Queens. His son visits him every week, but his dad has no clue who he is.'

'I'm sorry to hear that.'

'Right,' the detective said again. He seemed like a man who'd boiled his vocal responses down to simple units, which he could deploy as and when necessary. He put something on the arm of Kristina's chair and walked toward the door, but stopped as he reached the corridor.

'The third person died. Hard. Of course, we

can't tie that to Reinhart, or I wouldn't be here trying to get sense out of the next asshole in line.'

I didn't say anything.

'This person was a woman,' the cop added, more wearily. 'And your friend was smart enough to cut away the parts of her that might have held traces of his DNA. So the bottom line is, we got three people who can't help get this guy what he deserves . . . and one who can. You.'

He flicked his thumb at Kristina. 'Your friend has my card. She's probably got the smarts to be able to read the words on it, too. If *you* grow a brain anytime soon, Mr Henderson, give me a call.'

He left.

'I'm leaving,' I said.

'No, you're not.'

I pulled the sheet off the lower half of my body. This triggered ricochets of pains across my chest and back. My first attempt to swing my legs off the bed did not go smoothly and made me feel nauseous. 'Yeah, I am.'

'Stay *there*.'

'Kris, you heard the guy.'

'Yes, I *did*. I was worried you hadn't. I was wondering if maybe you'd got hit in the head so often that you lost all ability to hear what the hell people are saying to you, you *asshole*.'

Then she had her hands on my shoulder and was either shaking me or trying to push me back down. It wasn't easy to tell which, but I held her until the first rage or fear was spent and eventually got my arms around her back and pulled her in to me. That hurt too, but it was a different kind of pain, and I held her as long as she'd let me, until she'd stopped trying to shout in my ear and was letting me kiss her on the cheek, and then doing the same thing back, reluctantly, and still angrily, but hard.

Finally she pulled away, and I was shocked to see her eyes were wet. I have never seen Kris cry.

'I'm sorry,' I said.

'It's not your fault.'

'Pushing Reinhart's buttons today was dumb. But that cop sounded serious and that's why I'm out of here. It won't be hard for Reinhart to find out where I am and right now I'm not in a position to—'

'John, you haven't seen what you look like. You haven't talked to the nurse. You're *concussed*.'

'All the more reason to get home.'

'He's right,' said a voice.

I looked at the door to discover a tall girl in a black coat standing out in the dark corridor, the girl who seemed to have been the catalyst to pull us into all of this, whatever 'this' was.

Kristina looked as guilty as hell and I guessed I knew where she'd been that evening. 'Lizzie – what are you *doing* here?'

'I followed you,' the woman said. 'It's what we do.'

'John should *stay here*. And talk to that policeman.'

Lizzie shook her head. 'Those would be mistakes.'

Kristina went out into the corridor. They went back and forth for a while, which gave me the opportunity to slide awkwardly out of bed, wrench myself out of the gown, find my clothes, and get dressed. Getting out of the gown revealed how bruised and scuffed my chest was. Climbing into my clothes suggested that in my current state I could probably be knocked over by a toddler, or a boisterous mouse. I stuck to the task, however, moving like a puppet with tangled strings. I picked up the cop's business card and stuffed that in my pocket, too.

'So,' I said when I was done and had lurched out into the corridor to join them. 'How do we get out of this place? I'm afraid I have no idea.'

'John, for God's *sake* . . .'

'I'm dressed and it hurt and I'm not getting undressed again.' I meant to say more but got light-headed and had to lean against the wall.

'Christ,' she said. 'Okay, let's go.'

The corridor was in night mode, periodically lit by dim lights. There was no sign of the nurse. Lizzie held up a hand to tell us to stay where we were. She hurried to the intersection and looked both ways, then gestured for us to follow. I wasn't sure why I was taking direction from her, but if it meant I could get out of the hospital I was prepared to go along with it for now.

At the intersection we found a nurse's station,

empty, and a sign pointing down a long corridor toward the elevators. The longest of the corridors, of course.

We started along it, but then Lizzie slowed, twisting her head around in short, abrupt movements, as if listening for something. Whatever it was, she eventually seemed to catch it.

She bit her lip. 'Go,' she said.

Kris hesitated, caught between wanting to get me out and wanting to know what was going on. 'What is it?'

'It's . . . just go,' Lizzie muttered, setting off down the side corridor. 'Go somewhere safe.'

But Kristina followed the girl as she hurried away, and I limped after her. Every three yards along this corridor was a door to an individual room. All had been left slightly ajar, presumably to allow monitoring staff to poke their heads in during the night. For no obvious reason, Lizzie approached the door about halfway along and then froze outside, hand held up toward the door as if about to push it open.

She was so unnaturally still that for a moment it seemed as if she could never have moved at all, but was something seen as a layer over the world, like a particular vivid memory or daydream. Then she was in movement again, gently pushing.

We reached the doorway as she stepped in. It was dark inside, with only a low glow from a short fluorescent tube halfway up the far wall.

On the left was a bed. In it lay a man, propped

up. He was asleep, breathing raggedly. He was pale and bloated and had plastic tubes going into one wrist and one nostril and it did not seem likely that he was in the hospital for something minor. This was a man whose body was at war against him. His body, and time.

I turned to go, feeling bad for intruding on his sickness and while he was asleep, but realized there was someone else in the room. There was a chair in the corner, pointed toward the bed. Another man, younger than the other or in better health and shape, was sitting there. He had his elbows on his knees and his hands clasped tightly together, intently watching the man in the bed. He was rocking back and forth.

'Oh, Billy,' Lizzie said.

He didn't answer. Lizzie put her hand on his shoulder. 'How long have you been here?'

He licked his lips. 'Two days.'

'What happened?'

'Heart attack.'

'But he's only . . .'

'I know. I *know*. But it's been coming. I realize that now. I hadn't seen him in years. I didn't understand how he'd become. I thought it was me losing faith, slowly going hollow. But it was him all along.'

The figure in the bed pulled in a rasping breath. 'No,' Billy said, leaning forward. 'No . . .'

After a few seconds the man in the bed breathed out again, and the rhythm of his chest's rise and fall seemed to settle. Lizzie stood by the bed, looking down. 'Why isn't anybody here with him?'

'They were. I've been standing at the end of the bed all day, out of their way. The doctors say he's stable, so they've gone home to get some rest and change their clothes and, I don't know, that kind of thing.'

'Well, if the doctor says that then . . . it could all be okay.'

The man shook his head. In the weak light his face looked pinched, almost translucent. I don't think he had any idea that Kristina and I were even in the room.

'I felt it. I didn't realize it, but I *felt* it. That's why . . . that's why. It *wasn't* my fault.'

Lizzie looked at us. 'Go,' she said. She no longer looked elfin, or distant. She looked like if we didn't go then bad things would happen to us.

'Kris,' I said . . . but then the man on the bed made a quiet, terrible sound, as if he'd tried to pull in another breath and found the world withholding it.

He tried again, and this time it sounded like he'd succeeded but the air had gone the wrong way inside his body, as if there was no longer any proper place in there for it. His eyes opened, staring up at the ceiling, and in them was all possible knowledge of what was happening to him. He knew, and because he knew it was impossible for the rest of us not to know too.

'Get a nurse,' Kristina said. 'John, get a—'

A final exhale, an out breath that seemed to last far longer than it should for a pair of lungs to void themselves of air – as if instead it was clearing out the stale remains of every single inhale, back through thirty years of in-and-outs and sneezes, to childhood breaths in fields and classrooms, breaths sucked in to blow out birthday candles, back even to the first breath scrabbled out of a cold new world, to give the power to wail.

The man on the chair – Billy – was standing now, coming closer to the bed, arms held down and rigid by his sides. He closed his eyes.

'Goodbye, my friend.'

The breath finished, or came to a point where it was no longer going on. In the life of the person in the bed, nothing ever happened again.

The man standing next to him seemed to condense. It was as if something had shifted in the lighting, making a shape that had been so inconsequential when we entered that I hadn't even noticed him, into something more substantial. Not bigger, exactly, but much more *there*.

He was motionless for a moment, then took in a *huge* jagged breath, his eyes flying open. 'Ha,' he said.

He breathed out massively, then back in again. 'Ha!' He started walking around the room, faster and faster, arms and legs jerking robotically. 'Oh, yes,' he said, starting to laugh. '*That's* what I'm talking about.'

He pulled another monstrous breath in through mouth and nose, and held it down, as if savoring it.

'Billy,' Lizzie said. 'Billy, slow down.'

He paid no attention to her. He completed one more chaotic circuit of the room and nearly knocked me down as he went striding out the door, arms thrashing.

Lizzie ran after him, leaving us in a hospital room with a cooling body and no clue what was going on.

'What the hell just happened?'

'Let's get you home,' Kristina said, with a final glance at the dead man in the bed. 'There's . . . stuff we need to talk about.'

CHAPTER 47

We didn't go home, however. In the cab we realized that if Reinhart did decide to come back and finish the discussion tonight, then directly after the hospital he'd come hunting where we lived. Both of us believed he'd already have that information or be able to obtain it, and that being trapped up at the top of a five-story building was a bad defensive position.

I hated the feeling of hiding from him, but on the other hand – and perhaps contrary to appearances – I'm not a total fool. If we were going to meet again, it needed to be in circumstances of my choosing, or at least at a time when I could straighten my back and move my limbs without feeling like I was going to pass out. Merely lolling in the back of a yellow cab felt like someone was still hitting me, and my brain was so washy and vague that I wasn't completely convinced of what I thought I'd seen in the private room in the hospital.

Trying to work out where to hide in the middle of the night is a good way to focus the mind on the relationships in your life. The news that came back was not good. The restaurant made no sense and neither did the apartments of any staff members. Even if we'd been close enough to impose upon them, their connection to the Adriatico would rule them out. I'd traced Reinhart to his lunch via this kind of link and I had no doubt he'd be able to do the same in reverse. The only other person we could think of was Catherine, which clearly wasn't an option either. Once we'd run out of ideas and sat in silence for a few minutes, Kristina took my hand.

'We don't really live here, do we?'

'No,' I said. 'Maybe you're right. Maybe we should move. Live in a neighborhood. Try to hang with some real people for a change.'

She shook her head.

'Why? I thought that's what you wanted.'

'Throwing money at a more expensive apartment isn't going to solve anything.'

'It might help.' She shook her head again, with a finality I found unnerving. 'Kris, what?'

'How much cash do you have on you now?'

'Not enough for a hotel room, if that's what you're thinking. And I didn't bring any cards out with me.'

'How much?'

Wincing, I managed to lever my wallet out of my pocket and check the contents. 'About eighty bucks.'

She took the bills and shoved them through the slot in the glass toward the driver.

'That's what we have,' she said to him.

The driver, an elderly man in a turban, looked surprised – but didn't give the money back. 'Where to?'

'Just drive.'

'I need a destination.'

'Take us to wherever forty bucks gets us, and then come back. In the meantime, shut this slot thing, please, and then turn your radio up.'

The guy decided the money was worth the attitude, and did what he'd been asked. Kristina sat back in the seat, and – after a couple of false starts – told me what had happened to her before she turned up at the hospital.

I listened, and tried not to interrupt.

The money bought us half an hour, enough for me to get Kristina to repeat the sections of her story that I found hardest to believe and also to establish that she at least half believed what Lizzie had told her as they sat together in the park. I spent the last five minutes in silence, watching out the window as smeared neon and streetlights flowed across the pane like bright horizontal raindrops. It was hard to push focus past these and other reflections in the glass and out onto the people on the sidewalks, leaning in doorways, sitting on benches, the people who are always out there, on their way somewhere or back, glimpsed from the side or behind, people whose identity and business you'll never know and who really, in your heart of hearts, you afford no more reality than the shadows of birds flying overhead.

Yes, clearly they represent something. But something real? Something as substantial as you and me? I didn't understand how what Kristina had told me could possibly work, but that did not mean it could not be so. There had been a time when I didn't understand how I could live in a world where my eldest son was dead, in which I could look at the woman I married and see someone I didn't recognize, or how I could now be living three thousand miles from Tyler, my remaining boy, and not have seen him in a year or have the faintest idea of what he was like now that he was six years old and older than Scott ever got to be. It had seemed impossible that I could find or take the steps that would lead me from a previous reality to these new ones without breaking apart on the journey. I did not, in fact, handle the events well – except perhaps in that I did ultimately survive, and woke up one morning and understood that this new world I lived in was real, and that therefore I must be real too.

Did that mean that the previous one had been *un*real? That reality in which Scott walked the earth, or my mother, come to that – where did it stand now? It did not feel as if it lay back in time, that a mere sequence of events was what had moved it away from me. It felt like it still existed to one side, through a glass wall a hundred feet thick. I could see the land on the other side in my

mind's eye, and sometimes in melancholy fantasy or sleeping dream it came closer than that, as if when I poured my soul and all the emotional energy I had into it these shades on the other side of alive/not alive and true/not true remained far more proximal than I'd thought. Close, in fact, to still being real.

If you believe life is worth living, it is. If you believe you are fat, you are. And if you believe for long enough, and strongly enough, that someone imaginary is real, and they were to come to believe it too . . .

Kris waited as patiently as she could, but in the end dug me in the ribs. 'Well?'

'Ow.'

'Sorry. But . . . *well*? Talk to me. Say something.'

I leaned forward and opened the slot to the driver's compartment. 'How much we got left?'

He glanced at the meter. 'About five bucks.'

'Take us to Chelsea,' I said.

I leaned against the railing at the bottom of the steps as Kristina hesitated at the door.

'John, it's two o'clock in the morning.'

'Push the thing.'

She pressed quickly on the door buzzer, trying to make a noise that should be audible to someone already awake, but hopefully not enough to raise the sleeping.

At first nothing seemed to happen, but then we heard the slow tramp of footsteps coming down

the staircase inside. There was a pause, then the sound of a bolt and a chain being slid across. The door opened.

Father Jeffers stood in yellow glow inside. He looked me up and down. 'What on earth happened to you?'

'Not what,' I said. 'Who.'

CHAPTER 48

An hour later, three things had happened. I'd been given several cups of strong coffee, which had helped. I'd seen myself in a mirror, which had not. Though I felt Kristina's and Jeffers's reactions had been extreme, a look at my face would leave you in no doubt that I'd been in a fight and lost. Apart from a few stitches in a cut under my left cheekbone, it was mainly bruising and scrapes, however. I wouldn't want to have to apply for a job in childcare or public relations, but I've seen worse, and the coffee and a fistful of painkillers from the priest's bathroom cabinet had made me feel better.

The third thing was that Kristina had told the priest what she'd told me, and I'd sketched out other events of the last week. Jeffers had listened impassively, as though withstanding a parishioner's doleful recitation of excessive drinking or unwholesome thoughts toward his neighbor's ass, in preparation for trotting out the prescribed means of atoning for such deviations from accepted moral practice. Only at one point did he seem more affected, when Kristina confirmed that Lizzie had been our first point of contact.

'You're absolutely sure she was taking an interest in this friend of yours?'

'Yes,' I said. 'I told you the time I disturbed your piano practice. It's been going on for some time.'

'What do you mean by "some time"?'

'I'm not sure,' I admitted. 'Certainly a few weeks, and that's what had been freaking Catherine out. But she also seems to think it happened a long time ago too.'

Jeffers didn't appear surprised. We were in his study, dimly lit by a couple of yellow lamps. He and Kristina had insisted that I take the comfortable chair, and were perched on wooden ones.

'I'm sorry to hear that,' he said eventually. 'Lizzie starting to follow again is a backward step. I shall need to discuss it with her.'

Kris was watching him, as if beginning to get an idea about something. 'Fine,' she said. 'But it's not just about Lizzie. There are others, too. Flaxon, the other ones that call themselves Angels. Lizzie's friend Maj, too. And she mentioned another . . . Golzen?'

Jeffers smiled stiffly. 'I'm aware of him, yes.'

'How many of these people *are* there?'

'I must have met fifty over the last three years, perhaps closer to a hundred. I suspect there are many, many more. I have been trying to work with some of them.'

'Work how?'

'Develop a program of recovery. Help them to move from their current state to a more positive one.'

'But who *are* they?' I asked. 'They're basically people who've fallen between the cracks, right?'

'No,' he said. 'It's . . . more complicated than that, and you're not going to believe it.'

'Try us,' Kris said.

'You really want to know?'

'Yes.'

'They're dead.'

Kristina and I stared at him.

'I told you.' He sighed. 'One of the biggest problems with my job is that "dead" is a word that startles people.'

'It's a big word,' I said.

'Of course. Because these days it says a world-changing event has happened. It didn't use to. People had a relationship with those who had gone before. Some believe one of the reasons our species turned from a nomadic lifestyle was we started to bury the departed, housing them before we even housed ourselves. If you have an ongoing dialogue with the dead then you don't want to leave them behind. Heaven was a way of getting around this – a realm that is always "above," wherever you are and from which the deceased can be benignly looking down even if you keep moving. For thousands of years religion supported people's grief by telling them the dead remained in reach,

411

but now science says that when someone dies they're gone forever except in memory, and that those memories are merely electrical impulses in a bundle of fragile flesh, and so death has become the big divide. The bigger the chasm, the more terrifying it becomes.'

'But how does that relate to Lizzie and her friends?'

'They're ghosts,' he said. 'People who died in the city but haven't moved on.'

'Lizzie is *not* a ghost,' Kristina said. 'She's *there*. Her friends are, too. I spent two hours with them stealing drinks off people in bars, for God's sake.'

'Nobody said ghosts can't interact with the physical world,' Jeffers said. 'There's all the stories about them passing through walls and vanishing at will, but the ability to disappear is just about whether you're *noticed* or not. Real people can do that too. And for every story like those there's another about poltergeists – spirits that *can* manipulate objects, however crudely – or elves or pixies that take things and move them around, or phantoms that run cold fingers across the back of your neck.'

'You're saying these are all the same thing?'

'The same *kind* of thing. We're able to see some of these spirits, once in a while, in the right conditions. With others we only experience their effects, but that holds true of normal life too. If someone claps their hands together out of our sight, we still *hear* the event; we don't need to see it or suffer the hand smacking against our own body to prove it. Just as there are many types of human, with different abilities and ways of being, so it is with souls, too.'

I couldn't work out whether the guy was serious or if this was some weird priest metaphor that I was too tired to get. 'So *why* are these spirits still here?'

'Unfinished business. Or because there's someone still alive, refusing to let go, maintaining a relationship that is too strong for the departed to progress according to the natural order of things.'

I remembered giving the priest's address to Lydia earlier that evening – an event that felt like it had taken place about two weeks ago – and wondered if that had been such a smart idea after all. 'But how would that *work*?'

'Strange,' Jeffers said. 'I wouldn't have taken you for a staunch defender of science.'

'I'm not. That doesn't mean I'll believe any old crap. Seriously. How *would it work*?'

'Do you know how love works? Or hate? Or hope? Yet you wouldn't deny their existence or power to change human behavior.'

'Those are emotions, not states of being.'

'I'm aware it's a category error in the minds of a philosopher, but they're seldom the most practical of thinkers and I'm not sure there's a big distinction in the real world. The universe is a different place to someone who's in love than it is to one who is withstanding grief – different worlds that exist side by side, brought into being by emotion. If emotion can structure reality then why shouldn't it enable an individual soul to persist beyond its intended span?'

I shook my head, knowing there were a million flaws in this but not being able to nail them.

'It's not a permanent state,' he said. 'It's unstable, precisely because it relies upon emotion. Some of their number, the ones they call Hollows, they're closer to moving on. They retreat from the world, often settling in graveyards, as if they dimly remember the circumstance of their interment and wish to rejoin the process of transition. There are others who appear not to even realize they're dead – the Dozenos. On the other side of the spectrum, the strong and self-actualized dead, there are Fingermen, who possess a poltergeist-style ability to manipulate objects. There are especially restless spirits called Journeymen, who have no desire to remain near the person holding them here, and there are Cornermen, who remain stationary for long periods – as if tied to one particular locale – and pass messages among the other ghosts. There are more of these souls on the loose than there ever used to be. The dead have always been with us. There have always been spirits that lost their way. But now that our society has taken down the signposts it will happen more and more.'

'Surely it doesn't matter if we pull the plug on ways of understanding death. Doesn't *God* call them home?'

Jeffers looked at me as though I were a member of a Sunday school class who, having previously shown promise, had revealed himself to have understood nothing at all.

I wanted a cigarette but couldn't face the four-floor trek downstairs to the outdoors. I felt exhausted and in pain. But I wanted to understand.

'So according to you, Reinhart has built himself a team of *ghosts* to help him steal shit?'

'Yes. These souls, or "friends" as they tend to call themselves, are in moral danger. Many may still be here as a result of shortcomings in their lives. To encourage them to engage in further acts of turpitude is to damn them forever. I am not prepared to let that happen.'

'Speaking as someone with recent experience in the field,' I said, 'you may not have a lot of choice over what Reinhart does. Unless you're prepared to get biblical on it in ways different to the ones you're accustomed to.'

Jeffers reached to the desk in the corner, opened the drawer, and pulled out an ashtray. 'Another leaving from my predecessor. Open the window, please.'

I stared at him. 'How did you know?'

'People's feelings and desires are often visible, sometimes even tangible,' he said. 'That's precisely what I've been trying to tell you.'

'What I still don't understand,' Kristina said, 'is why some of the friends work with Reinhart.'

'His main contact among them is this Golzen person. Every now and then one of these souls tries to raise themselves above the others. Usually that's been a positive thing. But Golzen has . . . a different take.'

'Different how?'

'More militant. There's a widespread misapprehension among the friends about their state of being. This "imaginary friends" delusion that Lizzie told Kristina about – unfortunately, she believes it. A great many of them do. Golzen has exploited this, along with legends and stories that have gained credence over the years, including one concerning a promised land.'

I laughed. 'Dead people have their own *myths*?'

'Gather three individuals together and by the end of the evening part of their relationship will rest upon something supposed, rather than demonstrably true.'

'But what if they *are* imaginary?' Kristina said. 'Are you *sure* they're not?'

The priest stood. 'I've told you what I believe. I have a spare room. It's never been used, so I daresay it's rather dusty, but you're welcome to it.'

Kris and I looked at each other, and knew that given the chance not to have to go back home, we'd take it.

'Thank you,' I said.

'They're dead,' he said flatly. 'Don't believe it if they tell you differently. Sometimes the dead lie.'

CHAPTER 49

David sat with his back to the wall. He could smell clean carpet – Dawn had gone ahead and vacuumed around the boxes that evening, not pointedly, but the point was still made. He couldn't see much. That wasn't because it was the middle of the night and the spare room was dark. It wasn't that there wasn't much to see in the room even during the day.

He just wasn't seeing anything outside his own head.

When he got back he'd tried to work, of course. Nothing had come of it – of course. He'd read more of Talia's book and glumly accepted that the further she'd gotten into her stride the better it became. Her writing possessed authenticity and directness and a simple pleasure in the act of creation, something he doubted he'd be able to replicate. For him it was always going to be more complicated. Talia was a real person and made things up for fun. For him the act of imagination was more deep-seated. It was who he was, and that made it harder; if you'd made your own self up, written yourself, reality will always seem compromised.

417

At dinner he and Dawn talked of inconsequential things. She seemed distracted but when asked said she was fine. It could be concerns about the pregnancy, he supposed, or wondering how his book was going but not wanting to ask because she knew it would stress him out to have to admit it wasn't going well. It could more likely be that David was finding it hard to mesh with the world, and as a consequence everything seemed off balance and skewed – even positive things like going to an ATM and knowing there would be money in their account. After such a long time where they'd been scraping by, being solvent made the world strange.

The thing with Maj was the same. He'd tried to forget about it, to run with the idea it was something he didn't need and could thus be excised. It didn't work. It was like trying to put a looming tax bill out of your mind. You keep pretending it'll be okay and think furiously about other things – about anything else at all – but it's there in the twist in your stomach and in the way you hold your shoulders.

As he got into bed with Dawn, David finally decided to try to talk to her about it, tell her about the stranger who'd come to visit and what had happened in New York. He couldn't keep burying it, and he knew himself well enough to realize that when he had something on his mind he behaved awkwardly – and it might be this that was making Dawn quiet.

He lay next to her trying to think of a non-crazy way of bringing the subject up, but took too long; her breathing settled into the rhythms that meant the god of sleep had gathered her in his arms. So he lay there, mind spinning faster and faster, stomach cramping, until he decided he may as well get up.

As he padded out into the hallway, he passed the door to the spare room. Maybe he could use the time to sort through the stuff, if he did it quietly – at least get one positive thing out of the day. He went in and shut the door. He didn't bother to turn on the light. There was enough moonlight coming through the window.

He pulled the lids of the boxes open and took everything out, arranging it around where he sat. It was the same stuff he'd seen before. Nothing surprising. Nothing he'd forgotten about. No big reveals. A few souvenirs of once having had parents, books that a much younger version of himself had loved. The only interesting thing about these was the authors. Ray Bradbury. Philip K. Dick. Stephen King. These were the kind of stories he'd enjoyed and yet he'd gone on to sell a literary novel. He knew why that was – but what next? Did he carry on pretending to be that guy when he had no right, or should he to try to find a route back to who he was? Was there even anything left to return to?

The books felt like they belonged to someone else. The house felt like it did, too.

There was a noise from downstairs.

★ ★ ★

He walked quietly out onto the landing. The noise had seemed to come from directly beneath the spare room. The kitchen. A scraping sound.

He went to the bedroom and poked his head around the door to check that it wasn't Dawn waking and going downstairs to see what he was up to. She was fast asleep. So what did he do now? Stay where he was, at the top of the stairs, and wait to see if someone came up them?

He started slowly down the staircase, carefully lowering each foot, using years of familiarity with the house to stick to the outside of the treads so as not to set off any creaks. He hesitated before turning the corner at the return, listening as hard as he could. All he could hear was the sound of rushing in his ears.

He quickly took the next step, bending at the waist so as to be able to see down into the hallway right away. Something was off about the light. He couldn't tell what, but he knew now that he hadn't imagined the sound.

He waited, motionless, expecting to see a shape or shadow crossing the hallway. Nothing happened.

Very slowly, holding on to the banister to help him get around the corner soundlessly, he started down the lower flight. By the time he got to the bottom it was obvious what was unusual about the light in the hallway.

The front door was open.

Knowing now that he was dealing with a very

real situation, David stopped. The door was open. Only nine inches or so, but open is open.

But did that mean someone *was* inside, or *had* been inside? You had to work on the assumption someone was still inside, surely.

So . . . did he creep back upstairs, use the phone in his study to call the cops? What if the intruder came up the stairs when he was doing that, or before the police arrived? Presumably they'd left the door open to make it easier to escape. Would it be better to make as much noise as possible now, in the hope of scaring them off?

The front door closed.

David blinked at it. It looked like a hand had pulled it shut – from the outside. That's all he'd seen – a hand pulling the handle.

The hand hadn't been there, and then it was.

He waited, poised awkwardly with his feet on two different stairs, strain settling into the muscles in his legs. Nothing else happened.

He walked down the last two steps. He crept over to the tall and narrow window next to the front door. He kept well back in the darkness, craning his neck to see if there was anyone out there on the path.

He couldn't see anyone. He turned his head and checked the sidewalk down on the street. No one there either. He waited and heard nothing.

So he reached out for the door and opened it.

Cold air came in, along with moonlight, the

factor that had keyed him in to the door being open in the first place. He went out onto the step. The stone was very cold underfoot. The street was silent, dead, and empty. He looked left and he looked right. He saw no one.

He did not look up, and so he did not see the three tall, thin people lying on the roof, their faces hanging over the edge, grinning down at him.

When he had the door shut behind him again David stood in the hallway. He didn't know for sure that the house was empty, of course. The fact that (he thought) he'd seen a hand pulling the door from the outside didn't prove there was no one left in the interior. It didn't *feel* like it. He realized that while he'd been on the stairs he'd *known* there was someone in the house. He could feel it.

He could *then*, anyhow. Now it felt otherwise. Was he prepared to trust that intuition?

He walked to the sitting room, took a breath, and slipped his head around the door. An empty room, looking staged, as they did in the night, familiar objects and furniture turned into sets.

He didn't think it likely that someone would be in the half bathroom, but he checked anyway. Then he walked toward the kitchen.

It was obvious from the doorway that something was wrong, but in the darkness it took him a moment to work out what. It was something about the color and texture, and it was all over the place.

He turned on the light. The room was covered in pieces of paper. It jumped into his head that it must be Talia's book, but then he remembered that he'd never printed it out. There were sheets on the table, across the floor, on the counters. Literally all over the place.

He bent down and picked up the nearest. It was blank. He pulled another few pieces toward him and saw they were the same. Blank. On both sides.

He moved around the kitchen, gathering up pieces of typing paper until he'd gotten them all.

CHAPTER 50

Waking the morning after a serious fight is not good. My body felt like it had been dismantled in my sleep and put back together in basically the right shape, but without whatever cushioning substance normally stops the parts from scraping against one another. My head was no better, but I woke up with a resolution fully formed. I was going home. It might be a crappy apartment with barely enough room to swing a cat (soon after we'd moved in, somewhat drunk, Kris and I had established this was technically possible using a cardboard mock-up), but it was mine.

I opened my eyes to find I was alone in the narrow bed. Kris was perched on the arm of the comfortable chair, looking out the window.

'What time is it?'

'Just after seven,' she said.

'How long have you been awake?'

'Didn't sleep.'

'At all? Why?'

'Keeping an eye on the bare-knuckle fighter. I woke you a couple of times to make sure you didn't think you were Napoleon. Don't you remember?'

I shook my head, found the movement hurt, and said no instead. 'So am I out of the woods?'

'Search me. I'm a barmaid, not a neurologist. Check this out, though.'

I hauled myself over to the window. From there you could see down and across to the church. Father Jeffers was standing there alone.

'What's he doing?'

'Nothing,' she said. 'I heard him leave the building – about two minutes after the phone downstairs rang. He's been there half an hour.'

'Waiting for?'

'That would be the question.'

Not sure I needed to know the answer, I went into the bathroom. This showed no sign of recent habitation. It was clean but otherwise could have been in a museum. White tiles, an unsmeared mirror, a neatly folded fawn towel hanging off a rail, and a white sink and shower stall. I established that the last of these functioned, and undressed gingerly. There were a lot of bruises but they were hurting less as my body warmed up, and the sight of each just made me more resolved.

I was out of the shower and halfway back into my clothes when Kristina called out, 'Quick – come here!'

We pressed our faces up against the glass. At first I could only see one person coming up the street, intermittently visible through the trees. A slim man, in a suit. He was running up the middle of the road. He ran for a while, at least, then stopped and whirled around. Then he was running again.

'Is that the guy from the hospital?'

'Yes,' I said. 'And look who else.'

Two people were following in his wake, one on either sidewalk as if to shepherd him. A woman in a red dress under a black coat and a man in jeans.

'Lizzie,' I said. 'I've seen the guy before, too.'

'I think that's Maj,' Kris said.

By the time we stepped out of the house Lizzie and the other guy had managed to coral Billy toward the church. He was still fighting it – not with aggression or ill will, but hectic enthusiasm. He was like a child on a sugar rush, right at the moment when it's all just uncontrollably fantastic and the best possible way to feel and you believe everybody else *must* be finding all this as hilarious as you are. He kept darting toward the other two as if about to make a getaway up the street, but then turning back in a circle, arms held out like a bird. He didn't really want to escape. He was happy where he was. He would, by the look of it, be happy just about anywhere.

As we got closer we realized that wasn't the whole story. He was very pale, with a slick of perspiration over his face. As we got in range, he stopped whirling and stared at me, blinking rapidly.

426

'I know you,' he said. 'I know you. I know you.'

He laughed loudly before trying to dart off down the road again. Maj moved to put himself in his way, effectively forcing him through the gate and into the church enclosure. Once there, Billy seemed to recognize his surroundings and looked up at the stairs.

'Hey, Father,' he called. 'Look at me!'

'I see you,' Jeffers said. 'I've always seen you.'

'But not like now, huh?'

'You're certainly very visible this morning.'

'Ha!'

'You look a little worn-out, though. Why don't you come inside. Catch your breath.'

'Aha, no,' Billy said, with a smile of low cunning. 'I've been in there *before*. I want to see *new* things.'

'Of course you do,' the priest said. 'I have new things inside.'

'What kind of things?' Billy said. 'Are they green? Are they sand-papery?'

'Not especially. But I have pastries. And coffee.'

'Ooh.'

Billy hesitated. When he stopped moving, I realized the damp glow over his face did not look like sweat. It looked like something viscous seeping from the pores. His fingers were twitching. His hair looked like straw, and he was scrawny inside his disheveled suit.

Maj remained outside the gate, ready to bar an escape. Lizzie stood farther back, one hand in front of her mouth. She looked composed in sadness, as

427

if happening upon a photograph of somebody now gone, someone she hadn't realized how much she missed.

Billy was breathing more heavily. The power that had seemed to thrum through him was abating. He blinked, his eyes staying closed for a beat too long.

'I feel silly,' he said distractedly. 'I . . . I've forgotten something. What is it?'

'Come inside,' Jeffers said softly.

Billy seemed to be having second thoughts, but he looked weary now. He didn't look as if he could make it up the stairs, never mind go haring off down the street.

Maj walked into the enclosed area and came up behind him. He leaned forward and said something in Billy's ear. Whatever it was, it seemed to perk the other man up.

'Really?' he said, looking round. The look broke my heart. It was the kind a boy might give his father if, some sunny afternoon, the man had decided to treat his son to an ice cream cone out of the blue.

Maj nodded. Billy smiled, a small boy's grin that changed his face so much it was hard to remember what it had looked like before. He waved to Lizzie before running off up the stairs, past the priest, and into the church.

Maj followed, more slowly. Jeffers walked down the steps past him and over to the gate.

'Thank you, Lizzie,' he said.

'You asked,' she said. 'So I did it. That's all.'

She looked upset, as though she wanted no part of whatever was about to happen.

'It's the right thing,' Jeffers said. 'Will you come by later?'

She walked away without answering. Jeffers watched for a moment, then hurried up the stairs and into the church, closing the door behind him.

'I'm going after her,' Kris said. She pecked me on the cheek.

I let myself in through the church gate.

Jeffers was a man of his word. There was a tray on the table by the wall under the lackluster stained-glass windows. Billy was stuffing baked goods into his mouth. Jeffers meanwhile busied himself with moving prayer books from one neat pile into another.

Maj had turned around one of the chairs in the back row and was watching Billy with a complicated expression. There was something of the look Lizzie had given the priest in it, but a touch of envy, too.

Jeffers smiled. 'How's that taste, Billy?'

'Great,' Billy said, voice indistinct. 'Fucking *great*.'

'That's good. Would you like some coffee?'

'Hell yes.'

Billy reached for a thermos that Jeffers had placed next to the tray. He tried to pick it up but fumbled the handle. He frowned, and tried again.

'It's pretty heavy,' Jeffers said. 'Why don't you let me help you with it?'

'I can do it.' Billy tried again, but he couldn't. Frustrated, he made a growling sound.

'Let the father do it,' Maj said. 'He's had more practice, that's all.'

'Exactly,' Jeffers said, picking it up and pouring a careful stream of coffee into a white mug. Billy watched the process avidly, still chewing on a *pain au chocolat*.

The priest glanced at me. 'Do you remember John, Billy? He was there in the hospital with you last night.'

Billy looked at me. 'Yeah. Maybe.'

Maj was looking at me too. 'What's he doing here now?'

'He's run into problems with someone we know,' Jeffers said. He held a pot of cream in front of Billy, who nodded enthusiastically. 'Which is why he looks like he got pulled through a hedge backward.'

Maj came to look me up and down. Being that close to him made the conversations of last night seem absurd. He was a man in his early thirties, with strong bone structure and stubble across his jawline. His hair was brown, mid-length. His eyes were brown too, with a touch of green around the irises. He was there. He took up space. He was substantial, and his presence was strong.

'Yes, you could touch me,' he said, as if he knew what I'd been thinking.

430

He was also, however, wearing exactly the same outfit as when I'd last glimpsed him. Battered jeans and the untucked shirt. Of course, someone living as he did – however that might precisely be – wouldn't change their outfit often. The clothes did not look tired, however, as if at the end of several days' use. There was no hint of sweat. In fact, there was no odor to him at all. We underestimate the importance of that sense, but once you've noticed its absence, you keep noticing it.

It made me wonder whether the clothes he was wearing were independent objects in their own right, or if they were just part of the idea of him.

'I've heard two different theories that say I *shouldn't* be able to touch you.'

'I don't know what you've been told,' Maj said. 'Don't care, either. I'm sorry you've run into Reinhart. He's a bad man. But our world is none of your business. The best thing to do would be to leave.'

'I'll do that,' I said. 'But that doesn't mean Reinhart's going to leave me alone. A cop told me last night that Reinhart tends to finish what he starts. Two days ago he threatened my girl-friend. I don't like that. And I don't like that this mess came from you people.'

'No, it didn't.'

'Yeah, it did. If we hadn't been trying to find out who was following one of Kristina's friends, we'd never have even seen your friend Lizzie.'

His eyes narrowed. This felt strangely noticeable,

as if I was admiring the realism of a special effect. 'Lizzie was following someone?'

'Catherine Warren. Do you know her?'

I don't know what I'd said, or why it meant something to him, but the man's whole attitude changed.

'It happens,' Jeffers said quickly. 'Look at you and David. You've even *talked* to him.'

'That's different. And I told her about it,' Maj said. 'She didn't say anything to me about this.'

'It's just following,' Jeffers said. 'Not trying to make contact. I'm sure it's fine.'

There was a violent coughing sound.

Billy was still at the table, cup of coffee in one hand and yet another pastry in the other. A mouthful of this had gone down the wrong way. He was trying to clear it, hacking up like a cat with a hairball. At first it didn't seem such a big deal – flakey pastry down the windpipe – but the cough got deeper, wrenching.

'Aren't you going to do something?' I said. 'He's choking.'

Maj watched. 'No, he's not.'

Billy turned from the table. His eyes were bulging, his face white. Even through his coughing he was still trying to shove some more of the pastry into his mouth.

'It's too late, Billy,' Jeffers said.

Billy didn't seem to hear. He raised the coffee to his mouth, chewing manically. The blockage seemed to clear, and he smiled. 'Got it,' he said.

As the mug got to his lips, something fell to the floor near his feet. I stared at it. It was brown, damp.

'What the hell is that?'

The others ignored me. I looked closer and saw that it was a mouthful of chewed pastry. Other things were floating down to join it now, flakes, drifting down through the air. Through Billy's body.

He tipped the cup back and poured coffee into his mouth. The liquid fell out and through his face and the length of his body to splatter onto the wooden floor.

Jeffers started murmuring something, a stream of words that sounded formalized. Maj put his hand out to Billy. Billy stared at it and then up at Maj's face.

'Is that *it?*'

'Afraid so.'

'But that wasn't . . . Oh, no, that's not *fair.*'

'Your friend was very sick when he died,' Maj said. 'Maybe there just wasn't that much left to have.'

'Not *fair.*' Billy stared wildly around, but not for an escape. He looked as if he were trying to drink things in. 'That's not *fair.*'

Jeffers kept up his words, nodding gently.

'Go *fuck yourself*,' Billy shouted. 'You don't understand *shit.*' He tried to throw the mug at the priest, but it clattered to the floor and broke. Jeffers didn't flinch.

433

'Go well,' Maj said, and shook Billy's hand.

'I don't want to.'

'But you'll see your friend.'

Billy hesitated. 'Do you think? Am I going home?'

Maj looked awkward. 'To be honest, I don't know. But that's what they say. He died last night. So there's a chance he'll be wherever you're going, right?'

'Can you come with me?'

'Not now. But one day.'

Jeffers put his hand on my shoulder. 'I'd like you to go now.'

I didn't feel like fighting a priest, and I didn't feel like I had any place there. But I couldn't help glancing back before I went through the door.

Jeffers had his hand on Billy's head. Billy was trembling, weeping. The words coming out of Jeffers's mouth were soothing.

I left. I have no idea what happened next.

CHAPTER 51

Lizzie moved fast – faster than Kris had ever seen before. Soon she was having to trot to even keep her in sight. When Lizzie seemed to jump cut to the other side of 14th without crossing the road, Kris shouted the girl's name and ran across the street after her, and kept shouting in the hope that it would embarrass the girl into stopping. At first Lizzie ignored her, but slowly she drew to a halt. She didn't turn.

'What do you want?'

Kris came around the front. Lizzie didn't look friendly. 'To *talk* to you.'

'What about?'

'What was happening to Billy?'

'What comes to all of us.'

'He was dying?'

'The end of the Bloom. What else did you think was on the horizon? Even for you? Did you have some other destination in mind?'

'Jeffers thinks you're already dead, Lizzie.'

'He's a nice man. But he's wrong.'

'He's kind of sweet on you too, isn't he?'

'Come, come. How could anyone be sweet on a *ghost*?'

'Because he's lonely and bored and has found something where he believes he can make a difference. And because you're not a ghost.'

'So what am I?'

'I don't *know*. I want you to explain. *Properly*.'

Lizzie looked away, seemingly at people walking up and down the street. A middle-aged couple, bickering good-naturedly. A mother smiling down at a child in a stroller. A man standing on the corner and sipping from a coffee, looking vaguely into space as if he'd forgotten what he was supposed to be doing. She breathed out, slow and long, and some of the tension seemed to dissipate.

'You really want to know? What it's like?'

'Yes.'

Pretty soon Kristina got an inkling of where they might be headed. The idea didn't make her feel comfortable, and she asked if that's where Lizzie was going. She spoke the question in a low tone, moving her lips as little as possible, sticking to the rules.

Lizzie didn't answer.

Kristina kept following – though she knew the girl's silence probably meant she was right – tucking behind and walking in Lizzie's wake. Nobody looked at the other girl as they cut through the Village, though a few glanced at Kristina, seeing a woman on a mission, striding out, looking neither left nor right – one of the extras that cities and towns are wallpapered with, shadows put on the streets by God to stop everywhere seeming empty.

Five minutes later Lizzie turned onto Greenwich Avenue and headed along the south side, straight toward the café where Kristina had met with Catherine several times and where she'd introduced her to John, for better or worse. For a ten-yard stretch there was no one close by and Kristina spoke at her normal volume.

'I don't know what you've got in mind, Lizzie, but can't you just tell me instead? I've spent a lot of time following you around.'

'Telling won't work. You have to walk this life yourself.'

Then they were level with the café. Lizzie glanced to the right. Kristina did the same, cringing, and saw Catherine at one of the tables inside with two women she'd never seen before.

She turned her head away quickly, her heart doing a double-thump, hoping to God Catherine hadn't seen her.

But she found herself slowing over her next stride, stealing another glance. The other women looked a lot like Catherine. Not physically – both had dark hair and their weights and heights were distributed along the spectrum of social norms for this time and place – but in every other way. They were well dressed and accessorized. Their hair had been recently cut and styled. They were armed with expensive purses and boutique iPhone cases. There was an ease about the angles at which they sat to one another, too – one leaning forward, the other back, the last turned slightly to the side – that made them look like a matching set.

And there was something about the way they laughed.

As Lizzie and Kristina passed, one of the trio evidently said something uproarious. You couldn't hear the cackling out on the sidewalk, but stripping it of sound merely made it more arresting. The nearest threw her head back. The other sniggered into her hand. Catherine started with a smile but upgraded to a reluctant oh-you-are-bad guffaw. They looked like equals in a warm, shared moment – or, Kristina found herself thinking, like . . . witches. Three hearty, well-groomed witches of the West Village, gathered together where it cost five bucks for a flat white and the dainty cakes and cookies had been fashioned from ingredients so tightly optimized that eating them made you *more* healthy.

When shall we three meet again? Tomorrow, dear sisters, or else the next day, whenever our busy, fulfilling lives allow. Let's synchronize smart-phones. Get something in the virtual diary. Let's write the next verse of this everlasting song, the Ballad of the Urban Supermom.

Then Kristina was past the café and it was as if a light had gone out, turning her and Lizzie back into two random women on a shadowy sidewalk with nowhere in particular to go on a cold fall morning.

Lizzie led Kris across the road before coming back along the other side. When she was opposite the café once again she stopped, taking Kristina by surprise. Lizzie was *never* stationary in public. Even when apparently standing in one spot, she constantly turned back and forth, taking a step backward or forward or to the side.

For this moment, however, she was absolutely still.

'What?'

'Wait,' Lizzie said.

'For *what*?'

'. . . this.'

At that moment, Catherine glanced up and looked directly at them.

Kristina froze.

She *so* did not want to be caught gawking across the street – even though she lived a twenty-minute walk away and could legitimately be taking a stroll through the Village. She could be heading for this very café. She lived in New York City too. It wasn't like she needed a membership card or qualified sponsor to gain access to coffee shops. And if she'd happened to see her book club pal Catherine inside, what could be more natural than to stop – maybe even wave, go in and say hi?

She felt horribly caught out nonetheless, and had no desire to wave, much less walk over and strike up a conversation with Catherine in front of those two other women. Those *better* women.

The women who were more real than she was.

Catherine meanwhile gazed out at the exact spot where they were standing – Kristina could have *sworn* she did, that she looked her right in the eyes – but her gaze floated past, as if she'd glanced up to check whether the sky held sign of rain and found it did not. She turned back to one of her companions and started nodding vigorously at whatever she was saying.

'See?' Lizzie said quietly.

'See what?'

'How do you feel?'

Kristina felt embarrassed, insubstantial. 'So what?' she snapped. 'She wasn't *looking*. She's got her mind on what's been said or how long it is until school's out or whatever. No big deal.'

'That's what you feel?'

'Yes. Because anything else would be dumb.'

'Right,' Lizzie said, as she turned to head up the street. 'Keep telling yourself that.'

'I don't want to do this,' Kristina said, several hours later. They were outside Catherine's daughters' school. In the meantime they'd walked. Just that. They had gone in no stores or cafés. As Lizzie pointed out, she had no money and no one would serve her anyway. So they walked, an endless communion with the streets. Sometimes Lizzie pointed other people out to Kristina, people on corners, lying in park bushes, standing outside restaurants watching the people inside – usually watching one person in particular, it seemed, like a obsessive fan club of one. She pointed also at a few rooftops, both low and high, where men and women were sometimes to be found perching, looking up at the sky or down at the streets or apparently at nothing at all. She pointed out someone dressed as a clown, riding by on the top of a bus. She pointed out a very large ginger cat wearing striped trousers, sitting in the middle of the street as traffic passed by on either side. They all looked lost and alone.

By the time they got to the school, it was five minutes before dismissal, and the tribe of mothers was swelling in the street. Kristina felt cold and tired and sad. 'Seriously. I don't feel comfortable being here.'

'That's up to you,' Lizzie said. She was under a tree, holding on to the trunk with one hand and slowly circling around. '*You* can do whatever you like.'

'If she spots us, she's going to call the cops.'

'Spots *you*, you mean.'

'Lizzie, let's go. Let's do something else.'

But Lizzie wouldn't leave, and Kristina stayed. She faded back up the street and stuck close to the railings in front of one of the houses, and kept her head down, but she stayed. She saw Catherine stride confidently into the street. Saw her stop to exchange words with other mothers, mostly fly-bys but one longer conversation, more serious, concluded with mutual smiles. Saw her put her hand on a few arms as she passed through the crowd and saw the owners of those arms turn and acknowledge her passing and her right to be there.

When Catherine got to the gates she was greeted by the teacher on duty, who chatted cheerfully before remembering something and reaching into a folder. She pulled out a piece of colored paper and stood close to Catherine to discuss it. Catherine turned her head to ask a considered question. What was the document about? Probably nothing so important. A concert, school trip, book drive. It was something *they* knew about, however, and you did not. You got that message all the way down the street. That piece of pale blue paper held a world in it, a universe you did not know and never would.

Lizzie still held the tree with one hand but had stopped circling. She was watching Catherine, her face expressionless, absorbing every little thing that happened, every inconsequential thing she did.

Ella and Isabella came running across the playground. As they were released back into the wild, the youngest, Isabella, threw herself up at Catherine without checking arms were in place to catch her – as you did, when you were confident your mother loved you and would always be there to halt your fall. Kristina's mother had not been that way. Kristina's mother was dead, and her daughter was broadly content with the arrangement. That didn't mean it wouldn't have been nice for things to have been otherwise.

Still Lizzie watched, silent.

Catherine strolled off up the road with a child holding each hand, turning her head to one side and then the other to listen to their updates and speculations and questions, a woman at the center of her world.

Kristina realized Lizzie was no longer beside her. She followed the girl as she walked up the street.

They eventually stopped at the grassy area beside the Hudson River, past where the Riverwalk ended. They leaned together against the railing, looking out over the water. Kristina had lost count of the times her phone had buzzed. More than four. John, texting to find out where the hell she was; texting again subsequently because he was smart and considerate enough to realize that if she hadn't responded the first time she was busy doing what-ever she was doing and wouldn't welcome a call. That was John. He thought things through, even if there came a point when he then decided to *stop* thinking and start acting instead. She could picture him, waiting for her somewhere, wanting to talk about what happened next, and maybe also whether they were going to head over to the restaurant later, given that they still had jobs.

Because Kristina *did* have a place in the world. For a few hours most nights she was a fixture in the firmament of strangers: the woman who made the alcohol happen and kept the banter flowing when a couple hours in the company of intoxicating liquors was all these men (and women) had to look forward to. Many were divorced or notoriously single. Others did apparently have a home to go to, but when someone's ordering another drink at ten thirty you wonder whether the place where they're not is really home, no matter how long and hard they work to keep paying the bills and regardless of who's there waiting for them. Kristina had more than once thought that she'd rather end up like Lydia than one of these banished ghosts, people with homes that were not a home.

In the end they went, however, and she did too, with John. Where is home? Where you're allowed without question, where your right to be is accepted. What must it be like to not have that? To have no direction home because home doesn't exist anywhere; to be like an electrical device with a plug that fits no socket in the entire world.

'What are you going to do?'

Lizzie's face was somewhere between thoughtful and confused. 'What do you mean?'

'I get it. I understand what you've been showing me. The question is what you're going to do about it.'

'There's nothing I *can* do.'

'Really?'

Kristina watched as the girl turned the question

over in her mind. She looked thinner this afternoon, less substantial. Just plain unhappy, perhaps.

'I used to think I was the lucky one,' Lizzie said. 'Compared to Maj. He had nothing. I could watch, at least. Though for a long, long time I stopped myself. When Catherine moved in with Mark I knew it was over between us. I kept away. But then a month or two ago . . . I fell off the wagon. I started following her again.'

'Are you jealous?'

'Of Maj?' Lizzie shook her head. 'I'm glad for him. Any good thing that happens is good for everyone. This isn't about him. It's about me. I'm just . . . I'm tired.'

'Of what?'

Lizzie raised her hands in a gesture that meant everything, and the absence of it. She was tired of lack, of making do in the hope of better tomorrows.

'Isn't there *anything* you can do?'

The girl laughed, the first bitter sound Kristina had heard her utter. 'Sure. I can go sit against the wall in old St Pat's or some unpopular park, or in one of the old tunnels where trains don't run anymore. They say it doesn't take long once you've decided to hollow out.'

Kris was shocked. 'Is that what you *want*?'

'No. I want a home.'

'Good. Because if I heard you were even *considering* something like that, I'd come kick your ass.'

Lizzie smiled. 'You can't kick imaginary ass.'

'You'd be surprised what I can do. That solution sucks. It's not happening. What's the alternative?'

Lizzie shrugged, but not in a way that said she didn't know the answer. She knew, all right.

'So do that instead,' Kristina said, knowing she was out on a limb and speaking of things she didn't understand well enough. Sometimes you do that, though. Sometimes that's what friends are for: to watch from the outside of your life, and listen, and say the thing you need to hear said.

Lizzie was still, so motionless that she looked like a painting. 'Really?'

'I think it's time for a reunion. Don't you?'

Lizzie went back to staring out over the water toward the unknown land and buildings on the other side.

Kristina left her to it, walking off down the street to rejoin life as she knew it.

She saw Lizzie only one more time.

CHAPTER 52

The first David knew about it was when he went into Roast Me. He got up at the usual hour. He made Dawn breakfast. He almost always did this, but that morning he especially wanted to get to the kitchen before her. In case he'd missed one of the blank sheets of paper. In case something else had happened there, something silent, while he lay unsleeping next to his wife. Just in case.

The kitchen was fine. Which meant everything else was fine, right? Right. Until something else happened, everything was fine.

You bet.

Dawn seemed chirpier than the night before and drove off to school in good humor. David went straight upstairs to the spare room. The contents of his boxes lay on the floor where he'd left them in the night. He decided he was done being bullied by inanimate objects and methodically destroyed the cardboard crates to force himself to do something about the items in them *right now*.

It took only half an hour, as he basically moved almost all of their contents into his study. So what had the fuss been about? Why had it taken him so long to do this?

Why was he not thinking about the paper in the kitchen the night before, and the open door?

He knew at least that he had not imagined or dreamed that incident, because the pile of paper was where he'd left it after gathering the pieces from the kitchen, on the lower shelf on the table in the front hallway. He wasn't sure whether it would have been better to have imagined an inexplicable incident so clearly that it felt real, or for it to have actually happened, and felt rising hysteria when he tried to make the choice.

In daylight it was easier to see that the sheets of paper didn't look like they'd been sold recently. They were dry and slightly yellowed. He knew why that was. That didn't help him understand them any better.

He took one of his childhood books back out of the bookcase where he'd just stacked it, a bookcase that would – six months from now – hold author copies of his own work. This morning that did not feel like anything to be proud of. The book he picked was *I Sing the Body Electric*. It was a paperback, and obviously well read. He didn't remember it, however. He knew it was his, could recall owning it, but it got cloudy after that.

He flicked through the pages, smelling old paper. Old paper in books, old paper in a pile. All he had was old paper and secondhand words.

Something caught his eye near the end of the

book. It was another piece of paper, folded over, wedged between the pages. He unfolded it.

Something was written in pencil, faint and scratchy. It wasn't David's handwriting, even as it had been back in his early teens. It wasn't in either of his parents' hands either. It looked like the work of someone struggling to manipulate a physical object.

David held it up and squinted. It said:

why am I called maj?

He dropped it in the trash and left the house thinking firmly about other things.

He could tell something was off from the moment he walked into the coffeehouse. Dylan was behind the counter, failing to cope. Nobody was tutting or giving him grief, however. Dylan was nineteen and, as Talia put it, 'dozy like a fucking mouse' – very much the barista B or C team, drafted in only when one of the main servers was sick. Regulars tended to feel able to give him a certain amount of good-natured ribbing in recompense for the guaranteed inaccuracy and scaldedness of the coffees they'd receive by his hand. This afternoon everyone in line seemed subdued, and silent.

As David got closer to the counter he noticed Dylan wasn't merely being slow. His hands were shaking. Sylvia, the owner, was back there too, turned from the room, on the phone.

'You okay?' David asked. He was reconciled to the idea that his coffee would be completely wrong.

Dylan looked at him. 'Shit,' he said, after a moment. 'You don't know?'

'Don't know what?'

'Talia's dead.'

'She's . . . *what*?'

'Yeah.' Dylan started nodding and swallowing compulsively. 'They found her a couple hours ago.'

'Where?'

'By the creek. The cops came by a while back to let us know – Sylvia called me in when Talia didn't show and wasn't answering her phone.'

'Well, did she fall, or . . .'

'I don't know, dude. That's all they told us.'

David pushed back from the counter, unable to process this information. He'd stood *right here* and blurted out his and Dawn's news to Talia only two days ago. How could she be . . . 'Jesus.'

'It's fucked up,' Dylan agreed.

David walked stiff-legged out of the coffeehouse. When he hit the cold outside he became aware his mouth was hanging open, and shut it. He should call Dawn – she'd known Talia longer, having been born and bred in Rockbridge – but he didn't know what he could say to her. The news would arrive at the school soon enough and probably she'd call him. He wasn't sure what he'd say then either. Quite apart from her having been a friend, he'd spent a lot of the last week buried in her novel. The idea that the mind that had created it was now gone doubled the effect. She'd taken a world with her.

'I want to talk to you,' someone said.

It was George Lofland. His face was red and he wasn't wearing a jacket, despite the chill.

'What abou—'

Then George was right in his face. His breath smelled of stale alcohol. He shoved a hand into David's chest, knocking him backward.

'Hey,' David said. 'What's the—'

'What's the *problem*? Have you heard about Talia?'

'Dylan just told me. But—'

'Someone killed her.' George had stopped trying to push David back down the sidewalk and was standing hands on hips. When he was in front of you like that you realized he was kind of a big guy.

'What? What makes you even *say* that?'

'I've just been up to her place,' he said. 'The cops are there. One of them is Bedloe's son. I've known him since he was a kid.'

'Are *they* saying somebody killed her?'

'No. But they didn't know her like I did. Talia was never going to kill herself, and even if she *did*, she'd have left instructions about her cats. And plenty of food. Which she did not. I just fed them myself.'

'But no one's *saying* she killed herself, are they? Surely it was an accident.'

'An accident she got herself dressed up for, in fancy clothes?'

David was uncomfortably aware that someone would be able to tell that a confrontation was going on from right across the street. 'What are you talking about?'

'The Bedloe kid told me how she was found. At the bottom of the creek, neck broken. Wearing a dress smarter than anything else they found in the trailer, something that didn't even fit. That make any sense to you?'

It didn't, but nothing about Talia's death had made sense. He could tell Lofland was one step from taking a swing at him, however, so he tried to speak calmly.

'So . . . what do you think happened?'

'I don't *know* what happened, David. What I *do* know is she called me on the phone yesterday afternoon, asking questions about that guy I picked up in my car. A guy who disappeared into thin air – just like the guy you were talking with in Kendricks.'

'I . . . was there by myself. I told you that.'

'I know that's what you *said*, but it was bullshit. I know I saw a guy sitting opposite you, and then he wasn't there. Talia kept me on the line for twenty minutes trying to get me to remember things about the guy I picked up. Now, why do you think she would do that?'

'I have no idea.'

'Me neither. Then that same night she gets dolled up and goes out to meet someone and . . .' He swallowed. 'And she doesn't come back.'

452

David tried to get these pieces to fit together and couldn't. 'I don't know what to tell you,' he said.

'I can see that. But I'll tell *you* this. If I find your 'friend' had anything to do with what happened to her, anything *at all*, I'm going to come find you. Understand?'

David realized that George meant what he said and that there lurked years of pent-up anger and frustration in the man that would help him carry the job through. Denying anything – everything – wasn't going to help.

He nodded. George stormed away.

David had no desire to go home. Home – the house he owned with Dawn, where they kept their stuff – did not feel like a place he needed to be. If anywhere, he felt he needed to go back to his hometown – something he'd never felt since leaving it years before. He didn't understand why. There was nothing for him there. No closure to be had. Nothing that could be said or done. No parents.

No friends.

He knew this was the reality of Talia's death sinking in. Where you live is not your world. What you own isn't either. The people you know . . . *that's* the world you live in, and that's why living a life is like building a house on an emotional fault line. Places persist, but every living thing is going to die.

Die, or leave you.

He recalled an acquaintance who went on a

contract to a country eight hours' time difference away; the guy said living that far out of sync with everyone he knew felt like being a ghost. Maybe that's all being a ghost *is* – finding yourself out of step with everything and everyone you knew. David had never been sociable (total loner geek – thanks, Dad), so the few people he cared about loomed large. Talia had been one, even though they'd never gone for a drink, eaten together, even visited each other's houses. Losing her was bad enough. That someone might think he was somehow *involved* or implicated . . . was terrible.

And how *could* he be? He thought back to the last conversation they'd had, outside Roast Me. She'd been talking very strangely, yes. He'd blown straight past the concern he should probably have felt for her state of mind because of the part where she reprised the story of George and the hitch-hiker. Was there something he'd missed, something he could have talked her down from, a difference he could have made?

He tried to remember. There'd been something about how people when they died might not actually have gone, or something . . . Christ.

She'd got it into her head that the guy George picked up on the forest road was a ghost.

Not just any ghost, either. Talia had believed in signs and portents. It was all over her novel – there was even a mawkish and credibility stretching moment where one of her key characters, the slim and plucky heroine, was given fresh strength to continue life's struggle after seeing a shooting star. Yes, this was fiction, but what people write reflects what they believe – fiction is where you go to tell or read the truth that people will stare or laugh at you for expressing in real life. She'd latched on to George's hitchhiker story right from the start, telling David about it the same day in the coffee shop. It had spoken to her, and maybe something *else* had then happened that had given her some bizarre cause to add two and two together to make seventy-five . . .

The person George picked up *must* have been Maj, as he'd already realized. But how did that explain what had happened? There was no evidence Maj was in town now, or had been last night. What motive would he have for hassling other people, never mind setting up a situation in which one of them might *die*?

Except . . . *someone* had been in David's house, hadn't they? That was evidence of *someone* being on his case in however inexplicable a manner, even if it wasn't Maj.

And if Maj or these others were unable to get anywhere with David, what might be the obvious next step?

Lean on his friends.

Isn't that what the crazy or vindictive *did* in these circumstances – bring pressure on their victim in any way they can, threatening him from the outside? Talia wasn't in a position to force David to do anything, though – and Maj had already

455

made contact with David. Why would he resort to doing things secondhand?

What if it hadn't been Maj, but *someone like him*?

It had been clear from the night in the city that Maj had friends, people who lived the same kind of life. Might he have sent some of them to try to lean on David? Or . . .

Maj also had enemies.

David remembered the people in Bid's. The unfriendly looking guy in the old-fashioned suit and the fucked-up thin people who'd been with him in the bar. He recalled that, as he'd hurried away from the church later, he'd thought he'd been followed for at least some of the way to the train station. By whom, he wasn't sure. He thought he'd lost them.

But what if he'd been followed all the way home?

When he got to the house he knew at once that someone had been inside again. The paper he'd stowed on the hall table had been thrown all over the hallway. He hurried around, picking them up. He knew where the paper had come from. He'd known last night. It was old stock from one of the boxes he'd unpacked in the study, one of the things he'd kept from the upstairs room in his parents' house, his father's much-discussed 'study.' Paper his father had never typed anything on. A secondhand blank slate.

He had to get rid of it. He gathered the sheets and went back out the door to the side of the house where the recycling was kept. The paper felt like it was symbolic of everything that needed purging from his life, and he lifted the lid of the container and raised his arm high, ready to hurl the paper into it.

There was something in there.

Something other than tin cans and cardboard and glass bottles that had held organic ice tea. He pulled it out, feeling the skin all over his scalp crawling. It was obvious what it was. He just didn't understand it.

It was a laptop. He turned it over in his hands. It was battered, cheap-looking. He'd never seen it before. So what the hell was it doing in his recycling?

He hurried back indoors. Once inside, he popped the catch on the laptop and opened it. After a pause the screen blinked into life. There was so much unfamiliarity there – smaller screen, Windows instead of Mac, someone else's lunatic idea of how to organize a desktop – that it took him a few moments to spot something he recognized. In the middle of the desktop (a fuzzy picture of a lot of cats) was a file called ALEGORIA II.

No no no . . .

Within a minute he'd confirmed it beyond doubt. This was Talia's laptop. He closed the machine and put it on the floor, so hard he probably came close to damaging it, but he had to get it out of his hands.

He felt like vomiting.

He had a dead woman's computer in his house. If he was right and someone *had* followed him home from the city, there could be no doubt that they were now systematically persecuting him.

Coming into the house.

Attacking his friends.

Even trying to implicate him in Talia's death. What else would be the point of putting the computer here?

It had to stop.

He had to deal with it.

He stared at the machine as if it could leap up and bite him – knowing that, for now, job number one was finding somewhere in the house to hide it – and it randomly struck him that he didn't have to finish reading Talia's book now. The idea felt bad. He felt he owed it to her to get to the end, out of respect. Nobody else ever would. He also wanted to know what happened. On that most basic of levels the book worked, and worked well.

As he carried the laptop upstairs another thought dropped into his mind.

Had anybody else seen Talia's book?

Anybody apart from him?

It was only when he straightened from stowing the laptop in his closet that he realized if he *was* right, and someone *was* attacking him through those closest to him, there was one obvious person they would target next.

CHAPTER 53

Lizzie went downtown first and left a message. After that she kept in movement, spiraling around the deed and building her concentration. If she was going to break her own rules it had to be worth it. She had to get it right.

With the girls it was hard to be specific and bringing something for the sake of it wouldn't work – so she dropped the idea. Catherine was hard too, but in different ways. She had so much already. It seemed hard to believe she could want for more. We do, though. Lizzie understood that. There's always something new to add to the pile. We want more stuff and the comfort that comes with it. We want to surround ourselves with a nest, a cocoon. It's one of the reasons we have friends, and there's nothing necessarily wrong with the arrangement . . . assuming you can *get* the stuff. If you can't then all you have is no stuff, and after a while the lack of things starts to suffocate you.

She avoided the parks. She might chance upon Maj in one and, though she really wanted to see him, she knew he'd realize something was up. It was too late for her to be dissuaded and she did not want to argue with him.

So she remained in perpetual movement, as throughout her life. Walking, walking, with nowhere to sit down at the end of it. She realized how tired her feet were. Not physically, but emotionally. Her legs were the idea of tired. That's all they really were if you got down to it, ideas and dreams, and while people poured so much time and energy into both they were also liable to drop them at a moment's notice. Most of the time it doesn't matter whether dreams come to fruition. It only matters whether they cheer you up. Except, perhaps, to the dreams themselves, who might yearn to come true, to become more than a comforting pattern of thought that eventually lapses into an emotional line of least resistance.

That's why change sometimes had to come to those who weren't looking for it – who'd done everything they could to *avoid* it. They could squat there in their great big warm houses with their big warm lives, ignoring everything outside their window. You could do that if you had enough stuff inside with you, if you *had* an inside to start off with. That didn't mean the situation couldn't change. Lizzie had tried hard not to need, very hard, but after so many years it still hadn't worked. If Kristina could take Lizzie seriously and seem to want to be her friend, what was to say others could not?

Was there any law that said dreams could not dream too?

Lizzie felt dumb and childish for having followed and watched and been a good girl. For accepting her lot. The time for being dumb and childish was over.

It ended this afternoon.

It ended now.

She was close to settling on Bloomingdale's when she had a better idea. She hurried back down Fifth Avenue. Going to Bloomingdale's would have felt too much like the bad old days. Instead she'd try the street where she'd followed Kristina the first time they'd spoken to each other. That felt appropriate. It was following the signs, and Lizzie was a believer in story-maker events. Why else would she have met Kristina – and come to believe in the possibility of a real friendship there – if not for the idea of today to come into her mind? You put thoughts out into the universe and God gives them form and sets them down. So Father Jeffers said, and on that he might even be right.

She walked along 47th, peering in windows. Within a few minutes she'd found a store that looked like a possibility. It had interesting things in the window and was a little larger than most of the others, which would make it easier too. She picked her moment, moving in a meandering figure eight over a forty-yard radius, waiting until she'd seen a few people enter the store – a couple

461

of men who looked like dealers, a handful of civilians too.

Then she slipped inside.

The interior was lined on three sides by display units filled with tray cases, turned into a U shape by a central island, within which a fat-faced man in an expensive suit prowled. The walls were mirrored to help ricochet light around the space and make the diamonds and other precious stones sparkle, but that was all to the good. Lots of reflections made it harder for people to see, confusing their sense of space.

At the back of the store the two men in homburgs were involved in a voluble price negotiation with another employee, who was listening with the stoic expression of someone who'd been down this road many times and generally ended up receiving a price very close to what he'd originally had in mind. Lizzie drifted past and saw the two men were buying rings in quantity – plain, functional things that would not suit her purpose.

She paused by a pair of German tourists (gawking at thick gold bracelets, also wholly inappropriate), before glancing over the shoulders of a group at the central island: three whip-thin English women giving serious consideration to a tray that Lizzie could immediately tell was far more interesting. It held five pieces of silver jewelry in arts-and-crafts style, each given plenty of space on a cushion to showcase their individuality – and to broadcast the message that they weren't going to be cheap. They looked good. They looked right.

One of them in particular, the brooch in the middle, would be *perfect*.

The fat-faced man was being attentive, having judged the ladies weren't just killing time but could have their interest parleyed up into acquisition. He unlocked the unit and brought the tray up onto the counter.

The women bent at the waist to inspect the treasures a little closer. Lizzie felt her insides start to churn.

It felt like being a teenager again, and not in a good way. It felt dirty.

She kept moving around the U shape. She knew that when she got to the other side she should keep walking, go back out into the world and forget the idea. But she knew also that you go to your god or goddess with offerings, and that she'd been locked on this course from the moment she'd seen Billy's Bloom, and probably before. He wasn't the first she'd seen burn out, but for some reason it had hit her much, much harder.

If she walked out now, what came next? Would her heart heal for the hundredth time, or would it be forever suspended in a moment of blackness?

She ground to a halt, feeling out of practice and drained of hope, fully lost.

One of the men in homburgs turned around.

His colleague was still haggling vigorously, but this man had become distracted, as if he'd smelled something unexpected. He peered peevishly around the store, face creasing into a frown.

Lizzie realized she had to be quick. Sometimes people felt something. You could never predict who, and once they'd done so the atmosphere would change and it would be harder.

The need for speed made the decision for her. She waited until the man had turned back to re-engage with the negotiations, and then she coughed.

Two of the English women glanced up – distractedly, minds still on the goodies on the counter. Their eyes skated across the apparently empty space behind them, unable to see Lizzie, and then returned to the matter at hand – the display cushion.

Lizzie moved decisively toward the window. This was constructed of a pair of sliding panels of glass on runners, locked in the middle, protecting the goods in the window from people inside the store.

She placed her hands on the left pane of glass, widely spread apart. The head is the hardest part of your body. It's where all the thinking is. That makes it tough. Fragile, too, of course, the place where all the real and lasting pain is born, and stays – but hard enough for her purposes in the physical world.

Lizzie summoned all her concentration, and smashed her forehead into the glass.

It wasn't anything like the impact Maj or another Fingerman could have achieved, but it was enough.

The glass cracked loudly, splintering diagonally across the large pane.

Everyone in the store heard it. The Germans took a defensive step backward. Two of the English ladies did the same, pulling the third – who was still obliviously inspecting jewelry – with them.

The store owner started bellowing in a foreign language, gesturing at the underling in back to come and do something about the situation. He came hurrying, leaving the men in homburgs wide-eyed.

The top half of the window slowly tilted forward, then fell to the ground with a tremendous splintering crash. There was screaming and running.

Lizzie swept past the velvet cushion with her hand out, weaved through the chaos, and ran from the store.

When she got back onto Fifth Avenue she slowed, however, knowing she had to go back. This was a betrayal of everything she'd come to believe, turning the clock back too far and too hard and in a way that could only lead to bad things.

But without it . . .

As she hesitated, she saw a couple coming up the street. Mid-twenties, hand in hand, the man wearing a baby papoose. The child inside it could only be weeks old. The couple looked exhausted but so happy, adrift on the bleary seas of early parenthood, adapting to the changes inaugurated by this new phase in their lives.

Lizzie felt her heart stiffen. She'd been born – as they all had – before their friends had any conception of the process of conception. They were a sterile race. Just one more thing that none of them would ever have.

Unaware that she'd come to a standstill – and that a man in his early thirties and a girl of six had caught split-second glimpses of her, this tall woman wearing a red velvet dress under a black coat, and that trying to discuss the Ghost Lady of Fifth Avenue would earn the child a telling off for making up stories and bring the man a step closer to finally being diagnosed schizophrenic – Lizzie decided the time for sinning had come. It's how we broke out of the cozy prison of the Garden of Eden, after all. Father Jeffers wouldn't approve, but then he didn't really understand anything except dead composers, and death is too safe a haven for those who want to live.

Lizzie clasped the brooch tightly in her hand, where passersby would hopefully not see it, and started to walk quickly down the street. She felt bad. She felt scared. She felt excited.

It was time to go home.

CHAPTER 54

When Kristina finally answered her phone I told her to meet me at the apartment but didn't go into detail. It took her a long time to get home and I decided in the meantime to get out of the place and wait on the street. With Reinhart at large, I realized it wouldn't be smart to hang around right outside and so I went forty yards up the sidewalk and sat in a shadowed doorway for nearly three hours and smoked and drank a series of coffees from the deli and watched leaves wandering along the street and didn't try too hard to get everything to line up in my mind. My body and head still hurt, but it was settling into a set of sturdy aches now, rather than urgent yelps. My brain felt clear. I wanted it to stay that way because it was evident my life was changing for good today. You seldom get warnings so obvious, and I figured I'd better be ready for what came next with an open mind.

Kristina eventually came wandering down the street. I whistled and she spotted me in the doorway and came over.

She looked down at me in silence, then held out

her hand. I passed her a cigarette. Kristina smokes only about once a month, and it's always a portent of storm clouds.

'So what happened with you and Lizzie?'

She sat on the step next to me and took a light. 'How do you know something happened?'

'The way you look, plus the fact that you've been gone a very long time and wouldn't answer the phone. This isn't a time for holding back, Kris.'

'I know.'

'So what happened?'

'She showed me some things.'

'What kind of things?'

She shrugged. 'What her life is like. What *all* their lives are like.'

'Who *are* these people?'

'Lizzie's adamant she's not dead. I believe her. I don't get why ghosts would attach to other people the way she is with Catherine. It doesn't make sense.'

'Make *sense*? You realize we're sitting discussing whether someone we've both spoken to is dead? So, what – are we back to them being imaginary friends?'

'I don't know, John. That's what Lizzie told me. I don't see why she'd lie.'

'Did you ever have one? When you were a kid?'

'An imaginary friend? No. At least not that I remember.'

'Me neither,' I said. 'But . . . I guess that's their whole point.'

'What happened back at the church, with Billy?'

Now it was my turn to shrug. 'I have no idea.'

'Didn't you see?'

'I saw. I just don't know *what* I saw, in that I have no way of explaining or understanding it.'

I described what had happened, up to the point where coffee and bits of Danish started falling through Billy's body and splatting on the floor. After I'd left the church I'd stood on the street for a few moments. The guy/ghost/friend/whatever called Maj walked away without saying another word. His head was down. He looked like a person who had a mission in mind.

Kris listened and was silent for a while. 'There's only two options here, John. Either we're screwed up in the head or this stuff is real – whatever the explanation is. Sitting with cold sun shining down on us, the first option seems more credible, maybe, but it's not. You know that. If it were *just* me, or just *you*, that'd be one thing. But we've both seen these people, spoken to them.'

'How did the conversation with Lizzie end?'

Kris looked uncomfortable. 'She's unhappy.'

'About what?'

'Everything. She has a friend. Had one, anyway. That relationship is more important to her than anything else in the world – even more than the one with Maj. Maj managed to make contact with his friend. They've spoken, even hung out for a few hours. Lizzie's glad for him, but it's brought home how unhappy she is about her own life.'

'So?'

'What?'

'So what did you tell her?'

'That maybe she needed to do something about it.'

'Kristina, I don't think we want to start interfering in these people's lives.'

'I wasn't interfering.'

'Okay, bad word. I meant, we understand nowhere near enough about their world to offer advice.'

'She's my friend, John.'

'Friend? How many times have you even met her?'

'What difference does *that* make?'

'Friend's a big word, Kris.'

'It's big because it's a tiny step and the tiny steps are the hardest to understand. The first time you came into the bar in Black Ridge I knew we could be friends – whatever else might happen. Didn't you?'

I thought about it. 'Yes.'

'That's not shared time. That's not interests in common or dating agency profiling. That's something that passes through the air in an instant, that comes out of people's minds and is real and you have to say yes to.'

'I see where you're going, but I don't think it's enough to explain Lizzie, or Maj.'

'I'm not trying to explain them,' she said, stubbing out her cigarette. 'I don't have to. We've had

470

conversations with these people. They exist. We're out the other side of having to explain how or why. The question is what we *do*. That's what I've been trying to work out. I left Lizzie hours ago and I still don't have an answer. I've been alternating between thinking I'm crazy and knowing I'm not. It doesn't make much difference. I still don't know what to do.'

She was right. The problem of how something works is of little importance outside laboratories. The question is what happens next.

'I still think it's a mistake to get between Lizzie and Catherine,' I said. 'Other people's relationships are written in a different language, especially when they're broken.'

'You're right,' she said reluctantly. 'Next time I see her I'll back off on the idea.'

'Okay,' I said. 'Well, the next thing—'

I was interrupted by someone cheerfully shouting my name, and started – suddenly realizing how wrapped up I'd been and that Reinhart could have come strolling up and shot me in the head before I'd known what was happening. Thankfully, it was only Lydia heading down the road.

'Hey, Lyds,' I said, standing painfully and trying not to sound tense. 'How are you?'

'Well, you know,' she said thoughtfully, 'I've been better. But, matter of fact, I've been worse.'

She looked okay. Certainly better than she had when I'd seen her the night before. 'That's good.'

'*You* look like shit, though.'

471

'Thanks,' I said, as she leaned forward to peer at my face. 'I had a disagreement with someone.'

'They kicked your ass, by the look of it.'

'It may not be over yet.'

'Wasn't Krissie here, was it?'

'No.'

She cackled merrily for a moment. 'I talked to him,' she said, for a moment making me think she'd somehow run in to Reinhart. 'Thanks for that.'

'Frankie? He's back?'

'No. Don't know where that asshole's got to, and today I don't care. Fuck him. I mean, I went and talked to the other guy. This morning. That priest.'

Kristina was looking question marks at me. 'I gave Lyds his address last night,' I muttered. 'This was before I knew Jeffers believed in ghosts.'

Lydia laughed, completely normally, a sound I'd never heard from her before. 'He really does, doesn't he? Good listener, though. I went around thinking I didn't know why I was wasting my time, but I'd been feeling so shitty in my soul lately maybe it was time to try anything. Next thing I know I'm telling him about Frankie and all *manner* of crap, and he's kind of like you are about it. He listens. He heard me out and went with it, and I only had to explain to him about three times that Frankie ain't dead. Didn't ask me to pray with him or nothing either. Gave me a pastry, too.'

'That's great,' Kristina said thoughtfully. I could see her trying to make something of this, to work out whether Lyds maybe wasn't crazy after all, and if for all these years she'd been trying to make contact with something that actually existed; if perhaps this was a case of a real person trying to reconnect with a friend, one who'd decided he didn't want to play ball.

'Jeffers seems like a good guy,' I said, to forestall this. I felt Lydia's world was complicated enough and that if an hour of being taken seriously had made a difference then there was no need to get it tangled up with other stuff.

Lyds sniffed, losing interest, and wandered off down the street. 'You put that ugly mug of yours indoors,' she yelled back as a parting shot. 'You're going to scare people looking like that.'

'You need to come upstairs now,' I told Kristina, when Lydia had finally turned the corner. Kris was about to crack wise, but then she saw the expression on my face.

She stood in the middle of the room, not saying anything. I think she'd started to guess what was up from the way I double-locked the street door, but there's no substitute for seeing something in the flesh.

The apartment had been destroyed. Not just turned over, not merely vandalized. They – or he – had been extremely thorough. Every drawer had been turned out and its contents broken or torn. Every plate, bowl, and piece of glassware had been smashed. The fridge had been opened and pulled over onto its front, turning the floor into a sea of liquids. Everything from the cupboards had been broken, thrown around. Every lightbulb in the apartment was smashed, along with the mirror in the bathroom and the two wooden chairs we'd bought for good money at a nice store in SoHo in the first flush of living in the city. Cards we'd written to each other, along with a few pieces of cheap art we'd picked up in local thrift stores, had been set fire to. The ashes from these had been thrown onto a pile of Kristina's clothes and the sheets from our bed in the middle of the living room.

It had been meticulous. I'd had plenty of time to go through it in the hours while Kristina wasn't answering her phone, and yet coming back into the apartment after a couple of hours was a shock. The apartment as it had been yesterday was still alive in my mind. It takes a while for your mind to understand something's gone.

Eventually Kris looked at me. Her eyes were dry, but she was blinking rapidly. 'Other rooms the same?'

'Yes.'

'Guess we did right not coming home last night, huh?'

'Guess so,' I said. 'And I don't think we should stay here now. He's going to come back. He only did this because he couldn't do it to me.'

'Jesus.'

'FYI, he didn't tear or burn *everything*, unfortunately. I can't find your diary or that notebook you insist on keeping stuff in. Like your passwords and ATM numbers. And your credit card.'

'He's a psycho, isn't he.' This was a statement, not a question. 'I mean, a real one.'

'Yes. An angry man just trashes the place. This is dismantlement. He went back and forth, breaking everything that could be broken, and then he went back through it and broke it some more. I don't want to think what the equivalent would be when committed upon a person. I especially do not want it to happen to us. So let's go.'

'Where?'

'I don't know. Not back to Jeffers. He's in deep enough already, and I don't think him being a priest will stay Reinhart's hand.'

'Well then, where?' Kristina said, her voice rising. The reality of what surrounded her was beginning to sink in. There were spots of high color on her cheeks. 'Where else can we *go*, John? Are we going to be fucking *street people* now? Should we chase after Lydia and see if she knows some good parks to sleep in?'

'The first thing we should do is leave, Kris. Seriously. Let's talk about this outside.'

'Outside? Oh – you mean *where we live*, right?'

I put my arms around her. 'We'll find somewhere for tonight. We can sleep in the bar if we have to – Mario's got some serious locks on that place. After that . . .'

I trailed off, not knowing what would happen after that. I'd even wondered if it was excessively insane to consider talking to Lizzie or Maj or one of these other people. They evidently had places to roost at night. Maybe there'd be room for us, maybe not.

Kristina didn't say anything. She was looking past my shoulder, and I figured she'd noticed something else that was broken or missing or was maybe trying to see past all the chaos entirely.

'What times were you in here? From when until when?'

'Don't know,' I said. 'I got here around ten. Why?'

'Then what? When did you go outside? Right after we spoke on the phone?'

'Yeah, pretty much. I was certainly down there a few hours. Why?'

She disengaged from me and pointed. I turned and looked at the window. There was writing on it, scrawled in the dust and rain dirt on the other side.

'Was that there when you were here?'

'No,' I said, going closer. 'I remember being amazed he hadn't broken the window too. There was nothing on it then.'

We angled our heads to catch the light against the dirt. It was easier to read than the first time, as if whoever had left this had tried a lot harder, pouring all their concentration into it.

It said:

GOING TO TALK TO MY FRIEND
THANK YOU :-)
LXXx

'Oh no,' Kristina said. She ran out the door.

CHAPTER 55

Catherine turned from unlocking the front door to find Ella and Isabella weren't waiting on the steps behind her as she'd assumed, but were still down on the sidewalk. More than that, they were arguing. This had been brewing from the moment she'd picked them up from school. Usually the girls got along as well as you could expect of life-long competitors for parental attention and resources, but once in a while something (or someone) snapped. It was almost always Isabella. She had stronger opinions than Ella on just about everything, and no compunction about taking incisive action to ensure they were widely understood. Ella took life as it came. Isabella regarded the world as a work in progress and herself as a one-person focus group of infinite power. In that, Catherine privately believed, she took after her mother.

'Hey, hey, *hey*,' she said, as Isa abruptly escalated to shock and awe mode and punched her elder sister in the chest. 'Isa – *stop* that!'

The girls turned as one and launched into high-pitched mutual denunciations. Catherine hurried down the steps to sort it out, leaving the door open behind her.

An hour later, homework was done. Pretty much. Isabella had been flogged through memorizing her six spelling words of the week and writing extremely short sentences showcasing them. Ella had done enough work on her project on Chad to feel honor had been served. Catherine was at a loss to understand why her daughter had to do a project on Chad – nobody's idea of an A- or even C-list country – but that wasn't the point, and hers had been the easier ride. Ella, though less sharp, accepted homework as another aspect of the world in the face of which she was essentially powerless. Isa resisted enforced learning with passion, imagination, and a capacity for self-distraction that bordered on genius. Catherine had largely managed to ignore the fact that this was an hour of her life she was never going to get back, for which one daughter's newfound ability to spell 'beach' and the other's shadowy understanding of the whereabouts of N'Djamena, Chad's capital (and home of its only cinema, apparently), might never seem sufficient recompense.

There was more to be done, but she sensed none of the team were in the right place for it. Ella appeared listless, Isa closer to the edge than usual. When Catherine ran out of steam as works foreman at the homework mines, both children looked at her with tired and grumpy faces.

'That's enough for today,' she said. 'Go on, shoo.'

'Can we watch television?'

Catherine opened her mouth to say no, of course not, then realized she was feeling pretty listless herself and screw the developmental implications. This was precisely what television had been invented for – or would have been, if women had been allowed to do the inventing back then. 'Okay,' she said. 'For a little while.'

'Can we have a cookie?'

'I'll see what I can find.'

'Yay!'

Much cheered, the girls ran out of the kitchen and into the family room. Feeling the wash of relief that comes from completing some trivially arduous but potentially volatile session of child-wrangling, Catherine started to gather up the books and papers strewn over the table – but then decided the smarter tactician would get the girls settled with a snack first. As she turned toward the cupboard, her gaze skated across the antique mirror propped up over the mantelpiece.

She frowned and looked back. For a moment it had looked like there was a shadow in the corner, the kind of thing a passing figure might cast on the white walls. A cloud passing outside the window, presumably.

Luckily it turned out there were two oatmeal cookies left. She took these and two glasses of apple juice through to the other room.

★   ★   ★

When she came back into the kitchen, something felt different. She looked around. Everything was as it should be. A quiet, airy kitchen, the sound of wholesome entertainment from the other room. Catherine had a little time, too – Mark was heading straight from work to a business dinner (again). Except for getting the kids bathed and into bed and read to and asleep, the evening was her own, and amen to that. People drain you – of time, energy, even the will to live sometimes. Being able to ride the rails by yourself for once is a good way to recharge. Catherine thought a cup of Earl Grey tea might be a nice way to start, and reached for the kettle.

She noticed the table and stopped. She put the kettle down.

There was a clamor from the next room, distracting her. She quickly walked through the door to find the girls pointing at the television set.

Catherine saw a blank screen. 'Yes, so?'

'It stopped.'

'Well, was it the end?'

'No,' Isa said firmly. 'It was *not* finished yet.'

'So press PLAY again. It's probably just a glitch.'

Emma got the remote from the end of the sofa, held it out like she was afraid it was going to explode in her face, and pressed the button. Nothing happened.

Isa asked: 'What's a glitch?'

Catherine took the remote. 'When the world does something odd.' She stabbed at the PLAY,

STOP and PAUSE buttons. 'Well, maybe you've watched enough already.'

'No! It's only been on for a second!'

'Well there's something wrong with it and Daddy's not here so—'

The DVD suddenly came on again, in mid-scene. The sound was *way* too loud, grotesquely so. Ella let out a squeal of surprise. Isa cackled in strange glee.

Catherine hurriedly wrestled the volume back to a sane level. 'Did you mess with the remote? I've *told* you about doing that.'

Both girls denied it immediately and in unison. In the face of potential punishment, they deserted the ship of sisterhood faster than the eye could blink, ratting the other out immediately. Taking the same side was a reliable indicator of joint innocence.

'Well, just don't touch it, okay?'

She'd lost them already. Both were munching their cookies, staring at the cartoon. Catherine put the remote out of reach and went back into the kitchen, where she stood and looked at the table.

When she'd stopped to sort out cookies and juice, the table had held two exercise books, seventeen pencils in a rainbow of colors, printouts from Wikipedia, a sharpener, and two erasers. They'd been spread across the artfully distressed Restoration Hardware table with the randomness only children can cause.

Now everything was down at one end.

The papers were in a pile, the exercise books on top. The pencils were lined up next to one another, perfectly aligned at the unsharpened end.

She hadn't done that. She was sure of it.

She noticed what wasn't on the table – a mess – before noticing what *was* there. Something was lying in the middle of the table. A small object, metallic, but not shiny. What the hell was it?

She took cautious steps forward. Was it a *brooch*? Unconsciously her hand reached up to her chest before she remembered that she hadn't put on anything that morning. So it couldn't have fallen off.

Was it even hers? She looked more closely. The piece was two inches wide and one inch tall, a muted pewter. The detailing had the sinuous lines you'd associate with early Tiffany, or Liberty, and with Archibald Knox in particular. It was the kind of thing that, had she seen it in a store, she'd have bought in a flash.

But she didn't recognize it.

An upcoming gift from Mark – stashed in a drawer, found by the girls and played with before being dumped here? They'd been through her jewelry any number of times in the past, despite stern warnings, and one pair of earrings had disappeared never to be seen again.

But this hadn't been on the table when they'd gone into the living room, and neither of the girls had been back in the kitchen since. They wouldn't have tidied the table up, either.

She picked up the brooch. It was heavy. And beautiful. But it shouldn't be here, and the cool weight of it in her hand reminded her of something. Of feelings of guilt and pleasure, inextricably mingled. Of needs and desires that felt personal, rather than domestic, a long time ago. Of being younger.

'I hope you like it,' said a voice.

Catherine whirled around.

There was no one there.

She backed away. She realized the brooch was still in her hand and dropped it on the table. Threw it almost. Part of her had been hoping it was some kind of illusion or daydream. It wasn't. Imaginary brooches do not go *thunk*.

There was no one in the kitchen. She could see that. The only other place the voice could have come from was the DVD the kids were watching. The voices on the soundtrack were high-pitched, squeaky. The voice she thought she'd heard was different. Female. Adult.

Familiar?

She went to the hallway and stuck her head out. No one there, of course.

She leaned over to the staircase and peered up and down, seeing nothing but dust-free floorboards, white walls, black-and-white photos, and restrained art.

She turned back to the kitchen but decided now that she was out here she may as well make a proper fool of herself. She trotted upstairs and checked the bedrooms and bathrooms, then back down past the kitchen and into the formal sitting room, before going right down to the lower hallway, which was empty too.

The front door was shut. Catherine stood by it, relieved and yet not relieved. The house was empty. Just her and the girls. She'd demonstrated it.

That should be a good thing. So why had proving it made her feel worse?

She looked around the hallway, realizing how much of being at home was an unspoken contract with the building. It's yours, and you belong to it. There was a bond there, surely. Or maybe not. Maybe it was just a structure that a dead person had built out of insensate materials as cheaply as possible. Maybe it didn't care about you at all, and could be accommodating to the passage of others.

Christ, she thought. *What* others? There were no others. She'd just *proved* it.

She breathed out heavily. Gathered herself.

And that's when the girls began to scream.

CHAPTER 56

They were huddled tightly together at the end of the sofa in the living room, eyes wide, utterly silent.

Ella leapt up and ran to her mother as soon as she came in the room, nearly knocking her off her feet. The television was showing an innocuous scene from the DVD. There was no sound, however.

'What?' Catherine said. 'What's wrong?'

She was freaked out, and spoke too sharply. Ella started crying, clinging to her, burying her face in her stomach. 'Ella,' she said. 'Calm down. What—'

Then the television went off.

The screen went black. Catherine heard the sound of the button being depressed. Not the button on the remote – the actual plastic button on the unit itself.

Isa was motionless on the sofa. She looked very scared but also curious. 'There's a lady,' she said.

Catherine stared at her. 'What?'

Isa lifted her arm and pointed to an area near the television set. There was nothing there.

'Isa – what are you *talking* about?'

'A pretty lady.'

'There's no one there, Isa. Stop making up stories.'

Isa started to move her arm. She held it up at the same height, moving it slowly to the left as if following something changing position from beside the television to the far end of the room, near the fireplace.

The back of Catherine's neck felt very cold. 'Isa . . . what are you pointing at?'

'For heaven's sake,' said a voice. 'Can't you see me *at all*?'

It was the voice Catherine had heard in the kitchen. It sounded now as though the speaker was trying to remain cheerful in the face of high odds.

Catherine grabbed the TV remote and stabbed at the off button and the volume button. Nothing happened.

'It's not the television, Cathy. She's pointing at *me*. Why can't you see?'

Ella started to wail, a hitching cry. Isa remained silent, staring avidly at the end of the room, her head moving from left to right, as if watching something. Something large, too – her head was tilted backward – and perhaps something that was pacing up and down. Catherine couldn't see anything at all.

'Catherine.'

And then . . . she could. Down at the far end of the room, in front of the bookcase. A shadow, like the one she thought she'd seen in the kitchen.

She took a step back, pulling Ella with her. 'Isa – come here.'

'Who is it, Mama?' Isa didn't move. 'Who is the lady?'

Then finally Catherine saw her, standing in front of the fireplace.

A tall woman, wearing a red velvet full-length dress under a long black coat. Her face was bone pale. Red lips and dark eyes, thick hair gathered up, like . . .

'How did you get in here?'

'It's *me*, Catherine.'

The woman disappeared again, as though a shutter had come down between them, or as if she was there only when Catherine blinked, painted on the inside of her eyelids.

'What the hell is happening?'

'Who's the lady, Mama?' Isa asked. She could evidently still see the woman. 'Why is she so mad at you?'

'Mommy knows,' said the voice.

'Who the hell *are* you?'

'Come on, Catherine. It's *Lizzie*.'

Catherine's stomach rolled over. All the blood felt like it dropped out of her head, as if she'd been sucked down a snake to being five years old, as if everything she'd ever done had been found out.

Lizzie.

Oh holy God.

'Get . . . get out of my house,' Catherine said,

trying to keep her voice steady, turning blindly toward the spot the voice had come from.

Suddenly the woman was visible again, stronger and more concrete this time.

Lizzie took a step toward her, hands held out, and finally Isa lost it and started screaming too.

'It's okay,' Lizzie said to the children, trying to smile in a reassuring way. 'I'm not going to hurt you.'

Catherine screamed at her. '*Get out.*'

'But . . . I brought you something.'

'What are you *talking* about?'

'The brooch. You like it, don't you?'

'That was *you*?'

'Of course.'

'Take it back. Take it and *get out of my house.*'

'But . . . that's what you always wanted,' Lizzie said, confused. 'I thought . . . I thought you stopped seeing me because I stopped doing what you wanted.'

'I didn't want you to steal.'

'Yes . . . you *did*. You asked me to. You *told* me to. In school you wanted me to do other stuff, like the Kelly thing, but when we came to the city that's all you ever *talked* about. Things you wanted me to *get* for you.'

Catherine was clutched by a vertiginous twist of guilt, so strong it felt like nausea.

She hadn't thought of Kelly Marshall in twenty years, but all it took was hearing the name to take her back to the afternoon when she'd seen the girl

488

who'd been her best friend, talking in class with a boy Catherine had decided she might fall in love with. She didn't want to be taken back there, didn't want to remember how Kelly had lost that boy (to Catherine) after she'd been accused of stealing from other girls, or how she'd wound up losing weight and getting thinner and thinner until she was a full-blown anorexic who got taken out of the school by her parents, never to be seen again.

'Get out of here,' she said as firmly as she could, not liking the cracking sound in her voice.

'This was a mistake, wasn't it?' Lizzie said forlornly. 'I should have been happy with what we'd had. Or what I thought we'd had.'

'You're not real,' Catherine shouted. 'You've *never* been real.'

'I was real from the moment you first saw me,' Lizzie shouted, clenching her fists. 'I *am* real, and *I was your friend*. I've stayed your friend, keeping an eye, keeping you safe when you walk home at night. I never forgot you. You forgot *me*. You *threw me away*.'

'You can't throw away something that doesn't exist.'

'I *do* exist.'

'You don't. You're *nothing*.'

'No – I *have* nothing. While you've got *everything*. The house, husband, the daughters. That's you and that's *always* been you. Pretty Cathy's got to have whatever she wants, even if she has to make her friend steal it for her.'

Catherine was trying to retreat, drawing the girls with her. Ella seemed to be slipping into a catatonic state, eyes wide, chest rising and falling in silent sobs. Isa was staring at the pretty lady who kept disappearing and coming back, who was saying all these interesting things and advancing toward them.

'*That's* what your lovely mama is like underneath, girls. A thief and a liar and a cheat – and not even brave enough to do it on her own.'

Catherine abruptly pushed the kids to one side and swung her hand toward the woman in front of her.

Isa saw the pretty lady's hand whip up and grab her mother's wrist, however, far too fast. Lizzie held on to it with all her might, moving her face closer and closer to Catherine's.

'Remember me,' she said. '*Remember how much you loved me.*'

'I never loved you.'

'Yes, you did. You *did*.'

Catherine shoved her own face forward until they were nose to nose. 'You were *nothing* to me. Ever. You were just me talking to myself, the make-believe of a little girl who didn't have a *real* friend when she needed one and made up a pathetic excuse for one instead.'

'You *needed* me.'

'No. You were just a game.'

'You made me do things.'

'And how pathetic is *that*? You were just the bits

of me I didn't want festering in my own head. You followed me here to the city and wouldn't let go, *long* after you should have been forgotten. *You* kept stealing on your own because that's *all you knew how to do.*'

Lizzie tried to grip Catherine's wrist harder, tried to hurt her, tried to grind the bones together until they broke – but she couldn't get enough purchase.

Meanwhile the children screamed and cried.

'If you didn't get the message back then,' Catherine said, 'then get it now. I *don't* remember you, I *don't* want you, and I have to look after my children now – something you'll never have. Why? Oh yeah, that's right – *because you're not real.*'

Catherine shoved out, but the other woman didn't let go and so she found herself off balance. Lizzie discovered she did have further strength of purpose after all, a strength that came out of a mist of outraged hurt and black fury.

She lashed her arm, throwing Catherine sideways to smack into the wall next to the television. Catherine crumpled to the ground.

'Oh, I'll go,' Lizzie said. 'And I know just the way to make that happen. You ever hear of the Bloom, Cathy? It involves you, I'm afraid. And involves you *giving*, for once. Giving your perfect life.'

She started toward Catherine, who was dazedly trying to push herself upright against the wall. She saw a very heavy glass vase on the bookcase above Catherine's head. She knew she had the will left to knock it over, and gravity would do the rest, gravity and time, bringing an end to this prison.

Catherine looked up and saw what Lizzie had seen.

'Mama,' Isa said.

Ella was screaming, off in another world. But Isa had stopped and was crawling toward her mother.

Lizzie hesitated, seeing the girl reach her hand out toward Catherine, toward her mother, the shining star at the center of her world. She saw Catherine, who knew Lizzie was coming for her and what might happen if she got to her, decide that it was more important that she reach back and take her daughter's hand.

Lizzie realized that *this* was love, not what she'd thought she'd had from Catherine all the long years ago.

Catherine was right. Lizzie had never been loved.

She'd never been anything at all.

CHAPTER 57

It began to rain and traffic was crazy all the way through the Village and within minutes of getting in a cab I wished we'd stuck to going on foot. Kristina got on the driver's case about taking some other route, but I knew it wouldn't make any difference and tried to ease her back into the seat. She fought me hard but eventually saw the guy just wasn't paying attention anyway. As soon as we started making headway I called ahead to Jeffers. It rang and rang and I was about to give up when he came on the line, sounding distracted. I told him we were headed in his direction and to be out on the street waiting for us.

'Is it Reinhart?'

'No,' I said. 'It's Lizzie.'

Now I had him. 'What's wrong?'

'Nothing, I hope. We're in a cab. Just be outside.'

Kristina rocked in the seat next to me, her body rigid, willing the traffic to part.

Five minutes later it'd become clear that it wasn't going to and so we got the guy to let us out on the corner of 14th Street and Seventh Avenue. As we started to run up the avenue, I called Jeffers again.

'I'm here,' he said. He sounded freaked out. 'I'm standing outside. Where *are* you?'

'Change of plan. We're on foot. Come to the corner of Eighth.'

The sidewalks were black and wet, clogged with bad-tempered people with umbrellas and apparently no desire to *get the hell out of other people's way*, and soon I gave up trying to be dignified or polite and simply ran straight at anyone who was in my path.

Kristina was just behind as we reached the end of the stretch of 16th that intersected with Eighth, and I saw Jeffers on the other side looking all around. The street was wall-to-wall traffic, but here it was moving fast.

'Is that Maj with him?'

'Oh thank God,' Kristina said. 'He'll be able to talk to her.'

She shouted across, telling them to run up toward 18th. Jeffers looked confused, but Maj got it right away – he evidently knew where Catherine lived. They started running up the street, and rather than confront the traffic and cross over, we ran up the side we were on. It wasn't as busy as Seventh, but there were plenty of people hurrying home or heading to bars and restaurants or trying to get somewhere out of the rain.

Jeffers was having a hard time trying to follow Maj. Maj was running *fast*, weaving through people far more quickly than I could have done, than anyone should even be able to. He'd seen something up ahead, too.

'No,' he shouted. 'No!'

He ran faster, shouting Lizzie's name over and over. He went straight past 18th, sprinting now, arms pistoning forward and back. At first I couldn't understand why he hadn't turned in there, gone toward Catherine's house.

Then I realized what he was running toward.

Lizzie was half a block ahead, staggering along the middle of the road, cars flashing past her on either side. Her head was down, hair loose and straggled and wet. Her shoulders were bent.

I don't know why she was heading back toward us. Perhaps she'd gone up the other way first, lost track, found herself coming back down the road by accident.

She was flicker-lit by car headlights and signs, red, white, and yellow. She didn't look like she had any destination in mind. She looked wholly lost. She looked like a child slipping beneath the surface of a lake.

Maj was closer now, still shouting her name. Nobody saw him running past. Nobody cared. They did see Jeffers come up behind and jumped out of the way, but they didn't care about anything except the inconvenience.

Kristina lunged across the next street, nearly

getting taken out by a car. I got caught trying to follow her and was forced diagonally against the traffic until I was trapped in the middle of the avenue.

'Lizzie,' I shouted. '*Stay where you are.*'

She raised her head, but I don't think it was because she'd heard me. Her face was glowing white and dripping wet and it was not from the rain.

Kristina called her name over and over.

Maj ran into the traffic toward her, shouting too. I don't think she heard them either. I don't think she knew where she was, and I don't believe she cared.

She tilted her head back and howled.

Nobody heard. Nobody in the cars streaming past her on either side, no one on the sidewalks. No one but us, and we were too slow, though I don't believe it would have made any difference if we'd been quicker.

At the last moment she did see us, saw Maj at least, and Kristina too. She saw them, but she remained alone. I saw her eyes narrow, saw her summon all the concentration and substance she could muster, using pure force of will to make herself as concrete as possible.

I saw her smile fiercely as she did this, and maybe she *did* see me then, because she was looking at someone – or perhaps she saw through me to some other and better place and time.

There was a beat, and then she became much

brighter. That's the wrong word. She became more *there*.

An instant later a cab ran straight into her.

Nothing happened. Nothing flew up into the air. The driver slammed on the brakes and skidded thirty feet, tires fighting the wet surface. Other cars barked and honked and swerved.

The cab came to a juddering halt as I sprinted toward it. A skinny man leapt out. He stared all around, whirling on the spot, terrified, knowing he'd just hit someone – but wherever he looked, he saw exactly the same as I did. Nothing.

When he'd spun around five times he seemed to realize I was ten feet away, doing the same thing. 'What the fuck?' he said. 'Did you *see* her?'

People honked. People shouted at him, at me.

'There was no one there,' I said.

'*Bullshit*, man!'

'Just a trick of the light.'

'No fucking way. No *way*. There was a woman. I saw her. There was no one there, and *then there was*. I fucking ran straight into her, man.'

'You didn't hit anyone,' I said.

Maj stood in the middle of the traffic, frozen, staring at the spot where Lizzie had last been. Kristina had reeled off up the sidewalk, head in hands. Jeffers was motionless, mouth open, face blank.

'I was right here,' I told the driver. 'I saw everything. You did nothing wrong.'

'What the fuck?' he kept saying. 'What the *fuck*?'

As I walked back over to the sidewalk, wanting to go to Kristina, I saw something on the side of the road.

A twist of red velvet cloth, something that could once have been a dress. Not recently – it was faded and filthy from years of rain and dirt – but once. It was screwed up into the side of the gutter, and looked like it had been trodden on and rained on and ignored ten thousand times.

When I reached down for it, it had gone.

And when I looked up and tried to find Kristina, she'd gone too.

CHAPTER 58

Dawn was closing out the day. The last of her kids had just left – Eddie Moscone, who always hung around the school grounds for at least an hour, playing on the climbing frame with focus and concentration while his mother piggy-backed school Wi-Fi to send e-mails or update her status or whatever the heck it was people did with their phones the whole damned day. Dawn had a phone, sure. She used it for phone calls, old-school. The rest of the time she preferred to spend with people who were *there*.

Dawn had a guilty secret. She hated the Internet. Sure it was useful for shopping, but the rest of the time she watched family and friends putting it out there – updating constantly, being passionate and sincere, putting up heartfelt blogs when someone died. And what came back? Nothing. Nobody cared. Your follower count – a more critical indicator of your worth than anything you did in real life – would stay the same, or maybe even dip because you were being too serious, not hip or smart or ironic enough. Followers are not friends. Friends are different and do not come cheap. So why not *forget* the constant attention seeking . . . and just be?

That was one of the things Dawn liked about her kids – their ability to exist. Most of them, anyway. She paused in tidying books in her classroom's library of battered classics and watched Eddie on the bars. Eddie was a decent kid, intelligent, polite and responsive most of the time. At other times he retreated. Sometimes it took two or three nudges to bring him back to the world. God knows Dawn saw David doing the same thing often enough – and it could take more than two or three prods to re-center her husband if he'd really got his vague on – but when you watched Eddie you realized how much of his universe came out of his own head and how very real it was to him.

Eventually Eddie's mother got serious about hauling her kid away, and they left. A few older children would be wandering about the campus, engaged in projects, some teachers too, but otherwise it had the calm you find only during downtime in places that take hard usage during the day. Dawn worked her way around the classroom, putting everything in order. She privately believed this was her key role in the children's lives, whatever the job description might say. Yes, she had to teach them a bunch of stuff, but providing a predictable environment in which to grow a little older – while absorbing all the weird crap the world threw at them – was just as important. And someday in the not so distant future, another woman (or man, possibly, though the lower grades tend to attract the feminine touch) would be doing this for her child, too. Child*ren*, of course – part of her still hadn't gotten around that twist.

Container loads of supplements were on the way. A vast bounty of advice about the best ways to maintain your body and mind during pregnancy had been downloaded (okay, the web was good for that stuff), with further hard-copy manuals expected any day in the mail. The attic room was nearly done and . . . would be finished soon.

She shelved the questions that came from that last point, sticking to a decision made as she'd brushed her teeth that morning, and contented herself with the bottom-line declaration that Dawn and David's babies would be born into an orderly world, inside and out.

Of that, my embryonic beings, have no doubt.

She decided she could call the classroom done. All the art equipment was where it were supposed to be, bar a couple of crayons on the counter, which she'd tidy on the way out; chairs were under tables; circle time mats in a neat pile; and there was picture of a face on the door.

Dawn did a double take.

The door to the classroom was made of wood and painted a cheerful green except for a glass panel in the upper half. A sheet of paper was stuck to this, the kind she handed out many times a day for pupils to inexpertly mark in one way or another.

This one had also been marked, but it didn't look like it had been done by a child. The face was rendered in black crayon – an irregular oval, a few lines inside evoking eyes, nose, and ears, a hooked one below that looked something like a smile.

As she looked more closely, however, she saw the lines were labored and ragged, drawn far more arduously than their freedom implied, as if even holding the crayon had been a struggle.

Dawn had seen a lot of face drawings. One of the first exercises she gave pupils each year was a self-portrait. The amount you could tell about a child – signs ranging from the level of competence and dexterity to the use of color, and even the size of the face relative to the page – was remarkable. She'd never seen one like this, though. Strong, flowing lines suggested long and unkempt hair – whereas children tended to render it either as unfeasibly neat or in wild scribbles. The facial expression, though technically a smile, was not one you'd want to see coming at you. The eyes were too knowing. The line of the mouth seemed cruel.

Dawn knew that any child who'd seen a countenance like this in real life needed an appointment with the school counselor. Urgently. It was horrible.

She took it down. None too gently, either – the top of the sheet tore, leaving a fragment still attached with the blob of tack that had been used to put it up there.

But by whom, and when? Dawn hadn't left the classroom since the end of school. Had somebody sneaked in and stuck it up when she wasn't looking? Would that even have been *possible*?

Dawn went to the window. For a moment the playground was empty, and then she saw Jeff – school handyman, gardener, general factotum – in the distance, going about his endless tasks. He didn't glance over and of course it wouldn't have been him.

Neither could Dawn imagine any of the older kids doing this. It was a good school. Sneaking into a classroom behind a female teacher's back and putting up a picture . . . that was pretty creepy.

She turned from the window. And let out a shriek.

There were three pictures on the blackboard now.

All were faces. Two obviously female, the other male. One of the women's faces was substantially rounder than the other. The expressions were muted and blank. Whoever had drawn them hadn't been trying to imbue them with life. They'd been trying to say something else.

A threat.

The door was shut. It would have been impossible for anyone to open it without her noticing, much less get to the blackboard and stick pictures up in a neat row.

Dawn looked at the opposite corner of the classroom.

The library was arranged in a four-foot-high bookcase, behind which was an area two feet deep. This was where she left her bag and sweater during the day, the closest she had to a backstage area.

It struck her now that it was also big enough, just about, for someone to hide. For a person – a smallish person – to have lurked, darting out while she'd been looking at Jeff to stick the papers to the board before scurrying back again.

Maybe big enough. Just about.

Dawn knew the sensible thing to do was run to the door, get Jeff, and have him to come take a look – but this was her classroom, dammit. If some older kid got away with something like this, then . . .

She put the drawing in her hand down on the counter and squared up to the opposite corner.

'Okay – who's back there?' Her voice was clear and strong. It was met with silence.

You're going to be a mother, Dawn reminded herself. *Now is the time to start making sure you don't take any shit.* 'Seriously, this isn't funny. Come out here.'

Still nothing. No quiet, explosive giggling or the intake of breath you might expect from a little prankster who'd realized the game was up.

Abruptly Dawn decided the hell with it and walked over.

There was no one behind the bookcase.

She blinked, not realizing how convinced she'd been that she'd find someone there until she didn't.

Someone tapped her in the middle of the back.

She whirled around. The classroom was empty. Of course. She would have heard the door – it was impossible to open it without a loud click. It must just have been a twitch between her shoulder blades, a reaction to discovering nothing behind the library bookcase.

Except . . . Dawn knelt and picked the black crayon off the floor. She straightened and looked over toward the counter near the door. There were two other crayons there now. Hadn't there been three before?

She wasn't sure. She wasn't sure *enough*, anyway.

She saw that there were no longer any pictures on the blackboard. Moving in a calm and sedate manner, and electing to leave any stray crayons wherever they damned well were, Dawn left the classroom.

She locked the door and walked toward the lot without a glance back.

She sat in the car for ten minutes before turning the ignition. By then she'd worked it all out.

She was pregnant. Duh. Everybody knew the hormones screwed with your head. She knew damned well that she'd seen the pictures – but there was seeing and *seeing*. You saw things in daydreams and imagination, too. It didn't mean they'd actually been there. If the pictures were no longer in the classroom, then they could not have been there in the first place.

Weird. Yes. But . . . explained.

She'd tell David about it, of course – but not right away. He'd been very twitchy since he got back from New York, a lot more Eddie Moscone than usual. Dawn wasn't sure how he'd react to the reveal that pregnancy hormones might be messing with his wife's head more than was probably normal.

Not to mention that when the time came for a big talk, there was something else they needed to discuss, something a lot more concrete. She didn't want that water muddied with this.

She breathed out, a hard and active exhale. She started the car feeling shaken but confident that the world was broadly okay, and hurrah for that.

She didn't realize that all the time she'd been tidying the classroom, three people had been there with her – two men, one woman, all of them thin and very tall, sometimes watching from the edges of the room, sometimes behind her, sometimes right up close, surrounding her, grinning, peeking down her blouse.

And she also didn't know that all three of them were now sitting in the backseat of her car.

CHAPTER 59

As David sprinted up the road toward the school, he saw Dawn's car coming the other way. He jumped into the street and waved, trying not to look too frantic, trying to make this look like it was a normal thing to do. He could see Dawn through the windshield staring into the middle distance, mind on something else; then he saw her clocking the fact that some idiot was in middle of the road, then finally that the idiot was her husband.

She braked, too hard. The wheels spun and the car skidded toward him. David got his arm out between his body and the car, sidestepping out of the way at the last moment.

He yanked open the passenger door. 'Are you okay?'

'What are you *doing*, David?'

He got in. 'Has anything weird happened?'

'I could have *killed* you.' He kept staring at her. 'David . . . what? Why are you here? And why are you looking so weird? You're scaring me.'

'Are you *sure* nothing strange has happened to you? Or around you?'

507

'David – what's this about?'

'Didn't you hear about Talia?'

'Heard *what*, David? I've been in the classroom all day, and the last two hours I've been marking and . . .'

She broke off. David kept trying to work what was strange about her. The atmosphere in the car felt wrong, as if there was something that wasn't being spoken about.

'What?' he said. 'What aren't you telling me?'

'*Nothing*. What's the big deal?'

'Talia's dead.'

'*What?*'

He pulled his seat belt tight. 'Drive.'

'Drive? Where?'

'New York.'

'New *York*? Are you *joking*?'

He looked at her. 'Dawn, do I look like I'm joking?'

She drove.

He told her everything.

At first, just what had happened in the days after their trip to the city. Bumping into the man outside Bryant Park and in the train station. The matchbook left outside their house in the night, the same day she'd come back from school to find a pile of small change on the step. The meeting in Kendricks.

Dawn kept trying to interrupt, but he pleaded with her to let him speak until he got it all out.

508

Then it got harder, because he moved into the realm of lies. He had to start telling her about things he'd misled her over, or hidden by omission. The fact that when he'd hooked up with the guy in the city, it hadn't been a simple case of meeting an old friend. That this was the same guy who'd bumped into him and come to their town to talk. That David hadn't come home from the city to make sure he was there in time for the scan, but because *very weird shit* had started happening.

'But . . .' Dawn interrupted finally. She was piloting the car quickly but with care. That's why David usually let her drive. She possessed a sense of being in control – of a car, of herself, of life – that he'd never felt. 'Who *is* this guy? I thought you said he was a friend.'

David hesitated. Could he tell her this? Could he tell the woman who was carrying his child – children – that he believed a phantom from his childhood had somehow come back into his life?

'It's difficult to explain,' he said.

'Wait.' She concentrated for a moment, negotiating the car into the fast-moving traffic on the freeway. Then she glanced at him. 'Do you love me?'

'Of course,' he said, baffled. 'Why do you ask that?'

She told him what had just happened in the classroom. He felt his stomach lurch. He'd known *something* had happened as soon as he opened the car door. That explained the atmosphere, the sense of things unsaid. He hoped it did, anyhow, though her telling it hadn't dissipated what he was feeling.

'So,' she said. 'Am I going nuts?'

'No,' he said. 'But what else?'

'What do you mean?'

'Is there something you're not telling me?'

'No.' She seemed irritable. 'But there's something *you're* not saying.'

'I'm getting to it,' he snapped. This was going wrong. He could feel it curdling, but he didn't understand why. He felt a non-specific crankiness, bad temper, a pervading sense of something dark and broken, a desire to nurture conflict out of curiosity, to see how far it could go – or be pushed. It felt like something black and gleefully bad was creeping up behind, something that wanted nothing less than his misery for all time.

'I know about the manuscript,' Dawn said.

She had decided to see if there was anything she could do to help, she said. She knew he was busy, caught up in the new book. It was the way their relationship always worked – her marshaling the real world, him standing on the ledge outside the window, bringing home the dreams.

So she'd gone upstairs and had a look through his boxes. Pretty quickly it had become clear that he'd want to keep most of it, and he had to decide where it went (because the obvious and only acceptable answer would be 'in your study, dude'). By the time she got to the third box she'd lost focus and was peering into it with little more than mild curiosity.

When she spotted the pile of paper, she'd snapped back to attention. How cool, she thought – the manuscript for David's novel. That shouldn't be hidden away in a box. That should be . . . well, not actually on display (a pile of paper was never going to look acceptable in the living room) but at least safely stowed. She pulled it out and leafed through the first few pages, smiling, before realizing there was something strange about it.

Yes, it was the book, but it was different. Not only in the way a first draft will always be different – the raw material, hacked like a block of stone out of the quarry of random words and events, ready to be shaped into meaning by subsequent drafts – but *wholly* different. David's handwriting was all over it, in pencil and ballpoint pen, hundreds of corrections and changes. But the stuff underneath, the typed material, not to mention the very paper it was typed on . . .

'What was it, David? Where did it come from?'

David had been listening without any attempt to speak, eyes on the growing traffic through the windshield, as they came into Newark. He looked down at his hands. Lying hands, hands that . . .

'It was my father's,' he said.

'What?'

'The place where I grew up wasn't very different from Rockbridge. It was called Palmerston, in Pennsylvania. There was a weird shooting there back in the 1990s, but otherwise it was your regular small town. My parents lived there all their lives. They loved each other, but they argued. A lot. Viciously sometimes. One of the things they used to argue about was a little room my father used as his study. It was a hobby. He . . .'

David found he couldn't finish. He didn't have to. Dawn already knew, and she said the words for him. 'He wrote the book I found.'

'Yes.'

'But it wasn't finished,' she said 'There was only half a novel there, and the prose was *terrible*, and . . .'

'He was still working on it when they died, I guess. He tinkered with it for years. Maybe he would have finished it, maybe not. When I packed up stuff to bring to Rockbridge, I found the manu-script. I didn't think about it for a long time, but one day I wondered whether I should try to do something with it. At first it was supposed to be something for him, a way of getting to know him better, or . . . But as I worked at it and changed it and added things and took stuff out, I stopped seeing it as his book and started seeing it as mine. And when I finished it and gave it to you and you said you loved it . . . I didn't want to admit it hadn't been.'

'David, you could have told me.'

'I know. I fucked up. And . . . I wonder whether Maj coming back into my life has to do with all of that. He bumped into me on the day I met with my publishers for the first time. That can't be a coincidence, can it?'

'David, who *is* Maj?'

'He was the first thing I ever wrote, my first big make-believe. I just made him up a little too well.'

CHAPTER 60

When Golzen got to the club he found the street door ajar. From that moment he realized that things were running differently, that something was afoot. Maybe he even started to hope tonight was going to be the night. You follow the signs, unclear though they may be.

Follow signs, until Jedburgh appears.

There was no one behind the bar, though cold blue light shone from the bulbs behind the bottles. Chalk up another hint that all was not business as usual. By now tattooed staff would normally be checking that the beer fridges were stocked, racking backup spirits on the high shelves. Golzen walked across the big empty space to the office.

Reinhart was waiting, arms folded, leaning back against the desk. Golzen noticed immediately that the phone was not in its customary place, but lying in six pieces against the wall and over the floor.

'What happened to that?'

'It broke.'

Reinhart spoke as if the event had nothing to do with him, as though whatever cataclysm had befallen the device had occurred at its own hands and been its own fault. Though trivial – Golzen had seen the man do far worse to foes both inanimate and animate – he found this disquieting. It reminded him of the kind of thoughts that sometimes needled at him from the cloudy depths of his own mind: the thoughts that said everything was a game, and the darker and bloodier it got, the better. The ones that said there was no responsibility, no fault, no damage, no rules. The thoughts that didn't have the slightest understanding of what those words even meant.

'Who was it?'

'The priest. I don't know how he got this number, but he's crazier than usual tonight. Ratfuck insane.'

'Something happened over in Chelsea an hour ago, in the street near his church. One of the friends canceled herself out. She was very popular. A lot of people are upset. He's probably one of them.'

Golzen considered mentioning that Lizzie had been very close to Maj, too, but elected not to. Since the encounter the day before, Reinhart had been silent about Maj. Golzen was content to let that remain so.

'Whatever. The priest has gone past the point of no return. He needs dealing with.'

'He's not our only problem.'

'I'm aware that other people are trying to make our business their business.'

'Don't we need to do something about them, too?'

515

'I will. Have no doubt. But they're no threat.'

There was something wrong here. It was as if Reinhart had turned some part of himself up. Some not-good part. 'To you, maybe. But to *us*. These people know who we are, *what* we are. They may try to do something.'

'Let them. When the enemy comes at you, the smart tactician does not retreat. He doesn't even stand and fight unless absolutely necessary. You know why?'

'Why?'

Reinhart smiled serenely. 'The enemy is at their weakest at the moment when they advance. They're off balance, head full of plans and impulses and leaping ahead to their victory . . . instead of watching what *you're* doing. That makes it the ideal time to vault straight over them in the direction you were already going.'

Golzen blinked, feeling caught out, as if he couldn't keep up. 'But . . . what direction is that?'

'You don't get it. That's why I am me and you are you. You don't even realize who the enemy *is*. It's not these new people, the tough guy and his witchy girlfriend. We kill them, they're gone. But that's not the end of it. The enemy is *everyone*, my friend. You must start at your own front door, but after that, there is no end to it. That's who we're fighting all the time, and today is Day Zero of the new deal.'

'You mean . . .'

'Yes. We're doing it. Right now.'

Golzen's heart leapt. 'We're leaving for Perfect?'

'Not us, no.'

'But you said . . .'

Reinhart shook his head. 'I said nothing. You didn't listen properly and so you heard things that were never said. Nobody's going anywhere.'

'We're going to Perfect,' Golzen said stubbornly.

'Perfect isn't a place. It's a *state*.'

'Like . . . Colorado?'

'No, you dumb asshole. A state of *being*. You can't change anything by altering where you are. You have to change *what* you are. That option is unavailable to you because of the situation with your own friend. You should have had the presence of mind to do something about that way back in the day. I'm sorry.'

He didn't look remotely sorry.

'I'm not *going*?'

'No one's going anywhere. Are you even *listening*?'

'What are you . . . Perfect is a *place*.'

'Jesus. So tell me – where do you think this place even is? Utah? Texas? Fucking California? You think you were going on some Mormon adventure, prancing off into the wilderness to find the promised fucking land?'

Golzen stared at him. That's exactly what he'd thought would happen, what he'd believed lay in his future and destiny since the night many years ago when he dreamed of a place where they could all live like normal people. Perfect had been Reinhart's name for it. In Golzen's dream it had

517

been announced to him as Jedburgh, and in the confines of his head he still thought of it that way. He'd thought Reinhart believed in it too, but now he was saying something else . . . and Golzen couldn't even work out what it was.

'So . . . what *is* going to happen? When?'

Reinhart bounced off the desk and strode out into the main club room. Golzen hurried after him.

'It's already started,' Reinhart said. 'A broadcast was passed to all available Cornermen' – he checked his watch – 'nearly forty minutes ago. It won't happen all at once. It depends when the chosen happen to get the message. That's okay. That's the *other* secret to success in battle, my friend. No events. Only evolution.'

'I don't . . . understand.'

'No, you don't. Let's leave it at that.'

Golzen became aware of someone coming toward them out of the shadows. 'Wait up,' said a girl's voice.

'Hey,' Reinhart said. 'You ready?'

It was the girl Golzen had brought to Reinhart – the ditzy teen he'd turned a few days before. She looked different, though. She was dressed the same, was still the kind of random hoodie girl that no one would look twice at in the street, but there was a new confidence about her. She looked like she had a destination now.

She grinned. 'You bet.'

Golzen glared at her. 'What's *she* doing here?'

'I always liked your idea of there being twelve initial warriors,' Reinhart said. 'It has a ring to it, you know? Twelve holy ghosts, ha-ha. So she's doing this thing in your place.'

'*What?*'

'She's got what it takes. Fingerskills and an accessible friend. You have neither. Maj would have been perfect, of course. He's a weapon already. He took the step long ago. You're no good for this.'

'But . . . but she's *nobody*.'

'Screw you,' the girl said with amusement. 'My name's Jessica. Or it's gonna be.'

Reinhart laughed. 'That's my girl. Go and be.'

He tossed something to her. She caught it deftly in one hand and held it up in front of Golzen, taunting him.

A matchbook.

'Later,' she said, and walked quickly toward the street. By the time she got through the door, she was running.

Reinhart chuckled. Then he stopped, just like that, as if tiring of doing an impersonation of a normal person. His face darkened. 'There's a thing I'm going to do,' he said. 'Then we need to talk. The fun starts here, but we have much still to do, my friend.'

Golzen's head was buzzing. He felt sickened, disgusted with himself. Christmas day had come and there was nothing under the tree. There never had been. There wasn't even a tree. Just lies. Always lies.

'No,' he said numbly.

He turned his back on Reinhart and walked out into the twilight.

CHAPTER 61

I'd run up and down the avenue all the way from 14th to 23rd. I'd searched down it again, this time along every side street to the next avenues. I had the phone to my ear throughout, hitting redial time and again.

I couldn't find Kristina anywhere. After forty minutes I realized this wasn't working and I stopped running around like a fool. I thought it very unlikely she'd have gone to work, but I called the restaurant to eliminate the possibility. Mario's sister answered and tartly said no, she hadn't seen her and she didn't want to either, because we were both fired.

'What? Why?'

'She never here. You a fighting man. Mario, he had enough.'

I knew it would have been Maria who made the decision rather than her brother, but I was too wound up to take the problem seriously right now and said fine, but if Kris happened by could they tell her to call me, please. Mario's sister sniffed and said maybe and put the phone down, which I had to hope meant yes.

I went back up to 18th and rang the bell of Catherine Warren's house. There was no response, but I saw the drapes move on the second floor so I put my thumb back on the buzzer and kept it there until I saw a shape in the hallway. Catherine kept the chain on but opened the door, a tear-stained child in her arms.

Catherine's face was hard and set. 'Go away.'

'Have you seen Kristina?'

'No. Now go, or I'll call the police.'

She was so self-possessed, so impregnable, that I couldn't help myself. 'So how'd it go with Lizzie? Not well, by the look of it.'

Her eyes didn't even flicker. 'I don't know anyone by that name,' she said. 'I never have.'

She slammed the door in my face.

Our apartment – or the remains of it – was a possibility, but I believed that however upset Kristina was, she'd have the sense to avoid going back there. I'd seen the look in her eyes as she surveyed the devastation and knew the place was dead to her. She hadn't liked it much before, and whatever we'd built there was gone.

I realized that despite spending every day with this woman for six months, we remained separate. I knew where *our* places were – the cafés and delis and bars where we spent time – but there was some whole different Kristina-based map of Manhattan, and I didn't have a copy. I didn't know where she went when I wasn't there. She didn't know where I went, either, and this finally proved to me that we'd never really lived here. Our tracks were faint pencil lines on the city's plan. It was too big and old for us to make lasting marks upon it. We needed to find somewhere we could start to write ourselves in ink, together, a place where our lives would become part of the object itself – otherwise we were just shades, haunting street corners, passing time.

I kept walking fast and running, trying her phone.

She kept not answering.

I spun around like a headless chicken for another hour – checking bars, calling people we knew from late-night drinking sessions – before I had a better idea. I'd gotten myself way up in Midtown and it took another twenty minutes to get back from there to the place I'd thought of.

Union Square Park was empty. It was cold and dark and the drizzle had settled in. No one would have any good reason to be there – no one with a normal life, anyway. But this is where Kris and I had first encountered the friends en masse and where she'd met up with Lizzie and the Angels. Maybe she'd come here to mourn her. I didn't know. I couldn't think of anywhere else.

I finally slowed down – partly because my lungs and legs were aching, and also because I didn't think I'd stand any chance of finding what I was looking for if I came into the area loud and fast.

I walked down the central path. The grass and bushes and trees on either side of it were empty apart from a few sleeping street people on benches. I got to the bottom and there were others in evidence – but just regular humans, striding between wherever they'd been and whoever they were going to. Each looked like they had sensible lives where things were joined with straight lines and everything had a beginning, middle, and an end. I did not feel a part of that world.

It would take only ten minutes to run to the apartment, but I still believed that would be a waste of time. I decided to give the park one more circuit, just in case. This time I forsook the path and stepped over low hedges, looking around the bushes and under trees – even under the benches. By the time I got back up to the northern section I was beginning to lose hope.

Then I spotted something over in the kids' playground. It was closed, but two figures, adult size, were standing in the open area between the slides and climbing frames. One had his back to me. He was wearing a shirt and jeans.

The other was a man with short, ginger hair, wearing an ill-matched suit. As I watched, this second guy reached out and put a hand on the other's shoulder. His face said he knew he ought to be saying something and he had absolutely no idea what it might be. The other guy shook it off and started shouting. I could hear the noise, feel the anger, but couldn't make out the words.

I ran to the wooden fence. 'Hey,' I said.

They ignored me. The man in jeans was losing it now, shouting louder and louder, arms flailing by his sides. I was close enough that what he was saying should have been audible, but all I got was misery and fury.

I let myself in the gate, aware I could be approaching a drug deal going wrong and setting myself up for another trip to the hospital. I didn't care.

'Turn the fuck around,' I shouted, my voice spiraling out of my control.

The man turned. It was Maj, of course. His face was pure white. His eyes were black. He seemed condensed and powerful and yet on the verge of blowing apart, a dark kernel of terrible anger and violence.

'Have you seen Kristina?'

The other man glanced at me but was far more concerned with trying to talk Maj down.

'Do you *know where she is*?'

'Look, I don't know, mate,' said the man in the suit. 'Never met her. And we've got bigger—'

Maj ran off. The other guy went after him. By the time I got outside the enclosure, they'd become lost in shadows.

'*Assholes*,' I shouted. 'She tried to *help*. She tried to stop it happening. Lizzie was her *friend*.'

All I heard in reply were the sounds of leaves in the trees around the park and traffic out on the streets.

As I stormed back toward the road I saw someone standing in the bushes by the side of the playground, however. She might even have been there all along – from the angle I'd approached, I wouldn't have seen her.

She was dressed in black but with a vibrant green skirt. She was plump with pure white hair. She was watching me.

But then she wasn't there.

Two minutes later my phone rang. I yanked it out of my pocket so fast that it spun out of my fingers. I snatched it off the floor and got it to my ear.

'Kris? Where are you?'

'Not her,' a voice said – an older, croaky voice. 'It's Lydia. You got to come, John.'

'Where? Are you with Kris?'

'No, I don't know where your girl is. But you got to come to the church. Right now.'

'What? Why?'

'There's a bad man here.'

CHAPTER 62

Streets slick with rain and reflecting lights and blackness a purple-blue oil in puddles. Cars flashing by on their way from nowhere to nowhere else, spraying cold, dirty water. Windows and houses and stores and bars. Distant shouts, honks, half a laugh at some circumstance out of sight. People, real and imagined, standing, walking, turning – still or in movement.

So many strangers, so few friends; among the millions of people in the world, barely a handful you'd rather be with than be alone. You could pass through all this like a shadow and never be a part of it.

You can pass like that, and Kristina did. She walked. Her head was empty but for one thought.

Eventually she ended up somewhere. She had been standing in it for five minutes before she realized where she even was. She became aware of trees and bushes and a dark open space. Bryant Park.

Of course. Her feet had brought her here – her feet and the part of the mind that keeps moving even when the thinking portions have absolved responsibility and dived into a black hole. Her feet had brought her to the first place where she and Lizzie had spoken.

Why would they do that? How could it help?

Kristina had thought she had no more tears. She was wrong. She'd kept finding she was wrong about this, discovering herself doubled up, stomach clenched in the kind of spasm the body resorts to when poisoned. Events can poison, too. If you cry on the streets people will avoid you. They will step past and look the other way. They know the kind of things that cause people to break down in public and are scared it might be contagious. The only times Kris could remember something this huge was the death of her father. A bulletproof world of beings and love had split along a seam, leaving a gap for some force outside to suck someone out of the circle and into permanent darkness beyond.

She was aware her response was out of proportion. As John had pointed out with characteristic bluntness, she hadn't known Lizzie long or well. It was like being knocked sideways by the death of a celebrity. Ridiculous. Self-indulgent. And yet real. People can define your world and emotional space without having sat at the same table. You build your own universe, and if you choose to cover some of its walls with pictures of someone you've never met – patching over your need for love and attention and meaning when there's no real person to fit the bill – then the tearing of their image from reality will uncover cracks just as real as the death of someone you've known all your life.

Somehow, Lizzie's death did exactly that. Not to mention . . . it was Kris's fault.

She knew she needed to talk to John, that he was the only person who might be able to make her feel better, but every time her phone buzzed she let it go. She didn't deserve help. Her dumb speech to Lizzie about how it was time for a reunion – what the hell had she thought she was doing? What had made her think she had the perspective to talk that way?

She slumped onto a bench, mercifully obscured from the rest of the world by an overhanging tree. Her head was splitting, nose dripping, her face a puddle of hot tears and cold drizzle, and still it kept coming, pumped out by the fiercest and most terrible motor of grief – the idea that something could have been done differently and none of this would have happened; that you have been the engine of your own destruction. It's the moment that the smoker with lung cancer realizes they could have gone through with giving up twenty years ago; the moment the sole survivor of a car crash realizes he could have double-checked in the mirror before changing lanes on the interstate; the agonizing moment someone on a rusty fire escape has to think yeah, maybe they could have checked how stable the thing felt before climbing out . . . and meanwhile the old bolt pulls free of crumbling brick and the entire contraption of life tilts away from the wall of reality on a one-way trip into blackness.

Regret is the poison that kills for all eternity, because no matter how violently the mind and body spasms, it cannot be expelled. Lizzie was dead because of something Kristina had said.

That was a deed that would never be repaired.

'It's not your fault.'

Kristina jerked her head up. She had no idea how long she'd been on the bench, lost in silent screams of self-recrimination. For a moment she couldn't see who had spoken. Then she realized the Angel girl, Flaxon, was standing in front of her, body as straight as the rain. It was coming down harder now and the girl looked soaked. This fact cut through Kristina's confusion.

'How . . . are you wet?'

'The more you feel, the harder you are. A person could break bricks on you right now. I heard you half the way from Union Square.'

She came and sat next to Kristina. Kristina sniffed, wiped her nose on her sleeve, unsure how seriously to take what the girl had said.

'For real,' Flaxon said, as if in answer. Her face was pinched-looking. She seemed thinner than the night before, and smaller and younger – though also stronger. She held up her hand, and Kristina saw that a few of the raindrops seemed to bounce, rather than passing through. 'I can hear what you're thinking, too, a bit. Only because you're loud. And because you think like my friend did. She was a dismal bitch too.'

Kristina was surprised into something like a laugh. 'What . . . happened to her?'

'No idea. She dropped me. End of story.'

Kristina remembered Lizzie saying how hard it had been for this girl to accept her place in the world, and suspected that *wasn't* the end of the story, but she was done trying to wheedle information out of people.

'I'm sorry.'

'I need to talk to you,' Flaxon said.

Kristina felt another surge of guilt, certain she was about to be brought to account and that she deserved it. 'I'm sorry,' she said again.

The girl shook her head curtly. 'Get over yourself. Just because you're real doesn't mean everything starts and ends with you. Lizzie was a strong person. She acted. *She* did the thing. Don't try to take that away from her.'

'Then . . . what?'

'I was down in Union Square and I overheard something and I see a dark cloud over it.'

'What do you mean?'

'Maj was there with that Cornerman buddy of his, Fictitious Bob, and he was losing it. Badly. Not sure if you're aware, but Maj knows where his real friend lives.'

'I heard.'

'Okay. Well, if you're looking for what pushed

Lizzie over the edge this afternoon, that's more likely it than anything you said or did.'

'No. She said she was happy for Maj.'

'I'm sure she was. She had a lot of good and happy thoughts and she spread them around. That's how she rolled. But it was also like a knife to her.'

'Why?'

'Everybody wants to feel they're the center of creation, not just someone's friend. But you get used to it. Kinda. Not everybody gets to be a rock star, right? It's hard for us to love, though. One another, anyway.'

'Because of what you feel for your real friend?'

'It's like a first love, I think. From what I've heard. That sound right?'

Kristina thought about it. That first love, the one that changes you, striking like an arrow or axe into your adolescent heart, the one that will (despite decades of dating and far deeper and more meaningful affairs) define your emotional landscape forever. You won't spend the rest of your life trying to replicate it – you may do just the opposite – but it's there nonetheless, a ghost in your heart. She nodded.

'Maj and Lizzie got close, though,' Flaxon said. 'He is *very* broken up by what happened and *almighty* pissed at the world of real people right now.'

Aware that she was deflecting some of her anger at her own actions, Kristina said: 'So maybe him talking to his friend is exactly what needs to happen.'

'No,' Flaxon said patiently. 'No good comes of it. Ever. I don't think it would be his friend he'd be looking for anyway. He was ranting about the priest.'

'Jeffers? Why? He's been trying to *help*.'

'Maybe. But Maj thinks he screwed with Lizzie's thinking and maybe it was part of what made her . . . do what she did today. It's a really bad idea for them to talk right now.'

'Are you sure? Real people have to *learn*. They have to take responsibility for what they say and do.'

'You don't get it. Maj is different.'

'I know. He's a Fingerman. A good one.'

'Oh, he's that. The best that ever was, people say. But that's not what I'm talking about.' Her voice dropped to a whisper, a tangled mixture of distaste, respect, and dark excitement. 'He killed someone once. A real person.'

Kristina stared. 'How would that even be *possible?*'

'I don't know. I don't know who it was or when or how. But they say it's true. It's why Reinhart wanted him to work for him so bad – he'd already crossed that line. My point is, if Maj gets the brush-off from Jeffers then people could get hurt. You think Lizzie would have wanted that? For Maj to do something black because of her?'

'But what can I do?'

'At least talk to Maj. He knows Lizzie dug you. It might make a difference.'

'I don't know where he is.'

'First place to try would be the church, duh?'

Kristina didn't know what to say. She didn't know whether going after someone she'd barely met would make a difference, or if she even had the courage to try after what had happened.

'Still hearing you, babe,' Flaxon said. She shook her head like a dog, spreading rain flying in all directions. 'There's something else Lizzie used to say, and it's what stopped me running with the bad guys and made me want to be an Angel instead. She said regret is the only thing that kills forever and also the only poison that you feed yourself.'

Kristina blinked at her. This was exactly what she'd thought earlier, almost word for word. It couldn't be coincidence, and she knew Lizzie hadn't said it to her.

Was part of Lizzie here now, in this park?

Was part of her *inside* Kristina now?

'Let's get on this,' Flaxon said, standing. 'And page your boyfriend, too.'

'I don't even know whether he'll come.'

'Make him. He seems like a guy who'd be useful in this type of situation.' She winked. 'Also, he's kind of hot, for a real person.'

Flaxon started running. Aware she was stopping the other girl from moving much faster, Kristina did her best to keep up, and ran after Flaxon as fast as she could.

CHAPTER 63

David kept talking as Dawn drove in through the outskirts of the city. He talked longer than ever before in his life, dredging up out of memory and hidden spaces. He told her everything he could remember from the time he crawled under a kitchen table in the midst of a fight that was breaking his heart, to find a boy there with him. He told her about the hours and days spent in the woods by himself – except for the friend he'd conjured up; the times in his bedroom with him playing the endless made-up games that neither parent could seem to stomach or understand; the long talks they would take together as David – a solitary boy, the total loner geek – explored the small town where he grew up. Told her, too, how Maj was there into his early teens and beyond, long after he'd heard about the idea of imaginary friends and realized most people had forgotten about them by then. How when he was at some other kid's birthday party at a roller-skating rink or bigger house, Maj would be there in the background, giving him a wink every now and then to reassure him he wasn't alone.

How the boy kept pace with him in age while always looking and dressing differently, always that bit more daring than David and naughtier *(what nobody sees, nobody knows)* – sometimes lifting a dollar bill from dresser tables or small change from the tips people left in restaurants and putting them where David would find them, dropping them out of the air to be discovered on the floor or on the path outside his parents' house. Money that David saved and eventually used to buy the basic word processor on which he tentatively started to write, in secret, keeping silent about this lest his mother find out and hate the endeavor in him as much as she evidently hated it in his father; also in case his father poured scorn upon it as he did with most everything else his son did, scorn mixed with the pungent jealousy that's born of the realization that too many years have passed without achievement and there's a new generation coming to elbow you aside and take the things you assumed one day would be yours.

Dawn listened in silence apart from when they got close to the bridge over to Manhattan, when she asked him where they were going. He got out the map from the glove compartment and told her to head toward Chelsea.

He told her how Maj had remained a constant into his late teens, well past the point where David had realized this was an abnormal state of affairs and had begun to become embarrassed by seeing his old friend in the background in bars or keg parties or outside the windows of diners in which David was muddling through his first, terrified dates. David had started to fight back against his father's character summation by then, trying to reinvent himself as someone who *could* function sociably, and was making progress, too – to the point where he'd stopped wanting to be reminded of the terribly lonely little boy who'd once hidden under the kitchen table.

You want to be different than everyone else and then you want to be the same, and finally you need to be different again. That means being *you*, and nobody else. Old friends become an encumbrance, a reminder of the buggy beta version of you. The magnets started to repel, and the move to New York turned up the charge a hundredfold. Eventually David pushed hard enough and grew up enough, and the idea of Maj fell out of his head.

'I just didn't remember,' David said, as he sat flicker-lit by neon in the passenger seat, eyes glazed with an avalanche of things that had been lost. 'I forgot Maj. I have to remember him again now, or he's never going to leave me alone.'

Five minutes later Dawn made the turn onto 16th. She drove along the dark, tree-lined street until David indicated for her to pull over to the curb.

'Why are we here?'

'See the church? That's the one Maj brought me to. The priest knows about him and his friends.

He may know where Maj is now. I don't know what else to try.'

Dawn turned off the engine. She sat in silence with her hands in her lap. Apart from asking directions, she had not spoken for forty minutes. She seemed in no hurry to say anything now.

'Well?'

'Well what?' she said.

'Do you believe me?'

She pursed her lips. 'I don't know.'

'I'm telling the truth.'

'How could you have forgotten all of this?'

'I didn't forget. I just . . . didn't think about it.'

'But how?'

He shrugged. 'The way you forget what you did any given afternoon when you were five or ten. The way you lose track of things you used to feel or understand or dream of when you were fourteen. The way you'll find your favorite toy in a drawer and stare at this tired, dusty thing and find it impossible to understand how there were months when you couldn't go to sleep at night without it. You change and you forget and you leave behind. You abandon things.'

'I had an imaginary friend too,' Dawn said. 'It's why I leave a couple of mouthfuls at the end of a meal.'

'So you know what I'm talking about.'

'No. I was six years old. All this . . . It's very hard to believe.'

'Oh, believe it,' said a voice from the backseat.

There was a low chuckle, and David realized, far too late, that this had been the source of the swirling blackness he'd felt from the moment he got into the car.

Then all the doors locked.

CHAPTER 64

It took ten minutes to get back to Chelsea. On the way, I fumbled a card out of my wallet and made a call to the cops. I got an answering machine on Raul Brooke's number, but I figured leaving a message was better than nothing.

That done, I concentrated on moving fast. Lyds had been insistent I shouldn't go straight to the church but instead should meet her at the junction of Eighth Avenue and 13th. There was no sign of her. I'd tried to get her to be more specific about what was going down, but she was both more together and even crazier than usual, and making the call from a phone box in a noisy bar. I didn't know what to do but wait to see if she appeared.

I tried Kristina yet again in the meantime. 'Kris,' I said, fighting to keep my voice fairly calm. 'Please call me back. I'm sorry about what happened. I'm sorry you couldn't stop it. But *we have to talk*.'

I ended the message feeling I'd once again failed to say anything that would make a difference. On an afterthought I called back and added: 'Plus I saw Maj and some other guy in Union Square.

Maj looks upset and very angry. I don't know whether he'd try to do anything to Catherine, but if you're near where she lives and see him, bear it in mind. And *please call me.*'

Someone emerged from a shadowed doorway. It was Lydia. Her eyes were wide. She was swallowing compulsively. She approached warily.

'Is . . . that you?'

'Of course it's me, Lyds. How long have you been watching?'

She took cautious steps toward me, peering like a mole. 'I had to be sure. Lot of liars out tonight.'

'A lot of what?'

She swept her hand to indicate the busy avenue. 'You see them too, right? I know you do. Mirror people in windows and puddles, and then the assholes aren't even really there. They're always around. But tonight . . .'

'Lyds . . .'

She kept looking around suspiciously. 'All *over* the place. Liars. Never *seen* so many. I saw a shadow man run away down the street and climb up a wall like a spider. I saw a hefty girl with white hair screaming and punching a store window and it didn't even break. Five minutes ago I saw another guy, running up 16th. You believe me?'

'Yes, probably, whatever. Lyds, I don't know where Kris is and everything is badly fucked up. Can you *just tell me what's going on?*'

'I went to the church a couple hours ago. Wanted to talk to the priest. He wasn't there and I was going to leave, but then he came back. He looked worse than you do. Not beat up, but *fucked* up. Thought he was drunk, he was staggering up the road so bad. Face wet and smeared and like, I don't know what. He gets his shit together and lets me into the church, but he's shaking and so messed up he can't hold his hands steady. There's a thing of coffee on a table and I pour some for him, and even though it's cold he drinks it and drinks some more and he starts pacing around the place and talking to himself.'

'About what?'

She started hurrying up the avenue, and I followed. 'I have no idea. It's just word and then word and they ain't connected, but he's getting angrier and angrier. All this shit about his life and I don't know what. I mean, Jesus fuck, I ain't so fucking happy about how the dice has rolled for me the last few decades, but this guy has *really* got his hate on. He's hurting bad.'

I put together how many times Jeffers had dropped Lizzie's name when he'd been discussing the people he'd been trying to help. I wondered if, while he'd been trying to assist them all toward whatever light he felt beckoned to them, perhaps he'd been reaching out to one in particular – reaching out *for*, even. I didn't know how to reconcile that with what he'd told us he believed, but I was giving up on the idea of things making sense. Maybe things don't *have* to make sense. Maybe we should just let everything be.

'And then what?'

'Suddenly he stops shouting. When he starts talking again, he's calm but in a bad way. Tells me he has done wrong, got distracted. Then he goes downstairs and I hear him yelling on the phone. He's even weirder when he comes back up. I tried to talk him down, but he's not hearing. He tells me the whole time he's been there there's been ghosts downstairs under the church. He says it's another priest or some shit like that. The guy never left and is watching him the whole time, watching, watching. He says the ghost's never going to leave unless he steps up and does the thing. The man is . . . this priest has got serious issues, John, is what I'm saying. I left him to it because I don't need this kind of crap in my life right now, but as I'm coming out another guy turns up in the street, heading for the church, and he *reeks* of bad.'

'What did he look like?'

'Tough-looking, coat, head like a bullet.'

'Shit,' I said wearily. We were now at the corner of 16th. 'Okay, Lyds, you did the right thing.'

'I know. But what are you going to do about it?'

'I'm going to the church. You're going to walk away.'

'I hear you.'

I started up the street, feeling exhausted and scared. I'll admit I was wondering why I would risk contact with a man who'd already beaten the crap out of me. Because another man had been kind to us and taken us in during the middle of the night, I guess. I hoped that was a good enough reason.

I realized Lydia was trotting along right behind me. 'Lyds . . .'

'Said I heard you,' she rasped. 'Didn't say I was going to do what you fucking said.'

CHAPTER 65

When I got to the church I heard the sound of shouting from inside the building and so I ran through the gates and up the stairs, Lydia close behind.

'More liars,' Lydia whispered loudly as I hurried down the corridor toward the sound of pain. 'Fake people. You *listen* to me, John.'

The hall was barely lit but for a couple of lamps and a row of candles down at the far end and it felt like a damp mausoleum. Reinhart was right in the middle, chairs in chaos all around him. Maj was leaning against the wall, watching, face like thunder.

Jeffers lay in a slumped position against the far wall, near the remains of the altar, blood dripping from his nose. He lifted his head when he saw me, but I didn't see anyone I recognized in his eyes.

'Wow, déjà vu,' I said to Reinhart, feeling my fists bunch hard and tight. 'You really get a kick out of messing up a church, huh?'

He did a double take. 'Jesus, *you're* here? How fucking dumb *are* you, Henderson? Haven't you been back to your shitty little apartment yet?'

'That's what I'm here about. I want my girl-friend's credit card back.'

Lydia scuttled around me and toward the priest. Reinhart made a grab for her as she passed, but his attention was on me and she eluded him.

'Actually you don't,' he said. 'I already used it to buy some pretty funky stuff.'

'You and I need to talk sometime,' I told Reinhart. 'But that's not why I'm here. I want the priest.'

'You want . . . the priest?'

'I'm going to get him out of your face, okay?'

Reinhart walked over to me. 'I checked you out,' he said thoughtfully. 'You used to do some intelligence shit for the government, right?'

'Long time ago.'

'Must have been. I find it hard to believe intelligence *ever* figured in your life. You honestly think you're walking out of here, with the praise Jesus fuckhead or without? Then you're even dumber than you look. You've saved me time by presenting your-self, though, so thank you. I think it's important to be polite to people, don't you, if they've done a good thing?'

I didn't say anything.

'I really do,' he mused. 'Because that way they understand that when you kill them, you mean that too.'

He pistoned his hand out into my chest, knocking me backward. 'You trying to take over my action? You really think you can do that?'

'I just want the priest,' I said doggedly. 'I don't even understand what these people are.'

I heard Lydia bellowing from the end wall, asking me to help. She was trying to keep Jeffers down. He was hauling himself to his feet and in the direction of the broken altar. I wasn't in a position to influence their debate because Reinhart was right up in my face now and thrumming with the desire to hurt.

'You don't?' he sneered. 'I'll explain. It's simple. They're children. Without attention they're nothing – like all the other losers in this city, in this whole country. It's *look at me, look at me* all fucking day. If no one's looking then they're just empty space, like ninety-nine percent of people in the world.'

'See,' I said. 'You don't know either. Aren't you even curious?'

'I just told you, asshole.'

'No. You just told me about yourself.'

The street door slammed open behind me and I turned with relief to see a man I'd been hoping would arrive – the person I'd called on the way from Union Square. Raul, the detective who'd come to see me in the hospital.

'S'up, Mr Henderson,' he said.

He looked alert and ready for action, and my stomach flipped over with relief. Reinhart looked perplexed.

'What the fuck are you doing here?'

The cop came and stood next to him. 'Mr Henderson called for assistance. I'm here to help.'

Reinhart laughed. 'I love it. I just been telling him how dumb he is.'

I realized he was right.

CHAPTER 66

Things happened fast, and this time I was the first to move. It'd been brewing since I woke up in the hospital smarting with the ego of a man who's been physically dominated by another. The cop just happened to be at the head of the line. I decided to cut the next few exchanges and hammered my fist straight up into his gut as hard as I could. He staggered, reaching into his jacket.

Reinhart was very fast to rotate about the waist and throw a blow up toward my face, but I'd been caught out by his speed before and had already stepped to the side and around the cop in anticipation.

I knew he'd be straight after me and that I couldn't fight them both at once, so I focused on smacking hard on the cop, trying to keep him between me and Reinhart long enough to at least get one of them down.

Raul was sucking breath trying to recover from the first punch at the same time as having to duck from further punches from me, and he messed up pulling his hand out of his coat. I ducked another incoming blow from Reinhart and kicked out to the side, catching him below the knee hard enough to knock him back. I was aware of Maj pushing himself off the wall and heading our way and I didn't know what, if anything, he'd be able to do, but I knew it wouldn't be on my side, so I went for broke and smacked my forehead down into the cop's nose, slashing out with my left elbow and connecting with Reinhart's throat more by luck than judgment.

The cop staggered backward. I grabbed his arm. The hand holding the gun tore free from his inside pocket and I let him drop. He slammed onto the floor semi-sideways, head connecting with the boards, and I stamped on his wrist with all my weight.

The fingers spasmed, letting go of the gun.

Reinhart was too strong though, and my blow to the face hadn't done more than delay him for a second. He slammed into me from the side as I was reaching for the cop's weapon, throwing me off balance to tumble toward Raul, too twisted to try to roll out of it.

A kick caught me under the arm where he'd hit me time and again in the restaurant, sending a vast bloom of pain across my ribs, unusually sharp and pointed, but in my head it was like being winged on the leg by the hood of a car while running across a highway – I knew I absolutely could not stop driving forward, no matter how much it hurt, or Reinhart would tag me time and again until I couldn't move anymore . . . and this time he'd leave me dead on the floor.

I scrabbled out with my fingers and got ahold of the gun while Reinhart pulled back for another kick, and as I rolled onto my back I could see in his face that this one was coming at my head and would stop me cold. His eyes were already seeing a world in which I was deceased and all that remained was finding a chainsaw.

I swung my arm around to the front and pulled the trigger. I saw his eyes fly open.

Then he was gone.

Not run, not ducked, not sidestepped. He disappeared.

I jumped up, gun gripped in both hands, raking it around in a shaky circle. I panned past Jeffers, who'd finally made it to his feet and was heading to the end of the hall, shambling like an old man.

'Where'd he go?'

Maj looked dumbfounded.

'Where did he go?'

'He's one of us,' he said, slowly, as the penny dropped.

'What do you mean? How *can* he be?'

'Well, what did you think?' the cop muttered. He'd pushed himself up onto his elbows. There was blood on his face and his eyes looked groggy but were refocusing fast.

I pointed the gun at him. 'Are you one too?'

'Me? I'm just a regular guy.'

'So . . . are you Reinhart's friend? His real person?'

'Hell no. Way he tells it, he killed that guy years ago, before he came to the city. Whacked him in a motel room in the back of beyond, somewhere out West. He's killed a lot of people since, like I tried to tell you in the hospital, but you wouldn't fucking listen. Every one has made him stronger. I did *try* to warn you, asshole.'

Maj looked like a person whose world had sheared apart in front of his eyes. 'But . . . how can he have killed his friend and still . . . be?'

'Search me. You're the freaks. You figure it out. All I know is he's got a dozen of you people heading into the streets tonight to do the same thing.'

Maj walked quickly away toward the door. I shouted to him, 'What does this mean?'

The cop took his chance and started to get up. He looked like a man who knew he'd been playing the wrong side of the fence for a long time and if he didn't get rid of me, he was about to pay for it.

'Stay the fuck down,' I said, bearing down on him. 'Where's Reinhart now?'

'I have no idea. He comes and goes. I did start out trying to nail the guy, you know, like a real policeman. I worked out that wasn't going to be possible, and well, you know how the song goes. If you can't beat them . . .'

I realized I'd read him wrong. 'Why aren't you scared I'm going to call you in?'

'Because you've got a girlfriend and you have

no idea where Reinhart is right now. Or where he'll be tomorrow night when you're sleeping.'

'If he wants to hurt us he'll do it anyway.'

'That's true,' the cop said cheerfully. 'You've made some bad life choices recently, huh.'

'Where *is he*?'

'Downstairs,' Jeffers said.

Keeping the gun on the cop, I stepped back to widen the angle and saw Jeffers re-emerging from the door at the end of the hall. He shut it behind him and set off toward the street door, limping. His nose was at an angle, there was blood at the corners of his mouth, and his breathing was ragged. Reinhart had hurt him badly, inside, and he needed a hospital – and yet the priest looked lighter than I'd ever seen him before.

'How do you know? Did you see him down there?'

'I don't need to.'

Jeffers got to the end of the hall and pulled the main door shut. He gave it a tug to make sure – a man trying to set in order the parts of the world over which he feels he has control. 'He won't have run. The devil never does. He bides his time; he entreats and entices. He'll wait until you're off guard and then reappear, and this time he'll kill you.'

'What's downstairs?'

'Don't go down there.'

'*What's downstairs?*'

'Cellars. They stretch under the church and the

houses on each side. Full of chairs that need repairing and Bibles and prayer books that seem to be surplus to requirements these days. And dead people.'

'*What?*'

'The previous father knew about the ghosts too. He allowed some to rest here, as they waited the call home. I didn't work that out until today. I thought it was just *his* spirit down there, restless, unsatisfied with my work. In a way it's a relief to know it's not.'

'Excuse me – *who's* downstairs?'

He ignored me. 'It's not working, though. They do not fade and will not leave. Either God isn't calling them loudly enough or they're just not listening. It's my job to lead them home. To lead you all.'

With a great deal of effort he fumbled something out of his trouser pocket. It was a key. He locked the door, then started doggedly back the other way.

'Jeffers – what are you doing?'

'Don't worry. I don't think any of them will aid Reinhart. They're Hollows. You can feel their presence but they don't move much anymore and they don't care enough about anything to help. He wants *you* to go down there, though. Can't you feel that?'

I could. I didn't know whether it was merely my desire to finish the business with Reinhart, or something else, but there was an undeniable draw to go downstairs.

'You must not,' the priest said. 'In the darkness he will win. Evil always thrives in the dark, whether it is literal lack of light, or mere ignorance.'

'John,' Lydia said. She was bending down, her hand on the floor. 'You getting this?'

I didn't understand what she meant and ignored her, focusing on the cop – who showed every sign of wanting to get back into it – and trying to make sense of what the priest was saying. 'We can't leave Reinhart down there,' I said. 'I'm not going to just let him go.'

'Oh, neither am I. There's only one thing that has always worked,' Jeffers said, as he got to the remains of the altar. 'It purges and transforms.'

'Jeffers – what the fuck are you doing?'

'*John,*' Lydia said more insistently, but by then I'd already realized what she was talking about. The floor was getting hot under foot.

The priest opened the door in the wall behind the altar and threw the key through it, threw it hard, as smoke came billowing out.

CHAPTER 67

David and Dawn sat with their arms wrapped around each other's heads. Of course they'd tried to unlock the doors and smash the windows, but cars aren't designed to allow this. The designers of modern automobiles do not realize that someday you may have to try to escape from things you cannot touch and can barely see. David had tried talking to the people in the back. The more he talked, the clearer they became, though this was not a good thing. There were two men, one woman. He recognized them.

The woman in back giggled, and the car locks went back up. 'You can get out now,' she said.

Her voice sounded like the strange friend of your mother's who one night said, 'Go on, try it, just this one time; you may even like it.'

Dawn kept her head buried in David's shoulder. She couldn't see the people in the back. She'd tried, but all that happened was that her vision went blurry and she felt twists of fury and vicious misery, like tiny arrows of pre-menstrual tension. She could make out their voices, like snatches of a radio in the next street, but she didn't try to hear what they were saying. Dawn wasn't having any of this. It wasn't lack of strength, and her husband understood that. It was a simple refusal to deal.

David envied her that. He'd always accommodated, always had his doors open too wide. Things had come in. Things had gone out, too – and stayed alive. 'No,' he said, however. 'I'm not opening anything.'

'This is our whole problem, you see,' the girl in the back muttered. 'All your heavy, heavy things. And *Christ* does it piss us off. *Open the door.*'

'No,' David said. 'You can't do anything to us.'

'You're very wrong. As your fat friend Talia would tell you, assuming she could still talk.'

'You . . . What did you do to her?'

'A little game. Real people play in make-believe. *We* get to play with real life – so *much* more fun. Dreams can bite – and they draw real blood. Now open that door or I'm going to slip into your wife's head and scare her so badly she'll abort right here and now.'

Dawn jerked her head off David's shoulder. 'Who said that?' she whispered. 'Who's *back* there?'

'See?' The thin woman laughed. 'She can hear *some* things. She'll hear enough when I tell her secrets about what people do to other people sometimes. And especially to little children.'

'What do you *want*?' David pleaded, knowing he was fighting a losing battle. 'We've done nothing to you.'

557

'You all do something to *all* of us. And we're done putting up with it.'

'Open the door,' one of the men in the backseat said, the one with straggly hair.

'Open it. Open it,' chanted the man with the shaved head, leaning to put his face next to the woman's, 'or I'll take the ride into your wife's tidy little soul too. It'll be some trip, dude. I've always been the most imaginative when it comes to breaking things.'

'Oh, nonsense,' said the woman. 'Though impersonating the trailer whale's dead beau *was* your idea, I'll admit. Open the door, David.'

Then her expression changed. She hissed: '*Quickly*.'

David heard shouting and saw Maj running up the street. It was like feeling every lie you've ever told and every mistake you've made coming bubbling up out of your subconscious at once, as if someone had found the hidden notebook in which you've written your worst deeds and thoughts and started to read it out loud.

And David realized things had gotten even worse.

Maj stopped at the car. He took a deep breath. Then he reached out and opened the door. David stared up at him: caught, guilty, powerless.

'David,' Maj said, years of hurt and loneliness starting to burn. 'We really need to talk.'

Dawn turned to see a man in jeans and an

558

untucked shirt. His hair was tousled and his jaw stubbled. It was a look she knew David could pull off, though she'd given up trying to lead him toward it.

'I can see you,' she said.

'Makes sense,' the man said. 'You probably know him better than anyone but me.'

'No,' Dawn said, pushing herself away from David and getting out of the car. 'I know him *better*.'

'Dawn . . .' David said, getting out the other side.

Maj stared her down. 'You don't even know who I am.'

'You're Maj. He just told me everything.'

'I doubt it.'

'So you're his friend – I get that. You were kids together. I get that too. But he's not yours anymore. He's my *husband*.'

David came around the front. 'Dawn, let me—'

'No!' she shouted. 'I'm *not* going to let you handle this. That's not the way it's going to be, sunshine.'

Maj wasn't getting drawn into the discussion. When he'd seen the car, he'd known this was meant to be, that David arriving in town so soon after Lizzie had gone – and moments after realizing Reinhart had never been real – meant it was time for this joke to be put to bed. Either David was going to put him back into his rightful place in his life, or Maj would take it from him.

Dawn saw this in his eyes, or felt it, and stepped in front of David, keeping him back with her arm.

'I don't want to hurt you,' Maj said, taking a step toward them. 'So get out of the way.'

'No,' Dawn said. 'Not doing it.'

'He's mine.'

'Mine.'

'I *deserve his life*. I was always the one who made things happen. He's a liar and a taker. You *all* are.'

'He's not,' Dawn shouted.

'If you don't know that about him,' Maj said, in wonder, 'then you don't know him at all.'

'I know who he is. You just know who he *was*. People change and friendships end. Deal with it.'

David kept trying to pull Dawn away, but she was strong, and furious like he'd never seen her before. Meanwhile, the three skinny people had slipped out of the car and were crowding around, laughing at him in the way he'd always suspected people did when he wasn't looking.

'I'm having a real life,' Maj said. 'It's time.'

He pushed Dawn aside. David backed up, trying to get away around the side of the car. He couldn't get past the skinny people. They blocked him, rubbing their bodies against him. They possessed no substance except for the disgust they made you feel, but that was enough.

Maybe he shouldn't *try* to get away.

Maybe this had been coming all his life, or at least since he got a phone call in the middle of the night a decade ago telling him that his mother

560

and father were dead. If it had *always* felt like a struggle to live, to make friends, to write, to be alive, perhaps it would be easier to let it all go.

'Yes,' a voice said, close to his ear. The red-haired woman had pushed even closer to him, letting the front of her dress fall open. It smelled bad in there. 'You're right, Davey. It would be *so* much easier that way. You won't be lonely anymore. Do it. Just let go.'

David's mind filled with a flash image seen through some other boy's eyes, a scene from many years ago. It was so brief that he couldn't register what it showed – only that the boy in question had been broken into pieces one dark winter's afternoon in a house somewhere up in Wisconsin twenty years ago, and that this woman and her three brothers had been that boy's attempt to surround himself with something he could under-stand – though it turned out that even the people out of his own head were not his friends. It all got very badly away from him, and there arrived the week when he murdered his family, slowly, one at a time, along with several other people he'd never admitted to and whose bodies have never been found.

David lost the strength in his legs and crashed down to his knees.

'No!' Dawn shouted. 'David – *get up.*'

But . . . why would he? Would it be worth it? Yes, he was going to be a father, probably. So what? He'd screw that up too, carrying on the genetic line. A bad father and a bad writer, a thief and a cheat. Was it worth slogging through the next forty years to prove the fact? If a character was destined to mess up every plotline you tried to put him in, why not let him go, cut him out?

'Do it then,' he mumbled, looking up to see Maj standing over him. 'Have my life, if you want.'

Dawn tried to get to David but couldn't get past the end of the car. There was something in her way, or someone, *more* than one – she could feel their unpleasant pressure forcing against her like a field of anxiety and temptation, though she couldn't see anyone but Maj. She tried to shout out, to call for help – surely there would be *someone* in the houses on the street who would hear – but blank despair strangled the noise in her throat.

Then, thank God, she heard someone else shouting.

She pulled her eyes from the sight of David on his knees in the gutter next to the car (her car, *their* car, the car she'd already pictured with two little car seats in the back, and years from now, the sound of singing and are-we-there-yet and I-Spy games) and saw two people running down the road.

At least . . . for a moment she thought it was two, but then it was only one – a woman, skinny and tall.

★　★　★

562

Kristina knew right away what Maj had in mind.

'Maj, *no*,' she shouted. Maj was pulling in long, deep breaths and punching them back out again. Each time this happened it seemed like the hairs on his head were more visible. 'You think Lizzie can't see you?'

'Don't try to—'

'Oh, shut up,' she snapped. 'Lizzie's dead. That doesn't mean she's gone. And she *loved* you.'

'She didn't love me,' he said. 'She loved Catherine. Which is how it should—'

'Catherine was her friend and that never goes away. But Lizzie loved *you*. She told me so.'

'Listen to her, Maj,' Flaxon said.

Kristina saw a great flatness in Maj's eyes that said he knew he should care about what was being said but didn't understand it. 'It doesn't matter. She's gone.'

'Don't do it, Maj,' another voice said, urgently. A squat man in a strange suit was hurrying toward them – the man Kristina had seen in SoHo with Reinhart the first time she went for a walk with Lizzie.

Flaxon snarled at him. 'Fuck off, Golzen.'

'No, listen to him,' Kristina said. 'He's trying to stop—'

'It'll just be some trick,' Flaxon said. 'This is the asshole who told me I wasn't real and got me into a whole load of shit that I only escaped because Lizzie showed me another way. Him and his putrid-ass brothers and sister are groomer slime.'

563

'Brothers?' Kristina said.

Flaxon pointed at the three tall, thin people looming over the man who was on his knees in the gutter. 'They've all got the same real person – a world-class sicko called Simon Jedburgh, who's been locked in a psych ward twenty years for . . . what was it? Oh yeah – dismembering his entire fucking family.'

'I've made mistakes,' Golzen said. 'I'm trying to put them right.'

'I don't believe you,' Flaxon spat. 'There's no promised land either, FYI. That's more bullshit, probably the crazy crap your psycho friend is screaming in his padded cell.'

Golzen turned from her and focused on Maj. 'Don't harm your friend,' he said. 'No good will come of it.'

'Reinhart's one of us,' Maj said.

Golzen stared at him. '*What*?'

'He killed his friend. Look what it did for *him*.'

Golzen looked like he was putting ten things together at once. 'That's what he's been planning,' he said quietly. 'That's what he meant by 'Perfect' all along. Evolving to another state. Getting us to kill our real people, to become more like him.'

'Suits me,' Maj said. 'Bring it on.'

But Flaxon threw herself at him and started ranting in his face, and then all of them were shouting at once.

Dawn meanwhile kept trying to get through to David, to get his eyes to refocus on her. 'Please,

564

David,' she said. 'Please get up. These things aren't real. They can't do this to you.'

The woman called Kristina turned her head. 'What the hell is that?'

Dawn realized she could smell something, and heard a crackling sound. 'Is that from the church?'

The others turned to look. 'Who's in there?' Kristina screamed at Maj. '*Who's in there?*'

'The priest and Reinhart,' Maj said. 'Some old woman. And . . . your man.'

Kristina grabbed David by the scruff of the neck. She hauled him to his feet, shoving him toward Dawn. 'Get him out of here,' she said, and then sprinted up the street toward the church.

After a beat, Maj and the others followed.

CHAPTER 68

Some people are always going to look after themselves – first, foremost, and always. The cop was one of them. He latched on to what Lydia and I had realized – that the priest had set fire to the building, for *the love of Christ* – and that my attention was drawn. He threw himself into me, clattering us into a pile of overturned chairs. He wasn't in Reinhart's league, but he was desperate and focused on one task – getting his gun back.

I got tangled in a mess of broken wood and was finding it impossible to strike back. After ten seconds I started to be afraid that he was going to win. He got his hands around my wrist and began smacking it against anything he could find, sticking terrier-like to the task despite me kicking and kneeing him as hard as I could. Then there was a crunching blow that took us both on the shoulders and smacked us down onto the ground.

'Jesus,' Lydia said.

I crawled away to see her holding the remains of the chair she'd brought down on us. 'Men are all the same,' she muttered. 'Get us *out* of here, you assholes. Then you can beat each other to death for all I care.'

The cop had taken more of the impact and was still on hands and knees, trying to raise his head. Smoke was billowing in through the door at the end. Jeffers sat on the chair facing the congregation. He looked composed.

'Jeffers,' I said. 'What have you done?'

He smiled with the maddening peacefulness of someone who is so far out the other side of present circumstances that he finds it hard to understand what you're saying.

I pulled out my phone, but the screen was blank and cracked, and I knew there'd be a phone-shaped bruise on my ribs where Reinhart's shoe had connected with it before I pulled the gun on him. I pressed buttons and nothing happened.

'Call 911,' I shouted to the cop, who was getting back to his feet.

'Left it in the car,' he muttered.

I ran to the main door and yanked at the handle. It was locked. I knew that. I'd stood and watched Jeffers do it but had been too caught up in Reinhart's disappearance and keeping the gun on the cop that I hadn't processed the implications.

I looked up at the big glass windows, knowing I'd noticed the first time I'd been in the room that they were covered with wire. I jumped onto the table with the scattered remains of Billy's last meal, and tried to see if the wire could be gotten off. Maybe – if you had a few hours and a selection of tools. Some very thorough person had bedded it into the sides of the window frames. There were no other windows in the church because there were buildings on both sides. The roof was thirty feet above my head.

I got down and went back to the front door. I kicked it. Banged my shoulder against it. I realized the cop was heading toward me again and rounded on him.

'Fuck with me and I'll shoot you,' I said. 'We don't have time for this.'

'I know,' he said – and threw his own shoulder against the door. Nothing happened. He did it again.

I left him to it and headed back to where Jeffers was sitting. 'Is there any way out through the basement?'

'There's no way out of anywhere.'

'Listen to me,' I said. 'I understand that you're in pain of various kinds and have things you feel you need to do. You've got three other people in here with you, though. You don't get to make that call.'

'A bad cop, a crazy lady, and a man trying to find his path,' the priest said.

'Is that supposed to be me, or you?'

'Oh, both, don't you think?'

The cop had given up on battering the door. 'Look, you fucking whacko—'

'If Reinhart's a ghost,' I said, holding my hand out to keep the cop back, 'then how is this going to help?'

568

'He's not a ghost. I thought we covered that. He's the reason these souls are trapped in the city.'

I could hear the crackling of wood and old paper from below. Smoke was pouring out of the basement door. 'At least shut that,' I yelled at the cop.

Meanwhile Lyds had come closer. She seemed the calmest person in the room. 'But why us?' she asked.

'I had to move quickly,' the priest said. 'The battle always turns on a moment of decisive action. History shows this. Any one of you could decide to help him. It's better this way.'

'Reinhart's just one of these . . . people,' I said. 'Somehow he's found a way of getting to the other side of the Bloom and surviving, that's all. How do you know he didn't put the idea for this into your head? How do you know he can't just flip himself out of here, leaving us to burn to death?'

'He can't.'

'How do you know?'

'He's right,' the cop said. 'Reinhart can't do that. He can hide himself in plain sight, but he can't magic himself through walls. He's too solid.'

I hesitated, trying to stop myself from doing the wrong thing. When there's a fire, you want to run. Senses shriek with how crucial it is that you get yourself away as fast as possible. I knew there was no point just running around the room. I knew also that Jeffers wouldn't help us even if he could.

So I grabbed a chair and went back to the street end of the room for one last try.

I gathered all my strength and smashed the chair into the bottom of the lowest window. The chair shattered into pieces that rained all around me. The window didn't even crack. Not just covered with wire, it turned out, but reinforced. It wouldn't break until the temperature in here got high enough to override the pressure treatment, by which time we'd be a charred memory.

I pulled out the gun and pointed it at the door. I emptied it into the frame and around the handle. Afterward the door looked like shit, but neither tugging or kicking made anything move.

I became aware that Lydia was standing right next to me. She looked scared but also brave.

'Come on,' she said, holding out her hand. 'I'll go with you.'

'Go where?'

'Where the key is.'

Jeffers got to his feet. 'Turn your face from her,' he commanded, his voice low and hard. 'She lies. He is inside her now.'

'You should do it,' the cop said to me. 'She's right. That's where the key is. That's the only chance.'

'So why don't *you* go down there?' Lydia said. 'You're the cop, right?'

He went back to banging on the front door. He started shouting, too, to make it look more like he was doing something of substance rather than turning away from the only road that went anywhere but death.

Lydia took my hand, and I let her lead me toward the far end of the room. Jeffers got there first. He positioned himself in front of the doorway.

'Every second you screw around just makes it more likely that people are going to die,' I said. 'I know very little about your God and his value system, but I don't see how that's ever going to be a good thing.'

'You will not pass,' he said.

I grabbed his head and threw him aside. I pulled open the door to the basement. 'You've done enough,' I told Lydia, and put her gently to one side.

Then I went through the door.

CHAPTER 69

Kristina had her phone out and was on with 911.

'Fire at a church on 16th,' she said, struggling to keep her voice calm and intelligible. 'There are people inside. Please be fast.' The woman on the other end kept trying to getting her to stay on the line, but once Kris knew she'd communicated the information and the urgency she hung up and ran with Flaxon to the church.

The smell was strong and smoke was curling out of ventilation gaps in the brickwork down near the floor inside the gates.

'*Shit*,' Flaxon wailed. 'What are we going to do?'

Maj vaulted straight over the gate. He ran up the stairs to the door on the right, then came back and over to the other side. 'Locked,' he said.

Kris ran back into the street, listening for the sound of sirens and hoping to see a truck – but saw nothing other than the couple that had been at the car down the street, hurrying toward her. With early-evening traffic there was no knowing how long it would take for help to arrive. Could be five minutes. Could be twenty.

Could be long enough for everyone to die.

The guy called David seemed to have gotten himself together now, a little. 'What's happening?'

'The church is on fire,' Kris said, feeling dream-like. 'And my boyfriend is inside.'

There was a muted crash as a shadow came and went against the lowest of the colored panes of glass on the upper floor. John throwing something against it, Kristina guessed, and though it made her feel sick to realize that whatever he'd tried had failed, at least he was still trying things.

'Can you get inside?' she shouted to Flaxon, who was hopping from foot to foot, desperate to do something.

'No,' she said. 'We climb well. But we can't just go through walls.'

Smoke was billowing out of the lower grills; then heat from below starting to build and build. Then there was the sound of eight shots. It sounded like they were coming from close to the right doorway.

Dawn screamed. Kris listened and heard something being struck near the same position. And a shout of frustration that she *knew* was John.

'Has somebody been shot?'

'I don't think so,' she said, but she wasn't sure and she could feel herself panicking.

Maj turned to David. 'Tell me,' he said.

'Tell you what?'

'What to do.'

David had no idea what he meant. Maj leaned

forward and tapped his finger in the middle of David's forehead. '*Focus*. What do you do now? What do *we* do?'

'I don't *know*.'

'So *make it up*, David. You know the question.'

'What question?'

'The only one that ever mattered to you. *What happens next*?'

David looked up at the church, thinking furiously. The doors were locked and too tough to break. The windows on the second story were too high and reinforced and someone had just tried to break through them from the inside and failed. Obviously there was an air route into a basement where the smoke was coming from, but they didn't have the tools to break through, and anyway *that was where the fire was*. 'I don't know,' he said. 'I can't . . .'

Then he stopped, let himself out of the gate and stepped out onto the sidewalk, looking back at the church. He felt something coming at him, opening the door in the back of his mind.

'What?' Maj came after him, followed by Flaxon. 'What have you seen?'

'It's the only thing I can think of.'

Flaxon saw where he was looking. 'The roof.'

Kristina looked up at the shallow-pitched roof, and then downward, tracing a route down the wall. Ornamental bricks stuck out at irregular intervals. *Maybe* you could climb that way, if you scrambled up the head-height columns either side of the doorway and then onto the roof above it. Maybe. And maybe you'd fall and die.

'It's all I've got,' David said. 'I'm sorry.'

Maj ran back into the courtyard. Flaxon followed, looking dubious. Smoke from the basement was curling up the front of the building now. Kris heard more shouting from inside. Maj reached for the column on the left side of the door and pulled himself up, then used both hands to haul himself up onto the roof.

'But we won't be able to break through the roof when we get there,' Flaxon said as she scaled the other column, bracing her toes on the outcrop at the bottom and pulling herself up onto the little roof, moving more quickly and with greater surety than Maj. 'Even you don't have the fingerskills for that, do you?'

Maj shook his head. 'There's nothing else to try. We have to get up there and then see what we can do.'

'I can do it,' David said.

'No, David,' Dawn said firmly.

David turned to Kris. 'Keep her back,' he said. 'She's pregnant.'

He reached for the column by the side of the doorway and started pulling himself up.

'No!' Dawn screamed. She started to run up the stairs, but Kristina held her arms tight. 'Don't!'

'Come back and I'll go,' Kris said, but David had already hauled himself up onto the roof above the doorway and was reaching for the brickwork above.

Maj climbed quickly, but Flaxon was faster. She moved up the upper face of the church like a lizard, hands and feet reaching out for the bricks that poked out. She was up and over onto the roof while Maj was still ten feet down and David had barely made it halfway.

Dawn shook Kristina off. 'But then what?' she shouted.

The same thing had just occurred to Kristina. It was all very well getting up there and maybe even breaking through the roof, but unless there happened to be a thirty-foot ladder in the church all this would achieve was a bird's-eye view of people being burned alive.

She knew also that John wouldn't be waiting for the fates to step in on his behalf. He'd be trying to break down the walls of the reality he found himself in, kicking toward some better place on the other side, even if that place didn't exist, and even if running toward it might bring the end upon him quicker than it might otherwise have done.

'Please, John,' she prayed, silently, but as deep and loud as she could. 'I love you. Please don't do something brave.'

David nearly fell, twice. The bricks were cold and wet and he'd realized before he was halfway to the roof that this was an insane thing to try and he just wasn't strong enough for it. He knew also that he wasn't strong enough to spend the rest of his life aware that he'd stood on the sidewalk and done nothing, however. He already had too much guilt and regret socked away.

He reached up with hand after hand and scrabbled for enough purchase under his fingers to feel he stood a chance. He was terrified. His insides were twisted so tightly that he could barely breathe. But when he felt he'd gotten enough traction with his fingertips he pushed carefully up with his right leg, straightening it, until his head was poking up over the roof.

Maj and Flaxon were standing halfway down, as if being up here was the most natural thing in the world.

Somehow this made David realize it was only the *idea* of standing on a roof that was frightening. Apart from the knowledge of what will happen to you if you fall, it's no different from being on a slope a couple of feet off the ground. The idea felt precarious in his mind, but it was enough to get him moving again.

He brought his left arm over and reached as far as he could, pushing up with the other leg at the same time . . . until he could start to haul himself up onto the tiles.

Maj was stamping at the roof, but nothing was happening. As David pulled himself up far enough that the balance of his weight was over the roof, he realized that wasn't going to change. He could barely feel the vibration of the other man's foot striking the tiles, even though he was doing it time after time with all his force.

Which meant it was down to David. He hauled himself up using his left hand to grab on to the capstone at the peak of the gable. The pitch of the roof was thankfully shallow, designed to make the space inside seem as big and impressive as possible.

He pulled himself along the tiles toward Maj and Flaxon, using his other hand to scoot himself across the wet tiles. They were slippery and a few were missing. The second time he came across a hole he lowered his head and looked into the gap beyond.

'Need more than that,' Maj said, shouting against the wind. David saw that he was right. Beyond the hole was a narrow space, then beams and tight-fitting planks of wood.

Making sure he had a good hold on the capstone, he used his other hand to bang against the boards. They were very solid. Levering off tiles wasn't going to be enough.

'*Now* what?' the girl asked. She'd come over and was squatted down beside him, looking into the hole.

'What about the other end?' Maj said. 'Maybe there's a window on the other side of the church.'

'So what? We're not going to be able to get to it – and even if we can, it's obviously too high for whoever's in there to get to, or they'd have tried it already.'

Maj looked down at David. 'This was a crap idea,' he said, not unkindly.

Then his foot slipped on a broken tile, and he started to fall.

From below all they saw was a shadow standing at the apex of the roof, right at the end. The sound of flames in the basement was now clearly audible, and the smoke coming out had turned black and choking. There had been no more noises from inside the building itself.

Dawn heard sirens and turned to look up the street. She missed the moment where Maj lost his footing, slipped, and started to topple over the edge of the roof.

She also missed seeing David's hand lash out.

CHAPTER 70

The other side of the door was a space barely big enough to turn around in, a narrow set of stairs leading down on the left. Within seconds of starting down it was almost impossible to see anything through the smoke.

I didn't want to go down there.

I didn't see any choice.

I held my arm up against my nose and mouth, trying not to breathe deeply despite my lungs' panicky insistence that they needed more air. I felt out with my foot, taking one step at a time. I'd seen the priest throw the key. Surely it couldn't have gone far.

Each time I went down a step I carefully swept my other foot across it, listening for the sound of something small and metal moving against wood.

There was a split-second breeze or change of wind direction and for a moment I could see a little more of where I was – a staircase with a second landing leading down, and below that, reflections of fire on a wall. I thought that I glimpsed something down there, small and dark on the bigger step, and that it *might* be a key.

It was enough to keep me going. But for how long and how far? Could I keep going if it got hotter and if I couldn't see anything?

I had a heavy urge to give up and turn around. It felt as if there was a voice in my head, pleading with me to stop, to turn around – not a bad voice, I didn't think it was Reinhart; it felt like someone who had only love for me and wanted me out of harm's way and for me not to do something dumb.

But if I *didn't* do this, what then?

I made it down to the landing and dropped to a crouch, feeling around on the wooden floor with my hand, trying to stay calm. I couldn't find anything, though I was sure this was the right step. Then my fingers caught on something and by leaning right over and squinting through the smoke I realized it was just a knot in the old wood. That's all I'd seen.

I coughed so hard I went dizzy, caught in a chain of retching spasms that threatened to knock me off balance.

I had to keep going. If Jeffers had thrown the key straight down from the door above, it would have hit the wall over my head and bounced down the next landing. After that it couldn't have gone far. It had to be within twenty feet of where I was. In the growing heat and blackness, that was a long way, but if it meant the difference between living and dying it was close enough.

I lowered myself to a sitting position and started to shuffle down the final set of stairs one at a time.

I heard something ahead. Something new, that is. The crackle of flames from the corner was ever-present. The smoke around me was shot with light from the burning. Some other sound was growing. I got down to the lower level.

Then I saw it. I saw the key.

It was only ten feet away. I dropped onto my hands and knees and felt my way through smoke that had redoubled in thickness. There were splinters in the wood under my hand, but I kept sweeping it back and forth, side to side, reaching out as far ahead of me as I could, until finally they banged into something.

It was hot, the key – the air had heated up to the point where grabbing hold of it made me wince, and then cough again.

I was reaching out too far. The wrenching cough cost me my balance and I tipped onto my face and shoulder, falling to lie halfway around the corner.

My face immediately felt like someone had turned a blowtorch on it. My eyes clamped against the heat, shocked into closure. I was paralyzed, body going into seizure, unable to move in any direction at all.

Above the roar of flames the new noise was getting louder and louder. I'd never heard anything like it in my life before.

Holding my hand out as a block, I cracked open my eyes. All I could see was flame and smoke, alternately black and searing bright, and maybe that's what caused patterns to spark across my brain, as if my eyes were trying to make sense of the insensible.

I felt Reinhart coming toward the corner from the other side. He was at ease. He was glad I'd come. He was happy there was fire. It held no fear for him. He knew it's what you need to transform.

Between us there was the smoke and it was full of people now. It seemed like the flames were high-lighting things that lay and sat along this stretch of corridor, scrunched into fetal balls or standing with their faces against the walls. There was a figure with a grotesquely large head and a woman dressed like a dolly, her hair in braids. There were children, or things shaped like them. There was a lion with golden eyes.

The sound . . . I don't know what it was. I will never know. I couldn't tell whether it was the noise of beings dying, or being born, of horror or a fierce and mindless kind of joy, of a huge dark door being slammed shut forever, or a white one being opened as fifty souls woke from dusty sleep together and moved their fading limbs.

It was horrible. It was beautiful. It held my attention a moment too long.

When I coughed again it didn't feel like all of it came back out. Certainly not enough. My chest locked, full of smoke and heat and unable to expel.

My mind filled with a face, nothing to do with anything down here. It was the face of my remaining son, Tyler, as I'd last seen him, and I realized with terrible sadness that I had abandoned him like some imaginary boy, presenting my back as I walked out of his life. I'd turned my back on him in pain, and to keep myself sane, but he wasn't to understand that. All he knew was that he'd been forgotten and left behind.

The shapes in the smoke still moved. I couldn't get up. My cheek was flat against the boards and I could feel the heat rising from them and hear the sound of whatever beings lined the corridor ahead.

I could also feel Reinhart getting closer to where I lay sprawled, my mind fluttering, splitting into black and white and heat. It did not feel like a single person coming toward me, but I couldn't tell whether that was because of all the others around the corridor or if Reinhart's power and concentration came from a gathering of the people he'd caused to die, lost souls corralled into one vessel and bent now to a single will. Each one of us contains multitudes, after all: who we are and who we've been, and perhaps also who we love or kill.

He squatted down in front of me. His clothes were on fire. He put a finger under my chin and lifted my head.

'I got plans,' he said. 'I don't need you running around my head like some big black dog without a home. You . . . can just die. It's my gift to you.'

He looked up, as if hearing something. He smiled and stood back up and backed away into the flames and smoke until he became part of them.

I knew that getting the key wasn't enough.

I had to get him, too.

I tried to push myself up. Nothing happened. Once again I heard that other voice, the one deep in my mind, telling me not to do anything rash, not to be a hero. I realized it was Kristina.

'It's okay,' I whispered. 'I'll be fine.' I'm not sure if the words made it out of my head.

I pulled my arm around and tried to get it in front of my face before pulling in another breath. This time I got just enough air into my lungs to experience a moment of jagged clarity, and knew I had to get out of here, *right now*, or Reinhart was going to get what he wanted.

I tried to shift all my limbs at once, hoping to get at least one of them to achieve concerted movement. Nothing happened, again, and I realized that's all I had left. It had been my last shot.

I coughed and I coughed and I coughed, each time with less and less strength.

Then someone yanked my arm, hard – so hard that I felt my chest pulled off the floor and my body dragged up into a slumped position, and beyond.

I heard a voice in my ear, speaking with extraordinary calm. Strong hands hauled me up onto my knees, and this time I knew the hands were real.

I looked up through the smoke, as the hands shoved me back along the corridor, and saw Jeffers's face.

'Go,' he said.

The priest stepped over me to walk into the smoke and down through the slowly moving shapes and toward the turning at the end, beyond which lay the fire and whatever now waited there for him, the man or being or thing that called itself Reinhart.

As I crawled toward the stairs I heard the sound of breakage from above, as though a door had been smashed into pieces. Then a lot of shouting.

I made it halfway up.

CHAPTER 71

What happened in the next hour is patchy. I remember sitting on the curb with an oxygen mask on my face and a blanket around my shoulders, Kristina perched alongside and holding me so tightly she was making it harder to breathe than all the smoke I'd inhaled. I didn't hold that against her, not least because she'd saved my life.

I remember watching a stream of the firefighters she'd summoned going in and out of the church. At first it seemed they'd got it under control, but then something new caught fire in the basement and it started to get away from them. There was a lot of shouting and running. Eventually it died back.

I had told them about seeing the priest in the cellar. I heard one later saying to a colleague that he'd tried to make his way through the blaze down there and thought he saw two people in the distance at the far end before the heat forced him to retreat, though according to the papers the next morning the remains of only one body was eventually retrieved from the wreckage. The picce took

587

the line that Father Robert Jeffers had died in defense of his church, trying to save something he believed in. I think that is a fair assessment.

In the meantime I saw Lydia being loaded into the back of an ambulance on a stretcher, deadly pale but alive. A portion of the floor in the church had given way while I was downstairs, and she and the cop got it almost as bad as I did. The cop ran, fleeing the scene the moment the door was opened. He was standing there waiting for his chance, and had been since the moment he realized help had arrived outside. He did nothing to aid the old woman who'd been trapped with him.

I know his name. There will come a reckoning for him. It may arrive via official channels. It may not.

As my head started to clear I became aware of other people in the street. I saw the guy David standing with a woman Kristina explained to me was his wife. Maj came walking diffidently toward David, and Dawn stepped away, coming to where we sat, to give them space.

There was a pause, long and full, as if between two people who'd known each other a long time ago meeting again, people trying to bridge a gulf a hundred years wide but only a couple of feet deep.

'It was short for "imaginary,"' David said, as if he'd been asked a question.

Maj nodded. 'Okay.'

'I'm sorry. I was just a kid, but I should have come up with a better name. You deserved more than that.'

'I'm used to it,' Maj said 'And it's better than having no name at all.'

They stood awkwardly for a moment.

'You didn't have to do that up there,' Maj said. 'Grabbing my hand.'

'I know.'

'No. I mean I wouldn't have died if I fell.'

'That doesn't mean you let people fall.'

Maj nodded, and they looked each other full in the face for the first time. 'Goodbye, David.'

'What are you going to do?'

'Don't know. May try being a Journeyman for a while. There's a great big world outside the city. None of it's perfect. But it's there.'

'Will I see you again?'

'Do you want to?'

'Yes.'

'Then maybe.'

David watched as Maj walked away up the street. He passed the three siblings who had been in Dawn's car. Maj paused, then suddenly lunged at them, for a moment seeming bigger or brighter. They disappeared. Then at the corner he saw Maj pause once more, to exchange words with a squat man in a striped suit.

He started off again and turned the corner, the other man walking by his side, as though they had decided to travel together for now.

Kristina glanced up at Dawn. 'So David's a writer, huh?'

'Yes,' she said proudly. 'He's got a novel coming out soon.'

'Any good?'

'He's awesome. And he'll get even better, too.'

'When's the baby due?'

'Bab*ies*. Not for a while. I can't wait. It'll be so good for David to have a family again. He needs roots to keep him from floating away.'

'Isn't there anyone else but you?'

She shook her head. 'He's an only child, and his parents died in an accident years ago. It was awful for him. It was their fault, too. Well, the people in the car coming up the other side said they thought they *maybe* saw someone stepping into the road before it happened. That David's father swerved to avoid him and lost control. But they never found anyone, and David's always been very sure it was his father's fault.'

'Where was David at the time?'

'Here in the city.'

I saw Kris thinking about this. I knew her well enough to know she could see a door in her mind, one that would open onto things that hadn't been known before; I knew she wanted to ask questions about how far a friend would be prepared to go for their real person if they feared they were losing them, and whether that real person might even have known what had been done on his behalf, and have been living with it ever since.

'Let's go,' I said, pushing myself up to my feet. 'Bad things happen. Leave it at that.'

Some guy from the ambulance shouted at us as we left, but they were sufficiently busy dealing with Lydia – who was trying to sit and cussing up a storm – that we were able to walk away without someone dragging me off to the hospital.

When we got to the corner I looked back at David and Dawn. They were standing with their foreheads touching, hands together. He loved her – I could see that – and she loved him. Sometimes that's all you need to know.

We spent the night at a hotel. I let Kristina do the talking at reception and stood well out of the way and tried not to smell of wood smoke. I had a long shower and we sat in bathrobes on a balcony fifteen floors up and watched the lights and listened to the cars below. You could see people down on the sidewalks, too, walking up and down, back and forth, standing, waiting, living. I've no doubt that some of them were real. I'm unsure now how to tell which, or of how much difference it makes.

Reinhart was still in the city somewhere, alive. I could feel it. I don't know whether I truly believe he killed his friend and became something new, or that he is like the rest of them, or ever was. It could be that Jeffers was right. Reinhart might simply be the unholy ghost, the shadow in our minds, that thing that has always existed wherever

591

humans congregate, something born out of our behaviors and desires and yet which takes on a life of its own. We try to find words to cage this thing, to help us understand, but it is beyond comprehension. All you can do is fight, wherever you find it, and hope that someday your kind will win – the kind that does the best it can, rather than the worst it is capable of.

The next morning we didn't have to discuss what to do. We left the hotel and walked down to Penn Station and bought two tickets for the first long-distance service due to leave. We sat together as the train started to whirr and chug, ready to start out toward the countryside, where there are fewer people, wider spaces, and it's easier to work out who you are. In the fullness of time we may get all the way to the other side of the country, and when that happens I will try to see my ex-wife and my boy. He may never view me as his father. I may always be just some guy. But he needs to know that I did not forget him and never will.

Out of the corner of my eye, as we pulled up out of the tunnels and light flooded into the carriage through the windows, I saw a girl slip into an empty seat six rows behind us. White hair, tough-looking.

Kristina told me her name is Flaxon. I didn't turn and stare. If need be, we'll work out what to do about it somewhere down the line. And she's welcome, anyhow.

We have no idea where we're going. I've got no problem with a friend coming along for the ride.

The church was not the only thing that burned that night. It appears from news reports that there were twelve arson attacks at other locations in the city. Twenty-seven people died, including one in a house on the Upper West Side, where a girl called Jessica Markham suffocated in her bed. Her parents survived. The fire was apparently started by a lit matchbook pushed through the letterbox.

A witness claimed to have seen a teenage girl wearing a gray hoodie standing in the street and watching the flames, before running away into the city.

She was laughing.

She looked very alive.

EPILOGUE

Ten days later a woman found herself wandering the city in the early afternoon, walking streets she knew and streets she did not, walking because it felt like the only thing to do. Eventually she came to rest in a grassed area at the end of the Riverwalk, overlooking the Hudson. Despite living only ten or fifteen minutes from this little park, she'd never stood on this spot and didn't know what might have drawn her to it now.

Catherine Warren had found herself feeling unaccountably lonely over the last few days. She'd discovered that meeting with friends in the Village, keeping up her end at dinner parties, or chatting with other mothers outside the school gate had started to feel flat. Nothing had changed about these people or about the structures of her existence . . . and yet something had. There was a lack. A hole, even if she'd long ago stopped being aware of what had filled it.

It felt specific.

It was like someone was missing in her life.

But she supposed everybody feels that way

sometimes. You enter adulthood on the promise of becoming full, of achieving one hundred percent and three-sixty degrees and 24–7/365 – but slowly come to accept there'll always be a gap somewhere. She knew this intellectually but still couldn't shake the feeling of melancholy. She was old enough to know it would pass, however. The world keeps serving up stuff and you deal with it and sooner or later it's either okay or overlaid with something else – like adding layer after layer of paint onto a canvas until one day you have the finished picture. It may not be what you had in mind when you started. But it is what it is.

She couldn't seem to leave the spot, this park, though she knew she needed to get back to Chelsea and her life. She had to be in good form tonight, too. Mark would be tired. He was busy at work. He was always busy. Work stood behind him, hands on his shoulders, holding him down. He would need nurturing and looking after, and probably – if he had a glass of wine too many again – a great deal of reassurance that everything was okay.

Catherine actually had no idea if everything was okay. She didn't recall being promised it would be, either. She remembered coming to the city convinced she was going to be a journalist, that one day people would pick up the *New York Times* and her byline would be there, fighting the good fight and pulling aside the veil. It didn't happen. She worked hard at it for a while, but the world fought back, with its good-natured persistence and slow but constant cavalcade of events and demands: in the battle between you and reality – as she'd once read somewhere – you should always offer to hold reality's coat.

One day she woke up to realize that she was a mother, not a Pulitzer hopeful, and so she'd decided that she would be the best damned mother she could instead.

These days she barely remembered the other things she'd wanted, and she didn't care. What would be the point? Dreams are supposed to support and succor us, not to make us feel bad. Catherine had always been good at pushing aside things that no longer worked. It was the best way, the adult way, the sensible way – and she had wanted to be adult and sensible since she was a little girl.

She remembered that, at least. She would never remember, because it was buried too deeply, the evenings back then during which someone who should have loved her in better ways had done inappropriate things. She would never recall – except in the shape of the formless but very strong distaste she now held for the work of certain artists from the turn of the previous century – the way in which during these events she had fastened her attention on a reproduction picture on the wall in this man's house, a pre-Raphaelite painting of a young woman standing alone and drinking out of a glass bowl the color of irises, in front of a window showing sailing ships in the distance; a tall, slim girl with thick dark hair and pale skin, wearing a red velvet dress. The girl had looked thoughtful, and kind, the sort of friend that would not allow what was happening to be happening.

But happen it did.

And so what? What matters in life is what *you* do, not what's done to you by someone else.

Catherine frowned, finding herself remembering Thomas Clark, the guy she'd dated before Mark. Though he would never be anything more than part of a superseded past, she found herself wondering how he was and how he dealt with the dreams that had faded around them. He'd had big plans once, too. Maybe she should try to get in touch, say sorry, or hi, or something like that.

She put a pin in the idea.

Eventually she pushed away from the railing and started the walk down to Chelsea. It was time to pick up the girls. She walked slowly at first, then gradually with more enthusiasm, finding that her mood, if not cured, was a little lighter. She thought of her two little girls, happy to have them, and glimpsing for a moment the road that lay in front of these young women – the road of school and college, of living in apartments and having good sex and bad hangovers and working hard and goofing off and meeting a guy (or girl, whatever) and eventually starting to settle, moving in smaller circles like balls rattling around a pinball table, before finally finding the place they were meant to land. Maybe they'd be housewives. Maybe one would be president.

Dreams are dreams and real is real. Somewhere in between is what you get, and that's good enough.

Catherine picked up her step and strode down into the bustle and noise. If she got a move on she might even have time to pick up a tub of shrimp salad. The fact that Mark liked it wasn't the point, and never had been.

The point was this was her life.

Ian Rankin:
Three Great Novels

Rebus: The St Leonard's Years

Also by Ian Rankin

The Inspector Rebus Series

Knots & Crosses

Hide & Seek

Tooth & Nail (previously published as Wolfman)

A Good Hanging and Other Stories

Strip Jack

The Black Book

Mortal Causes

Let It Bleed

Black & Blue

The Hanging Garden

Death Is Not The End (a novella)

Dead Souls

Rebus: The Early Years

Set In Darkness

The Falls

Other Novels

The Flood

Watchman

Westwind

Writing as Jack Harvey

Witch Hunt

Bleeding Hearts

Blood Hunt

Ian Rankin:
Three Great Novels

Rebus: The St Leonard's Years

■

Strip Jack
The Black Book
Mortal Causes

ORION

Strip Jack Copyright © 1992 Ian Rankin
The Black Book Copyright © 1993 Ian Rankin
Mortal Causes Copyright © 1994 Ian Rankin

This omnibus edition first published as *Rebus: The St Leonard's Years*
in Great Britain in 2001 by Orion,
an imprint of the Orion Publishing Group Ltd.

Fifth impression 2003

A CIP catalogue record for this book is available
from the British Library.

ISBN 0 75284 656 6

Printed in Great Britain by
Clays Ltd, St Ives plc

The Orion Publishing Group Ltd
Orion House
5 Upper Saint Martin's Lane
London WC2H 9EA

Contents

Introduction

Well, by now I had three Rebus novels under my belt, plus a collection of short stories. I had finally decided to give up the day job (magazine journalism). My wife had persuaded me that if I was going to write full-time, we couldn't afford to stay put in London, so she found us a house in south-west France. Sounds romantic, but it wasn't. The house hadn't been lived in for eight years. It had broken windows, woodworm and no bath. In other words, just perfect for two foolhardy young adults with no DIY skills. We moved in.

I wrote *Strip Jack* in France – along with the other two books in this collection. Back in Scotland there was rising mistrust of the Thatcher administration, and talk of devolution. I wanted to write a novel about a politician. In keeping with the game-playing motif of the first two Rebus novels, I started reading a book of card games, and came across Strip Jack Naked. This appealed to me, but when I wrote it down it seemed too long. I deleted the 'naked' and suddenly it was punchier.

Maybe it helped that our first son was about to be born, and we'd already decided to name him Jack (hence the book's dedication). As Jack was born in real life, so the fictional MP Gregor Jack began to take shape in my mind. I think the resulting novel is one of the lighter additions to the series. There's not too much darkness; not too much blood. It was my attempt at a more traditional whodunnit. Maybe my surroundings were to blame. I'd exchanged high-pressure London and its daily grind for rolling hills, time and space. It couldn't last and it didn't.

The Black Book is altogether darker fare. When I'd lived and worked in Edinburgh, the smell of the brewery in the city's west end had seemed omnipresent. I decided to bring a brewing family into this story. Then I remembered something I'd been told in the Oxford Bar. It was a rumour about a hotel on Princes Street, which had burned down in mysterious circumstances. So that went into the mix, too. Meantime, I'd won one of the world's largest literary prizes: the Chandler–Fulbright Award. This presented me with a sum of money, the only stipulation being that I spend it during a six-month jaunt to the USA. We got someone to look after the place in France, and booked ourselves onto the first flight out.

I didn't do any writing in the States. We flew into Seattle, bought a beaten-up VW Camper, strapped the infant Jack into the back, and headed south ... then east ... then north. I think we clocked up 14,000 miles. During those long drives, I thought about *The Black Book*, and in New Orleans we wandered into a dive which happened to have an Elvis theme. Tatty, faded photos of the star were pinned to the walls; his early music crooned in the background. I started dreaming up dishes the place might serve. Then I decided to transplant it to Edinburgh, complete with all my bad puns – the Love Me Tenderloin and King Shrimp Creole.

By this time I'd made the decision to stop trying to create a purely fictional Edinburgh. Up until the end of *Strip Jack*, Rebus had worked in a police station in a street whose name and location I dreamed up. In *The Black Book*, he has been transferred to a real cop-shop, St Leonard's. Around the same time, I took him out of the fictional pubs he'd been drinking in and gave him some real ones to enjoy. Maybe my physical isolation from the city had given me this licence. I still went back, on what I euphemistically referred to as 'research trips'. These were spent mostly in the Oxford Bar, always a good source of gossip and stories. Cops, councillors and lawyers supped there, and still do. I was there for the Festival one August, and decided it was something I should write about. I imagined how the curmudgeonly Rebus would feel, surrounded by all the youth and enthusiasm of the Fringe. I was also growing in confidence, coming to realise that I could tackle serious issues in my stories.

It's hard to live in Scotland without at some time coming into contact with religious bigotry. Added to this, my wife had been brought up in Belfast at the height of 'the Troubles'. We went back from time to time, visiting her family. I had got a feel for the umbilical cord between Northern Ireland and Scotland. I wanted to write about it.

I think the resulting book, *Mortal Causes*, is the first 'grown-up' Rebus story, its themes salient, addressing contemporary problems. I had a lot of trouble finding the title. I'd tried researching the names of games, but couldn't find anything suitable. It was my wife who, having read the completed manuscript, suggested *Mortal Causes*. I liked that immediately. In Scotland, 'getting mortal' means getting drunk, and I knew that Rebus's drinking was going to prove a growing problem both in his personal life and in his professional one.

Mary King's Close exists, by the way. It has now been opened to tour groups. And for those who've been asking, here's the punchline to the book's running joke: 'For Hans that does dishes can feel soft as Gervase with mild, green hairy-lipped squid.' My pal George told it to me. Cheers, George.

To everyone else, welcome to the grown-up world of John Rebus. The St Leonard's Years.

Ian Rankin
Edinburgh, 2001

Strip Jack

To the only Jack I've ever stripped

He knows nothing; and he thinks he knows
everything. That points clearly to a political career.

Shaw, *Major Barbara*

The habit of friendship is matured by constant
intercourse.

Libianus, 4th century AD, quoted in *Edinburgh*

by Charles McKean

Acknowledgements

The first thing to acknowledge is that the constituency of North and South Esk is the author's creation. However, you don't need to be Mungo Park to work out that there must be some correlation between North and South Esk and the real world, Edinburgh being a real place, and 'south and east of Edinburgh' being a vaguely definable geographical area.

In fact, North and South Esk bears *some* resemblance to the Midlothian parliamentary constituency – prior to 1983's Boundary Commission changes – but also bites a small southernmost chunk out of the present Edinburgh Pentlands constituency and a westerly chunk out of East Lothian constituency.

Gregor Jack, too, is fiction, and bears no resemblance to any MP.

Thanks are due to the following for their inestimable help: Alex Eadie, who was until his retirement the MP for Midlothian; John Home Robertson MP; Professor Busuttil, Regius Professor of Forensic Medicine, University of Edinburgh; Lothian and Borders Police; City of Edinburgh Police; the staff of the Edinburgh Room, Edinburgh Central Library; the staff of the National Library of Scotland; staff and customers of Sandy Bell's, the Oxford Bar, Mather's (West End), Clark's Bar and the Green Tree.

Contents

1

The Milking Shed

The wonder of it was that the neighbours hadn't complained, hadn't
even – as many of them later told the newsmen – realized. Not until
that night, the night their sleep was disturbed by sudden activity in the
street. Cars, vans, policemen, the static chatter of radios. Not that the
noise ever got out of hand. The whole operation was directed with such
speed and, yes, even good humour that there were those who slept
through the excitement.

'I want courtesy,' Chief Superintendent 'Farmer' Watson had
explained to his men in the briefing room that evening. 'It may be a
hoor-hoose, but it's on the right side of town, if you take my meaning.
No telling who might be in there. We might even come across our own
dear Chief Constable.'

Watson grinned, to let them know he was joking. But some of the
officers in the room, knowing the CC better than Watson himself apparently did, exchanged glances and wry smiles.

'Right,' said Watson, 'let's go through the plan of attack one more
time...'

Christ, he's loving this, thought Detective Inspector John Rebus. He's
loving every minute. And why not? This was Watson's baby after all,
and it was to be a home birth. Which was to say, Watson was going to
be in charge all the way from immaculate conception to immaculate
delivery.

Maybe it was a male menopause thing, this need to flex a bit of
muscle. Most of the chief supers Rebus had known in his twenty years
on the force had been content to push pens over paper and wait for
retirement day. But not Watson. Watson was like Channel Four: full of
independent programmes of minority interest. He didn't make waves
exactly, but by Christ he splashed like hell.

And now he even seemed to have an informer, an invisible somebody
who had whispered in his ear the word 'brothel'. Sin and debauchery!
Watson's hard Presbyterian heart had been stirred to righteous indig-
nation. He was the kind of Highland Christian who found sex within
marriage just about acceptable – his son and daughter were proof – but

who baulked at anything and everything else. If there was an active brothel in Edinburgh, Watson wanted it shut down with prejudice.

But then the informer had provided an address, and this caused a certain hesitation. The brothel was in one of the better streets of the New Town, quiet Georgian terraces, lined with trees and Saabs and Volvos, the houses filled with professional people: lawyers, surgeons, university professors. This was no seaman's bawdy-house, no series of damp, dark rooms above a dockside pub. This was, as Rebus himself had offered, an Establishment establishment. Watson hadn't seen the joke.

Watch had been kept for several days and nights, courtesy of unmarked cars and unremarkable plainclothes men. Until there could be little doubt: whatever was happening inside the shuttered rooms, it was happening after midnight and it was happening briskly. Interestingly, few of the many men arrived by car. But a watchful detective constable, taking a leak in the dead of night, discovered why. The men were parking their cars in side streets and walking the hundred yards or so to the front door of the four-storey house. Perhaps this was house policy: the slamming of after-hours car doors would arouse suspicion in the street. Or perhaps it was in the visitors' own interests not to leave their cars in broad street-light, where they might be recognized ...

Registration numbers were taken and checked, as were photographs of visitors to the house. The owner of the house itself was traced. He owned half a French vineyard as well as several properties in Edinburgh, and lived in Bordeaux the year through. His solicitor had been responsible for letting the house to a Mrs Croft, a very genteel lady in her fifties. According to the solicitor, she paid her rent promptly and in cash. Was there any problem ...?

No problem, he was assured, but if he could keep the conversation to himself ...

Meantime, the car owners had turned out to be businessmen, some local, but the majority visiting the city from south of the border. Heartened by this, Watson had started planning the raid. With his usual blend of wit and acumen, he chose to call it Operation Creeper.

'Brothel creepers, you see, John.'

'Yes sir,' Rebus answered. 'I used to own a pair myself. I've often wondered how they got the name.'

Watson shrugged. He was not a man to be sidetracked. 'Never mind the creepers,' he said. 'Let's just get the creeps.'

The house, it was reckoned, would be doing good business by midnight. One o'clock Saturday morning was chosen as the time of the raid. The warrants were ready. Every man in the team knew his place. And the solicitor had even come up with plans of the house, which had been memorized by the officers.

'It's a bloody warren,' Watson had said.

'No problem, sir, so long as we've got enough ferrets.'

In truth, Rebus wasn't looking forward to this evening's work. Brothels might be illegal, but they fulfilled a need and if they veered towards respectability, as this one certainly did, then what was the problem? He could see some of this doubt reflected in Watson's eyes. But Watson had been enthusiastic from the first, and to pull back now was unthinkable, would seem a sign of weakness. So, with nobody really keen for it, Operation Creeper went ahead. While other, meaner streets went unpatrolled. While domestic violence took its toll. While the Water of Leith drowning still remained to be solved...

'Okay, in we go.'

They left their cars and vans and marched towards the front door. Knocked quietly. The door was opened from within, and then things began to move like a video on double-speed. Other doors were opened ... how many doors could a house have? Knock first, then open. Yes, they were being courteous.

'If you wouldn't mind getting dressed, please...'

'If you could just come downstairs now...'

'You can put your trousers on first, sir, if you like...'

Then: 'Christ, sir, come and take a look at this.' Rebus followed the flushed, youthful face of the detective constable. 'Here we are, sir. Feast your peepers on this lot.'

Ah yes, the punishment room. Chains and thongs and whips. A couple of full-length mirrors, a wardrobe full of gear.

'There's more leather here than in a bloody milking shed.'

'You seem to know a lot about cows, son,' Rebus said. He was just thankful the room wasn't in use. But there were more surprises to come.

In parts, the house resembled nothing more lewd than a fancy-dress party – nurses and matrons, wimples and high heels. Except that most of the costumes revealed more than they hid. One young woman seemed to be wearing a rubber diving suit with the nipples and crotch cut away. Another looked like a cross between Heidi and Eva Braun. Watson watched the parade, righteous fury filling him. He had no doubts now: it was absolutely proper that this sort of place be closed down. Then he turned back to the conversation he was having with Mrs Croft, while Chief Inspector Lauderdale lingered only a short distance away. He had insisted on coming alone, knowing his superior and fearing some almighty cock-up. Well, thought Rebus with a smile, no cock-ups in sight yet.

Mrs Croft spoke in a kind of gentrified Cockney, which became less gentrified as time went on and more couples spilled down the stairs and into the large, sofa-crammed living room. A room smelling of expensive perfume and proprietary whisky. Mrs Croft was denying everything.

She was even denying that they were standing in a brothel at all.

I am not my brothel's keeper, thought Rebus. All the same, he had to admire her performance. She was a businesswoman, she kept saying, a taxpayer, she had rights ... and where was her solicitor?

'I thought it was her that was doing the soliciting,' Lauderdale muttered to Rebus: a rare moment of humour from one of the dourest buggers Rebus had ever worked with. And as such, it deserved a smile.

'What are you grinning at? I didn't know there was an interval. Get back to work.'

'Yes, sir.' Rebus waited till Lauderdale had turned away from him, the better to hear what Watson was saying, and then flicked a quick v-sign at him. Mrs Croft, though, caught the gesture and, perhaps thinking it intended at her, returned it. Lauderdale and Watson both turned towards where Rebus was standing, but by then he was already on his way ...

Officers who had been posted in the back garden now marched a few pale-faced souls back into the house. One man had leapt from a first-floor window, and was hobbling as a result. But he was insistent, too, that no doctor was necessary, that no ambulance be called. The women seemed to find the whole thing amusing, and appeared especially taken by the looks on their clients' faces, looks ranging from the ashamed and embarrassed to the furious and embarrassed. There was some short-lived bravado of the I-know-my-rights variety. But in the main, everybody did as they were told: that is, they shut up and tried to be patient.

Some of the shame and embarrassment started to lift when one of the men recalled that it wasn't illegal to visit a brothel; it was only illegal to run one or work in one. And this was true, though it didn't mean the men present were going to escape into the anonymous night. Give them a scare first, then send them away. Starve the brothels of clients, and you'd have no brothels. That was the logic. So the officers were prepared with their usual stories, the ones they used with kerb-crawlers and the like.

'Just a quiet word, sir, between you and me, like. If I were you, I'd have myself checked over for AIDS. I'm serious. Most of these women could well be carrying the disease, even if it doesn't show. Mostly, it doesn't show till it's too late anyway. Are you married, sir? Any girl-friends? Best tell them to have a test, too. Otherwise, you never know, do you ...?'

It was cruel stuff, but necessary; and as with most cruel words, there was a truth to it. Mrs Croft seemed to use a small back room as an office. A cash-box was found. So was a credit-card machine. A receipt-book was headed Crofter Guest House. As far as Rebus could tell, the cost of a single room was seventy-five pounds. Dear for a B&B, but how many company accountants would take the trouble to check? If wouldn't surprise Rebus if the place was VAT registered to boot ...

'Sir?' It was Detective Sergeant Brian Holmes, newly promoted and bristling with efficiency. He was halfway up one of the flights of stairs, and calling down to Rebus. 'I think you better come up here...'

Rebus wasn't keen. Holmes looked to be a long way up, and Rebus, who lived on the second floor of a tenement, had a natural antipathy to stairs. Edinburgh, of course, was full of them, just as it was full of hills, biting winds, and people who liked to girn about things like hills and stairs and the wind...

'Coming.'

Outside a bedroom door, a detective constable stood in quiet discussion with Holmes. When Holmes saw Rebus reaching the landing, he dismissed the DC.

'Well, Sergeant?'

'Take a look, sir.'

'Anything you want to tell me first?'

Holmes shook his head. 'You've seen the male member before, sir, haven't you?'

Rebus opened the bedroom door. What was he expecting to find? A mock-up dungeon, with someone stretched out naked on the rack? A farmyard scene with a few chickens and sheep? The male member. Maybe Mrs Croft had a collection of them displayed on her bedroom wall. *And here's one I caught in '73. Put up a tough fight, but I had it in the end...*

But no, it was worse than that. Much worse. It was an ordinary bedroom, albeit with red lightbulbs in its several lamps. And in an ordinary bed lay an ordinary enough looking woman, her elbow pressed into the pillow, head resting at an angle on her clenched fist. And on that bed, dressed and staring at the floor, sat someone Rebus recognized: the Member of Parliament for North and South Esk.

'Jesus Christ,' said Rebus. Holmes put his head round the door.

'I can't work in front of a fucking audience!' yelled the woman. Her accent, Rebus noted, was English. Holmes ignored her.

'This is a bit of a coincidence,' he said to Gregor Jack MP. 'Only, my girlfriend and me have just moved into your constituency.'

The MP raised his eyes more in sorrow than in anger.

'This is a mistake,' he said. 'A terrible mistake.'

'Just doing a bit of canvassing, eh, sir?'

The woman had begun to laugh, head still resting on her hand. The red lamplight seemed to fill her gaping mouth. Gregor Jack looked for a moment as though he might be about to throw a punch in her general direction. Instead he tried a slap with his open hand, but succeeded only in catching her arm, so that her head fell back on to the pillow. She was still laughing, almost girl-like. She lifted her legs high into the air, the bedcovers falling away. Her hands thumped the mattress with glee. Jack had risen to his feet and was scratching nervously at one finger.

'Jesus Christ,' Rebus said again. Then: 'Come on, let's get you down-stairs.'

Not the Farmer. The Farmer might go to pieces. Lauderdale then. Rebus approached with as much humility as he could muster.

'Sir, we've got a bit of a problem.'

'I know. It must have been that bugger Watson. Wanted his moment of glory captured. He's always been keen on publicity, you should know that.' Was that a sneer on Lauderdale's face? With his gaunt figure and bloodless face, he reminded Rebus of a painting he'd once seen of some Calvinists or Seceders ... some grim bunch like that. Ready to burn anyone who came to hand. Rebus kept his distance, all the time shaking his head.

'I'm not sure I –'

'The bloody papers are here,' hissed Lauderdale. 'Quick off the mark, eh? Even for our friends in the press. Bloody Watson must have tipped them off. He's out there now. I tried to stop him.'

Rebus went to one of the windows and peeped out. Sure enough, there were three or four reporters gathered at the bottom of the steps up to the front door. Watson had finished his spiel and was answering a couple of questions, at the same time retreating slowly back up the steps.

'Oh dear,' Rebus said, admiring his own sense of understatement. 'That only makes it worse.'

'Makes what worse?'

So Rebus told him. And was rewarded with the biggest smile he'd ever seen flit across Lauderdale's face.

'Well, well, who's been a naughty boy then? But I still don't see the problem.'

Rebus shrugged. 'Well, sir, it's just that it doesn't do anyone any good.' Outside, the vans were arriving. Two to take the women to the station, two to take the men. The men would be asked a few questions, names and addresses taken, then released. The women ... well, that was another thing entirely. There would be charges. Rebus's colleague Gill Templer would call it another sign of the phallocentric society, something like that. She'd never been the same since she'd got her hands on those psychology books ...

'Nonsense,' Lauderdale was saying. 'He's only got himself to blame. What do you want us to do? Sneak him out the back door with a blanket over his head?'

'No, sir, it's just –'

'He gets treated the same as the rest of them, Inspector. You know the score.'

'Yes, sir, but –'

'But what?'

But what? Well, that was the question. What? Why was Rebus feeling so uncomfortable? The answer was complicatedly simple: because it *was* Gregor Jack. Most MPs, Rebus wouldn't have given the time of day. But Gregor Jack was ... well, he was *Gregor Jack*.

'Vans are here, Inspector. Let's round 'em up and ship 'em out.'

Lauderdale's hand on his back was cold and firm.

'Yes, sir,' said Rebus.

So it was out into the cool dark night, lit by orange sodium lights, the glare of headlamps, and the dimmer light from open doors and twitching windows. The natives were restless. Some had come out on to their doorsteps, wrapped in paisley dressing gowns or wearing hastily found clothes, not quite hanging right.

Police, natives, and of course the reporters. Flash-guns. Christ, there were photographers too, of course. No camera crews, no video machines. That was something: Watson hadn't persuaded the TV companies to attend his little soirée.

'Into the van, quick as you can,' called Brian Holmes. Was that a new firmness, a new authority in his voice? Funny what promotion could do to the young. But by God they *were* quick. Not so much following Holmes' orders, Rebus knew, as keen to escape the cameras. One or two of the women posed, trying a lopsided glamour learned from page three, before being persuaded by WPCs that this was neither the time nor the place.

But the reporters were hanging back. Rebus wondered why. Indeed, he wondered what they were doing here at all. Was it such a big story? Would it provide Watson with useful publicity? One reporter even grabbed at a photographer's arm and seemed to warn him about shooting off too many pictures. But now they were keening, now they were shouting. And the flashbulbs were going off like flak. All because they'd recognized a face. All because Gregor Jack was being escorted down the steps, across the narrow pavement, and into a van.

'Christ, it's Gregor Jack!'

'Mr Jack! A word!'

'Any comment to make?'

'What were you doing –'

'Any comment?'

The doors were closing. A thump with the constabulary hand on the side of the van, and it moved slowly away, the reporters jogging after it. Well, Rebus had to admit it: Jack had held his head high. No, that wasn't being accurate. He had, rather, held his head just low enough, suggesting penitence but not shame, humility but not embarrassment.

'Seven days he's been my MP,' Holmes was saying by Rebus's side. 'Seven days.'

'You must have been a bad influence on him, Brian.'

'Bit of a shock though, wasn't it?'

Rebus shrugged noncommittally. The woman from the bedroom was being brought out now, having pulled on jeans and a t-shirt. She saw the reporters and suddenly lifted the t-shirt high over her naked breasts.

'Get a load of this then!'

But the reporters were busy comparing notes, the photographers loading new film. They'd be off to the station next, ready to catch Gregor Jack as he left. Nobody paid her any attention, and eventually she let her t-shirt fall back down and climbed into the waiting van.

'He's not choosy, is he?' said Holmes.

'But then again, Brian,' answered Rebus, 'maybe he is.'

Watson was rubbing at his gleaming forehead. It was a lot of work for only one hand, since the forehead seemed to extend as far as Watson's crown.

'Mission accomplished,' he said. 'Well done.'

'Thank you, sir,' Holmes said smartly.

'No problems then?'

'Not at all, sir,' said Rebus casually. 'Unless you count Gregor Jack.'

Watson nodded, then frowned. 'Who?' he asked.

'Brian here can tell you all about him, sir,' said Rebus, patting Holmes' back. 'Brian's your man for anything smacking of politics.'

Watson, hovering now somewhere between elation and dread, turned to Holmes.

'Politics?' he asked. He was smiling. *Please be gentle with me.*

Holmes watched Rebus moving back inside the house. He felt like sobbing. Because, after all, that's what John Rebus was – an s.o.b.

2

Scratching the Surface

It is a truth universally acknowledged that some Members of Parliament have trouble keeping their trousers on. But Gregor Jack was not thought to be one of these. Indeed, he often eschewed troose altogether, opting for the kilt on election nights and at many a public function. In London, he took the jibes in good part, his responses matching the old questions with the accuracy of catechism.

'Tell us now, Gregor, what's worn beneath the kilt?'

'Oh nothing, nothing at all. It's all in perfect working order.'

Gregor Jack was not a member of the SNP, though he had flirted with the party in his youth. He *had* joined the Labour Party, but had resigned for never specified reasons. He was not a Liberal Democrat, nor was he that rare breed – a Scots Tory MP. Gregor Jack was an Independent, and as an Independent had held the seat of North and South Esk, south and east of Edinburgh, since his mildly surprising by-election win of 1985. 'Mild' was an adjective often used about Jack. So were 'honest', 'legal' and 'decent'.

All this John Rebus knew from memory, from old newspapers, magazines and radio interviews. There had to be something wrong with the man, some chink in his shining armour. Trust Operation Creeper to find the flaw. Rebus scanned the Saturday newsprint, seeking a story. He didn't find it. Curious that; the press had seemed keen enough last night. A story breaking at one thirty ... plenty of time, surely, to see it into print by the final morning edition. Unless, of course, the reporters hadn't been local. But they must have been, mustn't they? Having said which, he hadn't recognized any faces. Did Watson really have the front to get the London papers involved? Rebus smiled. The man had plenty of 'front' all right: his wife saw to that. Three meals a day, three courses each.

'Feed the body,' Watson was fond of saying, 'and you feed the spirit.' Something like that. Which was another thing: bible-basher or no, Watson was starting to put away a fair amount of spirits. A rosy glow to the cheeks and chins, and the unmistakable scent of extra-strong mints. When Lauderdale walked into his superior's room these days, he sniffed and sniffed, like a bloodhound. Only it wasn't bloody he was sniffing, it was promotion.

Lose a Farmer, gain a Fart.

The nickname had perhaps been unavoidable. Word association. Lauderdale became Fort Lauderdale, and Fort quickly turned into Fart. Oh, but it was an apt name, too. For wherever Chief Inspector Lauderdale went, he left a bad smell. Take the Case of the Lifted Literature. Rebus had known the minute Lauderdale walked into his office that there would soon be a need to open the windows.

'I want you to stick close to this one, John. Professor Costello is highly thought of, an international figure in this field . . .'

'And?'

'And,' Lauderdale tried to look as though his next utterance meant nothing to him, 'he's a close personal friend of Chief Superintendent Watson.'

'Ah.'

'What is this – Monosyllable Week?'

'Monosyllable?' Rebus frowned. 'Sorry, sir, I'll have to ask D S Holmes what that means.'

'Don't try to be funny –'

'I'm not, sir, honest. It's just that D S Holmes has had the benefit of a university education. Well . . . five months' worth or thereabouts. He'd be the very man to coordinate the officers working on this highly sensitive case.'

Lauderdale stared at the seated figure for what seemed – to Rebus at least – a very long time. God, was the man really that stupid? Did no one appreciate irony these days?

'Look,' Lauderdale said at last, 'I need someone a bit more senior than a recently promoted D S. And I'm sorry to say that you, Inspector, God help us all, are that bit more senior.'

'You're flattering me, sir.'

A file landed with a dull thud on Rebus's desk. The chief inspector turned and left. Rebus rose from his chair and turned to his sash window, tugging at it with all his might. But the thing was stuck tight. There was no escape. With a sigh, he turned back and sat down at his desk. Then he opened the folder.

It was a straightforward case of theft. Professor James Aloysius Costello was Professor of Divinity at the University of Edinburgh. One day someone had walked into his office, then walked out again taking with them several rare books. Priceless, according to the Professor, though not to the city's various booksellers and auction rooms. The list seemed eclectic: an early edition of Knox's *Treatise on Predestination*, a couple of Sir Walter Scott first editions, Swedenborg's *Wisdom of Angels*, a signed early edition of *Tristram Shandy*, and editions of Montaigne and Voltaire.

None of which meant much to Rebus until he saw the estimates at auction, provided by one of the George Street auction houses. The question then was: what were they doing in an unlocked office in the first place?

'To be read,' answered Professor Costello blithely. 'To be enjoyed, admired. What good would they be locked up in a safe or in some old library display case?'

'Did anyone else know about them? I mean, about how valuable they are?'

The Professor shrugged. 'I had thought, Inspector, that I was amongst friends.'

He had a voice like a peat bog and eyes that gleamed like crystal. A Dublin education, but a life spent, as he put it, 'cloistered' in the likes of Cambridge, Oxford, St Andrews, and now Edinburgh. A life spent collecting books, too. Those left in his office – still kept unlocked – were worth at least as much as the stolen volumes, perhaps more.

'They say lightning never strikes twice,' he assured Rebus.

'Maybe not, but villains do. Try to lock your door when you step out, eh, sir? If nothing else.'

The Professor had shrugged. Was this, Rebus wondered, a kind of stoicism? He felt nervous sitting there in the office in Buccleuch Place. For one thing, he was a kind of Christian himself, and would have liked to be able to talk the subject through with this wise-seeming man. *Wise?* Well, perhaps not worldly-wise, not wise enough to know how snib locks and human minds worked, but wise in other ways. But Rebus was nervous, too, because he knew himself for a clever man who could have been cleverer, given the breaks. He had never gone to university, and never would. He wondered how different he would be if he had or could . . .

The Professor was staring out of his window, down on to the cobble-stoned street. On one side of Buccleuch Place sat a row of neat tenements, owned by the university and used by various departments. The Professor called it Botany Bay. And across the road uglier shapes reared up, the modern tone mausoleums of the main university complex. If this side of the road was Botany Bay, Rebus was all for transportation.

He left the Professor to his muses and musings. Had the books been filched at random? Or was this designer theft, the thief stealing to order? There might well be unscrupulous collectors who would pay – no questions asked – for an early *Tristram Shandy*. Though the authors' names had rung bells, only that particular title had meant anything to Rebus. He owned a paperback copy of the book, bought at a car-boot sale on The Meadows for tenpence. Maybe the Professor would like to borrow it . . .

And so the Case of the Lifted Literature had, for Inspector John Rebus, begun. The ground had been covered before, as the case-notes showed, but it could be covered again. There were the auction houses, the bookshops, the private collectors . . . all to be talked to. And all to satisfy an unlikely friendship between a police chief superintendent and a professor of Divinity. A waste of time, of course. The books had disappeared the previous Tuesday. It was now Saturday, and they would doubtless be under lock and key in some dark and secret corner.

What a way to spend a Saturday. Actually, if the time had been his own, this would have been a nice afternoon, which was perhaps why he hadn't balked at the task. Rebus collected books. Well, that was putting it strongly. He *bought* books. Bought more of them than he had time to read, attracted by this cover or that title or the fact that he'd heard good things about the author. No, on second thoughts it was just as well these were business calls he was making, otherwise he'd be bankrupting himself in record time.

In any case, he didn't have books on his mind. He kept thinking about a certain MP. Was Gregor Jack married? Rebus thought so. Hadn't there been some big society wedding several years previous? Well, married men were bread and butter to prostitutes. They just gobbled them up. Shame though, about Jack. Rebus had always respected the man – which was to say, now that he thought about it, that he'd been taken in by Jack's public image. But it wasn't all image, was it? Jack really had come from a working-class background, had clawed his way upwards, and *was* a good MP. North and South Esk was difficult territory, part mining villages, part country homes. Jack seemed to glide easily between the two hemispheres. He'd managed to get an ugly new road rerouted well away from his well-heeled constituents, but had also fought hard to bring new high-tech industry to the area, retraining the miners so that they could do the jobs.

Too good to be true. Too bloody good to be true . . .

Bookshops. He had to keep his mind on bookshops. There were only a few to check, the ones that had not been open earlier in the week. Footwork really, the stuff he should have been doling out to more junior men. But all that meant was that he'd feel bound to come round after them, double checking what they'd done. This way, he saved himself some grief.

Buccleuch Street was an odd mixture of grimy junk shops and bright vegetarian takeaways. Student turf. Not far from Rebus's own flat, yet he seldom ventured into this part of town. Only on business. Only ever on business.

Ah, this was it. Suey Books. And for once the shop looked to be open. Even in the spring sunshine there was a need for a light inside. It was a tiny shop, boasting an unenthusiastic window display of old hardbacks, mostly with a Scottish theme. An enormous black cat had made a home for itself in the centre of the display, and blinked slowly if malignly up at Rebus. The window itself needed washing. You couldn't make out the titles of the books without pressing your nose to the glass, and this was made difficult by the presence of an old black bicycle resting against the front of the shop. Rebus pushed open the door. If anything, the shop's interior was less pristine than its exterior. There was a bristle-mat just inside the door. Rebus made a note to wipe his feet before he went back into the street . . .

The shelves, a few of them glass-fronted, were crammed, and the smell was of old relatives' houses, of attics and the insides of school desks. The aisles were narrow. Hardly enough room to swing a . . . There was a thump somewhere behind him, and he feared one of the books had fallen, but when he turned he saw that it was the cat. It swerved past him and made for the desk situated to the rear of the shop, the desk with a bare lightbulb dangling above it.

'Anything in particular you're looking for?'

She was seated at the desk, a pile of books in front of her. She held a pencil in one hand and appeared to be writing prices on the inside leaves of the books. From a distance, it was a scene out of Dickens. Close up was a different story. Still in her teens, she had hennaed her short spiked hair. The eyes behind the circular tinted glasses were themselves round and dark, and she sported three earrings in either ear, with another curling from her left nostril. Rebus didn't doubt she'd have a pale boyfriend with lank dreadlocks and a whippet on a length of clothes-rope.

'I'm looking for the manager,' he said.

'He's not here. Can I help?'

Rebus shrugged, his eyes on the cat. It had leapt silently on to the desk and was now rubbing itself against the books. The girl held her pencil out towards it, and the cat brushed the tip with its jaw.

'Inspector Rebus,' said Rebus. 'I'm interested in some stolen books. I was wondering if anyone had been in trying to sell them.'

'Do you have a list?'

Rebus did. He drew it out of his pocket and handed it over. 'You can keep it,' he said. 'Just in case.'

She glanced down the typed list of titles and editions, her lips pursed. 'I don't think Ronald could afford them, even if he was tempted.'

'Ronald being the manager?'

'That's right. Where were they stolen from?'

'Round the corner in Buccleuch Place.'

'Round the corner? They'd hardly be likely to bring them here then, would they?'

Rebus smiled. 'True,' he said, 'but we have to check.'

'Well, I'll hang on to this anyway,' she said, folding the list. As she pushed it into a desk drawer, Rebus reached out a hand and stroked the cat. Like lightning, a paw flicked up and caught his wrist. He drew back his hand with a sharp intake of breath.

'Oh dear,' said the girl. 'Rasputin's not very good with strangers.'

'So I see.' Rebus studied his wrist. There were inch-long claw marks there, three of them. Whitened scratches, they were already rising, the skin swelling and breaking. Beads of blood appeared. 'Jesus,' he said, sucking on the damaged wrist. He glared at the cat. It glared back, then dropped from the desk and was gone.

'Are you all right?'

'Just about. You should keep that thing on a chain.'

She smiled. 'Do you know anything about that raid last night?'

Rebus blinked, still sucking. 'What raid?'

'I heard the police raided a brothel.'

'Oh?'

'I heard they caught an MP, Gregor Jack.'

'Oh?'

She smiled again. 'Word gets about.' Rebus thought, not for the first time, I don't live in a city, I live in a bloody village . . .

'I just wondered,' the girl was saying, 'if you knew anything about it. I mean, if it's true. I mean, if it is . . .' she sighed. 'Poor Beggar.'

Rebus frowned now.

'That's his nickname,' she explained. 'Beggar. That's what Ronald calls him.'

'Your boss knows Mr Jack then?'

'Oh yes, they were at school together. Beggar owns half of this. She waved a hand around her, as though she were proprietress of some Princes Street department store. She saw that the policeman didn't seem impressed. 'We do a lot of business behind the scenes,' she said defensively. 'A lot of buying and selling. It might not look much, but this place is a goldmine.'

Rebus nodded. 'Actually,' he said, 'now that you mention it, it *does* look a bit like a mine.' His wrist was crackling now, as though stung by nettles. Bloody cat. 'Right, keep an eye out for those books, won't you?'

She didn't answer. Hurt, he didn't doubt, by the 'mine' jibe. She was opening a book, ready to pencil in a price. Rebus nodded to himself, walked to the door, and rubbed his feet noisily on the mat before leaving the shop. The cat was back in the window, licking its tail.

'Fuck you too, pal,' muttered Rebus. Pets, after all, were his pet hate.

Dr Patience Aitken had pets. Too many pets. Tiny tropical fish . . . a tame hedgehog in the back garden . . . two budgies in a cage in the living room . . . and, yes, a cat. A stray which, to Rebus's relief, still liked to spend much of its time on the prowl. It was a tortoiseshell and it was called Lucky. It liked Rebus.

'It's funny,' Patience had said, 'how they always seem to go for the people who don't like them, don't want them, or are allergic to them. Don't ask me why.'

As she said this, Lucky was climbing across Rebus's shoulders. He snarled and shrugged it off. It fell to the floor, landing on its feet.

'You've got to have patience, John.'

Yes, she was right. If he did not have patience, he might lose Patience. So he'd been trying. He'd been trying. Which was perhaps why he'd been tricked into trying to stroke Rasputin. *Rasputin*! Why was it pets always seemed to be called either Lucky, Goldie, Beauty, Flossie, Spot, or else Rasputin, Beelzebub, Fang, Nirvana, Bodhisattva? Blame the breed of owner.

Rebus was in the Rutherford, nursing a half of eight-shilling and watching the full-time scores on TV, when he remembered that he was expected at Brian Holmes' new house this evening, expected for a meal with Holmes and Nell Stapleton. He groaned. Then remembered that his only clean suit was at Patience Aitken's flat. It was a worrying fact. Was he *really* moving in with Patience? He seemed to be spending an awful lot of time there these days. Well, he liked her, even if she did treat him like yet another pet. And he liked her flat. He even liked the fact that it was underground.

Well, not quite underground. In some parts of town, it might once have been described as the 'basement' flat, but in Oxford Terrace, well-appointed Oxford Terrace, Stockbridge's Oxford Terrace, it was a *garden* flat. And sure enough it had a garden, a narrow isosceles triangle of land. But the flat itself was what interested Rebus. It was like a shelter, like a children's encampment. You could stand in either of the front bedrooms and stare up out of the window to where feet and legs moved along the pavement above you. People seldom looked down. Rebus, whose own flat was on the second floor of a Marchmont tenement, enjoyed this new perspective. While other men his age were moving out of the city and into bungalows, Rebus found a sort of amused thrill from walking *downstairs* to the front door instead of walking *up*. More than novelty, it was a reversal, a major shift, and his life felt full of promise as a result.

Patience, too, was full of promise. She was keen for him to move more of his things in, to 'make himself at home'. And she had given him a key. So, beer finished, and car persuaded to make the five-minute trip, he was able to let himself in. His suit, newly cleaned, was lying on the bed in the spare bedroom. So was Lucky. In fact, Lucky was lying on the suit, was rolling on it, plucking at it with his claws, was shedding on it and marking it. Rebus saw Rasputin in his mind's eye as he swiped the cat off the bed. Then he picked up the suit and took it to the bathroom, where he locked the door behind him before running a bath.

The parliamentary constituency of North and South Esk was large but not populous. The population, however, was growing. New housing estates grew in tight clusters on the outskirts of the mining towns and villages. Commuter belt. Yes, the region was changing. New roads, new railway stations even. New kinds of people doing new kinds of jobs. Brian Holmes and Nell Stapleton, however, had chosen to buy an old terraced house in the heart of one of the smallest of the villages, Eskwell. Actually, it was all about Edinburgh in the end. The city was growing, spreading out. It was the city that swallowed villages and spawned new estates. People weren't moving *into* Edinburgh; the city was moving into *them* ...

But by the time Rebus reached Eskwell he was in no mood to contemplate the changing face of country living. He'd had trouble starting the car. He was *always* having trouble starting the car. But wearing a suit and shirt and tie had made it that bit more difficult to tinker beneath the bonnet. One fine weekend he'd strip the engine down. Of course he would. Then he'd give up and phone for a tow truck.

The house was easy to find, Eskwell boasting one main street and only a few back roads. Rebus walked up the garden path and stood on the doorstep, a bottle of wine gripped in one hand. He clenched his free fist and rapped on the door. It opened almost at once.

'You're late,' said Brian Holmes.

'Perogative of rank, Brian. I'm allowed to be late.'

Holmes ushered him into the hall. 'I did say informal, didn't I?'

Rebus puzzled for a moment, then saw that this was a comment on his suit. He noticed now that Holmes himself was dressed in open-necked shirt and denims, with a pair of moccasins covering his bare feet.

'Ah,' said Rebus.

'Never mind, I'll nip upstairs and change.'

'Not on my account. This is your house, Brian. You do as you please.'

Holmes nodded to himself, suddenly looking pleased. Rebus was right: this *was* his house. Well, the mortgage was his ... *half* the mortgage. 'Go on through,' he said, gesturing to a door at the end of the hall.

'I think I'll nip upstairs myself first,' Rebus said, handing over the bottle. He spread his hands out palms upwards, then turned them over. Even Holmes could see the traces of oil and dirt.

'Car trouble,' he said, nodding. 'The bathroom's to the right of the landing.'

'Right.'

'And those are nasty scratches, too. I'd see a doctor about them,'

Holmes' tone told Rebus that the young man assumed a certain doctor had been responsible for them in the first place.

'A cat,' Rebus explained. 'A cat with eight lives left.'

Upstairs, he felt particularly clumsy. He rinsed the wash-hand-basin after him, then had to rinse the muck off the soap, then rinsed the basin again. A towel was hanging over the bath, but when he started to dry his hands he found he was drying them not on a towel but on a foot-mat. The real towel was on a hook behind the door. Relax, John, he told himself. But he couldn't. Socializing was just one more skill he'd never really mastered.

He peered round the door downstairs.

'Come in, come in.'

Holmes was holding out a glass of whisky towards him. 'Here you go, cheers.'

'Cheers.'

They drank, and Rebus felt the better for it.

'I'll give you the tour of the house later,' Holmes said. 'Sit down.'

Rebus did so, and looked around him. 'A real Holmes from home,' he commented. There were good smells in the air, and cooking and clattering noises from the kitchen, which seemed to be through another door off the living room. The living room was almost cuboid, with a table in one corner set with three places for dinner, a chair in another corner, a TV in the third, and a standard lamp in the fourth.

'Very nice,' commented Rebus. Holmes was sitting on a two-person sofa against one wall. Behind him was a decent-sized window looking on to the back garden. He shrugged modestly.

'It'll do us,' he said.

'I'm sure it will.'

Now Nell Stapleton strode into the room. As imposing as ever, she seemed almost too tall for her surroundings, Alice after the 'Eat Me' cake. She was wiping her hands on a dishcloth, and smiled at Rebus.

'Hello there.'

Rebus had risen to his feet. She came over and pecked him on his cheek.

'Hello, Nell.'

Now she was standing over Holmes, and had lifted the glass out of his hand. There was sweat on her forehead, and she too was dressed casually. She took a swallow of whisky, exhaled noisily, and handed the glass back.

'Ready in five minutes,' she announced. 'Shame your doctor friend couldn't make it, John.'

He shrugged. 'Prior engagement. A medical dinner party. I was glad of an excuse to get out of it.'

She gave him rather too fixed a smile. 'Well,' she said, 'I'll leave you two to talk about whatever it is boys talk about.'

And then she was gone, the room seeming suddenly empty. Shit, what had he said? Rebus had tried to find words to describe Nell when speaking about her to Patience Aitken. But somehow the words never told the story. Bossy, stroppy, lively, canny, big, bright, a handful . . . like another set of seven dwarves. Certainly, she didn't fit the stereotype of a university librarian. Which seemed to suit Brian Holmes just fine. He was smiling, studying what was left of his drink. He got up for a refill – Rebus refusing the offer – and came back with a manilla folder.

'Here,' he said.

Rebus accepted the folder. 'What is it?'

'Take a look.'

Newspaper cuttings mostly, magazine articles, press releases . . . all concerning Gregor Jack MP.

'Where did you . . . ?'

Holmes shrugged. 'Innate curiosity. When I knew I was moving into his constituency, I thought I'd like to know more.'

'The papers seem to have kept quiet about last night.'

'Maybe they've been warned off.' Holmes sounded sceptical. 'Or maybe they're just biding their time.' Having just reseated himself, he now leapt up again. 'I'll see if Nell needs a hand.'

Leaving Rebus with little to do but read. There wasn't much he didn't already know. Working-class background. Comprehensive school in Fife, then Edinburgh University. Degree in Economics and Accounting. Chartered accountant. Married Elizabeth Ferrie. They'd met at university. She, the daughter of Sir Hugh Ferrie the businessman. She was his only daughter, his only child. He doted on her, could refuse her nothing, all, it was said, because she reminded him of his wife, dead these past twenty-three years. Sir Hugh's most recent 'companion' was an ex-model less than half his age. Maybe she, too, reminded him of his wife . . .

Funny though. Elizabeth Jack was an attractive woman, beautiful even. Yet you never heard much about her. Since when was an attractive wife an asset not to be used by canny politicians? Maybe she wanted her own life. Skiing holidays and health resorts, rather than an MP's round of factory openings, tea parties, all that.

Rebus recalled now what it was that he liked about Gregor Jack. It was the background – so similar to his own. Born in Fife, and given a comprehensive education. Except that back then they'd been called secondary and high schools. Both Rebus and Gregor Jack had gone to a high school, Rebus because he passed his eleven-plus, the younger Jack because of good grades at his junior high. Rebus's school had been in Cowdenbeath, Jack's in Kirkcaldy. No distance at all, really.

The only muck that had ever been thrown at Jack seemed to be over the siting of a new electronics factory just inside his constituency. Rumours that his father-in-law had pulled a few strings ... It had all died down quickly enough. No evidence, and a whiff of writs for libel. How old was Jack? Rebus studied a recent newspaper photograph. He looked younger on paper than he did in real life. People in the media always did. Thirty-seven, thirty-eight, something like that. Beautiful wife, plenty of money.

And he ends up caught on a tart's bed during a brothel raid. Rebus shook his head. It was a cruel world. Then he smiled: serve the bugger right for not sticking to his wife.

Holmes was coming back in. He nodded towards the file. 'Makes you wonder, doesn't it?'

Rebus shrugged. 'Not really, Brian. Not really.'

'Well, finish your whisky and sit at the table. I'm informed by the management that dinner is about to be served.'

It was a good dinner, too. Rebus insisted on making three toasts: one to the couple's happiness, one to their new home, and one to Holmes' promotion. By then, they were on to their second bottle of wine and the evening's main course – roast beef. After that there was cheese, and after the cheese, crannachan. And after all that there was coffee and Laphroaig and drowsiness in the armchair and on the sofa for all concerned. It hadn't taken long for Rebus to relax – the alcohol had seen to that. But it had been a nervous kind of relaxation, so that he felt he'd said too much, most of it rubbish.

There was some shop talk, of course, and Nell allowed it so long as it was interesting. She thought Farmer Watson's drinking habit was interesting. ('Maybe he doesn't drink at all. Maybe he's just addicted to strong mints.') She thought Chief Inspector Lauderdale's ambition was interesting. And she thought the brothel raid sounded interesting, too. She wanted to know where the fun was in being whipped, or dressed in nappies, or having sex with a scuba-diver. Rebus admitted he'd no answer. 'Suck it and see,' was Brian Holmes' contribution. It earned him a cushion over the head.

By quarter past eleven, Rebus knew two things. One was that he was too drunk to drive. The other was that even if he could drive (or be driven) he'd not know his destination – Oxford Terrace or his own flat in Marchmont? Where, these days, did he live? He imagined himself parking the car on Lothian Road, halfway between the two addresses, and kipping there. But the decision was made for him by Nell.

'The bed in the spare room's made up. We need someone to christen it so we can start calling it the guest bedroom. Might as well be you.'

Her quiet authority was not to be challenged. Rebus shrugged his acceptance. A little later, she went to bed herself. Holmes switched on the TV but found nothing there worth watching, so he turned on the hi-fi instead.

'I haven't got any jazz,' he admitted, knowing Rebus's tastes. 'But how about this . . .?'

It was *Sergeant Pepper*. Rebus nodded. 'If I can't get the Rolling Stones, I'll always settle for second best.'

So they argued 60s pop music, then talked football for a little while and shop for a bit longer still.

'How much more time do you think Doctor Curt will take?'

Holmes was referring to one of the pathologists regularly used by the police. A body had been fished out of the Water of Leith, just below Dean Bridge. Suicide, accident or murder? They were hoping Dr Curt's findings would point the way.

Rebus shrugged. 'Some of those tests take weeks, Brian. But actually, from what I hear, he won't be much longer. A day or two maybe.'

'And what will he say?'

'God knows.' They shared a smile; Curt was notorious for his fund of bad jokes and ill-timed levity.

'Should we stand by to repel puns?' asked Holmes. 'How about this: deceased was found near waterfall. However, study of eyes showed no signs of cataracts.'

Rebus laughed. 'That's not bad. Bit too clever maybe, but still not bad.'

They spent a quarter of an hour recalling some of Curt's true gems, before, somehow, turning the talk to politics. Rebus admitted that he'd voted only three times in his adult life.

'Once Labour, once SNP, and once Tory.'

Holmes seemed to find this funny. He asked what the chronological order had been, but Rebus couldn't remember. This, too, seemed worth a laugh.

'Maybe you should try an Independent next time.'

'Like Gregor Jack you mean?' Rebus shook his head. 'I don't think there's any such thing as an "Independent" in Scotland. It's like living in Ireland and trying not to take sides. Damned hard work. And speaking of work . . . some of us have been working today. If you don't mind, Brian, I think I'll join Nell . . .' More laughter. 'If you see what I mean.'

'Sure,' said Holmes, 'on you go. I don't feel so bad. I might watch a video or something. See you in the morning.'

'Mind you don't keep me awake,' said Rebus with a wink.

In fact, meltdown at the Torness reactor couldn't have kept him awake. His dreams were full of pastoral scenes, skin-divers, kittens, and last-minute goals. But when he opened his eyes there was a dark shadowy figure looming over him. He pushed himself up on his elbows. It was Holmes, dressed and wearing a denim jacket. There was a jangle of car keys from one hand; the other hand held a selection of newspapers which he now threw down on to the bed.

'Sleep all right? Oh, by the way, I don't usually buy these rags but I thought you'd be interested. Breakfast'll be ready in ten minutes.'

Rebus managed to mumble a few syllables. He heaved himself upright and studied the front page of the tabloid in front of him. This was what he'd been waiting for, and he actually felt some of the tension leave his body and his brain. The headline was actually subtle – JACK THE LAD! – but the sub-head was blunt enough – MP NICKED IN SEX-DEN SWOOP. And there was the photograph, showing Gregor Jack on his way down the steps to the waiting van. More photos were promised inside. Rebus turned to the relevant pages. A pasty-faced Farmer Watson; a couple of the 'escorts' posing for the cameras; and another four shots of Jack, showing his progress all the way into the van. None from the cop-shop aftermath, so presumably he'd been spirited away. You couldn't hope to spirit this away though, photogenic or no. Ha! In the background of one of the photos Rebus could make out the cherubic features of Detective Sergeant Brian Holmes. One for the scrapbook and no mistake.

There were two more newspapers, both telling a similar tale graced by similar (sometimes even identical) photos. THE DISHONOURABLE MEMBER; MP'S VICE SHAME. Ah, the great British Sunday headline, coined by an elect of teetotal virgins boasting the combined wisdom of Solomon and the magnanimity of a zealot. Rebus could be as prurient as the next man, but this stuff was a class above. He prised himself out of bed and stood up. The alcohol inside him stood up too; then it began to pogostick its way around his head. Red wine and whisky. Bad news and a chaser. What was the phrase? Never mix the grain and the grape. Never mind, a couple of litres of orange juice would sort him out.

But first there was the little matter of the fry-up. Nell looked as though she'd spent all night in the kitchen. She had washed up the debris of the previous night, and now was providing a breakfast of hotel proportions. Cereal, toast, bacon, sausage and egg. With a pot of coffee taking pride of place on the dining table. Only one thing was missing.

'Any orange juice?' Rebus suggested.

'Sorry,' said Brian. 'I thought the paper shop would have some, but they'd run out. There's plenty of coffee though. Tuck in.' He was busy with another paper, a broadsheet this time. 'Didn't take them long to stick the knife in, did it?'

'You mean Gregor Jack? No, well, what can you expect?'

Holmes turned a page. 'Strange though,' he said, and let it lie at that, wondering whether Rebus would know . . .

'You mean,' Rebus replied, 'it's strange that the London Sunday's knew about Operation Creeper.'

Another page was turned. It didn't take long to read a newspaper these days, not unless you were interested in the adverts. Holmes folded the paper into four and laid it down on the table beside him.

'Yes,' he said, lifting a piece of toast. 'Like I say, it's strange.'

'Come on, Brian. Papers are always getting tip-offs to juicy stories. A copper looking for beer money, something like that. Chances are, you raid a posh brothel you're going to come out with some weel-kent faces.'

Hold on though . . . Even as he spoke, Rebus knew there was something more. That night, the reporters had been biding their time, hadn't they? Like they knew *exactly* who or what might be walking out of the door and down the steps. Holmes was staring at him now.

'What are you thinking?' Rebus asked.

'Nothing. No, nothing at all . . . yet. Not our business, is it? And besides, this is Sunday.'

'You're a sly bugger, Brian Holmes.'

'I've got a good tutor, haven't I?'

Nell came into the room carrying two plates, filled with glistening fried food. Rebus's stomach pleaded with its owner not to do anything rash, anything he would regret later on in the day.

'You're working too hard,' Rebus told Nell. 'Don't let him treat you like a skivvy.'

'Don't worry,' she said, 'I don't. But fair's fair. Brian did wash last night's dishes. And he'll wash this morning's too.'

Holmes groaned. Rebus opened one of the tabloids and tapped his finger against a photograph.

'Better not work him too hard, Nell, not now he's in pictures.'

Nell took the paper from him, studied it for a moment, then shrieked. 'My God, Brian! You look like something off the *Muppet Show*.'

Holmes was on his feet now, too, staring over her shoulder. 'And is that what Chief Superintendent Watson looks like? He could pass for an Aberdeen Angus.'

Rebus and Holmes shared a smile at that. He wasn't called Farmer for nothing . . .

Rebus wished the young couple well. They had made a commitment to living together. They had bought a house together and set up home. They seemed content. Yes, he wished them well with all his heart.

But his brain gave them two or three years at most.

A policeman's lot was not entirely a happy one. Striving towards inspectorship, Brian Holmes would find himself working still longer hours. If he could shut it all out when he got home of an evening or morning, fine. But Rebus doubted the young man would. Holmes was the type to get involved in a case, to let it rule his thinking hours whether on duty or off, and that was bad for a relationship.

Bad, and often terminal. Rebus knew more divorced and separated policemen (himself included) than happily married ones. It wasn't just the hours worked, it was the way police work itself gnawed into you like a worm, burrowing deep. Eating away from the inside. As protection against the worm, you wore armour plating – more of it, perhaps, than was necessary. And that armour set you apart from friends and family, from the 'civilians' ...

Ach. Pleasant thoughts for a Sunday morning. After all, it wasn't *all* gloom. The car had started without a hitch (that is, without him having to hitch a ride to the nearest garage), and there was just enough blue in the sky to send hardy day-trippers off into the country. Rebus was going on a drive, too. An aimless tour, he told himself. A nice day for a drive. But he knew where he was headed. Knew where, if not exactly *why.*

Gregor Jack and his wife lived in a large, old, detached and walled residence on the outskirts of Rosebridge, a little further south than Eskwell, a little bit more rural. Gentry country. Fields and rolling hills and an apparent moratorium on new building work. Rebus had no excuse save curiosity for this detour, but he was not, it seemed, alone. The Jacks' house was recognizable by the half dozen cars parked outside its gates and by the posse of reporters who were lounging around, chatting to each other or instructing fed-up-looking photographers on how far they should go (morally rather than geographically) for that elusive picture. Clamber on to the wall? Climb that nearby tree? Try the back of the house? The photographers didn't seem keen. But just then something seemed to galvanize them.

By this time, Rebus had parked his own car further along the road. To one side of the road was a line of perhaps half a dozen houses, none of them spectacular in terms of design or size, but wonderfully isolated by those high walls, long driveways, and (doubtless) vast back gardens. The other side of the road was pasture. Bemused cows and fat-looking sheep. Some sizeable lambs, their voices not yet quite broken. The view ended at some steepish hills, three or so miles distant. It was nice. Even the troglodyte Rebus could appreciate that.

Which was perhaps why the reporters left a more bitter taste than usual beneath his tongue. He stood behind them, an observer. The house was dark-stoned, reddish from this distance. A two-storey construction, probably built in the early 1900s. Tacked on to it at one side was a large garage, and in front of the house at the top of the drive sat a white Saab, one of the 9000 series. Sturdy and reliable, not cheap but not show-offish. Distinctive though: a car of distinction.

A youngish man, early thirties, a sneer creasing his face, was unlocking the gates just wide enough so that a younger woman, out of her teens but trying to look ten years older, could hand a silver tray to the reporters. She spoke louder than she needed to.

'Gregor thought you might like some tea. There may not be enough cups, you'll just have to share. There are biscuits in the tin. No ginger nuts, I'm afraid. We've run out.'

There were smiles at this, nods of appreciation. But throughout questions were being fired off.

'Any chance of a word with Mr Jack?'

'Can we expect a statement?'

'How's he taking it?'

'Is Mrs Jack in the house?'

'Any chance of a word?'

'Ian, is he going to be saying *any*thing?'

This last question was directed at the sneering man, who now held up one hand for silence. He waited patiently, and the silence came. Then:

'No comment,' he said. And with that he began to close the gates. Rebus pushed through the good-natured crush until he was face to face with Mr Sneer.

'Inspector Rebus,' he said. 'Could I have a word with Mr Jack?'

Mr Sneer and Miss Teatray seemed highly suspicious, even when they accepted and examined Rebus's ID. Fair enough: he'd known of reporters who'd try a stunt just like this, fake ID and all. But eventually there was a curt nod, and the gates opened again wide enough to allow him to squeeze through. The gates were shut again, locked. With Rebus on the inside.

He had a sudden thought: What the hell am I doing? The answer was: He wasn't sure. Something about the scene at the gates had made him want to be on the other side of those gates. Well, here he was. Being led back up the gravel driveway towards the large car, the larger house behind it, and the garage off to the side. Being led towards Gregor Jack MP, with whom, apparently, he wanted a word.

I believe you want a word, Inspector?

No, sir, just being nosey.

It wasn't much of an opening line, was it? Watson had warned him before about this ... this ... was it a character flaw? This need to push his way into the centre of things, to become involved, to find out for himself rather than accepting somebody's word, no matter who that somebody was.

Just passing, thought I'd pay my respects. Jesus, and Jack would recognize him, wouldn't he? From the brothel. Sitting on the bed, while the woman in the bed kicked up her legs, screeching with laughter. No, maybe not. He'd had other things on his mind after all.

'I'm Ian Urquhart, Gregor's constituency agent.' Now that he had his back to the reporters, the sneer had left Urquhart's face. What was left was a mixture of worry and bewilderment. 'We got word last night of what was coming. I've been here ever since.'

Rebus nodded. Urquhart was compact, a bunching of well-kept muscles inside a tailored suit. A bit smaller than the MP, and a bit less good-looking. In other words, just right for an agent. He also looked efficient, which Rebus would say was a bonus.

'This is Helen Greig, Gregor's secretary.' Urquhart was nodding towards the young woman. She gave a quick smile towards Rebus. 'Helen came over this morning to see if there was anything she could do.'

'The tea was my idea actually,' she said.

Urquhart glanced towards her. 'Gregor's idea, Helen,' he warned.

'Oh yes,' she said, reddening.

Efficient and faithful, thought Rebus. Rare qualities indeed. Helen Greig, like Urquhart himself, spoke in an educated Scots accent which did not really betray county of origin. He would hazard at east coast for both of them, but couldn't narrow things down any further. Helen looked either like she'd been to an early Kirk service, or was planning to attend one later on. She was wearing a pale woollen two-piece with plain white blouse offset by a simple gold chain around her neck. Sensible black shoes on her feet and thick black tights. She was Urquhart's height, five feet six or seven, and shared something of his build. You wouldn't call her beautiful: you'd call her handsome, in the way Nell Stapleton was handsome, though the two women were dissimilar in many ways.

They were passing the Saab now, Urquhart leading. 'Was there anything in particular, Inspector? Only, I'm sure you can appreciate that Gregor's hardly in a state...'

'It won't take long, Mr Urquhart.'

'Well, in you come then.' The front door opened, and Urquhart ushered both Rebus and Helen Greig into the house before him. Rebus was immediately surprised by how modern the interior was. Polished pine flooring, scatter rugs, Mackintosh-style chairs and low-slung Italian-looking tables. They passed through the hall and into a large room boasting more modern furnishings still. Pride of place went to a long angular sofa constructed from leather and chrome. On which sat, in much the same position as when Rebus had first met him, Gregor Jack. The MP was scratching absent-mindedly at a finger and staring at the floor. Urquhart cleared his throat.

'We have a visitor, Gregor.'

The effect was that of a talented actor changing roles – tragedy to comedy. Gregor Jack stood up and fixed a smile on to his face. His eyes now sparkled, looking interested, his whole face speaking sincerity. Rebus marvelled at the ease of the transformation.

'Detective Inspector Rebus,' he said, taking the proffered hand.

'Inspector, what can we do for you? Here, sit down.' Jack gestured towards a squat black chair, matching the sofa in design. It was like sinking into marshmallow. 'Something to drink?' Now Jack seemed to remember something and turned to Helen Greig. 'Helen, you took the tea out to our friends?'

She nodded.

'Excellent. Can't have the gentlemen of the press going without their elevenses.' He smiled towards Rebus, then lowered himself on to the edge of the sofa, arms resting on his knees so that the hands remained mobile. 'Now, Inspector, what's the problem?'

'Well, sir, it's really just that I happened to be passing, and saw that gang at the gates, so I stopped.'

'You know why they're here, though?'

Rebus was obliged to nod. Urquhart cleared his throat again.

'We're going to prepare a statement for them over lunch,' he said. 'It probably won't be enough to see them off, but it might help.'

'You know, of course,' said Rebus, aware that he had to tread carefully, 'that you've done nothing wrong, sir. I mean, nothing illegal.'

Jack smiled again and shrugged. 'It doesn't need to be illegal, Inspector. It just has to be news.' His hands kept fluttering, as did his eyes and head. It was as though his mind were elsewhere. Then something seemed to click. 'You didn't say, Inspector,' he said, 'tea or coffee? Something stronger perhaps?'

Rebus shook his head slowly. His hangover was a dull presence now. No point swaddling it. Jack raised his soulful eyes to Helen Greig.

'I'd love a cup of tea, Helen. Inspector, you're sure you won't...?'

'No, thank you.'

'Ian?'

Urquhart nodded towards Helen Greig.

'Would you, Helen?' said Gregor Jack. What woman, Rebus wondered, would refuse? Which reminded him...

'Your wife's not here then, Mr Jack?'

'On holiday,' Jack said quickly. 'We've a cottage in the Highlands. Not much of a place, but we like it. She's probably there.'

'Probably? Then you don't know for sure?'·

'She didn't make out an itinerary, Inspector.'

'So does she know...?'

Jack shrugged. 'I've no idea, Inspector. Maybe she does. She's an insatiable reader of newsprint. There's a village nearby stocks the Sundays.'

'But she hasn't been in touch?'

Urquhart didn't bother clearing his throat this time before interrupting. 'There's no phone at the lodge.'

'That's what we like about it,' Jack explained. 'Cut off from the world.'

'But if she knew,' Rebus persisted, 'surely she'd get in touch?'

Jack sighed, and began scratching at his finger again. He caught himself doing it and stopped. 'Eczema,' he explained. 'Just on the one finger, but it's annoying all the same.' He paused. 'Liz ... my wife ... she's very much a law unto herself, Inspector. Maybe she'd get in touch, maybe she wouldn't. She's just as likely not to want to talk about it. Do you see what I mean?' Another smile, a weaker one, seeking the sympathy vote. Jack ran his fingers through his thick dark hair. Rebus wondered idly whether the perfect teeth were capped. Maybe the thatch was capped, too. The open-necked shirt didn't look like chain-store stuff ...

Urquhart was still standing. Or, rather, was on his feet but in constant movement. Over to the window to peer through the net curtains. Over to a glass-topped table to examine some papers lying there. Over to a smaller table where the telephone sat, disconnected at the wall. So that even if Mrs Jack *did* try to call ... Neither Urquhart nor Jack seemed to have thought of that. Curious. The room, the taste it displayed, seemed to Rebus not Jack's but his wife's. Jack looked like a man for older established pieces of furniture, safe comfy armchairs and a chesterfield sofa. A conservative taste. Look at the car he chose to drive ...

Yes, Jack's car: now there was an idea, or rather an excuse, an excuse for Rebus's presence.

'Maybe if we could get that statement out *by* lunchtime, Gregor,' Urquhart was saying. 'Sooner we dampen things down the better, really.'

Not very subtle, thought Rebus. The message was: state your business and leave. Rebus knew the question he wanted to ask: Do you think you were set up? Wanted to ask, but daren't. He wasn't here officially, was a tourist merely.

'About your car, Mr Jack,' he began. 'Only, I noticed when I stopped that it's sitting there in the drive, on full view so as to speak. And there are photographers out there. If any pictures of your car get into the papers ...'

'Everyone will recognize it in future?' Jack nodded. 'I see what you're getting at, Inspector. Yes, thank you. We hadn't thought of that, had we, Ian?' Better put it in the garage. We don't want everyone who reads a newspaper to know what kind of car I drive.'

'And its registration,' Rebus added. 'There are all sorts of people out there ... terrorists ... people with a grudge ... plain nutters. Doesn't do any good.'

'Thank you, Inspector.' The door swung open and Helen Greig entered, carrying two large mugs of tea. A far cry from the silver salver routine at the gates. She handed one to Urquhart and one to Gregor Jack, then removed a slim box from where it had been held between her arm and her side. It was a fresh box of ginger nuts. Rebus smiled.

'Lovely, Helen, thanks,' said Gregor Jack. He eased two biscuits from the packet.

Rebus rose to his feet. 'Well,' he said. 'I'd better be going. Like I say, I only dropped in . . .'

'I do appreciate it, Inspector.' Jack had placed mug and biscuits on the floor and was now standing, too, hand held out again towards Rebus. A warm, strong and unflawed hand. 'I meant to ask, do you live in the constituency?'

Rebus shook his head. 'One of my colleagues does. I was staying with him last night.'

Jack raised his head slowly before nodding. The gesture could have meant anything. 'I'll open the gates for you,' Ian Urquhart was saying.

'Stay here and drink your tea,' Helen Greig said. 'I'll see the Inspector out.'

'If you like, Helen,' Urquhart said slowly. Was there a warning in his voice? If there was, Helen Greig seemed not to sense it. He fished in his pocket for the keys and handed them to her.

'Right then,' Rebus said. 'Goodbye, Mr Jack . . . Mr Urquhart.' He took Urquhart's hand for a moment and squeezed it. But his attention was on the man's left hand. Wedding ring on one finger, and a signet ring on another. Gregor Jack's left hand sported just the one thick band of gold. Not, however, on his wedding finger, but on the finger next to it. The wedding finger was the one with the eczema . . .

And Helen Greig? A few trinket rings on both hands, but she was neither married nor engaged.

'Goodbye.'

Helen Greig was first out of the house, but waited for him beside the car, jangling the keys in her right hand.

'Have you worked for Mr Jack long?'

'Long enough.'

'Hard work, being an MP, isn't it? I expect he needs to unwind from time to time –'

She stopped and glared at him. 'Not you too! You're as bad as that lot!' She gestured with the keys towards the gates and the figures beyond. 'I won't hear a word said against Gregor.' She started walking again, more briskly now.

'He's a good employer then?'

'He's not *like* an employer at all. My mother's been ill. He gave me a bonus in the autumn so I could take her for a wee holiday down the coast. *That's* the sort of man he is.' There were tears in her eyes, but she forced them back. The reporters were passing cups between them, complaining about sugar or the lack of it. They didn't seem to expect much from the approach of the two figures.

'Talk to us, Helen.'

'A word with Gregor and we can all go home. We've got families to think of, you know.'

'I'm missing communion,' joked one of them.

'Yes, communion with your lunchtime pint,' returned another.

One of the local reporters – by the accents, there weren't many of them present – had recognized Rebus.

'Inspector, anything to tell us?' A few ears pricked up at that 'Inspector'.

'Yes,' said Rebus, causing Helen Greig to stiffen. 'Bugger off.'

There were smiles at this and a few groans. The gates opened and were about to close, leaving Rebus on the outside again. But he pressed his weight against the gate and leaned towards the young woman, his mouth close to her ear.

'I forgot, I'll have to go back in.'

'What?'

'I forgot, or rather Mr Jack did. He wanted me to check on his wife, in case she was taking the news badly ...'

He waited for the notion of this to sink in. Helen Greig puckered her lips in a silent *O*. The notion had sunk in.

'Only,' Rebus went on, 'I forgot to get the address ...'

She stood on her toes and, so the newsmen wouldn't hear, whispered into his ear: 'Deer Lodge. It's between Knockandhu and Tomnavoulin.'

Rebus nodded, and allowed her to close and lock the gates. His curiosity was not exactly dispelled. In fact, he was more curious now than when he'd gone in. Knockandhu and Tomnavoulin: the names of a couple of malt whiskies. His head told him never to drink again. His heart told him differently ...

Damn, he'd meant to phone Patience from Holmes' house, just to let her know he was on his way. Not that she kept him to an itinerary or anything ... but all the same. He made for the reporter he recognized, the local lad. Chris Kemp.

'Hello, Chris. Got a phone in your car? Mind if I make a call ...?'

'So,' said Dr Patience Aitken, 'how was your *ménage à trois*?'

'Not bad,' said Rebus, before kissing her loudly on the lips. 'How was your orgy?'

She rolled her eyes. 'Shop talk and overcooked lasagne. You didn't manage home then?' Rebus looked blank. 'I tried phoning Marchmont, and you weren't there either. Your suit looks like you slept in it.'

'Blame the bloody cat.'

'Lucky?'

'He was doing the twist all over the jacket till I rescued it.'

'The *twist*? Nothing shows a man's true age more than his choice of dance step.'

Rebus was shedding the suit now. 'You haven't got any orange juice, have you?'

'Bit of a sore head? Time to stop the drinking, John.'

'Time to settle down, you mean.' He pulled off his trousers. 'All right if I take a bath?'

She was studying him. 'You know you don't have to ask.'

'No, but all the same, I like to ask.'

'Permission granted ... as always. Did Lucky do that, too?' She was pointing to the scratches on his wrist.

'He'd be in the microwave if he had.'

She smiled. 'I'll see about the orange juice.'

Rebus watched her make for the kitchen. He attempted a dry-mouthed, wolf-whistle. From nearby, one of the budgies showed him how to do it properly. Patience turned towards the budgie and smiled.

He lay down in the foaming bath and closed his eyes, breathing deeply, the way his doctor had told him to. Relaxation technique, he'd called it. He wanted Rebus to relax a bit more. High blood pressure, nothing serious, but all the same ... Of course, there were pills he could take, beta-blockers. But the doctor was in favour of self-help. Deep relaxation. Self-hypnosis. Rebus had had half a mind to tell the doctor that his own father had been a hypnotist, that his brother still might be a professional hypnotist somewhere ...

Deep breathing ... emptying the mind ... relaxing the head, the forehead, the jaw, the neck muscles, the chest, the arms. Counting backwards down to zero ... no stress, no strain ...

At first, Rebus had accused the doctor of penny-pinching, of not wanting to give out costly drugs. But the damned thing seemed to work. He *could* help himself. He could help himself to Patience Aitken ...

'Here you go,' she said, coming into the bathroom. She was holding a long thin glass of orange juice. 'As squeezed by Dr Aitken.'

Rebus slipped a sudsy arm around her buttocks. 'As squeezed by Inspector Rebus.'

She bent down and kissed him on his head. Then touched a finger to his hair. 'You need to start using a conditioner, John. All the life's going out of your follicles.'

'That's because it's headed somewhere else.'

She narrowed her eyes. 'Down, boy,' she said. Then, before he could make a grab for her again, she fled from the bathroom. Rebus, smiling, settled further into the bath.

Deep breathing ... emptying the mind ... *Had* Gregor Jack been set up. If so, who by? And to what purpose? A scandal, of course. A political scandal, a front-page scandal. But the atmosphere in the Jack household had been ... well, *strange*. Strained, certainly, but also cold and edgy, as though the worst were still to happen.

The wife ... Elizabeth ... something didn't seem right there. Something seemed very odd indeed. Background, he needed more background. He needed to be *sure*. The lodge address was fixed in his mind, but from what he knew of Highland police stations little good would come of phoning on a Sunday. Background ... He thought again of Chris Kemp, the reporter. Yes, why not? Wake up, arms, wake up, chest, neck and head. Sunday was no time to be resting. For some people, Sunday was a day of work.

Patience stuck her head round the door. 'Quiet night in this evening?' she suggested. 'I'll cook us a –'

'Quiet night be damned,' Rebus said, rising impressively from the water. 'Let's go out for a drink.'

'You know me, John. I don't *mind* a bit of sleaze, but this place is cheapskate sleaze. Don't you think I'm worth better?'

Rebus pecked Patience's cheek, placed their drinks on the table, and sat down beside her. 'I got you a double,' he said.

'So I see.' She picked up the glass. 'Not much room for the tonic, is there?'

They were seated in the back room of the Horsehair public house on Broughton Street. Through the doorway could be seen the bar itself, noisy as ever. People who wanted to have a conversation seemed to place themselves like duellists a good ten paces away from the person they wanted to talk with. The result was that a lot of shouting went on, producing much crossfire and more crossed wires. It was noisy, but it was fun. The back room was quieter. It was a U-shaped arrangement of squashy seating (around the walls) and rickety chairs. The narrow lozenge-shaped tables were fixed to the floor. Rumour had it that the squashy seating had been stuffed with horsehair in the 1920s and not restuffed since. Thus the Horsehair, whose real and prosaic name had long since been discarded.

Patience poured half a small bottle of tonic water into her gin, while Rebus supped on a pint of IPA.

'Cheers,' she said, without enthusiasm. Then: 'I know damned fine that there's got to be a reason for this. I mean, a reason why we're here. I *suppose* it's to do with your work?'

Rebus put down the glass. 'Yes,' he said.

She raised her eyes to the nicotine-coloured ceiling. 'Give me strength,' she said.

'It won't take long,' Rebus said. 'I thought afterwards we could go somewhere ... a bit more your style.'

'Don't patronize me, you pig.'

Rebus stared into his drink, thinking about that statement's various meanings. Then he caught sight of a new customer in the bar, and waved through the doorway. A young man came forwards, smiling tiredly.

'Don't often see you in here, Inspector Rebus,' he said.

'Sit down,' said Rebus. 'It's my round. Patience, let me introduce you to one of Scotland's finest young reporters, Chris Kemp.'

Rebus got up and headed for the bar. Chris Kemp pulled over a chair and, having tested it first, eased himself on to it. 'He must want something,' he said to Patience, nodding towards the bar. 'He knows I'm a sucker for a bit of flattery.'

Not that it *was* flattery. Chris Kemp had won awards for his early work on an Aberdeen evening paper, and had then moved to Glasgow, there to be voted Young Journalist of the Year, before arriving in Edinburgh, where he had spent the past year and a half 'stirring it' (as he said himself). Everyone knew he'd one day head south. He knew it himself. It was inescapable. There didn't seem to be much left for him to stir in Scotland. The only problem was his student girlfriend, who wouldn't graduate for another year and wouldn't think of moving south before then, if ever . . .

By the time Rebus returned from the bar, Patience had been told all of this and more. There was a film over her eyes which Chris Kemp, for all his qualities, could not see. He talked, and as he talked she was thinking: Is John Rebus worth all this? Is he worth the effort I seem to have to make? She didn't love him: that was understood. 'Love' was something that had happened to her a few times in her teens and twenties and even, yes, in her thirties. Always with inconclusive or atrocious results. So that nowadays it seemed to her 'love' could as easily spell the end of a relationship as its beginning.

She saw it in her surgery. She saw men and women (but mostly women) made ill from love, from loving too much and not being loved enough in return. They were every bit as sick as the child with earache or the pensioner suffering angina. She had pity and words for them, but no medicines.

Time heals, she might say in an unguarded moment. Yes, heals into a callus over the wound, hard and protective. Just like she felt: hard and protective. But did John Rebus need her solidity, her protection?

'Here we are,' he said on his return. 'The barman's slow tonight, sorry.'

Chris Kemp accepted the drink with a thin smile. 'I've just been telling Patience . . .'

Oh God, Rebus thought as he sat down. She looks like a bucketful of ice. I shouldn't have brought her. But if I'd said I was popping out for the evening on my own ... well, she'd have been the same. Get this over and done with, maybe the night can be rescued.

'So, Chris,' he said, interrupting the young man, 'what's the dirt on Gregor Jack?'

Chris Kemp seemed to think there was plenty, and the introduction of Gregor Jack into the conversation perked Patience up a bit, so that she forgot for a time that she wasn't enjoying herself.

Rebus was interested mostly in Elizabeth Jack, but Kemp started with the MP himself, and what he had to say was interesting. Here was a different Jack, different from the public image, the received opinion, but different too from Rebus's own ideas having met with the man. He would not, for example, have taken Jack for a drinker.

'Terrible one for the whisky,' Kemp was saying. 'Probably more than half a bottle a day, more when he's in London by all accounts.'

'He never looks drunk.'

'That's because he doesn't *get* drunk. But he drinks all the same.'

'What else?'

There was more, plenty more. 'He's a smooth operator, but cunning. Deep down cunning. I wouldn't trust him further than I can spit. I know someone who knew him at university. Says Gregor Jack never did anything in his life that wasn't premeditated. And that goes for capturing *Mrs* Gregor Jack.'

'How do you mean?'

'Story is, they met at university, at a party. Gregor had seen her around before, but hadn't paid much attention. Once he knew she was *rich* though, that was another matter. He went at it full throttle, charmed the pants off her.' He turned to Patience. 'Sorry, poor choice of words.'

Patience, on her second g and t, merely bowed her head a little.

'He's calculating, you see. Remember, he was trained as an accountant, and he's got an accountant's mind all right. What are you having?'

But Rebus was rising. 'No, Chris, let me get them.'

But Kemp wouldn't hear of it. 'Don't think I'm telling you all this for the price of a couple of beers, Inspector ...'

And when the drinks had been bought and brought to the table, it was this train of thought which seemed to occupy Kemp.

'Why do you want to know anyway?'

Rebus shrugged.

'Is there a story?'

'Could be. Early days.'

They were talking now as professionals: the meaning was all in what was left unsaid.

'But there might be a story?'

'If there is, Chris, as far as I'm concerned it's yours.'

Kemp gulped at his beer. 'I was out there all day, you know. And all we got was a statement. Plain and simple. No further comment to make, et cetera. The story ties in with Jack?'

Rebus shrugged again. 'Early days. That was interesting, what you were saying about Mrs Jack . . .'

But Kemp's eyes were cool. 'I get the story first?'

Rebus massaged his neck. 'As far as I'm concerned.'

Kemp seemed to size the offer up. As Rebus himself knew, there was almost no offer *there* for the sizing. Then Kemp placed his glass on the table. He was ready to say a little more.

'What Jack didn't know about Liz Ferrie was that she ran with a *very* fast crowd. A rich fast crowd. People like her. It took Gregor quite a while before he was able to insinuate his way into the group. A working-class kid, remember. Still gangly and a bit awkward. But it happened, he had Liz hooked. Where he went, she would et cetera. And Jack had his own gang. Still does.'

'I don't follow.'

'Old schoolfriends mostly, a few people he met at university. His circle, you could call it.'

'One of them runs a bookshop, doesn't he?'

Kemp nodded. 'That's Ronald Steele. Known to the gang as Suey. That's why his shop's called Suey Books.'

'Funny nickname,' said Patience.

'I don't know how he came by it,' admitted Kemp. 'I'd *like* to know, but I don't.'

'Who else is there?' asked Rebus.

'I'm not sure how many there are altogether. The interesting ones are Rab Kinnoul and Andrew Macmillan.'

'Rab Kinnoul the actor?'

'The very same.'

'That's funny, I've got to talk to him. Or rather, to his wife.'

'Oh?'

Kemp was sniffing his story, but Rebus shook his head. 'Nothing to do with Jack. Some stolen books. Mrs Kinnoul is a bit of a collector.'

'Not Prof Costello's missing hoard?'

'That's it.'

Kemp was nothing if not a newsman. 'Any progress?'

Rebus shrugged.

'Don't tell me,' said Kemp, 'it's early days yet.'

And he laughed, and Patience laughed with him. But something had just struck Rebus.

'Not *the* Andrew Macmillan, surely?'

Kemp nodded. 'They were at school together.'

'Christ.' Rebus stared at the plastic-topped table. Kemp was explaining to Patience who Andrew Macmillan was.

'A very successful something-or-other. Went off his head one day. Toddled off home and sawed off his wife's head.'

Patience gasped. 'I remember that,' she said. 'They never found the head, did they?'

Kemp shook his own firmly fixed head. 'He'd have done his daughter in, too, but the kid ran for her life. She's a bit dotty now herself, and no wonder.'

'Whatever happened to him?' Rebus wondered aloud. It had been several years ago, and in Glasgow not Edinburgh. Not his territory.

'Oh,' said Kemp, 'he's in that new psychiatric place, the one they've just built.'

'You mean Duthil?' said Patience.

'That's it. Up in the Highlands. Near Grantown, isn't it?'

Well, thought Rebus, curiouser and curiouser. His geography wasn't brilliant, but he didn't think Grantown was *too* far from Deer Lodge. 'Is Jack still in touch with him?'

It was Kemp's turn to shrug. 'No idea.'

'And they were at school together?'

'That's the story. To be honest, I think Liz Jack is the more interesting character by far. Jack's sidekicks are scrupulous in keeping her out of the way.'

'Yes, why is that?'

'Because she's still the proverbial wild child. Still runs around with her old crowd. Jamie Kilpatrick, Matilda Merriman, all that sort. Parties, booze, drugs, orgies ... God knows. The press never gets a sniff.' He turned again to Patience. 'If you'll pardon the phrase. Not a sniff do we get. And anything we *do* get is blue pencilled with a fair amount of prejudice.'

'Oh?'

'Well, editors are nervous at the best of times, aren't they? And you've got to remember that Sir Hugh Ferrie is never slow with a libel suit where his family's concerned.'

'You mean that electronics factory?'

'Case in point.'

'So what about this "old crowd" of Mrs Jack's?'

'Aristos, mostly old money, some new money.'

'What about the lady herself?'

'Well, she certainly spurred Jack on in the early days. I think he always wanted to go into politics, and MPs can hardly afford not to be married. People start to suspect a shirt-lifting tendency. My guess is he looked for someone pretty, with money, and with a father of influence. Found her and wasn't going to let go. And it's been a successful marriage, so far as the public's concerned. Liz gets wheeled out for the photo opportunities and looks just right, then she disappears again. Completely different to Gregor, you see. Fire and ice. She's the fire, he's the ice, usually with whisky added . . .'

Kemp was in a talkative mood tonight. There was more, but it was speculation. Still, it was interesting to be given a different perspective, wasn't it? Rebus considered this as he excused himself and visited the gents'. The Horsehair's trough-like urinal was brimful of liquid, as had always, to Rebus's knowledge, been the case. The condensation on the overhead cistern dripped unerringly on to the heads of those unwise enough to get too close, and the graffiti was mostly the work of a dyslexic bigot: REMEMBER 1960. There was some new stuff though, written in biro. 'The Drunk as a Lord's Prayer,' Rebus read. 'Our Father which are in heavy, Alloa'd be they name . . .'

Rebus reckoned that if he didn't have all he needed, he had all Chris Kemp was able to give. No reason to linger then. No reason at all. He came out of the gents' briskly, and saw that a young man had stopped at the table to chat with Patience. He was moving away now, back to the main bar, while Patience smiled a farewell in his direction.

'Who was that?' Rebus asked, not sitting down.

'He lives next door in Oxford Terrace,' Patience said casually. 'Works in Trading Standards. I'm surprised you haven't met him.'

Rebus murmured something, then tapped his watch with his finger.

'Chris,' he said, 'this is all your fault. You're too interesting by half. We were supposed to be at the restaurant twenty minutes ago. Kevin and Myra will kill us. Come on, Patience. Listen, Chris, I'll be in touch. Meantime . . .' he leaned closer to the reporter, lowering his voice. 'See if you can find who tipped off the papers about the brothel raid. *That* might be the start of the story.' He straightened up again. 'See you soon, eh? Cheers.'

'Cheerio, Chris,' said Patience, sliding out of her seat.

'Oh, right, bye then. See you.' And Chris Kemp found himself alone, wondering if it was something that he'd said.

Outside, Patience turned to Rebus. 'Kevin and Myra?' she said.

'Our oldest friends,' explained Rebus. 'And as good a get-out clause as anything. Besides, I *did* promise you dinner. You can tell me all about our next-door neighbour.'

He took her arm in his and they walked back to the car – her car. Patience had never seen John Rebus jealous before, so it was hard to tell, but she could have sworn he was jealous now. Well well, wonders would never cease . . .

3

Treacherous Steps

Springtime in Edinburgh. A freezing wind, and near-horizontal rain. Ah, the Edinburgh wind, that joke of a wind, that black farce of a wind. Making everyone walk like mime artists, making eyes water and then drying the tears to a crust on red-nipped cheeks. And throughout it all, that slightly sour yeasty smell in the air, the smell of not-so-distant breweries. There had been a frost overnight. Even the prowling, fur-coated Lucky had yowled at the bedroom window, demanding entry. The birds had been chirping as Rebus let him in. He checked his watch: two thirty. Why the hell were the birds singing so early? When he next awoke, at six, they'd stopped. Maybe they were trying to avoid the rush hour...

This sub-zero morning, it had taken him a full five minutes to start his clown of a car. Maybe it was time to get one of those red noses for the radiator grille. And the frost had swollen the cracks in the steps up to Great London Road police station, swollen and then fissured, so that Rebus stepped warily over wafers of stone.

Treacherous steps. Nothing would be done about them. The rumours were still rife anyway; rumours that Great London Road was shagged out, wabbit, past its sell-by. Rumours that it would be shut down. A prime site, after all. Prime land for another hotel or office block. And the staff? Split up, so the rumours went. With most of them being transferred to St Leonard's, the Divisional HQ (Central). Much closer to Rebus's flat in Marchmont; but much further from Oxford Terrace and Dr Patience Aitken. Rebus had made himself a little pact, a sort of contract in his head: if, within the next month or two, the rumours became fact, then it was a message from on high, a message that he should not move in with Patience. But if Great London Road remained a going concern, or if they were moved to Fettes HQ (five minutes from Oxford Terrace) ... what then? What then? The fine print on the contract was still being decided.

'Morning, John.'

'Hello, Arthur. Any messages?'

The duty desk sergeant shook his head. Rebus rubbed his hands over his ears and face, thawing them out, and climbed the stairs towards his room, where treacherous linoleum replaced treacherous stone. And then there was the treacherous telephone . . .

'Rebus here.'

'John?' It was the voice of Chief Superintendent Watson. 'Can you spare a minute?'

Rebus made noisy show of rustling some papers on his desk, hoping Watson would think he'd been in the office for hours, hard at work.

'Well, sir . . .'

'Don't piss about, John. I tried you five minutes ago.'

Rebus stopped shuffling papers. 'I'll be right along, sir.'

'That's right, you will.' And with that the phone went dead. Rebus shrugged off his weatherproof jacket, the one which always let water in at the shoulders. He felt the shoulders of his suit-jacket. Sure enough, they were damp, matching his enthusiasm for a Monday-morning meeting with the Farmer. He took a deep breath and spread his hands in front of him like an old-time song and dance man.

'It's showtime,' he told himself. Only five working days till the weekend. Then he made a quick phone call to Dufftown Police Station and asked them to check on Deer Lodge.

'Is that d-e-a-r?' asked the voice.

'D-double e-r,' corrected Rebus, thinking: But it probably *was* dear enough when they bought it.

'Anything we're looking for in particular?'

An MP's wife . . . leftovers from a sex orgy . . . flour bags full of cocaine . . . 'No,' said Rebus, 'nothing special. Just let me know what you find.'

'Right you are. It might take a while.'

'Soon as you can, eh?' And so saying, Rebus remembered that he should be elsewhere. 'Soon as you can.'

Chief Superintendent Watson was as blunt as a tramp's razor blade.

'What the hell were you doing at Gregor Jack's yesterday?'

Rebus was almost caught off guard. Almost. 'Who's been telling tales?'

'Never mind that. Just give me a bloody answer.' Pause. 'Coffee?'

'I wouldn't say no.'

Watson's wife had bought him the coffee-maker as a Christmas present. Maybe as a hint that he should cut down his consumption of Teacher's whisky. Maybe so that he'd stand a chance of being sober when he returned home of an evening. All it had done so far though was make Watson hyperactive of a morning. In the afternoon, however, after a few lunchtime nips, drowsiness would take over. Best, therefore, to avoid Watson in the mornings. Best to wait until afternoon to ask him about that leave you were thinking of taking or to tell him the news of the latest bodged operation. If you were lucky, you'd get off with a 'tut-tut'. But the mornings . . . the mornings were different.

Rebus accepted the mug of strong coffee. Half a packet of espresso looked as though it had been tipped into the generous filter. Now, it tipped itself into Rebus's bloodstream.

'Sounds stupid, sir, but I was just passing.'

'You're right,' said Watson, settling down behind his desk, 'it *does* sound stupid. Even supposing you *were* just passing . . .'

'Well, sir, to be honest, there was a little more to it than that.' Watson sat back in his chair, holding the mug in both hands, and waited for the story. Doubtless he was thinking: this'll be good. But Rebus had nothing to gain by lying. 'I like Gregor Jack,' he said. 'I mean, I like him as an MP. He's always seemed to me to be a bloody good MP. I felt a bit . . . well, I thought it was bad timing, us happening to bust that brothel the same time he was there . . .' Bad timing? Did he really believe that was all there was to it? 'So, when I *did* happen to be passing – I'd stayed the night at Sergeant Holmes' new house . . . he lives in Jack's constituency – I thought I'd stop and take a look. There were a lot of reporters about the place. I don't know exactly why I stopped, but then I saw that Jack's car was sitting out on the drive in full view. I reckoned that was dangerous. I mean, if a photo of it got into the papers. Everybody'd know Jack's car, right down to its number plate. You can't be too safe, can you? So I went in and suggested the car be moved into the garage.'

Rebus stopped. That was all there was to it, wasn't it? Well, it was enough to be going on with. Watson was looking thoughtful. He took another injection of coffee before speaking.

'You're not alone, John. I feel guilty myself about Operation Creeper. Not that there's anything to feel guilty *about*, you understand, but all the same . . . and now the press are on to the story, they'll keep on it till the poor bugger's forced to resign.'

Rebus doubted this. Jack hadn't looked like a man ready or willing or about to resign.

'If we can help Jack . . .' Watson paused again, wanting to catch Rebus's eye. He was warning Rebus that this was all unofficial, all unwritten, but that it had already been *discussed*, at some level far above Rebus himself. Perhaps, even, above Watson. Had the Chief Super been rapped over the knuckles by the high heidyins themselves? 'If we can help him,' he was saying, 'I'd like him to get that help. If you see what I mean, John.'

'I think so, sir.' Sir Hugh Ferrie had powerful friends. Rebus was beginning to wonder just *how* powerful . . .

'Right then.'

'Just the one thing, sir. Who gave you the info about the brothel?'

Watson was shaking his head even before Rebus had finished the question. 'Can't tell you that, John. I know what you're thinking. You're wondering if Jack was set up. Well, if he was, it had nothing to do with my informant. I can promise you that. No, if Jack *was* set up, the question that needs answering is why *he* was there in the first place, not why *we* were there.'

'But the papers knew, too. I mean, they knew about Operation Creeper.'

Watson was nodding now. 'Again, nothing to do with my informant. But yes, I've been thinking about that. It had to be one of us, hadn't it? Someone on the team.'

'So nobody else knew when it was planned for?'

Watson seemed to hold his breath for a moment, then shook his head. He was lying, of course. Rebus could see that. No point probing further, not yet at any rate. There would be a reason behind the lie, and that reason would come out in good time. Right now, and for no reason he could put his finger on, Rebus was more worried about *Mrs* Jack. Worried? Well, maybe not quite worried. Maybe not even *concerned*. Call it . . . call it *interested*. Yes, that was it. He was interested in her.

'Any progress on those missing books?'

What missing books? Oh, *those* missing books. He shrugged. 'We've talked to all the booksellers. The list is doing the rounds. We might even get a mention in the trade magazines. I shouldn't think any bookseller is going to touch them. Meantime . . . well, there are the private collectors still to be interviewed. One of them's the wife of Rab Kinnoul.'

'The actor?'

'The very same. Lives out towards South Queensferry. His wife collects first editions.'

'Better try to get out there yourself, John. Don't want to send a constable out to see Rab Kinnoul.'

'Right, sir.' It was the answer he'd wanted. He drained his mug. His nerves were already sizzling like bacon in a pan. 'Anything else?'

But Watson had finished with him, and was rising to replenish his own mug. 'This stuff's addictive,' he was saying as Rebus left the office. 'But by God, it makes me feel full of beans.'

Rebus didn't know whether to laugh or cry . . .

Rab Kinnoul was a professional hit man.

He had made his name initially through a series of roles on television: the Scottish immigrant in a London sitcom, the young village doctor in a farming serial, with the occasional guest spot on more substantial fare such as *The Sweeney* (playing a Glasgow runaway) or the drama series *Knife Ledge*, where he played a hired killer.

It was this last part which swung things for Kinnoul. Noticed by a London-based casting director, he was approached and screen-tested for the part of the assassin in a low-budget British thriller, which went on to do surprising business, picking up good notices in the USA as well as in Europe. The film's director was soon persuaded to move to Hollywood, and he in turn persuaded his producers that Rab Kinnoul would be ideal for the part of the gangster in an Elmore Leonard adaptation.

So, Kinnoul went to Hollywood, played minor roles in a series of major and minor murder flicks, and was again a success. He possessed a face and eyes into which could be read anything, simply anything. If you thought he should be evil, he *was* evil; if you thought he should be psychotic, he *was* psychotic. He was cast in these roles and he fitted them, but if things had taken a different turning in his career he might just as easily have ended up as the romantic lead, the sympathetic friend, the hero of the piece.

Now he'd settled back in Scotland. There was talk that he was reading scripts, was about to set up his own film company, was retiring. Rebus couldn't quite imagine retiring at thirty-nine. At fifty, maybe, but not at thirty-nine. What would you do all day? Driving towards Kinnoul's home just outside South Queensferry, the answer came to him. You could spend all day every day painting the exterior of your house; supposing, that is, it was the size of Rab Kinnoul's house. Like the Forth Rail Bridge, by the time you'd finished painting it, the first bit would be dirty again.

Which was to say that it was a very large house, even from a distance. It sat on a hillside, its surroundings fairly bleak. Long grass and a few blasted trees. A river ran nearby, discharging into the Firth of Forth. Since there was no sign of a fence separating house from surroundings, Rebus reckoned Kinnoul must own the lot.

The house was modern, if the 1960s could still be considered 'modern', styled like a bungalow but about five times the scale. It reminded Rebus mostly of those Swiss chalets you saw on postcards, except that the chalets were always finished in wood, whereas this house was finished in harling.

'I've seen better council houses,' he whispered to himself as he parked on the pebbled driveway. Getting out of the car he did, however, begin to see one of the house's attractions. The view. Both spectacular Forth Bridges not too far away at all, the firth itself sparkling and calm, and the sun shining on green and pleasant Fife across the water. You couldn't see Rosyth, but over to the east could just about be made out the seaside town of Kirkcaldy, where Gregor Jack and, presumably, Rab Kinnoul, had been schooled.

'No,' said Mrs Kinnoul – Cath Kinnoul – as she walked, a little later, into the sitting room. 'People are always making that mistake.'

She had come to the door while Rebus was still staring.

'Admiring the view?'

He grinned back at her. 'Is that Kirkcaldy over there?'

'I think so, yes.'

Rebus turned and started up the steps towards the front door. There were rockeries and neat borders to either side of them. Mrs Kinnoul looked the type to enjoy gardening. She wore homely clothes and a homely smile. Her hair had been permed into waves, but pulled back and held with a clasp at the back. There was something of the 1950s about her. He didn't know what he'd been expecting – some Hollywood blonde, perhaps – but certainly he'd not been expecting this.

'I'm Cath Kinnoul.' She held out a hand. 'I'm sorry, I've forgotten your name.'

He'd phoned, of course, to warn of his visit, to make sure someone would be at home. 'Detective Inspector Rebus,' he said.

'That's right,' she said. 'Well, come in.'

Of course, the whole thing could have been done by telephone. The following rare books have been stolen ... has anyone approached you ...? If anyone should, please contact us immediately. But like any other policeman, Rebus liked to *see* who and what he was dealing with. People often gave something away when you were there in person. They were flustered, edgy. Not that Cath Kinnoul looked flustered. She came into the sitting room with a tray of tea things. Rebus had been staring out of the picture window, drinking in the scene.

'Your husband went to school in Kirkcaldy, didn't he?'

And then she'd said: 'No, people are always making that mistake. I think because of Gregor Jack. You know, the MP.' She placed the tray on a coffee table. Rebus had turned from the window and was studying the room. There were framed photographs of Rab Kinnoul on the walls, stills from his movies. There were also photos of actors and actresses Rebus supposed he should know. The photos were signed. The room seemed to be dominated by a thirty-eight-inch television, atop which sat a video recorder. To either side of the TV, piled high on the floor, were videotapes.

'Sit down, Inspector. Sugar?'

'Just milk, please. You were saying about your husband and Gregor Jack ...?'

'Oh yes. Well, I suppose because they're both in the media, on television I mean, people tend to think they must know one another.'

'And don't they?'

She laughed. 'Oh yes, yes, they know one another. But only through me. People get their stories mixed up, I suppose, so it started to appear in the papers and magazines that Rab and Gregor went to school together, which is nonsense. Rab went to school in Dundee. It was *me* that went to school with Gregor. And we went to university together, too.'

So not even the cream of young Scottish reporters always got it right.

Rebus accepted the china cup and saucer with a nod of thanks.

'I was plain Catherine Gow then, of course. I met Rab later, when he was already working in television. He was doing a play in Edinburgh. I bumped into him in the bar after a performance.'

She was stirring her tea absent-mindedly. 'I'm Cath Kinnoul now, Rab Kinnoul's wife. Hardly anyone calls me Gowk any more.'

'Gowk?' Rebus thought he'd misheard. She looked up at him.

'That was my nickname. We all had nicknames. Gregor was Beggar . . .'

'And Ronald Steele was Suey.'

She stopped stirring, and looked at him as though seeing him for the first time. 'That's right. But how . . . ?'

'It's what his shop's called,' Rebus explained, this being the truth.

'Oh yes,' she said. 'Well, anyway, about these books . . .'

Three things struck Rebus. One was that there seemed precious few books around, for someone who was supposedly a collector. The second was that he'd rather talk some more about Gregor Jack. The third was that Cath Kinnoul was on drugs, tranquillizers of some kind. It was taking a second too long for her lips to form each word, and her eyelids had a droop to them. Valium? Moggies even?

'Yes,' he said, 'the books.' Then he looked around him. Any actor would have known it for a cheap effect. 'Mr Kinnoul's not at home just now?'

She smiled. 'Most people just call him Rab. They think if they've seen him on television, they know him, and knowing him gives them the right to call him Rab. Mr Kinnoul . . . I can see you're a policeman.' She almost wagged a finger at him, but thought better of it and drank her tea instead. She held the delicate cup by its body rather than by the awkward handle, drained it absolutely dry, and exhaled.

'Thirsty this morning,' she said. 'I'm sorry, what were you saying?'

'You were telling me about Gregor Jack.'

She looked surprised. 'Was I?'

Rebus nodded.

'Yes, that's right, I read about it in the papers. Horrible things they were saying. About him and Liz.'

'Mrs Jack?'

'Liz, yes.'

'What's she like?'

Cath Kinnoul seemed to shiver. She got up slowly and placed her empty cup on the tray. 'More tea?' Rebus shook his head. She poured milk, lots of sugar, and then a trickle of tea into her cup. 'Thirsty,' she said, 'this morning.' She went to the window, holding the cup in both hands. 'Liz is her own woman. You've got to admire her for that. It can't be easy, living with a man who's in the public eye. He hardly sees her.'

'He's away a lot, you mean?'

'Well, yes. But she's away a lot, too. She has her own life, her own friends.'

'Do you know her well?'

'No, no, I wouldn't say that. You wouldn't believe what we got up to at school. Who'd have thought ...' She touched the window. 'Do you like the house, Inspector?'

This was an unexpected turn in the conversation. 'It's ... er, big, isn't it?' Rebus answered. 'Plenty of room.'

'Seven bedrooms,' she said. 'Rab bought it from some rock star. I don't think he'd have bothered if it hadn't been a *star*'s home. What do we need seven bedrooms for? There's only the two of us ... Oh, here's Rab now.'

Rebus came to the window. A Land-Rover was bumping up the driveway. There was a heavy figure in the front, hands clenching the wheel. The Land-Rover gave a squeal as it stopped.

'About these books,' said Rebus, suddenly an efficient official. 'You collect books, I believe?'

'Rare books, yes. First editions, mostly.' Cath Kinnoul, too, was starting to play another part, this time the woman who's helping police with their ...

The front door opened and closed. 'Cath? Whose car's that in the drive?'

Rab Kinnoul came massively into the room. He was six feet two tall, and probably weighed fifteen stone. His chest was huge, a predominantly red tartan shirt stretched across it. He wore baggy brown corduroys tied at the waist with a thin, straining belt. He'd started growing a reddish beard, and his brown hair was longer than Rebus remembered, curling over his ears. He looked expectantly at Rebus, who came towards him.

'Inspector Rebus, sir.'

Kinnoul looked surprised, then relieved, then, Rebus thought, worried. The problem was those eyes; they didn't seem to change, did they? So that Rebus began to wonder whether the surprise, relief and worry were in Kinnoul's mind or in his own.

'Inspector, what's ... I mean, is there something wrong?'

'No, no, sir. It's just that some books have been stolen, rare books, and we're going around talking to private collectors.'

'Oh.' Now Kinnoul broke into a grin. Rebus didn't think he'd seen him grin in any of his TV or film roles. He could see why. The grin changed Kinnoul from ominous heavy into overgrown teenager, lighting his face, making it innocent and benign. 'So it's Cath you want then?' He looked over Rebus's shoulder at his wife. 'All right, Cath?'

'Fine, Rab.'

Kinnoul looked at Rebus again. The grin had disappeared. 'Maybe you'd like to see the library, Inspector? Cath and you can have a chat in there.'

'Thank you, sir.'

Rebus took the back roads on his way into Edinburgh. They were nicer, certainly quieter. He'd learned very little in the Kinnoul's library, except that Kinnoul felt protective towards his wife, so protective that he'd felt unable to leave Rebus alone with her. What was he afraid of? He had stalked the library, had pretended to browse, and sat down with a book, all the time listening as Rebus asked his simple questions and left the simple list and asked Cath Kinnoul to be on the lookout. And she'd nodded, fingering the xeroxed sheet of paper.

The 'library' in fact was an upper room of the house, probably intended at one time as a bedroom. Two walls had been fitted with shelves, most of them sheeted with sliding glass doors. And behind these sheets of glass sat a dull collection of books – dull to Rebus's eyes, but they seemed enough to bring Cath Kinnoul out of her daydreams. She pointed out some of the exhibits to Rebus.

'Fine first edition ... rebound in calfskin ... some pages still uncut. Just think, that book was printed in 1789, but if I cut open those pages I'd be the first person ever to read them. Oh, and that's a Creech edition of Burns ... first time Burns was published in Edinburgh. And I've some modern books, too. There's Muriel Spark ... *Midnight's Children* ... George Orwell ...'

'Have you read them all?'

She looked at Rebus as though he'd asked her about her sexual preferences. Kinnoul interrupted.

'Cath's a collector, Inspector.' He came over and put his arm around her. 'It could have been stamps or porcelain or old china dolls, couldn't it, love? But it's books. She collects books.' He gave her a squeeze. 'She doesn't read them. She collects them.'

Rebus shook his head now, tapping his fingers against the steering wheel. He'd shoved a Rolling Stones tape into the car's cassette player. An aid to constructive thought. On the one hand, you had Professor Costello, with his marvellous library, the books read and reread, worth a fortune but still there for the borrowing ... for the *reading*. And on the other hand there was Cath Kinnoul. He didn't quite know why he felt so sorry for her. It couldn't be easy being married to ... well, she'd said it herself, hadn't she? Except that she'd been talking about Elizabeth Jack. Rebus was intrigued by Mrs Jack. More, he was becoming *fascinated* by her. He hoped he would meet her soon ...

The call from Dufftown came just as he got into the office. On the stairs, he'd been told of another rumour. By the middle of next week, there would be official notification that Great London Road was to close. Then back I go to Marchmont, Rebus thought.

The telephone was ringing. It was always ringing either just as he was coming in, or else just as he was about to go out. He could sit in his chair for hours and never once...

'Hello, Rebus here.'

There was a pause, and enough snap-crackle over the line for the call to be trans-Siberian.

'Is that Inspector Rebus?'

Rebus sighed and fell into his chair. 'Speaking.'

'Hello, sir. This is a terrible line. It's Constable Moffat. You wanted someone to go to Deer Lodge.'

Rebus perked up. 'That's right.'

'Well, sir, I've just been over there and –' And there was a noise like an excited geiger counter. Rebus held the receiver away from his ear. When the noise had stopped, the constable was still speaking. 'I don't know what more I can tell you, sir.'

'You can tell me the whole bloody lot again for a start,' Rebus said. 'The line went supernova for a minute there.'

Constable Moffat began again, articulating his words as though in conversation with a retard. 'I was saying, sir, that I went over to Deer Lodge, but there's no one at home. No car outside. I had a look through the windows. I'd say someone *had* been there at some time. Looked like there'd been a bit of a party. Wine bottles and glasses and stuff. But there's no one there at the minute.'

'Did you ask any of the neighbours ...?' As he said it, Rebus knew this to be a stupid question. The constable was already laughing.

'There *aren't* any neighbours, sir. The nearest would be Mr and Mrs Kennoway, but they're a mile hike the other side of the hills.'

'I see. And there's nothing else you can tell me?'

'Not that I can think of. If there was anything in particular ...? I mean, I know the lodge is owned by that MP, and I saw in the papers...'

'No,' Rebus was quick to say, 'nothing to do with that.' He didn't want *more* rumours being tossed around like so many cabers at a Highland games. 'Just wanted a word with Mrs Jack. We thought she might be up there.'

'Aye, she's up this way occasionally, so I hear.'

'Well, if you hear anything else, let me know, won't you?'

'Goes without saying, sir.' Which, Rebus supposed, it did. The constable sounded a bit hurt.

'And thanks for your help,' Rebus added, but received only a curt 'Aye' before the phone went dead.

'Fuck you too, pal,' he said to himself, before going off in search of Gregor Jack's home telephone number.

Of course, there was an almighty chance that the phone would still be unplugged. Still, it was worth a try. The number itself would be on computer, but Rebus reckoned he'd be quicker looking for it in the filing cabinet. And sure enough, he found a sheet of paper headed 'Parliamentary Constituencies in Edinburgh and Lothians' on which were given the home addresses and telephone numbers of the area's eleven MPs. He punched in the ten numbers, waited, and was rewarded with the ringing tone. Not that that meant –
    'Hello?'
    'Is that Mr Urquhart?'
    'I'm sorry, Mr Urquhart's not here right at the moment –'
    But of course by now Rebus recognized the voice. 'Is that you, Mr Jack? It's Inspector Rebus here. We met yester–'
    'Why yes, hello, Inspector. You're in luck. We plugged the phone back in this morning, and Ian's spent all day taking calls. He's just taken a break. He thought we should unplug the thing again, but I plugged it back in myself when he'd gone. I hate to think I'm completely cut off. My constituents, after all, might need to get–'
    'What about Miss Greig?'
    'She's working. Work must go on, Inspector. There's an office to the back of the house where she does the typing and so on. Helen's really been a–'
    'And Mrs Jack? Any news?'
    Now the flow seemed to have dried up. There was a parched cough. Rebus could visualize a readjustment of facial features, maybe even a scratching of finger, a running of fingers through hair . . .
    'Why . . . yes, funny you should mention it. She phoned this morning.'
    'Oh?'
    'Yes, poor love. Said she'd been trying for hours, but of course the phone was disconnected all day Sunday and busy most of today –'
    'She's at your cottage then?'
    'That's right, yes. Spending a week there. I told her to stay put. No point in her getting dragged into all this rubbish, is there? It'll soon blow over. My solicitor –'
    'We've checked Deer Lodge, Mr Jack.'
    Another pause. Then: 'Oh?'
    'She doesn't seem to be there. No sign of life.'
    There was sweat beneath the collar of Rebus's shirt. He could blame it on the heating of course. But he knew the heating wasn't *all* to blame. Where was this leading? What was he wandering into?
    'Oh.' A statement this time, a deflated sound. 'I see.'

'Mr Jack, is there anything you'd like to tell me?'

'Yes, Inspector, there is, I suppose.'

Carefully: 'Would you like me to come over?'

'Yes.'

'All right. I'll be there as soon as I can. Just sit tight, all right?'

No answer.

'All right, Mr Jack?'

'Yes.'

But Gregor Jack didn't sound it.

Of course, Rebus's car wouldn't start. The sound it made was more and more like an emphysema patient's last hacking laugh. Herka-herka-herka-ka. Herka-herka-her.

'Having trouble?' This was yelled from across the car park by Brian Holmes, waving and about to get into his own car. Rebus slammed his car door shut and walked briskly over to where Holmes was just – with a first-time turn of the ignition – starting his Metro.

'Off home?'

'Yes.' A nod towards Rebus's doomed car. 'Doesn't sound as if you are. Want a lift?'

'As it happens, Brian, yes. And you can come along for the ride if you like.'

'I don't get it.'

Rebus was trying to open the passenger-side door, without success. Holmes hesitated a moment before unlocking it.

'It's my turn to cook tonight,' he said. 'Nell'll be up to high doh if I'm late . . .'

Rebus settled into the passenger seat and pulled the seatbelt down across his chest.

'I'll tell you all about it on the way.'

'The way where?'

'Not far from where you live. You won't be late, honest. I'll get a car to bring me back into town. But I'd quite like your attendance.'

Holmes wasn't slow; careful – yes, but never slow. 'You mean the male member,' he said. 'What's he done this time?'

'I shudder to think, Brian. Believe me, I shudder to think.'

There were no pressmen patrolling the gates, and the gates themselves were unlocked. The car had been put away in the garage, leaving the driveway clear. They left Holmes' car sitting on the main road outside.

'Quite a place,' Holmes commented.

'Wait till you see inside. It's like a film set, Ingmar Bergman or something.'

Holmes shook his head. 'I still can't believe it,' he said. 'You, coming out here yesterday, barging your way in –'

'Hardly barging, Brian. Now listen, I'm going to have a word with Jack. You sniff around, see if anything smells rotten.'

'You mean literally rotten?'

'I'm not expecting to find decomposing bodies in the flower beds, if that's what you're thinking. No, just keep your eyes open and your ears keen.'

'And my nose wet?'

'If you haven't got a handkerchief on you, yes.'

They separated, Rebus to the front door, Holmes around to the side of the house, towards the garage. Rebus rang the doorbell. It was nearly six. No doubt Helen Greig would be on her way home . . .

But it was Helen Greig who answered the door.

'Hello,' she said. 'Come in. Gregor's in the living room. You know the way.'

'Indeed I do. Keeping you busy, is he?' He laid a finger on the face of his wristwatch.

'Oh yes,' she said smiling, 'he's a real slavemaster.'

An unkind image came to Rebus then, of Jack in leather gear and Helen Greig on a leash . . . He blinked it away. 'Does he seem all right?'

'Who? Gregor?' She gave a quiet laugh. 'He seems fine, under the circumstances. Why?'

'Just wondering, that's all.'

She thought for a moment, seemed about to say something, then remembered her place. 'Can I get you anything?'

'No, thanks.'

'Right, see you later then.' And off she went, back past the curving staircase, back to her office to the rear of the house. Damn, he hadn't told Holmes about her. If Holmes peered in through the office window . . . Oh well. If he heard a scream, he'd know what had happened. He opened the living room door.

Gregor Jack was alone. Alone and listening to his hi-fi. The volume was low, but Rebus recognized the Rolling Stones. It was the album he'd been listening to earlier, *Let It Bleed*.

Jack rose from his leather sofa, a glass of whisky in one hand. 'Inspector, you didn't take long. You've caught me indulging in my secret vice. Well, we all have *one* secret vice, don't we?'

Rebus thought again of the scene at the brothel. And Jack seemed to read his mind, for he gave an embarrassed smile. Rebus shook the proffered hand. He noticed that a plaster had been stuck on the left hand's offending finger. One secret vice, and one tiny flaw . . .

Jack saw him noticing. 'Eczema,' he explained, and seemed about to say more.

'Yes, you said.'

'Did I?'

'Yesterday.'

'You'll have to forgive me, Inspector. I don't usually repeat myself. But what with yesterday and everything...'

'Understood.' Past Jack, Rebus noticed a card standing on the mantelpiece. It hadn't been there yesterday.

Jack realized he had a glass in his hand. 'Can I offer you a drink?'

'You can, sir, and I accept.'

'Whisky all right? I don't think there's much else...'

'Whatever you're having, Mr Jack.' And for some reason he added: 'I like the Rolling Stones myself, their earlier stuff.'

'Agreed,' said Jack. 'The music scene these days, it's all rubbish, isn't it?' He'd gone over to the wall to the left of the fireplace, where glass shelves held a series of bottles and glasses. As he poured, Rebus walked over to the table where yesterday Urquhart had been fussing with some papers. There were letters, waiting to be signed (all with the House of Commons portcullis at the head), and some notes relating to parliamentary business.

'This job,' Jack was saying, approaching with Rebus's drink, 'really is what you make of it. There are some MPs who do the minimum necessary, and believe me that's still plenty. Cheers.'

'Cheers.' They both drank.

'Then there are those,' said Jack, 'who go for the maximum. They do their constituency work, and they become involved in the parliamentary process, the wider world. They debate, they write, they attend...'

'And which camp do you belong to, sir?' He talks too much, Rebus was thinking, and yet he says so little...

'Straight down the middle,' said Jack, steering a course with his flattened hand. 'Here, sit down.'

'Thank you, sir.' They both sat, Rebus on the chair, Jack on the sofa. Rebus had noticed straight away that the whisky was watered, and he wondered by whom? And did Jack know about it? 'Now then,' said Rebus, 'you said on the phone that there was something –'

Jack used a remote control to switch off the music. He aimed the remote at the wall, it seemed to Rebus. There was no hi-fi system in sight. 'I want to get things straight about my wife, Inspector,' he said. 'About Liz. I *am* worried about her, I admit it. I didn't want to say anything before...'

'Why not, sir?' So far, the speech sounded well prepared. But then he'd had over an hour in which to prepare it. Soon enough, it would run out. Rebus could be patient. He wondered where Urquhart was...

'Publicity, Inspector. Ian calls Liz my liability. I happen to think he's going a bit far, but Liz is ... well, not quite temperamental...'

56

'You think she saw the newspapers?'

'Almost certainly. She always buys the tabloids. It's the gossip she likes.'

'But she hasn't been in touch?'

'No, no, she hasn't.'

'And that's a bit strange, wouldn't you say?'

Jack creased his face. 'Yes and no, Inspector. I mean, I don't know what to think. She's capable of just laughing the whole thing off. But then again . . .'

'You think she might harm herself, sir?'

'Harm herself?' Jack was slow to understand. 'You mean suicide? No, I don't think so, no, not that. But if she felt embarrassed, she might simply disappear. Or something could have happened to her, an accident . . . God knows what. If she got angry enough . . . it's just possible . . .' He bowed his head again, elbows resting on his knees.

'Do you think it's police business, sir?'

Jack looked up with glinting eyes. 'That's the crux, isn't it? If I report her missing . . . I mean report her *officially* . . . and she's found, and it turns out she was simply keeping out of things . . .'

'Does she seem the type who *would* stay out of things, sir?' Rebus's thoughts were spinning now. Someone had set Jack up . . . but not his wife, surely? Sunday newspaper thoughts, but still they worried him.

Jack shrugged. 'Not really. It's hard to tell with Liz. She's changeable.'

'Well, sir, we could make a few discreet inquiries up north. Check hotels, guest houses –'

'It would have to be hotels, Inspector, where Liz is concerned. *Expensive* hotels.'

'Okay then, we check hotels, ask around. Any friends she might visit?'

'Not many.'

Rebus waited, wondering if Jack would change his mind. After all, there was always Andrew Macmillan, the murderer. Someone she probably knew, someone nearby. But Jack merely shrugged and repeated, 'Not many.'

'Well, a list would help, sir. You might even contact them yourself. You know, just phoning for a chat. If Mrs Jack was there, they'd be bound to tell you.'

'Unless she'd told them not to.'

Well, that was true.

'But then,' Jack was saying, 'if it turned out she'd been off to one of the islands and hadn't heard a thing . . .'

Politics, it was all about politics in the end. Rebus was coming to respect Gregor Jack less, but, in a strange way, like him more. He rose and walked over towards the shelf unit, ostensibly to put his glass there. At the mantelpiece, he stopped by the card and picked it up. The front was a cartoon showing a young man in an open-topped sports car, champagne in an ice bucket on the passenger seat. The message above read GOOD LUCK! Inside was another message, written in felt pen: 'Never fear, The Pack is with you'. There were six signatures.

'Schoolfriends,' Jack was saying. He came over to stand beside Rebus. 'And a couple from university days. We've stuck pretty close over the years.'

A few of the names Rebus recognized, but he was happy to look puzzled and let Jack provide the information.

'Gowk, that's Cathy Gow. She's Cath Kinnoul now, Kinnoul as in Rab, the actor.' His finger drifted to the next signature. 'Tampon is Tom Pond. He's an architect in Edinburgh. Bilbo, that's Bill Fisher, works in London for some magazine. He was always daft on Tolkien.' Jack's voice had become soft with sentiment. Rebus was thinking of the schoolfriends *he'd* kept up with – a grand total of none. 'Suey is Ronnie Steele...'

'Why Suey?'

Jack smiled. 'I'm not sure I should tell you. Ronnie would kill me.' He considered for a moment, gave a mellow shrug. 'Well, we were on a school trip to Switzerland, and a girl went into Ronnie's room and found him ... doing something. She went and told everyone about it, and Ronnie was so embarrassed that he ran outside and lay down in the road. He said he was going to kill himself, only no cars came past, so eventually he got up.'

'And suicide abbreviates to Suey?'

'That's right.' Jack studied the card again. 'Sexton, that's Alice Blake. Sexton Blake, you see. A detective like yourself.' Jack smiled. 'Alice works in London, too. Something to do with PR.'

'And what about ...?' Rebus was pointing to the last secret name, Mack. Jack's face changed.

'Oh, that's ... Andy Macmillan.'

'And what does Mr Macmillan do these days?' Mack, Rebus was thinking. As in Mack the Knife, grimly apt ...

Jack was aloof. 'He's in prison, I believe. Tragic story, tragic.'

'In prison?' Rebus was keen to pursue the subject, but Jack had other ideas. He pointed to the names on the card.

'Notice anything, Inspector?'

Yes, Rebus had, though he hadn't been going to mention it. Now he did. 'The names are all written by the same person.'

Jack gave a quick smile. 'Bravo.'

'Well, Mr Macmillan's in prison, and Mr Fisher and Miss Blake could hardly have signed, could they, living in London? The story only broke yesterday...'

'Ah yes, good point.'

'So who...?'

'Cathy. She used to be an expert forger, though you might not think it to look at her. She used to have all our signatures off by heart.'

'But Mr Pond lives in Edinburgh . . . couldn't he have signed his own?'

'I think he's in the States on business.'

'And Mr Steele . . . ?' Rebus tapped the 'Suey' scrawl.

'Well, Suey's a hard man to catch, Inspector.'

'Is that so,' mused Rebus, 'is that so.'

There was a knock at the door.

'Come in, Helen.'

Helen Greig put her head round the door. She was dressed in a raincoat, the belt of which she was tying. 'I'm just off, Gregor. Ian not back yet?'

'Not yet. Catching up on his sleep, I expect.'

Rebus was replacing the card on the mantelpiece. He was wondering, too, whether Gregor Jack was surrounded by friends or by something else entirely . . .

'Oh,' said Helen Greig, 'and there's another policeman here. He was at the back door . . .'

The door opened to its full extent, and Brian Holmes walked into the room. Awkwardly, it seemed to Rebus. It struck him that Holmes was awkward in the presence of Gregor Jack MP.

'Thank you, Helen. See you tomorrow.'

'You're at Westminster tomorrow, Gregor.'

'God, so I am. Right, see you the day after.'

Helen Greig left, and Rebus introduced Jack to Brian Holmes. Holmes still seemed unnaturally awkward. What the hell was the matter? It couldn't just be Jack could it? Then Holmes cleared his throat. He was looking at his superior, avoiding eye contact with the MP altogether.

'Sir, er . . . there's something maybe you should see. Round the back. In the dustbin. I had some rubbish in my pockets and I thought I'd get rid of it, and I happened to lift the lid off the bin . . .'

Gregor Jack's face turned stark white.

'Right,' said Rebus briskly, 'lead the way, Brian.' He made a sweeping motion with his arm. 'After you, Mr Jack.'

The back of the house was well lit. Two sturdy black plastic bins sat beside a bushy rhododendron. Each bin had attached inside it a black plastic refuse bag. Holmes lifted the lid off the left-hand bin and held it open so that Rebus could peer inside. He was staring at a flattened cornflake packet and the wrapping from some biscuits.

'Beneath,' Holmes stated simply. Rebus lifted the cornflake packet. It had been concealing a little treasure chest. Two video cassettes, their casings broken, tape spewing from them . . . a packet of photographs . . . two small gold-coloured vibrators . . . two pairs of flimsy-looking handcuffs ... and clothing, body-stockings, knickers with zips. Rebus couldn't help wondering what the hacks would have done if they'd found this lot first ...

'I can explain,' said Jack brokenly.

'You don't have to, sir. It's none of our business.' Rebus said this in such a way that his meaning was clear: it might not be our business, but you'd better tell us anyway.

'I ... I panicked. No, not really a panic. It's just, what with that story about the brothel, and now Liz is off somewhere ... and I knew you were on your way ... I just wanted rid of the lot of it.' He was perspiring. 'I mean, I know it must look strange, that's precisely why I wanted rid of it all. Not my stuff, you see, it's Liz's. Her friends ... the parties they have ... well, I didn't want you to get the wrong impression.'

Or the right impression, thought Rebus. He picked up the packet of photographs, which just happened to burst open. 'Sorry,' he said, making a show of gathering them up. They were polaroids, taken at a party it was true. Quite a party, by the look of it. And who was this?

Rebus held the photograph up so that Jack could see it. It showed Gregor Jack having his shirt removed by two women. Everyone's eyes were red.

'The first and last party I ever went to,' Jack stated.

'Yes, sir,' said Rebus.

'Look, Inspector, my wife's life is her *own*. What she chooses to get up to ... well, it's out of my hands.' Anger was replacing embarrassment. 'I might not *like* it, I might not like her *friends*, but it's *her* choice.'

'Right, sir.' Rebus threw the photographs back into the bin. 'Well, maybe your wife's ... friends will know where she is, eh? Meantime, I wouldn't leave that lot in there, not unless you want to see yourself on the front pages again. The bins are the first place some journalists look. It's not called "getting the dirt" for nothing. And as I say, Mr Jack, it's none of *our* business ... not yet.'

But it would be soon enough; Rebus felt it in his gut, which tumbled at the thought.

It would be soon enough.

Back inside the house, Rebus tried to concentrate on one thing at a time. Not easy, not at all easy. Jack wrote down the names and addresses of a few of his wife's friends. If not quite high society, they were certainly more than a few rungs above the Horsehair. Then Rebus asked about Liz Jack's car.

'A black BMW,' said Jack. 'The 3-series. My birthday present to her last year.'

Rebus thought of his own car. 'Very nice too, sir. And the registration?' Jack reeled it off. Rebus looked a little surprised, but Jack smiled weakly.

'I'm an accountant by training,' he explained. 'I never forget figures.'

'Of course, sir. Well, we'd better be –'

There was a sound, the sound of the front door opening and closing. Voices in the hall. Had the prodigal wife returned? All three men turned towards the living room door, which now swung open.

'Gregor? Look who I found coming up the drive . . .'

Ian Urquhart saw that Gregor Jack had visitors. He paused, startled. Behind him, a tired-looking man was shuffling into the room. He was tall and skinny, with lank black hair and round NHS-style spectacles.

'Gregor,' the man said. He walked up to Gregor Jack and they shook hands. Then Jack placed a hand on the man's shoulder.

'Meant to look in before now,' the man was saying, 'but you know how it is.' He really did look exhausted, with dark-ringed eyes and a stoop to his posture. His speech and movements were slow. 'I think I've clinched a nice collection of Italian art books . . .'

He now seemed ready to acknowledge the visitors' presence. Rebus had been given Urquhart's hand and was shaking it. The visitor nodded towards Rebus's right hand.

'You,' he said, 'must be Inspector Rebus.'

'That's right.'

'How do you know that?' said Gregor Jack, suitably impressed.

'Scratch marks on the wrist,' the visitor explained. 'Vanessa told me an Inspector Rebus had been in, and that Rasputin had made his mark . . . his considerable mark, by the look of things.'

'You must be Mr Steele,' said Rebus, shaking hands.

'The very same,' said Steele. 'Sorry I wasn't in when you called. As Gregor here will tell you, I'm a hard man to –'

'Catch,' interrupted Jack. 'Yes, Ronnie, I've already told the Inspector.'

'No sign of those books then, sir?' Rebus asked Steele. He shrugged.

'Too hot to handle, Inspector. Do you have any idea how much that lot would fetch? My guess would be a private collector.'

'Stolen to order?'

'Maybe. A fairly broad range though . . .' Steele seemed to tire quickly of the topic. He turned again to Gregor Jack and held his arms wide open, half shrugging. 'Gregor, what the hell are they trying to do to you?'

'Obviously,' said Urquhart, who was helping himself unasked to a drink, 'someone somewhere is looking for a resignation.'

'But what were you doing there in the first place?'

Steele had asked *the* question. He asked it into a silence which lasted for a very long time. Urquhart had poured him a drink, and handed it over, while Gregor Jack seemed to study the four men in the room, as though one of them might have the answer. Rebus noticed that Brian Holmes was studying a painting on one wall, seemingly oblivious to the whole conversation. At last, Jack made an exasperated sound and shook his head.

'I think,' Rebus said, into the general silence, 'we'd better be off.'

'Remember to empty your dustbin, sir,' was his final message to Jack, before he led Holmes down the driveway towards the main road. Holmes agreed to give him a lift into Bonnyrigg, from where Rebus could pick up a ride back into town, but otherwise reached, opened and started the car without comment. As he moved up into second gear, however, Holmes finally said: 'Nice guy. Do you think maybe he'd give us an invite to one of those parties?'

'Brian,' Rebus said warningly. Then: 'Not *his* parties, parties attended by his wife. It didn't look like their house in those photos.'

'Really? I didn't get that good a look. All I saw was my MP being stripped by a couple of eager ladies.' Holmes gave a sudden chuckle.

'What?'

'Strip Jack Naked,' he said.

'Pardon?'

'It's a card game,' Holmes explained. 'Strip Jack Naked. You might know it as Beggar My Neighbour.'

'Really?' Rebus said, trying not to sound interested. But was that precisely what someone was trying to do, strip Jack of his constituency, his clean-cut image, perhaps even his marriage? Were they trying to beggar the man whose nickname also was Beggar?

Or was Jack not quite as innocent as he seemed? No, hell, be honest: he didn't *seem* all that innocent anyway. Fact: he had visited a brothel. Fact: he had tried to get rid of evidence that he himself had attended at least one fairly 'high-spirited' party. Fact: his wife hadn't been in touch. Big deal. Rebus's money was still on the man. In religion, he might be more Pessimisterian than Presbyterian, but in some things John Rebus still clung to faith.

Faith and hope. It was charity he usually lacked.

4
Tips

'We've got to keep this away from the papers,' said Chief Superintendent Watson. 'For as long as we can.'

'Right, sir,' said Lauderdale, while Rebus stayed silent. They were not talking about Gregor Jack, they were discussing a suspect in the Water of Leith drowning. He was in an interview room now with two officers and a tape recorder. He was helping with inquiries. Apparently, he was saying little.

'Could be nothing, after all.'

'Yes, sir.'

There was an afternoon smell of strong mints in the room, and perhaps this was why Chief Inspector Lauderdale sounded and looked more starched than ever. His nose twitched whenever Watson wasn't looking at him. Rebus all of a sudden felt sorry for his Chief Superintendent, in the way that he felt sorry for the Scotland squad whenever it was facing defeat at the hands of third-world part-timers. There but for the grace of complete inability go I . . .

'Just a bit of bragging, perhaps, overheard in a pub. The man was drunk. You know how it is.'

'Quite so, sir.'

'All the same . . .'

All the same, they had a man in the interview room, a man who had told anyone who'd listen in a packed Leith pub that he had dumped that body under Dean Bridge.

'It wis me! Eh? How 'bout that, eh? Me! Me! I did it. She deserved worse. They all do.'

And more of the same, all of it reported to the police by a fearful barmaid, nineteen next month and this was her first bar job.

Deserved worse, she did . . . they *all* do . . . Only when the police had come into the pub, he'd quietened down, gone all sulky in a corner, standing there with head bent under the weight of a cigarette. The pint glass seemed heavy, too, so that his wrist sagged beneath it, beer dripping down on to his shoes and the wooden floor.

'Now then, sir, what's all this you've been telling these people, eh?

Mind telling us about it? Down at the station, eh? We've got seats down there. You can have a seat while you tell us all about it . . .'

He was sitting, but he wasn't telling. No name, no address, nobody in the pub seemed to know anything about him. Rebus had taken a look at him, as had most of the CID and uniformed men in the building, but the face meant nothing. A sad, weak example of the species. In his late thirties, his hair was already grey and thin, the face lined, bristly with stubble, and the knuckles had grazes and scabs on them.

'How did you get them then? Been in a fight? Hit her a few times before you chucked her in?'

Nothing. He looked scared, but he was resilient. Their chances of keeping him in were, to put it mildly, not good. He didn't need a solicitor; he knew he just had to keep his mouth shut.

'Been in trouble before, eh? You know the score, don't you? That's why you're keeping quiet. Much good will it do you, pal. Much good.'

Indeed. The pathologist, Dr Curt, was now being harried. They needed to know: accident, suicide, or murder? They desperately needed to know. But before any news arrived, the man began to talk.

'I was drunk,' he told them, 'didn't know what I was saying. I don't know what made me say it.' This was the story he stuck to, repeating it and refining it. They pressed for his name and address. 'I was drunk,' he said. 'That's all there is to it. I'm sober now, and I'd like to go. I'm sorry I said what I did. Can I go now?'

Nobody at the pub had been keen to press charges, not once the offending body was removed from the premises. Unpaid bouncers, thought Rebus, that's all we are. Was the man going to walk? Were they going to lose him? Not without a fight.

'We need a name and address before we can let you go.'

'I was drunk. Can I go now, please?'

'Your name!'

'Please, can I go?'

Curt still wasn't ready to pronounce. An hour or two. Some results he was waiting for . . .

'Just give us a name, eh? Stop pissing about.'

'My name's William Glass. I live at 48 Semple Street in Granton.'

There was silence, then sighs. 'Check that, will you?' one officer asked the other. Then: 'Now that wasn't so painful, was it, Mr Glass?'

The other officer grinned, then had to explain why. 'Painful . . . Glass . . . pane of glass, see?'

'Just do that check, eh?' said his colleague, rubbing at a headache which, these days, never seemed to leave him.

'They've let him go,' Holmes informed Rebus.

'About time. A wild haggis chase and no mistake.'

Holmes came into the office and made himself comfortable on the spare chair.

'Don't stand on ceremony,' said Rebus from his desk, 'just because I'm the senior officer. Why not take a seat, Sergeant?'

'Thank you, sir,' said Holmes from the chair. 'I don't mind if I do. He gave his address as Semple Street, Granton.'

'Off Granton Road?'

'That's the one.' Holmes looked around. 'It's like an oven in here. Can't you open a window?'

'Jammed shut, and the heating's –'

'I know, either on full blast or nothing. This place . . .' Holmes shook his head.

'Nothing a bit of maintenance wouldn't fix.'

'Funny,' said Holmes, 'I've never seen you as the sentimental sort . . .'

'Sentimental?'

'About this place. Give me St Leonard's or Fettes any day.'

Rebus wrinkled his nose. 'No character,' he said.

'Speaking of which, what news of the male member?'

'That joke's worn as thin as my hair, Brian. Why not part-ex it against a new one?' Rebus breathed out noisily through his nose and threw down the pen he'd been playing with. 'What you mean,' he said, 'is what news of *Mrs* Jack, and the answer is none, nada, zero. I've put out the description of her car, and all the posh hotels are being checked. But so far, nothing.'

'From which we infer . . .?'

'Same answer: nothing. She could still be off at some Iona spiritual retreat, or shacked up with a Gaelic crofter, or doing the Munros. She could be pissed-off at her hubby, or not know a thing about any of it.'

'And all that kit I found, the sex-shop stock clearance?'

'What about it?'

'Well . . .' Holmes seemed stuck for an answer. 'Nothing really.'

'And there you've put your finger on it, Sergeant. Nothing really. Meantime, I've got work enough to be getting on with.' Rebus laid a solemn hand on the pile of reports and case-notes in front of him. 'How about you?'

Holmes was out of his chair now. 'Oh, I've plenty keeping me busy, sir. Please, don't worry yourself about me.'

'It's natural for me to worry, Brian. You're like a son to me.'

'And you're like a father to me,' Holmes replied, heading for the door. 'The fa-ther I get from you, the easier my life seems to be.'

Rebus screwed a piece of paper into a ball, but the door closed before he had time to take aim. Ach, some days the job could be a laugh. Well, okay, a grin at least. If he forgot all about Gregor Jack, the load would be lighter still. Where would Jack be now? At the House of Commons? Sitting on some committee? Being fêted by businesses and lobbyists? It all seemed a long way from Rebus's office, and from his life.

William Glass ... no, the name meant nothing to him. Bill Glass, Billy Glass, Willie Glass, Will Glass ... nothing. Living at 48 Semple Street. Hold on ... Semple Street in Granton. He went to his filing cabinet and pulled out the file. Yes, just last month. Stabbing incident in Granton. A serious wounding, but not fatal. The victim had lived at 48 Semple Street. Rebus remembered it now. Bedsits carved from a house, all of them rented. A rented bedsit. If William Glass was living at 48 Semple Street, then he was staying in a rented bedsit. Rebus reached for his telephone and called Lauderdale, to whom he told his story.

'Well, someone there vouched for him when the patrol car dropped him off. The officers were told to be sure he did live there, and apparently he does. Name's William Glass, like he said.'

'Yes, but those bedsits are short-let. Tenants get their social security cheque, hand half the cash over to the landlord, maybe more than half for all I know. What I'm saying is, it's not much of an address. He could disappear from there any time he liked.'

'Why so suspicious all of a sudden, John? I thought you were of the opinion we were wasting our time in the first place?'

Oh, but Lauderdale always knew the question to ask, the question to which, as a rule, Rebus did not have an answer.

'True, sir,' he said. 'Just thought I'd let you know.'

'I appreciate it, John. It's nice to be kept informed.' There was a slight pause there, an invitation for Rebus to join Lauderdale's 'camp'. And after the pause: 'Any progress on Professor Costello's books?'

Rebus sighed. 'No, sir.'

'Oh well. Mustn't keep you chatting then. Bye, John.'

'Goodbye, sir.' Rebus wiped his palm across his forehead. It *was* hot in here, like a dress rehearsal for the Calvinist hell.

The fan had been installed and turned on, and an hour or so later Dr Curt provided the shit to toss at it.

'Murder, yes,' he said. 'Almost definitely murder. I've discussed my findings with my colleagues, and we're of a mind.' And he went on to explain about froth and unclenched hands and diatoms. About problems of differentiating immersion from drowning. The deceased, a woman in her late twenties or early thirties, had imbibed a good deal of drink prior to death. But she had been dead before she'd hit the water, and the cause of death was probably a blow to the back of the head, carried out by a right-handed attacker (the blow itself having come from the right of the head).

But who was she? They had a photograph of the dead woman's face, but it wasn't exactly breakfast-time viewing. And though her description and a description of her clothes had been given out, nobody had been able to identify her. No identification on the body, no handbag or purse, nothing in her pockets . . .

'Better search the area again, see if we can come up with a bag or a purse. She must have had *some*thing.'

'And search the river, sir?'

'A bit late for that probably, but yes, better give it a shot.'

'The alcohol,' Dr Curt was telling anyone who would listen, had 'muddied the water, you see', after which he smiled his slow smile. 'And the fish had eaten their fill: fish fingers, fish feet, fish stomach . . .'

'Yes, sir. I see, sir.'

All of which Rebus mercifully avoided. He had once made the mistake of making a sicker pun than Dr Curt, and as a result found himself in the doctor's favour. One day, he knew, Holmes would make a better pun yet, and then Curt would have himself a new pupil and confidant . . . So, skirting around the doctor, Rebus made for Lauderdale's office. Lauderdale himself was just getting off the phone. When he saw Rebus, he turned stony. Rebus could guess why.

'I just sent someone round to Glass's bedsit.'

'And he's gone,' Rebus added.

'Yes,' Lauderdale said, his hand still on the receiver. 'Leaving little or nothing behind him.'

'Should be easy enough to pick him up, sir.'

'Get on to it, will you, John? He must still be in the city. What is it? – an hour since he left here. Probably somewhere in the Granton area.'

'We'll get out there right away, sir,' said Rebus, glad of this excuse for a little action.

'Oh, and John . . .?'

'Sir?'

'No need to look so smug, okay?'

So the day filled itself, evening coming upon him with surprising speed. But still they had not found William Glass. Not in Granton, Pilmuir, Newhaven, Inverleith, Canonmills, Leith, Davidson's Mains . . . Not on buses or in pubs, not by the shore, not in the Botanic Gardens, not in chip shops or wandering on playing fields. They had found no friends, no family, just bare details so far from the DHSS. And at the end of it all, Rebus knew, the man might be innocent. But for now he was their straw, to be clutched at. Not the most tasteful metaphor under the circumstances, but then, as Dr Curt himself might have said, it was all water under the bridge so far as the victim was concerned.

'Nothing, sir,' Rebus reported to Lauderdale at the end of play. It had been one of those days. Nothing was the sum total of Rebus's endeavours, yet he felt weary, bone and brain weary. So that he turned down Holmes' kindly offer of a drink, and didn't even debate over his destination. He headed for Oxford Terrace and the ministrations of Dr Patience Aitken, not forgetting Lucky the cat, the wolf-whistling budgies, the tropical fish, and the tame hedgehog he'd yet to see.

Rebus telephoned Gregor Jack's home first thing Wednesday morning. Jack sounded tired, having spent yesterday in Parliament and the evening at some 'grotesque function, and you can quote me on that'. There was a new and altogether fake heartiness about him, occasioned, Rebus didn't doubt, by the shared knowledge of the contents of that dustbin.

Well, Rebus was tired, too. The real difference between them was a question of pay scales . . .

'Have you heard anything from your wife yet, Mr Jack?'

'Nothing.'

There was that word again. Nothing.

'What about you, Inspector? Any news?'

'No, sir.'

'Well, no news is better than bad news, so they say. Speaking of which, I read this morning that that poor woman at Dean Bridge was murder.'

'I'm afraid so.'

'Puts my own troubles into perspective, doesn't it? Mind you, there's a constituency meeting this morning, so my troubles may just be starting. Let me know, won't you? If you hear anything, I mean.'

'Of course, Mr Jack.'

'Thank you, Inspector. Goodbye.'

'Goodbye, sir.'

All very formal and correct, as their relationship had to be. Not even room for a 'Good luck with the meeting'. He knew what the meeting would be about. People didn't like it when their MP got himself into a scandal. There would be questions. There would need to be answers . . .

Rebus opened his desk drawer and lifted out the list of Elizabeth Jack's friends, her 'circle'. Jamie Kilpatrick the antique dealer (and apparent black sheep of his titled family); the Hon. Matilda Merriman, notorious for her alleged night of non-stop rogering with a one-time cabinet member; Julian Kaymer, some sort of artist; Martin Inman, professional landowner; Louise Patterson-Scott, separated wife of the retail millionaire . . .

The 'names' just kept on coming, most of them, as Jack himself had put it while making out the list, 'seasoned dissolutes and hangers-on'. Mainly old money, as Chris Kemp had said, and a long way away from Gregor Jack's own 'pack'. But there was one curio among them, one seeming exception. Even Rebus had recognized it as Gregor Jack scratched it on to the list.

'What? *The* Barney Byars? The original dirty trucker?'

'The haulier, yes.'

'A bit out of place in that sort of company, isn't he?'

Jack had owned up. 'Actually, Barney's an old school-pal of mine. But as time's gone on, he's grown friendlier with Liz. It happens sometimes.'

'Still, somehow I can't see him fitting in with that lot –'

'You'd be surprised, Inspector Rebus. Believe me, you would be surprised.' Jack gave each word equal weight, leaving Rebus in no doubt that he meant what he said. Still . . . Byars was another fly Fifer, another famous son. While at school, he'd made his name as a hitchhiker, often claiming he'd spent the weekend in London without paying a penny to get there. After school, he made the news again by hitching his way across France, Italy, Germany, Spain. He'd fallen in love with the lorries themselves, with the whole business of them, so he'd saved, got his HGV licence, bought himself a lorry . . . and now was the largest independent haulier that Rebus could think of. Even on last year's trip to London, Rebus had been confronted by a Byars Haulage artic trying to steer its way through Piccadilly Circus.

Well, it was Rebus's job to ask if anyone had seen hide or hair of Liz Jack. He'd gladly let others do the hard work with the likes of Jamie Kilpatrick and the grim-sounding Julian Kaymer; but he was keeping Barney Byars for himself. Another week or two of this, he thought, and I'll have to buy an autograph book.

As it happened, Byars was in Edinburgh, 'drumming up custom', as the girl in his office put it. Rebus gave her his telephone number, and an hour later Byars himself called back. He would be busy all afternoon, and he'd to go to dinner that evening 'with a few fat bastards', but he could see Rebus for a drink at six if that was convenient. Rebus wondered which luxury hotel would be the base for their drink, and was stunned, perhaps even disappointed, when Byars named the Sutherland Bar, one of Rebus's own watering holes.

'Right you are,' he called. 'Six o'clock.'

Which meant that the day stretched ahead of him. There was the Case of the Lifted Literature, of course. Well, he wasn't going to hold his breath waiting for a result there. They would turn up or they would not. His bet would be that by now they'd be on the other side of the Atlantic. Then there was William Glass, suspect in a murder inquiry, somewhere out there in a back close or a cobbled side street. Well, he'd turn up come giro day. If, that is, he was more stupid than so far he'd proved to be. No, maybe he was full of cunning. In which case he wouldn't go near a DHSS office or back to his digs. In which case he would have to get money from somewhere.

So – go talk to the tramps, the city's dispossessed. Glass would steal, or else he would resort to begging. And where he begged, there would be others begging, too. Put his description about, maybe with a tenner as a reward, and let others do your work for you. Yes, it was definitely worth mentioning to Lauderdale. Except that Rebus didn't want to do the Chief Inspector *too* many good turns, otherwise Lauderdale would think he was currying favour.

'I'd rather curry an alsatian,' he said to himself.

With a nice sense of timing, Brian Holmes came into the office carrying a white paper bag and a polystyrene beaker.

'What've you got there?' Rebus asked, suddenly hungry.

'You're the policeman, you tell me.' Holmes produced a sandwich from the bag and held it in front of Rebus.

'Corned chuck?' Rebus guessed.

'Wrong. Pastrami on rye bread.'

'What?'

'And decaffeinated filter coffee.' Holmes prised the lid from the beaker and sniffed the contents with a contented smile. 'From that new delicatessen next to the traffic lights.'

'Doesn't Nell make you up a sandwich?'

'Women have equal rights these days.'

Rebus believed it. He thought of Inspector Gill Templer and her psychology books and her feminism. He thought of the demanding Dr Patience Aitken. He even thought of the free-living Elizabeth Jack. Strong women to a man ... But then he remembered Cath Kinnoul. There were still casualties out there.

'What's it like?' he asked.

Holmes had taken a bite from the sandwich and was studying what was left. 'Okay,' he said. 'Interesting.'

Pastrami – now there was a sandwich filling that would be a long time coming to the Sutherland Bar.

Barney Byars, too, was a long time coming to the Sutherland. Rebus arrived at five minutes to six. Byars at twenty-five past. But he was well worth waiting for.

'Inspector, sorry I'm late. Some cunt was trying to knock me down five per cent on a four-grand contract, *and* he wanted sixty days to pay. Know what that does to a cash flow? I told him I ran a lorry firm, not fuckin' rickshaws.'

All of which was delivered in a thick Fife tongue and at a volume appreciably above that of the bar's early evening rumble of TV and conversation. Rebus was seated at one of the bar stools, but stood and suggested they take a table. Byars, however, was already making himself comfortable on the stool next to the policeman, laying his brawny arms along the bar-top and examining the array of taps. He pointed to Rebus's glass.

'That any good?'

'Not bad.'

'I'll have a pint of that then.' Whether from awe, fear, or just good management of his customers, the barman was on hand to pour the requested pint.

'Another yourself, Inspector?'

'I'm okay, thanks.'

'And a whisky, too,' ordered Byars. 'A double, mind, not the usual smear-test.'

Byars handed a fifty-pound note to the barman. 'Keep the change,' he said. Then he roared with laughter. 'Only joking, son, only joking.'

The barman was new and young. He held the note as though it were likely to ignite. 'Ehh ... you haven't got anything smaller on you?' His accent was effeminate west coast. Rebus wondered how long he'd last in the Sutherland.

Byars exasperated but rejecting Rebus's offer of help, dug into his pockets and found two crumpled one-pound notes and some change. He accepted his fifty back and pushed the coins towards the barman, then he winked at Rebus.

'I'll tell you a secret, Inspector, if I had to choose between having five tenners or one fifty, I'd go for the one fifty every time. Want to know why? Tenners in your pocket, people think nothing of it. But whip a fifty out, and they think you're Crœsus.' He turned to the barman, who was counting the coins out into the open till. 'Hey, son, got anything for eating?' The barman jerked round as though hit by a pellet.

'Ehh ... I think there's some Scotch broth left over from lunch.' His vowels turned broth into 'braw-wrath'. The braw wrath of the Scots, Rebus thought to himself. Byars was shaking his head. 'A pie or a sandwich,' he demanded.

The barman proffered the last lonely sandwich in the place. It looked unnervingly like pastrami, but turned out to be, as Byars put it, 'the guid roast beef'.

'One pound ten,' the barman said. Byars got out the fifty-pound note again, snorted, and produced a fiver instead. He turned back to Rebus and lifted his glass.

'Cheers.' Both men drank.

'Not bad at all,' Byars said of the beer.

Rebus gestured towards the sandwich. 'I thought you were going to dinner later on?'

'I am, but more importantly, *I'm* paying. This way, I won't eat as much and won't cost myself so much.' He winked again. 'Maybe I should write a book, eh? Business tips for sole traders, that sort of thing. Heh, speaking of tips, I once asked a waiter what "tips" meant. Know what he said?'

Rebus hazarded a wild guess. 'To insure prompt service?'

'No, to insure I don't piss in the soup!' Byars' voice was back to the level of megaphone diplomacy. He laughed, then took a bite of sandwich, still chortling as he chomped. He was not a tall man, five seven or thereabouts. And he was stocky. He wore newish denims and a black leather jacket, beneath which he sported a white polo-shirt. In a bar like this, you'd take him for ... well, just about anybody. Rebus could imagine him ruffling feathers in plush hotels and business bars. Image, he told himself. It's just another image: the hard man, the no-nonsense man, a man who worked hard and who expected others to work hard, too – always in his favour.

He had finished the sandwich, and was brushing crumbs from his lamp. 'You're from Fife,' he said casually, sniffing the whisky.

'Yes,' Rebus admitted.

'I could tell. Gregor Jack's from Fife too, you know. You said you wanted to talk about him. Is it to do with that brothel story? I found that a bit hard to swallow.' He nodded towards the empty plate in front of him. 'Not as hard as that sandwich though.'

'No, it's not really to do with the ... with Mr Jack's ... no, it's more to do with Mrs Jack.'

'Lizzie? What about her?'

'We're not sure where she is. Any ideas?'

Byars looked blank. 'Knowing Lizzie, you'd better get Interpol on the case. She's as likely to be in Istanbul as Inverness.'

'What makes you say Inverness?'

Byars looked stuck for an answer. 'It was the first place that came to mind.' Then he nodded. 'I see what you mean though. You were thinking she might be at Deer Lodge, it being up that way. Have you looked?'

Rebus nodded. 'When did you last see Mrs Jack?'

'A couple of weeks ago. Maybe three weekends ago, I can check. Funnily enough, it was at the lodge. A weekend party. The Pack mostly.' He looked up from his drink. 'I better explain that ...'

'It's all right, I know who The Pack are. Three weekends ago, you say?'

'Aye, but I can check if you like.'

'A weekend party ... you mean a party lasting the whole weekend?'

'Well, just a few friends ... all very civilized.' A light came on behind his eyes. 'Ah-ha, I know what you're getting at. You know about Liz's parties then? No, no, this was tame stuff, dinner and a few drinks and a brisk country walk on the Sunday. Not really my mug of gin, but Liz had invited me, so ...'

'You prefer her other kinds of party?'

Byars laughed. 'Of course! You're only young once, Inspector. I mean, it's all above board ... isn't it?'

He seemed genuinely curious, not without reason. Why should a policeman know about 'those' parties? Who could have told him if not Gregor, and what exactly *would* Gregor have said?

'As far as I know, sir. So you don't know any reason why Mrs Jack might want to disappear?'

'I can think of a few.' Byars had finished both drinks, but didn't look like he was hanging around for another. He kept shifting on the stool, as if unable to get comfortable. 'That newspaper story for a start. I think I'd want to be well away from it, wouldn't you? I mean, I can see how it's bad for Gregor's image, not having his wife beside him, but at the same time . . .'

'Any other reasons?'

Byars was half standing now. 'A lover,' he suggested. 'Maybe he's whisked her off to Tenerife for a bit of pash under the sun.' He winked again, then his face became serious, as though he'd just remembered something. 'There were those phone calls,' he said.

'Phone calls?'

Now he was standing. 'Anonymous phone calls. Lizzie told me about them. Not to her, to Gregor. Bound to happen, the game he's in. Caller would phone up and say he was Sir Somebody-Somebody or Lord This 'n' That, and Gregor would be fetched to the phone. Soon as he got to it, the line would go dead. That's what she told me.'

'Did these calls worry her?'

'Oh yes, you could see she was upset. She tried to hide it, but you could see. Gregor just laughed it off, of course. Can't afford to let something like that rattle him. She might even have mentioned letters. Something about Gregor getting these letters, but tearing them up before anyone could see them. But you'd have to ask Lizzie about that.' He paused. 'Or Gregor, of course.'

'Of course.'

'Right . . .' Byars stuck out his hand. 'You've got my number if you need me, Inspector.'

'Yes.' Rebus shook hands. 'Thanks for your help, Mr Byars.'

'Any time, Inspector. Oh, and if you ever need a lift to London, I've got lorries make that trip four times a week. Won't cost you a penny, and you can still claim the journey on expenses.'

He gave another wink, smiled generally around the bar, and marched back out as noticeably as he'd marched in. The barman came to clear away plate and glass. Rebus saw that the tie the young man was wearing was a clip-on, standard issue in the Sutherland. If a punter tried to grab you, the tie came away in his hand . . .

'Was he talking about me?'

Rebus blinked. 'Eh? What makes you think that?'

'I thought I heard him mention my name.'

Rebus poured the dregs from his glass into his mouth and swallowed. Don't say the kid was called Gregor ... Lizzie maybe ... 'What name is that then?'

'Lawrie.'

Rebus was more than halfway there before he realized he was headed not for Stockbridge comforts and Patience Aitken, but for Marchmont and his own neglected flat. So be it. Inside the flat, the atmosphere managed to be both chill and stale. A coffee mug beside the telephone resembled Glasgow insofar as it, too, was a city of culture, an interesting green and white culture.

But if the living room was growing mould, surely the kitchen would be worse. Rebus sat himself down in his favourite chair, stretched for the answering machine, and settled to listen to his calls. There weren't many. Gill Templer, wondering where he was keeping himself these days ... as if she didn't know. His daughter Samantha, phoning from her new flat in London, giving him her address and telephone number. Then a couple of calls where the speaker had decided not to say anything.

'Be like that then.' Rebus turned off the machine, drew a notebook from his pocket, and, reading the number from it, telephoned Gregor Jack. He wanted to know why Jack hadn't said anything about his own anonymous calls. Strip Jack ... beggar my neighbour ... Well, if someone *were* out to beggar Gregor Jack, Jack himself didn't seem overly concerned. He didn't exactly seem resigned, but he did seem unbothered. Unless he was playing a game with Rebus ... And what about Rab Kinnoul, on-screen assassin? What was he up to all the time he was away from his wife? And Ronald Steele, too, a 'hard man to catch'. Were they *all* up to something? It wasn't that Rebus distrusted the human race ... wasn't just that he was brought up a Pessimisterian. He was sure there was something happening here; he just didn't know what it was.

There was nobody home. Or nobody was answering. Or the apparatus had been unplugged. Or ...

'Hello?'

Rebus glanced at his watch. Just after quarter past seven. 'Miss Greig?' he said. 'Inspector Rebus here. He does keep you working late, doesn't he?'

'You seem to work fairly late hours yourself, Inspector. What is it this time?'

Impatience in her voice. Perhaps Urquhart had warned her against being friendly. Perhaps it had been discovered that she'd given Rebus the address of Deer Lodge ...

'A word with Mr Jack, if possible.'

'Not possible, I'm afraid.' She didn't sound afraid; she sounded if anything a bit smug. 'He's speaking at a function this evening.'

'Oh. How did his meeting go this morning?'

'Meeting?'

'I thought he had some meeting in his constituency...?'

'Oh, that. I think it went very well.'

'So he's not for the chop then?'

She attempted a laugh. 'North and South Esk would be mad to get rid of him.'

'All the same, he must be relieved.'

'I wouldn't know. He was on the golf course all afternoon.'

'Nice.'

'I *think* an MP is allowed one afternoon off a week, don't you, Inspector?'

'Oh yes, absolutely. That's what I meant,' Rebus paused. He had nothing to say, really; he was just hoping that if he kept her talking Helen Greig herself might tell him something, something he didn't know ... 'Oh,' he said, 'about those telephone calls...'

'What calls?'

'The ones Mr Jack was getting. The anonymous ones.'

'I don't know what you're talking about. Sorry, I've got to go now. My mum's expecting me home at quarter to eight.'

'Right you are then, Miss Gr – ' But she had already put the phone down.

Golf? This afternoon? Jack must be keen. The rain had been falling steadily in Edinburgh since midday. He looked out of his unwashed window. It wasn't falling now, but the streets were glistening. The flat felt suddenly empty, and colder than ever. Rebus picked up the phone and made one more call. To Patience Aitken. To say he was on his way. She asked him where he was.

'I'm at home.'

'Oh? Picking up some more of your stuff?'

'That's right.'

'You could do with bringing a spare suit if you've got one.'

'Right.'

'And some of your precious books, since you don't seem to approve of my taste.'

'Romances were never my thing, Patience.' In fiction as in life, he thought to himself. On the floor around him were strewn some of his 'precious books'. He picked one up, tried to remember buying it, couldn't.

'Well, bring whatever you like, John, and as much as you like. You know how much room we've got here.'

We. We've got.

'Okay, Patience. See you later.' He replaced the receiver with a sigh and took a look around him. After all these years, there were *still* gaps on the wall-shelves from where his wife Rhona had removed her things. Still gaps in the kitchen, too, where the tumble-drier had sat, and her precious dishwasher. Still clean rectangular spaces on the walls where her posters and prints had been hung. The flat had last been redecorated – when? – in '81 or '82. Ach, it still didn't look too bad though. Who was he kidding? It looked like a squat.

'What have you done with your life, John Rebus?' The answer was: Not much. Gregor Jack was younger than him, and more successful. Barney Byars was younger than him, and more successful. Who did he know who was *older* than him and *less* successful? Not a single soul, discounting the beggars in the city centre, the ones he'd spent the afternoon with – without a result, but with a certain uncomfortable sense of belonging . . .

What was he thinking about? 'You're becoming a morbid old bugger.' Self-pity wasn't the answer. Moving in with Patience was the answer . . . so why didn't it feel like one? Why did it feel like just another problem?

He rested his head against the back of the chair. I'm caught, he thought, between a cushion and a soft place. He sat there for a long time, staring up at the ceiling. It was dark outside, and foggy, too, a haar drifting in across the city from the North Sea. In a haar, Edinburgh seemed to shift backwards through time. You half expected to see press-gangs on the streets of Leith, hear coaches clattering over cobblestones and cries of gardy-loo in the High Street.

If he sold the flat, he could buy himself a new car, send some money to Samantha. *If* he sold the flat . . . *if* he moved in with Patience . . .

'If shit was gold,' his father used to say, 'you'd have a tyke at yer erse.' The old bugger had never explained exactly what a tyke was . . .

Jesus, what made him think of that?

It was no good. He couldn't think straight, not here. Perhaps it was that his flat held too many memories, good and bad. Perhaps it was just the mood of the evening.

Or perhaps it was that the image of Gill Templar's face kept appearing unbidden (he told himself unbidden) in his mind . . .

5

Up the River

Burglary with violent assault: just the thing for a dreich Thursday morning. The victim was in hospital, head bandaged and face bruised. Rebus had been to talk with her, and was at the house in Jock's Lodge, overseeing the dusting for prints and the taking of statements, when word reached him from Great London Road. The call came from Brian Holmes.

'Yes, Brian?'

'There's been another drowning.'

'Drowning?'

'Another body in the river.'

'Oh Christ. Whereabouts this time?'

'Out of town, up towards Queensferry. Another woman. She was found this morning by someone out for a walk.' He paused while someone handed him something. Rebus heard a muted 'thanks' as the person moved away. 'It could be our Mr Glass, couldn't it?' Holmes said now, pausing again to slurp coffee. 'We expected him to stick around the city, but he could as easily have headed north. Queensferry's an easy walk, and mostly across open land, well away from roads where he might be spotted. If I was on the run, that's the way I'd do it . . .'

Yes, Rebus knew that country. Hadn't he been out there just the other day? Quiet back roads, no traffic, nobody to notice . . . Hang on, there was a stream – no, more a river – running past the Kinnouls' house.

'Brian . . .' he started.

'And that's another thing,' Holmes interrupted. 'The woman who found the body . . . guess who it was?'

'Cathy Gow,' Rebus said casually.

Holmes seemed puzzled. 'Who? Anyway, no, it was Rab Kinnoul's wife. You know, Rab Kinnoul . . . the actor. Who's this Cathy Gow . . .?'

It was uphill from the Kinnoul house, and along the side of the hill, too. Not too far a walk, but the country grew if anything bleaker still. Fifty yards from the fast-flowing river there was a narrow road, leading eventually to a wider road which meandered down to the coast. For someone to get here, they either had to walk past the Kinnoul house, or else walk down from the road.

'No sign of a car?' Rebus asked Holmes. Both men had zippered their jackets against the snell wind and the occasional smirr.

'Any car in particular?' Holmes asked. 'The road's tarmac, I've had a look for myself. No tyre tracks.'

'Where does it lead?'

'It peters out into a farm track, then, surprise surprise, a farm.' Holmes was moving his weight from one foot to the other, trying in vain to keep warm.

'Better check at the farm and see –'

'Someone's up there doing precisely that.'

Rebus nodded. Holmes knew this routine well enough by now: he would do something, and Rebus would double check that it had been done.

'And Mrs Kinnoul?'

'She's in the house with a WPC, drinking sweet tea.'

'Don't let her take too many downers. We'll need a statement.'

Holmes was lost, until Rebus explained about his previous visit here. 'What about Mr Kinnoul?'

'He went off somewhere this morning early. That's why Mrs Kinnoul went for a walk. She said she always went for a walk in the morning when she was on her own.'

'Do we know where he's gone?'

Holmes shrugged. 'Just on business, that's all she could tell us. Couldn't say where or how long he'd be. But he should be back this evening, according to Mrs Kinnoul.'

Rebus nodded again. They were standing above the river, near the roadway. The others were down by the river itself. It was in spate after the recent rain. Just about wide enough and deep enough to be classed a river rather than a stream. The 'others' included police officers, dressed in waders and plunging their arms into the icy water, feeling for evidence which would long have been flushed away, forensics men, hovering above the body, the Identification Unit, similarly hovering but armed with cameras and video equipment, and Dr Curt, dressed in a long flapping raincoat, its collar turned up. He trudged towards Rebus and Holmes, reciting as he came.

'When shall we three meet again ... blasted heath et cetera. Good morning, Inspector.'

'Morning, Dr Curt. What have you got for us?'

Curt removed his glasses and wiped spots of water from them. 'Double pneumonia, I shouldn't wonder,' he answered, replacing them.

'Accident, suicide, or murder?' asked Rebus.

Curt tut-tutted him, shaking his head sadly. 'You know I can't make snap decisions, Inspector. Granted, this poor woman hasn't been in the water as long as the previous one, but all the same . . .'

'How long?'

'A day at most. But with the weight of water and all . . . debris and so on . . . she's taken a bit of a battering. Lucky she was found at all, really.'

'How do you mean?'

'Didn't the sergeant say? Her wrist caught in a dead branch. Otherwise, she'd almost certainly have been swept down into the river and out into the sea.'

Rebus thought about the direction the river would take, bypassing the only settlements . . . yes, a body falling into the stream here might well have disappeared without trace . . .

'Any idea who she is?'

'No identification on the body. Plenty of rings on her fingers though, and she's wearing quite a nice dress, too. Care to take a look?'

'Why not, eh? Come on, Brian.'

But Holmes stood his ground. 'I had a look earlier, sir. Don't let me stop you though . . .'

So Rebus followed the pathologist down the slope. He was thinking: difficult to bring a body down here . . . but you could always roll it from the top . . . yes, roll it . . . hear the splash and assume it had fallen into the river . . . you might not know the wrist had caught in a branch. But to get a body up here in the first place – dead *or* alive – surely you'd need a car. Was William Glass capable of stealing a car? Why not, everyone else seemed to know how to do it these days. Kids in primary school could show you how to do it . . .

'Like I say,' Curt was saying, 'she's been bashed about a bit . . . can't tell yet whether post- or ante-mortem. Oh, about that other drowning at Dean Bridge . . .'

'Yes?'

'Recent sexual intercourse. Traces of semen in the vagina. We should be able to get a DNA profile. Ah, here we go . . .'

The body had been laid out on a plastic sheet. Yes, it was a nice dress, distinctive, summery, though torn now and smeared with mud. The face was muddy, too . . . and cut . . . and swollen . . . the hair drawn back and part of the skull exposed. Rebus swallowed hard. Had he been expecting this? He wasn't sure. But the photographs he'd seen made him sure in his mind.

'I know her,' he said.

'What?' Even the forensics men looked up at him in disbelief. The tableau must have alerted Brian Holmes, for he came stumbling down the slope to join them.

'I said I know her. At least, I think I do. No, I'm *sure* I do. Her name is Elizabeth Jack. Her friends call her Liz or Lizzie. She's ... she *was* married to Gregor Jack MP.'

'Good God,' said Dr Curt. Rebus looked at Holmes, and Holmes stared back at him, and neither seemed to know what to say.

There was more to identification than that, of course. Much more. Death was certainly suspicious, but this had to be decided *officially* by the gentleman from the Procurator Fiscal's office, the gentleman who now stood talking with Dr Curt, nodding his head gravely while Curt made hand gestures which would not have disgraced an excited Italian. He was explaining – explaining tirelessly, explaining for the thousandth time – about the movement of diatoms within the body, while his listener grew paler still.

The Identification Unit was still busy shooting off photographs and some video film, wiping their camera lenses every thirty seconds or so. The rain had, if anything, grown heavier, the sky an unbroken shading of grey-black. An autopsy was needed, agreed the Procurator Fiscal. The body would be transported to the mortuary in Edinburgh's Cowgate, and there formal identification would take place, involving two people who knew the deceased in life, and two police officers who had known her in death. If it turned out *not* to be Elizabeth Jack, Rebus was in a dung-pile of trouble. Watching the body being taken away, Rebus allowed himself a muffled sneeze. Perhaps Dr Curt's diagnosis of pneumonia was right. He knew where he was headed: the Kinnoul house. With luck, he might find hot tea there. The forensics team squeezed wetly into their car and headed back to police headquarters at Fettes.

'Come on, Brian,' said Rebus, 'let's see how Mrs Kinnoul's getting on.'

Cath Kinnoul seemed in a state of shock. A doctor had been to the house, but had left by the time Rebus and Holmes reached the scene. They shed their sodden jackets in the hall, while Rebus had a quiet word with the WPC.

'No sign of the husband?'

'No, sir.'

'How is she?'

'Comfortably numb.'

Rebus tried to look bedraggled and pathetic. It wasn't difficult. The WPC read his mind and smiled.

'I'll make some tea, shall I?'

'Anything hot would hit the spot, believe me.'

Cath Kinnoul was sitting in one of the living room's huge armchairs. The chair itself looked like it was in the process of consuming her, while she looked about half the size and a quarter of the age she'd been when Rebus had last seen her.

'Hello again,' he said, mock-cheerily.

'Inspector ... Rebus?'

'That's it. And this is Sergeant Holmes. No jokes, please, he's heard them all before, haven't you, Sergeant?'

Holmes saw that they were playing the comedy duo, trying to bring some life back into Mrs Kinnoul. He nodded encouragingly. In fact, he was glancing around wistfully, hoping to find a roaring log or coal fire. But there wasn't even a roaring gas fire for him to stand in front of. Instead, there was a one-bar electric job, just about glowing with warmth, and there were two radiators. He went and stood in front of one of these, separating his trousers from his legs. He pretended to be admiring the pictures on the wall in front of him. Rab Kinnoul with a TV actor ... with a TV comedian ... with a gameshow host ...

'My husband,' Mrs Kinnoul explained. 'He works in television.'

Rebus spoke. 'No idea what he's up to today though, Mrs Kinnoul?'

'No,' she said quietly, 'no idea.'

Two witnesses who had known the deceased in life ... Well, thought Rebus, you can scrub Cath Kinnoul. She'd fall apart if she *knew* it was Liz Jack out there, never mind having to identify the body. Even now, someone was trying to get in touch with Gregor Jack, and Jack would probably arrive at the mortuary with Ian Urquhart or Helen Greig, either of whom would do as the second nod of the head. No need to bother Cath Kinnoul.

'You look soaked,' she was saying. 'Something to drink?'

'The WPC's making some tea ...' But as he spoke, Rebus knew this was not what she was suggesting. 'A drop of the cratur wouldn't go amiss though, if it's not too much trouble.'

She nodded towards a sideboard. 'Right-hand cupboard,' she said. 'Please help yourself.'

Rebus thought of suggesting that she join them. But what pills had the doctor given her? And what pills had she taken of her own? He poured Glenmorangie into two long slim glasses and handed one to Holmes, who had taken up a canny position in front of a radiator.

'Mind you don't get steaming,' Rebus said in a murmur. Just then, the WPC appeared, carrying a tray of tea things. She saw the alcohol and almost frowned.

'Here's tae us,' said Rebus, downing the drink in one.

At the mortuary, Gregor Jack seemed hardly to recognize Rebus at all. Jack had been holding his weekly constituency surgery, Ian Urquhart explained to Rebus in a conspiratorial whisper. This was usually held on a Friday, but there was a Private Member's Bill in the Commons this

Friday, and Gregor Jack wanted to be part of the debate. So, Gregor having been in the area on Wednesday anyway, they'd decided to hold the surgery on Thursday, leaving Friday free.

Listening to all this in silence, Rebus thought: Why are you telling me? But Urquhart was clearly nervous and felt the need to talk. Well, mortuaries could have that effect, never mind the fact that your employer was about to see scandal heaped upon scandal. Never mind the fact that your job was about to be made more difficult than ever.

'How did the golf game go?' Rebus asked back.

'What golf game?'

'Yesterday.'

'Oh.' Urquhart nodded. 'You mean Gregor's game. I don't know. I haven't asked him yet.'

So Urquhart himself hadn't been involved. He paused for so long that Rebus thought a dead end had been reached, but the need to speak was too great.

'That's a regular date,' Urquhart went on. 'Gregor and Ronnie Steele. Most Wednesday afternoons.'

Ah, Suey, Mr would-be teenage suicide ...

Rebus tried to make his next question sound like a joke. 'Doesn't Gregor *ever* do any work?'

Urquhart looked stunned. 'He's always working. That game of golf ... it's about the only free time I've ever known him have.'

'But he doesn't seem to be in London very often.'

'Ah well, the constituency comes first, that's Gregor's way.'

'Look after the folk who voted you in, and they'll look after you?'

'Something like that,' Urquhart allowed. There was no more time for talk. The identification was about to take place. And if Gregor Jack looked bad before he saw the body, he looked like a half-filled rag doll afterwards.

'Oh Christ, that dress ...' He seemed about to collapse, but Ian Urquhart had a firm grip on him.

'If you'll look at the face,' someone was saying, 'We need to be definite ...'

They all looked at the face. Yes, thought Rebus, that's the person I saw beside the stream.

'Yes,' said Gregor Jack, his voice wavering, 'that's my ... that's Liz.'

Rebus actually breathed a sigh of relief.

What nobody had expected, what nobody had really considered, was Sir Hugh Ferrie.

'Let's just say,' said Chief Superintendent Watson, 'that a certain amount of ... pressure ... is being applied.'

As ever, Rebus couldn't hold his tongue. 'There's nothing to apply pressure *to*! What are we supposed to do that we're not already doing?'

'Sir Hugh considers that we should have caught William Glass by now.'

'But we don't even know –'

'Now, we all know Sir Hugh can be a bit hot-headed. But he's got a point . . .'

Meaning, thought Rebus, he's got friends in high places.

'He's got a point, and we can do without the media interest that's bound to erupt. All I'm saying is that we should give the investigation an extra *push* whenever and wherever we can. Let's get Glass in custody, let's make sure we keep everyone informed, and let's get that autopsy report as soon as humanly possible.'

'Not so easy with a drowning.'

'John, you know Dr Curt fairly well, don't you?'

'We're on second-name terms.'

'How about giving him that extra little nudge?'

'What happens if he nudges me back, sir?'

Watson looked like a kindly uncle suddenly tiring of a precocious nephew. 'Nudge him harder. I *know* he's busy. I *know* he's got lectures to give, university work to do, God knows what else. But the longer we have to wait, the more the media are going to fill the gaps with specu-lation. Go have a word, John, eh? Just make sure he gets the message.'

Message? What message? Dr Curt told Rebus what he'd always told him. I can't be rushed . . . delicate business, deciding an actual drowning from mere immersion . . . professional reputation . . . daren't make mis-takes . . . more haste, less speed . . . patience is a virtue . . . many a mickle maks a muckle . . .

All of this delivered between appointments in the doctor's Teviot Place office. The Department of Pathology's Forensic Medicine Unit, divided in loyalties between the Faculty of Medicine and the Faculty of Law, had its offices within the University Medical School in Teviot Place. Which seemed, to Rebus, natural enough. You didn't want your Com-mercial Law students mixing with people who keened over cadavers . . .

'Diatoms . . .' Dr Curt was saying. 'Washerwoman's skin . . . blood-tinged froth . . . distended lungs . . .' Almost a litany now, and none of it got them any further. Tests on tissue . . . examination . . . diatoms . . . toxicology . . . fractures . . . diatoms. Curt really did have a thing about those tiny algae.

'Unicellular algae,' he corrected.

Rebus bowed his head to the correction. 'Well,' he said, rising to his feet, 'fast as you can, eh, Doctor? If you can't catch me in the office, you can always try me by unicellular phone.'

'Fast as I can,' agreed Doctor Curt, chuckling. He too got to his feet.

'Oh, one thing I can tell you straight away.' He opened his office door for Rebus.

'Yes?'

'Mrs Jack was depilated. There'd be no getting *her* by the short-and-curlies...'

Because Teviot Place wasn't far from Buccleuch Street, Rebus thought he'd wander along to Suey Books. Not that he was expecting to catch Ronald Steele, for Ronald Steele was a hard man to catch. Busy behind the scenes, busy out of sight. The shop itself was open, the rickety bicycle chained up outside. Rebus pushed the door open warily.

'It's okay,' called a voice from the back of the shop. 'Rasputin's gone out for a wander.'

Rebus closed the door and approached the desk. The same girl was sitting there, and her duties still seemed to entail the pricing of books. There wasn't any room for any more books on the shelves. Rebus wondered where these new titles were headed...

'How did you know it was me?' he asked.

'That window.' She nodded towards the front-of-shop. 'It might look filthy from the outside, but you can see out of it all right. Like one of those two-way mirrors.'

Rebus looked. Yes, because the shop's interior was darker than the street, you could see out all right, you just couldn't see in.

'No sign of your books, if that's what you're wondering.'

Rebus nodded slowly. It was *not* what he was wondering...

'And Ronald's not here.' She checked the oversized face of her wrist-watch. 'Should have been in half an hour ago. Must have got held up.'

Rebus kept on nodding. Steele had told him this girl's name. What was it again...? 'Was he in yesterday?'

She shook her head. 'We were shut. All day. I was a bit off colour, couldn't come in. At the start of the university year, we do okay business on a Wednesday, Wednesday being a half-teaching day, but not just now...'

Rebus thought of Vaseline ... vanishing cream ... Vanessa! That was it.

'Well, thanks anyway. Keep an eye out for those books...'

'Oh! Here's Ronald now.'

Rebus turned round, just as the door rattled open. Ronald Steele closed it heavily behind him, started up the central aisle of books, but then almost lost balance and had to rest against a bookcase. His eyes caught a particular spine, and he levered the book out from the others around it.

'*Fish out of Water*,' he said. 'Out of water ...' He threw the book as far as he could – a matter of a yard or so. It crashed into a bookcase and fell open on to the floor. Then he began picking books out at random and throwing them with force, his eyes red with tears.

Vanessa screamed at him and came round from her desk, making towards him, but Steele pushed past her and stumbled past Rebus, past the desk, and through a doorway at the very back of the shop. There was the sound of another door closing.

'What's back there?'

'The loo,' said Vanessa, stooping to recover a few of the books. 'What the hell's the matter with him?'

'Maybe he's had a bit of bad news,' Rebus speculated. He was helping her retrieve books. He stood up and examined the blurb on the back jacket of *Fish out of Water*. The front cover illustration showed a woman seated more or less demurely on a chaise longue, while a rugged suitor leant over her from behind, his lips just short of her bared shoulder. 'I think I might buy this,' he said. 'Looks like just my sort of thing.'

Vanessa accepted the book, then stared up from it to him, her disbelief not quite showing through the shock of the scene she'd just witnessed. 'Fifty pence,' she told him quietly.

'Fifty pence it is,' said Rebus.

And after the formal identification, while the autopsy took its defined and painstaking course, there were the questions. There were an awful lot of questions.

Cath Kinnoul had to be questioned. Gently questioned, with her husband by her side and a bloodstream dulled by tranqs. No, she hadn't really taken a close look at the body. She'd known from a good way off what it was. She could see the dress, could see that it *was* a dress. She'd run back to the house and telephoned for the police. Nine-nine-nine, the way they told you to in emergencies. No, she hadn't gone back out to the river. She doubted she'd ever go there again.

And, turning to Mr Kinnoul, where had *he* been this morning? Business meetings, he said. Meetings with potential partners and potential backers. He was trying to set up an independent television company, though he'd be grateful if the information went no further. And the previous evening? He'd spent it at home with his wife. And they hadn't seen or heard anything? Not a thing. They'd been watching TV all night, not current TV but old stuff kept on video, stuff featuring Mr Kinnoul himself . . . *Knife Ledge*. The on-screen assassin.

'You must have learned a few tricks of the trade in your time, Mr Kinnoul.'

'You mean acting?'

'No, I mean about how to kill . . .'

And then there was Gregor Jack . . . Rebus kept out of that altogether. He'd look at any notes and transcripts later. He didn't want to get involved. There was too much he already knew, too much pre-judgement, which was another way of saying potential prejudice. He let other CID men deal with Mr Jack, and with Ian Urquhart, and with Helen Greig, and with *all* Elizabeth Jack's cronies and cohorts. For this wasn't merely a case of the lady vanishing; this was a matter of death. Jamie Kilpatrick, the Hon. Matilda Merriman, Julian Kaymer, Martin Inman, Louise Patterson-Scott, even Barney Byars. They'd all either been questioned, or were about to be. Perhaps they'd all be questioned again at a later date. There were missing days to be filled. Huge gaps in Liz Jack's life, the whole final week of her life. Where had she been? Who had she seen? When had she died? (Hurry up, please, Dr Curt. Chop-chop.) *How* had she died? (Ditto.) Where was her car?

But Rebus read all the transcripts, all the notes. He read through the interview with Gregor Jack, and the interview with Ronald Steele. A Detective Constable was sent to Braidwater Golf Course to check the story of the Wednesday afternoon game. The interview with Steele, Rebus read very carefully indeed. Asked about Elizabeth Jack, Steele admitted that 'she always accused me of not being enough fun. She was right, I suppose. I'm not exactly what you'd call a "party animal". And I never had enough money. She liked people with money to throw around, or who threw it around even if they couldn't afford it.'

A touch of bitterness there? Or just the bitter truth?

To all of which Rebus added one other question – had Elizabeth Jack ever left Edinburgh in the first place?

Then there was the separate hunt, the hunt for William Glass. If he *had* gone to Queensferry, where would be next? West, towards Bathgate, Linlithgow, or Bo'ness? Or north, across the Forth to Fife? Police forces were mobilized. Descriptions were issued. *Had* Liz Jack spent any time at all at Deer Lodge? How could William Glass simply disappear? Was there any connection between Mrs Jack's death and her husband's 'night out' at an Edinburgh brothel?

This last line was the one pursued most eagerly by the newspapers. They seemed to be favouring a verdict of suicide in the case of Elizabeth Jack. Husband's shame . . . discovered after she's been on retreat . . . on her way home she decides she can't face things . . . sets off perhaps to visit her friend the actor Rab Kinnoul . . . but grows more desperate and, having read the details of the Dean Bridge murder, decides to end it all. Throws herself into the river above Rab Kinnoul's house. End of story.

Except that it wasn't the end of the story. As far as the papers were concerned, it was just the beginning. After all, this one had it all – a TV actor, an MP, a sex scandal, a death. The headline writers were boggled, trying to decide which order to put things in. Sex Scandal MP's Wife Drowns in TV Star's Stream? Or TV Star's Agony at MP Friend's Wife's Suicide Act? You could see the problem . . . All those possessives . . .

And the grieving husband? Kept well away from the media by protective friends and colleagues. But he was always available for interview by the police, when clarification of some point was required. While his father-in-law gave the media as many interviews as they needed, but kept his comments to the police succinct and scathing.

'What do you want to talk to me for? Find the bugger who did it, then you can talk all you want. I want the animal who did this put behind bars! Better make them bloody strong bars, too, otherwise I might just pull them apart and strangle the life out of the bugger myself!'

'We're doing what we can, believe me, Sir Hugh.'

'Is it enough though, that's what I want to know!'

'Everything we can . . .'

Yes, everything. Leaving just the one final question: Did *anyone* do it? Only Dr Curt could answer that.

6
Highland Games

Rebus packed an overnight bag. It was a large sports holdall, bought for him by Patience Aitken when she'd decided he should get fit. They'd enrolled together in a health club, bought all the gear, and had attended the club four or five times together. They'd played squash, been massaged, had saunas, encountered the plunge pool, gone swimming, survived the expensively equipped gymnasium, tried jogging ... but ended up spending more and more time in the health club bar, which was stupid, the drinks being double the price they were at the pleasant-enough pub round the corner.

No longer a sports bag then, but these days an overnight bag. Not that Rebus was taking much this trip. He packed a change of shirt, socks and underwear, toothbrush, camera, notebook, a kagoul. Would he require a phrase book? Probably, but he doubted if one existed. Something to read though ... bedtime reading. He found the copy of *Fish out of Water* and threw it in on top of everything else. The phone was ringing. But he was in Patience's flat, and she had her own answering machine. All the same ...

He went through to the living room and listened as the message played. Then the caller's voice. 'This is Brian Holmes, trying to get in touch with –'

Rebus picked up the receiver. 'Brian, what's up?'

'Ah, caught you. Thought maybe you'd already headed for the hills.'

'I was just leaving.'

'Sure you don't want to drop by the station first?'

'Why should I?'

'Because Dr Curt is about to pronounce ...'

The problem with drowning was that drowning and immersion were two entirely different things. A body (conscious or unconscious) might fall (or be pushed) into water and drown. Or an already dead body might be dumped into water as a means of concealment or to lead the police astray. Cause of death became problematical, as did time of death. Rigor mortis might or might not be present. Bruising on and damage to the body might be the result of rocks or other objects in the water itself.

However, froth from mouth and nose when the chest was pumped down on was a sign that the body was alive when it entered the water. So was the presence in the brain, marrow, kidney and so forth of diatoms. Diatoms, Dr Curt never tired of explaining, were micro-organisms which penetrated the lung membrane and would be pumped around the blood-stream by a still-beating heart.

But there were other signs, too. Silted matter in the bronchial tubes provided evidence of inhalation of water. A living person falling into water made attempts to grip something (a true-life 'clutching at straws') and so the hands of the corpse would be clenched. Washerwoman's skin, the shedding of nails and hair, the swelling of the body – all these could lead to an estimate of the amount of time the corpse had spent in the water.

As Curt pointed out, not all the relevant tests had been completed yet. It would be a few more days before the toxicology tests would yield results, so they couldn't be sure yet whether the deceased had taken any drink or drugs prior to death. No semen had been found in the vagina, but then the deceased's husband had provided information that the deceased 'had trouble' with the pill, and that her preferred method of contraception had always been the sheath...

Christ, thought Rebus, imagine poor old Jack being asked about that. Still, there might be even less pleasant questions to answer...

'What we have so far,' Curt said, while everyone begged him silently to get on with it, 'is a series of negatives. No froth from the mouth and nose ... no silted matter ... no clenched hands. What's more, rigor mortis would suggest that the body was dead prior to immersion, and that it had been kept in a confined space. You'll see from the photographs that the legs are bent quite unnaturally.'

At that moment, they knew ... but still he hadn't said it.

'I'd say the body was in the water not less than eight hours and not more than twenty-four. As to when death occurred, well, some time before that, obviously, but not too long, a matter of hours...'

'And cause of death?'

Dr Curt smiled. 'The photographs of the skull show a clear fracture to the right-hand side of the head. She was hit very hard from behind, gentlemen. I'd say death was almost instantaneous...'

There was more, but not much more. And much mumbling between officers. Rebus knew what they were thinking and saying: it was the same M.O. as the Dean Bridge killing. But it wasn't. The woman found at Dean Bridge had been murdered at that spot, not transported there, and she had been murdered on a riverside path in the middle of a city, not ... well, where *had* Liz Jack died? Anywhere. It could be anywhere. While people were muttering that William Glass had to be found, Rebus was thinking in a different direction: Mrs Jack's BMW had to be found, and found quickly. Well, he was already packed, and he'd okayed the trip with Lauderdale. Constable Moffat would be there to meet him, and Gregor Jack had provided the keys.

'So there it is, ladies and gentlemen.' Curt was saying. 'Murder would be my opinion. Yes, murder. The rest is down to your forensic scientists and yourselves.'

'Off are you?' Lauderdale commented, seeing Rebus toting his bag.

'That's right, sir.'

'Good hunting, Inspector.' Lauderdale paused. 'What's the name of the place again?'

'Where is it expensive to be a Mason, sir?'

'I don't follow ... ah right, a dear lodge.'

Rebus winked at his superior and made his way out towards his car.

It was very pleasing the way Scotland changed every thirty miles or so – changed in landscape, in character, and in dialect. Mind you, stick in a car and you'd hardly guess. The roads all seemed much the same. So did the roadside petrol stations. Even the towns, long, straight main streets with their supermarkets and shoe shops and wool shops and chip shops ... even these seemed to blur one into the other. But it was possible to look beyond them; possible, too, to look further *into* them. A small country, thought Rebus, yet so various. At school, his geography teacher had taught that Scotland could be divided into three distinct regions: Southern Uplands, Lowlands, and Highlands ... something like that. Geography didn't begin to tell the story. Well, maybe it did actually. He was heading due north, towards a people very different to those found in the southern cities or the coastal towns.

He stopped in Perth and bought some supplies – apples, chocolate, a half bottle of whisky, chewing gum, a box of dates, a pint of milk ... You never knew what might not be available further north. It was all very well on the tourist trail, but if he stepped off that trail ...

In Blairgowrie he stopped for fish and chips, which he ate at a Formica-topped table in the chip shop. Lashings of salt, vinegar and brown sauce on the chips. Two slices of white pan bread thinly spread with margarine. And a cup of dark-brown tea. The haddock was covered in batter, which Rebus picked off, eating it first before starting on the fish.

'You look as if you enjoyed that,' the frier's wife said, wiping down the table next to him. He had enjoyed it. All the more so since Patience wouldn't be smelling his breath this evening, checking for cholesterol and sodium and starch ... He looked at the list of delights printed above the counter. Red, white and black puddings, haggis, smoked sausage,

sausage in batter, steak pie, mince pie, chicken ... with pickled onions or pickled eggs on the side. Rebus couldn't resist. He bought another bag of chips to eat while he drove ...

Today was Tuesday. Five days since Elizabeth Jack's body was found, probably six days since she died. Memories were short, Rebus knew. Her photograph had been in all the newspapers, had appeared on television and on several hundred police posters. And still no one had come forward with information. He'd worked through the weekend, seeing little of Patience, and he'd come up with this notion, this latest straw to be clutched at.

The scenery deepened around him, growing wilder and quieter. He was in Glenshee. In it and through it as quickly as he could. There was something sinister and empty about the place, a louring sense of disease. The Devil's Elbow wasn't the treacherous spot it had seemed in his youth; the road had somehow been levelled, or the corner straightened. Braemar ... Balmoral ... turning off just before Ballater towards Cockbridge and Tomintoul, that stretch of road which always seemed to be the first of the winter to close for snow. Bleak? Yes, he'd call it bleak. But it was impressive, too. It just went on and on and on. Deep valleys hewn by glaciers, collections of scree. Rebus's geography teacher had been an enthusiast.

He was close now, close to his destination. He turned to the directions which he had scribbled down, an amalgam of notes from Constable Moffat and Gregor Jack. Gregor Jack ...

Jack had wanted to talk with him about something, but Rebus hadn't given him the chance. Too dangerous to get involved. Not that Rebus believed for one second that Jack had anything to hide. All the same ... The others though, the Rab Kinnouls and Ronald Steeles and Ian Urquharts ... there was definitely ... well, maybe not definitely ... but there was ... ach, no, he couldn't put it into words. He didn't really want to think about it even. Thinking about it, about all those permutations and possibilities, all those what ifs ... well, they just made his head birl.

'Left and then right ... along the track beside a fir plantation ... up to the top of the rise ... through a gateway. It's like *Treasure Hunt*.' The car was behaving impeccably (touch wood). Touch wood? He only had to stop the car and stretch his arm out of the window. No plantation now, but a wild wood. The track was heavily rutted, with grass growing high along a strip between the ruts. Some of the larger potholes had been filled in with gravel, and Rebus's speed was down to five miles an hour or less, but that didn't seem to stop his bones being shaken, his head snapped from side to side. It didn't seem possible that there could be a habitation ahead. Maybe he'd taken a wrong turning. But the tyre tracks he was following were fresh enough, and besides, he didn't fancy reversing all the way back along the trail, and there was no spot wide enough for a three-point turn.

At last, the surface improved, and he was driving on gravel. As he turned a long, high-cambered bend, he found himself suddenly in front of a house. On the grass outside was parked a police Mini Metro. A narrow stream trickled past the front entrance. There was no garden to speak of, just meadow and then forest, and a smell of wet pine in the air. In the distance, beyond the back of the house, the land climbed and climbed. Rebus got out of the car, feeling his nerves jangle back into position. The door of the Metro had already opened, and out stepped a farm labourer in police uniform.

It was like some sort of Guinness challenge: how large a man can you get in the front of a Mini Metro? He was also young, late teens or early twenties. He gave a big rubicund smile.

'Inspector Rebus? Constable Moffat.' The hand Rebus shook was as large as a coal shovel but surprisingly smooth, almost delicate. 'Detective Sergeant Knox was going to be here, but something came up. He sends his apologies and hopes I'll do instead, this being my neck of the woods, so to speak.'

Rebus, who was rubbing his neck at this point, smiled at the joke. Then he pressed a thumb either side of his spine and straightened up, exhaling noisily. Vertebrae clicked and crunched.

'Long drive, eh?' Constable Moffat commented. 'But you've made not bad time. I've only been here five minutes myself.'

'Have you had another look round?'

'Not yet, no. Thought I'd best wait.'

Rebus nodded. 'Let's start with the outside. Big place, isn't it? I mean, after that road up to it I was expecting something a bit more basic.'

'Well, the house was here first, that's the point. Used to have a fine garden, well-kept drive, and that forest was hardly there at all. Before my time, of course. I think the place was built in the 1920s. Part of the Kelman estate. The estate got sold off bit by bit. There used to be estate workers to keep the place in check. Not these days, and this is what happens.'

'Still, the house looks in good nick.'

'Oh, aye, but you'll see there's a few slates missing, and the gutters could do with patching up.'

Moffat spoke with the confidence of the DIYer. They were circling the house. It was a two-storey affair of solid-looking stone. To Rebus's mind, it wouldn't have been out of place on the outskirts of Edinburgh; it was just a bit odd to find it in a clearing in the wilderness. There was a back door, beside which sat a solitary dustbin.

'Do the bins get emptied around here?'

'They do if you can get them down to the roadside.'

Rebus lifted the lid. The smell was truly awful. A rotting side of salmon, by the shape of it, and some chicken or duck bones.

'I'm surprised the animals haven't been at those,' Moffat said. 'The deer or the wildcats . . .'

'Looks as though it's been in the bin long enough, doesn't it?'

'I wouldn't say they were last week's leavings, sir, if that's what you're getting at.'

Rebus looked at Moffat. 'That's what I'm getting at,' he agreed. 'The whole of last week, and for a few days before that, Mrs Jack was away from home. Driving a black BMW. Supposedly staying here.'

'Well, if she did, nobody I've spoken to saw her.'

Rebus held up a door key. 'Let's see if the inside of the house tells a different story, eh?' But first he returned to his car and produced two pairs of clear polythene gloves. He handed one pair to the constable. 'I'm not even sure these'll fit you,' he told him. But they did. 'Right, try not to touch anything, even though you're wearing gloves. It might be you could smear or wipe a fingerprint. Remember, this is murder we're talking about, not joyriding or cattle rustling. Okay?'

'Yes, sir.' Moffat sniffed the air. 'Did you enjoy your chips? I can smell the vinegar from here.'

Rebus slammed shut the car door. 'Let's go.'

The house smelt damp. At least, the narrow hallway did. The doors off this hallway were wide open, and Rebus stepped through the first, into a room which stretched from the front of the house to the back. The room had been decorated with comfort in mind. There were three sofas, a couple of armchairs, and beanbags and scatter cushions. There were TV and video, and a hi-fi system sitting on the floor, one of its speakers lying side on. There was also mess.

Mugs, cups and glasses for a start. Rebus sniffed one of the mugs. Wine. Well, the vinegary stuff left in it had once been wine. Empty bottles of burgundy, champagne, armagnac. And stains – on the carpet, on the scatter cushions, and on one wall, where a glass had landed with some force, shattering on impact. Ashtrays overflowed, and there was a small hand-mirror half hidden under one of the floor cushions. Rebus bent down over it. Traces of white powder around its rim. Cocaine. He left it where it was and approached the hi-fi, examining the choice of music. Cassettes, mostly. Fleetwood Mac, Eric Clapton, Simple Minds . . . and opera. *Don Giovanni* and *The Marriage of Figaro*.

'A party, sir?'

'Yes, but how recent?' Rebus got the feeling that this wasn't all the result of a single evening. A load of bottles looked to have been pushed to one side, making a little oasis of space on the floor, in the midst of which sat a solitary bottle – still upright – and two mugs, one with lipstick on its rim.

'And how many people, do you reckon?'

'Half a dozen, sir.'

'You could be right. A lot of booze for six people.'

'Maybe they don't bother clearing up between parties.'

Just what Rebus was thinking. 'Let's have a look around.'

Across the hall there was a front room which had probably once been dining room or lounge, but now served as a makeshift bedroom. A mattress took up half the floor space, sleeping bags covering the other half. There were a couple of empty bottles in here, too, but nothing to drink out of. A few art prints had been pinned to the walls. On the mattress sat a pair of shoes, men's, size nine, into one of which had been stuffed a blue sock.

The only room left was the kitchen. Pride of place seemed to go to a microwave oven, beside which sat empty tins, and packets of something called Microwave Popcorn. The tins had contained lobster bisque and venison stew. The double sink was filled with dishes and grey, speckled water. On a foldaway table sat unopened bottles of lemonade, packs of orange juice, and a bottle of cider. There was a larger pine breakfast table, its surface dotted with soup droppings but free from dishes and other detritus. On the floor around it, however, lay empty crisp packets, a knocked-over ashtray, bread-sticks, cutlery, a plastic apron and some serviettes.

'Quick way of clearing a table,' said Moffat.

'Yes,' said Rebus. 'Have you ever seen *The Postman Always Rings Twice*? The later version, with Jack Nicholson?'

Moffat shook his head. 'I saw him in *The Shining* though.'

'Not the same thing at all, Constable. Only, there's a bit in the film where ... you must have heard about it ... where Jack Nicholson and the boss's wife clear the kitchen table so they can have a spot of you-know-what on it.'

Moffat looked at the table suspiciously. 'No,' he said. Clearly, this idea was new to him. 'What did you say the film was called...?'

'It's only an idea,' said Rebus.

Then there was upstairs. A bathroom, the cleanest room in the house. Beside the toilet sat a pile of magazines, but they were old, too old to yield any clue. And two more bedrooms, one a makeshift attempt like the one downstairs, the other altogether more serious, with a newish-looking wooden four-poster, wardrobe, chest of drawers and dressing table. Improbably, above the bed had been mounted the head of a Highland cow. Rebus stared at the stuff on the dressing table: powders, lipsticks, scents and paints. There were clothes in the wardrobe – mostly women's clothes, but also men's denims and cords. Gregor Jack could give no description of what clothing his wife had taken with her when she left. He couldn't even be sure that she'd taken any until he noticed that her small green suitcase was missing.

The green suitcase jutting out from beneath the bed. Rebus pulled it out and opened it. It was empty. So were most of the drawers.

'We keep a change of clothes up there,' Jack had told detectives. 'Enough for emergencies, that's all.'

Rebus stared at the bed. Its pillows had been fluffed up, and the duvet lay straight and smooth across it. A sign of recent habitation? God knows. This was it, the last room in the house. What had he learned at the end of his hundred-odd-mile drive? He'd learned that Mrs Jack's suitcase – the one Mr Jack *said* she'd taken with her – was here. Anything else? Nothing. He sat down on the bed. It crackled beneath him. He stood up again and pulled back the duvet. The bed was covered in newspapers, Sunday newspapers, all of them open at the same story.

MP Found in Sex Den Raid.

So she'd been here, and she knew. Knew about the raid, about Operation Creeper. Unless someone else had been here and planted this stuff ... No, keep to the obvious. His eye caught something else. He moved aside one of the pillows. Tied to the post behind it was a pair of black tights. Another pair had been tied to the opposite post. Moffat was staring quizzically, but Rebus thought the young man had learned enough for one day. It was an interesting scenario all the same. Tied to her bed and left there. Moffat could have come, looked the house over, and gone, without ever being aware of her presence upstairs. But it wouldn't work. If you were *really* going to restrain someone, you wouldn't use tights. Too easy to escape. Tights were for sex-games. For restraint, you'd use something stronger, twine or handcuffs ... Like the handcuffs in Gregor Jack's dustbin?

At least now Rebus knew that she'd known. So why hadn't she got in touch with her husband? There was no telephone at the lodge.

'Where's the nearest call-box?' he asked Moffat, who still seemed interested in the tights.

'About a mile and a half away, on the road outside Cragstone Farm.'

Rebus checked his watch. It was four o'clock. 'Okay, I'd like to take a look at it, then we'll call it a day. But I want this place gone over for fingerprints. Christ knows, there should be enough of them. Then we need to check and double check the shops, petrol stations, pubs, hotels. Say, within a twenty-mile radius.'

Moffat looked doubtful. 'That's an awful lot of places.'

Rebus ignored him. 'A black BMW. I think some more handouts are being printed today. There's a photo of Mrs Jack, and the car description and registration. If she was up this way – and she *was* – *some*body must have seen her.'

'Well . . . folk keep to themselves, you know.'

'Yes, but they're not blind, are they? And if we're lucky, they won't be suffering from amnesia either. Come on, sooner we look at that phone-box, the sooner I can get to my digs.'

Actually, Rebus's original plan had been to sleep in the car and claim the price of a B&B, pocketing the money. But the weather looked uninviting, and the thought of spending a night cramped in his car like a half-shut knife . . . So, on the way to the phone-box, he signalled to a stop outside a roadside cottage advertising bed & breakfast and knocked on the door. The elderly woman seemed suspicious at first, but finally agreed that she had a vacancy. Rebus told her he'd be back in an hour, giving her time to 'air' the room. Then he returned to his car and followed Moffat's careful driving all the way to Cragstone Farm.

It wasn't much of a farm actually. A short track led from the main road to a cluster of buildings: house, byre, some sheds and a barn. The phone-box was by the side of the main road, fifty yards along from the farm and on the other side of the road, next to a lay-by big enough to allow them to park their two cars. It was one of the original red boxes.

'They daren't change it,' said Moffat. 'Mrs Corbie up at the farm would have a fit.' Rebus didn't understand this at first, but then he opened the door to the phone-box – and he understood. For one thing, it had a carpet a good carpet, too, a thick-piled offcut. There was a smell of air freshener, and a posy of field flowers had been placed in a small glass jar on the shelf beside the apparatus.

'It's better kept than my flat,' Rebus said. 'When can I move in?'

'It's Mrs Corbie,' Moffat said with a grin. 'She reckons a dirty phone-box would reflect badly on her, seeing her house is closest. She's been keeping it spick and span since God knows when.'

A pity though. Rebus had been hoping for something, some hint or clue. But supposing there had been anything, it must certainly have been tidied away . . .

'I'd like to talk to Mrs Corbie.'

'It's a Tuesday,' said Moffat. 'She's at her sister's on a Tuesday.' Rebus pointed back along the road to where a car was braking hard, signalling to pull into the farm's driveway. 'What about him?'

Moffat looked, then smiled coldly. 'Her son, Alec. A bit of a tearaway. He won't tell us anything.'

'Gets into trouble, does he?'

'Speeding mostly. He's one of the local boy racers. Can't say I blame him. There's not much to occupy the teenagers round here.'

'You can't be much more than a teenager yourself, Constable. *You* didn't get into trouble.'

'I had the Church, sir. Believe me, the fear of God is something to reckon with . . .'

Rebus's landlady, Mrs Wilkie, was something to reckon with, too. It started when he was changing in his bedroom. It was a nice bedroom, a bit overdone on the frills and finery, but with a comfortable bed and a twelve-inch black and white television. Mrs Wilkie had shown him the kitchen, and told him he should feel free to make himself tea and coffee whenever he felt like it. Then she had shown him the bathroom, and told him the water was hot if he felt like a bath. Then she had led him back to the kitchen and told him that he could make himself a cup of tea or coffee whenever he felt like it.

Rebus didn't have the heart to tell her he'd heard it all before. She was tiny, with a tiny voice. Between his first visit and his second, she had dressed in her best B&B-keeper's clothes and tied some pearls around her neck. He reckoned her to be in her late seventies. She was a widow, her husband Andrew having died in 1982, and she did the B&B 'as much for the company as the money'. She always seemed to get nice guests, interesting people like the German jam-buyer who had stayed for a few nights last autumn . . .

'And here's your bedroom. I've given it a bit of an airing and –'

'It's very nice, thank you.' Rebus put his bag on the bed, saw her ominous look, and shifted it off the bed and on to the floor.

'I made the bedspread myself,' she said with a smile. 'I was once advised to go professional, selling my bedspreads. But at my age . . .' She gave a chuckle. 'It was a German gentleman told me that. He was in Scotland to buy jam. Would you credit it? He stayed here a few nights . . .'

Eventually, she recalled her duties. She'd just go and make them a spot of supper. Supper. Rebus glanced at his watch. Unless it had stopped, it was not yet five thirty. But then, he'd booked bed and breakfast, and any hot meal tonight would be a bonus. Moffat had given him directions to the closest pub – 'tourist place, tourist prices' – before leaving him for the undoubted delights of Dufftown. The fear of God . . .

He had just slipped off his trousers when the door opened and Mrs Wilkie stood there.

'Is that you, Andrew? I thought I heard a noise.' Her eyes had a glassy, faraway look. Rebus stood there, frozen, then swallowed.

'Go and make us some supper,' he said quietly.

'Oh yes,' Mrs Wilkie said. 'You must be hungry. You've been gone such a long time . . .'

Then, the idea of a quick bath appealed. He looked into the kitchen first, and saw that Mrs Wilkie was busy at the stove, humming to herself.

So he headed for the bathroom. There was no lock on the door. Or rather, there was a lock, but half of it was hanging loose. He looked around him, but saw nothing he could wedge against the door. He decided to take his chance and started both taps running. There was a furious pressure to the water, and the bath filled quickly and hotly. Rebus undressed and sank beneath the surface. His shoulders were stiff from the drive, and he massaged them as best he could. Then he lifted his knees so that his shoulders, neck and head slid into the water. Immersion. He thought of Dr Curt, of drowning and immersion. Skin wrinkling . . . hair and nails shedding . . . slit in the bronchial . . .

A noise brought him to the surface. He cleared his eyes, blinked, and saw that Mrs Wilkie was staring down at him, a dish towel in her hands.

'Oh!' she said. 'Oh dear, I'm sorry.' And she retreated behind the door, calling through it: 'I quite forgot you were here! I was just going to . . . well . . . never mind, it can wait.'

Rebus screwed shut his eyes and sank beneath the waves . . .

The meal was, to his surprise, good, if a bit odd. Cheese pudding, boiled potatoes, and carrots. Followed by tinned steamed pudding and packet custard.

'So convenient,' as Mrs Wilkie commented. The shock of seeing a naked man in her bathtub seemed to have brought her into the here and now, and they talked about the weather, the tourists and the government until the meal was over. Rebus asked if he could wash the dishes, and was told he could not – much to his relief. Instead, he asked Mrs Wilkie for a front-door key, then set off, stomach full, clean of body and underwear, for the Heather Hoose.

Not a name he would have chosen for his own pub. He entered by the lounge door, but, the place being dead, pushed through another door into the public bar. Two men and a woman stood at the bar and shared a joke, while a barman studiously filled glasses from a whisky optic. The group looked round at Rebus as he came and stood not too far from them.

'Evening.'

They nodded back, almost without seeing him, and the barman returned the greeting, setting down three double measures of whisky on the bar.

'And one for yourself,' said one of the customers, handing across a ten-pound note.

'Thanks,' said the barman, 'I'll have a nip myself for later on.'

Behind the array of optics, bottles and glasses, the wall was mirrored, so Rebus was able to study the group without seeming to. The man who had spoken sounded English. There had been only two cars in the pub's courtyard, a beaten-up Renault 5 and a Daimler. Rebus reckoned he knew who owned which . . .

'Yes, sir?' asked the barman and Renault 5 owner.

'Pint of export, please.'

'Certainly.'

The wonder of it was that three well-off English tourists would drink in the public bar. Maybe they just hadn't noticed that the Heather Hoose possessed such an amenity as a lounge. All three looked a bit the worse for wear, mostly from drink. The woman had a formidable face, framed by dyed platinum hair. Her cheeks were too red and her eyelashes too black. When she sucked on her cigarette, she arched her head up to blow the smoke ceilingwards. Rebus tried counting the lines on her neck. Maybe it worked the way it did with tree-rings . . .

'There you are.' The pint glass was placed on a mat in front of him. He handed over a fiver.

'Quiet tonight.'

'Midweek and not quite the season,' recited the barman, who had obviously just said the same thing to the other group. 'It'll get busier later on.' Then he retreated to the till.

'Another round here when you're ready,' said the Englishman, the only one of the three to have finished his whisky. He was in his late thirties, younger than the woman. He looked fit, prosperous, but somehow faintly disreputable. It had something to do with the way he stood, slightly slouched and looming, as though he might be about either to fall down or else pounce. And his head swayed a little from side to side in time with his sleepy eyelids.

The third member of the group was younger still, mid-thirties. He was smoking French cigarettes and staring at the bottles above the bar. Either that, thought Rebus, or he's looking at *me* in the mirror, the way I'm looking at *him*. Certainly, it was a possibility. The man had an affected way of tapping the ash from his affected cigarette. Rebus noticed that he smoked without inhaling, holding the smoke in his mouth and releasing it in a single belch. While his companions stood, he rested on one of the high bar stools.

Rebus had to admit, he was intrigued. An unlikely little threesome. And about to become more unlikely still . . .

A couple of people had entered the lounge bar, and looked like staying there. The barman slipped through a doorway between rooms to serve these new customers, and this seemed to start off a conversation between the two men and the woman.

'God, the nerve. He hasn't served *us* yet.'

'Well, Jamie, we're not exactly gasping, are we?'

'Speak for yourself. I hardly felt that first one slip down. Should have asked for quadruples in the first place.'

'Have mine,' said the woman, 'if you're going to become ratty.'

'I am not becoming ratty,' said the slouching pouncer, becoming very ratty indeed.

'Well fuck you then.'

Rebus had to stifle a grin. The woman had said this as though it were part of any polite conversation.

'And fuck you, too, Louise.'

'Ssh,' the French-smoker warned. 'Remember, we're not alone.'

The other man and woman looked towards Rebus, who sat staring straight ahead, glass to lips.

'Yes we are,' said the man. 'We're all alone.'

This utterance seemed to signal the end of the conversation. The barman reappeared.

'Same again, barman, if you'll be so kind . . .'

The evening hotted up quickly. Three locals appeared and started to play dominoes at a nearby table. Rebus wondered if they were paid to come in and add the requisite local colour. There was probably more colour in a Meadowbank Thistle-Raith Rovers friendly. Two other drinkers appeared, wedging themselves in between Rebus and the threesome. They seemed to take it as an insult that there were other drinkers in the bar before them, and that some of those drinkers were standing next to *their* space at the bar. So they drank in dour silence, merely exchanging looks whenever the Englishman or his two friends said anything.

'Look,' said the woman, 'are we heading back tonight? If not, we'd better think about accommodation.'

'We could sleep at the lodge.'

Rebus put down his glass.

'Don't be so sick,' the woman retorted.

'I thought that was why we came.'

'I wouldn't be able to sleep.'

'Maybe that's why they call it a wake.'

The Englishman's laughter filled the silent bar, then died. A domino clacked on to a table. Another chapped. Rebus left his glass where it was and approached the group.

'Did I hear you mention a lodge?'

The Englishman blinked slowly. 'What's it to you?'

'I'm a police officer.' Rebus brought out his ID. The two dour regulars finished their drinks and left the bar. Funny how an ID had that effect sometimes . . .

'Detective Inspector Rebus. Which lodge did you mean?'

All three looked sober now. It was an act, but a good act, years in the learning.

'Well, officer,' said the Englishman, 'now what business is that of yours?'

'Depends which lodge you were talking about, sir. There's a nice police station at Dufftown if you'd prefer to go there...'

'Deer Lodge,' said the French-smoker. 'A friend of ours owns it.'

'Owned it,' corrected the woman.

'You were friends of Mrs Jack then?'

They were. Introductions were made. The Englishman was actually a Scot, Jamie Kilpatrick the antique dealer. The woman was Louise Patterson-Scott, wife (separated) of the retail tycoon. The other man was Julian Kaymer, the painter.

'I've already spoken with the police,' Julian Kaymer said. 'They telephoned me yesterday.'

Yes, they had *all* been questioned, asked if they knew Mrs Jack's movements. But they hadn't seen her for weeks.

'I spoke to her on the telephone,' Mrs Patterson-Scott announced, 'a few days before she went off on holiday. She didn't say where she was going, just that she fancied a few days away by herself.'

'So what are you all doing here?' Rebus asked.

'This is a wake,' said Kilpatrick. 'Our little token of friendship, our time of mourning. So why don't you bugger off and let us get on with it.'

'Ignore him, Inspector,' said Julian Kaymer. 'He's a bit pissed.'

'What I am,' stated Kilpatrick, 'is a bit *upset.*'

'Emotional,' Rebus offered.

'Exactly, Inspector.'

Kaymer carried on the story. 'It was my idea. We'd all been on the phone to each other, none of us really able to take it in. Devastated. So I said why don't we take a run to the lodge? That was where we all met last.'

'At a party?' asked Rebus.

Kaymer nodded. 'A month back.'

'A great bloody big piss-up it was,' confirmed Kilpatrick.

'So,' said Kaymer, 'the plan was to drive here, have a few drinks in memory of Lizzie, and drive back. Not everybody could make it. Prior commitments and so on. But here we are.'

'Well,' said Rebus, 'I *would* like you to look inside the house. But there's no point going out there in the dark. What I *don't* want is the three of you going out there on your own. The place still has to be gone over for fingerprints.'

They looked a bit puzzled at this. 'You haven't heard?' Rebus said, recalling that Curt had only revealed his findings that morning. 'It's a murder hunt now. Mrs Jack was murdered.'

'Oh no!'

'Christ...'

'I'm going to be –'

And Louise Patterson-Scott, wife of the et cetera, threw up on to the carpeted floor. Julian Kaymer was weeping, and Jamie Kilpatrick was losing all the blood from his face. The barman stared in horror, while the domino players stopped their game. One of them had to restrain his dog from investigating further. It cowered under the table and licked its whiskery chops . . .

Local colour, as provided by John Rebus.

Finally, a hotel was found, not far out of Dufftown. It was arranged that the three would spend the night there. Rebus had considered asking Mrs Wilkie if she had any spare rooms, but thought better of it. They would stay at the hotel, and meet Rebus at the lodge in the morning. Bright and early: some of them had jobs to get back to.

When Rebus returned to the cottage, Mrs Wilkie was knitting by her gas fire and watching a film on the TV. He put his head round the living room door.

'I'll say goodnight, Mrs Wilkie.'

'Night-night, son. Mind, say your prayers. I'll be up to tuck you in a bit later on . . .'

Rebus made himself a mug of tea, went to his room, and wedged the chair against the door handle. He opened the window to let in some air, switched on his own little television, and fell on to the bed. There was something wrong with the picture on the TV, and he couldn't fix it. The vertical hold had gone. So he switched it off again and dug into his bag, coming up with *Fish out of Water*. Well, he'd nothing else to read, and he certainly didn't feel tired. He opened the book at chapter one.

Rebus woke up the next morning with a bad feeling. He half expected to turn and see Mrs Wilkie lying beside him, saying 'Come on, Andrew, time for the conjugals'. He turned. Mrs Wilkie was not lying beside him. She was outside his door and trying to get in.

'Mr Rebus, Mr Rebus.' A soft knock, then a hard. 'The door seems to be jammed, Mr Rebus! Are you awake? I've brought you a cup of tea.'

During which time Rebus was out of bed and half dressed. 'Coming, Mrs Wilkie.'

But the old lady was panicking. 'You're locked in, Mr Rebus. The door's stuck! Shall I call for a carpenter? Oh dear.'

'Hold on, Mrs Wilkie, I think I've got it.' His shirt still unbuttoned. Rebus put his weight to the door, keeping it shut, and at the same time lifted the chair away, stretching so as to place it nearer the bed. Then he made show of thumping the edges of the door before pulling it open.

'Are you all right, Mr Rebus? Oh dear, that's never happened before. Dear me no . . .'

Rebus lifted the cup and saucer from her hand and began pouring the tea back from saucer into cup. 'Thank you, Mrs Wilkie.' He made show of sniffing. 'Is something cooking?'

'Oh dear, yes. Breakfast.' And off she toddled, back down the stairs. Rebus felt a bit guilty for having pulled the 'locked-door' stunt. He'd show her after breakfast that the door was all right really, that she didn't need to phone for cowboy carpenters to put it right. But for now he had to continue the process of waking up. It was seven thirty. The tea was cold but the day seemed unseasonally warm. He sat on the bed for a moment, collecting his thoughts. What day was it? It was Wednesday. What needed to be done today? What was the best order to do it in? He'd to return to the cottage with the Three Stooges. Then there was Mrs Corbie to speak to. And something else ... something he'd been thinking about last night, in the melting moment between waking and sleep. Well, why not? He was in the area anyway. He'd telephone after breakfast. A fry-up by the smell of it, rather than Patience's usual choice of muesli or Bran Crunch. Ah, that was another thing. He'd meant to phone Patience last night. He'd do it today, just to say hello. He thought about her for a little while, Patience and her collection of pets. Then he finished dressing and made his way downstairs ...

He was first to arrive at the lodge. He let himself in and wandered into the living room. Immediately, he knew something was different. The place was tidier. Tidier? Well, say then that there was less debris around than before. Half the bottles looked to have disappeared. He wondered what else had vanished. He lifted the scatter cushions, searching in vain for the hand-mirror. Damn. He fairly flew through to the kitchen. The back window was lying in shards in the sink and on the floor. Here, the mess was as bad as before. Except that the microwave had gone. He went upstairs ... slowly. The place seemed deserted, but you never could tell. The bathroom and small bedroom were as before. So was the main bedroom. No, hold on. The tights had been untied from their bedposts and were now lying innocently on the floor. Rebus crouched and picked one up. Then dropped it again. Thoughtfully, he made his way back downstairs.

A burglary, yes. Break in and steal the microwave. That was the way it was supposed to look. But no petty thief would take empty bottles and a mirror with him, no petty thief would have reason to untie pairs of tights from bedposts. That didn't matter though, did it? What mattered was that the evidence had to disappear. Now it would merely be Rebus's word.

'Yes, sir, I'm sure there was a mirror in the living room. Lying on the floor, a small mirror with traces of white powder on it ...'

'And you're sure you're not merely *imagining* this, Inspector? You could be wrong, couldn't you?'

No, no, he couldn't. But it was too late for all that. Why take the bottles ... and only some of them, not all? Obviously, because some bottles had certain prints on them. Why take the mirror? Maybe fingerprints again ...

Should have thought of all this yesterday, John. Stupid, stupid, stupid.

'Stupid, stupid, stupid.'

And he'd done the damage himself. Hadn't he told the Three Stooges not to go near the lodge? Because it hadn't been fingerprinted. Then he'd let them wander off, with no guard left on the house. A constable should have been here all night.

'Stupid, stupid.'

It had to be one of them, didn't it? The woman, or one of the men. But why? Why had they done it? So it couldn't be proved they'd been there in the first place? Again, why? It didn't make much sense. Not much sense at all.

'Stupid.'

He heard a car approaching, pulling up outside, and went to meet it. It was the Daimler, Kilpatrick driving, Patterson-Scott in the passenger seat, and Julian Kaymer emerging from the rear. Kilpatrick looked a lot breezier than before.

'Inspector, good morning to you.'

'Morning, sir. How was the hotel?'

'Fair, I'd say. Only fair.'

'Better than average,' added Kaymer.

Kilpatrick turned to him. 'Julian, when you're used to excellence as I am, you no longer recognize "average" and "better than".'

Kaymer stuck his tongue out.

'Children, children,' chided Louise Patterson-Scott. But they all seemed light of heart.

'You sound chirpy,' Rebus said.

'A decent night's sleep and a long breakfast,' said Kilpatrick, patting his stomach.

'You stayed at the hotel last night?'

They seemed not to understand his question.

'You didn't go for a drive or anything?'

'No,' Kilpatrick said, his tone wary.

'It's your car, isn't it, Mr Kilpatrick?'

'Yes ...'

'And you kept the keys with you last night?'

'Look, Inspector ...'

'Did you or didn't you?'

'I suppose I did. In my jacket pocket.'

'Hanging up in your bedroom?'

'Correct. Look, can we go ins –'

'Any visitors to your room?'

'Inspector,' interrupted Louise Patterson-Scott, 'perhaps if you'd tell us . . .?'

'Someone broke into the lodge during the night, disturbing potential evidence. That's a serious crime, madam.'

'And you think one of us –?'

'I don't think anything yet, madam. But whoever did it must have come by car. Mr Kilpatrick here has a car.'

'Both Julian and I are capable of driving, Inspector.'

'Yes,' said Kaymer, 'and besides, we all went to Jamie's room for a late-night brandy . . .'

'So any one of you could have taken the car?'

Kilpatrick shrugged mightily. 'I still don't see,' he said, 'why you think we should want –'

'As I say, Mr Kilpatrick, I don't think anything. All I know is that a murder inquiry is under way, Mrs Jack's last known whereabouts remain this lodge, and now someone's trying to tamper with evidence.' Rebus paused. 'That's all I know. You can come inside now, but, please, don't touch anything. I'd like to ask you all a few questions.'

Really, what he wanted to ask was: Is the house pretty much in the state you remember it from the last party here? But he was asking too much. Yes, they remembered drinking champagne and armagnac and a lot of wine. They remembered cooking popcorn in the microwave. Some people drove off – recklessly, no doubt – into the night, while others slept where they lay or staggered off into the various bedrooms. No, Gregor hadn't been present. He didn't enjoy parties. Not his wife's, at any rate.

'A bit of a bore, old Gregor,' commented Jamie Kilpatrick. 'At least, I thought he was till I saw that story about the brothel. Just goes to show . . .'

But there had been another party, hadn't there? A more recent party. Barney Byars had told Rebus about it that night in the pub. A party of Gregor's friends, of The Pack. Who else knew Rebus was on his way up here? Who else knew what he might find? Who else might want to stop him finding anything? Well, Gregor Jack knew. And what he knew, The Pack might know, too. Maybe not one of these three then; maybe someone entirely different.

'Seems funny,' said Louise Patterson-Scott, 'to think we won't be having parties here any more . . . to think Liz won't be here . . . to think she's gone . . .' She began to cry, loudly and tearfully. Jamie Kilpatrick put an arm around her, and she buried her face in his chest. She reached out a hand and found Julian Kaymer, pulling him to her so that he, too, could be embraced.

And that's pretty much how they were when Constable Moffat arrived...

Rebus, with a real sense of bolting the stable door, left Moffat to stand guard, much against the young man's will. But the forensics team would be arriving before lunchtime, and Detective Sergeant Knox with them.

'There are some magazines in the bathroom, if you need something to read,' Rebus told Moffat. 'Or, better still, here ...' And he opened the car, reached into his bag, and took out *Fish out of Water*. 'Don't bother returning it. Think of it as a sort of present.'

Then, the Daimler having already left, Rebus got into his own car, waved back at Constable Moffat, and was off. He'd read *Fish out of Water* last night, every fraught sentence of it. It was a dreadful romantic tale of doomed love between a young Italian sculptor and a wealthy but bored married woman. The sculptor had come to England to work on a commission for the woman's husband. At first, she uses him like a plaything, but then falls in love. Meantime, the sculptor, bowled over by her at first, has moved his attentions to her niece. And so on.

It looked to Rebus as though the title alone had been what had made Ronald Steele pluck it from the shelf and throw it with such venom. Yes, just that title (the title, too, of the young sculptor's statue). The fish out of water was Liz Jack. But Rebus wondered whether she'd been out of water, or just out of her depth...

He drove to Cragstone Farm, parking in the yard to the rear of the farmhouse, scattering chickens and ducks before him. Mrs Corbie was at home, and took him into the kitchen, when there was a wondrous smell of baking. The large kitchen table was white with flour, but only a few globes of leftover pastry remained. Rebus couldn't help recalling that scene in *The Postman Always Rings Twice*...

'Sit yourself down,' she ordered. 'I've just made a pot...'

Rebus was given tea, and some of yesterday's batch of fruit scones, with fresh butter and thick strawberry jam.

'Ever thought about doing B&B, Mrs Corbie?'

'Me? I wouldn't have the patience.' She was wiping her hands on her white cotton apron. She seemed always to be wiping her hands. 'Mind you, it's not for shortage of space. My husband passed away last year, so now there's just Alec and me.'

'What? Running the whole farm?'

She made a face. 'Running it *down* would be more like it. Alec just isn't interested. It's a sin, but there you are. We've got a couple of workers, but when they see *he's* not interested, they can't see why *they* should be. We'd be as well selling up. That's what Alec would like. Maybe that's the only thing that stops me from doing it ...' She was looking at her hands. Then she slapped them against her thighs. 'Good-ness, would you listen to me! Now, Inspector, what was it you wanted?'

After all his years on the force, Rebus reckoned that at last he was in the presence of someone with a genuinely clear conscience. It didn't usually take so long for people to ask what a policeman was after. When it *did* take so long, the person either knew already what was wanted, or else had absolutely nothing to fear or to hide. So Rebus asked his question.

'I notice you keep the telephone kiosk sparkling, Mrs Corbie. I was wondering if you'd noticed anything suspicious recently? I mean, any-thing up at the box?'

'Oh, well, let me think.' She placed the flat of one hand against her cheek. 'I can't say ... what sort of thing exactly, Inspector?'

Rebus couldn't look her in the eye – for he knew that she had started to lie to him.

'A woman perhaps. Making a telephone call. Something left in the box ... a note or a telephone number ... anything at all.'

'No, no, nothing in the box.'

His voice hardened a little. 'Well, outside the box then, Mrs Corbie. I'm thinking specifically of a week ago, last Wednesday or maybe the Tuesday...?'

She was shaking her head. 'Have another scone, Inspector.'

He did, and chewed slowly, in silence. Mrs Corbie looked to be doing some thinking. She got up and checked in her oven. Then she poured the last of the tea from the pot, and returned to her seat, studying her hands again, laying them against her lap for inspection.

But she didn't say anything. So Rebus did.

'You *were* here last Wednesday?'

She nodded. 'But not the Tuesday. I go to my sister's on a Tuesday. I was here all day Wednesday though.'

'What about your son?'

She shrugged. 'He might have been here. Or maybe he was in Duff-town. He spends a lot of time off gallivanting...'

'He's not here just now?'

'No, he's gone to town.'

'Which town?'

'He didn't say. Just said he was off...'

Rebus stood up and went to the kitchen window. It faced on to the yard, where chickens now pecked at Rebus's tyres. One of them was sitting on the bonnet of the car.

'Is it possible to see the kiosk from the house, Mrs Corbie?'

'Eh ... yes, from the sitting room. But we don't spend much time in there. That is, I don't. I prefer here in the kitchen.'

'Could I take a look?'

Well, it was clear enough who *did* spend time in the living room. There was a direct line between sofa, coffee table and television set. The coffee table was marked with rings made by too many hot mugs. On the floor by the sofa there was an ashtray and the remains of a huge bag of crisps. Three empty beer cans lay on their sides beneath the coffee table. Mrs Corbie tut-tutted and went to work, lifting the cans. Rebus went to the window and peered out.

He could make out the kiosk in the distance, but only just. It was possible Alec Corbie might have seen something. Possible, but doubtful. Not worth sticking around for. He'd let DS Knox come and ask Corbie the questions.

'Well,' he said, 'thanks for your help, Mrs Corbie.'

'Oh.' Her relief was palpable. 'Right you are, Inspector. I'll see you out.'

But Rebus knew he had one last bet worth laying. He stood with Mrs Corbie in the yard and looked around him.

'I used to love farms when I was a lad. A pal of mine lived on one,' he glibly lied. 'I used to go up there every evening after tea. It was great.' He turned his wide-eyed nostalgic smile towards her. 'Mind if I take a wander round?'

'Oh.' No relief now; rather sheer terror. Which didn't stop Rebus. No, it pushed him on. So that before she knew it, he was walking up to the hutches and sties, looking in, moving on. On past the chickens and the roused ducks, into the barn. Straw underfoot and a strong smell of cattle. Concrete cubicles, coiled hosepipes, and a leaking tap. There were pools of water underfoot. One sick-looking cow blinked slowly at him from its enclosure. But the livestock wasn't his concern. The tarpaulin in the corner was.

'What's under here, Mrs Corbie?'

'That's Alec's property!' she shrieked. 'Don't touch it! It's nothing to do with –'

But he'd already yanked the tarpaulin off. What was he expecting to find? Something . . . nothing. What he *did* find was a black BMW 3-series bearing Elizabeth Jack's registration. It was Rebus's turn to tut-tut, but only after he'd sucked in his breath and held back a whoop of delight.

'Dear me, Mrs Corbie,' he said. 'This is just the very car I've been looking for.'

But Mrs Corbie wasn't listening. 'He's a good laddie, he doesn't mean any harm. I don't know what I'd do without him.' And so on. While Rebus circled the car, looking but not touching. Lucky the forensics team was on its way. They'd be kept busy . . .

Wait, what was that? On the back seat. A huddled shape. He peered in through the tinted glass.

'Expect the unexpected, John,' he muttered to himself.

It was a microwave.

7

Duthil

Rebus telephoned Edinburgh to make his report and request an extra day's stay up north. Lauderdale sounded so impressed that the car had been found that Rebus forgot to tell him about the break-in at the lodge. Then, once Alec Corbie had arrived home (drunk and in charge of a vehicle – but let that pass), he'd been arrested and taken to Dufftown. Rebus seemed to be stretching the local police like they'd never been stretched before, so that Detective Sergeant Knox had to be diverted from the lodge and brought to the farm instead. He looked like an older brother of Constable Moffat, or perhaps a close cousin.

'I want forensics to go over that car,' Rebus told him. 'Priority, the lodge can wait.'

Knox rubbed his chin. 'It'll take a tow-truck.'

'A trailer would be better.'

'I'll see what I can do. Where will you want it taken?'

'Anywhere secure and with a roof.'

'The police garage?'

'It'll do.'

'What exactly are we looking for?'

'Christ knows.'

Rebus went back into the kitchen, where Mrs Corbie was sitting at the table studying an array of burnt cakes. He opened his mouth to speak, but kept his silence. She was an accessory, of course. She'd lied to him to protect her son. Well, they had the son now, and *he* was the one that mattered. As quietly as he could, Rebus left the farmhouse and started his car, staring through the windscreen at his bonnet, where one of the chickens had left him a little gift . . .

He was able to avail himself of Dufftown police station for the interview with Alec Corbie.

'You're in keech up to your chin, son. Start at the beginning and leave nothing out.'

Rebus and Corbie, seated across the table from one another, were smoking, DS Knox, resting against the wall behind Rebus, was not.

Corbie had prepared an extremely thin veneer of macho indifference, which Rebus was quick to wipe off.

'This is a murder investigation. The victim's car has been found in your barn. It'll be dusted for prints, and if we find yours I'm going to have to charge you with murder. Anything you think you know that might help your case, you'd better talk.'

Then, seeing the effect of these words: 'You're in keep up to your chin, son. Start at the beginning and leave nothing out.'

Corbie sang like his namesake: it didn't make for edifying listening, but it had an honest sound. First, though, he asked for some paracetamol.

'I've got a hell of a headache.'

'That's what daytime drinking does to you,' said Rebus, knowing it wasn't the drinking that was to blame – it was the stopping. The tablets were brought and swallowed, washed down with water. Corbie coughed a little, then lit another cigarette. Rebus had stubbed his out. He just couldn't deal with them any more.

'The car was in the lay-by,' Corbie began. 'It was there for hours, so I went and took a look. The keys were still in the ignition. I started her up and brought her back to the farm.'

'Why?'

He shrugged. 'Never refuse a gift horse.' He grinned 'Or gift horse-power, eh?' The two detectives were not impressed. 'No, well, it was, you know, like with treasure. Finders keepers.'

'You didn't think the owner was coming back?'

He shrugged again. 'Never really thought about it. All I knew was that there were going to be some gey jealous looks if I turned up in town driving a BMW.'

'You planned to race it?' The question came from DS Knox.

'Sure.'

Knox explained to Rebus. 'They take cars out on to the back roads and race them one against one.'

Rebus remembered the phrase Moffat had used: boy racer. 'You didn't see the owner then?' he asked.

Corbie shrugged.

'What does that mean?'

'It means maybe. There was another car in the lay-by. Looked like a couple were in it, having an argument. I heard them from the yard.'

'What did you see?'

'Just that the BMW was parked, and this other car was in front of it.'

'You didn't get a look at the other car?'

'No. But I could hear the shouting, sounded like a man and a woman.'

'What were they arguing about?'

'No idea.'

'No?'

Corbie shook his head firmly.

'Okay,' said Rebus, 'and this was on . . .?'

'Wednesday. Wednesday morning. Maybe around lunchtime.'

Rebus nodded thoughtfully. Alibis would need re-checking . . . 'Where was your mother all this time?'

'In the kitchen, same as always.'

'Did you mention the argument to her?'

Corbie shook his head. 'No point.'

Rebus nodded again. Wednesday morning: Elizabeth Jack was killed that day. An argument in a lay-by . . .

'You're sure it was an argument?'

'I've been *in* enough in my time, it was an argument all right. The woman was screeching.'

'Anything else, Alec?'

Corbie seemed to relax at the use of his first name. Maybe he wouldn't be in trouble after all, so long as he told them . . .

'Well, the other car disappeared, but the BMW was still there. Couldn't tell if there was anyone in it, windows being tinted. But a radio was playing. Then in the afternoon –'

'So the car had been there all morning?'

'That's right. Then in the afternoon –'

'What time precisely?'

'No idea. I think there was horse-racing or something on the telly.'

'Go on.'

'Well, I looked out and there was *another* car had turned up. Or maybe it was the same one come back.'

'You still couldn't see?'

'I saw it better the second time. Don't know what make it was, but it was blue, light blue. I'm fairly sure of that.'

Cars would need checking . . . Jamie Kilpatrick's Daimler wasn't blue. Gregor Jack's Saab wasn't blue. Rab Kinnoul's Land-Rover wasn't blue.

'Anyway,' Corbie was saying, 'then there was *more* shouting the odds. I reckon it was coming from the BMW, because at one point the volume went right up on the radio.'

Rebus nodded appreciation of the observation.

'Then what?'

Corbie shrugged. 'It went quiet again. Next time I looked out, the other car was gone and the BMW was still there. Later on, I took a wander into the yard and through the field. Took a closer look. The passenger door was a bit open. Didn't look as though anyone was there, so I crossed the road. Keys were in the ignition . . .' He gave a final shrug. He had told his all.

And an interesting all it was. Two other cars? Or had the car from the morning returned in the afternoon? Who had Liz Jack been calling from the phone-box? What had she been arguing about? The volume rising on the radio ... to mask an argument, or because, in the course of a struggle, the knob had been moved? His head was beginning to birl again. He suggested they have some coffee. Three plastic cups were brought, with sugar and a plate containing four digestive biscuits.

Corbie seemed relaxed in the hard-back chair, one leg slung over the other, and smoking yet another cigarette. So far Knox had eaten all the biscuits ...

'Right,' said Rebus, 'now what about the microwave ...?'

The microwave was easy. The microwave was more treasure, again found by the side of the road.

'You don't expect us to believe that?' Knox sneered. But Rebus could believe it.

'It's the truth,' Corbie said easily, 'whether you believe it or not, Sergeant Knox. I was out in the car this morning, and saw it lying in a ditch. I couldn't believe it. Someone had just dumped it there. Well, it looked good enough, so I thought I'd take it home.'

'But why did you hide it?'

Corbie shifted in his seat. 'I knew my mum would think I'd nicked it. Well, anyway, she'd never believe I just *found* it. So I decided to keep it out of her way till I could come up with a story ...'

'There was a break-in last night,' Rebus said, 'at Deer Lodge. Do you know it?'

'That MP owns it, the one from the brothel.'

'You know it then. I think that microwave was stolen during the break-in.'

'Not by me it wasn't.'

'Well, we'll know soon enough. The place is being dusted for prints.'

'Lot of dusting going on,' Corbie commented. 'You lot are worse than my mum.'

'Believe it,' Rebus said, rising to his feet. 'One last thing, Alec. The car, what did you tell your mum about *it*?'

'Nothing much. Said I was storing it for a friend.'

Not that she'd have believed it. But if she lost her son, she lost her farm, too.

'All right, Alec,' said Rebus, 'it's time to get it all down on paper. Just what you've told us. Sergeant Knox will help you.' He paused by the door. 'Then, if we're *still* not happy that you've told us the truth and nothing but, maybe it'll be time to talk about drunk driving, eh?'

It was a long drive back to Mrs Wilkie's, and Rebus regretted not having taken a room in Dufftown. Still, it gave him time to think. He had made a telephone call from the station, putting back a certain appointment until tomorrow morning. So the rest of today was free. Clouds had settled low over the hills. So much for the nice weather. This was how Rebus remembered the Highlands – louring and forbidding. Terrible things had happened here in the past, massacres and forced migrations, blood feuds as vicious as any. Cases of cannibalism, too, he seemed to recall. Terrible things.

Who had killed Liz Jack? And why? The husband was always the first to fall under suspicion. Well, others could do the suspecting. Rebus, for one, didn't believe it. Why not?

Why not?

Well, look at the evidence. That Wednesday morning, Jack had been at a constituency meeting, then a game of golf, and in the evening he'd attended some function ... according to whom? According to Jack himself and to Helen Greig. Plus, his car was white. There could be no mistaking it for blue. Plus, someone was out to get Jack into terrible trouble. And *that* was the person Rebus needed to find ... unless it had been Liz Jack herself. He'd thought about that, too. But then there were the anonymous phone calls ... according to whom? Only Barney Byars. Helen Greig had been unable (or unwilling) to confirm their existence. Rebus realized now that he really did need to talk to Gregor Jack again. Did his wife have any lovers? Judging by what Rebus had learned of her, the question needed changing to: how many did she have? One? Two? More? Or was he guilty of judging what he did not know? After all, he knew next to nothing about Elizabeth Jack. He knew what her allies and her critics thought of her. But he knew nothing *of her*. Except that, judging by her tastes in friends and furnishings, she hadn't had much taste ...

Thursday morning. A week since the body had been found.

He woke up early, but was in no hurry to rise, and this time he let Mrs Wilkie bring him his tea in bed. She'd had a good night, never once thinking him her long-dead husband or long-lost son, so he reckoned she deserved not to be kept out of the bedroom. Not only tea this morning, but ginger nuts, too. And the tea was hot. But the day was cool, still grey and drizzly. Well, never mind. He'd be heading back to civilization, just as soon as he'd paid his respects elsewhere.

He ate a hurried breakfast, and received a peck on the cheek from Mrs Wilkie before leaving.

'Come back again some time,' she called, waving to him from the door. 'And I hope the jam sells all right ...'

The rain came on at its heaviest just as his windscreen wipers gave up. He stopped the car to study his map, then dashed outside to give the wipers a quick shake. It had happened before: they just stuck, and could be righted with a bit of force. Except this time they really had packed in. And not a garage in sight. So he drove slowly, and found after a while that the heavier the rain fell, the clearer his windscreen became. It was the slow fine rain that was the problem, blotting out all but the vaguest shapes and outlines. The heavy dollops of rain came and went so fast that they seemed to clear the windscreen rather than obscuring it.

Which was just as well, for the rain stayed heavy all the way to Duthil.

Duthil Special Hospital had been planned and built to act as a show-piece for treatment of the criminally insane. Like the other 'special hospitals' dotted around the British Isles, it was just that – a hospital. It wasn't a prison, and patients who arrived in its care were treated like patients, not prisoners. Treatment, not punishment, was its function, and with the brand new buildings came up-to-date methods and under-standings.

All this the hospital's medical director, Dr Frank Forster, told Rebus in his pleasant but purposeful office. Rebus had spent a long time last night on the telephone with Patience, and she'd told him much the same thing. Fine, thought Rebus. But it was still a place of detention. The people who came here came with no time limit attached, no 'sentence' that had to be served. The main gates were operated electronically and by guards, and everywhere Rebus had gone so far the doors had been locked again behind him. But now Dr Forster was talking about recreation facilities, staff/patient ratios, the weekly disco ... He was obviously proud. He was also obviously overdoing it. Rebus saw him for what he was: the front-man whose job it was to publicize the benefits of this particular special hospital, the caring attitude, the role of treat-ment. The likes of Broadmoor had come in for a lot of criticism in previous years. To avoid criticism, you needed good PR. And Dr Forster looked good PR. He was young for a start, a good few years younger than Rebus. And he had a healthy, scrupulous look to him, with a smile always just around the corner.

He reminded Rebus of Gregor Jack. That enthusiasm and energy, that public image. It used to be the sort of stuff Rebus associated with American presidential campaigns; now it was everywhere. Even in the asylums. The lunatics hadn't taken over; the image-men had.

'We have just over three hundred patients here,' Forster was saying, 'and we like the staff to get to know as many of them as possible. I don't just mean faces, I mean names. First names at that. This isn't Bedlam, Inspector Rebus. Those days are long past, thank God.'

'But you're a secure unit.'

'Yes.'

'You deal with the criminally insane.'

Forster smiled again. 'You wouldn't know it to look at most of our patients. Do you know, the majority of them – over sixty per cent, I believe – have above-average IQs? I think some of them are brighter than I am!' A laugh this time, then the serious face again, the caring face. 'A lot of our patients are confused, deluded. They're depressed, or schizophrenic. But they're not, I assure you, anything like the lunatics you see in the movies. Take Andrew Macmillan, for example.' The file had been on Forster's desk all along. He now opened it. 'He's been with us since the hospital opened. Before that, he was in much less ... savoury surroundings. He was making no progress at all before he came here. Now, he's becoming more talkative, and he seems about ready to participate in some of the available activities. I believe he plays a very good game of chess.'

'But is he still dangerous?'

Forster chose not to answer. 'He suffers occasional panic attacks ... hyperventilation, but nothing like the frenzies he went into before.' He closed the file. 'I would say, Inspector, that Andrew Macmillan is on his way to a complete recovery. Now, why do you want to talk to him?'

So Rebus explained about The Pack, about the friendship between 'Mack' Macmillan and Gregor Jack, about Elizabeth Jack's murder and the fact that she had been staying not forty miles from Duthil.

'I just wondered if she'd visited.'

'Well, we can check that for you.' Forster was flipping through the file again. 'Interesting, there's nothing in here about Mr Macmillan knowing Mr Jack, or about his having that nickname. Mack, did you say?' He reached for a pencil. 'I'll just make a note ...' He did so, then flicked through the file again. 'Apparently, Mr Macmillan has written to several MPs in the past ... and to other public figures. Mr Jack is mentioned ...' He read a little more in silence, then closed the file and picked up the telephone. 'Audrey, can you bring me the records of recent visitors ... say in the last month? Thanks.'

Duthil wasn't exactly a tourist attraction, and, out of sight being out of mind, there were few enough entries in the book. So it was the work of minutes to find what Rebus was looking for. The visit took place on Saturday, the day after Operation Creeper, but before the story became public knowledge.

' "Eliza Ferrie," ' he read. ' "Patient visited: Andrew Macmillan. Relation to patient: friend." Signed in at three o'clock and out again at four thirty.'

'Our regular visiting hours,' Forster explained. 'Patients can have visitors in the main recreation room. But I've arranged for you to see Andrew in his ward.'

'His ward?'

'Just a large room, really. Four beds to a room. But we call them wards to enforce ... perhaps enhance would be a better word ... to enhance the hospital atmosphere. Andrew's in the Kinnoul Ward.'

Rebus started. 'Why Kinnoul?'

'Pardon?'

'Why call the ward Kinnoul?'

Forster smiled. 'After the actor. You must have heard of Rab Kinnoul? He and his wife are among the hospital's patrons.'

Rebus decided not to say anything about Cath Kinnoul being one of The Pack, about her having known Macmillan at school ... It was no business of his. But the Kinnouls went up in his estimation; well, Cath did. She had not, it seemed, forgotten her one-time friend. *Nobody calls me Gowk any more.* And Liz Jack, too, had visited, albeit under her maiden name and with a twist to her Christian name to boot. He could understand that: the papers would have had a field day. MP's Wife's Visits to Crazed Killer. All those possessives. She couldn't have known that the papers were about to have their story anyway ...

'Perhaps at the end of your visit,' Dr Forster said, 'you'd like to see some of our facilities? Pool, gym, workshops ...'

'Workshops?'

'Simple mechanics. Car maintenance, that sort of thing.'

'You mean you give the patients spanners and screwdrivers?'

Forster laughed. 'And we count them in again at the end of the session.'

Rebus had thought of something. 'Did you say *car* maintenance? I don't suppose somebody could take a look at my windscreen wipers?'

Forster started to laugh again, but Rebus shook his head.

'I'm serious,' he said.

'Then I'll see what we can do.' Forster rose to his feet. 'Ready when you are, Inspector.'

'I'm ready,' said Rebus, not at all sure that he was.

There was much passing through corridors, and the nurse who was to show Rebus to Kinnoul Ward had to unlock and relock countless doors. A heavy chain of keys swung from his waistband. Rebus attempted conversation, but the nurse replied with short measures. There was just the one incident. They were passing along a corridor when from an open doorway a hand appeared, grabbing at Rebus. A small, elderly man was trying to say something, eyes shining, mouth making tiny movements.

'Back into your room, Homer,' said the nurse, prising the fingers from Rebus's jacket. The man scuttled back inside. Rebus waited a moment for his heart rate to ease, then asked: 'Why do you call him Homer?'

The nurse looked at him. 'Because that's his name.' They walked on in silence.

Forster had been right. There were few moans or groans or sudden curdling shrieks, and few enough signs of movement, never mind *violent* movement. They passed through a large room where people were watching TV. Forster had explained that actual television wasn't allowed, since it couldn't be pre-determined. Instead, there was a daily diet of specially chosen video titles. *The Sound of Music* seemed to be a particular favourite. The patients watched in mute fascination.

'Are they on drugs?' Rebus hazarded.

The nurse suddenly became talkative. 'As many as we can stick down their throats. Keep them out of mischief.'

So much for the caring face . . .

'Nothing wrong with it,' the nurse was saying, 'giving them drugs. It's all in the MHA.'

'MHA?'

'Mental Health Act. Allows for sedation as part of the treatment process.'

Rebus got the feeling the nurse was reciting a little defence he'd prepared to deal with visitors who asked. He was a big bugger: not tall, but broad, with bulging arms.

'Do any weight training?' Rebus asked.

'Who? That lot?'

Rebus smiled. 'I meant you.'

'Oh.' A grin. 'Yeah, I push some weights. Most of these places, the patients get all the facilities and there's nothing for the staff. But we've got a pretty good gym. Yeah, pretty good. In here . . .'

Another door was unlocked, another corridor beckoned, but off this corridor a sign pointed through yet another door – unlocked – to the Kinnoul Ward. 'In there,' the guard commanded, pushing open the door. His voice became firm. 'Okay, walk to the wall.'

Rebus thought for a moment the nurse was talking to *him*, but he saw that the object of the command was a tall, thin man, who now rose from his bed and walked to the far wall, where he turned to face them.

'Hands against the wall,' the nurse commanded. Andrew Macmillan placed the palms of his hands against the wall behind him.

'Look,' began Rebus, 'is this really –?'

Macmillan smiled wryly. 'Don't worry,' the nurse told Rebus. 'He won't bite. Not after what we've pumped into him. You can sit there.' He was pointing to a table on which a board had been set for chess. There were two chairs. Rebus sat on the one which faced Andrew Macmillan. There were four beds, but they were all empty. The room was light, its walls painted lemon. There were three narrow barred windows, through which some rare sunshine poured. The nurse looked to be staying, and took up position behind Rebus, so that he was reminded of the scene in Dufftown interview room, with himself and Corbie and Knox.

'Good morning,' Macmillan said quietly. He was balding, and looked to have been doing so for some years. He had a long face, but it was not gaunt. Rebus would have called the face 'kindly'.

'Good morning, Mr Macmillan. My name's Inspector Rebus.'

This news seemed to excite Macmillan. He took half a step forward.

'Against the wall,' said the nurse. Macmillan paused, then retreated.

'Are you an Inspector of Hospitals?' he asked.

'No, sir, I'm a police inspector.'

'Oh.' His face dulled a little. 'I thought maybe you'd come to . . . they don't treat us well here, you know.' He paused. 'There, because I've told you that I'll probably be disciplined, maybe even put into solitary. Everything, any dissension, gets reported back. But I've got to keep telling people, or nothing will be done. I have some influential friends, Inspector.' Rebus thought this was for the nurse's ears more than his own. 'Friends in high places . . .'

Well, Dr Forster knew that now, thanks to Rebus.

'. . . friends I can trust. People need to be told, you see. They censor our mail. They decide what we can read. They won't even let me read *Das Kapital*. And they give us drugs. The mentally ill, you know, by whom I mean those who have been *judged* to be mentally ill, we have less rights than the most hardened mass murderer . . . hardened but *sane* mass murderer. Is that fair? Is that . . . humane?'

Rebus had no ready answer. Besides, he didn't want to be sidetracked.

'You had a visit from Elizabeth Jack.'

Macmillan seemed to think back, then nodded. 'So I did. But when she visits me she's Ferrie, not Jack. It's our secret.'

'What did you talk about?'

'Why are you interested?'

Rebus decided that Macmillan did not know of Liz Jack's murder. How could he know? There was no access to news in this place. Rebus's fingers toyed with the chessmen.

'It's to do with an investigation . . . to do with Mr Jack.'

'What has he done?'

Rebus shrugged. 'That's what I'm trying to find out, Mr Macmillan.'

Macmillan had turned his face towards the ray of sunshine. 'I miss the world,' he said, his voice dropping to a murmur. 'I had so many – friends.'

'Do you keep in touch with them?'

'Oh yes,' Macmillan said. 'They come and take me home with them for the weekend. We enjoy evenings out at the cinema, the theatre, drinking in bars. Oh, we have some wonderful times together.' He smiled ruefully, and tapped his head. 'But only in here.'

'Hands against the wall.'

'Why?' he spat. 'Why do I have to keep my hands against the wall? Why can't I just sit down and have a normal conversation like . . . a . . .

normal ... person.' The angrier he got, the lower his voice dropped. There were flecks of saliva either side of his mouth, and a vein bulged above his right eye. He took a deep breath, then another, then bowed his head slightly. 'I'm sorry, Inspector. They give me drugs, you know. God knows what they are. They have this ... effect on me.'

'That's all right, Mr Macmillan,' Rebus said, but inside he was quivering. Was this madness or sanity? What happened to sanity when you chained it to a wall? Chained it, moreover, with chains that weren't real.

'You were asking,' Macmillan went on, breathless now, 'you were asking about ... Eliza ... Ferrie. You're right, she did come and visit. Quite a surprise. I know they have a home near here, yet they've never visited before. Lizzie ... Eliza ... did visit once, a long time ago. But Gregor ... Well, he's a busy man, isn't he? And she's a busy woman. I hear about these things...'

From Cath Kinnoul, Rebus didn't doubt.

'Yes, she visited. A very pleasant hour we spent. We talked about the past, about ... friends. Friendship. Is their marriage in trouble?'

'Why do you say that?'

Another creased smile. 'She came alone, Inspector. She told me she was on holiday alone. Yet a man was waiting for her outside. Either it was Gregor, and he didn't want to see me, or else it was one of her ... friends.'

'How do you know?'

'Nursie here told me. If you don't want to sleep tonight, Inspector, get him to show you the punishment block. I bet Doc Forster didn't mention the punishment block. Maybe that's where they'll throw me for talking like this.'

'Shut it, Macmillan.'

Rebus turned to the nurse. 'Is it true?' he asked. 'Was someone waiting outside for Mrs Jack?'

'Yeah, there was somebody in the car. Some guy. I only saw him from one of the windows. He'd got out of the car to stretch his legs.'

'What did he look like?'

But the nurse was shaking his head. 'He was getting back in when I saw him. I just saw his back.'

'What kind of car was it?'

'Black 3-series, no mistake about that.'

'Oh, he's very good at noticing things, Inspector, except when it suits him.'

'Shut it, Macmillan.'

'Ask yourself this, Inspector. If this is a *hospital*, why are all the so-called "nurses" members of the Prison Officers' Association? This isn't a hospital, it's a warehouse, but full of headcases rather than packing cases. The twist is, the headcases are the ones *in charge*!'

He was moving away from the wall now, walking on slow, doped legs, but his energy was unmistakable. Every nerve was blazing.

'Against the wall –'

'Headcases! I took her head off! God knows, I did –'

'Macmillan!' The nurse was moving too.

'But it was so long ago ... a different –'

'Warning you –'

'And I want so much ... so much to –'

'Right, that's it.' The nurse had him by the arms.

'– touch the earth.'

In the end, Macmillan offered little resistance, as the straps were attached to his arms and legs. The guard laid him out on the floor. 'If I leave him on the bed,' he told Rebus, 'he just rolls off and injures himself.'

'And you wouldn't want that,' said Macmillan, sounding almost peaceful now that he'd been restrained. 'No, nurse, you wouldn't want that.'

Rebus opened the door, making to leave.

'Inspector!'

He turned. 'Yes, Mr Macmillan?'

Macmillan had twisted his head so it was facing the door. 'Touch the earth for me ... please.'

Rebus left the hospital on shakier legs than he'd entered it. He didn't want the tour of the pool and the gym. Instead, he'd asked the nurse to show him the punishment block, but the nurse had refused.

'Look,' he'd said, 'you might not like what goes on here, *I* might not like some of what goes on, but you've seen how it is. They're supposed to be "patients", but you can't turn your back on them, you can't leave them alone. They'll swallow lightbulbs, they'll be shitting pens and pencils and crayons, they'll try to put their head through the television. I mean, they might *not*, but you just can't ever be sure ... ever. Try to keep an open mind, Inspector. I know it's not easy, but try.'

And Rebus had wished the young man luck with his weight training before making his exit. Into the courtyard. He stooped by a flowerbed and plunged his fingers deep into it, rubbing the soil between forefinger and thumb. It felt good. It felt good to be outside. Funny the things he took for granted, like earth and fresh air and free movement.

He looked up at the hospital windows, but couldn't be sure which, if any, belonged to Macmillan's ward. There were no faces staring at him, no signs of life at all. He rose to his feet, went to his car and got in, staring out through the windscreen. The brief sunshine had vanished. There was drizzle again, obscuring the view. Rebus pressed the button ... and the windscreen wipers came on, came on and stayed on, their blades moving smoothly. He smiled, hands resting on the steering wheel, and asked himself a question.

'What happens to sanity when you chain it to a wall?'

He took a detour on his way back south, coming off the dual carriageway at Kinross. He passed Loch Leven (scene of many a family picnic when Rebus had been a kid), took a right at the next junction, and headed towards the tired mining villages of Fife. He knew this territory well. He'd been born and brought up here. He knew the grey housing schemes and the corner shops and the utilitarian pubs. The people cautious with strangers, and almost as cautious with friends and neighbours. Street-corner dialogues like bare-knuckle fights. His parents had taken his brother and him away from it at weekends, travelling to Kirkcaldy for shopping on the Saturday, and Loch Leven for those long Sunday picnics, sitting cramped in the back of the car with salmon-paste sandwiches and orange juice, flasks of tea smelling of hot plastic.

And for summer holidays there had been a caravan in St Andrews, or bed and breakfast in Blackpool, where Michael would always get into trouble and have to be hauled out by his older brother.

'And a lot of bloody thanks I got for it.'

Rebus kept driving.

Byars Haulage was sited halfway up a steep hill in one of the villages. Across the road was a school. The kids were on their way home, swinging satchels at each other and swearing choicely. Some things never changed. The yard of Byars Haulage contained a neat row of artics, a couple of nondescript cars, and a Porsche Carrera. None of the cars was blue. The offices were actually Portakabins. He went to the one marked 'Main Office' (below which someone had crayoned 'The Boss') and knocked.

Inside a secretary looked up from her word-processor. The room was stifling, a calor-gas heater roaring away by the side of the desk. There was another door behind the secretary. Rebus could hear Byars talking fast and loud and uproariously behind the door. Since no one answered him back, Rebus reckoned it was a phone call.

'Well tell Shite-for-brains to get off his arse and get over here.' (Pause.) 'Sick? *Sick?* Sick means he's shagging that missus of his. Can't blame him, mind . . .'

'Yes?' the secretary said to Rebus. 'Can I help you?'

'Well never mind what he says,' came Byars' voice, 'I've got a load here that's got to be in Liverpool yesterday.'

'I'd like to see Mr Byars, please,' said Rebus.

'If you'll take a seat, I'll see whether Mr Byars is available. What's the name, please?'

'Rebus, Detective Inspector Rebus.'

At that moment, the door of Byars' office opened and Byars himself came out. He was holding a portable phone in one hand and a sheet of paper in the other. He handed the paper to his secretary.

'That's right, wee man, and there's a load coming up from London the day after.' Byars' voice was louder than ever. Rebus noticed that, unseen by her, Byars was staring at his secretary's legs. He wondered if this whole performance was for her benefit . . .

But now Byars had spotted Rebus. It took Byars a second to place him, then he nodded a greeting in Rebus's direction. 'Aye, you give him big licks, wee man,' he said into the telephone. 'If he's got a sick-note, fine, if not tell him I'm looking out his cards, okay?' He termined the call and shot out a hand.

'Inspector Rebus, what the hell brings you to this blighted neck of the bings?'

'Well,' said Rebus, 'I was passing, and –'

'Passing my arse! Plenty of people pass through, but nobody stops unless they want something. Even then, I'd advise them to keep on going. But you come from round here, don't you? Into the office then, I can spare you five minutes.' He turned to the secretary and rested a hand on her shoulder. 'Sheena, hen, get on to tadger-breath in Liverpool and tell him tomorrow morning definite.'

'Will do, Mr Byars. Will I make a cup of coffee?'

'No, don't bother, Sheena. I know what the polis like to drink.' He gave Rebus a wink. 'In you go, Inspector. In you go.'

Byars' office was like the back room of a dirty bookshop, its walls apparently held together by nude calendars and centrefolds. The calendars all seemed to be gifts donated by garages and suppliers. Byars saw Rebus looking.

'Goes with the image,' he said. 'A hairy-arsed truck driver with tattoos on his neck comes in here, he thinks he knows the sort of man he's dealing with.'

'And what if a woman comes in?'

Byars clucked. '*She*'d think she knew, too. I'm not saying she'd be all wrong either.' Byars didn't keep his whisky in the filing cabinet. He kept it inside a wellington boot. From the other boot he produced two glasses, which he sniffed. 'Fresh as the morning dew,' he said, pouring the drinks.

'Thanks,' said Rebus. 'Nice car.'

'Eh? Oh, outside you mean? Aye, it's no' bad. Nary a dent in it either. You should see the insurance payments though. Talk about steep. They make this brae look like a billiard table. Good health.' He sank the measure in one gulp, then noisily exhaled.

Rebus, having taken a sip, examined the glass, then the bottle. Byars chuckled.

'Think I'd give Glenlivet to the ba'-heids I get in here? I'm a businessman, not the Samaritans. They look at the bottle, think they know what they're getting, and they're impressed. Image again, like the scuddy pics on the wall. But it's really just cheap stuff I pour into the bottle. Not many folk notice.'

Rebus thought this was meant as a compliment. Image, that's what Byars was, all surface and appearance. Was he so different from MPs and actors? Or policemen come to that. All of them hiding their ulterior motives behind a set of gimmicks.

'So what is it you want to see me about?'

That was easily explained. He wanted to ask Byars a little more about the party at Deer Lodge, seemingly the last party to be held there.

'Not many of us there,' Byars told him. 'A few cried off pretty late. I don't think Tom Pond was there, though he was expected. That's right, he was off to the States by then. Suey was there.'

'Ronald Steele?'

'That's the man. And Liz and Gregor, of course. And me. Cathy Kinnoul was there, but her husband wasn't. Let's see ... who else? Oh, a couple who worked for Gregor. Urquhart ...'

'Ian Urquhart?'

'Yes, and some young girl ...'

'Helen Greig?'

Byars laughed. 'Why bother to ask if you already know? I think that was about it.'

'You said a *couple* who worked for Gregor. Did you get the impression that they *were* a couple?'

'Christ, no. I think everybody *but* Urquhart tried to get the girl into the sack.'

'Did anyone succeed?'

'Not that I noticed, but after a couple of bottles of champagne I tend not to notice very much. It wasn't like one of Liz's parties. You know, not wild. I mean, everybody had plenty to drink, but that was all.'

'All?'

'Well, you know ... Liz's crowd was *wild*.' Byars stared towards one of the calendars, seemingly reminiscing. 'A real wild bunch and no mistake ...'

Rebus could imagine Barney Byars lapping it up, mixing with Patterson-Scott, Kilpatrick and the rest. And he could imagine them ... tolerating Byars, a bit of nouveau rough. No doubt Byars was the life and soul of the party, a laugh a minute. Only they were laughing *at* him rather than with him ...

'How was the lodge when you arrived?' Rebus asked.

Byars wrinkled his nose. 'Disgusting. It hadn't been cleaned since the last party a fortnight before. One of Liz's parties, not one of Gregor's.

Gregor was going spare. Liz or somebody was supposed to have had it cleaned. It looked like a bloody sixties squat or something.' He smiled. 'Actually, I probably shouldn't be telling you this, you being a member of the constabulary and all, but I don't bother staying the night. Drove back about four in the morning. Absolutely guttered, but there was nobody about on the roads for me to be a menace to. Wait till you hear this though. I thought my feet were cold when I stopped the car. Got out to open the garage ... and I didn't have any shoes on! Just the one sock and no fucking shoes! Christ knows how come I didn't notice...'

8

Spite and Malice

Did John Rebus receive a hero's welcome? He did not. There were some who felt he'd merely added to the chaos of the case. Perhaps he had. Chief Superintendent Watson, for example, still felt William Glass was the man they were looking for. He sat and listened to Rebus's report, while Chief Inspector Lauderdale rocked to and fro on another chair, sometimes staring ruminatively at the ceiling, sometimes studying the one immaculate crease down either trouser-leg. It was Friday morning. There was coffee in the air. There was coffee, too, coursing through Rebus's nervous system as he spoke. Watson interrupted from time to time, asking questions in a voice as thin as an after-dinner mint. And at the end of it all, he asked the obvious question.

'What do you make of it, John?'

And Rebus gave the obvious, if only mostly truthful, answer.

'I don't know, sir.'

'Let's get this straight,' said Lauderdale, raising his eyes from a trouser-crease. 'She's at a telephone box. She meets a man in a car. They're arguing. The man drives off. She hangs around for some time. Another car, maybe the same car, arrives. Another argument. The car goes off, leaving her car still in the lay-by. And next thing we know of her, she's turning up dumped in a river next to the house owned by a friend of her husband's.' Lauderdale paused, as though inviting Rebus to contradict him. 'We still don't know when or where she died, only that she managed to end up in Queensferry. Now, you say this actor's wife is an old friend of Gregor Jack's?'

'Yes.'

'Any hint that they were a bit *more* than friends?'

Rebus shrugged. 'Not that I know of.'

'What about the actor, Rab Kinnoul? Maybe he and Mrs Jack . . .?'

'Maybe.'

'Convenient, isn't it?' said the Chief Superintendent, rising to pour himself another cup of black death. 'I mean, if Mr Kinnoul *did* ever want to dispose of a body, what better place than his own fast-flowing river, discharging into the sea, body turning up weeks later, or perhaps never

125

at all. *And* he's always played killers on the TV and in films. Maybe it's all gone to his head ...'

'Except,' said Lauderdale, 'that Kinnoul was in a series of meetings all day that Wednesday.'

'And Wednesday night?'

'At home with his wife.'

Watson nodded. 'We come back to Mrs Kinnoul again. Could she be lying?'

'She's certainly under his thumb,' said Rebus. 'And she's on all sorts of anti-depressants. I'd be surprised if she could tell Wednesday night at home in Queensferry from the twelfth of July in Londonderry.'

Watson smiled. 'Nicely put, John, but let's *try* to stick to facts.'

'What precious few there are,' said Lauderdale. 'I mean, we all *know* who the obvious candidate is: Mrs Jack's husband. She finds out he's been caught trousers-down in a brothel, they have a row, he may not mean to kill her but he strikes her. Next thing, she's dead.'

'He was caught trousers-up,' Rebus reminded his superior.

'Besides,' added Watson, 'Mr Jack, too, has his alibis.' He read from a sheet of paper. 'Constituency meeting in the morning. Round of golf in the afternoon – corroborated by his playing partner and checked by Detective Constable Broome. Then a dinner appointment where he made a speech to eighty or so fine upstanding members of the business community in Central Edinburgh.'

'And he drives a white Saab,' Rebus stated. 'We need to check car colours for everyone involved in the case, all Mrs Jack's friends and all Mr Jack's.'

'I've already put DS Holmes on to it,' said Lauderdale. 'And forensics say they'll have a report on the BMW ready by morning. I've another question though.' He turned to Rebus. 'Mrs Jack was, apparently, up north for anything up to a week. Did she stay all that time at Deer Lodge?'

Rebus had to give Lauderdale credit, the bugger had his thinking cap on today. Watson was nodding as though he'd been about to ask the selfsame thing, but of course he hadn't. Rebus *had* thought about it though.

'I don't think so,' he said. 'I *do* think she spent some time there, otherwise where did the Sunday papers and the green suitcase come from? But a whole week ...? I doubt it. No signs of recent cooking. All the food and cartons and stuff I found were either from one party or another. There *had* been an attempt to clear a space on the living room floor, so one person or maybe two could sit and have a drink. But maybe that goes back to the last party, too. I suppose we could ask the guests while we're fingerprinting them ...'

'Fingerprinting them?' asked Watson.

Lauderdale sounded like an exasperated parent. 'Purposes of elim-ination, sir. To see if any prints are left that can't be identified.'

'What would that tell us?' Watson said.

'The point is, sir,' commented Lauderdale, 'if Mrs Jack didn't stay at Deer Lodge, then *who* was she with and where *did* she stay? Was she even up north all that time?'

'Ah ...' said Watson, nodding again as though understanding every-thing.

'She visited Andrew Macmillan on the Saturday,' added Rebus.

'Yes,' said Lauderdale, getting into his stride, 'but then she's next seen on the Wednesday by that yob at the farm. What about the days in between?'

'She was at Deer Lodge on the Sunday with her newspapers,' Rebus said. Then he realized the point Lauderdale was making. 'When she saw the story,' he continued, 'you think she may have headed south again?'

Lauderdale spread out his hands, examining the nails. 'It's a theory,' he said, merely.

'Well, we've plenty bloody theories,' said Watson, slapping one of his own much meatier hands down on the desk. 'We need something concrete. And let's not forget friend Glass. We still want to talk to him. About Dean Bridge if nothing else. Meanwhile ...' he seemed to be trying to think of some path they might take, of some instructions or inspiration he might give. But he gave up and swigged back his coffee instead. 'Meanwhile,' he said at last, while Rebus and Lauderdale waited for the imparted wisdom, 'let's be careful out there.'

The old man's really showing his age now, thought Rebus, as he waited to follow Lauderdale out of the office. *Hill Street Blues* was a long, long time ago. In the corridor, after the door was closed behind them, Lauderdale grasped Rebus's arm. His voice was an excited hiss.

'Looks like the Chief Super's on the way out, doesn't it? Can't be long before the high heidyins see what's going on and pension him off.' He was trying to control his glee. Yes, Rebus was thinking, one or two very public foul-ups, that's all it would take. And he wondered ... he wondered if Lauderdale was capable of engineering a balls-up with this in mind. Someone had tipped off the papers about Operation Creeper. Christ, it seemed such a long time ago. But wasn't Chris Kemp supposed to be doing some digging into that? He'd have to remember to ask Kemp what he'd found. So much still needed to be done ...

He was shrugging his arm free of Lauderdale when Watson's door opened again, and Watson stood there staring at the two of them. Rebus wondered if they looked as guilty and conspiratorial as he himself felt. Then Watson's eyes settled on him.

'John,' he said, 'telephone call. It's Mr Jack. He says he'd be grateful if you'd go and see him. Apparently, there's something he'd like to talk to you about . . .'

Rebus pressed the bell at the locked gate. The voice over the intercom was Urquhart's.

'Yes?'

'Inspector Rebus to see Mr Jack.'

'Yes, Inspector, be right with you.'

Rebus peered through the bars. The white Saab was parked outside the house. He shook his head slowly. Some people never learned. A reporter had been sent from one of the line of cars to ask who Rebus was. The other reporters and photographers took shelter in the cars themselves, listening to the radio, reading newspapers. Soup or coffee was poured from flasks. They were here for the duration. And they were bored. As he waited, the wind sliced against Rebus, squeezing through a gap between jacket and shirt collar, trickling down his neck like ice water. He watched Urquhart emerge from the house, apparently trying to sort out the tangle of keys in his hand. The reconnaissance reporter still stood beside Rebus, twitching, readying himself to ask Urquhart his questions.

'I shouldn't bother, son,' advised Rebus.

Urquhart was at the gate now.

'Mr Urquhart,' blurted the reporter, 'anything to add to your previous statement?'

'No,' said Urquhart coolly, opening the gate. 'But I'll repeat it for you if you like – bugger off!'

And with that, Rebus safely through the gate, he slammed it shut and locked it, giving the bars an extra shake to make sure they were secure. The reporter, smiling sourly, was heading back to one of the cars.

'You're under siege,' Rebus observed.

Urquhart looked like he'd done without sleep for a night or two too many. 'It's diabolical,' he confided as they walked towards the house. 'Day and night they're out there. God knows what they think they're going to get.'

'A confession?' Rebus hazarded. He was rewarded with a weak smile.

'That, Inspector, they'll never get.' The smile left his face. 'But I *am* worried about Gregor . . . what all this is doing to him. He's . . . well, you'll see for yourself.'

'Any idea what this meeting's all about?'

'He wouldn't say. Inspector . . .' Urquhart had stopped. 'He's very fragile. I mean, he might say *any*thing. I just hope you can tell truth from fantasy.' Then he started to walk again.

'Are you still diluting his whisky?' Rebus asked.

Urquhart gave him an appraising look, then nodded. 'That's not the answer, Inspector. That's not what he needs. He needs friends.'

Andrew Macmillan, too, had gone on about friends. Rebus wanted to talk to Jack about Andrew Macmillan. But he wasn't in a hurry. He had paused beside the Saab, causing Urquhart to pause too.

'What is it?'

'You know,' said Rebus, 'I've always like Saabs, but I've never had the money around to buy one. Do you think Mr Jack would mind if I just sat in the driver's seat for a minute?'

Urquhart looked at a loss for an answer. He ended up making a gesture somewhere between a shrug and a shake of the head. Rebus tried the driver's door. It was unlocked. He slid into the seat and rested his hands on the steering wheel, leaving the door itself open so Urquhart could stand there and watch.

'Very comfortable,' Rebus said.

'So I believe.'

'You've never driven it yourself then?'

'No.'

'Oh.' Rebus stared out of the windscreen, then at the passenger seat and the floor. 'Yes, well designed, comfortable. Plenty of room, eh?' And he turned in his seat, twisting his whole body round to examine the rear seat . . . the rear floor. 'Heaps of room,' he commented. 'Lovely.'

'Maybe Gregor would let you take her for a spin?'

Rebus looked up keenly. 'Do you think so? I mean, when this has all blown over, of course.' He started to get out of the car. Urquhart snorted.

'Blown over? This sort of thing doesn't "blow over", not when you're an MP. The broth – . . . those allegations in the newspapers, they were bad enough, but now murder? No.' He shook his head. 'This won't just blow over, Inspector. It's not a raincloud, it's a mud bath, and mud sticks.'

Rebus closed the door. 'Nice solid clunk, too, when you shut it, isn't there? How well did you know Mrs Jack?'

'Pretty well. I used to see her most days.'

'But I believe Mr and Mrs Jack led fairly separate lives?'

'I wouldn't go that far. They *were* married.'

'And in love?'

Urquhart thought for a moment. 'I'd say so, yes.'

'Despite everything?' Rebus was walking around the car now, as though deciding whether or not to buy it.

'I'm not sure I understand.'

'Oh, you know, different sorts of friends, different lifestyles, separate holidays . . .'

'Gregor is an MP, Inspector. He can't always get away at the drop of a hat.'

'Whereas,' Rebus said, 'Mrs Jack was . . . what would you say? Spontaneous? Flighty, maybe even? The sort who'd say, let's just up and go?'

'Actually, yes, that's fairly accurate.'

Rebus nodded and tapped the boot. 'What about luggage room?'

Urquhart himself actually came forward and opened the boot.

'Goodness,' said Rebus, 'yes, there's plenty of room. Quite deep, isn't it?'

It was also immaculately clean. No mud or scuff marks, no crumbs of earth. It looked as though it had never been used. Inside were a small reserve petrol tank, a red warning triangle, and a half-set of golf clubs.

'He's keen on golf, isn't he?'

'Oh yes.'

Rebus closed the boot shut. 'I've never seen the attraction myself. The ball's too small and the pitch is too big. Shall we go in?'

Gregor Jack looked like he'd been to hell and back on an LRT bus. He'd probably combed his hair yesterday or the day before, and last changed his clothes then, too. He was shaven, but there were small patches of dark stubble the razor had missed. He didn't bother rising when Rebus entered the room. He just nodded a greeting and gestured with his glass to a vacant chair, one of the infamous marshmallow chairs. Rebus approached with care.

There was whisky in Jack's crystal tumbler, and a bottle of the stuff – three quarters empty – on the rug beside him. The room smelt unaired and unpolished. Jack took a gulp of liquid, then used the edge of the glass to scratch at his raw red finger.

'I want to talk to you, Inspector Rebus.'

Rebus sat down, sinking, sinking . . . 'Yes, sir?'

'I want to say a few things about me . . . and maybe about Liz, too, in a roundabout way.'

It was another prepared speech, another well-considered opening. There were just the two of them in the room. Urquhart had said he'd make a pot of coffee. Rebus, still jumpy from his meeting with Watson, had begged for tea. Helen Greig, it seemed, was at home, her mother having been taken ill – 'again', as Urquhart put it, before marching off kitchenwards. Faithful women: Helen Greig and Cath Kinnoul. Doggedly faithful. And Elizabeth Jack? Doggie-style faithful maybe . . . Christ, that was a terrible thing to think! And especially of the dead, especially of a woman he'd never met! A woman who liked to be tied to bedposts for a spot of . . .

'It's nothing to do with . . . well, I don't know, maybe it is.' Jack paused for thought. 'You see, Inspector, I can't help feeling that *if* Liz saw those stories about me, and *if* they upset her, then maybe she did something . . . or stayed away . . . and maybe . . .' He leapt to his feet and wandered over towards the window, looking out at nothing. 'What I'm trying to say is, what if I'm responsible?'

'Responsible, sir?'

'For Liz's ... murder. If we'd been together, if we'd been *here* together, it might never have happened. It *wouldn't* have happened. Do you see what I mean?'

'No good blaming yourself, sir –'

Jack whirled towards him. 'But that's just it, I *do* blame myself.'

'Why don't you sit down, Mr Jack –'

'Gregor, please.'

'All right ... Gregor. Now why don't you sit down and calm down.'

Jack did as he was told. Bereavement affected different people in different ways, the weak becoming strong and the strong becoming weak. Ronald Steele hurled books around, Gregor Jack became ... pathetic. He was scratching at the finger again. 'But it's all so ironic,' he spat.

'How's that?' Rebus wished the tea would hurry up. Maybe Jack would pull himself together in Urquhart's presence.

'That brothel,' Jack said, fixing Rebus's eyes with his own. 'That's what started it all. And the reason I was there ...'

Rebus sat forward. 'Why *were* you there, Gregor?'

Gregor Jack paused, swallowed, seemed to take a breath while he thought about whether to answer or not. Then he answered.

'To see my sister.'

There was silence in the room, so profound that Rebus could hear his watch ticking. Then the door flew open.

'Tea,' said Ian Urquhart, sidling into the room.

Rebus, who had been so eager for Urquhart's arrival, now couldn't wait for the man to leave. He rose from the chair and walked to the mantelpiece. The card from The Pack was still there, but it had been joined by over a dozen condolence cards – some from other MPs, some from family and friends, some from the public.

Urquhart seemed to sense the atmosphere in the room. He left the tray on a table and, without a word, made his exit. The door had barely closed before Rebus said, 'What do you mean, your sister?'

'I mean just that. My sister was working in that brothel. Well, I suspected she was, I'd been *told* she was. I thought maybe it was a joke, a sick joke. Maybe a trap, to get me to a brothel. A trap and a trick. I thought long and hard before I went, but I still went. He'd sounded so confident.'

'Who had?'

'The caller. I'd been getting these calls ...' Ah yes, Rebus had meant to ask about those. 'By the time I got to the phone, the caller would have hung up. But one night, the caller got me straight away, and he told me: "Your sister's working in a brothel in the New Town." He gave me the address, and said if I went around midnight she'd just be starting her ... shift.' The words were like some food he didn't enjoy, but given him at a banquet so that he didn't dare spit it out, but had to go on chewing, trying hard not to swallow ... He swallowed. 'So along I went, and she *was* there. The caller had been telling the truth. I was trying to talk to her when the police came in. But it was a trap, too. The newsmen were there...'

Rebus was remembering the woman in the bed, the way she kicked her legs in the air, the way she'd lifted her t-shirt for the photographers to see...

'Why didn't you say anything at the time, Gregor?'

Jack laughed shrilly. 'It was bad enough as it was. Would it have been any better if I'd let everyone know my sister's a tart?'

'Well then, why tell me now?'

His voice was calm. 'It looks to me, Inspector, like I'm in deep water. I'm just jettisoning what I don't need.'

'You must know then, sir ... you must have known all along, that someone is setting you up to take a very big fall.'

Jack smiled. 'Oh yes.'

'Any idea who? I mean, any enemies?'

The smile again. 'I'm an MP, Inspector. The wonder is that I have any *friends*.'

'Ah yes, The Pack. Could one of them...?'

'Inspector, I've racked my brain and I'm no nearer finding out.' He looked up at Rebus. 'Honest.'

'You didn't recognize the caller's voice?'

'It was heavily muffled. Gruff. A man probably, but to be honest it could have been a woman.'

'Okay then, what about your sister? Tell me about her.'

It was soon told. She'd left home young, and never been heard of. Vague rumours of London and marriage had drifted north over the years, but that was all. Then the phone call...

'How could the caller know? How might they have found out?'

'Now *that's* a mystery, because I've never told anybody about Gail.'

'But your schoolfriends would know of her?'

'Slightly, I suppose. I doubt any of them remember her. She was two years below us at school.'

'You think maybe she came back up here looking for revenge?'

Jack spread his palms. 'Revenge for what?'

'Well, jealousy then.'

'Why didn't she just get in touch?'

It was a point. Rebus made a mental note to get in touch with *her*, supposing she was still around. 'You haven't heard from her since?'

'Not before, not since.'

'Why *did* you want to see her, Gregor?'

'One, I really was interested.' He broke off.

'And two?'

'Two . . . I don't know, maybe to talk her out of what she was doing.'

'For her own good, or for yours?'

Jack smiled. 'You're right, of course, bad for the image having a sister on the game.'

'There are worse forms of prostitution than whoring.'

Jack nodded, impressed. 'Very deep, Inspector. Can I use that in one of my speeches? Not that I'll be making many of *those* from now on. Whichever way you look at it, my career's down the Swanny.'

'Never give up, sir. Think of Robert the Bruce.'

'And the spider, you mean? I hate spiders. So does Liz.' He halted. '*Did* Liz.'

Rebus wanted to keep the conversation moving. The amount of whisky Jack had drunk, he might tip over any minute. 'Can I ask you about that last party up at Deer Lodge?'

'What about it?'

'For a start, who was present?'

Having to use his memory seemed to sober Jack up. Not that he could add much to what Barney Byars had already told Rebus. It was a boozy, sit-around-and-chat evening, followed by a morning hike up some nearby mountain, lunch – at the Heather Hoose – and then home. Jack's only regret was inviting Helen Greig to go.

'I'm not sure she saw any of us in a decent light. Barney Byars was doing elephant impressions, you know, where you pull out your trouser pockets and –'

'Yes, I know.'

'Well, Helen took it in good enough part, but all the same . . .'

'Nice girl, isn't she?'

'The sort my mum would have wanted me to marry.'

Mine too, thought Rebus. The whisky wasn't just loosening Jack's tongue, it was also loosening his accent. The polish was fading fast, leaving the raw wood of towns like Kirkcaldy, Leven, Methil.

'This party was a couple of weeks ago, wasn't it?'

'Three weeks ago. We were back here five days when Liz decided she needed a holiday. Packed a case and off she went. Never saw her again . . .' He raised a fist and punched the soft leather of the sofa, making hardly a sound and no discernible mark. 'Why are they doing this to me? I'm the best MP this constituency's ever had. Don't take my word for it. Go out and talk to them. Go to a mining village or a farm or a factory or a fucking afternoon tea party. They tell me the same thing:

well done, Gregor, keep up the good work.' He was on his feet again now, feet holding their ground but the rest of the body in motion. 'Keep up the good work, the hard work. Hard work! It bloody is hard work, I can tell you.' His voice was rising steadily. 'Worked my balls off for them! Now somebody's trying to piss on my whole life from a very high place. Why me? Why me? Liz and me . . . Liz . . .'

Urquhart tapped twice before putting his head round the door. 'Everything all right?'

Jack put on a grotesque mask of a smile. 'Everything's fine, Ian. Listening behind the door, are you? Good, wouldn't want you to miss a word, would we?'

Urquhart glanced at Rebus. Rebus nodded: everything's okay in here, really it is. Urquhart retreated and closed the door. Gregor Jack collapsed into the sofa. 'I'm making such a mess of everything,' he said, rubbing his face with his hand. 'Ian's such a good friend . . .'

Ah yes, friends.

'I believe,' said Rebus, 'that you haven't just been receiving anonymous calls.'

'What?'

'Someone said something about letters, too.'

'Oh . . . oh yes, letters. Crank letters.'

'Do you still have them?'

Jack shook his head. 'Not worth keeping.'

'Did you let anyone see them?'

'Not worth reading.'

'What exactly was in them, Mr Jack?'

'Gregor,' Jack reminded him. 'Please, call me Gregor. What was in them? Rubbish. Garbled nonsense. Ravings . . .'

'I don't think so.'

'What?'

'Someone told me you'd refuse to let anyone open them. He thought they might be love letters.'

Jack hooted. 'Love letters!'

'I don't think they were either. But it strikes me, how could Ian Urquhart or anyone else *know* which letters they were to hand to you unopened? The handwriting? Difficult to tell though, isn't it? No, it had to be the postmark. It had to be what was on the envelope. I'll tell you where those letters came from, Mr Jack. They came from Duthil. They came from your old friend Andrew Macmillan. And they weren't raving, were they? They weren't garbled or nonsense or rubbish. They were asking you to do something about the system in the special hospitals. Isn't that right?'

Jack sat and studied his glass, mouth set petulantly, a kid who's been caught out.

'Isn't that right?'

Jack gave a curt nod. Rebus nodded, too. Embarrassing to have a sister who's a prostitute. But how much *more* embarrassing to have an old friend who's a murderer? And mad, to boot. Gregor Jack had worked hard to form his public image, and harder still to preserve it. Rushing around with his vacuously sincere grin and strong-enough-for-the-occasion handshake. Working hard in his constituency, working hard in *public*. But his private life ... well, Rebus wouldn't have wanted to swop. It was a mess. And what made it so messy was that Jack had tried to hide it. He didn't have skeletons in his closet; he had a crematorium.

'Wanted me to start a campaign,' Jack was muttering. 'Couldn't do that. Why did you start this crusade, Mr Jack? To help an old friend. Which old friend is that, Mr Jack? The one who cut his wife's head off. Now, if you'll excuse me. Oh, and please remember to vote for me next time round ...' And he began a drunken, wailing laugh, near-manic, near-crying. Finally actually becoming crying, tears streaming down his cheeks, dripping into the glass he still held.

'Gregor,' Rebus said quietly. He repeated the name, and again, and again, always quietly. Jack sniffed back more tears and looked blurrily towards him. 'Gregor,' said Rebus, 'did you kill your wife?'

Jack wiped his eyes on his shirt-sleeve, sniffed, wiped again. He began to shake his head.

'No,' he said. 'No, I didn't kill my wife.'

No, because William Glass killed her. He killed the woman under Dean Bridge, and he killed Elizabeth Jack.

Rebus had missed all the excitement. He had driven back into town unaware of it. He had climbed the steps up to Great London Road station without knowing. And he had entered a place of jumpy, jittery clamour. Christ, what did it mean? Was the station definitely staying open? No move to St Leonard's? Which meant, if he remembered his bet, that he'd set up home with Patience Aitken. But no, it was nothing to do with the station staying open or being reduced to rubble. It was William Glass. A beat constable had come across him sleeping amidst the dustbins behind a supermarket in Barnton. He was in custody. He was talking. They were feeding him soup and giving him endless cups of tea and fresh cigarettes, and he was talking.

'But what's he saying?'

'He's saying he did them – both of them!'

'He's saying *what*?'

Rebus started calculating. Barnton ... not so far from Queensferry when you thought about it. They were thinking he'd have headed north or west, but in fact he'd started crawling back into town ... supposing he'd ever got as far as Queensferry in the first place.

'He's admitting both murders.'

'Who's with him?'

'Chief Inspector Lauderdale and Inspector Dick.'

Lauderdale! Christ, he'd be loving it. This would be the making of him, the final nail in the Chief Super's coffee-maker. But Rebus had other things to be doing. He wanted Jack's sister found, for a start. Gail Jack, but she wouldn't be calling herself that, would she? He went through the Operation Creeper case-notes. Gail Crawley. That was her. She'd been released, of course. And had given a London address. He found one of the officers who'd interviewed her.

'Yes, she said she was heading south. Couldn't keep her, could we? Didn't want to either. Just gave her a kick up the arse and told her not to come back up here again. Isn't it incredible? Catching Glass like that!'

'Incredible, yes,' said Rebus. He photocopied what notes there were, along with Gail Crawley's photograph, and scribbled some further notes of his own on to the copy. Then he telephoned an old friend, an old friend in London.

'Inspector Flight speaking.'

'Hello George. When's the retirement party then?'

There was laughter. 'You tell me, you were the one who persuaded me to stay on.'

'Can't afford to lose you.'

'Meaning you want a favour?'

'Official business, George, but speed is of the –'

'As usual. All right, what is it?'

'Give me your fax number and I'll send you the details. If she's at the address, I'd like you to talk to her. I've put down a couple of phone numbers. You can reach me anytime on one or the other.'

'Two numbers, eh? Got yourself in deep, have you?'

In deep ... jettisoning what I don't need ...

'You could say that, George.'

'What's she like?' By which he meant Patience, not Gail.

'She likes domesticity, George. Pets and nights in, candles and fire-light.'

'Sounds perfect.' George Flight paused. 'I'll give it three months max.'

'Sod you,' said Rebus, grinning. Flight was laughing again.

'Four months then,' he said. 'But that's my final offer.'

That done, Rebus headed for the nerve centre, the one place he needed to station himself – the gents' toilets. Part of the ceiling had fallen down and had been replaced with a piece of brown cardboard on which some joker had drawn a huge eyeball. Rebus washed his hands, dried them, chatted to one of the other detectives, shared a cigarette. In a public toilet, he'd have been picked up for loitering. He *was* loitering, too, loitering with intent. The door opened. Bingo. It was Lauderdale, a frequent user of rest rooms when he was on an interrogation.

'All the time you're coming and going,' he'd told Rebus, 'the suspect's sweating that bit more, wondering what's up, what's happened that's new.'

'What's up?' Rebus asked now. Lauderdale smiled and went to splash water on his face, patting his temples and the back of his neck. He looked pleased with himself. More worrying, he didn't smell.

'Looks like our Chief Super may have got it right for once,' Lauderdale admitted. 'He said we should be concentrating on Glass.'

'He's confessed?'

'As good as. Looks as though he's sorting his defence out first.'

'What's that then?'

'The media,' said Lauderdale, drying himself. 'The media pushed him into doing it. I mean, killing again. He says it was *expected* of him.'

'Sounds to me like he's one domino shy of a set.'

'I'm not putting any words into his mouth, if that's what you're thinking. It's all on tape.'

Rebus shook his head. 'No, no, I mean, if he says he did it, then fair enough. That's fine. And by the way, it was me that shot JFK.'

Lauderdale was examining himself in the spattered mirror. He still looked triumphal, his neck rising from his shirt collar so that his head sat on it like a golf ball on its tee.

'A confession, John,' he was saying, 'it's a powerful thing is a confession.'

'Even when the guy's been sleeping rough for nights on end? Strung out on Brasso and hunted by Edinburgh's finest? Confession might be good for the soul, sir, but sometimes all it's worth is a bowl of soup and some hot tea.'

Lauderdale tidied himself, then turned towards Rebus. 'You're just a pessimist, John.'

'Think of all the questions Glass *can't* answer. Ask him some of them. How did Mrs Jack get to Queensferry? How come he dumped her *there*? Just ask him, sir. I'll be interested to read the transcript. I think you'll find the conversation's all one way.'

Exit the Inspector Rebus, leaving behind the Chief Inspector Lauderdale, brushing himself down like a statue examining itself for chips. He seems to find one, too, for he frowns suddenly, and spends longer in the washroom than intended...

'I need just a little bit more, John.'

They were lying in bed together, just the three of them: Rebus. Patience, and Lucky the cat. Rebus affected an American accent.

'I gave ya everything I got, baby.'

Patience smiled, but wasn't to be placated. She thumped her pillows and sat up, drawing her knees up to her chin. 'I mean,' she said, 'I need to know what you're going to do ... what *we're* going to do. I can't decide whether you're moving in with me, or else moving out.'

'In and out,' he said, a final attempt at humour and escape. She punched him on the shoulder. Punched him hard. He sucked in his breath. 'I bruise easily,' he said.

'So do I!' There were almost tears in her eyes, but she wasn't going to give him the satisfaction. 'Is there anybody else?'

He looked surprised. 'No, what makes you think that?'

The cat had crawled up the bed to lie in Patience's lap, plucking at the duvet with its claws. As it settled, she started stroking its head. 'It's just that I keep thinking there's something you're about to tell me. You look as though you're gathering up the strength to say it, but then you never quite manage. I'd rather *know*, whatever it is.'

What was there to know? That he still hadn't made up his mind about moving in? That he still carried if not a flame then at least an unstruck Scottish Bluebell for Gill Templer? What was there to know?

'You know how it is, Patience. A policeman's lot is not a happy one, and all that.'

'Why do you have to get involved?'

'What?'

'In all these bloody cases, why do *you* have to get involved, John? It's just a job like any other. I manage to forget about my patients for a few hours at a stretch, why can't you?'

He gave her just about his only honest answer of the evening. 'I don't know.'

The telephone rang. Patience picked the extension up off the floor and held it between them. 'Yours or mine?' she asked.

'Yours.'

She picked up the receiver. 'Hello? Yes, this is Doctor Aitken. Yes, hello, Mrs Laird. Is he now? Is that right? It isn't maybe just flu?'

Rebus checked his watch. Nine thirty. It was Patience's turn to do standby emergency for her group practice.

'A-ha,' she was saying, 'a-ha,' as the caller talked on. She held the receiver away from her for a second and hurled a silent scream towards the ceiling. 'Okay, Mrs Laird. No, just leave him be. I'll be there as soon as I can. What was your address again?'

At the end of the call, she stomped out of bed and started to dress. 'Mrs Laird's husband says he's on the way out this time,' she said. 'That's the third time in as many months, damn the man.'

'Do you want me to drive you?'

'No, it's all right, I'll go myself.' She paused, came over and pecked him on the cheek. 'But thanks for the offer.'

138

'You're welcome.' Lucky, disturbed from his rest, was now kneading Rebus's half of the duvet. Rebus made to stroke its head, but the cat shied away.

'See you later then,' said Patience, giving him another kiss. 'We'll have a talk, eh?'

'If you like.'

'I like.' And with that she was gone. He could hear her in the living room, getting together her stuff, then the front door opening and closing. The cat had left Rebus and was investigating the warm section of mattress from which Patience had lately risen. Rebus thought about getting up, then thought about not. The phone rang again. Another patient? Well, he wouldn't answer. It kept on ringing. He answered with a non-committal 'Hello'.

'Took your time,' said George Flight. 'Haven't interrupted anything, have I?'

'What have you got, George?'

'Well, I've got the trots, since you ask. I blame it on that curry I had at Gunga's last night. I've also got the information you requested, Inspector.'

'Is that so, Inspector? Well would you mind passing it the hell on!'

Flight snorted. 'That's all the thanks I get, after a hard day's graft.'

'We all know the kind of graft the Met's interested in, George.'

Flight tut-tutted. 'Wires have ears, John. Anyway, the address was a no-show. Yes, a friend of Miss Crawley's lives there. But she hasn't seen her for weeks. Last she heard, Crawley was in Edinburgh.' He pronounced it head-in-burrow.

'Is that it?'

'I tried, asking a couple of sleazebags connected with Croft.'

'Who's Croft?'

Flight sighed. 'The woman who ran the brothel.'

'Oh, right.'

'Only, we've had dealings with her before, you see. Maybe that's why she moved her operation north. So I talked to a couple of her "former associates".'

'And?'

'Nothing. Not even a trade discount on French with spanking.'

'Right. Well, thanks anyway, George.'

'Sorry, John. When are we going to see you down here?'

'When are we going to see you up *here*?'

'No offence, John, but it's all that square sausage and fizzy beer. It doesn't agree with me.'

'I'll let you get back to your smoked salmon and Scotch then. Night, George.'

He put the phone down, and considered for a moment. Then he

got out of bed and started to dress. The cat looked satisfied with this arrangement, and stretched himself out. Rebus searched for paper and a pen and scribbled a note to Patience. 'Lonely without you. Gone for a drive, John.' He thought about adding a few kisses. Yes, a few kisses were definitely in order.

'xxx'

Checking that he had car keys, flat keys and money, he let himself out, locking the door behind him.

If you didn't know, you wouldn't see.

It was a pleasant enough night for a drive, as it happened. The cloud cover kept the air mild, but there was no sign of rain or wind. It wasn't at all a bad night for a drive. Inverleith, then Granton, an easy descent to the coast. Past what had been William Glass's digs . . . then Granton Road . . . then Newhaven. The docks.

If you didn't know, you wouldn't see.

He was a lonely man, just out driving, just out driving slowly. They stepped out of shadowy doorways, or else crossed and recrossed at the traffic lights, like a sodium-lit fashion show. Crossed and recrossed. While drivers slowly drove, and slower yet, and slower. He saw nothing he wanted, so he took the car the length of Salamander Street, then turned it. Oh, he was a keen one. Shy, lonely, quiet and keen. Driving his beaten-up old car around the night-time streets, looking for . . . well, maybe just looking *at*, unless he could be tempted . . .

He stopped the car. She came walking smartly towards him. Not that her clothes were smart. Her clothes were cheap and cheerless, a pale raincoat, one size too big, and beneath it a bright red blouse and a mini-skirt. The mini-skirt, Rebus felt, was her big mistake, since her legs were bare and thinly unattractive. She looked cold; she looked as if she *had* a cold. But she tried him with a smile.

'Get in,' he said.

'Hand-job's fifteen, blow's twenty-five, thirty-five the other.'

Naïve. He could have arrested her on the spot. You never, *never* talked money till you were sure the punter was straight.

'Get in,' he repeated. She had a lot to learn. She got in. Rebus fished out his ID. 'Detective Inspector Rebus. I'd like a word, Gail.'

'You lot never give up, do you?' There was still Cockney in the accent, but she'd been back north long enough for her native Fife to start reasserting itself. A few more weeks, and that final 'you' would be a 'yiz': youse lot nivir gie up, dae yiz . . . ?

She was a slow learner. 'How come you know my name?' she asked at last. 'Were you on that raid? After a freebie, are you, is that it?'

That wasn't it at all. 'I want to talk about Gregor.'

The colour drained from her face, leaving only eye make-up and slick red lipstick. 'Who's he when he's at home?'

'He's your brother. We can talk down the station, or we can talk at your flat, either suits me.' She made a perfunctory attempt at getting out of the car. It only needed a touch of his hand to restrain her.

'The flat then,' she said levelly. 'Just don't be all night about it, eh?'

It was a small room in a flat full of bed-sits. Rebus got the feeling she never brought men back here. There was too much of her about the place; it wasn't anonymous enough. For a start, there was a picture of a baby on the dressing table. Then there were newspaper cuttings pinned to the walls, all of them detailing the fall of Gregor Jack. He tried not to look at them, and instead picked up the photograph.

'Put that down!'

He did so. 'Who is it?'

'If you must know, it's me.' She was sitting on the bed, her two arms stretched out behind her, her mottled legs crossed. The room was cold, but there was no sign of any means of heating it. Clothes spilled from an open chest of drawers, and the floor was littered with bits and pieces of make-up. 'Get on with it then,' she said.

There being nowhere to sit, he stood, keeping his hands in his jacket pockets. 'You know that the only reason your brother was in that brothel was so he could talk to you?'

'Yeah?'

'And that if you'd told this to anyone –'

'Why should I?' she spat. 'Why the fuck should I? I don't owe him no favours!'

'Why not?'

'Why not? Because he's an oily git's why not. Always was. He's got it made, hasn't he? Mum and Dad always liked him better than me ...' Her voice trailed off into silence.

'Is that why you left home?'

'None of your business why I left home.'

'Ever see any old friends?'

'I don't have any "old friends".'

'You came back north. You must have known there was a chance you'd bump into your brother.'

She snorted. 'We don't exactly move in the same circles.'

'No? I thought prostitutes always reckoned MPs and judges were their best clients?'

'They're just johns to me, that's all.'

'How long have you been on the game?'

She folded her arms tight. 'Just sod off, will you?' And there they were again, the not-quite-tears. Twice tonight he'd just failed to reduce a woman to tears. He wanted to go home and have a bath. But where was home?

'Just one more question, Gail.'

'Ms Crawley to you.'

'Just one more question, *Ms* Crawley.'

'Yeah?'

'Someone knew you were working in that brothel. Someone who then told your brother. Any idea who it might be?'

There was a moment's thought. 'Not a clue.'

She was lying, obviously. Rebus nodded towards the clippings. 'Still, you're interested in him, aren't you? You know he came to see you that night because he cares –'

'Don't give me that crap!'

Rebus shrugged. It *was* crap, too. But if he didn't get this woman on to Gregor Jack's side, then he might never find out who was behind this whole ugly thing.

'Suit yourself, Gail. Listen, if you want to talk, I'm at Great London Road police station.' He fished out a card with his name and phone number on it.

'That'll be the day.'

'Well . . .' He headed for the door, a matter of two and a half strides.

'The more trouble that piss-pot's in, the better I'll like it.' But her words had lost their force. It wasn't quite indecision, but perhaps it was a start . . .

9
Within Range

On Monday morning, first findings started filtering down from Duff-town, where the forensic tests of Elizabeth Jack's BMW were under way. Specks of blood found on the driver's-side carpet matched Mrs Jack's type, and there were signs of what might have been a struggle: marks on the dashboard, scuff-marks on the interiors of both front doors, and damage to the radio-cassette, as though it had been hit with the heel of a shoe.

Rebus read the notes in Chief Inspector Lauderdale's office, then handed them back across the desk.

'What do you think?' Lauderdale asked, stifling a Monday morning yawn.

'You know what I think,' said Rebus. 'I think Mrs Jack was murdered in that lay-by, inside her car or outside it. Maybe she tried to run away and was hit from behind. Or maybe her assailant knocked her unconscious first, *then* hit her from behind to make it look like the work of the Dean Bridge murderer. However it happened, I don't think William Glass did it.'

Lauderdale shrugged and rubbed his chin, checking the closeness of the shave. 'He still says he did. You can read the transcripts any time you like. He says he was lying low, knowing we were after him. He needed money for food. He came upon Mrs Jack and hit her over the head.'

'What with?'

'A rock.'

'And what did he do with all her stuff?'

'Threw it into the river.'

'Come on, sir . . .'

'She didn't have any money. That's what made him so angry.'

'He's making it up.'

'Sounds plausible to me –'

'No! With respect, sir, what it sounds like is a quick solution, one that'll please Sir Hugh Ferrie. Doesn't it matter to you that it isn't the truth?'

'Now look here ...' Lauderdale's face was reddening with anger. 'Look here, Inspector, all I've had from you so far is ... well, what is it? It's nothing really, is it? Nothing solid or concrete. Nothing you could hang a shirt on, never mind a case in a court of law. Nothing.'

'How did she get to Queensferry? Who drove her there? What sort of state was she in?'

'For Christ's sake, I *know* it's not cut and dried. There are still gaps –'

'Gaps! You could fit Hampden into them three times over!'

Lauderdale smiled. 'There you go again, John, exaggerating. Why can't you just accept there's less to this than meets your eye?'

'Look, sir ... fine, charge Glass with the Dean Bridge murder, that's okay by me. But let's keep an open mind on Mrs Jack, eh? At least until forensics are finished with the car.'

Lauderdale thought about it.

'Just till they finish the car,' Rebus pressed. He wasn't about to give up: Monday mornings were hell for Lauderdale, and the man would agree to just about anything if it meant getting Rebus out of his office.

'All right, John,' Lauderdale said, 'have it your way. But don't get bogged down in it. Remember, *I'll* keep an open mind if *you* will. Okay?'

'Okay.'

Lauderdale seemed to relax a little. 'Have you seen the Chief Superintendent this morning?' Rebus had not. 'I'm not even sure he's in yet. Maybe he had a heavy weekend, eh?'

'None of our business really, sir.'

Lauderdale stared at him. 'Of course, none of our business. But if the Chief Super's *personal* problems start interfering with his –'

The phone rang. Lauderdale picked up the receiver. 'Yes?' He straightened suddenly in his chair. 'Yes, sir. Was I, sir?' He flipped open his desk diary. 'Oh yes, ten.' He checked his watch. 'Well, I'll be there right away. Yes, sir, sorry about that.' He had the good grace to blush as he put down the receiver.

'The Chief Super?' guessed Rebus. Lauderdale nodded.

'I was supposed to be in a meeting with him five minutes ago. Forgot all about the bloody thing.' Lauderdale got to his feet. 'Plenty to keep you occupied, John?'

'Plenty. I believe DS Holmes has some cars for me to look at.'

'Oh? Thinking of getting rid of that wreck of yours? About time, eh?'

And, this being his idea of wit, Lauderdale actually laughed.

Brian Holmes had cars for him, cars aplenty. Well actually, a Detective Constable seemed to have done the work. Holmes, it appeared, was already learning to delegate. A list of the cars owned and run by friends of the Jacks. Make, registration, and colour. Rebus glanced down it quickly. Oh great, the only possessor of a colour blue was Alice Blake

(The Pack's Sexton Blake), but she lived and worked in London. There were whites, reds, blacks, and a green. Yes, Ronald Steele drove a green Citroën BX. Rebus had seen it parked outside Gregor Jack's house the night Holmes had gone through the bins ... Green? Well, yes, green. He remembered it more as a greeny-blue, a bluey-green. *Keep an open mind.* Okay, it was green. But it was easier to mistake green for blue than, say, red for blue, or white, or black. Wasn't it?

Then there was the question of that particular Wednesday. Everyone had been asked: where were you that morning, that afternoon? Some of the answers were vaguer than others. In fact, Gregor Jack's alibis were more watertight than most. Steele, for example, had been uncertain about the morning. His assistant, Vanessa, had been off work that day, and Steele himself couldn't recall whether or not he'd gone into the shop. There was nothing in his diary to help him remember either. Jamie Kilpatrick had been sleeping off a hangover all day – no visitors, no phone calls – while Julian Kaymer had been 'creating' in his studio. Rab Kinnoul, too, was hesitant; he recalled meetings, but not necessarily the people he'd met. He could check, but it would take time ...

Time, the one thing Rebus didn't have. He, too, needed all the friends he could get. So far, he'd ruled out two suspects: Tom Pond, who was abroad, and Andrew Macmillan, who was in Duthil. Pond was a nuisance. He wasn't back from the States yet. He had been questioned by telephone of course, and he knew all about the tragedy, but he had yet to be fingerprinted.

Anyone who might have been at Deer Lodge had been, or was being, or would be, fingerprinted. Just, so they were reassured, for processes of elimination. Just in case there were any fingerprints left in the lodge, any that couldn't be accounted for. It was painstaking work, this collection and collation of tiny facts and tiny figures. But it was how murder cases worked. Mind you, they worked more easily when there was a distinct scene of crime, a locus. Rebus wasn't in much doubt that Elizabeth Jack had been killed, or as good as, in the lay-by. Had Alec Corbie seen something, something he was holding back? Was there something he might know, without knowing he knew? Maybe something he didn't think was important. What if Liz Jack had said something to Andrew Macmillan, something he didn't realize might be a clue? Christ, Macmillan still didn't know she was *dead*. How would he react were Rebus to tell him? Maybe it would jog his memory. Then again, maybe it would have an altogether different effect. And besides, could anything he said be trusted? Wasn't it possible that he held a grudge against Gregor Jack, the way Gail Crawley did? The way others might, too ...

Who, really, was Gregor Jack? Was he merely a tarnished saint, or was he a bastard? He'd ignored Macmillan's letters; he'd tried to keep his sister from disgracing him; he was embarrassed by his wife. Were his friends really friends? Or were they truly a 'pack'? Wolves ran in packs. Hounds ran in packs. And so did newshounds. Rebus remembered that he'd still to track down Chris Kemp. Maybe he was clutching at straws, but it felt more as if they were clutching at *him* . . .

And speaking of clutch, that was something else to be added to his car's list of woes. There was a worrying whirring and grinding as he pushed the gear-shift from neutral into first. But the car wasn't behaving badly (windscreen wipers aside – they'd begun sticking again). It had taken him north and back without so much as a splutter. All of which worried Rebus even more. It was like a terminal patient's final rally, that last gleam of life before the support machines took over.

Maybe next time he'd take the bus. After all, Chris Kemp's flat was only a quarter of an hour from Great London Road. The harassed-sounding woman on the news desk had given him the address as soon as he asked for it. And he had asked for it only when told that Kemp was on his day off. She'd given him the reporter's home phone number fist, and, recognizing the first three digits as designating a local code, Rebus had asked for the address.

'You could just as easily have looked in the book,' she'd said before ringing off.

'Thank you, too,' he answered to the dead connection.

It was a second-floor flat. He pressed the intercom button beside the main door of the tenement, and waited. And waited. Should have phoned first, John. But then a crackle, and after the crackle: 'Yeah?' The voice groggy. Rebus glanced at his watch. Quarter to two.

'Didn't wake you, did I, Chris?'

'Who is that?'

'John Rebus. Get your breeks on and I'll buy you a pie and a pint.'

A groan. 'What time is it?'

'Nearly two.'

'Christ . . . Never mind the alcohol, I need coffee. There's a shop at the corner. Fetch some milk, will you? I'll put the kettle on.'

'Back in two ticks.'

The intercom crackled into silence. Rebus went and fetched the milk, then buzzed the intercom again. There was a louder buzz from behind the door, and he pushed it open, entering the dim stairwell. By the time he reached the second floor, he was peching and remembering exactly why he liked living in Patience's basement. The door to Kemp's flat was ajar. Another name had been fixed to the door with Sellotape, just below Kemp's own. V. Christie. The girlfriend, Rebus supposed. A bicycle wheel, missing its tyre, rested against the hall wall. So did books, dozens of them, rickety, towering piles of them. He tiptoed past.

'Milkman!' he called.

'In here.'

The living room was at the end of the hall. It was large, but contained almost no space. Kemp, dressed in last week's t-shirt and the week before's denims, ran his fingers through his hair.

'Morning, Inspector. A timely alarm call. I'm supposed to be meeting someone at three o'clock.'

'Hint taken. I was just passing and –'

Kemp threw him a disbelieving glance, then busied himself at the sink, where he was trying his damnedest to get the stains off two mug-rims. The room served as living room and kitchen both. There was a fine old cooking range in the fireplace, but it had become a display case for pot plants and ornamental boxes. The actual cooker was a greasy-looking electrical device sited just next to the sink. On a dining table sat a word processor, boxes of paper, files, and next to the table stood a green metal filing cabinet, four drawers high, its bottom drawer open to show more files. Books, magazines, and newspapers were stacked on most of the available floor space, but there was room for a sofa, one armchair, TV and video, and a hi-fi.

'Cosy,' said Rebus. He actually thought he meant it. But Kemp looked around and made a face.

'I'm supposed to be cleaning this place up today.'

'Good luck.'

Coffee was spooned into the mugs, the milk splashed in after it. The kettle came to the boil and switched itself off, and Kemp poured.

'Sugar?'

'No thanks.' Rebus had settled on the arm of the sofa, as if to say: don't worry, I'm not about to linger. He accepted the mug with a nod. Kemp threw himself on to the armchair and gulped at the coffee, screwing up his face as it burned his mouth and throat.

'Christ,' he gasped.

'Heavy night?'

'Heavy week.'

Rebus wandered over in the direction of the dining table. 'It's a terrible thing, drink.'

'Maybe it is, but I was talking about *work*.'

'Oh. Sorry.' He turned from the table and headed over to the sink . . . the cooker . . . stopping beside the fridge. Kemp had left the carton of milk sitting on top of the fridge, next to the kettle. 'I'd better put this away,' he said, lifting the carton. He opened the fridge. 'Oh, look,' he said, pointing. 'There already *is* milk in the fridge. Looks fresh enough, doesn't it? I needn't have bothered going to the shop.'

He put the new carton of milk in beside the other, slammed shut the door, and returned to the arm of the sofa. Kemp was attempting something like a grin.

'You're sharp for a Monday.'

'But I can be blunt when I need to. What were you hiding from old Uncle Rebus, Chris? Or did you just need the time to check there was nothing *to* hide? A bit of blaw? That sort of thing. Or maybe something else, eh? Some story you're working on ... working on late into the night. Something *I* should know about. How about it?'

'Come on, Inspector. I'm the one who's doing *you* a favour, remember?'

'You'll have to refresh my memory.'

'You wanted me to see what I could find about the brothel story, about how the Sundays knew it was breaking.'

'But you never got back to me, Chris.'

'Well, I've been pressed for time.'

'You still are. Remember, you've got that meeting at three. Better tell me what you know, then I can be on my way.' Now Rebus slid off the arm and on to the sofa proper. He could feel the springs probing at him through what was left of the patterned covering.

'Well,' said Kemp, sitting forward in his chair, 'it looks like there was a kind of mass tip-off. All the papers thought they were getting an exclusive. Then, when they all turned up they knew they'd been had.'

'How do you mean?'

'Well, if there *was* a story, they had to publish. If they didn't, and their rivals did ...'

'Editors would be asking questions about how come they got scooped?'

'Exactly. So whoever set the story up was guaranteed maximum exposure.'

'But who did set it up?'

Kemp shook his head. 'Nobody knows. It was anonymous. A telephone call on the Thursday to all the news desks. Police are going to raid a brothel in Edinburgh on Friday night ... here's the address ... if you're there around midnight, you're guaranteed to bag an MP.'

'The caller said that?'

'Apparently, his exact words were "at least one MP will be inside".'

'But he didn't name any names?'

'He didn't have to. Royalty, MPs, actors and singers – give those papers a sniff of any category and you've got them hooked. I'm probably mixing metaphors there, but you get the gist.'

'Oh yes, Chris, I get the gist. So what do you make of it?'

'Looks like Jack was set up to take a fall. But note, his name wasn't mentioned by the caller.'

'All the same ...'

'Yes, all the same.'

Rebus was thinking furiously. If he hadn't been slouching on the sofa, he might have said he was thinking on his feet. Actually, he was debating with himself. About whether or not to do Gregor Jack a huge favour. Points against: he didn't owe Jack any favours; besides, he should try to remain objective – wasn't that what Lauderdale had been getting at? Points for: one really – he wouldn't just be doing Jack a favour, he might also flush out the rat who'd set Jack up. He made his decision.

'Chris, I want to tell you something . . .'

Kemp caught the whiff of a story. 'Attributable?'

But Rebus shook his head. 'Afraid not.'

'Accurate then?'

'Oh yes, I can guarantee it's accurate.'

'Go on, I'm listening.'

Last chance to bottle out. No, he wasn't going to bottle out. 'I can tell you why Gregor Jack was at that brothel.'

'Yes?'

'But I want to know something first – *are* you holding something back?'

Kemp shrugged. 'I don't think so.'

Rebus still didn't believe him. But then Kemp had no reason to tell Rebus anything. It wasn't as if Rebus was going to tell *him* anything that he didn't want him to know. They sat in silence for half a minute, neither friends nor enemies; more like trench soldiers on a Christmas Day kickabout. At any moment, the sirens might sound and shrapnel pierce the peace. Rebus recalled that he knew *one* thing Kemp wanted to know: how Ronald Steele got his nickname . . .

'So,' Kemp said, 'why *was* he there?'

'Because someone told him him his sister was working there.'

Kemp pursed his lips.

'Working as a prostitute,' Rebus explained. 'Someone phoned him – anonymously – and told him. So he went along.'

'That was stupid.'

'Agreed.'

'And *was* she there?'

'Yes. She calls herself Gail Crawley.'

'How do you spell that?'

'C-r-a-w-l-e-y.'

'And you're sure of this?'

'I'm sure. I've spoken with her. She's still in Edinburgh, still working.'

Kempt kept his voice level, but his eyes were gleaming. 'You know this is a story?'

Rebus shrugged, saying nothing.

'You want me to place it?'

Another shrug.

'Why?'

Rebus stared at the empty mug in his hands. Why? Because once it was public knowledge, the caller would have failed, at least in his or her own terms. And, having failed, maybe they'd feel compelled to try something else. If they did, Rebus would be ready . . .

Kemp was nodding. 'Okay, thanks. I'll think it over.'

Rebus nodded too. He was already regretting the decision to tell Kemp. The man was a reporter, and one with a reputation to make. There was no way of knowing what he'd do with the story. It could be twisted to make Jack sound like samaritan or slime . . .

'Meantime,' Kemp was saying, rising from his chair, 'I better take a bath if I'm going to make that meeting . . .'

'Right.' Rebus rose, too, and placed his mug in the sink. 'Thanks for the coffee.'

'Thanks for the milk.'

The bathroom was on the way to the front door. Rebus made show of looking at his watch. 'Go get into your bath,' he said. 'I'll let myself out.'

'Bye then.'

'See you, Chris.' He walked to the door, checking that his weight on the floorboards did not make them creak, then glanced round and saw that Kemp had disappeared into the bathroom. Water started splashing. Gently, Rebus turned the snib and locked it at the off position. Then he opened the door and slammed it noisily behind him. He stood in the stairwell, pulling the door by its handle so that it couldn't swing back open. There was a spy-hole, but he kept himself tucked in against the wall. Anyway, if Kemp came to the door he'd notice the snib was off . . . A minute passed. Nobody came to the door. More fortuitously, perhaps, nobody came into the stairwell. He didn't fancy explaining what he was doing standing there holding on to a door handle . . .

After two minutes, he crouched down and opened the letter box, peering in. The bathroom door was slightly ajar. The water was still running, but he could hear Kemp humming, then a-ha-hee-ha-ing as he got into the bath. The water continued to run, giving the noise-cover he needed. He opened the door quietly, slipped back indoors, and closed it, jamming it shut with a hardback book from the top of one of the stacks. The remaining books looked as though they might topple, but they steadied again. Rebus exhaled and crept along the corridor, past the door. Taps pouring . . . Kemp still humming. This part was easy; getting back out would be the hard part, *if* he had nothing to show for the deception.

He crossed the living room and studied the desk. The files gave nothing away. No sign of the 'big story' Kemp was working on. The computer disks were marked numerically – no clues there. Nothing interesting in the open drawer of the filing cabinet. He turned back to the desk. No scribbled sheets of notes had been tucked beneath other, blank sheets. He flipped through the pile of LPs beside the stereo, but no sheets had been hidden there either. Under the sofa ... no. Cupboards ... drawers ... no. Bugger it. He went to the great iron range. Tucked away at the back, behind three or four pot plants, sat an ugly-looking trophy, Kemp's Young Journalist of the Year Prize. Along the front of the range sat the row of ornamental boxes. He opened one. It contained a CND badge and a pair of ANC earrings. In another box was a 'Free Nelson Mandela' badge and a ring which looked to be carved out of ivory. The girlfriend's stuff, obviously. And in the third box ... a tiny cellophane package of dope. He smiled. Hardly enough to run someone in for, half a quarter at most. Was this what Kemp had been so eager to conceal? Well, Rebus supposed a conviction wouldn't do the 'campaigning journalist' tag much good. Difficult to chastise public figures for their small vices when you'd been done for possession.

Bugger it. And on top of everything, he'd now to get out of the flat without being seen or heard. The taps had stopped running. No noise to cover his retreat ... He crouched by the range and considered. The bold as brass approach might be best. Just go marching past saying something about having left behind your keys ... Aye, sure, Kemp would fall for *that*. Might as well put five bar on Cowdenbeath for the league and cup double.

He found that, as he thought, he was staring at the range's small oven, or rather at the closed door of that oven. A spider-plant sat above it, with two of its fronds trapped in the door. Dear me, he couldn't have that, could he? So he pulled open the door, releasing the leaves. Sitting in the oven itself were some books. Old hardbacks. He lifted one and examined its spine.

John Knox on predestination. Well, wasn't *that* a coincidence.

The bathroom door flew in.

'Christ's sake!' Chris Kemp, who had been lying with his head floating on the surface of the water, now shot up. Rebus marched over to the toilet, lowered its lid, and made himself comfortable.

'Carry on, Chris. Don't mind me. Just thought I might borrow a few of your books.' He slapped the pile he was holding. They were resting on his knees, all seven of them. 'I like a good read.'

Kemp actually blushed. 'Where's your search warrant?'

Rebus looked stunned. 'Search warrant? Why should I need a search warrant? I'm just borrowing a few books, that's all. Thought I might show them to my old friend Professor Costello. You know Professor Costello, don't you? Only this stuff's right up his street. No reason why you should mind me borrowing them . . . is there? If you like, I'll go get that search warrant and –'

'Fuck off.'

'Language, son,' Rebus reprimanded. 'Don't forget, you're a journalist. You're the protector of our language. Don't go cheapening it. You just cheapen yourself.'

'I thought you wanted me to do you a favour?'

'What? You mean the story about Jack and his sister?' Rebus shrugged. 'I thought *I* was doing *you* a favour. I know keen young reporters who'd give their eye teeth for –'

'What do you want?'

Now Rebus sat forward. 'Where did you get them, Chris?'

'The books?' Kemp ran his hands down his sleek hair. 'They're my girlfriend's. As far as I know, she borrowed them from her university library . . .'

Rebus nodded. 'It's a fair story. I doubt it would get you off the hook, but it's a fair story. For a start, it won't explain why you hid them when you knew I was on my way up to see you.'

'Hid them? I don't know what you're talking about.'

Rebus chuckled. 'Fine, Chris, fine. There I was, thinking I could do you a favour. *Another* favour, I should say . . .'

'What favour?'

Rebus slapped the books again. 'Seeing these get back to their rightful owner without anyone needing to know where they've been in the interim.'

Kemp considered this. 'In exchange for what?'

'Whatever it is you're keeping from me. I *know* you know something, or you think you do. I just want to help you do your duty.'

'My duty?'

'Helping the police. It *is* your duty, Chris.'

'Like it's *your* duty to go creeping around people's flats without their permission.'

Rebus didn't bother replying. He didn't need to reply; he just needed to bide his time. Now that he had the books, he had the reporter in his pocket, too. Safe and snug for future use . . .

Kemp sighed. 'The water's getting cold. Mind if I get out?'

'Any time you like. I'll go wait next door.'

Kemp came into the living room wearing a blue towelling robe and using a matching towel to rub at his hair.

'Tell me about your girlfriend,' Rebus said. Kemp filled the kettle again. He had used the minute's solitary time to do a little thinking, and he was ready now to talk.

'Vanessa?' he said. 'She's a student.'

'A divinity student? With access to Professor Costello's room?'

'*Everybody*'s got access to Prof Costello's room. He told you that himself.'

'But not everyone knows a rare book when they see it . . .'

'Vanessa also works part time in Suey Books.'

'Ah.' Rebus nodded. Pencilling in her prices. Earrings and a bicycle . . .

'Old Costello's a customer, so Vanessa knows him fairly well,' Kemp added.

'Well enough to steal from him, at any rate.'

Chris Kemp sighed. 'Don't ask me why she did it. Was she planning to sell them? I don't know. Did she want to keep them for herself? I don't know. I've asked her, believe me. Maybe she just had a . . . a brainstorm.'

'Yes, maybe.'

'Whatever, she reckoned Costello might not even miss them. Books are books to him. Maybe she thought he'd be as happy with the latest paperback editions . . .'

'But she, presumably, wouldn't be?'

'Look, just take them back, okay? Or keep them for yourself. Anything.'

The kettle clicked off. Rebus refused the offer of more coffee. 'So,' he said, as Kemp made himself a mug, 'what have you got to tell me, Chris?'

'It's just something Vanessa told me about her employer.'

'Ronald Steele?'

'Yes.'

'What about him?'

'He's having an affair with Mrs Rab Kinnoul.'

'Really?'

'Yes. Not your business, you see, Inspector. Nothing to do with law and order.'

'But a juicy story nevertheless, eh?' Rebus found it hard to talk. His head was birling again. New possibilities, new configurations. 'So how did she come to this conclusion?'

'It started a while back. Our entertainment correspondent on the paper had gone to interview *Mr* Kinnoul. But there'd been a cock-up over the dates. He turned up on a Wednesday afternoon when it should have been Thursday. Anyway, Kinnoul wasn't there, but Mrs Kinnoul was, and she had a friend with her, a friend introduced as Ronald Steele.'

'One friend visits another . . . I don't see —'

'But then Vanessa told me something. A couple of Wednesdays back, there was an emergency at the shop. Well, not exactly an *emergency*. Some old dear wanted to sell some of her deceased husband's books. She brought a list to the shop. Vanessa could see there were a few gems in there, but she needed to talk to the boss first. He doesn't trust her when it comes to the buying. Now, Wednesday afternoons are sacrosanct...'

'The weekly round of golf –'

'With Gregor Jack. Yes, precisely. But Vanessa thought, he'll kill me if this lot get away. So she rang the golf club, out at Braidwater.'

'I know it.'

'And they told her that Messrs Steele and Jack had cancelled.'

'Yes?'

'Well, I started to put two and two together. Steele's supposed to be playing golf every Wednesday, yet one Wednesday my colleague finds him out at the Kinnoul house, and another Wednesday there's no sign of him on the golf course. Rab Kinnoul's known to have a temper, Inspector. He's known as a very *possessive* man. Do you think he knows that Steele's visiting his wife when he's not there?'

Rebus's heart was racing. 'You might have a point, Chris. You might have a point.'

'But like I say, it's hardly police business, is it?'

Hardly! It was *absolutely* police business. Two alibis chipped into the same bunker. Was Rebus nearer the end of the course than he'd suspected? Was he playing nine holes rather than eighteen? He got up from the sofa.

'Chris, I've got to be going.' Like spokes on a bicycle wheel, turning in his head: Liz Jack, Gregor Jack, Rab Kinnoul, Cath Kinnoul, Ronald Steele, Ian Urquhart, Helen Greig, Andrew Macmillan, Barney Byars, Louise Patterson-Scott, Julian Kaymer, Jamie Kilpatrick, William Glass. Like spokes on a bicycle wheel.

'Inspector Rebus?'

He paused by the door. 'What?'

Kemp pointed to the sofa. 'Don't forget to take your books with you.'

Rebus stared at them as though seeing them for the first time. 'Right,' he said, heading back towards the sofa. 'By the way,' he said, picking up the bundle, 'I *know* why Steele's called Suey.' Then he winked. 'Remind me to tell you about it some time, when this is all over...'

He returned to the station, intending to share some of what he knew with his superiors. But Brian Holmes stopped him outside the Chief Superintendent's door.

'I wouldn't do that.'

Rebus, his fist raised high, ready to knock, paused. 'Why not?' he asked, every bit as quietly as Holmes himself had spoken.

'Mrs Jack's father's in there.'

Sir Hugh Ferrie! Rebus lowered his hand carefully, then began backing away from the door. The last thing he wanted was to be dragged into a discussion with Ferrie. Why haven't you found ... what are you doing about ... when will you ...? No, life was too short, and the hours too long.

'Thanks, Brian. I owe you one. Who else is in there?'

'Just the Farmer and the Fart.'

'Best leave them to it, eh?' They moved a safe distance from the door. 'That list of cars you made up was pretty comprehensive. Well done.'

'Thanks. Lauderdale never told me exactly what it was –'

'Anything else happening?'

'What? No, quiet as the grave. Oh, Nell thinks she might be pregnant.'

'What?'

Holmes gave a bemused smile. 'We're not sure yet ...'

'Were you ... you know, *expecting* it?'

The smiled stayed. 'Expect the unexpected, as they say.'

Rebus whistled. 'How does she feel about it?'

'I think she's holding back on the feelings till we know one way or the other.'

'What about you?'

'Me? If it's a boy he'll be called Stuart and grow up to be a doctor and a Scottish international.'

Rebus laughed. 'And if it's a girl?'

'Katherine, actress.'

'I'll keep my fingers crossed for you.'

'Thanks. Oh, and another bit of news – Pond's back.'

'Tom Pond?'

'The very one. Back from across the pond. We reached him this morning. I thought I'd go have a talk with him, unless you want to?'

Rebus shook his head. 'He's all yours, Brian, for what he's worth. Right now, he's about the only bugger I think is in the clear. Him and Macmillan and Mr Glass.'

'Have you seen the interview transcript?'

'No.'

'Well, I know you and Chief Inspector Lauderdale don't always get on, but I'll say this for him, he's sharp.'

'A Glass-cutter, you might say?'

Holmes sighed. 'I might, but you always seem to beat me to the pun.'

Edinburgh was surrounded by golf courses catering to every taste and presenting every possible degree of difficulty. There were links courses, where the wind was as likely to blow your ball backwards as forwards. And there were hilly courses, all slope and gully, with greens and flags positioned on this or that handkerchief-sized plateau. The Braidwater course belonged to the latter category. Players made the majority of their shots trusting either to instinct or fortune, since the flag would often be hidden from view behind a rise or the brow of a hill. A cruel course designer would have tucked sand traps just the other side of these obstacles, and indeed a cruel course designer had.

People who didn't know the course often started their round with high hopes of a spot of exercise and fresh air, but finished with high blood pressure and the dire need of a couple of drams. The club house comprised two contrasting sections. There was the original building, old and solid and grey, but to which had been added an oversized extension of breeze block and pebbledash. The old building housed committee rooms, offices and the like, but the bar was in the new building. The club secretary led Rebus into the bar, where he thought one of the committee members might be found.

The bar itself was on the first floor. One wall was all window, looking out over the eighteenth green and beyond to the rolling course itself. On another wall were framed photos, rolls of honour, mock-parchment scrolls and a pair of very old putters looking like emaciated crossbones. The club's trophies – the small trophies – were arrayed on a shelf above the bar. The larger, the more ancient, the more valuable trophies were kept in the committee room in the old building. Rebus knew this because some of them had been stolen three years before, and he'd been one of the investigating officers. They had been recovered, too, though utterly by accident, found lying in an open suitcase by officers called out to a domestic.

The club secretary remembered Rebus though. 'Can't recall the name,' he'd said, 'but I know the face.' He showed Rebus the new alarm system and the toughened glass case the trophies were kept in. Rebus hadn't the heart to tell him that even an amateur burglar could still be in and out of the place in two minutes flat.

'What will you have to drink, Inspector?'

'I'll have a small whisky, if it's no trouble.'

'No trouble at all.'

The bar wasn't exactly busy. A late-afternoon hiatus, as the secretary had explained. Those who played in the afternoon usually liked to get started before three, while those who came for an early evening round arrived around five thirty.

Two men in identical yellow V-neck pullovers sat at a table by the window and stared out in silence, sipping from time to time at identical bloody marys. Two more men sat at the bar, one with a flat-looking half pint of beer, the other with what looked suspiciously like a glass of milk. They were all in their forties, or slightly older; all my contemporaries, thought Rebus.

'Bill here could tell you a few stories, Inspector,' the club secretary said, nodding towards the barman. Bill nodded back, half in greeting, half in agreement. His own V-neck was cherry red, and did nothing to hide his bulging stomach. He didn't look like a professional barman, but took a slow, conspicuous pride in the job. Rebus reckoned him for just another member, doing his stint of duty.

Nobody had twitched at the secretary's mention of 'Inspector'. These men were law-abiding; or, if not, they were certainly law-*abetting*. They believed in law and order and that criminals should be punished. They just didn't think fiddling your tax was a criminal act. They looked ... secure. They thought of themselves as secure. But Rebus knew *he* held the skeleton keys.

'Water, Inspector?' The secretary pushed a jug towards him.

'Thank you.' Rebus adulterated the whisky. The secretary was looking around him, as though surrounded by bodies.

'Hector's not here. I thought he was.'

Bill the Barman chipped in: 'He'll be back in a sec.'

'Gone for the proverbial jimmy,' added the drinker of milk, while Rebus pondered which proverb he meant.

'Ah, here he comes.'

Rebus had imagined a large Hector, curly hair, distended gut, tangerine V-neck. But this man was small and had thinning, Brylcreemed black hair. He, too, was in his forties, and peered at the world through thick-lensed, thick-rimmed glasses. His mouth was set in a defiance at odds with his appearance, and he examined Rebus thoroughly while the introductions were made.

'How do you do?' he said, slipping a small, damp hand into Rebus's paw. It was like shaking hands with a well-brought-up child. His V-neck was camel-coloured but expensive-looking. Cashmere ...?

'Inspector Rebus,' the secretary said, 'is wondering about a particular round which was either played or was not played a couple of Wednesdays ago.'

'Yes.'

'I told him you're the brains of the set-up, Hector.'

'Yes.'

The secretary seemed to be struggling. 'We thought maybe you'd –'

But Hector now had enough information, and had digested it. 'First thing to do,' he said, 'is look at the bookings. They may not tell us the whole story, but they're the place to start. Who was playing?'

The question was directed at Rebus. 'Two players, sir,' he replied. 'A Mr Ronald Steele and a Mr Gregor Jack.'

Hector glanced behind Rebus to where the two drinkers sat at the bar. The room hadn't exactly grown quieter, but there was a palpable change of atmosphere. The drinker of milk spoke first.

'Those two!'

Rebus turned to him. 'Yes, sir, those two. How do you mean?'

But it was Hector's place to answer. 'Messrs Jack and Steele have a regular booking. Mr Jack was an MP, you know.'

'He still is, sir, so far as I know.'

'Not for much longer,' muttered the milk-drinker's companion.

'I'm not aware that Mr Jack has committed any crime.'

'I should think not,' snapped Hector.

'He's still a royal pain in the arse,' commented the milk-drinker.

'How's that, sir?'

'Books and never shows. Him and his cronies.' Rebus became aware that this was a long-festering sore, and that the man's words were directed more towards the club secretary and Hector than towards him. 'Gets away with it, too. Just because he's an MP.'

'Mr Jack has been warned,' Hector said.

'Reprimanded,' corrected the club secretary. The milk-drinker just screwed up his face.

'You kissed his bloody arse and you know it.'

'Now then, Colin,' said Bill the Barman, 'no need to –'

'It's about time *some*body said it out loud!'

'Hear hear,' said the beer-drinker. 'Colin's right.'

An argument wasn't much use to Rebus. 'Do I take it,' he said, 'that Mr Jack and Mr Steele had a regular booking, but then wouldn't turn up?'

'You take it absolutely right,' said Colin.

'Let's not exaggerate or misrepresent,' said Hector quietly. 'Let us deal in facts.'

'Well, sir,' said Rebus, 'while we're dealing in facts, it's a fact that a colleague of mine, Detective Constable Broome, came out here last week to check on whether that particular round of golf had been played. I believe he dealt with *you*, seeing how the club secretary here was ill that day.'

'Remember, Hector,' the secretary interrupted nervously, 'one of my migraines.'

Hector nodded curtly. 'I remember.'

'You weren't exactly honest with DC Broome, were you, sir?' said Rebus. Colin was licking his lips, enjoying the confrontation.

'On the contrary, Inspector,' said Hector. 'I was *scrupulously* honest in answering the detective constable's questions. He just didn't ask the right ones. In fact, he was very sloppy indeed. Took one look at the bookings and seemed satisfied. I recall he was in a hurry ... he had to meet his wife.'

Right, thought Rebus, Broome was for a carpeting then. Even so ...

'Even so, sir, it was your duty –'

'I answered his questions, Inspector. I did not lie.'

'Well then, let's say that you were "economical with the truth".'

Colin snorted. Hector gave him a cold look, but his words were for Rebus. 'He wasn't thorough enough, Inspector. It's as simple as that. I don't expect my patients to help me if I'm not thorough enough in my treatment of them. *You* shouldn't expect *me* to do your work for you.'

'This is a serious criminal case, sir.'

'Then why are we arguing? Ask your questions.'

The barman interrupted. 'Hold on, before you start, *I've* got a question.' He looked at each of them in turn. 'What are you having?'

Bill the Barman poured the drinks. The round was on him, and he totted up the amount and scribbled it into a small notebook kept beside the till. The bloody marys from the window came over to join in. The beer-drinker was introduced to Rebus as David Cassidy – 'No jokes, please. How were my parents supposed to know?' – and the man called Colin was indeed drinking milk – 'ulcer, doctor's orders'.

Hector accepted a thin, delicate glass filled to the lip with dry sherry. He toasted 'our general health'.

'But not the National Health, eh, Hector?' added Colin, going on to explain to Rebus that Hector was a dentist.

'Private,' Cassidy added.

'Which,' Hector retorted, 'is what this club is supposed to be. Private. Members' private business should be none of our concern.'

'Which is why,' Rebus speculated, 'you've been acting as alibi for Jack and Steele?'

Hector merely sighed. '"Alibi" is rather strong, Inspector. As club members, they are allowed to book *and* to cancel at short notice.'

'And that's what happened?'

'Sometimes, yes.'

'But not all the time?'

'They played occasionally.'

'How occasionally?'

'I'd have to check.'

'About once a month,' Barman Bill said. He held on to the glass-towel as if it were a talisman.

'So,' said Rebus, 'three weeks out of four they'd cancel? How did they cancel?'

'By telephone,' said Hector. 'Usually Mr Jack. Always very apologetic. Constituency business ... or Mr Steele was ill ... or, well, there were a number of reasons.'

'Excuses you mean,' Cassidy said.

'Mind you,' said Bill, 'sometimes Gregor'd turn up anyway, wouldn't he?'

Colin conceded that this was so. 'I went a round with him myself one Wednesday when Steele hadn't shown up.'

'So,' said Rebus, 'Mr Jack came to the club more often than Mr Steele?'

There were nods at this. Sometimes he'd cancel, then turn up. He wouldn't play, just sit in the bar. Never the other way round: Steele never turned up without Jack. And on the Wednesday in question, the Wednesday Rebus was interested in?

'It bucketed down,' Colin said. 'Hardly any bugger went out that day, never mind those two.'

'They cancelled then?'

Oh yes, they cancelled. And no, not even Mr Jack had turned up. Not that day, and not since.

The lull was over. Members were coming in, either for a quick one before starting out or for a quick one before heading home. They came over to the little group, shook hands, swopped stories, and the group itself started to fragment, until only Rebus and Hector were left. The dentist laid a hand on Rebus's arm.

'One more thing, Inspector,' he said.

'Yes?'

'I hope you won't think I'm being unsubtle . . .'

'Yes?'

'But you really should get your teeth seen to.'

'So I've been told, sir,' Rebus said. 'So I've been told. Incidentally, I hope you won't think *I'm* being unsubtle . . .?'

'Yes, Inspector?'

Rebus leaned close to the man, the better to hiss into his ear. 'I'm going to try my damnedest to see you on a charge for obstruction.' He placed his empty glass on the bar.

'Cheers then,' said Barman Bill. He took the glass and rinsed it in the machine, then placed it on the plastic dripmat. When he looked up, Hector was still standing where the policeman had left him, his sherry glass rigid in his hand.

'You told me on Friday,' Rebus said, 'that you were jettisoning what you didn't need.'

'Yes.'

'Then I take it you *did* feel you needed the alibi of your golf game?'

'What?'

'Your weekly round with your friend Ronald Steele.'

'What about it?'

'Funny isn't it? *I'm* making the statements and *you're* asking the questions. Should be the other way round.'

'Should it?'

Gregor Jack looked like a war casualty who could still hear and see the battle, no matter how far from the front he was dragged. The

160

newsmen were still outside his gates, while Ian Urquhart and Helen Greig were still inside. The sounds of a printer doing its business came from the distant back office. Urquhart was ensconced in there with Helen. Another day, another press release.

'Do I need a solicitor?' Jack asked now, his eyes dark and sleepless.

'That's entirely up to you, sir. I just want to know why you've lied to us about this round of golf.'

Jack swallowed. There was an empty whisky bottle on the coffee table, and three empty coffee mugs. 'Friendship, Inspector,' he said, 'is . . . it's . . .'

'An excuse? You need more than excuses, sir. What *I* need right now are some facts.' He thought of Hector as he said the word. 'Facts,' he repeated.

But Jack was still mumbling something about friendship. Rebus rose awkwardly from his ill-fitting marshmallow-chair. He stood over the MP. MP? This wasn't an MP. This wasn't *the* Gregor Jack. Where was the confidence, the charisma? Where the voteworthy face and that clear, honest voice? He was like one of those sauces they make on cookery programmes – reduce and reduce and reduce . . .

Rebus reached down and grabbed him by his shoulders. He actually shook him. Jack looked up in surprise. Rebus's voice was cold and sharp like rain.

'Where were you that Wednesday?'

'I was . . . I . . . was . . . nowhere. Nowhere really. Everywhere.'

'Everywhere except where you were supposed to be.'

'I went for a drive.'

'Where?'

'Down the coast. I think I ended up in Eyemouth, one of those fishing villages, somewhere like that. It rained. I walked along the sea front. I walked a lot. Drove back inland. Everywhere and nowhere.' He began to sing. 'You're everywhere and nowhere, baby.' Rebus shook him again and he stopped.

'Did anyone see you? Did you speak to anyone?'

'I went into a pub . . . two pubs. One in Eyemouth, one somewhere else.'

'Why? Where was . . . Suey? What was he up to?'

'Suey.' Jack smiled at the name. 'Good old Suey. Friends, you see, Inspector. Where was he? He was where he always was – with some woman. I'm his cover. If anyone asks, we're out playing golf. And sometimes we are. But the rest of the time, I'm covering for him. Not that I mind. It's quite nice really, having that time to myself. I go off on my own, walking . . . thinking.'

'Who's the woman?'

'What? I don't know. I'm not even sure it's just the one . . .'

'You can't think of any candidates?'

'Who?' Jack blinked. 'You mean Liz? My Liz? No, Inspector, no.' He smiled briefly. 'No.'

'All right, what about Mrs Kinnoul?'

'Gowk?' Now he laughed. 'Gowk and Suey? Maybe when they were fifteen, Inspector, but not now. Have you seen Rab Kinnoul? He's like a mountain. Suey wouldn't dare.'

'Well, maybe Suey will be good enough to tell me.'

'You'll apologize, won't you? Tell him I *had* to tell you.'

'I'd be grateful,' Rebus said stonily, 'if you'd think back on that afternoon. Try to remember where you stopped, the names of the pubs, anyone who *might* remember seeing you. Write it all down.'

'Like a statement.'

'Just to help you remember. It often helps when you write things down.'

'That's true.'

'Meantime, I'm going to have to think about charging you with obstruction.'

'What?'

The door opened. It was Urquhart. He came in and closed it behind him. 'That's that done,' he said.

'Good,' Jack said casually. Urquhart, too, looked like he was just hanging on. His eyes were on Rebus, even when he was speaking to his employer.

'I told Helen to run off a hundred copies.'

'As many as that? Well, whatever you think, Ian.'

Now Urquhart looked towards Gregor Jack. He wants to shake him, too, Rebus thought. But he won't.

'You've got to be strong, Gregor. You've got to *look* strong.'

'You're right, Ian. Yes, look strong.'

Like wet tissue paper, Rebus thought. Like an infestation of woodworm. Like an old person's bones.

Ronald Steele was a hard man to catch. Rebus even went to his home, a bungalow on the edge of Morningside. No sign of life. Rebus went on trying the rest of the day. At the fourth ring of Steele's telephone, an answering machine came into play. At eight o'clock, he stopped trying. What he didn't want was Gregor Jack warning Steele that their story had come apart as its badly stitched seams. Given the means, he'd have kept Steele's answering machine busy all night. But instead his own telephone rang. He was in the Marchmont flat, slumped in his own chair, with nothing to eat or drink, and nothing to take his mind off the case.

He knew who it would be. It would be Patience. She would just be wondering if and when he intended making an appearance. She would just have been worried, that was all. They'd spent a rare weekend together: shopping on Saturday afternoon, a film at night. A drive to Cramond on Sunday, wine and backgammon on Sunday night. Rare . . . He picked up the receiver.

'Rebus.'

'Jesus, you're a hard man to catch.' It was a male voice. It was not Patience. It was Holmes.

'Hello, Brian.'

'I've been trying you for hours. Always engaged or else not answering. You should get an answering machine.'

'I've *got* an answering machine. I just sometimes forget to plug it in. What do you want anyway? Don't tell me, you're telephone-selling as a sideline? How's Nell?'

'As well as can be not expecting.'

'She's negative then?'

'I'm positive she is.'

'Maybe next time, eh?'

'Listen, thanks for the interest, but that's not why I'm calling. I thought you'd want to know. I had a very interesting chat with Mr Pond.'

A.k.a. Tampon, thought Rebus. 'Oh yes?' he said.

'You're not going to believe it . . .' said Brian Holmes. For once, he was right.

10
Brothel Creepers

The way Tom Pond explained it to Rebus, architects were either doomed to failure or else doomed to success. He had no doubt at all that he came into the latter category.

'I know architects my age, guys I went to college with, they've been on the dole for the past half dozen years. Or else they give up and do something sensible like working on a building site or living on a kibbutz. Then there are some of us, for a time we can't put a foot wrong. This prize leads to that contract, and that contract gets noticed by an American corporation, and we start calling ourselves "international". Note, I say "for a time". It can all turn sour. You get in a rut, or the economic situation can't support your new ideas. I'll tell you, the best architectural designs are sitting locked away in drawers – nobody can afford to build the buildings, not yet anyway, maybe not ever. So I'm just enjoying my lucky break. That's all I'm doing.'

It was not *quite* all Tom Pond was doing. He was also crossing the Forth Road Bridge doing something in excess of one hundred miles an hour. Rebus daren't look at the speedo.

'After all,' Pond had explained, 'it's not every day I can go breaking the speed limit with a policeman in the car to explain it away if we get stopped.' And he laughed. Rebus didn't. Rebus didn't say much after they hit the ton.

Tom Pond owned a forty-grand Italian racing job that looked like a kit-car and sounded like a lawnmower. The last time Rebus had been sitting this close to ground level, he'd just slipped on some ice outside his flat.

'I've got three habits, Inspector: fast cars, fast women, and slow horses.' And he laughed again.

'If you don't slow down, son,' Rebus yelled above the engine's whine, 'I'm going to have to book you for speeding myself!'

Pond looked hurt, but eased back on the accelerator. And after all, he *was* doing them all a favour, wasn't he?

'Thank you,' Rebus conceded.

Holmes had told him he wouldn't believe it. Rebus was still trying.

Pond had arrived back the previous day from the States, only to find a message waiting for him on his answering machine.

'It was Mrs Heggarty.'

'Mrs Heggarty being...?'

'She looks after my cottage. I've got a cottage up near Kingussie. Mrs Heggarty goes in now and again to give it a clean and check everything's okay.'

'And this time everything *wasn't?*'

'That's right. At first, she said there'd been a break-in, but then I called her back and from what she said they'd used my spare key to get in. I keep a key under a rock beside the front door. Hadn't made any mess or anything, not really. But Mrs Heggarty knew somebody'd been there and it hadn't been me. Anyway, I happened to mention it to the detective sergeant...'

The detective sergeant whose geography was better than fair. Kingussie wasn't far from Deer Lodge. It certainly wasn't far from Duthil. Holes had asked the obvious question.

'Would Mrs Jack have known about the key?'

'Maybe. Beggar knew about it. I suppose *everybody* knew about it, really.'

All of which Holmes had relayed to Rebus. Rebus had gone to see Pond, their conversation lasting just over half an hour, at the end of which he had announced a wish to see the cottage.

'Be my guest,' Pond had said. And so Rebus was trapped in this narrow metal box, travelling so fast at times that his eyeballs were aching. It was well after midnight, but Pond seemed neither to notice nor to mind. 'I'm still in New York,' he said. 'Brain and body still disconnected. You know, this all sounds incredible, all this stuff about Gregor and Liz and her being found by Gowk. Just incredible.'

Pond had been in the United States for a month; already he was hooked. He was testing out the language, the intonation, even some of the mannerisms. Rebus studied him. Thick, wavy blond hair (dyed? highlighted?) atop a beefy face, the face of someone who had been good-looking in youth. He wasn't tall, but he *seemed* taller than he was. A trick of posture; yes, to a certain extent, but he also had that confidence, that aura Gregor Jack had once possessed. He was firing on all cylinders.

'Can this car take a corner or what? Say what you like about the Italians, they build a mean ice cream and a meaner car.'

Rebus gritted his lower intestine. He was determined to talk seriously with Pond. It was too good a chance to miss, the two of them trapped like this. He tried to talk without his teeth knocking each other out of his mouth.

'So, you've known Mr Jack since school?'

'I know, I know, it's hard to believe, isn't it? I look so much younger than him. But yes, we only lived three streets apart. I think Bilbo lived in the same street as Beggar. Sexton and Mack lived in the same street too. I mean, the same street as one another, not the same as Beggar and Bilbo. Suey and Gowk lived a bit further away, other side of the school from the rest of us.'

'So what drew you all together?'

'I don't know. Funny, I've never really thought about it. I mean, we were all pretty clever, I suppose. Down a gear for this corner ... and ... *like shit off a goddamned shovel*!'

Rebus felt as though his seat was trying to push its way through his body.

'More like a motorbike than a car. What do you think, Inspector?'

'Do you keep in touch with Mack?' Rebus asked at last.

'Oh, you know about Mack? Well ... no, not really. Beggar was the catalyst. I think it was only because I kept in touch with him that I kept in touch with everybody else. But after Mack ... well, when he went into the nuthouse ... no, I don't keep in touch. I think Gowk does. You know, she was the cleverest of the lot of us, and look what happened to her.'

'What did happen to her?'

'She married that spunk-head and started shovelling Valium because it was the only way she could cope.'

'Is her problem common knowledge then?'

He shrugged. 'I only know because I've seen it happen to other people ... other times.'

'Have you tried talking to her?'

'It's her life, Inspector. I've got enough trouble keeping myself together.'

The Pack. What did a pack do when one of its number grew lame or sick? They left it to die, the fittest trotting along at the head...

Pond seemed to sense Rebus's thoughts. 'Sorry if that sounds callous. I was never one for tea and sympathy.'

'Who was?'

'Sexton was always ready with a willing ear. But then she buggered off south. Suey, too, I suppose. You could talk to him. He never had any answers, mind, but he was a good listener.'

Rebus hoped he'd be as good a talker. There were more and more questions to be answered. He decided – how would an American phrase it? – yes, to throw Pond a few curve-balls.

'If Elizabeth Jack had a lover, who would be your guess?'

Pond actually slowed down a little. He thought for a moment. 'Me,' he said at last. 'After all, she'd be stupid to plump for anybody else, wouldn't she?' And he grinned again.

'Second choice?'

'Well, there were rumours . . . there were *always* rumours.'

'Yes?'

'Jesus, you want me to list them? Okay, Barney Byars for a start. Do you know him?'

'I know him.'

'Well, Barney's all right I suppose. Bit screwed up about class, but otherwise he's fine. The two of them were pretty close for a while . . .'

'Who else?'

'Jamie Kilpatrick . . . Julian Kaymer . . . I think that fat bastard Kinnoul even tried his luck. Then she was supposed to have had a fling with that grocer's ex.'

'You mean Louise Patterson-Scott?'

'Can you imagine it? Story was, the morning after a party they were found together in bed. But so what?'

'Anyone else?'

'Probably hundreds.'

'You never . . . ?'

'Me?' Pond shrugged. 'We had a kiss and a cuddle a few times.' He smiled at the memory. 'It could have gone anywhere . . . but it didn't. The thing with Liz was . . . generosity.'

Pond nodded to himself, pleased that he had found the right word, the fitting epitaph.

Here lies Elizabeth Jack.
She gave.

'Can I use your telephone?' Rebus asked.

'Sure.'

He called Patience. He had tried twice before in the course of the evening – no reply. But there was a reply this time. This time, he got her out of bed.

'Where are you?' she asked.

'Heading north.'

'When will I see you?' Her voice had lost all emotion, all interest. Rebus wondered if it was merely a trick of the telephone.

'Tomorrow. Definitely tomorrow.'

'It can't keep on like this, John. Really, it can't.'

He sought for words which would reassure her while not embarrassing him in front of Pond. He sought too long.

'Bye, John.' And the receiver went dead.

They reached Kingussie well before dawn, having met little enough traffic and not a single patrol car. They had brought torches, though these weren't really necessary. The cottage was situated at the far corner of a village, a little off the main road but still receiving a good share of what street-lighting there was. Rebus was surprised to find that the 'cottage' was quite a modern bungalow, surrounded by a high hedge on all four sides, excepting the necessary gates which opened on to a short gravel drive leading up to the house itself.

'When Gregor and Liz got their place,' Pond explained, 'I thought what the hell, only I couldn't bear to rough it the way they do. I wanted something a bit more modern. Less charm, better amenities.'

'Nice neighbours?'

Pond shrugged. 'Hardly ever seen them. The place next door is a holiday home, too. Half the houses in the village are.' He shrugged again.

'What about Mrs Heggarty?'

'Lives the other side of the main drag.'

'So whoever's been living here . . . ?'

'They could have come and gone without anyone noticing, no doubt about that.'

Pond left his headlights on while he opened the front door of the house. Suddenly, hallway and porch were illuminated. Rebus, freed from the cage, was stretching and trying to stop his knees from folding in on him.

'Is that the stone?'

'That's the one,' Pond said. It was a huge pebble-shaped piece of pinkish rock. He lifted it, showing that the spare key was still there. 'Nice of them to leave it when they went. Come on, I'll show you around.'

'Just a second, Mr Pond. Could you try not to touch anything? We might want to check for fingerprints later on.'

Pond smiled. 'Sure, but my prints'll be everywhere anyway.'

'Of course, but all the same . . .'

'Besides, if Mrs Heggarty's tied up after our "guests", the place'll be polished and tidied from ceiling to floor.'

Rebus's heart sank as he followed Pond into the cottage. There was certainly a smell of furniture polish, mingling with air-freshener. In the living room, not a cushion or an executive toy looked to be out of place.

'Looks the same as when I left it,' Pond said.

'You're sure?'

'Pretty sure. I'm not like Liz and her crew, Inspector. I don't go in for parties. I don't mind other people's, but the last thing I want to have to do is clean salmon mousse off the ceiling or explain to the village that the woman with her arse hanging out of a Bentley back window is actually an Hon.'

'You wouldn't be thinking of the Hon. Matilda Merriman?'

'The same. Christ, you know them all, don't you?'

'I've yet to meet the Hon. Matilda actually.'

'Take my advice: defer the moment. Life's too short.'

And the hours too long, thought Rebus. Today's hours had certainly been way too long. The kitchen was neat. Glasses sat sparkling on the draining board.

'Shouldn't think you'll get many prints off them, Inspector.'

'Mrs Heggarty's very thorough, isn't she?'

'Not always so thorough upstairs. Come on, let's see.'

Well, someone had been thorough. The beds in both bedrooms had been made. There were no cups or glasses on display, no newspapers or magazines or unfinished books. Pond made show of sniffing the air.

'No,' he said, 'it's no good. I can't even smell her perfume.'

'Whose?'

'Liz's. She always wore the same brand, I forget what it was. She always smelt beautiful. Beautiful. Do you think she was here?'

'Someone was here. And we think she was in this area.'

'But who was she with – that's what you're wondering?'

Rebus nodded.

'Well, it wasn't me, more's the pity. I was having to make do with call girls. And get this – they want to check your medical certificate before they start.'

'AIDS?'

'AIDS. Okay, finished up here? Beginning to look like a wasted journey, isn't it?'

'Maybe. There's still the bathroom ...'

Pond pushed open the bathroom door and ushered Rebus inside. 'Ah-ha,' he said, 'looks like Mrs Heggarty was running out of time.' He nodded towards where a towel lay in a heap on the floor. 'Usually, that would go straight in the laundry.' The shower curtain had been pulled across the bath. Rebus drew it back. The bath was drained, but one or two long hairs were sticking to the enamel. Rebus was thinking: We can check those. A hair's enough for an ID. Then he noticed the two glasses, sitting together on a corner of the bath. He leaned over and sniffed. White wine. Just a trickle of it left in one glass.

Two glasses! For two people. Two people in the bath and enjoying a drink. 'Your telephone's downstairs, isn't it?'

'That's right.'

'Come on then. This room's out of bounds until further notice. And I'm about to become a forensic scientist's nightmare.'

Sure enough, the person Rebus ended up speaking to on the telephone did not sound pleased.

'We've been working our bums off on that car and that other cottage.'

'I appreciate that, but this could be just as important. It could be *more* important.' Rebus was standing in the small dining room. He couldn't quite tie up these furnishings to Pond's personality. But then he saw a framed photograph of a couple young and in love, captured some time in the 1950s. Then he understood: Pond's parents. The furniture here had once belonged to them. Pond had probably inherited it but decided it didn't go with his fast women/slow horses lifestyle. Perfect, though, for filling the spaces in his holiday home. Pond himself, who had been sitting on a dining chair, rose to his feet. Rebus placed a hand over the receiver.

'Where are you going?'

'For a pee. Don't panic, I'll go out the back.'

'Just don't go upstairs, okay?'

'Fine.'

The voice on the telephone was still complaining. Rebus shivered. He was cold. No, he was tired. Body temperature dropping. 'Look,' he said, 'bugger off back to bed then, but be here first thing in the morning. I'll give you the address. And I *mean* first thing. All right?'

'You're a generous man, Inspector.'

'They'll put it on my gravestone: he gave.'

Pond slept, with Rebus's envious blessing, in the master bedroom, while Rebus himself kept vigil outside the bathroom door. Once bitten ... He didn't want a repetition of the Deer Lodge 'break-in'. This evidence, if evidence it was, would stay intact. So he sat in the upstairs hallway, his back against the bathroom door, a blanket wrapped around him, and dozed. Then he slid down the door, so that he was lying in front of it on the carpet, curled into a foetus. He dreamed that he was drunk ... that he was being driven around in a Bentley. The chauffeur was managing to drive and at the same time stick his backside out of the window. There was a party in the back of the Bentley. Holmes and Nell were there, copulating discreetly and hoping for a boy. Gill Templer was there, and attempting to undo Rebus's zip, but he didn't want Patience to catch them ... Lauderdale seemed to be there, too. Watching, just watching. Someone opened the drinks cabinet, but it was full of books. Rebus picked one out and started to read it. It was the best book he'd ever read. He couldn't put it down. It had everything ...

In the morning, when he awoke, stiff and cold, he couldn't recall a line or a word of the book. He rose and stretched, twisting himself back into human shape. Then he opened the bathroom door and stepped inside, and looked towards where the glasses should be.

The glasses were still there. Rebus, despite his aches, almost smiled.

He stood in the shower for a long time, letting the water trampoline on his head, his chest and his shoulders. Where was he? He was in the Oxford Terrace flat. He should be at work by now, but that could be explained away. He felt rough, but not as rough as he'd feared. Amazingly, he'd been able to sleep on the journey back, a journey taken at a more sedate pace than that of the previous night.

'Clutch trouble,' Pond had said, only twenty miles out of Kingussie. He'd pulled into the side of the road and had a look under the bonnet. There was a lot of engine under the bonnet. 'I wouldn't know where to start looking,' he'd admitted. The trouble with these fancy cars was that capable mechanics were few and far between. In fact, he had to take the car to London for every service. So they'd ambled, an early-morning amble, having left the cottage under the stewardship of a bemused Detective Sergeant Knox and two overworked forensics people.

And Rebus had slept. Not enough, admittedly, which was why he'd resisted the temptation to run a bath and had opted for the shower instead. Difficult to nod off in a shower; all too easy in a hot morning bath. And he had chosen Patience's flat over his own – an easy choice, since Oxford Terrace was the right side of Edinburgh after the drive. They'd had a hellish crossing of the Forth Bridge: commuter traffic crawling citywards. Sales reps in Astras gave the Italian car the once-over, and comforted themselves with the thought that its crew looked like crooks of some kind, pimps or moneylenders . . .

He turned off the shower and towelled himself dry, changed into some clean clothes, and began the process of becoming a human being again. Shaving, brushing his teeth, then a mug of fresh-brewed coffee. Lucky pleaded at a window, and Rebus let the cat in. He even tipped some food into a bowl. The cat looked up at him, full of suspicion. This wasn't the Rebus he knew.

'Just be thankful while it lasts.'

What day was it? It was Tuesday. Over a fortnight since the brothel raid, nearly two weeks since Alec Corbie heard the lay-by argument and saw either two or three cars. There had been progress, most of it thanks to Rebus himself. If only he could shake his superiors' minds free of William Glass . . .

There was a note on the mantelpiece, propped up against the clock: 'Why don't we try meeting some time? Dinner tonight, or else – Patience.' No kisses: always a bad sign. No crosses meant she was cross. She had every right to be. He really had to make up his mind one way or the other. Move in or move out. Stop using the place as a public amenity, somewhere to have a shower, a shave, a shit, and, on occasions, a shag. Was he any better than Liz Jack and her mysterious companion, making use of Tom Pond's cottage? Hell, in some ways he was worse.

Dinner tonight, or else. Meaning, or else I lose Patience. He took the biro out of his pocket and turned the note over.

'If not dinner, then just desserts,' he wrote. Utterly ambiguous, of course, but it sounded clever. He added his name and a row of kisses.

Chris Kemp had his scoop. A front-page scoop at that. The young reporter had worked hard after the visit from John Rebus. He'd tracked down Gail Crawley, a photographer in tow. She hadn't exactly been forthcoming, but there was a photograph of her alongside a slightly blurred picture of a teenage girl: Gail Jack, aged fourteen or so. The story itself was riddled with get-out clauses, just in case it proved to be false. The reader was left more or less to make up his or her own mind. MP's Visit to Mystery Prostitute – His Secret Sister? But the photos were the clincher. They were definitely of the same person, same nose, same eyes and chin. Definitely. The photo of Gail Jack in her youth was a stroke of genius, and Rebus didn't doubt that the genius behind it was Ian Urquhart. How else could Kemp have found, and so quickly found, the photograph he needed? A call to Urquhart, explaining that the story was worth his cooperation. Either Urquhart himself searched out the picture, or else he persuaded Gregor Jack to find it.

It was in the morning edition. By tomorrow, the other papers would have their own versions; they could hardly afford not to. Rebus, having recovered his car from outside Pond's flat, idling at traffic lights had seen the paper-seller's board: Brothel MP Exclusive. He'd crossed the lights, and parked by the roadside, then jogged back to the newspaper booth. Returned to the car and read the story through twice, admiring it as a piece of work. Then he'd started the car again and continued towards his destination. I should have bought two copies, he thought to himself. He won't have seen it yet . . .

The green Citroën BX was in its drive, the garage doors open behind it. As Rebus brought his own car to a halt, blocking the end of the driveway, the garage doors were being pulled to. Rebus got out of the car, the folded newspaper in one hand.

'Looks like I just caught you,' he called.

Ronald Steele turned from the garage. 'What?' He saw the car parked across his driveway. 'Look, would you mind? I'm in a –' Then he recognised Rebus. 'Oh, it's Inspector . . .?'

'Rebus.'

'Rebus, yes. Rasputin's friend.'

Rebus turned his wrist towards Steele. 'Healing nicely,' he said.

'Look, Inspector . . .' Steele glanced at his wristwatch. 'Was it anything important? Only I'm meeting a customer and I've already overslept.'

'Nothing too important, sir,' Rebus said breezily. 'It's just that we've found out your alibi for the Wednesday Mrs Jack died is a pack of lies. Wondered if you'd anything to say to that?'

Steele's face, already long, grew longer. 'Oh.' He looked down at the toes of his well-scuffed shoes. 'I thought it was bound to come out.' He tried a smile. 'Not much you can keep hidden from a murder inquiry, eh?'

'Not much you *should* keep hidden, sir.'

'Do you want me to come down to the station?'

'Maybe later, sir. Just so we can get everything on record. But for the moment your living room would do.'

'Right.' Steele started to walk slowly back towards the bungalow.

'Nice area this,' commented Rebus.

'What? Oh, yes, yes it is.'

'Lived here long?' Rebus wasn't interested in Steele's answers. His only interest was in keeping the man talking. The more he talked, the less time he had in which to think, and the less time he had to think, the better the chances of him coming out with the truth.

'Three years. Before that I had a flat in the Grassmarket.'

'They used to hang people down there, did you know that?'

'Did they? Hard to imagine it these days.'

'Oh, I don't know...'

They were indoors now. Steele pointed to the hall phone. 'Do you mind if I call the customer? Make my apologies?'

'Whatever you like, sir. I'll wait in the living room, if that's all right.'

'Through there.'

'Fine.'

Rebus went into the room but left the door wide open. He heard Steele dialling. It was an old bakelite telephone, the kind with a little drawer in the bottom containing a notepad. People used to want rid of them; now they wanted them back, and were willing to pay. The conversation was short and innocent. An apology and a rescheduling of the meeting. Rebus opened his morning paper wide in front of him and made show of reading the inside pages. The receiver clattered back into its cradle.

'That's that,' said Steele, entering the room. Rebus read on for a moment, then lowered the paper and began to fold it.

'Good,' he said. Steele, as he had hoped, was staring at the paper.

'What's that about Gregor?' he said.

'Hm? Oh, you mean you haven't seen it yet?' Rebus handed over the paper. Steele, still standing, devoured the story. 'What do you reckon, sir?'

He shrugged. 'Christ knows. I suppose it makes sense. I mean, none of us could think *what* Gregor was doing in a place like that. I can't think of a much better reason. The photos certainly look similar ... I don't remember Gail at all. Well, I mean, she was always *around*, but I never paid much attention. She never mixed with us.' He folded the paper. 'So Gregor's off the hook then?'

Rebus shrugged. Steele made to hand the paper back. 'No, no, you can keep it if you like. Now, Mr Steele, about this non-existent golfing fixture . . .'

Steele sat down. It was a pleasant, book-lined room. In fact, it reminded Rebus strongly of another room, a room he'd been in recently . . .

'Gregor would do anything for his friends,' Steele said candidly, 'including the odd telling of a lie. We made up the golf game. Well, that's not strictly true. At first, there *was* a weekly game. But then I started seeing a . . . a lady. On Wednesdays. I explained it to Gregor. He didn't see why we shouldn't just go on telling everyone we were playing golf.' He looked up at Rebus for the first time. 'A jealous husband is involved, Inspector, and an alibi was always welcome.'

Rebus nodded. 'You're being very honest, Mr Steele.'

Steele shrugged. 'I don't want Gregor getting into trouble because of me.'

'And you were with this woman on the Wednesday afternoon in question? The afternoon Mrs Jack died?'

Steele nodded solemnly.

'And will she back you up?'

Steele smiled grimly. 'Not a hope in hell.'

'The husband again?'

'The husband,' Steele acknowledged.

'But he's bound to find out sooner or later, isn't he?' Rebus said. 'So many people seem to know already about you and Mrs Kinnoul.'

Steele twitched, as though a small electric shock had been administered to his shoulder blades. He stared down at the floor, willing it to become a pit he might jump into. Then he sat back.

'How did you . . .?'

'A guess, Mr Steele.'

'A bloody inspired guess. But you say other people . . .?'

'Other people are guessing too. You persuaded Mrs Kinnoul to take up an interest in rare books. It makes a good cover, after all, doesn't it? I mean, if you're ever found there with her. I even notice that she's modelled her library on your own room here.'

'It's not what you think, Inspector.'

'I don't think anything, sir.'

'Cathy just needs someone to listen to her. Rab never has time. The only time he has is for himself. Gowk was the cleverest of the lot of us.'

'Yes, so Mr Pond was telling me.'

'Tom? He's back from the States then?'

Rebus nodded. 'I was with him just this morning . . . at his cottage.'

Rebus waited for a reaction, but Steele's mind was still fixed on Cath Kinnoul. 'It breaks my heart to see her . . . to see what she's . . .'

'She's a friend,' Rebus stated.

'Yes, she is.'

'Well then, she's sure to back up your story; a friend in need and all that . . . ?'

Steele was shaking his head. 'You don't understand, Inspector. Rab Kinnoul is . . . he *can* be . . . a violent man. Mental violence and physical violence. He terrifies her.'

Rebus sighed. 'Then we've only your own word for your whereabouts?'

Steele shrugged. He looked as though he might cry – tears of frustration rather than anything else. He took a deep breath. 'You think I killed Liz?'

'Did you?'

Steele shook his head. 'No.'

'Well then, you've nothing to worry about, have you, sir?'

Steele managed that grim smile again. 'Not a worry in the world,' he said.

Rebus rose to his feet. 'That's the spirit, Mr Steele.' But Ronald Steele looked like there was just about enough spirit left in him to fill a teaspoon. 'All the same, you're not making it easy for yourself . . .'

'Have you spoken to Gregor?' Steele asked.

Rebus nodded.

'Does *he* know about Cathy and me?'

'I couldn't say.' They were both heading for the front door now. 'Would it make any difference if he did?'

'Christ knows. No, maybe not.'

The day was turning sunny. Rebus waited while Steele closed and double locked the door.

'Just one more thing . . . ?'

'Yes, Inspector?'

'Would you mind if I took a look in the boot of your car?'

'What?' Steele stared at Rebus, but saw that the policeman was not about to explain. He sighed. 'Why not?' he said.

Steele unlocked the boot and Rebus peered inside, peered at a pair of mud-crusted wellingtons. There was muck on the floor, too.

'Tell you what, sir,' said Rebus, closing the boot. 'Maybe it'd be best if you came down to the station just now. Sooner we get everything cleared up the better, eh?'

Steele stood up very straight. Two women were walking past, gossiping. 'Am I under arrest, Inspector?'

'I just want to make sure we get *your* side of things, Mr Steele. That's all.'

But Rebus was wondering: Were there *any* forensics people left spare? Or had he tied each and every one of them up already? If so, Steele's car might have to wait. If not, well, here was another little job for them. It really was turning into *Guinness Book of Records* stuff, wasn't it? How many forensic scientists can one detective squeeze into a case?

'What case?'

'I've just told you, sir.'

Lauderdale looked unimpressed. 'You haven't told me *anything* about the murder of Mrs Jack. You've told me about mysterious lovers, alibis for assignations, a whole barrel-load of mixed-up yuppies but not a blind thing about *murder*.' He pointed to the floor. 'I've got someone downstairs who swears he committed both murders.'

'Yes sir,' Rebus said calmly, 'and you've also got a psychiatrist who says Glass could just as easily admit the murders of Gandhi or Rudolf Hess.'

'How do you know that?'

'What?'

'About the psychiatric report?'

'Call it an inspired guess, sir.'

Lauderdale began to look a little dispirited. He licked his lips thoughtfully. 'All right,' he said at last. 'Go through it one more time for me.'

So Rebus went through it one more time. It was like a giant collage to him now: different textures but the same theme. But it was also like a kind of artist's trick: the closer he moved towards it, the further away it seemed. He was just finishing, and Lauderdale was still looking sceptical, when the telephone rang. Lauderdale picked it up, listened and sighed.

'It's for you,' he said, holding the receiver towards Rebus.

'Yes?' Rebus said.

'Woman for you,' explained the switchboard operator. 'Says it's urgent.'

'Put her through.' He waited till the connection was made. 'Rebus here,' he said.

He could hear background noise, announcements. A railway station. Then: 'About bleedin' time. I'm at Waverley. My train goes in forty-five minutes. Get here before it leaves and I'll tell you something.' The line went dead. Short and sour, but intriguing for all that. Rebus checked his watch.

'I've got to go to Waverley Station,' he told Lauderdale. 'Why don't you talk to Steele yourself meantime, sir? See what you make of him?'

'Thank you,' said Lauderdale. 'Maybe I will...'

She was sitting on a bench in the concourse, conspicuous in sunglasses which were supposed to disguise her identity.

'That bastard,' she said, 'putting the papers on to me like that.' She was talking of her brother, Gregor Jack. Rebus didn't say anything. 'One yesterday,' she went on, 'then this morning, half a dozen of the bastards. Picture plastered all over the front pages . . .'

'Maybe it wasn't your brother,' Rebus said.

'What? Who else could it be?' Behind the dark lenses, Rebus could still make out Gail Crawley's tired eyes. She was dressed as though in a hurry – tight jeans, high heels, baggy t-shirt. Her luggage seemed to consist of a large suitcase and two carrier bags. In one hand she clutched her ticket to London, in the other she held a cigarette.

'Maybe,' Rebus suggested, 'it was the person who knew who you were, the person who told Gregor where to find you.'

She shivered. 'That's what I wanted to tell you about. God knows why. I don't owe the bastard any favours . . .'

Nor do I, thought Rebus, yet I always seem to be doing them for him.

'What about a drink?' she suggested.

'Sure,' said Rebus. He picked up her suitcase, while she clip-clopped along carrying the bags. Her shoes made a lot of noise, and attracted glances from some of the men, lolling about. Rebus was quite relieved to reach the safety of the bar, where he bought a half of export for himself and a Bacardi and Coke for her. They found a corner not too near the gaming machine or the frazzled loudspeaker of the jukebox.

'Cheers,' she said, trying to drink and inhale at much the same time. She spluttered and swore, then stubbed out the cigarette, only seconds later to light another.

'Good health,' said Rebus, sipping his own drink. 'So, what was it you wanted to get off your chest?'

She snorted. 'I like that: get off your chest.' This time she remembered to swallow her mouthful of rum before drawing on the cigarette. 'Only,' she said, 'what you were saying, about how somebody might have known who I was . . .'

'Yes?'

'Well, I remembered. It was a night a while back. Like, a couple of months. Six weeks . . . something like that. I hadn't been up here long. Anyway, the usual trio of pissed punters comes in. Funny how they usually come in threes . . .' She paused, snorted. 'If you'll pardon the expression.'

'So three men came to the brothel?'

'Just said so, didn't I? Anyway, one of them liked the look of me, so off we went upstairs. I told him my name was Gail. I can't see the point of all those stupid names everybody else uses – Candy and Mandy and

Claudette and Tina and Suzy and Jasmine and Roberta. I'd just forget who I was supposed to be.'

Rebus glanced at his watch. A little over ten minutes left ... She seemed to understand.

'So, anyway, I asked him if *he* had a name. And he laughed. He said, "You mean you don't recognize the face?" I shook my head, and he said, "Of course, you're a Londoner, aren't you? Well hen," he said, "I'm weel kent up here." Something stupid like that. Then he says, "I'm Gregor Jack." Well, I just started laughing, don't ask me why. He *did* ask me why. So I said, "No, you're not. *I know* Gregor Jack." That seemed to put him off his stroke. In the end, he buggered off back to his pals. All the usual winks and slaps on the back, and I didn't say anything...'

'What did he look like?'

'Big. Like a Highlander. One of the other girls said she thought she *had* seen him on the telly...'

Rab Kinnoul. Rebus described him briefly.

'Sounds about right,' she conceded.

'What about the men who were with him?'

'Didn't pay much attention. One of them was the shy type, tall and skinny like a beanpole. The other was fat and had on a leather jacket.'

'You didn't catch their names?'

'No.'

Well, it didn't matter. Rebus would bet she could pick them out from a line-up. Ronald Steele and Barney Byars. A night out on the town. Byars, Steele, and Rab Kinnoul. A curious little assembly, and another incendiary he could toss in Steele's direction.

'Finish your drink, Gail,' he said. 'Then let's get you on to that train.'

But on the way, he extracted an address from her, the same one she had given before, the one he'd had George Flight check on.

'That's where I'll be,' she said. She took a final look around her. The train was idling, filling with people. Rebus lifted her suitcase in through one of the doors. She was still staring up at the glass roof of the station. Then she lowered her gaze to Rebus. 'I should never have left London, should I? Maybe nothing would have happened if I'd stayed where I was.'

Rebus tilted his head slightly. 'You're not to blame, Gail.' But all the same, he couldn't help feeling that she had a point. *If* she'd stayed away from Edinburgh, *if* she hadn't come out with that "*I know* Gregor Jack" ... who could say? She stepped up on to the train, then turned back towards him.

'If you see Gregor ...' she began. But there wasn't anything else. She shrugged and turned away, carrying her case and her bags with her. Rebus, never one for emotional farewells where prostitutes were concerned, turned briskly on his heels and headed back towards his car.

'You've what?'

'I've let him go.'

'You've let Steele go?' Rebus couldn't believe it. He paced what there was of Lauderdale's floor. 'Why?'

Now Lauderdale smiled coldly. 'What was the charge, John? Be realistic, for Christ's sake.'

'Did you talk to him?'

'Yes.'

'And?'

'He seems very plausible.'

'In other words, you believe him?'

'I think I do, yes.'

'What about his car boot?'

'You mean the mud? He told you himself, John, Mrs Kinnoul and he go for walks. That hillside's hardly what you'd call paved. You need wellies, and wellies get muddy. It's their *purpose*.'

'He admitted he was seeing Cath Kinnoul?'

'He admitted nothing of the sort. He just said there was a "woman".'

'That's all he'd say when *I* brought him in. But he admitted it back in his house.'

'I think it's quite noble of him, trying to protect her.'

'Or could it be that he knows she couldn't back up his story anyway?'

'You mean it's a pack of lies?'

Rebus sighed. 'No, I think *I* believe it, too.'

'Well then.' Lauderdale sounded – for Lauderdale – genuinely gentle. 'Sit down, John. You've had a hard twenty-four hours.'

Rebus sat down. 'I've had a hard twenty-four years.'

Lauderdale smiled. 'Tea?'

'I think some of the Chief Superintendent's coffee would be a better idea.'

Lauderdale laughed. 'Kill or cure, certainly. Now look, you've just admitted yourself that you believe Steele's story –'

'Up to a point.'

Lauderdale accepted the clause. 'But still, the man wanted to leave. How the hell was I going to hold him?'

'On suspicion. We're allowed to hang on to suspects a bit longer than ninety minutes.'

'Thank you, Inspector, I'm aware of that.'

'So now he toddles back home and gives the boot of his car a damned good clean.'

'You need more than mucky wellies for a conviction, John.'

'You'd be surprised what forensics can do . . .'

'Ah, now that's another thing. I hear you've been getting up people's noses faster than a Vick's inhaler.'

179

'Anybody in particular?'

'*Everybody* in the field of forensic science, it seems. Stop hassling them, John.'

'Yes, sir.'

'Take a break. Just for the afternoon, say. What about the Professor's missing tomes?'

'Back with their owner.'

'Oh?' Lauderdale waited for elucidation.

'A turn-up for the books, sir,' Rebus said instead. He stood up. 'Well, if there's nothing else –'

The telephone rang. 'Hold on,' Lauderdale ordered. 'The way things have been going, that'll probably be for you.' He picked up the receiver. 'Lauderdale.' Then he listened. 'I'll be right down,' he said at last, before replacing the receiver. 'Well, well, well. Take a guess who's downstairs.'

'The Dundonald and Dysart Pipe Band?'

'Close. Jeanette Oliphant.'

Rebus frowned. 'I know the name . . .'

'She's Sir Hugh Ferrie's solicitor. And also, it seems, Mr Jack's. They're both down there with her.' Lauderdale had risen from his chair and was straightening his jacket. 'Let's see what they want, eh?'

Gregor Jack wanted to make a statement, a statement regarding his movements on the day his wife was murdered. But the prime mover was Sir Hugh Ferrie; that much was obvious from the start.

'I saw that piece in the paper this morning,' he explained. 'Phoned Gregor to ask if it was true. He says it was. I felt a sight better for knowing it, though I told him he's a bloody fool for not telling anyone sooner.' He turned to Gregor Jack. 'A bloody fool.'

They were seated around a table in one of the conference rooms – Lauderdale's idea. No doubt an interview room wasn't good enough for Sir Hugh Ferrie. Gregor Jack had been smartened up for the occasion: crisp suit, tidied hair, sparkling eyes. Seated, however, between Sir Hugh and Jeanette Oliphant, he was always going to come home third in the projection stakes.

'The point is,' said Jeanette Oliphant, 'Mr Jack told Sir Hugh about something else he'd been keeping secret, namely that his Wednesday round of golf was a concoction.'

'Bloody fool –'

'And,' Oliphant went on, a little more loudly, 'Sir Hugh contacted me. We feel that the sooner Mr Jack makes a statement regarding his genuine actions on the day in question, the less doubt there will be.' Jeanette Oliphant was in her mid-fifties, a tall, elegant, but stern-faced woman. Her mouth was a thin slash of lipstick, her eyes piercing, missing nothing. Her ears stuck out ever so slightly from her short permed hair, as though ready to catch any nuance or ambiguity, any wrong word or overlong pause.

Sir Hugh, on the other hand, was stocky and pugnacious, a man more used to speaking than listening. His hands lay flat against the table top, as though they were attempting to push *through* it.

'Let's get everything sorted out,' he said.

'If that's what Mr Jack wants,' Lauderdale said quietly.

'It's what he wants,' replied Ferrie.

The door opened. It was Detective Sergeant Brian Holmes, carrying a tray of cups. Rebus looked up at him, but Holmes refused to meet his eyes. Not normally a DS's job, playing waiter, but Rebus could just see Holmes waylaying the *real* tea-boy. He wanted to know what was going on. So, it seemed, did Chief Superintendent Watson, who came into the room behind him. Ferrie actually half rose from his chair.

'Ah, Chief Superintendent.' They shook hands. Watson glanced from Lauderdale to Rebus and back, but there was nothing they could tell him, not yet. Holmes, having laid the tray on the table, was lingering.

'Thank you, Sergeant,' said Lauderdale, dismissing him from the room. In the general mêlée, Rebus saw that Gregor Jack was looking at him, looking with his sparkling eyes and his little boy's smile. Here we are again, he was saying. Here we are again.

Watson decided to stay. Another cup would be needed, but then Rebus declined the offer of tea, so there was a cup for Watson after all. It was obvious from his face that he would have preferred coffee, his own coffee. But he accepted the cup from Rebus with a nodded thanks. Then Gregor Jack spoke.

'After Inspector Rebus's last visit, I did some thinking. I was able to recall the names of some of the places I went to that Wednesday ...' He reached into his jacket's inside pocket and drew out a piece of paper. 'I looked in on a bar in Eyemouth itself, but it was packed. I didn't stay. I *did* have a tomato juice at a hotel outside the town, but again the bar there was packed, so I can't be sure anyone will remember me. And I bought chewing gum at a newsagent's in Dunbar on the way down. Apart from that, I'm afraid it's pretty vague.' He handed the list to the Chief Superintendent. 'A walk along the front at Eyemouth ... a stop in a lay-by just north of Berwick ... there was another car in the lay-by, a rep or something, but he seemed more interested in his maps than he did in me ... That's about it.'

Watson nodded, studying the list as though it contained exam questions. Then he handed it on to Lauderdale.

'It's certainly a start,' said Watson.

'The thing is, Chief Superintendent,' said Sir Hugh, 'the boy knows he's in trouble, but it seems to me the only trouble he's in stems from trying to help other people.'

Watson nodded thoughtfully. Rebus stood up. 'If you'll excuse me a moment ...' And he made for the door, closing it behind him with a real sense of escape. He had no intention of returning. There might be a slap on the wrist later from Lauderdale or Watson – bad manners that, John – but no way could he sit in that stifling room with all those stifling people. Holmes was loitering at the far end of the corridor.

'What's up?' he asked when Rebus approached.

'Nothing to get excited about.'

'Oh.' Holmes looked deflated. 'Only we all thought ...'

'You all thought he was coming in to confess? Quite the opposite, Brian.'

'Is Glass going to end up going down for both murders then?'

Rebus shrugged. 'Nothing would surprise me,' he said. Despite his morning shower, he felt grimy and unhealthy.

'Makes it nice and neat, doesn't it?'

'We're the police, Brian, we're not meant to be char ladies.'

'Sorry I spoke.'

Rebus sighed. 'Sorry, Brian. I didn't mean to dust you off.' They stared at one another for a second, then laughed. It wasn't much, but it was better than nothing. 'Right, I'm off to Queensferry.'

'Autograph-hunting?'

'Something like that.'

'Need a chauffeur?'

'Why not. Come on then.'

A snap decision. Rebus was later to think, which probably saved his life.

11

Old School Ties

They managed not to speak about work on the way out to Queensferry. Instead, they spoke about women.

'What about the four of us going out some night?' Brian Holmes suggested at one point.

'I'm not sure Patience and Nell would get on,' Rebus mused.

'What, different personalities, you mean?'

'No, similar personalities. That's the problem.'

Rebus was thinking of tonight's dinner with Patience. Of trying to take time off from the Jack case. Of not making a Jack-ass of himself. Of jacking it all in . . .

'It was only a thought,' said Holmes. 'That's all, only a thought.'

The rain was starting as they neared the Kinnoul house. The sky had been darkening for the duration of the drive, until now, it seemed, evening had come early. Rab Kinnoul's Land-Rover was parked outside the front door. Curiously, the door to the house was open. Rain bounced off the car bonnet, becoming heavier by the second.

'Better make a run for it,' said Rebus. They opened their doors and ran. Rebus, however, was on the right side for the house, while Holmes had to skirt around the car first. So Rebus was first up the steps, and first through the doorway and into the hall. He shook his hair free of water, then opened his eyes.

And saw the carving knife swooping down on him.

And heard the shriek behind it.

'*Bastard!*'

Then someone pushed him sideways. It was Holmes, flying through the doorway. The knife fell into space and kept falling floorwards. Cath Kinnoul fell after it, her weight propelling her. Holmes was on her in an instant, pulling her wrist round, twisting it up against her back. He had his knee firmly on her spine, just below the shoulder blades.

'Christ almighty!' gasped Rebus. 'Jesus Christ almighty.'

Holmes was examining the sprawled figure. 'She took a knock when she fell,' he said. 'She's out cold.' He prised the knife from her grasp and released her arm. It flopped on to the carpet. Holmes stood up. He seemed wonderfully calm, but his face was unnaturally pale. Rebus, meantime, was shaking like a sick mongrel. He rested against the hallway wall and closed his eyes for a moment, breathing deeply. There was a noise at the door.

'Who the –?' Rab Kinnoul saw them, then looked down at the unconscious figure of his wife. 'Oh hell,' he said. He knelt down beside her, dripping rainwater on to her back, her head. He was drenched.

'She's all right, Mr Kinnoul,' Holmes stated. 'Knocked herself out, that's all.'

Kinnoul saw the knife Holmes was holding. 'She had that?' he said, his eyes opening wide. 'Dear God, Cathy.' He touched a trembling hand to her head. 'Cathy, Cathy.'

Rebus had recovered a little. He swallowed. 'She didn't get those bruises from falling though.' Yes, there were bruises on her arms, fresh-looking. Kinnoul nodded.

'We had a bit of a row,' he said. 'She went for me, so I . . . I was just trying to push her away. But she was hysterical. I decided to go for a walk until she calmed down.'

Rebus had been looking at Kinnoul's shoes. They were caked with mud. There were splashes, too, on his trousers. Go for a walk? In *that* rain? No, he'd run for it, pure and simple. He'd turned tail and run . . .

'Doesn't look as though she calmed down,' Rebus said matter of factly. Matter of factly, she had almost murdered him, mistaking him for her husband, or so incensed by then that any man – any victim – would do. 'Tell you what, Mr Kinnoul, I could do with a drink.'

'I'll see what there is,' said Kinnoul, rising to his feet.

Holmes phoned for the doctor. Cath Kinnoul was still unconscious. They'd left her lying in the hall, just to be on the safe side. It was best not to move fall victims anyway; and besides, this way they could keep an eye on her through the open door of the living room.

'She needs treatment,' Rebus said. He was sitting on the sofa, nursing a whisky and what were left of his nerves.

'What she needs,' Kinnoul said quietly, 'is to be away from me. We're useless together, Inspector, but then we're just as useless apart.' He was standing with his hands resting against the window sill, his head against the glass.

'What was the fight about?'

Kinnoul shook his head. 'It seems stupid now. They always start with something petty, and it just builds and builds . . .'

'And this time?'

Kinnoul turned from the window. 'The amount of time I'm spending away from home. She didn't believe there were any "projects". She thinks it'll all just an excuse so I can get out of the house.'

'And is she right?'

'Partly, yes, I suppose. She's a shrewd one ... a bit slow sometimes, but she gets there.'

'And what about evenings.'

'What about them?'

'You don't always, spend *them* at home either, do you? Sometimes you have a night out with friends.'

'Do I?'

'Say, with Barney Byars ... with Ronald Steele.'

Kinnoul stared at Rebus, appearing not to understand, then he snapped his fingers. 'Christ, you mean *that* night. Jesus, the night ...' He shook his head. 'Who told you? Never mind, it must have been one or the other. What about it?'

'I just thought you made an unlikely trio.'

Kinnoul smiled. 'You're right there. I don't know Byars all that well, hardly at all really. But that day he'd been in Edinburgh and he'd sewn up a deal ... a *big* deal. We bumped into each other at the Eyrie. I was in the bar having a drink, drowning my sorrows, and he was on his way up to the restaurant. Somehow I got roped in. Him and the firm he'd done the deal with. After a while ... well, it was good fun.'

'What about Steele?'

'Well ... Barney was planning on taking these guys to a brothel he knew about, but they weren't interested. They went their way, and Barney and me nipped into the Strawman for another drink. That's where we picked up Ronnie. He was a bit pissed, too. Something to do with the lady in his life ...' Kinnoul was thoughtful for a moment. 'Anyway, he's usually a bit of a boring fart, but that night he seemed all right.'

Rebus was wondering: Did Kinnoul know about Steele and Cathy? It didn't look like it, but then the man was an actor, a pro.

'And,' Kinnoul was saying, 'we all ended up going on to the ill-famed house.'

'Did you have a good time?'

Kinnoul seemed to think this an unusual question. 'I suppose so,' he said. 'I can't really remember too clearly.'

Oh, thought Rebus, you can remember clearly enough. You can remember, all right. But now Kinnoul was looking through the hallway at Cathy's still figure.

'You must think I'm a bit of a shite,' he said in a level tone. 'You're probably right. But, Christ ...' The actor had run out of words. He looked around the room, looked out of the window at what, weather willing, would have been the view, then looked towards the door again. He exhaled noisily, then shook his head.

'Did you tell the others what the prostitute told you?'

Now Kinnoul looked startled.

185

'I mean,' said Rebus, 'did you tell them what she said about Gregor Jack?'

'How the hell do you know about that?' Kinnoul fell onto one of the chairs.

'An inspired guess. Did you?'

'I suppose so.' He thought about it. 'Yes, definitely. Well, it was such a strange thing for her to say.'

'A strange thing for you to say, too, Mr Kinnoul.'

Kinnoul shrugged his huge shoulders. 'Just a laugh, Inspector. I was a bit pissed. I thought it would be funny to pretend to be Gregor. To be honest, I was a bit hurt that she didn't recognize Rab Kinnoul. Look at the photos on the wall. I've met all of them.' He was up on his feet again now, studying the pictures of himself, like he was in an art gallery and not seeing them for the thousandth, the ten thousandth time.

'Bog Wagner ... Larry Hagman ... I knew them all once.' The litany continued. 'Martin Scorsese ... the top director, absolutely the top ... John Hurt ... Robbie Coltrane and Eric Idle ...'

Holmes was motioning for Rebus to come into the hall. Cathy Kinnoul was coming round. Rab Kinnoul stood in front of his photographs, his mementoes, the list of names sloshing around in his mouth.

'Take it easy,' Holmes was telling Cathy Kinnoul. 'How do you feel?'

Her speech was slurred to incoherence.

'How many have you taken, Cathy?' Rebus asked. 'Tell us how many?'

She was trying to focus. 'I've checked all the rooms,' Holmes said. 'No sign of any empty bottles.'

'Well, she's taken something.'

'Maybe the doctor will know.'

'Yes, maybe.' Rebus leaned down close to Cathy Kinnoul, his mouth two inches from her ear. 'Gowk,' he said quietly, 'tell me about Suey.'

The names registered with her, but the question seemed not to.

'You and Suey,' Rebus went on. 'Have you been seeing Suey? Just the two of you, eh? Like the old days? Have you and Suey been seeing one another?'

She opened her mouth, paused, then closed it again, and slowly began to shake her head. She mumbled something.

'What was that, Gowk?'

Clearly this time: 'Rab mussn know.'

'He won't know, Gowk. Trust me, he won't know.'

She was sitting up now, holding her head in one hand while the other hand rested on the floor.

'So,' Rebus persisted, 'you and Suey have been seeing one another, eh? Gowk and Suey?'

She smiled drunkenly. 'Gow' an' Suey,' she said, enjoying the words. 'Gow' an' Suey.'

'Remember, Gowk, remember the day before you found the body? Remember that Wednesday, that Wednesday afternoon? Did Suey come and see you? Did he, Gowk? Did Suey pay a visit that Wednesday?'

'Wensay? Wensay?' She was shaking her head. 'Poor Lizzie ... poor, poor ...' Now she held her hand palm upwards. 'Gi' me th' knife,' she said. 'Rab'll never know. Gi' me th' knife.'

Rebus glanced at Holmes. 'We can't let you do that, Gowk. That would be murder.'

She nodded. 'Thas right, murder.' She said the final word very carefully, enunciating each letter, then repeated it. 'Cut off his head,' she said. 'An' they'll put me beside Mack.' She smiled again, the thought pleasing her. And all the time Rab Kinnoul's names were drifting from the other room ...

'... best, absolutely ... like to work with him again. Consummate professionalism ... and good old George Cole, too ... the old school ... yes, the old school ... the old school ...'

'Mack ...' Cathy Kinnoul was saying. 'Mack ... Suey ... Sexton ... Beggar ... Poor Beggar ...'

'The old school.'

Some school ties you just kept too long. Way after they should have been thrown out.

Rebus telephoned Baney Byars. The secretary put him through.

'Inspector,' came Byars' voice, all energy and business, 'I just can't shake you off, can I?'

'You're too easy to catch,' Rebus said.

Byars laughed. 'I've got to be,' he said, 'otherwise the clients can't catch me. I always like to make myself available. Now, what's your beef this time?'

'It's about an evening you spent not so long ago with Rab Kinnoul and Ronald Steele ...'

Byars was able to substantiate the story in all but the most crucial details. Rebus explained about Kinnoul coming downstairs and repeating what Gail had said to him.

'I don't remember that,' Byars said. 'I was well on by then, mind. So well on I think I stumped up for the three of us.' He chuckled. 'Suey had his usual excuse of being flat broke, and Rab was carrying not more than ten bar by then.' Another chuckle. 'See, I always remember my sums, especially when it's money.'

'But you're sure you don't recall Mr Kinnoul telling you what the prostitute told him?'

'I'm not saying he *didn't* say it, mind, but no, I can't for the life of me remember it.'

Which made it Kinnoul's word against Byars' memory. The only thing for it was to talk to Steele again. Rebus could call in on the way to Patience's. It was a long way round for a shortcut, but it shouldn't take too long. Cathy Kinnoul was another problem. It didn't do to have knife-wielding pill-poppers running around at large. The family doctor, summoned by Holmes, had listened to their story and suggested that Mrs Kinnoul be admitted to a hospital on the outskirts of the city. Would there be any criminal charges . . .?

'Of course,' said Holmes testily. 'Attempted murder for starters.'

But Rebus was thinking. He was thinking of how badly Cath Kinnoul had been treated. Thinking, too, of all those obstruction charges he might be filing – Hector, Steele, Jack himself. And, most of all, thinking of Andrew Macmillan. He'd seen what 'special hospitals' did with the criminally insane. Cath Kinnoul would be treated anyway. So long as she underwent treatment, what was the point of pressing a charge of attempted murder on her?

So he shook his head – to Brian Holmes' astonishment. No, no charges, not if she was admitted straight away. The doctor checked that the paperwork would be a mere formality, and Kinnoul, who had come back to something like his senses by this time, agreed to the whole thing.

'In that case,' said the doctor, 'she can be admitted today.'

Rebus made one more call. To Chief Inspector Lauderdale.

'Where the hell did you disappear to?'

'It's a long story, sir.'

'It usually is.'

'How did the meeting go?'

'It went. Listen, John, we're formally charging William Glass.'

'What?'

'The Dean Bridge victim had had intercourse just before she died. Forensics tell me the DNA-test matches our man Glass.' Lauderdale paused, but Rebus said nothing. 'Don't worry, John, we'll start with the Dean Bridge murder. But really, just between us . . . do you think you're getting anywhere?'

'Really, sir, just between us . . . I don't know.'

'Well, you'd better get a move on, otherwise I'm going to charge Glass with Mrs Jack, too. Ferrie and that solicitor are going to start asking awkward questions any minute now. It's on a knife edge, John, understand?'

'Yes, sir, oh yes, I understand all about knife edges, believe me . . .'

Rebus didn't walk up to Ronald Steele's front door – not straight away. First, he stood in front of the garage and peered in through a crack between the two doors. Steele's Citroën was at home, which presumably meant the man himself was at home. Rebus went to the door and pushed the bell. He could hear it sounding in the hall. Halls: he could write a book on them. My night sleeping in a hallway; the day I was almost stabbed in a hallway ... He rang again. It was a loud and unpleasant bell, not the kind you could easily ignore.

So he rang one more time. Then he tried the door. It was locked. He walked on to the little strip of grass running in front of the bungalow and pressed his face against the living room window. The room was empty. Maybe he'd just popped out for a pint of milk ... Rebus tried the gate to the side of the garage, the gate giving access to the back garden. It, too, was locked. He walked back to the front gate and stood beside it, looking up and down the silent street. Then he checked his watch. He could give it five minutes, ten at most. The last thing he felt like was sitting down to dinner with Patience. But he didn't want to lose her either ... Quarter of an hour to get back to Oxford Terrace ... twenty minutes to be on the safe side. Yes, he could still be there by seven thirty. Time enough. *Well, you'd better get a move on.* Why bother? Why not give Glass his moment of infamy, his second – his *famous* – victim?

Why bother with anything? Not for the praise of a pat on the back; not for the rightness of it; maybe, then, from sheer stubbornness. Yes, that would just about fit the bill. Someone was coming ... His car was pointing the wrong way, but he could see in his rearview. Not a man but a woman. Nice legs. Carrying two carrier bags of shopping. She walked well but she was tired. It couldn't be ...? What the ...?

He rolled down his window. 'Hello, Gill.'

Gill Templer stopped, stared, smiled. 'You know, I thought I recognized that heap of junk.'

'Ssh! Cars have feelings, too.' He patted the steering wheel. She put down her bags.

'What are you doing here?'

He nodded towards Steele's house. 'Waiting to talk to someone who isn't going to show.'

'Trust you.'

'Me? I *live* here. Well, next street on the right to be honest. You *knew* I'd moved.'

He shrugged. 'I didn't realize it was round here.'

She gave him an unconvinced smile.

'No, honest,' he said. 'But now I *am* here, can I give you a lift?'

She laughed. 'It's only a hundred yards.'

'Please yourself.'

She looked down at her bags. 'Oh, go on then.'

He opened the door for her and she put the bags down on the floor, squeezing her feet in beside them. Rebus started the car. It spluttered, wheezed, died. He tried again, choke full out. The car gasped, whinnied, then got the general idea.

'Like I said, heap of junk.'

'*That's* why it's behaving like this,' Rebus warned. 'Temperamental, like a thoroughbred horse.'

But the field of an egg-and-spoon race could probably have beaten them over the distance. Finally, they reached the house unscathed. Rebus looked out.

'Nice,' he said. It was a double-fronted affair with bay windows either side of the front door. There were three floors all told, with a small and steep garden dissected by the stone steps which led from gate to doorway.

'I haven't got the whole house, of course. Just the ground floor.'

'Nice all the same.'

'Thanks.' She pushed open the door and manoeuvred her bags out on to the pavement. She gestured towards them. 'Vegetable stir-fry. Interested?'

It took him a moment's eternity to decide. 'Thanks, Gill. I'm tied up tonight.'

She had the grace to look disappointed. 'Maybe another time then.'

'Yes,' said Rebus, as she pushed the passenger door shut. 'Maybe another time.'

The car crawled back along her road. If it gives out on me, he thought, I'll go back and take her up on her offer. It'll be a sign. But the car actually began to sound healthier as it passed Steele's bungalow. There was still no sign of life, so Rebus kept going. He was thinking of a set of weighing scales. On one side sat Gill Templer, on the other Dr Patience Aitken. The scales rose and fell, while Rebus did some hard thinking. Christ, it was hard too. He wished he had more time, but the traffic lights were with him most of the way, and he was back at Patience's by half past.

'I don't believe it,' she said as he walked into the kitchen. 'I really don't believe you actually kept a date.' She was standing beside the microwave. Inside, something was cooking. Rebus pulled her to him and gave her a wet kiss on the lips.

'Patience,' he said, 'I think I love you.'

She pulled back from him a little, the better to look at him. 'And there's not a drop of alcohol in the man either. What a night for surprises. Well, I think I should tell you that I've had a *foul* day and as a result I'm in a *foul* mood ... that's why we're eating chicken.' She smiled and kissed him. ' "I think I love you." ' she mimicked. 'You should have seen the look on your face when you said that. A picture of sheer puzzlement. You're not exactly the last of the red-hot romantics, are you, John Rebus?'

'So teach me,' said Rebus, kissing her again.

'I think,' said Patience ... 'I think we'll have that chicken cold.'

*

He was up early next morning. More unusually, he was up before Patience herself, who lay with a satisfied, debauched look on her sleeping face and with her hair wild around her on the pillow. He let Lucky in and gave him a bigger than normal bowl of food, then made tea and toast for himself and Patience.

'Pinch me, I must be dreaming,' she said when he woke her up. She gulped at the tea, then took a small bite from one buttered triangle. Rebus half refilled his own cup, drained it, and got up from the bed.

'Right,' he said, 'I'm off.'

'What?' She looked at her clock. 'Night shift is it this week?

'It's morning, Patience. And I've a lot on today.' He bent over her to peck her forehead, but she pulled at his tie, tugging him further down so that she could give him a salty, crumbly kiss on the mouth.

'See you later?' she asked.

'Count on it.'

'It would be nice to be able to.' But he was already on his way. Lucky came into the room and leapt on to the bed. The cat was licking his lips.

'Me too, Lucky,' said Patience. 'Me too.'

He drove straight to Ronald Steele's bungalow. The traffic was heavy coming into town, but Rebus was heading out. It wasn't yet quite eight. He didn't take Steele for an early riser. This was a grim anniversary: two weeks to the day since Liz Jack was murdered. Time to get things straight.

Steele's car was still in its garage. Rebus went to the front door and pressed the bell, attempting a jaunty rhythm of rings – a friend, or the postman ... someone you'd want to open your door to.

'Come on, Suey, chop-chop.'

But there was no answer. He peered through the letter box. Nothing. He looked in through the living room window. Exactly as it had been yesterday evening. The curtains hadn't even been pulled shut. No sign of life.

'I hope you haven't done a runner,' Rebus muttered. Though maybe it would be better if he *had*. At least it would be an action of some kind, a sign of fear or of something to hide. He could ask the neighbours if they'd seen anything, but a wall separated Steele's bungalow from theirs. He decided against it. It might only serve to alert Steele to Rebus's interest, an interest strong enough to bring him here at breakfast time. Instead, he got back into the car and drove to Suey Books. A hundred-to-one shot this. As he'd suspected, the shop was barred and meshed and padlocked. Rasputin lay asleep in the window. Rebus made a fist and pounded it against the glass. The cat's head shot up and it let out a sharp, shocked yowl.

'Remember me?' said Rebus, grinning.

191

Traffic was slower now, treacle through the sieve of the road system. He slipped down on to the Cowgate to avoid the worst of it. If Steele couldn't be found, there was only one thing for it. He'd have to change Farmer Watson's mind. What's more, he'd have to do it this morning, while the old boy was bristling with caffeine. Now there was a thought . . . what time did that deli just off Leith Walk open . . .?

'Well thank you, John.'

Rebus shrugged. 'We drink enough of *your* coffee, sir. I just thought it was time someone else did the buying for a change.'

Watson opened the bag and sniffed. 'Mmm, freshly ground.' He started to tip the dark powder into his filter. The machine was already full of water. 'What kind did you say?'

'Breakfast blend, sir, I think. Robustica and Arabica . . . something like that. I'm not exactly an expert . . .'

But Watson waved the apology aside. He put the jug in position and flipped the switch. 'Takes a couple of minutes,' he said, sitting down behind his desk. 'Right, John.' He put his hands together in front of him. 'What can I do for you?'

'Well, sir, it's about Gregor Jack.'

'Yes . . .?'

'You know how you told me we'd to help Mr Jack if possible? How you felt he'd perhaps been set up?' Watson merely nodded. 'Well, sir, I'm close to proving not only that he was, but *who* did it.'

'Oh? Go on.'

So Rebus told his story, the story of a chance meeting in a red-lit bedroom. And of three men. 'What I was wondering was . . . I know you said you couldn't divulge your source, sir . . . but was it one of them?'

Watson shook his head. 'Way off, I'm afraid, John. Mmmm, do you smell that?' The room was filling with the aroma. How could Rebus *not* smell it?

'Yes, sir, very nice. So it wasn't –?'

'It wasn't anyone who *knows* Gregor Jack. If pro –' He stuttered to a halt. 'Can't wait for that coffee,' he said, rather too eagerly.

'You were about to say, sir?' But what? What? Providence? Provost? Prodigal? Problem?

Provost? No, no. Not provost. Protestant? Proprietor? A name or a title.

'Nothing, John, nothing. I wonder if I've any clean cups . . .?'

A name or a title. Professor. *Professor!*

'You weren't about to mention a professor then?'

Watson's lips were sealed. But Rebus was thinking fast now.

'Professor Costello, for instance. He's a friend of yours, isn't he, sir? He doesn't know Mr Jack then?'

Watson's ears were turning red. Got you, thought Rebus. Got you, got you, got you. That coffee was worth every last penny.

'Interesting though,' mused Rebus, 'that the Professor would know about a brothel.'

Watson slapped the desk. 'Enough.' His light morning mood had vanished. His whole face was red now, except for two small white patches, one on either cheek. 'All right,' he said. 'You might as well know, it *was* Professor Costello who told me.'

'And how did the Professor know?'

'He said . . . he *said* he had a *friend* who'd visited the place one night, and now felt ashamed. Of course,' Watson lowered his voice to a hiss, 'there isn't any *friend*. It's the old chap himself. He just can't bring himself to admit it. Well,' his voice rising again, 'we're all tempted some time, aren't we?' Rebus thought of Gill Templer last night. Yes, tempted indeed. 'So I promised the Professor I'd have the place closed down.'

Rebus was thoughtful. 'And did you let him know when Operation Creeper was set for?'

It was Watson's turn to be thoughtful. Then he nodded. 'But he's . . . he's a *professor* . . . of *divinity*. He wouldn't have been the one to tip off the papers. And he doesn't *know* Gregor bloody Jack.'

'But you told him? Date *and* time?'

'More or less.'

'Why? Why did he need to know?'

'His "friend" . . . The "friend" needed to know so he could warn anyone he knew from going there.'

Rebus leapt to his feet. 'Jesus Christ, sir!' He paused. 'With respect. But don't you see? There *was* a friend. There *was* someone who needed to be warned. But not so they could stop their friends being caught . . . so they could *ensure* Gregor Jack walked straight into the trap. As soon as they knew when we were going in, all they had to do was phone Jack and tell him his sister was there. They knew he couldn't *not* go and check it out for himself.' He tugged open the door.

'Where are you off to?'

'To see Professor Costello. Not that I need to, not really, but I want to hear him say the name, I want to hear it for myself. Enjoy your coffee, sir.'

But Watson didn't. It tasted like charred wood. Too bitter, too strong. For some time now he'd been wavering; now he made the decision. He'd stop drinking coffee altogether. It would be his penance. Just like Inspector John Rebus was his comforter . . .

'Good morning, Inspector.'

'Morning, sir. Not disturbing you?'

Professor Costello waved his arm airily around the empty room. 'Not

193

a student in Edinburgh's awake at this – to them – ungodly hour. Not the divinity students at any rate. No, Inspector, you're not disturbing me.'

'You got the books all right, sir?'

Costello pointed towards his glass-fronted bookshelves. 'Safe and sound. The officer who delivered them said something about them being found abandoned...?'

'Something like that, sir.' Rebus glanced back at the door. 'You haven't had a proper lock fitted yet.'

'*Mea culpa*, Inspector. Fear not, one's on its way.'

'Only I wouldn't like you to lose your books again...'

'Point taken, Inspector. Sit down, won't you? Coffee?' The hand this time was directed towards an evil-looking percolator sitting smoking on a hotplate in a corner of the room.

'No thanks, sir. Bit early for me.'

Costello bowed his head slightly. He slid into the comfortable leather chair behind his comfortable oaken desk. Rebus sat on one of the modern, spindly metal-framed chairs the other side of it. 'So, Inspector, social niceties dispensed with ... what can I do for you?'

'You gave some information to Chief Superintendent Watson, sir.'

Costello pursed his lips. 'Confidential information, Inspector.'

'At one time perhaps, but it may help us with a murder inquiry.'

'Surely not!'

Rebus nodded. 'So you see, sir, that changes things slightly. We need to know who your "friend" was, the one who told you about the ... er...'

'I believe the phrase is "hoor-hoose". Almost poetic, much nicer at any rate than "brothel".' Costello almost squirmed in his chair. 'My friend, Inspector, I did promise him...'

'Murder, sir. I'd advise against withholding information.'

'Oh yes, agreed, agreed. But one's conscience...'

'Was it Ronald Steele?'

Costello's eyes opened wide. 'Then you already know.'

'Just an inspired guess, sir. You're a frequent customer in his shop, aren't you?'

'Well, I do like to browse...'

'And you were in his shop when he told you.'

'That's right. It was a lunchtime. Vanessa, his assistant, she was on her break. She's a student here, actually. Lovely girl...'

If only you knew, thought Rebus.

'Anyway, yes, Ronald told me his little guilty secret. He'd been taken to this hoor-hoose one night by some friends. He really was *very* embarrassed about it all.'

'Was he?'

'Oh, terribly. He knew I knew Superintendent Watson, and he wondered if I could pass word on about the establishment.'

'So we could close it down?'

'Yes.'

'But he needed to know the night?'

'He was *desperate* to know. His friends, you see, the ones who'd taken him. He wanted to warn them off.'

'You know Mr Steele is a friend of Gregor Jack's?'

'Who?'

'The MP.'

'I'm sorry, the name doesn't . . . Gregor Jack?' Costello frowned, shook his head. 'No.'

'He's been in all the newspapers.'

'Really?'

Rebus sighed. The real world, it seemed, stopped at the door to Costello's office. This was a lighter realm altogether. He was almost startled by the sudden electronic twittering of the high-tech telephone. Costello apologized and picked up the receiver.

'Yes? Speaking. Yes, he is. Wait one moment, please.' He held the receiver out towards Rebus. 'It's for you, Inspector.' Somehow, Rebus wasn't surprised . . .

'Hello?'

'The Chief Superintendent said I'd find you there.' It was Lauderdale.

'Good morning to you too, sir.'

'Cut the crap, John. I'm just in and already a bit of the ceiling's fallen off and missed my head by inches. I'm not in the mood for it okay?'

'Understood, sir.'

'I'm only phoning because I thought you'd be interested.'

'Yes, sir?'

'Forensics didn't take long with those two glasses you found in Mr Pond's bathroom.'

Of course they didn't. They had all the match-up prints they needed, taken so as to eliminate people from Deer Lodge.

'Guess who they belong to?' Lauderdale asked.

'One set will be Mrs Jack, the other set Ronald Steele.'

There was silence on the other end of the telephone.

'Was I close?' asked Rebus.

'How the hell did you know?'

'What if I told you it was an inspired guess?'

'I'd tell you you're a liar. Get back here. We need to talk.'

'Right you are, sir. Just one more thing . . .?'

'What?'

'Mr Glass . . . is he still on for the double?'

The line went dead.

12

Escort Service

The way Rebus saw it . . .

Well, it didn't take too much brain activity once the name had been established. The way he saw it, Ronald Steele and Elizabeth Jack had been lovers, probably for some time. (Christ, Sir Hugh was going to *love* this when it came out.) Maybe nobody knew. Maybe everybody but Gregor Jack knew. Anyway, Liz Jack decided to head north, and Steele joined her whenever he could. (Deer Lodge and back every day? A superhuman effort. No wonder Steele looked ready to drop all the time . . .) Deer Lodge itself though was a tip, a heap. So they moved into Pond's cottage, only using Deer Lodge itself for fetching changes of clothes. Maybe Liz Jack had been fetching clean clothes when she'd stopped and bought the Sunday rags . . . and found out all about her husband's apparently naughty night.

Steele, though, had plans way above the occasional legover scenario. He wanted Liz. He *wanted* her to himself. The quiet ones always got intense about that sort of thing, didn't they? He'd been making anonymous calls maybe. And sending letters. Anything to throw a spanner in the works of the marriage, anything to unsettle Gregor. Maybe that's why Liz had headed north, to get away from it all. Steele saw his chance. He'd already been to the brothel, and he'd already discovered just who Gail Crawley was. (All it took was a halfway decent memory, and maybe a question or two asked of the likes of Cathy Kinnoul.) Ah, Cathy . . . Yes, maybe Steele *was* seeing her too. But Rebus doubted it was for anything but conversation and counselling. There was that side to Steele, too.

Which didn't do anything to stop him trying to strip Gregor Jack, his lifelong friend, ally in his bookshop, all-round good guy, to strip him completely and utterly naked. The brothel plan was simple and knife-sharp. Find out the time of the planned raid . . . a call to Gregor Jack . . . and calls beforehand to the Docklands dirt-diggers.

The set-up. And Gregor Jack shed his first layer.

Did Steele try to keep it from Liz? Maybe, maybe not. He thought it would be the final screw in the marriage-coffin. It nearly was. But he couldn't be north with her all the time, telling her how great they could be together, what a shit Gregor was, et cetera, et cetera. And during the time she was alone, Liz Jack wavered, until finally she made up her mind not to leave Gregor but to leave Steele. Something like that. She was unpredictable after all. She was fire. And they argued. In his interview, he'd alluded to the argument itself: *She always accused me of not being enough fun . . . and I never had enough money either . . .* So they argued, and he stormed off, leaving her in the lay-by. Alec Corbie's blue car had been a green car, the green Citroën BX. Steele had sped off, only to return and continue the argument, an argument which became violent, violence which went a little too far . . .

The next bit was, to Rebus's mind, the cleverest, either that or the most fortuitous. Steele had to dump the body. The first thing to do was to get it away from the Highlands: there were too many clues up there to the fact that they'd spent time together. So he headed back towards Edinburgh with her in the boot. But what to do with her? Wait, there had been another killing, hadn't there? A body dumped in a river. He could make it look the same. Better still, he could send her body out to sea. So he headed for someplace he knew: the hill above the Kinnoul house. He'd walked up there with Cathy so many times. He knew the small road, a road never used. And he knew that even if the body *were* found, the first suspect would be the Dean Bridge killer. So, at some point, he gave her that blow to the head, the blow so like the one administered to the Dean Bridge victim.

And the beautifully irony was: his alibi for the afternoon was provided by Gregor Jack himself.

'And that's how you see it, is it?'

The meeting was in Watson's office: Watson, Lauderdale and Rebus. On the way in, Rebus had passed Brian Holmes.

'I hear there's a meeting in the Farmhouse.'

'You've got good hearing.'

'What's it about?'

'You mean you're not on the guest list, Brian?' Rebus winked. 'Too bad. I'll try to bring you a doggie-bag.'

'Big of you.'

Rebus turned. 'Look, Brian, the paint's hardly dry on your promotion as it is. Relax, take it easy. If you're looking for a quick road to Detective Inspector, go track down Lord Lucan. Meantime, I'm expected else-where, okay?'

'Okay.'

Too cocky by half, thought Rebus. But speaking of cocky, he was doing a bit of strutting himself, wasn't he? Sitting here in Watson's office, spouting forth, while Lauderdale looked worriedly towards his suddenly caffeine-free superior.

'And that's how you see it, is it?' The question was Watson's. Rebus merely shrugged.

'It sounds plausible,' said Lauderdale. Rebus raised half an eyebrow: having Lauderdale's support was a bit like locking yourself in with a starved alsatian . . .

'What about Mr Glass?' asked Watson.

'Well, sir,' said Lauderdale, shifting a little in his seat, 'psychiatric reports don't show him to be the most stable individual. He lives in a sort of fantasy world, you might say.'

'You mean he made it up?'

'Very probably.'

'Which brings us back to Mr Steele. I think we'd better have him in for a word, hadn't we. Did you say you brought him in yesterday, John?'

'That's right, sir. I thought we might give the boot of his car a once-over. But Mr Lauderdale seemed convinced by Steele's story and let him go.'

The look on Lauderdale's face would remain long in Rebus's memory. Man bites alsatian.

'Is that so?' said Watson, also seeming to enjoy Lauderdale's discomfort.

'We'd no reason to hold him *then*, sir. It's only information received this morning which has allowed us –'

'All right, all right. So have we picked him up again?'

'He's not at home, sir,' said Rebus. 'I checked last night and then again this morning.'

Both men looked at him. Watson's look said: Very efficient. Lauderdale's look said: You bastard.

'Well,' said Watson, 'we'd better get a warrant out, hadn't we? I think there's quite enough that needs explaining by Mr Steele.'

'His car's still in its garage, sir. We could get forensics to take a look at it. Most probably he'll have cleaned it, but you never know . . .'

Forensics? They loved Rebus. He was their patron saint.

'Right you are, John,' said Watson. 'See to it, will you?' He turned to Lauderdale. 'Another cup of coffee? There's plenty in the pot, and you seem to be the only one drinking it . . .'

Strut, strut, strut. He was the little red rooster. He was the cock of the north. He'd felt it all along, of course: Ronald Steele. Suey, who had once tried to commit suicide when found by a girl masturbating in his hotel room.

'Bound to be a bit screwed up.' Who needed a psychology degree? What Rebus needed now was a combination of orienteering skills and old-fashioned man-hunting. His instincts told him that Steele would have headed south, leaving the car behind. (What use was it, after all?

The police already had its description and licence number, and he'd known they were closing in. Or rather, he'd known *Rebus* was closing in.)

'Ain't nothing but a bloodhound,' he sang to himself. He'd just phoned the hospital where Cathy Kinnoul was now a patient. Early days, he'd been told, but she'd had a peaceful night. Rab Kinnoul, however, hadn't been near. Maybe this was understandable. It could be that she'd go for him with a broken water jug or try to strangle him with pyjama cord. All the same, Kinnoul was as shitty as the rest of them. Gregor Jack, too, risking all for a career in politics, a career he'd planned from birth, it seemed. Marrying Liz Ferrie not for herself but for her father. Completely unable to control her, so that he just stuffed her into a compartment, dusting her off for photo-shoots and the occasional public engagement. Yes, shitty. Only one person, to Rebus's mind, came out of this with anything like dignity intact, and that person was a burglar.

The forensics team had come up with a match for the prints on the microwave: Julian Kaymer. He'd swiped Jamie Kilpatrick's keys and driven to Deer Lodge in the dead of night, smashing the window to gain entry.

Why? To tidy away evidence of anything *too* scandalous. Which meant the cocaine-stained hand-mirror and two pairs of tights tied to a four-poster. Why? Simple: to protect what he could of a friend's reputation . . . a dead friend's reputation. Pathetic, but noble, too, in a way. Stealing the microwave was outrageous really. PC Plod was supposed to put the whole thing down to kids, smashing their way into an empty house on the off-chance . . . and making off not with the hi-fi (always a favourite), but with the microwave. He'd driven off with it, then thrown it away, only to have it found by the magpie himself, Alec Corbie.

Yes, Steele would be in London by now. His shop operated in the sphere of cash. There would have been some hidden somewhere; perhaps quite a lot. He might be on a flight out of Heathrow or Gatwick, a train to the coast and the boat over to France.

'Trains and boats and planes . . .'

'Somebody sounds happy.' It was Brian Holmes, standing in the doorway to Rebus's office. Rebus was seated at his desk, feet resting on the desk itself, hands behind his head. 'Mind if I come in, or do we need to reserve tickets to touch your hem?'

'You leave my hem out of this. Sit down.' Holmes was halfway to the chair when he tripped over a gash in the linoleum. He put his hands out to save himself, and found himself sprawled on Rebus's desktop, an inch from one of the shoes.

'Yes,' said Rebus, 'you may kiss them.'

Holmes managed something between a smile and a grimace. 'This place really should be condemned.' He slumped into the chair.

'Mind out for the shoogly leg,' warned Rebus. 'Any progress on Steele?'

'Not much.' Holmes paused. 'None at all, really. Why didn't he take his car?'

'We know it too well, remember? I thought *you* were responsible for putting together that list? Everybody in the world's car make, colour and registration number. Oh no, I forgot, you delegated the work to a detective constable.'

'What was it for anyway?' Rebus stared at him. 'Seriously. I'm just a *sergeant*, as you'll recall. Nobody tells me anything. Lauderdale was vaguer even than usual.'

'Mrs Jack's BMW was parked in a lay-by,' explained Rebus.

'That much I knew.'

'So was another car. An eye witness said it might be blue. It wasn't, it was green.'

'That reminds me,' said Holmes, 'I meant to ask you: what was she waiting around for?'

'Who?'

'Mrs Jack. At that lay-by, what was she hanging around there for?' While Rebus considered this, Holmes thought of another question. 'What about *Mr* Jack's car?'

Rebus sighed. 'What about it?'

'Well, I didn't get a good look at it that night you dragged me out there . . . I mean, it was in the garage, and there were lights to the front and back of the house, but not to the side. But you did say to have a snoop. The side door to the garage was open, so I wandered in. Too dark really, and I couldn't find the light switch . . .'

'Jesus Christ, Brian, get on with it!'

'Well, I was only going to ask: what about the car in Jack's garage? It was blue. At least, I *think* it was blue.'

This time, Rebus rubbed his temples. 'It's white,' he explained, slowly. 'It's a white Saab.'

But Holmes was shaking his head. 'Blue,' he said. 'It could never have been white, it was blue. And it was an Escort, *definitely* an Escort.'

Rebus stopped rubbing his temples. 'What?'

'There was some stuff on the passenger seat, too. I peered in through the side window. All that bumpf they give you with hire cars. That sort of thing. Yes, the more I think back on it, the clearer it comes. A blue Ford Escort. And whatever else was in that garage, there certainly wasn't room to swing a Saab . . .'

No rooster now, no strutting cock, no bloodhound. But rather cowed, sheepish, with his tail between his legs . . . Rebus took Holmes and his story to Watson first, and Watson called for Lauderdale.

'I thought,' Lauderdale said to Rebus, 'you told us Mr Jack's car was *white?*'

'It *is* white, sir.'

'You're sure it was a hire car?' Watson asked Holmes. Holmes thought again before nodding. This was serious. He was where he wanted to be, in the thick of things, but he was realizing, too, that here one mistake – one slightest error – could send him to limbo.

'We can check,' said Rebus.

'How?'

'Phone Gregor Jack's house and ask.'

'And warn him off?'

'We don't have to talk to *Jack*. Ian Urquhart or Helen Greig would know.'

'They could still tip him off.'

'Maybe. Of course, there's another possibility. The car Brian saw could have been Urquhart's or even Miss Greig's.'

'Miss Greig doesn't drive,' said Holmes. 'And Urquhart's car's nothing like the one I saw. Remember, they've all been checked.'

'Well, whatever,' said Watson, 'let's tread carefully, eh? Get on to the hire firms first.'

'What about Steele?' Rebus asked.

'Until we know what we're dealing with, we still want to talk to him.'

'Agreed,' said Lauderdale. He seemed aware that Watson was back in control, at least for now.

'Well,' said Watson, 'what are you all waiting for? Jump to it!'

They jumped.

There weren't that many hire firms in Edinburgh, and the third call brought a result. Yes, Mr Jack had hired a car for a few days. Yes, a blue Ford Escort. Did he give any reason for the hire? Yes, his own car was going in for a service.

And, thought Rebus, he needed a change of cars so he could escape the attentions of the press. Christ, hadn't Rebus put the idea into his head himself? Your car's out there . . . being photographed . . . everyone'll know what it looks like. So Jack had hired another car for a few days, just to help him get around incognito.

Rebus stared at the office wall. Stupid, stupid, stupid. He would have banged his head against the wall if he could have been sure it wouldn't fall down . . .

It had been a devil of a job, the man from the hire firm said. The client had wanted his car-phone transferred from his own car to the hire car.

Of course: how else could Liz Jack have contacted him? He had been on the move all day, hadn't he?

Had the hire car been cleaned since its return? Naturally, a full valet service. What about the boot? The boot? The boot, had it been cleaned too? A bit of a wipe maybe ... Where was the car now? On hire again, a London businessman. A forty-eight-hour hire only, and due back by six o'clock. It was now a quarter to five. Two CID men would be waiting to drive it from the car-hire offices to the police pound. Were there any forensics people available at Fettes HQ ...?

Stupid, stupid, stupid. Not the same car returning to the lay-by, but another car. Holmes had asked the question: what had Liz Jack been waiting for? She'd been waiting for her husband. She must have telephoned him from the box in the lay-by. She'd just had the argument with Steele. Too upset to drive herself home maybe. So he'd told her to wait there and he'd pick her up. He had a free afternoon anyway. He'd pick her up in the blue Escort. But when he'd arrived there had been another argument. About what? It could have been anything. What would it take to smash the ice that was Gregor Jack? The original newspaper story? The police finding evidence of his wife's lifestyle? Shame and embarrassment? The thought of further public scrutiny, of losing his precious constituency?

There was enough there to be going on with.

'Okay,' said Lauderdale, 'so we've got the car. Let's see if Jack's at home.' He turned to Rebus. 'You phone, John.'

Rebus phoned. Helen Greig answered.

'Hello, Miss Greig. It's Inspector Rebus.'

'He's not here,' she blurted out. 'I haven't seen him all day, or yesterday come to that.'

'But he's not in London?'

'We don't know where he is. He was with you yesterday morning, wasn't he?'

'He came into the station, yes.'

'Ian's going up the wall.'

'What about the Saab?'

'It's not here either. Hold on ...' She placed her hand over the mouthpiece, but not very effectively. 'It's that Inspector Rebus,' he heard her say. Then a frantic hiss: 'Don't tell him anything!' And Helen again: 'Too late, Ian.' Followed by a sort of snarl. She removed her hand.

'Miss Greig,' said Rebus, 'how has Gregor seemed?'

'Same as you might expect of a man whose wife's been murdered.'

'And how's that?'

'Depressed. He's been sitting around in the living room, just staring into space, not saying much. Like he was thinking. Funny, the only time I got a conversation out of him was when he asked me about last year's holiday.'

'The one you went on with your mum?'

'Yes.'

'Remind me, where did you go again?'

'Down the coast,' she said. 'Eyemouth, round there.'

Yes, of course. Jack had uttered the name of the first town that had come to mind. Then he'd pumped Helen for details so he could prop up his rickety story...

He put down the receiver.

'Well?' asked Watson.

'His car's gone, and Gregor Jack with it. All that stuff he told us about Eyemouth ... eye *wash* more like ... he got it all from his secretary. She went there on holiday last year.'

The room was stuffy, the late afternoon outside preparing itself for thunder. Watson spoke first.

'What a mess.'

'Yes,' said Lauderdale.

Holmes nodded. He was a relieved man; more than that, inwardly he was rejoicing: the hire car had turned out to be fact. He'd proved his worth.

'What now?'

'I'm just thinking,' said Rebus, 'about that lay-by. Liz Jack has an argument with Steele. She tells him she's going back to her husband. Steele buggers off. What's the next he hears of her?'

'That she's dead,' answered Holmes.

Rebus nodded. Throwing all those books around the shop in his grief and his anger ... 'Not only dead, but murdered. And the *last* he saw of her, she was waiting for Gregor.'

'So,' said Watson, 'he must know Jack did it? Is that what you're suggesting?'

'You think,' Lauderdale said, 'Steele's run off to *protect* Gregor Jack?'

'I don't think anything of the sort,' said Rebus. 'But *if* Gregor Jack is the murderer, then Ronald Steele has known for some time that he is. Why hasn't he done anything? Think about it: how could he come to the police? He was in way too deep himself. It would mean explaining everything, and explaining it would make him if anything a bigger suspect than Gregor Jack himself!'

'So what *would* he do?'

Rebus shrugged. 'He might try persuading Jack to come forward.'

'But that would mean admitting to Jack that –'

'Exactly, that *he* was Elizabeth Jack's lover. What would you do in Jack's position?'

Holmes dared to supply the answer. 'I'd kill him. I'd kill Ronald Steele.'

Rebus sat all that evening in Patience's living room, an arm around her as they both watched a video. A romantic comedy; only there wasn't much romance and precious little comedy. You knew from reel one that the secretary would go off with the bucktoothed student and not with her bloodsucking boss. But you kept on watching anyway. Not that he was taking much of it in. He was thinking about Gregor Jack, about the person he'd seemed to be and the person he really was. You peeled away layer after layer, stripped the man to the bone and beyond . . . and never found the truth. Strip Jack Naked: a card game, also known as Beggar My Neighbour. Patience was a card game, too. He stroked her neck, her hair, her forehead.

'That's nice.'

Patience was a game easily won.

The film rolled past him. Another foil had entered the picture, a big-hearted con man. Rebus had yet to meet a con man in real life who was anything but the most predatory shark. What was the phrase? – they'd steel your false teeth and drink the water out of the glass. Well, maybe *this* con man was in with a chance. The secretary was interested, but she was loyal to her boss too, and *he* was doing everything short of whipping his sausage out and slapping it on her desk . . .

'A penny for them.'

'They're not worth it, Patience.' They'd find Steele, they'd find Jack. Why couldn't he relax? He kept thinking of a set of clothes and a note, left on a beach. Stonehouse. Lucan had done it, hadn't he, disappeared without trace? It wasn't easy, but all the same . . .

The next thing he knew, Patience was shaking him by the shoulder.

'Wake up, John. Time for bed.'

He'd been asleep for an hour. 'The con man or the student?' he asked.

'Neither,' she said. 'The boss changed his ways and gave her a part-nership in the firm. Now come on, partner . . .' She held her hands out to help him up on to his feet. 'After all, tomorrow *is* another day . . .'

Another day, another dolour. Thursday. Two weeks since they'd found Elizabeth Jack's body. Now all they could do was wait . . . and hope no more bodies turned up. Rebus picked up his office phone. It was Lauderdale.

'The Chief Super's bitten the bullet,' he told Rebus. 'We're holding a press conference, putting out wanteds on both of them, Steele and Jack.'

'Does Sir Hugh know yet?'

'I wouldn't want to be the one who tells him. He marches in here with his son-in-law, not knowing the bugger killed his daughter? No, I wouldn't want to be the one who tells him.'

'Am I supposed to be there?'

'Of course, and bring Holmes, too. After all, *he's* the one who spotted the car . . .'

The line went dead. Rebus stared at the receiver. Alsatian bites man after all . . .

*

Spotted it *and* told Nell about it all last night. Repeating the story, adding missed details, hardly able to sit down. Until she'd screeched at him to stop or else she'd go off her head. That calmed him down a little, but not much.

'You see, Nell, if they'd told me earlier, if they'd let me in on the whole story of the car colours, of *why* they were needed, well, we'd have nailed him all the sooner, wouldn't we? I don't want to, but really I blame John. It was him who . . .'

'I thought you said it was Lauderdale who gave you the job in the first place?'

'Yes, true, but even so John should have –'

'Shut up! For God's sake, just shut up!'

'Mind you, you're right, Laud –'

'*Shut up!*'

He shut up.

And now here he was at the press conference, and there was Inspector Gill Templer, who had such a rapport with the press, handing out sheets of paper – the official release – and generally making sure that everyone knew what was going on. And Rebus, of course, looking the same as ever. Which was to say, tired and suspicious. Watson and Lauderdale hadn't made their entrance yet, but would do so soon.

'Well, Brian,' said Rebus quietly, 'reckon they'll promote you to Inspector for this?'

'No.'

'What then? You look like a kid who's about to get the school prize.'

'Come on, be fair. We all know you did most of the work.'

'Yes, but *you* stopped me haring after the wrong man.'

'So?'

'So now I owe you a favour.' Rebus grinned. 'I *hate* owing favours.'

'Ladies and gentlemen,' came Gill Templer's voice, 'if you'll find yourselves a seat we can start . . .'

A moment later Watson and Lauderdale entered the room. Watson was first to speak.

'I think you all know why we've called this conference.' He paused. 'We're looking for two men we think may be able to help us with a certain inquiry, a murder inquiry. The names are Ronald Adam Steele and Gregor Gordon Jack . . .'

The local evening paper had it in by its lunchtime edition. The radio stations were broadcasting the names in their hourly news slots. The early evening TV news carried the story. The usual questions were being asked, to which the usual 'no comment's were being appended. But the phone call itself came only at half past six. The call was from Dr Frank Forster.

'I'd have known sooner, Inspector, only we don't like to let the patients listen to the news. It just upsets them. It's only when I was getting ready to go home that I turned on the radio in my office . . .'

Rebus was tired. Rebus was terribly, terribly tired. 'What is it, Dr Forster?'

'It's your man Jack, Gregor Jack. He was here this afternoon. He was visiting Andrew Macmillan.'

13

Hot-Head

It was nine that evening when Rebus reached Duthil Hospital. Andrew Macmillan was sitting in Forster's office, arms folded, waiting.

'Hello again,' he said.

'Hello, Mr Macmillan.'

There were five of them: two 'nurses', Dr Forster, Macmillan and Rebus. The nurses stood behind Macmillan's chair, their bodies less than two inches from his.

'We've sedated him,' Forster had explained to Rebus. 'He may not be as talkative as usual, but he should stay calm. I heard about what happened last time ...'

'Nothing happened last time, Dr Forster. He just wanted to have a normal conversation. What's wrong with that?'

Macmillan looked on the verge of sleep. His eyes were heavy-lidded, his smile fixed. He unfolded his arms and rested the hands delicately on his knees, reminding Rebus at that moment of Mrs Corbie ...

'Inspector Rebus wants to ask you about Mr Jack,' explained Forster.

'That's right,' said Rebus, resting against the edge of the desk. There was a chair for him, but he was stiff after the drive. 'I was wondering why he visited. It's unusual after all, isn't it?'

'It's a first,' corrected Macmillan. 'They should put up a plaque. When I saw him come in, I thought he must be here to open an extension or something. But no, he just walked right up to me ...' His hands were moving now, carving air, his eyes held by the movements they made. 'Walked right up to *me*, and he said ... he said, "Hello, Mack." Just like that. Like we'd seen one another the day before, like we saw one another *every* day.'

'What did you talk about?'

'Old friends. Yes, old friends ... old friend*ships*. We'd always be friends, he told me. We couldn't *not* be friends. We went back *all the way*. Yes, all the way back ... All of us. Suey and Gowk, Beggar and me, Bilbo, Tampon, Sexton Blake ... Friends are important, that's what he said. I told him about Gowk, about how she visited sometimes ... about the money she gives this place ... He didn't know about any of that. He was interested. He works too hard though, you can see that. He doesn't look healthy any more. Not enough sunlight. Have you ever seen the House of Commons? Hardly any windows. They work away in there like moles ...'

'Did he say anything else?'

'I asked him why he never answered my letters. Do you know what he said? He said he *never even received them!* He said he'd take it up with the post office, but I know who it is.' He turned to Forster. 'It's you, Dr Forster. You're not letting out any of my mail. You're steaming off the stamps and using them for yourself! Well, be warned, Gregor Jack MP knows all about it now. Something'll be done now.' He remembered something and turned quickly to Rebus. 'Did you touch the earth for me?'

Rebus nodded. 'I touched the earth for you.'

Macmillan nodded too, satisfied. 'How did it feel, Inspector?'

'It felt fine. Funny, it's something I've always taken for granted –'

'Never take *anything* for granted, Inspector,' said Macmillan. He was calming a little. All the same, you could see him fighting against the soporifics in his bloodstream, fighting for the right to get angry, to get ... to get mad. 'I asked him about Liz,' he said. 'He told me she's the same as ever. But I didn't believe *that.* I'm sure their marriage is in trouble. In-com-pat-ible. My wife and I were just the same ...' His voice trailed off. He swallowed, laid his hands flat against his knees again and studied them. 'Liz was never one of The Pack. He should have married Gowk, only Kinnoul got to her first.' He looked up. 'Now *there's* a man who needs treatment. If Gowk knew what she was about, she'd have him see a psychiatrist. All those roles he's played ... bound to have an effect, aren't they? I'll tell Gowk next time I see her. I haven't seen her for a while ...'

Rebus shifted his weight a little. 'Did Beggar say anything else, Mack? Anything about where he was headed or why he was here?'

Macmillan shook his head. Then he sniggered. 'Headed, did you say? *Headed?*' He chuckled to himself for a few moments, then stopped as abruptly as he'd started. 'He just wanted to let me know we were friends.' He laughed quietly. 'As if I needed reminding. And one other thing. Guess what he wanted to know? Guess what he asked? After all these years ...'

'What?'

'He wanted to know what I'd done with her head.'

Rebus swallowed. Forster was licking his lips. 'And what did you tell him, Mack?'

'I told him the truth. I told him I couldn't remember.' He brought the palms of his hands together as if in prayer and touched the fingertips to his lips. Then he closed his eyes. The eyes were still closed when he spoke. 'Is it true about Suey?'

'What about him, Mack?'

'That he's emigrated, that he might not be coming back?'

'Is that what Beggar told you?'

Macmillan nodded, opening his eyes to gaze at Rebus. 'He said Suey might not be coming back . . .'

The nurses had taken Macmillan back to his ward, and Forster was putting on his coat, getting ready to lock up and see Rebus out to the car park, when the telephone rang.

'At this time of night?'

'It might be for me,' said Rebus. He picked up the receiver. 'Hello?'

It was DS Knox from Dufftown. 'Inspector Rebus? I did as you said and had someone stake out Deer Lodge.'

'And?'

'A white Saab drove in through the gateway not ten minutes ago.'

There were two cars parked by the side of the road. One of them was blocking the entrance to Deer Lodge's long driveway. Rebus got out of his own car. DS Knox introduced him to Detective Constable Wright and Constable Moffat.

'We've already met,' Rebus said, shaking Moffat's hand.

'Oh yes,' said Knox. 'How could I forget, you've been keeping us so busy? So, what do you think, sir?'

Rebus thought it was cold. Cold and wet. It wasn't raining now, but any minute it might be on again. 'You've called for reinforcements?'

Knox nodded. 'As many as can be mustered.'

'Well, we could wait it out till they arrive.'

'Yes?'

Rebus was sizing Knox up. He didn't seem the kind of man who enjoyed waiting. 'Or,' he said, 'we could go in, three of us, one standing guard on the gate. After all, he's either got a corpse or a hostage in there. If Steele's alive, the sooner we go in, the better chance he's got.'

'So what are we waiting for?'

Rebus looked to DC Wright and Constable Moffat, who nodded approval of the plan.

'It's a long walk up to the house, mind,' Knox was saying.

'But if we take a car, he's bound to hear it.'

'We can take one up so far and walk the rest,' suggested Moffat. 'That way the exit road's good and blocked. I wouldn't fancy wandering up that bloody road in the dark only to have him come racing towards me in that car of his.'

'Okay, agreed, we'll take a car.' Rebus turned to DC Wright. 'You stay on the gate, son. Moffat here knows the layout of the house.' Wright looked snubbed, but Moffat perked up at the news. 'Right,' said Rebus, 'let's go.'

They took Knox's car, leaving Moffat's parked across the entrance. Knox had taken one look at Rebus's heap and then shaken his head.

'Best take mine, eh?'

He drove slowly, Rebus in the front beside him, Moffat in the back. The car had a nice quiet engine, but all the same ... all around was silence. Any noise would travel. Rebus actually began to pray for a sudden storm, thunder and rain, for anything that would give them sound-cover.

'I enjoyed that book,' said Moffat, his head just behind Rebus's.

'What book?'

'*Fish out of Water.*'

'Christ, I'd forgotten all about it.'

'Cracking story,' said Moffat.

'How much further?' asked Knox. 'I can't remember.'

'There's a bend to the left then another to the right,' said Moffat. 'We better stop after the second one. It's only another couple of hundred yards.'

They parked, opening the doors and leaving them open. Knox produced two large rubber torches from the glove compartment. 'I was a cub scout,' he explained. 'Be prepared and all that.' He handed one torch to Rebus and kept the other. 'Moffat here eats his carrots, he doesn't need one. Right, what's the plan now?'

'Let's see how things look at the house, then I'll tell you.'

'Fair enough.'

They set off in a line. After about fifty yards, Rebus turned off his torch. It was no longer necessary: all the lights in and around the lodge seemed to be burning. They stopped just before the clearing, peering through what cover there was. The Saab was parked outside the front door. Its boot was open. Rebus turned to Moffat.

'Remember, there's a back door? Circle around and cover it.'

'Right.' The constable moved off the road and into the forest, disappearing from sight.

'Meantime, let's check the car first, then take a look through the windows.'

Knox nodded. They left their cover and crept forwards. The boot itself was empty. Nothing on the car's back seat either. Lights were on in the living room and the front bedroom, but there was no sign of anyone. Knox pointed with his torch towards the door. He tried the handle. The door opened a crack. He pushed it a little further. The hall was empty. They waited a moment, listening. There was a sudden eruption of noise, drums and guitar chords. Knox jumped back. Rebus rested a calming hand on his shoulder, then retreated to look again through the living room window. The stereo. He could see its LEDs pulsing. The cassette player, probably on automatic replay. A tape had been winding back while they'd approached the house. Now it was playing.

Early Stones. 'Paint It Black'. Rebus nodded. 'He's in there,' he said to himself. *My secret vice, Inspector.* One of many. At any rate, it meant he might not have heard the car's approach, and now the music was on again he might not even hear them entering the house.

So they entered. Moffat was covering the kitchen, so Rebus headed directly upstairs, Knox behind him. There was fine white powder on the wooden banister, leftovers from the dusting the house had been given by forensics. Up the stairs ... and on to the landing. What was that smell? *What was that smell?*

'Petrol,' whispered Knox.

Yes, petrol. The bedroom door was closed. The music seemed louder up here than downstairs. Thump-thump-thump of drum and bass. Clashing guitar and sitar. And those cheesegrater vocals.

Petrol.

Rebus leaned back and kicked in the door. It swung open and stayed open. Rebus took in the scene. Gregor Jack standing there, and against the wall a bound and gagged figure, its face puffy, forehead bloody. Ronald Steele. Gagged? No, not exactly a gag. Scraps of paper seemed to fill his mouth, scraps torn from the Sunday papers on the bed, all the stories which had started with his plotting. Well, Jack had made him eat his words.

Petrol.

The can lay empty on its side. The room was reeking. Steele looked to have been drenched in the stuff, or was it just sweat? And Gregor Jack standing there, his face at first full of mischief, but then turning, turning, softening, softening into shame. Shame and guilt. Guilt at being caught.

All of this Rebus took in in a second. But it took less time than that for Jack to strike the match and drop it.

The carpet caught immediately, and then Jack was flying forwards, knocking Rebus off balance, powering past Knox, heading for the stairs. The flames were moving too fast. Too fast to do anything. Rebus grabbed Steele by his feet and started to drag him towards the door. Dragging him of necessity *through* the fire itself. If Steele *was* soaked in petrol ... Well, no time to think about that. But it was sweat, that was all. The fire licked at him, but it didn't suddenly engulf the body.

Out into the hallway. Knox was already pounding down the stairs, following Jack. The bedroom was an inferno now, the bed like a kind of pyre in the centre of it. Rebus went back and glanced in. The mounted cow's head above the bed had caught and was crackling. He grabbed the door handle and dragged the door shut, thanking God he hadn't kicked it off its hinges in the first place . . .

It was a struggle, but he managed to haul Steele to his feet. Blood was caked on the face, and one eye had swollen shut. The other eye had tears in it. Paper was spilling from his mouth as he tried to speak. Rebus made a perfunctory attempt at loosening the knots. It was baler twine, and tight as tight could be. Christ, his head was hurting. He couldn't think why. He hefted the taller man on to his shoulder and started down the stairs.

At some point, Steele disgorged the paper from his mouth. His first words were: 'Your hair's on fire!'

So it was, at the nape of the neck. Rebus patted his head with his free hand. The back of his head was crispy, like strands of breakfast cereal. And something else: it was hurting like blazes.

They were at the bottom of the stairs now. Rebus dumped Steele on to the floor then straightened up. There was a tidal sound in his ears, and his eyes fogged over for a moment. His heart was thumping in sympathy with the rock music. 'I'll get a knife from the kitchen,' he said. Entering the kitchen, he saw that the back door was wide open. There were noises from outside, shouts, but indistinct. Then a figure stumbled into view. It was Moffat. He was holding both hands to his nose, covering the nose like a protective mask. Blood was pouring down his wrists and chin. He lifted the mask away to speak.

'The bastard butted me!' Flecks of blood flew from his mouth and his nostrils. 'Butted me!' You could tell he thought it wasn't fair play.

'You'll live,' said Rebus.

'The sergeant's gone after him.'

Rebus pointed to the hall behind him. 'Steele's in there. Find a knife and cut him loose, then both of you get out.' He pushed past Moffat and out of the back door. Light from the kitchen flooded the immediate scene, but beyond that was darkness. He'd dropped his torch up in the bedroom, and now cursed the fact. Then, eyes adjusting to the changing light, he ran across the small clearing and into the forest beyond.

More haste, less speed. He moved carefully past trunks and bushes and saplings. Briars tugged at him, but they were a minor nuisance. His main worry was that he didn't know where he was heading. The ground was sloping upwards, that much he could tell. As long as he kept moving upwards with it, he wouldn't be chasing his own tail. His foot caught on something and he fell against a tree. The breath left him. His shirt was wringing wet, his eyes stinging from a mixture of recent smoke and present sweat. He paused. He listened.

'Jack! Don't be stupid! Jack!'

It was Knox. Up ahead. A good distance ahead, but not impossible. Rebus took a deep breath and started walking. Miraculously, he came out of the forest and into a larger clearing. The slope seemed steeper here, the ground sprawling with bracken and gorse and other low spiky plants. He caught a sudden flash of light: Knox's torch. Way over to the right of him and slightly uphill. Rebus began jogging, lifting his legs high to avoid the worst of the undergrowth. All the same, something kept tearing at his trouser-legs and his ankles. Stinging and scratching. Then there were patches of short grass, areas where quicker progress was possible – or would have been possible if he'd been fitter and younger. Ahead of him, the torch moved in a circle. The meaning was clear: Knox had lost his quarry. Instead of continuing to head for the beam of light, Rebus swung away from it. If it were possible for only two men to fan out, then that's what Rebus was trying to ensure they did, widening the arc of the search.

He came to the top of the rise, and the ground levelled out. He got the feeling that in daytime it would make a bleak picture. There was nothing here but stunted wilderness, hardly fit for the hardiest sheep. Way ahead a shadow rose into the sky, some hill-range or other. The wind, which had dried his shirt but chilled him to the marrow, now dropped. Jesus, his head was hurting. Like sunburn but a hundred times worse. He stared up at the sky. The outlines of the clouds were visible. The weather was clearing. A sound had replaced the whistling of the wind in his ears.

The sound of running water.

It grew louder as he moved forwards. He had lost Knox's torchlight now, and was conscious of being alone; conscious, too, that if he strayed too far, he might not find his way back. A route wrongly taken could leave him heading towards nothing but hill and forest. He glanced back. The line of trees was still just about visible, though the house lights beyond were not.

'Jack! Jack!' Knox's voice seemed miles away. Rebus decided that he would skirt round towards it. If Gregor Jack was out there, let him freeze to death. The rescue services would find him tomorrow . . .

The running water was much closer now, and the ground beneath his feet was becoming rockier, the vegetation sparse. The water was somewhere below him. He stopped again. The shapes and shades in front of him . . . they didn't make sense. It was as if the land were folding in on itself. Just then, a huge chunk of cloud moved away from the moon, the large, nearly full moon. There was light now, and Rebus saw that he was standing not four feet from a sheer drop of five or six yards, a drop into a dark, twisting river. There was a noise to his right. He turned his head towards it. A figure was staggering forwards, bent over nearly double from exhaustion, its arms swinging loose and almost touching the ground. An ape, he thought at first. He looks just like an ape.

Gregor Jack was panting hoarsely, almost moaning from effort. He wasn't watching where he was going; all he knew was that he had to keep moving.

'Gregor.'

The figure wheezed, the head jerking up. It came to a stop. Gregor Jack rose to his full height, arching his head to the sky. He lifted his tired arms and rested his hands on his waist, for all the world like a runner at the end of his race. One hand went instinctively to his hair, tidying it back into place. Then he bent forwards and put his hands on his knees, and the hair flopped forwards again. But his breathing was becoming steadier. Eventually he straightened up again. Rebus saw that he was smiling, showing his perfect teeth. He began shaking his head and chuckling. Rebus had heard the sound before from people who'd lost: lost everything from their freedom to a big bet or a game of five-a-side. They were laughing at circumstance.

Gregor's laughter collapsed into a cough. He slapped at his chest, then looked at Rebus and smiled again.

Then sprang.

Rebus's instinct was to dodge, but Jack was moving away from him. And both of them knew precisely where he was headed. As his foot touched the last inch of earth, he leapt out into the air, jumping feet first. A couple of seconds later came the sound of his body hitting the water. Rebus toed his way to the edge of the rock and looked down, but the cloud was closing in again overhead. The moonlight was lost. There was nothing to see.

Making their way back to Deer Lodge, there was no need for Knox's torch. The flames lit up the surrounding countryside. Glowing ash landed on the trees as they made their way through the woods. Rebus ran his fingers over the back of his head. The skin was stinging. But he got the feeling shock might have set in: the pain wasn't quite so bad as before. His ankles stung too – thistles, probably. He'd run through what had turned out to be a field full of them. There was no one near the house. Moffat and Steele were waiting by Knox's car.

'How good a swimmer is he?' Rebus asked Steele.

'Beggar?' Steele was massaging his untethered arms. 'Can't swim a stroke. We all learned at school, but his mum used to give him a note excusing him.'

'Why?'

Steele shrugged. 'She was scared he'd catch verrucas. How's the head, Inspector?'

'I won't need a haircut for a while.'

'What about Jack?' Moffat asked.

'He won't be needing one either.'

They searched for Gregor Jack's body the following morning. Not that Rebus was there to participate. He was in hospital and feeling dirty and unshaven – except for his head.

'If you have a problem with baldness,' one senior doctor told him, 'you could always wear a toupee till it grows back. Or a hat. Your scalp will be sensitive, too, so try to keep out of the sun.'

'Sun? What sun?'

But there was sun, during his time off work there was plenty of it. He stayed indoors, stayed underground, reading book after book, emerging for brief forays to the Royal Infirmary to have his dressings changed.

'I could do that for you,' Patience had told him.

'Never mix business and pleasure,' was Rebus's enigmatic response. In fact, there was a nurse up at the infirmary who had taken a shine to him, and he to her ... Ach, it wouldn't go anywhere; it was just a bit of flirting. He wouldn't hurt Patience for the world.

Holmes visited, always with a dozen cans of something gassy. 'Hiya, baldie,' was the perennial greeting, even when the skinhead had become a suedehead, the suedehead longer still.

'What's the news?' asked Rebus.

Apart from the fact that Gregor Jack's body had still not been recovered, the big news was that the Farmer was off the booze after having been 'visited by the Lord' at some revivalist Baptist meeting.

'It's communion wine only from now on,' said Holmes. 'Mind you –' pointing to Rebus's head, 'for a while there I thought maybe *you* were going to go Buddhist on us.'

'I might yet,' said Rebus. 'I might yet.'

The media clung to the Jack story, clung to the idea that he might still be alive. Rebus wondered about that, too. More, he still wondered why Jack had killed Elizabeth. Ronald Steele could shed no light on the problem. Apparently, Jack had spoken hardly a word to him all the time he'd held him captive ... Well, that was Steele's story. Whatever *had* been said, it wasn't going any further.

All of which left Rebus with scenarios, with guesswork. He played out the scene time after time in his head – Jack arriving at the lay-by, and arguing with Elizabeth. Maybe she'd told him she wanted a divorce. Maybe the argument was over the brothel story. Or maybe there'd been something else. All Steele would say was that when he'd left her, she'd been waiting for her husband.

'I thought about hanging around and confronting him...'

'But?'

Steele shrugged. 'Cowardice. It's not doing something "wrong" that's the problem, Inspector, it's getting caught. Wouldn't you agree?'

'But if you *had* stayed . . .?'

Steele nodded. 'I know. Maybe Liz would have told Gregor to bugger off and have stuck with me instead. Maybe they'd both still be alive.'

If Steele hadn't fled from the lay-by . . . *if* Gail Jack hadn't come north in the first place . . . What then? Rebus was in no doubt: it would have worked out some other way, not necessarily any less painful a way. Fire and ice and skeletons in the closet. He wished he could have met Elizabeth Jack, just once, even though he had the feeling they wouldn't have got on . . .

There was one more news story. It started as another rumour, but the rumour turned out to be a leak, and the leak was followed by notification: Great London Road was to undergo a programme of repair and refurbishment.

Which means, thought Rebus, I move in with Patience. To all intents, he already had.

'You don't have to sell your flat,' she told him. 'You could always rent it.'

'Rent it?'

'To students. Your street's half full of them as it is.' This was true. You saw the migration in the morning, down towards The Meadows carrying their satchels and ringbinders and supermarket carriers; back in the late afternoon (or late night) laden with books and ideas. The notion appealed. If he rented out his flat, he could pay Patience something towards living here with her.

'You're on,' he said.

He was back at work one full day when Great London Road police station caught fire. The building was razed to the ground.

The Black Book

'To the wicked, all things are wicked; but to the just, all things are just and right.'

James Hogg, *The Private Memoirs and Confessions of a Justified Sinner*

Acknowledgements

The author wishes to acknowledge the assistance of the Chandler-Fulbright Award in the writing of this book.

Prologue

There were two of them in the van that early morning, lights on to combat the haar which blew in from the North Sea. It was thick and white like smoke. They drove carefully, being under strict instructions.

'Why does it have to be us?' said the driver, stifling a yawn. 'What's wrong with the other two?'

The passenger was much larger than his companion. Though in his forties, he kept his hair long, cut in the shape of a German military helmet. He kept pulling at the hair on the left side of his head, straightening it out. At the moment, however, he was gripping the sides of his seat. He didn't like the way the driver screwed shut his eyes for the duration of each too-frequent yawn. The passenger was not a conversationalist, but maybe talk would keep the driver awake.

'It's just temporary,' he said. 'Besides, it's not as if it's a daily chore.'

'Thank God for that.' The driver shut his eyes again and yawned. The van glided in towards the grass verge.

'Do you want me to drive?' asked the passenger. Then he smiled. 'You could always kip in the back.'

'Very funny. That's another thing, Jimmy, the stink!'

'Meat always smells after a while.'

'Got an answer for everything, eh?'

'Yes.'

'Are we nearly there?'

'I thought you knew the way.'

'On the main roads I do. But with this mist.'

'If we're hugging the coast it can't be far.' The passenger was also thinking: if we're hugging the coast, then two wheels past the verge and we're over a cliff face. It wasn't just this that made him nervous. They'd never used the east coast before, but there was too much attention on the west coast now. So it was an untried run, and *that* made him nervous.

'Here's a road sign.' They braked to peer through the haar. 'Next right.' The driver jolted forwards again. He signalled and pulled in through a low iron gate which was padlocked open. 'What if it had been locked?' he offered.

'I've got cutters in the back.'

'A bloody answer for everything.'

They drove into a small gravelled car park. Though they could not see them, there were wooden tables and benches to one side, where Sunday families could picnic and do battle with the midges. The spot was popular for its view, an uninterrupted spread of sea and sky. When they opened their doors, they could smell and hear the sea. Gulls were already shrieking overhead.

'Must be later than we thought if the birds are up.' They readied themselves for opening the back of the van, then did so. The smell really was foul. Even the stoical passenger wrinkled his nose and tried hard not to breathe.

'Quicker the better,' he said in a rush. The body had been placed in two thick plastic fertiliser sacks, one pulled over the feet and one over the head, so that they overlapped in the middle. Tape and string had been used to join them. Inside the bags were also a number of breeze blocks, making for a heavy and awkward load. They carried the grotesque parcel low, brushing the wet grass. Their shoes were squelching by the time they passed the sign warning about the cliff face ahead. Even more difficult was the climb over the fence, though it was rickety enough to start with.

'Wouldn't stop a bloody kid,' the driver commented. He was peching, the saliva like glue in his mouth.

'Ca' canny,' said the passenger. They shuffled forwards two inches at a time, until they could all too clearly make out the edge. There was no more land after that, just a vertical fall to the agitated sea. 'Right,' he said. Without ceremony, they heaved the thing out into space, glad immediately to be rid of it. 'Let's go.'

'Man, but that air smells good.' The driver reached into his pocket for a quarter-bottle of whisky. They were halfway back to the van when they heard a car on the road, and the crunch of tyres on gravel.

'Aw, hell's bells.'

The headlights caught them as they reached the van.

'The fuckin' polis!' choked the driver.

'Keep the heid,' warned the passenger. His voice was quiet, but his eyes burned ahead of him. They heard a handbrake being engaged, and the car door opened. A uniformed officer appeared. He was carrying a torch. The headlights and engine had been left on. There was no one else in the car.

The passenger knew the score. This wasn't a set-up. Probably the copper came here towards the end of his night shift. There'd be a flask or a blanket in the car. Coffee or a snooze before signing off for the day.

'Morning,' the uniform said. He wasn't young, and he wasn't used to trouble. A Saturday night punch-up maybe, or disputes between neighbouring farmers. It had been another long boring night for him, another night nearer his pension.

'Morning,' the passenger said. He knew they could bluff this one, if the driver stayed calm. But then he thought, *I'm* the conspicuous one.

'A right pea-souper, eh?' said the policeman.

The passenger nodded.

'That's why we stopped,' explained the driver. 'Thought we'd wait it out.'

'Very sensible.'

The driver watched as the passenger turned to the van and started inspecting its rear driver-side tyre, giving it a kick. He then walked to the rear passenger-side and did the same, before getting down on his knees to peer beneath the vehicle. The policeman watched the performance too.

'Got a bit of trouble?'

'Not really,' the driver said nervously. 'But it's best to be safe.'

'I see you've come a ways.'

The driver nodded. 'Off up to Dundee.'

The policeman frowned. 'From Edinburgh? Why didn't you just stick to the motorway or the A914?'

The driver thought quickly. 'We've a drop-off in Tayport first.'

'Even so,' the policeman started. The driver watched as the passenger rose from his inspection, now sited behind the policeman. He was holding a rock in his hand. The driver kept his eyes glued to the policeman's as the rock rose, then fell. The monologue finished mid-sentence as the body slumped to the ground.

'That's just beautiful.'

'What else could we do?' The passenger was already making for his door. 'Come on, vamoose!'

'Aye,' said the driver, 'another minute and he'd have spotted your ... er ...'

The passenger glowered at him. 'What you mean is, another minute and he'd've smelt the booze on your breath.' He didn't stop glowering until the driver shrugged his agreement.

They turned the van and drove out of the car park. The gulls were still noisy in the distance. The police car's engine was turning over. The headlights picked out the prone unconscious figure. But the torch had broken in the fall.

1

It all happened because John Rebus was in his favourite massage parlour reading the Bible.

It all happened because a man walked in through the door in the mistaken belief that any massage parlour sited so close to a brewery and half a dozen good pubs had to be catering to Friday night pay packets and anytime drunks; and therefore had to be bent as a paper-clip.

But the Organ Grinder, God-fearing tenant of the set-up, ran a clean shop, a place where tired muscles were beaten mellow. Rebus was tired: tired of arguments with Patience Aitken, tired of the fact that his brother had turned up seeking shelter in a flat filled to the gunwales with students, and most of all tired of his job.

It had been that kind of week.

On the Monday evening, he'd had a call from his Arden Street flat. The students he'd rented to had Patience's number and knew they could reach him there, but this was the first time they'd ever had reason. The reason was Michael Rebus.

'Hello, John.'

Rebus recognised the voice at once. 'Mickey?'

'How are you, John?'

'Christ, Mickey. Where are you? No, scratch that, I know where you are. I mean —' Michael was laughing softly. 'It's just I heard you'd gone south.'

'Didn't work out.' His voice dropped. 'Thing is, John, can we talk? I've been dreading this, but I really need to talk to you.'

'Okay.'

'Shall I come round there?'

Rebus thought quickly. Patience was picking up her two nieces from Waverley Station, but all the same . . . 'No, stay where you are. I'll come over. The students are a good lot, maybe they'll fix you a cup of tea or a joint while you're waiting.'

There was silence on the line, then Michael's voice: 'I could have done without that.' The line went dead.

Michael Rebus had served three years of a five-year sentence for drug dealing. During that time, John Rebus had visited his brother fewer than half a dozen times. He'd felt relief more than anything when, upon release, Michael had taken a bus to London. That was two years ago, and the brothers had not exchanged a word since. But now Michael was back, bringing with him bad memories of a period in John Rebus's life he'd rather not remember.

The Arden Street flat was suspiciously tidy when he arrived. Only two of the student tenants were around, the couple who slept in what had been Rebus's bedroom. He talked to them in the hallway. They were just going out to the pub, but handed over to him another letter from the Inland Revenue. Really, Rebus would have liked them to stay. When they left, there was silence in the flat. Rebus knew that Michael would be in the living room and he was, crouched in front of the stereo and flipping through stacks of records.

'Look at this lot,' Michael said, his back still to Rebus. 'The Beatles and the Stones, same stuff you used to listen to. Remember how you drove dad daft? What was that record player again . . .?'

'A Dansette.'

'That's it. Dad got it saving cigarette coupons.' Michael stood up and turned towards his brother. 'Hello, John.'

'Hello, Michael.'

They didn't hug or shake hands. They just sat down, Rebus on the chair, Michael on the sofa.

'This place has changed,' Michael said.

'I had to buy a few sticks of furniture before I could rent it out.' Already Rebus had noticed a few things – cigarette burns on the carpet, posters (against his explicit instructions) sellotaped to the wallpaper. He opened the taxman's letter.

'You should have seen them leap into action when I told them you were coming round. Hoovering and washing dishes. Who says students are lazy?'

'They're okay.'

'So when did this all happen?'

'A few months ago.'

'They told me you're living with a doctor.'

'Her name's Patience.'

Michael nodded. He looked pale and ill. Rebus tried not to be interested, but he was. The letter from the tax office hinted strongly that they knew he was renting his flat, and didn't he want to declare the income? The back of his head was tingling. It did that when he was fractious, ever since it had been burned in the fire. The doctors said there was nothing he or they could do about it.

Except, of course, not get fractious.

He stuffed the letter into his pocket. 'What do you want, Mickey?'

'Bottom line, John, I need a place to stay. Just for a week or two, till I can get on my feet.' Rebus stared stonily at the posters on the walls as

Michael ran on. He wanted to find work ... money was tight ... he'd take any job ... he just needed a chance.

'That's all, John, just one chance.'

Rebus was thinking. Patience had room in her flat, of course. There was space enough there even with the nieces staying. But no way was Rebus going to take his brother back to Oxford Terrace. Things weren't going that well as it was. His late hours and her late hours, his exhaustion and hers, his job involvement and hers. Rebus couldn't see Michael improving things. He thought: I am not my brother's keeper. But all the same.

'We might squeeze you into the box room. I'd have to talk to the students about it.' He couldn't see them saying no, but it seemed polite to ask. How *could* they say no? He was their landlord and flats were hard to find. Especially good flats, especially in Marchmont.

'That would be great.' Michael sounded relieved. He got up from the sofa and walked over to the door of the box room. This was a large ventilated cupboard off the living room. Just big enough for a single bed and a chest of drawers, if you took all the boxes and the rubbish out of it.

'We could probably store all that stuff in the cellar,' said Rebus, standing just behind his brother.

'John,' said Michael, 'the way I feel, I'd be happy enough sleeping in the cellar myself.' And when he turned towards his brother, there were tears in Michael Rebus's eyes.

On Wednesday, Rebus began to realise that his world was a black comedy.

Michael had been moved into the Arden Street flat without any fuss. Rebus had informed Patience of his brother's return, but had said little more than that. She was spending a lot of time with her sister's girls anyway. She'd taken a few days off work to show them Edinburgh. It looked like hard going. Susan at fifteen wanted to do all the things which Jenny, aged eight, didn't or couldn't. Rebus felt almost totally excluded from this female triumvirate, though he would sneak into Jenny's room at night just to re-live the magic and innocence of a child asleep. He also spent time trying to avoid Susan, who seemed only too aware of the differences between women and men.

He was kept busy at work, which meant he didn't think about Michael more than a few dozen times each day. Ah, work, now there was a thing. When Great London Road police station had burnt down, Rebus had been moved to St Leonard's, which was Central District's divisional HQ.

With him had come Detective Sergeant Brian Holmes and, to both their dismays, Chief Superintendent 'Farmer' Watson and Chief

Inspector 'Fart' Lauderdale. There had been compensations – newer offices and furniture, better amenities and equipment – but not enough. Rebus was still trying to come to terms with his new workplace. Everything was so tidy, he could never find anything, as a result of which he was always keen to get out of the office and onto the street.

Which was why he ended up at a butcher's shop on South Clerk Street, staring down at a stabbed man.

The man had already been tended to by a local doctor, who'd been standing in line waiting for some pork chops and gammon steaks when the man staggered into the shop. The wound had been dressed initially with a clean butcher's apron, and now everyone was waiting for a stretcher to be unloaded from the ambulance outside.

A constable was filling Rebus in.

'I was only just up the road, so he couldn't have been here more than five minutes when somebody told me, and I came straight here. That's when I radioed in.'

Rebus had picked up the constable's radio message in his car, and had decided to stop by. He kind of wished he hadn't. There was blood smeared across the floor, colouring the sawdust which lay there. Why some butchers still scattered sawdust on their floors he couldn't say. There was also a palm-shaped daub of blood on the white-tiled wall, and another less conclusive splash of the stuff below this.

The wounded man had also left a trail of gleaming drips outside, all the way along and halfway up Lutton Place (insultingly close to St Leonard's), where they suddenly stopped kerbside.

The man's name was Rory Kintoul, and he had been stabbed in the abdomen. This much they knew. They didn't know much more, because Rory Kintoul was refusing to speak about the incident. This was not an attitude shared by those who had been in the butcher's at the time. They were outside now, passing on news of the excitement to the crowd who had stopped to gawp through the shop window. It reminded Rebus of Saturday afternoon in the St James Centre, when pockets of men would gather outside the TV rental shops, hoping to catch the football scores.

Rebus crouched over Kintoul, just a little intimidatingly.

'And where do you live, Mr Kintoul?'

But the man was not about to answer. A voice came from the other side of the glass display case.

'Duncton Terrace.' The speaker was wearing a bloodied butcher's apron and cleaning a heavy knife on a towel. 'That's in Dalkeith.'

Rebus looked at the butcher. 'And you are . . .?'

'Jim Bone. This is my shop.'

'And you know Mr Kintoul?'

Kintoul had turned his head awkwardly, seeking the butcher's face, as if trying to influence his answer. But, slouched as he was against the display case, he would have required demonic possession to effect such a move.

'I ought to,' said the butcher. 'He's my cousin.'

Rebus was about to say something, but at that moment the stretcher was trolleyed in by two ambulancemen, one of whom almost skited on the slippery floor. It was as they positioned the stretcher in front of Kintoul that Rebus saw something which would stay with him. There were two signs in the display cabinet, one pinned into a side of corned beef, the other into a slab of red sirloin.

Cold Cuts, one said. The other stated simply, Fleshing. A large fresh patch of blood was left on the floor as they lifted the butcher's cousin. Cold Cuts and Fleshing. Rebus shivered and made for the door.

On the Friday after work, Rebus decided on a massage. He had promised Patience he'd be in by eight, and it was only six now. Besides, a brutal pummelling always seemed to set him up for the weekend.

But first he wandered into the Broadsword for a pint of the local brew. They didn't come more local than Gibson's Dark, a heavy beer made only six hundred yards away at the Gibson Brewery. A brewery, a pub and a massage parlour: Rebus reckoned if you threw in a good Indian restaurant and a corner shop open till midnight he could live happily here for ever and a day.

Not that he didn't like living with Patience in her Oxford Terrace garden flat. It represented the other side of the tracks, so to speak. Certainly, it seemed a world away from this disreputable corner of Edinburgh, one of many such corners. Rebus wondered why he was so drawn to them.

The air outside was filled with the yeasty smell of beer-making, vying with the even stronger aromas from the city's other much larger breweries. The Broadsword was a popular watering hole, and like most of Edinburgh's popular pubs, it boasted a mixed clientele: students and low lifes with the occasional businessman. The bar had few pretensions; all it had in its favour were good beer and a good cellar. The weekend had already started, and Rebus was squeezed in at the bar, next to a man whose immense alsatian dog was sleeping on the floor behind the barstools. It took up the standing room of at least two adult men, but nobody was asking it to shift. Further along the bar, someone was drinking with one hand and keeping another proprietorial hand on a coatstand which Rebus assumed they'd just bought at one of the nearby secondhand shops. Everyone at the bar was drinking the same dark brew.

Though there were half a dozen pubs within a five-minute walk of here, only the Broadsword stocked draught Gibson's, the other pubs being tied to one or other of the big breweries. Rebus started to wonder, as the beer slipped down, what effect it would have on his metabolism once the Organ Grinder got to work. He decided against a refill, and instead made for O-Gee's, which was what the Organ Grinder had called his shop. Rebus liked the name; it made the same sound customers made once the Grinder himself got to work – 'Oh Jeez!' But they were always careful not to say anything out loud. The Organ Grinder didn't like to hear blasphemy on the massage table. It upset him, and nobody wanted to be in the hands of an upset Organ Grinder. Nobody wanted to be his monkey.

So, there he was sitting with the Bible in his lap, waiting for his six-thirty appointment. The Bible was the only reading matter on the premises, courtesy of the Organ Grinder himself. Rebus had read it before, but didn't mind reading it again.

Then the front door burst open.

'Where's the girls, eh?' This new client was not only misinformed, but also considerably drunk. There was no way the Grinder would handle drunks.

'Wrong place, pal.' Rebus was about to make mention of a couple of nearby parlours which would be certain to offer the necessary Thai assisted sauna and rub-down, but the man stopped him with a thick pointed finger.

'John bloody Rebus, you son of a shite-breeks!'

Rebus frowned, trying to place the face. His mind flipped through two decades of mug shots. The man saw Rebus's confusion, and spread his hands wide. 'Deek Torrance, you don't remember?'

Rebus shook his head. Torrance was walking determinedly forward. Rebus clenched his fists, ready for anything.

'We went through parachute training together,' said Torrance. 'Christ, you must remember!'

And suddenly Rebus did remember. He remembered everything, the whole black comedy of his past.

They drank in the Broadsword, swopping stories. Deek hadn't lasted in the Parachute Regiment. After a year he'd had enough, and not too long after that he'd bought his way out of the Army altogether.

'Too restless, John, that was my problem. What was yours?'

Rebus shook his head and drank some more beer. 'My problem, Deek? You couldn't put a name to it.' But a name *had* been put to it, first by Mickey's sudden appearance, and now by Deek Torrance. Ghosts, both of them, but Rebus didn't want to be their Scrooge. He bought another round.

'You always said you were going to try for the SAS,' Torrance said.

Rebus shrugged. 'It didn't work out.'

The bar was busier than ever, and at one point Torrance was jostled by a young man trying to manoeuvre a double bass through the mêlée.

'Could you no' leave that outside?'

'Not around here.'

Torrance turned back to Rebus. 'Did you see thon?'

Rebus merely smiled. He felt good after the massage. 'No one brings anything small into a bar around here.' He watched Deek Torrance grunt. Yes, he remembered him now, all right. He'd gotten fatter and balder, his face was roughened and much fleshier than it had been. He didn't even sound the same, not exactly. But there was that one characteristic: the Torrance grunt. A man of few words, Deek Torrance had been. Not now, though, now he had plenty to say.

'So what do you do, Deek?'

Torrance grinned. 'Seeing you're a copper I better not say.' Rebus bided his time. Torrance was drunk to the point of slavering. Sure enough, he couldn't resist. 'I'm in buying and selling, mostly selling.'

'And what do you sell?'

Torrance leaned closer. 'Am I talking to the polis or an old pal?'

'A pal,' said Rebus. 'Strictly off-duty. So what do you sell?'

Torrance grunted. 'Anything you like, John. I'm sort of like Jenners department store . . . only I can get things they can't.'

'Such as?' Rebus was looking at the clock above the bar. It couldn't be that late, surely. They always ran the clock ten minutes fast here, but even so.

'Anything at all,' said Torrance. 'Anything from a shag to a shooter. You name it.'

'How about a watch?' Rebus started winding his own. 'Mine only seems to go for a couple of hours at a stretch.'

Torrance looked at it. 'Longines,' he said, pronouncing the word correctly, 'you don't want to chuck that. Get it cleaned, it'll be fine. Mind you, I could probably part-ex it against a Rolex . . .?'

'So you sell dodgy watches.'

'Did I say that? I don't recall saying that. *Anything*, John. Whatever the client wants, I'll fetch it for him.' Torrance winked.

'Listen, what time do you make it?'

Torrance shrugged and pulled up the sleeve of his jacket. He wasn't wearing a watch. Rebus was thinking. He'd kept his appointment with the Grinder, Deek happy to wait for him in the anteroom. And afterwards they'd still had time for a pint or two before he had to make his way home. They'd had two . . . no, three drinks so far. Maybe he was running a bit late. He caught the barman's attention and tapped at his wrist.

'Twenty past eight,' called the barman.

'I'd better phone Patience,' said Rebus.

But someone was using the public phone to cement some romance. What's more, they'd dragged the receiver into the ladies' toilet so that they could hear above the noise from the bar. The telephone cord was stretched taut, ready to garotte anyone trying to use the toilets. Rebus bided his time, then began staring at the wall-mounted telephone cradle. What the hell. He pushed his finger down on the cradle, released it, then moved back into the throng of drinkers. A young man appeared from inside the ladies' toilet and slammed the receiver hard back into its cradle. He checked for change in his pocket, had none, and started to make for the bar.

Rebus moved in on the phone. He picked it up, but could hear no tone. He tried again, then tried dialling. Nothing. Something had obviously come loose when the man had slammed the receiver home. Shite on a stick. It was nearly half past eight now, and it would take fifteen minutes to drive back to Oxford Terrace. He was going to pay dearly for this.

'You look like you could use a drink,' said Deek Torrance when Rebus joined him at the bar.

'Know what, Deek?' said Rebus. 'My life's a black comedy.'

'Oh well, better than a tragedy, eh?'

Rebus was beginning to wonder what the difference was.

He got back to the flat at twenty past nine. Probably Patience had cooked a meal for the four of them. Probably she'd waited fifteen minutes or so before eating. She'd have kept his meal warm for another fifteen minutes, then dumped it. If it was fish, the cat would have eaten it. Otherwise its destination would be the compost heap in the garden. This had happened before, too many times, really. Yet it kept on happening, and Rebus wasn't sure the excuses of an old friend or a broken watch would work any kind of spell.

The steps down to the garden flat were worn and slippery. Rebus took them carefully, and so was slow to notice the large sports holdall which, illuminated by the orange street-lamp, was sitting on the rattan mat outside the front door of the flat. It was his bag. He unzipped it and looked in. On top of some clothes and a pair of shoes there was a note. He read it through twice.

Don't bother trying the door, I've bolted it. I've also disconnected the doorbell, and the phone is off the hook for the weekend. I'll leave another load of your stuff on the front step Monday morning.

The note needed no signature. Rebus whistled a long breathy note, then tried his key in the lock. It didn't budge. He pressed the doorbell. No sound. As a last resort, he crouched down and peered in through the letterbox. The hall was in darkness, no sign of light from any of the rooms.

'Something came up,' he called. No response. 'I tried phoning, I couldn't get through.' Still nothing. He waited a few more moments, half-expecting Jenny at least to break the silence. Or Susan, she was a right stirrer of trouble. And a heartbreaker too, by the look of her. 'Bye, Patience,' he called. 'Bye, Susan. Bye, Jenny.' Still silence. 'I'm sorry.'

He truly was.

'Just one of those weeks,' he said to himself, picking up the bag.

On Sunday morning, in weak sunshine and a snell wind, Andrew McPhail sneaked back into Edinburgh. He'd been away a long time, and the city had changed. Everywhere and everything had changed. He was still jetlagged from several days ago, and poorer than he should have been due to London's inflated prices. He walked from the bus station to the Broughton area of town, just off Leith Walk. It wasn't a long walk, but every step seemed heavy, though his bags were light. He'd slept badly on the bus, but that was nothing new: he couldn't remember when he'd last had a good night's sleep, sleep without dreams.

The sun looked as though it might disappear at any minute. Thick clouds were pushing in over Leith. McPhail tried to walk faster. He had an address in his pocket, the address of a boarding house. He'd phoned last night, and his landlady was expecting him. She sounded nice on the phone, but it was difficult to tell. He wouldn't mind, no matter what she was like, so long as she kept quiet. He knew that his leaving Canada had been in the Canadian newspapers, and even in some of the American ones, and he supposed that journalists here would be after him for a story. He'd been surprised at slipping so quietly into Heathrow. No one seemed to know who he was, and that was good.

He wanted nothing but a quiet life, though perhaps not as quiet as a few of the past years.

He'd phoned his sister from London and asked her to check directory enquiries for a Mrs MacKenzie in the Bellevue area. (Directory enquiries in London hadn't gone out of their way to help.) Melanie and her mother had lodged with Mrs MacKenzie when he'd first met them, before they moved in together. Alexis was a single parent, a DSS case. Mrs MacKenzie had been a more sympathetic landlady than most. Not that he'd ever visited Melanie and her mum there – Mrs MacKenzie wouldn't have liked it.

She didn't take lodgers much these days, but she was a good Christian and McPhail was persuasive.

He stood outside the house. It was a plain two-storey construction finished off in grey pebbledash and ugly double glazing. It looked just the same as the houses either side of it. Mrs MacKenzie answered the door as though she'd been ready for him for some time. She fussed about in the living room and kitchen, then led him upstairs to show him the bathroom, and then finally his own bedroom. It was no larger than a prison cell, but had been nicely decorated (sometime in the mid-1960s, he'd guess). It was fine, he'd no complaints.

'It's lovely,' he told Mrs MacKenzie, who shrugged her shoulders as if to say, of course it is.

'There's tea in the pot,' she said. 'I'll just go make us a cuppy.' Then she remembered something. 'No cooking in the room, mind.'

Andrew McPhail shook his head. 'I don't cook,' he said. She thought of something else and crossed to the window, where the net curtains were still closed.

'Here, I'll open these. You can open a window too, if you want some fresh air.'

'Fresh air would be nice,' he agreed. They both looked out of the window down onto the street.

'It's quiet,' she said. 'Not too much traffic. Of course, there's always a wee bit of noise during the day.'

McPhail could see what she was referring to: there was an old school building across the road with a black iron fence in front of it. It wasn't a large school, probably primary. McPhail's window looked down onto the school gates, just to the right of the main building. Directly behind the gates was the deserted playground.

'I'll get that tea,' said Mrs MacKenzie. When she'd gone, McPhail placed his cases on the springy single bed. Beside the bed was a small writing desk and chair. He lifted the chair and placed it in front of the window, then sat down. He moved a small glass clown further along the sill so that he could rest his chin where it had been. Nothing obscured his view. He sat there in a dream, looking at the playground, until Mrs MacKenzie called to him that the tea was in the living room. 'And a Madeira cake, too.' Andrew McPhail got up with a sigh. He didn't really want the tea now, but he supposed he could always bring it up to his room and leave it untouched till later. He felt tired, bone tired, but he was home and something told him that tonight he would sleep the sleep of the dead.

'Coming, Mrs MacKenzie,' he called, tearing his gaze away from the school.

2

On Monday morning word went around St Leonard's police station that Inspector John Rebus was in an impressively worse mood than usual. Some found this hard to believe, and were almost willing to get close enough to Rebus to find out for themselves . . . almost.

Others had no choice.

DS Brian Holmes and DC Siobhan Clarke, seated with Rebus in their sectioned-off chunk of the CID room, had the look of people who were resting their backsides on soft-boiled eggs.

'So,' Rebus was saying, 'what about Rory Kintoul?'

'He's out of hospital, sir,' said Siobhan Clarke.

Rebus nodded impatiently. He was waiting for her to put a foot wrong. It wasn't because she was English, or a graduate, or had wealthy parents who'd bought her a flat in the New Town. It wasn't because she was a she. It was just Rebus's way of dealing with young officers.

'And he's still not talking,' said Holmes. 'He won't say what happened, and he's certainly not pressing any charges.'

Brian Holmes looked tired. Rebus noticed this from the corner of his eye. He didn't want to make eye-contact with Holmes, didn't want Holmes to realise that they now had something in common.

Both had been kicked out by their girlfriends.

It had happened to Holmes just over a month ago. As Holmes revealed later, once he'd moved in with an aunt in Barnton, it was all to do with children. He hadn't realised how strongly Nell wanted a baby, and had started to joke about it. Then one day, she'd blown up – an awesome sight – and kicked him out, watched by most of the female neighbours in their mining village south of Edinburgh. Apparently the women neighbours had applauded as Holmes scurried off.

Now, he was working harder than ever. (This also had been a cause of strife between the couple: her hours were fairly regular, his anything but.) He reminded Rebus of a frayed and faded pair of work denims, not far from the end of their life.

'What are you saying?' Rebus asked.

'I'm saying I think we should drop it, sir, with all respect.'

' "With all respect", Brian? That's what people say when they mean "you fucking idiot".' Rebus still wasn't looking at Holmes, but he could feel the young man blushing. Clarke was looking down at her lap.

'Listen,' said Rebus, 'this guy, he staggers a couple of hundred yards with a two-inch gash in his gut. Why?' No answer was forthcoming. 'Why,' Rebus persisted, 'does he walk past a dozen shops, only stopping at his cousin's?'

'Maybe he was making for a doctor's, but had to stop,' Clarke suggested.

'Maybe,' said Rebus dismissively. 'Funny that he can make it into his *cousin's* shop, though.'

'You think it's something to do with the cousin, sir?'

'Let me ask the both of you something else.' Rebus stood up and took a few paces, then retraced his steps, catching Holmes and Clarke exchanging a glance. It set Rebus wondering. At first, there had been sparks between them, sparks of antagonism. But now they were working well together. He just hoped the relationship didn't go further than that. 'Let me ask you this,' he said. 'What do we know about the victim?'

'Not much,' said Holmes.

'He lives in Dalkeith,' Clarke offered. 'Works as a lab technician in the Infirmary. Married, one son.' She shrugged.

'That's it?' asked Rebus.

'That's it, sir.'

'Exactly,' said Rebus. 'He's nobody, a nothing. Not one person we've talked to has had a bad word to say about him. So tell me this: how did he end up getting stabbed? And in the middle of a Wednesday morning? If it had been a mugger, surely he'd tell us about it. As it is, he's clammed up as tight as an Aberdonian's purse at a church collection. He's got something to hide. Christ knows what, but it involves a car.'

'How do you work that out, sir?'

'The blood starts at the kerb, Holmes. Looks to me like he got out of a car and at that point he was already wounded.'

'He drives, sir, but doesn't own a car at present.'

'Smart girl, Clarke.' She prickled at 'girl', but Rebus was talking again. 'And he'd taken a half day off work without telling his wife.' He sat down again. 'Why, why, why? I want the two of you to have another go at him. Tell him we're not happy with his lack of a story. If he can't think of one, we'll pester him till he does. Let him know we mean business.' Rebus paused. 'And after that, do a check on the butcher.'

'Chop chop, sir,' commented Holmes. He was saved by the phone ringing. Rebus picked up the receiver. Maybe it would be Patience.

'DI Rebus.'

'John, can you come to my office?'

It wasn't Patience, it was the Chief Super. 'Two minutes, sir,' said Rebus, putting down the phone. Then, to Holmes and Clarke: 'Get onto it.'

'Yes, sir.'

'You think I'm making too much of this, Brian?'

'Yes, sir.'

'Well, maybe I am. But I don't like a mystery, no matter how small. So bugger off and satisfy my curiosity.'

As they rose, Holmes nodded towards the large suitcase which Rebus had placed behind his desk, supposedly out of view. 'Something I should know about?'

'Yes,' said Rebus. 'It's where I keep all my graft payments. Yours still probably fit in your back pooch.' Holmes didn't look like budging, though Clarke had already retreated to her own desk. Rebus expelled air and lowered his voice. 'I've just joined the ranks of the dispossessed.' Holmes' face became animated. 'Not a bloody word, mind. This is between you and me.'

'Understood.' Holmes thought of something. 'You know, most evenings I eat at the Heartbreak Cafe . . .'

'I'll know where to find you then, if I ever need to hear any early Elvis.'

Holmes nodded. 'And Vegas Elvis too. All I mean is, if there's anything I can do . . .'

'You could start by disguising yourself as me and trotting along to see Farmer Watson.'

But Holmes was shaking his head. 'I meant anything within reason.'

Within reason. Rebus wondered if it was within reason to be asking the students to put up with him sleeping on the sofa while his brother slept in the box room. Maybe he should offer to lower the rent. When he'd arrived at the flat unannounced on Friday night, three of the students and Michael had been sitting cross-legged on the floor rolling joints and listening to mid-period Rolling Stones. Rebus stared in horror at the cigarette papers in Michael's hand.

'For fuck's sake, Mickey!' So at last Michael Rebus had elicited a reaction from his big brother. The students at least had the grace to look like the criminals they were. 'You're lucky,' Rebus told them all, 'that at this exact second I don't give a shit.'

'Go on, John,' said Michael, offering a half-smoked cigarette. 'It can't do any harm.'

'That's what I mean.' Rebus drew a bottle of whisky out of the carrier-bag he was holding. 'But this can.'

He had proceeded to spend the final hours of the evening sprawled across the sofa supping whisky and singing along to any old record that was put on the turntable. He'd spent much of the weekend in the same spot, too. The students hadn't seemed to mind, though he'd made them put away the drugs for the duration. They cleaned the flat around him, with Michael pitching in, and everyone trooped out to the pub on Saturday night leaving Rebus with the TV and some cans of beer. It didn't look as though Michael had told the students about his prison record; Rebus hoped he'd keep it that way. Michael had offered to move out, or at least give his brother the box room, but Rebus refused. He wasn't sure why.

On Sunday he went to Oxford Terrace, but there didn't seem to be anyone home, and his key still wouldn't open the door. So either the lock had been changed or Patience was hiding in there somewhere, going through her own version of cold turkey with the kids for company.

Now he stood outside Farmer Watson's door and looked down at himself. Sure enough, when he'd gone to Oxford Terrace this morning Patience had left a suitcase of stuff for him outside the door. No note, just the case. He'd changed into the clean suit in the police station toilets. It was a bit crumpled but no more so than anything he usually wore. He hadn't a tie to match, though: Patience had included two horrible brown ties (were they really *his*?) along with the dark blue suit. Brown ties don't make it. He knocked once on the door before opening it.

'Come in, John, come in.' It seemed to Rebus that the Farmer too was having trouble making St Leonard's fit his ways. The place just didn't feel right. 'Take a seat.' Rebus looked around for a chair. There was one beside the wall, loaded high with files. He lifted these off and tried to find space for them on the floor. If anything, the Chief Super had less space in his office than Rebus himself. 'Still waiting for those bloody filing cabinets,' he admitted. Rebus swung the chair over to the desk and sat down.

'What's up, sir?'

'How are things?'

'Things?'

'Yes.'

'Things are fine, sir.' Rebus wondered if the Farmer knew about Patience. Surely not.

'DC Clarke getting on all right, is she?'

'I've no complaints.'

'Good. We've got a bit of a job coming up, joint operation with Trading Standards.'

'Oh?'

'Chief Inspector Lauderdale will fill in the details, but I wanted to sound you out first, check how things are going.'

'What sort of joint operation?'

'Money lending,' said Watson. 'I forgot to ask, do you want coffee?' Rebus shook his head and watched as Watson bent over in his chair. There being so little space in the room, he'd taken to keeping his coffee-maker on the floor behind his desk, where twice so far to Rebus's knowledge he'd spilt it all across the new beige carpet. When Watson sat up again, he held in his meaty fist a cup of the devil's own drink. The Chief Super's coffee was a minor legend in Edinburgh.

'Money lending with some protection on the side,' Watson corrected. 'But mostly money lending.'

The same old sad story, in other words. People who wouldn't stand a chance in any bank, and with nothing worth pawning, could still borrow money, no matter how bad a risk. The problem was, of course, that the interest ran into the hundreds per cent and arrears could soon mount, bringing more prohibitive interest. It was the most vicious circle of all, vicious because at the end of it all lay intimidation, beatings and worse.

Suddenly, Rebus knew why the Chief Super had wanted this little chat. 'It's not Big Ger, is it?' he asked.

Watson nodded. 'In a way,' he said.

Rebus sprang to his feet. 'This'll be the fourth time in as many years! He always gets off. You know that, I know that!' Normally, he would have recited this on the move, but there was no floorspace worth the name, so he just stood there like a Sunday ranter at the foot of The Mound. 'It's a waste of time trying to pin him on money lending. I thought we'd been through all this a dozen times and decided it was useless going after him without trying another tack.'

'I know, John, I know, but the Trading Standards people are worried. The problem seems bigger than they thought.'

'Bloody Trading Standards.'

'Now, John . . .'

'But,' Rebus paused, 'with respect, sir, it's a complete waste of time and manpower. There'll be a surveillance, we'll take a few photos, we'll arrest a couple of the poor saps who act as runners, and nobody'll testify. If the Procurator Fiscal wants Big Ger nailed, then they should give us the resources so we can mount a decent size of operation.'

The problem, of course, was that nobody wanted to nail Morris Gerald Cafferty (known to all as Big Ger) as badly as John Rebus did. He wanted a full scale crucifixion. He wanted to be holding the spear, giving one last poke just to make sure the bastard really was dead. Cafferty was scum, but clever scum. There were always flunkies around to go to jail on his behalf. Because Rebus had failed so often to put the man away, he would rather not think of him at all. Now the Farmer was telling him that there was to be an 'operation'. That would mean long days and nights of surveillance, a lot of paperwork, and the arrests of a few pimply apprentice hardmen at the end of it all.

'John,' said Watson, summoning his powers of character analysis, 'I know how you feel. But let's give it one more shot, eh?'

'I know the kind of shot I'd take at Cafferty given half a chance.' Rebus turned his fist into a gun and mimed the recoil.

Watson smiled. 'Then it's lucky we won't be issuing firearms, isn't it?'

After a moment, Rebus smiled too. He sat down again. 'Go on then, sir,' he said, 'I'm listening.'

At eleven o'clock that evening, Rebus was watching TV in the flat. As usual, there was no one else about. They were either still studying in the University library, or else down at the pub. Since Michael wasn't around either, the pub seemed an odds-on bet. He knew the students were wary, expecting him to kick at least one of them out so he could claim a bedroom. They moved around the flat like eviction notices.

He'd phoned Patience three times, getting the answering machine on each occasion and telling it that he knew she was there and why didn't she pick up the phone?

As a result, the phone was on the floor beside the sofa, and when it rang he dangled an arm, picked up the receiver, and held it to his ear.

'Hello?'

'John?'

Rebus sat up fast. 'Patience, thank Christ you –'

'Listen, this is important.'

'I know it is. I know I was stupid, but you've got to believe –'

'Just listen, will you!' Rebus shut up and listened. He would do whatever she told him, no question. 'They thought you'd be here, so someone from the station just phoned. It's Brian Holmes.'

'What did he want?'

'No, they were phoning about him.'

'What about him?'

'He's been in some sort of . . . I don't know. Anyway, he's hurt.'

Still holding the receiver, Rebus stood up, hauling the whole apparatus off the floor with him. 'Where is he?'

'Somewhere in Haymarket, some bar . . .'

'The Heartbreak Cafe?'

'That's it. And listen, John?'

'Yes?'

'We will talk. But not yet. Just give me time.'

'Whatever you say, Patience. Bye.' John Rebus dropped the phone from his hand and grabbed his jacket.

Rebus was parking outside the Heartbreak Cafe barely seven minutes later. That was the beauty of Edinburgh when you could avoid traffic lights. The Heartbreak Cafe had been opened just over a year before by a chef who also happened to be an Elvis Presley fan. He had used some of his extensive memorabilia to decorate the interior, and his cooking skills to come up with a menu which was almost worth a visit even if, like Rebus, you'd never liked Elvis. Holmes had raved about the place since its opening, drooling for hours over the dessert called Blue Suede Choux. The Cafe operated as a bar too, with garish cocktails and 1950s music, plus bottled American beers whose prices would have caused convulsions in the Broadsword pub. Rebus got the idea that Holmes had become friends with the owner; certainly, he'd been spending a lot of time there since the split from Nell, and had put on a fair few pounds as a result.

From the outside, the place looked nothing special: pale cement front wall with a narrow rectangular window in the middle, most of which was filled with neon signs advertising beers. And above this a larger neon sign flashing the name of the restaurant. The action wasn't here, however. Holmes had been set on around the back of the place. A narrow alley, just about able to accommodate the width of a Ford Cortina, led to the patrons' car park. This was small by any restaurant's standards, and was also where the overflowing refuse bins were kept. Most clients, Rebus guessed, would park on the street out front. Holmes only parked back here because he spent so much time in the bar, and because his car had once been scratched when he'd left it out front.

There were two cars in the car park. One was Holmes', and the other almost certainly belonged to the owner of the Heartbreak Cafe. It was an old Ford Capri with a painting of Elvis on its bonnet. Brian Holmes lay between the two cars. So far no one had moved him. He would be moved soon, though, after the doctor had finished his examination. One of the officers present recognised Rebus and came over.

'Nasty blow to the back of the head. He's been out cold for at least twenty minutes. That's how long ago he was found. The owner of the place – that's who found him – recognised him and called in. Could be a fractured skull.'

Rebus nodded, saying nothing, his eyes on the prone figure of his colleague. The other detective was still talking, going on about how Holmes' breathing was regular, the usual reassurances. Rebus walked towards the body, standing over the kneeling doctor. The doctor didn't even glance up, but ordered a uniformed constable, who was holding a flashlight over Brian Holmes, to move it a bit to the left. He then started examining that section of Holmes' skull.

Rebus couldn't see any blood, but that didn't mean much. People died all the time without losing any blood over it. Christ, Brian looked so at peace. It was almost like staring into a casket. He turned to the detective.

'What's the owner's name again?'

'Eddie Ringan.'

'Is he inside?'

The detective nodded. 'Propping up the bar.'

That figured. 'I'll just go have a word,' said Rebus.

*

Eddie Ringan had nursed what was euphemistically called a drinking problem for several years, long before he'd opened the Heartbreak Cafe. For this reason, people reckoned the venture would fail, as other ventures of his had. But they reckoned wrong, for the sole reason that Eddie managed to find a manager, a manager who not only was some kind of financial guru but was also as straight and as strong as a construction girder. He didn't rip Eddie off, and he kept Eddie where Eddie belonged during working hours – in the kitchen.

Eddie still drank, but he could cook and drink; that wasn't a problem. Especially when there were one or two apprentice chefs around to do the stuff which required focused eyes or rock steady hands. And so, according to Brian Holmes, the Heartbreak Cafe thrived. He still hadn't managed to persuade Rebus to join him there for a meal of King Shrimp Creole or Love Me Tenderloin. Rebus wasn't persuaded to walk through the front door . . . until tonight.

The lights were still on. It was like walking into some teenager's shrine to his idol. There were Elvis posters on the walls, Elvis record covers, a life-size cut-out figure of the performer, even an Elvis clock, with the King's arms pointing to the time. The TV was on, an item on the late news. Some oversized charity cheque was being handed over in front of Gibson's Brewery.

There was no one in the place except Eddie Ringan slumped on a barstool, and another man behind the bar, pouring two shots of Jim Beam. Rebus introduced himself and was invited to take a seat. The bartender introduced himself as Pat Calder.

'I'm Mr Ringan's partner.' The way he said it made Rebus wonder if the two young men were more than merely business partners. Holmes hadn't mentioned Eddie was gay. He turned his attention to the chef.

Eddie Ringan was probably in his late twenties, but looked ten years older. He had straight, thinning hair over a large oval-shaped head, all of which sat uneasily above the larger oval of his body. Rebus had seen fat chefs and fatter chefs, and Ringan surely was a living advertisement for *some*body's cooking. His doughy face was showing signs of wear from the drink; not just this evening's scoop, but the weeks and months of steady, heavy consumption. Rebus watched him drain the inch of amber fire in a single savouring swallow.

'Gimme another.'

But Pat Calder shook his head. 'Not if you're driving.' Then, in clear and precise tones: 'This man is a police officer, Eddie. He's come to talk about Brian.'

Eddie Ringan nodded. 'He fell down, hit his head.'

'Is that what you think?' asked Rebus.

'Not really.' For the first time, Ringan looked up from the bartop and into Rebus's eyes. 'Maybe it was a mugger, or maybe it was a warning.'

'What sort of a warning?'

'Eddie's had too many tonight, Inspector,' said Pat Calder. 'He starts imagining –'

'I'm not bloody imagining.' Ringan slapped his palm down on the bartop for emphasis. He was still looking at Rebus. 'You know what it's like. It's either protection money – insurance, they like to call it – or it's the other restaurants ganging up because they don't like the business you're doing and they're not. You make a lot of enemies in this game.'

Rebus was nodding. 'So do you have anyone in mind, Eddie? Anyone in particular?'

But Ringan shook his head in a slow swing. 'Not really. No, not really.'

'But you think maybe *you* were the intended victim?'

Ringan signalled for another drink, and Calder poured. He drank before answering. 'Maybe. I don't know. They could be trying to scare off the customers. Times are hard.'

Rebus turned to Calder, who was staring at Eddie Ringan with a fair amount of revulsion. 'What about you, Mr Calder, any ideas?'

'I think it was just a mugging.'

'Doesn't look like they took anything.'

'Maybe they were interrupted.'

'By someone coming up the alley? Then how did they escape? That car park's a dead end.'

'I don't know.' Rebus kept watching Pat Calder. He was a few years older than Ringan, but looked younger. He'd drawn his dark hair back into what Rebus supposed was a fashionable ponytail, and had kept long straight sideburns reaching down past his ears. He was tall and thin. Indeed, he looked like he could use a good meal. Rebus had seen more meat on a butcher's pencil. 'Maybe,' Calder was saying, 'maybe he did fall after all. It's pretty dark out there. We'll get some lighting put in.'

'Very commendable of you, sir.' Rebus rose from the uncomfortable barstool. 'Meantime, if anything *does* come to mind, and especially if any *names* come to mind, you can always call us.'

'Yes, of course.'

Rebus paused in the doorway. 'Oh, and Mr Calder?'

'Yes?'

'If you let Mr Ringan drive tonight, I'll have him pulled over before he reaches Haymarket. Can't you drive him home?'

'I don't drive.'

'Then I suggest you put your hand in the till for cab fare. Otherwise Mr Ringan's next creation might be Jailhouse Roquefort.'

As Rebus left the restaurant, he could actually hear Eddie Ringan starting to laugh.

*

He didn't laugh for long. Drink was demanding his attention. 'Gimme another,' he ordered. Pat Calder silently poured to the level of the shot-glass. They'd bought the glasses on a trip to Miami, along with a lot of other stuff. Much of the money had come out of Pat Calder's own pockets, as well as those of his parents. He held the glass in front of Ringan, then toasted him before draining the contents himself. When Ringan started to complain, Calder slapped him across the face.

Ringan looked neither surprised nor hurt. Calder slapped him again.

'You stupid bugger!' he hissed. 'You stupid, stupid bugger!'

'I can't help it,' said Ringan, proffering his empty glass. 'I'm all shook up. Now give me a drink before I do something *really* stupid.'

Pat Calder thought about it for a moment. Then he gave Eddie Ringan the drink.

The ambulance took Brian Holmes to the Royal Infirmary.

Rebus had never been persuaded by this hospital. It seemed full of good intentions and unfilled staff rosters. So he stood close by Brian Holmes' bed, as close as they'd let him stand. And as the night wore on, he didn't flinch; he just slid a little lower down the wall. He was crouching with his head resting against his knees, arms cold against the floor, when he sensed someone towering over him. It was Nell Stapleton. Rebus recognised her by her very height, long before his eyes had reached her tear-stained face.

'Hello there, Nell.'

'Christ, John.' And the tears started again. He pulled himself upright, embracing her quickly. She was throwing words into his ear. 'We talked only this evening. I was horrible. And now this happens . . .'

'Hush, Nell. It's not your fault. This sort of thing can happen anytime.'

'Yes, but I can't help remembering, the last time we spoke it was an argument. If we hadn't argued . . .'

'Sshh, pet. Calm down now.' He held her tight. Christ, it felt good. He didn't like to think about how good it felt. It felt good all the same. Her perfume, her shape, the way she moulded against him.

'We argued, and he went to that bar, and then . . .'

'Sshh, Nell. It's not your fault.'

He believed it, too, though he wasn't sure whose fault it was: protection racketeers? Jealous restaurant owners? Simple neds? A difficult one to call.

'Can I see him?'

'By all means.' Rebus gestured with his arm towards Holmes' bed. He turned away as Nell Stapleton approached it, giving the couple some privacy. Not that the gesture meant anything; Holmes was still unconscious, hooked up to some monitor and with his head heavily bandaged. But he could almost make out the words Nell used when she spoke to her estranged lover. The tone she used made him think of Dr Patience Aitken, made him half-wish *he* were lying unconscious. It was nice to think people were saying nice things about you.

After five minutes, she came tiredly back. 'Hard work?' Rebus offered.

Nell Stapleton nodded. 'You know,' she said quietly, 'I think I've an idea why this happened.'

'Oh?'

She was speaking in a near-whisper, though the ward was quiet. They were the only two souls about on two legs. She sighed loudly. Rebus wondered if she'd ever taken drama classes.

'The black book,' she said. Rebus nodded as though understanding her, then frowned.

'What black book?' he asked.

'I probably shouldn't be telling you, but you're not just someone he works with, are you? You're a friend.' She let out another whistle of air. 'It was Brian's notebook. Nothing official, this was stuff he was looking into on his own.'

Rebus, wary of waking anyone, led her out of the ward. 'A diary?' he asked.

'Not really. It was just that sometimes he used to hear rumours, bits of pub gossip. He'd write them down in the black book. Then he might take things further. It was sort of a hobby with him, but maybe he thought it was also a way to an early promotion. I don't know. We used to argue about that, too. I was hardly seeing him, he was so busy.'

Rebus was staring at the wall of the corridor. The overhead lighting stung his eyes. He'd never heard Holmes mention any kind of notebook.

'What about it?'

Nell was shaking her head. 'It was just something he said, something before we ...' Her hand went to her mouth, as though she were about to cry. 'Before we split up.'

'What was it, Nell?'

'I'm not sure exactly.' Her eyes met Rebus's. 'I just know Brian was scared, and I'd never seen him scared before.'

'Scared of what?'

She shrugged. 'Something in the book.' Then she shook her head again. 'I'm not sure what. I can't help feeling ... feeling I'm somehow responsible. If we'd never ...'

Rebus pulled her to him again. 'There there, pet. It's not your fault.'

'But it *is*! It *is*!'

'No it isn't.' Rebus made his voice sound determined. 'Now, tell me, where did Brian keep this wee black book of his?'

About his person, was the answer. Brian Holmes' clothes and possessions had been removed when the ambulance delivered him to the Infirmary.

But Rebus's ID was enough to gain access to the hospital's property department, even at this grim hour. He plucked the notebook out of an A4 envelope's worth of belongings, and had a look at the other contents. Wallet, diary, ID. Watch, keys, small change. Stuff without personality, now that it had been separated from its owner, but strengthening Rebus's conviction that this was no mere mugging.

Nell had gone home still crying, leaving no message to be passed along to Brian. All Rebus knew was that she suspected the beating was something to do with the notebook. And maybe she was right. He sat in the corridor outside Holmes' ward, sipping water and skipping through the cheap leatherette book. Holmes had employed a kind of shorthand, but the code was not nearly complex enough to puzzle another copper. Much of the information had come from a single night and a single action: the night an animal rights group had broken into Fettes HQ's records room. Amongst other things, they'd uncovered evidence of a rent-boy scandal among Edinburgh's most respectable citizens. *This* didn't come as news to John Rebus, but some other entries were intriguing, and especially the one referring to the Central Hotel.

The Central Hotel had been an Edinburgh institution until five years ago, when it had been razed to the ground. An insurance scam was rumoured, and £5,000 had been hoisted by the insurance company involved as a reward for proof that just such a scam had really taken place. But the reward had gone uncollected.

The hotel had once been a traveller's paradise. It was sited on Princes Street, no distance at all from Waverley Station, and so had become a travelling businessman's home-from-home. But in its latter years, the Central had seen business decline. And as genuine business declined, so disingenuous business took over. It was no real secret that the Central's stuffy rooms could be hired by the hour or the afternoon. Room service would provide a bottle of champagne and as much talcum powder as any room's tenants required.

In other words, the Central had become a knocking-shop, and by no means a subtle one. It also catered to the town's shadier elements in all shapes and forms. Wedding parties and stag nights were held for a spread of the city's villains, and underage drinkers could loll in the lounge bar for hours, safe in the knowledge that no honest copper would stray inside the doors. Familiarity bred further contempt, and the lounge bar started to be used for drug deals, and other even less savoury deals too, so that the Central Hotel became something more than a mere knocking-shop. It turned into a swamp.

A swamp with an eviction order over its head.

The police couldn't turn a blind eye forever and a day, especially when complaints from the public were rising by the month. And the more trash was introduced to the Central, the more trash was produced by the place. Until almost no real drinkers went there at all. If you ventured into the Central, you were looking for a woman, cheap drugs, or a fight. And God help you if you weren't.

Then, as had to happen, one night the Central burnt down. This came as no surprise to anyone; so much so that reporters on the local paper hardly bothered to cover the blaze. The police, of course, were delighted. The fire saved them having to raid the joint.

But the next morning there was a solitary surprise: for though all the hotel's staff and customers had been accounted for, a body turned up amongst the charred ceilings and roofbeams. A body that had been burnt out of all recognition.

A body that had been dead when the fire started.

These scant details Rebus knew. He would not have been a City of Edinburgh detective if he hadn't known. Yet here was Holmes' black book, throwing up tantalising clues. Or what looked like tantalising clues. Rebus read the relevant section through again.

Central fire. El was there! Poker game on 1st floor. R. Brothers involved (so maybe Mork too??). Try finding.

He studied Holmes' handwriting, trying to decide whether the journal said El or E1; the letter l or the number 1. And if it was the letter l, did he mean El to stand as the phonetic equivalent of a single letter l? Why the exclamation mark? It seemed that the presence of El (or L or E-One) was some kind of revelation to Brian Holmes. And who the hell were the R. Brothers? Rebus thought at once of Michael and him, the Rebus brothers, but shook the picture from his mind. As for Mork, a bad TV show came to mind, nothing else.

No, he was too tired for this. Tomorrow would be time enough. Maybe by tomorrow Brian would be up and talking. Rebus decided he'd say a little prayer for him before he went to sleep.

3

A prayer which went unanswered. Brian Holmes had still not regained consciousness when Rebus phoned the Infirmary at seven o'clock.

'Is he in a coma or something, then?'

The voice on the other end of the phone was cold and factual. 'There will be tests this morning.'

'What sorts of tests?'

'Are you part of Mr Holmes' immediate family?'

'No, I'm bloody not. I'm ...' A police officer? His boss? Just a friend? 'Never mind.' He put down the receiver. One of the students put her head around the living-room door.

'Want some herbal tea?'

'No thanks.'

'A bowl of muesli?'

Rebus shook his head. She smiled at him and disappeared. Herbal tea and muesli, great God almighty. What sort of way was that to start the day? The door of the box room opened from within, and Rebus was startled when a teenage girl dressed only in a man's shirt came out into the daylight, rubbing at her eyes. She smiled at him as she passed, making for the living-room door. She walked on tiptoe, trying not to put too much bare foot on the cold linoleum.

Rebus stared at the living-room door for another ten seconds, then walked over to the box room. Michael was lying naked on the narrow single bed, the bed Rebus had bought secondhand at the weekend. He was rubbing a hand over his chest and staring at the ceiling. The air inside the box room was foetid.

'What the hell do you think you're doing?' Rebus asked.

'She's eighteen, John.'

'That's not what I meant.'

'Oh? What did you mean?'

But Rebus wasn't sure any more. There was just something plain ugly about his brother sharing a box room bed with some student while he slept on the sofa not eight feet away. It was all ugly, all of it. Michael would have to go. Rebus would have to move into a hotel or something. None of it could go on like this much longer. It wasn't fair on the students.

'You should come to the pub more often,' Michael offered. 'That's what's wrong you know.'

'What?'

'You just don't see life, John. It's time you started to live a little.'

Michael was still smiling when his brother slammed the door on him.

'I've just heard about Brian.'

DC Siobhan Clarke looked in some distress. She had lost all colour from her face except for two dots of red high on her cheeks and the paler red of her lips. Rebus nodded for her to sit down. She pulled a chair over to his desk.

'What happened?'

'Somebody hit him over the head.'

'What with?'

Now *that* was a good question, the sort of question a detective would ask. It was also a question Rebus had forgotten to ask last night. 'We don't know,' he said. 'Nor do we have any motive, not yet.'

'It happened outside the Heartbreak Cafe?'

Rebus nodded. 'In the car park out back.'

'He kept saying he was going to take me there for a meal.'

'Brian always keeps his word. Don't worry, Siobhan, he'll be all right.'

She nodded, trying to believe this. 'I'll go see him later.'

'If you like,' said Rebus, not sure quite what his tone was supposed to mean. She looked at him again.

'I like,' she said.

After she'd gone, Rebus read through a message from Chief Inspector Lauderdale. It detailed the initial surveillance plans for the money lending operation. Rebus was asked for questions and 'useful comments'. He smiled at that phrase, knowing Lauderdale had used it hoping to deter Rebus from his usual basic critique of anything put in front of him. Then someone delivered a hefty package, the package he had been waiting for. He lifted the flaps of the cardboard box and started to pull out bulging files. These were the notes referring to the Central Hotel, its history and final sorry end. He knew he had a morning's reading ahead of him, so he found Lauderdale's letter, penned a large OK on it, scrawled his signature beneath, and tossed it into his out tray. Lauderdale wouldn't believe it, wouldn't believe Rebus had accepted the surveillance without so much as a murmur. It was bound to perplex the Chief Inspector.

Not a bad start to the working day.

Rebus sat down with the first file from the box and started to read.

He was filling a second page with his own notes when the telephone rang. It was Nell Stapleton.

249

'Nell, where are you?' Rebus continued writing, finishing a sentence.

'I'm at work. Just thought I'd call and see if you'd found anything.'

He finished the sentence. 'Such as?'

'Well, what happened to Brian.'

'I'm not sure yet. Maybe he'll tell us when he wakes up. Have you talked to the hospital?'

'First thing.'

'Me too.' Rebus started writing again. There was a nervous silence on the other end of the line.

'What about the black book?'

'Oh, that. Yes, I had a wee read of it.'

'Did you find whatever Brian was afraid of?'

'Maybe and maybe not. Don't worry, Nell, I'm working on it.'

'That's good.' There was genuine relief in her voice. 'Only, when Brian wakes up, don't tell him I told you, will you?'

'Why not? I think it's . . . it shows you care about him.'

'Of course I care!'

'That didn't stop you chucking him out.' He wished he hadn't said it, but he had. He could hear her anguish, and imagined her in the University library, trying not to let any of the other staff see her face.

'John,' she said at last, 'you don't know the whole story. You've only heard Brian's side.'

'That's true. Want to tell me yours?'

She thought it over. 'Not like this, on the telephone. Maybe some other time.'

'Any time you like, Nell.'

'I'd better get back to work. Are you going to see Brian today?'

'Maybe tonight. They're running tests all morning. What about you?'

'Oh yes, I'll drop by. It's only two minutes away.'

So it was. Rebus thought of Siobhan Clarke. For some reason, he didn't want the two women to meet at Brian's bedside. 'What time are you thinking of going?'

'Lunchtime, I suppose.'

'One last thing, Nell.'

'Yes?'

'Does Brian have any enemies?'

It took her a little while to answer. 'No.'

Rebus waited to see if she had anything to add. 'Well, take care, Nell.'

'You too, John. Bye.'

After he'd put down the receiver, Rebus started back to his note-taking. But after half a sentence he stopped, tapping his pen thoughtfully against his mouth. He stayed that way for a considerable time, then made some phone calls to his contacts (he didn't like the word 'grasses'), telling them to keep ears open regarding an assault behind the Heart-break Cafe.

'A colleague of mine, which means it's serious, okay?'

He'd ended up saying 'colleague' but had meant to say 'friend'.

At lunchtime, he walked over to the University and paid his respects at the Department of Pathology. He had called ahead and Dr Curt was ready in his office, wearing a cream-coloured raincoat and humming some piece of classical music which Rebus annoyingly could recognise but not name.

'Ah, Inspector, what a pleasant surprise.'

Rebus blinked. 'Really?'

'Of course. Usually when you're pestering me, it's because of some current and pressing case. But today ...' Curt opened his arms wide. 'No case! And yet you phone me up and invite me to lunch. It can't be very busy along at St Leonard's.'

On the contrary, but Rebus knew the workload was in good hands. Before leaving, he'd loaded enough work onto Siobhan Clarke that she wouldn't have time for a lunch-break, beyond a sandwich and a drink from the cafeteria. When she'd complained, he'd told her she could take time off later in the afternoon to visit Brian Holmes.

'How have you settled in there, by the way?'

Rebus shrugged. 'It doesn't matter to me where they put me. Where do you want to eat?'

'I've taken the liberty of reserving a table at the University Staff Club.'

'What, some sort of canteen?'

Curt laughed, shaking his head. He had ushered Rebus out of his office and was locking the door. 'No,' said Curt. 'There is a canteen, of course, but as you're buying I thought we'd opt for something a little bit more refined.'

'Then lead on to the refinery.'

The dining-room was on the ground floor, near the main door of the Staff Club on Chambers Street. They'd walked the short walk, talking about nothing in particular when they could hear one another above the traffic noise. Curt always walked as though he were late for some engagement. Well, he was a busy man: a full teaching load, plus the extra duties heaped on him at one time or another by most of the police forces in Scotland, and most onerously by the City of Edinburgh Police.

The dining-room was small but with plenty of space between the tables. Rebus was pleased to see that the prices were reasonable, though the tally was upped when Curt ordered a bottle of wine.

'My treat,' he said. But Rebus shook his head.

'The Chief Constable's treat,' he corrected. After all, he had every intention of claiming it as a legitimate expense. The wine arrived before the soup. As the waitress poured, Rebus wondered when would be the right moment to open the *real* conversation.

'Slainte!' said Curt, raising his glass. Then: 'So what's this all about? You're not the kind for lunch with a friend, not unless there's something you want, and can't get by buying pints and bridies in some smoky saloon.'

Rebus smiled at this. 'Do you remember the Central Hotel?'

'A dive of a place on Princes Street. It burnt down six or seven years ago.'

'Five years ago actually.'

Curt took another sip of wine. 'There was a smouldering body as I recall. "Crispy batter" we call those.'

'But when you examined the corpse, he hadn't died in the fire, had he?'

'Some new evidence has come to light?'

'Not exactly. I just wanted to ask what you remember about the case.'

'Well, let's see.' Curt broke off as the soup arrived. He took three or four mouthfuls, then wiped a napkin around his lips. 'The body was never identified. I know that we tried dental checks, but to no avail. There was no external evidence, of course, but people stupidly believe that a burned body tells no tales. I cut the deceased open and found, as I'd known I would, that the internal organs were in pretty good shape. Cooked on the outside, raw within, like a good French steak.'

A couple at a nearby table were soundlessly chewing their food, and staring hard at their tabletop. Curt seemed either not to notice or not to mind.

'DNA fingerprinting had been around for four years, but though we got some blood from the heart, we were never given anything to match it against. Of course, the heart was the clincher.'

'Because of the bullet wound.'

'Two wounds, Inspector, entrance and exit. That set you lot scurrying back to the scene, didn't it?'

Rebus nodded. They'd searched the immediate vicinity of the body, then widened the search until a cadet found the bullet. Its calibre was eight millimetre, matching the wound to the heart, but it offered no other clues.

'You also found,' said Rebus, 'that the deceased had suffered a broken arm at some time in the past.'

'Did I?'

'But again it didn't get us any further forward.'

'Especially,' said Curt, mopping his bowl with bread, 'bearing in mind the reputation of the Central. Probably every second person in the place had been in a fight and suffered *some* breakages.'

Rebus was nodding. 'Agreed, yet he was never identified. If he'd been a regular, or one of the staff, surely someone would have come forward. But nobody ever did.'

'Well, it was a long time ago. Are you about to start dusting off some ghosts?'

'There was nothing ghostly about whoever brained Brian Holmes.'

'Sergeant Holmes? What happened?'

Rebus was hoping to spend some of the afternoon reading through more of the case-notes. He'd thought it would take half a day; but this had been optimistic from the start. He was now thinking in terms of half a week, including some evening reading in the flat. There was so much stuff. Lengthy reports from the fire department, the council's building department, news clippings, police reports, interview statements ...

But when he got back to St Leonard's, Lauderdale was waiting. He had received Rebus's hasty comment on the money-lending surveillance, and now wanted to push things on. Which meant that Rebus was trapped in the Chief Inspector's office for the best part of two hours, an hour of it head-to-head stuff. For the other hour, they were joined by Detective Inspector Alister Flower, who had worked out of St Leonard's since its opening day back in September 1989 and bragged continually that when he had shaken hands with the main dignitary at the occasion, they had both turned out to be Masons, with Flower's being the older clan.

Flower resented the incomers from Great London Road. If there were friction and factions within the station, you could be sure Flower was at the back of them somewhere. If anything united Lauderdale and Rebus it was a dislike of Flower, though Lauderdale was slowly being drawn into the Flower camp.

Rebus, however, had contempt even for the funny way the man spelt his first name. He called him 'Little Weed' and thought probably Flower had something to do with the taxman's sudden inquiries.

In the operation against the money lenders, Flower was to lead the other surveillance team. Typically, in an effort to appease the man, Lauderdale offered him the pick of the surveillances. One would be of a pub where the lenders were said to hang out and take payments. The other would be of what looked like the nominal HQ of the gang, an office attached to a mini-cab firm on Gorgie Road.

'I've okayed the Gorgie surveillance with Divisional HQ West,' said Lauderdale, as ever efficient behind a desk. Take him out onto the streets, Rebus knew, and he was about as efficient as pepper on a vindaloo.

'Well,' said Flower, 'if it's okay with Inspector Rebus, I think I'd prefer the watch on the pub. It's a bit closer to home.' And Flower smiled.

'Interesting choice,' said Rebus, his arms folded, legs stretched out in front of him.

Lauderdale was nodding, his eyes flitting between the two men. 'Well, that's settled then. Now, let's get down to details.'

The same details, in fact, that Rebus and he had gone through in the hour prior to Flower's arrival. Rebus tried to concentrate but couldn't. He was desperate to get back to the Central Hotel records. But the more agitated he grew, the slower things moved.

The plan itself was simple. The money lenders worked out of the Firth Pub in Tollcross. They picked up business there, and generally hung around waiting for debtors to come and pay the weekly dues. The money was taken at some point to the office in Gorgie. This office also was used as a drop-off point by debtors, and here the leading visible player could be found.

The men working out of the Firth were bit-parts. They collected cash, and maybe even used some verbal persuasion when payment was late. But when it came to the crunch, everyone paid dues to Davey Dougary. Davey turned up every morning at the office as prompt as any businessman, parking his BMW 635CSi beside the battered mini-cabs. On the way from car to office, if the weather was warm he would slip his jacket off and roll up his shirt-sleeves. Yes, Trading Standards had been watching Davey for quite some time.

There would be Trading Standards officers involved in both surveillances. The police were really only there to enforce the law; it was a Trading Standards operation in name. The name they had chosen was Moneybags. Another interesting choice, thought Rebus, so original. Keeping surveillance in the pub would mean sitting around reading newspapers, circling the names of horses on the betting sheet, playing pool or the jukebox or dominoes. Oh yes, and drinking beer; after all, they didn't want to stand out in the crowd.

Keeping surveillance on the office meant sitting in the window of a disused first floor room in the tenement block across the road. The place was without charm, toilet facilities, or heating. (The bathroom fittings had been stolen during a break-in earlier in the year, down to the very toilet-pan.) A happy prospect, especially for Holmes and Clarke who would bear the burden of the surveillance, always supposing Holmes recovered in time. He thought of his two junior officers spending long days huddling for warmth in a double sleeping-bag. Hell's bells. Thank God Dougary didn't work nights. And thank God there'd be some Trading Standards bodies around too.

Still, the thought of nabbing Davey Dougary warmed Rebus's heart. Dougary was bad the way a rotten apple was. There was no repairing the damage, though the surface might seem untainted. Of course, Dougary was one of Big Ger Cafferty's 'lieutenants'. Cafferty had even turned up once at the office, captured on film. Much good would it do; he'd have a thousand good reasons for that visit. There'd be no pinning him in court. They might get Dougary, but Cafferty was a long way off, so far ahead of them they looked like they were pushing their heap of a car while he cruised in fifth gear.

'So,' Lauderdale was saying. 'We can start with this as of next Monday, yes?'

Rebus awoke from his reverie. It was clear that much had been discussed in his spiritual absence. He wondered if he'd agreed to any of it. (His silence had no doubt been received as tacit consent.)

'I've no problem with that,' said Flower.

Rebus moved again in his seat, knowing that escape was close now. 'I'll probably need someone to fill in for DS Holmes.'

'Ah yes, how is he doing?'

'I haven't heard today, sir,' Rebus admitted. 'I'll call before I clock off.'

'Well, let me know.'

'We're putting together a collection,' Flower said.

'For Christ's sake, he's no' deid yet!'

Flower took the explosion without flinching. 'Well, all the same.'

'It's a nice gesture,' Lauderdale said. Flower shrugged his shoulders modestly. Lauderdale opened his wallet and dug out a reluctant fiver, which he handed to Flower.

Hey, big spender, thought Rebus. Even Flower looked startled.

'Five quid,' he said, unnecessarily.

Lauderdale didn't want any thanks. He just wanted Flower to take the money. His wallet had disappeared back into its cave. Flower stuck the note in his shirt pocket and rose from his chair. Rebus stood too, not looking forward to being in the corridor alone with Flower. But Lauderdale stopped him.

'A word, John.'

Flower sniffed as he left, probably thinking Rebus was to receive a dressing down for his outburst. In fact, this wasn't what Lauderdale had in mind.

'I was passing your desk earlier. I see you've got the files on the Central Hotel fire. Old news, surely?' Rebus said nothing. 'Anything I should know about?'

'No, sir,' said Rebus, rising and making for the door. He reckoned Flower would be on his way by now. 'Nothing you should know about. Just some reading of mine. You could call it a history project.'

'Archaeology, more like.'

True enough: old bones and hieroglyphs; trying to make the dead come to life.

'The past is important, sir,' said Rebus, taking his leave.

4

The past was certainly important to Edinburgh. The city fed on its past like a serpent with its tail in its mouth. And Rebus's past seemed to be circling around again too. There was a message on his desk in Clarke's handwriting. Obviously she'd gone to visit Holmes, but not before taking a telephone call intended for her superior.

> DI Morton called from Falkirk. He'll try again another time. He wouldn't say what it's about. Very cagey. I'll be back in two hours.

She was the sort who would make up the two hours by staying late a few nights, even though Rebus had deprived her of a reasonable lunch-break. Despite being English, there was something of the Scottish Protestant in Siobhan Clarke. It wasn't her fault she was called Siobhan either. Her parents had been English Literature lecturers at Edinburgh University back in the 1960s. They'd lumbered her with the Gaelic name, then moved south again, taking her to be schooled in Nottingham and London. But she'd come back to Edinburgh to go to college, and fallen in love (her story) with Edinburgh. Then she'd decided on the police as a career (alienating her friends and, Rebus suspected, her liberal parents). Still, the parents had bought her a New Town flat, so it couldn't be all strife.

Rebus suspected she'd do well in the police, despite people like him. Women did have to work harder in the force to progress at the same pace as their male colleagues: everyone knew it. But Siobhan worked hard enough, and by Christ did she have a memory. A month from now, he could ask her about this note on his desk, and she'd remember the telephone conversation word for word. It was scary.

It was slightly scary too that Jack Morton's name had come up at this particular time. Another ghost from Rebus's past. When they'd worked together six years ago, Rebus wouldn't have given the younger Morton more than four or five years to live, such was his steady consumption of booze and cigarettes.

There was no contact phone number. It would have taken only a few minutes to find the number of Morton's nick, but Rebus didn't feel like it. He felt like getting back to the files on his desk. But first he phoned the Infirmary to check on Brian Holmes' progress, only to be told that there wasn't any, though there was also no decline.

'That sounds cheery.'

'It's just an expression,' the person on the phone said.

The test results wouldn't be known until next morning. He thought for a moment, then made another call, this time to Patience Aitken's group practice. But Patience was out on a call, so Rebus left a message. He got the receptionist to read it back so he could be sure it sounded right.

'"Thought I'd call to let you know how Brian's doing. Sorry you weren't in. You can call me at Arden Street if you like. John."'

Yes, that would do. She'd have to call *him* now, just to show she wasn't uncaring about Brian's condition. With a speck of hope in his heart, Rebus went back to work.

He got back to the flat at six, having done some shopping en route. Though he'd proposed taking the files home, he really couldn't be bothered. He was tired, his head ached, and his nose was stuffy from the old dust which rose from their pages. He climbed the flights of stairs wearily, opened the door, and took the grocery bags into the kitchen, where one of the students was spreading peanut butter onto a thick slice of brown bread.

'Hiya, Mr Rebus. You got a phone call.'

'Oh?'

'Some woman doctor.'

'When?'

'Ten minutes ago, something like that.'

'What did she say?'

'She said if she wanted to find out about ...'

'Brian? Brian Holmes?'

'Aye, that's it. If she wanted to find out about him, she could call the hospital, and that's exactly what she'd done twice today already.' The student beamed, pleased at having remembered the whole message. So Patience had seen through his scheme. He should have known. Her intelligence, amongst other things, had attracted him to her. Also, they were very much alike in many ways. Rebus should have learned long ago, never try to put one over on someone who knows the way your mind works. He lifted a box of eggs, tin of beans, and packet of bacon out of the bag.

'Oh my God,' said the student in disgust. 'Do you know just how intelligent pigs *are*, Mr Rebus?'

Rebus looked at the student's sandwich. 'A damned sight more intelligent than peanuts,' he said. Then: 'Where's the frying-pan?'

*

Later, Rebus sat watching TV. He'd nipped over to the Infirmary to visit Brian Holmes. He reckoned it was quicker to walk rather than driving around The Meadows. So he'd walked, letting his head clear. But the visit itself had been depressing. Not a bit of progress.

'How long can he stay conked out?'

'It can take a while,' a nurse had consoled.

'It's *been* a while.'

She touched his arm. 'Patience, patience.'

Patience! He almost took a taxi to her flat, but dropped the idea. Instead, he walked back to Arden Street, climbed the same old weary stairs, and flopped onto the sofa. He had spent so many evenings deep in thought in this room, but that had been back when the flat was his, only his.

Michael came into the living room, fresh from a shave and a shower. He wore a towel tight around his flat stomach. He was in good shape; Rebus hadn't noticed before. But Michael saw him noticing now, and patted his stomach.

'One thing about Peterhead, plenty of exercise.'

'I suppose you've got to get fit in there,' Rebus drawled, 'so you can fight back when someone's after your arse.'

Michael shook off the remark like it was so much water. 'Oh, there's plenty of that too. Never interested me.' Whistling, he went into the box room and started to dress.

'Going out?' Rebus called.

'Why stay in?'

'Seeing that wee girl again?'

Michael put his head around the door. 'She's a consenting adult.'

Rebus got to his feet. 'She's a wee girl.' He walked over to the box room and stared at Michael, forcing him to stop what he was doing.

'What, John? You want me to stop going out with women? If you don't like it, tough.'

Rebus thought of all the remarks he could make. This is my flat ... I'm your big brother ... you should know better ... He knew Mickey would laugh – quite rightly – at any and all of them. So he thought of something else to say.

'Fuck you, Mickey.'

Michael Rebus recommended dressing. 'I'm sorry I'm such a disappointment, but what's the alternative? Sit here all night watching you stew or sulk or whatever it is you do inside your head? Thanks but no thanks.'

'I thought you were going to look for a job.'

Michael Rebus grabbed a book from the bed and threw it at his brother. 'I'm looking for a fucking job! What do you think I do all day?

Just give it a rest, will you?' He picked up his jacket and pushed past Rebus. 'Don't wait up for me, eh?'

That was a laugh: Rebus was asleep, and alone in the flat, before the ten o'clock news. But it wasn't a sound sleep. It was a sleep filled with dreams. He was chasing Patience through some office block, always just losing her. He was eating in a restaurant with a teenage girl while the Rolling Stones entertained unnoticed on the small stage in the corner. He was watching a hotel burn to the ground, wondering if Brian Holmes, still unaccounted for, had gotten out alive ...

And then he was awake and shivering, the room illuminated only by the street-lamp outside, burning through a chink in the curtains. He'd been reading the book Michael had thrown at him. It was about hypno-therapy and still lay in his lap, beneath the blanket someone had thrown over him. There were noises nearby, noises of pleasure. They were coming from the box room. Some therapy, no doubt. Rebus listened to them for what seemed like hours until the light outside grew pale.

5

Andrew McPhail sat beside his bedroom window. Across the road, the children were being lined up two by two outside the school doors. The boys had to hold hands with the girls, the whole thing supervised by two female staff members, looking hardly old enough to be parents, never mind teachers. McPhail sipped cold tea from his mug and watched. He paid very close attention to the children. Any one of the girls might have been Melanie. Except, of course, that Melanie would be older. Not much older, but older. He wasn't kidding himself. He knew the odds were Melanie wouldn't be at this school, probably wasn't even in Edinburgh any more. But he watched all the same, and imagined her down there, her hand touching the cool wet hand of one of the boys. Small delicate fingers, the beginning of fine lines on the palm. One girl was really quite similar: short straight hair curling in towards her ears and the nape of her neck. The height was familiar, too, but the face, what he could see of the face, was nothing like Melanie. Really, nothing like her. And besides, what did it matter to McPhail?

They were marching into the building now, leaving him behind with his cold tea and his memories. He could hear Mrs MacKenzie downstairs, washing dishes and probably chipping and breaking as much crockery as she got clean. Not her fault, her eyesight was failing. Everything about the old woman was failing. The house was bound to be worth £40,000, as good as money in the bank. And what did he have? Only memories of the way things had been in Canada and before Canada.

A plate crashed onto the kitchen floor. It couldn't go on like this, really it couldn't. There'd be nothing left. He didn't like to think about the budgie in the living-room . . .

McPhail drained the strong tea. The caffeine made him slightly giddy, sweat breaking out on his forehead. The playground was empty, the school doors closed. He couldn't see anything through the building's few visible windows. There might be a late-arriving straggler, but he didn't have time to waste. He had work to do. It was good to keep busy. Keeping busy kept you sane.

'Big Ger,' Rebus was saying, 'real name Morris Gerald Cafferty.'

Dutifully, and despite her good memory, DC Siobhan Clarke wrote these words on her notepad. Rebus didn't mind her taking notes. It was good exercise. When she lowered her head to write, Rebus had a view of the crown of her head, light-brown hair falling forward. She was good looking in a homely sort of way. Indeed, she reminded him a bit of Nell Stapleton.

'He's the prime mover, and if we're offered him we'll take him. But Operation Moneybags will actually be focusing on David Charles Dougary, known as Davey.' Again, the words went onto the paper. 'Dougary rents office space from a dodgy mini-cab service in Gorgie Road.'

'Not far from the Heartbreak Cafe?'

The question surprised him. 'No,' he said, 'not too far.'

'And the restaurant owner hinted at a protection pay-off?'

Rebus shook his head. 'Don't get carried away, Clarke.'

'And these men are involved in protection money too, aren't they?'

'There's not much Big Ger Cafferty *isn't* involved in: money laundering, prostitution. He's a big bad bastard, but that isn't the point. The point is, this operation will concentrate on loan-sharking, period.'

'All I'm saying is maybe Sergeant Holmes was attacked by mistake instead of the Cafe's owner.'

'It's a possibility,' said Rebus. And if it's true, he thought, I'm wasting a lot of time and effort on an old case. But as Nell said, Brian was frightened of something in his black book. And all because he'd started trying to track down the mysterious R. Brothers.

'But to get back to business, we'll be setting up a surveillance across the road from the taxi firm.'

'Round the clock?'

'We'll start with working hours. Dougary has a fairly fixed routine by all accounts.'

'What's he supposed to be doing in that office?'

'The way he tells it, everything from basic entrepreneurship to arranging food parcels for the Third World. Don't get me wrong, Dougary's clever. He's lasted longer than most of Big Ger's "associates". He's also a maniac, it's worth bearing that in mind. We once arrested him after a pub brawl. He'd torn the ear off another man with his teeth. When we got there, Dougary was chomping away. The ear was never recovered.'

Rebus always expected some reaction from his favourite stories, but all Siobhan Clarke did was smile and say, 'I love this city.' Then: 'Are there files on Mr Cafferty?'

'Oh aye, there are files. By all means, plough through them. They'll give you some idea what you're up against.'

She nodded. 'I'll do that. And when do we start the surveillance, sir?'

'First thing Monday morning. Everything will be set up on Sunday. I just hope they give us a decent camera.' He noticed Clarke was looking relieved. Then the penny dropped. 'Don't worry, you won't miss the Hibs game.'

She smiled. 'They're away to Aberdeen.'

'And you're still going?'

'Absolutely.' She tried never to miss a game.

Rebus was shaking his head. He didn't know that many Hibs fans. 'I wouldn't travel that far for the Second Coming.'

'Yes you would.'

Now Rebus smiled. 'Who's been talking? Right, what's on the agenda for today?'

'I've talked to the butcher. He was no help at all. I think I'd have more chance of getting a complete sentence out of the carcases in his deep freeze. But he does drive a Merc. That's an expensive car. Butchers aren't well known for high salaries, are they?'

Rebus shrugged. 'The prices they charge, I wouldn't be so sure.'

'Anyway, I'm planning to drop in on him at home this morning, just to clear up a couple of points.'

'But he'll be at work.'

'Unfortunately yes.'

Rebus caught on. 'His wife will be home?'

'That's what I'm hoping. The offer of a cup of tea, a little chat in the living room. Wasn't it terrible about Rory? That sort of thing.'

'So you can size up his home life, and maybe get a talkative wife thrown in for good measure.' Rebus was nodding slowly. It was so devious he should have thought of it himself.

'Get tae it, lass,' he said, and she did, leaving him to reach down onto the floor and lift one of the Central Hotel files onto his desk.

He started reading, but soon froze at a certain page. It listed the Hotel's customers on the night it burnt down. One name fairly flew off the page.

'Would you credit that?' Rebus got up from the desk and put his jacket on. Another ghost. And another excuse to get out of the office.

The ghost was Matthew Vanderhyde.

6

The house next to Vanderhyde's was as mad as ever. Owned by an ancient Nationalist, it sported the saltire flag on its gate and what looked like thirty-year-old tracts taped to its windows. The owner couldn't get much light, but then the house Rebus was approaching had its curtains drawn closed.

He rang the doorbell and waited. It struck him that Vanderhyde might well be dead. He would be in his early- to mid-seventies, and though he'd seemed healthy enough the last time they'd met, well, that was over two years ago.

He had consulted Vanderhyde in an earlier case. After the case was closed, Rebus used to drop in on Vanderhyde from time to time, just casually. They only lived six streets apart, after all. But then he'd started to get serious with Dr Patience Aitken, and hadn't found time for a visit since.

The door opened, and there stood Matthew Vanderhyde, looking just the same as ever. His sightless eyes were hidden behind dark green spectacles, above which sat a high shiny forehead and long swept-back yellow hair. He was wearing a suit of beige cord with a brown waistcoat, from the pocket of which hung a watch-chain. He leaned lightly on his silver-topped cane, waiting for the caller to speak.

'Hello there, Mr Vanderhyde.'

'Ah, Inspector Rebus. I was wondering when I'd see you. Come in, come in.'

From Vanderhyde's tone, it sounded like they'd last met two weeks before. He led Rebus through the dark hallway and into the darker living room. Rebus took in the shapes of bookshelves, paintings, the large mantelpiece covered in mementoes from trips abroad.

'As you can see, Inspector, nothing has changed in your absence.'

'I'm glad to see you looking so well, sir.'

Vanderhyde shrugged aside the remark. 'Some tea?'

'No thanks.'

'I'm really quite thrilled that you've come. It must mean there's something I can do for you.'

Rebus smiled. 'I'm sorry I stopped visiting.'

'It's a free country, I didn't pine away.'

'I can see that.'

'So what sort of thing is it? Witchcraft? Devilment in the city streets?'

Rebus was still smiling. In his day, Matthew Vanderhyde had been an active white witch. At least, Rebus hoped he'd been white. It had never been discussed between them.

'I don't *think* this is anything to do with magic,' Rebus said. 'It's about the Central Hotel.'

'The Central? Ah, happy memories, Inspector. I used to go there as a young man. Tea dances, a very acceptable luncheon – they had an excellent kitchen in those days, you know – even once or twice to an evening ball.'

'I'm thinking of more recent times. You were at the hotel the night it was torched.'

'I don't recall arson was proven.'

As usual, Vanderhyde's memory was sharp enough when it suited him. 'That's true. All the same, you were there.'

'Yes, I was. But I left several hours before the fire started. Not guilty, your honour.'

'Why were you there in the first place?'

'To meet a friend for a drink.'

'A seedy place for a drink.'

'Was it? You'll have to remember, Inspector, I couldn't *see* anything. It certainly didn't *smell* or *feel* particularly disreputable.'

'Point taken.'

'I had my memories. To me, it was the same old Central Hotel I'd lunched in and danced in. I quite enjoyed the evening.'

'Was the Central your choice, then?'

'No, my friend's.'

'Your friend being . . .?'

Vanderhyde considered. 'No secret, I suppose. Aengus Gibson.'

Rebus sifted through the name's connotations. 'You don't mean Black Aengus?'

Vanderhyde laughed, showing small blackened teeth. 'You'd better not let him hear you calling him that these days.'

Yes, Aengus Gibson was a reformed character, that much was public knowledge. He was also, so Rebus presumed, still one of Scotland's most eligible young men, if thirty-two could be considered young in these times. Black Aengus, after all, was sole heir to the Gibson Brewery and all that came with it.

'Aengus Gibson,' said Rebus.

'The same.'

'And this was five years ago, when he was still . . .'

'High spirited?' Vanderhyde gave a low chuckle. 'Oh, he deserved the name Black Aengus then, all right. The newspapers got it just right when they came up with *that* nickname.'

Rebus was thinking. 'I didn't see his name in the records. Your name was there, but his wasn't.'

'I'm sure his family saw to it that his name never appeared in any records, Inspector. It would have given the media even more fuel than they needed at the time.'

Yes, Christ, Black Aengus had been a wild one all right, so wild even the London papers took an interest. He'd looked to be spiralling out of control on ever-new excesses, but then suddenly all that stopped. He'd been rehabilitated, and was now as respectable as could be, involved in the brewing business and several prominent charities besides.

'The leopard changed its spots, Inspector. I know you policemen are dubious about such things. Every offender is a potential repeat offender. I suppose you have to be cynical in your job, but with young Aengus the leopard really *did* change.'

'Do you know why?'

Vanderhyde shrugged. 'Maybe because of our chat.'

'That night in the Central Hotel?'

'His father had asked me to talk to him.'

'You know them, then?'

'Oh, from long ago. Aengus regarded me more as an uncle than anything else. Indeed, when I heard that the Central had been razed to the ground, I saw it as symbolic. Perhaps he did too. Of course I knew the reputation it had garnered – an altogether unsavoury reputation. When it happened to burn down that night, well, I thought of the phoenix Aengus rising cleansed from its ashes. And it turned out to be true.' He paused. 'Yet now here you are, Inspector, asking questions about long forgotten events.'

'There was a body.'

'Ah yes, never identified.'

'A murdered body.'

'And somehow you've reopened that particular investigation? Interesting.'

'I wanted to ask you what you remembered from that night. Anyone you met, anything that seemed at all suspicious.'

Vanderhyde tilted his head to one side. 'There were many people in the hotel that night, Inspector. You have a list of them. Yet you choose to come to a blind man?'

'That's right,' said Rebus. 'A blind man with a photographic memory.'

Vanderhyde laughed. 'Certainly, I can give ... impressions.' He thought for a moment. 'Very well, Inspector. For you, I'll do my best. I only ask one thing.'

'What's that?'

'I've been stuck here too long. Take me out, will you?'

'Anywhere in particular?'

Vanderhyde looked surprised that he needed to ask. 'Why, Inspector, to the Central Hotel, of course!'

'Well,' said Rebus, 'this is where it used to stand. You're facing it now.' He could feel the stares of passers-by. Princes Street was lunchtime busy, office workers trying to make the most of their limited time. A few looked genuinely annoyed at having to manoeuvre past two people *daring* to stand still on the pavement! But most could see that one man was blind, the other his helper in some way, so they found charity in their souls and didn't complain.

'And what has it become, Inspector?'

'A burger joint.'

Vanderhyde nodded. 'I thought I could smell meat. Franchised, doubtless, from some American corporation. Princes Street has seen better days, Inspector. Did you know that when Scottish Sword and Shield was started up, they used to meet in the Central's ballroom? Dozens and dozens of people, all vowing to restore Dalriada to its former glory.'

Rebus remained silent.

'You don't recall Sword and Shield?'

'It must have been before my time.'

'Now that I think of it, it probably was. This was in the 1950s, an offshoot of the National Party. I attended a couple of the meetings myself. There would be some furious call to arms, followed by tea and scones. It didn't last long. Broderick Gibson was the president one year.'

'Aengus's father?'

'Yes.' Vanderhyde was remembering. 'There used to be a pub near here, famous for politics and poetry. A few of us went there after the meetings.'

'I thought you said you only went to two?'

'Perhaps a few more than two.'

Rebus grinned. If he looked into it, he knew he would probably find that a certain M. Vanderhyde had been president of Sword and Shield at some time.

'It was a fine pub,' Vanderhyde reminisced.

'In its day,' said Rebus.

Vanderhyde sighed. 'Edinburgh, Inspector. Turn your back and they change the name of a pub or the purpose of a shop.' He pointed behind him with his stick, nearly tripping someone up in the process. 'They can't change that though. *That's* Edinburgh too.' The stick was wavering in the direction of the Castle Rock. It rapped someone against their leg. Rebus tried to smile an apology, the victim being a woman.

'Maybe we should go sit across the road,' he suggested. Vanderhyde nodded, so they crossed at the traffic lights to the quieter side of the street. There were benches here, their backs to the gardens, each dedicated to someone's memory. Vanderhyde got Rebus to read the plaque on their bench.

'No,' he said, shaking his head. 'I don't recognise either of those names.'

'Mr Vanderhyde,' said Rebus, 'I'm beginning to suspect you got me to bring you here for no other reason than the outing itself.' Vanderhyde smiled but said nothing. 'What time did you go to the bar that night?'

'Seven sharp, that was the arrangement. Of course, Aengus being Aengus, he was late. I think he turned up at half past, by which time I was seated in a corner with a whisky and water. I think it was J and B whisky.' He seemed pleased by this small feat of memory.

'Anyone you knew in the bar?'

'I can hear bagpipes,' Vanderhyde said.

Rebus could too, though he couldn't see the piper. 'They play for the tourists,' he explained. 'It can be a big earner in the summer.'

'He's not very good. I should imagine he's wearing a kilt but that the tartan isn't correct.'

'Anyone in the bar you knew?' Rebus persisted.

'Oh, let me think . . .'

'With respect, sir, you don't *need* to think. You either know or you don't.'

'Well, I think Tom Hendry was in that night and stopped by the table to say hello. He used to work for the newspapers.'

Yes, Rebus had seen the name on the list.

'And there was someone else . . . I didn't know them, and they didn't speak. But I recall a scent of lemon. It was very vivid. I thought maybe it was a perfume, but when I mentioned it to Aengus he laughed and said it didn't belong to a woman. He wouldn't say any more, but I got the feeling it was a huge joke to him that I'd made the initial comment. I'm not sure any of this is relevant.'

'Me neither.' Rebus's stomach was growling. There was a sudden explosion behind them. Vanderhyde slipped his watch from his waistcoat pocket, opened the glass, and felt with his fingers over the dial.

'One o'clock sharp,' he said. 'As I said, Inspector, some things about our precipitous city remain immutable.'

Rebus nodded. 'Such as the precipitation, for instance?' It was beginning to drizzle, the morning sun having disappeared like a conjurer's trick. 'Anything else you can tell me?'

'Aengus and I talked. I tried to persuade him that he was on a very dangerous path. His health was failing, and so was the family's wealth. If anything, the latter argument was the more persuasive.'

'So there and then he renounced the bawdy life?'

'I wouldn't go that far. The Edinburgh establishment has never bided too far from the stews. When we parted he was setting off to meet some woman.' Vanderhyde was thoughtful. 'But if I do say so myself, my words had an effect on him.' He nodded. 'I ate alone that evening in The Eyrie.'

'I've been there myself,' said Rebus. His stomach growled again. 'Fancy a burger?'

After he'd dropped Vanderhyde home he drove back to St Leonard's – not a lot wiser for the whole exercise. Siobhan sprang from her desk when she saw him. She looked pleased with herself.

'I take it the butcher's wife was a talker,' Rebus said, dropping into his chair. There was another note on his desk telling him Jack Morton had called. But this time there was also a number where Rebus could reach him.

'A right little gossip, sir. I had trouble getting away.'

'And?'

'Something and nothing.'

'So give me the something.' Rebus rubbed his stomach. He'd enjoyed the burger, but it hadn't quite filled him up. There was always the canteen, but he was a bit worried about getting a 'dough-ring', as he termed the gut policemen specialised in.

'The something is this.' Siobhan Clarke sat down. 'Bone won the Merc in a bet.'

'A bet?'

Clarke nodded. 'He put his share of the butcher's business up against it. But he won the bet.'

'Bloody hell.'

'His wife actually sounded quite proud. Anyway, she told me he's a great one for betting. Maybe he is, but it doesn't look like he's got a winning formula.'

'How do you mean?'

She was warming to her subject. Rebus liked to see it, the gleam of successful detection. 'There were a few things not quite right in the living room. For instance, they'd videotapes but no video, though you could see where the machine used to sit. And though they had a large unit for storing the TV and video, the TV itself was one of those portable types.'

'So they've got rid of their video and their big television.'

'I'd guess to pay off a debt or debts.'

'And your money would be on gambling dues?'

'If I were the betting kind, which I'm not.'

He smiled. 'Maybe they had the stuff on tick and couldn't keep up the payments.'

Siobhan sounded doubtful. 'Maybe,' she conceded.

'Okay, well, it's interesting so far as it goes, but it doesn't go very far ... not yet. And it doesn't tell us anything about Rory Kintoul, does it?' She was frowning. 'Remember him, Clarke? He's the one who was stabbed in the street then wouldn't talk about it. *He's* the one we're interested in.'

'So what do you suggest, sir?' There was a tinge of ire to that 'sir'. She didn't like it that her good detection had not been better rewarded. 'We've already spoken to him.'

'And you're going to speak to him again.' She looked ready to protest. 'Only this time,' Rebus went on, 'you're going to be asking about his cousin, Mr Bone the butcher. I'm not sure what we're looking for exactly, so you'll have to feel your way. Just see whether anything hits the marrow.'

'Yes, sir.' She stood up. 'Oh, by the way, I got the files on Cafferty.'

'Plenty of reading in there, most of it x-rated.'

'I know, I've already started. And there's no x-rating nowadays. It's called "eighteen" instead.'

Rebus blinked. 'It's just an expression.' As she was turning away, he stopped her. 'Look, take some notes, will you? On Cafferty and his gang, I mean. Then when you're finished you can refresh my memory. I've spent a long time shutting that monster out of my thoughts; it's about time I opened the door again.'

'No problem.'

And with that she was off. Rebus wondered if he should have told her she'd done well at Bone's house. Ach, too late now. Besides, if she thought she were pleasing him, maybe she'd stop trying so hard. He picked up his phone and called Jack Morton.

'Jack? Long time no hear. It's John Rebus.'

'John, how are you?'

'No' bad, how's yourself?'

'Fine. I made Inspector.'

'Aye, me too.'

'So I heard.' Jack Morton choked off his words as he gave a huge hacking cough.

'Still on the fags, eh, Jack?'

'I've cut down.'

'Remind me to sell my tobacco shares. So listen, what's the problem?'

'It's your problem, not mine. Only I saw something from Scotland Yard about Andrew McPhail.'

Rebus tried the name out in his head. 'No,' he admitted, 'you've got me there.'

'We had him on file as a sex offender. He'd had a go at the daughter of the woman he was living with. This was about eight years back. But we never got the charge to stick.'

Rebus was remembering a little of it. 'We interviewed him when those wee girls started to disappear?' Rebus shivered at the memory: his own daughter had been one of the 'wee girls'.

'That's it, just routine. We started with convicted and suspected child offenders and went on from there.'

'Stocky guy with wiry hair?'

'You've got him.'

'So what's the point, Jack?'

'The point is, you really have got him. He's in Edinburgh.'

'So?'

'Christ, John, I thought you'd know. He buggered off to Canada after that last time we hassled him. Set himself up as a photographer, doing shots for fashion catalogues. He'd approach the parents of kids he fancied. He had business cards, camera equipment, the works, rented a studio and used to take shots of the children, promising they'd be in some catalogue or other. They'd get to dress up in fancy dresses, or sometimes maybe just in underwear . . .'

'I get the picture, Jack.'

'Well, they nabbed him. He'd been touching the girls, that was all. A lot of girls, so they put him inside.'

'And?'

'And now they've let him out. But they've also deported him.'

'He's in Edinburgh?'

'I started checking. I wanted to find out where he'd ended up, because I knew if it was anywhere near my patch I'd pay him a visit some dark night. But he's on your patch instead. I've got an address.'

'Wait a second.' Rebus found a pen and copied it down.

'How did you get his address anyway? The DSS?'

'No, the files said he had a sister in Ayr. She told me he'd had her get a phone number for him, a boarding house. Know what else she said? She said we should lock him in a cellar and forget about the key.'

'Sounds like a lovely lass.'

'She's my kind of woman, all right. Of course, he's probably been rehabilitated.'

That word – rehabilitated. A word Vanderhyde had used about Aengus Gibson. 'Probably,' said Rebus, believing it about as much as Morton himself. They were professional disbelievers, after all. It was a policeman's lot.

'Still, it's good to know about. Thanks, Jack.'

'You're welcome. Any chance we'll be seeing you in Falkirk some day? It'd be good to have a drink.'

'Yes, it would. Tell you what, I might be over that way soon.'

'Oh?'

'Dropping McPhail off in the town centre.'

Morton laughed. 'Ya shite, ye.' And with that he put down the phone.

Jack Morton stared at the phone for the best part of a minute, still grinning. Then the grin melted away. He unwrapped a stick of chewing gum and started gnawing it. It's better than a cigarette, he kept telling himself. He looked at the scribbled sheet of notes in front of him on the desk. The girl McPhail had assaulted was called Melanie Maclean these days. Her mother had married, and Melanie lived with the couple in Haddington, far enough from Edinburgh so that she probably wouldn't bump into McPhail. Nor, in all probability, would McPhail be able to find her. He'd have to know the stepfather's name, and that wouldn't be easy for him. It hadn't been *that* easy for Jack Morton. But the name was here. Alex Maclean. Jack Morton had a home address, home phone number, and work number. He wondered ...

He knew too that Alex Maclean was a carpenter, and Haddington police were able to inform him that Maclean had a temper on him, and had twice (long before his marriage) been arrested after some flare-up or other. He wondered, but he knew he was going to do it. He picked up the receiver and punched in the numbers. Then waited.

'Hello, can I speak to Mr Maclean please? Mr Maclean? You don't know me, but I have some information I'd like to share with you. It concerns a man called Andrew McPhail ...'

Matthew Vanderhyde too made a telephone call that afternoon, but only after long thought in his favourite armchair. He held the cordless phone in his hand, tapping it with a long fingernail. He could hear a dog outside, the one from down the street with the nasal whine. The clock on the mantelpiece ticked, the tick seeming to slow as he concentrated on it. Time's heartbeat. At last he made the call. There was no preamble.

'I've just had a policeman here,' he said. 'He was asking about the night the Central Hotel caught fire.' He hesitated slightly. 'I told him about Aengus.' He could pause now, listening with a weary smile to the fury on the other end of the line, a fury he knew so well. 'Broderick,' he interrupted, 'if any skeletons are being uncloseted, *I* don't want to be the only one shivering.'

When the fury began afresh, Matthew Vanderhyde terminated the call.

7

Rebus noticed the man for the first time that evening. He thought he'd seen him outside St Leonard's in the afternoon. A young man, tall and broad-shouldered. He was standing outside the entrance to Rebus's communal stairwell in Arden Street. Rebus parked his car across the street, so that he could watch the man in his rearview mirror. The man looked agitated, pumped up about something. Maybe he was only waiting for his date. Maybe.

Rebus wasn't scared, but he started the car again and drove off anyway. He'd give it an hour and see if the man was still there. If he was, then he wasn't waiting on any date, no matter how bonny the girl. He drove along the Meadows to Tollcross, then took a right down Lothian Road. It was slow going, as per. The number of vehicles needing to get through the city of an evening seemed to grow every week. Edinburgh in the twilight looked much the same as any other place: shops and offices and crowded pavements. Nobody looked particularly happy.

He crossed Princes Street, cut into Charlotte Square, and began the crawl along Queensferry Street and Queensferry Road until he could take a merciful (if awkward) right turn into Oxford Terrace. But Patience wasn't home. He knew Patience's sister was expected this week, staying a few days then taking the girls home. Patience's cat, Lucky, sat outside, demanding entry, and Rebus for once was almost sympathetic.

'Nae luck,' he told it, before starting back up the steps.

When he got back to Arden Street, there was no sign of the skulking hulk. But Rebus would recognise him if he saw him again. Oh yes, he'd know him, all right.

Indoors, he had another argument with Michael, the two of them in the living room, everyone else in the kitchen. That was another thing: how many tenants did he have? There seemed to be a shifting population of about a dozen, where he'd rented to three with a possible fourth. He could swear he saw different faces every morning, and as a result could never remember anyone's name.

So there was another row about that, this time with the students in the kitchen while Michael sat in the box room, at the end of which Rebus said, 'Away to hell,' and proceeded to follow his own instructions by getting back in his car and making for one of the city's least respectable quarters, there to dine on pies and pints while staring at a soundless TV. He spoke with a few of his contacts, who had nothing to report regarding the assault on Brian Holmes.

So it was just another evening, really.

He got back purposely late, hoping everyone else would have gone to bed. He fumbled with the door-catch of the tenement and let the door swing shut loudly behind him, searching in his pockets for the flat key, eyes to the ground. So he didn't see the man, who must have been sitting on the bottom step of the stairs.

'Hello there.'

Rebus looked up, startled, recognised the figure, and sent small change and keys scattering as he threw a punch. He wasn't that drunk, but then his target was stone cold sober and twenty years younger. The man palmed the punch easily. He looked surprised at the attack, but also somehow excited by it. Rebus cut short the thrill of it all by sharply raising his knee into unprotected groin. The man expelled air noisily, and started to double over, which gave Rebus the opportunity to punch down onto the back of his neck. He felt his knuckles crackle with the force of the blow.

'Jesus,' the man gasped. 'Stop it.'

Rebus stopped it and wagged his aching hand. But he wasn't about to offer help. He kept his distance, and asked 'Who are you?'

The man managed to stop retching for a moment. 'Andy Steele.'

'Nice to meet you, Andy. What the fuck do you want?'

The man looked up at Rebus with tears in his eyes. It took him a while to catch his breath. When he spoke, Rebus either couldn't understand the accent or else just didn't believe what he was saying. He asked Steele to repeat himself.

'Your auntie sent me,' said Steele. 'She's got a message for you.'

Rebus sat Andy Steele down on the sofa with a cup of tea, including the four sugars Steele himself had requested.

'Can't be good for your teeth.'

'They're not my own,' Steele replied, huddled over the hot mug.

'Then whose are they?' asked Rebus. Steele gave the flicker of a smile. 'You've been following me all day.'

'Not exactly. Maybe if I had a car, but I don't.'

'You don't have a car?' Steele shook his head. 'Some private detective.'

'I didn't say I was a private detective exactly. I mean, I *want* to be one.'

'A sort of trainee, then?'

'Aye, that's right. Testing the water, so to speak.'

'And how's the water, Andy?'

273

Another smile, a sip of tea. 'A bit hot. But I'll be more careful next time.'

'I didn't even know I had an aunt. Not up north.' Steele's accent was a giveaway.

Andy Steele nodded. 'She lives next door to my mum and dad, just across the road from Pittodrie.'

'Aberdeen?' Rebus nodded to himself. 'It's coming back to me. Yes, an uncle and aunt in Aberdeen.'

'Your dad and Jimmy – that's your uncle – fell out years ago. You're probably too young to remember.'

'Thanks for the compliment.'

'It's just what Ena told me.'

'And now Uncle Jimmy's dead?'

'Three weeks past.'

'And Aunt Ena wants to see me?' Steele nodded. 'What about?'

'I don't know. She was just talking about how she'd like to see you again.'

'Just me? No mention of my brother?'

Steele shook his head. Rebus had checked to see if Michael was in the box room. He wasn't. But the other bedrooms seemed to be occupied.

'Right enough,' said Rebus, 'if they argued when I was wee, maybe it was before Michael was born.'

'They might no' even know about him,' Steele conceded. Well, that was families for you. 'Anyway, Ena kept harping on about you, so I told her I'd come south and have a look. I got laid off from the fishing boats six months ago, and I've been going up the wall ever since. Besides, I told you I've always fancied being a private eye. I love all those films.'

'Films don't get you a knee in the balls.'

'True enough.'

'So how *did* you find me?'

Steele's face brightened. 'I went to the address Ena gave me, where you and your dad used to live. All the neighbours knew was that you were a policeman in Edinburgh. So I got the directory out and phoned every station I could find, asking for John Rebus.' He shrugged and returned to his tea.

'But how did you get my home address?'

'Someone in CID gave it to me.'

'Don't tell me, Inspector Flower?'

'A name like that, aye.'

Seated on the sofa, Andy Steele looked to be in his mid-twenties. He had the sort of large frame which could be kept in shape only through hard work, such as that found on a North Sea fishing boat. But already, deprived of work for six months, that frame was growing heavy with disuse. Rebus felt sorry for Andy Steele and his dreams of becoming a private eye. The way he stared into space as he drank the tea, he looked lost, his immediate life without form or plan.

'So are you going to go and see her?'

'Maybe at the weekend,' said Rebus.

'She'd like that.'

'I can give you a lift back.'

But the young man was shaking his head. 'No, I'd like to stay in Edinburgh for a bit.'

'Suit yourself,' said Rebus. 'Just be careful.'

'Careful? I could tell you stories about Aberdeen that would make your hair stand on end.'

'And could they thicken it a bit at the temples while they're at it?'

It took Andy Steele a minute to get the joke.

The next day, Rebus paid a visit to Andrew McPhail. But McPhail wasn't home, and his landlady hadn't seen him since the previous evening.

'Usually he comes down at seven sharp for a wee bitty breakfast. So I went upstairs and there was no sign of him. Is he in any trouble, Inspector?'

'No, nothing like that, Mrs MacKenzie. This is a lovely Madiera by the way.'

'Ach, it's a few days since I made it, it's probably a bit dry by now.'

Rebus shook his head and gulped at the tea, hoping to wash the crumbs down his throat. But they merely formed into a huge solid lump which he had to force down by degrees, and without a public show of gagging.

There was a bird-cage standing in one corner of the room, boasting mirrors and cuttle-fish and millet spray. But no sign of any bird. Maybe it had escaped.

He left his card with Mrs MacKenzie, telling her to pass it on to Mr McPhail when she saw him. He didn't doubt that she would. It had been unfair of him to introduce himself as a policeman to the landlady. She would probably become suspicious, and might even give McPhail a week's notice on the strength of those suspicions. That would be a terrible shame.

Actually, it didn't look to Rebus as though Mrs MacKenzie would twig. And McPhail would doubtless come up with some reason for Rebus's visit. Probably the City of Edinburgh Police were about to award him a commendation for saving some puppies from the raging torrents of the Water of Leith. McPhail was good at making up stories, after all. Children just loved to hear stories.

Rebus stood outside Mrs MacKenzie's house and looked across the road. It had to be coincidence that McPhail had chosen a boarding house within ogling distance of a primary school. Rebus had seen it on his arrival; it had been enough to decide him on identifying himself to the landlady. After all, he didn't believe in coincidence.

And if McPhail couldn't be persuaded to move, well, maybe the neighbours would find out the true story of Mrs MacKenzie's lodger. Rebus got into his car. He didn't always like himself or his job.

But some bits were okay.

Back at St Leonard's, Siobhan Clarke had nothing new to report on the stabbing. Rory Kintoul was being very cagey about another interview. He'd cancelled one arranged meeting, and she'd not been able to contact him since.

'His son's seventeen and unemployed, spends most of the day at home, I could try talking to him.'

'You could.' But it was a lot of trouble. Maybe Holmes was right. 'Just do your best,' said Rebus. 'After you've talked with Kintoul, if we're no further forward we'll drop the whole thing. If Kintoul wants to get himself stabbed, that's fine with me.'

She nodded and turned away.

'Any news on Brian?'

She turned back. 'He's been talking.'

'Talking?'

'In his sleep. I thought you'd know.'

'What's he been saying?'

'Nothing they can make out, but it means he's slowly regaining consciousness.'

'Good.'

She started to turn away again, but Rebus thought of something. 'How are you getting to Aberdeen on Saturday?'

'Driving, why?'

'Any room in the car?'

'There's just me.'

'Then you won't mind giving me a lift.'

She looked startled. 'Not at all. Where to?'

'Pittodrie.'

Now she looked even more surprised. 'I wouldn't have taken you for a Hibs fan, sir.'

Rebus screwed up his face. 'No, you're all alone in that category. I just need a lift, that's all.'

'Fine.'

'And on the way, you can tell me what you've learned from the files on Big Ger.'

8

By Saturday, Rebus had argued three times with Michael (who was talking about moving out anyway), once with the students (also talking about moving), and once with the receptionist at Patience's surgery when she wouldn't put Rebus through. Brian Holmes had opened his eyes briefly, and it was reckoned by the doctors that he was on his way to recovery. None of them, however, hazarded the phrase 'full recovery'. Still, the news had cheered Siobhan Clarke, and she was in a good mood when she arrived at Rebus's Arden Street flat. He was waiting for her at street level. She drove a two-year-old cherry-red Renault 5. It looked young and full of life, while Rebus's car (parked next to it) looked to be in terminal condition. But Rebus's car had been looking like this for three or four years now, and just when he'd determined to get rid of it it always seemed to go into remission. Rebus had the feeling the car could read his mind.

'Morning, sir,' said Siobhan Clarke. There was pop music coming from the stereo. She saw Rebus cringe as he got into the passenger seat, and turned the volume down. 'Bad night?'

'People always seem to ask me that.'

'Now why could that be?'

They stopped at a bakery so Rebus could buy some breakfast. There had been nothing in the flat worth the description 'food', but then Rebus couldn't really complain. His contribution to the larder so far had filled a single shopping basket. And most of that had been meat, something the students didn't touch. He noticed Michael had gone vegetarian too, at least in public.

'It's healthier, John,' he'd told his brother, slapping his stomach.

'What's that supposed to mean?' Rebus had snapped.

Michael had merely shaken his head sadly. 'Too much caffeine.'

That was another thing, the kitchen cupboards were full of jars of what looked like coffee but turned out to be 'infusions' of crushed tree bark and chicory. At the bakery, Rebus bought a polystyrene beaker of coffee and two sausage rolls. The sausage rolls turned out to be a bad mistake, the flakes of pastry breaking off and covering the otherwise pristine car interior – despite Rebus's best attempts with the paper bag.

'Sorry about the mess,' he offered to Siobhan, who was driving with her window conspicuously open. 'You're not vegetarian, are you?'

She laughed. 'You mean you haven't noticed?'

'Can't say I have.'

She nodded towards a sausage roll. 'Well, have you heard of mechanically recovered meat?'

'Don't,' warned Rebus. He finished the sausage rolls quickly, and cleared his throat.

'Anything I should know about between you and Brian?'

The look on her face told him this was not the year's most successful conversational gambit. 'Not that I know of.'

'It's just that he and Nell were ... well, there's still a good chance –'

'I'm not a monster, sir. And I know the score between Brian and Nell. Brian's just a nice guy. We get along.' She glanced away from the windscreen. 'That's all there is to it.' Rebus was about to say something. 'But if there *was* more to it than that,' she went on, 'I don't see that it would be any of your business, with respect, sir. Not unless it was interfering with our work, which I wouldn't let happen. I don't suppose Brian would either.'

Rebus stayed silent.

'I'm sorry, I shouldn't have said that.'

'What you said was fair enough. The problem was the *way* you said it. A police officer's never off duty, and I'm your boss – even on a jaunt like this. Don't forget that.'

There was more silence in the car, until Siobhan broke it. 'It's a nice part of town, Marchmont.'

'Almost as nice as the New Town.'

She glared at him, her grip on the steering-wheel as determined as any strangler's.

'I thought,' she said slyly, 'you lived in Oxford Terrace these days, sir.'

'You thought wrong. Now, what about turning that bloody music off? After all, we've got a lot to talk about.'

The 'lot', of course, being Morris Gerald Cafferty.

Siobhan Clarke hadn't brought her notes with her. She didn't need them. She could recite the salient details from memory, along with a lot of detail that might not be salient but was certainly interesting. Certainly she'd done her homework. Rebus thought how frustrating the job could be. She'd swotted up on Big Ger as background to Operation Moneybags, but Operation Moneybags almost certainly wouldn't trap Cafferty. And she'd spent a lot of hours on the Kintoul stabbing, which might also turn out to be nothing.

'And another thing,' she said. 'Apparently Cafferty's got a little diary of sorts, all of it in code. We've never been able to crack his code, which means it must be highly personal.'

Yes, Rebus remembered. Whenever they brought Big Ger into custody, the diary would be collected along with his other possessions. Then they'd photocopy the pages of the diary and try to decipher them. They'd never been successful.

'Rumour has it,' Siobhan was saying, 'the diary's a record of bad debts, debts Cafferty takes care of personally.'

'A man like that garners a lot of rumours. They help make him larger than life. In life, he's just another witless gangster.'

'A code takes wits.'

'Maybe.'

'In the file, there's a recent clipping from the *Sun*. It's all about how bodies keep washing up on the coastline.'

Rebus nodded. 'On the Solway coast, not far from Stranraer.'

'You think it's Cafferty's doing?'

Rebus shrugged. 'The bodies have never been identified. Could be anything. Could be people pushed off the Larne ferry. Could be some connection with Ulster. There are some weird currents between Larne and Stranraer.' He paused. 'Could be anything.'

'Could be Cafferty, in other words.'

'Could be.'

'It's a long way to go to dispose of a body.'

'Well, he's not going to shit in his own nest, is he?'

She considered this. 'There was mention in one of the papers of a van spotted on that coastline, too early in the morning to be delivering anything.'

Rebus nodded. 'And there was nowhere along the road for it to be delivering *to*. I read the papers sometimes, Clarke. The Dumfries and Galloway Police have patrols along there now.'

Siobhan drove for a while, gathering her thoughts. 'He's just been lucky so far, hasn't he, sir? I mean, I can understand that he's a clever villain, and clever villains are harder to catch. But he has to delegate, and usually even though a villain's clever his underlings are so stupid or lazy they *would* shit in the nest.'

'Language, Clarke, language.' He got a smile from her. 'Point taken, though.'

'Reading all about Cafferty's "associates" I didn't get an impression of many "O" Grades. They've all got names like Slink and Codge and the Radiator.'

Rebus grinned. 'Radiator McCallum, I remember him. He was supposed to be descended from a family of Highland cannibals. He did research and everything, he was so proud of his ancestors.'

'He disappeared from the scene, though.'

'Yes, three or four years ago.'

'Four and a half, according to the records. I wonder what happened to him.'

Rebus shrugged. 'He tried to doublecross Big Ger, got scared and ran off.'

'Or didn't get the chance to run off.'

'That too, of course. Or else he just got fed up, or had another job offer. It's a very mobile profession, being a thug. Wherever the work is . . .'

'Cafferty certainly gets through the personnel. McCallum's cousins disappeared from view just before McCallum himself did.'

Rebus frowned. 'I didn't know he had any cousins.'

'Known colloquially as the Bru-head Brothers. Something to do with a penchant for Irn-Bru.'

'Altogether understandable. What were their real names, though?'

She thought for a moment. 'Tam and Eck Robertson.'

Rebus nodded. 'Eck Robertson, yes. I didn't know about the other one, though. Hang on a minute . . .'

Tam and Eck Robertson. The R. Brothers. Which would mean that Mork was . . .

'Morris bloody Cafferty!' Rebus slapped the dashboard. Brian short-ened the name and used a k for the c. Christ . . . If Brian Holmes was on to something involving Cafferty and his gang, no wonder he was scared. Something to do with the night the Central Hotel caught fire. Did they start the blaze because the hotel hadn't been paying its protection dues? What about the body, maybe it'd been some debtor or other. And soon afterwards, Radiator McCallum and his cousins left the scene. Bloody hell.

'If you're going to have a seizure,' said Siobhan, 'I'm trained in cardiac resuscitation.'

Rebus wasn't listening. He stared at the road ahead, one fist around the coffee cup, the other pounding his knee. He was thinking of Brian's note. He hadn't said for sure that Cafferty was there that night, only that the brothers were. And something about a poker game. He was going to try to find the Robertson brothers; that was his final comment. After which, someone came along and hit him on the head. Maybe it was beginning to come together.

'I'm not sure I can deal with catatonia though.'

'What?'

'Was it something that I said?'

'Yes, it was.'

'The Bru-Head Brothers?'

'The very same. What else can you tell me about them?'

'Born in Niddrie, petty thieves from the time they left the pram –'

'They probably stole the pram, too. Anything else?'

Siobhan knew that she'd hit some nerve. 'Plenty. Both had long records. Eck liked flashy clothes, Tam always wore jeans and a T-shirt.

The funny thing is, though, Tam kept scrupulously clean. He even took his own soap everywhere with him. I thought that was strange.'

'If I were the gambling kind,' said Rebus, 'I'd bet the soap was lemon-scented.'

'How did you know that?'

'Instinct. Not mine, someone else's.' Rebus frowned. 'How come I never heard of Tam?'

'He moved to Dundee when he left school, or rather when he was *asked* to leave school. He only came back to Edinburgh years later. The records have him down as working for the gang for about six months, maybe even less.' She waited. 'Are you going to tell me what this is all about?'

'It's all about a hotel fire.'

'You mean those files on the floor behind your desk?'

'I mean those files on the floor behind my desk.'

'I couldn't help taking a peek.'

'They might tie in with the attack on Brian.' She turned to him. 'Keep your eyes on the road. You concentrate on the driving, and I'll tell you a story. It might even keep us going till Aberdeen.'

And it did.

'In ye come, Jock. My, my, I wouldn't have recognised ye.'

'I was in shorts the last time you saw me, Auntie Ena.'

The old woman laughed. She used a zimmer frame to walk back through the narrow musty hall and into a small back room. The room was crammed with furniture. There would be a front room, too, another lounge kept for the most special occasions. But Rebus was family, and family were greeted in the back room.

She was frail-looking and hunch-backed and wore a shawl over her angular shoulders. Her silver hair had been pulled back severely and pinned tight against her head, and her eyes were sunken dots in a parchment face. Rebus couldn't remember her at all.

'You must have been three when we were last in Fife. You could talk the hind legs off a donkey, but with such a thick accent, I could hardly make out a word of it. Always wanting to tell a joke or sing a song.'

'I've changed,' Rebus said.

'Eh?' She had dumped herself into a chair beside the fireplace, and craned her head forward. 'My hearing's not so good, Jock.'

'I said, nobody calls me Jock!' Rebus called. 'It's John.'

'Oh aye, John. Right you are.' She pulled a travel-rug over her legs. In the fireplace stood an electric fire, the kind with fake coals, fake flames, and, so far as Rebus could tell, fake heat. There was one pale orange bar on, but he couldn't feel anything.

'Danny found you, then?'

'You mean Andy?'

'He's a good laddie. Such a shame he got made redundant. Did he come back with you?'

'No, he's still in Edinburgh.' She was resting her head against the back of the chair. Rebus got the impression she was about to drift off to sleep. The walk to the front door and back had probably exhausted her.

'His parents are nice folk, always so kind to me.'

'You wanted to see me about something, Auntie Ena?'

'Eh?'

He crouched down in front of her, resting his hands on the side of the chair. 'You wanted to see me.' Well, she could see him . . . and then she couldn't, as her eyes glazed over and, mouth wide open, she started to snore.

Rebus stood up and gave a loud sigh. The clock over the mantelpiece had stopped, but he knew he had at least two hours to kill. Talking over the Central Hotel case with Siobhan had made him agitated. He wanted to get back to work on it. And here he was, trapped in this miniature museum. He looked around, wrinkling his nose at a chrome commode in one dark corner. There were photos inside a glass-fronted china cabinet. He went over and examined them. He recognised a picture of his grandparents on his father's side, but there were no photos of his father. The feud, or whatever it had been, had seen to that.

The Scots never forgot. It was a burden and a gift. The living-room led directly onto a small scullery. Rebus looked in the antique fridge and found a piece of brisket, which he sniffed. There was bread in a large tin in the pantry, and butter in a dish on the draining-board. It took him ten minutes to make the sandwiches, and five minutes to find out which of the many caddies contained the tea.

He found a radio beside the sink and tried to find commentary on a football game, but the batteries were weaker than his tea. So he tiptoed back through to where Auntie Ena was still sleeping and sat down in the chair opposite her. He hadn't come up here expecting an inheritance, exactly, but he had bargained for more than this. A particularly loud snore brought Auntie Ena wriggling towards consciousness.

'Eh? Is that you, Jimmy?'

'It's John, your nephew.'

'Gracious, John, did I nod off?'

'Just forty winks.'

'Isn't that terrible of me, with a visitor here and everything.'

'I'm not a visitor, Auntie Ena, I'm family.'

'Aye, son, so you are. Now, listen to me. There's some beef in the fridge. Shall I go and –?'

'They're already made.'

'Eh?'

'The sandwiches. I've made them up.'

'You have? You always were a bright one. Now what about some tea?'

'Sit where you are, I'll make some fresh.'

He made a pot of tea and brought the sandwiches through on a plate, setting them in front of her on a footstool. 'There we are.' He was about to hand her one, when she made a grab for his wrists, nearly toppling the plate. He saw that her eyes were shut, and though she looked frail enough her grip was strong. She'd started speaking before Rebus realised she was saying grace.

'Some hae meat and cannae eat, and some hae nane that want it. But we hae meat and we can eat, so let the Lord be thankit.'

Rebus almost burst out laughing. Almost. But inside, he was touched too. He handed her a smile along with her sandwich, then went to fetch the tea.

The meal revived her, and she seemed to remember why she'd wanted to see him.

'Your faither and my husband fell out very many years ago. Maybe forty or more years ago. They never exchanged a letter, a Christmas card, or a civil word ever again. Now, don't you think that's stupid? And do you know what it was about? It was about the fact that though we invited your faither and mither to our Ishbel's wedding, we didn't invite you. We'd decided there would be no children, you see. But then a friend of mine, Peggy Callaghan, brought her son along uninvited, and we could hardly turn him away, since there was no way for him to get back home on his own. When your faither saw this, he argued with Jimmy. A real blazing row. And then your faither stormed out, leaving your mither to follow him. A sweet woman she was. So that's that.'

She sat back in her chair, breadcrumbs prominent on her lower lip.

'That was all?'

She nodded. 'Doesn't seem like much, does it? Not from this distance. But it was enough. And the both of them were too stubborn ever to make it up.'

'And you wanted to see me so you could tell me this?'

'Partly, yes. But also, I wanted to give you something.' She rose slowly from her chair, using the zimmer-frame for support, and leaned up towards the mantelpiece. Rebus half-rose to help her, but she didn't need his help. She found the photograph and handed it down to him. He looked at it. In fading black and white, it showed two grinning schoolboys, not exactly dressed to the nines. They had their arms casually slung around one another's necks, and their faces were close together. Best friends, but more than that: brothers.

'He kept that, you see. He told me once that he'd thrown out all the photos of your faither. But when we were going through his things, we found that in the bottom of a shoebox. I wanted you to have it, Jock.'

'It's not Jock, it's John,' said Rebus, his eyes not entirely dry.

'Of course it is,' said his Auntie Ena. 'Of course it is.'

Earlier that afternoon, Michael Rebus had lain along the couch asleep and unaware that he was missing one of his favourite films, *Double Indemnity*, on BBC2. He'd gone to the pub for a lunchtime drink: alone, as it turned out. The students weren't into it. Instead, they'd gone shopping, or to the laundrette, or home for the weekend to see parents and friends. So Michael drank only two lagers topped with lemonade and returned to the flat, where he promptly fell asleep in front of the TV.

He'd been thinking about John recently. He knew he was imposing on his big brother, but didn't reckon on doing so much longer. He had spoken on the phone to Chrissie. She was still in Kirkcaldy with the kids. She'd wanted nothing to do with him after the bust, and was especially disgusted that his own brother had given evidence against him. But Michael didn't blame John for that. John had principles. And besides, some of the evidence had worked – deliberately, he was sure – in Michael's favour.

Now Chrissie was talking to him again. He'd written to her all through his incarceration, then had written from London too; not knowing whether she'd received any of his letters. But she had. She told him that when they spoke. And she didn't have a boyfriend, and the kids were fine, and did he want to see them some time?

'I want to see you,' he'd told her. It sounded right.

He was dreaming about her when the doorbell went. Well . . . her and Gail the student, if truth be told. He staggered to his feet. The bell was insistent.

It took a second to turn the snib-lock, after which Michael's world imploded.

With another Hibernian defeat behind her, Siobhan Clarke was quiet on the way home, which suited Rebus. He had some thinking to do, and not about work, for a change. He thought about the job too much as it was, gave himself to it the way he had never given himself to any *person* in his life. Not his ex-wife, not his daughter, not Patience, not Michael.

He'd come into the police prematurely weary and cynical. Then he watched recruits like Holmes and Clarke and saw their best intentions thwarted by the system and the public's attitude. There were times you'd feel more welcome if you were painting plague markers on people's doors.

'A penny for them,' said Siobhan Clarke.

'Don't waste your money.'

'Why not? Look how much I've wasted already today.'

Rebus smiled at that. 'Aye,' he said, 'I keep forgetting, there's always someone in the world worse off than yourself . . . Unless you're a Hibs supporter.'

'Ha bloody ha.'

Siobhan Clarke reached for the stereo and tried to find a station that didn't run the day's classified results.

9

Full of good intentions, Rebus opened the door of the flat, sensing immediately that nobody was home. Well, it was Saturday night, after all. But they might at least have turned the TV off.

He went into the box room and placed the old photograph on Michael's unmade bed. The room smelt faintly of perfume, reminding Rebus of Patience. He missed her more than he liked to admit. When they'd first started seeing one another, they'd agreed that they were both too old for anything that could be called 'love'. They'd also agreed that they were more than ready for lashings of sex. Then, when Rebus had moved in, they'd talked again. It didn't really mean commitment, they were agreed on that; it was just handier for the moment. Ah, but when Rebus had rented out his own flat . . . *that* had meant commitment, commitment to sleeping on the sofa should Patience ever kick him out.

He lay along the sofa now, noticing that he had all but annexed what had been the flat's main communal space. The students tended to sit around in the kitchen now, talking quietly with the door closed. Rebus didn't blame them. It was all a mess in here, and all *his* mess. His suitcase lay wide open on the floor beside the window, ties and socks trickling from it. The holdall was tucked behind the sofa. His two suits hung limply from the picture-rail next to the box room, partially blocking out a psychedelic poster which had been making Rebus's eyes hurt. The place had a feral smell from lack of fresh air. The smell suited it, though. After all, wasn't this Rebus's lair?

He picked up the telephone and rang Patience. Her taped voice spoke to him; the message was new.

'I'm going with Susan and Jenny back to their mother's. Any messages, leave them after the tone.'

Rebus's first thought was how stupid Patience had been. The message let any caller – *any* caller – know she wasn't home. He knew that burglars often telephoned first. They might even go through the phone book more or less at random, finding phones that rang and rang, or answering machines. You had to make your message vague.

He guessed that if she'd gone to her sister's, she wouldn't be back until tomorrow night at the earliest, and might even stay over on the Monday.

'Hi, Patience,' he said to the machine. 'It's me. I'm ready to talk when you are. I . . . miss you. Bye.'

So, the girls had gone. Maybe now things could get back to normal. No more smouldering Susan, no more gentle Jenny. They weren't the cause of the rift between Rebus and Patience, but maybe they hadn't helped. No, they definitely hadn't helped.

He made himself a cup of 'coffee substitute', all the time thinking of wandering down to the late-opening shop at the corner of Marchmont Road. But their coffee was instant and expensive, and besides, maybe this stuff would taste okay.

It tasted awful, and was absolutely caffeine-free, which was probably why he fell asleep during a dreary mid-evening movie on the television.

And awoke to a ringing telephone. Someone had switched the TV off, and perhaps that same person had thrown the blanket over him. It was getting to be a regular thing. He was stiff as he sat up and reached for the receiver. His watch told him it was one-fifteen a.m.

'Hello?'

'Is that Inspector Rebus?'

'Speaking.' Rebus rubbed at his hair.

'Inspector, this is PC Hart. I'm in South Queensferry.'

'Yes?'

'There's someone here claims he's your brother.'

'Michael?'

'That's the name he gave.'

'What's up? Is he guttered?'

'Nothing like that, sir.'

'What is it then?'

'Well, sir, we've just found him . . .'

Rebus was very awake now. 'Found him where?'

'He was hanging from the Forth Rail Bridge.'

'What?' Rebus felt his hand squeezing the telephone receiver to death. '*Hanging?*'

'I don't mean like that, sir. Sorry if I . . .' Rebus's grip relaxed.

'No, I mean he was hanging by his feet, sort of suspended, like. Just hanging in mid-air.'

'We thought it was some sort of joke gone wrong at first. You know, bungee jumper, that kind of thing.' PC Hart was leading Rebus to a hut on the quayside at South Queensferry. The Firth of Forth was dark and quiet in front of them, but Rebus could make out the rail bridge lowering far above them. 'But that's not the story he gave us. Besides, it was clear he hadn't taken the dive on his own.'

'How clear?'

287

'His hands were tied together, sir. And his mouth had been taped shut.'

'Christ.'

'Doctor says he'll be all right. If they'd tipped him over the side, his legs could've come out of the sockets, but the doc reckons they must have lowered him over.'

'How did they get onto the bridge in the first place?'

'It's easy enough, if you've a head for heights.'

Rebus, who had no head for heights, had already declined the offer of a visit to the spot where Michael had been found, up on the ochre-coloured iron construction.

'Looks like they waited till they knew there'd be no trains about. But a boat was going under the bridge, and the skipper thought he saw something, so he radioed in. Otherwise, well, he could have been up there all night.' Hart shook his head. 'A cold night, I can't say I'd fancy it.'

They were at the hut now. There was only enough room inside for two men. One of these, seated with a blanket over his shoulders, was Michael. The other was a local doctor, called from his bed by the look of him. Other men stood around: police, the proprietor of a hotel on the waterfront, and the boat skipper who might just have saved Michael's life, or at the very least his sanity.

'John, thank Christ.' Michael was trembling, and seemed to have no colour in him at all. The doctor was holding a hot cup of something, from which he was coaxing Michael to drink.

'Drink up, Mickey,' said Rebus. Michael looked pathetic, like the victim of some terrible tragedy. Rebus felt a tremendous sadness overwhelm him. Michael had spent years in jail, where God knows what had happened to him. Then, released, he'd had no luck at all until he'd come to Edinburgh. The bravado, the nights out with the students – Rebus suddenly saw it for what it really was, a front, an attempt to put behind him all that Michael had feared these past few years. And now this had happened, reducing him to the crouched shivering animal in the hut.

'I'll be back in a second, Mickey.' Rebus pulled Hart around the side of the hut. 'What has he told you?' He was trying to control the fury inside him.

'He said he was in your flat, sir, on his own.'

'When?'

'This afternoon, about four. There was a ring at the doorbell, so he answered, and three men pushed their way in. The first thing they did was put a cloth bag over his head. Then they held him down and tied him up, took the bag off and taped shut his mouth, then put the bag back.'

'He didn't see them?'

'They kept his face against the hall carpet. He just got the quick glimpse of them when he opened the door.'

'Go on.' Rebus was trying not to look up at the rail bridge. Instead, he focused on the flashing red lights on top of the more distant road bridge.

'They seem to have wrapped something like a carpet around him and taken him downstairs and into a van. It was pretty cramped in there, according to your brother. Narrow, like. He reckoned there were boxes either side of him.' Hart paused. He didn't like the look of concentration on the Inspector's face.

'Well?' Rebus snapped.

'He says they drove around for hours, not saying anything. Then he was lifted out of the van and taken into something like a cellar or a storeroom. They never took the bag off his head, so he can't be sure.' Hart paused. 'I didn't want to question him too closely, sir, in his present condition.'

Rebus nodded.

'Anyway, finally they brought him up here. Tied him to the side of the bridge, and lowered him over it. They still hadn't said anything. But when they started to lower away, they finally took the bag off his head.'

'Christ.' Rebus screwed shut his eyes. It brought back the grimmest memories of his own SAS training, the way they'd tried to get him to hand over information. Taking him up in a helicopter with a bag over his head, then threatening to drop him out, and carrying out their threat ... But only eight feet off the ground, not the hundreds of feet he'd visualised. Horrible, all of it. He pushed past Hart, pulled the doctor out of the way, and bent down to hug Michael, keeping him close against his chest as he heard Michael start to bawl. The crying lasted for many minutes, but Rebus wasn't about to let go.

And then at last, it was over. Racking dry coughs, the breathing slowing, and a sort of calm. Michael's face was a mess of tear tracks and mucus. Rebus handed him a handkerchief.

'The ambulance is waiting,' the doctor said quietly. Rebus nodded. Michael was obviously in shock; they'd keep him in the Infirmary overnight.

Two patients to visit, thought Rebus. What was more, he suspected similar motives behind the attacks. Very similar motives, if it came down to it. The rage began in him all over again, and his scalp prickled like hell. But he calmed a little as he helped Michael over to the ambulance.

'Do you want me to come with you?' he asked.

'Absolutely not,' said Michael. 'Just go home, eh?'

Part of the way to the ambulance, Michael's legs gave way, his knees refusing to lock. They carried him instead, like taking an injured player off the field, closed the door on him, and took him away. Rebus thanked the doctor, the skipper, and Hart.

'Hellish thing to happen,' Hart said. 'Any idea why it did?'

'A few,' said Rebus.

He went home to brood in his darkened living room. His whole life seemed shot to hell. Someone had been sending him a message tonight. They'd either decided to send it *via* Michael, or else they'd simply mistaken Michael for him. After all, people said they looked alike. Since the men had come to Arden Street, they were either working on very old information, or else they knew all about his separation from Patience, which meant they were very well-informed indeed. But Rebus suspected the former. The name on the doorbell still said Rebus, though it also listed on a scrap of paper four other names. That must have confused them for a minute. Yet they'd decided to attack anyway. Why? Did it mean they were desperate? Or was it just that any hostage would do to get the message across?

Message received.

And almost understood. Almost. This was serious, deadly serious. First Brian, now Michael. He had so few doubts that the two were connected. It felt like it was time to do something, not just wait for their next move. He knew what he wanted to do, too. That one phrase had brought it to mind: *shot to hell*. A part of him wanted to be holding a gun. A gun would even the odds very nicely indeed. He even knew where he could get one, didn't he? *Anything from a shag to a shooter*. He found that he'd been pacing the floor in front of the window. He felt caged, unwilling to sleep and unable to act against his invisible foe. But he had to do *some*thing . . . so he went for a drive.

He drove to Perth. It didn't take long on the motorway in the middle of the night. In the city itself, he got lost once or twice (with no one about to ask directions of, not even a policeman) before finding the street he wanted. It was sited on a ridge of land, with houses on the one side only. This was where Patience's sister lived. Rebus spotted Patience's car and found a parking space two cars away from it. He turned off his lights and engine and reached into the back seat for the blanket he'd brought, pulling the blanket over as much of him as it would cover. He sat for a while, feeling more relaxed than in ages. He'd thought of bringing some whisky with him, but knew the kind of head it would give him in the morning. And tomorrow he wanted to be clear-headed if nothing else. He thought of Patience asleep in the spare room, just through the wall from Susan. She slept soundly, the moon lighting her forehead and her cheeks. It seemed a long way from Edinburgh, a long way from the shadow of the Forth Rail Bridge. John Rebus drifted into sleep, and slept well for once.

When he awoke, it was six-thirty on Sunday morning. He threw aside the blanket and started the car, turning the heating all the way up. He felt chilled but rested. The street was quiet, except for a man walking his ugly white poodle. The man seemed to find Rebus's presence there curious. Rebus smiled steadily at him as he shifted the gearstick into first and drove away.

10

He went straight to the Infirmary where, despite the early hour, pre-breakfast tea was being served. Michael was sitting up in bed with the cup on the tray in front of him. He seemed like a statue, staring at the surface of the dark brown liquid, his face blank. He didn't move as Rebus approached, pulled a chair noisily from a pile beside one wall, and sat down.

'Hiya, Mickey.'

'Hello, John.' Michael continued to stare. Rebus hadn't seen him blink yet.

'Going through it again and again, eh?' Michael didn't answer. 'I've been there myself, Mickey. Something terrible happens, you play it over in your mind. Eventually it fades. You might not believe that just now.'

'I'm trying to understand who did it, *why* they did it.'

'They wanted you scared, Mickey. I think it was a message for me.'

'Couldn't they have written instead? They got me scared all right. I could have shit through a Polo mint.'

Rebus laughed loudly at this. If Michael was getting back a sense of humour, the rest couldn't be far behind. 'I brought you this,' he said.

It was the photograph from Aberdeen. Rebus placed it on the tray beside the untouched tea.

'Who are they?'

'Dad and Uncle Jimmy.'

'Uncle Jimmy? I don't remember an Uncle Jimmy.'

'They fell out a long time ago, never spoke again.'

'That's a shame.'

'Uncle Jimmy died a few weeks ago. His widow – Auntie Ena – wanted us to have this photo.'

'Why?'

'Maybe because we're blood,' Rebus said.

Michael smiled. 'You wouldn't always know it.' He looked up at Rebus with wet shining eyes.

'We'll know it from now on,' said Rebus. He nodded towards the cup. 'Can I have that tea if you're not drinking it? My tongue feels like a happy hour's welcome-mat.'

'Help yourself.'

Rebus drank the tea in two swallows. 'Jesus,' he said, 'I was doing you a favour, believe me.'

'I know all about the tea they serve in institutions.'

'You're not as daft as you look then.' Rebus paused. 'You didn't see much of them, eh?'

'Who?'

'The men who grabbed you.'

'I saw bodies coming through the door. The first one was about my height, but a lot broader. The others, who knows. I never saw any faces. Sorry.'

'No problem. Can you tell me *any*thing?'

'No more than I told the constable last night. What was his name again?'

'Hart.'

'That's it. He thought I'd been bungee-jumping.' Michael gave a low laugh. 'I told him, no, I was just hanging around.'

Rebus smiled. 'But thankfully not at a loose end, eh?'

But Michael had stopped laughing. 'I had a nightmare about it. They had to give me something to make me sleep. I don't know what it was, but I still feel doped.'

'Get them to give you a prescription, you can sell tabs to the students.'

'They're good kids, John.'

'I know.'

'It'd be a shame if they moved out.'

'I know that, too.'

'You remember Gail?'

'The girl you've been seeing?'

'I've seen every inch of her. Strictly past tense now. But she has a boyfriend in Auchterarder. You don't suppose he's the jealous type?'

'I don't think he's behind last night.'

'No? Only, I've not been around Edinburgh long enough to make any enemies.'

'Don't worry,' said Rebus. 'I've got enemies enough for both of us.'

'That's very reassuring. Meanwhile . . .'

'Yes?'

'What about getting a spyhole for your door? Just think if one of the lassies had answered.'

Oh, Rebus had thought about it. 'And a chain,' he said. 'I'm getting them this afternoon.' He paused. 'Hart said something about the van.'

'When they pushed me in, it was like I was fitting into a narrow space. Yet I got the feeling the van itself was a decent size.'

'So it had stuff in the back then?'

'Maybe. Bloody solid, whatever it was. I bruised both knees.' Michael shrugged. 'That's about it.' Then he thought of something. 'Oh yes, and it had a bad smell. Either that or something had died in the carpet they wrapped me in . . .'

They sat talking for another quarter of an hour or so, until Michael closed his eyes and went to sleep. He wouldn't be asleep for long: they were starting to serve breakfast. Rebus got up and moved the chair back, then placed the photograph on Michael's bedside cabinet. He had another call to pay, while he was here.

But there were doctors with Brian Holmes, and the nurse didn't know how long they'd be. She only knew that Brian had woken again in the night for almost a minute. Rebus wished he'd been there: a minute would be long enough for the question he wanted to ask. Brian had also been talking in his sleep, but his words had been mumbled at best, and no one had any record of what he'd said. So Rebus gave up and went off to do some shopping. If he phoned around noon they'd let him know when Michael was likely to be getting home.

He went back to the flat by way of the corner shop, where he bought a week's worth of groceries. He was finishing breakfast when the first student wandered into the kitchen and drank three glassfuls of water.

'You're supposed to do that *before* you go to bed,' Rebus advised.

'Thank you, Sherlock.' The young man groaned. 'Got any paracetamol?' Rebus shook his head. 'Definitely a bad keg of beer last night. I thought the first pint tasted ropey.'

'Aye, but I'll bet the second tasted better and the sixth tasted great.'

The student laughed. 'What're you eating?'

'Toast and jam.'

'No bacon or sausages?'

Rebus shook his head. 'I've decided to lay off meat for a while.'

The student seemed unnaturally pleased.

'There's orange juice in the fridge,' Rebus continued. The student opened the fridge door and gave a gasp.

'There's enough stuff in here to feed a lecture hall!'

'Which is why,' said Rebus, 'I reckon it'll do us for at least a day or two.'

The student lifted a letter from the top of the fridge. 'This came for you yesterday.'

It was from the Inland Revenue. They were thinking of coming to check on the flat.

'Remember,' Rebus told the student, 'anyone asks, you're my nephews and nieces.'

'Yes, uncle.' The student recommenced rummaging in the refrigerator. 'Where did Mickey and you get to last night?' he asked. 'I crept in at two and there was no sign of life.'

'Oh, we were just . . .' But Rebus couldn't find any words. So the student supplied them for him.

'Shooting the breeze?'

'Shooting the breeze,' agreed Rebus.

He drove to a DIY superstore on the edge of the city and bought a chain for the door, a spy-hole, and the tools a helpful assistant suggested would be needed for both jobs. (A lot more tools than Rebus used, as it turned out.) Since there was a supermarket nearby, Rebus did a bit more grocery shopping, by which time the pubs were open for business. He looked in a few places, but couldn't find who he was looking for. But he was able to put word out with a couple of useful barmen, who said they would pass the message along.

Back at the flat, he called the Infirmary, who told him Michael could come home this afternoon. Rebus arranged to pick him up at four. He then got to work. He drilled the necessary hole in the door, only to find he'd drilled it too high for the girl student, who had to stand on tiptoe even to get close. So he drilled another hole, filled in the first with wood putty, and then fitted the spy-hole. It was a bit askew, but it would work. Fitting the sliding chain was easier, and left him with two tools and a drill-bit unused. He wondered if the DIY store would take them back.

Next he tidied the box room and put Michael's stuff into the washing machine, after which he shared the macaroni cheese which the students had prepared for lunch. He didn't quite apologise to them for the past week, but he insisted they use the living room whenever they liked, and he told them also that he was reducing their rent – news they took unsurprisingly well. He didn't say anything about Michael; he didn't reckon Michael would want them to know. And he'd already explained away the extra security on the door by citing several recent burglaries in the locality.

He brought Michael and a large bottle of sleeping tablets back from the hospital, having first bribed the students to be out of the flat for the rest of the afternoon and evening. If Michael needed to cry again, he wouldn't want an audience.

'Look, our new peephole,' said Rebus at the door of the flat.

'That was quick.'

'Protestant work ethic. Or is it Calvinist guilt? I can never remember.' Rebus opened the door. 'Please also note the security chain on the inside.'

'You can tell it's a rush job, look where the paint's all scored.'

'Don't push your luck, brother.'

Michael sat in the living room while Rebus made two mugs of tea. The stairwell had seemed full of menace for both brothers, each sensing the other's disquiet. And even now Rebus didn't feel completely safe.

This was not, however, something he wished to share with Michael.

'Just the way you like it,' he said, bringing the tea in. He could see Michael was weepy again, though trying to hide it.

'Thanks, John.'

The phone rang before Rebus could say anything. It was Siobhan Clarke, checking details of the following morning's surveillance operation.

Rebus assured her that everything was in hand; all she had to do was turn up and freeze her bum off for a few hours.

'You're a great one for motivation, sir,' was her final comment.

'So,' Rebus asked Michael, 'what do you want to do?'

Michael was shaking a large round pill out of the brown bottle. He put it on his tongue with a wavering hand, and washed it down with tea.

'A quiet night in would suit me fine,' he said.

'A quiet night in it is,' agreed Rebus.

11

Operation Moneybags began quietly enough at eight-thirty on Monday morning, thirty minutes before Davey Dougary's BMW bumped its way into the pot-holed parking lot of the taxi-cab firm. Alister Flower and his team, of course, wouldn't be starting work till eleven or a little after, but it was best not to think about that, especially if, like Siobhan Clarke, you were already cold and stiff by opening time, and dreading your next visit to the chemical toilet which had been installed, for want of any other facilities, in a broom closet.

She was bored, too. DC Peter Petrie (from St Leonard's) and Elsa-Beth Jardine from Trading Standards appeared to be nursing post-weekend hangovers and resultant blues. She got the feeling that Jardine and her might actually have a lot to talk about – both were women fighting for recognition in what was perceived as a male profession – but the presence of Petrie ruled out discussion.

Peter Petrie was one of those basically intelligent but not exactly perceptive officers who climbed the ladder by passing the exams (though never with brilliant marks) and not getting in anyone's way. Petrie was quiet and methodical; she didn't doubt his competence, it was just that he lacked any spark of inspiration or instinct. And probably, she thought, he was sitting there with his thermos summing her up as an over-talkative smart-arse with a university degree. Well, whatever he was he was no John Rebus.

She had accused her superior of not exactly motivating those who worked for him, but this was a lie. He could draw you into a case, and into his way of thinking about a case, merely by being so narrow-minded about the investigation. He was secretive – and that drew you in. He was tenacious – and that drew you in. Above all, though, he had the air of knowing exactly where he was going. And he wasn't all that bad looking either. She'd learned a lot about him by sticking close to Brian Holmes, who had been only too willing to chat about past cases and what he knew of his boss's history.

Poor Brian. She hoped he was going to be all right. She had thought a lot last night about Brian, but even more about Cafferty and his gang. She hoped she could be of help to Inspector John Rebus. She already had a few ideas about the fire at the Central Hotel ...

'Here comes someone,' said Petrie. He was squatting behind the tripod and busily adjusting the focus on the camera. He fired off half a dozen shots. 'Unidentified male. Denim jacket and light-coloured trousers. Approaching the office on foot.'

Siobhan took up her pad and copied down Petrie's description, noting the time alongside.

'He's entering the office . . . now.' Petrie turned away from the camera and grinned. 'This is what I joined the police for: a life of adventure.' Having said which, he poured more hot chocolate from his thermos into a cup.

'I can't use that loo,' said Elsa-Beth Jardine. 'I'll have to go out.'

'No can do,' said Petrie, 'it would attract too much attention, you tripping in and out every time you needed a piss.'

Jardine turned to Siobhan. 'He's got a way with words, your colleague.'

'Oh, he's a right old romantic. But it's true enough about going to the toilet.' The bathroom had flooded during the previous year's break-in, leaving the floor unsafe. Hence the broom closet.

Jardine flipped over a page of her magazine. 'Burt Reynolds has seven bathrooms in his home,' she commented.

'One for every dwarf,' muttered Petrie.

Rebus might, in Siobhan's phrase, have an air of knowing exactly where he was going, but in fact he felt like he was going round in circles. He'd visited a few early-opening pubs (near the offices of the daily newspaper; down towards the docks at Leith), social clubs and betting shops, and had asked his question and left his message in all of them. Deek Torrance was either keeping a low profile, or else he'd left the city. If still around, it was unfeasible that he wouldn't at some point stagger into a bar and loudly introduce himself and his thirst. Few people, once introduced, could forget Deek Torrance.

He'd also opened communications with hospitals in Edinburgh and Dundee, to see if either of the Robertson brothers had received surgery for a broken right arm, the old injury found on the Central Hotel corpse.

But now it was time to give up and go check out Operation Moneybags. He'd left Michael still asleep this morning, and likely to remain asleep for quite some time if those pills were anything to go by. The students had tiptoed in at a minute past midnight, 'well kettled' as one of them termed it, having spent Rebus's thirty quid on beverages at a local hostelry. They too had been asleep when Rebus had let himself out of the flat. He hardly dared admit to himself that he liked sleeping rough in his own living-room.

The whole weekend seemed like a strange bad dream now. The drive to Aberdeen, Auntie Ena, Michael . . . then the drive to Perth, the lock-fitting, and too much spare time (even after all that) in which to brood. He wondered how Patience's weekend had gone. She'd be back later today for sure. He'd try phoning again.

He parked in one of the many side streets off Gorgie Road and locked his car. This was not one of the city's safest areas. He hoped Siobhan hadn't worn a green and white scarf to work this morning . . . He walked down onto Gorgie Road, where buses were spraying the pavement with some of the morning's rainwater, and was careful not to pause outside the door, careful not to glance across the street at the cab offices. He just pushed the door open and climbed the stairs, then knocked at another door.

Siobhan Clarke herself opened it. 'Morning, sir.' She looked cold, though she had wrapped up well enough. 'Coffee?'

The offer was from her thermos, and Rebus shook his head. Normally during a surveillance, drinks and food could be brought in, but not to *this* surveillance. There wasn't supposed to be any activity in the building, so it would look more than a mite suspicious if someone suddenly appeared at the door with three beakers of tea and a home-delivery pizza. There wasn't even a back entrance to the building.

'How's it going?'

'Slow.' This from Elsa-Beth Jardine, who didn't look at all comfortable. There was an open magazine on her lap. 'Thank God I'm relieved at one o'clock.'

'Think yourself lucky, then,' commented DC Petrie.

Ah, how Rebus liked to see a happy crew. 'It's not supposed to be fun,' he told them. 'It's supposed to be work. If and when we nab Dougary and Co., *that's* when the party begins.' They had nothing to add to this, and neither did Rebus. He walked over to the window and peered out. The window itself was so grimy he doubted anyone could see them through it, and especially not from across the street. But a square had been cleaned off just a little, enough so that any photos would be recognisable. 'Camera working okay?'

'So far,' said Petrie. 'I don't really trust these motorised jobs. If the motor goes, you're buggered. You can't wind on by hand.'

'Got enough batteries?'

'Two back-up sets. They're not going to be a problem.'

Rebus nodded. He knew Petrie's reputation as a solid detective who might climb a little higher up the ladder yet. 'How about the phone?'

'It's connected, sir,' said Siobhan Clarke.

Usually, there would be radio contact between any stake-out and headquarters, but not for Moneybags. The problem was the cab company. The cabs and their home base were equipped with two-way radios, so it was possible that communications from Moneybags to HQ could actually be picked up across the road. There was the added complication, too, that the cab radios might interfere with Moneybags' transmissions.

To avoid these potential disasters, a telephone line had been installed early on Sunday morning. The telephone apparatus sat on the floor near the door. So far it had been used twice: once by Jardine to make a hairdresser's appointment; and once by Petrie to make a bet after he'd checked the day's horse-racing tips in his tabloid. Siobhan intended using it this afternoon to check on Brian's condition. But now Rebus was actually using it to phone St Leonard's.

'Any messages for me?' He waited. 'Oh? That's interesting. Anything else? *What?* Why the hell didn't you tell me that first?' He slammed the phone down. 'Brian's awake,' he said. 'He's sitting up in bed eating chicken soup and watching daytime TV.'

'Either of which could give him a relapse,' said Siobhan. She was wondering what the other message had been.

'Hello, Brian.'

'Hello, sir.' Holmes had been listening to a personal hi-fi. He switched it off and slipped the headphones down around his neck. 'Patsy Cline,' he said. 'I've been listening to a lot of her since Nell booted me out.'

'Where did the tape come from?'

'My aunt brought it in, bless her. She knows what I like. It was waiting for me when I woke up.'

Rebus had a sudden thought. They played music to coma victims, didn't they? Maybe they'd been playing Patsy Cline to Holmes. No wonder he'd been a long time waking up.

'I'm finding it hard to take in, though,' Holmes went on. 'I mean, whole days of my life, just gone like that. I wouldn't mind, I mean I like a good sleep. Only I can't remember a bloody thing I dreamt about.'

Rebus sat down by the bedside. The chair was already in place. 'Been having visitors?'

'Just the one. Nell looked in.'

'That's nice.'

'She spent the whole time crying. My face isn't horribly scarred and no one's telling me?'

'Looks as ugly as ever. What about amnesia?'

Holmes smiled. 'Oh no, I remember the whole thing, not that it'll help.'

Holmes really did look fine. It was like the doctors said, the brain shuts all systems down, thinks what damage has been done, effects repairs, and then you wake up. Policeman heal thyself.

'So?'

'So,' said Holmes, 'I'd spent the evening in the Heartbreak Cafe. I can even tell you what I ate.'

'Whatever it was, I'll bet you finished with Blue Suede Choux.'

Holmes shook his head. 'They'd none left. Like Eddie said, it's the fastest mover since the King himself.'

'So what happened after you ate?'

'The usual, I sat at the bar drinking and chatting, wondering if any gorgeous young ladies were going to slip onto the stool beside mine and ask if I came there often. I talked with Pat for a while. He was on bar duty that night.' Holmes paused. 'I should explain, Pat is –'

'Eddie's business partner, and maybe a *sleeping* partner too.'

'Now now, no homophobia.'

'Some of my best friends know gays,' Rebus said. 'You've mentioned Calder in the past. I can also tell you he doesn't drive.'

'That's right, Eddie does.'

'Even when he's shit-faced.'

Holmes shrugged. 'I've never made it my business.'

'You will when he knocks some poor old lady down.'

Holmes smiled. 'That car of his might look like a hot-rod, but it's in terrible shape. It barely does forty on the open road. Besides, Eddie's the most, if you will, *pedestrian* driver I know. He's so slow I've seen him overtaken by a skateboard – and that was being carried under somebody's arm at the time.'

'So it was just you and Calder at the bar?'

'Until Eddie joined us, after he'd finished cooking. I mean, there were other people in the place, but no obvious villains.'

'Pray continue.'

'Well, I went to go home. Someone must have been waiting behind the dustbins. Next thing I knew there was a draught up my kilt. I opened my eyes and saw these two nurses washing my tadger.'

'What?'

'That's what woke me up, I swear.'

'It's a medical miracle.'

'The magic sponge,' said Holmes.

'So who thumped you, any ideas?'

'I've been mulling it over. Maybe they were after Eddie or Pat.'

'And why would that be?'

Holmes shrugged.

'Don't keep secrets from old Uncle Rebus, Brian. You forget, I can read your mind.'

'Well, you tell *me* then.'

'Could be they've not been paying their dues.'

'You mean protection?'

'Insurance, as people like to call it.'

'Well, maybe.'

'The dynamic duo at the Heartbreak Cafe seem to think maybe it's an

301

unholy alliance of curry house owners disgruntled at the fall-off in trade.'

'I can't see that.'

'Neither can I. Maybe it was nobody, Brian. Maybe nobody was after Eddie and Pat. Maybe they were after *you*. Now why would that be?'

The pink in Holmes' cheeks grew slightly redder. 'You've seen the Black Book?'

'Of course I have. I was looking for clues, so I had a rifle through your stuff. And there it was, all in code, too. Or at least in shorthand, so nobody but another copper would know what you were on about. But I'm another copper, Brian. Now there were a lot of cases in there, but only one that stood out.'

'The Central Hotel.'

'Give the man a cigar. Yes, the Central. A poker game took place, and in attendance were Tam and Eck Robertson, neither of whom crop up in the list of punters at the Central that night. You've been trying to find them. No luck so far?' Holmes shook his head. 'But someone told you all this, didn't they? There's no mention in the files of any poker game. Now,' Rebus leaned closer, 'would I be right in thinking that the person who told you is the mysterious El?' Holmes nodded. 'Then that's all you need to tell me, Brian. Who the hell is El?'

At that moment, a nurse pushed open the door and came in bearing medicine and a lunch tray for Holmes.

'I'm starving,' he explained to Rebus. 'This is my second meal since I woke up.' He lifted the metal cover from the plate. A pale pink slice of meat, watery mashed spuds, and sliced green beans.

'Yum yum,' said Rebus. But Holmes looked keen enough. He scooped some mash and gravy into his mouth and swallowed it down.

'I'd have thought,' he said, 'that since you've figured out the hard part, you wouldn't have had any trouble with El.'

'Sorry to disappoint you. Who is he?'

'It's Elvis,' said Brian Holmes. 'Elvis himself told me.' He lifted another forkful of mush to his lips and started to slurp it down.

12

Rebus studied the menu, finding little to his liking beyond the often painful puns. The Heartbreak Cafe was open all day, but he'd arrived just in time for the special luncheon menu. A foot-long sausage on a roll was predictably if unappetisingly a 'Hound Dog'. Rebus could only hope that there was no literal truth to the appelation. More obscure was the drinks list, with one wine called 'Mama Liked the Rosé'. Rebus decided that he wasn't so hungry after all. Instead, he nursed his 'Teddy' beer at the bar and handed the menu back to the teenage barman.

'Pat's not in then?' he asked casually.

'Doing some shopping. He'll be back later.'

Rebus nodded. 'But Eddie's around?'

'In the kitchen, yeah.' The barman glanced towards the restaurant area. He wore three gold studs in his left ear. 'He won't be much longer, unless he's making something special for tonight.'

'Right,' said Rebus. A few minutes later, he picked up his beer glass and wandered over to a huge jukebox near the toilets. Finding it to be ornamental only, he studied some of the Presley mementoes on the walls, including a signed photograph of the Vegas Elvis and what looked like a rare Sun Records pressing. Both were protected by thick framed glass, and both were picked out by spotlights from the surrounding gloom. Finding himself, as if by chance, at the door to the kitchen, Rebus pushed it open with his shoulder and let it swing shut behind him.

Eddie Ringan was creating. Sweat glistened on his face, thin strands of hair sticking to his brow, as he shook a small frying pan over a gas flame. The set-up was impressive: cleaner than Rebus had expected, with many more cookers and pots and work surfaces. A lot of money had been spent; the Cafe wasn't just a designer façade. Amusingly, it seemed to Rebus, there was different music here from the constant diet of Presley served at the bar. Eddie Ringan was listening to Miles Davis.

The chef hadn't noticed Rebus yet, and Rebus hadn't noticed a trainee chef who'd been fetching something from one of several fridges at the back of the kitchen.

Rebus watched as Eddie, pausing from his work, grabbed a bottle of Jim Beam by its neck and upended it into his mouth, taking it away again with a satisfied exhalation.

'Hey,' said the trainee chef, 'no one's allowed in here.' Eddie looked up from the pan and gave a whoop.

'You're just the man!' he cried. 'The very man! Come over here.'

If anything, he sounded drunker than at their first meeting. But then, at their first meeting there had been the civilising (or at least restricting) presence of Pat Calder, as well as the sobering fact of Brian Holmes' attack.

Rebus walked over to the cooker. He too was starting to sweat in the heat.

'This,' said Eddie Ringan, nodding towards the pan, 'is my latest dish. Pieces of Roquefort cheese imprisoned in breadcrumb and spice and fried. Either pan-fried or deep-fried, that's what I'm deciding.'

'Jailhouse Roquefort,' Rebus guessed. Ringan whooped again, losing his balance slightly and sliding back with one foot.

'*Your* idea, Inspector Rabies.'

'I'm flattered, but the name's Rebus.'

'Aye, well, you should be flattered. Maybe we'll gie you a wee mention on the menu. How about that, eh?' He studied the golden nuggets, turning them expertly with a fork. 'I'm giving this lot six minutes. Willie!'

'I'm right here.'

'How long's that been?'

The protégé checked his watch. 'Three and a half. I've put the butter down there next to the eggs.'

'Willie's my assistant, Inspector.'

The exasperation in Willie's voice and expressions made Rebus doubt he would be assisting for much longer. Though younger than Ringan, Willie was about the same size. You wouldn't call him slender. Rebus reckoned chefs were partial to too much R&D. 'Can we talk for a minute?'

'Two and a half minutes if you like.'

'I'd like to know about the Central Hotel.' Ringan didn't seem to hear this, his attention on the contents of the frying-pan. 'You were there the night it burned down.'

El was short for Elvis, and Elvis was code for Eddie Ringan. Holmes hadn't wanted the wrong people getting hold of the Black Book and being able to identify the person who'd been talking. That's why he'd gone an extra step in disguising Ringan's identity.

He'd also made Rebus promise that he wouldn't tell the chef Holmes had shared their secret. It *was* to have been a secret, a little tale spilt from a bottle of bourbon. But Ringan hadn't poured out nearly enough, he'd just given Holmes a taste.

'Did you hear me, Eddie?'

'A minute left, Inspector.'

'You never cropped up on the list of staff because you were moon-lighting, working there some nights without the other place you worked at knowing anything about it. So you were able to give a false name, and nobody ever found out it was you there that night, the night of the poker game.'

'Nearly done.' There was more sweat on Eddie Ringan's face now, and his mouth seemed stiff with suppressed anger.

'I'm nearly done too, Eddie. When did you start on the booze, eh? Just after that night, wasn't it? Because something happened in that hotel. I wonder what it was. Whatever it was, you saw it, and if you don't tell me about it, I'm going to find out anyway, and then I'm going to come back here for you.' To emphasise this, Rebus pushed a finger against the chef's arm.

Ringan snatched the frying-pan and swung it at Rebus, sending bits of Jailhouse Roquefort flying in arcs across the kitchen.

'Get the fuck away from me!'

Rebus dodged the frying-pan, but Ringan was still holding it in front of him, ready to lunge.

'Just you get the fuck out of here! Who told you, anyway?'

'Nobody needed to tell me, Eddie. I worked it out for myself.'

Willie meantime was down on one knee. A hot cube of cheese had caught him smack in the eye.

'I'm dying!' he called. 'Get an ambulance, get a lawyer! This is an industrial injury.'

Eddie Ringan glanced towards the trainee chef, then back at the frying-pan in his hand, then at Rebus, and he began to laugh, the laughter becoming uproarious, hysterical. But at least he put down the pan. He even picked up one of the cheese cubes and took a bite out of it.

'Tastes like shite,' he said, still laughing and spluttering bits of bread-crumb at Rebus.

'Are you going to tell me, Eddie?' Rebus asked calmly.

'I'm going to tell you this: get the fuck out.'

Rebus stood his ground, though Eddie had already turned his back. 'Tell me where I can find the Bru-Head Brothers.'

This brought more laughter.

'Just give me a start, Eddie. Then it'll be off your conscience.'

'I lost my conscience a long time ago, Inspector. Willie, let's get a fresh batch going.'

The young man was still checking for damage. He held one hand across his good eye like a patch. 'I cannae see a thing,' he complained. 'I think the retina's cracked.'

'And the cornea's melted,' added Ringan. 'Come on, I'm hoping to have this on the menu tonight.' He turned to Rebus, making a show of astonishment. 'Still here? A definite case of too many cooks.'

Rebus looked at him with sad, steady eyes. 'Just a start, Eddie.'

'Away tae fuck.'

Slowly, Rebus turned around and pushed open the door.

'Inspector!' He turned his head towards the chef. 'There's a pub in Cowdenbeath called The Midtown. The locals call it the Midden. I wouldn't eat the food there.'

Rebus nodded slowly. 'Thanks for the tip.'

'It's *you* that's supposed to give *me* the tip!' he heard Ringan roar as he exited from the kitchen. He placed his empty glass on the bartop.

'Kitchen's off limits,' the barman informed him.

'More like the outer bloody limits.'

But no, he knew that only now would he be going to the outer limits, back to the haunts of his youth.

13

He had only dropped into St Leonard's to pick up a few things from his desk, but the duty sergeant stopped him short.

'Gentleman here has been waiting to see you. He seems a bit anxious.'

The 'gentleman' in question had been standing in a corner, but was now directly in front of Rebus. 'You don't recognise me?'

Rebus studied the man for a moment longer, and felt an old loathing. 'Oh yes,' he said, 'I recognise you all right.'

'Didn't you get my message?'

This had been the other message relayed to him when he'd called in from Gorgie Road. He nodded.

'Well, what are you going to do?'

'What would you like me to do, Mr McPhail?'

'You've got to stop him!'

'Stop who exactly? And from what?'

'You said you got the message.'

'All I was told was that someone called Andrew McPhail had phoned wanting to speak to me.'

'What I want is bloody protection!'

'Calm down now.' Rebus saw that the desk sergeant was getting ready for action, but he didn't think there would be any need for that.

'What have I got to do?' McPhail was saying. 'You want me to hit you? That'd get me a night in the cells, wouldn't it? I'd be safe there.'

Rebus nodded. 'You'd be safe all right, until we told your cell mates about your past escapades.'

This seemed to calm McPhail down like a bucket of ice. Maybe he was remembering particular incidents during his spell in the Canadian prison. Or maybe it was a less localised fear. Whatever it was, it worked. His tone became quietly plaintive. 'But he'll kill me.'

'Who will?'

'Stop pretending! I know you set him on to me. It had to be you.'

'Humour me,' said Rebus.

'Maclean,' said McPhail. 'Alex Maclean.'

'And who is Alex Maclean?'

McPhail looked disgusted. He spoke in an undertone. 'The wee girl's stepfather. Melanie's stepfather.'

'Ah,' said Rebus, nodding now. He knew immediately what Jack Morton had done, bugger that he was. No wonder McPhail got in touch. And as Rebus had been round to see Mrs MacKenzie, he'd thought Rebus must be behind the whole scheme.

'Has he threatened you?'

McPhail nodded.

'In what way?'

'He came to the house. I wasn't there. He told Mrs MacKenzie he'd be back to get me. Poor woman's in a terrible state.'

'You could always move, get out of Edinburgh.'

'Christ, is that what you want? That's why you've set Maclean on me. Well, I'm staying put.'

'Heroic of you, Mr McPhail.'

'Look, I know what I've done, but that's behind me.'

Rebus nodded. 'And all you've got in front of you is the view from your bedroom.'

'Jesus, *I* didn't know Mrs MacKenzie lived across from a primary school!'

'Still, you could move. A location like that, it's bound to rile Maclean further.'

McPhail stared at Rebus. 'You're repulsive,' he said. 'Whatever I've done in my life, I'm willing to bet you've done worse. Never mind about me, I'll look after myself.' McPhail made show of pushing past Rebus towards the door.

'Ca' canny, Mr McPhail,' Rebus called after him.

'Christ,' said the desk sergeant, 'who was that?'

'That,' said Rebus, 'was someone finding out how it feels to be a victim.'

All the same, he felt a bit guilty. What if McPhail *had* been rehabilitated, and Maclean *did* do him some damage? Scared as he was, McPhail might even decide a first strike was his only form of defence. Well, Rebus had slightly more pressing concerns, hadn't he?

In the CID room, he studied the only available mug-shots of Tam and Eck Robertson, taken over five years ago. He got a DC to make him some photocopies, but then had a better idea. There was no police artist around, but that didn't bother Rebus. He knew where an artist could always be found.

It was five o'clock when he got to McShane's Bar near the bottom of the Royal Mile. McShane's was a haven for bearded folk fans and their woolly sweaters. Upstairs, there was always music, be it a professional performer or some punter who'd taken the stage to belt out 'Will Ye Go Lassie Go' or 'Both Sides O' The Tweed'.

Midgie McNair did good business in McShane's sketching flattering likenesses of acquiescent customers, who paid for the privilege and often bought the drinks as well.

At this early hour, Midgie was downstairs, reading a paperback at a corner table. His sketch-pad sat on the table beside him, along with half a dozen pencils. Rebus placed two pints on the table, then sat down and produced the photos of the Bru-Head Brothers.

'Not exactly Butch and Sundance, are they?' said Midgie McNair.

'Not exactly,' said Rebus.

14

John Rebus had once known Cowdenbeath very well indeed, having gone to school there. It was one of those Fife mining communities which had grown from a hamlet in the late nineteenth or early twentieth centuries when coal was in great demand, such demand that the cost of digging it out of the ground hardly entered the equation. But the coalfields of Fife didn't last long. There was still plenty of coal deep underground, but the thin warped strata were difficult (and therefore costly) to mine. He supposed some opencast mining might still be going on – at one time west central Fife had boasted Europe's biggest hole in the ground – but the deep pitshafts had all been filled in. In Rebus's youth there had been three obvious career choices for a fifteen-year-old boy: the pits, Rosyth Dockyard, or the Army. Rebus had chosen the last of these. Nowadays, it was probably the only choice on offer.

Like the towns and villages around it, Cowdenbeath looked and felt depressed: closed down shops and drab chainstore clothes. But he knew that the people were stronger than their situation might suggest. Hardship bred a bitter, quickfire humour and a resilience to all but the most terminal of life's tragedies. He didn't like to think about it too deeply, but inside he felt like he really was 'coming home'. Edinburgh might have been his base for twenty years, but he was a Fifer. 'Fly Fifers', some people called them. Rebus was ready to do battle with some very fly people indeed.

Monday night was the quietest of the week for pubs across the land. The pay packets or dole money had disappeared over the course of the weekend. Monday was for staying in. Not that you would know this from the scene that greeted Rebus as he pushed open the door to the Midden. Its name belittled it; its interior was no worse than many a bar in Edinburgh and elsewhere. Basic, yes, with a red linoleum floor spotted black from hundreds of cigarette dowps. The tables and chairs were functional, and though the bar was not large enough space had been found for a pool table and dartboard. A game of darts was in progress when Rebus entered, and one young man marched around the pool table, potting shot after shot as he squinted through the smoke which rose from the cigarette in his mouth. At a corner table three old men, all wearing flat bunnets, were playing a tense game of dominoes, groups of steady drinkers filling the other tables.

So Rebus had no choice but to stand at the bar. There was just room for one more, and he nodded a greeting to the pint drinkers either side of him. A greeting no one bothered to return.

'Pint of special, please,' he said to the slick-haired barman.

'Special, son, right you are.'

Rebus got the feeling this fiftyish bartender would call even the domino players 'son'. The drink was poured with the proper amount of care, like the ritual it was in this part of the world.

'Special, son, there you are.'

Rebus paid for the beer. It was the cheapest pint he'd bought in months. He started to think about how easy it would be to commute to work from Fife . . .

'Pint of spesh, Dod.'

'Spesh, son, right you are.'

The pool player stood just behind Rebus, not quite menacingly. He placed his empty glass on the bartop and waited for it to be refilled. Rebus knew the youth was interested, maybe waiting to see whether Rebus would speak. But Rebus didn't say anything. He just took photocopies of the two drawings out of his jacket pocket and unfolded them. He'd had ten copies of each made up at a newsagent's on the Royal Mile. The originals were safe in the glove compartment of his car; though how safe his car itself was, parked on the poorly lit street outside, was another matter.

He could feel the drinkers either side of him glance at the drawings, and didn't doubt that the youth was having a look too. Still nobody said anything.

'Spesh, son, there you are.' The pool player picked up the glass, spilling some beer onto the sheets of paper. Rebus turned his head towards him.

'Sorry about that.'

Rebus had seldom heard a less sincere tone of voice. 'That's all right,' he said, matching the tone. 'I've got plenty more copies.'

'Oh aye?' The youth took his change from the barman and went back to the pool table, crouching to load coins into the slot. The balls fell with a dull rumble and he started to rack them up, staring at Rebus.

'You do a bit of drawing, eh?'

Rebus, who had been wiping the drawings with his hand, turned to Dod the barman. 'Not me, no. Good though, aren't they?' He turned the drawings around slowly so Dod could get a better look.

'Oh aye, no' bad. I'm no' an expert, like. The only things anybody around here draws are the pension or the dole.' There was laughter at this.

'Or a bowl,' added one drinker. He made the word sound like 'bowel', but Rebus knew what he meant.

'Or a cigarette,' somebody else suggested, but the joke was by now history. The barman nodded towards the drawings. 'Anybody in particular, like?'

Rebus shrugged.

'Could be brothers, eh?'

Rebus turned to the drinker on his left, who had just spoken. 'What makes you say that?'

The drinker twitched and turned to stare at the row of optics behind the bar. 'They look similar.'

Rebus examined the two drawings. As requested, Midgie had aged the brothers five or six years. 'You could be right.'

'Or cousins maybe,' said the drinker on his right.

'Related, though,' Rebus mused.

'I cannae see it myself,' said Dod the barman.

'Look a bit closer,' Rebus advised. He ran his finger over the sheets of paper. 'Same chins, eyes look the same too. Maybe they *are* brothers.'

'Who are they, then?' asked the drinker on his right, a middle-aged man with square unshaven jaw and lively blue eyes.

But Rebus just shrugged again. One of the domino players came to the bar to order a round. He looked like he'd just won a rubber, and clapped his hands together.

'How's it going then, James?' he asked the drinker on Rebus's right.

'No' bad, Matt. Yourself?'

'Ach, just the same.' He smiled at Rebus. 'Havenae seen you in here afore, son.'

Rebus shook his head. 'I've been away.'

'Oh aye?' Three pints had appeared on a metal tray.

'There you go, Matt.'

'Thanks, Dod.' Matt handed over a ten-pound note. As he waited for change, he saw the drawings. 'Butch and Sundance, eh?' He laughed. Rebus smiled warmly. 'Or more like Steptoe and Son.'

'Steptoe and Brother,' Rebus suggested.

'Brothers?' Matt studied the drawings. He was still studying them when he asked, 'Are you the polis then, son?'

'Do I look like the polis?'

'No' exactly.'

'No' fat enough for a start,' said Dod. 'Eh, son?'

'You get skinny polis, though,' argued James. 'What about Stecky Jamieson?'

'Right enough,' said Dod. 'Thon bugger could hide behind a lamp post.'

Matt had picked up the tray of drinks. The other domino players at his table called out that they were 'gasping'. Matt nodded towards the drawings. 'I've seen yon buggers afore,' he said, before moving off.

Rebus drained his glass and ordered another. The drinker on his left finished and, fixing a bunnet to his head, started to make his goodbyes.

'Cheerio then, Dod.'

'Aye, cheerio.'

'Cheerio, James.'

This went on for minutes. The long cheerio. Rebus folded the drawings and put them in his pocket. He took his time over the second pint. There was some talk of football, extra-marital affairs, the nonexistent job market. Mind you, the amount of affairs that seemed to be going on, Rebus was surprised anyone found the time or energy for a job.

'You know what this part of Fife's become?' offered James. 'A giant DIY store. You either work in one, or you shop there. That's about it.'

'True enough,' said Dod, though there was little conviction in his voice.

Rebus finished the second pint and went to visit the gents'. The place stank to high heaven, and the graffiti was poor. Nobody came in for a quiet word, not that he'd been expecting it. On his way back from bathroom to bar he stopped at the dominoes game.

'Matt?' he asked. 'Sorry to interrupt. You didn't say where you thought you'd seen Butch and Sundance.'

'Maybe just the one o' them,' said Matt. The doms had been shuffled and he picked up seven, three in one hand and four in the other. 'It wasnae here, though. Maybe Lochgelly. For some reason, I think it was Lochgelly.' He put the dominoes face down on the tabletop and picked out the one he wished to play. The man next to him chapped.

'Bad sign that, Tam, this early on.'

Bad sign indeed. Rebus would have to go to Lochgelly. He returned to the bar and said his own brief cheerio.

'Or you could draw a fire,' someone at the bar was saying, poking the embers of that long-dead joke.

The drive from Cowdenbeath to Lochgelly took Rebus through Lumphinnans. His father had always made jokes about Lumphinnans; Rebus wasn't sure why, and certainly couldn't recall any of them. When he'd been young, the skies had been full of smoke, every house heated by a coal fire in the sitting room. The chimneys sent up a grey plume into the evening air, but not now. Now, central heating and gas had displaced Old King Coal.

It saddened Rebus, this silence of the lums.

It saddened him, too, that he would have to repeat his performance with the drawings. He'd hoped the Midden would be the start and finish of his quest. Of course, it was always possible Eddie had been setting a false trail in the first place. If so, Rebus would see he got his just desserts, and it wouldn't be Blue Suede Choux.

He did his act in three pubs nursing three half-pints, with no reaction save the usual bad jokes including the 'drawing the pension' line. But in the fourth bar, an understandably understated shack near the railway station, he drew the attention of a keen-eyed old man who had been cadging drinks all round the pub. At the time, Rebus was showing the drawings to a cluster of painters and decorators at the corner of the L-shaped bar. He knew they were decorators because they'd asked him if he needed any work doing. 'On the fly, like. Cheaper that way.' Rebus shook his head and showed them the drawings.

The old man pushed his way into the group. He looked up at all the faces around him. 'All right, lads? Here, I was decorated in the war.' He cackled at his joke.

'So you keep telling us, Jock.'

'Every fuckin' night.'

'Without fuckin' fail.'

'Sorry, lads,' Jock apologised. He thrust a short thick finger at one of the drawings. 'Looks familiar.'

'Must be a bloody jockey then.' The decorator winked at Rebus. 'I'm no' joking, mister. Jock would recognise a racehorse's bahookey quicker than a human face.'

'Ach,' said Jock dismissively, 'away tae hell wi' you.' And to Rebus: 'Sure you dinnae owe me a drink fae last week ...?'

Five minutes after Rebus glumly left this last pub, a young man arrived. It had taken him some time, visiting all the bars between the Midden and here, asking whether a man had been in with some drawings. He was annoyed, too, at having to break off his pool practice so early. His screwball needed work. There was a competition on Sunday, and he had every intention of winning the £100 prize. If he didn't, there'd be trouble. But meantime, he knew he could do someone a favour by trailing this man who claimed not to be a copper. He knew it because he'd made a phone call from the Midden.

'You'd be doing me a favour,' the person on the other end of the line had said, when the pool player had finally been put through to him, having had to relate his story to two other people first.

It was useful to be owed a favour, so he'd taken off from the Midden, knowing that the man with the drawings was on his way to Lochgelly. But now here he was at the far end of the town; there were no pubs after this until Lochore. And the man had gone. So the pool player made another call and gave his report. It wasn't much, he knew, but it had been time-consuming work all the same.

'I owe you one, Sharky,' the voice said.

Sharky felt elated as he got back into his rusty Datsun. And with luck, he'd still have time for a few games of pool before closing time.

John Rebus drove back to Edinburgh with just desserts on his mind. And Andrew McPhail, and Michael with his tranquillisers, and Patience, and Operation Moneybags, and many other things besides.

Michael was sound asleep when he arrived at the flat. He checked with the students, who were worried that his brother was maybe on some sort of drugs. He assured them the drugs were prescribed rather than proscribed. Then he telephoned Siobhan Clarke at home.

'How did it go today?'

'You had to be there, sir – I could write the book on boredom. Dougary had five visitors all day. He had pizza delivered lunch. Drove home at five-thirty.'

'Any of the visitors interesting?'

'I'll let you see the photographs. Customers, maybe. But they came out with as many limbs as they went in with. Will you be joining us tomorrow?'

'Probably.'

'Only I thought maybe we could talk about the Central Hotel.'

'Speaking of which, have you seen Brian?'

'I popped in after work. He looks great.' She paused. 'You sound tired. Have you been working?'

'Yes.'

'The Central?'

'Christ knows, I suppose so.' Rebus rubbed the back of his neck. The hangover was starting already.

'You had to buy a few drinks?' Siobhan guessed.

'Yes.'

'And drink a few?'

'Right again, Sherlock.'

She laughed, then tutted. 'And afterwards you drove home. I'd be happy to chauffeur you if it would help.' She sounded like she meant it.

'Thanks, Clarke. I'll bear it in mind.' He paused. 'Know what I'd like for Christmas?'

'It's a long way off.'

'I'd like someone to *prove* that the corpse belongs to one of the Bru-Head Brothers.'

'The body had a broken –'

'I know, I've checked. The hospitals came up with spit.' He paused again. 'Not your problem,' he said. 'I'll see you tomorrow.'

'Good night, sir.'

Rebus sat in silence for a minute or two. Something about his conversation with Siobhan Clarke made him want to talk with Patience. He picked up the receiver again and rang her.

'Hello?'

Ye Gods, not an answering machine!

'Hello, Patience.'

'John.'

'I'd like to talk. Are you ready?'

There was silence, then: 'Yes, I think so. Let's talk.'

John Rebus lay down on the sofa, one hand behind his head. Nobody else used the phone that night.

15

John Rebus was in a good mood that Tuesday morning, for no other reason than that he'd spent what seemed like half the previous night on the phone with Patience. They were going to meet for a drink; he just had to wait for her to get back to him with a place and a time. He was still in a good mood when he opened the ground floor door and started up the stairs towards Operation Moneybags' Gorgie centre of operations.

He could hear voices; nothing unusual about that. But the voices grew in intensity as he climbed, and he opened the door just in time to see a man lunge at DC Petrie and butt him square on the nose. Petrie fell back against the window, knocking over the camera tripod. Blood gushed from his nostrils. Rebus only half took in that two small boys were watching, along with Siobhan Clarke and Elsa-Beth Jardine. The man was pulling Petrie upright when Rebus got an arm lock around him, pinning the man's arms to his side. He pulled Rebus to right and left, trying to throw him off, all the time yelling so loudly it was a wonder nobody on the street below could hear the commotion.

Rebus heaved the man backwards and turned him, so that he lost balance and fell to the floor, where Rebus sat on top of him. Petrie started forward, but the man lashed out with his legs and sent Petrie back into the window, where his elbow smashed the glass. Rebus did what he had to do. He punched the man in the throat.

'What the hell's going on here?' he asked. The man was gasping but still struggling. 'You, stop it!' Then something hit Rebus on the back of his head. It was the clenched fist of one of the boys, and it hit him right on his burnt patch of scalp. He screwed shut his eyes, fighting the stinging pain of the blow and a nausea in his gut, right where his muesli and tea with honey were sitting.

'Leave my dad alone!'

Siobhan Clarke grabbed the boy and dragged him off.

'Arrest that little bugger,' Rebus said. Then, to the boy's father: 'I mean it, too. If you don't calm down, I'm going to have *him* charged with assault. How would you like that?'

'He's too young,' gasped the man.

'Is he?' said Rebus. 'Are you sure?'

317

The man thought about it and calmed down.

'That's better.' Rebus rose from the man's chest. 'Now is *someone* going to explain all this to me?'

It was quickly explained, once Petrie had been sent off to find a doctor for his nose and the boys had been sent home. The man was called Bill Chilton, and Bill Chilton didn't like squatters.

'Squatters?'

'That's what Wee Neilly told me.'

'Squatters?' Rebus turned to Siobhan Clarke. She'd been downstairs to check no passers-by had been injured by falling glass, and more importantly to explain the 'accident'.

'The two boys,' she said now, 'came barging in. They said they sometimes played here.'

Rebus stopped her and turned to Chilton. 'Why isn't Neil at school?'

'He's been suspended for fighting.'

Rebus nodded. 'He's got a fair punch on him.' The back of his head throbbed agreement. He turned back to Siobhan.

'They asked us what we were doing, and Ms Jardine' – at this Elsa-Beth Jardine lowered her head – 'told them we were squatters.'

'Just joking,' Jardine found it necessary to add. Rebus feigned surprise, and she lowered her eyes again, blushing furiously.

'DC Petrie joined in, the boys cleared out, and we all had a laugh about it.'

'A laugh?' Rebus said. 'It wasn't a laugh, it was a breach of security.' He sounded as furious as he looked, so that even Siobhan turned her eyes away from his. He now turned his gaze on Bill Chilton.

'Well,' Chilton continued, 'Neil came home and told me there were squatters here. We've had a lot of that going on this past year or two, deserted tenement flats being broken open and used for all sorts of things ... drug pushing and that. Some of us are doing something about it.'

'What are we talking about here, Mr Chilton? Vigilante tactics? Pickaxe handles at dawn?'

Chilton was unabashed. '*You* lot are doing bugger all!'

'So you came up here looking to scare the squatters off?'

'Before they got a toe-hold, aye.'

'And?'

Chilton said nothing.

'And,' Rebus said for him, 'you started shouting the odds at DC Petrie, who started shouting back that he was a police officer and you'd better bugger off. Only by that time you were too fired up to back off. Got a bit of a temper, Mr Chilton? Maybe it's rubbed off on Neilly, eh? Did *you* get into a lot of fights at school?'

'What the hell's that got to do with anything?' Chilton's anger was rising again. Rebus raised a pacifying hand.

'It's a serious offence, assaulting a police officer.'

'Mistaken identity,' said Chilton.

'Even after he'd identified himself?'

Chilton shrugged. 'He never showed me any ID.'

Rebus raised an eyebrow. 'You're very knowledgeable about procedure. Maybe you've been in this sort of trouble before, eh?' This shut Chilton's mouth. 'Maybe if I go down the station and look you up on the computer ... what would this be, second offence? Third? Might we be talking about a wee trip to Saughton jail?' Chilton was looking decidedly uncomfortable, which was exactly what Rebus wanted.

'Of course,' he said, 'we could always shut the book on this one.' Chilton looked interested. 'If,' Rebus warned, 'you could keep your gob shut about it. *And* get Neil and his pal to forget they saw anything.'

Chilton nodded towards the camera. 'You're watching somebody, eh? A stake-out?'

'Best if you don't know, Mr Chilton. Do we have a deal?'

Chilton thought about it, then nodded.

'Good,' said Rebus, 'now get the fuck out of here.'

Chilton knew when he was being made an offer. He got the fuck out of there. Rebus shook his head.

'Sir –'

'Shut up and listen,' Rebus told Siobhan Clarke. 'This could've blown the whole thing. Maybe it has, we won't know for a day or two. Meanwhile, get that camera set up again and get back to work. Phone HQ and get someone in here to board up the window, leaving a big enough hole for the camera. Either that or we need a new pane of glass.

'And listen to me, the two of you.' He raised a warning finger. 'Nobody gets to know about this, *nobody*. It's forgotten as of now, understand?'

They understood. What they did not understand perhaps was exactly why Rebus wanted it kept quiet. It wasn't that he feared the early termination of Operation Moneybags – as far as he was concerned, the whole project was doomed to failure anyway. No, it was another fear altogether, the fear that Detective Inspector Alister Flower, safe and snug in the Firth Pub with his own surveillance crew, would find out. By God, that would mean trouble, more trouble than Rebus was willing to contemplate.

A pity then that he hadn't managed to say anything to DC Peter Petrie, who went back to St Leonard's for a change of shirt. The blood on his T-shirt might have been mistaken for tomato sauce or old tea, but there was no doubting the cause of the white gauze pad which had been taped across his nose and half his face. And when questioned, Peter Petrie quite gladly told his story, embellishing it only a little – as, for example, in exaggerating his assailant's size, skill, and speed of attack. There were sympathetic smiles and shakes of the head, and the same comment was uttered by more than one fellow officer.

'Wait till Flower hears about this.'

By lunchtime, Flower had heard from several sources about the giant who had wreaked such havoc to the Gorgie surveillance.

'Dearie me,' he said, sipping an orange juice laced with blue label vodka. 'That's terrible. I wonder if Chief Inspector Lauderdale knows? Ach, of course he does, Rebus wouldn't try to keep a thing like that from him, would he?' And he smiled so warmly at the DC seated beside him that the DC got quite worried, really quite worried about his boss . . .

Siobhan picked up the telephone.

'Hello?' She watched John Rebus staring out of the broken window. He'd been watching the taxi offices for half an hour, so deep in thought that neither she nor Jardine had uttered a word to one another above a whisper. 'It's for you, sir.'

Rebus took the receiver from her. It was CID with a message to relay.

'Go ahead.'

'From someone called Pat Calder. He says a Mr Ringan has disappeared.'

'Disappeared?'

'Yes, and he wanted you to know. Do you want us to do anything this end?'

'No thanks, I'll go have a word myself. Thanks for letting me know.' Rebus put down the phone.

'Who's disappeared?' Siobhan asked.

'Eddie Ringan.'

'The Heartbreak Cafe?'

Rebus nodded. 'I was only speaking to him yesterday. He threatened me with a panful of hot cheese.' Siobhan was looking interested, but Rebus shook his head. 'You stay here, at least until Petrie gets back.' The Heartbreak Cafe was only five minutes away. Rebus wondered if Calder would be there. A kitchen without a chef, after all, it was hardly worth opening for the day . . .

But when Rebus arrived, the Cafe was doing a brisk trade in early lunches. Calder, acting as maitre d', waved to Rebus when he entered. Passing the same young barman as yesterday, Rebus gave him a wink. Calder was looking frantic.

'What the hell did you say to Eddie yesterday?'

'What do you mean?'

'Come off it, you had a stand-up row, didn't you? I knew something was wrong. He was edgy as hell all last night, and his cooking went to pot.' Calder saw no humour in this. 'You must have said *some*thing.'

'Who told you?'

Calder cocked his head towards the kitchen. 'Willie.'

Rebus nodded understanding. 'And today, Willie gets his chance for fame and fortune.'

'He's doing the lunches, if that's what you mean.'

'So when did Eddie go missing?'

'After we closed last night, he went off to look for some club or other. One of those moveable feasts that takes over a warehouse for one night a week.'

'You didn't fancy it yourself?'

Calder wrinkled his nose in distaste.

'Would this be a club for gentlemen, Mr Calder?'

'A gay club, yes. No secret there, Inspector. It's all quite legit.'

'I'm sure it is. And Mr Ringan didn't come home?'

'No.'

'So maybe he found someone else to go home with ...?'

'Eddie's not that type.'

'Then what type is he?'

'The *faithful* type, believe me. He often goes out drinking, but he always comes back.'

'Until now.'

'Yes.'

Rebus considered. 'Bit early yet to start a missing person file. We usually give it at least forty-eight hours, if there's no other evidence.'

'What sort of evidence?'

'Well, a body, for example.'

Calder turned his head away. 'Christ,' he said.

'Look, I'm sure there's nothing to worry about.'

'I'm not,' said Pat Calder.

No, and neither was John Rebus.

Calder slapped a smile on his face as a couple entered the Cafe. He picked up two menus and asked them to follow him to a table. They were in their early twenties and dressed fashionably, the man looking like he'd walked out of a 1930s gangster flick, the woman like she'd put on her wee sister's skirt by mistake.

When Calder came back he spoke in an undertone. 'Someone should tell her you can't hide acne with panstick. You know, Eddie hasn't been the same since the night Brian was attacked.'

'Brian's okay now, by the way.'

'Yes, Eddie rang the hospital yesterday.'

'He didn't visit, though?'

'We hate hospitals, too many friends dying in them lately.'

'The news about Brian didn't cheer him up?'

Calder pursed his lips. 'I suppose it did for a little while.' He pulled a notebook and pen out of his pocket. 'Must go and see what they want to drink.'

Rebus nodded. 'I'll just have a word with Willie and your barman, see what they think.'

'Fine. Lunch is on the house.' Rebus shook his head. 'We won't poison you, Inspector.'

'It's not that,' said Rebus. 'It's all this Presley stuff on the walls. It fair takes away my appetite.'

Willie the trainee chef looked like he was enjoying his day as ruler of all he surveyed. Flustered as he was, with no one to help him, still he gave off an air of never wanting things to change.

'Remember me, Willie?'

Willie glanced up. 'Jailhouse Roquefort?' He went back to shimmying pans, then started to chop a bunch of fresh parsley. Rebus marvelled at how speedily he worked with the knife mere millimetres from his fingertips.

'You here about Eddie? He's a mad bastard that, but a brilliant chef.'

'Must be fun to be in charge though?'

'It would be if I got the credit, but those buggers out there probably think the great Eduardo's prepared each dish of the day. Like Pat says, if they knew he wisnae here, they'd go off for a tandoori businessman's lunch at half the price.'

Rebus smiled. 'Still, being in charge . . .'

Willie stopped chopping. 'What? You think I've got Eddie stashed away in my coal bunker? Just so I can have a day of tearing around like a mad-arsed fly?' He waved his knife towards the kitchen door. 'Pat might lend a hand, but no, he's got to be out there buttering up the clientele. Butter Pat, that's his name. If I was going to do away with either one of them, it'd be the one right outside that door.'

'You're taking it very seriously, Willie. Eddie's only been missing overnight. Could be sleeping it off in the gutter somewhere.'

'That's not what Pat thinks.'

'And what do *you* think?'

Willie tasted from a steaming vat. 'I think I've put too much cream in the *potage*.'

'It's the way Elvis would have wanted it,' commented Rebus.

The barman, whose name was Toni ('with an i'), poured Rebus a murky half pint of Cask Conditioned.

'This looks as conditioned as my hair.'

'I know a good hairdresser if you're interested.'

Rebus ignored the remark, then decided to ignore the beer too. He waited while Toni chattily served two student types at the other end of the bar.

'How did Eddie seem after I left yesterday?'

'What's the name of that Scorsese film?'

'*Taxi Driver*?'

The barman shook his head. '*Raging Bull*. That was Eddie.'

'He was like that all evening?'

'I didn't see him much. By the time he comes out of the kitchen, I'm putting on my coat to go home.'

'Was there anyone ... *unusual* in the bar last night?'

'You get a mixed crowd in here. Any particular *type* of unusual?'

'Forget it.'

It looked like Toni-with-an-i already had.

16

It was beginning to look like the circle was now complete. Eddie told Holmes something about the body in the Central Hotel. Holmes tried to find out more, by going after the Bru-Head Brothers. Then Rebus came along to offer help. Now all three had been warned off in some way or other. Well, he *hoped* Eddie was just being warned off. He hoped it wasn't more drastic. Everyone knew the chef had trouble keeping his mouth shut after a drink, and 'after a drink' seemed to be his permanent state. Yes, Rebus was worried. They'd tried scaring him off and only made him more determined. So would they now pull another stunt? Or would they perhaps revert to more certain means of silence?

Rebus's face was as dark as the sky when he walked back into St Leonard's, only to be ordered immediately to Lauderdale's office. Lauderdale was pouring whisky into three glasses.

'Ah, there you are.'

Rebus could not deny it. 'Summoned by Bell's, sir.' He accepted the glass, trying not to look at Alister Flower's beaming face. The three men sat down.

'Cheers,' offered Lauderdale.

'Here's tae us,' said Flower.

Rebus just drank.

'Been having a bit of bother, John?' Lauderdale was positioning his half-empty glass on the desk. When he used Rebus's first name, Rebus knew he was in trouble.

'I don't know about that, sir. There was a minor hiccup this morning, all taken care of.'

Lauderdale nodded, still seeming affable. Flower had crossed his legs, at ease with the world. When Lauderdale next spoke, he held up a finger to accompany each point.

'Two schoolkids barge in on you. Then DC Petrie gets into a punch-up with a complete stranger. A window is smashed, and so is Petrie's nose. DC Clarke's down at street level trying to brush away broken glass and curious passers-by.' He looked up from his full hand. 'Any possibility, John, that Operation Moneybags has been placed in jeopardy?'

'No possibility, sir.' Rebus held up one finger. 'The man won't talk, because if he does we'll charge him with assault.' A second finger. 'And the boys won't talk because the father will warn them not to.' He held his two fingers in the air, then lowered his hand.

'With all due respect, sir,' the Little Weed was saying, 'we've got a fight and a broken window in what was supposed to be a deserted building. People are nosy, it's human nature. They'll be looking up at that window tomorrow, and they'll be wondering. Any movement behind the window will be noticed.'

Lauderdale turned to Rebus. 'John?'

'What Inspector Flower says is true, sir, as far as it goes. But people are quick to forget. What they'll see tomorrow is a new window, end of story. Nobody saw anything from the taxi offices, and even if they heard the glass, it's not like it doesn't happen every day along Gorgie.'

'Even so, John . . .'

'Even so, sir, it was a mistake. I've already made that clear to DC Clarke.' He could have told them that it was all the fault of the woman from Trading Standards, but making excuses made you seem weak. Rebus could take this on the chin. He'd even take it on the back of his scalp if it would get him out of the office any faster. The aromas of whisky and body odour were making him slightly queasy.

'Alister?'

'Well, sir, you know my view on the subject.'

Lauderdale nodded. 'John,' he said, 'a lot of planning has gone into Operation Moneybags, and there's a lot at stake. If you're going to let a couple of kids wander into the middle of the surveillance, maybe it's time you rethought your priorities. For example, those files beside your desk. That stuff's five years old. Get your brain back to the here and now, understand?'

'Yes, sir.'

'We know you must have been affected by the attack on DS Holmes. What I'm asking is, are you up to helping run Operation Moneybags?'

Ah, here it was. The Little Weed wanted the surveillance for himself. He wanted to be the one to bring in Dougary.

'I'm up to it, sir.'

'No more fuck-ups then, understood?'

'Understood, sir.'

Rebus would have said anything to shorten the meeting; well, just about anything. But he was damned if he was going to hand *anything* to Flower, least of all a case like this, even if he *did* think it a waste of time. Get back to the here and now, Lauderdale had said. But when Rebus left the office, he knew exactly where his brain was heading: back to the there and then.

By late afternoon, he decided that he had only two options regarding the Central Hotel, only two people left who might help. He telephoned one, and after a little persuasion was able to arrange an immediate interview.

'There may be interruptions,' the secretary warned. 'We're very busy just now.'

'I can put up with interruptions.'

Twenty minutes later, he was ushered into a small wood-panelled office in a well-maintained old stone building. The windows looked out onto uglier new constructions of corrugated metal and shining steel. Steam billowed from pipes, but indoors you miraculously lost that strong brewery smell.

The door opened and a thirtyish man ambled into the room.

'Inspector Rebus?'

They shook hands. 'Good of you to see me at such short notice, sir.'

'Your call was intriguing. I still like a bit of intrigue.'

Close up, Rebus saw that Aengus Gibson was probably still in his twenties. The sober suit, the spectacles and short sleek hair made him seem older. He went to his desk, slipped off his jacket, and placed it carefully over the back of a large padded chair. Then he sat down and began rolling up his shirtsleeves.

'Sit yourself down, Inspector, please. Now, something to do with the Central Hotel, you said?'

There were papers laid out on the desk, and Gibson appeared to be browsing through them as Rebus spoke, but Rebus knew the man was taking in every word.

'As you know, Mr Gibson, the Central burnt down five years ago. The cause of the fire was never satisfactorily explained, but more disturbing still was the finding of a body, a body with a bullet-hole through the heart. The body has never been identified.'

Rebus paused. Gibson took off his glasses and laid them on top of the papers. 'I knew the Central quite well, Inspector. I'm sure my reputation precedes you into this office.'

'Past and present reputations, sir.'

Gibson made no show of hearing this. 'I was a bit wild in my youth, and a wilder crowd you'd be hard pressed to find than that congregating in the Central Hotel in *those* days.'

'You'd be in your early twenties, sir, hardly a "youth".'

'Some of us take longer to grow up than others.'

'Why did you arrange to meet Matthew Vanderhyde there?'

Gibson sat back in his chair. 'Ah, now I see why you're here. Well, I thought Uncle Matthew might appreciate the seedy glory of the Central. He was wild himself in years past.'

'And maybe also you thought it might shock him?'

'Nobody could shock Matthew Vanderhyde, Inspector.' He smiled. 'But perhaps you're right. Yes, I'm sure there was an element of that. I knew damned fine that my father had asked him to talk to me. So I arranged to meet in the worst place I could think of.'

'I could probably have helped find a few worse places than the Central.'

'Me too, really. But the Central was . . . well, *central*.'

'And the two of you talked?'

'He talked. I was supposed to listen. But when you're with a blind man, Inspector, you don't need to put up any pretence. No need for glazed eyes and all that. I think I read the paper, tried the crossword, watched the TV. It didn't seem to matter to him. He was doing my father a favour, that was all.'

'But pretty soon afterwards you put your "Black Aengus" days behind you.'

'That's true, yes. Maybe Uncle Matthew's words had an effect after all.'

'And after the meeting?'

'We thought of having dinner together – not, I might add, in the Central. Filthiest kitchens I've ever seen. But I think I had a prior appointment with a young lady. Well, not that young, actually. Married, I seem to recall. Sometimes I miss those days. The media call me a reformed character. It's an easy cliché, but damned hard to live up to.'

'Your name never appeared on the official list of the Central's customers that night.'

'An oversight.'

'One you could have corrected by coming forward.'

'Giving yet more fuel to the newspapers.'

'What if they found out now that you *were* there?'

'Well, Inspector, that wouldn't be fuel.' Aengus Gibson's eyes were warm and clear. 'That would be an incendiary.'

'Is there anything you can tell me about that night, sir?'

'You seem to know all of it. I was in the bar with Matthew Vanderhyde. We left hours before the place caught fire.'

Rebus nodded. 'Have you ever been on the hotel's first floor, sir?'

'What an extraordinary question. It was *five years ago*.'

'A long time, certainly.'

'And now the case is being reopened?'

'In a way, sir, yes. We can't give too many details.'

'That's all right, I'll get my father to ask the Chief Constable. They're good friends, you know.'

Rebus kept silent. There was no case. Nothing he could present to his superiors would cause them to reopen it. He knew he was in this all on his own, and for not very good reasons. There was a brisk tap at the door, and an older man came into the office. His face strongly resembled Aengus Gibson's, but both face and body were much leaner. Ascetic was the word that came to mind. Broderick Gibson would rarely loosen his tight-knotted tie or undo the top button of his shirt. He wore a woollen V-neck below his suit jacket. Rebus had seen church elders like him. Their faces persuaded more guilt-money into the collection.

'Sorry to butt in,' Broderick Gibson said. 'These need a look-over before tomorrow morning.' He placed a folder on the desk.

'Father, this is Inspector Rebus. Inspector, Broderick Gibson, my father.'

And the man who had started Gibson's Brewing from his garden shed back in the 1950s. Rebus shook the firm hand.

'No trouble I hope, Inspector?'

'None at all, sir,' replied Rebus.

Broderick Gibson turned to his son. 'You haven't forgotten that do tonight for the SSPCC?'

'No, father. Eight o'clock?'

'Damned if I can remember.'

'I think it's eight o'clock.'

'You're right, sir,' said Rebus.

'Oh?' Aengus Gibson looked surprised. 'Will you be there yourself?'

But Rebus shook his head. 'I read a piece about it in the paper.' He was so far below these people on the social ladder, he wondered if they could see him at all. As they'd climbed, they'd sawn off the rungs behind them. Rebus could only peer up into the clouds, catching a glimpse every now and then. But they *all* liked to be liked by the police. Which was probably why Broderick Gibson insisted on shaking Rebus's hand again before leaving.

With his father gone, Aengus Gibson seemed to relax. 'I'm sorry, I should have asked you before – would you like tea or coffee? I know you're on duty, so I won't ask if you'd like to try a beer.'

'Actually, sir,' said Rebus, glancing at the clock on the wall, 'I finished work five minutes ago.'

Aengus Gibson laughed and went to a large cupboard which, when opened, revealed three bar-pumps and a gathering of sparkling pint and half-pint glasses. 'The Dark is very good today,' he said.

'Dark's fine, but just a half.'

'A half of Dark it is.'

In fact, Rebus managed another half, this time of the pale ale. But it was the taste of the Dark that stayed with him as he drove back out through the brewery's wrought-iron gates. Gibson's Dark. The Gibsons, father and son, were dark, all right. You had to look beneath the surface to see it, but it was there. To the outside world, Aengus Gibson might be a changed man, but Rebus could see the young man was just barely in control of himself. He even wondered if Gibson might be on mood control drugs of some kind. He had spent some time in a private 'nursing' home – euphemism for psychiatric care. At least, that was the story Rebus had heard. He thought maybe he'd do a bit of digging, just to satisfy his curiosity. He was curious about one small detail in particular, one thing Aengus Gibson had said. He not only knew the kitchens of the Central Hotel were filthy – he'd *seen* them.

John Rebus found that very interesting indeed.

He returned to St Leonard's and was relieved to find no sign of Lauderdale or Little Weed. He'd forgotten to visit Holmes, so telephoned the hospital instead. He knew how it went at the Infirmary; they could wheel a payphone to your bed.

'Brian?'

'Hello there. I've just had a visit from Nell.' He sounded bright. Rebus hoped he wasn't just getting her sympathy vote.

'How is she?'

'She's okay. Any progress?'

Rebus thought about the past twenty-four hours. A lot of work. 'No,' he said, 'no progress.' He decided not to tell Holmes that Eddie Ringan was missing: he might worry himself back into relapse.

'Are you thinking of giving up?'

'I've got a lot on my plate, Brian, but no, I'm not giving up.'

'Thanks.'

Rebus almost blurted out, It's not just for you now, it's for my brother too. Instead, he told Holmes to take care, and promised him a visit soon.

'Better make it *very* soon, they're letting me out tomorrow or the day after.'

'That's good.'

'I don't know ... there's this nurse in here ...'

'Ach, away with ye!' But Rebus remembered a nurse who had treated his scalp, a nurse he'd become too friendly with. That had been the start of the trouble with Patience. 'Be careful,' he ordered, putting down the phone.

His next call was to the local newspaper. He spoke to someone there for a few minutes, after which he tried calling Siobhan Clarke in Gorgie. But there was no answer. Obviously Dougary had clocked off for the day, and with him her surveillance. Well, it was time for Inspector Rebus to clock off too. On his way out, he heard the unmistakable brag of Alister Flower's voice heading towards him. Rebus dodged into another office and waited for Flower and his underlings to pass. They hadn't been talking about him, which was something. He felt only a little ashamed at hiding. Every good soldier knew when to hide.

17

Michael was up and about that evening, doing a fair imitation of a telly addict. He held the remote control like it was a pacemaker, and stared deeply at anything on the screen. Rebus began to wonder about the dosages he'd been taking. But there still seemed to be a fair number of tablets in the bottle.

He went out and bought fish suppers from the local chip shop. It wasn't the best of stuff, but Rebus didn't feel like driving the distance to anywhere better. He remembered the chip shop in their home town, where the fryer would spit into the fat to check how hot it was. Michael smiled at the story, but his eyes never left the TV. He pushed chips into his mouth, chewing slowly, picking batter off the fish and eating that before attacking the fatty white flesh.

'Not bad chips,' Rebus commented, pouring Irn-Bru for both of them. He was waiting for Patience's phone call, giving the time and place for their meet. But whenever the phone did ring, it was for the students.

It rang for a fifth or sixth time, and Rebus picked up the receiver. 'Edinburgh University answering service?'

'It's me,' said Siobhan Clarke.

'Oh, hello there.'

'Don't sound *too* excited.'

'What can I do for you, Clarke?'

'I wanted to apologise for this morning.'

'Not entirely your fault.'

'I should have told those boys who we really were. I've been going over it again and again in my head, what I should have done.'

'Well, you won't do it again.'

'No, sir.' She paused. 'I heard you were carpeted.'

'You mean by the Chief Inspector?' Rebus smiled. 'More like a fireside rug than a length of Wilton. How's the window?'

'Boarded up. The glass'll be replaced overnight.'

'Anything of interest today?'

'You were there for it, sir. Petrie came back in the afternoon.'

'Oh yes, how was he?'

'Bandaged up like the Elephant Man.'

Rebus knew that if anyone had talked about the morning's incident –

330

and someone had – it must be Petrie. He'd little sympathy. 'I'll see you tomorrow.'

'Yes, sir. Goodnight.'

'What was all that about?' asked Michael.

'Nothing.'

'I thought that's what you'd say. Is there any more Irn-Bru?'

Rebus passed him the bottle.

When Patience hadn't phoned by ten, he gave up and started to concentrate on the TV. He had half a mind to leave the receiver off its cradle. The next call came ten minutes later. There was tremendous background noise, a party or a pub. A bad song was being badly sung nearby.

'Turn that down a bit, Mickey.' Michael hit the mute button, silencing a politician on the news. 'Hello?'

'Is that you, Mr Rebus?'

'It's me.'

'Chick Muir here.' Chick was one of Rebus's contacts.

'What is it, Chick?' The song had come to an end, and Rebus heard clapping, laughter, and whistles.

'That fellow you were wanting to see, he's about twenty feet away from me with a treble whisky up at his nose.'

'Thanks, Chick. I'll be right there.'

'Wait a second, don't you want to know where I am?'

'Don't be stupid, Chick. I *know* where you are.'

Rebus put the receiver down and looked over at Mickey, who seemed to have fallen asleep. He switched off the television, and went to get his jacket.

It was a nap Chick Muir had been calling from the Bowery, a late-opening dive near the bottom of Easter Road. The pub had been called Finnegan's until a year ago, when a new owner had come up with the 'inspired' change of name, because, as he explained, he wanted to see loads of bums on seats.

He got bums all right, some of whom wouldn't have looked amiss in the original Bowery. He also got some students and perennial hard drinkers, partly because of the pub's location but mostly because of the late licence. There had never been any trouble though, well, none to speak of. Half the drinkers in the Bowery feared the other half, who meantime were busy fearing *them*. Besides which, it was rumoured Big Ger gave round-the-clock insurance – for a price.

Chick Muir often drank there, though he managed not to participate in what was reckoned to be Edinburgh's least musical karaoke. Eddie Ringan for one would have died on the spot at the various awful deaths suffered by 'Hound Dog' and 'Wooden Heart'. Off-key and out of condition, the singers could transform a simple word like 'crying' into a multi-syllabled meaningless drawl. Huh-kuh-rye-a-yeng was an approximation of the sound that greeted Rebus as he pulled at the double doors to the pub and slitted his eyes against the cigarette fug.

As 'Crying in the Chapel' came to its tearful end, Rebus felt a hand squeeze his arm.

'You made it then.'

'Hullo, Chick. What are you having?'

'A double Grouse would hit the spot, not that I believe they keep real Grouse in their Grouse bottles.' Chick Muir grinned, showing two rows of dull gold teeth. He was a foot and a half shorter than Rebus, and looked in this crowd like a wee boy lost in the woods. 'Still,' he said, 'it might not be Grouse, but it's a quarter gill.'

Well, there was logic in that somewhere. So Rebus pushed his way to the bar and shouted his order. There was applause all around as a favourite son of song took the stage. Rebus glanced along the bar and saw Deek Torrance, looking no more drunk or sober than the last time they'd met. As Rebus was paying for his drinks (he'd never to wait; they knew him in here) Torrance saw him, and gave a nod and a wave. Rebus indicated that he had to take the drinks but would be back, and Torrance nodded again.

The music had started up. Oh please, no, thought Rebus. Not 'Little Red Rooster'. On the video, a cockerel seemed to be taking an interest in the blonde farm-girl who had come out to collect the morning eggs.

'Here you are, Chick. Cheers.'

'Slainte.' Chick took a sip, savoured, then shook his head. 'I'm sure this isn't Grouse. Did you see him?'

'I saw him.'

'And it's the right chap?'

Rebus handed over a folded tenner, which Chick pocketed. 'It's him, all right.'

And indeed, Deek Torrance was squeezing his way towards them through the crush. But he stopped short and leaned over another drinker to tap Rebus's shoulder.

'John, just going –' He yanked his head towards the toilets at the side of the stage. 'Back in a min.' Rebus nodded his understanding and Torrance moved away again through the tide. Chick Muir sank his whisky. 'I'll make myself scarce,' he said.

'Aye, see you around, Chick.' Chick nodded and, placing his glass on a table, made for the exit. Rebus tried to shut out 'Little Red Rooster', and when this failed he followed Torrance to the toilets. He saw Deek having a word with the DJ on the stage, then pushing open the door of the gents'. Rebus glared at the singer as he passed, but the crowd was whipping the middle-aged man to greater and greater depths.

Deek was at the communal urinal, laughing at a cartoon on the wall. It showed two football players in Hearts strips involved in an act of buggery, and above it was the caption 'Jam Tarts – Well Stuffed!' It was the sort of thing you had to expect on Easter Road. In a pub somewhere in Gorgie there would be a similar cartoon portraying two Hibernian players. Rebus checked that no one else was in the gents'. Deek, looking over his shoulder, spotted him.

'John, I thought for a minute you were a willie-watcher.'

But Rebus was in serious mood. 'I need you to get me something, Deek.'

Torrance grunted.

'Remember when you said you could lay your hands on anything?'

'Anything from a shag to a shooter,' quoted Deek.

'The latter,' Rebus said simply. Deek Torrance looked like he might be about to comment. Instead, he grunted, zipped his fly, and went over to the washbasin.

'You could get into trouble.'

'I could.'

Torrance dried his hands on the filthy roller-towel. 'When would you need it?'

'ASAP.'

'Any particular model?' They were both serious now, talking in quiet, level tones.

'Whatever you can get will be fine. How much?'

'Anything up to a couple of hundred. You sure you want to do this?'

'I'm sure.'

'You could get a licence, make it legit.'

'I could.'

'But you probably won't.'

'You don't want to know, Deek.'

Deek grunted again. The door swung open and a young man, grinning from one side of his mouth while holding a cigarette in the other, breezed in. He ignored the two men and made for the urinal.

'Give me a phone number.' The youth half-glanced over his shoulder at them. 'Eyes front, son!' Torrance snarled at him. 'Guide dogs are gey expensive these days!'

Rebus tore a sheet from his notepad. 'Two numbers,' he said. 'Home and work.'

'I'll be in touch.'

Rebus pulled open the door. 'Buy you a drink?'

Torrance shook his head. 'I'm heading off.' He paused. 'You're sure about this?'

John Rebus nodded.

When Deek had gone, he bought himself another drink. He was

shaking, his heart racing. A good-looking woman had been singing 'Band of Gold', and adequately too. She got the biggest cheer of the night. The DJ came to the microphone and repeated her name. There were more cheers as her boyfriend helped her down from the stage. His fingers were covered with gold rings. Now the DJ was introducing the next act.

'He's chosen to sing for us that great old number "King of the Road". So let's have a big hand for John Rebus!'

There was some applause, and the people who knew him lowered their drinks and looked towards where Rebus stood at the bar.

'You bastard, Deek!' he hissed. The DJ was looking out over the crowd.

'John, are you still with us?' The audience were looking around too. Someone, Rebus realised later, must have pointed him out, for suddenly the DJ was announcing that John was a shy one but he was standing at the bar with the black padded jacket on and his head buried in his glass. 'So let's coax him up here with an extra big hand.'

There was an extra big hand for John Rebus as he turned to face the crowd. It was fortunate indeed, he later decided, that Deek hadn't given him a gun then and there. Just the one bullet would have done.

Deek Torrance hated himself, but he made the phone call anyway. He made it from a public box beside a patch of waste ground. Despite the late hour, some children were riding their bikes noisily across the churned-up tarmac. They had set up a ramp from two planks and a milk crate, and launched themselves into darkness, landing heavily on their suffering tyres.

'It's Deek Torrance,' he said when the telephone was answered. He knew he would have to wait while his name was passed along. He rested his forehead against the side of the call-box. The plastic was cool. We all grow up, he said to himself. It's not much fun, but we all do it. No Peter Pans around these days.

Someone was on the line now. The telephone had been picked up at the other end.

'It's Deek Torrance,' he repeated, quite unnecessarily. 'I've got a bit of news . . .'

18

Rebus was at work surprisingly early on Wednesday morning. He'd never been known as the earliest of arrivals, and his presence in the CID room made his more punctual colleagues look twice, just to be sure they weren't still warm and safe and dreaming in their beds.

They didn't get too close though, an early morning Rebus not being in the best of humours. But he'd wanted to get here before the day's swarm began: he didn't want too many people seeing just what information he was calling up on the computer.

Not that there was much on Aengus Grahame Fairmile Gibson. Public drunkenness mostly, usually with associated high jinks. Knocking the policeman's helmet off seemed to be a game enjoyed by youthful Gibson and his cronies. Other indiscretions included kerb-crawling in a part of town not renowned for its prostitutes, and an attempt to enter a friend's flat by the window (the key having been lost) which landed him in the wrong flat.

But it all came to a stop five years ago. From then till now, Gibson had received not so much as a parking ticket or a speeding fine. So much for his police files. Rebus punched in Broderick Gibson, too, not expecting anything. His expectations were fulfilled. The elder Gibson's 'youthful indiscretions' would be the stuff of musty old files in an annexe somewhere – always supposing there were any to begin with. Rebus had the feeling that anyone associated with Scottish Sword & Shield would probably have been arrested for disorderly conduct or breach of the peace at *some* point in their career. The possible exception, perhaps, being Matthew Vanderhyde.

He made a phone call to check that the meeting he'd arranged yesterday was still on, then switched off the computer and headed out of the building, just as a bleary Chief Superintendent Watson was coming in.

He waited in the newspaper office's public area, flipping through the past week's editions. A few early punters came in with Spot the Ball coupons or the like, and a few more hopefuls were checking copy with the people on the classified ads desk.

'Inspector Rebus.' She'd come from behind the main desk, where a

335

stern security man had been keeping a watchful eye on Rebus. She was already wearing her raincoat, so there was to be no tour of the premises today, though she'd been promising him for weeks.

Her name was Mairie Henderson and she was in her early twenties. Rebus had come up against her when she was compiling a postmortem feature on the Gregor Jack case. Rebus had just wanted to forget about the whole ugly episode, but she'd been persistent . . . and persuasive. She was just out of college, where she'd won awards for her student journalism and for pieces she'd contributed to the daily and weekly press. She hadn't yet forgotten how to be hungry; Rebus liked that.

'Come on,' she said. 'I'm starving. I'll buy you breakfast.'

So they went to a little cafe/bakery on South Bridge, where there were difficult choices to be made. Was it too early for pies and bridies? Too early for a fruit scone? Well then, they'd be like everyone else and settle for sliced sausage, black pudding and fried eggs.

'No haggis or dumpling?' Mairie was so imploring, the woman at the counter went off to ask the chef. Which made Rebus make a mental note to phone Pat Calder sometime today. But there was no haggis or dumpling, not even for ready money. So they took their trays to the cash till, where Mairie insisted on paying.

'After all, you're going to give me the story of the decade.'

'I don't know about that.'

'One of these days you will, trust me.'

They squeezed into a booth and she reached for the brown sauce, then for the ketchup. 'I can never decide between the two. Shame about the fried dumpling, that's my favourite.'

She was about five feet five inches and had about as much fat on her as a rabbit in a butcher's window. Rebus looked down at his fry-up and suddenly didn't feel very hungry. He sipped the weak coffee.

'So what's it all about?' she asked, having made a good start into the food on her plate.

'You tell me.'

She waved a no-no with her knife. 'Not till you tell me why you want to know.'

'That's not the way the game's played.'

'We'll change the rules, then.' She scooped up some egg-white with her fork. She had her coat wrapped tight around her, though it was steamy in the cafe. Good legs too; Rebus missed seeing her legs. He blew on the coffee, then sipped again. She'd be willing to wait all day for him to say something.

'Remember the fire at the Central Hotel?' he said at last.

'I was still at school.'

'A body turned up in the ruins.' She nodded encouragement. 'Well, maybe there's new evidence . . . no, not new evidence. It's just that some things have been happening, and I think they've got something to do with that fire and that shooting.'

'This isn't an official investigation, then?'

'Not yet.'

'And there's no story?'

Rebus shook his head. 'Nothing that wouldn't get you pasted in a libel court.'

'I could live with that, if the story was good enough.'

'It isn't, not yet.'

She began mopping-up operations with a triangle of buttered bread. 'So let me get this straight: you're on your own looking into a fire from five years ago?'

A fire which turned one man to drink, he could have said, and led another to the path of self-righteousness. But all he did was nod.

'And what's Gibson got to do with it?'

'Strictly between us, he was there that night. Yet he was kept off the list of the hotel's customers.'

'His father pulled some strings?'

'Could be.'

'Well, that's already a story.'

'I've nothing to back it up.' This was a lie, there was always Vanderhyde; but he wasn't going to tell her that. He didn't want her getting ideas. The way she was staring, she was getting plenty of those anyway.

'Nothing?'

'Nothing,' he repeated.

'Well, I don't know that this will help.' She opened her coat and pulled out the file which she'd been hiding, tucked down the front of her fashion-cut denims. He accepted the file from her, looking around the cafe. Nobody seemed to be paying attention.

'A bit cloak and dagger,' he told her. She shrugged.

'So I've seen too many films.'

Rebus opened the file. It bore no title, but inside were cuttings and 'spiked' stories concerning Aengus Gibson.

'Those are only from five years ago to the present. There isn't much, mostly charity work, giving to good causes. A little bit about the brewery's rising image and ditto profits.'

He glanced through the stuff. It was worthless. 'I was hoping to find out something about him from just after the fire.'

Mairie nodded. 'So you said on the phone. That's why I talked to a few people, including our chief sub. He says Gibson went into a psychiatric hospital. Nervous breakdown was the word.'

'Were the words,' corrected Rebus.

'Depends,' she said cryptically. Then: 'He was there the best part of three months. There was never a story, the father kept it out of the papers. When Aengus reappeared, *that's* when he started working in the business, and that's when he started all the do-gooding.'

'Shouldn't that be good-doing?'

She smiled. 'Depends,' she said. Then, of the file, 'It's not much, is it?' Rebus shook his head. 'I thought not. Still, it's all there was.'

'What about your chief sub? Would he be able to say *exactly* when Gibson went into that hospital?'

'I don't know. No harm in asking. Do you want me to?'

'Yes, I do.'

'All right then. And one more question.'

'Yes?'

'Aren't you going to eat any of that?'

Rebus pushed his plate across to her and watched her take her fill.

When he got back to St Leonard's, there was a call from the Chief Super's office. Chief Superintendent Watson wanted to see him straight away, as in ten minutes ago. Rebus checked that there were no messages for him, and called Siobhan Clarke in Gorgie to make sure the new window had been fitted.

'It's perfect,' she told him. 'It's got white gunk on it, window polish or something. We just didn't bother wiping it off. We can take shots through it, but from the outside it just looks like a new window that's waiting to be cleaned.'

'Fine,' said Rebus. He wanted to make sure he was up to date. If Watson intended to carpet him over yesterday, it would be considerably more than Lauderdale's fireside rug.

But Rebus had got it way wrong.

'What the hell are you up to?' Watson looked like he'd run a half-marathon gobbling down chilli peppers all the way. His breathing was raspy, his cheeks a dark cherry colour. If he walked into a hospital, they'd have him whisked to emergency on a two-man stretcher.

No, better make that a four-man.

'I'm not sure what you mean, sir.'

Watson fairly pounded the desk with his fist. A pencil dropped onto the floor. 'You're not sure what I mean!'

Rebus moved forward to pick up the pencil.

'Leave it! Just sit down.' Rebus went to sit. 'No, better yet, keep standing.' Rebus stood up. 'Now, just tell me why.' Rebus remembered a science teacher at his secondary school, a man with an evil temper who had spoken to the teenage Rebus just like this. 'Just tell me why.'

'Yes, sir.'

'Go on then.'

'With respect, sir, why what?'

The words came out through gritted teeth. 'Why you've seen fit to start pestering Broderick Gibson.'

'With respect, sir –'

'Stop all that "with respect" shite! Just give me an answer.'

'I'm not pestering Broderick Gibson, sir.'

'Then what *are* you doing, wooing him? The Chief Constable phoned me this morning in absolute fucking apoplexy!' Watson, being a Christian of no mean persuasion, didn't swear often. It was a bad sign.

Rebus saw it all. The bash for the SSPCC. Yes, and Broderick Gibson collaring his friend the Chief Constable. One of your minions has been on to me, what's it all about? The Chief Constable not knowing anything about it, stuttering and spluttering and saying he'd get to the bottom of it. Just give me the officer's name . . .

'It's his son I'm interested in, sir.'

'But you looked both of them up on the computer this morning.'

Ah, so *some*one had taken notice of his early shift. 'Yes, I did, but I was really only interested in Aengus.'

'You still haven't explained why.'

'No, sir, well, it's a bit . . . nebulous.'

Watson frowned. '*Nebulous?* When's the graduation party?' Rebus didn't get it. 'Since you've obviously,' Watson was happy to explain, 'just got your astronomy degree!' He poured himself coffee from the machine on the floor, offering none to Rebus who could just use a cup.

'It was the word that came to mind, sir,' he said.

'I can think of a few words too, Rebus. Your mother wouldn't like to hear them.'

No, thought Rebus, and yours would wash your mouth out with soap.

The Chief Super slurped his coffee. They didn't call him 'Farmer' for nothing; he had many ways and predilections that could only be described as agricultural.

'But before I say any of them,' he went on, 'I'm a generous enough man to say that I'll listen to your explanation. Just make it bloody convincing.'

'Yes, sir,' said Rebus. How could he make *any* of it sound convincing? He supposed he'd have to try.

So he tried, and halfway through Watson even told him he could sit if he liked. At the end of fifteen minutes, Rebus placed his hands out in front of him, palms up, as if to say: that's all, folks.

Watson poured another cup of coffee and placed it on the desk in front of Rebus.

'Thank you, sir.' Rebus gulped it down black.

'John, have you ever thought you might be paranoid?'

'All the time, sir. Show me two men shaking hands and I'll show you a Masonic conspiracy.'

Watson almost smiled, before recalling that this was no joking matter. 'Look, let me put it like this. What you've got so far is . . . well, it's . . .'

'Nebulous, sir?'

'Piss and wind,' corrected Watson. 'Somebody died five years ago. Was it anyone important? Obviously not, or we'd know who they were by now. So we assume it was somebody the world had hardly known and was happy to forget. No grieving widow or weans, no family asking questions.'

'You're saying let it die, sir? Let somebody get away with murder?'

Watson looked exasperated. 'I'm saying we're stretched as it is.'

'All Brian Holmes did was ask a few questions. Somebody brained him for it. I take over, my flat's invaded and my brother half scared to death.'

'My point exactly, it's all become *personal*. You can't allow that to happen. Look at the other stuff on your plate. Operation Moneybags for a start, and I'm sure there's more besides.'

'You're asking me to drop it, sir? Might I ask if you're under any personal pressure?'

There was personal pressure aplenty as Watson's blood rose, his face purpling. 'Now wait just one second, that's not the sort of comment I can tolerate.'

'No, sir. Sorry, sir.' But Rebus had made his point. The clever soldier knows when to duck. Rebus had taken his shot, and now he was ducking.

'I should think so,' said Watson, wriggling in his chair as though his trousers were lined with scouring-pads. 'Now here's what I think. I think that if you can bring me something concrete, the dead man's identity perhaps, within twenty-four hours, then we'll reopen the case. Otherwise, I want the whole thing dropped until such time as new evidence *does* come forward.'

'Fair enough, sir,' said Rebus. It wasn't much good arguing the point. Maybe twenty-four hours would be enough. And maybe Charlie Chan had a clan tartan. 'Thanks for the coffee, much appreciated.'

When Watson started to make his joke about feeling 'full of beans', Rebus made his excuses and left.

19

He was seated at his desk, glumly examining all the dead ends in the case, when he happened to catch word of an 'altercation' at a house in Broughton. He caught the address, but it took a few seconds for it to register with him. Minutes later, he was in his car heading into the east end of town. The traffic was its usual self, with agonisingly slow pockets at the major junctions. Rebus blamed the traffic lights. Why couldn't they just do away with them and let the pedestrians take their chances? No, there'd only be more hold-ups, what with all the ambulances they'd need to ferry away the injured and the dead.

Still, why was he hurrying? He thought he knew what he was going to find. He was wrong. (It was turning out to be one of those weeks.) A police car and an ambulance sat outside Mrs MacKenzie's two-storey house, and the neighbours were out in a show of conspicuous curiosity. Even the kids across the road were interested. It must be a break-time, and some of them pushed their heads between the vertical iron bars and stared open-mouthed at the brightly marked vehicles.

Rebus thought about those railings. Their intention was to keep the kids *in*, keep them safe. But could they keep anybody *out*?

Rebus flashed his ID at the constable on door duty and entered Mrs MacKenzie's house. She was wailing loudly, so that Rebus started to think of murder. A WPC comforted her, while trying to have a conversation with her own over-amplified shoulder radio. The WPC saw Rebus.

'Make her some tea, will you?' she pleaded.

'Sorry, hen, I'm only CID. Needs someone a bit more senior to mash a pot of Brooke Bond.' Rebus had his hands in his pockets, the casually informed observer, distanced from the mayhem into which he walked. He wandered over to the bird cage and peered in. On the sand floor, amidst feathers and husks and droppings, lay a mummified budgie.

'Away the crow road,' he muttered to himself, moving out of the living room. He saw the ambulancemen in the kitchen, and followed them. There was a body on the floor, hands and face heavily bandaged. He couldn't see any blood, though. He nearly skited on wet linoleum, and steadied himself by gripping the edge of the antiquated gas cooker. It was warm to the touch. A police constable stood by the open back door, looking out to right and left. Rebus squeezed past the carers and their patient and joined the PC.

'Nice day, eh?'

'What?'

'I see you're admiring the weather.' Rebus showed his ID again.

'No, not that. Just seeing the way he went.'

Rebus nodded. 'How do you mean?'

'The neighbours say he climbed three fences, then ran down a close and away.' The PC pointed. 'That close there, just past the line full of washing.'

'Behind the clothes-pole?'

'Aye, that must be the one. Three fences ... one, two, three. It's got to be that close over there.'

'Well done, son, that really gets us a long way.'

The constable stared at him. 'My Inspector's a stickler for notes. You're from St Leonard's? Not quite your patch is it, sir?'

'Everywhere's my patch, son, and everybody's my constable. Now what happened here?'

'The gentleman on the floor was attacked. The attacker ran off.'

Rebus nodded. 'I can tell you the how and the who already.' The PC looked dubious. 'The attacker was a man called Alex Maclean, and he almost certainly punched or headbutted Mr McPhail there.'

The constable blinked, then shook his head. '*That's* Maclean lying there.' Rebus looked down, and for the first time took in the size of the man, a good forty pounds heavier than McPhail. 'And he wasn't punched or butted. He had a pot of boiling water thrown over him.'

Just a little abashed, Rebus listened without comment to the PC's version of events. McPhail, who had been steering well clear of the house, had at last telephoned to say he'd be popping over for some clothes and things. He'd fobbed Mrs MacKenzie off with some story about working long shifts in a supermarket. He'd arrived, and was in the kitchen chatting to his landlady while she put on the water for her boiled eggs (boiled eggs every Wednesday lunchtime; poached on Thursdays – this was one part of Mrs MacKenzie's statement she wanted to get absolutely clear). But Maclean had been watching the house, and saw McPhail go in. He opened the unlocked front door and ran into the kitchen. 'A terrifying sight,' according to Mrs MacKenzie. 'I'll never forget it if I live to be a hundred.'

It was at this point that McPhail lifted the pan and swung it at Maclean, showering him with boiling water. Then he'd opened the back door and fled. Over three fences and through a close. End of melodrama.

Rebus watched them lift Maclean into the back of the ambulance. They'd be taking him to the Infirmary. Soon everyone Rebus knew in

Edinburgh would be lying in the Infirmary. McPhail had been lucky this time. If he knew what was good for him, he would now take Rebus's advice and flee the city, dodging the police who would be looking for him.

Rebus wondered if McPhail really did know what was good for him. This, after all, was a man who thought little girls were good for him. He wondered this as he sat in heavy lunchtime traffic, slowly oozing towards St Leonard's. The route he'd taken to Broughton had been so slow, he saw little to lose by sticking to the bigger roads – Leith Street, The Bridges, and Nicolson Street. Something made him stay on this road till he came to the butcher's shop where Rory Kintoul had ended up, bleeding beneath the meat counter.

He registered only slight surprise at the wooden board which had been placed across the entire front window of the shop. Pinned to the board was a large white sheet of paper with thick felt-pen writing. The sign said simply 'Business as Usual'. Interesting, thought Rebus, parking his car. He noticed that rain or general wear underfoot had done away with the splashes of blood which had once left a crimson trail along the pavement.

Mr Bone the butcher was slicing corned beef with a manual machine whose circular blade hissed through the meat. He was smaller and thinner than most butchers Rebus had come across, his face all cheek-bone and worry line, hair thinning and grey. There was no one else in the front of the shop, though Rebus could hear someone whistling as they worked in the back. Bone noticed that he had a customer.

'And what'll it be today, sir?'

Rebus noticed that the display cases just inside the front window were empty, doubtless waiting to be checked for slivers of glass before restocking. He nodded towards the wooden board. 'When did that happen?'

'Ach, last night.' Bone placed the sliced corned beef in an unsullied section of the display case, then skewered the price marker into it. He wiped his hands on his white apron. 'Kids or drunks.'

'What was it, a brick?'

'Search me.'

'Well, if there was nothing lying in the shop it must have been a sledgehammer. I can't see a kick with a steel toecap doing that sort of damage.'

Now Bone looked at him properly, and recognised him. 'You were here when Rory ...'

'That's right, Mr Bone. They didn't use a sledgehammer on him though, did they?'

'I don't know what you mean.'

'Pound of beef links, by the way.'

Bone hesitated, then took out the string of sausages and cut a length from it.

'You could be right, of course,' Rebus continued. 'Could have been kids or drunks. Did anyone see anything?'

'I don't know.'

'You didn't report it?'

'Didn't have to. Police phoned me at two this morning to tell me about it.' He sounded disgruntled.

'All part of the service, Mr Bone.'

'That's just over the pound,' Bone said, looking at the weighing scales. He wrapped the sausages in white paper, then in brown, marking the price with a pencil on this outer wrapper. Rebus handed over a five-pound note.

'Insurance will take care of it, I suppose,' he said.

'Bloody hope so, the money they charge.'

Rebus accepted his change, and made sure to catch Bone's eye. 'But I meant the *real* insurance people, Mr Bone.' An elderly couple were coming into the shop.

'What happened, Mr Bone?' the woman asked, her husband shuffling along behind her.

'Just kids, Mrs Dowie,' said Bone in the voice he used with customers, a voice he hadn't been using with Rebus. He was staring at Rebus, who gave him a wink, picked up his package, and left. Outside, he looked down at the brown paper parcel. It was chill in his hand. He was supposed to be cutting down on meat, wasn't he? Not that there was much meat in sausages anyway. Another passing shopper stopped to examine the boarded-up window, then went into the shop. Jim Bone would do good business today. Everyone would want to know what had happened. Rebus was different; he *knew* what had happened, though proving it wasn't going to be easy. Siobhan Clarke hadn't managed to talk to the stabbing victim yet. Maybe Rebus should push her along, especially now that she could tell Rory Kintoul all about his cousin's broken window.

Next to his car someone had parked a Land Rover-style 4×4, inside which a huge black dog was ravening to get out. Pedestrians were giving the car a wide berth, and quite right too: the whole vehicle rocked on its axle when the dog lunged at the back window. Rebus noticed that the considerate owner had left the window open an inch. Maybe it was a trap intended for a particularly stupid car thief.

Rebus stopped in front of the open window and unrolled the package of sausages into the car. They fell onto the seat where the dog sniffed them for a nanosecond before starting to dine.

The street was blessedly quiet as Rebus unlocked his own car.

'All part of the service,' he said to himself.

At the station, he telephoned the Heartbreak Cafe, where what sounded like a hastily recorded message told him the place would be shut 'due to convalescence'. In Brian Holmes' desk drawer, he found a print-out of names and phone numbers, those most often used by Holmes himself. Some numbers had been added at the bottom in blue biro, including one for Eddie Ringan marked (h).

Rebus returned to his desk and made the call. Pat Calder answered on the third ring.

'Mr Calder, it's DI Rebus.'

'Oh.' The hope left Calder's voice.

'No sign of him then?'

'None.'

'Right, let's make it official, then. He's a missing person. I'll have someone come over and –'

'Why can't you come?'

Rebus thought about it. 'No reason at all, sir.'

'Make it anytime you like, we're shut today.'

'What happened to wonderchef Willie?'

'We had a busy night, busier than usual.'

'He cracked up?'

'Came flying out of the kitchen yelling, "I'm the chef! I'm the chef!" Lifted some poor woman's entrée and started eating it himself with his face in the bowl. I think he'd been taking drugs.'

'Sounds like he was just doing a good impersonation of late-period Elvis. I'll be there in half an hour, if that's all right.'

Stockbridge's 'Colonies' had been constructed to house the working poor, but were now much desired by young professional types. They were designed as maisonettes, with steep flights of stone stairs leading to the first floor properties. Rebus found the proportions mean in comparison with his Marchmont tenement. No high ceilings here, and no huge rooms with splendid windows and original shutters.

But he could see miners and their families being cosy here a hundred years ago. His own father had been born in a miners' row in Fife. Rebus imagined it must have been very like this . . . at least on the outside.

On the inside, Pat Calder had done incredible things. (Rebus didn't doubt that his was the designing and decorating hand.) There were wooden and brass ship's trunks, black anglepoise lamps, Japanese prints in ornate frames, a dinner table whose candelabra resembled some Jewish icon, and a huge TV/hi-fi centre. But of Elvis there was nary a jot. Rebus, seated in a black leather sofa, nodded towards one of the coffin-sized loudspeakers.

'Neighbours ever complain?'

'All the time,' admitted Calder. 'Eddie's proudest moment was when the guy from four doors down phoned to tell us he couldn't hear his TV.'

'Considerate, eh?'

Calder smiled. 'Eddie's never been exactly "politic".'

'Have you known one another long?'

Calder, lying stretched on the floor with his bum on a beanbag, blew nervous smoke from a black Sobranie cigarette. 'Two years casually. We moved in together about the time we had the idea for the Heart-break.'

'What's he like? I mean, outside the restaurant?'

'Brilliant one minute, a spoilt brat the next.'

'Do you spoil him?'

'I buffer him from the world. At least, I used to.'

'So what was he like when you met?'

'Drinking more than he does now, if you can believe that.'

'Ever tell you why he started?' Rebus had refused a cigarette, but the smoke was getting to him. Maybe he'd have to change his mind.

'He said he drank to forget. Now you're going to ask, Forget what? And I'm going to say that he never told me.'

'He never even hinted?'

'I think he told Brian Holmes more than he told me.'

Jesus, was there a hint of jealousy there? Rebus had a sudden vision of Calder bashing Holmes on the napper . . . and maybe even doing away with Fast Eddie too . . .?

Calder laughed. 'I couldn't hurt him, Inspector. I know what you're thinking.'

'It must be frustrating, though? This genius, you call him, wasting it all for booze. People like that take a lot of looking after.'

'And you're right, it *can* become frustrating.'

'Especially when they're gassed all the time.'

Calder frowned, peering through the smoke from his nostrils. 'Why do you say "gassed"?'

'It means drunk.'

'I know it does. So do a lot of other words. It's just that Eddie used to have these nightmares. About being gassed or gassing people. You know, with *real* gas, like in the concentration camps.'

'He told you about these dreams?'

'Oh no, but he used to shout out in his sleep. A lot of gays went to the gas chambers, Inspector.'

'You think that's what he meant?'

Calder stubbed out the cigarette into a porcelain bedpan beside the fireplace. He got up awkwardly from the floor. 'Come on, I want to show you something.'

Rebus had already seen the kitchen and the bathroom, and so realised that the door Calder was leading him towards must be to the only bedroom. He didn't know quite what to expect.

'I know what you've been thinking,' Calder said, swinging the door wide open. 'This is all Eddie's work.'

And what a work it was. A huge double bed covered with what looked like several zebra-skins. And on the walls, several large paintings of the rhinestone Elvis at work, the face an intentional blur of pink and sheen. Rebus looked up. There was a mirror on the ceiling. He guessed that pretty much any position you took on that bed, you'd be able to watch a white one-piece suit at work with a microphone-hand raised high.

'Whatever turns you on,' he commented.

He visited Clarke and Petrie for a couple of hours, just to show willing. Unsurprisingly, Jardine had been replaced by a young man called Madden with a stock of puns not heard since the days of valve radio.

'Madden by name,' the Trading Standards officer said by way of introduction, 'mad 'un by nature.'

Make that *steam* radio. Rebus began to wonder if it had been such a good idea, phoning Jardine's boss and swearing exotically at him for twenty minutes.

'I make the jokes around here, son,' he warned.

Rebus had spent more exciting afternoons in his life. For example, being taken by his father to watch Cowdenbeath reserves at home to Dundee. He managed to break the monotony only by stepping out to buy buns at a nearby bakery, though this sort of activity was supposed to be *verboten*. He kept the custard slice for himself, peeling away and discarding the icing. Madden asked if he could have it, and Rebus nodded.

Siobhan Clarke looked like she'd stepped under a gardy-loo bucket. She tried not to show it, and smiled whenever she saw him looking in her direction, but there was definitely something up with her. Rebus couldn't be bothered asking what. He got the idea it was to do with Brian ... maybe Brian and Nell. He told her about Bone's window.

'Make some time,' he said. 'Track down Kintoul, if not at home then at the Infirmary. He works in the labs there, right?'

'Right.' Definitely something up with her.

As was his prerogative, Rebus eventually made his excuses and left. Back at St Leonard's, there was a message for him to call Mairie Henderson at work.

'Mairie?'

'Inspector, that didn't take long.'

'You're about the only lead I've got.'

'It's nice to feel wanted.' She had one of those accents that could sound sarcastic without really flexing any muscle. 'Don't get too excited, though.'

'Your Chief Sub didn't remember?'

'Only that it was around August, making it three months after the Central burnt down.'

'Could mean something or nothing.'

'I did my best.'

'Yes, thanks, Mairie.'

'Hold on, don't hang up!' Rebus wasn't about to. 'He did tell me something. Apparently some snippet that's stuck with him.' She paused.

'In your own time, Mairie.'

'This *is* my time, Inspector.' She paused again.

'Are you drawing on a fag?'

'What if I am?'

'Since when did you start smoking?'

'It beats chewing the ends off pencils.'

'You'll stunt your growth.'

'You sound like my dad.'

Well, that brought him back to earth. Here he'd thought they were . . . what? Chatting away? Chatting one another *up*? Aye, in your dreams, John Rebus. Now she'd reminded him of the not insignificant age gap between them.

'Are you still there, Inspector?'

'Sorry, my hearing aid slipped out. What did the Chief Sub say?'

'Remember that story about Aengus Gibson entering the wrong flat?'

'I remember.'

'Well, the woman whose flat he broke into was called Mo Johnson.'

Rebus smiled. But then the smile faded. 'That name almost rings a bell.'

'He's a football player.'

'I *know* he's a football player. But a female Mo Johnson, *that's* what rings bells.' But they were faint, too faint.

'Let me know if you come up with anything.'

'I will, Mairie. And Mairie?'

'What?'

'Don't stay out too late.' Rebus terminated the call.

Mo Johnson. He supposed it must be short for Maureen. Where had he come across that name? He knew how he might check. But if Watson found out, it would mean more trouble. Ach, to hell with Watson anyway. He wasn't much more than slave to a coffee bean. Rebus went to the computer console and punched in the details, bringing up Aengus Gibson's record. The anecdote was there, but no charges had ever been pressed. The woman was not mentioned by name, and there was no sign of her address. But, since Gibson was involved, CID had taken an interest. You couldn't always depend on the lower ranks to hush things up properly.

And look who the investigating officer was: DS Jack Morton. Rebus closed the file and got back on the phone. The receiver was still warm.

'You're in luck, he got back from the pub five minutes ago.'

'Away, ya gobshite,' Rebus heard Morton say as he grabbed at the receiver. 'Hello?' Two minutes later, thanks to what was left of Jack Morton's memory, Rebus had an address for Mo Johnson.

A day of contrasts. From bakery to butchery, from The Colonies to Gorgie Road. And now to the edge of Dean Village. Rebus hadn't been down this way since the Water of Leith drowning. He had forgotten how beautiful it was. Tucked down a steep hill from Dean Bridge, the Village gave a good impression of rural peace. Yet it was a five-minute walk from the West End and Princes Street.

They were spoiling it, of course. The developers had squeezed their hands around vacant lots and decaying buildings and choked them into submission. The prices asked for the resultant 'apartments', prices as steep as Bell's Brae, boggled Rebus's mind. Not that Mo Johnson lived in one of the new buildings. No, her flat was a chunk of an older property at the bottom of the brae, with a view of the Water of Leith and Dean Bridge. But she no longer lived there, and the people who did were reluctant to allow Rebus in. They didn't think they had a new address for her. There had been another owner between her moving out and their moving in. They might still have *that* owner's new address, though it would go back a couple of years.

Did they know when Ms Johnson herself moved out?

Four years ago, maybe five.

Which brought Rebus back to the fire at the Central Hotel. Everything he did in this case seemed to bounce straight back to a period five years ago, when something had happened which had changed a lot of people's lives, and taken away at least one life too. He sat in his car wondering what to do next. He knew what to do, but had been putting it off. If tangling with the Gibsons could earn him minus points, he dreaded to think what he might earn by talking with the only other person he could think of who might be able to help.

Help? That was a laugh. But Rebus wanted to meet him all the same. Christ, Flower would have a field day if he found out. He'd hire tents and food and drink and invite everyone to the biggest party in town. Right up from Lauderdale to the Chief Constable, they'd be blowing fuses that could have run hydro stations.

Yes, the more Rebus thought about it, the more he knew it was the right thing to do. The right thing? He had so few openings left, it was the *only* thing. And looking on the bright side, if he did get caught, at least the celebration would bankrupt Little Weed . . .

20

He telephoned first, Morris Cafferty not being a man you just dropped in on.

'Will I need my lawyer?' Cafferty growled, sounding amused. 'I'll answer that for you, Strawman, no I fucking won't. Because I've got something better than a lawyer here, better than a fucking judge in my pocket. I've got a dog that'll rip your oesophagus out if I tell it to lick your chops. Be here at six.' The phone went dead, leaving Rebus dry-mouthed and persuading himself all over again that this jumped-up bastard didn't scare him.

What scared him more was the realisation that someone somewhere in the ranks of the Lothian and Borders Police was probably listening in to Cafferty's telephone conversations. Rebus felt like he was in a corridor with doors locking behind him all the time. He saw a gas chamber in his mind and shivered, changing the picture.

Six o'clock wasn't very far away. And at least in dentists' waiting rooms they gave you magazines to pass the time.

Morris Gerald Cafferty lived in a mansion house in the expensive suburb of Duddingston. Duddingston was a 'suburb' by dint of having Arthur's Seat and Salisbury Crags between it and central Edinburgh. Cafferty liked living in Duddingston because it annoyed his neighbours, most of whom were lawyers, doctors and bankers, and also because it wasn't far from his actual and spiritual birthplace, Craigmillar. Craigmillar was one of the tougher Edinburgh housing schemes. Cafferty grew up there, seeing his first trouble there and in neighbouring Niddrie. He'd led a gang of Craigmillar youths into Niddrie to sort out their rivals. There was a stabbing . . . with an uprooted iron railing. Police discovered that the teenage Cafferty had already been in trouble at school for 'accidentally' jamming a ballpoint pen into the corner of a fellow pupil's eye.

It was the quiet start to a long career.

The wrought iron gates at the bottom of the driveway opened automatically as Rebus approached. He drove his car along a well-gritted private road with mature trees either side. You caught a glimpse of the house from the main road, nothing more. But Rebus had been here before; to ask questions, to make an arrest. He knew there was another smaller house behind the main house, linked by a covered walkway. This smaller house had been staff quarters in the days when a city merchant might have lived here. The gravel road forked to the front and back of the main house. A man directed Rebus towards the back: the servants' entrance. The man was very big with a biker helmet haircut, cut high at the fringe but falling over the ears. Where did Cafferty get them, these throwbacks?

The man followed him to the back of the house. Rebus knew where to park. There were three spaces, two vacant and one taken up by a Volvo estate. Rebus thought he recognised the Volvo, though it wasn't Cafferty's. Cafferty's collection of cars was kept in the vast garage. He had a Bentley and a cherry-red '63 T-Bird, neither of which he ever drove. For daily use, there was always the Jag, an XJS-HE. And for weekends there was a dependable Roller which Cafferty had owned for at least fifteen years.

The man opened Rebus's door for him, and pointed towards the small house. Rebus got out.

'Vidal Sassoon was booked up then,' he said.

'Uh?' The man turned his head right-side towards Rebus.

'Never mind.' He was about to walk away, but paused. 'Ever been in a fight with a man called Dougary?'

'Nane i' your business.'

Rebus shrugged. The big man closed the car door and stood watching Rebus walk away. So there was no chance to check the tax disc or anything else about the Volvo; nothing to do except memorise the number plate.

Rebus pulled open the door to the small house and was greeted by a wave of heat and steam. The whole structure had been gutted, so that a swimming pool and gymnasium could be installed. The pool was kidney-shaped, with a small circular pool off it – a jacuzzi, presumably. Rebus had always hated kidney pools: it was impossible to do laps in them. Not that he was much of a swimmer.

'Strawman! About bastardin' time!'

He didn't see Cafferty at first, though he had no trouble seeing who was standing over him. Cafferty lay on a massage table, head resting on a pile of towels. His back was being kneaded by none other than the Organ Grinder, who just happened to own a Volvo estate. The Organ Grinder sensibly pretended not to know Rebus; and when Cafferty wasn't looking, Rebus nodded almost imperceptibly his agreement with the pretence.

Cafferty had spun around on his backside and was now easing himself into a standing position. He tested his back and shoulders. 'That's magic,' he said. He removed the towel from around his loins and padded towards Rebus on bare feet.

'See, Strawman, no concealed weapons.' His laughter was like an apprentice with a rasp-file.

Rebus looked around. 'I don't see the –'

But suddenly there it was, pulling itself massively out of the swimming pool. Rebus hadn't even noticed it in there, retrieving a bone. Not a plastic bone either. The black beast dropped the bone at Cafferty's feet, sniffed at Rebus's legs, then shook itself dry onto him.

'Good boy, Kaiser,' said Cafferty. The parking attendant had joined them in the sticky heat. Rebus nodded nowhere in particular.

'I hope you got planning permission for this.'

'All above board, Strawman. Come on, you'd better get changed.'

'Changed for what?'

Laughter again. 'Don't worry, you're not staying to dinner. I'm going for a run, and so are you – if you want to talk to me.'

A run, Jesus! Cafferty turned and walked away towards what looked like a changing cubicle. He slapped the Organ Grinder as he passed him.

'Magic. Same time next week?'

He was hairily muscular, with a chest a borders farmer would be proud to own. There was flab, of course, but not as much as Rebus would have guessed. There was no doubt: Big Ger had got himself in shape. The backside and upper thighs were pockmarked, but the gut had been tightened. Rebus tried to remember when he'd last seen Cafferty. Probably in court . . .

Rebus would have enjoyed a quiet word with the Organ Grinder, but now that the parking attendant gorilla was in spying distance, it just wasn't feasible. You couldn't be sure how much the one-eared man could hear.

'There's some stuff here, it should fit.'

The 'stuff ' consisted of sweatshirt, running shorts, socks and trainers . . . and a headband. There was no way Rebus was going to wear a headband. But when Cafferty emerged from his cubicle, *he* was wearing one, along with a white running vest and immaculate white shorts. He started to limber up while Rebus entered the cubicle to change.

What the hell am I doing? he asked himself. He had imagined a lot of things, but not this. Some things might be painful in life, but this, he had no doubt, was going to be torture.

'Where to?' he asked when they emerged from the overheated gym into the cool twilit evening. He wasn't wearing the headband. And he had put the sweatshirt on inside out. The legend across its front had read 'Kick me if I stop'. He supposed it represented Cafferty's idea of a joke.

'Sometimes I run to Duddingston Loch, sometimes up to the top of the Seat. You choose.' Big Ger was bouncing on the spot.

'The loch.'

'Right,' said Big Ger, and off they set.

Rebus spent the first few minutes checking that his body could take this sort of thing, which was why he was slow to spot the car following them. It was the Jag, driven by the parking attendant at a steady 0–5 mph.

'Remember the last time you gave evidence against me?' Big Ger said. As a conversational opening, it had its merits. Rebus merely nodded. They were running side by side, the pavements being all but deserted. He wondered if any undercover officers would be snapping photographs of this. 'Over in Glasgow, it was.'

'I remember.'

'Not guilty, of course.' Big Ger grinned. He looked like he'd had his teeth seen to as well. Rebus remembered them being greyish-green. Now they were a brilliantly capped white. And his hair . . . was it thicker? One of those hair-weaves, maybe? 'Anyway, I heard afterwards you went back down to London and had a bit of a time.'

'You could say that.'

They ran another minute in silence. The pace wasn't exactly taxing, but then neither was Rebus in condition. His lungs were already passing him warnings of the red hot and burning varieties.

'You're getting thin at the back,' Cafferty noticed. 'A hair weave would sort that out.'

It was Rebus's turn to smile. 'You know damned fine I got burned.'

'Aye, and I know who burned you, too.'

Still, Rebus reckoned his own guess about the hair weave had been confirmed.

'Actually,' he said, 'I wanted to talk to you about another fire.'

'Oh aye?'

'At the Central.'

'The Central Hotel?' Rebus was pleased to notice that the words weren't coming so easily from Big Ger either now. 'That's prehistory.'

'Not as far as I'm concerned.'

'But what's it to do with me?'

'Two of your men were there that night, playing in a poker game.'

Cafferty shook his head. 'That can't be right. I won't have gamblers working for me. It's against the Bible.'

'Everything you do from waking till sleeping is against *somebody's* Bible, Cafferty.'

'Please, Strawman, call me Mr Cafferty.'

'I'll call you what I like.'

'And I'll call you the Strawman.'

The name jarred . . . every time. It had been at the Glasgow trial, a sheet of notes wrongly glanced at by the prosecution, mistaking Rebus for the only other witness, a pub landlord called Stroman.

'Now then, Inspector Stroman . . .' Oh, Cafferty had laughed at that, laughed from the dock so hard that he was in danger of contempt. His eyes had bored into Rebus like fat woodworm, and he'd mouthed the word one final time the way he'd heard it – Strawman.

'Like I say,' Rebus went on, 'two of your hired heid-the-ba's. Eck and Tam Robertson.'

They had just passed the Sheep's Heid pub, Rebus sorely tempted to veer inside, Cafferty knowing it.

'There'll be herbal tea when we get back. Watch out there!' His warning saved Rebus from stepping in a discreet dog turd.

'Thanks,' Rebus said grudgingly.

'I was thinking of the shoes,' Cafferty replied. 'Know what "flowers of Edinburgh" are?'

'A rock band?'

'Keech. They used to chuck all their keech out of the windows and onto the street. There was so much of it lying around, the locals called it the flowers of Edinburgh. I read that in a book.'

Rebus thought of Alister Flower and smiled. 'Makes you glad you're living in a decent society.'

'So it does,' said Cafferty, with no trace of irony. 'Eck and Tam Robertson, eh? The Bru-Heid Brothers. I won't lie to you, they used to work for me. Tam for just a few weeks, Eck for longer.'

'I won't ask what they did.'

Cafferty shrugged. 'They were general employees.'

'Covers a multitude of sins.'

'Look, I didn't ask you to come out here. But now that you are, I'm answering your questions, all right?'

'I appreciate it, really. You say you didn't know they were at the Central that night?'

'No.'

'Do you know what happened to them afterwards?'

'They stopped working for me. Not at the same time, Tam left first, I think. Tam then Eck. Tam was a dunderheid, Strawman, a real loser. I can't abide losers. I only hired him because Eck asked me to. Eck was a good worker.' He seemed lost in thought for a minute. 'You're looking for them?'

'That's it.'

'Sorry, I can't help.' Rebus wondered if Cafferty's cheeks were half as red as his felt. He had a piercing stitch in his side, and didn't know how he was going to make the run back. 'You think they had something to do with the body?'

Rebus merely nodded.

'What makes you so sure?'

'I'm not sure. But if they *did* have something to do with it, I'm willing to bet you weren't a hundred miles behind.'

'Me?' Cafferty laughed again, but the laugh was strained. 'As I recall, I was on holiday in Malta with some friends.'

'You always seem to be with friends when anything happens.'

'I'm a gregarious man, I can't help it if I'm popular. Know something else I read about Scotland? The Pope called it "the arse of Europe".' Cafferty slowed to a stop. They'd come to near the top of Duddingston Loch, the city just visible down below them. 'Hard to believe, isn't it? The arse of Europe, it doesn't look like one to me.'

'Oh, I don't know,' said Rebus, bent over with hands on knees. 'If this is the arse . . .' he looked up, 'I'd know where to stick the enema.'

Cafferty's laughter roared out all around. He was breathing deeply, trying to slow things down. When he spoke, it was in an undertone, though there was no one around to hear them. 'But we're a cruel people, Strawman. All of us, you and me. And we're ghouls.' His face was very close to Rebus's, both of them bent over. Rebus kept his eyes on the grass below him. 'When they killed the grave-robber Burke, they made souvenirs from his skin. I've got one in the house, I'll show it to you.' The voice might have been inside Rebus's own head. 'We *like* to watch, and that's the truth. I bet even you've got a taste for pain, Strawman. You're hurting all over, but you ran with me, you didn't give up. Why? Because you *like* the pain. It's what makes you a Calvinist.'

'It's what makes you a public menace.'

'Me? A simple businessman who has managed to survive this disease called recession.'

'No, you're more than that,' said Rebus, straightening up. 'You're the disease.'

Cafferty looked like he might throw a punch, but instead he pounded Rebus on the back. 'Come on, time to go.'

Rebus was about to plead another minute's rest, but saw Cafferty walking to the Jag. 'What?' Cafferty said. 'You think I'd run it both ways? Come on now, your herbal tea is waiting.'

And herbal tea it was, served up poolside after Rebus had showered and changed back into his clothes. He had the feeling someone had been through his wallet and diary in his absence, but knew they wouldn't have found much there. For one thing, he'd tucked his ID and credit cards into the front of his running shorts; for another, he'd about as much cash as would buy an evening paper and a packet of mints.

'Sorry I couldn't be more help,' said Cafferty after Rebus had sat himself down.

'You could if you tried,' Rebus replied. He was trying to stop his legs from shaking. They hadn't had this much exercise since the last time he'd flitted.

Cafferty just shrugged. He was now wearing baggy and wildly coloured swimming trunks, and had just had a dip. As he dried himself off, he showed enough anal cleavage to qualify as a construction worker.

The devil dog meantime sat by the pool licking its chops. Of the bone it had been chewing, there was not the slightest trace. Rebus suddenly placed the dog.

'Do you own a 4x4?' Cafferty nodded. 'I saw it parked across from Bone's the Butcher on South Clerk Street. This mutt was in the back.'

Cafferty shrugged. 'It's my wife's car.'

'And she often takes the dog into town?'

'She gets Kaiser's bones there. Besides, he's cheaper than a car alarm.' Cafferty smiled fondly at the dog. 'And I've never known anyone bypass him.'

'Maybe sausages would do it.' But this was lost on Cafferty. Rebus decided he was getting nowhere. It was time to try one final tactic. He finished the brew. It tasted like spearmint chewing gum. 'A colleague of mine was trying to track down the Robertson brothers. Someone put him in hospital.'

'Really?' Cafferty looked genuinely surprised. 'What happened?'

'He was attacked behind a restaurant called the Heartbreak Cafe.'

'Dear me. Did he find them, Tam and Eck?'

'If he'd found them, I wouldn't have had to come here.'

'I thought maybe it was just an excuse for a blether about the good old days.'

'What good old days?'

'True enough, you look about as bad as ever. Not me, though. My wild days are behind me.' He sipped his tea to prove the point. 'I'm a changed man.'

Rebus nearly laughed. 'You tell that line so often in court, you're beginning to believe it.'

'No, it's true.'

'Then you wouldn't be trying to put the frighteners on me?'

Cafferty shook his head. He was crouching beside the dog, rubbing its head briskly. 'Oh no, Strawman, the day's long past when I'd take a set of six-inch carpentry nails and fix you to the floorboards in some derelict house. Or tickle your tonsils with jump-leads connected to a generator.' He was warming to his subject, looking almost as ready to pounce as his dog.

Rebus stayed nonchalant. Indeed, he had one to add to the list. 'Or hang me over the Forth Rail Bridge?' There was silence, except for the hum of the jacuzzi and the snuffling of the dog. Then the door swung open and a woman's head smiled heedlessly towards them.

'Morris, dinner in ten minutes.'

'Thanks, Mo.'

The door closed again, and Cafferty got up. So did the dog. 'Well, Strawman, it's been lovely chatting away like this, but I better take a shower before I eat. Mo's always complaining I smell like chlorine. I keep telling her, we wouldn't have to put chlorine in the pool if the visitors didn't piss in it, but she blames Kaiser!'

'She's your ... er ...?'

'My wife. As of four years and three months.'

Rebus was nodding. He knew Cafferty was married, of course. He'd just forgotten the name of the lucky bride.

'She's the one who's changed me if anyone has,' Cafferty was saying. 'She makes me read all these books.'

Rebus knew the Nazis had read books too. 'Just one thing, Cafferty.'

'*Mr* Cafferty. Go on, indulge me.'

Rebus swallowed hard. 'Mr Cafferty. What's your wife's maiden name?'

'Morag,' said Cafferty, puzzled by the question. 'Morag Johnson.' Then he padded away towards the shower, kicking off his trunks, mooning mightily at Rebus as he did so.

Morag Johnson. Yes, of course. Rebus would bet that not many people tried the 'Mo Johnson' gag in front of Big Ger. But that's where he'd heard the name before. The woman into whose flat Aengus Gibson had trespassed had soon afterwards married Big Ger Cafferty. So soon after, in fact, that they *must* have been going out together at the time the break-in had occurred.

Rebus had his link between Aengus Gibson, the Bru-Head Brothers and Big Ger.

Now all he had to do was figure out what the hell it meant.

He rose from his chair, eliciting a low growl from the devil dog. Slowly and quietly he made for the door, knowing all Big Ger had to do was call from the shower, and Kaiser would be on Rebus faster than piss on a lamp post. As he made his exit, he was remembering those scenarios for his painful execution, so lovingly described by Big Ger.

John Rebus was once again grateful he didn't yet have the gun.

But there was something else. The way Big Ger had seemed surprised when told about Holmes. As if he *really* hadn't known about it. Added to which how keen he'd been to find out if Holmes had had any success tracking down Tam and Eck Roberston.

Rebus drove away with more mysteries than answers. But one question he was sure had been answered: Cafferty had been behind Michael's abduction. He was certain of it now.

21

'You can't have,' said Siobhan Clarke.

'And yet I have,' said Peter Petrie. He had run out of film. Plenty of spare batteries. Of batteries there were plenty. But film was there none. It was first thing Thursday morning, and the last thing Clarke needed. 'So you'd better go and fetch some pronto.'

'Why me?'

'Because *I* am in pain.' This was true. He was on painkillers for his nose, and had complained about nothing else all day yesterday. So much so that the maddening Madden had lost all sense of good fun and bad puns and had told Petrie to 'shut the fuck up'. Now they weren't talking. Siobhan wondered if it was a good idea to leave them alone.

'It's special film,' Petrie was telling her. He rummaged in the camera case and came out with an empty film-box, the flap of which he tore off and handed to her. 'This is the stuff.'

'This,' she said to him, grabbing the scrap of card, 'is a pain in the arse.'

'Try Pyle's,' said Madden.

She turned on him. 'Are you being funny?'

'It's the name of a camera shop on Morrison Street.'

'That's miles away!'

'Take your car,' Petrie suggested.

Siobhan grabbed her bag. 'Stuff that, I'll find somewhere before Morrison Street.'

However, after ten filmless minutes she began to realise that there was no great demand for special high-speed film in Gorgie Road. It wasn't as if you needed high-speed to take a photo of Hearts in action. She consoled herself with this thought and resigned herself to the walk to Morrison Street. Maybe she could catch a bus back.

She saw that she was nearing the Heartbreak Cafe, and crossed the road to look at it. It had looked closed yesterday when she drove past, and there was a sign in the window. She read now that the place was closed 'due to convalescence'. Strange, though, the door was open a couple of inches. And was there a funny smell, a smell like gas? She pushed the door open and peered in.

'Hello?'

Yes, definitely gas, and there was no one around. A woman on the street stopped to watch.

'Awfy smell o' gas, hen.'

Siobhan nodded and walked into the Heartbreak Cafe.

Without its lights on, and with little natural light, the place was all darkness and shadows. But the last thing she planned to do was flick an electric switch. She could see chinks of light through the kitchen door, and made towards it. Yes, there were windows in the kitchen, and the smell was much stronger here. She could hear the unmistakable hiss of escaping gas. With a hankie stuffed to her nose, she made for the emergency exit, and pushed at the bar which should release it. But the thing was sticking, or else ... She gave a mighty heave and the door grunted open an inch. Dustbins were being stored right against it on the outside. Fresh air started trickling in, the welcome smells of traffic exhaust and beer hops.

Now she had to find whichever cooker had been left on. Only as she turned did she see the legs and body which were lying on the floor, the head hidden inside a huge oven. She walked over and turned off the gas, then peered down. The body lay on its side, dressed in black and white check trousers and a white chef's jacket. She didn't recognise the man from his face, but the elaborately stitched name on his left breast made identification easy.

It was Eddie Ringan.

The place was still choking with gas, so she walked back to the emergency door and gave it another heave. This time it opened most of the way, scattering clanking dustbins onto the ground outside. It was then that a curious passer-by pushed open the door from the restaurant to the kitchen. His hand went to the light-switch.

'Don't touch tha –!'

There was a tremendous blast and fireball. The shock sent Siobhan Clarke flying backwards into the parking lot, where her landing was softened by the rubbish she'd scattered only seconds earlier. She didn't even suffer the same minor burns as the hapless passer-by, who went crashing back into the restaurant pursued by a blue ball of flame. But Eddie Ringan, well, he looked like he'd been done to a turn inside an oven which wasn't even hot.

By the time Rebus got there, aching after last night's exertions, the scene was one of immaculate chaos. Pat Calder had arrived in time to see his lover being carted away in a blue plastic bag. The bag was deemed necessary to stop bits of charred face breaking off and messing up the floor. The bagging itself had been overseen by a police doctor, but Rebus knew where Eddie would eventually end up: under the all-seeing scalpel of Dr Curt.

'All right, Clarke?'

Rebus affected the usual inspectorial nonchalance, hands in pockets and an air of having seen it all before.

'Apart from my coccyx, sir.' And she gave the bone a rub for luck.

'What happened?'

So she filled in the details, all the way from having no film (yes, why not drop Petrie in it?) to the passer-by who had nearly killed her. He had been seen to by the doctor too: frizzled eyebrows and lashes, some bruising from the fall. Rebus's scalp tingled at the thought. There was no smell of gas in the kitchen now. But there was a smell of cooked meat, almost inviting till you remembered its source.

Calder was seated at the bar, watching the world move past him in and out of the dream he had built with Eddie Ringan. Rebus sat down beside him, glad to take the weight off his legs.

'Those nightmares,' Calder said immediately, 'looks like he made them come true, eh?'

'Looks like it. Any idea why he'd kill himself?'

Calder shook his head. He was bearing up, but only just. 'I suppose it all got too much for him.'

'All what?'

Calder continued shaking his head. 'Perhaps we'll never know.'

'Don't you believe it,' Rebus said, trying not to make it sound like a threat. He must have failed, for suddenly Calder turned towards him.

'Can't you let it rest?' The pale eyes were glistening.

'No rest for the wicked, Mr Calder,' said Rebus. He slid off the barstool and went back into the kitchen. Siobhan was standing beside a shelf filled with basic cookery books.

'Most chefs,' she said, 'would rather die than keep this lot out on display.'

'He wasn't any ordinary chef.'

'Look at this one.' It was a school jotter, with ruled red lines about half an inch apart and an inch-wide margin. The margins were full of doodles and sketches, mostly of food and men with large quiffs. Neatly written in a large hand inside the margins were recipes. 'His own creations.' She flipped to the end. 'Oh look, here's Jailhouse Roquefort.' She quoted from the recipe. ' "With thanks to Inspector John Rebus for the idea." Well, well.' She was about to put the book back, but Rebus took it from her. He opened it at the inside cover, where he'd spotted a copious collection of doodles. Something had been written in the midst of the drawings (some of them gayly rude). But it had been scored out again with a darker pen.

'Can you make that out?'

They took the jotter to the back door and stood in the parking lot, where so recently someone had thumped Brian Holmes on the head.

361

Siobhan started things off. 'Looks like the first word's "All".'

'And that's "turn",' said Rebus of a later word. 'Or maybe "tum".' But the rest remained beyond them. Rebus pocketed the recipe book.

'Thinking of a new career, sir?' Siobhan asked.

Rebus pondered a suitable comeback line. 'Shut up, Clarke,' he said.

Rebus dropped the jotter off at Fettes HQ, where they had people whose job it was to recover legibility from defaced and damaged writing. They were known as 'pen pals', the sort of boffins who liked to do really difficult crosswords.

'This won't take long,' one of them told Rebus. 'We'll just put it on the machine.'

'Great,' said Rebus. 'I'll come back in quarter of an hour.'

'Make it twenty minutes.'

Twenty minutes was fine by Rebus. While he was here and at a loose end, he might as well pay his respects to DI Gill Templer.

'Hello, Gill.' Her office smelt of expensive perfume. He'd forgotten what kind she wore. Chanel, was it? She slipped off her glasses and blinked at him.

'John, long time no see. Sit down.'

Rebus shook his head. 'I can't stay, the lab's going to have something for me in a minute. Just thought I'd see how you're doing.'

She nodded her answer. 'I'm doing fine. How about you?'

'Aw, not bad. You know how it is.'

'How's the doctor?'

'She's fine, aye.' He shuffled his feet. He hadn't expected this to be so awkward.

'It's not true she kicked you out, then?'

'How the hell do you know about that?'

Gill was smiling her lipsticked smile; a thin mouth, made for irony. 'Come on, John, this is *Edinburgh*. You want to keep secrets, move somewhere bigger than a village.'

'Who told you, though? How many people know?'

'Well, if they know here at Fettes, they're bound to know at St Leonard's.'

Christ. That meant Watson knew, Lauderdale knew, Flower knew. And none of them had said anything.

'It's only a temporary thing,' he muttered, shuffling his feet again. 'Patience has her nieces staying, so I moved back into my flat. Plus Michael's there just now.'

It was Gill Templer's turn to look surprised. 'Since when?'

'Ten days or so.'

'Is he back for good?'

Rebus shrugged. 'Depends, I suppose. Gill, I wouldn't want word getting round . . .'

'Of course not! I can keep a secret.' She smiled again. 'Remember, I'm *not* from Edinburgh.'

'Me neither,' said Rebus. 'I just get screwed around here.' He checked his watch.

'Are my five minutes up?'

'Sorry.'

'Don't be, I've got plenty of work to be getting on with.'

He turned to leave.

'John? Come up and see me again sometime.'

Rebus nodded. 'Mae West, right?'

'Right.'

'Bye, Gill.'

Halfway along her corridor, Rebus recalled that a Mae West was also the name for a life-jacket. He considered this, but shook his head. 'My life's complicated enough.'

He returned to the lab.

'You're a bit early,' he was told.

'Keen's the word you're looking for.'

'Well, speaking of words we're looking for, come and have a peek.' He was led to a computer console. The scribble had been OCR'd and fed into the computer, where it was now displayed on the large colour monitor. A lot of the overpenning had been 'erased', leaving the original message hopefully intact. The pen pal picked up a sheet of paper. 'Here are my ideas so far.' As he read them off, Rebus tried to see them in the message on the screen.

' "Ale I did, tum on the gum", "Ole I did man, term on the gam" . . .' Rebus gazed up at him, and the pen pal grinned. 'Or maybe this,' he said. ' "All I did was turn on the gas".'

'What?'

' "All I did was turn on the gas".'

Rebus stared at the message on the screen. Yes, he could see it . . . well, most of it. The pen pal was talking again.

'It helped that you told me he'd gassed himself. I still had that half in mind when I started working, and spotted "gas" straight off. A suicide note, maybe?'

Rebus looked disbelieving. 'What, scored out and surrounded by doodles on the inside cover of a jotter he tucked away on a shelf? Stick to what you know and you'll do fine.'

What Rebus knew was that Eddie Ringan had suffered nightmares during which he cried out the word 'gas'. Was this scribble the remnant from one of his bad nights? But then why score it out so heavily? Rebus picked up the jotter from the OCR machine. The inside cover looked old, the stuff there going back a year or more. Some of the doodles looked more recent than the defaced message. Whenever Eddie had written this, it wasn't last night. Which meant, presumably, that it had no direct connection to his gassing himself. Making it . . . a coincidence? Rebus didn't believe in coincidence, but he did believe in serendipity. He turned to the pen pal, who was looking not happy at Rebus's put-down.

'Thanks,' he said.

'You're welcome.'

Each was sure the other was being less than sincere.

Brian Holmes was waiting for him at St Leonard's, waiting to be welcomed back into the world.

'What the hell are you doing here?'

'Don't worry,' said Holmes, 'I'm just visiting. I've got another week on the sick.'

'How are you feeling?' Rebus was glancing nervously around, wondering if anyone had told Holmes about Eddie. He knew in his heart they hadn't, of course; if they had, Brian wouldn't be half as chipper.

'I get thumping headaches, but that apart I feel like I've had a holiday.' He patted his pocket. 'And DI Flower got up a collection. Nearly fifty quid.'

'The man's a saint,' said Rebus. 'I had a present I was going to bring you.'

'What?'

'A tape, the Stones' *Let it Bleed*.'

'Thanks a lot.'

'Something to cheer you up after Patsy De-Cline.'

'At least she can sing.'

Rebus smiled. 'You're fired. Are you at your aunt's?'

This quietened Holmes, as Rebus had hoped it would. Bring him down slowly, then drop the real news into his lap. 'For the meantime. Nell's . . . well, she says she's not quite ready yet.'

Rebus knew the feeling; he wondered when Patience would be ready for that drink. 'Still,' he offered, 'things sound a bit brighter between the two of you.'

'Ach.' Holmes sat down opposite his superior. 'She wants me to leave the police.'

'That's a bit drastic.'

'So is separation.'

Rebus exhaled. 'I suppose so, but all the same . . . What are you going to do?'

'Think it over, what else can I do?' He got back to his feet. 'Listen, I'd better get going. I only came in to –'

'Brian, sit down.' Holmes, recognising Rebus's tone, sat. 'I've got some bad news about Eddie.'

'Chef Eddie?' Rebus nodded. 'What about him?'

'There's been an accident. Well, sort of. Eddie was involved.'

There was no mistaking Rebus's meaning. He'd become good at this sort of speech through repetition over the years to the families of car crash victims, accidents at work, murders ...

'He's dead?' Holmes asked quietly. Rebus, lips pursed, nodded. 'Christ, I was going to drop in and see him. What happened?'

'We're not sure yet. The post-mortem will probably be this afternoon.'

Holmes was no fool; again he caught the gist. 'Accident, suicide or murder?'

'One of those last two.'

'And your money'd be on murder?'

'My money stays in my pocket till I've spoken to the tipster.'

'Meaning Dr Curt?'

Rebus nodded. 'Till then, there's not much we can do. Listen, let me get a car to take you home ...'

'No, no, I'll be all right.' He rose to his feet slowly, as though checking his bones for solidity. 'I'll be fine really. It's just ... poor Eddie. He was a friend of mine, you know?'

'I know,' said Rebus.

After Holmes had gone, Rebus was able to reflect that he'd gotten off lightly. Brian still wasn't operating at full throttle; partly the convalescence, partly the shock. So he hadn't asked Rebus any difficult questions. Questions like, does Eddie's death have anything to do with the person who nearly killed *me*? It was something Rebus had been wondering himself. Last night Eddie was missing, and Rebus had gone to see Cafferty. Today, first thing, Eddie was dead. Meaning one less person who could say anything about the night the Central burnt down; one less person who'd been there. But Rebus still had the gut feeling Cafferty had been surprised to learn of Holmes' attack. So what was the answer?

'I'm buggered if I know,' John Rebus said quietly to himself. His phone rang. He picked it up and heard pub noises, then Flower's voice.

'That's some team you've got there, Inspector. One gets his face mashed in, and now the other falls on her arse.' The connection was briskly severed.

'And bugger you, too, Flower,' Rebus said, all too aware that no one was listening.

22

Edinburgh's public mortuary was sited on the Cowgate, named for the route cattle would take when being brought into the city to be sold. It was a narrow canyon of a street with few businesses and only passing traffic. Way up above it were much busier streets, South Bridge for instance. They seemed so far from the Cowgate, it might as well have been underground.

Rebus wasn't sure the area had ever been anything other than a desperate meeting place for Edinburgh's poorest denizens, who often seemed like cattle themselves, dull-witted from lack of sunlight and grazing on begged handouts from passers-by. The Cowgate was ripe for redevelopment these days, but who would slaughter the cattle?

A fine setting for the understated mortuary where, when he wasn't teaching at the University, Dr Curt plied his trade.

'Look on the bright side,' he told Rebus. 'The Cowgate's got a couple of fine pubs.'

'And a few more you could shave a dead man with.'

Curt chuckled. 'Colourful, though I'm not sure the image conjured actually *means* anything.'

'I bow to your superior knowledge. Now, what have you got on Mr Ringan?'

'Ah, poor Orphan Eddie.' Curt liked to find names for all his cadavers. Rebus got the feeling the 'Orphan' prefix had been used many a time before. In Eddie Ringan's case, though, it was accurate. He had no living relations that anyone knew of, and so had been identified by Patrick Calder, and by Siobhan Clarke, since she'd been the one to find the body.

'Yes, that's the man I found,' she had said.

'Yes, that's Edward Ringan,' Pat Calder had said, before being led away by Toni the barman.

Rebus now stood with Curt beside the slab on which what was left of the corpse was being tidied up by an assistant. The assistant was whistling 'Those Were the Days' as he scraped miscellany into a bucket of offal. Rebus was reading through a list. He'd been through it three times already, trying to take his mind off the scene around him. Curt was smoking a cigarette. At the age of fifty-five, he'd decided he might as well start, since nothing else had so far managed to kill him. Rebus might have taken a cigarette from him, but they were Player's untipped, the smoking equivalent of paint stripper.

Maybe because he'd perused the list so often, something clicked at last. 'You know,' he said, 'we never found a suicide note.'

'They don't always leave them.'

'Eddie would have. *And* he'd have had Elvis singing *Heartbreak Hotel* on a tape player beside the oven.'

'Now that's style,' Curt said disingenuously.

'And now,' Rebus went on, 'from this list of the contents of his pockets, I see he didn't have any keys on him.'

'No keys, eh.' Curt was enjoying his break too much to bother trying to work it out. He knew Rebus would tell him anyway.

'So,' Rebus obliged, 'how did he get in? Or if he *did* use his keys to get in, where are they now?'

'Where indeed.' The attendant frowned as Curt stubbed his cigarette into the floor.

Rebus knew when he'd lost an audience. He put the list away. 'So what have you got for me?'

'Well, the usual tests will have to be carried out, of course.'

'Of course, but in the meantime . . .?'

'In the meantime, a few points of interest.' Curt turned to the cadaver, forcing Rebus to do the same. There was a cover over the charred face, and the attendant had roughly sewn up the chest and stomach, now empty of their major organs, with thick black thread. The face had been badly burnt, but the rest of the body remained unaffected. The plump flesh was pale and shiny.

'Well,' Curt began, 'the burns were superficial merely. The internal organs were untouched by the blast. That made things easier. I would say he probably asphyxiated through inhalation of North Sea gas.' He turned to Rebus. 'That "North Sea" is pure conjecture.' Then he grinned again, a lopsided grin that meant one side of his mouth stayed closed. 'There was evidence of alcoholic intake. We'll have to wait for the test results to determine how much. A lot, I'd guess.'

'I'll bet his liver was a treat. He's been putting the stuff away for years.'

Curt seemed doubtful. He went to another table and returned with the organ itself, which had already been cross-sectioned. 'It's actually in pretty good shape. You said he was a spirits drinker?'

Rebus kept his eyes out of focus. It was something you learned. 'A bottle a day easy.'

'Well, it doesn't show from this.' Curt tossed the liver a few inches into the air. It slapped back down into his palm. He reminded Rebus of a butcher showing off to a potential buyer. 'There was also a bump to the head and bruising and minor burns to the arms.'

'Oh?'

'I'd imagine these are injuries often incurred by chefs in their daily duties. Hot fat spitting, pots and pans everywhere ...'

'Maybe,' said Rebus.

'And now we come to the section of the programme Hamish has been waiting for.' Curt nodded towards his assistant, who straightened his back in anticipation. 'I call him Hamish,' Curt confided, 'because he comes from the Hebrides. Hamish here spotted something *I* didn't. I've been putting off talking about it lest he become encephalitic.' He looked at Rebus. 'A little pathologist's joke.'

'You're not so small,' said Rebus.

'You need to know, Inspector, that Hamish has a fascination with teeth. Probably because his own as a child were terribly bad and he has memories of long days spent under the dentist's drill.'

Hamish looked as though this might actually be true.

'As a result, Hamish always looks in people's mouths, and this time he saw fit to inform me that there was some damage.'

'What sort of damage?'

'Scarring of the tissues lining the throat. Recent damage, too.'

'Like he'd been singing too loud?'

'Or screaming. But much more likely that something has been forced down his throat.'

Rebus's mind boggled. Curt always seemed able to do this to him. He swallowed, feeling how dry his own throat was. 'What sort of thing?'

Curt shrugged. 'Hamish suggested ... You understand, this is entirely conjecture – usually *your* field of expertise. Hamish suggested a pipe of some kind, something solid. I myself would add the possibility of a rubber or plastic tube.'

Rebus coughed. 'Not anything ... er, organic then?'

'You mean like a courgette? A banana?'

'You know damned well what I mean.'

Curt smiled and bowed his head. 'Of course I do, I'm sorry.' Then he shrugged. 'I wouldn't rule anything out. But if you're suggesting a penis, it must have been sheathed in sandpaper.'

Behind them, Rebus heard Hamish stifle a laugh.

Rebus telephoned Pat Calder and asked if they might meet. Calder thought it over before agreeing.

'At the Colonies?' Rebus asked.

'Make it the Cafe, I'm heading over there anyway.'

So the Cafe it was. When Rebus arrived, the 'convalescence' sign had

368

been replaced with one stating, 'Due to bereavement, this establishment has ceased trading.' It was signed Pat Calder.

As Rebus entered, he heard Calder roar, 'Do fuck off!' It was not, however, aimed at Rebus but at a young woman in a raincoat.

'Trouble, Mr Calder?' Rebus walked into the restaurant. Calder was busy taking the mementoes down off the walls and packing them in newspaper. Rebus noticed three tea chests on the floor between the tables.

'This bloody reporter wants some blood and grief for her newspaper.'

'Is that right, miss?' Rebus gave Mairie Henderson a disapproving but, yes, almost *fatherly* look. The kind that let her know she should be ashamed.

'Mr Ringan was a popular figure in the city,' she told Rebus. 'I'm sure he'd have wanted our readers to know –'

Calder interrupted. 'He'd have wanted them to stuff their faces here, leave a fat cheque, then get the fuck out. Print *that*!'

'Quite an epitaph,' Mairie commented.

Calder looked like he'd brain her with the Elvis clock, the one with the King's arms replacing the usual clock hands. He thought better of it, and lifted the Elvis mirror (one of several) off the wall instead. He wouldn't dare smash that: seven years' bad junk food.

'I think you'd better go, miss,' Rebus said calmly.

'All right, I'm going.' She slung her bag over her shoulder and stalked past Rebus. She was wearing a skirt today, a short one too. But a good soldier knew when to keep eyes front. He smiled at Pat Calder, whose anguish was all too evident.

'Bit soon for all this, isn't it?'

'You can cook, can you, Inspector? Without Eddie, this place is ... it's nothing.'

'Looks like the local restaurants can sleep easy, then.'

'How do you mean?'

'Remember, Eddie thought the attack on Brian was a warning.'

'Yes, but what's that ...' Calder froze. 'You think someone ...? It was suicide, wasn't it?'

'Looked that way, certainly.'

'You mean you're not sure?'

'Did he seem the type who would kill himself?'

Calder's reply was cold. 'He was killing himself every day with drink. Maybe it all got too much. Like I said, Inspector, the attack on Brian affected Eddie. Maybe more than we knew.' He paused, still with the mirror gripped in both hands. 'You think it was murder?'

'I didn't say that, Mr Calder.'

'Who would do it?'

'Maybe you were behind with your payments.'

'What payments?'

'Protection payments, sir. Don't tell me it doesn't go on.'

Calder stared at him unblinking. 'You forget, I was in charge of finances, and we always paid our bills on time. All of them.'

Rebus took this information in, wondering exactly what it meant. 'If you think you know who might have wanted Eddie dead, best tell me, all right? Don't go doing anything rash.'

'Like what?'

Like buying a gun, Rebus thought, but he said nothing. Calder started to wrap the mirror. 'This is about all a newspaper's worth,' he said.

'She was only doing her job. You wouldn't have turned down a good review, would you?'

Calder smiled. 'We got plenty.'

'What will you do now?'

'I haven't thought about it. I'll go away, that's all I know.'

Rebus nodded towards the tea chests. 'And you'll keep all that stuff?'

'I couldn't throw it away, Inspector. It's all there is.'

Well, thought Rebus, there's the bedroom too. But he didn't say anything. He just watched Pat Calder pack everything away.

Hamish, real name Alasdair McDougall, had more or less been chased from his native Barra by his contemporaries, one of whom tried to drown him during a midnight boat crossing from South Uist after a party. Two minutes in the freezing waters of the Sound of Barra and he'd have been fit for nothing but fish-food, but they'd hauled him back into the boat and explained the whole thing away as an accident. Which is also what it would have been had he actually drowned.

He went to Oban first, then south to Glasgow before crossing to the east coast. Glasgow suited him in some respects, but not in others. Edinburgh suited him better. His parents had always denied to themselves that their son was homosexual, even when he'd stood there in front of them and said it. His father had quoted the Bible at him, the same way he'd been quoting it for seventeen years, a believer's righteous tremble in his voice. It had once been a powerful and persuasive performance; but now it seemed laughable.

'Just because it's in the Bible,' he'd told his father, 'doesn't mean you should take it as gospel.'

But to his father it was and always would be the literal truth. The Bible had been in the old man's hand as he'd shooed his youngest son out of the door of the croft house. 'Never dare to blacken our name!' he'd called. And Alasdair reckoned he'd lived up to this through introducing himself as Dougall and almost never passing on a last name. He had been Dougall to the gay community in Glasgow, and he was Dougall here in Edinburgh. He liked the life he'd made for himself (there was never a dull night), and he'd only been kicked-in twice. He had his clubs and pubs, his bunch of friends and a wider circle of acquaintances. He was even beginning to think of writing to his parents. He would tell them, By the time my boss gets through with a body, believe me there isn't very much left for Heaven to take.

He thought again of the plump young man who'd been gassed, and he laughed. He should have said something at the time, but hadn't. Why not? Was it because he still had one foot in the closet? He'd been accused of it before, when he'd refused to wear a pink triangle on his lapel. Certainly, he wasn't sure he wanted a policeman to know he was gay. And what would Dr Curt do? There was all sorts of homophobia about, an almost medieval fear of AIDS and its transmission. It wasn't that he couldn't live without the job, but he liked it well enough. He'd seen plenty of sheep and cattle slaughtered and quartered in his time on the island. This wasn't so very different.

No, he would keep his secret to himself. He wouldn't let on that he *knew* Eddie Ringan. He remembered the evening a week or so back. They went to Dougall's place and Eddie cooked up a chilli from stuff he found in the cupboards. Hot stuff. It really made you sweat. He wouldn't stay the night, though, wasn't that type. There'd been a long kiss before parting, and half-promises of further trysts.

Yes, he knew Eddie, knew him well enough to be sure of one thing.

Whoever it was on the slab, it wasn't the guy who'd shared chilli in Dougall's bed.

Siobhan Clarke felt unnaturally calm and in control the rest of the day. She'd been given the day off from Operation Moneybags to get over the shock of her experience at the Heartbreak Cafe, but by late afternoon was itching to do *some*thing. So she drove out to Rory Kintoul's house on the half-chance. It was a neat and quite recent council semi in a cul-de-sac. The front garden was the size of a beer-mat but probably more hygienic; she reckoned she could eat her dinner off the trimmed weed-less lawn without fear of food poisoning. She couldn't even say that of the plates in most police canteens. One gate led her down the path, and another brought her to Kintoul's front door. It was painted dark blue. Every fourth door in the street was dark blue. The others were plum-red, custard yellow, and battleship grey. Not exactly a riot of colour, but somehow in keeping with the pebbledash and tarmac. Some kids had chalked a complex hopscotch grid on the pavement and were now playing noisily. She'd smiled towards them, but they hadn't looked up from their game. A dog barked in a back garden a few doors down, but otherwise the street was quiet.

She rang the doorbell and waited. Nobody, it seemed, was home. She thought of the phrase 'gallus besom' as she took the liberty of peering in through the front window. A living room stretched to the back of the house. The dog was barking louder now, and through the far window she caught sight of a figure. She opened the garden gate and turned right, running through the close separating Kintoul's house from its neighbour. This led to the back gardens. Kintoul had left his kitchen door open so as not to make a noise. He had one leg over his neighbour's fence, and was trying to shush the leashed mongrel.

'Mr Kintoul!' Siobhan called. When he looked up, she waved her hand. 'Sitting on the fence, I see. How about the two of us going inside for a word?'

She wasn't about to spare him any blushes. As he slouched towards her across the back green, she grinned. 'Running away from the police, eh? What've you got to hide?'

'Nuthin'.'

'You should be careful,' she warned. 'A stunt like that could open those stitches in your side.'

'Do you want everyone to hear? Get inside.' He almost pushed her through the kitchen door. It was exactly the invitation Siobhan wanted.

Rebus got the call at six-fifteen and arranged the meeting for ten. At eight, Patience called him. He knew he wouldn't sound right to her, would sound like his thoughts were elsewhere (which they were), but he wanted to keep her talking. He was filling the time till ten o'clock and didn't want any of it left vacant. He might start to think about it otherwise, might change his mind.

Eventually, for want of other topics, he told Patience all about Michael (who was asleep in the box room). At last they were on the same wavelength. Patience suggested counselling, and was amazed no one at the hospital had mentioned the possibility. She would look into it and get back to Rebus. Meantime, he'd have to watch Michael didn't go into clinical depression. The problem with those drugs was that they not only killed your fears, they could kill your emotions stone dead.

'He was so lively when he moved in,' Rebus said. 'The students are wondering what the hell's happened to him. I think they're as worried as I am.'

Michael's self-proclaimed 'girlfriend' had spent time trying to talk to him, coaxing him out to pubs and clubs. But Michael had fought against it, and she hadn't shown her face for at least a day. One of the male students had approached Rebus in the kitchen and asked, in tones of deepest sympathy, if a bit of 'blaw' might help Mickey. Rebus had shaken his head. Christ, it might not be a bad idea, though.

But Patience was against it. 'Mix the stuff he's on with cannabis and God knows what sort of reaction you'd get: paranoia or a complete downer would be my guess.'

She was anti-drugs anyway, and not just the proscribed kinds. She knew that the easy way out for doctors was to fill out a form for the pharmacy. Valium, moggies, whatever it took. People all over Scotland, and especially the people who needed most help, were eating tablets like they were nourishment. And the doctors pointed to their workloads and said, What else can we do?

'Want me to come over?' she was asking now. It was a big step. Yes, Rebus wanted her to come over, but it was nearly nine.

'No, but I appreciate the thought.'

'Well, try not to leave him too long on his own. He's sleeping to escape something he needs to confront.'

'Bye, Patience.' Rebus put down the phone and made ready to leave the flat.

Why had he chosen the waterfront at North Queensferry for the meeting? Well, wasn't it obvious? He stood near the same hut they'd taken Michael to, and he got cold. He'd arrived early, and Deek naturally was late. Rebus didn't really mind. It gave him time to stare up at the rail bridge, wondering how it would feel to be lowered over the side at the dead of night. Screaming dumbly into your gag as they took the bag from your face. Looking all the way down. That's where Rebus was now, though he was at sea level. He was looking all the way down.

'Cold though, eh?' Deek Torrance rubbed his hands together.

'Thanks for setting me up the other night.'

'Eh?'

' "Sailor for trade or rent".'

'Oh aye, that.' Torrance grinned. ' "King of the Road". That's not the way it goes, though . . .'

'You've got it?'

Deek patted his coat pocket. He was jittery, with good cause. It wasn't every day you sold an illegal firearm to a policeman.

'Let's see it, then.'

'What? Out here?'

Rebus looked around. 'There's nobody here.'

Deek bit his lip, then resigned himself to lifting the handgun out of his pocket and placing it in John Rebus's palm.

The thing was a lifeless weight, but comfortable to hold. Rebus placed it in his own capacious pocket. 'Ammo?'

The bullets shook in their box like a baby's toy. Rebus pocketed them too, then reached into the back pocket of his trousers for the cash.

'Want to count it?'

Deek shook his head, then nodded across the road. 'I'll buy you a drink though, if you like.'

A drink sounded good to Rebus. 'I'll just get rid of this first.' He unlocked his car and slipped the gun and ammo underneath the driver's seat. He noticed he was trembling and a little dizzy as he stood back up. A drink would be good. He was hungry, too, but the thought of food made him want to boak. He looked again at the bridge. 'Come on, then,' he said to Deek Torrance.

Minus gun and with money in its place, Torrance was more relaxed and loquacious. They sat in the Hawes Inn with their drinks. Torrance was explaining how the guns came into the country.

'See, it's easy to buy a gun in France. They even come around the towns in vans and flog them off the back. Stick a catalogue through your door to let you know what they'll have. I got to meet this French guy, not bad to say he's French. He's back and forth over the Channel, some sort of business he's in. He brings the guns with him, and I buy them. He brings Mace too, if you're interested.'

'Why didn't you say?' Rebus muttered into his pint. 'I wouldn't have needed the gun.'

'Eh?' Deek saw he was making a joke and laughed.

'So what have I got?' asked Rebus. 'It was a bit dark out there to see.'

'Well, they're all copies. Don't worry, I file off any identifiers myself. Yours is a Colt 45. It'll take ten rounds.'

'Eight millimetre?'

Deek nodded. 'There are twenty in the box. It's not the most lethal weapon around. I can get replica Uzis too.'

'Christ.' Rebus finished his pint. He suddenly wanted to be out of there.

'It's a living,' said Deek Torrance.

'Aye, right, a living,' said Rebus, getting up to go.

23

Next morning Rebus forced himself into the usual routine. He checked to see if there had been any sign of Andrew McPhail. There had not. Maclean hadn't been too badly hurt by the boiled water, most of which he'd deflected with his arms. Nobody was yet treating McPhail like a dangerous criminal. His description had been issued to bus and train stations, motorway service areas, and the like. If the manpower were available, Rebus knew *exactly* where he would start looking for him.

A shadow fell over his desk. It was the Little Weed.

'So,' Flower said, 'you lose a DS to a blow on the napper, and a DC to a gas explosion. What's for an encore?'

Rebus saw that they had an audience. Half the station had been waiting for a confrontation between the two inspectors. Now more detectives than usual seemed interested in the filing cabinets near Rebus's desk.

'It's easier if you do a handstand,' commented Rebus.

'What is?'

'Talking out of your arse.'

There were a few covering coughs from the filing cabinets. 'I've got some throat pastilles if you want them,' Rebus called. The cabinet doors slid shut. The audience moved away.

'You think you're God's gift, don't you?' Flower said. 'You think you're all it takes.'

'I'm better than some.'

'And a lot worse than others.'

Rebus picked up the previous evening's arrest sheet and started to read it. 'If you're finished . . .?'

Flower smiled. 'Rebus, I thought your kind went out with the dinosaurs.'

'Aye, but only because they turned *you* down when you asked them.'

Which made it two-nil as Alister Flower walked off the field. But Rebus knew there'd be another leg to the match, and another after that.

He looked again at the arrest sheet, checking he'd seen the name right, then sighed and went down to the cells. A cluster of young constables stood outside cell one, taking turns at the peephole.

'It's that guy with the tattoos,' one of them explained to Rebus.

'The Pincushion?'

The constable nodded. The Pincushion was tattooed from head to foot, not an inch unblemished. 'He's been brought in for questioning.'

Rebus nodded. Whenever they had reason to bring the Pincushion into a station, he always ended up naked.

'It's a good name, isn't it, sir?'

'What, Pincushion? It's better than my name for him, I suppose.'

'What's that.'

'Just another prick,' said Rebus, unlocking cell number two. He closed the door behind him. A young man was sitting on the bunk, unshaven and sorry-eyed.

'What happened to you, then?'

Andy Steele looked up at him, then away. The city of Edinburgh had not been kind to him during his visit. He ran a handful of fingers through his tousled hair.

'Did you go see your Auntie Ena?' he asked.

Rebus nodded. 'I didn't see your mum and dad, though.'

'Ach well, at least I managed that, eh? I managed to track you down and put you in touch with her.'

'So what have you been up to since?'

Flakes of scalp were being clawed from the surface of Andy Steele's head. They floated down onto his trousers. 'Well, I did a bit of sightseeing.'

'They don't arrest you for that these days, though.'

Steele sighed and stopped scratching. 'Depends what sights you see. I told a man in a pub I was a private detective. He said he had a case for me.'

'Oh aye?' Rebus's attention was momentarily drawn to a crude game of noughts and crosses on the cell wall.

'His wife was cheating him. He told me where he thought I could find her, and he gave me a description. I got ten quid, with more when I reported back.'

'Go on.'

Andy Steele stared up at the ceiling. He knew he wasn't making himself look good, but it was a bit late for that anyway. 'It was a ground floor flat. I watched all evening. I saw the woman, she was there, all right. But no man. So I went round the back to get a better look. Someone must have spotted me and phoned the police.'

'You told them your story?'

Steele nodded. 'They even took me back to the bar. He wasn't there, of course, and nobody knew him. I didn't even know his name.'

'But his description of the woman was accurate?'

'Oh aye.'

'Probably an ex-wife or some old flame. He wanted to give them a scare, and it was worth ten notes to do it.'

'Except now the woman's pressing charges. Not a very good start to my career, is it, Inspector?'

'Depends,' said Rebus. 'Your career as a private dick may not be much cop, but as a peeping-tom your star is definitely in the ascendant.' Seeing Steele's misery, Rebus winked. 'Cheer up, I'll see what I can do.'

In fact, before he could do anything, Siobhan Clarke was on the telephone from Gorgie to tell him about her meeting with Rory Kintoul.

'I asked him if he knew anything about his cousin's heavy betting. He wouldn't say, but I get the feeling they're a close-knit family. There were hundreds of photos in the living room: aunties and uncles, brothers and sisters, nieces, cousins, grannies . . .'

'I get the idea. Did you mention the broken window?'

'Oh yes. He was so interested, he had to clamp himself to the chair to stop from jumping out of it. Not a great talker, though. He reckoned it must have been a drunk.'

'The same drunk who took a knife to his gut?'

'I didn't put it quite like that, and neither did he. I don't know whether it's relevant or not, but he did say he'd driven the butcher's van for his cousin.'

'What, full time?'

'Yes. Up until about a year ago.'

'I didn't know Bone's had a van. That'll be the next to go.'

'Sir?'

'The van. Smash the shop window, and if that doesn't work, torch the van.'

'You're saying it's all about protection?'

'Maybe protection, more likely money owing on bad bets. What do you think?'

'Well, I did raise that possibility with Kintoul.'

'And?'

'He laughed.'

'That's strong language coming from him.'

'Agreed, he's not exactly the emotional type.'

'So it's not betting money. I'll have another think.'

'His son came in while we were talking.'

'Refresh my memory.'

'Seventeen and unemployed, name's Jason. When Kintoul told him I was CID, the son looked worried.'

'A natural reaction in a teenager on the dole. They think we're press-ganging these days.'

'There was more to it than that.'

'How much more?'

'I don't know. Could be the usual, drugs and gangs.'

'We'll see if he's got a record. How's Moneybags?'

'Frankly, I'd rather be sewing mailbags.'

Rebus smiled. 'All part of the learning curve, Clarke,' he said, putting down the phone.

Somehow yesterday he'd forgotten to ask Pat Calder about the message on the inside of the recipe book. He didn't like to think it had been jostled from his mind by Mairie's legs or the sight of all those Elvises. Rebus had checked before leaving the station. Jason Kintoul was not on the files. Somehow the gun beneath the driver's seat helped keep Rebus's mind sharp. The drive to the Colonies didn't take long.

Pat Calder seemed quite shocked to see him.

'Morning,' said Rebus. 'Thought I'd find you at home.'

'Come in, Inspector.'

Rebus went in. The living room was much less tidy than on his previous visit, and he began to wonder which of the couple had been the tidier. Certainly, Eddie Ringan looked and acted like a slob, but you couldn't always tell.

'Sorry for the mess.'

'Well, you've got a lot on your mind just now.' The place was stuffy, with that heavy male smell you got sometimes in shared flats and locker-rooms. But usually it took more than one person to create it. Rebus began to wonder about the lean young bartender who'd accompanied Calder to the mortuary . . .

'I've just been arranging the funeral,' Pat Calder was saying. 'It's on Monday. They asked if it would be family and friends. I had to tell them Eddie didn't have any family.'

'He had good friends, though.'

Calder smiled. 'Thank you, Inspector. Thank you for that. Was there something in particular . . .?'

'It was just something we found at the scene.'

'Oh?'

'A sort of a message. It said, "I only turned on the gas".'

Calder froze. 'Christ, it *was* suicide, then?'

Rebus shrugged. 'It wasn't that kind of note. We found it on the inside of a school jotter.'

'Eddie's recipe book?'

'Yes.'

'I wondered where that had got to.'

'The message had been heavily scored out. I took it away for analysis.'

'Maybe it's something to do with the nightmares.'

'That's just what I was thinking. Depends what he was dreaming *about*, though, doesn't it? Nightmares can be about things you fear, *or* things you've done.'

'I'm no psychologist.'

'Me neither,' Rebus admitted. 'I take it Eddie had keys to the restaurant?'

'Yes.'

'We didn't find any on his body. Did you come across them when you were packing things up?'

'I don't think so. But how did he get in without keys?'

'You should be in CID, Mr Calder. That's what I've been wondering.' Rebus got up from the sofa. 'Well, sorry I had to come by.'

'Oh, that's all right. Can you tell Brian about the funeral arrangements? Warriston Cemetery at two o'clock.'

'Monday at two, I'll tell him. Oh, one last thing. You keep a record of table bookings, don't you?'

Calder seemed puzzled. 'Of course.'

'Only, I'd like to take a look. There might be some names there that don't mean anything to you but might mean something to a policeman.'

Calder nodded. 'I see what you're getting at. I'll drop it into the station. I'm going to the Heartbreak at lunchtime, I'll pick it up then.'

'Still clearing stuff away?'

'No, it's a potential buyer. One of the pizza restaurants is looking to expand . . .'

Whatever it was Pat Calder was hiding, he was doing only a fair job. But Rebus really didn't have the heart to start digging. There was way too much for him to worry about as it was. Starting with the gun. He'd sat with it in his car last night, his finger on the trigger. Just the way his instructor had taught him back in the Army: firm, but not tense. Like it was an erection, one you wanted to sustain.

He had been thinking too of goodies and baddies. If you thought bad things – dreams of cruelty and lust – that didn't make you bad. But if your head was full of civilised thoughts and you spent all day as a torturer . . . It came down to the fact that you were judged by your actions in society, not by the inside of your head. So he'd no reason to feel bad about thinking grim and bloody thoughts. Not unless he turned thoughts into deeds. Yet going beyond thought would feel so good. More than that, it would feel *right*.

He stopped his car at the first church he came to. He hadn't attended any kind of worship for several months, always managing to make excuses and promises to himself that he'd try harder. It was just that Patience had made Sunday mornings so good.

Someone had been busy with a marker-pen on the wooden signboard in the churchyard, turning 'Our Lady of Perpetual Help' into 'Our Lady of Perpetual Hell'. Not the greatest of omens, but Rebus went inside anyway. He sat in a pew for a while. There weren't many souls in there with him. He had picked up a prayer book on the way in, and stared long and hard at its unjudgmental black cover, wondering why it made him feel so guilty. Eventually, a woman left the confessional, pulling up her headscarf. Rebus stood up and made himself enter the small box. He sat there in silence for a minute, trying to think what it was you were supposed to say.

'Forgive me, father, I'm about to sin.'

'We'll see about that, son,' came a gruff Irish voice from the other side of the grille. There was such assurance in the voice, Rebus almost smiled.

Instead he said, 'I'm not even a Catholic.'

'I'm sure that's true. But you're a Christian?'

'I suppose so. I used to go to church.'

'Do you believe?'

'I can't not believe.' He didn't add how hard he'd tried.

'Then tell me your problem.'

'Someone's been threatening me, my friends and family.'

'Have you gone to the police?'

'I am the police.'

'Ah. And now you're thinking of taking the law into your own hands, as they say in the films.'

'How did you know?'

'You're not the first bobby I've had in this confessional. There are a *few* Catholics in the police force.' This time Rebus did smile. 'So what is it you're going to do?'

'I've got a gun.'

There was an intake of breath. 'Now that's serious. Oh yes, that's serious. But you must see that if you use a gun, you turn into that which you despise so much. You turn into *them*.' The priest managed to hiss this last word.

'So what?' Rebus asked.

'So, ask yourself this. Can you live the rest of your life with the memories and the guilt?' The voice paused. 'I know what you Calvinists think. You think you're doomed from the start, so why not raise some hell before you get there? But I'm talking about *this* life, not the next. Do you want to live in Purgatory *before* you die?'

'No.'

'You'd be a bloody eejit to say anything else. Tie that gun to a rock and chuck it in the Forth, that's where it belongs.'

'Thank you, father.'

'You're more than welcome. And son?'

'Yes, father?'

'Come back and talk to me again. I like to know what madness you Prods are thinking. It gives me something to chew on when there's nothing good on the telly.'

Rebus didn't spend long at Gorgie Road. They weren't getting anywhere. The photos taken so far had been developed, and some of the faces identified. Those identified were all small-timers, old cons, or up-and-comers. They weren't so much small fish as spawn in a corner of the pond. It wasn't as if Flower was having better luck, which was just as well for Rebus. He couldn't wait for the Little Weed to put in his reimbursement claim. All those rounds of drinks . . .

He felt revived by his talk with the priest, whose name he now realised he didn't even know. But then that was part of the deal, wasn't it? Sinners Anonymous. He might even grant the priest's wish and go back sometime. And tonight he'd drive out to the coast and get rid of the gun. It had been madness all along. In a sense, buying it had been enough. He'd never have used it, would he?

He parked at St Leonard's and went inside. There was a package for him at the front desk – the reservations book for the Heartbreak Cafe. Calder had put a note in with it.

'Well, Elvis ate pizza, didn't he?' So it looked like the Heartbreak was about to go Italian.

While he'd been reading the note, the desk officer had been phoning upstairs, keeping his voice low.

'What's all that about?' Rebus asked. He thought he'd overheard the distinct words 'He's here'.

'Nothing, sir,' said the desk officer. Rebus tried to stare an answer out of him, then turned away, just as the inner doors were pushed open in businesslike fashion by the Uglybug Sisters, Lauderdale and Flower.

'Can I have your car-keys?' Lauderdale demanded.

'What's going on?' Rebus looked to Flower, who resembled a preacher at a burning.

'The keys, please.' Lauderdale's hand was so steady, Rebus thought if he walked away and left the two men standing there, it would stay stretched out for hours. He handed over his keys.

'It's a pile of junk. If you don't kick it in the right place, you won't even get it to start.' He was following the two men through the doors and into the car park.

'I don't want to drive it,' Lauderdale said. He sounded threatening, but it was Flower's serene silence that most worried Rebus. Then it hit him: the gun! They knew about the gun. And yes, it was still under his driver's seat. Where else was he going to hide it – in the flat, where Michael might find it? In his trousers, where it would raise eyebrows? No, he'd left it in the car.

The door of which Lauderdale was now opening. Lauderdale turned towards him, his hand out again. 'The gun, Inspector Rebus.' And when Rebus didn't move: 'Give me the gun.'

24

He raised the gun and fired it – one, two, three shots. Then lowered it again.

They all took off their ear-protectors. The forensics man had fired the gun into what looked like a simple wooden crate. The bullets would be retrieved from its interior and could then be analysed. The scientist had been holding the gun's butt with a polythene glove over his hand. He dropped the gun into a polythene bag of its own before slipping off the glove.

'We'll let you know as soon as we can,' he told Chief Superintendent Watson, who nodded the man's dismissal. After he'd left the room, Watson turned to Lauderdale.

'Give it to me again, Frank.'

Lauderdale took a deep breath. This was the third time he'd told Watson the story, but he didn't mind. He didn't mind at all. 'Inspector Flower came to me late this morning and told me he'd received information –'

'What sort of information?'

'A phone call.'

'Anonymous, naturally.'

'Naturally.' Lauderdale took another breath. 'The caller told him the gun that had been used in the Central Hotel shooting five years ago was in Inspector Rebus's possession. Then he rang off.'

'And we're supposed to believe Rebus shot that man five years ago?'

Lauderdale didn't know. 'All I know is, there *was* a gun in Rebus's car. And he says himself, it'll have his prints all over it. Whether it's the same gun or not, we'll know by the end of play today.'

'Don't sound so fucking cheerful! We both know this is a stitch-up.'

'What we know, sir,' said Lauderdale, ignoring Watson's outburst, 'is that Inspector Rebus has been carrying on a little private investigation of his own into the Central Hotel. The files are by the side of his desk. He wouldn't tell anyone why.'

'So he found something out and now somebody's worried. That's why they've planted the –'

'With respect, sir,' Lauderdale paused, 'nobody planted anything. Rebus has admitted he bought the gun from someone he calls "a

382

stranger". He specifically *asked* this "stranger" to get a gun for him.'

'What for?'

'He says he was being threatened. Of course, he could be lying.'

'How do you mean?'

'Maybe the gun was the clue he found, the one that started him back into the Central files. Now he's spinning this story because at least then we can't accuse him of withholding evidence.'

Watson took this in. 'What do you think?'

'Without prejudice, sir –'

'Come on, Frank, we all know you hate Rebus's guts. When he saw you and Flower coming for him, he must have thought the lynch-mob had arrived.'

Lauderdale tried an easy laugh. 'Personalities aside, sir, even if we stick to the bare *facts*, Inspector Rebus is in serious trouble. Even supposing he did buy the gun, it's obviously a nasty piece of goods – it's had a file taken to it in the past.'

'He's worse than ever,' Watson mused, 'now that his girlfriend's kicked him out. I had high hopes there.'

'Sir?'

'She'd got him wearing decent clothes. Rebus was beginning to look . . . promotable.'

Lauderdale nearly swallowed his tongue.

'Stupid bugger,' Watson went on. Lauderdale decided he was talking about Rebus. 'I suppose I'd better talk to him.'

'Do you want me to . . .?'

'I want you to stay here and wait for those results. Where's Flower?'

'Back on duty, sir.'

'You mean back in the pub. I'll want to talk to him too. Funny how this anonymous Deep Throat just manages to talk to the one person in St Leonard's who loves Rebus as much as you do.'

'Loves, sir?'

'I said "loathes".'

But actually, as Rebus already knew, the call had been taken not by Flower himself but by a DC who just happened to know how Flower felt about Inspector John Rebus. He'd called Flower at the pub, and Flower had raced Jackie Stewart-style back to St Leonard's to tell Lauderdale.

Rebus knew this because he had time to kill at St Leonard's while everyone else was up at the forensic lab in Fettes. And he knew he had to be quick, because Watson would suspend him as soon as he came back. He found some carrier bags and put the Central Hotel files in them, along with the reservations book from the Heartbreak Cafe. Then he took the whole lot down to his car and threw them in the boot ... probably the first place Watson would want to look.

Christ, he'd been planning to get rid of that gun tonight.

Lauderdale had said it was 'suspected' of being the gun used in the Central Hotel murder. Well, that would be easy enough to prove or disprove. They still had the original bullet. Rebus wished he'd given the gun closer scrutiny. It had looked shiny new, but then maybe it had only ever been fired that one fatal time.

He didn't doubt that it *was* the gun. He just wondered how the hell they'd managed to set him up. The only answer was to work backwards. Deek had handed him the gun. So somehow they'd gotten to Deek. Well, Rebus himself had put word out that he was looking for Deek Torrance. And word got around. Someone had heard and been interested enough to track down Deek too. They'd asked him what his connection was with John Rebus. And when Rebus had then asked Deek for a gun, Deek had reported back to them.

Oh yes, that was it, all right. Rebus had set *himself* up by asking for the gun in the first place. Because then they'd known exactly what to do with him. Planting the gun was a bit *too* obvious, wasn't it? No one was going to be taken in. But it would have to be investigated, and investigations like that could take months, during which time he'd be suspended. They wanted him out of the way, that was all. Because he was getting close.

Rebus smiled to himself. He was no closer than Alaska ... unless he'd stumbled upon something without realising it. He needed to go over everything again, down to the last detail. But this would take time: time he was sure Watson would unwittingly be about to offer him.

So, when he walked into the Chief Superintendent's office, he surprised even Watson with his ease.

'John,' said Watson, after motioning for Rebus to sit, 'how come you always seem to have a banana skin up your sleeve?'

'Because I say the magic word, sir?' Rebus offered.

'And what is the magic word?'

Rebus looked surprised Watson didn't know. 'Abracadabra, sir.'

'John,' said Watson, 'I'm suspending you.'

'Thank you, sir,' said Rebus.

He spent that evening on the trail of Deek Torrance, even driving out to South Queensferry – the most forlorn hope of a forlorn night. Deek would have been paid plenty to get well away from the city. By now, he might not even be in the western hemisphere. Then again, maybe they'd have silenced him in some other more permanent way.

'Some pal you turned out to be,' Rebus muttered to himself more than once. And to complete the circle, he headed out to his favourite massage parlour. He always seemed to be the only customer, and had wondered how the Organ Grinder made his money. But now of course he knew: the Organ Grinder would come to your home. Always supposing you were wealthy enough ... or had reputation enough.

'How long have you been going out there?' Rebus asked. Prone on the table, he was aware that the Organ Grinder could break his neck or his back with consummate ease. But he didn't think he would. He hoped his instincts weren't wrong in this at least.

'Just a couple of months. Someone at a health club told his wife about me.'

'Know her, do you?'

'Not really. She thinks I'm too rough.'

'That's droll, coming from the wife of Big Ger Cafferty.'

'He's a villain, then?'

'Whatever gave you that idea?'

'You forget, I've not been up here that long.'

True, Rebus had forgotten the Organ Grinder's north London pedigree. When in the mood, he told wonderful stories of that city.

'Anything about him you want to tell me?' Rebus ventured, despite the thick hands on his neck.

'Nothing to tell,' said the Organ Grinder. 'Silence is a virtue, Inspector.'

'And there's too much of it around. You ever seen anyone out at his house?'

'Just his wife and the chauffeur.'

'Chauffeur? You mean the man mountain with the knob of gristle for a left ear?'

'That explains the haircut,' mused the Organ Grinder.

'Precious little else would,' said Rebus.

After the Organ Grinder had finished with him, Rebus went back to the flat. Michael was watching a late film, the glow from the TV set flicking across his rapt face. Rebus went over to the TV and switched it off. Michael still stared at the screen, not blinking. There was a cup of cold tea in his hand. Gently, Rebus took it from him.

'Mickey,' he said. 'I need someone to talk to.'

Michael blinked and looked up at him. 'You can always talk to me,' he said. 'You know that.'

'I know that,' said Rebus. 'We've got something else in common now.'

'What's that?'

Rebus sat down. 'We've both been recently suspended.'

25

Chief Superintendent Watson dreaded these Saturday mornings, when his wife would try to entice him to go shopping with her. Dreary hours in department stores and clothes shops, not to mention the supermarket, where he'd be guinea-pig for the latest microwavable Malaysian meal or some rude looking unpronounceable fruit. Worst of all, of course, he saw other men in exactly the same predicament. It was a wonder one of them didn't lose the rag and start screaming about how they used to be the hunters, fierce and proud.

But this morning he had the excuse of work. He always tried to have an excuse either for nipping into St Leonard's or else bringing work home with him. He sat in his study, listening to Radio Scotland and reading the newspaper, the house quiet and still around him. Then the telephone rang, annoying him until he remembered he was waiting for just this call. It was Ballistics at Fettes. After he took the call, he looked up a number in his card index and made another.

'I want you in my office Monday morning,' he told Rebus, 'for formal questioning.'

'From which I take it,' said Rebus, 'that I bought a lulu of a gun.'

'Lulu *and* her backing band.'

'They were called the Luvvers, sir. The bullets matched up?'

'Yes.'

'You knew they would,' said Rebus. 'And so did I.'

'It's awkward, John.'

'It's supposed to be.'

'For you as well as me.'

'With all respect, sir, I wasn't thinking of you . . .'

When Siobhan Clarke woke up that morning, she glanced at the clock then shot out of bed. Christ, it was nearly nine! She had just run water for a bath, and was looking for clean underwear in the bathroom, when it hit her. It was the weekend! Nothing to rush for. In fact, quite the opposite. The relief team had taken over Moneybags, just for this first weekend, to see if there was any sign of life at Dougary's office. According to Trading Standards, Dougary's weekends were sacrosanct. He wouldn't go anywhere near Gorgie. But they had to be sure, so for this weekend only Operation Moneybags had a relief retinue, keeping an eye on the place. If nothing happened, next weekend they wouldn't bother. Dougary was blessedly fixed in his ways. She hadn't had to hang about too often on the surveillance past five-thirty, more often a bit earlier. Which suited Siobhan fine. It meant she'd managed a couple of useful trips to Dundee out of hours.

She'd arranged another trip for this morning, but didn't need to leave Edinburgh for an hour or so yet. And she was sure to be home before the Hibees kicked off.

Time now for some coffee. The living room was messy, but she didn't mind. She usually set aside Sunday morning for all the chores. That was the nice thing about living by yourself: your mess was your own. There was no one to comment on it or be disturbed by it. Crisp bags, pizza boxes, three-quarters-empty bottles of wine, old newspapers and magazines, CD cases, items of clothing, opened and unopened mail, plates and cutlery and every mug in the flat – these could all be found in her fourteen-by-twelve living room. Somewhere under the debris there was a futon and a cordless telephone.

The telephone was ringing. She reached under a pizza carton, picked up the receiver, and yanked up the aerial.

'Is that you, Clarke?'

'Yes, sir.' The last person she'd been expecting: John Rebus. She wandered through to the bathroom.

'Terrible interference,' said Rebus.

'I was just turning off the bath.'

'Christ, you're in the –'

'No, sir, not yet. Cordless phone.'

'I hate those things. You're talking for five minutes, then you hear the toilet flushing. Well, sorry to . . . what time is it?'

'Just turned nine.'

'Really?' He sounded dead beat.

'Sir, I heard about your suspension.'

'That figures.'

'I know it's none of my business, but what were you doing with a gun in the first place?'

'Psychic protection.'

'Sorry?'

'That's what my brother calls it. He should know, he used to be a hypnotist.'

'Sir, are you all right?'

'I'm fine. Are you going to the game?'

'Not if you need me for anything else.'

'Well, I was wondering . . . do you still have the Cafferty files?'

She had walked back into the living room. Oh, she still had the files, all right. Their contents were spread across her coffee table, her desk, and half the breakfast bar.

'Yes, sir.'

'Any chance you could bring them over to my flat? Only I've got the Central Hotel files here. Somewhere in them there's a clue I'm missing.'

'You want to cross-reference with the Cafferty files? That's a big job.'

'Not if two people are working on it.'

'What time do you want me there?'

Saturday at Brian Holmes' aunt's house in Barnton was a bit like Sunday, except that on Saturday he didn't have to deny her his company at the local presbyterian kirk. Was it any wonder that, having found the Heartbreak Cafe such a welcoming spot, he should have spent so long there? But those days were over. He tried to accept the fact that 'Elvis' was dead, but it was difficult. No more King Shrimp Creole or Blue Suede Choux or In the Gateau, no more Blue Hawaii cocktails. No more late nights of tequila slammers (with Jose Cuervo Gold, naturally) or Jim Beam (Eddie's preferred bourbon).

' "Keep on the Beam," he used to say.'

'There there, pet.' Oh great, now his aunt had caught him talking to himself. She'd brought him a cup of Ovaltine.

'This stuff's for bedtime,' he told her. 'It's not even noon.'

'It'll calm you down, Brian.'

He took a sip. Ach, it didn't taste bad anyway. Pat had dropped round to ask if he'd be a pall-bearer on Monday.

'It'd be an honour,' Holmes had told him, meaning it. Pat hadn't wanted to meet his eyes. Maybe he too was thinking of the nights they'd all spent slurring after-hours gossip at the bar. On one of those nights, when they'd been talking about great Scottish disasters, Eddie had suddenly announced that he'd been there when the Central Hotel caught fire.

'I was filling in for a guy, cash in the hand and no questions. Dead on my feet after the day-shift at the Eyrie.'

'I didn't know you'd worked at the Eyrie.'

'Assistant to the head man himself. If he doesn't get a Michelin recommendation this year, he'd be as well giving up.'

'So what happened at the Central?' Holmes' head hadn't been entirely befuddled by spirits.

'Some poker game was going on, up in one of the rooms on the first floor.' He seemed to be losing it, drifting towards sleep. 'Tam and Eck were looking for players . . .'

'Tam and Eck?'

'Tam and Eck Robertson . . .'

'But what happened?'

'It's no good, Brian,' said Pat Calder, 'look at him.'

Though Eddie's eyes were open, head resting on his arms, arms spread across the bar, he was asleep.

'A cousin of mine was at Ibrox the day of the big crush,' Pat revealed, cleaning a pint glass.

'But do you remember where you were the night Jock Stein died?' Holmes asked. More stories had followed, Eddie sleeping through all of them.

Permanently asleep now. And Holmes was to be pall-bearer number four. He'd asked Pat a few questions.

'Funny,' Pat had said, 'your man Rebus asked me just the same.'

So Brian knew the case was in good hands.

Rebus drove around the lunchtime streets. On a Saturday, providing you steered clear of Princes Street, the city had a more relaxed feel. At least until about two-thirty, when either the east end or the west of the city (depending who was playing home) would fill with football fans. And on derby match days, best stay away from the centre altogether. But today wasn't a derby match, and Hibs were at home, so the town was quiet.

'You asked about him just the other week,' a barman told Rebus.

'And I'm asking again.'

He was again on the lookout for Deek Torrance; a seek and destroy mission. He doubted Deek would be around, but sometimes money and alcohol did terrible things to a man, boosting his confidence, making him unwary of danger and vengeance. Rebus's hope was that Deek was still mingin' somewhere on the money he'd paid for the gun. As hopes went, it was more forlorn than most. But he did stumble upon Chick Muir in a Leith social club, and was able to tell him the news.

'That's just awfy,' Chick consoled. 'I'll keep my nose to the ground.'

Rebus appreciated the muddled sentiment. In Chick's case, it wouldn't be hard anyway. Informers were sometimes called snitches, and Chick's snitch was about as big as they came.

One-thirty found him leaving a dingy betting shop. He'd seen more hope and smiles in a hospice, and fewer tears too. Ten minutes later he was sitting down to microwaved haggis, neeps and tatties in the Sutherland Bar. Someone had left a newspaper on his chair, and he started to read it. By luck, it was open at a piece by Mairie Henderson.

'You're late,' he said as Mairie herself sat down. She nearly stood up again in anger.

'I was in here half an hour ago! Quarter past one, we arranged. I stayed till half past.'

'I thought half past was the agreement,' he said blithely.

'You weren't *here* at half past. You're lucky I came back.'

'Why did you?'

She tore the newspaper from him. 'I left my paper.'

'Not much in it anyway.' He scooped more haggis into his mouth.

'I thought you were buying me lunch.'

Rebus nodded towards the food counter. 'Help yourself. They'll add it to my tab.'

It took her a moment to decide that she was hungrier than she was angry. She came back from the food counter with a plate of quiche and bean salad, and grabbed her purse. 'They don't *have* tabs here!' she informed him. Rebus winked.

'Just my little joke.' He tried to hand her some money, but she turned on her heels. Low heels, funny little shoes like children's Doc Marten's. And black tights. Rebus rolled the food around with his tongue. She sat down at last and took off her coat. It took her a moment to get comfortable.

'Anything to drink?' asked Rebus.

'I suppose it's my round?' she snapped.

He shook his head, so she asked for a gin and fresh orange. Rebus got the drinks, a half of Guinness for himself. There was probably more nutrition in the Guinness than in the meal he'd just consumed.

'So,' said Mairie, 'what's the big secret?'

Rebus used his little finger to draw his initials on the thick head of his drink, knowing they'd still be there when he reached the bottom. 'I've been shown the red card.'

That made her look up. 'What? Suspended?' She wasn't angry with him any more. She was a reporter, sniffing a story. He nodded. 'What happened?' Excitedly she forked up a mouthful of kidney bean and chickpea. Rebus had had a crash-course in pulses from his tenants. Never mind red kids and chicks, he could tell a borlotti from a pinto at fifty yards downwind.

'I came into possession of a handgun, a Colt 45. May or may not have been a copy.'

'And?' She nearly spattered him with pastry in her haste.

'And it was the gun used in the Central Hotel shooting.'

'No!' Her screech caused several drinkers to pause before their next swallow. The Sutherland was that kind of place. Riots in the streets would have merited a single measured comment. Rebus could see Mairie's head fairly filling to the brim with questions.

'Do you still write for the Sunday edition?' he asked her. She nodded, still busy trying to find an order for all the questions she had. 'What about doing me a favour, then? I've always wanted to be on the front page ...'

Not that he'd any intention of seeing his *own* name in the story. They went through it carefully together, back at the newspaper office. So Rebus got his tour of the building at last. It was a bit disappointing, all stairwell and open-plan and not much action. What action there was centred exclusively on Mairie's desk and its up-to-date word processor.

There was even a discussion with the editor of the Sunday. They needed to be sure of a few things. It was always like this with unattributed stories. In Scots law, there was no place for uncorroborated evidence. The press seemed to be following suit. But Rebus had a staunch defender in the woman whose byline would appear with the story. After a conference call with the paper's well-remunerated lawyer, the nod was given and Mairie started to hammer the keyboard into submission.

'I can't promise front page,' the editor warned. 'Beware the breaking story! As it is, you've just knocked a car crash and its three victims to the inside.'

Rebus stayed to watch the whole process. A series of commands on Mairie's computer sent the text to typesetting, which was done elsewhere in the building. Soon a laser printer was delivering a rough copy of how the front page might look tomorrow morning. And there along the bottom was the headline: GUN RECOVERED IN FIVE-YEAR-OLD MURDER MYSTERY.

'That'll change,' said Mairie. 'The sub will have a go at it once he's read the story.'

'Why?'

'Well, for one thing, it looks like the murder victim is a five-year-old.'

So it did. Rebus hadn't noticed. Mairie was staring at him.

'Isn't this going to get you in even *more* trouble?'

'Who's going to know it was me gave you the story?'

She smiled. 'Well, let's start with everyone in the City of Edinburgh Police.'

Rebus smiled too. He'd bought some caffeine pills this morning to keep him moving. They were working fine. 'If anyone asks,' he said, 'I'll just have to tell them the truth.'

'Which is what exactly?'

'That it wisnae me.'

26

Rebus dished out yet more money to the students that afternoon to get them out of the flat until midnight. He wondered if it were unique in Scottish social history for a landlord to be paying his own tenants. There were only two of them there, the other two (he'd now established that he had four permanent tenants, whose names he still had trouble with so never tried using) having headed home for purposes of cosseting and feeding-up.

Michael, however, stayed put. Rebus knew he wouldn't be any bother. He'd either be dozing in the box room or else watching the TV. He didn't seem to mind if the sound were turned off, just so long as there was a picture to stare at.

Rebus bought a bag of provisions: real coffee, milk, beer, soft drinks, and snacks. Back in the flat he remembered Siobhan was a vegetarian, and cursed himself for buying smoky bacon crisps. Bound to be artificial flavourings though, so maybe it didn't matter. She arrived at five-thirty.

'Come in, come in.' Rebus led her through the long dark hallway to the living room. 'This is my brother Michael.'

'Hello, Michael.'

'Mickey, this is DC Siobhan Clarke.' Michael nodded his head, blinking slowly. 'Here, let me take your jacket. How was the game, by the way?'

'Goalless.' Siobhan put down her two carrier-bags and slipped off her black leather jacket. Rebus took the jacket into the hall and hung it up. When he came back, he noticed her studying the living room doubtfully.

'Bit of a tip,' he said, though he'd spent quarter of an hour tidying it.

'Big, though.' She didn't deny it was a tip. You could hardly see out of the huge sash window. And the carpet looked like it had moulted from a buffalo's back. As for the wallpaper . . . she could well understand why the students had tried covering every inch with kd lang and Jesus & Mary Chain posters.

'Something to drink?'

She shook her head. 'Let's get on with it.' This wasn't quite what she'd imagined. The zombie brother didn't help, of course. But he wasn't much of a distraction either. They got down to work.

An hour later, they had scraped the surface of the files. Siobhan was lying on her side on the floor, legs curled up, one arm supporting her head. She was on her second can of cola. The file was on the floor in front of her. Rebus sat near her on the sofa, files on his lap and in a heap beside him. He had a pen behind his ear, just like a butcher or a turf accountant. Siobhan held her pen in her mouth, tapping it against her teeth when she was thinking. Some bad quiz show was playing to silent hysterics on the TV. For all the reaction on his face, Michael could have been watching a war trial.

He pulled himself out of the chair. 'I'm going to take forty winks,' he informed them. Siobhan tried not to look surprised when he made not for the living-room door but for the box room. He closed the door behind him.

'I'd like two things,' said Rebus. 'To identify the murder victim, once and for all.'

'And to identify the killer?' Siobhan guessed.

But Rebus shook his head. 'To place Big Ger at the scene.'

'There's no evidence he was anywhere near.'

'And maybe there never will be. But all the same ... We still don't know who was at the poker game. It can't just have been the Bru-Head Brothers.'

'We could talk to all the hotel's customers that night.'

'Yes, we could.' Rebus didn't sound enthusiastic.

'Or we could find the brothers – always supposing they're still alive – and ask them.'

'Their cousin might know where they are.'

'Who? Radiator McCallum?'

Rebus nodded. 'But then we don't know where he is either. Eddie Ringan was there, but he was never on the official list. Black Aengus wasn't on the list, and neither were the Bru-Head Brothers. I'm surprised we got any names at all.'

'We *are* talking about a long time ago.' Siobhan sounded more relaxed with Michael out of the room.

'We're also talking about long memories. Maybe I should have another go at Black Aengus.'

'Not if you know what's good for you.' Siobhan could have said something about Dundee, but she wanted it to be confirmed first, and she wanted it to be a surprise. She'd know by Monday.

The phone rang. Rebus picked it up.

'John? It's Patience.'

'Oh, hello there.'

'Hello yourself. I thought maybe we'd fix up that date.'

'Oh, right. For a drink?'

'Don't tell me you've forgotten? No, I know what it is: you're just playing hard to get. Don't push it *too* far, Rebus.'

'No, it's not that, I'm just a bit busy right this minute.' Siobhan seemed to take a hint, and got up, motioning that she'd make some coffee in the kitchen. Rebus nodded.

'Well, I'm sorry to interrupt whatever it is you're –'

'Don't take it the wrong way, Patience. I've just got things on my mind.'

'And I'm not included?'

Rebus made an exasperated sound. From the kitchen there came the louder sound of a sneeze. Aye, those Easter Road terraces could be snell.

'John,' said Patience, 'is there a woman in the flat?'

'Yes,' he said.

'One of the students?'

He seldom lied to her. 'No, a colleague. We're working through some case-notes.'

'I see.'

Christ, he should have tried lying. His head was too full of the Central Hotel to be able to cope with Patience's jousting. 'Look,' he said, 'have you got a time and place in mind for that drink?'

But Patience had rung off. Rebus stared at the receiver, shrugged, and placed it on the carpet. He didn't want any more interruptions.

'Coffee's on,' said Siobhan.

'Great.'

'Was it something I said?'

'What? No, no, just ... nothing.'

But Siobhan was canny. 'She heard me sneeze and thought you had another woman here.'

'I *do* have another woman here. It's just the way her mind works ... She doesn't exactly trust me.'

'And she should trust you?'

Rebus sighed. 'Tell me about the Robertson brothers again.'

Siobhan sat down on the floor and started to read from the file. From the sofa, Rebus looked down on her. The top of her head, the nape of her neck with its fine pale hairs disappearing into her collar. Small pierced ears ...

'We know they get on well. It was a close family, six kids in a one-bedroom cottage.'

'What happened to the other brothers and sisters?'

'Four sisters,' Siobhan read. 'Law-abiding wives and mothers these days. The boys were the only wild ones. Both like gambling, especially cards and the horses. Tam is the better card player of the two, but Eck has more luck on the horses ... Remember this stuff is six years old, and all hearsay in the first place.'

Rebus nodded. He was remembering the old man in that last pub in Lochgelly, the one who'd come cadging drinks from the painters and decorators. He'd said one of the drawings looked familiar. Then one of the painters had cut him short with a story about how he'd recognise a horse easier than a man. So the old guy was keen on the gee-gees, and so were Eck and Tam.

'Maybe he saw him in a bookie's,' Rebus wondered aloud.

'Sorry?'

So Rebus told her.

'It's worth a try,' she conceded. 'What else do we have to go on?'

Rebus had one good contact at Dunfermline CID, Detective Sergeant Hendry. It was rumoured that Hendry was too good at his job ever to merit promotion. Only the incompetent were promoted. It shuffled them out of the way. As a DI, Rebus didn't necessarily agree. But he knew Hendry should have been an Inspector long ago, and wondered what or who was blocking him. It couldn't be that Hendry was too abrasive: he was one of the calmest people Rebus had ever met. His hobby, bird-watching, reflected his nature. They'd exchanged home phone numbers once on a case. Yes, it was worth a try.

'Hello there, Hendry,' he said. 'It's Rebus here.'

'Rebus, trust you to disturb a working man's rest.'

'Been bird-watching?'

'I saw a spotted woodpecker this morning.'

'I saw a spotted dick once.'

'Ah, but I'm not a man of the world like you. So what do you want?'

'I want you to look in your local phone directory. I'm after bookie's shops.'

'Any one in particular?'

'No, I'm not picky. I need the names and addresses of all of them.'

'Which towns?'

Rebus thought. 'Dunfermline, Cowdenbeath, Lochgelly, Cardenden, Kelty, Ballingry. That'll do for starters.'

'This could take a bit of time. Can I phone you back?'

'Aye, sure. And ponder on two names for me. Tom and Eck Robertson. They're brothers.'

'Okay. You're at Arden Street, I hear.'

'What?'

'You got the heave from the doctor. What was it, your bedside manner?'

'Who told you?'

'Word gets around. Isn't it true then?'

'No, it's not. It's just that my brother's here for a ... ach, forget it.'

'Talk to you later.'

Rebus put down the phone. 'Would you credit that? Every bugger seems to know about Patience and me. Was there a notice in the papers, or something?'

Siobhan smiled. 'What now?'

'Hendry's going to get back with the details. Meantime, we could nip out and get a curry or something.'

'What if he phones while we're out?'

'He'll try again.'

'Haven't you got an answering machine?'

'I could never get it to work, so I chucked it out. Besides, there are that many bookie's shops in Fife, Hendry'd be on it for hours.'

They walked to Tollcross, Siobhan insistent that she could do with some fresh air.

'I thought you'd have had enough of that at the game.'

'Are you joking? *Fresh air?* Between the smoking and the smells of dead beer and pie-grease ...'

'You're putting me off my curry.'

'I bet you're the vindaloo type too.'

'Strictly Madras,' said Rebus.

During the meal, he reasoned that Siobhan might as well toddle off home afterwards. It wasn't as if they could do anything tonight with the list of betting shops. And tomorrow the shops would be closed. But Siobhan wanted to stick around at least until Hendry phoned.

'We haven't covered all the files yet,' she argued.

'True enough,' said Rebus. After the meal, while Siobhan drank a cup of coffee Rebus ordered some takeaway for Michael.

'Is he all right?' Siobhan asked.

'He's getting better,' Rebus insisted. 'Those pills are nearly finished. He'll be fine once he's shot of them.'

As if to prove the point, when they got back to the flat Michael was in the kitchen, dunking a teabag in a mug of hot milky water. He looked like he'd just had a shower. He'd also shaved.

'I fetched you a curry,' Rebus said.

'You must be a mind reader.' Michael sniffed into the brown paper bag. 'Rogan Josh?' Rebus nodded and turned to Siobhan. 'Michael is the city's Rogan Josh expert.'

'There was a call while you were out.' Michael lifted the cardboard containers out of the bag.

'Hendry?'

'That was the name.'

'Did he leave a message?'

Michael unpeeled both cartons, meat and rice. 'He said you should get a pen and a lot of paper ready.'

Rebus smiled at Siobhan. 'Come on,' he said, 'let's save Hendry's phone bill.'

'I'm glad you phoned back,' were Hendry's first words. 'For one thing,

I'm due at an indoor bowls tourney in half an hour. For another, this is a big list.'

'So let's have it,' said Rebus.

'I could fax it to you at the station?'

'No you couldn't, I'm out of the game.'

'I hadn't heard.'

'Funny, that; you hear about my love life fast enough. Ready when you are.'

As Hendry reeled off the names, addresses and phone numbers, Rebus relayed them to Siobhan. She claimed to be a fast writer, so was given the job of transcribing. But after ten minutes they switched over, her hand being sore. The final list covered three sides of A4. As well as the basic information, Hendry dropped in snippets of his own, such as licensing wrangles, suspected handling of stolen goods, hangouts for ne'er-do-wells and the like. Rebus was grateful for all of it.

'A fine institution, the bookie's,' he commented, when Siobhan handed him the receiver.

'You bet,' said Hendry. 'Can I go now?'

'Sure, and thanks for everything.'

'So long as it helps you get back in the game. We need all the fly-halfs we can get. Those two names didn't click with me, by the way. And Rebus?'

'What?'

'She sounds a right wee smasher.'

Hendry severed the connection before Rebus could explain. When it came to gossip, Hendry was a regular sweetie-wife. Rebus dreaded to think what stories he'd be hearing about himself in the next week or two.

'What was he saying?' Siobhan asked.

'Nothing.'

She'd been running through the list for herself. 'Well,' she said, 'no names there that mean anything to me.' Rebus took the list from her.

'Me neither.'

'Next stop Fife?'

'For me, yes. On Monday, I suppose.' Except that on Monday he'd to report to Chief Superintendent Watson *and* attend Eddie Ringan's funeral. 'You,' he said, 'are going to be busy shoring up our side of Operation Moneybags.'

'Oh, I thought I might go to the funeral. That'd give us the excuse for a couple of hours' work in Fife.'

Rebus shook his head. 'I appreciate the thought, but *you're* still on the force. I'm the one with time for this sort of legwork.' She looked bitterly disappointed. 'And that's an order,' Rebus told her.

'Yes, sir,' said Siobhan.

27

The thought of another interminable Sunday bothered Rebus so much that, after attending Mass, he drove across the Forth Road Bridge back into Fife.

He'd been to Our Lady of Perpetual Hell, sitting at the back, watching and wondering if the priest who led the worship was *his* priest. The accent was Scots-Irish; hard to tell. His priest had spoken quietly, while this one belted everything out at the top of his voice. Maybe some of the congregation were deaf. But at least there were a fair number of young folk in attendance. He was almost alone in not accepting communion.

West-central Fife could use a spot of communion itself. It would drink the wine and pawn the chalice. He decided to leave Dunfermline till last; it was the biggest town with the most locations. He'd start small. He couldn't recall whether it was quicker to get to Ballingry by coming off the motorway at Kinross, but certainly it was a much bonnier drive. He was tempted to stop at Loch Leven, site of many a childhood picnic and game of football. He still had a lump below his knee where Michael had kicked him once. The narrow, meandering roads were busy with Sunday drivers, their cars polished like medals. There was half a chance Hendry would be at the Loch Leven bird sanctuary, but Rebus didn't stop. Soon enough he was in the glummer confines of Ballingry. He didn't loiter longer than he needed to.

He wasn't sure what this trip was supposed to accomplish. All the betting shops would be tight shut. Maybe he'd find someone he could gossip with about this or that bookie's, but he doubted it. He knew what he was doing. He was killing time, and this was a good place for it. At least here there was the illusion that he was doing something constructive about the case. So he parked outside the closed shop and constructively marked a tick against the address on his three-page list.

Of course, there *was* one more reason for his early rise this morning and his early exit from the house. In the car with him he had the Sunday paper. The Central Hotel story had stuck tenaciously to the front page, now with the headline CENTRAL MURDER BLAZE: GUN FOUND. Once Watson and co. saw it, they'd be on the phone to each other and, naturally, to John Rebus. But for once the students would have to field *his* calls. He'd read the story through twice to himself, knowing every word by heart. He was hoping that somewhere *some*body was reading it and starting to panic . . .

Next stops: Lochore, Lochgelly, Cardenden. Rebus had been born and raised in Cardenden. Well, Bowhill actually, back when there had been four parishes: Auchterderran, Bowhill, Cardenden, and Dundonald. The ABCD, people called it. Then the post office had termed it all the one town, Cardenden. It wasn't so very much changed from the place Rebus had known. He stopped the car at the cemetery and spent a few minutes by the grave of his father and mother. A woman in her forties placed some flowers against a headstone nearby and smiled at Rebus as she passed him. When Rebus got back to the cemetery gates, she was waiting there.

'Johnny Rebus?'

It was so unexpected he grinned, the grin dissolving years from his face.

'I went to school with you,' the woman stated. 'Heather Cranston.'

'Heather . . .?' He stared at her face. '*Cranny?*'

She put a hand to her mouth, blocking laughter. 'Nobody's called me that in twenty-odd years.'

He remembered her now. The way she always stifled laughs with her hand, embarrassed because her laugh sounded so funny to her. Now she nodded into the cemetery.

'I walk past your mum and dad most weeks.'

'It's more than I do.'

'Aye, but you're in Edinburgh or someplace now, aren't you?'

'That's right.'

'Just visiting?'

'Passing through.' They had come out of the cemetery now, and were walking downhill into Bowhill. They passed by Rebus's car, but he'd no wish to break off the conversation. So they walked.

'Aye,' she said, 'plenty of folk pass through. Never many stay put. I used to ken everybody in the place, but not now . . .'

A yistiken awb-di. Listening to her, Rebus realised how much of the accent and the dialect he'd lost over the years.

'Come round for a cup of tea,' she was saying now. He'd looked in vain for an engagement or wedding ring on her hand. She was by no means an unlovely woman. Big, whereas at school she'd been tiny and shy. Or maybe Rebus wasn't remembering right. Her cheeks were shining and there was mascara round her eyes. She was wearing black shoes with inch and a half heels, and tea-coloured tights on muscular legs. Rebus, who hadn't had breakfast or lunch, would bet that she had a pantry full of cakes and biscuits.

'Aye, why not?' he said.

She lived in a house along Craigside Road. They'd passed one betting shop on the way from the cemetery. It was as dead as the rest of the street.

'Are you going to take a look at the old house?' She meant the house he'd grown up in. He shrugged and watched her unlock her door. In the lobby, she listened for a second then yelled, 'Shug! Are you up there?' But there was no sound from upstairs. 'It's a miracle,' she said. 'Out of his bed before four o'clock. He must've gone out somewhere.' She saw the look on Rebus's face, and her hand went to her mouth. 'Don't worry, it's not a husband or boyfriend or anything. Hugh's my son.'

'Oh?'

She took off her coat. 'Away through you go.' She opened the living room door for him. It was a small room, choked with a huge three-piece suite, dining-table and chairs, wall-unit and TV. She'd had the chimney blocked off and central heating installed.

Rebus sank into one of the fireside chairs. 'But you're not married?'

She had slung her coat over the banister. 'Never really saw the point,' she said, entering the room. She devoured space as she moved, first to the radiator to check it was warm, then to the mantelpiece for cigarettes and her lighter. She offered one to Rebus.

'I've stopped,' he said. 'Doctor's orders.' Which was, in a sense, the truth.

'I tried stopping once or twice, but the weight I put on, you wouldn't credit it.' She inhaled deeply.

'So, Hugh's father . . .?'

She blew the smoke out of her nostrils. 'Never knew him, really.' She saw the look on Rebus's face. 'Have I shocked you, Johnny?'

'Just a bit, Cranny. You used to be . . . well . . .'

'Quiet? That was a lifetime ago. What do you fancy, coffee, tea or me?' And she laughed behind her cigarette hand.

'Coffee's fine,' said John Rebus, shifting in his chair.

She brought in two mugs of bitter instant. 'No biscuits, sorry, I'm all out.' She handed him his mug. 'I've already sugared it, hope that's all right.'

'Fine,' said Rebus, who did not take sugar. The mug was a souvenir of Blackpool. They talked about people they'd known at school. Sitting opposite him, she decided at one point to cross one leg over the other. But her skirt was too tight, so she gave up and tugged at the hem of the garment.

'So what brings you here? Passing through, you said?'

'Well, sort of. I'm actually looking for a bookie's shop.'

'We passed one on the –'

'This is a particular business. It's probably either new in the past five or so years, or else has been taken over by a new operator during that time.'

'Then you're after Hutchy's.' She said this nonchalantly, sucking on her cigarette afterwards.

'Hutchy's? But that place was around when *we* were growing up.'

She nodded. 'Named after Joe Hutchinson, he started it. Then he died and his son Howie took over. Tried changing the name of the place, but everybody kept calling it Hutchy's, so he gave up. About, oh, five years ago, maybe a bit less, he sold up and buggered off to Spain. Imagine, same age as us and he's made his pile. Retired to the sun. Nearest we get to the sun here is when the toaster's on.'

'So who did he sell the business to?'

She had to think about this. 'Greenwood, I think his name is. But the place is still called Hutchy's. That's what the sign says above the door. Aye, Tommy Greenwood.'

'Tommy? You're sure of that. Not Tom or Tam?'

She shook her permed head. She'd had a salt-and-pepper dye done quite recently. Rebus supposed it was to hide some authentic grey. The style itself could only be termed Bouffant Junior. It took Rebus back in time . . .

'Tommy Greenwood,' she said. 'Friend of mine used to go out with him.'

'Had he been around Cardenden for long before he bought Hutchy's?'

'No time at all. We didn't know him from Adam. Then in short order he'd bought Hutchy's *and* the old doctor's house down near the river. The story goes, he paid Howie from a suitcase stacked with cash. The story goes, he *still* doesn't have a bank account.'

'So where did the money come from?'

'Aye, now you're asking a good question.' She nodded her head slowly. 'A few folk would like to know the answer to *that* one.'

He asked a few more questions about Greenwood, but there wasn't more she could tell. He kept himself to himself, walked between his house and the bookie's every day. Didn't own a flash car. No wife, no kids. Didn't do much in the way of socialising or drinking.

'He'd be quite a catch for some woman,' she said, in tones that let Rebus know she'd tried with the rod and line. 'Oh aye, quite a catch.'

Rebus escaped twenty minutes later, but not without an exchange of addresses and phone numbers and promises to keep in touch. He walked back slowly past Hutchy's – an uninspiring little double-front with peeling paint and smoky windows – and then briskly up the brae to the cemetery. At the cemetery, he saw that another car had been parked tight in behind his. A cherry-red Renault 5. He passed his own car and tapped on the window of the Renault. Siobhan Clarke put down her newspaper and wound open the window.

'What the hell are you doing here?' Rebus demanded.

'Following a hunch.'

'I don't have a hunch.'

'Took me a while. Did you start with Ballingry?' He nodded. 'That's what threw me. I came off the motorway at Kelty.'

'Listen,' Rebus said, 'I've found a contender.'

She didn't seem interested. 'Have you seen this morning's paper?'

'Oh that, I meant to tell you about it.'

'No, not the front page, the inside.'

'Inside?'

She tapped a headline and handed the paper through the window to him. THREE INJURED IN M8 SMASH. The story told how on Saturday morning a BMW left the motorway heading towards Glasgow and ended up in a field. The family in the car had all been hospitalised – wife, teenage son, and 'Edinburgh businessman David Dougary, 41'.

'Christ,' gasped Rebus, 'I knocked that off the front page.'

'Pity you didn't read it at the time. What'll happen now?'

Rebus read the story through again. 'I don't know. It'll depend. If they shut down or transfer the Gorgie operation, either we shut down or we follow it.'

' "We"? You're suspended, remember.'

'Or else Cafferty brings someone else in to take over while Dougary's on the mend.'

'It would be short notice.'

'Which means he'll hand pick someone.'

'Or fill in for Dougary himself?'

'I doubt it,' said Rebus, 'but wouldn't it be just magic if he did? The only way of knowing is to keep the surveillance going till *something* happens one way or the other.'

'And meantime?'

'Meantime, we've got a ton more bookie's shops to check.' Rebus turned and gave Bowhill a smiling glance. 'But something tells me we've already had a yankee come up.'

'What's a yankee?' Siobhan asked, as Rebus unlocked and got into his car.

When they stopped for a bite to eat and some tea in Dunfermline, Rebus told her the story of Hutchy's and the man with the case full of cash. Her face twitched a little, as though her tea were too hot or the egg mayonnaise sandwich too strong.

'What was that name again?' she asked.

'Tommy Greenwood.'

'But he's in the Cafferty file.'

'What?' It was Rebus's turn to twitch.

'Tommy Greenwood, I'm sure it is. He's ... he *was* one of Cafferty's associates years ago. Then he disappeared from the scene, like so many others. They'd quarrelled about equal shares, or something.'

'Sounds like a boulder round the balls and the old heave-ho off a bridge.'

'As you say, it's a mobile profession.'

'Glub, glub, glub, all the way to the bottom.'

Siobhan smiled. 'So is it the real Tommy Greenwood or not?'

Rebus shrugged. 'If the bugger's had plastic surgery, it could be hard to tell. All the same, there are ways.' He was nodding to himself. 'Oh yes, there are ways.'

Ways which started with a friendly taxman . . .

More than one person that Sunday read the story on the front page of their morning paper with a mixture of anguish, fear, guilt, and fury. Telephone calls were made. Words were exchanged like bullets. But being Sunday, there wasn't much anyone could do about the situation except, if they were of a mind, pray. If the off-licences had been open, or the supermarkets and grocer's shops allowed to sell alcohol, they might have drowned their sorrows or assuaged their anger. As it was, the anger just built, and so did the anguish. Block by block, the structure neared completion. A roof, that was all it lacked. Something to keep the pressure in, or nature's forces out.

And it was all because of John Rebus. This was more or less agreed. John Rebus was out there with a battering ram, and more than one person was of a mind to unlock the door and let him in – let him into *their* lair. And then lock the door after him.

28

The meeting in Farmer Watson's office had been arranged for nine in the morning. Presumably, they wanted Rebus at his groggiest and most supine. He might growl loudly in the morning, but he didn't normally start biting till afternoon. That everyone from Watson to the canteen staff knew he was being fitted up didn't make things any less awkward. For a start, the investigation into the Central Hotel murder wasn't official, and Watson still wasn't keen to sanction it. So Rebus had been working rogue anyway. Give the Farmer his due, he looked after his team. They managed between them to concoct a story whereby Rebus had been given permission to do some digging into the files on his own time.

'With a view towards the case perhaps being reopened at a later date as fresh evidence allowed,' said the Farmer. His secretary, a smart woman with a scary taste in hair colourants, copied down these closing words. 'And date it a couple of weeks ago.'

'Yes, sir,' she said.

When she'd left the room, Rebus said, 'Thank you, sir.' He'd been standing throughout the proceedings, there being space for just the one chair, the one the secretary had been seated on. He now stepped gingerly over piles of files and placed his bum where hers had latterly been.

'I'm covering *my* hide as well as yours, John. And not a word to anyone, understand?'

'Yes, sir. What about Inspector Flower, won't he suspect? He's bound to complain to Chief Inspector Lauderdale at least.'

'Good. Him and Lauderdale can have a chinwag. There's something you've got to understand, John.' Watson clasped his hands together on the desk, his head sinking into huge rounded shoulders. He spoke softly. 'I *know* Lauderdale's after my job. I know I can trust him as far as I'd trust an Irish scoor-oot.' He paused. 'Do *you* want my job, Inspector?'

'No fear.'

Watson nodded. 'That's what I mean. Now, I know you're not going to be sitting on your hands for the next week or two, so take some advice. The law can't be tinkered with the way you tinker with an old car. *Think* before you do anything. And remember, stunts like buying a gun can get you thrown off the force.'

'But I didn't buy it, sir,' said Rebus, reciting the story they'd thought up, 'it came into my possession as a potential piece of evidence.'

Watson nodded. 'Quite a mouthful, eh? But it might just save your bacon.'

'I'm vegetarian, sir,' Rebus said. A statement which caused Watson to laugh very loudly indeed.

They were both more than a little interested in what was happening in Gorgie. The initial news had not seemed promising. Nobody had turned up at the office, nobody at all. An extra detail was now keeping a watch on the hospital where Dougary lay in traction. If nothing happened at the Gorgie end, they'd switch to the hospital until Dougary was up and about. Maybe he'd keep working from his bedside. Stranger things had happened.

But at eleven-thirty, a brightly polished Jag pulled into the taxi lot. The chauffeur, a huge man with long straight hair, got out, and when he opened the back door, out stepped Morris Gerald Cafferty.

'Got you, you bastard,' hissed DS Petrie, firing off a whole roll of film in the excitement. Siobhan was already telephoning St Leonard's. And after talking with CI Lauderdale, as instructed (though *not* by Lauderdale) she phoned Arden Street. Rebus picked up the phone on its second ring.

'Bingo,' she said. 'Cafferty's come calling.'

'Make sure the photographs are dated and timed.'

'Yes, sir. How did the meeting go?'

'I think the Farmer's in love with me.'

'They're both going in,' said Petrie, at last lifting his finger from the shutter release. The camera motor stopped. Madden, who had come over to the window to watch, asked who they were.

At the same time, Rebus was asking a similar question. 'Who's with Big Ger?'

'His driver.'

'Man mountain with long hair?'

'That's him.'

'That's also the guy who got his ear eaten by Davey Dougary.'

'No love lost there, then?'

'Except now the man mountain's working for Big Ger.' He thought for a moment. 'Knowing Big Ger, I'd say he put him on the payroll just to piss off Dougary.'

'Why would he do that?'

'His idea of a joke. Let me know when they come out again.'

'Will do.'

She phoned him back half an hour later. 'Cafferty's taken off again.'

'He didn't stay long.'

'But listen, the chauffeur stayed put.'

'What?'

'Cafferty drove off alone.'

'Well, I'll be buggered. He's putting the man mountain in charge of Dougary's accounts!'

'He must trust him.'

'I suppose he must. But I can't see the big chap having much experience running a book. He's strictly a guard dog.'

'Meaning?'

'Meaning Big Ger will have to nurse him along. Meaning Big Ger will be down at that office practically every day. It couldn't be better!'

'We'd better get in some more film, then.'

'Aye, don't let that stupid bugger Petrie run out again. How's his face by the way?'

'Itchy, but it hurts when he scratches.' Petrie glanced over, so she told him, 'Inspector Rebus was just asking after you.'

'Was I buggery,' said Rebus. 'I hope his nose drops off and falls in his thermos.'

'I'll pass your good wishes on, sir,' said Siobhan.

'Do that,' replied Rebus. 'And don't be shy about it either. Right, I'm off to a funeral.'

'I was talking to Brian, he said he's a pall-bearer.'

'Good,' said Rebus. 'That means I'll have a shoulder to cry on.'

Warriston Cemetery is a sprawling mix of graves, from the ancient (and sometimes desecrated) to the brand new. There are stones there whose messages have been eroded away to faint indents only. On a sunny day, it can be an educational walk, but at nights the local Hell's Angels chapter have been known to party hard, recreating scenes more like New Orleans voodoo than Scottish country dancing.

Rebus felt Eddie would have approved. The ceremony itself was simple and dignified, if you ignored the wreath in the shape of an electric guitar and the fact that he was to be buried with an Elvis LP cover inside the casket.

Rebus stood at a distance from proceedings, and had turned down an invitation by Pat Calder to attend the reception afterwards, which was to be held not in the hollow Heartbreak Cafe but in the upstairs room of a nearby hostelry. Rebus was tempted for a moment – the chosen pub served Gibson's – but shook his head the way he'd shaken Calder's hand: with regrets.

Poor Eddie. For all that Rebus hadn't really known him, for all that the chef had tried scalping him with a panful of appetisers, Rebus had liked the man. He saw them all the time, people who could have made so much of their lives, yet hadn't. He knew he belonged with them. The losers.

But at least I'm still alive, he thought. And God willing nobody will dispatch me by funneling alcohol down my throat before turning on the gas. It struck him again: why the need for the funnel? All you had to do was take Eddie to any bar and he'd willingly render himself unconscious on tequila and bourbon. You didn't *need* to force him. Yet Dr Curt had tossed his liver in the air and proclaimed it a fair specimen. That was difficult to accept, except that he'd seen it with his own eyes.

Or had he?

He peered across the distance to where Pat Calder was taking hold of rope number one, testing it for tensile strength. Brian was number four, which meant he stood across the casket from Calder and sandwiched between two men Rebus didn't know. The barman Toni was number six. But Rebus's eyes were on Calder. Oh Jesus, you bastard, he thought. You didn't, did you? Then again, maybe you did.

He turned and ran, back to where his car was parked out on the road outside the cemetery. His destination was Arden Street.

Arden Street and the reservations book for the Heartbreak Cafe.

As he saw it, Rebus had two choices. He could kick the door down, or he could try to open it quietly. It was a snib lock, the kind a stiff piece of plastic could sometimes open. Of course, there was a mortice deadlock too, but probably not engaged. When he pushed and pulled the door, there was enough give in it to suggest this was probably true. Only the snib then. But the gap where door met jamb was covered by a long strip of ornamental wood. This normally wouldn't deter a burglar, who would take a crowbar to it until he had access to the gap.

But Rebus had forgotten to pack his crowbar.

A rap with the door-knocker wouldn't elicit a response, would it? But he didn't fancy his chances of shouldering or kicking the door down, snib-lock or not. So he crouched down, opened the letterbox with one hand, put his eyes level with it, and reached up his other hand to the black iron ring, giving it five loud raps: shave-and-a-haircut, some people called it. It signalled a friend; at least, that's what Rebus hoped. There was neither sound nor movement from the inside of the maisonette. The Colonies was daytime quiet. He could probably crowbar the door open without anyone noticing. Instead, he tried the knocker again. The door had a spy-hole, and he was hoping someone might be intrigued enough to want to creep to the spy-hole and take a look.

Movement now, a shadow moving slowly from the living area towards the hall. Moving stealthily. And then a head sticking out of the doorway. It was all Rebus needed.

'Hello, Eddie,' he called. 'I've got your wreath here.'

Eddie Ringan let him in.

He was dressed in a red silk kimono-style gown with a fierce dragon crawling all down its back. On the arms were symbols Rebus didn't understand. They didn't worry him. Eddie flopped onto the sofa, usually Rebus's perch, so Rebus made do with standing.

'I was lying about the wreath,' he said.

'It's the thought that counts. Nice suit, too.'

'I had to borrow the tie,' said Rebus.

'Black ties are cool.' Eddie looked like death warmed up. His eyes were dark-ringed and bloodshot, and his face resembled a prisoner's: sunless grey, lacking hope. He scratched himself under the armpit. 'So how did it go?'

'I left just as they were lowering you away.'

'They'll be at the reception now. Wish I could have done the catering myself, but you know how it is.'

Rebus nodded. 'It's not easy being a corpse. You'd have found that out.'

'Some people have managed quite nicely in the past.'

'Like Radiator McCallum and the Robertson brothers?'

Eddie produced a grim smile. 'One of those, yes.'

'You must be pretty desperate to stage your own death.'

'I'm not saying anything.'

'That's fine.' There was silence for a minute until Eddie broke it.

'How did you find out?'

Rebus absent-mindedly took a cigarette from the pack on the mantelpiece. 'It was Pat. He made up this unnecessarily exaggerated story.'

'That's Pat for you. Amateur fucking dramatics all the way.'

'He said Willie stormed out of the restaurant after sticking his face in some poor punter's plate. I checked with a couple of the people who ate there that night. A quick phone call was all it took. Nobody saw anything of the sort. Then there was the dead man's liver. It was in good nick, so it couldn't possibly have been yours.'

'You can say that again.'

Rebus was about to light up. He caught himself, lifted the cigarette from his mouth, and placed it beside the packet.

'Then I checked missing persons. Seems Willie hasn't been back to his digs in a few days. The whole thing was amateurish, Eddie. If the poor bugger hadn't got his face blown away in the explosion, we'd've known straight away it wasn't you.'

'Would you? We wondered about that, we reckoned with Brian off the scene and Haymarket not your territory, it might just work.'

Rebus shook his head. 'For a start, we take photographs, and I'd have seen them sooner or later. I always do.' He paused. 'So why did you kill him?'

'It was an accident.'

'Let me guess, you came back late to the restaurant after a pretty good bender. You were angry as hell to see Willie had coped. You had a fight, he smashed his head. Then you had an idea.'

'Maybe.'

'There's only one rotten thing about the whole story,' said Rebus. Eddie shifted on the sofa. He looked ridiculous in the kimono, and had folded his arms protectively. He was staring at the fireplace, avoiding Rebus altogether.

'What?' he said finally.

'Pat said Willie ran out of the Cafe on *Tuesday* night. His body wasn't found until Thursday morning. If he'd died in a fight on Tuesday, lividity and rigor mortis would have told the pathologist the body was old. But it wasn't, it was fresh. Which means you didn't booze him up and gas him until early Thursday morning. You must've kept him alive all day Wednesday, knowing pretty well what you were going to do with him.'

'I'm not saying anything.'

'No, *I'm* saying it. Like I say, a desperate remedy, Eddie. About as desperate as they come. Now come on.'

'What?'

'We're taking a drive.'

'Where to?'

'Down to the station, of course. Get some clothes on.' Rebus watched him try to stand up. His legs took a while to lock upright. Yes, murder could do that to you. It was the opposite of rigor mortis. It was lique-faction, the jelly effect. It took him a long time to dress, Rebus watching throughout. There were tears in Eddie's eyes when he finished, and his lips were wet with saliva.

Rebus nodded. 'You'll do,' he said. He fully intended taking Eddie to St Leonard's.

But they'd be taking the scenic route.

'Where are we going?'

'A little drive. Nice day for it.'

Eddie looked out of the windscreen. It was a uniform grey outside, buildings and sky, with rain threatening and the breeze gaining force. He started to get the idea when they turned up Holyrood Park Road, heading straight for Arthur's Seat. And when Rebus took a right, away from Holyrood and in the direction of Duddingston, Eddie started to look very worried indeed.

'You know where we're going?' Rebus suggested.

'No.'

'Oh well.'

He kept driving, drove all the way up to the gates of the house and signalled with his indicator that he was turning into the drive.

'Christ, no!' yelped Eddie Ringan. He tucked his knees in front of him, wedging them against the dashboard like he thought they were about to crash. Instead of turning in at the gates, Rebus cruised past them and stopped kerbside. You caught a glimpse of Cafferty's mansion from here. Presumably, if someone up at the house were looking out of the right window, they could see the car.

'No, no.' Eddie was weeping.

'You *do* know where we are,' Rebus said, voicing surprise. 'You know Big Ger, then?' He waited till Eddie nodded. The chef had assumed a foetal position, feet on the seat beneath him, head tucked into his knees. 'Are you scared of him?' Eddie nodded again. 'Why?' Slowly, Eddie shook his head. 'Is it because of the Central Hotel?'

'Why did I have to tell Brian?' It was a loud yell, all the louder for being confined by the car. 'Why the fuck am I so stupid?'

'They've found the gun, you know.'

'I don't know anything about that.'

'You never saw the gun?'

Eddie shook his head. Damn, Rebus had been expecting more. 'So what did you see?'

'I was in the kitchens.'

'Yes?'

'This guy came running in, screaming at me to turn on the gas. He looked crazy, spots of blood on his face ... in his eyelashes.' Eddie was calming as the exorcism took effect. 'He started to turn on all the gas rings. Not lighting them. He looked so crazy, I helped him. I turned on the gas, just like he told me to.'

'And then?'

'I got out of there. I wasn't sticking around. I thought the same as everybody else: it was for the insurance money. Till they found the body. A week later, I got a visit from Big Ger. A *painful* visit. The message was: never say a word, not a word about what happened.'

'Was Big Ger there that night?'

Eddie shrugged. Damn him again! 'I was in the kitchens. I only saw the crazy guy.'

Well, Rebus knew who *that* was – someone who'd seen the state of the Central kitchens. 'Black Aengus?' he asked.

Eddie didn't say anything for a few minutes, just stared blearily out of the windscreen. Then: 'Big Ger's bound to find out I said something. Every now and then he sends another warning. Nothing physical ... not to me, at least. Just to let me know he remembers. He'll kill me.' He turned his head to Rebus. 'He'll kill me, and all I did was turn on the gas.'

'The man with the blood, it was Aengus Gibson, wasn't it?'

Eddie nodded slowly, screwing shut his eyes and wringing out tears. Rebus started the car. As he was driving off, he saw the 4x4 coming towards him from the opposite direction. It was signalling to pull into the gates, and the gates themselves were opening compliantly. The car was driven by a thug whose face was new to Rebus. In the back seat sat Mo Cafferty.

It bothered him, during the short drive back to St Leonard's, with Eddie bawling and huddled in the passenger seat. It bothered him. Could Mo Cafferty drive at all? That would be easy enough to check: a quick chat with DVLC. If she couldn't, if she needed a chauffeur, then who was driving the 4x4 that day Rebus had seen it parked outside Bone's? And wasn't *that* quite a coincidence anyway? John Rebus didn't believe in coincidences.

'The Heartbreak Cafe didn't get its meat from Bone's, did it?' he asked Eddie, who misinterpreted the question. 'I mean Bone's the butcher's shop,' Rebus explained. But Eddie shook his head. 'Never mind,' said Rebus.

Back at St Leonard's, the very person he wanted to see was waiting for him.

'Why aren't you out at Gorgie?' he asked.

'Why aren't you on suspension?' Siobhan Clarke asked back.

'That's below the belt. Besides, I asked first.'

'I had to come and pick up these.' She waved a huge brown envelope at him.

'Well, listen, I've got a little job for you. Several, in fact. First, we need to have Eddie Ringan's casket back up out of the ground.'

'What?'

'It's not Eddie inside, I've just put him in the cells. You'll need to interview and book him. I'll tell you all about it.'

'I'm going to need to write all this down.'

'No you won't, your memory's good enough.'

'Not when my brain's in shock. You mean that wasn't Eddie in the oven?'

'That's what I mean. Next, check and see if Mo Cafferty has a driving licence.'

'What for?'

'Just do it. And do you remember telling me that when Bone won his Merc, he put up *his share* of the business to cover the bet? Your words: his share.'

'I remember. His wife told me.'

Rebus nodded. 'I want to know who owns the other half.'

'Is that all, sir?'

Rebus thought. 'No, not quite. Check Bone's Merc. See if anyone owned it before him. That way, we'll know who he won it from.' He looked at her unblinking. 'Quick as you can, eh?'

'Quick as I can, sir. Now, do you want to know what's in the envelope? It's for the man who has everything.'

'Go on then, surprise me.'

So she did.

Rebus was so surprised, he bought her coffee and a dough-ring in the canteen. The X-rays lay on the table between them.

'I don't believe this,' he kept saying. 'I really don't believe this. I put out a search for these *ages* ago.'

'They were in the records office at Ninewells.'

'But I *asked* them!'

'But did you ask nicely?'

Siobhan had explained that she'd been able to take a few trips to Dundee, chatting up anyone who might be useful, and especially in the chaotic records department, which had been moved and reorganised a few years before, leaving older records an ignored shambles. It had taken time. More than that, she'd had to promise a date to the young man who'd finally come up with the goods.

Rebus held up one of the X-rays again.

'Broken right arm,' Siobhan confirmed. 'Twelve years ago. While he was living and working in Dundee.'

'Tam Roberston,' Rebus said simply. That was that then: the dead man, the man with the bullet wound through his heart, the bullet from Rebus's Colt 45, was Tam Robertson.

'Difficult to prove in a court of law,' Siobhan suggested. True enough, you'd need more than hearsay and an X-ray to prove identity to a jury.

'There are ways,' said Rebus. 'We can try dental records again, now we've got an idea who the corpse is. Then there's superimposition. For the moment, it's enough for me that *I'm* satisfied.' He nodded. 'Well done, Clarke.' He started to get up.

'Sir?'

'Yes?'

She was smiling. 'Merry Christmas, sir.'

29

He phoned Gibson's Brewery, only to be told that 'Mr Aengus' was attending an ale competition in Newcastle, due back later tonight. So he called the Inland Revenue and spoke for a while to the inspector in charge of his case. If he was going to confront Tommy Greenwood, he'd need all the ammo he could gather ... bad metaphor considering, but true all the same. He left his car at St Leonard's while he went for a walk, trying to clear his head. Everything was coming together now. Aengus Gibson had been playing cards with Tam Robertson, and had shot him. Then set fire to the hotel to cover up the murder. It should all be tied up, but Rebus's brain was posing more questions than answers. Was it likely Aengus carried a gun around with him, even in his wild days? Why didn't Eck, also present, seek revenge for his brother? Wouldn't Aengus have had to shut him up somehow? Was it likely that only three of them were involved in the poker game? And who had delivered the gun to Deek Torrance? So many questions.

As he came down onto South Clerk Street, he saw that a van was parked outside Bone's. A new plate-glass window was being installed in the shop itself, and the van door was open at the back. Rebus walked over to the van and looked in the back. It had been a proper butcher's van at one time, and nobody had bothered changing it. You climbed a step into the back, where there were counters and cupboards and a small fridge-freezer. The van would have had its usual rounds of the housing schemes in the city, housewives and retired folk queuing for meat rather than travelling to a shop. A man in a white apron came out of Bone's with an ex-pig hoisted on his shoulder.

'Excuse me,' he said, carrying the carcass into the van.

'You use this for deliveries?' Rebus asked.

The man nodded. 'Just to restaurants.'

'I remember when a butcher's van used to come by our way,' Rebus reminisced.

'Aye, it's not economic these days, though.'

'Everything changes,' said Rebus. The man nodded agreement. Rebus was examining the interior again. To get behind the counter, you climbed into the van, pulled a hinged section of the counter up, and pushed open a narrow little door. Narrow: that's what the back of the van was.

He remembered Michael's description of the van he'd been shunted about in. A narrow van with a smell. As the man came out of the van, he disturbed something with his foot. It was a piece of straw. Straw in a butcher's van? None of the animals carried in here had seen straw for a while.

Rebus looked into the shop. A young assistant was watching the glass being installed.

'Open for business, sir,' he informed Rebus cheerily.

'I was looking for Mr Bone.'

'He's not in this afternoon.'

Rebus nodded towards the van. 'Do you still do runs?'

'What, house-to-house?' The young man shook his head. 'Just general deliveries, bulk stuff.'

Yes, Rebus would agree with that.

He walked back up to St Leonard's, and caught Siobhan again. 'I forgot to say . . .'

'More work?'

'Not much more. Pat Calder, you'll need to bring him in for questioning too. He'll be back home by now and getting frantic wondering where Eddie's sloped off to. I'm just sorry I won't be around for the reunion. I suppose I can always catch it in court . . .'

It had been quite a day already, and it wasn't yet six o'clock. Back in the flat, the students were cooking a lentil curry while Michael sat in the living room reading another book on hypnotherapy. It had all become very settled in the flat, very . . . well, the word that came to mind was *homely*. It was a strange word to use about a bunch of teenage students, a copper and an ex-con, yet it seemed just about right.

Michael had finished the tablets, and looked the better for it. He was supposed to arrange a check-up, but Rebus was dubious: they'd probably only stick him on more tablets. The scars would heal over naturally. All it took was time. He'd certainly regained his appetite: two helpings of curry.

After the meal they all sat around in the living room, the students drinking wine, Michael refusing it, Rebus supping beer from a can. There was music, the kind that never went away: the Stones and the Doors, Janis Joplin, very early Pink Floyd. It was one of those evenings. Rebus felt absolutely shattered, and blamed it on the caffeine tablets he'd been taking. Here he'd been worrying about Michael, and all the time he'd been swallowing down his own bad medicine. They'd seen him through the weekend, sleeping little and thinking lots. But you couldn't go on like that forever. And what with the music and the beer and the relaxed conversation, he'd almost certainly fall asleep here on the sofa . . .

'What was that?'

'Sounds like somebody smashed a bottle or something.'

The students got up to look out of the window. 'Can't see anything.'

'No, look, there's glass on the road.' They turned to Rebus. 'Someone's broken your windshield.'

Someone had indeed broken his windshield, as he found when he wandered downstairs and into the street. Other neighbours had gathered at doors and windows to check the scene. But most of them were retreating now. There was a chunk of rock on the passenger seat, surrounded by jewels of shattered glass. Nearby a car was reversing lazily out of its parking spot. It stopped in the road beside him. The passenger side window went down.

'What happened?'

'Nothing. Just a rock through the windscreen.'

'What?' The passenger turned to his driver. 'Wait here a second.' He got out to examine the damage. 'Who the hell would want to do that?'

'How many names do you want?' Rebus reached into the car to pull out the rock, and felt something collide with the back of his head. It didn't make sense for a moment, but by then he was being dragged away from the car into the road. He heard a car reverse and stop. He tried to resist, clawing at the unyielding tarmac with his fingernails. Jesus, he was going to pass out. His head was trying to close all channels. Each thud of his heart brought intense new pain to his skull. Someone had opened a window and was shouting something, some warning or complaint. He was alone in the middle of the road now. The passenger had run back to the car and slammed the door shut. Rebus pushed himself onto all fours, a baby resisting gravity for the first time. He blinked, trying to see out of cloudy eyes. He saw headlights, and knew what they were going to do.

They were going to drive straight over him.

Sucker punch, and he'd fallen for it. The offer of help from your attacker routine. Older than Arthur's Seat itself. The car's engine roared, and the tyres squealed towards him, dragging the body of the car with them. Rebus wondered if he'd get the licence number before he died.

A hand grabbed the neck of his shirt and hauled, pulling him backwards out of the road. The car caught his legs, tossing one shoe up off his foot and into the air. The car didn't stop, or even slow down, just kept on up the slope to the top of the road, where it took a right and disappeared.

'Are you okay, John?'

It was Michael. 'You saved my life there, Mickey.' Adrenalin was mixing with pain in Rebus's body, making him feel sick. He threw up undigested lentil curry onto the pavement.

'Try to stand up,' said Michael. Rebus tried and failed.

'My legs hurt,' he said. 'Christ, do my legs hurt!'

The X-rays showed no breaks or fractures, not even a bone chipped. 'Just bad bruising, Inspector,' said the woman doctor at the Infirmary. 'You were lucky. A hit like that could have done a lot of damage.'

Rebus nodded. 'I suppose I should have known,' he said. 'I've been due a visit here as a patient. Christ knows I've been here enough recently as a visitor.'

'I'll just fetch you something,' said the doctor.

'Wait a second, doctor. Are your labs open in the evening?'

She shook her head. 'Why do you ask?'

'Nothing.'

She left the room. Michael came closer. 'How do you feel?'

'I don't know which hurts worse, my head or my left leg.'

'No great loss to association football.'

Rebus almost smiled, but grimaced instead. Any movement of his face muscles sent electric spurts through his brain. The doctor came back into the room. 'Here you are,' she said. This should help.'

Rebus had been expecting painkillers. But she was holding a walking stick.

It was an aluminium walking stick, hollow and therefore lightweight, with a large rubberised grip and adjustable height courtesy of a series of holes in its shaft, into which a locking-pin could be placed. It looked like some strange wind instrument, but Rebus was glad of it as he walked out of the hospital.

Back at the flat, however, one of the solicitous students said he had something better, and came back from his bedroom with a black wooden cane with a silver and bone handle. Rebus tried it. It was a good height for him.

'I bought it in a junk shop,' the student said, 'don't ask me why.'

'Looks like it should have a concealed sword,' said Rebus. He tried twisting and pulling at the handle, but nothing happened. 'So much for that.'

The police, who had talked to Rebus at the Infirmary, had also spoken to the students.

'This constable,' related the walking-stick owner, whose name Rebus was sure was Ed, 'I mean, he was looking at us like we were squatters, and he was asking, was Inspector Rebus in here with you? And we were nodding, yes he was. And the constable couldn't figure it out at all.' He started laughing. Even Michael smiled. Someone else made a pot of herbal tea.

Great, thought Rebus. Another story that would be doing the rounds:

Rebus fills his flat with students, then sits around with them of an evening with wine and beer. At the Infirmary, they'd asked if he'd recognised either of the men. The answer was no. It was a mobile profession, after all ... One of the neighbours had caught the car's number plate. It was a Ford Escort, stolen only an hour or so before from a car park near the Sheraton on Lothian Road. They would find it abandoned quite soon, probably not far from Marchmont. There wouldn't be any fingerprints.

'They must've been crazy,' Michael said on the way home, Rebus having got them a lift in the back of a patrol car. 'Thinking they could pull a stunt like that.'

'It wasn't a stunt, Michael. Somebody's desperate. That story in yesterday's paper has really shaken them up.' After all, wasn't that exactly what he'd wanted? He'd sought a reaction, and here it was.

From the flat he telephoned an emergency windscreen replacement firm. It would cost the earth, but he needed the car first thing in the morning. He just prayed his leg wouldn't seize up in the night.

30

Which of course it did. He was up at five, practising walking across the living room, trying to unstiffen the joints and tendons. He looked at his left leg. A spectacular blood-filled bruise stretched across his calf, wrapping itself around most of the front of the leg too. If the bony front of his leg had taken the impact rather than the fleshy back, there would have been at the very least a clean break. He swallowed two paracetamol – recommended for the pain by the Infirmary doctor – and waited for morning proper to arrive. He'd needed sleep last night, but hadn't got much. Today he'd be living on his wits. He just hoped those wits would be sharp enough.

At six-thirty he managed the tenement stairs and hobbled to his car, now boasting a windscreen worth more than the rest of it put together. Traffic wasn't quite heavy yet coming into town, and non-existent heading out, so the drive itself was mercifully shortened. Pressing down on the clutch hurt all the way up into his groin. He took the coast road out to North Berwick, letting the engine labour rather than changing gears too often. Just the other side of the town, he found the house he was looking for. Well, an estate, actually, and not a housing estate. It must have been about thirty or forty acres, with an uninterrupted view across the mouth of the Forth to the dark lump of Bass Rock. Rebus wasn't much good at architecture; Georgian, he'd guess. It looked like a lot of the houses in Edinburgh's New Town, with fluted stone columns either side of the doorway and large sash windows, nine panes of glass to each half.

Broderick Gibson had come a long way since those days in his garden shed, pottering with homebrew recipes. Rebus parked outside the front door and rang the bell. The door was opened by Mrs Gibson. Rebus introduced himself.

'It's a bit early, Inspector. Is anything wrong?'

'If I could just speak to your son, please.'

'He's eating breakfast. Why don't you wait in the sitting-room and I'll bring you –'

'It's all right, mother.' Aengus Gibson was still chewing and wiping his chin with a cloth napkin. He stood in the dining-room doorway. 'Come in here, Inspector.'

Rebus smiled at the defeated Mrs Gibson as he passed her.

'What's happened to your leg?' Gibson asked.

'I thought you might know, sir.'

'Oh? Why?' Aengus had seated himself at the table. Rebus had been entertaining an image of silver service – tureens and hot-plates, kedgeree or kippers, Wedgewood plates, and tea poured by a manservant. But all he saw was a plain white plate with greasy sausage and eggs on it. Buttered toast on the side and a mug of coffee. There were two newspapers folded beside Aengus – Mairie's paper and the *Financial Times* – and enough crumbs around the table to suggest that mother and father had eaten already.

Mrs Gibson put her head round the door. 'A cup of coffee, Inspector?'

'No, thank you, Mrs Gibson.' She smiled and retreated.

'I just thought,' Rebus said to Aengus, 'you might have arranged it.'

'I don't understand.'

'Trying to shut me up before I can ask a few questions about the Central Hotel.'

'That again!' Aengus bit into a piece of toast.

'Yes, that again.' Rebus sat down at the table, stretching his left leg out in front of him. 'You see, I *know* you were there that night, long after Mr Vanderhyde left. I know you were at a poker game set up by two villains called Tam and Eck Robertson. I know someone shot and killed Tam, and I know you ran into the kitchens covered in blood and screaming for all the gas rings to be turned on. That, Mr Gibson, is what I know.'

Gibson seemed to have trouble swallowing the chewed toast. He gulped coffee, and wiped his mouth again.

'Well, Inspector,' he said, 'if that's what you know, I suggest you don't know very much.'

'Maybe you'd like to tell me the rest, sir?'

They sat in silence. Aengus toyed with the empty mug, Rebus waiting for him to speak. The door burst open.

'Get out of here!' roared Broderick Gibson. He was wearing trousers and an open-necked shirt, whose cuffs flapped for want of their links. Obviously, his wife had disturbed him halfway through dressing. 'I could have you arrested right this minute!' he said. 'The Chief Constable tells me you've been suspended.'

Rebus stood up slowly, making much of his injured leg. But there was no charity in Broderick Gibson.

'And stay away from us, unless you have the authority! I'll be talking to my solicitor this morning.'

Rebus was at the door now. He stopped and looked into Broderick Gibson's eyes. 'I suggest you do that, sir. And you might care to tell him where *you* were the night the Central Hotel burnt down. Your son's in serious trouble, Mr Gibson. You can't hide him from the fact forever.'

'Just get out,' Gibson hissed.

'You haven't asked about my leg.'

'What?'

'Nothing, sir, just wondering aloud ...'

As Rebus walked back across the large hallway, with its paintings and candelabra and fine curving stairwell, he felt how cold the house was. It wasn't just its age or the tiled floor either; the place was cold at its heart.

He arrived in Gorgie just as Siobhan was pouring her first cup of decaf of the day.

'What happened to your leg?' she asked.

Rebus pointed with his stick to the man stationed behind the camera. 'What the hell are you doing here?'

'I'm relieving Petrie,' said Brian Holmes.

'I wonder what any of us is doing here,' said Siobhan. Rebus ignored her.

'You're off sick.'

'I was bored, I came back early. I spoke to the Chief Super yesterday and he okayed it. So here I am.' Holmes looked fine but sounded dour. 'There was an ulterior motive, though,' he said. 'I wanted to hear from Siobhan herself the story of Eddie and Pat. It all sounds so ... incredible. I mean, I *cried* at that cemetery yesterday, and the bastard I was crying for was sitting at home playing with himself.'

'He'll be playing with himself in jail soon,' said Rebus. Then, to Siobhan: 'Give me some of that coffee.' He drank two scalding swallows before passing the plastic cup back. 'Thanks. Any progress?'

'No one's arrived yet. Not even our Trading Standards companion.'

'I meant those other things.'

'What *did* happen to your leg?' Holmes asked. So Rebus told them all about it.

'It's my fault,' Holmes said, 'for getting you into this in the first place.'

'That's right, it is,' said Rebus, 'and as penance you can keep your eyes glued to that window.' He turned to Siobhan. 'So?'

She took a deep breath. 'So I interviewed Ringan and Calder yesterday afternoon. They've both been charged. I also checked and Mrs Cafferty doesn't have a driving licence, not under her married or her maiden name. Bone's Mercedes belonged to –'

'Big Ger Cafferty.'

'You already knew?'

'I guessed,' said Rebus. 'What about the other half of Bone's business?'

'Owned by a company called Geronimo Holdings.'

'Which in turn is owned by Big Ger?'

'And sweetly, the word Geronimo includes both his and his wife's names. So what do you make of it?'

'Looks to me like Ger probably won his half of the business in a bet with Bone.'

'Either that,' added Holmes, 'or he got it in lieu of protection money Bone couldn't afford.'

'Maybe,' said Rebus. 'But the bet's more likely.'

'After all,' said Siobhan, 'Bone won the car in a bet with Cafferty. They've gambled together in the past.'

Rebus nodded. 'Well, it all adds up to a tight connection between the two of them. And there's a tighter connection too, though I can't prove it just yet.'

'Hang on,' said Siobhan, 'if the stabbing and the smashed window are to do with protection or gambling, then they're to do with Cafferty. Which means, since Cafferty owns half the business, that Cafferty smashed his *own* window.'

Rebus was shaking his head. 'I didn't say they were to do with protection or gambling.'

'And where does the cousin fit in?' Holmes interrupted.

'My my,' commented Rebus, 'you *are* keen to be back, aren't you? I'm not sure exactly where Kintoul fits in, but I'm getting a fair idea.'

'Hold on,' said Holmes, 'here we are.'

They all watched as a battered purple mini drove up to the taxi offices. When the driver's door opened, the man mountain squeezed himself out.

'Like toothpaste from the tube,' said Rebus.

'Christ,' added Holmes, 'he must've taken out the front seats.'

'All alone today,' Siobhan noted.

'I'll bet Cafferty drops in sometime, though,' said Rebus, 'just to check. He's been ripped off badly in the past, he won't want it happening again.'

'Ripped off badly?' Siobhan echoed. 'How do you know that?'

Rebus winked at her. 'It's an odds-on bet,' he said.

He had to wait till after lunch for the information he needed. He had it faxed to him at a local newsagent's. During the long wait in Gorgie, he'd discussed the case with Holmes and Siobhan. They both were of the same mind in one particular: nobody would testify against Cafferty. And of like minds in another: they couldn't even be sure Cafferty had anything to do with it.

'I'll find out this afternoon,' Rebus told them, heading out to pick up the fax.

He was getting used to walking with the cane, and as long as he kept moving, the leg itself didn't stiffen up. But he knew the drive to Cardenden wouldn't do him much good. He considered the train, but ruled it out in short order. He might want to escape from Fife in a hurry; and Scotrail's timetables just didn't fit the bill.

It was just after two-thirty when he pushed open the door of Hutchy's betting shop. The place was airless, smelling old and undusted. The cigarette butts on the floor were probably last week's. There was a two-thirty-five race, and a few punters lined the walls waiting for the commentary. Rebus didn't let the look of the place put him off. Nobody wanted to bet in a plush establishment: it meant the bookie was making too much money. These tawdry surroundings were all psychology. You might not be winning, the bookmaker was saying, but look at me, I'm not doing any better.

Except that he was.

Rebus noticed a half-familiar face studying the form on one of the newspapers pinned to the wall. But then this town was full of half-familiar faces. He approached the glass-partitioned desk. 'I'd like a word with Mr Greenwood, please.'

'Do you have an appointment?'

But Rebus was no longer talking to the woman. His attention was on the man who'd looked up from a desk behind her. 'Mr Greenwood, I'm a police officer. Can we have a word?'

Greenwood thought about it, then got up, unlocked the door of the booth, and came out. 'Round here,' he said, leading Rebus to the rear of the shop. He unlocked another door, letting them into a much cosier and more private office.

'Any trouble?' he asked immediately, sitting down and reaching into his desk drawer for a bottle of whisky.

'Not for me, sir,' Rebus said. He sat down opposite Greenwood and stared at him. Christ, it was difficult after all these years. But Midge's portrait wasn't so far off the mark. A chess player would be making ready to play a pawn; Rebus decided to sacrifice his queen. 'So, Eck,' he said, getting comfortable, 'how've things been?'

Greenwood looked around. 'Are you talking to me?'

'I suppose I must be. My name's not Eck. Do you want to keep playing games? Fine then, let's play games.' Greenwood was pouring himself a large whisky. 'Your name is Eck Robertson. You fled from the Cafferty gang taking with you quite a lot of Big Ger's money. You also took another man's identity – Thomas Greenwood. You knew Tommy wouldn't complain because he was dead. Another one of Big Ger's incredible disappearing acts. You took his name and his identity, and you set up for yourself in the arse-end of Fife, living out of a suitcase full of money till you got this place in profit.' Rebus paused. 'How am I doing?'

Greenwood, *aka* Eck Robertson, swallowed loudly and refilled his glass.

'You took too much of Greenwood's identity, though. When you set up here, Inland Revenue got onto you for an unpaid income tax bill. You wrote to them, and eventually you paid up.' Rebus brought the faxed sheets from his pocket. 'I've got a copy of your letter here, along with some earlier stuff from the *real* Thomas Greenwood. Wait till a handwriting expert gets hold of them in court. Have you ever seen those guys work on a jury? It's like Perry Mason. Even I can see the signatures aren't the same.'

'I changed my writing style.'

Rebus smiled. 'Changed your face too. Dyed hair, shaved off your moustache, contact lenses ... tinted. Your eyes used to be hazel, didn't they, Eck?'

'I keep telling you, my name's –'

Rebus got up. 'Whatever you say. I'm sure Big Ger will recognise you quick enough.'

'Wait a minute, sit down.' Rebus sat and waited. Eck Robertson tried to smile. He flicked on his radio for a moment and listened to the race, then flicked it off again. A six-to-one shot had romped home.

'Another win for the bookies,' Rebus said. 'Always liked the horses, didn't you? Not as much as Tam, though, Tam just loved betting. He bet you he could screw money out of Big Ger without Ger noticing. Creaming it off just a little at a time, but it all mounted up. Here.' Rebus tossed the drawing of Tam Robertson onto the desk. 'Here's what he might look like these days if Big Ger hadn't found out.'

Eck Robertson stared at the drawing, tracing a finger over it.

'You had to do a runner before Big Ger caught you, so you took the money. Then Radiator ran too. After all, he'd introduced the two of you into the gang. He'd be in for punishment too.' Rebus paused again. 'Or did Big Ger catch up with him?'

Robertson, eyes still on the drawing, shrugged.

'Well, whatever,' said Rebus. 'I think I'll have that whisky now.' His leg was hurting like blazes, his knuckles white on the handle of the cane. It took Robertson a while to pour the drink. 'So,' Rebus asked him, 'anything you want to add?'

'How did you find me?'

'Somebody spotted you.'

Robertson nodded. 'The chef, what's his name? Ringan? I saw him in some pub in Cowdenbeath. He looked like he was on a bender, so I got out fast. I didn't think he'd seen me, and if he had I didn't think he'd recognise me. I was wrong, eh?'

'You were wrong.' Rebus sipped the whisky like it was medicine on a spoon.

'It was Aengus Gibson,' Robertson said suddenly. 'Aengus Gibson had the gun.'

And then he told the rest of the story. Tam had been cheating at poker, as usual. But Aengus was on to him, and drew the gun. Shot Tam dead.

'We scarpered.'

'What?' Rebus was disbelieving. 'No thoughts of revenge? That young drunk had just killed your brother!'

'Nobody touched Black Aengus. He was Big Ger's pal. They got friendly after some misunderstanding, a break-in at Mo's flat. Big Ger had plans for him.'

'What sort of plans?'

Robertson shrugged. 'Just plans. You're right about the money. I knew I had to run while I could.'

'Why here, though?'

Robertson blinked. 'It was the last station on the line. Big Ger's never had much interest in Fife. It would mean tackling the Italians and the Orangemen.'

Rebus was doing some quick thinking. 'So what did Ger do when Aengus shot Tam?'

'How do you mean?'

'Eck, I *know* Big Ger was at the poker game. So what did he do?'

'He scarpered the same as the rest of us.'

So Big Ger *had* been there! Robertson's eyes were on his brother's portrait again. Rebus had a very good idea, too, what Cafferty's 'plans' for Aengus must have been. Imagine, having such a hold over someone who'd one day control the Gibson Brewing business. Such a hold all these years . . .

'Who took away the gun, Eck?'

Eck shrugged again. Rebus got the idea he'd stopped listening. He rapped the edge of the desk with his cane. 'You went to a lot of trouble, Eck. Eddie Ringan appreciated that. He learned from you that it's possible to disappear. A handy lesson when Big Ger's after you. He *really* makes people disappear, doesn't he? Dumping them at sea like that. That's what he does, isn't it?'

'After a while, aye.'

Rebus frowned at this. But then Eck Robertson's next words hit him.

'Nobody notices a butcher's van.'

Rebus nodded, smiling. 'You're right about that.' He wet his lips. 'Eck, would you testify against him? In closed court, keep your new identity secret? Would you?'

But Eck Robertson was shaking his head. He was still shaking it when the door burst open. Ah, the half-remembered face from the form sheets. It was the pool player from the Midden.

'All right, Tommy?'

424

'Fine, Sharky, fine.' But 'Tommy Greenwood' didn't look it.

'Out you go, son,' said Rebus, 'Mr Greenwood and me have got business.'

Sharky ignored him. 'Want me to chuck him out, Tommy?'

Tommy Greenwood never got a chance to answer. Rebus pushed the handle of his cane hard up under Sharky's nose and then whipped it harder still against his knees. The young man crumpled. Rebus stood up. 'Handy thing, this,' he said. He pointed it at Eck Robertson. 'You can keep the picture as a reminder, Eck. Meantime, I'll be back. I want you to testify against Cafferty. Not now, not yet. Sometime after I've got him firm on a charge. And if you won't testify, I can always resurrect Eck Robertson. Think about it. One way or the other, Big Ger'll know.'

He was crossing the Forth Road Bridge when he heard the news on the radio.

'Aw Christ,' he said, stepping on the accelerator.

31

Rebus showed his ID as he drove through the brewery gates. There was only the one police car left at the scene, and no sign of an ambulance. Workers stood around in huddled, low-talking groups, passing round cigarettes and stories.

Rebus knew the detective sergeant. He worked out of Edinburgh West, and his unfortunate name was Robert Burns. This Burns was tall and bulky and red-haired, with freckles on his face. On Sunday afternoons, he could sometimes be found at the foot of the Mound, where he would lambast the strolling heathens. Rebus was glad to see Burns. You might get fire and brimstone with him, but you'd never get waffle.

Burns pointed to the huge aluminium tank. 'He climbed to the top.' Yes, Rebus could see all too clearly the metal stairwell which reached to the top of the tank, with walkways circling the tank every thirty feet or so. 'And when he got to the top, he jumped. A lot of the workers saw him, and they all said the same thing. He just climbed steadily till there were no more stairs, and then he threw himself off, arms stretched out. One of them said the dive was better than anything he'd seen in the Olympics.'

'That good, eh?' They weren't the only ones staring at the tank. Some of the workforce glanced up from time to time, then traced Aengus Gibson's descent. He'd hit the tarmac and crumpled like a concertina. There was a dent in the ground as though a boulder had been lifted from the spot.

'His father tried chasing after him,' Burns was saying. 'Didn't get very far. Old boy like that, it's a wonder his heart didn't give out. They had to help him down from the third circle.'

Rebus counted up three walkways. 'A bit of Dante, eh?' he said, winking at Burns.

'The old boy's saying it was an accident.'

'Of course he is.'

'It wasn't, though.'

'Of course it wasn't.'

'I've got a dozen witnesses who say he jumped.'

'A dozen witnesses,' Rebus corrected, 'who'll change their minds if their jobs are on the line.'

'Aye, right enough.'

Rebus breathed in. He'd always liked that smell of hops, but from now on he knew it would smell differently to him. It would smell like this moment, played over time and time again.

'The Lord giveth and the Lord taketh away,' said Burns. 'What happened to your leg, by the way?'

'Ingrown toenails,' said Rebus. 'The Lord gave them, the Infirmary took them away.'

Burns was shaking his head at this easy blasphemy when a window in the building behind them opened.

'You!' shouted Broderick Gibson. 'You killed him! You did it!' His crooked finger, a finger he seemed unable to straighten, was mostly pointed at Rebus. His eyes were like wet glass, his breathing strained. Someone was trying to coax him gently back into the office, hands on his shoulders. 'There'll be a reckoning!' he called to Rebus. 'Mark my words. There'll come a reckoning!'

The old man was finally pulled inside, the window falling shut after him. The workers were looking over towards the two policemen.

'He must be one of yours,' said Rebus, making for his car.

That was that then. Aengus Gibson had shot and killed Tam Robertson, and now Aengus was dead. End of story. Rebus could think of one person not in Aengus's family who was going to be very upset: Big Ger Cafferty. Cafferty had protected Black Aengus, maybe even blackmailed him, all the time waiting for the day when the young man would take over the brewery. With Aengus dead, the whole edifice fell, and good riddance to it.

Still, there was no comeback for Cafferty, no punishment.

Back at the flat, Michael had some news.

'The doc's been trying to get you.'

'Which one? I've seen so many recently.'

'Dr Patience Aitken. She seems to think you're avoiding her. Sounds like the ploy's working, too.'

'It's not a ploy. I've just had a lot on my plate.'

'And if you don't finish it, you won't get afters.' Michael smiled. 'She sounds nice, by the way.'

'She *is* nice. I'm the arsehole.'

'So go see her.'

Rebus flopped onto the sofa. 'Maybe I will. What are you reading?' Michael showed him the cover. 'Another book on hypnotherapy. You must have exhausted the field.'

'I've just been scratching the surface.' Michael paused. 'I'm going to take a course.'

'Oh?'

'I'm going to become a hypnotherapist. I mean, I know I can hypnotise people.'

'You can certainly get them to take their trousers off and bark like dogs.'

'Exactly, it's about time I put it to better use.'

'They say laughter is the best medicine.'

'Shut up, John, I'm trying to be serious. And I'm moving back in with Chrissie and the kids.'

'Oh?'

'I've talked with her. We've decided to try again.'

'Sounds romantic.'

'Well, one of us has got to have some romance in his soul.' Michael picked up the telephone and handed it to Rebus. 'Now phone the doctor.'

'Yes, sir,' said Rebus.

Broderick Gibson had clout, there was no denying it. On Wednesday morning the newspapers reported the 'tragic accident' at the Gibson Brewery near Fountainbridge, Edinburgh. There were photos of Aengus, some in his Black Aengus days, others showing the later model at charity events. There wasn't a whisper of suicide. It was another cover-up by Aengus's father, another distortion of the truth. It had become just something Broderick Gibson did, a part of the routine.

At ten-fifteen, Rebus received a phone call. It was Chief Super-intendent Watson.

'There's someone here to see you,' he said. 'I told him you're under suspension, but he's bloody insistent.'

'Who is it?' asked Rebus.

'Some blind old duffer called Vanderhyde.'

Vanderhyde was still waiting when Rebus arrived. He looked quite at ease, concentrating on the sounds around him. Chatter and phone calls and the clacking of keyboards. He was seated on a chair facing Rebus's desk. Rebus tiptoed painfully around him and sat down. He watched Matthew Vanderhyde for a couple of minutes. He was dressed in a dark suit, white shirt and black tie: mourning clothes. He carried a blue cardboard folder, which he rested on his thighs. His walking-stick rested against the side of his chair.

'Well, Inspector,' said Vanderhyde suddenly, 'seen enough?'

Rebus gave a wry smile. 'Good morning, Mr Vanderhyde. What gave me away?'

'You're carrying a cane of some kind. It hit the corner of your desk.'

Rebus nodded. 'I was sorry to hear –'

'No sorrier than his parents. They've worked hard over the years with Aengus. He has *been* hard work. Devilish hard at times. Now it's all gone to waste.' Vanderhyde leaned forward in his chair. Had he been sighted, his eyes would have been boring into Rebus's. As it was, Rebus could see his own face reflected in the double mirror of Vanderhyde's glasses. 'Did he deserve to die, Inspector?'

'He had a choice.'

'Did he?'

Rebus was remembering the priest's words. *Can you live the rest of your life with the memories and the guilt?* Vanderhyde knew Rebus wasn't about to answer. He nodded slowly, and sat back a little in his chair.

'You were there that night, weren't you?' Rebus asked.

'Where?'

'At the card game.'

'Blind men make poor card-players, Inspector.'

'A sighted person could help them.' Rebus waited. Vanderhyde sat stiff and straight like the wax figure of a Victorian. 'Maybe someone like Broderick Gibson.'

Vanderhyde's fingers played over the blue folder, gripped it, and passed it over the desk.

'Broderick wanted you to have this.'

'What is it?'

'He wouldn't say. All he did say was, he hoped you'll think it was worth it, though he himself doubts it.' Vanderhyde paused. 'Of course, I was curious enough to study it in my own particular way. It's a book of some kind.' Rebus accepted the heavy folder, and Vanderhyde took his own hand away, finding his walking-stick and resting the hand there. 'Some keys were found on Aengus. They didn't seem to match any known lock. Last night, Broderick found some bank statements detailing monthly payments to an estate office. He knows the head of the office, so he phoned him. Aengus, it seems, had been leasing a flat in Blair Street.'

Rebus knew it, a narrow passage between the High Street and the Cowgate, balanced precariously between respectability and low living. 'Nobody knew about it?'

Vanderhyde shook his head. 'It was his little den, Inspector. A real rat's nest, according to Broderick. Mouldering food and empty bottles, pornographic videos ...'

'A regular bachelor pad.'

Vanderhyde ignored his levity. 'This book was found there.'

Rebus had already opened the folder. Inside was a large ring-bound notebook. It bore no title, but its narrow lines were filled with writing. A few sentences told Rebus what it was: Aengus Gibson's journal.

32

Rebus sat at his desk reading. Nobody bothered him, despite the fact that he was supposed to be suspended. The day grew sunless, and the office emptied slowly. He might as well have been in solitary confinement for all the notice he took. His phone was off its hook and his head, bowed over the journal, was hidden by his hands; a clear sign that he did not want to be disturbed.

He read the journal quickly first time through. After all, only some of the pages were germane. The early entries were full of wild parties, illicit coitus in country mansions with married women who were still 'names' even today, and more often with the daughters of those women. Arguments with father and mother, usually over money. Money. There was a lot of money in these early entries, money spent on travel, cars, champagne, clothes. However, the journal itself opened quite strangely:

> Sometimes, mostly when I'm alone, but occasionally in company, I catch a glimpse of someone from the corner of my eye. Or think I do. When I look properly, there's nobody there. There may be some shape there, some interesting, unconscious arrangement of the edge of an open door and the window frame beyond it, or whatever, which gives the hint of a human shape. I mention the door and the window frame because it is the most recent example.
>
> I am becoming convinced, however, that I really am seeing things. And what I am seeing – being shown, to be more accurate – is myself. That other part of me. I went to church when I was a child, and believed in ghosts. I still believe in ghosts . . .

Rebus skipped to the start of the next entry:

> I can write this journal safe in the knowledge that whoever is reading it – yes you, dear reader – does so after my death. Nobody knows it is here, and since I have no friends, no confidants or confidantes, it is unlikely that anyone will sneak a look at it. A burglar may carry it off, of course. If so, shame on you: it is the least valuable thing in this flat, though it may become more valuable the longer I write . . .

There were huge gaps in the chronology. A single year might garner half a dozen dated entries. Black Aengus, it seemed, was no more regular in keeping a diary than he was in anything else. Five years ago, though, there had been a spate of entries. The accidental break-in at Mo Johnson's flat; Aengus becoming friendly with Mo and being introduced by her to a certain Morris Cafferty. After a while, Cafferty became simply 'Big Ger' as Aengus and he met at parties and in pubs and clubs.

By far the longest entry, however, belonged to the one day Rebus was really interested in:

This isn't a bad place really. The nursing staff are understanding and ready with jokes and stories. They carry me with all gentleness back to my room when I find I've wandered from it. The corridors are long and mazey. I thought I saw a tree once in one corridor, but it was a painting on the window. A nurse placed my hand on the cold glass so I could be sure in my mind.

Like the rest of them, she refused to smuggle in any vodka.

From my window I can see a squirrel – a red squirrel, I think – leaping between trees, and beyond that hills covered with stunted foliage, like a bad school haircut.

But I'm not really seeing this pastoral scene. I'm looking into a room, a room where I think I'll be spending a great deal of my time, even after I've left this hospital.

Why did I ever try to talk my father into going to the poker game? I know the answer now. Because Cafferty wanted him there. And father was keen enough – there's still a spark in him, a spark of the wildness that has been his legacy to me. But he couldn't come. Had he been there, I wonder if things would have turned out differently.

I met Uncle Matthew in the bar. God, what a bore. He thinks that because he has dabbled with demons and the hobgoblins of nationalism he has some import in the world. I could have told him, men like Cafferty have import. They are the hidden movers and shakers, the deal-makers. Simply, they get things done. And God, what things!

Tam Robertson suggested that I join the poker game which was happening upstairs. The stake money required was not high, and I knew I could always nip over to Blair Street for more cash if needed. Of course, I knew Tam Robertson's reputation. He dealt cards in a strange manner, elbow jutting out and up. Though I couldn't fathom how, some people reckoned he was able to see the underside of the cards as he dealt. His brother, Eck, explained it away by saying Tam had broken his arm as a young man. Well, I'm no card sharp, and I expected to lose a few quid, but I was sure I'd know if anyone tried to cheat me.

But then the other two players arrived, and I knew I would not be cheated. One was Cafferty. He was with a man called Jimmy Bone, a butcher by trade. He looked like a butcher, too – puffy-faced, red-cheeked, with fingers as fat as link sausages. He had a just-scrubbed look too. You often get that with butchers, surgeons, workers in the slaughterhouse. They like to look cleaner than clean.

Now that I think of it, Cafferty looked like that too. And Eck. And Tam. Tam was always rubbing his hands, giving off an aroma of lemon soap. Or he would examine his fingernails and pick beneath them. To look at his clothes, you would never guess, but he was pathologically hygienic. I realise now – blessed hindsight! – that the Robertson brothers were not pleased to see Cafferty. Nor did the butcher look happy at having been cajoled into playing. He kept complaining that he owed too much as it was, but Cafferty wouldn't hear of it.

The butcher was a dreadful poker player. He mimed dejection whenever he had a bad hand, and fidgeted, shuffling his feet, when he had a good one. As the game wore on, it was obvious there was an undercurrent between Cafferty and the Robertsons. Cafferty kept complaining about business. It was slow, money wasn't what it was. Then he turned to me abruptly and slapped his palm against the back of my hand.

'How many dead men have you seen?'

In Cafferty's company, I affected more bravado even than usual, an effect achieved in most part by seeming preternaturally relaxed.

'Not many,' I said (or something offhand like that).

'Any at all?' he persisted. He didn't wait for an answer. 'I've seen dozens. Yes, dozens. What's more, Black Aengus, I've killed my fair share of them.'

He lifted his hand away, sat back and said nothing. The next hand was dealt in silence. I wished Mo were around. She had a way of calming him down. He was drinking whisky from the bottle, sloshing it around in his mouth before swallowing noisily. Sober, he is unpredictable; drunk, he is dangerous. That's why I like him. I even admire him, in a strange sort of way. He gets what he wants by any means necessary. There is something magnetic about that singularity of mind. And of course, in his company I am someone to be respected, respected by people who would normally call me a stuck-up snob and, as one person did, 'a pissed-up piece of shite'. Cafferty took exception when I told him I'd been called this. He paid the man responsible a visit.

What makes him want to spend time with me? Before that night, I'd thought maybe we saw fire in one another's eyes. But now I know differently. He spent time with me because I was going to be another means to an end. A final, bitter end.

I was drinking vodka, at first with orange, later neat – but always from a glass and always with ice. The Robertsons drank beer. They had a crate of bottles on the floor between them. The butcher drank whisky, whenever Cafferty deigned to pour him some, which wasn't often enough for the poor butcher. I was twenty quid down within a matter of minutes, and sixty quid down after a quarter of an hour. Cafferty placed his hand on mine again.

'If I'd not strayed along,' he said, 'they'd have had the shirt off your back and the breeks off your arse.'

'I never cheat,' said Tam Robertson. I got the feeling Cafferty had been wanting him to say something all along. Robertson acknowledged this by biting his lip.

Cafferty asked him if he was sure he didn't cheat. Robertson said nothing. His brother tried to calm things down, putting our minds back onto the game. But Cafferty grinned at Tam Robertson as he picked up his cards. Later, he started again.

'I've killed a lot of men,' he said, directing his eyes at me but his voice at the Robertsons. 'But not one of those killings wasn't justified. People who owed me, people who'd done me wrong, people who'd cheated. The way I look at it, everybody knows what he's getting into. Doesn't he?'

For want of any other answer, I agreed.

'And once you're into something, there are consequences to be faced, aren't there?' I nodded again. 'Black Aengus,' he said, 'have you ever *thought* about killing someone?'

'Many a time.'

This was true, though I wish now I'd held my tongue. I'd wanted to kill men wealthier than me, more handsome than me, men possessing beautiful women, and women who rejected my advances. I'd wanted to kill people who refused me service when drunk, people who didn't smile back when I smiled at them, people who were paged in hotels and made movies in Hollywood and owned ranches and castles and their own private armies. So my answer was accurate.

'Many a time.'

Cafferty was nodding. He'd almost finished the whisky. I thought something must be about to happen, some act of violence, and I was prepared for it – or thought I was. The Robertsons looked ready either to explode or implode. Tam had his hands on the edge of the table, ready to jump to his feet. And then the door opened. It was someone from the kitchens, bringing us up the sandwiches we'd ordered earlier. Smoked salmon and roast beef. The man waited to be paid.

'Go on, Tam,' said Cafferty quietly, 'you're the one with the luck tonight. Pay the man.'

Grudgingly, Tam counted out some notes and handed them over.

'And a tip,' said Cafferty. Another note was handed over. The waiter left the room. 'A very nice gesture,' said Cafferty. It was his turn to deal. 'How much are you down now, Black Aengus?'

'I'm not bad,' I said.

'I asked how much.'

'About forty.' I'd been a hundred down at one stage, but two decent hands had repaired some of the damage. Plus – there could be no doubt about it – the best card players around the table, by which I mean the Robertson brothers, were finding it hard to concentrate. The room was not warm, but there was sweat trickling down from Eck's sideburns. He kept rubbing the sweat away.

'You're letting them cheat you out of forty?' Cafferty said conversationally.

Tam Robertson leapt to his feet, his chair tipping over behind him.

'I've heard just about enough!'

But Eck righted the chair and pulled him down into it. Cafferty had finished dealing and was studying his cards, as though oblivious to the whole scene. The butcher got up suddenly, anouncing that he was going to be sick. He walked quickly out of the room.

'He won't be back,' Cafferty announced.

I said something lame to the effect that I was thinking of an early night myself. When Cafferty turned to me, he looked and sounded unlike any of his many personalities, the many I'd encountered so far.

'You wouldn't know an early night if it kicked you in the cunt.' He had started to gather up the cards for a redeal. I could feel blood tingling in my cheeks. He'd spoken with something close to revulsion. I told myself that he'd just drunk too much. People often said things ... etc. Look at me, I was one to be upset about the nasty things drunks could say!

He dealt the hand again. When it came time for him to make his initial bet, he threw a note into the pot, then laid his cards face down on the table. He reached into the waistband of his trousers. He'd worn a suit throughout; he always looks smart. He says the police are warier of picking up people wearing good clothes, and certainly more wary about punching or kicking them.

'They don't like to see good material ruined,' he told me. 'Canny Scots, you see.'

Now, when he withdrew his hand from the waistband, it was holding a pistol of some kind. The Robertsons started to object, while I just stared at the gun. I'd seen guns before, but never this close and in this kind of situation. Suddenly, the vodka, which had been having little or no effect all night, swam through me like waste through a sewer-pipe. I thought I was going to be sick, but swallowed it down. I even thought I might pass out. And all the time Cafferty was talking calm as you like about how Tam had been cheating him and where was the money.

'And you've been cheating Black Aengus too,' he said. I wanted to protest that this wasn't true, but still thought I might be sick if I opened my mouth, so I just shook my head, after which I felt even dizzier. You can't know the pain and frustration I'm feeling as I try to write this down candidly and exactly. Fourteen weeks have passed since that night, but every night it comes back to me, waking and sleeping. They're giving me drugs here, and strictly no alcohol. During the day I can walk in the grounds. There are 'encounter groups' where I'm supposed to talk my way out of my problem. Christ, if it were only that easy! The first thing my father did was get me out of the way. I am tempted to say *his* way. His answer was to send me on holiday. Mother chaperoned me around New England, where an aunt has a house in Bar Harbor. I tried talking to mother, but didn't seem to make much sense. She had that stupid sympathetic smile pasted onto her face.

I digress, not that it matters. Back to the poker game. You've perhaps guessed what happened next. I felt Cafferty's hand on mine, only this time he lifted my hand up in his. Then he placed the gun in my hand. I can feel it now, cold and hard. Half of me thought the gun was fake and he was just going to scare the Robertsons. The other half knew the gun was real, but didn't think he would use it.

Then I felt his fingers pushing mine until my index finger was around the trigger. His hand now fully enclosed mine, and aimed the gun. He squeezed his finger against mine, and there was an explosion in the room, and wisps of acrid powder. Blood freckled us all. It was warm for a moment, then cold against my skin. Eck was leaning over his brother, speaking to him. The gun clattered onto the table. Though I didn't take it in at the time, Cafferty proceeded to wrap the gun in a polythene bag. I know that any prints on it must be mine.

I flew up from the table, panicking, hysterical. Cafferty was seated still, and looking pacified. His calm had the opposite effect on me. I threw the vodka bottle against the wall, where it smashed, dousing wallpaper and curtains in alcohol. Seeing an idea, I grabbed a lighter from the table and ignited the vodka. Only now did Cafferty get up. He was swearing at me, and tried to douse the flames, but they were licking up the curtains out of our reach, scudding across the fabric wallcovering on the ceiling. He saw the fire was moving quicker than we could. I think Eck had already forsaken his brother and fled before I ran out of the room. I took the stairs three at a time and burst into the kitchens, demanding that all the gas be turned on. If the Central was going to burn, let it take the evidence with it.

I must have looked crazy enough, for the chef followed my instructions. I think he was the same person who served us the sandwiches, only he'd changed jackets. It was late, and he was alone in the kitchen, writing something down in a book. I told him to get out. He left by the back way, and I followed, keeping my head low as I jogged back to Blair Street.

I think that's everything. It doesn't feel any better for the writing down. There's no exorcism or catharsis. Maybe there never will be. You see, they've found the body. More than that, they know the man was shot. I don't see how the devil they can know, but they do. Maybe someone told them. Eck Robertson would have reason to. He's the only one who could tell. It's all my fault. I know that Cafferty started swearing at me because I'd mucked things up by setting fire to the room. If I hadn't, he would have seen to it that Tam Robertson's body disappeared in the usual way. No one would have known. We would have gotten away with murder.

But 'getting away with it' isn't always getting away with it. The corpse haunts me. Last night I dreamt it came back to me, charred, smouldering. Pointing a finger towards me and squeezing the trigger. Oh Christ, this is agony. And they think I'm here for alcoholism. I still haven't told father all of it, not yet. He knows, though. He knows I was there. But he's not saying anything. Sometimes I wish he'd hit me more as a child and not let me misbehave. He *liked* me to misbehave! 'We'll make a man of you,' he used to say. Father, I am made.

That was that. Rebus sat back in his chair and stared at the ceiling. Eddie Ringan knew a little more than he'd been telling. He'd been a witness at the card game and could place Cafferty there. No wonder he'd been running scared. Cafferty probably hadn't known him back then, hadn't paid attention to a waiter who was moonlighting anyway and not one of the regular staff.

Rebus rubbed his eyes and returned to the journal. There was a bit about a holiday, then about the hospital again. And then a few months later:

I saw Cafferty today (Sunday). Not my idea. He must have been following me. He caught up on Blackford Hill. I'd come through the Hermitage, climbing the steep face of the hill. He must have thought I was trying to get away from him. He pulled on my arm, swinging me around. I think I nearly jumped out of my skin.

He told me I had to keep my nose clean from now on. He said it was a good idea, going into that hospital. I think he was trying to let me know that he knew everything I'd been up to. I think I know what he's doing. He's biding his time. Watching me as I take instructions in the business. Waiting for the day when I take over from my father. I think he wants it all, body and soul.

Yes, body and soul.

There was a lot more, the style and substance of the entries changing as Aengus too tried to change. He'd found it hard work. The public face, the charity face, masked a yearning for some of that wild past. Rebus flipped to the final entry, undated:

You know, dear friend or foe, I liked the feel of that gun in my hand. And when Cafferty put my finger on the trigger . . . he *did* squeeze it. I'm certain of that. But supposing he hadn't? Would I still have fired, with his strong unfailing hand on mine? After all these years, all the bad dreams, the cold sweats and sudden surges, something has happened. The case is being reopened. I've spoken with Cafferty who tells me not to worry. He says I should concentrate my energies on the brewery. He seems to know more about our finances than I do. Father is talking of retiring next year. The business will be all mine, and all Cafferty's. I've seen him at charity functions, accompanied by Mo, and at various public occasions. We've talked, but never since that night have we enjoyed one another's company. I lost my usefulness that night. Perhaps I just showed my weakness by smashing the bottle. Or perhaps that had been the plan all along. He always gives me a wink when he sees me. But then he winks at just about everyone. But when he winks at me, when he closes his eye for that second, it's as if he's taking aim, setting me in his sights. Christ, is there no end in sight? If I weren't so scared, I'd be praying the police would find me. But Cafferty won't let them. He never will let them, never.

Rebus closed the journal. His heart was beating fast, hands trembling. You poor bugger, Aengus. When you read we'd got the gun, you thought we'd fingerprint it and then we'd come looking for you.

But instead, Cafferty had blown his trump trying to incriminate Rebus, just to keep him out of the picture for a while. And the irony of it all was, with the prints messed up, Black Aengus was in the clear – in the clear for a murder he didn't really commit.

Again, though, it was all uncorroborated. Rebus imagined the field day the defence would have if he walked into the Royal Mile courts with nothing more than the journal of a recovering dipsomaniac. The Edinburgh law courts were notoriously tough at the best of times. With the sort of advocate Cafferty could afford, it was a definite loser from the word go.

Yet Rebus *knew* he had to do something about Cafferty. The man deserved punishment, a million punishments. Let the punishment fit the crime, he thought. But he shook the notion away. No more guns.

He didn't go home, not right away. He walked out of the now-empty office and got into his car. And sat there, in the car park. The key was in the ignition, but he let it sit there. His hands rested lightly on the steering-wheel. After almost an hour, he started the engine, mostly because he was getting cold. He didn't go anywhere, except inside his head, and slowly but surely, with backtracking and rerouting along the way, the idea came to him. Let the punishment fit the crime. Yes, but not Cafferty's punishment. No, not Cafferty's.

Andrew McPhail's.

33

Rebus didn't go near St Leonard's for a couple of days, though he did get a message from Farmer Watson that Broderick Gibson was considering bringing an action against him, for harrying his son.

'He's been harrying himself for years,' was Rebus's only comment.

But he was waiting in his car when they released Andy Steele. The fisherman cum private eye blinked into the sun. Rebus sounded his horn, and Steele approached warily. Rebus wound down his window.

'Oh, it's you,' said Steele. There was disappointment in his voice. Rebus had said he'd see what he could do for the young man, then had left him to languish, never coming near.

'They let you out, then,' said Rebus.

'Aye, on bail.'

'That's because someone put up the money for you.'

Steele nodded, then started. 'You?'

'Me,' said Rebus. 'Now get in, I've got a job for you.'

'What sort of job?'

'Get in and I'll tell you.'

There was a bit more life in Steele as he walked round to the passenger side and opened the door.

'You want to be a private eye,' stated Rebus. 'Fair enough. I've got a job for you.'

Steele seemed unable to take it in for a moment, then cleared his head by shaking it briskly, rubbing his hands through his hair.

'Great,' he said. 'So long as it's not against the law.'

'Oh, it's nothing illicit. All I want you to do is talk to a few folk. They're good listeners too, shouldn't be any problem.'

'What am I going to tell them?'

Rebus started the car. 'That there's a contract out on a certain individual.'

'A contract?'

'Come on, Andy, you've seen the films. A contract.'

'A contract,' Andy Steele mouthed, as Rebus pulled into the traffic.

There was still no sign of Andrew McPhail. Alex Maclean, Rebus discovered, was back in circulation though not yet back at work. When

Rebus visited Mrs Mackenzie, she said she hadn't seen a man with bandaged hands and face hanging around. But one of the neighbours had. Well, it didn't matter, McPhail wouldn't be coming back here again. He would probably write or telephone with a forwarding address, asking his landlady to send on his stuff. Rebus looked towards the school as he got back into his car. The children were in their own little world . . . and safe.

He did a lot of driving, visiting schools and playparks. He knew McPhail must be sleeping rough. Maybe he was well away from Edinburgh by now. Rebus had a vision of him climbing up onto a coal train headed slowly south. A hand reached out and helped McPhail into the wagon. It was Deek Torrance. The opening credits began to roll . . .

It didn't matter if he couldn't find McPhail; it would just be a nice touch. A nicely cruel touch.

Wester Hailes was a good place to get lost, meaning it was an easy place to get lost. Sited to the far west of the city, visible from the bypass which gave Edinburgh such a wide berth, Wester Hailes was somewhere the city put people so it could forget about them. The architecture was unenthusiastic, the walls of the flat-blocks finished off with damp and cracks.

People might leave Wester Hailes, or stay there all their lives, surrounded by roads and industrial estates and empty green spaces. It had never before struck Rebus that it would make a good hiding place. You could walk the streets, or the Kingsknowe golf course, or the roads around Sighthill, and as long as you didn't look out of place you would be safe. There were places you could sleep without being discovered. And if you were of a mind, there was a school. A school and quite a few play-parks.

This was where, on the second day, he found Andrew McPhail. Never mind watching the bus and railway stations, Rebus had known where to look. He followed McPhail for three-quarters of an hour, at first in the car and then, when McPhail took a pedestrian shortcut, awkwardly on foot. McPhail kept moving, his gait brisk. A man out for a walk, that was all. A bit shabby maybe, but these days with unemployment what it was, you lost the will to shave every morning, didn't you?

McPhail was careful not to draw attention to himself. He didn't pause to stare at any children he saw. He just smiled towards them and went on his way. When Rebus had seen enough, he gained quickly and tapped him on the shoulder. He might as well have used a cattle-prod.

'Jesus, it's you!' McPhail's hand went to his chest. 'You nearly gave me a heart attack.'

'That would have saved Alex Maclean a job.'

'How is he?'

'Minor burns. He's up and about and on the warpath.'

'Christ's sake! We're talking about something that happened *years* ago!'

'And it's not going to happen again?'

'No!'

'And it was an accident you ended up living across from a primary school?'

'Yes.'

'And I was wrong to think I'd find you somewhere near a school or a playground ...?'

McPhail opened his mouth, then closed it again. He shook his head. 'No, you weren't wrong. I still like kids. But I never ... I'd never do anything to them. I won't even speak to them these days.' He looked up at Rebus. 'I'm *trying*, Inspector.'

Everyone wanted a second chance: Michael, McPhail, even Black Aengus. Sometimes, Rebus could help. 'Tell you what,' he said. 'There are programmes for past offenders. You could go into one of them, not in Edinburgh, somewhere else. You could sign on for social security and look for a job.' McPhail looked ready to say something. 'I know it takes money, a wee bit of cash to get you on your feet. But I can help with that too.'

McPhail blinked, one eye staying half closed. 'Why?'

'Because I want to. And afterwards, you'll be left alone, I promise. I won't tell anyone where you are or what's happened to you. Is it a deal?'

McPhail thought about it – for two seconds. 'A deal,' he said.

'Fine then.' Rebus put his hand on McPhail's shoulder again, drawing him a little closer. 'There's just one small thing I'd like you to do for me first ...'

It had been quiet in the social club, and Chick Muir was thinking of heading home when the young chap at the bar asked if he could buy him a drink. Chick readily agreed.

'I don't like drinking on my own,' the young man explained.

'Who can blame you?' said Chick agreeably, handing his empty glass to the barman. 'Not from round here?'

'Aberdeen,' said the young man.

'A long way from home. Is it still like Dallas up there?'

Chick meant the oil-boom, which had actually disappeared almost as quickly as it had begun, except in the mythology of those people not living in Aberdeen.

'Maybe it is,' said the young man, 'but that didn't stop them sacking me.'

'Sorry to hear it.' Chick really was too. He'd been hoping the young man was off the oil rigs with cash to burn. He was planning to tap him for a tenner, but now shrugged away the idea.

'I'm Andy Steele, by the way.'

'Chick Muir.' Chick placed his cigarette in his mouth so he could shake Andy Steele's hand. The grip was like a rubbish-crusher.

'The money didn't bring much luck to Aberdeen, you know,' Steele was reminiscing. 'Just a load of sharks and gangsters.'

'I'll believe it.' Muir was already halfway through his drink. He wished he'd been drinking a whisky instead of the half-pint when he'd been asked about another. It didn't look good exchanging a half-pint for a nip, so he was stuck with a half.

'That's mostly why I'm here,' said Steele.

'What? Gangsters?' Muir sounded amused.

'In a way. I'm visiting a friend, too, but I thought while I was here I might pick up a few bob.'

'How's that?' Chick was beginning to feel uncomfortable, but also distinctly curious.

Steele dropped his voice, though they were alone at the bar. 'There's word going around Aberdeen that someone's out to get a certain individual in Edinburgh.'

The barman had turned on the tape machine behind the bar. The low-ceilinged room was promptly filled with a folk duet. They'd played the club last week, and the barman had made a tape of them. It sounded worse now than it had then.

'In the name of Auld Nick, turn that down!' Chick didn't have a loud voice, but no one could say it lacked authority. The barman turned the sound down a bit, and when Chick still glared at him turned it even lower. 'What was that?' he asked Andy Steele. Andy Steele, who had been enjoying his drink, put down the glass and told Chick Muir again. And a little while later, mission accomplished, he bought Chick a final drink and then left.

Chick Muir didn't touch this fresh half pint. He stared past it at his own reflection in the mirror behind the row of optics. Then he made a few phone calls, again roaring at the barman to 'turn that shite off!' The third call he made was to St Leonard's, where he was informed, a bit too light-heartedly, he thought, that Inspector Rebus had been suspended from duty pending enquiries. He tried Rebus at his flat, but no joy there either. Ach well, it wasn't so important. What mattered was that he'd talked to the big man. Now the big man owed him, and that was quite enough for the penniless Chick Muir to be going on with.

Andy Steele gave the same performance in a meanly lit pub and a betting shop, and that evening was at Powderhall for the greyhound racing. He recited to himself the description Rebus had given him, and eventually spotted the man tucking into a meal of potato crisps at a window-seat in the bar.

'Are you Shuggie Oliphant?' he asked.

'That's me,' said the huge thirtyish man. He was poking a finger into the farthest corner of the crisp-bag in search of salt.

'Somebody told me you might be interested in a bit of information I've got.'

Oliphant still hadn't looked at him. The bag emptied, he folded it into a thin strip, then tied it in a knot and placed it on the table. There were four other granny knots just like it in a row. 'You don't get paid till I do,' Oliphant informed him, sucking on a greasy finger and smacking his lips.

Andy Steele sat down across from him. 'That's okay by me,' he said.

On Sunday morning Rebus waited at the top of a blustery Calton Hill. He walked around the observatory, as the other Sunday strollers were doing. His leg was definitely improving. People were pointing out distant landmarks. Broken clouds were moving rapidly over a pale blue sky. Nowhere else in the world, he reckoned, had this geography of bumps and valleys and outcrops. The volcanic plug beneath Edinburgh Castle had been the start of it. Too good a place *not* to build a fortress. And the town had grown around it, grown out as far as Wester Hailes and beyond.

The observatory was an odd building, if functional. The folly, on the other hand, was just that, and served no function at all save as a thing to clamber over and a place to spraypaint your name. It was one side of a projected Greek temple (Edinburgh, after all, being 'the Athens of the north'). The all-too-eccentric brain behind the scheme had run out of money after completion of this first side. And there it stood, a series of pillars on a plinth so tall kids had to stand on each other's shoulders to climb aboard.

When Rebus looked towards it, he saw a woman there swinging her legs from the plinth and waving towards him. It was Siobhan Clarke. He walked over to her.

'How long have you been here?' he called up.

'Not long. Where's your stick?'

'I can manage fine without it.' This was true, though by 'fine' he meant that he could hobble along at a reasonable pace. 'I see Hibs got a result yesterday.'

'About time.'

'No sign of himself?'

But Siobhan pointed to the car park. 'Here he comes now.'

A Mini Metro had climbed the road to the top of the hill and was squeezing into a space between two shinier larger cars. 'Give me a hand down,' said Siobhan.

'Watch for my leg,' Rebus complained. But she felt almost weightless as he lifted her down.

'Thanks,' she said. Brian Holmes had watched the performance before locking his car and coming towards them.

'A regular Baryshnikov,' he commented.

'Bless you,' said Rebus.

'So what's this all about, sir?' Siobhan asked. 'Why the secrecy?'

'There's nothing secret,' Rebus said, starting to walk, 'about an Inspector wanting to talk with two of his junior colleagues. *Trusted* junior colleagues.'

Siobhan caught Holmes' eye. Holmes shook his head: he wants something from us. As if she didn't know.

They leaned against a railing, enjoying the view, Rebus doing most of the talking. Siobhan and Holmes added occasional questions, mostly rhetorical.

'So this would be off our own bats?'

'Of course,' Rebus answered. 'Just two keen coppers with a little bit of initiative.' He had a question of his own. 'Will the lighting be difficult?'

Holmes shrugged. 'I'll ask Jimmy Hutton about that. He's a professional photographer. Does calendars and that sort of thing.'

'It's not going to be wee kittens or a Highland glen,' replied Rebus.

'No, sir,' said Holmes.

'And you think this'll work?' asked Siobhan.

Rebus shrugged. 'Let's wait and see.'

'We haven't said we'll do it, sir.'

'No,' said Rebus, turning away, 'but you will.'

34

Off their own initiative then, Holmes and Siobhan decided to spend Monday evening doing a surveillance shift on Operation Moneybags. Without heating, the room they crouched in was cold and damp, and dark enough to attract the odd mouse. Holmes had set the camera up, after taking advice from the calendar man. He'd even borrowed a special lens for the occasion, telephoto and night-sighted. He hadn't bothered with his Walkman and his Patsy Cline tapes: in the past, there'd always been more than enough to talk about with Siobhan. But tonight she didn't seem in the mood. She kept gnawing on her top and bottom lips, and got up every now and then to do stretching exercises.

'Don't you get stiff?' she asked him.

'Not me,' said Holmes quietly. 'I've been in training for this – years of being a couch potato.'

'I thought you kept pretty fit.'

He watched her bend forward and lay her arms down the length of one leg. 'And you must be double-jointed.'

'Not quite. You should've seen me in my teens.' Holmes' grin was illuminated by the street light's diffuse orange glow. 'Down, Rover,' said Siobhan. There was a scuttling overhead.

'A rat,' said Holmes. 'Ever cornered one?' She shook her head. 'They can jump like a Tummel salmon.'

'My parents took me to the hydro dam when I was a kid.'

'At Pitlochry?' She nodded. 'So you've seen the salmon leaping?' She nodded again. 'Well,' said Holmes, 'imagine one of those with hair and fangs and a long thick tail.'

'I'd rather not.' She watched from the window. 'Do you think he'll come.'

'I don't know. John Rebus isn't often wrong.'

'Is that why everyone hates him?'

Holmes seemed a little surprised. 'Who hates him?'

She shrugged. 'People I've talked to at St Leonard's ... and other places. They don't trust him.'

'He wouldn't have it any other way.'

'Why not?'

'Because he's thrawn.' He was remembering the first time Rebus had

444

used him in a case. He'd spent a cold frustrating evening watching for a dog-fight that never took place. He was hoping tonight would be better.

The rat was moving again, to the back of the room now, over by the door.

'*Do* you think he'll come?' Siobhan asked again.

'He'll come, lass.' They both turned towards the shape in the doorway. It was Rebus. 'You two,' he said, 'blethering like sweetiewives. I could have climbed those stairs in pit boots and you'd not have heard me.' He came over to the window. 'Anything?'

'Nothing, sir.'

Rebus angled his watch towards the light. 'I make it five to.'

The display on Siobhan's digital watch was backlit. 'Ten to, sir.'

'Bloody watch,' muttered Rebus. 'Not long now. There'll be some action by the top of the hour. Unless that daft Aberdonian's put the kibosh on it.'

But the 'daft Aberdonian' wasn't so daft. Big Ger Cafferty paid for information. Even if it was information he already knew, he tended to pay: it was a cheap way of making sure *everything* got back to him. For example, even though he'd already heard from two sources that the teuchters were planning to muscle in on him, he still paid Shug Oliphant a few notes for his effort. And Oliphant, who liked to keep his own sources sweet, handed over ten quid to Andy Steele, this representing two-fifths of Oliphant's reward.

'There you go,' he said.

'Cheers,' said Andy Steele, genuinely pleased.

'Found anything you like?'

Oliphant was referring to the videotapes which surrounded them in the small rental shop which he operated. The area behind the narrow counter was so small, Oliphant only just squeezed in there. Every time he moved he seemed to knock something off a shelf onto the floor, where it remained, since there was also no room for him to bend over.

'I've got some bits and pieces under the counter,' he went on, 'if you're interested.'

'No, I don't want a video.'

Oliphant grinned unpleasantly. 'I'm not sure the gentleman really believed your story,' Oliphant told Andy. 'But I've heard the rumour a few times since, so maybe there's something in it.'

'There is,' said Andy Steele. Rebus was right, if you told a deaf man something on Monday, by Tuesday it was in the evening paper. 'They've got a watch on his hang-outs, including the operation in Gorgie.'

Oliphant looked mightily suspicious. 'How do you know?'

'Luck, really. I bumped into one of them. I knew him in Aberdeen. He told me to get out if I didn't want to get mixed up in it.'

'But you're still here.'

'I'm on the mail train tomorrow morning.'

'So something's happening tonight?' Oliphant still sounded highly sceptical, but then that was his way.

Steele shrugged. 'All I know is, they're keeping watch. I think maybe they just want to talk.'

Oliphant considered, running his fingers over a video-box. 'There were two pubs last night got their windows smashed.' Steele didn't blink. 'Pubs where the gentleman drank. Could be a connection?'

Steele shrugged. 'Could be.' If he were being honest, he'd have told how he acted as getaway driver while Rebus himself tossed the large rocks through the glass. One of the pubs had been the Firth at Tollcross, the other the Bowery at the bottom of Easter Road.

But instead he said, 'Loon called McPhail, he's the one watching Gorgie. He's in charge.'

Oliphant nodded. 'You know the way it works, come back in a day or two. There'll be money if the gen's on the nail.'

But Steele shook his head. 'I'm off up to Aberdeen.'

'So you are,' said Oliphant. 'Tell you what,' he tore a sheet from a pad, 'give me your address and I'll send on the cash.'

Andy Steele had fun inventing the address.

Cafferty was playing snooker when he got the message. He had a quarter share in an upmarket snooker hall and leisure complex in Leith. The intended market had been yuppies, working class lads scraping their way up the greasy pole. But the yuppies had vanished in a puff of smoke. So now the complex was shifting cannily downmarket with video bingo, happy hour, an arcade full of electronic machines, and plans for a bowling alley. Teenagers always seemed to have money in their pockets. They would carve the bowling alley out of the little-used gymnasium, the restaurant next to it, and the aerobics room beyond that.

Staying in business, Cafferty had found, was all about remaining flexible. If the wind changed, you didn't try to steer in the opposite direction. Mooted future plans included a soul club and a 1940s ball-room, the latter complete with tea dances and 'blackout nights'. Groping nights, Cafferty called them.

He knew he was crap at snooker, but he liked the game. His theory was fine; it was the practice that was lacking. Vanity prevented him taking lessons, and his renowned lack of patience would have dissuaded all but the most foolhardy from giving them. On Mo's advice, he'd tried a few other sports – tennis, squash, even skiing one time. The only one he'd enjoyed was golf. He loved thwacking that ball all over the place. Problem was, he didn't know when to hold back, he was always overshooting. If he hadn't split at least a couple of balls after nine holes, he wasn't happy.

Snooker suited him. It had everything. Tactics, ciggies, booze, and a few sidebets. So here he was again in the hall, overhead lights flooding the green tables, dusk everywhere else. Quiet, too, therapeutic; just the clack of the balls, the occasional comment or joke, a floor-stomp with the cue to signal a worthy shot. Then Jimmy the Ear was coming towards him.

'Phone call from the house,' he told Cafferty. Then he gave him Oliphant's message.

Andrew McPhail trusted Rebus about as far as he could toss a caber into a gale. He knew he should be running for cover right now, let the caber land where it might. There were several ways it could go. Rebus might be setting up a meeting between McPhail and Maclean. Well, McPhail could prepare himself against this. Or it might be some other kind of ruse, probably ending up with a beating and the clear message to get the fuck out of Edinburgh.

Or it could be straight. Aye, if the spirit-level was bent. Rebus had asked McPhail to deliver a message, a letter. He'd even handed over the envelope. The message was for a man called Cafferty, who would be leaving the taxi office on Gorgie Road around ten.

'So what's the message?'

'Never you mind,' Rebus had said.

'Why me?'

'It can't come from me, that's all you need to know. Just make sure it's him, and give him the envelope.'

'This stinks.'

'I can't make it any simpler. We'll meet afterwards and fix up your new future. The ball's already rolling.'

'Aye,' said McPhail, 'but where the fuck's the net?'

Yet here he was, walking up Gorgie Road. A bit cold, threatening rain. Rebus had taken him to St Leonard's this afternoon, let him shower and shave, even provided some clean clothes which he'd picked up from Mrs Mackenzie's.

'I don't want a tramp delivering my post,' he'd explained. Ah, the letter. McPhail wasn't donnert; he'd torn the envelope open earlier this evening. Inside was a smaller brown envelope with some writing on the front: NO PEEKING NOW, McPHAIL!

He'd thought about opening it anyway. It didn't feel like there was much inside, a single sheet of paper. But something stopped him, a pale spark of hope, the hope that everything was going to be all right.

He didn't have a watch, but was a good judge of time. It felt like ten o'clock. And here he was in front of the taxi office. There were lights on inside, and cabs ready and waiting outside. Their busiest shift would be starting soon, the rides home after closing time. The night air smelt like ten o'clock. Diesel from the railway lines, rain close by. Andrew McPhail waited.

He saw the headlights, and when the car – a Jag – swerved and mounted the pavement his first thought was: drunk driver. But the car braked smoothly, stopping beside him, almost pinning him to the wire fence. The driver got out. He was big. A gust of wind flapped his long hair, and McPhail saw that one ear was missing.

'You McPhail?' he demanded. The back door of the Jag was opening slowly, another man getting out. He wasn't as big as the driver, but he somehow *seemed* larger. He was smiling unkindly.

The letter was in McPhail's pocket. 'Cafferty?' he asked, forcing the word from his lungs.

The smiling man blinked lazily in acknowledgement. In McPhail's other pocket was the broken neck of a whisky bottle he'd found beside an overflowing bottle bank. It wasn't much of a weapon, but it was all he could afford. Even so, he didn't rate his chances. His bladder felt painfully full. He reached for the letter.

The driver pinned his arms to his side and swung him around, so he was face to face with Cafferty, who swung a kick into his groin. The butt of a three-section snooker cue slipped expertly from Cafferty's coat sleeve into his hand. As McPhail doubled over, the cue caught him on the side of the jaw, fracturing it, dislodging teeth. He fell further forwards and was rewarded with the cue on the back of his neck. His whole body went numb. Now the driver was pulling his head up by the hair and Cafferty was forcing his mouth open with the cue, working it past his tongue and into his throat.

'Hold it there!' Two of them, a man and a woman, running from across the street and holding open their IDs. 'Police officers.'

Cafferty lifted both hands away, raising them head high. He had left the cue in McPhail's mouth. The driver released the battered man, who remained upright on his knees. Shakily, Andrew McPhail started to pull the snooker cue out of his throat. There were sirens close by as a police car approached.

'It's nothing, officer,' Cafferty was saying, 'a misunderstanding.'

'Some misunderstanding,' said the male police officer. His sidekick slipped her hand into McPhail's pocket. She felt a broken bottle. Wrong pocket. From the other pocket she produced the letter, crumpled now. She handed it to Cafferty.

'Open this, please, sir,' she said.

Cafferty stared at it. 'Is this a set-up?' But he opened it anyway. Inside was a scrap of paper, which he unfolded. The note was unsigned. He knew who it was from anyway. 'Rebus!' he spat. 'That bastard Rebus!'

A few minutes later, as Cafferty and his driver were being taken away, and the ambulance was arriving for Andrew McPhail, Siobhan picked up the note which Cafferty had dropped. It said simply, 'I hope they sell your skin for souvenirs.' She frowned and looked up at the surveillance window, but couldn't see anyone there.

Had she seen anything, it would have been the outline of a man making the shape of a gun from his fist, lining up the thumb so Cafferty was in its sights, and pulling the imaginary trigger.

Bang!

35

Nobody at St Leonard's believed Holmes and Siobhan were there that night simply out of an exaggerated sense of duty. The more credible version had them meeting for a clandestine shag and just happening upon the beating. Lucky there was film in the surveillance camera. And didn't the photos come out well?

With Cafferty in custody, they got the chance to take away his things and have yet another look at them ... including the infamous coded diary. Watson and Lauderdale were poring over xeroxed sheets from it when there was a knock at the Chief Super's door.

'Come!' called Watson.

John Rebus walked in and looked around admiringly at the sudden floorspace. 'I see you got your cabinets, sir.'

Lauderdale pulled himself up straight. 'What the hell are you doing here? You're suspended from duty.'

'It's all right, Frank,' said Watson, 'I asked Inspector Rebus to come in.' He turned the xeroxed pages towards Rebus. 'Take a look.'

It didn't take long. The problem with the code in the past was that they hadn't known *what* to look for. But now Rebus had a more than fair idea. He stabbed one entry. 'There,' he said. '3TUB SCS.'

'Yes?'

'It means the butcher on South Clerk Street owes three thousand. He's abbreviated 'butcher' and written it backwards.'

Lauderdale looked disbelieving. 'Are you sure?'

Rebus shrugged. 'Put the experts at Fettes onto it. They should be able to find at least a few more late-payers.'

'Thank you, John,' said Watson. Rebus turned smartly and left the room. Lauderdale stared at his superior.

'I get the feeling,' he said, 'something's going on here I don't know about.'

'Well, Frank,' said Watson, 'why should today be different from any other?'

Which, as the saying went, put CI Lauderdale's gas at a very low peep.

It was Siobhan Clarke who came up with the most important piece of information in the whole case.

It *was* a case now. Rebus didn't mind that the machine was in operation without him. Holmes and Clarke reported back to him at the end of each day. The code-breakers had been hard at work, as a result of which detectives were talking to Cafferty's black book victims. It would only take one or two of them in court, and Cafferty would be going down. So far, though, no one was talking. Rebus had an idea of one person who, given enough persuasion, might.

Then Siobhan mentioned that Cafferty's company Geronimo Holdings held a seventy-nine per cent share in a large farm in the south-west Borders, not so very far from the coastline where the bodies had been washing up until recently. A party was sent to the farm. They found plenty for the forensic scientists to start working on ... especially the pigsties. The sties themselves were clean enough, but there was an enclosed area of storage space above each ramshackle sty. Most of the farm had turned itself over to the latest in high-tech agriculture, but not the sties. It was this which initially alerted the police. Above the pigsties, in the dark enclosures strewn with rank straw, there was a tangible reek of something unwholesome, something putrid. Strips of cloth were found; in one corner there lay a man's trouser-belt. The area was photographed and picked over for its least congruous particles. Upstairs in the farmhouse, meanwhile, a man who claimed initially to be an agricultural labourer eventually admitted to being Derek Torrance, better known as Deek.

At the same time, Rebus was driving out to Dalkeith, to Duncton Terrace, to be precise. It was early evening, and the Kintoul family was at home. Mother, father and son took up three sides of a fold-down table in the kitchen. The chip-pan was still smouldering and spitting on the greasy gas cooker. The vinyl wallpaper was slick with condensation. Most of the food on the plates was disguised by brown sauce. Rebus could smell vinegar and washing-up liquid. Rory Kintoul excused himself and went with Rebus into the living room. Kitchen and living room were connected by a serving hatch. Rebus wondered if wife and son would be listening at the hatch.

Rebus sat in one fireside chair, Kintoul opposite him.

'Sorry if it's a bad time,' Rebus began. There was a ritual to be followed, after all.

'What is it, Inspector?'

'You'll have heard, Mr Kintoul, we've arrested Morris Cafferty. He'll be going away for quite a while.' Rebus looked at the photos on the mantelpiece, snapshots of gap-toothed kids, nephews and nieces. He smiled at them. 'I just thought maybe it was time you got it off your chest.'

He kept silent for a moment, still examining the framed photos. Kintoul said nothing.

'Only,' said Rebus, 'I know you're a good man. I mean, a *good* man.

You put family first, am I right?' Kintoul nodded uncertainly. 'Your wife and son, you'd do anything for them. Same goes for your other family, parents, sisters, brothers, cousins ...' Rebus trailed off.

'I know Cafferty's going away,' said Kintoul.

'And?'

Kintoul shrugged.

'It's like this,' said Rebus. 'We know just about all there is to know. We just need a little corroboration.'

'That means testifying?'

Rebus nodded. Eddie Ringan would be testifying too, telling all he knew about the Central Hotel, in return for a good word from the police come his own trial. 'Mr Kintoul, you've got to accept something. You've got to accept that you've changed, you're not the same man you were a year or two ago. Why did you do it?' Rebus asked the way a friend would, just curious.

Kintoul wiped a smear of sauce from his chin. 'It was a favour. Jim always needed favours.'

'So you drove the van?'

'Yes, I did his rounds.'

'But you were a lab technician!'

Kintoul smiled. 'And I could earn more on the butcher's round.' He shrugged again. 'Like you say, Inspector, I put family first, especially where money's concerned.'

'Go on.'

'How much do you know?'

'We know the van was used to dump the bodies.'

'Nobody ever notices a butcher's van.'

'Except a poor constable in north-east Fife. He ended up with concussion.'

'That was after my time. I was shot of it by then.' He waited till Rebus nodded agreement, then went on. 'Only, when I wanted out Cafferty didn't want me out. He was putting pressure on.'

'That's how you got stabbed?'

'It was that bodyguard of his, Jimmy the Ear. He lost the head. Knifed me as I was getting out of the car. Crazy bastard.' Kintoul glanced towards the serving-hatch. 'You know what Cafferty did when I said I wanted to stop driving the van? He offered Jason a job "driving" for him. Jason's my son.'

Rebus nodded. 'But why all this fuss? Cafferty could get a hundred guys to drive a van for him.'

'I thought you knew him, Inspector. Cafferty's like that. He's ... particular about his flesh.'

'He's off his head,' commented Rebus. 'How did you get sucked in in the first place?'

'I was still driving full-time when Cafferty won half the business from Jimmy. One evening, one of Cafferty's men turned up all smarmy, told me we'd be taking a run to the coast early next morning. Via some farm in the Borders.'

'You went to the farm?' So that's why there was straw in the van.

The colour was seeping from Kintoul's face like blood from a cut of meat.

'Oh aye. There was something in the pigsties, tied up in fertiliser bags. Stank to high heaven. I'd been working in a butcher's long enough to know it had been rotting in that sty for a good few weeks, months, even.'

'A corpse?'

'Easy to tell, isn't it? I threw my guts up. Cafferty's man said what a waste, I should've done it into the trough.' Kintoul paused. He was still wiping at his chin, though the sauce mark had long ago been erased. 'Cafferty liked the bodies to be rotten, less chance of them washing ashore in any recognisable state.'

'Christ.'

'I haven't come to the worst part yet.' In the next room, Kintoul's wife and son were speaking in undertones. Rebus was in no hurry, and merely watched as Kintoul got up to stare from his back window. There was a patch of garden out there he could call his own. It was small, but it was his. He came back and stood in front of the gas fire, not looking at Rebus.

'I was there one day when he killed someone,' he said baldly. Then he screwed shut his eyes. Rebus was trying to control his own breathing. This guy would make a gem of a witness.

'Killed them how?' Still not pressing; still the friend.

Kintoul tipped his head back, feeding tears back where they had come from. 'How? With his bare hands. We'd arrived late. The van had broken down in the middle of nowhere. It was about ten in the morning. Mist all around the farm, like driving into Brigadoon. They were both wearing business suits, that's what got me. And they were up to their ankles in glaur.'

Rebus frowned, not quite comprehending. 'They were *in* the pigsty?'

Kintoul nodded. 'There's a fenced run. Cafferty was in there with this man. There were other people watching through the fence.' He swallowed. 'I swear Cafferty looked like he was enjoying it. There with the mud lapping at him, and the pigs squealing in their boxes wondering what the hell was happening, and all the silent onlookers.' Kintoul tried to shake the memory away, probably a daily event.

'They were fighting?'

'The other man looked like he'd been roughed up beforehand. Nobody'd call it a fair fight. And eventually, after Cafferty'd beaten the living shite out of him, he grabbed him by the neck and forced him down into the muck. He stood on the man's back, balancing there, and holding the face down with his hands. He looked like it was nothing new. Then the man stopped struggling . . .'

Rebus and Kintoul were silent, blood pounding through them, both trying to cope with the vision of an early morning pigsty . . . 'Afterwards,' said Kintoul, his voice lower than ever, 'he beamed at us like it was his coronation.'

Then, in complete grimacing silence, he started to weep.

Rebus was visiting the Infirmary so often he was considering taking out a season ticket. But he hadn't expected to see Flower there.

'Checking in? The psychiatric section's down the hall.'

'Ha ha,' said Flower.

'What are you doing here anyway?'

'I could ask you the same question.'

'I live here, what about you?'

'I came to ask some questions.'

'Of Andrew McPhail?' Flower nodded. 'Did nobody tell you his jaw's wired shut?' Flower twitched, producing a good wide grin from Rebus. 'How come it's your business anyway?'

'It involves Cafferty,' Flower said.

'Oh aye, so it does, I'd forgotten.'

'Looks like we've got him this time.'

'Looks like it. But you never know with Cafferty.' Rebus stared unblinking at Flower as he spoke. 'The reason he's lasted so long is he's clever. He's clever, and he's got the best lawyers. Plus he's got people scared of him, and he's got people in his pocket . . . maybe even a copper or three.'

Flower had stared out the gaze; now he blinked. 'You think I was in Cafferty's pocket?'

Rebus had been pondering this. He had Cafferty marked down for the attack on Michael and the scam with the gun. As for the clumsy hit-and-run attempt, that was so amateurish, he guessed at Broderick Gibson for its architect. Quite simply, Cafferty would have used better men.

He'd been silent long enough, so he shook his head. 'I don't think you're that smart. Cafferty likes smart people. But I *do* think you had a word with the Inland Revenue about me.'

'I don't know what you're talking about.'

Rebus grinned. 'I do like a cliché.' Then he walked on down the hall.

Andrew McPhail was easy to find. You just looked for the broken face. He was wired up like somebody's first attempt at a junction box. Rebus thought he could see where they'd used two wires where one would have sufficed. But then he was no doctor. McPhail had his eyes closed.

'Hello there,' said Rebus. The eyes opened. There was anger there, but Rebus could cope with it. He held up a hand. 'No,' he said, 'don't bother to thank me.' Then he smiled. 'It's all set up for when they let you out. Up north for rehabilitation, maybe a job, and bracing coastal walks. Man, I envy you.' He looked around the ward. Every bed had a body in it. The nurses looked like they could use a holiday or at the very least a gin and lime with some dry-roast peanuts.

'I said I'd leave you alone,' Rebus went on, 'and I keep my word. But a piece of advice.' He rested his hands on the edge of the bed and leaned towards McPhail. 'Cafferty's the biggest villain in town. You're probably the only bugger in Edinburgh who didn't know that. Now his men know a guy called McPhail set their boss up. So don't ever think of coming back, will you?' McPhail still glared at him. 'Good,' said Rebus. He straightened up, turned, and walked away, then paused and turned. 'Oh,' he said, 'and I meant to say something.' He returned to the bed and stood at its foot, where charts showed McPhail's temperature and medicaments. Rebus waited till McPhail's wet eyes were on his, then he smiled sympathetically again.

'Sorry,' he said. This time, when he turned he kept on walking.

Andy Steele had been the necessary go-between. It was too dangerous for Rebus to put the story out first-hand. The source of the tale might have got back to Cafferty, and that would have ruined everything. McPhail hadn't been necessary, but he'd been useful. Rebus explained the ruse twice to Andy Steele, and even then the young fisherman didn't seem to take it all in. He had the look of a man with a dozen unaskable questions.

'So what are you going to do now?' Rebus asked. He'd been hoping in fact that Steele might already have left for home.

'Oh, I'm applying for a grant,' said Steele.

'You mean like university?'

But Steele hooted. 'Not likely! It's one of those schemes to get the unemployed into business.'

'Oh aye?'

Steele nodded. 'I'm eligible.'

'So what's the business?'

'A detective agency, of course!'

'Where exactly?'

'Edinburgh. I've made more money since I came here than I made in six months in Aberdeen.'

'You cannot be serious,' said Rebus. But Andy Steele was.

36

He had one last meeting planned, and wasn't looking forward to it. He walked from St Leonard's to the University library at George Square. The indifferent security man on the door glanced at his ID and nodded him towards the front desk, where Nell Stapleton, tall and broad-shouldered, was taking returned books from a duffel-coated student. She caught his eye and looked surprised. Pleased at first; but as she went through the books, Rebus saw her mind wasn't wholly on the job. At last, she came over to him.

'Hello, John.'

'Nell.'

'What brings you here?'

'Can we have a word?'

She checked with the other assistant that it was okay to take a five-minute break. They walked as far as a book-lined corridor.

'Brian tells me you've closed the case, the one he was so worried about.'

Rebus nodded.

'That's great news. Thanks for your help.'

Rebus shrugged.

She tilted her head slightly. 'Is something the matter?'

'I'm not sure,' said Rebus. 'Do you want to tell me?'

'*Me*?'

Rebus nodded again.

'I don't understand.'

'You've lived with a policeman, Nell. You know we deal in motives. Sometimes there isn't much else to go on. I've been thinking about motives recently.' He shut up as a female student pulled open a door, came out into the corridor, smiled briefly at Nell, and went on her way. Nell watched her go. Rebus thought she would like to swop bodies for a few minutes.

'Motives?' she said. She was leaning against the wall, but Rebus got no notion of calmness from her stance.

'Remember,' he said, 'that night in the hospital, the night Brian was attacked. You said something about an argument, and him going off to the Heartbreak Cafe?'

She nodded. 'That's right. We met that night to talk over a drink. But we argued. I don't see –'

'Only, I've been thinking about the motive behind the attack. There were too many at first, but I've narrowed them down. They're all motives *you'd* have, Nell.'

'What?'

'You told me you were scared for him, scared because *he* was scared. And he was scared because he was poking into something that could nail Big Ger Cafferty. Wouldn't it be better if there was *another* body on the case, someone else to attract the fire? Me, in other words. So you got me involved.'

'Now wait a minute –'

But Rebus held his hand up and closed his eyes, begging silence. 'Then,' he said, 'there was DC Clarke. They were getting along so famously together. Jealousy maybe? Always a good motive.'

'I don't believe this.'

Rebus ignored her. 'And of course the simplest motive. The two of you had been rowing about whether or not to have kids. That and the fact that he was overworking, not paying you enough attention.'

'Did he tell you that?'

Rebus did not sound unkind. 'You told me yourself you'd had a row that evening. You knew where he was headed – same place as always. So why not wait near his car and brain him when he came out? A nice simple revenge.' Rebus paused. 'How many motives does that make? I've lost count. Enough to be going on with, eh?'

'I don't believe this.' Tears were rising into her eyes. Every time she blinked, more appeared. She ran a thumb and forefinger down her nose, clearing it, breathing in noisily. 'What are you going to do?' she asked at last.

'I'm going to lend you a hankie,' said Rebus.

'I don't want your fucking hankie!'

Rebus put a finger to his lips. 'This is a library, remember?'

She sniffed and wiped away tears.

'Nell,' he said quietly, 'I don't want you to say anything. I don't want to know. I just want *you* to know. All right?'

'You think you're so fucking smart.'

He shrugged. 'The offer of a hankie still stands.'

'Get stuffed.'

'Do you really want Brian to leave the force?'

But she was walking away from him, head held high, shoulders swinging just a little exaggeratedly. He watched her go behind the desk, where her co-worker saw something was wrong and put a comforting arm around her. Rebus examined the shelves of books in front of him in the corridor, but saw nothing to delay his leavetaking.

He sat on a bench in the Meadows, the back of the library rising up behind him. He had his hands in his pockets as he watched a hastily arranged game of football. Eight men against seven. They'd come over to him and asked if he fancied making up the numbers.

'You must be desperate,' he'd said, shaking his head. The goalposts comprised one orange and white traffic cone, one pile of coats, one pile of folders and books, and a branch stuck in the ground. Rebus glanced at his watch more often than necessary. No one on the field was worrying too much about the time taken to play the first half. Two of the players looked like brothers though they played on opposing sides. Mickey had left the flat that morning, taking the photo of their dad and Uncle Jimmy with him.

'To remind me,' he'd said.

A woman in a Burberry trenchcoat sat down on the bench beside him.

'Are they any good?' she asked.

'They'd give Hibs a run for their money.'

'How good does that make them?' she asked.

Rebus turned towards Dr Patience Aitken and smiled, reaching out to take her hand in his. 'What kept you so long?' he asked.

'Just the usual,' she said. 'Work.'

'I tried phoning you so often.'

'Put my mind at rest then,' she said.

'How?'

She moved closer. 'Tell me I'm not just a number in your little black book . . .'

Mortal Causes

Acknowledgements

A lot of people helped me with this book. I'd like to thank the people of Northern Ireland for their generosity and their 'crack'. Particular thanks need to go to a few people who can't be named or wouldn't thank me for naming them. You know who you are.

Thanks also to: Colin and Liz Stevenson, for trying; Gerald Hammond, for his gun expertise; the officers of the City of Edinburgh Police and Lothian and Borders Police, who never seem to mind me telling stories about them; David and Pauline, for help at the Festival.

The best book on the subject of Protestant paramilitaries is Professor Steve Bruce's *The Red Hand* (OUP, 1992). One quote from the book: 'There is no "Northern Ireland problem" for which there is a solution. There is only a conflict in which there must be winners and losers.'

The action of *Mortal Causes* takes place in a fictionalised summer, 1993, before the Shankill Road bombing and its bloody aftermath.

Perhaps Edinburgh's terrible inability to speak out,
Edinburgh's silence with regard to all it should be saying,
Is but the hush that precedes the thunder,
The liberating detonation so oppressively imminent now?

Hugh MacDiarmid

We're all gonna be just dirt in the ground.

Tom Waits

He could scream all he liked.

They were underground, a place he didn't know, a cool ancient place but lit by electricity. And he was being punished. The blood dripped off him onto the earth floor. He could hear sounds like distant voices, something beyond the breathing of the men who stood around him. Ghosts, he thought. Shrieks and laughter, the sounds of a good night out. He must be mistaken: he was having a very bad night in.

His bare toes just touched the ground. His shoes had come off as they'd scraped him down the flights of steps. His socks had followed sometime after. He was in agony, but agony could be cured. Agony wasn't eternal. He wondered if he would walk again. He remembered the barrel of the gun touching the back of his knee, sending waves of energy up and down his leg.

His eyes were closed. If he opened them he knew he would see flecks of his own blood against the whitewashed wall, the wall which seemed to arch towards him. His toes were still moving against the ground, dabbling in warm blood. Whenever he tried to speak, he could feel his face cracking: dried salt tears and sweat.

It was strange, the shape your life could take. You might be loved as a child but still go bad. You might have monsters for parents but grow up pure. His life had been neither one nor the other. Or rather, it had been both, for he'd been cherished and abandoned in equal measure. He was six, and shaking hands with a large man. There should have been more affection between them, but somehow there wasn't. He was ten, and his mother was looking tired, bowed down, as she leaned over the sink washing dishes. Not knowing he was in the doorway, she paused to rest her hands on the rim of the sink. He was thirteen, and being initiated into his first gang. They took a pack of cards and skinned his knuckles with the edge of the pack. They took it in turns, all eleven of them. It hurt until he belonged.

Now there was a shuffling sound. And the gun barrel was touching the back of his neck, sending out more waves. How could something be so cold? He took a deep breath, feeling the effort in his shoulder-blades. There couldn't be more pain than he already felt. Heavy breathing close to his ear, and then the words again.

463

'*Nemo me impune lacessit.*'

He opened his eyes to the ghosts. They were in a smoke-filled tavern, seated around a long rectangular table, their goblets of wine and ale held high. A young woman was slouching from the lap of a one-legged man. The goblets had stems but no bases: you couldn't put them back on the table until they'd been emptied. A toast was being raised. Those in fine dress rubbed shoulders with beggars. There were no divisions, not in the tavern's gloom. Then they looked towards him, and he tried to smile.

He felt but did not hear the final explosion.

1

Probably the worst Saturday night of the year, which was why Inspector John Rebus had landed the shift. God was in his heaven, just making sure. There had been a derby match in the afternoon, Hibs versus Hearts at Easter Road. Fans making their way back to the west end and beyond had stopped in the city centre to drink to excess and take in some of the sights and sounds of the Festival.

The Edinburgh Festival was the bane of Rebus's life. He'd spent years confronting it, trying to avoid it, cursing it, being caught up in it. There were those who said that it was somehow atypical of Edinburgh, a city which for most of the year seemed sleepy, moderate, bridled. But that was nonsense; Edinburgh's history was full of licence and riotous behaviour. But the Festival, especially the Festival Fringe, was different. Tourism was its lifeblood, and where there were tourists there was trouble. Pickpockets and housebreakers came to town as to a convention, while those football supporters who normally steered clear of the city centre suddenly became its passionate defenders, challenging the foreign invaders who could be found at tables outside short-lease cafes up and down the High Street.

Tonight the two might clash in a big way.

'It's hell out there,' one constable had already commented as he paused for rest in the canteen. Rebus believed him all too readily. The cells were filling nicely along with the CID in-trays. A woman had pushed her drunken husband's fingers into the kitchen mincer. Someone was applying superglue to cashpoint machines then chiselling the flap open later to get at the money. Several bags had been snatched around Princes Street. And the Can Gang were on the go again.

The Can Gang had a simple recipe. They stood at bus stops and offered a drink from their can. They were imposing figures, and the victim would take the proffered drink, not knowing that the beer or cola contained crushed up Mogadon tablets, or similar fast-acting tranquillisers. When the victim passed out, the gang would strip them of cash and valuables. You woke up with a gummy head, or in one severe case with your stomach pumped dry. And you woke up poor.

Meantime, there had been another bomb threat, this time phoned to the newspaper rather than Lowland Radio. Rebus had gone to the

465

newspaper offices to take a statement from the journalist who'd taken the call. The place was a madhouse of Festival and Fringe critics filing their reviews. The journalist read from his notes.

'He just said, if we didn't shut the Festival down, we'd be sorry.'

'Did he sound serious?'

'Oh, yes, definitely.'

'And he had an Irish accent?'

'Sounded like it.'

'Not just a fake?'

The reporter shrugged. He was keen to file his story, so Rebus let him go. That made three calls in the past week, each one threatening to bomb or otherwise disrupt the Festival. The police were taking the threat seriously. How could they afford not to? So far, the tourists hadn't been scared off, but venues were being urged to make security checks before and after each performance.

Back at St Leonard's, Rebus reported to his Chief Superintendent, then tried to finish another piece of paperwork. Masochist that he was, he quite liked the Saturday back-shift. You saw the city in its many guises. It allowed a salutory peek into Edinburgh's grey soul. Sin and evil weren't black – he'd argued the point with a priest – but were greyly anonymous. You saw them all night long, the grey peering faces of the wrongdoers and malcontents, the wife beaters and the knife boys. Unfocused eyes, drained of all concern save for themselves. And you prayed, if you were John Rebus, prayed that as few people as possible ever had to get as close as this to the massive grey nonentity.

Then you went to the canteen and had a joke with the lads, fixing a smile to your face whether you were listening or not.

'Here, Inspector, have you heard the one about the squid with the moustache? He goes into a restaurant and –'

Rebus turned away from the DC's story towards his ringing phone.

'DI Rebus.'

He listened for a moment, the smile melting from his face. Then he put down the receiver and lifted his jacket from the back of his chair.

'Bad news?' asked the DC.

'You're not joking, son.'

The High Street was packed with people, most of them just browsing. Young people bobbed up and down trying to instil enthusiasm in the Fringe productions they were supporting. Supporting them? They were probably the *leads* in them. They busily thrust flyers into hands already full of similar sheets.

'Only two quid, best value on the Fringe!'

'You won't see another show like it!'

There were jugglers and people with painted faces, and a cacophony of musical disharmonies. Where else in the world would bagpipes, banjos and kazoos meet to join in a busking battle from hell?

Locals said this Festival was quieter than the last. They'd been saying it for years. Rebus wondered if the thing had ever had a heyday. It was plenty busy enough for him.

Though it was a warm night, he kept his car windows shut. Even so, as he crawled along the setts flyers would be pushed beneath his windscreen wipers, all but blocking his vision. His scowl met impregnable drama student smiles. It was ten o'clock, not long dark; that was the beauty of a Scottish summer. He tried to imagine himself on a deserted beach, or crouched atop a mountain, alone with his thoughts. Who was he trying to kid? John Rebus was *always* alone with his thoughts. And just now he was thinking of drink. Another hour or two and the bars would sluice themselves out, unless they'd applied for (and been granted) the very late licences available at Festival time.

He was heading for the City Chambers, across the street from St Giles' Cathedral. You turned off the High Street and through one of two stone arches into a small parking area in front of the Chambers themselves. A uniformed constable was standing guard beneath one of the arches. He recognised Rebus and nodded, stepping out of the way. Rebus parked his own car beside a marked patrol car, stopped the engine and got out.

'Evening, sir.'

'Where is it?'

The constable nodded towards a door near one of the arches, attached to the side wall of the Chambers. They walked towards it. A young woman was standing next to the door.

'Inspector,' she said.

'Hello, Mairie.'

'I've told her to move on, sir,' the constable apologised.

Mairie Henderson ignored him. Her eyes were on Rebus's. 'What's going on?'

Rebus winked at her. 'The Lodge, Mairie. We always meet in secret, like.' She scowled. 'Well then, give me a chance. Off to a show, are you?'

'I was till I saw the commotion.'

'Saturday's your day off, isn't it?'

'Journalists don't get days off, Inspector. What's behind the door?'

'It's got glass panels, Mairie. Take a keek for yourself.'

But all you could see through the panels was a narrow landing with doors off. One door was open, allowing a glimpse of stairs leading down. Rebus turned to the constable.

'Let's get a proper cordon set up, son. Something across the arches to fend off the tourists before the show starts. Radio in for assistance if you need it. Excuse me, Mairie.'

'Then there *is* going to be a show?'

467

Rebus stepped past her and opened the door, closing it again behind him. He made for the stairs down, which were lit by a naked lightbulb. Ahead of him he could hear voices. At the bottom of this first flight he turned a corner and came upon the group. There were two teenage girls and a boy, all of them seated or crouching, the girls shaking and crying. Over them stood a uniformed constable and a man Rebus recognised as a local doctor. They all looked up at his approach.

'This is the Inspector,' the constable told the teenagers. 'Right, we're going back down there. You three stay here.'

Rebus, squeezing past the teenagers, saw the doctor give them a worried glance. He gave the doctor a wink, telling him they'd get over it. The doctor didn't seem so sure.

Together the three men set off down the next flight of stairs. The constable was carrying a torch.

'There's electricity,' he said. 'But a couple of the bulbs have gone.' They walked along a narrow passage, its low ceiling further reduced by air- and heating-ducts and other pipes. Tubes of scaffolding lay on the floor ready for assembly. There were more steps down.

'You know where we are?' the constable asked.

'Mary King's Close,' said Rebus.

Not that he'd ever been down here, not exactly. But he'd been in similar old buried streets beneath the High Street. He knew of Mary King's Close.

'Story goes,' said the constable, 'there was a plague in the 1600s, people died or moved out, never really moved back. Then there was a fire. They blocked off the ends of the street. When they rebuilt, they built over the top of the close.' He shone his torch towards the ceiling, which was now three or four storeys above them. 'See that marble slab? That's the floor of the City Chambers.' He smiled. 'I came on the tour last year.'

'Incredible,' the doctor said. Then to Rebus: 'I'm Dr Galloway.'

'Inspector Rebus. Thanks for getting here so quickly.'

The doctor ignored this. 'You're a friend of Dr Aitken's, aren't you?'

Ah, Patience Aitken. She'd be at home just now, feet tucked under her, a cat and an improving book on her lap, boring classical music in the background. Rebus nodded.

'I used to share a surgery with her,' Dr Galloway explained.

They were in the close proper now, a narrow and fairly steep roadway between stone buildings. A rough drainage channel ran down one side of the road. Passages led off to dark alcoves, one of which, according to the constable, housed a bakery, its ovens intact. The constable was beginning to get on Rebus's nerves.

There were more ducts and pipes, runs of electric cable. The far end of the close had been blocked off by an elevator shaft. Signs of renovation were all around: bags of cement, scaffolding, pails and shovels. Rebus pointed to an arc lamp.

'Can we plug that in?'

The constable thought they could. Rebus looked around. The place wasn't damp or chilled or cobwebbed. The air seemed fresh. Yet they were three or four storeys beneath road level. Rebus took the torch and shone it through a doorway. At the end of the hallway he could see a wooden toilet, its seat raised. The next door along led into a long vaulted room, its walls whitewashed, the floor earthen.

'That's the wine shop,' the constable said. 'The butcher's is next door.'

So it was. It too consisted of a vaulted room, again whitewashed and with a floor of packed earth. But in its ceiling were a great many iron hooks, short and blackened but obviously used at one time for hanging up meat.

Meat still hung from one of them.

It was the lifeless body of a young man. His hair was dark and slick, stuck to his forehead and neck. His hands had been tied and the rope slipped over a hook, so that he hung stretched with his knuckles near the ceiling and his toes barely touching the ground. His ankles had been tied together too. There was blood everywhere, a fact made all too plain as the arc lamp suddenly came on, sweeping light and shadows across the walls and roof. There was the faint smell of decay, but no flies, thank God. Dr Galloway swallowed hard, his Adam's apple seeming to duck for cover, then retreated into the close to be sick. Rebus tried to steady his own heart. He walked around the carcass, keeping his distance initially.

'Tell me,' he said.

'Well, sir,' the constable began, 'the three young people upstairs, they decided to come down here. The place had been closed to tours while the building work goes on, but they wanted to come down at night. There are a lot of ghost stories told about this place, headless dogs and –'

'How did they get a key?'

'The boy's great-uncle, he's one of the tour guides, a retired planner or something.'

'So they came looking for ghosts and they found this.'

'That's right, sir. They ran back up to the High Street and bumped into PC Andrews and me. We thought they were having us on at first, like.'

But Rebus was no longer listening, and when he spoke it wasn't to the constable.

'You poor little bastard, look what they did to you.'

Though it was against regulations, he leaned forward and touched the young man's hair. It was still slightly damp. He'd probably died on Friday night, and was meant to hang here over the weekend, enough time for any trail, any clues, to grow as cold as his bones.

'What do you reckon, sir?'

'Gunshots.' Rebus looked to where blood had sprayed the wall. 'Something high-velocity. Head, elbows, knees, and ankles.' He sucked in breath. 'He's been six-packed.'

There were shuffling noises in the close, and the wavering beam of another torch. Two figures stood in the doorway, their bodies silhouetted by the arc lamp.

'Cheer up, Dr Galloway,' a male voice boomed to the hapless figure still crouched in the close. Recognising the voice, Rebus smiled.

'Ready when you are, Dr Curt,' he said.

The pathologist stepped into the chamber and shook Rebus's hand. 'The hidden city, quite a revelation.' His companion, a woman, stepped forward to join them. 'Have the two of you met?' Dr Curt sounded like the host at a luncheon party. 'Inspector Rebus, this is Ms Rattray from the Procurator Fiscal's office.'

'Caroline Rattray.' She shook Rebus's hand. She was tall, as tall as either man, with long dark hair tied at the back.

'Caroline and I,' Curt was saying, 'were enjoying supper after the ballet when the call came. So I thought I'd drag her along, kill two birds with one stone . . . so to speak.'

Curt exhaled fumes of good food and good wine. Both he and the lawyer were dressed for an evening out, and already some white plaster-dust had smudged Caroline Rattray's black jacket. As Rebus moved to brush off the dust, she caught her first sight of the body, and looked away quickly. Rebus didn't blame her, but Curt was advancing on the figure as though towards another guest at the party. He paused to put on polythene overshoes.

'I always carry some in my car,' he explained. 'You never know when they'll be needed.'

He got close to the body and examined the head first, before looking back towards Rebus.

'Dr Galloway had a look, has he?'

Rebus shook his head slowly. He knew what was coming. He'd seen Curt examine headless bodies and mangled bodies and bodies that were little more than torsos or melted to the consistency of lard, and the pathologist always said the same thing.

'Poor chap's dead.'

'Thank you.'

'I take it the crew are on their way?'

Rebus nodded. The crew were on their way. A van to start with, loaded with everything they'd need for the initial scene of crime investigation. SOC officers, lights and cameras, strips of tape, evidence bags, and of course a bodybag. Sometimes a forensic team came too, if cause of death looked particularly murky or the scene was a mess.

'I think,' said Curt, 'the Procurator Fiscal's office will agree that foul play is suspected?'

Rattray nodded, still not looking.

'Well, it wasn't suicide,' commented Rebus. Caroline Rattray turned towards the wall, only to find herself facing the sprays of blood. She turned instead to the doorway, where Dr Galloway was dabbing his mouth with a handkerchief.

'We'd better get someone to fetch me my tools.' Curt was studying the ceiling. 'Any idea what this place was?'

'A butcher's shop, sir,' said the constable, only too happy to help. 'There's a wine shop too, and some houses. You can still go into them.' He turned to Rebus. 'Sir, what's a six-pack?'

'A six-pack?' echoed Curt.

Rebus stared at the hanging body. 'It's a punishment,' he said quietly. 'Only you're not supposed to die. What's that on the floor?' He was pointing to the dead man's feet, to the spot where they grazed the dark-stained ground.

'Looks like rats have been nibbling his toes,' said Curt.

'No, not that.' There were shallow grooves in the earth, so wide they must have been made with a big toe. Four crude capital letters were discernible.

'Is that Neno or Nemo?'

'Could even be Memo,' offered Dr Curt.

'Captain Nemo,' said the constable. 'He's the guy in *2,000 Leagues Beneath the Sea*.'

'Jules Verne,' said Curt, nodding.

The constable shook his head. 'No, sir, Walt Disney,' he said.

2

On Sunday morning Rebus and Dr Patience Aitken decided to get away from it all by staying in bed. He nipped out early for croissants and papers from the local corner shop, and they ate breakfast from a tray on top of the bedcovers, sharing sections of the newspapers, discarding more than they read.

There was no mention of the previous night's grisly find in Mary King's Close. The news had seeped out too late for publication. But Rebus knew there would be something about it on the local radio news, so he was quite content for once when Patience tuned the bedside radio to a classical station.

He should have come off his shift at midnight, but murder tended to disrupt the system of shifts. On a murder inquiry, you stopped working when you reasonably could. Rebus had hung around till two in the morning, consulting with the night shift about the corpse in Mary King's Close. He'd contacted his Chief Inspector and Chief Super, and kept in touch with Fettes HQ, where the forensic stuff had gone. DI Flower kept telling him to go home. Finally he'd taken the advice.

The real problem with back shifts was that Rebus couldn't sleep well after them anyway. He'd managed four hours since arriving home, and four hours would suffice. But there was a warm pleasure in slipping into bed as dawn neared, curling against the body already asleep there. And even more pleasure in pushing the cat off the bed as you did so.

Before retiring, he'd swallowed four measures of whisky. He told himself it was purely medicinal, but rinsed the glass and put it away, hoping Patience wouldn't notice. She complained often of his drinking, among other things.

'We're eating out,' she said now.

'When?'

'Lunch today.'

'Where?'

'That place out at Carlops.'

Rebus nodded. 'Witch's Leap,' he said.

'What?'

'That's what Carlops means. There's a big rock there. They used to throw suspected witches from it. If you didn't fly, you were innocent.'

'But also dead?'

'Their judicial system wasn't perfect, witness the ducking-stool. Same principle.'

'How do you know all this?'

'It's amazing what these young constables know nowadays.' He paused. 'About lunch . . . I should go into work.'

'Oh no, you don't.'

'Patience, there's been a –'

'John, there'll be a murder *here* if we don't start spending some time together. Phone in sick.'

'I can't do that.'

'Then *I'll* do it. I'm a doctor, they'll believe me.'

They believed her.

They walked off lunch by taking a look at Carlops Rock, and then braving a climb onto the Pentlands, despite the fierce horizontal winds. Back in Oxford Terrace, Patience eventually said she had some 'office things' to do, which meant filing or tax or flicking through the latest medical journals. So Rebus drove out along Queensferry Road and parked outside the Church of Our Lady of Perpetual Hell, noting with guilty pleasure that no one had yet corrected the mischievous graffiti on the noticeboard which turned 'Help' into 'Hell'.

Inside, the church was empty, cool and quiet and flooded with coloured light from the stained glass. Hoping his timing was good, he slipped into the confessional. There was someone on the other side of the grille.

'Forgive me, father,' said Rebus, 'I'm not even a Catholic.'

'Ah good, it's you, you heathen. I was hoping you'd come. I want your help.'

'Shouldn't that be my line?'

'Don't be bloody cheeky. Come on, let's have a drink.'

Father Conor Leary was between fifty-five and seventy and had told Rebus that he couldn't remember which he was nearer. He was a bulky barrelling figure with thick silver hair which sprouted not only from his head but also from ears, nose and the back of his neck. In civvies, Rebus guessed he would pass for a retired dockworker or skilled labourer of some kind who had also been handy as a boxer, and Father Leary had photos and trophies to prove that this last was incontrovertible truth. He often jabbed the air to make a point, finishing with an uppercut to show that there could be no comeback. In conversation between the two men, Rebus had often wished for a referee.

But today Father Leary sat comfortably and sedately enough in the deckchair in his garden. It was a beautiful early evening, warm and clear with the trace of a cool sea-borne breeze.

'A great day to go hot-air ballooning,' said Father Leary, taking a swig from his glass of Guinness. 'Or bungee jumping. I believe they've set up something of the sort on The Meadows, just for the duration of the Festival. Man, I'd like to try that.'

Rebus blinked but said nothing. His Guinness was cold enough to double as dental anaesthetic. He shifted in his own deckchair, which was by far the older of the two. Before sitting, he'd noticed how thread-bare the canvas was, how it had been rubbed away where it met the horizontal wooden spars. He hoped it would hold.

'Do you like my garden?'

Rebus looked at the bright blooms, the trim grass. 'I don't know much about gardens,' he admitted.

'Me neither. It's not a sin. But there's an old chap I know who does know about them, and he looks after this one for a few bob.' He raised his glass towards his lips. 'So how are you keeping?'

'I'm fine.'

'And Dr Aitken?'

'She's fine.'

'And the two of you are still . . . ?'

'Just about.'

Father Leary nodded. Rebus's tone was warning him off. 'Another bomb threat, eh? I heard on the radio.'

'It could be a crank.'

'But you're not sure?'

'The IRA usually use codewords, just so we know they're serious.'

Father Leary nodded to himself. 'And a murder too?'

Rebus gulped his drink. 'I was there.'

'They don't even stop for the Festival, do they? Whatever must the tourists think?' Father Leary's eyes were sparkling.

'It's about time the tourists learned the truth,' Rebus said, a bit too quickly. He sighed. 'It was pretty gruesome.'

'I'm sorry to hear that. I shouldn't have been so flippant.'

'That's all right. It's a defence.'

'You're right, it is.'

Rebus knew this. It was the reason behind his many little jokes with Dr Curt. It was their way of avoiding the obvious, the undeniable. Even so, since last night Rebus had held in his mind the picture of that sad strung-up figure, a young man they hadn't even identified yet. The picture would stay there forever. Everybody had a photographic memory for horror. He'd climbed back out of Mary King's Close to find the High Street aglow with a firework display, the streets thronged with people staring up open-mouthed at the blues and greens in the night sky. The

474

fireworks were coming from the Castle; the night's Tattoo display was ending. He hadn't felt much like talking to Mairie Henderson. In fact, he had snubbed her.

'This isn't very nice,' she'd said, standing her ground.

'This is very nice,' Father Leary said now, relaxing back further into his seat.

The whisky Rebus had drunk hadn't rubbed out the picture. If anything, it had smeared the corners and edges, which only served to highlight the central fact. More whisky would have made this image sharper still.

'We're not here for very long, are we?' he said now.

Father Leary frowned. 'You mean here on earth?'

'That's what I mean. We're not around long enough to make any difference.'

'Tell that to the man with a bomb in his pocket. Every one of us makes a difference just by being here.'

'I'm not talking about the man with the bomb, I'm talking about stopping him.'

'You're talking about being a policeman.'

'Ach, maybe I'm not talking about anything.'

Father Leary allowed a short-lived smile, his eyes never leaving Rebus's. 'A bit morbid for a Sunday, John?'

'Isn't that what Sundays are for?'

'Maybe for you sons of Calvin. You tell yourselves you're doomed, then spend all week trying to make a joke of it. Others of us give thanks for *this* day and its meaning.'

Rebus shifted in his chair. Lately, he didn't enjoy Father Leary's conversations so much. There was something proselytising about them. 'So when do we get down to business?' he said.

Father Leary smiled. 'The Protestant work ethic.'

'You haven't brought me here to convert me.'

'We wouldn't want a dour bugger like you. Besides, I'd more easily convert a fifty-yard penalty in a Murrayfield cross-wind.' He took a swipe at the air. 'Ach, it's not really your problem. Maybe it isn't a problem at all.' He ran a finger down the crease in his trouser-leg.

'You can still tell me about it.'

'A reversal of roles, eh? Well, I suppose that's what I had in mind all along.' He sat further forward in the deckchair, the material stretching and sounding a sharp note of complaint. 'Here it is then. You know Pilmuir?'

'Don't be daft.'

'Yes, stupid question. And Pilmuir's Garibaldi Estate?'

'The Gar-B, it's the roughest scheme in the city, maybe in the country.'

'There are good people there, but you're right. That's why the Church sent an outreach worker.'

'And now he's in trouble?'

'Maybe.' Father Leary finished his drink. 'It was my idea. There's a community hall on the estate, only it had been locked up for months. I thought we could reopen it as a youth club.'

'For Catholics?'

'For both faiths.' He sat back in his chair. 'Even for the faithless. The Garibaldi is predominantly Protestant, but there are Catholics there too. We got agreement, and set up some funds. I knew we needed someone special, someone really dynamic in charge.' He punched the air. 'Someone who might just draw the two sides together.'

Mission impossible, thought Rebus. This scheme will self-destruct in ten seconds.

Not least of the Gar-B's problems was the sectarian divide, or the lack of one, depending on how you looked at it. Protestants and Catholics lived in the same streets, the same tower blocks. Mostly, they lived in relative harmony and shared poverty. But, there being little to do on the estate, the youth of the place tended to organise into opposing gangs and wage warfare. Every year there was at least one pitched battle for police to contend with, usually in July, usually around the Protestant holy day of the 12th.

'So you brought in the SAS?' Rebus suggested. Father Leary was slow to get the joke.

'Not at all,' he said, 'just a young man, a very ordinary young man but with inner strength.' His fist cut the air. 'Spiritual strength. And for a while it looked like a disaster. Nobody came to the club, the windows were smashed as soon as we'd replaced them, the graffiti got worse and more personal. But then he started to break through. *That* seemed the miracle. Attendance at the club increased, and both sides were joining.'

'So what's gone wrong?'

Father Leary loosened his shoulders. 'It just wasn't quite right. I thought there'd be sports, maybe a football team or something. We bought the strips and applied to join a local league. But the lads weren't interested. All they wanted to do was hang around the hall itself. And the balance isn't there either, the Catholics have stopped joining. Most of them have even stopped attending.' He looked at Rebus. 'That's not just sour grapes, you understand.'

Rebus nodded. 'The Prod gangs have annnexed it?'

'I'm not saying that exactly.'

'Sounds like it to me. And your . . . outreach worker?'

'His name's Peter Cave. Oh, he's still there. Too often for my liking.'

'I still don't see the problem.' Actually he could, but he wanted it spelling out.

'John, I've talked to people on the estate, and all over Pilmuir. The gangs are as bad as ever, only now they seem to be working together, divvying the place up between them. All that's happened is that they've become more organised. They have meetings in the club and carve up the surrounding territory.'

'It keeps them off the street.' Father Leary didn't smile. 'So close the youth club.'

'That's not so easy. It would look bad for a start. And would it solve anything?'

'Have you talked with Mr Cave?'

'He doesn't listen. He's changed. That's what troubles me most of all.'

'You could kick him out.'

Father Leary shook his head. 'He's lay, John. I can't *order* him to do anything. We've cut the club's funding, but the money to keep it going comes from somewhere nevertheless.'

'Where from?'

'I don't know.'

'How much?'

'It doesn't take much.'

'So what do you want me to do?' The question Rebus had been trying not to ask.

Father Leary gave his weary smile again. 'To be honest, I don't know. Perhaps I just needed to tell someone.'

'Don't give me that. You want me to go out there.'

'Not if you don't want to.'

It was Rebus's turn to smile. 'I've been in safer places.'

'And a few worse ones, too.'

'I haven't told you about half of them, Father.' Rebus finished his drink.

'Another?'

He shook his head. 'It's nice and quiet here, isn't it?'

Father Leary nodded. 'That's the beauty of Edinburgh, you're never far from a peaceful spot.'

'And never far from a hellish one either. Thanks for the drink, Father.' Rebus got up.

'I see your team won yesterday.'

'What makes you think I support Hearts?'

'They're Prods, aren't they? And you're a Protestant yourself.'

'Away to hell, Father,' said John Rebus, laughing.

Father Leary pulled himself to his feet. He straightened his back with a grimace. He was acting purposely aged. Just an old man. 'About the Gar-B, John,' he said, opening his arms wide, 'I'm in your hands.'

Like nails, thought Rebus, like carpentry nails.

3

Monday morning saw Rebus back at work and in the Chief Super's office. 'Farmer' Watson was pouring coffee for himself and Chief Inspector Frank Lauderdale, Rebus having refused. He was strictly decaf these days, and the Farmer didn't know the meaning of the word.

'A busy Saturday night,' said the Farmer, handing Lauderdale a grubby mug. As inconspicuously as he could, Lauderdale started rubbing marks off the rim with the ball of his thumb. 'Feeling better, by the way, John?'

'Scads better, sir, thank you,' said Rebus, not even close to blushing.

'A grim business under the City Chambers.'

'Yes, sir.'

'So what do we have?'

It was Lauderdale's turn to speak. 'Victim was shot seven times with what looks like a nine-millimetre revolver. Ballistics will have a full report for us by day's end. Dr Curt tells us that the head wound actually killed the victim, and it was the last bullet delivered. They wanted him to suffer.'

Lauderdale sipped from the cleaned rim of his mug. A Murder Room had been set up along the hall, and he was in charge. Consequently, he was wearing his best suit. There would be press briefings, maybe a TV appearance or two. Lauderdale looked ready. Rebus would gladly have tipped the mug of coffee down the mauve shirt and paisley-pattern tie.

'Your thoughts, John,' said Farmer Watson. 'Someone mentioned the words "six-pack".'

'Yes, sir. It's a punishment routine in Northern Ireland, usually carried out by the IRA.'

'I've heard of kneecappings.'

Rebus nodded. 'For minor offences, there's a bullet in each elbow or ankle. For more serious crimes, there's a kneecapping on top. And finally there's the six-pack: both elbows, both knees, both ankles.'

'You know a lot about it.'

'I was in the army, sir. I still take an interest.'

'You were in Ulster?'

Rebus nodded slowly. 'In the early days.'

Chief Inspector Lauderdale placed his mug carefully on the desktop. 'But they normally wouldn't then kill the person?'

'Not normally.'

The three men sat in silence for a moment. The Farmer broke the spell. 'An IRA punishment gang? *Here?*'

Rebus shrugged. 'A copycat maybe. Gangs aping what they've seen in the papers or on TV.'

'But using serious guns.'

'Very serious,' said Lauderdale. 'Could be a tie-in with these bomb threats.'

The Farmer nodded. 'That's the line the media are taking. Maybe our would-be bomber had gone rogue, and they caught up with him.'

'There's something else, sir,' said Rebus. He'd phoned Dr Curt first thing, just to check. 'They did the knees from behind. Maximum damage. You sever the arteries before smashing kneecaps.'

'What's your point?'

'Two points, sir. One, they knew exactly what they were doing. Two, why bother when you're going to kill him anyway? Maybe whoever did it changed his mind at the last minute. Maybe the victim was meant to live. The probable handgun was a revolver. Six shots. Whoever did it must have stopped to reload before putting that final bullet in the head.'

Eyes were avoided as the three men considered this, putting themselves in the victim's place. You've been six-packed. You think it's over. Then you hear the gun being reloaded . . .

'Sweet Jesus,' said the Farmer.

'There are too many guns around,' Lauderdale said matter-of-factly. It was true: over the past few years there had been a steady increase in the number of firearms on the street.

'Why Mary King's Close?' asked the Farmer.

'You're not likely to be disturbed there,' Rebus guessed. 'Plus it's virtually soundproof.'

'You could say the same about a lot of places, most of them a long way from the High Street in the middle of the Festival. They were taking a big risk. Why bother?'

Rebus had wondered the same thing. He had no answer to offer.

'And Nemo or Memo?'

It was Lauderdale's turn, another respite from the coffee. 'I've got men on it, sir, checking libraries and phone directories, digging up meanings.'

'You've talked to the teenagers?'

'Yes, sir. They seem genuine enough.'

'And the person who gave them the key?'

'He didn't give it to them, sir, they took it without his knowledge. He's in his seventies and straighter than a plumb-line.'

'Some builders I know,' said the Farmer, 'could bend even a plumb-line.'

Rebus smiled. He knew those builders too.

'We're talking to everyone,' Lauderdale went on, 'who's been working in Mary King's Close.' It seemed he hadn't got the Farmer's joke.

'All right, John,' said the Farmer. 'You were in the army, what about the tattoo?'

Yes, the tattoo. Rebus had known the conclusion everyone would jump to. From the case notes, they'd spent most of Sunday jumping to it. The Farmer was examining a photograph. It had been taken during Sunday's post-mortem examination. The SOCOs on Saturday night had taken photos too, but those hadn't come out nearly as clearly.

The photo showed a tattoo on the victim's right forearm. It was a rough, self-inflicted affair, the kind you sometimes saw on teenagers, usually on the backs of hands. A needle and some blue ink, that's all you needed; that and a measure of luck that the thing wouldn't become infected. Those were all the victim had needed to prick the letters SaS into his skin.

'It's not the Special Air Service,' said Rebus.

'No?'

Rebus shook his head. 'For all sorts of reasons. You'd use a capital A for a start. More likely, if you wanted an SAS tattoo you'd go for the crest, the knife and wings and "Who dares wins", something like that.'

'Unless you didn't know anything about the regiment,' offered Lauderdale.

'Then why sport a tattoo?'

'Do we have any ideas?' asked the Farmer.

'We're checking,' said Lauderdale.

'And we still don't know who he is?'

'No, sir, we still don't know who he is.'

Farmer Watson sighed. 'Then that'll have to do for now. I know we're stretched just at the minute, with the Festival threat and everything else, but it goes without saying this takes priority. Use all the men you have to. We need to clean this up quickly. Special Branch and the Crime Squad are already taking an interest.'

Ah, thought Rebus, so that was why the Farmer was being a bit more thorough than usual. Normally, he'd just let Lauderdale get on with it. Lauderdale was good at running an office. You just didn't want him out there on the street with you. Watson was shuffling the papers on his desk.

'I see the Can Gang have been at it again.'

It was time to move on.

Rebus had had dealings in Pilmuir before. He'd seen a good policeman go wrong there. He'd tasted darkness there. The sour feeling returned as he drove past stunted grass verges and broken saplings. Though no tourists ever came here, there was a welcome sign. It comprised somebody's gable-end, with white painted letters four feet high: ENJOY YOUR VISIT TO THE GAR-B.

Gar-B was what the kids (for want of a better term) called the Garibaldi estate. It was a mish-mash of early-'60s terraced housing and late-'60s tower blocks, everything faced with grey harling, with boring swathes of grass separating the estate from the main road. There were a lot of orange plastic traffic cones lying around. They would make goalposts for a quick game of football, or chicanes for the bikers. Last year, some enterprising souls had put them to better use, using them to divert traffic off the main road and into the Gar-B, where youths lined the slip-road and pelted the cars with rocks and bottles. If the drivers ran from their vehicles, they were allowed to go, while the cars were stripped of anything of value, right down to tyres, seat-covers and engine parts.

Later in the year, when the road needed digging up, a lot of drivers ignored the genuine traffic cones and as a result drove into newly dug ditches. By next morning, their abandoned vehicles had been stripped to the bone. The Gar-B would have stripped the paint if they could.

You had to admire their ingenuity. Give these kids money and opportunity and they'd be the saviours of the capitalist state. Instead, the state gave them dole and daytime TV. Rebus was watched by a gang of pre-teens as he parked. One of them called out.

'Where's yir swanky car?'

'It's no' him,' said another, kicking the first lazily in the ankle. The two of them were on bicycles and looked like the leaders, being a good year or two older than their cohorts. Rebus waved them over.

'What is it?' But they came anyway.

'Keep an eye on my car,' he told them. 'Anyone touches it, you touch them, okay? There's a couple of quid for you when I get back.'

'Half now,' the first said quickly. The second nodded. Rebus handed over half the money, which they pocketed.

'Naebody'd touch *that* car anyway, mister,' said the second, producing a chorus of laughter from behind him.

Rebus shook his head slowly: the patter here was probably sharper than most of the stand-ups on the Fringe. The two boys could have been brothers. More than that, they could have been brothers in the 1930s. They were dressed in cheap modern style, but had shorn heads and wide ears and sallow faces with dark-ringed eyes. You saw them staring out from old photographs wearing boots too big for them and scowls too old. They didn't just seem older than the other kids; they seemed older than Rebus himself.

When he turned his back, he imagined them in sepia.

He wandered towards the community centre. He'd to pass some lock-up garages and one of the three twelve-storey blocks of flats. The community centre itself was no more than a hall, small and tired looking with boarded windows and the usual indecipherable graffiti. Surrounded by concrete, it had a low flat roof, asphalt black, on which lay four teenagers smoking cigarettes. Their chests were naked, their t-shirts tied around their waists. There was so much broken glass up there, they could have doubled as fakirs in a magic show. One of them had a pile of sheets of paper, and was folding them into paper planes which he released from the roof. Judging by the number of planes littering the grass, it had been a busy morning at the control tower.

Paint had peeled in long strips from the centre's doors, and one layer of the plywood beneath had been punctured by a foot or a fist. But the doors were locked fast by means of not one but two padlocks. Two more youths sat on the ground, backs against the doors, legs stretched in front of them and crossed at the ankles, for all the world like security guards on a break. Their trainers were in bad repair, their denims patched and torn and patched again. Maybe it was just the fashion. One wore a black t-shirt, the other an unbuttoned denim jacket with no shirt beneath.

'It's shut,' the denim jacket said.

'When does it open?'

'The night. No polis allowed though.'

Rebus smiled. 'I don't think I know you. What's your name?'

The smile back at him was a parody. Black t-shirt grunted an undeveloped laugh. Rebus noticed flecks of white scale in the youth's hair. Neither youth was about to say anything. The teenagers on the roof were standing now, ready to leap in should anything develop.

'Hard men,' said Rebus. He turned and started to walk away. Denim jacket got to his feet and came after him.

'What's up, Mr Polisman?'

Rebus didn't bother looking at the youth, but he stopped walking. 'Why should anything be up?' One of the paper planes, aimed or not, hit him on the leg. He picked it up. On the roof, they were laughing quietly. 'Why should anything be up?' he repeated.

'Behave. You're not our usual plod.'

'A change is as good as a rest.'

'Arrest? What for?'

Rebus smiled again. He turned to the youth. The face was just leaving acne behind it, and would be good looking for a few more years before it started to decline. Poor diet and alcohol would be its undoing if drugs or fights weren't. The hair was fair and curly, like a child's hair, but not thick. There was a quick intelligence to the eyes, but the eyes themselves were narrow. The intelligence would be narrow too, focusing only on the main chance, the next deal. There was quick anger in those eyes too, and something further back that Rebus didn't like to think about.

'With an act like yours,' he said, 'you should be on the Fringe.'

'I fuckn *hate* the Festival.'

'Join the club. What's your name, son?'

'You like names, don't you?'

'I can find out.'

The youth slipped his hands into his tight jeans pockets. 'You don't want to.'

'No?'

A slow shake of the head. 'Believe me, you really don't want to.' The youth turned, heading back to his friends. 'Or next time,' he said, 'your car might not be there at all.'

Sure enough, as Rebus approached he saw that his car was sinking into the ground. It looked like maybe it was taking cover. But it was only the tyres. They'd been generous; they'd only slashed two of them. He looked around him. There was no sign of the pre-teen gang, though they might be watching from the safe distance of a tower-block window.

He leaned against the car and unfolded the paper plane. It was the flyer for a Fringe show, and a blurb on the back explained that the theatre group in question were uprooting from the city centre in order to play the Garibaldi Community Centre for one night.

'You know not what you do,' Rebus said to himself.

Some young mothers were crossing the football pitch. A crying baby was being shaken on its buggy springs. A toddler was being dragged screaming by the arm, his legs frozen in protest so that they scraped the ground. Both baby and toddler were being brought back into the Gar-B. But not without a fight.

Rebus didn't blame them for resisting.

4

Detective Sergeant Brian Holmes was in the Murder Room, handing a polystyrene cup of tea to Detective Constable Siobhan Clarke, and laughing about something.

'What's the joke?' asked Rebus.

'The one about the hard-up squid,' Holmes answered.

'The one with the moustache?'

Holmes nodded, wiping an imaginary tear from his eye. 'And Gervase the waiter. Brilliant, eh, sir?'

'Brilliant.' Rebus looked around. The Murder Room was all purposeful activity. Photos of the victim and the locus had been pinned up on one wall, a staff rota not far from it. The staff rota was on a plastic wipe-board, and a WPC was checking names from a list against a series of duties and putting them on the board in thick blue marker-pen. Rebus went over to her. 'Keep DI Flower and me away from one another, eh? Even if it means a slip of the pen.'

'I could get into trouble for that, Inspector.' She was smiling, so Rebus winked at her. Everyone knew that having Rebus and Flower in close proximity, two detectives who hated one another, would be counter productive. But of course Lauderdale was in charge. It was Lauderdale's list, and Lauderdale liked to see sparks fly, so much so that he might have been happier in a foundry.

Holmes and Clarke knew what Rebus had been talking about with the WPC, but said nothing.

'I'm going back down Mary King's Close,' Rebus said quietly. 'Anyone want to tag along?'

He had two takers.

Rebus was keeping an eye on Brian Holmes. Holmes hadn't tendered his resignation yet, but you never knew when it might come. When you joined the police, of course, you signed on for the long haul, but Holmes's significant other was pulling on the other end of the rope, and it was hard to tell who'd win the tug o' war.

On the other hand, Rebus had stopped keeping an eye on Siobhan Clarke. She was past her probation, and was going to be a good detective. She was quick, clever and keen. Police officers were seldom all three. Rebus himself might pitch for thirty per cent on a good day.

The day was overcast and sticky, with lots of bugs in the air and no sign of a dispersing breeze.

'What are they, greenfly?'

'Maybe midges.'

'I'll tell you what they are, they're disgusting.'

The windscreen was smeared by the time they reached the City Chambers, and there being no fluid in the wiper bottle, the windscreen stayed that way. It struck Rebus that the Festival really was a High Street thing. Most of the city centre streets were as quiet or as busy as usual. The High Street was the hub. The Chambers' small car park being full, he parked on the High Street. When he got out, he brought a sheet of kitchen-towel with him, spat on it, and cleaned the windscreen.

'What we need is some rain.'

'Don't say that.'

A transit van and a flat-back trailer were parked outside the entrance to Mary King's Close, evidence that the builders were back at work. The butcher's shop would still be taped off, but that didn't stop the renovations.

'Inspector Rebus?'

An old man had been waiting for them. He was tall and fit looking and wore an open cream-coloured raincoat despite the day's heat. His hair had turned not grey or silver but a kind of custard yellow, and he wore half-moon glasses most of the way down his nose, as though he needed them only to check the cracks in the pavement.

'Mr Blair-Fish?' Rebus shook the brittle hand.

'I'd like to apologise again. My great-nephew can be such a –'

'No need to apologise, sir. Your great-nephew did us a favour. If he hadn't gone down there with those two lassies, we wouldn't have found the body so fast as we did. The quicker the better in a murder investigation.'

Blair-Fish inspected his oft-repaired shoes, then accepted this with a slow nod. 'Still, it's an embarrassment.'

'Not to us, sir.'

'No, I suppose not.'

'Now, if you'll lead the way ... ?'

Mr Blair-Fish led the way.

He took them in through the door and down the flights of stairs, out of daylight and into a world of low-wattage bulbs beyond which lay the halogen glare of the builders. It was like looking at a stage-set. The workers moved with the studied precision of actors. You could charge a couple of quid a time and get an audience, if not a Fringe First Award. The gaffer knew police when he saw them, and nodded a greeting. Otherwise, nobody paid much attention, except for the occasional sideways and appraising glance towards Siobhan Clarke. Builders were builders, below ground as above.

Blair-Fish was providing a running commentary. Rebus reckoned he'd been the guide when the constable had come on the tour. Rebus heard about how the close had been a thriving thoroughfare prior to the plague, only one of many such plagues to hit Edinburgh. When the denizens moved back, they swore the close was haunted by the spirits of those who had perished there. They all moved out again and the street fell into disuse. Then came a fire, leaving only the first few storeys untouched. (Edinburgh tenements back then could rise to a precarious twelve storeys or more.) After which, the city merely laid slabs across what remained and built again, burying Mary King's Close.

'The old town was a narrow place, you must remember, built along a ridge or, if you enjoy legend, on the back of a buried serpent. Long and narrow. Everyone was squeezed together, rich and poor living cheek by jowl. In a tenement like this you'd have your paupers at the top, your gentry in the middle floors, and your artisans and commercial people at street level.'

'So what happened?' asked Holmes, genuinely interested.

'The gentry got fed up,' said Blair-Fish. 'When the New Town was built on the other side of Nor' Loch, they were quick to move. With the gentry gone, the old town became dilapidated, and stayed that way for a long time.' He pointed down some steps into an alcove. 'That was the baker's. See those flat stones? That's where the oven was. If you touch them, they're still warmer than the stones around them.'

Siobhan Clarke had to test this. She came back shrugging. Rebus was glad he'd brought Holmes and Clarke with him. They kept Blair-Fish busy while he could keep a surreptitious eye on the builders. This had been his plan all along: to appear to be inspecting Mary King's Close, while really inspecting the builders. They didn't look nervous; well, no more nervous than you would expect. They kept their eyes away from the butcher's shop, and whistled quietly as they worked. They did not seem inclined to discuss the murder. Someone was up a ladder dismantling a run of pipes. Someone else was mending brickwork at the top of a scaffold.

Further into the tour, away from the builders, Blair-Fish took Siobhan Clarke aside to show her where a child had been bricked up in a chimney, a common complaint among eighteenth-century chimney sweeps.

'The Farmer asked a good question,' Rebus confided to Holmes. 'He said, why would you bring anyone down here? Think about it. It shows you must be local. Only locals know about Mary King's Close, and even then only a select few.' It was true, the public tour of the close was not common knowledge, and tours themselves were by no means frequent. 'They'd have to have been down here themselves, or know someone who had. If not, they'd more likely get lost than find the butcher's.'

Holmes nodded. 'A shame there's no record of the tour parties.' This had been checked, the tours were informal, parties of a dozen or more at a time. There was no written record. 'Could be they knew about the building work and reckoned the body would be down here for weeks.'

'Or maybe,' said Rebus, 'the building work is the reason they were down here in the first place. Someone might have tipped them off. We're checking everyone.'

'Is that why we're here just now? Giving the crew a once-over?' Rebus nodded, and Holmes nodded back. Then he had an idea. 'Maybe it was a way of sending a message.'

'That's what I've been wondering. But what kind of message, and who to?'

'You don't go for the IRA idea?'

'It's plausible and implausible at the same time,' Rebus said. 'We've got nothing here to interest the paramilitaries.'

'We've got Edinburgh Castle, Holyrood Palace, the Festival . . .'

'He has a point.'

They turned towards the voice. Two men were standing in torchlight. Rebus recognised neither of them. As the men came forwards, Rebus studied both. The man who had spoken, the slightly younger of the two, had an English accent and the look of a London copper. It was the hands in the trouser pockets that did it. That and the air of easy superiority that went with the gesture. Plus of course he was wearing old denims and a black leather bomber-jacket. He had close cropped brown hair spiked with gel, and a heavy pockmarked face. He was probably in his late-thirties but looked like a fortysomething with coronary problems. His eyes were a piercing blue. It was difficult to meet them. He didn't blink often, like he didn't want to miss any of the show.

The other man was well-built and fit, in his late-forties, with ruddy cheeks and a good head of black hair just turning silver at the edges. He looked as if he needed to shave two or even three times a day. His suit was dark blue and looked straight off the tailor's dummy. He was smiling.

'Inspector Rebus?'

'The same.'

'I'm DCI Kilpatrick.'

Rebus knew the name of course. It was interesting at last to have a face to put to it. If he remembered right, Kilpatrick was still in the SCS, the Scottish Crime Squad.

'I thought you worked out of Stuart Street, sir,' Rebus said, shaking hands.

'I moved back from Glasgow a few months ago. I don't suppose it made the front page of the *Scotsman*, but I'm heading the squad here now.'

Rebus nodded. The SCS took on serious crimes, where cross-force investigations were necessary. Drugs were their main concern, or had been. Rebus knew men who'd been seconded to the SCS. You stayed three or four years and came out two things: unwillingly, and tough as second-day bacon. Kilpatrick was introducing his companion.

'This is DI Abernethy from Special Branch. He's come all the way from London to see us.'

'That takes the biscuit,' said Rebus.

'My grandad was a Jock,' Abernethy answered, gripping Rebus's hand and not getting the joke. Rebus introduced Holmes and, when she returned, Siobhan Clarke. From the colouring in Clarke's cheeks, Rebus reckoned someone along the way had made a pass at her. He decided to rule out Mr Blair-Fish, which still left plenty of suspects.

'So,' said Abernethy at last, rubbing his hands, 'where's this slaughterhouse?'

'A butcher's actually,' Mr Blair-Fish explained.

'I know what I mean,' said Abernethy.

Mr Blair-Fish led the way. But Kilpatrick held Rebus back.

'Look,' he whispered, 'I don't like this bastard being here any more than you do, but if we're tolerant we'll get rid of him all the quicker, agreed?'

'Yes, sir.' Kilpatrick's was a Glaswegian accent, managing to be deeply nasal even when reduced to a whisper, and managing, too, to be full of irony and a belief that Glasgow was the centre of the universe. Usually, Glaswegians somehow added to all this a ubiquitous chip on their shoulder, but Kilpatrick didn't seem the type.

'So no more bloody cracks about biscuits.'

'Understood, sir.'

Kilpatrick waited a moment. 'It was you who noticed the paramilitary element, wasn't it?' Rebus nodded. 'Good work.'

'Thank you, sir.' Yes, and Glaswegians could be patronising bastards, too.

When they rejoined the group, Holmes gave Rebus a questioning look, to which Rebus replied with a shrug. At least the shrug was honest.

'So they strung him up here,' Abernethy was saying. He looked around at the setting. 'Bit melodramatic, eh? Not the IRA's style at all. Give them a lock-up or a warehouse, something like that. But someone who likes a bit of drama set this up.'

Rebus was impressed. It was another possible reason for the choice of venue.

'Bang-bang,' Abernethy continued, 'then back upstairs to melt into the crowd, maybe take in a late-night revue before toddling home.'

Clarke interrupted. 'You think there's some connection with the Festival?'

Abernethy studied her openly, causing Brian Holmes to straighten up. Not for the first time, Rebus wondered about Clarke and Holmes.

'Why not?' Abernethy said. 'It's every bit as feasible as anything else I've heard.'

'But it was a six-pack.' Rebus felt obliged to defend his corner.

'No,' Abernethy corrected, 'a *seven*-pack. And that's not paramilitary style at all. A waste of bullets for a start.' He looked to Kilpatrick. 'Could be a drug thing. Gangs like a bit of melodrama, it makes them look like they're in a film. Plus they do like to send messages to each other. Loud messages.'

Kilpatrick nodded. 'We're considering it.'

'My money'd still be on terrorists,' Rebus added. 'A gun like that –'

'Dealers use guns, too, Inspector. They *like* guns. Big ones to make a big loud noise. I'll tell you something, I'd hate to have been down here. The report from a nine-millimetre in an enclosed space like this. It could blow out your eardrums.'

'A silencer,' Siobhan Clarke offered. It wasn't her day. Abernethy just gave her a look, so Rebus provided the explanation.

'Revolvers don't take silencers.'

Abernethy pointed to Rebus, but his eyes were on Clarke's. 'Listen to your Inspector, darling, you might learn something.'

Rebus looked around the room. There were six people there, four of whom would gladly punch another's lights out.

He didn't think Mr Blair-Fish would enter the fray.

Abernethy meantime had sunk to his knees, rubbing his fingers over the floor, over ancient dirt and husks.

'The SOCOs took off the top inch of earth,' Rebus said, but Abernethy wasn't listening. Bags and bags of the stuff had been taken to the sixth floor of Fettes HQ to be sieved and analysed and God knew what else by the forensics lab.

It occurred to Rebus that all the group could now see of Abernethy was a fat arse and brilliant white Reeboks. Abernethy turned his face towards them and smiled. Then he got up, brushing his palms together.

'Was the deceased a drug user?'

'No signs.'

'Only I was thinking, SaS, could be Smack and Speed.'

Again, Rebus was impressed, thoroughly despite himself. Dust had settled in the gel of Abernethy's hair, small enough motes of comfort.

'Could be Scott and Sheena,' offered Rebus. In other words: could be anything. Abernethy just shrugged. He'd been giving them a display, and now the show was over.

'I think I've seen enough,' he said. Kilpatrick nodded with relief. It must be hard, Rebus reflected, being a top cop in your field, a man with

a rep, sent to act as tour guide for a junior officer ... and a Sassenach at
that.

Galling, that was the word.

Abernethy was speaking again. 'Might as well drop in on the Murder
Room while I'm here.'

'Why not?' said Rebus coldly.

'No reason I can think of,' replied Abernethy, all sweetness and bite.

5

St Leonard's police station, headquarters of the city's B Division, boasted a semi-permanent Murder Room. The present inquiry looked like it had been going on forever. Abernethy seemed to favour the scene. He browsed among the computer screens, telephones, wall charts and photographs. Kilpatrick touched Rebus's arm.

'Keep an eye on him, will you? I'll just go say hello to your Chief Super while I'm here.'

'Right, sir.'

Chief Inspector Lauderdale watched him leave. 'So that's Kilpatrick of the Crime Squad, eh? Funny, he looks almost mortal.'

It was true that Kilpatrick's reputation – a hard one to live up to – preceded him. He'd had spectacular successes in Glasgow, and some decidedly public failures too. Huge quantities of drugs had been seized, but a few terrorist suspects had managed to slip away.

'At least he looks human,' Lauderdale went on, 'which is more than can be said for our cockney friend.'

Abernethy couldn't have heard this – he was out of earshot – but he looked up suddenly towards them and grinned. Lauderdale went to take a phone call, and the Special Branch man sauntered back towards Rebus, hands stuffed into his jacket pockets.

'It's a good operation this, but there's not much to go on, is there?'

'Not much.'

'And what you've got doesn't make much sense.'

'Not yet.'

'You worked with Scotland Yard on a case, didn't you?'

'That's right.'

'With George Flight?'

'Right again.'

'He's gone for retraining, you know. I mean, at *his* age. Got interested in computers, I don't know, maybe he's got a point. They're the future of crime, aren't they? Day's coming, the big villains won't have to move from their living rooms.'

'The big villains never have.'

This earned a smile from Abernethy, or at least a lopsided sneer. 'Has my minder gone for a jimmy?'

'He's gone to say hello to someone.'

'Well tell him ta-ta from me.' Abernethy looked around, then lowered his voice. 'I don't think DCI Kilpatrick will be sorry to see the back of me.'

'What makes you say that?'

Abernethy chuckled. 'Listen to you. If your voice was any colder you could store cadavers in it. Still think you've got terrorists in Edinburgh?' Rebus said nothing. 'Well, it's *your* problem. I'm well shot of it. Tell Kilpatrick I'll talk to him before I head south.'

'You're supposed to stay here.'

'Just tell him I'll be in touch.'

There was no painless way of stopping Abernethy from leaving, so Rebus didn't even try. But he didn't think Kilpatrick would be happy. He picked up one of the phones. What did Abernethy mean about it being Rebus's problem? If there *was* a terrorist connection, it'd be out of CID's hands. It would become Special Branch's domain, M15's domain. So what did he mean?

He gave Kilpatrick the message, but Kilpatrick didn't seem bothered after all. There was relaxation in his voice, the sort that came with a large whisky. The Farmer had stopped drinking for a while, but was back off the wagon again. Rebus wouldn't mind a drop himself...

Lauderdale, who had also just put down a telephone, was staring at a pad on which he'd been writing as he took the call.

'Something?' Rebus asked.

'We may have a positive ID on the victim. Do you want to check it out?' Lauderdale tore the sheet from the pad.

'Do Hibs fans weep?' Rebus answered, accepting it.

Actually, not all Hibs fans were prone to tears. Siobhan Clarke supported Hibernian, which put her in a minority at St Leonard's. Being English-educated (another minority, much smaller) she didn't understand the finer points of Scottish bigotry, though one or two of her fellow officers had attempted to educate her. She wasn't Catholic, they explained patiently, so she should support Heart of Midlothian. Hibernian were the Catholic team. Look at their name, look at their green strip. They were Edinburgh's version of Glasgow Celtic, just as Hearts were like Glasgow Rangers.

'It's the same in England,' they'd tell her. 'Wherever you've got Catholics and Protestants in the same place.' Manchester had United (Catholic) and City (Protestant), Liverpool had Liverpool (Catholic) and Everton (Protestant). It only got complicated in London. London even had Jewish teams.

Siobhan Clarke just smiled, shaking her head. It was no use arguing, which didn't stop her trying. They just kept joking with her, teasing her, trying to convert her. It was light-hearted, but she couldn't always tell how light-hearted. The Scots tended to crack jokes with a straight face and be deadly serious when they smiled. When some officers at St Leonard's found out her birthday was coming, she found herself unwrapping half a dozen Hearts scarves. They all went to a charity shop.

She'd seen the darker side of football loyalty, too. The collection tins at certain games. Depending on where you were standing, you'd be asked to donate to either one cause or the other. Usually it was for 'families' or 'victims' or 'prisoners' aid', but everyone who gave knew they might be perpetuating the violence in Northern Ireland. Fearfully, most gave. One pound sterling towards the price of a gun.

She'd come across the same thing on Saturday when, with a couple of friends, she'd found herself standing at the Hearts end of the ground. The tin had come round, and she'd ignored it. Her friends were quiet after that.

'We should be doing something about it,' she complained to Rebus in his car.

'Such as?'

'Get an undercover team in there, arrest whoever's behind it.'

'Behave.'

'Well why not?'

'Because it wouldn't solve anything and there'd be no charge we could make stick other than something paltry like not having a licence. Besides, if you ask me most of that cash goes straight into the collector's pocket. It never reaches Northern Ireland.'

'But it's the *principle* of the thing.'

'Christ, listen to you.' Principles: they were slow to go, and some coppers never lost them entirely. 'Here we are.'

He reversed into a space in front of a tenement block on Mayfield Gardens. The address was a top floor flat.

'Why is it always the top floor?' Siobhan complained.

'Because that's where the poor people live.'

There were two doors on the top landing. The name on one doorbell read MURDOCK. There was a brown bristle welcome-mat just outside the door. The message on it was GET LOST!

'Charming.' Rebus pressed the bell. The door was opened by a bearded man wearing thick wire-framed glasses. The beard didn't help, but Rebus would guess the man's age at mid-twenties. He had thick shoulder-length black hair, through which he ran a hand.

'I'm Detective Inspector Rebus. This is –'

'Come in, come in. Mind out for the motorbike.'

'Yours, Mr Murdock?'

'No, it's Billy's. It hasn't worked since he moved in.'

The bike's frame was intact, but the engine lay disassembled along the hall carpet, lying on old newspapers turned black from oil. Smaller pieces were in polythene bags, each bag tied at the neck and marked with an identifying number.

'That's clever,' said Rebus.

'Oh aye,' said Murdock, 'he's organised is Billy. In here.' He led them into a cluttered living area. 'This is Millie, she lives here.'

'Hiya.'

Millie was sitting on the sofa swathed in a sleeping bag, despite the heat outside. She was watching the television and smoking a cigarette.

'You phoned us, Mr Murdock.'

'Aye, well, it's about Billy.' Murdock began to pad around the room. 'See, the description in the paper and on the telly, well . . . I didn't think about it at the time, but as Millie says, it's not like Billy to stay away so long. Like I say, he's organised. Usually he'd phone or something, just to let us know.'

'When did you last see him?'

Murdock looked to Millie. 'When was it, Thursday night?'

'I saw him Friday morning.'

'So you did.'

Rebus turned to Millie. She had short fair hair, dark at the roots, and dark eyebrows. Her face was long and plain, her chin highlighted by a protruding mole. Rebus reckoned she was a few years older than Murdock. 'Did he say where he was going?'

'He didn't say anything. There's not a lot of conversation in this flat at that hour.'

'What hour?'

She flicked ash into the ashtray which was balanced on her sleeping bag. It was a nervous habit, the cigarette being tapped even when there was no ash for it to surrender. 'Seven thirty, quarter to eight,' she said.

'Where does he work?'

'He doesn't,' said Murdock, resting his hand on the mantelpiece. 'He used to work in the Post Office, but they laid him off a few months back. He's on the dole now, along with half of Scotland.'

'And what do you do, Mr Murdock?'

'I'm a computer consultant.'

Sure enough, some of the living room's clutter was made up of keyboards and disk drives, some of them dismantled, piled on top of each other. There were piles of fat magazines too, and books, hefty operating manuals.

'Did either of you know Billy before he moved in?'

'I did,' said Millie. 'A friend of a friend, casual acquaintance sort of thing. I knew he was looking for a room, and there was a room going spare here, so I suggested him to Murdock.' She changed channels on the TV. She was watching with the sound turned off, watching through a squint of cigarette smoke.

'Can we see Billy's room?'

'Why not?' said Murdock. He'd been glancing nervously towards Millie all the time she'd been talking. He seemed relieved to be in movement. He took them back into where the narrow entrance hall became a wider rectangle, off which were three doors. One was a cupboard, one the kitchen. Back along the narrow hall they'd passed the bathroom on one side and Murdock's bedroom on the other. Which left just this last door.

It led them into a very small, very tidy bedroom. The room itself would be no more than ten feet by eight, yet it managed to contain single bed, wardrobe, a chest of drawers and a writing desk and chair. A hi-fi unit, including speakers, sat atop the chest of drawers. The bed had been made, and there was nothing left lying around.

'You haven't tidied up, have you?'

Murdock shook his head. 'Billy was always tidying. You should see the kitchen.'

'Do you have a photograph of Billy?' Rebus asked.

'I might have some from one of our parties. You want to look at them?'

'Just the best one will do.'

'I'll fetch it then.'

'Thank you.' When Murdock had gone, Siobhan squeezed into the room beside Rebus. Until then, she'd been forced to stay just outside the door.

'Initial thoughts?' Rebus asked.

'Neurotically tidy,' she said, the comment of one whose own flat looked like a cross between a pizza franchise and a bottle bank.

But Rebus was studying the walls. There was a Hearts pennant above the bed, and a Union Jack flag on which the Red Hand of Ulster was centrally prominent, with above it the words 'No Surrender' and below it the letters FTP. Even Siobhan Clarke knew what those stood for.

'Fuck the Pope,' she murmured.

Murdock was back. He didn't attempt to squeeze into the narrow aisle between bed and wardrobe, but stood in the doorway and handed the photo to Siobhan Clarke, who handed it to Rebus. It showed a young man smiling manically for the camera. Behind him you could see a can of beer held high, as though someone were about to pour it over his head.

'It's as good a photo as we've got,' Murdock said by way of apology.

'Thank you, Mr Murdock.' Rebus was almost sure. Almost. 'Billy had a tattoo?'

'On his arm, aye. It looked like one of those things you do yourself when you're a daft laddie.'

Rebus nodded. They'd released details of the tattoo, looking for a quick result.

'I never really looked at it close up,' Murdock went on, 'and Billy never talked about it.'

Millie had joined him in the doorway. She had discarded the sleeping bag and was wearing a modestly long t-shirt over bare legs. She put an arm around Murdock's waist. 'I remember it,' she said. 'SaS. Big S, small a.'

'Did he ever tell you what it stood for?'

She shook her head. Tears were welling in her eyes. 'It's him, isn't it? He's the one you found dead?'

Rebus tried to be non-committal, but his face gave him away. Millie started to bawl, and Murdock hugged her to him. Siobhan Clarke had lifted some cassette tapes from the chest of drawers and was studying them. She handed them silently to Rebus. They were collections of Orange songs, songs about the struggle in Ulster. Their titles said it all: *The Sash and other Glories*, *King Billy's Marching Tunes*, *No Surrender*. He stuck one of the tapes in his pocket.

They did some more searching of Billy Cunningham's room, but came up with little excepting a recent letter from his mother. There was no address on the letter, but it bore a Glasgow postmark, and Millie recalled Billy saying something about coming from Hillhead. Well, they'd let Glasgow deal with it. Let Glasgow break the news to some unsuspecting family.

In one of the drawers, Siobhan Clarke came up with a Fringe programme. It contained the usual meltdown of *Abigail's Party*s and *Krapp's Last Tape*s, revues called things like *Teenage Alsatian Orgy*, and comic turns on the run from London fatigue.

'He's ringed a show,' said Clarke.

So he had, a country and western act at the Crazy Hose Saloon. The act had appeared for three nights back at the start of the Festival.

'There's no country music in his collection,' Clarke commented.

'At least he showed taste,' said Rebus.

On the way back to the station, he pushed the Orange tape into his car's antiquated machine.

The tape played slow, which added to the grimness. Rebus had heard stuff like it before, but not for a wee while. Songs about King Billy and the Apprentice Boys, the Battle of the Boyne and the glory of 1690, songs about routing the Catholics and why the men of Ulster would struggle to the end. The singer had a pub vibrato and little else, and was backed by accordion, snare and the occasional flute. Only an Orange marching band could make the flute sound martial to the ears. Well, an Orange marching band or Iain Anderson from Jethro Tull. Rebus was reminded that he hadn't listened to Tull in an age. Anything would be better than these songs of ... the word 'hate' sprang to mind, but he dismissed it. There was no vitriol in the lyrics, just a stern refusal to compromise in any way, to give ground, to accept that things could change now that the 1690s had become the 1990s. It was all blinkered and backward-looking. How narrow a view could you get?

'The sod is,' said Siobhan Clarke, 'you find yourself humming the tunes after.'

'Aye,' said Rebus, 'bigotry's catchy enough all right.'

And he whistled Jethro Tull all the way back to St Leonard's.

Lauderdale had arranged a press conference and wanted to know what Rebus knew.

'I'm not positive,' was the answer. 'Not a hundred per cent.'

'How close?'

'Ninety, ninety-five.'

Lauderdale considered this. 'So should I say anything?'

'That's up to you, sir. A fingerprint team's on its way to the flat. We'll know soon enough one way or the other.'

One of the problems with the victim was that the last killing shot had blown away half his face, the bullet entering through the back of the neck and tearing up through the jaw. As Dr Curt had explained, they could do an ID covering up the bottom half of the face, allowing a friend or relative to see just the top half. But would that be enough? Before today's potential break, they'd been forced to consider dental work. The victim's teeth were the usual result of a Scottish childhood, eroded by sweets and shored up by dentistry. But as the forensic pathologist had said, the mouth was badly damaged, and what dental work remained was fairly routine. There was nothing unusual there for any dentist to spot definitively as his or her work.

Rebus arranged for the party photograph to be reprinted and sent to Glasgow with the relevant details. Then he went to Lauderdale's press conference.

Chief Inspector Lauderdale loved his duels with the media. But today he was more nervous than usual. Perhaps it was that he had a larger audience than he was used to, Chief Superintendent Watson and DCI Kilpatrick having emerged from somewhere to listen. Both sported faces too ruddy to be natural, whisky certainly the cause. While the journalists sat towards the front of the room, the police officers stood to the back. Kilpatrick saw Rebus and sidled over to him.

'You may have a positive ID?' he whispered.

'Maybe.'

'So is it drugs or the IRA?' There was a wry smile on his face. He didn't really expect an answer, it was the whisky asking, that was all. But Rebus had an answer for him anyway.

'If it's anybody,' he said, 'it's not the IRA but the other lot.' There were so many names for them he didn't even begin to list them: UDA, UVF, UFF, UR ... The U stood for Ulster in each case. They were proscribed organisations, and they were all Protestant. Kilpatrick rocked back a little on his heels. His face was full of questions, fighting their way to the surface past the burst blood vessels which cherried nose and cheeks. A drinker's face. Rebus had seen too many of them, including his own some nights in the bathroom mirror.

But Kilpatrick wasn't so far gone. He knew he was in no condition to ask questions, so he made his way back to the Farmer instead, where he spoke a few words. Farmer Watson glanced across to Rebus, then nodded to Kilpatrick. Then they turned their attention back to the press briefing.

Rebus knew the reporters. They were old hands mostly, and knew what to expect from Chief Inspector Lauderdale. You might walk into a Lauderdale session sniffing and baying like a bloodhound, but you shuffled out like a sleepy-faced pup. So they stayed quiet mostly, and let him have his insubstantial say.

Except for Mairie Henderson. She was down at the front, asking questions the others weren't bothering to ask; weren't bothering for the simple reason that they knew the answer the Chief Inspector would give.

'No comment,' he told Mairie for about the twentieth time. She gave up and slumped in her chair. Someone else asked a question, so she looked around, surveying the room. Rebus jerked his chin in greeting. Mairie glared and stuck her tongue out at him. A few of the other journalists looked around in his direction. Rebus smiled out their inquisitive stares.

The briefing over, Mairie caught up with him in the corridor. She was carrying a legal notepad, her usual blue fineliner pen, and a recording walkman.

'Thanks for your help the other night,' she said.

'No comment.'

She knew it was a waste of time getting angry at John Rebus, so exhaled noisily instead. 'I was first on the scene, I could have had a scoop.'

'Come to the pub with me and you can have as many scoops as you like.'

'That one's so weak it's got holes in its knees.' She turned and walked off, Rebus watching her. He never liked to pass up the opportunity of looking at her legs.

6

Edinburgh City Mortuary was sited on the Cowgate, at the bottom of High School Wynd and facing St Ann's Community Centre and Blackfriars Street. The building was low-built red brick and pebbledash, purposely anonymous and tucked in an out of the way place. Steep sloping roads led up towards the High Street. For a long time now, the Cowgate had been a thoroughfare for traffic, not pedestrians. It was narrow and deep like a canyon, its pavements offering scant shelter from the taxis and cars rumbling past. The place was not for the faint-hearted. Society's underclass could be found there, when it wasn't yet time to shuffle back to the hostel.

But the street was undergoing redevelopment, including a court annexe. First they'd cleaned up the Grassmarket, and now the city fathers had the Cowgate in their sights.

Rebus waited outside the mortuary for a couple of minutes, until a woman poked her head out of the door.

'Inspector Rebus?'

'That's right.'

'He told me to tell you he's already gone to Bannerman's.'

'Thanks.' Rebus headed off towards the pub.

Bannerman's had been just cellarage at one time, and hadn't been altered much since. Its vaulted rooms were unnervingly like those of the shops in Mary King's Close. Cellars like these formed connecting burrows beneath the Old Town, worming from the Lawnmarket down to the Canongate and beyond. The bar wasn't busy yet, and Dr Curt was sitting by the window, his beer glass resting on a barrel which served as table. Somehow, he'd found one of the few comfortable chairs in the place. It looked like a minor nobleman's perch, with armrests and high back. Rebus bought a double whisky for himself, dragged over a stool, and sat down.

'Your health, John.'

'And yours.'

'So what can I do for you?'

Even in a pub, Rebus would swear he could smell soap and surgical alcohol wafting up from Curt's hands. He took a swallow of whisky. Curt frowned.

'Looks like I might be examining your liver sooner than I'd hoped.'

Rebus nodded towards the pack of cigarettes on the table. They were Curt's and they were untipped. 'Not if you keep smoking those.'

Dr Curt smiled. He hadn't long taken up smoking, having decided to see just how indestructible he was. He wouldn't call it a death wish exactly; it was merely an exercise in mortality.

'How long have you and Ms Rattray been an item then?'

Curt laughed. 'Dear God, is that why I'm here? You want to ask me about Caroline?'

'Just making conversation. She's not bad though.'

'Oh, she's quite something.' Curt lit a cigarette and inhaled, nodding to himself. 'Quite something,' he repeated through a cloud of smoke.

'We may have a name for the victim in Mary King's Close. It's up to fingerprints now.'

'Is that why you wanted to see me? Not just to discuss Caro?'

'I want to talk about guns.'

'I'm no expert on guns.'

'Good. I'm not after an expert, I'm after someone I can talk to. Have you seen the ballistics report?' Curt shook his head. 'We're looking at something like a Smith and Wesson model 547, going by the rifling marks – five grooves, right-hand twist. It's a revolver, takes six rounds of nine millimetre parabellum.'

'You've lost me already.'

'Probably the version with the three-inch rather than four-inch barrel, which means a weight of thirty-two ounces.' Rebus sipped his drink. There were whisky fumes in his nostrils now, blocking any other smells. 'Revolvers don't accept silencers.'

'Ah.' Curt nodded. 'I begin to see some light.'

'A confined space like that, shaped the way it was . . .' Rebus nodded past the bar to the room beyond. 'Much the same size and shape as this.'

'It would have been loud.'

'Bloody loud. Deafening, you might say.'

'Meaning what exactly?'

Rebus shrugged. 'I'm just wondering how professional all of this really was. I mean, on the surface, if you look at the *style* of execution, then yes, it was a pro job, no question. But then things start to niggle.'

Curt considered. 'So what now? Do we scour the city for recent purchasers of hearing-aids?'

Rebus smiled. 'It's a thought.'

'All I can tell you, John, is that those bullets did damage. Whether meant to or not, they were messy. Now, we've both come up against messy killers before. Usually the facts of the mess make it easier to find them. But this time there doesn't seem to be much evidence left lying around, apart from the bullets.'

'I know.'

Curt slapped his hand on the barrel. 'Tell you what, I've got a suggestion.'

'What is it?'

He leaned forward, as if to impart a secret. 'Let me give you Caroline Rattray's phone number.'

'Bugger off,' said Rebus.

That evening, a marked patrol car picked him up from Patience's Oxford Terrace flat. The driver was a Detective Constable called Robert Burns, and Burns was doing Rebus a favour.

'I appreciate it,' said Rebus.

Though Burns was attached to C Division in the west end, he'd been born and raised in Pilmuir, and still had friends and enemies there. He was a known quantity in the Gar-B, which was what mattered to Rebus.

'I was born in one of the pre-fabs,' Burns explained. 'Before they levelled them to make way for the high-rises. The high-rises were supposed to be more "civilised", if you can believe that. Bloody architects and town planners. You never find one admitting he made a mistake, do you?' He smiled. 'They're a bit like us that way.'

'By "us" do you mean the police or the Wee Frees?' Burns was more than just a member of the Free Church of Scotland. On Sunday afternoons he took his religion to the foot of The Mound, where he spouted hellfire and brimstone to anyone who'd listen. Rebus had listened a few times. But Burns took a break during the Festival. As he'd pointed out, even his voice would be fighting a losing battle against steel bands and untuned guitars.

They were turning into the Gar-B, passing the gable end again with its sinister greeting.

'Drop me as close as you can, eh?'

'Sure,' said Burns. And when they came to the dead end near the garages, he slowed only fractionally as he bumped the car up first onto the pavement and then onto the grass. 'It's not my car,' he explained.

They drove beside the path past the garages and a high-rise, until there was nowhere else to go. When Burns stopped, the car was resting about twelve feet from the community centre.

'I can walk from here,' said Rebus.

Kids who'd been lying on the centre's roof were standing now, watching them, cigarettes hanging from open mouths. People watched from the path and from open windows, too. Burns turned to Rebus.

'Don't tell me you wanted to sneak up on them?'

'This is just fine.' He opened his door. 'Stay with the car. I don't want us losing any tyres.'

Rebus walked towards the community centre's wide open doors. The teenagers on the roof watched him with practised hostility. There were paper planes lying all around, some of them made airborne again temporarily by a gust of wind. As Rebus walked into the building, he heard grunting noises above him. His rooftop audience were pretending to be pigs.

There was no preliminary chamber, just the hall itself. At one end stood a high basketball hoop. Some teenagers were in a ruck around the grounded ball, feet scraping at ankles, hands pulling at arms and hair. So much for non-contact sports. On a makeshift stage sat a ghetto blaster, blaring out the fashion in heavy metal. Rebus didn't reckon he'd score many points by announcing that he'd been in at the birth. Most of these kids had been born after *Anarchy in the UK*, never mind *Communication Breakdown*.

There was a mix of ages, and it was impossible to pick out Peter Cave. He could be nodding his head to the distorted electric guitar. He could be smoking by the wall. Or in with the basketball brigade. But no, he was coming towards Rebus from the other direction, from a tight group which included black t-shirt from Rebus's first visit.

'Can I help?'

Father Leary had said he was in his mid-twenties, but he could pass for late-teens. The clothes helped, and he wore them well. Rebus had seen church people before when they wore denim. They usually looked as if they'd be more comfortable in something less comfortable. But Cave, in faded denim jeans and denim shirt, with half a dozen thin leather and metal bracelets around his wrists, he looked all right.

'Not many girls,' Rebus stated, playing for a little more time.

Peter Cave looked around. 'Not just now. Usually there are more than this, but on a nice night ...'

It was a nice night. He'd left Patience drinking cold rose wine in the garden. He had left her reluctantly. He got no initial bad feelings from Cave. The young man was fresh-faced and clear-eyed and looked level headed too. His hair was long but by no means untidy, and his face was square and honest with a deep cleft in the chin.

'I'm sorry,' Cave said, 'I'm Peter Cave. I run the youth club.' His hand shot out, bracelets sliding down his wrist. Rebus took the hand and smiled. Cave wanted to know who he was, a not unreasonable request.

'Detective Inspector Rebus.'

Cave nodded. 'Davey said a policeman had been round earlier. I thought probably he meant uniformed. What's the trouble, Inspector?'

'No trouble, Mr Cave.'

A circle of frowning onlookers had formed itself around the two of them. Rebus wasn't worried, not yet.

'Call me Peter.'

'Mr Cave,' Rebus licked his lips, 'how are things going here?'

'What do you mean?'

'A simple question, sir. Only, crime in Pilmuir hasn't exactly dropped since you started this place up.'

Cave bristled at that. 'There haven't been any gang fights.'

Rebus accepted this. 'But housebreaking, assaults ... there are still syringes in the playpark and aerosols lying –'

'Aerosols to you too.'

Rebus turned to see who had entered. It was the boy with the naked chest and denim jacket.

'Hello, Davey,' said Rebus. The ring had broken long enough to let denim jacket through.

The youth pointed a finger. 'I thought I said you didn't want to know my name?'

'I can't help it if people tell me things, Davey.'

'Davey Soutar,' Burns added. He was standing in the doorway, arms folded, looking like he was enjoying himself. He wasn't of course, it was just a necessary pose.

'Davey Soutar,' Rebus echoed.

Soutar had clenched his fists. Peter Cave attempted to intercede. 'Now, please. Is there a problem here, Inspector?'

'You tell me, Mr Cave.' He looked around him. 'Frankly, we're a little bit concerned about this gang hut.'

Colour flooded Cave's cheeks. 'It's a youth centre.'

Rebus was now studying the ceiling. Nobody was playing basketball any more. The music had been turned right down. 'If you say so, sir.'

'Look, you come barging in here –'

'I don't recall barging, Mr Cave. More of a saunter. I didn't ask for trouble. If Davey here can be persuaded to unclench his fists, maybe you and me can have a quiet chat outside.' He looked at the circle around them. 'I'm not one for playing to the cheap seats.'

Cave stared at Rebus, then at Soutar. He nodded slowly, his face drained of anger, and eventually Soutar let his hands relax. You could tell it was an effort. Burns hadn't put in an appearance for nothing.

'There now,' said Rebus. 'Come on, Mr Cave, let's you and me go for a walk.'

They walked across the playing fields. Burns had returned to the patrol car and moved it to a spot where he could watch them. Some teenagers watched from the back of the community centre and from its roof, but they didn't venture any closer than that.

'I really don't see, Inspector –'

'You think you're doing a good job here, sir?'

Cave thought about it before answering. 'Yes, I do.'

'You think the experiment is a success?'

'A limited success so far, but yes, once again.' He had his hands behind his back, head bowed a little. He looked like he didn't have a care in the world.

'No regrets?'

'None.'

'Funny then . . .'

'What?'

'Your church doesn't seem so sure.'

Cave stopped in his tracks. 'Is that what this is about? You're in Conor's congregation, is that it? He's sent you here to . . . what's the phrase? Come down heavy on me?'

'Nothing like that.'

'He's paranoid. *He* was the one who wanted me here. Now suddenly he's decided I should leave, *ipso facto* I *must* leave. He's used to getting his way after all. Well, I don't choose to leave. I like it fine here. Is that what he's afraid of? Well there's not much he can do about it, is there? And as far as I can see, Inspector, there's nothing you can do about it either, unless someone from the club is found breaking the law.' Cave's face had reddened, his hands coming from behind his back so he could gesture with them.

'That lot break the law every day.'

'Now just a –'

'No, listen for a minute. Okay, you got the Jaffas and the Tims together, but ask yourself why they were amenable. If they're not divided, they're united, and they're united for a *reason*. They're the same as before, only stronger. You must see that.'

'I see nothing of the sort. People can change, Inspector.'

Rebus had been hearing the line all his professional life. He sighed and toed the ground.

'You don't believe that?'

'Frankly, sir, not in this particular case, and the crime stats back me up. What you've got just now is a truce of sorts, and it suits them because while there's a truce they can get busy carving up territory between them. Anyone threatens them, they can retaliate in spades . . . or even *with* spades. But it won't last, and when they split back into their separate gangs, there's going to be blood spilled, no way round it. Because now there'll be more at stake. Tell me, in your club tonight, how many Catholics were there?'

Cave didn't answer, he was too busy shaking his head. 'I feel sorry for you, really I do. I can smell cynicism off you like sulphur. I don't happen to believe anything you've just said.'

'Then you're every bit as naive as I am cynical, and that means they're just using you. Which is good, because the only way of looking at this is that you've been sucked into it and you accept it, knowing the truth.'

Cave's cheeks were red again. 'How dare you say that!' And he punched Rebus in the stomach, hard. Rebus had been punched by professionals, but he was unprepared and felt himself double over for a moment, getting his wind back. There was a burning feeling in his gut, and it wasn't whisky. He could hear cheering in the distance. Tiny figures were dancing up and down on the community centre roof. Rebus hoped they'd fall through it. He straightened up again.

'Is that what you call setting a good example, Mr Cave?'

Then he punched Cave solidly on the jaw. The young man stumbled backwards and almost fell.

He heard a double roar from the community centre. The youth of the Gar-B were clambering down from the roof, starting to run in his direction. Burns had started the car and was bumping it across the football pitch towards him. The car was outpacing the crowd, but only just. An empty can bounced off its rear windscreen. Burns barely braked as he caught up with Rebus. Rebus yanked the door open and got in, grazing a knee and an elbow. Then they were off again, making for the roadway.

'Well,' Burns commented, checking the rearview, 'that seemed to go off okay.' Rebus was catching his breath and examining his elbow.

'How did you know Davey Soutar's name?'

'He's a maniac,' Burns said simply. 'I try to keep abreast of these things.'

Rebus exhaled loudly, rolling his sleeve back down. 'Never do a favour for a priest,' he said to himself.

'I'll bear that in mind, sir,' said Burns.

7

Rebus walked into the Murder Room next morning with a cup of delicatessen decaf and a tuna sandwich on wholemeal. He sat at his desk and peeled off the top from the styrofoam cup. From the corner of his eye he could see the fresh mound of paperwork which had appeared on his desk since yesterday. But he could ignore it for another five minutes.

The victim's fingerprints had been matched with those taken from items in Billy Cunningham's room. So now they had a name for the body, but precious little else. Murdock and Millie had been interviewed, and the Post Office were looking up their personnel files. Today, Billy's room would be searched again. They still didn't know who he was really. They still didn't know anything about where he came from or who his parents were. There was so much they didn't know.

In a murder investigation, Rebus had found, you didn't always need to know everything.

Chief Inspector Lauderdale was standing behind him. Rebus knew this because Lauderdale brought a smell with him. Not everyone could distinguish it, but Rebus could. It was as if talcum powder had been used in a bathroom to cover some less acceptable aroma. Then there was a click and the buzz of Lauderdale's battery-shaver. Rebus straightened at the sound.

'Chief wants to see you,' Lauderdale said. 'Breakfast can wait.'

Rebus stared at his sandwich.

'I said it can wait.'

Rebus nodded. 'I'll bring you back a mug of coffee, shall I, sir?'

He took his own coffee with him, sipping it as he listened for a moment at Farmer Watson's door. There were voices inside, one of them more nasal than the other. Rebus knocked and entered. DCI Kilpatrick was sitting across the desk from the Farmer.

'Morning, John,' said the Chief Super. 'Coffee?'

Rebus raised his cup. 'Got some, sir.'

'Well, sit down.'

He sat next to Kilpatrick. 'Morning, sir.'

'Good morning, John.' Kilpatrick was nursing a mug, but he wasn't drinking. The Farmer meantime was pouring himself a refill from his personal machine.

'Right, John,' he said at last, sitting down. 'Bottom line, you're being seconded to DCI Kilpatrick's section.' Watson took a gulp of coffee, swilling it around his mouth. Rebus looked to Kilpatrick, who obliged with a confirmation.

'You'll be based with us at Fettes, but you're going to be our eyes and ears on this murder inquiry, liaison if you like, so you'll still spend most of your time here at St Leonard's.'

'But why?'

'Well, Inspector, this case might concern the Crime Squad.'

'Yes, sir, but why me in particular?'

'You've been in the Army. I notice you served in Ulster in the late '60s.'

'That was quarter of a century ago,' Rebus protested. An age spent forgetting all about it.

'Nevertheless, you'll agree there seem to be paramilitary aspects to this case. As you commented, the gun is not your everyday hold-up weapon. It's a type of revolver used by terrorists. A lot of guns have been coming into the UK recently. Maybe this murder will connect us to them.'

'Wait a second, you're saying you're not interested in the shooting, you're interested in the *gun*?'

'I think it will become clearer when I show you our operation at Fettes. I'll be through here in –' he looked at his watch '– say twenty minutes. That should give you time to say goodbye to your loved ones.' He smiled.

Rebus nodded. He hadn't touched his coffee. A cooling scum had formed on its surface. 'All right, sir,' he said, getting to his feet.

He was still a little dazed when he got back to the Murder Room. Two detectives were being told a joke by a third. The joke was about a squid with no money, a restaurant bill, and the guy from the kitchen who washed up. The guy from the kitchen was called Hans.

Rebus was joining the SCS, the Bastard Brigade as some called it. He sat at his desk. It took him a minute to work out that something was missing.

'Which bollocks of you's eaten my sandwich?'

As he looked around the room, he saw that the joke had come to an untimely end. But no one was paying attention to him. A message was being passed through the place, changing the mood. Lauderdale came over to Rebus's desk. He was holding a sheet of fax paper.

'What is it?' Rebus asked.

'Glasgow have tracked down Billy Cunningham's mother.'

'Good. Is she coming here?'

Lauderdale nodded distractedly. 'She'll be here for the formal ID.'

'No father?'

'The father and mother split up a long time ago. Billy was still an infant. She told us his name though.' He handed over the fax sheet. 'It's Morris Cafferty.'

'What?' Rebus's hunger left him.

'Morris Gerald Cafferty.'

Rebus read the fax sheet. 'Say it ain't so. It's just Glasgow having a joke.' But Lauderdale was shaking his head.

'No joke,' he said.

Big Ger Cafferty was in prison, had been for several months, would be for many years to come. He was a dangerous man, runner of protection rackets, extortioner, murderer. They'd pinned only two counts of murder on him, but there had been others, Rebus knew there had been others.

'You think someone was sending him a message?' he asked.

Lauderdale shrugged. 'This changes the case slightly, certainly. According to Mrs Cunningham, Cafferty kept tabs on Billy all the time he was growing up, made sure he didn't want for anything. She still gets money from time to time.'

'But did Billy know who his father was?'

'Not according to Mrs Cunningham.'

'Then would anyone else have known?'

Lauderdale shrugged again. 'I wonder who'll tell Cafferty.'

'They better do it by phone. I wouldn't want to be in the same room with him.'

'Lucky my good suit's in my locker,' said Lauderdale. 'There'll have to be another press conference.'

'Best tell the Chief Super first though, eh?'

Lauderdale's eyes cleared. 'Of course.' He lifted Rebus's receiver to make the call. 'What did he want with you, by the way?'

'Nothing much,' said Rebus. He meant it too, now.

'But maybe this changes things,' he persisted to Kilpatrick in the car. They were seated in the back, a driver taking them the slow route to Fettes. He was sticking to the main roads, instead of the alleys and shortcuts and fast stretches unpoliced by traffic lights that Rebus would have used.

'Maybe,' said Kilpatrick. 'We'll see.'

Rebus had been telling Kilpatrick all about Big Ger Cafferty. 'I mean,' he went on, 'if it's a gang thing, then it's nothing to do with paramilitaries, is it? So I can't help you.'

Kilpatrick smiled at him. 'What is it, John? Most coppers I know would give their drinking arm for an assignment with SCS.'

'Yes, sir.'

'But you're not one of them?'

'I'm quite attached to my drinking arm. It comes in handy for other things.' Rebus looked out of the window. 'The thing is, I've been on secondment before, and I didn't like it much.'

'You mean London? The Chief Superintendent told me all about it.'

'I doubt that, sir,' Rebus said quietly. They turned off Queensferry Road, not a minute's walk from Patience's flat.

'Humour me,' said Kilpatrick stiffly. 'After all, it sounds like you're an expert on this man Cafferty too. I'd be daft not to use a man like you.'

'Yes, sir.'

And they left it at that, saying nothing as they turned into Fettes, Edinburgh's police HQ. At the end of the long road you got a good view of the Gothic spires of Fettes School, one of the city's most exclusive. Rebus didn't know which was uglier, the ornate school or the low anonymous building which housed police HQ. It could have been a comprehensive school, not so much a piece of design as a lack of it. It was one of the most unimaginative buildings Rebus had ever come across. Maybe it was making a statement about its purpose.

The Scottish Crime Squad's Edinburgh operation was run from a cramped office on the fifth floor, a floor shared with the city's Scene of Crime unit. One floor above worked the forensic scientists and the police photographers. There was a lot of interaction between the two floors.

The Crime Squad's real HQ was Stuart Street in Glasgow, with other branches in Stonehaven and Dunfermline, the latter being a technical support unit. Eighty-two officers in total, plus a dozen or so civilian staff.

'We've got our own surveillance and drugs teams,' Kilpatrick added. 'We recruit from all eight Scottish forces.' He kept his spiel going as he led Rebus through the SCS office. A few people looked up from their work, but by no means all of them. Two who did were a bald man and his freckle-faced neighbour. Their look wasn't welcoming, just interested.

Rebus and Kilpatrick were approaching a very large man who was standing in front of a wall-map. The map showed the British Isles and the north European mainland, stretching east as far as Russia. Some sea routes had been marked with long narrow strips of red material, like something you'd use in dressmaking. Only the big man didn't look the type for crimping-shears and tissue-paper cut-outs. On the map, the ports had been circled in black pen. One of the routes ended on the Scottish east coast. The man hadn't turned round at their approach.

'Inspector John Rebus,' said Kilpatrick, 'this is Inspector Ken Smylie. He never smiles, so don't bother joking with him about his name. He doesn't say much, but he's always thinking. And he's from Fife, so watch out. You know what they say about Fifers.'

'I'm from Fife myself,' said Rebus. Smylie had turned round to grip Rebus's hand. He was probably six feet three or four, and had the bulk to make the height work. The bulk was a mixture of muscle and fat, but mostly muscle. Rebus would bet the guy worked out every day. He was a few years younger than Rebus, with short thick fair hair and a small dark moustache. You'd take him for a farm labourer, maybe even a farmer. In the Borders, he'd definitely have played rugby.

'Ken,' Kilpatrick said to Smylie, 'I'd like you to show John around. He's going to be joining us temporarily. He's ex-Army, served in Ulster.' Kilpatrick winked. 'A good man.' Ken Smylie looked appraisingly at Rebus, who tried to stand up straight, inflating his chest. He didn't know why he wanted to impress Smylie, except that he didn't want him as an enemy. Smylie nodded slowly, sharing a look with Kilpatrick, a look Rebus didn't understand.

Kilpatrick touched Smylie's arm. 'I'll leave you to it.' He turned and called to another officer. 'Jim, any calls?' Then he walked away from them.

Rebus turned to the map. 'Ferry crossings?'

'There isn't a ferry sails from the east coast.'

'They go to Scandinavia.'

'This one doesn't.' He had a point. Rebus decided to try again. 'Boats then?'

'Boats, yes. We think boats.' Rebus had expected the voice to be *basso profondo*, but it was curiously high, as though it hadn't broken properly in Smylie's teens. Maybe it was the reason he didn't say much.

'You're interested in boats then?'

'Only if they're bringing in contraband.'

Rebus nodded. 'Guns.'

'Maybe guns.' He pointed to some of the east European ports. 'See, these days things being what they are, there are a lot of weapons in and around Russia. If you cut back your military, you get excess. And the economic situation there being what it is, you get people who need money.'

'So they steal guns and sell them?'

'If they need to steal them. A lot of the soldiers kept their guns. Plus they picked up souvenirs along the way, stuff from Afghanistan and wherever. Here, sit down.'

They sat at Smylie's desk, Smylie himself spilling from a moulded plastic chair. He brought some photographs out of a drawer. They showed machine guns, rocket launchers, grenades and missiles, armour-piercing shells, a whole dusty armoury.

'This is just some of the stuff that's been tracked down. Most of it in mainland Europe: Holland, Germany, France. But some of it in Northern Ireland of course, and some in England and Scotland.' He tapped a photo of an assault rifle. 'This AK 47 was used in a bank hold-up in Hillhead. You know Professor Kalashnikov is a travelling salesman these days?

Times are hard, so he goes to arms fairs around the world flogging his creations. Like this.' Smylie picked out another photograph. 'Later model, the AK 74. The magazine's made of plastic. This is actually the 74S, still quite rare on the market. A lot of the stuff travels across Europe courtesy of motorcycle gangs.'

'Hell's Angels?'

Smylie nodded. 'Some of them are in this up to their tattooed necks, and making a fortune. But there are other problems. A lot of stuff comes into the UK direct. The armed forces, they bring back souvenirs too, from the Falklands or Kuwait. Kalashnikovs, you name it. Not everyone gets searched, a lot of stuff gets in. Later, it's either sold or stolen, and the owners aren't about to report the theft, are they?'

Smylie paused and swallowed, maybe realising how much he'd been talking.

'I thought you were the strong silent type,' Rebus said.

'I get carried away sometimes.'

Rebus wouldn't fancy being on stretcher detail. Smylie began to tidy up the photographs.

'That's basically it,' he said. 'The material that's already here we can't do much about, but with the help of Interpol we're trying to stop the trafficking.'

'You're not saying Scotland is a target for this stuff?'

'A conduit, that's all. It comes through here on its way to Northern Ireland.'

'The IRA?'

'To whoever has the money to pay for it. Right now, we think it's more a Protestant thing. We just don't know why.'

'How much evidence do you have?'

'Not enough.'

Rebus was thinking. Kilpatrick had kept very quiet, but all along he'd thought there was a paramilitary angle to the murder, because it tied in with all of this.

'You're the one who spotted the six-pack?' Smylie asked. Rebus nodded. 'You might well be right about it. If so, the victim must've been involved.'

'Or just someone who got caught up in it.'

'That tends not to happen.'

'But there's another thing. The victim's father is a local gangster, Big Ger Cafferty.'

'You put him away a while back.'

'You're well informed.'

'Well,' said Smylie, 'Cafferty adds a certain symmetry, doesn't he?' He rose briskly from his chair. 'Come on, I'll give you the rest of the tour.'

Not that there was much to see. But Rebus was introduced to his colleagues. They didn't look like supermen, but you wouldn't want to fight them on their terms. They all looked like they'd gone the distance and beyond.

One man, a DS Claverhouse, was the exception. He was lanky and slow-moving and had dark cusps beneath his eyes.

'Don't let him fool you,' Smylie said. 'We don't call him Bloody Claverhouse for nothing.'

Claverhouse's smile took time forming. It wasn't that he was slow so much as that he had to calculate things before he carried them out. He was seated at his desk, Rebus and Smylie standing in front of him. He was tapping his fingers on a red cardboard file. The file was closed, but on its cover was printed the single word SHIELD. Rebus had just seen the word on another file lying on Smylie's desk.

'Shield?' he asked.

'The Shield,' Claverhouse corrected. 'It's something we keep hearing about. Maybe a gang, maybe with Irish connections.'

'But just now,' interrupted Smylie, 'all it is is a name.'

Shield, the word meant something to Rebus. Or rather, he knew it should mean something to him. As he turned from Claverhouse's desk, he caught something Claverhouse was saying to Smylie, saying in an undertone.

'We don't need him.'

Rebus didn't let on he'd heard. He knew nobody liked it when an outsider was brought in. Nor did he feel any happier when introduced to the bald man, a DS Blackwood, and the freckled one, DC Ormiston. They were as enthusiastic about him as dogs welcoming a new flea to the area. Rebus didn't linger; there was a small empty desk waiting for him in another part of the room, and a chair which had been found in some cupboard. The chair didn't quite have three legs, but Rebus got the idea: they hadn't exactly stretched themselves to provide him with a wholesome working environment. He took one look at desk and chair, made his excuses and left. He took a few deep breaths in the corridor, then descended a few floors. He had one friend at Fettes, and saw no reason why he shouldn't visit her.

But there was someone else in DI Gill Templer's office. The nameplate on the door told him so. Her name was DI Murchie and she too was a Liaison Officer. Rebus knocked on the door.

'Enter!'

It was like entering a headmistress's office. DI Murchie was young; at least, her face was. But she had made determined efforts to negate this fact.

'Yes?' she said.

'I was looking for DI Templer.'

Murchie put down her pen and slipped off her half-moon glasses.

They hung by a string around her neck. 'She's moved on,' she said. 'Dunfermline, I think.'

'Dunfermline? What's she doing there?'

'Dealing with rapes and sexual assaults, so far as I know. Do you have some business with Inspector Templer?'

'No, I just . . . I was passing and . . . Never mind.' He backed out of the room.

DI Murchie twitched her mouth and put her glasses back on. Rebus went back upstairs feeling worse than ever.

He spent the rest of the morning waiting for something to happen. Nothing did. Everyone kept their distance, even Smylie. And then the phone rang on Smylie's desk, and it was a call for him.

'Chief Inspector Lauderdale,' Smylie said, handing over the receiver. 'Hello?'

'I hear you've been poached from us.'

'Sort of, sir.'

'Well, tell them I want to poach you back.'

I'm not a fucking salmon, thought Rebus. 'I'm still on the investigation, sir,' he said.

'Yes, I know that. The Chief Super told me all about it.' He paused. 'We want you to talk to Cafferty.'

'He won't talk to me.'

'We think he might.'

'Does he know about Billy?'

'Yes, he knows.'

'And now he wants someone he can use as a punchbag?' Lauderdale didn't say anything to this. 'What good will it do talking to him?'

'I'm not sure.'

'Then why bother?'

'Because he's insisting. He wants to talk to CID, and not just any officer will do. He's asked to speak to *you*.' There was silence between them. 'John? Anything to say?'

'Yes, sir. This has been a very strange day.' He checked his watch. 'And it's not even one o'clock yet.'

8

Big Ger Cafferty was looking good.

He was fit and lean and had purpose to his gait. A white t-shirt was tight across his chest, flat over the stomach, and he wore faded work denims and new-looking tennis shoes. He walked into the Visiting Room like he was the visitor, Rebus the inmate. The warder beside him was no more than a hired flunkey, to be dismissed at any moment. Cafferty gripped Rebus's hand just a bit too hard, but he wasn't going to try tearing it off, not yet.

'Strawman.'

'Hello, Cafferty.' They sat down at opposite sides of the plastic table, the legs of which had been bolted to the floor. Otherwise, there was little to show that they were in Barlinnie Jail, a prison with a tough reputation from way back, but one which had striven to remake itself. The Visiting Room was clean and white, a few public safety posters decorating its walls. There was a flimsy aluminium ashtray, but also a No Smoking sign. The tabletop bore a few burn marks around its rim from cigarettes resting there too long.

'They made you come then, Strawman?' Cafferty seemed amused by Rebus's appearance. He knew, too, that as long as he kept using his nickname for Rebus, Rebus would be needled.

'I'm sorry about your son.'

Cafferty was no longer amused. 'Is it true they tortured him?'

'Sort of.'

'Sort of?' Cafferty's voice rose. 'There's no halfway house with torture!'

'You'd know all about that.'

Cafferty's eyes blazed. His breathing was shallow and noisy. He got to his feet.

'I can't complain about this place. You get a lot of freedom these days. I've found you can *buy* freedom, same as you can buy anything else.' He stopped beside the warder. 'Isn't that right, Mr Petrie?'

Wisely, Petrie said nothing.

'Wait for me outside,' Cafferty ordered. Rebus watched Petrie leave. Cafferty looked at him and grinned a humourless grin.

'Cosy,' he said, 'just the two of us.' He started to rub his stomach.

'What do you want, Cafferty?'

'Stomach's started giving me gyp. What's my point, Strawman? My point's this.' He was standing over Rebus, and now leant down, his hands pressing Rebus's shoulders. 'I want the bastard found.' Rebus found himself staring at Cafferty's bared teeth. 'See, I can't have people fucking with my family, it's bad for *my* reputation. Nobody gets away with something like that ... it'd be bad for business.'

'Nice to see the paternal instinct's so strong.'

Cafferty ignored this. 'My men are out there hunting, understood? And they'll be keeping an eye on *you*. I want a result, Strawman.'

Rebus shrugged off Cafferty's pressure and got to his feet. 'You think we're going to sit on our hands because the victim was your son?'

'You better not ... *that's* what I'm saying. Revenge, Strawman, I'll have it one way or the other. I'll have it on *some*body.'

'Not on me,' Rebus said quietly. He held Cafferty's stare, till Cafferty opened his arms wide and shrugged, then went to his chair and sat down. Rebus stayed standing.

'I need to ask you a few questions,' he said.

'Fire away.'

'Did you keep in touch with your son?'

Cafferty shook his head. 'I kept in touch with his mum. She's a good woman, too good for me, always was. I send her money for Billy, at least I did while he was growing up. I still send something from time to time.'

'By what means?'

'Someone I can trust.'

'Did Billy know who his father was?'

'Absolutely not. His mum wasn't exactly proud of me.' He started rubbing his stomach again.

'You should take something for that,' Rebus said. 'So, could anyone have got to him as a way of getting at you?'

Cafferty nodded. 'I've thought about it, Strawman. I've thought a lot about it.' Now he shook his head. 'I can't see it. I mean, it was my first thought, but nobody knew, nobody except his mum and me.'

'And the intermediary.'

'He didn't have anything to do with it. I've had people ask him.'

The way Cafferty said this sent a shiver through Rebus.

'Two more things,' he said. 'The word Nemo, mean anything?'

Cafferty shook his head. But Rebus knew that by tonight villains across the east of Scotland would be on the watch for the name. Maybe Cafferty's men *would* get to the killer first. Rebus had seen the body. He didn't much care who got the killer, so long as someone did. He guessed this was Cafferty's thinking too.

'Second thing,' he said, 'the letters SaS on a tattoo.'

Cafferty shook his head again, but more slowly this time. There was something there, some recognition.

'What is it, Cafferty?'

But Cafferty wasn't saying.

'What about gangs, was he in any gangs?'

'He wasn't the type.'

'He had the Red Hand of Ulster on his bedroom wall.'

'I've got a Pirelli calendar on mine, doesn't mean I use their tyres.'

Rebus walked towards the door. 'Not much fun being a victim, is it?'

Cafferty jumped to his feet. 'Remember,' he said, 'I'll be watching.'

'Cafferty, if one of your goons so much as asks me the time of day, I'll throw him in a cell.'

'You threw me in a cell, Strawman. Where did it get you?'

Unable to bear Cafferty's smile, the smile of a man who had drowned people in pigshit and shot them in cold blood, a cold devious manipulator, a man without morals or remorse, unable finally to bear any of this, Rebus left the room.

The prison officer, Petrie, was standing outside, shuffling his feet. His eyes couldn't meet Rebus's.

'You're an absolute disgrace,' Rebus told him, walking away.

While he was in Glasgow, Rebus could have talked to the boy's mother, only the boy's mother was in Edinburgh giving an official ID to the top half of her dead son's face. Dr Curt would be sure she never saw the bottom half. As he'd said to Rebus, if Billy had been a ventriloquist's dummy, he'd never have worked again.

'You're a sick man, doctor,' John Rebus had said.

He drove back to Edinburgh weary and trembling. Cafferty had that effect on him. He'd never thought he'd have to see the man again, at least not until both of them were of pensionable age. Cafferty had sent him a postcard the day he'd arrived in Barlinnie. But Siobhan Clarke had intercepted it and asked if he wanted to see it.

'Tear it up,' Rebus had told her. He still didn't know what the message had been.

Siobhan Clarke was still in the Murder Room when he got back.

'You're working hard,' he told her.

'It's a wonderful thing, overtime. Besides, we're a bit short of hands.'

'You've heard then?'

'Yes, congratulations.'

'What?'

'SCS, it's like a lateral promotion, isn't it?'

'It's only temporary, like a run of good games to Hibs. Where's Brian?'

'Out at Cunningham's digs, talking to Murdock and Millie again.'

'Was Mrs Cunningham up to questioning?'

'Just barely.'

'Who talked to her?'

'I did, the Chief Inspector's idea.'

'Then for once Lauderdale's had a good idea. Did you ask her about religion?'

'You mean all that Orange stuff in Billy's room? Yes, I asked. She just shrugged like it was nothing special.'

'It *is* nothing special. There are hundreds of people with the same flag, the same music-tapes. Christ, I've seen them.'

And this was the truth. He'd seen them at close quarters, not just as a kid, hearing the Sash sung by drunks on their way home, but more recently. He'd been visiting his brother in Fife, just over a month ago, the weekend before July 12th. There'd been an Orange march in Cowdenbeath. The pub they were in seemed to be hosting a crowd of the marchers in the dance hall upstairs. Sounds of drums, especially the huge drum they called the *lambeg*, and flutes and penny whistles, bad choruses repeated time and again. They'd gone upstairs to investigate, just as the thing was winding down. *God Save the Queen* was being destroyed on a dozen cheap flutes.

And some of the kids singing along, sweaty brows and shirts open, some of them had their arms raised, hands straight out in front of them. A Nazi-style salute.

'Nothing else?' he asked. Clarke shook her head. 'She didn't know about the tattoo?'

'She thinks he must have done it in the last year or so.'

'Well, that's interesting in itself. It means we're not dealing with some ancient gang or old flame. SaS was something recent in his life. What about Nemo?'

'It didn't mean anything to her.'

'I've just been talking to Cafferty, SaS meant something to him. Let's pull his records, see if they tell us anything.'

'*Now?*'

'We can make a start. By the way, remember that card he sent me?' Clarke nodded. 'What was on it?'

'It was a picture of a pig in its sty.'

'And the message?'

'There wasn't any message,' she said.

On the way back to Patience's he dropped into the video store and rented a couple of movies. It was the only video store nearby that he hadn't turned over at one time or another with vice or Trading Standards, looking for porn and splatter and various bootleg tapes. The owner was a middle-aged fatherly type, happy to tell you that some comedy was particularly good or some adventure film might prove a bit strong for 'the ladies'. He hadn't commented on Rebus's selections: *Terminator 2* and *All About Eve*. But Patience had a comment.

'Great,' she said, meaning the opposite.

'What's wrong?'

'You hate old movies and I hate violence.'

Rebus looked at the Schwarzenegger. 'It's not even an 18. And who says I don't like old films?'

'What's your favourite black and white movie?'

'There are hundreds of them.'

'Name me five. No, three, and don't say I'm not fair.'

He stared at her. They were standing a few feet apart in the living room, Rebus with the videos still in his hands, Patience with her arms folded, her back erect. He knew she could probably smell the whisky on his breath, even keeping his mouth shut and breathing through his nose. It was so quiet, he could hear the cat washing itself somewhere behind the sofa.

'What are we fighting about?' he asked.

She was ready for this. 'We're fighting about consideration, as usual. To wit, your lack of any.'

'*Ben Hur*.'

'Colour.'

'Well, that courtroom one then, with James Stewart.' She nodded. 'And that other one, with Orson Welles and the mandolin.'

'It was a zither.'

'Shite,' said John Rebus, throwing down the videos and making for the front door.

Millie Docherty waited until Murdock had been asleep for a good hour. She spent the hour thinking about the questions the police had asked both of them, and thinking further back to good days and bad days in her life. She spoke Murdock's name. His breathing remained regular. Only then did she slip out of bed and walk barefoot to Billy's bedroom door, touching the door with her fingertips. Christ, to think he wasn't there, would never be there again. She tried to control her breathing, fast in, slow out. Otherwise she might hyperventilate. Panic attacks, they called them. For years she'd suffered them not knowing she was not alone. There were lots of people out there like her. Billy had been one of them.

She turned the doorknob and slipped into his room. His mother had been round earlier on, hardly in a state to cope with any of it. There had been a policewoman with her, the same one who'd come to the flat that first time. Billy's mum had looked at his room, but then shook her head.

'I can't do this. Another time.'

'If you like,' Millie had offered, 'I can bag everything up for you. All you'd have to do is have his things collected.' The policewoman had nodded her gratitude at that. Well, it was the least ... She felt the tears coming and sat down on his narrow bed. Funny how a bed so narrow could be made wide enough for two, if the two were close. She did the breathing exercises again. Fast in, slow out, but those words, her instructions to herself, reminded her of other things, other times. Fast in, slow out.

'I've got this self-help book,' Billy had said. 'It's in my room.' He'd gone to find it for her, and she'd followed him into his room. Such a tidy room. 'Here it is,' he'd said, turning towards her quickly, not realising how close behind him she was.

'What's all this Red Hand stuff?' she'd asked, looking past him at his walls. He'd waited till her eyes returned to his, then he'd kissed her, tongue rubbing at her teeth till she opened her mouth to him.

'Billy,' she said now, her hands filling themselves with his bedcover. She stayed that way for a few minutes, part of her mind staying alert, listening for sounds from the room she shared with Murdock. Then she moved across the bed to where the Hearts pennant was pinned to the wall. She pushed it aside with a finger.

Underneath, taped flat against the wall, was a computer disk. She'd left it here, half hoping the police would find it when they searched the room. But they'd been hopeless. And watching them search, she'd become suddenly afraid for herself, and had started to hope they wouldn't find it. Now, she got her fingernails under it and unpeeled it, looking at the disk. Well, it was hers now, wasn't it? They might kill her for it, but she could never let it go. It was part of her memory of him. She rubbed her thumb across the label. The streetlight coming through the unwashed window wasn't quite enough for her to read by, but she knew what the label said anyway.

It was just those three letters, SaS.

Dark, dark, dark.

Rebus recalled that line at least. If Patience had asked him to quote from a poem instead of giving her movie titles, he'd have been all right. He was standing at a window of St Leonard's, taking a break from his deskful of work, all the paperwork on Morris Gerald Cafferty.

Dark, dark, dark.

She was trying to civilise him. Not that she'd admit it. What she said instead was that it would be nice if they liked the same things. It would give them things to talk about. So she gave him books of poetry, and played classical music at him, bought them tickets for ballet and modern dance. Rebus had been there before, other times, other women. Asking for something more, for commitment beyond the commitment.

He didn't like it. He enjoyed the basic, the feral. Cafferty had once accused him of liking cruelty, of being attracted to it; his natural right as a Celt. And hadn't Rebus accused Peter Cave of the same thing? It was coming back to him, pain on pain, crawling back along his tubes from some place deep within him.

His time in Northern Ireland.

He'd been there early in the history of 'the Troubles', 1969, just as it was all boiling over; so early that he hadn't really known what was going on, what the score was; none of them had, not on any side. The people were pleased to see them at first, Catholic and Protestant, offering food and drink and a genuine welcome. Then later the drinks were laced with weedkiller, and the welcome might be leading you into a 'honey trap'. The crunching in the sponge cake might only be hard seeds from the raspberry jam. Then again, it might be powdered glass.

Bottles flying through the dark, lit by an arc of flame. Petrol spinning and dripping from the rag wick. And when it fell on a littered road, it spread in an instant pool of hate. Nothing personal about it, it was just for a cause, a troubled cause, that was all.

And later still it was to defend the rackets which had grown up around that aged cause. The protection schemes, black taxis, gun-running, all the businesses which had spread so very far away from the ideal, creating their own pool.

He'd seen bullet wounds and shrapnel blasts and gashes left by hurled bricks, he'd tasted mortality and the flaws in both his character and his body. When not on duty, they used to hang around the barracks, knocking back whisky and playing cards. Maybe that was why whisky reminded him he was still alive, where other drinks couldn't.

There was shame too: a retaliatory strike against a drinking club which had gotten out of hand. He'd done nothing to stop it. He'd swung his baton and even his SLR with the rest of them. Yet in the middle of the commotion, the sound of a rifle being cocked was enough to bring silence and stillness...

He still kept an interest in events across the water. Part of his life had been left behind there. Something about his tour of duty there had made him apply to join the Special Air Service. He went back to his desk and lifted the glass of whisky.

Dark, dark, dark. The sky quiet save for the occasional drunken yell.

No one would ever know who called the police.

No one except the man himself and the police themselves. He'd given his name and address, and had made his complaint about the noise.

'And do you want us to come and see you afterwards, sir, after we've investigated?'

'That won't be necessary.' The phone went dead on the desk officer, who smiled. It was very seldom necessary. A visit from the police meant you were involved. He wrote on a pad then passed the note along to the Communications Room. The call went out at ten to one.

When the Rover patrol car got to the community centre, it was clear that things were winding down. The officers debated heading off again, but since they were here . . . Certainly there had been a party, a function of some kind. But as the two uniformed officers walked in through the open doors, only a dozen or so stragglers were left. The floor was a mess of bottles and cigarette butts, probably a few roaches in there too if they cared to look.

'Who's in charge?'

'Nobody,' came the sharp response.

There were flushing sounds from the toilets. Evidence being destroyed, perhaps.

'We've received complaints about the noise.'

'No noise here.'

The patrolman nodded. On a makeshift stage a ghetto-blaster had been hooked up to a guitar amplifier, a large Marshall job with separate amp and speaker-bin. Probably a hundred watts, none of it built for subtlety. The amplifier was still on, emitting an audible buzz. 'This thing belongs out at the Exhibition Centre.'

'Simple Minds let us borrow it.'

'Whose is it really though?'

'Where's your search warrant?'

The officer smiled again. He could see that his partner was itching for trouble, but though neither of them had a welter of experience, they weren't stupid either. They knew where they were, they knew the odds. So he stood there smiling, legs apart, arms by his side, not looking for aggro.

He seemed to be having a dialogue with one of the group, a guy with a denim jacket and no shirt underneath. He was wearing black square-toed biker boots with straps and a round silver buckle. The officer had always liked that style, had even considered buying himself a pair, just for the weekends.

Then maybe he'd start saving for the bike to go with them.

'Do we need a search warrant?' he said. 'We're called to a disturbance, doors wide open, no one barring our entry. Besides, this is a community centre. There are rules and regulations. Licences need to be applied for and granted. Do you have a licence for this . . . soirée?'

'Swaah-ray?' the youth said to his pals. 'Fuckin' listen to that! Swaaah-rrray!' And he came sashaying over towards the two uniforms, like he was doing some old-fashioned dance step. He turned behind and between them. 'Is that a dirty word? Something I'm not supposed to understand? This isn't your territory, you know. This is the Gar-B, and we're having our own wee festival, since nobody bothered inviting us to the other one. You're not in the real world now. You better be careful.'

The first officer could smell alcohol, like something from a chemistry lab or a surgery: gin, vodka, white rum.

'Look,' he said, 'there has to be someone running the show, and it isn't you.'

'Why not?'

'Because you're a short-arsed wee prick.'

There was stillness in the hall. The other officer had spoken, and now his partner swallowed, trying not to look at him, keeping all his concentration on the denim jacket. Denim jacket was considering, a finger to his lips, tapping them.

'Mmm,' he said at last, nodding. 'Interesting.' He started moving back towards the group. He seemed to be wiggling his bum as he moved. Then he stooped forward, pretending to tie a shoe-lace, and let rip with a loud fart. He straightened up as his gang enjoyed the joke, their laughter subsiding only when denim jacket spoke again.

'Well, sirs,' he said, 'we're just packing everything away.' He faked a yawn. 'It's well past our bedtimes and we'd like to go home. If you don't mind.' He opened his arms wide to them, even bowed a little.

'I'd like to –'

'That'll be fine.' The first officer touched his partner's arm and turned away towards the doors. They were going to get out. And when they got out, he was going to have words with his partner, no doubt about that.

'Right then, lads,' said denim jacket, 'let's get this place tidy. We'll need to put this somewhere for a start.'

The constables were near the door when, without warning, the ghetto-blaster caught both of them a glancing blow to the back of their skulls.

9

Rebus heard about it on the morning news. The radio came on at six twenty-five and there it was. It brought him out of bed and into his clothes. Patience was still trying to rouse herself as he placed a mug of tea on the bedside table and a kiss on her hot cheek.

'*Ace in the Hole* and *Casablanca*,' he said. Then he was out of the door and into his car.

At Drylaw police station, the day shift hadn't come on yet, which meant that he heard it from the horses' mouths, so to speak. Not a big station, Drylaw had requested reinforcements from all around, as what had started as an assault on two officers had turned into a miniature riot. Cars had been attacked, house windows smashed. One local shop had been ram-raided, with consequent looting (if the owner was to be believed). Five officers were injured, including the two men who had been coshed with a hi-fi machine. Those two constables had escaped the Gar-B by the skin of their arses.

'It was like Northern bloody Ireland,' one veteran said. Or Brixton, thought Rebus, or Newcastle, or Toxteth . . .

The TV news had it on now, and police heavy-handedness was being discussed. Peter Cave was being interviewed outside the youth club, saying that his had been the party's organising hand.

'But I had to leave early. I thought I had flu coming on or something.' To prove it, he blew his nose.

'At breakfast-time, too,' complained someone beside Rebus.

'I know,' Cave went on, 'that I bear a certain amount of responsibility for what happened.'

'That's big of him.'

Rebus smiled, thinking: we police invented irony, we live by its rules.

'But,' said Cave, 'there are still questions which need answering. The police seem to think they can rule by threat rather than law. I've talked to a dozen people who were in the club last night, and they've told me the same thing.'

'Surprise, surprise.'

'Namely, that the two police officers involved made threats and menacing actions.'

The interviewer waited for Cave to finish. Then: 'And what do you say, Mr Cave, to local people who claim the youth club is merely a sort of hang-out, a gang headquarters for juveniles on the estate?'

Juveniles: Rebus liked that.

Cave was shaking his head. They'd brought the camera in on him for the shot. 'I say rubbish.' And he blew his nose again. Wisely, the producer switched back to the studio.

Eventually, the police had managed to make five arrests. The youths had been brought to Drylaw. Less than an hour later, a mob from the Gar-B had gathered outside, demanding their release. More thrown bricks, more broken glass, until a massed charge by the police ranks dispersed the crowd. Cars and foot patrols had cruised Drylaw and the Gar-B for the rest of the night. There were still bricks and strewn glass on the road outside. Inside, a few of the officers involved looked shaken.

Rebus looked in on the five youths. They sported bruised faces, bandaged hands. The blood had dried to a crust on them, and they'd left it there, like war paint, like medals.

'Look,' one of them said to the others, 'it's the bastard who took a poke at Pete.'

'Keep talking,' retorted Rebus, 'and you'll be next.'

'I'm quaking.'

The police had stuck a video camera onto the rioters outside the station. The picture quality was poor, but after a few viewings Rebus made out that one of the stone throwers, face hidden by a football scarf, was wearing an open denim jacket and no shirt.

He stuck around the station a bit longer, then got back in his car and headed for the Gar-B. It didn't look so different. There was glass in the road, sounds of brittle crunching under his tyres. But the local shops were like fortresses: wire mesh, metal screens, padlocks, alarms. The would-be looters had run up and down the main road for a while in a hot-wired Ford Cortina, then had launched it at the least protected shop, a place specialising in shoe repairs and key-cutting. Inside, the owner's own brand of security, a sleepy-eyed Alsatian, had thrown itself into the fray before being beaten off and chased away. As far as anyone knew, it was still roaming the wide green spaces.

A few of the ground floor flats were having boards hammered into place across their broken windows. Maybe one of them had made the initial call. Rebus didn't blame the caller; he blamed the two officers. No, that wasn't fair. What would he have done if he'd been there? Yes, exactly. And there'd have been more trouble than this if he had . . .

He didn't bother stopping the car. He'd only be in the way of the other sight-seers and the media. With not much happening on the IRA story, reporters were here in numbers. Plus he knew he wasn't the Gar-B's most popular tourist. Though the constables couldn't swear who'd thrown the ghetto-blaster, they knew the most likely suspect. Rebus had seen the description back at Drylaw. It was Davey Soutar of course, the boy who couldn't afford a shirt. One of the CID men had asked Rebus what his interest was.

'Personal,' he'd said. A few years back, a riot like this would have prompted the permanent closure of the community hall. But these days it was more likely the Council would bung some more cash at the estate, guilt money. Shutting the hall down wouldn't do much good anyway. There were plenty of empty flats on the estate – flats termed 'unlettable'. They were kept boarded up and padlocked, but could soon be opened. Squatters and junkies used them; gangs could use them too. A couple of miles away in different directions, middle class Barnton and Inverleith were getting ready for work. A world away. They only ever took notice of Pilmuir when it exploded.

It wasn't much of a drive to Fettes either, even with the morning bottlenecks starting their day's business. He wondered if he'd be first in the office; that might show *too* willing. Well, he could check, then nip out to the canteen until everyone started arriving. But when he pushed open the office door, he saw that there was someone in before him. It was Smylie.

'Morning,' Rebus said. Smylie nodded back. He looked tired to Rebus, which was saying something, the amount of sleep Rebus himself had had. He rested against one of the desks and folded his arms. 'Do you know an Inspector called Abernethy?'

'Special Branch,' said Smylie.

'That's him. Is he still around?'

Smylie looked up. 'He went back yesterday, caught an evening plane. Did you want to see him?'

'Not really.'

'There was nothing here for him.'

'No?'

Smylie shook his head. 'We'd know about it if there was. We're the best, we'd've spotted it before him. QED.'

'*Quod erat demonstrandum.*'

Smylie looked at him. 'You're thinking of Nemo, aren't you? Latin for nobody.'

'I suppose I am.' Rebus shrugged. 'Nobody seems to think Billy Cunningham knew any Latin.' Smylie didn't say anything. 'I'm not wanted here, am I?'

'How do you mean?'

'I mean, you don't need me. So why did Kilpatrick bring me in? He must've known it'd cause nothing but aggro.'

'Best ask him yourself.'

'Maybe I will. Meantime, I'll be at St Leonard's.'

'We'll be pining away in your absence.'

'I don't doubt it, Smylie.'

'What does the woman do?'

'Her name's Millie Docherty,' said Siobhan Clarke. 'She works in a computer retailer's.'

'And her boyfriend's a computer consultant. And they shared their flat with an unemployed postie. An odd mix?'

'Not really, sir.'

'No? Well, maybe not.' They were in the canteen, facing one another across the small table. Rebus took occasional bites from a damp piece of toast. Siobhan had finished hers.

'What's it like over at Fettes?' she asked.

'Oh, you know: glamour, danger, intrigue.'

'Much the same as here then?'

'Much the same. I read some of Cafferty's notes last night. I've marked the place, so you can take over.'

'Three's more fun,' said Brian Holmes, dragging over a chair. He'd placed his tray on the table, taking up all the available room. Rebus gave Holmes's fry-up a longing look, knowing it wouldn't square with his diet. All the same . . . Sausage, bacon, eggs, tomato and fried bread.

'Ought to carry a government health warning,' said the vegetarian Clarke.

'Hear about the riot?' Holmes asked.

'I went out there this morning,' Rebus admitted. 'The place looked much the same.'

'I heard they threw an amplifier at a couple of our lads.'

The process of exaggeration had begun.

'So, about Billy Cunningham,' Rebus nudged, none too subtly.

Holmes forked up some tomato. 'What about him?'

'What have you found out?'

'Not a lot,' Holmes conceded. 'Unemployed deliverer of the royal mail, the only regular job he's ever had. Mum was overfond of him and kept gifting him money to get by on. Bit of a loyalist extremist, but no record of him belonging to the Orange Lodge. Son of a notorious gangster, but didn't know it.' Holmes thought for a second, decided this was all he had to say, and cut into his sliced sausage.

'Plus,' said Clarke, 'the anarchist stuff we found.'

'Ach, that's nothing,' Holmes said dismissively.

'What anarchist stuff?' asked Rebus.

'There were some magazines in his wardrobe,' Clarke explained. 'Soft porn, football programmes, a couple of those survivalist mags teenagers like to read to go with their diet of *Terminator* films.' Rebus almost said something, but stopped himself. 'And a flimsy little pamphlet called . . .' She sought the title. '*The Floating Anarchy Factfile.*'

'It was years old, sir,' said Holmes. 'Not relevant.'

'Do we have it here?'

'Yes, sir,' said Siobhan Clarke.

'It's from the Orkneys,' said Holmes. 'I think it's priced in old money. It belongs in a museum, not a police station.'

'Brian,' said Rebus, 'all that fat you're eating is going to your head. Since when do we dismiss *anything* in a murder inquiry?' He picked a thin rasher of streaky from the plate and dropped it into his mouth. It tasted wonderful.

The Floating Anarchy Factfile consisted of six sheets of A4 paper, folded over with a single staple through the middle to keep it from falling apart. It was typed on an old and irregular typewriter, with hand printed titles to its meagre articles and no photographs or drawings. It was priced not in old money but in new pence: five new pence to be exact, from which Rebus guessed it to be fifteen to twenty years old. There was no date, but it proclaimed itself 'issue number three'. To a large extent Brian Holmes was right: it belonged in a museum. The pieces were written in a style that could be termed 'Celtic hippy', and this style was so uniform (as were the spelling mistakes) that the whole thing looked to be the work of a single individual with access to a copying machine, something like an old Roneo.

As for the content, there were cries of nationalism and individualism in one paragraph, philosophical and moral lethargy the next. Anarcho-syndicalism was mentioned, but so were Bakunin, Rimbaud and Tolstoy. It wasn't, to Rebus's eye, the sort of stuff to boost advertising revenue. For example:

'What Dalriada needs is a new commitment, a new set of mores which look to the existent and emerging youth culture. What we need is action by the individual without recourse or prior thought to the rusted machinery of law, church, state.

'We need to be free to make our own decisions about our nation and then act self-consciously to make those decisions a reality. The sons and daughters of Alba are the future, but we are living in the mistakes of the past and must change those mistakes in the present. If you do not act then remember: Now is the first day of the rest of your strife. And remember too: inertia corrodes.'

Except that 'mores' was spelt 'moeres' and 'existent' as 'existant'. Rebus put the pamphlet down.

'A psychiatrist could have a field day,' he muttered. Holmes and Clarke were seated on the other side of his desk. He noticed that while he'd been at Fettes, people had been using his desktop as a dumping ground for sandwich wrappers and polystyrene cups. He ignored these and turned the pamphlet over. There was an address at the bottom of the back page: Zabriskie House, Brinyan, Rousay, Orkney Isles.

'Now that's what I call dropping out,' said Rebus. 'And look, the house is named after *Zabriskie Point*.'

'Is that in the Orkneys too?' asked Holmes.

'It's a film,' said Rebus. He'd gone to see it a long long time ago, just for the '60s soundtrack. He couldn't remember much about it, except for an explosion near the end. He tapped his finger against the pamphlet. 'I want to know more about this.'

'You're kidding, sir,' said Holmes.

'That's me,' said Rebus sourly, 'always a smile and a joke.'

Clarke turned to Holmes. 'I think that means he's serious.'

'In the land of the blind,' said Rebus, 'the one-eyed man is king. And even *I* can see there's more to this than meets your eyes, Brian.'

Holmes frowned. 'Such as, sir?'

'Such as its provenance, its advanced years. What would you say, 1973? '74? Billy Cunningham wasn't even born in 1974. So what's this doing in his wardrobe beside up-to-date scud mags and football programmes?' He waited. 'Answer came there none.'

Holmes looked sullen; an annoying trait whenever Rebus showed him up. But Clarke was ready. 'We'll get Orkney police to check, sir, always supposing the Orkneys possess any police.'

'Do that,' said Rebus.

10

Like a rubber ball, he thought as he drove, I'll come bouncing back to
you. He'd been summoned back to Fettes by DCI Kilpatrick. In his
pocket there was a message from Caroline Rattray, asking him to meet
her in Parliament House. He was curious about the message, which had
been taken over the phone by a Detective Constable in the Murder
Room. He saw Caroline Rattray as she'd been that night, all dressed up
and then dragged down into Mary King's Close by Dr Curt. He saw
her strong masculine face with its slanting nose and high prominent
cheekbones. He wondered if Curt had said anything to her about him
... He would definitely make time to see her.

Kilpatrick had an office of his own in a corner of the otherwise open-
plan room used by the SCS. Just outside it sat the secretary and the
clerical assistant, though Rebus couldn't work out which was which.
Both were civilians, and both operated computer consoles. They made
a kind of shield between Kilpatrick and everyone else, a barrier you
passed as you moved from your world into his. As Rebus passed them,
they were discussing the problems facing South Africa.

'It'll be like on Uist,' one of them said, causing Rebus to pause and
listen. 'North Uist is Protestant and South Uist is Catholic, and they can't
abide one another.'

Kilpatrick's office itself was flimsy enough, just plastic partitions, see-
through above waist height. The whole thing could be dismantled in
minutes, or wrecked by a few judicious kicks and shoulder-charges. But
it was definably an office. It had a door which Kilpatrick told Rebus to
close. There was a certain amount of sound insulation. There were two
filing-cabinets, maps and print-outs stuck to the walls with Blu-Tak, a
couple of calendars still showing July. And on the desk a framed photograph of three grinning gap-toothed children.

'Yours, sir?'

'My brother's. I'm not married.' Kilpatrick turned the photo around,
the better to study it. 'I try to be a good uncle.'

'Yes, sir.' Rebus sat down. Beside him sat Ken Smylie, hands crossed
in his lap. The skin on his wrists had wrinkled up like a bloodhound's
face.

'I'll get straight to the point, John,' said Kilpatrick. 'We've got a man undercover. He's posing as a long-distance lorry driver. We're trying to pick up information on arms shipments: who's selling, who's buying.'

'Something to do with The Shield, sir?'

Kilpatrick nodded. 'He's the one who's heard the name mentioned.'

'So who is he?'

'My brother,' Smylie said. 'His name's Calumn.'

Rebus took this in. 'Does he look like you, Ken?'

'A bit.'

'Then I dare say he'd pass as a lorry driver.'

There was almost a smile at one corner of Smylie's mouth.

'Sir,' Rebus said to Kilpatrick, 'does this mean you think the Mary King's Close killing had something to do with the paramilitaries?'

Kilpatrick smiled. 'Why do you think you're here, John? *You* spotted it straight off. We've got three men working on Billy Cunningham, trying to track down friends of his. For some reason they had to kill him, I'd like to know why.'

'Me too, sir. If you want to find out about Cunningham, try his flatmate first.'

'Murdock? Yes, we're talking to him.'

'No, not Murdock, Murdock's girlfriend. I went round there when they reported him missing. There was something about her, something not quite right. Like she was holding back, putting on an act.'

Smylie said, 'I'll take a look.'

'Her and her boyfriend both work with computers. Think that might mean something?'

'I'll take a look,' Smylie repeated. Rebus didn't doubt that he would.

'Ken thinks you should meet Calumn,' Kilpatrick said.

Rebus shrugged. 'Fine by me.'

'Good,' said Kilpatrick. 'Then we'll take a little drive.'

Out in the main office they all looked at him strangely, like they knew precisely what had been said to him in Kilpatrick's den. Well, of course they knew. Their looks told Rebus he was resented more than ever. Even Claverhouse, usually so laid back, was managing a snide little grin.

DI Blackwood rubbed a smooth hand over the hairless crown of his head, then tucked a stray hair back behind his ear. His tonsure was positively monasterial, and it bothered him. In his other hand he held his telephone receiver, listening to someone on the line. He ignored Rebus as Rebus walked past.

At the next desk along, DS Ormiston was squeezing spots on his forehead.

'You two make a picture,' Rebus said. Ormiston didn't appear to get it, but that wasn't Rebus's problem. His problem was that Kilpatrick was taking him into his confidence, and Rebus still didn't know why.

*

There are lots of warehouses in Sighthill, most of them anonymous. They weren't exactly advertising that one of them had been leased by the Scottish Crime Squad. It was a big old prefabricated building surrounded by a high wire fence and protected by a high barred gate. There was barbed wire strung out across the top of the fence and the gate, and the gatehouse was manned. The guard unlocked the gate and swung it open so they could drive in.

'We got this place for a song,' Kilpatrick explained. 'The market's not exactly thriving just now.' He smiled. 'They even offered to throw in the security, but we didn't think we'd need any help with that.'

Kilpatrick was sitting in the back with Rebus, Smylie acting as chauffeur. The steering wheel was like a frisbee in his paws. But he was a canny driver, slow and considerate. He even signalled as he turned into a parking bay, though there was only one other car in the whole forecourt, parked five bays away. When they got out, the Sierra's suspension groaned upwards. They were standing in front of a normal sized door whose nameplate had been removed. To its right were the much bigger doors of the loading bay. From the rubbish lying around, the impression was of a disused site. Kilpatrick took two keys from his pocket and unlocked the side door.

The warehouse was just that, no offices or partitions off, just one large space with an oily concrete floor and some empty packing cases. A pigeon, disturbed by their entrance, fluttered near the ceiling for a moment before settling again on one of the iron spars supporting the corrugated roof. It had left its mark more than once on the HGV's windshield.

'That's supposed to be lucky,' said Rebus. Not that the articulated lorry looked clean anyway. It was splashed with pale caked-on mud and dust. It was a Ford with a UK licence plate, K registration. The cab door opened and a large man heaved himself out.

He didn't have his brother's moustache and was probably a year or two younger. But he wasn't smiling, and when he spoke his voice was high-pitched, almost cracking from effort.

'You must be Rebus.'

They shook hands. Kilpatrick was doing the talking.

'We impounded this lorry two months back, or rather Scotland Yard did. They've kindly loaned it to us.'

Rebus hoisted himself onto the running-plate and peered in the driver's window. Behind the driving seat had been fixed a nude calendar and a dog-eared centrefold. There was space for a bunk, on which a sleeping bag was rolled up ready for use. The cab was bigger than some of the caravans Rebus had stayed in for holidays. He climbed back down.

'Why?'

There was a noise from the back of the lorry. Calumn Smylie was opening its container doors. By the time Rebus and Kilpatrick got there, the two Smylies had swung both doors wide and were standing inside the back, just in front of a series of wooden crates.

'We've taken a few liberties,' said Kilpatrick, hoisting himself into the back beside them, Rebus following. 'The stuff was originally hidden beneath the floor.'

'False fuel tanks,' explained Ken Smylie. 'Good ones too, welded and bolted shut.'

'The Yard cut into them from up here.' Kilpatrick stamped his foot. 'And inside they found what the tip-off had told them they'd find.'

Calumn Smylie lifted the lid off a crate so Rebus could look in. Inside, wrapped in oiled cloths, were eighteen or so AK 47 assault rifles. Rebus lifted one of them out by its folded metal butt. He knew how to handle a gun like this, even if he didn't like doing it. Rifles had gotten lighter since his Army days, but they hadn't gotten any more comfortable. They'd also gotten a deal more lethal. The wooden hand-grip was as cold as a coffin handle.

'We don't know exactly where they came from,' Kilpatrick explained. 'And we don't even know where they were headed. The driver wouldn't say anything, no matter how scary the Anti-Terrorist Branch got with him. He denied all knowledge of the load, and wasn't about to point a finger anywhere else.'

Rebus put the gun back in its crate. Calumn Smylie leaned past him to wipe off any fingerprints with a piece of rag.

'So what's the deal?' Rebus asked. Calumn Smylie gave the answer.

'When the driver was pulled in, there were some phone numbers in his pocket, two in Glasgow, one in Edinburgh. All three of them were bars.'

'Could mean nothing,' Rebus said.

'Or everything,' commented Ken Smylie.

'See,' Calumn added, 'could be those bars are his contacts, maybe his employers, or the people his employers are selling to.'

'So,' said Kilpatrick, leaning against one of the crates, 'we've got men watching all three pubs.'

'In the hope of what?'

It was Calumn's turn again. 'When Special Branch stopped the lorry, they managed to keep it quiet. It's never been reported, and the driver's tucked away somewhere under the Prevention of Terrorism Act and a few minor offences.'

Rebus nodded. 'So his employers or whoever won't know what's happened?' Calumn was nodding too. 'And they might get antsy?' Now Rebus shook his head. 'You should be a sniper.'

Calumn frowned. 'Why?'

'Because that's the longest shot I've ever heard.'

Neither Smylie seemed thrilled to hear this. 'I've already overheard a conversation mentioning The Shield,' Calumn said.

'But you've no idea what The Shield *is*,' Rebus countered. 'Which pub are we talking about anyway?'

'The Dell.'

It was Rebus's turn to frown. 'Just off the Garibaldi Estate?'

'That's the one.'

'We've had some aggro there.'

'Yes, so I hear.'

Rebus turned to Kilpatrick. 'Why do you need the lorry?'

'In case we can operate a sting.'

'How long are you going to give it?'

Calumn shrugged. His eyes were dark and heavy from tension and a lack of sleep. He rubbed a hand through his uncombed hair, then over his unshaven face.

'I can see it's been like a holiday for you,' Rebus said. He knew the plan must have been cooked up by the Smylie brothers. They seemed its real defenders. Kilpatrick's part in it was more uncertain.

'Better than that,' Calumn was saying.

'How so?'

'The holiday I'm having, you don't need to send postcards.'

Not many people know of Parliament House, home of the High Court of Justiciary, Scotland's highest court for criminal cases. There are few signposts or identifying markers outside, and the building itself is hidden behind St Giles, separated from it by a small anonymous car park containing a smattering of Jaguars and BMWs. Of the many doors facing the prospective visitor, only one normally stands open. This is the public entrance, and leads into Parliament Hall, from off which stretch the Signet Library and Advocates Library.

There were fourteen courts in all, and Rebus guessed he'd been in all of them over the years. He sat on one of the long wooden benches. The lawyers around him were wearing dark pinstripe suits, white shirts with raised collars and white bow ties, grey wigs, and long black cloaks like those his teachers had worn. Mostly the lawyers were talking, either with clients or with each other. If with each other, they might raise their voices, maybe even share a joke. But with clients they were more circumspect. One well-dressed woman was nodding as her advocate talked in an undertone, all the while trying to stop the many files under his arm from wriggling free.

Rebus knew that beneath the large stained glass window there were two corridors lined with old wooden boxes. Indeed, the first corridor was known as the Box Corridor. Each box was marked with a lawyer's name, and each had a slat in the top, though the vast majority of boxes were kept open more or less permanently. Here documents awaited collection and perusal. Rebus had wondered at the openness of the system, the opportunities for theft and espionage. But there had never been any reports of theft, and security men were in any case never far away. He got up now and walked over to the stained glass. He knew the King portrayed was supposed to be James V, but wasn't sure about the rest of it, all the figures or the coats of arms. To his right, through a wooden swing door with glass windows, he could see lawyers poring over books. Etched in gold on the glass were the words PRIVATE ROOM.

He knew another private room close to here. Indeed, just on the other side of St Giles and down some flights of stairs. Billy Cunningham had been murdered not fifty yards from the High Court.

He turned at the sound of heels clicking towards him. Caroline Rattray was dressed for work, from black shoes and stockings to powder-grey wig.

'I wouldn't have recognised you,' he said.

'Should I take that as a compliment?' She gave him a big smile, and held it as she held his gaze. Then she touched his arm. 'I see you've noticed.' She looked up at the stained glass. 'The royal arms of Scotland.' Rebus looked up too. Beneath the large picture there were five smaller square windows, each showing a coat of arms. Caroline Rattray's eyes were on the central panel. Two unicorns held the shield of the red Lion Rampant. Above on a scroll were the words IN DEFENCE, and at the bottom a Latin inscription. Rebus read it.

'*Nemo me impune lacessit.*' He turned to her. 'Never my best subject.'

'You might know it better as "Wha daur meddle wi' me?". It's the motto of Scotland, or rather, the motto of Scotland's kings.'

'A while since we've had any of them.'

'*And* of the Order of the Thistle. Sort of makes you the monarch's private soldier, except they only give it to crusty old sods. Sit down.' She led them back to the bench Rebus had been sitting on. She had files with her, which she placed on the floor rather than the bench, though there was space. Then she gave him her full attention. Rebus didn't say anything, so she smiled again, tipping her head slightly to one side. 'Don't you see?'

'Nemo,' he guessed.

'Yes! Latin for nobody.'

'We already know that, Miss Rattray. Also a character in Jules Verne and in Dickens, plus the letters make the word "omen" backwards.' He paused. 'We've been working, you see. But does it get us any further forward? I mean, was the victim trying to tell us that no one killed him?'

She seemed to puncture, her shoulders sagging. It was like watching an old balloon die after Christmas.

'It could be something,' he offered. 'But it's hard to know what.'

'I see.'

'You could have told me about it on the phone.'

'Yes, I could.' She straightened her back. 'But I wanted you to see for yourself.'

'You think the Order of the Thistle ganged up and murdered Billy Cunningham?' Her eyes were holding his again, no smile on her lips. He broke free, staring past her at the stained glass. 'How's the prosecution game?'

'It's a slow day,' she said. 'I hear the victim's father is a convicted murderer. Is there a connection?'

'Maybe.'

'No concrete motive yet?'

'No motive.' The longer Rebus looked at the royal arms, the more his focus was drawn to its central figure. It was definitely a shield. 'The Shield,' he said to himself.

'Sorry?'

'Nothing, it's just ...' He turned back to her. She was looking eager about something, and hopeful too. 'Miss Rattray,' he said, 'did you bring me here to chat me up?'

She looked horrified, her face reddening; not just her cheeks, but forehead and chin too, even her neck coloured. 'Inspector Rebus,' she said at last.

'Sorry, sorry.' He bowed his head and raised his hands. 'Sorry I said that.'

'Well, I don't know ...' She looked around. 'It's not every day I'm accused of being ... well, whatever. I think I need a drink.' Then, reverting to her normal voice: 'I think you'd better buy me one, don't you?'

They crossed the High Street, dodging the leafleters and mime artists and clowns on stilts, and threaded their way through a dark close and down some worn stone steps into Caro Rattray's preferred bar.

'I hate this time of year,' she said. 'It's such a hassle getting to and from work. And as for parking in town ...'

'It's a hard life, all right.'

She went to a table while Rebus stood at the bar. She had taken a couple of minutes to change out of her gown and wig, had brushed her hair out, though the sombre clothes that remained – the accent on black with touches of white – still marked her out as a lawyer in this lawyer's howff.

The place had one of the lowest ceilings of any pub Rebus had ever been in. When he considered, he thought they must be almost directly above some of the shops which led off Mary King's Close. The thought made him change his order.

'Make that whisky a double.' But he added plenty of water. Caroline Rattray had ordered lemonade with lots of ice and lemon. As Rebus placed her drink on the table, he laughed.

'What's so funny?'

He shook his head. 'Advocate and lemonade, that makes a snowball.' He didn't have to explain to her. She managed a weary smile. 'Heard it before, eh?' he said, sitting beside her.

'And every person who says it thinks they've just invented it. Cheers.'

'Aye, *slainte*.'

'*Slainte*. Do you speak Gaelic?'

'Just a couple of words.'

'I learnt it a few years ago, I've already forgotten most of it.'

'Ach, it's not much use anyway, is it?'

'You wouldn't mind if it died out?'

'I didn't say that.'

'I thought you just did.'

Rebus gulped at his drink. 'Never argue with a lawyer.'

Another smile. She lit a cigarette, Rebus declining.

'Don't tell me,' he said, 'you still see Mary King's Close in your head at night?'

She nodded slowly. 'And during the day. I can't seem to erase it.'

'So don't try. Just file it away, that's all you can do. Admit it to yourself, it happened, you were there, then file it away. You won't forget, but you won't harp on it either.'

'Police psychology?'

'Common sense, hard learnt. That's why you were so excited about the Latin inscription?'

'Yes, I thought I was . . . *involved*.'

'You'll be involved if we ever catch the buggers. It'll be your job to put them away.'

'I suppose so.'

'Until then, leave it to us.'

'Yes, I will.'

'I'm sorry though, sorry you had to see it. Typical of Curt, dragging you down there. There was no need to. Are you and him . . . ?'

Her whoop filled the bar. 'You don't think . . . ? We're just acquaintances. He had a spare ticket, I was on hand. Christ almighty, you think I could . . . with a *pathologist*?'

'They're human, despite rumours to the contrary.'

'Yes, but he's twenty years older than me.'

'That's not always a consideration.'

'The thought of those hands on me . . .' She shivered, sipped her drink. 'What did you say back there about a shield?'

He shook his head. He saw a shield in his mind, and you never got a shield without a sword. *With sword and shield*, that was a line from an Orange song. He slapped the table with his fist, so hard that Caroline Rattray looked frightened.

'Was it something I said?'

'Caroline, you're brilliant. I've got to go.' He got up and walked past the bar, then stopped and came back, taking her hand in his, holding it. 'I'll phone you,' he promised. Then: 'If you like.'

He waited till she'd nodded, then turned again and left. She finished her lemonade, smoked another cigarette, and stubbed it into the ashtray. His hand had been hot, not like a pathologist's at all. The barman came to empty her ashtray into a pail and wipe the table.

'Out hunting again I see,' he said quietly.

'You know too much about me, Dougie.'

'I know too much about everyone, hen,' said Dougie, picking up both glasses and taking them to the bar.

Several months back, Rebus had been talking to an acquaintance of his called Matthew Vanderhyde. Their conversation had concerned another case, one involving, as it turned out, Big Ger Cafferty, and apropos of very little Vanderhyde, blind for many years and with a reputation as a white witch, had mentioned a splinter group of the Scottish National Party. The splinter group had been called Sword and Shield, and they'd existed in the late 1950s and early 1960s.

But as a phone call to Vanderhyde revealed, Sword and Shield had ceased to exist around the same time the Rolling Stones were putting out their first album. And at no time, anyway, had they been known as SaS.

'I do believe,' Vanderhyde said, and Rebus could see him in his darkened living room, its curtains shut, slumped in an armchair with his portable phone, 'there exists in the United States an organisation called Sword and Shield, or even Scottish Sword and Shield, but I don't know anything about them. I don't think they're connected to the Scottish Rites Temple, which is a sort of North American Freemasons, but I'm a bit vague.'

Rebus was busy writing it all down. 'No you're not,' he said, 'you're a bloody encyclopaedia.' That was the problem with Vanderhyde: he seldom gave you just the one answer, leaving you more confused than before you'd asked your question.

'Is there anything I can read about Sword and Shield?' Rebus asked.

'You mean histories? I wouldn't know, I shouldn't think they'd bother to issue any as braille editions or talking books.'

'I suppose not, but there must have been something left when the organisation was wound up, papers, documents...?'

537

'Perhaps a local historian might know. Would you like me to do some sleuthing, Inspector?'

'I'd appreciate it,' said Rebus. 'Would Big Ger Cafferty have had anything to do with the group?'

'I shouldn't think so. Why do you ask?'

'Nothing, forget I said it.' He terminated the call with promises of a visit, then scratched his nose, wondering who to take all this to: Kilpatrick or Lauderdale? He'd been seconded to SCS, but Lauderdale was in charge of the murder inquiry. He asked himself a question: would Lauderdale protect me from Kilpatrick? The answer was no. Then he changed the names around. The answer this time was yes. So he took what he had to Kilpatrick.

And then had to admit that it wasn't much.

Kilpatrick had brought Smylie into the office to join them. Sometimes Rebus wasn't sure who was in charge. Calumn Smylie would be back undercover, maybe drinking in The Dell.

'So,' said Kilpatrick, 'summing up, John, we've got the word Nemo, we've got a Latin phrase –'

'Much quoted by nationalists,' Smylie added, 'at least in its Scots form.'

'And we've got a shield on this coat of arms, all of which reminds you of a group called Sword and Shield who were wound up in the early '60s. You think they've sprung up again?'

Rebus visualised a spring suddenly appearing through the worn covering of an old mattress. He shrugged. 'I don't know, sir.'

'And then this source of yours mentions an organisation in the USA called Sword and Shield.'

'Sir, all I know is, SaS must stand for something. Calumn Smylie's been hearing about an outfit called The Shield who might be in the market for arms. There's also a shield on the Scottish royal arms, as well as a phrase with the word Nemo. I know these are all pretty weak links, but all the same . . .'

Kilpatrick looked to Smylie, who gave a look indicating he was on Rebus's side.

'Maybe,' Smylie said in proof, 'we could ask our friends in the States to check for us. They'd be doing the work, there's nothing to lose, and with the back-up they've got they could probably give us an answer in a few days. As I say, we haven't lost anything.'

'I suppose not. All right then.' Kilpatrick's hands were ready for prayer. 'John, we'll give it a go.'

'Also, sir,' Rebus added, just pushing his luck a bit, 'we might do some digging into the original Sword and Shield. If the name's been revived, it wasn't just plucked out of the air.'

'Fair point, John. I'll put Blackwood and Ormiston onto it.'

Blackwood and Ormiston: they'd thank him for this, they'd bring him flowers and chocolates.

'Thank you, sir,' said Rebus.

11

Ever since the riot, Father Leary had been trying to contact Rebus, leaving message after message at St Leonard's. So when he got to St Leonard's, Rebus relented and called the priest.

'It hasn't gone too well, father,' he said gamely.

'Then it's God's will.'

For a second, Rebus heard it as God swill. He stuck in his own apostrophe and said, 'I knew you'd say that.' He was watching Siobhan Clarke striding towards him. She had her thumbs up and a big grin spread across her face.

'Got to go, father. Say one for me.'

'Don't I always?'

Rebus put down the receiver. 'What've you got?'

'Cafferty,' she said, throwing the file onto his desk. 'Buried way back.' She produced a sheet of paper and handed it to him. Rebus read through it quickly.

Yes, buried, because it was only a suspicion, one of hundreds that the police had been unable to prove over the course of Cafferty's career.

'Handling dirty money,' he said.

'For the Ulster Volunteer Force.'

Cafferty had formed an unholy alliance with a Glasgow villain called Jinky Johnson, and between them they'd offered a service, turning dirty money into clean at the behest of the UVF. Then Johnson disappeared. Rumour had it he'd either fled with the UVF's cash, or else he'd been skimming a bit and they'd found out and done away with him. Whatever, Cafferty broke his connection.

'What do you think?' Clarke asked.

'It ties Cafferty to the Protestant paramilitaries.'

'And if they thought he knew about Johnson, it'd mean there was no love lost.'

But Rebus had doubts about the time scale. 'They wouldn't wait ten years for revenge. Then again, Cafferty *did* know what SaS stood for. He's heard of it.'

'A new terrorist group?'

'I think so, definitely. And they're here in Edinburgh.' He looked up at Clarke. 'And if we're not careful, Cafferty's men are going to get to them first.' Then he smiled.

'You don't sound overly concerned.'

'I'm so bothered by it all, I think I'll buy you a drink.'

'Deal,' said Siobhan Clarke.

As he drove home, he could smell the cigarettes and booze on his clothes. More ammo for Patience. Christ, there were those videos to take back too. She wouldn't do it, it was up to him. There'd be extra to pay, and he hadn't even watched the bloody things yet.

To defer the inevitable, he stopped at a pub. They didn't come much smaller than the Oxford Bar, but the Ox managed to be cosy too. Most nights there was a party atmosphere, or at the very least some entertaining patter. And there were quarter gills too, of course. He drank just the one, drove the rest of the way to Patience's, and parked in his usual spot near the sports Merc. Someone on Queensferry Road was trying to sing *Tie a Yellow Ribbon*. Overhead, the streetlighting's orange glow picked out the top of the tenements, their chimney pots bristling. The warm air smelt faintly of breweries.

'Rebus?'

It wasn't dark yet, not quite. Rebus had seen the man waiting across the road. Now the man was approaching, hands deep in jacket pockets. Rebus tensed. The man saw the change and brought his hands out to show he was unarmed.

'Just a word,' the man said.

'What about?'

'Mr Cafferty's wondering how things are going.'

Rebus studied the man more closely. He looked like a weasel with misshapen teeth, his mouth constantly open in something that was either a sneer or a medical problem. He breathed in and out through his mouth in a series of small gasps. There was a smell from him that Rebus didn't want to place.

'You want a trip down the station, pal?'

The man grinned, showing his teeth again. Close up, Rebus saw that they were stained so brown from nicotine they might have been made of wood.

'What are the charges?' the weasel said.

Rebus looked him up and down. 'Offence against public decency for a start. They should have kept you in your cage, right at the back of the pet shop.'

'He said you had a way with words.'

'Not just with words.' Rebus started to cross the road to Patience's flat. The man followed, so close he might have been on a leash.

'I'm trying to be pleasant,' the weasel said.

'Tell the charm school to give you a refund.'

'He said you'd be difficult.'

Rebus turned on the man. 'Difficult? You don't know just how difficult I can get if I really try. If I see you here again, you'd better be ready to square off.'

The man narrowed his eyes. 'That'd suit me fine. I'll be sure to mention your co-operation to Mr Cafferty.'

'Do that.' Rebus started down the steps to the garden flat. The weasel leaned down over the rails.

'Nice flat.' Rebus stopped with his key in the lock. He looked up at the man. 'Shame if anything happened to it.'

By the time Rebus ran back up the steps, the weasel had disappeared.

12

'Have you heard from your brother?'

It was next morning, and Rebus was at Fettes, talking with Ken Smylie.

'He doesn't phone in that oftcn.'

Rebus was trying to turn Smylie into someone he could trust. Looking around him, he didn't see too many potential allies. Blackwood and Ormiston were giving him their double-act filthy look, from which he deduced two things. One, they'd been assigned to look into what, if anything, remained of the original Sword and Shield.

Two, they knew whose idea the job had been.

Rebus, pleased at their glower, decided he wouldn't bother mentioning that Matthew Vanderhyde was looking into Sword and Shield too. Why give them shortcuts when they'd have had him run the marathon?

Smylie didn't seem in the mood for conversation, but Rebus persisted. 'Have you talked to Billy Cunningham's flatmate?'

'She kept going on about his motorbike and what was she supposed to do with it?'

'Is that all?'

Smylie shrugged. 'Unless I want to buy a stripped down Honda.'

'Careful, Smylie, I think maybe you've caught something.'

'What?'

'A sense of humour.'

As Rebus drove to St Leonard's, he rubbed at his jaw and chin, enjoying the feel of the bristles under his fingertips. He was remembering the very different feel of the AK 47, and thinking of sectarianism. Scotland had enough problems without getting involved in Ireland's. They were like Siamese twins who'd refused the operation to separate them. Only one twin had been forced into a marriage with England, and the other was hooked on self-mutilation. They didn't need politicians to sort things out; they needed a psychiatrist.

The marching season, the season of the Protestant, was over for another year, give or take the occasional small fringe procession. Now it was the season of the International Festival, a festive time, a time to forget the small and insecure country you lived in. He thought again of the poor sods who'd decided to put on a show in the Gar-B.

St Leonard's looked to be joining in the fun. They'd even arranged for a pantomime. Someone had owned up to the Billy Cunningham murder. His name was Unstable from Dunstable.

The police called him that for two reasons. One, he was mentally unstable. Two, he claimed he came from Dunstable. He was a local tramp, but not without resources. With needle and thread he had fashioned for himself a coat constructed from bar towels, and so was a walking sandwich-board for the products which kept him alive and kept him dying.

There were a lot of people out there like him, shiftless until someone (usually the police) shifted them. They'd been 'returned to the community' – a euphemism for dumped – thanks to a tightening of the government's heart and purse-strings. Some of them couldn't tighten their shoe laces without bursting into tears. It was a crying shame.

Unstable was in an interview room now with DS Holmes, being fed hot sweet tea and cigarettes. Eventually they'd turf him out, maybe with a couple of quid in his hand, his technicolor beercoat having no pockets.

Siobhan Clarke was at her desk in the Murder Room. She was being talked at by DI Alister Flower.

So someone had forgotten Rebus's advice regarding the duty roster.

'Well,' Flower said loudly, spotting Rebus, 'if it isn't our man from the SCS. Have you brought the milk?'

Rebus was too slow getting the reference, so Flower obliged.

'The Scottish Co-Operative Society. SCS, same letters as the Scottish Crime Squad.'

'Wasn't Sean Connery a milkman with the Co-Op,' said Siobhan Clarke, 'before he got into acting?' Rebus smiled towards her, appreciating her effort to shift the gist of the conversation.

Flower looked like a man who had comebacks ready, so Rebus decided against a jibe. Instead he said, 'They think very highly of you.'

Flower blinked. 'Who?'

Rebus twitched his head. 'Over at SCS.'

Flower stared at him, then narrowed his eyes. 'Do tell.'

Rebus shrugged. 'What's to tell? I'm serious. The high hiedyins know your record, they've been keeping an eye on you . . . that's what I hear.'

Flower shuffled his feet, relaxing his posture. He almost became shy, colour showing in his cheeks.

'They told me to tell you . . .' Rebus leaned close, Flower doing likewise, '. . . that as soon as there's a milk round to spare, they'll give you a call.'

Flower showed two rows of narrow teeth as he growled. Then he stalked off in search of easier prey.

'He's easy to wind up, isn't he?' said Siobhan Clarke.

'That's why I call him the Clockwork Orangeman.'

'Is he an Orangeman?'

'He's been known to march on the 12th.' He considered. 'Maybe Orange Peeler would be a better name for him, eh?' Clarke groaned. 'What have you got for me from our teuchter friends?'

'You mean the Orkneys. I don't think they'd appreciate being called teuchters.' She tried hard to pronounce the word, but being mostly English, she just failed.

'Remember,' said Rebus, 'teuch is Scots for tough. I don't think they'd mind me calling them tough.' He dragged a chair over to her desk. 'So what did you get?'

She flicked open a paper pad, finding the relevant page. 'Zabriskie House is actually a croft. There's a small cottage, one bedroom and one other room doubling as –'

'I'm not thinking of buying the place.'

'No, sir. The current owners didn't know anything about its past history, but neighbours remembered a chap renting the place for a year or two back in the '70s. He called himself Cuchullain.'

'What?'

'A mythical warrior, Celtic I think.'

'And that was all he called himself?'

'That was all.'

It fitted with the tone of the *Floating Anarchy Factfile*: Celtic hippy. Rebus knew that in the early '70s a lot of young Scots had emulated their American and European cousins by 'dropping out'. But then years later they tended to drop back in again, and did well for themselves in business. He knew because he'd almost dropped out himself. But instead he'd gone to Northern Ireland.

'Anything else?' he asked.

'Bits and pieces. A description that's twenty-odd years old now from a woman who's been blind in one eye since birth.'

'This is your source, is it?'

'Mostly, yes. A police constable went sniffing. He also talked to the man who used to run the sub-post office, and a couple of boatmen. You need a boat to get provisions across to Rousay, and the postman comes by his own boat. He kept himself to himself, grew his own food. There was talk at the time, because people used to come and go at Zabriskie House, young women with no bras on, men with beards and long hair.'

'The locals must've been mortified.'

Clarke smiled. 'The lack of bras was mentioned more than once.'

'Well, a place like that, you have to make your own entertainment.'

'There's one lead the constable is still following up. He'll get back to me today.'

'I won't hold my breath. Have you ever been to the Orkneys?'

'You're not thinking of –' She was interrupted by her telephone. 'DC Clarke speaking. Yes.' She looked up at Rebus and pulled her notepad to her, starting to write. Presumably it was the Old Policeman of Hoy, so Rebus took a stroll around the room. He was reminded again just why he didn't fit, why he was so unsuited to the career life had chosen for him. The Murder Room was like a production line. You had your own little task, and you did it. Maybe someone else would follow up any lead you found, and then someone else after that might do the questioning of a suspect or potential witness. You were a small part of a very large team. It wasn't Rebus's way. He wanted to follow up every lead personally, cross referencing them all, taking them through from first principle to final reckoning. He'd been described, not unkindly, as a terrier, locking on with his jaws and not letting go.

Some dogs, you had to break the jaw to get them off.

Siobhan Clarke came up to him. 'Something?' he asked.

'My constable friend found out Cuchullain used to keep a cow and a pig, plus some chickens. Part of the self-sufficiency thing. He wondered what might have happened to them when Cuchullain moved away.'

'He sounds bright.'

'Turns out Cuchullain sold them on to another crofter, and this crofter keeps records. We got lucky, Cuchullain had to wait for his money, and he gave the crofter a forwarding address in the Borders.' She waved a piece of paper at him.

'Don't get too excited,' warned Rebus. 'We're still talking a twenty year old address for a man whose name we don't know.'

'But we do know. The crofter had a note of that too. It's Francis Lee.'

'Francis Lee?' Rebus sounded sceptical. 'Wasn't he playing for Manchester City in the '70s? Francis Lee ... as in Frank Lee? As in Frank Lee, my dear, I don't give a damn?'

'You think it's another alias?'

'I don't know. Let's get the Borders police to take a look.' He studied the Murder Room. 'Ach, no, on second thoughts, let's go take a look ourselves.'

13

Whenever John Rebus had cause or inclination to drive through any town in the Scottish Borders, one word came to his mind.

Neat.

The towns were simply laid out and almost pathologically tidy. The buildings were constructed from unadorned stone and had a square-built no-nonsense quality to them. The people walking briskly from bank to grocer's shop to chemist's were rosy cheeked and bursting with health, as though they scrubbed their faces with pumice every morning before sitting down to farmhouse fare. The men's limbs moved with the grace of farm machinery. You could present any of the women to your own mother. She'd tell them you weren't good enough for them.

Truth be told, the Borderers scared Rebus. He couldn't understand them. He understood though, that placed many more miles from any large Scottish conurbation than from the English border, there was bound to be some schizophrenia to the towns and their inhabitants.

Selkirk however was definably Scots in character, architecture, and language. Its annual Lammas Fair was not yet just a memory to see the townfolk through the winter. There were still rows of pennants waiting to be taken down, flapping in the slightest breeze. There were some outside the house which abutted the kirkyard wall. Siobhan Clarke checked the address and shrugged.

'It's the manse, isn't it?' Rebus repeated, sure that they had something wrong.

'It's the address I've got here.'

The house was large with several prominent gables. It was fashioned from dull grey stone, but boasted a lush and sweet-smelling garden. Siobhan Clarke pushed open the gate. She searched the front door for a bell but found none, so resorted to the iron knocker which was shaped like an open hand. No one answered. From nearby came the sound of a manual lawnmower, its pull and push as regular as a pendulum. Rebus looked in through the front window of the house, and saw no sign of movement.

'We're wasting our time,' he said. A waste of a long car journey too. 'Let's leave a note and get out of here.'

Clarke peered through the letterbox, then stood up again. 'Maybe we could ask around, now we're here.'

'Fine,' said Rebus, 'let's go talk to the lawnmower man.'

They walked round to the kirkyard gate and took the red gravel path around the perimeter of the church itself. At the back of the soot-blackened building they saw an old man pushing a mower which in Edinburgh might have graced a New Town antique shop.

The gentleman stopped his work when he saw them crossing the trimmed grass towards him. It was like walking on a carpet. The grass could not have been shorter if he'd been using nail scissors. He produced a voluminous handkerchief from his pocket and mopped his suntanned brow. His face and arms were as brown as oak, the face polished with sweat. The elderly skin was still tight across the skull, shiny like a beetle's back. He introduced himself as Willie McStay.

'Is it about the vandalism?' he asked.

'Vandalism? *Here?*'

'They've been desecrating the graves, daubing paint on the head-stones. It's the skinheads.'

'Skinheads in Selkirk?' Rebus was not convinced. 'How many skin-heads are there, Mr McStay?'

McStay thought about it, grinding his teeth together as though he were chewing tobacco or a particularly tough piece of phlegm. 'Well,' he said, 'there's Alec Tunnock's son for a start. His hair's cropped awful short and he wears those boots wi' the laces.'

'Boots with laces, eh?'

'He hasna had a job since he left school.'

Rebus was shaking his head. 'We're not here about the headstones, Mr McStay. We were wondering about that house.' He pointed towards it.

'The manse?'

'Who lives there, Mr McStay?'

'The minister, Reverend McKay.'

'How long has he lived there?'

'Gracious, I don't know. Fifteen years maybe. Before him it was Reverend Bothwell, and the Bothwells were here for a quarter century or more.'

Rebus looked to Siobhan Clarke. A waste of time.

'We're looking for a man called Francis Lee,' she said.

McStay chomped on the name, jaw chewing from side to side, cheek-bones working. He reminded Rebus of a sheep. The old man shook his head. 'Nobody I know of,' he said.

'Well, thanks anyway,' said Rebus.

'A minute,' McStay ordered. Meaning that he wanted to think about it for a minute more. Finally he nodded. 'You've got it the wrong way round.' He leant a hand against the mower's black rubber grip. 'The Bothwells were a lovely couple, Douglas and Ina. Couldn't do enough for this town. When they died, their son sold the house straight off. He wasn't supposed to, Reverend Bothwell told me that often enough. He was supposed to keep it in the family.'

'But it's a manse,' Clarke said. 'Church of Scotland property. How could he sell it?'

'The Bothwells loved the house so much, they bought it off the Church. They were going to live there when Reverend Bothwell retired. The thing is, the son sold it back to the Church. He was a wastrel, that one, took the money and ran. Nobody'd look after their grave if it wasn't for me and a few other old folk here who remember them fondly.' He shook his head. 'Young people, they've no sense of history or commitment.'

'What's this got to do with Francis Lee?' Siobhan Clarke asked. McStay looked at her like she was a child who'd spoken out of turn, and addressed his answer to Rebus.

'Their son was called Lee. I think his middle name was Francis.'

Lee Francis Bothwell: Francis Lee. It was too close to be mere coincidence. Rebus nodded slowly.

'I don't suppose you've any idea,' he said, 'where we might find –' He broke off. 'Frankie Bothwell? Thanks, Mr McStay, thanks for your help.' And he walked towards the gate. It took Siobhan Clarke a moment to catch up with him.

'So are you going to tell me?'

'You don't know Frankie Bothwell?' He watched her try out the name in her mind. She shook her head furiously. 'He owns the Crazy Hose Saloon.'

Now she nodded. 'That Fringe programme in Billy Cunningham's room.'

'Yes, with a show at the Crazy Hose circled. Nice coincidence, eh?' They were at the car now. Rebus opened the passenger door but didn't get in. Instead he rested his elbow on the roof and looked across at her. 'If you believe in coincidence.'

She'd driven them twenty or thirty yards when Rebus ordered her to stop. He'd been looking in his wing mirror, and now got out of the car and started back towards the gates. Siobhan cursed under her breath, drew the car in to the kerb, and followed him. Idling by the gates was a red estate car she'd seen parked further away when they were leaving. Rebus had stopped two men who'd been walking towards Willie McStay.

Neither of the two would have looked out of place in the back of a scrum. Siobhan was in time to catch the end of her superior's argument.

'– and if you don't lay off, so help me, I'll drop you so far in it you'll wish you'd brought a diving bell.' To reinforce this point, Rebus jabbed his finger into the larger man's gut, all the way up to the second joint. The man didn't look like he was enjoying it. His face was a huge ripe plum. But he kept his hands clasped behind his back throughout. He was showing such self control, Siobhan might have taken him for a Buddhist.

Only she'd yet to come across a Buddhist with razor scars carved down both cheeks.

'And what's more,' Rebus was saying, 'you can tell Cafferty we know all about him and the UVF, so he needn't go on acting the innocent about terrorism.'

The bigger of the two men spoke. 'Mr Cafferty's getting very impatient. He wants a result.'

'I don't care if he wants world peace. Now get out of here, and if I hear you've been back asking questions, I'll see you both put away, and I don't care what I've got to do, understood?'

They didn't look overly impressed, but the two men walked away anyway, back to the gates and through them.

'Your fan club?' Siobhan Clarke guessed.

'Ach, they only want me for my body.'

Which, in a sense, was true.

It was late afternoon, and the Crazy Hose was doing no trade at all.

Those in the know just called it the Hose; those not in the know would say, 'Shouldn't it be Horse?' But it was the Hose because its premises were an old decommissioned fire station, left vacant when they built a new edifice just up the street. And it was the Crazy Hose Saloon because it had a wild west theme and country and western music. The main doors were painted gloss black and boasted small square barred windows. Rebus knew the place was doing no trade, because Lee Francis Bothwell was sitting on the steps outside smoking a cigarette.

Although Rebus had never met Frankie Bothwell, he knew the reputation, and there was no mistaking the mess on the steps for anything else. He was dressed like a Las Vegas act, with the face and hair of McGarrett in *Hawaii 5–0*. The hair had to be fake, and Rebus would lay odds some of the face was fake too.

'Mr Bothwell?'

The head nodded without the hair moving one millimetre out of coiffeured place. He was wearing a tan-coloured leather safari jacket, tight white trousers, and an open-necked shirt. The shirt would offend all but the colour blind and the truly blind. It had so many rhinestones on it, Rebus was in no doubt the rhine mines were now exhausted as a result. Around Bothwell's neck hung a simple gold chain, but he would have been better off with a neck-cast. A neck-cast would have disguised the lines, the wrinkles and sags which gave away Bothwell's not insubstantial age.

'I'm Inspector Rebus, this is Detective Constable Clarke.' Rebus had briefed Clarke on the way here, and she didn't look too stunned by the figure in front of her.

'You want a bottle of rye for the police raffle?'

'No, sir. We're trying to complete a collection of magazines.'

'Huh?' Bothwell had been studying the empty street. Just along the road was Tollcross junction, but you couldn't see it from the front steps of the Crazy Hose. Now he looked up at Rebus.

'I'm serious,' Rebus said. 'We're missing a few back issues, maybe you can help.'

'I don't get it.'

'The Floating Anarchy Factfile.'

Frankie Bothwell took off his sunglasses and squinted at Rebus. Then he ground his cigarette-end under the heel of a cowboy boot. 'That was a lifetime ago. How do you know about it?' Rebus shrugged. Frankie Bothwell grinned. He was perking up again. 'Christ, that *was* a long time ago. Up in the Orkneys, peace and love, I had some fun back then. But what's it got to do with anything?'

'Do you know this man?' Rebus handed over a copy of the photo Murdock had given him, the one from the party. It had been cropped to show Billy Cunningham's face only. 'His name's Billy Cunningham.'

Bothwell took a while studying the photo, then shook his head.

'He came here to see a country and western show a couple of weeks back.'

'We're packed most nights, Inspector, especially this time of year. I can ask the bar staff, the bouncers, see if they know him. Is he a regular?'

'We don't know, sir.'

'See, if he's a regular, he'll carry the Cowpoke Card. You get one after three visits in any one month, entitles you to thirty per cent off the admission.' Rebus was shaking his head. 'What's he done anyway?'

'He's been murdered, Mr Bothwell.'

Bothwell screwed up his face. 'Bad one.' Then he looked at Rebus again. 'Not the kid in that underground street?'

Rebus nodded.

Bothwell stood up, brushing dirt from his backside. *'Floating Anarchy* hasn't been in circulation for twenty years. You say this kid had a copy?'

'Issue number three,' Siobhan Clarke confirmed.

Bothwell thought about it. 'Number three, that was a big printing, a thousand or so. There was momentum behind number three. After that ... not so much momentum.' He smiled ruefully. 'Can I keep the photo? Like I say, I'll ask around.'

'Fine, Mr Bothwell. We've got copies.'

'Secondhand shops maybe.'

'Pardon?'

'The magazine, maybe he got it secondhand.'

'That's a thought.'

'A kid that age, Christ.' He shook his head. 'I love kids, Inspector, that's what this place is all about. Giving kids a good time. There's nothing like it.'

'Really, sir?'

Bothwell spread his hands. 'I don't mean anything . . . you know . . . nothing like that. I've always liked kids. I used to run a football team, local youth club thing. Anything for kids.' He smiled again. 'That's because I'm still a kid myself, Inspector. Me, I'm Peter bloody Pan.'

Still holding the photo, he invited them in for a drink. Rebus was tempted, but declined. The bar would be an empty barn; no place for a drink. He handed Bothwell a card with his office number.

'I'll do my best,' Bothwell said.

Rebus nodded and turned away. He didn't say anything to Siobhan Clarke till they were back in her car.

'Well, what do you think?'

'Creepy,' she said. 'How can he dress like that?'

'Years of practice, I suppose.'

'So what do you reckon to him?'

Rebus thought about this. 'I'm not sure. Let me think about it over a drink.'

'That's very kind, sir, but I'm going out.' She made a show of checking her watch.

'A Fringe show?' She nodded.

'Early Tom Stoppard,' she said.

'Well,' Rebus sniffed, 'I didn't say you were invited anyway.' He paused. 'Who are you going with?'

She looked at him. 'I'm going on my own, not that it's any of your business . . . sir.'

Rebus shifted a little. 'You can drop me off at the Ox.'

As they drove past, there was no sign of Frankie Bothwell on the steps of the Crazy Hose Saloon.

The Ox gave Rebus a taste. He phoned Patience, but got the answerphone. He seemed to remember she was going out tonight, but couldn't recall where. He took the slow route home. In Daintry's Lounge, he stood at the bar listening in on its tough wit. The Festival only touched places like Daintry's insofar as providing posters to advertise the shows. These were as much decoration as the place ever had. He stared at a sign above the row of optics. It said, 'If arseholes could fly, this place would be an airport'.

'Ready for take-off,' he said to the barmaid, proffering his empty glass.

A little later, he found himself approaching Oxford Terrace from Lennox Street, so turned into Lennox Street Lane. What had once been stables in the Lane had now become first floor homes with ground floor garages. The place was always dead. Some of the tenements on Oxford Terrace backed onto the lane. Rebus had a key to Patience's garden gate. He'd let himself in the back door to the flat. As shortcuts went, it wasn't much of one, but he liked the lane.

He was about a dozen paces from the gate when somebody grabbed him. They got him from behind, pulling him by the coat, keeping the grip tight so that he might as well have been wearing a straitjacket. The coat came up over Rebus's head, trapping him, binding his arms. A knee came up into his groin. He lashed out with a foot, which only made it all the easier to unbalance him. He was shouting and swearing as he fell. The attacker had released his grip on the coat. While Rebus struggled to get out of it, a foot caught him on the side of the head. The foot was wearing a plimsoll, which explained why Rebus hadn't heard his attacker following him. It also explained why he was still conscious after the kick.

Another kick dug into his side. And then, just as his head was emerging from his coat, the foot caught him on the chin, and all he could see were the setts beneath him, slick and shining from what light there was. The attacker's hands were on him, rifling pockets. The man was breathing hard.

'Take the money,' Rebus said, trying to focus his eyes. He knew there wasn't much money to take, less than a fiver, all of it in small change. The man didn't seem happy with his haul. It wasn't much for a night's work.

'A'm gonny put you in the hospital.' The accent was Glaswegian. Rebus could make out the man's build – squat – but not yet his face. There was too much shadow. He was rearing up again, coins spilling from his hands to rain down on Rebus.

He'd given Rebus just enough time to shake off the alcohol. Rebus sprang from his crouch and hit the man square in the stomach with his head, propelling his assailant backwards. The man kept his balance, but Rebus was standing too now, and he was bigger than the Glaswegian. There was a glint in the man's hand. A cutthroat razor. Rebus hadn't seen one in years. It flashed in an arc towards him, but he dodged it, then saw that there were two other figures in the lane. They were watching, hands in pockets. He thought he recognised them as Cafferty's men, the ones from the churchyard.

The razor was swinging again, the Glaswegian almost smiling as he went about his business. Rebus slipped his coat all the way off and wrapped it around his left arm. He met the blade with his arm, feeling it cut into the cloth, and lashed out with the sole of his right foot, connecting with the man's knee. The man took a step back, and Rebus struck out again, connecting with a thigh this time. When the man attempted to come back at him, he was limping and easy to sidestep. But instead of aiming with the razor he barrelled into Rebus, pushing him hard against some garage doors. Then he turned and ran.

There was only one exit from the alley, and he took it, running past Cafferty's men. Rebus took a deep breath, then sank to his knees and threw up onto the ground. His coat was ruined, but that was the least of his problems. Cafferty's men were strolling towards him. They lifted him to his feet like he was a bag of shopping.

'You all right?' one asked.

'Winded,' Rebus said. His chin hurt too, but there was no blood. He puked up more alcohol, feeling better for it. The other man had stooped to pick up the money. Rebus didn't get it.

'Your man?' he said. They were shaking their heads. Then the bigger one spoke.

'He just saved us the bother.'

'He was trying to hospitalise me.'

'I think I'd have done the same,' said the big man, holding out Rebus's coins. 'If this is all I'd found.'

Rebus took the money and pocketed it. Then he took a swing at the man. It was slow and tired and didn't connect. But the big man connected all right. His punch took all the remaining fight out of Rebus. He fell to his knees again, palms on the cold ground.

'That's by way of an incentive,' the man said. 'Just in case you were needing one. Mr Cafferty'll be talking to you soon.'

'Not if I can help it,' spat Rebus, sitting with his back to the garage. They were walking away from him, back towards the mouth of the lane.

'He'll be talking to you.'

Then they were gone.

A Glaswegian with a razor, Rebus thought to himself, happy to sit here till the pain went away. If not Cafferty's man, then whose?

And why?

14

Rebus struggled towards consciousness, even as he picked up the telephone.

'Heathen!' he gasped into it.

'Pardon?'

'To call at this ungodly hour.' He'd recognised DCI Kilpatrick's voice. He ran the palm of his hand down his face, pulling open his eyelids. When he could focus, he tried finding the time on the clock, but in his struggle for the receiver he'd knocked it to the floor. 'What do you want ... sir?'

'I was hoping you could come in a bit early.'

'What? Cleaners on strike and you're looking for a relief?'

'He sounds like the dead, but he's still cracking jokes.'

'When do you want me?'

'Say, half an hour?'

'You say it, I'll do what I can.' He put down the receiver and found his watch. It was on his wrist. The time was five past six. He hadn't so much slept as drifted into coma. Maybe it was the drink or the vomiting or the beating. Maybe it was just too many late nights catching up with him. Whatever, he didn't feel the worse for it. He checked his side: it was bruised, but not badly. His chin and face didn't feel too bad either, just grazed.

'Who the hell was that?' Patience growled sleepily from beneath her pillow.

'Duty calls,' said Rebus, swinging his unwilling legs out of bed.

They were seated in Kilpatrick's office, Rebus and Ken Smylie. Rebus held his coffee cup the way a disaster victim would, cradling this smallest of comforts. He couldn't have looked worse if there'd been a blanket around his shoulders and a reporter in front of him asking how he felt about the plane crash. His early morning buzz had lasted all the way from the bed to the bathroom. It had been an effort to look in the mirror. Unshaven, you hardly noticed the bruises, but he could feel them on the inside.

Smylie seemed alert enough, not needing the caffeine. And Rebus shouldn't have been drinking it either; it would play merry hell with him later.

It was a minute short of seven o'clock, and they were watching Kilpatrick pretend to reread some fax sheets. At last he was ready. He put down the sheets and interlocked the fingers of both hands. Rebus and Smylie were trying to get a look at what the fax said.

'I've heard from the United States. You were right, Ken, they're quick workers. The gist is, there are two fairly widespread but above board organisations in the US, one's called the Scottish Rites Temple.'

'That's a kind of masonic lodge for Scots,' Rebus said, remembering Vanderhyde's words.

Kilpatrick nodded. 'The other is called Scottish Sword and Shield.' He watched Rebus and Smylie exchange a look. 'Don't get excited. It's much more low-key than Scottish Rites, but it's not into the financing of gun-running. However,' he picked up the fax again, 'there's one final group. It has its main headquarters in Toronto, Canada, but also has branches in the States, particularly in the south and the north-west. It's called The Shield, and you won't find it in any phone book. The FBI have been investigating the US operation for just over a year, as have the American tax people. I had a chat with an FBI agent at their headquarters in Washington.'

'And?'

'And, the Shield is a fund-raiser, only nobody's quite sure what for. Whatever it is, it isn't Catholic. The FBI agent said he'd already passed a lot of this information on to the Royal Ulster Constabulary, in the event of their becoming cognisant of the organisation.'

Ten minutes on the phone to Washington, and already Kilpatrick was aping American speech.

'So,' Rebus said, 'now we talk to the RUC.'

'I already have. That's why I called this meeting.'

'What did they say?'

'They were pretty damned cagey.'

'No surprises there, sir,' said Smylie.

'They did admit to having some information on what they called Sword and Shield.'

'Great.'

'But they won't release it. Usual RUC runaround. They don't like sharing things. Their line is, if we want to see it, we have to go there. Those bastards really are a law unto themselves.'

'No point going higher up with this, sir? *Some*one could order the information out of them.'

'Yes, and it could get lost, or they could lift out anything they didn't feel like letting us see. No, I think we show willing on this.'

'Belfast?'

Kilpatrick nodded. 'I'd like you both to go, it'll only be a day trip.' Kilpatrick checked his watch. 'There's a Loganair flight at seven-forty, so you'd best get going.'

'No time to pack my tour guides,' said Rebus. Inside, two old dreads were warming his gut.

They banked steeply coming down over Belfast harbour, like one of those fairground rides teenagers take to prove themselves. Rebus still had a hum of caffeine in his ears.

'Pretty good, eh?' said Smylie.

'Aye, pretty good.' Rebus hadn't flown in a few years. He'd had a fear of flying ever since his SAS training. Already he was dreading the return trip. It wasn't when he was high up, he didn't mind that. But the take-off and landing, that view of the ground, so near and yet far enough to kill you stone dead if you hit it. Here it came again, the plane dropping fast now, too fast. His fingers were sore against the armrests. There was every chance of them locking there. He could see a surgeon amputating at the wrists . . .

And then they were down. Smylie was quick to stand up. The seat had been too narrow for him, with not enough legroom. He worked his neck and shoulders, then rubbed his knees.

'Welcome to Belfast,' he said.

'We like to give visitors the tour,' Yates said.

He was Inspector Yates of the Royal Ulster Constabulary, and both he and his car were in mufti. He had a face formed of fist-fights or bad childhood infections, scar tissue and things not quite in their right place. His nose veered leftwards, one earlobe hung lower than the other, and his chin had been stitched together not altogether successfully. You'd look at him in a bar and then look away again quickly, not risking the stare he deserved. He had no neck, that was another thing. His head sat on his shoulders like a boulder on the top of a hill.

'That's very kind,' said Smylie, as they sped into town, 'but we'd –'

'Lets you see what we're dealing with.' Yates kept looking in his rearview, conducting a conversation with the mirror. 'The two cities. It's the same in any war zone. I knew this guy, height of the trouble in Beirut, he was recruited as a croupier there. Bombs falling, gunmen on the rampage, and the casinos were still open. Now these,' he nodded out of the windscreen, 'are the recruiting stations.'

They had left the City Airport behind, shaved the city's commercial centre, and were passing through a wasteland. Until now, you couldn't have said which British city you were in. A new road was being built down by the docks. Old flats, no worse than those in the Gar-B, were being demolished. As Yates had commented, sometimes the divide was hidden.

Not far away, a helicopter hovered high in the sky, watching someone or something. Around them, whole streets had been bulldozed. The kerbstones were painted green and white.

'You'll see red, white and blue ones in other areas.'

On the gable-end of a row of houses was an elaborate painting. Rebus could make out three masked figures, their automatic weapons raised high. There was a tricolour above them, and a phoenix rising from flames above this.

'A nice piece of propaganda,' said Rebus.

Yates turned to Smylie. 'Your man knows what he's talking about. It's a work of art. These are some of the poorest streets in Europe, by the way.'

They didn't look so bad to Rebus. The gable-end had reminded him again of the Gar-B. Only there was more rebuilding going on here. New housing developments were rising from the old.

'See that wall?' said Yates. 'That's called an environmental wall built and maintained by the Housing Executive.' It was a red brick wall, functional, with a pattern in the bricks. 'There used to be houses there. The other side of the wall is Protestant, once you get past the wasteland. They knock down the houses and extend the wall. There's the Peace Line too, that's an ugly old thing, made from iron rather than bricks. Streets like these, they're meat and drink to the paramilitaries. The loyalist areas are the same.'

Eyes were following their slow progress, the eyes of teenagers and children grouped at street corners. The eyes held neither fear nor hate, only mistrust. On a wall, someone had daubed painted messages, old references to the H Block and Bobby Sands, newer additions in praise of the IRA, and promising revenge against the loyalist paramilitaries, the UVF and UFF predominantly. Rebus saw himself patrolling these streets, or streets like them, back when there had been more houses, more people on the move. He'd often been the 'back walker', which meant he stayed at the back of the patrol and faced the rear, his gun pointing towards the people they'd just passed, men staring at the ground, kids making rude gestures, shows of bravado, and mothers pushing prams. The patrol moved as cautiously as in any jungle.

'See, here we are,' Yates was saying, 'we're coming into Protestant territory now.' More gable-ends, now painted with ten-foot-high Williams of Orange riding twenty-foot-high white horses. And then the cheaper displays, the graffiti, exhorting the locals to 'Fuck the Pope and the IRA'. The letters FTP were everywhere. Five minutes before, they had been FKB: Fuck King Billy. They were just routine, a reflex. But of course they were more. You couldn't laugh them off as name-calling, because the people who'd written them wouldn't let you. They kept shooting each other, and blowing each other up.

Smylie read one of the slogans aloud. ' "Irish Out".' He turned to Yates. 'What? All of them?'

Yates smiled. 'The Catholics write "Troops Out", so the loyalists write "Irish Out". They don't see themselves as Irish, they're British.' He looked in the mirror again. 'And they're getting more vicious, loyalist paramilitaries killed more civvies last year than the IRA did. That's a first, so far as I know. The loyalists hate us now, too.'

'Who's us?'

'The RUC. They weren't happy when the UDA was outlawed. Your man, Sir Patrick Mayhew, he lit the fuse.'

'I read about some riots.'

'Only last month, here in the Shankill and elsewhere. They say we're harassing them. We can't really win, can we?'

'I think we get the picture,' said Smylie, anxious to get to work. But Rebus knew the point the RUC man was making: this *was* their work.

'If you think you get the picture,' Yates said, 'then you're not getting the picture. You're to blame, you know.'

'Eh?'

'The Scots. You settled here in the seventeenth century, started pushing around the Catholics.'

'I don't think we need a history lesson,' Rebus said quietly. Smylie was looking like he might explode.

'But it's all about history,' Yates said levelly. 'On the surface at least.'

'And underneath?'

'Paramilitaries are in the business of making money. They can't exist without money. So now they've become gangsters, pure and simple, because that's the easy way to make the money they need. And then it becomes self-perpetuating. The IRA and UDA get together now and then and discuss things. They sit around a table together, just like the politicians want them to, but instead of talking about peace, they talk about carving up the country. You can extort from these taxi firms if we can extort from the building sites. You even get cases where the stuff the one side has stolen is passed on to the other for them to sell in their areas. You get times when the tension's high, then it's back to business as usual. It's like one of those mafia films, the money these bastards are making . . .' Yates shook his head. 'They can't *afford* peace. It'd be bad for business.'

'And bad for your business too.'

Yates laughed. 'Aye, right enough, overtime wouldn't be easy to come by. But then we might live to retirement age, too. That doesn't always happen just now.' Yates had lifted his radio transmitter. 'Two-Six-Zero, I'm about five minutes from base. Two passengers.' The radio spat static.

'Received and understood.'

He put down the receiver. 'Now this,' he said, 'this is Belfast too. South

Belfast, you don't hear much about it because hardly anything ever happens here. See what I mean about two cities?'

Rebus had been noticing the change in their surroundings. Suddenly it looked prosperous, safe. There were wide tree-lined avenues, detached houses, some of them very new-looking. They'd passed the university, a red-brick replica of some older college. Yet they were still only ten minutes from 'the Troubles'. Rebus knew this face of the city, too. He'd only spent the one tour of duty here, but he remembered the big houses, the busy city centre, the Victorian pubs whose interiors were regarded as national treasures. He knew the city was surrounded by lush green countryside, winding lanes and farm tracks, at the end of which might sit silent milk-churns packed with explosives.

The RUC station on the Malone Road was a well-disguised affair, tucked away behind a wooden fence, with a discreet lookout tower.

'We have to keep up appearances for the locals,' Yates explained. 'This is a nice part of town, no mesh fences and machine guns.'

The gates had been opened for them, and closed quickly again.

'Thanks for the tour,' Rebus said as they parked. He meant it, something Yates acknowledged with a nod. Smylie opened his door and prised himself out. Yates glanced at the upholstery, then opened the glove compartment and lifted out his holstered pistol, bringing it with him.

'Is your accent Irish?' Rebus asked.

'Mostly. There's a bit of Liverpool in there too. I was born in Bootle, we moved here when I was six.'

'What made you join the RUC?' Smylie asked.

'I've always been a stupid bastard, I suppose.'

He had to sign both visitors into the building, and their identities were checked. Later, Rebus knew, some clerical assistant would add them to a computer file.

Inside, the station looked much like any police station, except that the windows were heavily protected and the beat patrols carried padded vests with them and wore holsters. They'd seen policemen during their drive, but had acknowledged none of them. And they'd passed a single Army patrol, young squaddies sitting at the open rear door of their personnel carrier (known as a 'pig' in Rebus's day, and probably still), automatic rifles held lightly, faces trained not to show emotion. In the station, the windows might be well protected but there seemed little sign of a siege mentality. The jokes were just as blue, just as black, as the ones told in Edinburgh. People discussed TV and football and the weather. Smylie wasn't watching any of it. He wanted the job done and out again as quick as could be.

Rebus wasn't sure about Smylie. The man might be a wonder in the office, as efficient as the day was long, but here he seemed less sure of himself. He was nervous, and showed it. When he took his jacket off, complaining of the heat, there were large sweat marks spreading from beneath his arms. Rebus had thought *he'd* be the nervous one, yet he felt detached, his memories bringing back no new fears. He was all right.

Yates had a small office to himself. They'd bought beakers of tea at a machine, and now sat these on the desk. Yates put his gun into a desk drawer, draped his jacket over his chair, and sat down. Pinned above him on the wall behind the desk was a sheet of computer print-out bearing the oversized words *Nil Illegitimum Non Carborundum*. Smylie decided to take a poke.

'I thought Latin was for the Catholics?'

Yates stared at him. 'There *are* Catholics in the RUC. Don't get us confused with the UDR.' Then he unlocked another drawer and pulled out a file, pushing it across the desk towards Rebus. 'This doesn't leave the room.' Smylie drew his chair towards Rebus's, and they read the contents together, Smylie, the faster reader, fidgeting as he waited for Rebus to catch up.

'This is incredible,' Smylie said at one point. He was right. The RUC had evidence of a loyalist paramilitary force called Sword and Shield (usually just referred to as The Shield), and of a support group working out of the mainland, acting as a conduit through which money and arms could pass, and also raising funds independently.

'By mainland do you mean Scotland?' Rebus asked.

Yates shrugged. 'We're not really taking them seriously, it's just a cover name for the UVF or UFF, got to be. That's the way it works. There are so many of these wee groups, Ulster Resistance, the Red Hands Commando, Knights of the Red Hand, we can hardly keep up with them.'

'But this group is on the mainland,' Rebus said.

'Yes.'

'And we've maybe come up against them.' He tapped the folder. 'Yet nobody thought to tell us any of this.'

Yates shrugged again, his head falling further into his body. 'We leave that to Special Branch.'

'You mean Special Branch were told about this?'

'Special Branch here would inform Special Branch in London.'

'Any idea who the contact would be in London?'

'That's classified information, Inspector, sorry.'

'A man called Abernethy?'

Yates pushed his chair back so he could rock on it, the front two legs coming off the floor. He studied Rebus.

'That's answer enough,' Rebus said. He looked to Smylie, who nodded. They were being screwed around by Special Branch. But why?

'I see something's on your mind,' said Yates. 'Want to tell me about it? I'd like to hear what you know.'

Rebus placed the folder on the desk. 'Then come to Edinburgh some time, maybe we'll tell you.'

Yates placed all four legs of his chair on the floor. When he looked at Rebus, his face was stone, his eyes fire. 'No need to be like that,' he said quietly.

'Why not? We've wasted a whole day for four sheets of filing paper, all because you wouldn't send it to us!'

'It's nothing personal, Inspector, it's security. Wouldn't matter if you were the Chief fucking Constable. Perspectives tend to change when your arse is in the line of fire.'

If Yates was looking for the sympathy vote, Rebus wasn't about to place a cross in his box. 'The Prods haven't always been as keen as the Provos, have they? What's going on?'

'First off, they're loyalists, not Prods. Prods means Protestants, and we're dealing only with a select few, not with all of them. Second, they're Provies, not Provos. Third . . . we're not sure. There's a younger leadership, a keener leadership. Plus like I say, they're not happy just to let the security forces get on with it. See, the loyalist paramilitaries have always had a problem. They're supposed to be on the same side as the security forces, they're supposed to be law-abiding. That's changed. They feel threatened. Just now they're the majority, but it won't always be that way. Plus the British government's more concerned with its international image than with a few hard-line loyalists, so it's paying more attention to the Republic. Put all that together and you get disillusioned loyalists, and plenty of them. The loyalist paramilitaries used to have a bad image. A lot of their operations went wrong, they didn't have the manpower or the connections or the international support of the IRA.

'These days they seem to be better organised though, not so much blatant racketeering. A lot of the thugs have been put off the Road . . . that is, put off the Shankill Road, as in banished.'

'But at the same time they're arming themselves,' Rebus said.

'It's true,' added Smylie. 'In the past, whenever we caught them red-handed on the mainland, we used to find gelignite or sodium chlorate, now we're finding rocket launchers and armour-piercing shells.'

'Red-handed.' Yates smiled at that. 'Oh, it's getting heavy duty,' he agreed.

'But you don't know why?'

'I've given you all the reasons I can.'

Rebus wondered about that, but didn't say anything.

'Look, this is a new thing for us,' Yates said. 'We're used to facing off the Provies, not the loyalists. But now they've got Kalashnikovs, RPG-7s, frag grenades, Brownings.'

'And you're taking them seriously?'

'Oh yes, Inspector, we're taking them seriously. That's why I want to know what *you* know.'

'Maybe we'll tell you over a beer,' Rebus said.

Yates took them to the Crown Bar. Across the street, most of the windows in the Europa Hotel were boarded up, the result of another bomb. The bomb had damaged the Crown, too, but the damage hadn't been allowed to linger. It was a Victorian pub, well preserved, with gas lighting and a wall lined with snugs, each with its own table and its own door for privacy. The interior reminded Rebus of several Edinburgh bars, but here he drank stout rather than heavy, and whiskey rather than whisky.

'I know this place,' he said.

'Been here before, eh?'

'Inspector Rebus,' Smylie explained, 'was in the Army in Belfast.'

So then Rebus had to tell Yates all about it, all about 1969. He wasn't getting it out of his system; he could still feel the pressure inside him. He remembered the republican drinking club again, and the way they'd gone in there swinging wildly, some of the toms more enthusiastic than others. What would he say if he met any of the men they'd beaten? Sorry didn't seem enough. He wouldn't talk about it, but he told Yates a few other stories. Talking was okay, and drinking was okay too. The thought of the return flight didn't bother him so much after two pints and a nip. By the time they were in the Indian restaurant eating an early lunch in a private booth a long way from any other diners, Smylie had grown loquacious, but it was all mental arm-wrestling, comparing and contrasting the two police forces, discussing manpower, back-up, arrest sheets, drug problems.

As Yates pointed out, leaving aside terrorism, Northern Ireland had one of the lowest crime rates going, certainly for serious crimes. There were the usual housebreakings and car-jackings, but few rapes and murders. Even the rougher housing schemes were kept in check by the paramilitaries, whose punishments went beyond incarceration.

Which brought them back to Mary King's Close. Were they any nearer, Rebus wondered, to finding out why Billy Cunningham had been tortured and killed and who had killed him? The letters SaS on an arm, the word Nemo on the floor, the style of the assassination and Cunningham's own sympathies. What did it all add up to?

Yates meantime talked a little more freely, while helping Smylie polish off the remaining dishes. He admitted they weren't all angels in the RUC, which did not exactly surprise Rebus and Smylie, but Yates said they should see some of the men in the Ulster Defence Regiment, who were so fair-minded that their patrols had to be accompanied by RUC men keeping an eye on them.

'You were here in '69, Inspector, you'll remember the B Specials? The

UDR was formed to replace the B Spesh. The same madmen joined. See, if a loyalist wants to do something for his cause, all he has to do is join the UDR or the RUC Reserve. That fact has kept the UDA and UVF small.'

'Is there still collusion between the security forces and the loyalists?'

Yates pondered that one over a belch. 'Probably,' he said, reaching for his lager. 'The UDR used to be terrible, so did the Royal Irish Rangers. Now, it's not so widespread.'

'Either that or better hidden,' said Rebus.

'With cynicism like that, you should join the RUC.'

'I don't like guns.'

Yates wiped at his plate with a final sliver of nan bread. 'Ah yes,' he said, 'the essential difference between us. I get to shoot people.'

'It's a big difference,' Rebus suggested.

'All the difference in the world,' Yates agreed.

Smylie had gone quiet. He was wiping his own plate with bread.

'Do the loyalists get aid from overseas?' Rebus asked.

Yates sat back contentedly. 'Not as much as the republicans. The loyalists probably rake in £150,000 a year from the mainland, mostly to help families and convicted members. Two-thirds of that comes from Scotland. There are pockets of sympathisers abroad – Australia, South Africa, the US and Canada. Canada's the big one. The UVF have some Ingrams submachine guns just now that were shipped from Toronto. Why do you want to know?'

Rebus and Smylie shared a look, then Smylie started to talk. Rebus was happy to let him: this way, Yates only got to know what Smylie knew, rather than what Rebus suspected. Toronto: headquarters of The Shield. When Smylie had finished, Rebus asked Yates a question.

'This group, Sword and Shield, I didn't see any names on the file.'

'You mean individuals?' Rebus nodded. 'Well, it's all pretty low-key. We've got suspicions, but the names wouldn't mean anything to you.'

'Try me.'

Yates considered, then nodded slowly. 'Okay.'

'For instance, who's the leader?'

'We haven't breached their command structure ... not yet.'

'But you have your suspicions?'

Yates smiled. 'Oh yes. There's one bastard in particular.' His voice, already low, dropped lower still. 'Alan Fowler. He was UVF, but left after a disagreement. A right bad bastard, I think the UVF were glad to be shot of him.'

'Can I have a photo? A description?'

Yates shrugged. 'Why not? He's not my problem just now anyway.'

Rebus put down his glass. 'Why's that?'

'Because he took the ferry to Stranraer last week. A car picked him up and drove him to Glasgow.' Yates paused. 'And that's where we lost him.'

15

Ormiston was waiting at the airport with a car.

Rebus didn't like Ormiston. He had a huge round face marked with freckles, and a semi-permanent grin too close to a sneer for comfort. His hair was thickly brown, always in need of a comb or a cut. He reminded Rebus of an overgrown schoolboy. Seeing him at his desk next to the bald and schoolmasterly Blackwood was like seeing the classroom dunce placed next to the teacher so an eye could be kept on his work.

But there was something particularly wrong with Ormiston this afternoon. Not that Rebus really cared. All he cared about was the headache which had woken him on the approach to Edinburgh. A midday drinking headache, a glare behind the eyes and a stupor further back in the brain. He'd noticed at the airport, the way Ormiston was looking at Smylie, Smylie not realising it.

'Got any paracetamol on you?' Rebus asked.

'Sorry.' And he caught Rebus's eye again, as if trying to communicate something. Normally he was a nosy bugger, yet he hadn't asked about their trip. Even Smylie noticed this.

'What is it, Ormiston? A vow of *omerta* or something?'

Ormiston still wasn't talking. He concentrated on his driving, giving Rebus plenty of time for thought. He had things to tell Kilpatrick ... and things he wanted to keep to himself for the time being.

When Ormiston stopped the car at Fettes, he turned to Rebus.

'Not you. We've got to meet the Chief somewhere.'

'What?'

Smylie, half out of his door, stopped. 'What's up?'

Ormiston just shook his head. Rebus looked to Smylie. 'See you later then.'

'Aye, sure.' And Smylie got out, relieving the car's suspension. As soon as he'd closed the door, Ormiston moved off.

'What is it, Ormiston?'

'Best if the Chief tells you himself.'

'Give me a clue then.'

'A murder,' Ormiston said, changing up a gear. 'There's been a murder.'

*

565

The scene had been cordoned off.

It was a narrow street of tall tenements. St Stephen Street had always enjoyed a rakish reputation, something to do with its mix of student flats, cafes and junk shops. There were several bars, one of them catering mainly to bikers. Rebus had heard a story that Nico, ex-Velvet Underground, had lived here for a time. It could be true. St Stephen Street, connecting the New Town to Raeburn Place, was a quiet thoroughfare which still managed to exude charm and seediness in equal measures.

The tenements either side of the street boasted basements, and a lot of these were flats with their own separate stairwells and entrances. Patience lived in just such a flat not seven minutes' walk away. Rebus walked carefully down the stone steps. They were often worn and slippy. At the bottom, in a sort of damp courtyard, the owner or tenant of the flat had attempted to create a garden of terracotta pots and hanging baskets. But most of the plants had died, probably from lack of light, or perhaps from rough treatment at the hands of the builders. Scaffolding stretched up the front of the tenement, much of it covered with thick polythene, crackling in the breeze.

'Cleaning the façade,' someone said. Rebus nodded. The front door of the flat faced a whitewashed wall, and in the wall were set two doors. Rebus knew what these were, they were storage areas, burrowed out beneath the surface of the pavement. Patience had almost identical doors, but never used the space for anything; the cellars were too damp. One of the doors stood open. The floor was mostly moss, some of which was being scraped into an evidence-bag by a SOCO.

Kilpatrick, watching this, was listening to Blackwood, who ran his left hand across his pate, tucking an imaginary hair behind his ear. Kilpatrick saw Rebus.

'Hello, John.'

'Sir.'

'Where's Smylie?'

Ormiston was coming down the steps. Rebus nodded towards him. 'The Quiet Man there dropped him at HQ. So what's the big mystery?'

Blackwood answered. 'Flat's been on the market a few months, but not selling. Owner decided to tart it up a bit, see if that would do the trick. Builders turned up yesterday. Today one of them decided to take a look at the cellars. He found a body.'

'Been there long?'

Blackwood shook his head. 'They're doing the post-mortem this evening.'

'Any tattoos?'

'No tattoos,' said Kilpatrick. 'Thing is, John, it was Calumn.' The Chief Inspector looked genuinely troubled, almost ready for tears. His face had lost its colour, and had lengthened as though the muscles had lost all motivation. He massaged his forehead with a hand.

'Calumn?' Rebus shook away his hangover. 'Calumn Smylie?' He remembered the big man, in the back of the HGV with his brother. Tried to imagine him dead, but couldn't. Especially not here, in a cellar . . .

Kilpatrick blew his nose loudly, then wiped it. 'I suppose I'd better get back and tell Ken.'

'No need, sir.'

Ken Smylie was standing at street level, gripping the gloss-black railings. He looked like he might uproot the lot. Instead he arched back his head and gave a high-pitched howl, the sound swirling up into the sky as a smattering of rain began to fall.

Smylie had to be ordered to go home, they couldn't shift him otherwise. Everyone else in the office moved like automatons. DCI Kilpatrick had some decisions to make, chief among them whether or not to tie together the two murder inquiries.

'He was stabbed,' he told Rebus. 'No signs of a struggle, certainly no torture, nothing like that.' There was relief in his voice, a relief Rebus could understand. 'Stabbed and dumped. Whoever did it probably saw the For Sale sign outside the flat, didn't reckon on the body being found for a while.' He had produced a bottle of Laphroaig from the bottom drawer of his desk, and poured himself a glass.

'Medicinal,' he explained. But Rebus declined the offer of a glass. He'd taken three paracetamol washed down with Irn-Bru. He noticed that the level in the Laphroaig bottle was low. Kilpatrick must have a prescription.

'You think he was rumbled?'

'What else?' said Kilpatrick, dribbling more malt into his glass.

'I'd have expected another punishment killing, something with a bit of ritual about it.'

'Ritual?' Kilpatrick considered this. 'He wasn't killed there, you know. The pathologist said there wasn't enough blood. Maybe they held their "ritual" wherever they killed him. Christ, and I let him go out on a limb.' He took out a handkerchief and blew his nose, then took a deep breath. 'Well, I've got a murder inquiry to start up, the high hiedyins are going to be asking questions.'

'Yes, sir.' Rebus stood up, but stopped at the door. 'Two murders, two cellars, two lots of builders.'

Kilpatrick nodded, but said nothing. Rebus opened the door.

'Sir, who knew about Calumn?'

'How do you mean?'

'Who knew he was undercover? Just this office, or anyone else?'

Kilpatrick furrowed his brow. 'Such as?'

'Special Branch, say.'

'Just this office,' Kilpatrick said quietly. Rebus turned to leave. 'John, what did you find out in Belfast?'

'That Sword and Shield exists. That the RUC know it's operating here on the mainland. That they told Special Branch in London.' He paused. 'That DI Abernethy probably knows all about it.'

Having said which, Rebus left the room. Kilpatrick stared at the door for a full minute.

'Christ almighty,' he said. His telephone was ringing. He was slow to answer it.

'Is it true?' Brian Holmes asked. Siobhan Clarke was waiting for an answer too.

'It's true,' said Rebus. They were in the Murder Room at St Leonard's. 'He was working on something that might well be connected to Billy Cunningham.'

'So what now, sir?'

'We need to talk to Millie and Murdock again.'

'We've talked to them.'

'That's why I said "again". Don't you listen? And after that, let's fix up a little chat with some of the Jaffas.'

'Jaffas?'

Rebus tutted at Siobhan Clarke. 'How long have you lived here? Jaffas are Orangemen.'

'The Orange Lodge?' said Holmes. 'What can they tell us?'

'The date of the Battle of the Boyne for a start.'

'1690, Inspector.'

'Yes, sir.'

'The date, of course, means more than a mere *annus mirabilis*. One-six-nine-o. One and six make seven, nine plus nought equals nine, seven and nine being crucial numbers.' He paused. 'Do you know anything of numerology, Inspector?'

'No, sir.'

'What about the lassie?'

Siobhan Clarke bristled visibly. 'It's sort of a crank science, isn't it?' she offered. Rebus gave her a cooling look. Humour him, the look ordered.

'Not crank, no. It's ancient, with the ring of truth. Can I get you something to drink?'

'No, thanks, Mr Gowrie.'

They were seated in Arch Gowrie's 'front room', a parlour kept for visitors and special occasions. The real living room, with comfortable sofa, TV and video, drinks cabinet, was elsewhere on this sprawling ground floor. The house was at least three storeys high, and probably boasted an attic conversion too. It was sited in The Grange, a leafy backwater of the city's southern side. The Grange got few visitors, few strangers, and never much traffic, since it was not a well-known route between any two other areas of the city. A lot of the huge detached houses, one-time merchants' houses with walled grounds and high wooden or metal gates, had been bought by the Church of Scotland or other religious denominations. There was a retirement home to one side of Gowrie's own residence, and what Rebus thought was a convent on the other side.

Archibald Gowrie liked to be called 'Arch'. Everyone knew him as Arch. He was the public face of the Orange Lodge, an eloquent enough apologist (not that he thought there was anything to apologise for), but by no means that organisation's most senior figure. However, he was high enough, and he was easy to find – unlike Millie and Murdock, who weren't home.

Gowrie had agreed readily to a meeting, saying he'd be free between seven and quarter to eight.

'Plenty of time, sir,' Rebus had said.

He studied Arch Gowrie now. The man was big and fiftyish and probably attractive to women in that way older men could be. (Though Rebus noticed Siobhan Clarke didn't seem too enthralled.) Though his hair – thinning nicely – was silver, his thick moustache was black. He wore his shirt with the sleeves rolled up, showing darkly haired arms. He was always ready for business. In fact, 'open for business' had been his public motto, and he worked tirelessly whenever he got his teeth into a new development.

From what Rebus knew, Gowrie had made his money initially as director of a company which had nippily shifted its expertise from ships and pipelines to building exploration platforms and oil rigs for the North Sea. That was back in the early '70s. The company had been sold at vast profit, and Gowrie had disappeared for several years before reappearing in the guise of property developer and investment guru. He was still a property developer, his name on several projects around the city as well as further afield. But he had diversified into wildly different areas: film production, hi-fi design, edible algae, forestry, two country house hotels, a woollen mill, and the Eyrie restaurant in the New Town. Probably Arch was best known for his part-ownership of the Eyrie, the city's best restaurant, certainly its most exclusive, by far its most expensive. You wouldn't find nutritious Hebridean Blue Algae on its menu, not even written in French.

Rebus knew of only one large loss Gowrie had taken, as money man behind a film set predominantly in Scotland. Even boasting Rab Kinnoul as its star, the film had been an Easter turkey. Still, Gowrie wasn't shy: there was a framed poster for the film hanging in the entrance hall.

'*Annus mirabilis,*' Rebus mused. 'That's Latin, isn't it?'

Gowrie was horrified. 'Of course it's Latin! Don't tell me you never studied Latin at school? I though we Scots were an educated bunch. Miraculous year, that's what it means. Sure about that drink?'

'Maybe a small whisky, sir.' Kill or cure.

'Nothing for me, sir,' said Siobhan Clarke, her voice coming from the high moral ground.

'I won't be a minute,' said Gowrie. When he'd left the room, Rebus turned to her.

'Don't piss him off!' he hissed. 'Just keep your gob shut and your ears open.'

'Sorry, sir. Have you noticed?'

'What?'

'There's nothing green in this room, nothing at all.'

He nodded again. 'The inventor of red, white and blue grass will make a fortune.'

Gowrie came back into the room. He took a look at the two of them on the sofa, then smiled to himself and handed Rebus a crystal tumbler.

'I won't offend you by offering water or lemonade with that.'

Rebus sniffed the amber liquid. It was a West Highland malt, darker, more aromatic than the Speysides. Gowrie held his own glass up.

'*Slainte.*' He took a sip, then sat in a dark blue armchair. 'Well now,' he said, 'how exactly can I help you?'

'Well, sir –'

'It's nothing to do with us, you know. We've told the Chief Constable that. They're an offshoot of the Grand Lodge, less than that even, now that we've disbarred them.'

Rebus suddenly knew what Gowrie was talking about. There was to be a march along Princes Street on Saturday, organised by the Orange Loyal Brigade. He'd heard about it weeks ago, when the very idea had provoked attacks from republican sympathisers and anti-right wing associations. There were expected to be confrontations during the march.

'When did you disbar the group exactly, sir?'

'April 14th. That was the day we had the disciplinary hearing. They belonged to one of our district lodges, and at a dinner-dance they'd sent collecting tins round for the LPWA.' He turned to Siobhan Clarke. 'That's the Loyalist Prisoners' Welfare Association.' Then back to Rebus. 'We can't have that sort of thing, Inspector. We've denounced it in the past. We'll have no truck with the paramilitaries.'

'And the disbarred members set up the Orange Loyal Brigade?'

'Correct.'

Rebus was feeling his way. 'How many do you think will be on the march?'

'Ach, a couple of hundred at most, and that's including the bands. I think they've got bands coming from Glasgow and Liverpool.'

'You think there'll be trouble?'

'Don't you? Isn't that why you're here?'

'Who's the Brigade's leader?'

'Gavin MacMurray. But don't you know all this already? Your Chief Constable asked if I could intervene. But I told him, they're nothing to do with the Orange Lodge, nothing at all.'

'Do they have connections with the other right-wing groups?'

'You mean with fascists?' Gowrie shrugged. 'They deny it, of course, but I wouldn't be surprised to see a few skinheads on the march, even ones with Sassenach accents.'

Rebus left a pause before asking, 'Do you know if there's any link-up between the Orange Brigade and The Shield?'

Gowrie frowned. 'What shield?'

'Sword and Shield. It's another splinter group, isn't it?'

Gowrie shook his head. 'I've never heard of it.'

'No?'

'Never.'

Rebus placed his whisky glass on a table next to the sofa. 'I just assumed you'd know something about it.' He got to his feet, followed by Clarke. 'Sorry to have bothered you, sir.' Rebus held out his hand.

'Is that it?'

'That's all, sir, thanks for your help.'

'Well ...' Gowrie was clearly troubled. 'Shield ... no, means nothing to me.'

'Then don't worry about it, sir. Have a good evening now.'

At the front door, Clarke turned and smiled at Gowrie. 'We'll let you get back to your wee numbers. Goodbye, sir.'

They heard the door close behind them with a solid click as they walked back down the short gravel path to the driveway.

'I've only got one question, sir: what was all that about?'

'We're dealing with lunatics, Clarke, and Gowrie isn't a lunatic. A zealot maybe, but not a madman. Tell me, what do you call a haircut in an asylum?'

By now Clarke knew the way her boss's mind worked. 'A lunatic fringe?' she guessed.

'*That's* who I want to talk to.'

'You mean the Orange Loyal Brigade?'

Rebus nodded. 'And every one of them will be taking a stroll along Princes Street on Saturday.' He smiled without humour. 'I've always enjoyed a parade.'

16

Saturday was hot and clear, with a slight cooling breeze, just enough to make the day bearable. Shoppers were out on Princes Street in numbers, and the lawns of Princes Street Gardens were as packed as a seaside beach, every bench in full use, a carousel attracting the children. The atmosphere was festive if frayed, with the kids squealing and tiring as their ice-cream cones melted and dropped to the ground, turning instantly into food for the squirrels, pigeons, and panting dogs.

The parade was due to set off from Regent Road at three o'clock, and by two-fifteen the pubs behind Princes Street were emptying their cargo of brolly-toting white-gloved elders, bowler hats fixed onto their sweating heads, faces splotched from alcohol. There was a show of regalia, and a few large banners were being unfurled. Rebus couldn't remember what you called the guy at the front of the march, the one who threw up and caught the heavy ornamental staff. He'd probably known in his youth. The flute players were practising, and the snare drummers adjusted their straps and drank from cans of beer.

People outside the Post Office on Waterloo Place could hear the flutes and drums, and peered along towards Regent Road. That the march was to set off from outside the old Royal High School, mothballed site for a devolved Scottish parliament, added a certain something to the affair.

Rebus had been in a couple of the bars, taking a look at the Brigade members and supporters. They were a varied crew, taking in a few Doc Marten-wearing skinheads (just as Gowrie had predicted) as well as the bowler hats. There were also the dark suit/white shirt/dark tie types, their shoes as polished as their faces. Most of them were drinking like fury, though they didn't seem completely mortal yet. Empty cans were being kicked along Regent Road, or trodden on and left by the edges of the pavement. Rebus wasn't sure why these occasions always carried with them the air of threat, of barely suppressed violence, even before they started. Extra police had been drafted in, and were readying to stop traffic from coming down onto Princes Street. Metal-grilled barriers waited by the side of the road, as did the small groups of protesters, and the smaller group of protesters who were protesting against the protesters. Rebus wondered, not for the first time, which maniac on the Council had pushed through the okay for the parade.

The marching season of course had finished, the main parades being on and around the 12th of July, date of the Battle of the Boyne. Even then the biggest marches were in Glasgow. What was the point of this present parade? To stir things up, of course, to make a noise. To be noticed. The big drum, the *lambeg*, was being hammered now. There was competition from a few bagpipe buskers near Waverley Station, but they'd be silenced by the time the parade reached them.

Rebus wandered freely among the marchers as they drank and joked with each other and adjusted their uniforms. A Union Jack was unfurled, then ordered to be rolled up again, bearing as it did the initials of the British National Party. There didn't seem to be any collecting tins or buckets, the police having pressed for a quick march with as little interaction with the public as possible. Rebus knew this because he'd asked Farmer Watson, and the Farmer had confirmed that it would be so.

'Here's tae King Billy!' A can was raised. 'God bless the Queen and King William of Orange!'

'Well said, son.'

The bowler hats said little, standing with the tips of their umbrellas touching the ground, hands resting lightly on the curved wooden handles. It was easy to dismiss these unsmiling men too lightly. But God help you if you started an argument with one of them.

'Why dae yis hate Catholics?' a pedestrian yelled.

'We don't!' somebody yelled back, but she was already bustling away with her shopping bags. There were smiles, but she'd made her point. Rebus watched her go.

'Hey, Gavin, how long now?'

'Five minutes, just relax.'

Rebus looked towards the man who had just spoken, the man who was probably called Gavin MacMurray and therefore in charge. He seemed to have appeared from nowhere. Rebus had read the file on Gavin MacMurray: two arrests for breach of the peace and actual bodily harm, but a lot more information to his name than that. Rebus knew his age (38), that he was married and lived in Currie, and that he ran his own garage. He knew Inland Revenue had no complaints against him, that he drove a red Mercedes Benz (though he made his money from more prosaic Fords, Renaults and the like), and that his teenage son had been in trouble for fighting, with two arrests after pitched battles outside Rangers matches and one arrest after an incident on the train home from Glasgow.

So Rebus assumed the teenager standing close beside Gavin Mac-Murray must be the son, Jamesie. Jamesie had pretensions of all obvious kinds. He wore sunglasses and a tough look, seeing himself as his father's lieutenant. His legs were apart, shoulders back. Rebus had never seen anyone itching so badly for action of some kind. He had his father's low square jaw, the same black hair cut short at the front. But while Gavin MacMurray was dressed in chainstore anonymity, Jamesie wanted people to look at him. Biker boots, tight black jeans, white t-shirt and black leather jacket. He wore a red bandana around his right wrist, a studded leather strap around the left. His hair, long and curling at the back, had been shaved above both ears.

Turning from son to father was like turning from overt to covert strength. Rebus knew which he'd rather tackle. Gavin MacMurray was chewing gum with his front teeth, his head and eyes constantly in movement, checking things, keeping things in check. He kept his hands in his windcheater pockets, and wore silver-framed spectacles which magnified his eyes. There seemed little charisma about him, little of the rouser or orator. He looked chillingly ordinary.

Because he *was* ordinary, they all were, all these semi-inebriated working men and retired men, quiet family types who might belong to the British Legion or their local Ex-Servicemen's Club, who might inhabit the bowling green on summer evenings and go with their families on holiday to Spain or Florida or Largs. It was only when you saw them in groups like this that you caught a whiff of something else. Alone, they had nothing but a nagging complaint; together, they had a voice: the sound of the *lambeg*, dense as a heartbeat; the insistent flutes; the march. They always fascinated Rebus. He couldn't help it. It was in his blood. He'd marched in his youth. He'd done a lot of things back then.

There was a final gathering of lines, MacMurray readying his troops. A word with the policeman in charge, a conversation by two-way radio, then a nod from MacMurray. The opening fat-fry of snare drums, the *lambeg* pumping away, and then the flutes. They marched on the spot for a few moments, then moved off towards Princes Street, where traffic had been stopped for them, where the Castle glared down on them, where a lot of people but by no means everyone paused to watch.

A few months back, a pro-republican march had been banned from this route. That was why the protesters were particularly loud in their jeers, thumbs held down. Some of them were chanting Na-Zis, Na-Zis, and then being told to shut up by uniformed police. There would be a few arrests, there always were. You hadn't had a good day out at a march unless there'd been at least the threat of arrest.

Rebus followed the march from the pavement, sticking to the Gardens side, which was quieter. A few more marchers had joined in, but it was still small beer, hardly worth the bother. He was beginning to wonder what he'd thought would happen. His eyes moved back through the procession from the tosser at the front, busy with his muckle stick, through the flutes and drums, past bowler hats and suits, to the younger marchers and stragglers. A few pre-teenage kids had joined in on the edges, loving every minute. Jamesie, right near the back, told them in no uncertain terms that they should leave, but they didn't listen to him.

'Tough' always was a relative term.

But now one of the stragglers clutched Jamesie's arm and they shared a few words, both of them grinning. The straggler was wearing sunglasses with mirrored lenses, and a denim jacket with no shirt beneath.

'Hello,' said Rebus quietly. He watched Jamesie and Davey Soutar have their conversation, saw Jamesie pat Davey on the shoulder before Davey moved away again, falling back until he left the procession altogether, squeezing between two of the temporary barriers and vanishing into the crowd.

Jamesie seemed to relax a bit after this. His walk became looser, less of an act, and he swung his arms in time to the music. He seemed to be realising that it was a bright summer's day, and at last peeled off his leather jacket, slinging it over one shoulder, showing off his arm muscles and several tattoos. Rebus walked a bit faster, keeping close to the edge of the pavement. One of the tattoos was professional, and showed the ornately overlaid letters RFC: Rangers Football Club. But there was also the maroon emblem of Heart of Midlothian FC, so obviously Jamesie liked to play safe. Then there was a kilted, busby-wearing piper, and further down his arm towards the leather wristband a much more amateur job, the usual shaky greeny-blue ink.

The letters SaS.

Rebus blinked. It was almost too far away for him to be sure. Almost. But he *was* sure. And suddenly he didn't want to talk to Gavin Mac-Murray any more. He wanted a word with his son.

He stopped on the pavement, letting the march pull away from him. He knew where they were heading. A left turn into Lothian Road, passing the windows of the Caledonian Hotel. Something for the rich tourists to get a picture of. Then another left into King's Stables Road, stopping short of the Grassmarket. Afterwards, they'd probably head down into the Grassmarket itself for the post-march analysis and a few more beers. The Grassmarket being trendy these days, there'd be a lot of Fringe drinkers there too. A fine cocktail of cultures for a Saturday afternoon.

He followed the trail to one of the rougher pubs on the Cowgate, just the other side of Candlemaker Row from the Grassmarket. At one time, they'd hung miscreants from the gallows in the Grassmarket. It was a cheerier prospect these days, though you wouldn't necessarily know it from a visit to the Merchant's Bar where, at ten p.m. each night, the pint glasses were switched for flimsy plastic imposters, relieving the bar of ready weapons. It was that kind of place.

Inside, the bar was airless, a drinkers' fug of smoke and television heat. You didn't come here for a good time, you came out of necessity. The regulars were like dragons, each mouthful cooling the fire inside them. As he entered the bar, he saw no one he recognised, not even the barman. The barman was a new face, just out of his teens. He poured pints with an affected disdain, and took the money like it was a bribe. From the sounds of atonal song, Rebus knew the marchers were upstairs, probably emptying the place.

Rebus took his pint – still in a glass glass – and headed up to the dance hall. Sure enough, the marchers were about all there was. They'd shed jackets, ties, and inhibitions, and were milling around, singing to off-key flutes and downing pints and shorts. Getting the drink in had become a logistical nightmare, and more marchers were coming in all the time.

Rebus took a deep breath, carved a smile into his face, and waded in.

'Magic, lads.'

'Aye, ta, pal.'

'Nae bother, eh?'

'Aye, nae bother right enough.'

'All right there, lads?'

'Fine, aye. Magic.'

Gavin MacMurray hadn't arrived yet. Maybe he was off elsewhere with his generals. But his son was on the stage pretending he held a microphone stand and a crowd's attention. Another lad clambered onto the stage and played an invisible guitar, still managing to hold his pint glass. Lager splashed over his jeans, but he didn't notice. That was professionalism for you.

Rebus watched with the smile still on his face. Eventually they gave up, as he'd known they would, there being no audience, and leapt down from the stage. Jamesie landed just in front of Rebus. Rebus held his arms wide.

'Whoah there! That was brilliant.'

Jamesie grinned. 'Aye, ta.' Rebus slapped him on the shoulder.

'Get you another?'

'I think I'm all right, ta.'

'Fair enough.' Rebus looked around, then leant close to Jamesie's ear. 'I see you're one of us.' He winked.

'Eh?'

The tattoo had been covered by the leather jacket, but Rebus nodded towards it. 'The Shield,' he said slyly. Then he nodded again, catching Jamesie's eye, and moved away. He went back downstairs and ordered two pints. The bar was busy and noisy, both TV and jukebox blaring, a couple of arguments rising above even these. Half a minute later, Jamesie was standing beside him. The boy wasn't very bright, and Rebus weighed up how much he could get away with.

'How do you know?' Jamesie asked.

'There's not much I don't know, son.'

'But I don't know you.'

Rebus smiled into his drink. 'Best keep it that way.'

'Then how come you know me?'

Rebus turned towards him. 'I just do.' Jamesie looked around him, licking his lips. Rebus handed him one of the pints. 'Here, get this down you.'

'Ta.' He lowered his voice. 'You're in The Shield?'

'What makes you think that?' Now Jamesie smiled. 'How's Davey, by the way?'

'Davey?'

'Davey Soutar,' said Rebus. 'You two know each other, don't you?'

'I know Davey.' He blinked. 'Christ, you *are* in The Shield. Hang on, did I see you at the parade?'

'I bloody hope so.'

Now Jamesie nodded slowly. 'I thought I saw you.'

'You're a sharp lad, Jamesie. There's a bit of your dad in you.'

Jamesie started at this. 'He'll be here in five minutes. You don't want him to see us . . .'

'You're right. He doesn't know about The Shield then?'

'Of course not.' Jamesie looked slighted.

'Only sometimes the lads tell their dads.'

'Not me.'

Rebus nodded. 'You're a good one, Jamesie. We've got our eyes on you.'

'Really?'

'Absolutely.' Rebus supped from his pint. 'Shame about Billy.'

Jamesie became a statue, the glass inches from his lips. He recovered with effort. 'Pardon?'

'Good lad, say nothing.' Rebus took another sup. 'Good parade, wasn't it?'

'Oh aye, the best.'

'Ever been to Belfast?'

Jamesie looked like he was having trouble keeping up with the conversation. Rebus hoped he was. 'Naw,' he said at last.

'I was there a few days ago, Jamesie. It's a proud city, a lot of good people there, *our* people.' Rebus was wondering, how long can I keep this up? A couple of teenagers, probably a year or two beneath the legal drinking age, had already come to the stairs looking for Jamesie to join them.

'True,' Jamesie said.

'We can't let them down.'

'Absolutely not.'

'Remember Billy Cunningham.'

Jamesie put down his glass. 'Is this . . .' his voice had become a little less confident, 'is this a . . . some sort of warning?'

Rebus patted the young man's arm. 'No, no, you're all right, Jamesie. It's just that the polis are sniffing around.' It was amazing where a bit of confident bull's keech could get you.

'I'm no squealer,' said Jamesie.

The way he said it, Rebus knew. 'Not like Billy?'

'Definitely not.'

Rebus was nodding to himself when the doors burst open and Gavin MacMurray swaggered in, a couple of his generals squeezing through the doorway in his wake. Rebus became just another punter at the bar, as MacMurray slung a heavy arm around his son's neck.

'Awright, Jamesie boy?'

'Fine, Dad. My shout.'

'Three export then. Bring them up back, aye?'

'No bother, Dad.'

Jamesie watched the three men walk to the stairs. He turned towards his confidant, but John Rebus had already left the bar.

17

Every chain, no matter how strong, has one link weaker than the rest. Rebus had hopes of Jamesie MacMurray, as he walked out of the Merchant's. He was halfway to his car when he saw Caro Rattray walking towards him.

'You were going to call me,' she said.

'Work's been a bit hectic.'

She looked back at the pub. 'Call that work, do you?'

He smiled. 'Do you live here?'

'On the Canongate. I've just been walking my dog.'

'Your dog?' There was no sign of a leash, never mind the animal. She shrugged.

'I don't actually like dogs, I just like the idea of walking them. So I have an imaginary dog.'

'What's he called?'

'Sandy.'

Rebus looked down at her feet. 'Good boy, Sandy.'

'Actually, Sandy's a girl.'

'Hard to tell at this distance.'

'And I don't talk to her.' She smiled. 'I'm not mad, you know.'

'Right, you just go walking with a pretend dog. So what are you and Sandy doing now?'

'Going home and having a drink. Fancy joining us?'

Rebus thought about it. 'Sure,' he said. 'Drive or walk?'

'Let's walk,' said Caroline Rattray. 'I don't want Sandy shedding on your seats.'

She lived in a nicely furnished flat, tidy but not obsessive. There was a grandfather clock in the hall, a family heirloom. Her surname was engraved on the brass face.

A dividing wall had been taken away so that the living room had windows to front and back. A book lay open on the sofa, next to a half-finished box of shortbread. Solitary pleasures, thought Rebus.

'You're not married?' he said.

'God, no.'

'Boyfriend?'

She smiled again. 'Funny word that, isn't it? Especially when you get to my age. I mean, a boyfriend should be in his teens or twenties.'

'Gentleman friend then,' he persisted.

'Doesn't have the same connotations though, does it?' Rebus sighed. 'I know, I know,' she said, 'never argue with an advocate.'

Rebus looked out of the back window onto a drying-green. Overhead, the few clouds were basking in the space they had. 'Sandy's digging up your flower bed.'

'What do you want to drink?'

'Tea, please.'

'Sure? I've only got decaf.'

'That's perfect.' He meant it. While she made noises in the kitchen, he walked through the living room. Dining-table and chairs and wall units at the back, sofa, chairs, bookcases towards the front. It was a nice room. From the small front window, he looked down onto slow-walking tourists and a shop selling tartan teddy-bears.

'This is a nice part of town,' he said, not really meaning it.

'Are you kidding? Ever tried parking round here in the summer?'

'I never try parking anywhere in the summer.'

He moved away from the window. A flute and some sheet music sat on a spindly music-stand in one corner. On a unit were small framed photos of the usual gap-toothed kids and kind-looking old people.

'Family,' she said, coming back into the room. She lit a cigarette, took two deep puffs on it, then stubbed it into an ashtray, exhaling and wafting the smoke away with her hand. 'I hate smoking indoors,' she explained.

'Then why do it?'

'I smoke when I'm nervous.' She smiled slyly and returned to the kitchen, Rebus following. The aroma of the cigarette mingled with the richer aroma of the perfume she wore. Had she just applied some? It hadn't been this strong before.

The kitchen was small, functional. The whole flat had the look of recent but not radical redecoration.

'Milk?'

'Please. No sugar.' Their conversation, he realised, was assuming a studied banality.

The kettle clicked off. 'Can you take the mugs?'

She had already poured a splash of milk into either plain yellow mug. There wasn't much room at all in the kitchen, something Rebus realised as he went to pick up the mugs. He was right beside her as she stirred the teabags in the pot. Her head was bent down, affording a view of the long black hairs curling from her nape, and the nape of her neck itself. She half turned her face towards him, smiling, her eyes finally finding his. Then she moved her body around too. Rebus kissed her forehead first, then her cheek. She had closed her eyes. He burrowed his face in her neck, inhaling deeply: shampoo and perfume and skin. He kissed her again, then came up for air. Caroline opened her eyes slowly.

'Well now,' she said.

He felt suddenly as though he'd been flung down a tunnel, watching the circle of light at the entrance shrink to a full stop. He tried desperately to think of something to say. There was perfume in his lungs.

'Well now,' she repeated. What did that mean? Was she pleased, shocked, bemused? She turned back to the teapot and put its lid on.

'I better go,' Rebus said. She became very still. He couldn't see her face, not enough of it. 'Hadn't I?'

'I've no commitments, John.' Her hands were resting lightly on the work surface, either side of the pot. 'What about you?'

He knew what she meant; she meant Patience. 'There's someone,' he said.

'I know, Dr Curt told me.'

'I'm sorry, Caroline, I shouldn't have done that.'

'What?' She turned to him.

'Kissed you.'

'I didn't mind.' She gave him her smile again. 'I'll never drink a whole pot of tea on my own.'

He nodded, realising he was still holding the mugs. 'I'll take them through.'

He walked out of the kitchen on unsteady legs, his heart shimmying. He'd kissed her. Why had he kissed her? He hadn't meant to. But it had happened. It was real now. The photographs smiled at him as he put the mugs down on a small table which already had coffee-rings on it. What was she doing in the kitchen? He stared at the doorway, willing her to come, willing her not to come.

She came. The teapot was on a tray now, a tea-cosy in the shape of a King Charles spaniel keeping in the heat.

'Is Sandy a King Charles?'

'Some days. How strong do you like it?'

'As it comes.'

She smiled again and poured, handed him a mug, then took one herself and sat in her chair. She didn't look very comfortable. Rebus sat opposite her on the sofa, not resting against the back of it but leaning forward.

'There's some shortbread,' she said.

'No, thanks.'

'So,' she said, 'any progress on Nemo?'

'I think so.' This was good; they were talking. 'SaS is a loyalist support group. They're buying and shipping arms.'

'And the victim in Mary King's Close, he was killed by paramilitaries, nothing to do with his father?'

Rebus shrugged again. 'There's been another murder. It could be linked.'

'That man they found in the cellar?' Rebus nodded. 'Nobody told me they were connected.'

'It's being kept a bit quiet. He was working undercover.'

'How was he found?'

'The flat was having some building work done. One of the labourers opened the cellar door.'

'That's a coincidence.'

'What?'

'There was building work going on in Mary King's Close too.'

'Not the same firm.'

'You've checked?'

Rebus frowned. 'Not me personally, but yes, we've checked.'

'Oh well.' She took another cigarette from her packet and made to light it, but stopped herself. She took the cigarette from her mouth and examined it. 'John,' she said, 'if you'd like to, we can make love any time you want.'

There were none of Cafferty's men waiting for him outside Patience's flat, nothing to delay him. He'd been hoping for the Weasel. Right now, he felt ready for some hands-on with the Weasel.

But it wasn't Cafferty's man he was angry with.

Inside, the long hallway was cool and dark, the only light coming from three small panes of glass above the front door. 'Patience?' he called, hoping she'd be out. Her car was outside, but that didn't mean anything. He wanted to run a bath, steep in it. He turned on both taps, then went to the bedroom, picked up the phone, and rang Brian Holmes at home. Holmes's partner Nell picked up the call.

'It's John Rebus,' he told her. She said nothing, just put the receiver to one side and went off to fetch Brian. There was no love lost these days between Rebus and Nell Stapleton, something Holmes himself realised but couldn't bring himself to query . . .

'Yes, sir?'

'Brian, those two building companies.'

'Mary King's Close and St Stephen Street?'

'How thoroughly have we checked them?'

'Pretty well.'

'And we've cross-referenced? There's no connection between them.'

'No, why?'

'Can you check them again yourself?'

'I can.'

'Humour me then. Do it Monday.'

'Anything in particular I should be looking for?'

'No.' He paused. 'Yes, start with casual labour.'

'I thought you wanted Siobhan and me to go see Murdock?'

'I did. I'll take your place. Have a nice evening.' Rebus put down the phone and went back to the bathroom. There was good pressure in the pipes, and the bath was practically full already. He turned off the cold and reduced the hot to a trickle. The kitchen was through the living room, and he fancied some milk from the fridge.

Patience was in the kitchen, chopping vegetables.

'I didn't know you were here,' Rebus said.

'I live here, remember? This is my flat.'

'Yes, I know.' She was angry with him. He opened the fridge door, took out the milk, and managed to pass her without touching her. He put the milk on the breakfast table and got a glass from the draining board. 'What are you cooking?'

'Why the interest? You never eat here.'

'Patience . . .'

She came to the sink, scraping peelings into a plastic container. It would all go onto her compost heap. She turned to him. 'Running a bath?'

'Yes.'

'It's Giorgio, isn't it?'

'Sorry?'

'That perfume.' She leaned close, sniffed his shirt. 'Giorgio of Beverly Hills.'

'Patience . . .'

'You'll have to tell me about her one of these days.'

'You think I'm seeing someone?'

She threw the small sharp kitchen knife at the sink and ran from the room. Rebus stood there, listening until he heard the front door slam. He poured the milk down the sink.

He took back the videos – still unwatched – then went for a drive. The Dell Bar sat on an unlovely stretch of main road outside the Gar-B. It didn't get much passing trade, but there was a line of cars parked outside. Rebus slowed as he drove past. He could go in, but what good would it do? Then he saw something, and pulled his car up kerbside. Next to him a van was parked, with fly-posters pasted on its sides. The posters advertised the play which was soon to go on in the Gar-B gang hut. The theatre group was called Active Resistance. Some of them must be drinking inside. A few vehicles further on was the car he wanted. He bent down at the driver's side window. Ken Smylie tried to ignore him, then wound the window down angrily.

'What are you doing here?' he asked.

'I was about to ask the same,' said Rebus.

Smylie nodded towards the Dell. He had his hands on the steering-wheel. They weren't just resting on it, they were squeezing it. 'Maybe there's someone drinking in there killed Calumn.'

'Maybe there is,' Rebus said quietly: he didn't fancy being Smylie's punchbag. 'What are you going to do about it?'

Smylie stared at him. 'I'm going to sit here.'

'And then what? Break the neck of every man who comes out? You know the score, Ken.'

'Leave me alone.'

'Look, Ken –' Rebus broke off as the Dell's door swung open and two punters sauntered out, cigarettes in mouths, sharing some joke between them. 'Look,' he said, 'I know how you feel. I've got a brother too. But this isn't doing any good.'

'Just go away.'

Rebus sighed, straightened up. 'Fair enough then. But if there's any hassle, radio for assistance. Just do that for me, okay?'

Smylie almost smiled. 'There won't be any trouble, believe me.'

Rebus did, the way he believed TV advertising and weather reports. He walked back towards his car. The two drinkers were getting into their Vauxhall. As the passenger yanked open his door, it nearly caught Rebus.

The man didn't bother to apologise. He gave Rebus a look like it was Rebus's fault, then got into his seat.

Rebus had seen the man before. He was about five-ten, broad in the chest, wearing jeans and black t-shirt and a denim jacket. He had a face shiny with drink, sweat on his forehead and in his wavy brown hair. But it wasn't until Rebus was back in his own car and halfway home that he put a name to the face.

The man Yates had told him about, shown him a photo of, the ex-UVF man they'd lost in Glasgow. Alan Fowler. Drinking in the Gar-B like he owned the place.

Maybe he did at that.

Rebus retraced his route, cruising some of the narrow streets, checking parked cars. But he'd lost the Vauxhall. And Ken Smylie's car was no longer outside the Dell.

18

Monday morning at St Leonard's, Chief Inspector Lauderdale was having to explain a joke he'd just made.

'See, the squid's so meek, Hans can't bring himself to thump it either.' He caught sight of Rebus walking into the Murder Room. 'The prodigal returns! Tell us, what's it like working with the glamour boys?'

'It's all right,' said Rebus. 'I've already had one return flight out of them.'

Lauderdale clearly had not been expecting this . . .

'So it's true then,' he said, recovering well, 'they're all high flyers over at SCS.' He captured a few laughs for his trouble. Rebus didn't mind being the butt. He knew the way it was. In a murder inquiry, you worked as a team. Lauderdale, as team manager, had the job of boosting morale, keeping things lively. Rebus wasn't part of the team, not exactly, so he was open to the occasional low tackle with studs showing.

He went to his desk, which more than ever resembled a rubbish tip, and tried to see if any messages had been left for him. He had spent the rest of his weekend, when not avoiding Patience, trying to track down Abernethy or anyone else in Special Branch who'd talk to him. Rebus had left message after message, so far without success.

DI Flower, teeth showing, advanced on Rebus's desk.

'We've got a confession,' he said, 'to the stabbing in St Stephen Street. Want to talk to the man?'

Rebus was wary. 'Who is it?'

'Unstable from Dunstable. He's off his trolley this time, keeps asking for a curry and talking about cars. I told him he'd have to settle for a bridie and his bus fare.'

'You're all heart, Flower.' Rebus saw that Siobhan Clarke had finished getting ready. 'Excuse me.'

'Ready, sir?' Clarke asked.

'Plenty ready. Let's go before Lauderdale or Flower can think of another gag at my expense. Not that *their* jokes ever cost me more than small change.'

They took Clarke's cherry-red Renault 5, following bus after bus west through the slow streets until they could take a faster route by way of The Grange, passing the turn-off to Arch Gowrie's residence.

'And you said The Grange didn't lead anywhere,' Clarke said, powering through the gears. True enough, it was the quickest route between St Leonard's and Morningside. It was just that as a policeman, Rebus had never had much cause to heed Morningside, that genteel backwater where old ladies in white face powder, like something out of a Restoration play, sat in tea shops and pondered aloud their next choice from the cake-stand.

Morningside wasn't exclusive the way Grange was. There were students in Morningside, living at the top of roadside tenements, and people on the dole, in rented flats housing too many bodies, keeping the rent down. But when you thought of Morningside you thought of old ladies and that peculiar pronunciation they had, like they'd all understudied Maggie Smith in *The Prime of Miss Jean Brodie*. The Glaswegians joked about it. They said Morningside people thought sex was what the coal came in. Rebus doubted there were coal fires in Morningside any longer, though there would certainly be some wood-burning stoves, brought in by the young professionals who probably outnumbered the old ladies these days, though they weren't nearly so conspicuous.

It was to serve these young professionals, as well as to cater for local businesses, that a thriving little computer shop had opened near the corner of Comiston Road and Morningside Drive.

'Can I help you?' the male assistant asked, not looking up from his keyboard.

'Is Millie around?' Rebus asked.

'Through the arch.'

'Thanks.'

There was a single step up to the arch, through which was another part of the shop, specialising in contract work and business packages. Rebus almost didn't recognise Millie, though there was no one else there. She was seated at a terminal, thinking about something, tapping her finger against her lips. It took her a second to place Rebus. She hit a key, the screen went blank, and she rose from her seat.

She was dressed in an immaculate combination of brilliant white skirt and bright yellow blouse, with a single string of crystals around her neck.

'I just can't shake you lot off, can I?'

She did not sound unhappy. Indeed, she seemed almost *too* pleased to see them, her smile immense. 'Can I fix you some coffee?'

'Not for me, thanks.'

Millie looked to Siobhan Clarke, who shook her head. 'Mind if I make some for myself?' She went to the arch. 'Steve? Cuppa?'

'Wouldn't say no.'

She came back. 'No, but he might say please, just once.' There was a cubby-hole at the back of the shop, leading to a toilet cubicle. In the cubbyhole sat a percolator, a packet of ground coffee, and several grim-looking mugs. Millie got to work. While she was occupied, Rebus asked his first question.

'Billy's mum tells us you were good enough to pack up all his stuff.'

'It's still sitting in his room, three bin liners. Not a lot to show for a life, is it?'

'What about his motorbike?'

She smiled. 'That thing. You could hardly call it a bike. A friend of his asked if he could have it. Billy's mum said she didn't mind.'

'You liked Billy?'

'I liked him a lot. He was genuine. You never got bullshit with Billy. If he didn't like you, he'd tell you to your face. I hear his dad's some kind of villain.'

'They didn't know one another.'

She slapped the coffee-maker. 'This thing takes ages. Is that what you want to ask me about, Billy's dad?'

'Just a few general questions. Before he died, did Billy seem worried about anything?'

'I've been asked already, more than once.' She looked at Clarke. 'You first, and then that big bastard with the voice like something caught in a mousetrap.' Rebus smiled: it was a fair description of Ken Smylie. 'Billy was just the same as ever, that's all I can say.'

'Did he get along okay with Mr Murdock?'

'What sort of question is that? Christ, you're scraping the barrel if you think Murdock would've done anything to Billy.'

'You know what it's like in mixed flats though, where there's a couple plus one, jealousy can be a problem.'

An electric buzzer announced the arrival of a customer. They could hear Steve talking to someone.

'We've got to ask, Millie,' Clarke said soothingly.

'No you don't. It's just that you *like* asking!'

So much for the good mood. Even Steve and the customer seemed to be listening. The coffee machine started dolloping boiled water into the filter.

'Look,' said Rebus, 'let's calm down, eh? If you like, we can come back. We could come to the flat –'

'It never ends, does it? What is this? Trying to get a confession out of me?' She clasped her hands together. 'Yes, I killed him. It was me.'

She held her hands out, wrists prominent.

'I've forgotten my cuffs,' Rebus said, smiling. Millie looked to Siobhan Clarke, who shrugged.

'Great, I can't even get myself arrested.' She sloshed coffee into a mug. 'And I thought it was the easiest thing in the world.'

'Are we really so bad, Millie?'

She smiled, looked down at her mug. 'I suppose not, sorry about that.'

'You're under a lot of strain,' said Siobhan Clarke, 'we appreciate that. Maybe if we sit down, eh?'

So they sat at Millie's desk, like customers and assistant. Clarke, who liked computers, had actually picked up a couple of brochures.

'That's got a twenty-five megahertz microprocessor,' Millie said, pointing to one of the brochures.

'What size memory?'

'Four meg RAM, I think, but you can select a hard disk up to one-sixty.'

'Does this one have a 486 chip?'

Good girl, thought Rebus. Clarke was calming Millie down, taking her mind off both Billy Cunningham and her recent outburst. Steve brought the customer through to show him a certain screen. He gave the three of them a look full of curiosity.

'Sorry, Steve,' said Millie, 'forgot your coffee.' Her smile would not have passed a polygraph.

Rebus waited till Steve and the customer had retreated. 'Did Billy ever bring friends back to the flat?'

'I've given you a list.'

Rebus nodded. 'Nobody else you've thought of since?'

'No.'

'Can I try you with a couple of names? Davey Soutar and Jamesie MacMurray.'

'Last names don't mean much in our flat. Davey and Jamesie ... I don't think so.'

Rebus willed her to look at him. She did so, then looked away again quickly. You're lying, he thought.

They left the shop ten minutes later. Clarke looked up and down the pavement. 'Want to go see Murdock now?'

'I don't think so. What do you suppose it was she didn't want us to see?'

'Sorry?'

'You look up, see the police coming towards you, why do you blank your computer screen pronto and then come flying off your seat all bounce and flounce?'

'You think there was something on the computer she didn't want us to see?'

'I thought I just said that,' said Rebus. He got into the Renault's passenger seat and waited for Clarke. 'Jamesie MacMurray knows about The Shield. They killed Billy.'

'So why aren't we pulling him in?'

'We've nothing on him, nothing that would stick. That's not the way to work it.'

She looked at him. 'Too mundane?'

He shook his head. 'Like a golf course, too full of holes. We need to get him scared.'

She thought about this. 'Why did they kill Billy?'

'I think he was about to talk, maybe he'd threatened to come to us.'

'Could he be that stupid?'

'Maybe he had insurance, something he thought would save his skin.'

Siobhan Clarke looked at him. 'It didn't work,' she said.

Back at St Leonard's, there was a message for him to call Kilpatrick.

'Some magazine,' Kilpatrick said, 'is about to run with a story about Calumn Smylie's murder, specifically that he was working undercover at the time.'

'How did they get hold of that?'

'Maybe someone talked, maybe they just burrowed deep enough. Whatever, a certain local reporter has made no friends for herself.'

'Not Mairie Henderson?'

'That's the name. You know her, don't you?'

'Not particularly,' Rebus lied. He knew Kilpatrick was fishing. If someone in the notoriously tight-lipped SCS was blabbing, who better to point the finger at than the new boy?

He phoned the news desk while Siobhan fetched them coffee. 'Mairie Henderson, please. What? Since when? Right, thanks.' He put the phone down. 'She's resigned,' he said, not quite believing it. 'Since last week. She's gone freelance apparently.'

'Good for her,' said Siobhan, handing over a cup. But Rebus wasn't so sure. He called Mairie's home number, but got her answering machine. Its message was succinct:

'I'm busy with an assignment, so I can't promise a quick reply unless you're offering work. If you *are* offering work, leave your number. You can see how dedicated I am. Here comes the beep.'

Rebus waited for it. 'Mairie, it's John Rebus. Here are three numbers you can get me on.' He gave her St Leonard's, Fettes, and Patience's flat, not feeling entirely confident about this last, wondering if any message from a woman would reach him with Patience on the intercept.

Then he made an internal call to the station's liaison officer.

'Have you seen Mairie Henderson around?'

'Not for a wee while. The paper seems to have switched her for someone else, a right dozy wee nyaff.'

'Thanks.'

Rebus thought about the last time he'd seen her, in the corridor after Lauderdale's conference. She hadn't mentioned any story, or any plan of going freelance. He made one more call, external this time. It was to DCI Kilpatrick.

'What is it, John?'

'That magazine, sir, the one doing the story about Calumn Smylie, what's it called?'

'It's some London rag . . .' There were sounds of papers being shuffled. 'Yes, here it is. *Snoop.*'

'*Snoop?*' Rebus looked to Siobhan Clarke, who nodded, signalling she'd heard of it. 'Right, thank you, sir.' He put the receiver down before Kilpatrick could ask any questions.

'Want me to phone them and ask?'

Rebus nodded. He saw Brian Holmes come into the room. 'Just the man,' he said. Holmes saw them and wiped imaginary sweat from his brow.

'So,' said Rebus, 'what did you get from the builders?'

'Everything but an estimate for repointing my house.' He took out his notebook. 'Where do you want me to start?'

19

Davey Soutar had agreed to meet Rebus in the community hall.

On his way to the Gar-B, Rebus tried not to think about Soutar. He thought instead about building firms. All Brian Holmes had been able to tell him was that the two firms were no cowboys, and weren't admitting to use of casual, untaxed labour. Siobhan Clarke's call to the office of *Snoop* magazine had been more productive. Mairie Henderson's piece, which they intended publishing in their next issue, had not been commissioned specially. It was part of a larger story she was working on for an American magazine. Why, Rebus wondered, would an American magazine be interested in the death of an Edinburgh copper? He thought he had a pretty good idea.

He drove into the Gar-B car park, bumped his car up onto the grass, and headed slowly past the garages towards the community hall. The theatre group hadn't bothered with the car park either. Maybe someone had had a go at their van. It was now parked close by the hall's front doors. Rebus parked next to it.

'It's the filth,' someone said. There were half a dozen teenagers on the roof of the building, staring down at him. And more of them sitting and standing around the doors. Davey Soutar had not come alone.

They let Rebus past. It was like walking through hate. Inside the hall, there was an argument going on.

'I never touched it!'

'It was there a minute ago.'

'You calling me a liar, pal?'

Three men, who'd been constructing a set on the stage, had stopped to watch. Davey Soutar was talking with another man. They were standing close, faces inches apart. Clenched fists and puffed-out chests.

'Is there a problem?' Rebus said.

Peter Cave, who'd been sitting with head in hands, now stood up.

'No problem,' he said lightly.

The third man thought there was. 'The wee bastard,' he said, meaning Davey Soutar, 'just lifted a packet of fags.'

Soutar looked ready to hit something. It was interesting that he didn't hit his accuser. Rebus didn't know what he'd been expecting from the theatre company. He certainly hadn't been expecting this. The accuser was tall and wiry with long greasy hair and several days' growth of beard. He didn't look in the least scared of Soutar, whose reputation must surely have preceded him. Nor did the workers on the stage look unwilling to enter any fray. He reached into his pocket and brought out a fresh pack of twenty, which he handed to Davey Soutar.

'Here,' he said, 'take these, and give the gentleman back his ciggies.'

Soutar turned on him like a zoo leopard, not happy with its cage. 'I don't need your . . .' The roar faded. He looked at the faces around him. Then he laughed, a hysterical giggling laugh. He slapped his bare chest and shook his head, then took the cigarettes from Rebus and tossed another pack onto the stage.

Rebus turned to the accuser. 'What's your name?'

'Jim Hay.' The accent was west coast.

'Well, Jim, why don't you take those cigarettes outside, have a ten-minute break?'

Jim Hay looked ready to protest, but then thought better of it. He gestured to his crew and they followed him outside. Rebus could hear them getting into the van. He turned his attention to Davey Soutar and Peter Cave.

'I'm surprised you came,' said Soutar, lighting up.

'I'm full of surprises, me.'

'Only, last time I saw you here, you were heading for the hills. You owe Peter an apology, by the way.' Soutar had changed completely. He looked like he was enjoying himself, like he hadn't lost his temper in weeks.

'I don't think that's strictly necessary,' Peter Cave said into the silence.

'Apology accepted,' said Rebus. He dragged over a chair and sat down. Soutar decided this was a good idea. He found a chair for himself and sat with a hard man's slump, legs wide apart, hands stuffed into the tight pockets of his denims, cigarette hanging from his lips. Rebus wanted a cigarette, but he wasn't going to ask for one.

'So what's the problem, Inspector?'

Soutar had agreed to a meeting here, but hadn't mentioned Peter Cave would be present. Maybe it was coincidence. Whatever, Rebus didn't mind an audience. Cave looked tired, pale. There was no question who was in charge, who had power over whom.

'I just have a few things to ask, there's no question of charges or anything criminal, all right?' Soutar obliged with a grunt, examining the laces of his basketball boots. He was shirtless again, still wearing the worn denim jacket. It was filthy, and had been decorated with pen drawings and dark-inked words, names mostly. Grease and dirt were erasing most of the messages and symbols, a few of which had already been covered with fresh hieroglyphs in thicker, darker ink. Soutar slid a hand from his pocket and ran it down his chest, rubbing the few fair curling hairs over his breast bone. He was giving Rebus a friendly look, his lips slightly parted. Rebus wanted to smash him in the face.

'I can walk any time I want?' he said to Rebus.

'Any time.'

The chair grated against the floor as Soutar pushed it back and stood up. Then he laughed and sat down again, wriggling to get comfortable, making sure his crotch was visible. 'Ask me a question then,' he said.

'You know the Orange Loyal Brigade?'

'Sure. That was easy, try another.'

But Rebus had turned to Cave. 'Have you heard of it, too?'

'I can't say I –'

'Hey! It's me the questions are for!'

'In a second, Mr Soutar.' Davey Soutar liked that: *Mr* Soutar. Only the dole office and the census taker had ever called him Mr. 'The Orange Loyal Brigade, Mr Cave, is an extreme hardline Protestant group, a small force but an organised one, based in east central Scotland.'

Soutar confirmed this with a nod.

'The Brigade were kicked out of the Orange Lodge for being too extreme. This may give you some measure of them. Do you know what they're committed to, Mr Cave? Maybe Mr Soutar can answer.'

Mr again! Soutar chuckled. 'Hating the Papes,' he said.

'Mr Soutar's right.' Rebus's eyes hadn't moved from Cave's since he'd first turned to him. 'They hate Catholics.'

'Papes,' said Soutar. 'Left-footers, Tigs, bogmen, Paddies.'

'And a few more names beside,' added Rebus. He left a measured pause. 'You're a Roman Catholic, aren't you?' As if he'd forgotten. Cave merely nodded, while Soutar slid his eyes sideways to look at him. Suddenly Rebus turned to Soutar. 'Who's head of the Brigade, Davey?'

'Er . . . Ian Paisley!' He laughed, and got a smile from Rebus.

'No, but really.'

'I haven't a clue.'

'No? You don't know Gavin MacMurray?'

'MacMurray? Is he the one with the garage in Currie?'

'That's him. He's the Supreme Commander of the Orange Loyal Brigade.'

'I'll take your word for it.'

'And his son's the Provost-Marshall. Lad called Jamesie, be a year or two younger than you.'

'Oh aye?'

Rebus shook his head. 'Short term memory loss, that's what a bad diet does.'

'Eh?'

'All the chips and crisps, the booze you put away, not exactly brain food, is it? I know what it's like on estates like the Gar-B, you eat rubbish and you inject yourselves with anything you can get your paws on. Your body'll wither and die, probably before your brain does.'

The conversation had clearly taken an unexpected turn. 'What are you talking about?' Soutar yelled. 'I don't do drugs! I'm as fit as fuck, pal!'

Rebus looked at Soutar's exposed chest. 'Whatever you say, Davey.'

Soutar sprang to his feet, the chair tumbling behind him. He threw off his jacket and stood there, chest inflated, pulling both arms up and in to show the swell of muscle.

'You could punch me in the guts and I wouldn't flinch.'

Rebus could believe it, too. The stomach was flat except for ripples of musculature, looking so solid they might have been sculpted from marble. Soutar relaxed his arms, held them in front of him.

'Look, no tracks. Drugs are for mugs.'

Rebus held up a pacifying hand. 'You've proved your point, Davey.'

Soutar stared at him for a moment longer, then laughed and picked his jacket up off the floor.

'Interesting tattoos, by the way.'

They were the usual homemade jobs in blue ink, with one larger professional one on the right upper arm. It showed the Red Hand of Ulster, with the words No Surrender beneath. Below it the self-inflicted tattoos were just letters and messages: UVF, UDA, FTP, and SaS.

Rebus waited till Soutar had put on his jacket. 'You know Jamesie MacMurray,' he stated.

'Do I?'

'You bumped into him last Saturday when the Brigade was marching on Princes Street. You were there for the march, but you had to leave. However, you said hello to your old friend first. You knew Mr Cave was a Catholic right from the start, didn't you? I mean, he didn't hide the fact?'

Soutar was looking confused. The questions were all over the place, it was hard to keep up.

'Pete was straight with us,' he admitted. He was staying on his feet.

'And that didn't bother you? I mean, you came to his club, bringing your gang with you. And the Catholic gang came along too. What did Jamesie say about that?'

'It's nothing to do with him.'

'You could see it was a good thing though, eh? Meeting the Catholic gang, divvying up the ground between you. It's the way it works in Ulster, that's what you've heard. Who told you? Jamesie? His dad?'

'His *dad*?'

'Or was it The Shield?'

'I never even –' Davey Soutar stopped. He was breathing hard as he pointed at Rebus. 'You're in shite up past the point of breathing.'

'Then I must be standing on your shoulders. Come on, Davey.'

'It's *Mr* Soutar.'

'Mr Soutar then.' Rebus had his hands open, palms up. He was sitting back in his chair, rocking it on its back legs. 'Come on, sit down. It's no big deal. Everybody knows about The Shield, knows you're part of it. Everybody except Mr Cave here.' He turned to Peter Cave. 'Let's just say that The Shield is even more extreme than the Orange Loyal Brigade. The Shield collects money, mostly by violence and extortion, and it sends arms to Northern Ireland.' Soutar was shaking his head.

'You're nothing, you've *got* nothing.'

'But you've got something, Davey. You've got your hate and your anger.' He turned to Cave again. 'See, Mr Cave? You've got to be asking, how come Davey puts up with a committed worker for the Church of Rome, or the Whore of Rome as Davey himself might put it? A question that has to be answered.'

When he looked round, Soutar was on the stage. He pushed over the sets, kicking them, stomping them, then jumped down again and made for the doors. His face was orange with anger.

'Was Billy a friend too, Davey?' That stopped him dead. 'Billy Cunningham, I mean.'

Soutar was on the move.

'Davey! You've forgotten your fags!' But Davey Soutar was out the door and screaming things which were unintelligible. Rebus lit a cigarette for himself.

'That laddie's got too much testosterone for his own good,' he said to Cave.

'Look who's talking.'

Rebus shrugged. 'Just an act, Mr Cave. Method acting, you might say.' He blew out a plume of smoke. Cave was staring at his hands, which were clasped in his lap. 'You need to know what you've gotten into.'

Cave looked up. 'You think I condone sectarian hate?'

'No, my theory's much simpler. I think you get off on violence and young men.'

'You're sick.'

'Then maybe all you are, Mr Cave, is misguided. Get out while you can. A policeman's largesse never lasts.' He walked over to Cave and bent down, speaking quietly. 'They've swallowed you, you're in the pit of the Gar-B's stomach. You can still crawl out, but maybe there's not as much time as you think.' Rebus patted Cave's cheek. It was cold and soft, like chicken from the fridge.

'Look at yourself some time, Rebus. You might find you'd make a bloody good terrorist yourself.'

'Thing is, I'd never be tempted. What about you?'

Cave stood up and walked past him towards the doors. Then he walked through them and kept going. Rebus blew smoke from his nose, then sat on the edge of the stage, finishing the cigarette. Maybe he'd tripped Soutar's fuse too early. If it had come out right, he'd have learned something more about The Shield. At the moment, it was all cables and coiled springs, junctions from which spread different coloured wires. Hard to defuse when you didn't know which wire to attack first.

The doors were opening again, and he looked up. Davey Soutar was standing there. Behind him there were others, more than a dozen of them. Soutar was breathing hard. Rebus glanced at his watch and hoped it was right. There was an Emergency Exit at the other end of the hall, but where did Rebus go from there? Instead, he climbed onto the stage and watched them advance. Soutar wasn't saying anything. The whole procession took place in silence, except for breathing and the shuffle of feet on the floor. They were at the front of the stage now. Rebus picked up a length of wood, part of the broken set. Soutar, his eyes on the wood, began to climb onto the stage.

He stopped when he heard the sirens. He froze for a moment, staring up at Rebus. The policeman was smiling.

'Think I'd come here without my cavalry, Davey?' The sirens were drawing closer. 'Your call, Davey,' Rebus said, managing to sound relaxed. 'If you want another riot, here's your chance.'

But all Davey Soutar did was ease himself back off the stage. He stood there, eyes wide and unblinking, as if sheer will of thought might cause Rebus to implode. A final snarl, and he turned and walked away. They followed him, all of them. Some looked back at Rebus. He tried not to look too relieved, lit another cigarette instead. Soutar was crazy, a force gone mad, but he was strong too. Rebus was just beginning to realise how very strong he was.

He went home exhausted that evening, 'home' by now being a very loose term for Patience's flat.

He was still shaking a bit. When Soutar had left the hall that first time, he'd taken it all out on Rebus's car. There were fresh dents, a smashed headlamp, a chipped windscreen. The actors in the van looked like they'd witnessed a frenzy. Then Rebus had told them about their sets.

He'd thought about the theatre group on his way, under police escort, out of the Gar-B. They'd been parked outside the Dell the night he'd seen the Ulsterman there. He still had their flyer, the one that had doubled as a paper plane.

At St Leonard's, he found them in the Fringe programme, Active Resistance Theatre; active as opposed to passive, Rebus supposed. He placed a couple of calls to Glasgow. Someone would get back to him. The rest of the day was a blur.

As he was locking what was left of his car, he sensed a shape behind him.

'Damn you, weasel-face!'

But he turned to see Caroline Rattray.

'Weasel-face?'

'I thought you were someone else.'

She put her arms round him. 'Well I'm not, I'm me. Remember me? I'm the one who's being trying to phone you for God knows how long. I know you got my messages, because someone in your office told me.'

That would be Ormiston. Or Flower. Or anyone else with a grudge.

'Christ, Caro.' He pulled away from her. 'You must be crazy.'

'For coming here?' She looked around. 'This is where she lives?'

She sounded completely unconcerned. Rebus didn't need this. His head felt like it was splitting open above the eyes. He needed to bathe and to stop thinking, and it would take a great effort to stop him thinking about this case.

'You're tired,' she said. Rebus wasn't listening. He was too busy looking at Patience's parked car, at her gateway, then along the street, willing her not to appear. 'Well, I'm tired too, John.' Her voice was rising. 'But there's always room in the day for a little consideration!'

'Keep your voice down,' he hissed.

'Don't you dare tell me what to do!'

'Christ, Caro ...' He squeezed shut his eyes and she relented for a moment. It was long enough to appraise his physical and psychic state.

'You're exhausted,' she concluded. She smiled and touched his face. 'I'm sorry, John. I just thought you'd been avoiding me.'

'Who'd want to do that, Caro?' Though he was starting to wonder.

'What about a drink?' she said.

'Not tonight.'

'All right,' she said, pouting. A moment ago, she had been all tempest and cannon fire, and now she was a surface as calm as any doldrums could produce. 'Tomorrow?'

'Fine.'

'Eight o'clock then, in the Caly bar.' The Caly being the Caledonian Hotel. Rebus nodded assent.

'Great,' he said.

'See you then.' She leaned into him again, kissing his lips. He drew away as quickly as he could, remembering her perfume. One more waft of that, and Patience would go nuclear.

'See you, Caro.' He watched her get into her car, then walked quickly down the steps to the flat.

The first thing he did was run a bath. He looked at himself in the mirror and got a shock. He was looking at his father. In later years, his father had grown a short grey beard. There was grey in Rebus's stubble too.

'I look like an old man.'

There was a knock at the bathroom door. 'Have you eaten?' Patience called.

'Not yet. Have you?'

'No, shall I stick something in the microwave?'

'Sure, great.' He added foam-bath to the water.

'Pizza?'

'Whatever.' She didn't sound too bad. That was the thing about being a doctor, you saw so much pain every day, it was easy to shrug off the more minor ailments like arguments at home and suspected infidelities. Rebus stripped off his clothes and dumped them in the laundry basket. Patience knocked again.

'By the way, what are you doing tomorrow?'

'You mean tomorrow night?' he called back.

'Yes.'

'Nothing I know of. I might be working . . .'

'You better not be. I've invited the Bremners to dinner.'

'Oh, good,' said Rebus, putting his foot in the water without checking the temperature. The water was scalding. He lifted the foot out again and screamed silently at the mirror.

20

They had breakfast together, talking around things, their conversation that of acquaintances rather then lovers. Neither spoke his or her thoughts. We Scots, Rebus thought, we're not very good at going public. We store up our true feelings like fuel for long winter nights of whisky and recrimination. So little of us ever reaches the surface, it's a wonder we exist at all.

'Another cup?'

'Please, Patience.'

'You'll be here tonight,' she said. 'You won't be working.' It was neither question nor order, not explicitly.

So he tried phoning Caro from Fettes, but now she was the one having messages left for her: one on her answering machine at home, one with a colleague at her office. He couldn't just say, 'I'm not coming', not even to a piece of recording tape. So he'd just asked her to get in touch. Caro Rattray, elegant, apparently available, and mad about him. There *was* something of the mad in her, something vertiginous. You spent time with her and you were standing on a cliff edge. And where was Caro? She was standing right behind you.

When his phone rang, he leapt for it.

'Inspector Rebus?' The voice was male, familiar.

'Speaking.'

'It's Lachlan Murdock.' Lachlan: no wonder he used his last name.

'What can I do for you, Mr Murdock?'

'You saw Millie recently, didn't you?'

'Yes, why?'

'She's gone.'

'Gone where?'

'I don't know. What the hell did you say to her?'

'Are you at your flat?'

'Yes.'

'I'm coming over.'

He went alone, knowing he should take some back-up, but loath to approach anyone. Out of the four – Ormiston, Blackwood, 'Bloody' Claverhouse, Smylie – Smylie would still be his choice, but Smylie was as predictable as the Edinburgh weather, even now turning overcast.

The pavements were still Festival busy, but not for much longer, and as recompense September would be quiet. It was the city's secret month, a retreat from public into private.

As if to reassure him, the cloud swept away again and the sun appeared. He wound down his window, until the bus fumes made him roll it back up again. The back of the bus advertised the local newspaper, which led him to thoughts of Mairie Henderson. He needed to find her, and it wasn't often a policeman thought that about a reporter.

He parked the car as close to Murdock's tenement as he could find a space, pressed the intercom button beside the main door, and got the answering buzz which unlocked the door.

Your feet made the same sound on every tenement stairwell, like sandpaper on a church floor. Murdock had opened the door to his flat. Rebus walked in.

Lachlan Murdock did not look in good fettle. His hair was sprouting in clumps from his head, and he pulled on his beard like it was a fake he'd glued on too well. They were in the living room. Rebus sat down in front of the TV. It was where Millie had been sitting the first time he'd visited. The ashtray was still there, but the sleeping bag had gone. And so had Millie.

'I haven't seen her since yesterday.' Murdock was standing, and showed no sign of sitting down. He walked to the window, looked out, came back to the fireplace. His eyes were everywhere that wasn't Rebus.

'Morning or evening?'

'Morning. I got back last night and she'd packed and left.'

'Packed?'

'Not everything, just a holdall. I thought maybe she'd gone to see a pal, she does that sometimes.'

'Not this time?'

Murdock shook his head. 'I phoned Steve at her work this morning, and he said the police had been to see her yesterday, a young woman and an older man. I thought of you. Steve said she was in a terrible state afterwards, she'd to come home early. What did you say to her?'

'Just a few questions about Billy.'

'Billy.' The dismissive shake of the head told Rebus something.

'She got on better with Billy than you did, Mr Murdock?'

'I didn't dislike the guy.'

'Was there anything between the two of them?'

But Murdock wasn't about to answer that. He paced the room again, flapping his arms as though attempting flight. 'She hasn't been the same since he died.'

'It was upsetting for her.'

'Yes, it was. But to run off...'

'Can I see her room?'

'What?'

Rebus smiled. 'It's what we usually do when someone goes missing.'

Murdock shook his head again. 'She wouldn't want that. What if she comes back, and sees someone's been through her stuff? No, I can't let you do that.' Murdock looked ready for physical resistance if necessary.

'I can't force you,' Rebus said calmly. 'Tell me a bit more about Billy.'

This quietened Murdock. 'Like what?'

'Did he like computers?'

'Billy? He liked video games, so long as they were violent. I don't know, I suppose he was interested in computers.'

'He could work one?'

'Just about. What are you getting at?'

'Just interested. Three people sharing a flat, two of them work with computers, the third doesn't.'

Murdock nodded. 'You're wondering what we had in common. Look around the city, Inspector, you'll see flats full of people who're only there because they need a room or the rent money. In an ideal world, I wouldn't have needed someone in the spare room at all.'

Rebus nodded. 'So what should we do about Miss Docherty?'

'What?'

'You called me, I came, where do we go from here?' Murdock shrugged. 'Normally we'd wait another day or so before listing her missing.' He paused. 'Unless there's reason to suspect foul play.'

Murdock seemed lost in thought, then recovered. 'Let's wait another day then.' He started nodding. 'Maybe I'm overreacting. I just ... when Steve told me ...'

'I'm sure it wasn't anything I said to her,' Rebus lied, getting to his feet. 'Can I have another look at Billy's room while I'm here?'

'It's been gutted.'

'Just to refresh my memory.' Murdock said nothing. 'Thanks,' said Rebus.

The small room had indeed been gutted, the bed stripped of duvet and sheet and pillowcase, though the pillow still lay there. It was stained brown, leaking feathers. The bare mattress was pale blue with similar brown patches. There seemed a little more space in the room, but not much. Still, Rebus doubted Murdock would have any trouble finding a new tenant, not with the student season approaching.

He opened the wardrobe to a clanging of empty wire hangers. There was a fresh sheet of newspaper on the floor. He closed the wardrobe door. Between the corner of the bed and the wardrobe there was a clear patch of carpet. It lay hard up against the skirting-board beneath the still unwashed window. Rebus crouched down and tugged at the carpet's edge. It wasn't tacked, and lifted an inch or so. He ran his fingers underneath it, finding nothing. Still crouched, he lifted the mattress, but saw only bedsprings and the carpet beneath, thick balls of dust and hair marking the furthest reach of the hoover.

He stood up, glancing at the bare walls. There were small rips in the wallpaper where Blu-Tak had been removed. He looked more closely at one small pattern of these. The wallpaper had come away in two longer strips. Wasn't this where the pennant had hung? Yes, you could see the hole made by the drawing-pin. The pennant had hung from a maroon cord which had been pinned to the wall. Meaning the pennant had been hiding these marks. They didn't look so old. The lining paper beneath was clean and fresh, as though the Sellotape had been peeled off recently.

Rebus put his fingers to the two stripes. They were about three inches apart and three inches long. Whatever had been taped there, it had been square and thin. Rebus knew exactly what would fit that description.

Out in the hall, Murdock was waiting to leave.

'Sorry to keep you waiting, sir,' Rebus said.

The Carlton sounded like another old ladies' tea-room, but in fact was a transport cafe with famed large helpings. When Mairie Henderson finally got back to Rebus, he suggested taking her to lunch there. It was on the shore at Newhaven, facing the Firth of Forth just about where that broad inlet became inseparable from the North Sea.

Lorries bypassing Edinburgh or heading to Leith from the north would usually pause for a break outside the Carlton. You saw them in a line by the sea wall, between Starbank Road and Pier Place. The drivers thought the Carlton well worth a detour, even if other road users and the police didn't always appreciate their sentiments.

Inside, the Carlton was a clean well-lit place and as hot as a truck engine. For air conditioning, they kept the front door wedged open. You never ate alone, which was why Rebus phoned in advance and booked a table for two.

'The one between the counter and the toilets,' he specified.

'Did I hear you right? *Book* a table?'

'You heard me.'

'Nobody's *booked* a table all the years we've been open.' The chef held the phone away from his face. 'Hiy, Maggie, there's somebody here wants tae *book* a table.'

'Cut the shite, Sammy, it's John Rebus speaking.'

'Special occasion is it, Mr Rebus? Anniversary? I'll bake yis a cake.'

'Twelve o'clock,' said Rebus, 'and make sure it's the table I asked for, okay?'

'Yes, sir.'

So when Rebus walked into the Carlton, and Sammy saw him, Sammy whipped a dishtowel off the stove and came sauntering between the tables, the towel over his arm.

'Your table is ready, sir, if you'll follow me.'

The drivers were grinning, a few of them offering encouragement. Maggie stood there holding a pillar of empty white plates, and attempted a curtsy as Rebus went past. The small Formica-topped table was laid for two, with a bit of card folded in half and the word RESERVED written in blue biro. There was a clean sauce bottle, into the neck of which someone had pushed a plastic carnation.

He saw Mairie look through the cafe window, then come in through the door. The drivers looked up.

'Room here, sweetheart.'

'Hiy, hen, sit on my lap, no' his.'

They grinned through the smoke, cigarettes never leaving their mouths. One of them ate camel-style, lower jaw moving in sideways rotation while his upper jaw chewed down. He reminded Rebus so strongly of Ormiston, he had to look away. Instead he looked at Mairie. Why not, everyone else was. They were staring without shame at her bum as she moved between the tables. True to form, Mairie had worn her shortest skirt. At least, Rebus hoped it was her shortest. And it was tight, one of those black Lycra numbers. She wore it with a baggy white t-shirt and thick black tights whose vertical seams showed pin-pricks of white leg flesh. She'd pushed her sunglasses onto the top of her head, and swung her shoulder-bag onto the floor as she took her seat.

'I see we're in the members' enclosure.'

'It took money but I thought it was worth it.'

Rebus studied her while she studied the wall-board which constituted the Carlton's menu.

'You look good,' he lied. Actually, she looked exhausted.

'Thanks. I wish I could say the same.'

Rebus winced. 'I looked as good as you at your age.'

'Even in a mini-skirt?' She leaned down to lift a pack of cigarettes from her bag, giving Rebus a view of her lace-edged bra down the front of her t-shirt. When she came up again he was frowning.

'Okay, I won't smoke.'

'It stunts your growth. And speaking of health warnings, what about that story of yours?'

But Maggie came over, so they went through the intricacies of ordering. 'We're out of Moët Shandy,' Maggie said.

'What was that about?' Mairie asked after Maggie had gone.

'Nothing,' he said. 'You were about to tell me . . . ?'

'Was I?' She smiled. 'How much do you know?'

'I know you've been working on a story, a chunk of which you've sold to *Snoop* but the bulk of which is destined for some US magazine.'

'Well, you know quite a lot then.'

'You took the story to your own paper first?'

She sighed. 'Of course I did, but they wouldn't print it. The company lawyers thought it was close to libel.'

'Who were you libelling?'

'Organisations rather than individuals. I had a blow-up with my editor about it, and handed in my resignation. His line was that the lawyers were paid to be over-cautious.'

'I bet their fees aren't over-cautious.' Which reminded him: Caro Rattray. He still had to contact her.

'I was planning on going freelance anyway, just not quite so soon. But at least I'm starting with a strong story. A few months back I got a letter from a New York journalist. His name's Jump Cantona.'

'Sounds like a car.'

'Yes, a four-by-four, that's just what I thought. Anyway, Jump's a well known writer over there, investigations with a capital I. But then of course it's easier in the US.'

'How's that?'

'You can go further before someone starts issuing writs. Plus you've got more freedom of information. Jump needed someone this end, following up a few leads. His name comes first in the main article, but any spin-offs I write, I get sole billing.'

'So what have you found?'

'A can of worms.' Maggie was coming with their food. She heard Mairie's closing words and gave her a cold look as she placed the fry-up in front of her. For Rebus, there was a half-portion of lasagne and a green salad.

'How did Cantona find you?' Rebus asked.

'Someone I met when I was on a journalism course in New York. This guy knew Cantona was looking for someone who could do some digging in Scotland. I was the obvious choice.' She attacked four chips with her fork. Chewing, she reached for the salt, vinegar, and tomato sauce. After momentary consideration, she poured some brown sauce on as well.

'I knew you'd do that,' Rebus said. 'And it still disgusts me.'

'You should see me with mustard and mayonnaise. I hear you got moved to SCS.'

'It's true.'

'Why?'

'If I didn't know better, I'd say they were keeping an eye on me.'

'Only, they were there at Mary King's Close, a murder that looks like an execution. Then next thing you're off to SCS, and I know SCS are investigating gun-running with an Irish slant.' Maggie arrived with two cans of Irn-Bru. Mairie checked hers was cold enough before opening it. 'Are we working on the same story?'

'The police don't have stories, Mairie, we have cases. And it's hard to answer your question without seeing your story.'

She slipped a hand into her shoulder-bag and pulled out several sheets of neatly typed paper. The document had been stapled and folded in half. Rebus could see it was a photocopy.

'Not very long,' he said.

'You can read it while I eat.'

He did. But all it did was put a lot of speculative meat on the bones he already had. Mostly it concentrated on the North American angle, mentioning the IRA fundraising in passing, though the Orange Loyal Brigade was mentioned, as was Sword and Shield.

'No names,' Rebus commented.

'I can give you a few, off the record.'

'Gavin and Jamesie MacMurray?'

'You're stealing my best lines. Do you have anything on them?'

'What do you think we'll find, a garden shed full of grenade launchers?'

'That could be pretty close.'

'Tell me.'

She took a deep breath. 'We can't put anything in print yet, but we think there's an Army connection.'

'You mean stuff from the Falklands and the Gulf? Souvenirs?'

'There's too much of it for it to be souvenirs.'

'What then? The stuff from Russia?'

'Much closer to home. You know stuff walks out of Army bases in Northern Ireland?'

'I've heard of it happening.'

'Same thing happened in the '70s in Scotland, the Tartan Army got stuff from Army bases. We think it's happening again. At least, Jump thinks it is. He's spoken to someone who used to be in American Shield, sending money over here. It's easier to send money here than arms shipments. This guy told Jump the money was buying *British* armaments. See, the IRA has good links with the East and Libya, but the loyalist paramilitaries don't.'

'You're telling me they're buying guns from the Army?' Rebus laughed and shook his head. Mairie managed a small smile.

'There's another thing. I know there's nothing to back this up. Jump knows it too. It's just one man's word, and that man isn't even willing to go public. He's afraid American Shield would get to him. Anyway, who'd believe him: he's being paid to tell Jump this stuff. He could be making it all up. Journalists like a juicy conspiracy, we lap them up like cream.'

'What are you talking about, Mairie?'

'A policeman, a detective, someone high up in The Shield.'

'In America?'

She shook her head. 'At the UK end, no name or anything. Like I say, just a story.'

'Aye, just a story. How did you find out we had a man undercover?'

'That was strange. It was a phone call.'

'Anonymous of course?'

'Of course. But who could have known?'

'Another policeman, obviously.'

Mairie pushed her plate away. 'I can't eat all these chips.'

'They should put up a plaque above the table.'

Rebus needed a drink, and there was a good pub only a short walk away. Mairie went with him, though she complained she didn't have room for a drink. Still, when they got there she found space for a white wine and soda. Rebus had a half-pint and a nip. They sat by the window, with a view out over the Forth. The water was battleship grey, reflecting the sky overhead. Rebus had never seen the Forth look other than forbidding.

'What did you say?' He'd missed it completely.

'I said, I forgot to say.'

'Yes, but the bit after that?'

'A man called Moncur, Clyde Moncur.'

'What about him?'

'Jump has him pegged as one of The Shield's hierarchy in the US. He's also a big-time villain, only it's never been proven in a court of law.'

'And?'

'And he flies into Heathrow tomorrow.'

'To do what?'

'We don't know.'

'So why aren't you down in London waiting for him?'

'Because he's booked on a connecting flight to Edinburgh.'

Rebus narrowed his eyes. 'You weren't going to tell me.'

'No, I wasn't.'

'What changed your mind?'

She gnawed her bottom lip. 'It may be I'll need a friend sometime soon.'

'You're going to confront him?'

'Yes ... I suppose so.'

'Jesus, Mairie.'

'It's what journalists do.'

'Do you know anything about him? I mean *anything*?'

'I know he's supposed to run drugs into Canada, brings illegal immigrants in from the Far East, a real Renaissance man. But on the surface, all he does is own a fish-processing plant in Seattle.' Rebus was shaking his head. 'What's wrong?'

'I don't know,' he said. 'I suppose I just feel ... gutted.'

It took her a moment to get the joke.

21

'Caro, thank God.'

Rebus was back in Fettes, at his desk, on the phone, having finally tracked Caroline Rattray to ground.

'You're calling off our drink,' she said coldly.

'I'm sorry, something's cropped up. Work, you know how it is. The hours aren't always social.' The phone went dead in his hand. He replaced the receiver like it was spun sugar. Then, having requested five minutes of his boss's time, he went to Kilpatrick's office. As ever there was no need to knock; Kilpatrick waved him in through the glass door.

'Take a seat, John.'

'I'll stand, sir, thanks all the same.'

'What's on your mind?'

'When you spoke to the FBI, did they mention a man called Clyde Moncur?'

'I don't think any names were mentioned.' Kilpatrick wrote the name on his pad. 'Who is he?'

'He's a Seattle businessman, runs his own fish-processing plant. Possibly also a gangster. He's coming to Edinburgh on holiday.'

'Well, we need the tourist dollars.'

'And he may be high up in The Shield.'

'Oh?' Kilpatrick casually underlined the name. 'What's your source?'

'I'd rather not say.'

'I see.' Kilpatrick underlined the name one last time. 'I don't like secrets, John.'

'Yes, sir.'

'Well, what do you want to do?'

'Put a tail on him.'

'Ormiston and Blackwood are good.'

'I'd prefer someone else.'

Kilpatrick threw down his pen. 'Why?'

'I just would.'

'You can trust me, John.'

'I know that, sir.'

'Then tell me why you don't want Ormiston and Blackwood on the tail.'

'We don't get on. I get the feeling they might muck things up just to make me look bad.' Lying was easy with practice, and Rebus had years of practice at lying to superiors.

'That sounds like paranoia to me.'

'Maybe it is.'

'I've got a *team* here, John. I need to know that they can work as a team.'

'You brought me in, sir. I didn't ask for secondment. Teams always resent the new man, it just hasn't worn off yet.' Then Rebus played his ace. 'You could always move me back to St Leonard's.' Not that he wanted this. He liked the freedom he had, flitting between the two stations, neither Chief Inspector knowing where he was.

'Is that what you want?' Kilpatrick asked.

'It's not down to me, it's what *you* want that matters.'

'Quite right, and I want you in SCS, at least for the time being.'

'So you'll put someone else on the tail?'

'I take it you've got people in mind?'

'Two more from St Leonard's. DS Holmes and DC Clarke. They work well together, they've done this sort of thing before.'

'No, John, let's keep this to SCS.' Which was Kilpatrick's way of reasserting his authority. 'I know two good men over in Glasgow, no possible grudge against you. I'll get them over here.'

'Right, sir.'

'Sound all right to you, Inspector?'

'Whatever you think, sir.'

When Rebus left the office, the two typists were discussing famine and Third World debt.

'Ever thought of going into politics, ladies?'

'Myra's a local councillor,' one of them said, nodding to her partner.

'Any chance of getting my drains cleared?' Rebus asked Myra.

'Join the queue,' Myra said with a laugh.

Back at his desk Rebus phoned Brian Holmes to ask him a favour, then he went to the toilets down the hall. The toilet was one of those design miracles, like Dr Who's time machine. Somehow two urinals, a toilet cubicle, and washhand basin had been squeezed into a space smaller than their total cubic volume.

So Rebus wasn't thrilled when Ken Smylie joined him. Smylie was supposed to be taking time off work, only he insisted on coming in.

'How are you doing, Ken?'

'I'm all right.'

'Good.' Rebus turned from his urinal and headed for the sink.

'You seem to be working hard,' Smylie said.

'Do I?'

'You're never here, I assume you're working.'

'Oh, I'm working.' Rebus shook water from his hands.

'Only I never see any notes.'

'Notes?'

'You never write down your case notes.'

'Is that right?' Rebus dried his hands on the cotton roller-towel. This was his lucky day: a fresh roll had just been fitted. He still had his back to Smylie. 'Well, I like to keep my notes in my head.'

'That's not procedure.'

'Tough.'

He'd just got the word out, and was preparing for another intake of breath, when Smylie's arms gripped him with the force of a construction crane around his chest. He couldn't breathe, and felt himself being lifted off the ground. Smylie pushed his face against the wall next to the roller-towel. His whole weight was sandwiching Rebus against the wall.

'You're on to something, aren't you?' Smylie said in his high whistling voice. 'Tell me who it is.' He released his bear hug just enough so Rebus could speak.

'Get the fuck off me!'

The grip tightened again, Rebus's face pressing harder into the wall. I'll go through it in a minute, he thought. My head'll be sticking out into the corridor like a hunting trophy.

'He was my brother,' Smylie was saying. '*My* brother.'

Rebus's face was full of blood which wanted to be somewhere else. He could feel his eyes bulging out of their sockets, his eardrums straining. My last view, he thought, will be of this damned roller-towel. Then the door swung inwards, and Ormiston was standing there, cigarette gawping. The cigarette dropped to the floor as Ormiston flung his own arms around Smylie's. He couldn't reach all the way round, but enough to dig his thumbs into the soft flesh of the inner elbows.

'Let go, Smylie!'

'Get off me!'

Rebus felt the pressure on him ease, and used his own shoulders to throw Smylie off. There was barely room for all three men, and they danced awkwardly, Ormiston still holding Smylie's arms. Smylie threw him off with ease. He was on Rebus again, but now Rebus was ready. He kneed the big man in the groin. Smylie groaned and slumped to his knees. Ormiston was picking himself up.

'What the hell sparked this?'

Smylie pulled himself to his feet. He looked angry, frustrated. He nearly took the handle off the door as he pulled it open.

Rebus looked in the mirror. His face was that sunburnt cherry colour some fair-skinned people go, but at least his eyes had retreated back into their sockets.

'Wonder what my blood pressure got up to,' he said to himself. Then he thanked Ormiston.

'I was thinking of me, not you,' Ormiston retorted. 'With you two wrestling,' he stooped to pick up his cigarette, 'there wasn't room for me to have a quiet puff.'

The cigarette itself survived the mêlée, but after inspecting it Ormiston decided to flush it anyway and light up a fresh one.

Rebus joined him. 'That may be the first time smoking's saved someone's life.'

'My grandad smoked for sixty years, died in his sleep at eighty. Mind you, he was bedridden for thirty of them. So what was all that about?'

'Filing. Smylie doesn't like my system.'

'Smylie likes to know everything that's going on.'

'He shouldn't even be here. He should be at home, bereaving.'

'But that's what he *is* doing,' argued Ormiston. 'Just because he looks like a big cuddly bear, a gentle giant, don't be fooled.' He took a drag on his cigarette. 'Let me tell you about Smylie.'

And he did.

Rebus was home at six o'clock, much to Patience Aitken's surprise. He had a shower rather than a bath and came into the living room dressed in his best suit and wearing a shirt Patience had given him for Christmas. It wasn't till he'd tried it on that they both discovered it required cuff links, so then he'd had to buy some.

'I can never do these up by myself,' he said now, flapping his cuffs and brandishing the links. Patience smiled and came to help him. Close up, she smelt of perfume.

'Smells wonderful,' he said.

'Do you mean me or the kitchen?'

'Both,' said Rebus. 'Equally.'

'Something to drink?'

'What are you having?'

'Fizzy water till the cooking's done.'

'Same for me.' Though really he was dying for a whisky. He'd lost the shakes, but his ribs still hurt when he inflated his lungs. Ormiston said he'd once seen Smylie bear-hug a recalcitrant prisoner into unconsciousness. He also told Rebus that before Kilpatrick had come on the scene, the Smylie brothers had more or less run the Edinburgh Crime Squad.

He drank the water with ice and lime and it tasted fine. When the preparations were complete and the table laid and the dishwasher set to work on only the first of the evening's loads, they sat down together on the sofa and drank gin with tonic.

'Cheers.'

'Cheers.'

And then Patience led him by the hand out into the small back garden. The sun was low over the tops of the tenements, the birds easing off into evensong. She examined every plant as she passed it, like a general assessing her troops. She'd trained Lucky the cat well; it now went over the wall into the neighbouring garden when it needed the toilet. She named some of the flowers for him, like she always did. He could never remember them from one day to the next.

The ice clinked in Patience's glass as she moved. She had changed into a long patterned dress, all flowing folds and squares of colour. With her hair up at the back, the dress worked well, showing off her neck and shoulders and the contours of her body. It had short sleeves to show arms tanned from gardening.

Though the bell was a long way off, he heard it. 'Front door,' he said.

'They're early.' She looked at her watch. 'Well, not much actually. I'd better get the potatoes on.'

'I'll let them in.'

She squeezed his arm as they separated, and Rebus made his way down the hallway towards the front door. He straightened himself, readying the smile he'd be wearing all evening. Then he opened the door.

'Bastard!'

Something hissed, a spray-can, and his eyes stung. He'd closed them a moment too late, but could still feel the spray dotting his face. He thought it must be Mace or something similar, and swiped blindly, trying to knock the can out of his assailant's hand. But the feet were already on the stone steps, shuffling upwards and away. He didn't want to open his eyes, so staggered blindly towards the bathroom, his hands feeling the hallway walls, past the bedroom door then hitting the lightswitch. He slammed the door and locked it as Patience was coming into the hall.

'John? John, what is it?'

'Nothing,' he said through his teeth. 'It's all right.'

'Are you sure? Who was at the door?'

'They were looking for the upstairs neighbours.' He was running water into the sink. He got his jacket off and plunged his head into the warm water, letting the sink fill, wiping at his face with his hands.

Patience was still waiting on the other side of the bathroom door. 'Something's wrong, John, what is it?'

He didn't say anything. After a few moments, he pried open one eye, then shut it again. Shit, that stung! He swabbed again with the water, opening his eyes underwater this time. The water seemed murky to him. And when he looked at his hands, they were red and sticky.

Oh Christ, he thought. He forced himself to look in the mirror above the sink. He was bright red. It wasn't like earlier in the day when Smylie had attacked him. It was . . . paint. That's what it was, red paint. From an aerosol can. Jesus Christ. He staggered out of his clothes and got into the shower, turning his face up to the spray, shampooing his hair as hard as he could, then doing it again. He scrubbed at his face and neck. Patience was at the door again, asking him what the hell he was up to. And then he heard her voice change, rising on the final syllable of a name.

The Bremners had arrived.

He got out of the shower and rubbed himself down with a towel. When he looked at himself again, he'd managed to get a lot of the colour off, but by no means all of it. Then he looked at his clothes. His jacket was dark, and didn't show the paint too conspicuously; conspicuously enough though. As for his good shirt, it was ruined, no question about that. He unlocked the bathroom door and listened. Patience had taken the Bremners into the living room. He padded down the hall into the bedroom, noticing on the way that his hands had left red smears on the wallpaper. In the bedroom he changed quickly into chinos, yellow t-shirt and a linen jacket Patience had bought him for summer walks by the river which they never took.

He looked like a has-been trying to look trendy. It would do. The palms of his hands were still red, but he could say he'd been painting. He popped his head round the living room door.

'Chris, Jenny,' he said. The couple were seated on the sofa. Patience must be in the kitchen. 'Sorry, I'm running a bit late. I'll just dry my hair and I'll be with you.'

'No rush,' said Jenny as he retreated into the hall. He took the telephone into the bedroom and called Dr Curt at home.

'Hello?'

'It's John Rebus here, tell me about Caroline Rattray.'

'Pardon?'

'Tell me what you know about her.'

'You sound smitten,' Curt said, amusement in his voice.

'I'm smitten all right. She's just sprayed me with a can of paint.'

'I'm not sure I caught that.'

'Never mind, just tell me about her. Like for instance, is she the jealous type?'

'John, you've met her. Would you say she's attractive?'

'Yes.'

'And she has a very good career, plenty of money, a lifestyle many would envy?'

'Yes.'

'But does she have any beaux?'

'You mean boyfriends, and the answer is I don't know.'

'Then take it from me, she does not. That's why she can be at a loose end when I have ballet tickets to spare. Ask yourself, why should this be? Answer, because she scares men off. I don't know *what's* wrong with her, but I know that she's not very good at relationships with the opposite sex. I mean, she *has* relationships, but they never last very long.'

'You might have told me.'

'I didn't realise you two were an item.'

'We're not.'

'Oh?'

'Only she thinks we are.'

'Then you're in trouble.'

'It looks like it.'

'Sorry I can't be more help. She's always been all right with me, perhaps I could have a word with her ... ?'

'No thanks, that's my department.'

'Goodbye then, and good luck.'

Rebus waited till Curt had put his receiver down. He listened to the line, then heard another click. Patience had been listening on the kitchen extension. He sat on the bed, staring at his feet, till the door opened.

'I heard,' she said. She had an oven glove in one hand. She knelt down in front of him, her hands on his knees. 'You should have told me.'

He smiled. 'I just did.'

'Yes, but to my face.' She paused. 'There was nothing between the two of you, nothing happened?'

'Nothing happened,' he said without blinking. There was another moment's silence.

'What are we going to do?'

He took her hands. 'We,' he said, 'are going to join our guests.' Then he kissed her on the forehead and pulled her with him to her feet.

22

At nine-thirty next morning, Rebus was sitting in his car outside Lachlan Murdock's flat.

When he'd washed his eyes last night, it had been like washing behind them as well. Always it came to this, he tried to do things by the books and ended up cooking them instead. It was easier, that was all. Where would the crime detection rates be without a few shortcuts?

He had tried Murdock's number from a callbox at the end of the road. There was no one there, just an answering machine. Murdock was at work. Rebus got out of the car and tried Murdock's intercom. Again, no answer. So he picked the lock, the way he'd been taught by an old lag when he'd gone to the man for lessons. Once inside, he climbed the stairwell briskly, a regular visitor rather than an intruder. But no one was about.

Murdock's flat was on the Yale rather than a deadlock, so it was easy to open too. Rebus slipped inside and closed the door after him. He went straight to Murdock's bedroom. He didn't suppose Millie would have left the computer disk behind, but you never knew. People with no access to safe deposit boxes sometimes mistook their homes for one.

The postman had been, and Murdock had left the mail strewn on the unmade bed. Rebus glanced at it. There was a letter from Millie. The envelope was postmarked the previous day, the letter itself written on a single sheet of lined writing paper.

'Sorry I didn't say anything. Don't know how long I'll be away. If the police ask, say nothing. Can't say more just now. Love you. Millie.'

Rebus left the letter lying where it was and pulled on a pair of surgical gloves stolen from Patience. He walked over to Murdock's workdesk and switched on the computer, then started going through the computer disks. There were dozens of them, kept in plastic boxes, most of them neatly labelled. The majority had labels with spidery black handwriting, which Rebus guessed was Murdock's. The few that remained he took to be Millie's.

He went through these first, but found nothing to interest him. The unlabelled disks proved to be either blank or corrupted. He started searching through drawers for other disks. Parked on the floor one side of the bed were the plastic binliners containing Billy's things. He looked through these, too. Murdock's side of the bed was a chaos of books, ashtray, empty cigarette packets, but Millie's side was a lot neater. She had a bedside cupboard on which sat a lamp, alarm clock, and a packet of throat lozenges. Rebus crouched down and opened the cupboard door. Now he knew why Millie's side of the bed was so neat: the cupboard was like a wastepaper bin. He sifted through the rubbish. There were some crumpled yellow Post-It notes in amongst it. He picked them out and unpeeled them. They were messages from Murdock. The first one contained a seven-digit phone number and beneath it the words 'Why don't you call this bitch?' As Rebus unpeeled the others, he began to understand. There were half a dozen telephone messages, all from the same person. Rebus had thought he recognised the phone number, but on the rest of the messages the caller's name was printed alongside.

Mairie Henderson.

Back at St Leonard's he was pleased to find that both Holmes and Clarke were elsewhere. He went to the toilets and splashed water on his face. His eyes were still irritated, red at their rims and bloodshot. Patience had taken a close look at them last night and pronounced he'd live. After the Bremners had gone home happy, she'd also helped him scrub the rest of the red out of his hair and off his hands. Actually, there was still some on his right palm.

'Cuchullain of the Red Hand,' Patience had said. She'd been great really, considering. Trust a doctor to be calm in a crisis. She'd even managed to calm him down when, late in the evening, he'd considered going round to Caroline Rattray's flat and torching it.

'Here,' she'd said, handing him a whisky, 'set fire to yourself instead.'

He smiled at himself in the toilet mirror. There was no Smylie here, about to grope him to death, no jeering Ormiston or preening Black-wood. This was where he belonged. He wondered again just what he was doing at Fettes. Why had Kilpatrick scooped him up?

He thought now that he had a bloody good idea.

Edinburgh's Central Lending Library is situated on George IV Bridge, across the street from the National Library of Scotland. This was student territory, and just off the Royal Mile, and hence at the moment also Festival Fringe territory. Pamphleteers were out in force, still enthusing, sensing audiences to be had now that the least successful shows had packed up and headed home. For the sake of politeness, Rebus took a lurid green flyer from a teenage girl with long blonde hair, and read it as far as the first litter bin, where it joined many more identical flyers.

The Edinburgh Room was not so much a room as a gallery surrounding an open space. Far below, readers in another section of the library were at their desks or browsing among the bookshelves. Not that Mairie Henderson was reading books. She was poring over local newspapers, seated at one of the few readers' tables. Rebus stood beside Mairie, reading over her shoulder. She had a neat portable computer with her, flipped open and plugged into a socket in the library floor. Its screen was milky grey and filled with notes. It took her a minute to sense that there was someone standing over her. She looked round slowly, expecting a librarian.

'Let's talk,' said Rebus.

She saved what she'd been writing and followed him out onto the library's large main staircase. A sign told them not to sit on the window ledges, which were in a dangerous condition. Mairie sat on the top step, and Rebus sat a couple of steps down from her, leaving plenty of room for people to get past.

'I'm in a dangerous condition, too,' he said angrily.

'Why? What's happened?' She looked as innocent as stained glass.

'Millie Docherty.'

'Yes?'

'You didn't tell me about her.'

'What exactly should I have told you?'

'That you'd been trying to talk to her. Did you succeed?'

'No, why?'

'She's run off.'

'Really?' She considered this. 'Interesting.'

'What did you want to talk to her about?'

'The murder of one of her flatmates.'

'That's all?'

'Shouldn't it be?' She was looking interested.

'Funny she does a runner when you're after her. How's the research?' She'd told him over their drink in Newhaven that she was looking into what she called 'past loyalist activity' in Scotland.

'Slow,' she admitted. 'How's yours?'

'Dead stop,' he lied.

'Apart from Ms Docherty's disappearance. How did you know I wanted to talk to her?'

'None of your business.'

She raised her eyebrows. 'Her flatmate didn't tell you?'

'No comment at this time.'

She smiled.

'Come on,' said Rebus, 'maybe you'll talk over a coffee.'

'Interrogation by scone,' Mairie offered.

They walked the short walk to the High Street and took a right towards St Giles Cathedral. There was a coffee shop in the crypt of St Giles, reached by way of an entrance which faced Parliament House. Rebus glanced across the car park, but there was no sign of Caroline Rattray. The coffee shop though was packed, having not many tables to start with and this still being the height of the tourist season.

'Try somewhere else?' Mairie suggested.

'Actually,' said Rebus, 'I've gone off the idea. I've got a bit of business across the road.' Mairie tried not to look relieved. 'I'd caution you,' he warned her, 'not to piss me about.'

'Caution received and understood.'

She waved as she walked off back towards the library. Rebus watched her good legs recede from view. They stayed good-looking all the way out of his vision. Then he threaded his way between the lawyers' cars and entered the court building. He had an idea he was going to leave a note for Caroline Rattray in her box, always supposing she had one. But as he walked into Parliament Hall he saw her talking with another lawyer. There was no chance to retreat; she spotted him immediately. She kept up the conversation for a few more moments, then put her hand on her colleague's shoulder, said a brief farewell, and headed towards Rebus.

It was hard to reconcile her, in her professional garb, with the woman who had spray-painted him the previous night. She left her colleague with a faint smile on her lips, and met Rebus with that same smile. Under her arm were the regulation files and documents.

'Inspector, what brings you here?'

'Can't you guess?'

'Ah yes, of course, I'll send a cheque.'

He had kept telling himself all the way across the car park that he wasn't going to let her get under his skin. Now he found she was already there, like a half inch of syringe.

'Cheque?'

'For the dry cleaning or whatever.' A passing lawyer nodded to her. 'Hullo, Mansie. Oh, Mansie?' She spoke with the lawyer for a few moments, her hand on his elbow.

She was offering a cheque for the dry cleaning. Rebus was glad of a few moments in which to cool off. But now someone was tapping his shoulder. He turned to find Mairie Henderson standing there.

'I forgot,' she said, 'the American's in town.'

'Yes, I know. Have you done anything about him?'

She shook her head. 'Biding my time.'

'Good, no use scaring him off.' Caroline Rattray was looking interested in this new arrival, so much so that she was losing the thread of her own conversation. She dismissed Mansie halfway through a sentence and turned to Rebus and Mairie. Mairie smiled at her, the two women waiting for an introduction.

'See you then,' Rebus said to Mairie.

'Oh, right.' Mairie walked backwards a step or two, just in case he'd change his mind, then turned. As she turned, Caroline Rattray took a step forward, her hand out as though she were about to make her own introduction, but Rebus really didn't want her to, so he grabbed the hand and held her back. She shrugged his grip off and glared at him, then looked back through the doorway. Mairie had already left the building.

'You seem to have quite a little stable, Inspector.' She tried rubbing at her wrist. It wasn't easy with the files still precariously pressed between her elbow and stomach

'Better stable than unstable,' he said, regretting the dig immediately. He should just have denied the charge.

'Unstable?' she echoed. 'I don't know what you mean.'

'Look, let's forget it, eh? I mean, forget *everything*. I've told Patience all about it.'

'I find that difficult to believe.'

'That's your problem, not mine.'

'You think so?' She sounded amused.

'Yes.'

'Remember something, Inspector.' Her voice was level and quiet. '*You* started it. And then *you* told the lie. My conscience is clear, what about yours?'

She gave him a little smile before walking away. Rebus turned and found himself confronting a statue of Sir Walter Scott, seated with his feet crossed and a walking-cane held between his open knees. Scott looked as though he'd heard every word but wasn't about to pass judgment.

'Keep it that way,' Rebus warned, not caring who might hear.

He phoned Patience and invited her to an early evening drink at the Playfair Hotel on George Street.

'What's the occasion?' she asked.

'No occasion,' he said.

He was restless the rest of the day. Glasgow came back to him, but only to say that they'd nothing on either Jim Hay or Active Resistance Theatre. He turned up early at the Playfair, making across its entrance hall (all faded glory, but *studied* faded glory, almost too perfect) to the bar beyond. It called itself a 'wet bar', which was okay with Rebus. He ordered a Talisker, hoisted himself onto a well-padded barstool and dipped a hand into the bowl of peanuts which had appeared at his approach.

The bar was empty, but would be filled soon enough with prosperous businessmen on their way home, other businessmen who wanted to look prosperous and didn't mind spending money on it, and the hotel clientele, enjoying a snifter before a pre-dinner stroll. A waitress stood idly against the end of the bar, not far from the baby grand. The piano was kept covered with a dustsheet until evening, so for now there was wallpaper music, except that whoever was playing trumpet wasn't half bad. He wondered if it was Chet Baker.

Rebus paid for his drink and tried not to think about the amount of money he'd just been asked for. After a bit, he changed his mind and asked if he could have some ice. He wanted the drink to last. Eventually a middle-aged couple came into the bar and sat a couple of seats away from him. The woman put on elaborate glasses to study the cocktail list, while her husband ordered Drambuie, pronouncing it Dramboo-i. The husband was short but bulky, given to scowling. He was wearing a white golfing cap, and kept glancing at his watch. Rebus managed to catch his eye, and toasted him.

'*Slainte.*'

The man nodded, saying nothing, but the wife smiled. 'Tell me,' she said, 'are there many Gaelic speakers left in Scotland?'

Her husband hissed at her, but Rebus was happy to answer. 'Not many,' he conceded.

'Are you from Edinburgh?' Head-in-burrow, it sounded like.

'Pretty much.'

She noticed that Rebus's glass was now all melting ice. 'Will you join us?' The husband hissed again, something about her not bothering people who only wanted a quiet drink.

Rebus looked at his watch. He was calculating whether he could afford to buy a round back. 'Thank you, yes, I'll have a Talisker.'

'And what is that?'

'Malt whisky, it comes from Skye. There are some Gaelic speakers over there.'

The wife started humming the first few notes of the *Skye Boat Song*, all about a French Prince who dressed in drag. Her husband smiled to cover his embarrassment. It couldn't be easy, travelling with a madwoman.

'Maybe you can tell me something,' said Rebus. 'Why is a wet bar called a wet bar?'

'Could be because the beer's draught,' the husband offered grudgingly, 'not just bottled.'

The wife had perched her shiny handbag on the bar and now opened it, taking out a compact so she could check her face. 'You're not the mystery man, are you?' she asked.

Rebus put down his glass. 'Sorry?'

'Ellie!' her husband warned.

'Only,' she said, putting away her compact, 'Clyde had a message to meet someone in the bar, and you're the only person here. They didn't leave a name or anything.'

'A misunderstanding, that's all,' said Clyde. 'They got the wrong room.' But he looked at Rebus anyway. Rebus obliged with a nod.

'Mysterious, certainly.'

The fresh glass was put before Rebus, and the barman decided he merited another bowl of nuts too.

'*Slainte*,' said Rebus.

'*Slainte*,' said husband and wife.

'Am I late?' said Patience Aitken, running her hands up Rebus's spine. She slipped onto the stool which separated Rebus from the tourists. For some reason, the man now removed his cap, showing a good amount of hair slicked back from the forehead.

'Patience,' Rebus said, 'I'd like to introduce you to . . .'

'Clyde Moncur,' said the man, visibly relaxing. Rebus obviously posed no threat. 'This is my wife Eleanor.'

Rebus smiled. 'Dr Patience Aitken, and I'm John.'

Patience looked at him. He seldom used 'Dr' when introducing her, and why had he left out his own surname?

'Listen,' Rebus was saying, staring right past her, 'wouldn't we be more comfortable at a table?'

They took a table for four, the waitress appearing with a little tray of nibbles, not just nuts but green and black olives and chipsticks too. Rebus tucked in. The drinks might be expensive, but you had to say the food was cheap.

'You're on holiday?' Rebus said, opening the conversation.

'That's right,' said Eleanor Moncur. 'We just love Scotland.' She then went on to list everything they loved about it, from the skirl of the bagpipes to the windswept west coast. Clyde let her run on, taking sips from his drink, occasionally swirling the ice around. He sometimes looked up from the drink to John Rebus.

'Have you ever been to the United States?' Eleanor asked.

'No, never,' said Rebus.

'I've been a couple of times,' Patience said, surprising him. 'Once to California, and once to New England.'

'In the fall?' Patience nodded. 'Isn't that just heaven?'

'Do you live in New England?' Rebus asked.

Eleanor smiled. 'Oh no, we're way over the other side. Washington.'

'Washington?'

'She means the state,' her husband explained, 'not Washington DC.'

'Seattle,' said Eleanor. 'You'd like Washington, it's wild.'

'As in wilderness,' Clyde Moncur added. 'I'll put that on our room, miss.'

Patience had ordered lager and lime, which the waitress had just brought. Rebus watched as Moncur took a room key from his pocket. The waitress checked the room number.

'Clyde's ancestors came from Scotland,' Eleanor was saying. 'Some-where near Glasgow.'

'Kilmarnock.'

'That's right, Kilmarnock. There were four brothers, one went to Australia, two went to Northern Ireland, and Clyde's great-grandfather sailed from Glasgow to Canada with his wife and children. He worked his way across Canada and settled in Vancouver. It was Clyde's grand-father who came down into the United States. There are still offshoots of the family in Australia and Northern Ireland.'

'Where in Northern Ireland?' Rebus asked casually.

'Portadown, Londonderry,' she went on, though Rebus had directed the question at her husband.

'Ever visit them?'

'No,' said Clyde Moncur. He was interested in Rebus again. Rebus met the stare squarely.

'The north west's full of Scots,' Mrs Moncur rattled on. 'We have ceilidhs and clan gatherings and Highland Games in the summer.'

Rebus lifted his glass to his lips and seemed to notice it was empty. 'I think we need another round,' he said. The drinks arrived with their own scalloped paper coasters, and the waitress took away with her nearly all the money John Rebus had on him. He'd used the anonymous message to get Moncur down here, and Patience to put him off his guard. In the event, Moncur was sharper than Rebus had given him credit for. The man didn't need to say a word, his wife spoke enough for two, and nothing she said could prove remotely useful.

'So you're a doctor?' she asked Patience now.

'General practice, yes.'

'I admire doctors,' said Eleanor. 'They keep Clyde and me alive and ticking.' And she gave a big grin. Her husband had been watching Patience while she'd been speaking, but as soon as she finished he turned his gaze back to Rebus. Rebus lifted his glass to his lips.

'For some time,' Eleanor Moncur was saying now, 'Clyde's grandaddy was captain of a clipper. His wife gave birth on board while the boat was headed to pick up ... what was it, Clyde?'

'Timber,' Clyde said. 'From the Philippines. She was eighteen and he was in his forties. The baby died.'

'And know what?' said Eleanor. 'They preserved the body in brandy.'

'Embalmed it?' Patience offered.

Eleanor Moncur nodded. 'And if that boat had been a temperance vessel, they'd've used tar instead of brandy.'

Clyde Moncur spoke to Rebus. 'Now *that* was hard living. Those are the people who built America. You had to be tough. You might be conscientious, but there wasn't always room for a conscience.'

'A bit like in Ulster,' Rebus offered. 'They transplanted some pretty hard Scots there.'

'Really?' Moncur finished his drink in silence.

They decided against a third round, Clyde reminding his wife that they had yet to take their pre-prandial walk down to Princes Street Gardens and back. They exchanged handshakes outside, Rebus taking Patience's arm and leading her downhill, as though they were heading into the New Town.

'Where's your car?' he asked.

'Back on George Street. Where's yours?'

'Same place.'

'Then where are we going?'

He checked over his shoulder, but the Moncurs were out of sight. 'Nowhere,' he said, stopping.

'John,' said Patience, 'next time you need me as a cover, have the courtesy to ask first.'

'Can you lend me a few quid, save me finding a cashpoint?'

She sighed and dug into her bag. 'Twenty enough?'

'Hope so.'

'Unless you're thinking of returning to the Playfair bar.'

'I've been up braes that weren't as steep as that place.'

He told her he'd be back late, perhaps very late, and pecked her on the cheek. But she pulled him to her and took her fair share of mouth to mouth.

'By the way,' she said, 'did you talk to the action painter?'

'I told her to get lost. That doesn't mean she will.'

'She better,' said Patience, pecking him a last time on the cheek before walking away.

He was unlocking his car when a heavy hand landed on his own. Clyde Moncur was standing next to him.

'Who the fuck are you?' the American spat, looking around him.

'Nobody,' Rebus said, shaking off the hand.

'I don't know what all that shit was about at the hotel, but you better stay far away from me, friend.'

'That might not be easy,' said Rebus. 'This is a small place. *My* town, not yours.'

Moncur took a step back. He'd be in his late-60s, but the hand he'd placed on Rebus's had stung. There was strength there, and determination. He was the sort of man who normally got his own way, whatever the cost.

'Who *are* you?'

Rebus pulled open the car door. He drove away without saying anything at all. Moncur watched him go. The American stood legs apart, and raised a hand to pat his jacket at chest height, nodding slowly.

A gun, Rebus thought. He's telling me he's got a gun.

And he's telling me he'd use it, too.

23

Mairie Henderson had a flat in Portobello, on the coast east of the city. In Victorian times a genteel bathing resort, 'Porty' was still used by day trippers in summer. Mairie's tenement was on one of the streets between High Street and the Promenade. With his window rolled down, Rebus caught occasional wafts of salt air.

When his daughter Sammy was a kid they'd come to Porty beach for walks. The beach had been cleaned up by then, or at least covered with tons of sand from elsewhere. Rebus used to enjoy those walks, trouser legs rolled up past the ankles, feet treading the numbing water at the edge of the louring North Sea.

'If we kept walking, Daddy,' Sammy would say, pointing to the skyline, 'where would we go?'

'We'd go to the bottom of the sea.'

He could still see the dreadful look on her face. She'd be twenty this year. Twenty. He reached under his seat and let his hand wander till it touched his emergency pack of cigarettes. One wouldn't do any harm. Inside the pack, nestling amongst the cigarettes, was a slim disposable lighter.

The light was still on in Mairie's first-floor window. Her car was parked right outside the tenement's front door. He knew the back door led to a small enclosed drying-green. She'd have to come out the front. He hoped she'd bring Millie Docherty with her.

He didn't quite know why he thought Mairie was hiding Millie; it was enough that he thought it. He'd had wrong hunches before, enough for a convention of the Quasimodo fan club, but you always had to follow them up. If you stopped being true to instinct, you were lost. His stomach rumbled, reminding him that olives and chipsticks did not a meal make. He thought of the Portobello chip shops, but sucked on his cigarette instead. He was across the road from the tenement and about six cars down. It was eleven o'clock and dark; no chance of Mairie spotting him.

He thought he knew why Clyde Moncur was in town. Same reason the ex-UVF man was here. He just didn't want to go public with his thoughts, not when he didn't know who his friends were.

At quarter past eleven, the tenement door opened and Mairie came out. She was alone, wearing a Burberry-style raincoat and carrying a bulging shopping bag. She looked up and down the street before unlocking her car and getting in.

'What are you nervous about, kid?' Rebus asked, watching her headlights come on. He lit another cigarette, just to wash down the first, and started his engine.

She took the Portobello Road back into the city. He hoped she wasn't going far. Tailing a car, even in the dark, wasn't as easy as the movies made it look, especially when the person you were tailing knew your car. The roads were quiet, making things trickier still, but at least she stuck to the main routes. If she'd used side streets and rat runs, she'd have spotted him for sure.

On Princes Street, the bikers were out in summer-night force, hitting the late-opening burger bars and revving up and down the straight. He wondered if Clyde Moncur was out for a post-prandial stroll. With the burgers and bikes, he'd probably feel right at home. Moncur was tough the way old people could get; seeming to shrink as they got older but that was only because they were losing juice, becoming rock-hard as a result. There was nothing soft left of Clyde Moncur. He had a handshake like a saloon-bar challenge. Even Patience had complained of it.

The night was delicious, perfect for a walk, and that's what most people were enjoying. Too bad for the Fringe shows: who wanted to sit in an airless, dark theatre for two hours while the real show was outside, continuous and absolutely free?

Mairie turned left at the west end, heading up Lothian Road. The street was already reeling with drunks. They'd probably be heading for a curry house or pizza emporium. Later, they'd regret this move. You saw the evidence each morning on the pavements. Just past the Tollcross lights, Mairie signalled to cross the oncoming traffic. Rebus wondered where the hell she was headed. His question was soon answered. She parked by the side of the road and turned off her lights. Rebus hurried past while she was locking her door, then stopped at the junction ahead. There was no traffic coming, but he sat there anyway, watching in his rearview.

'Well, well,' he said as Mairie crossed the road and went into the Crazy Hose Saloon. He put the car into reverse, brought it back, and squeezed in a few cars ahead of Mairie. He looked across at the Crazy Hose. The sign above was yellow and red flashing neon, which must be fun for the people in the tenement outside which Rebus was parked. A short flight of steps led to the main doors, and on these steps stood two bouncers. The Hose's wild west theme had passed the bouncers by, and they were dressed in regulation black evening suits, white shirts and black bow ties. Both had cropped hair to match their IQs, and held their hands behind their backs, swelling already prodigious chests. Rebus watched them open the doors for a couple of stetson-tipping cowpokes and their mini-dressed partners.

'In for a dime, I suppose.' He locked his car and walked purposefully across the road, trying to look like a man looking for a good time. The bouncers eyed him suspiciously, and did not open the door. Rebus decided he'd played enough games today, so he opened his ID and stuck it in the tallest bouncer's face. He wondered if the man could read.

'Police,' he said helpfully. 'Don't I get the door opened for me?'

'Only on your way out,' the smaller bouncer said. So Rebus pulled open the door and went in. The admission desk had been done up like an old bank, with vertical wooden bars in front of the smiling female face.

'Platinum Cowpoke Card,' Rebus said, again showing his ID. Past the desk was a fair-sized hallway where people were playing one-armed bandits. There was a large crowd around an interactive video game, where some bearded actor on film invited you to shoot him dead if you were quick enough on the draw. Most of the kids in front of the machine were dressed in civvies, though a few sported cowboy boots and bootlace ties. Big belt-buckles seemed mandatory, and both males and females wore Levi and Wrangler denims with good-sized turn-ups. The toilets were out here too, always supposing you could work out which you were, a Honcho or Honchette.

A second set of doors led to the dance hall and four bars, one in each corner of the vast arena. Plenty of money had been spent on the decor, with the choicest pieces being spotlit behind Perspex high up out of reach on the walls. There was a life-size cigar-store Indian, a lot of native head-dresses and jackets and the like, and what Rebus hoped was a replica of a Gatling-gun. Old western films played silently on a bank of TV screens set into one wall, and there was a bucking bronco machine against another wall. This was disused now, ever since a teenager had fallen from it and been put in a coma. They'd nearly shut the place down for that. Rebus didn't like to think about why they hadn't. He kept coming up with friends in the right places and money changing hands. There was something that looked like a font near one of the bars, but Rebus knew it was a spittoon. He noticed that the bar closest to it wasn't doing great business.

Rebus wasn't hard to pick out in a crowd. Although there were people there his own age, they were all wearing western dress to some degree, and they were nearly all dancing. There was a stage which was spotlit and full of instruments but empty of bodies. Instead the music came through the PA. A DJ in an enclosed box next to the stage babbled between songs; you could have heard him halfway to Texas.

'Can I help you?'

Not hard to pick out in the crowd, and of course the bouncers had sent word to the floor manager. He was in his late-twenties with slick black hair and a rhinestone waistcoat. The accent was strictly Lothian.

'Is Frankie in tonight?' If Bothwell were in the dancehall, he'd have spotted him. Bothwell's clothes would have drowned out the PA.

'I'm in charge.' The smile told Rebus he was as welcome as haemorrhoids at a rodeo.

'Well, there's no trouble, son, so I can put your mind at rest straight off. I'm just looking for a friend, only I didn't fancy paying the admission.'

The manager looked relieved. You could see he hadn't been in the job long. He'd probably been promoted from behind the bar. 'My name's Lorne Strang,' he said.

'And mine's Lorne Sausage.'

Strang smiled. 'My real name's Kevin.'

'Don't apologise.'

'Drink on the house?'

'I'd rather drink on a bar-stool, if that's all right with you.'

Rebus had given the dance floor a good look, and Mairie wasn't there, which meant she was either trapped in the Honchettes' or was somewhere behind the scenes. He wondered what she could be doing behind the scenes at Frankie Bothwell's club.

'So,' said Kevin Strang, 'who are you looking for?'

'Like I say, a friend. She said she'd be here. Maybe I'm a bit late.'

'The place is only just picking up now. We're open another two hours. What'll you have?' They were at the bar. The bar staff wore white aprons covering chest and legs and gold-coloured bands around their sleeves to keep their cuffs out of the way.

'Is that so they can't palm any notes?' asked Rebus.

'Nobody cheats the bar here.' One of the staff broke off serving someone to attend to Kevin Strang.

'Just a beer, please,' Rebus said.

'Draught? We only serve half pints.'

'Why's that?'

'There's more profit in it.'

'An honest answer. I'll have a bottle of Beck's.' He looked back to the dance floor. 'The last time I saw this many cowboys was at a builders' convention.'

The record was fading out. Strang patted Rebus's back. 'That's my cue,' he said. 'Enjoy yourself.'

Rebus watched him move through the dancers. He climbed onto the stage and tapped the microphone, sending a whump through the on-stage PA. Rebus didn't know what he was expecting. Maybe Strang would call out the steps of the next barn dance. But instead all he did was speak in a quiet voice, so people had to be quiet to hear him. Rebus didn't think Kevin Strang had much future as floor manager at the Crazy Hose.

'Dudes and womenfolk, it's a pleasure to see you all here at the Crazy Hose Saloon. And now, please welcome onto the Deadwood Stage our band for this evening's hoedown ... Chaparral!'

There was generous applause as the band emerged through a door at the back of the stage. A few of the arcade junkies had come in from the foyer. The band was a six-piece, barely squeezing onto the stage. Guitar/vocals, bass, drums, another guitar and two backing singers. They started into their first number a little shakily, but had warmed up by the end, by which time Rebus was finishing his drink and thinking about heading back to the car.

Then he saw Mairie.

No wonder she'd had a raincoat around her. Underneath she must have been wearing a tasselled black skirt, brown leather waistcoat, white blouse cut just above the chest and up around the shoulders, leaving a lot of bare flesh. She wasn't wearing a stetson, but there was a red kerchief around her throat and she was singing her heart out.

She was one of the backing singers.

Rebus ordered another drink and gawped at the stage. After a few songs, he could differentiate between Mairie's voice and that of the other backing singer. He noticed that most of the men were watching this singer. She was much taller than Mairie and had long straight black hair, plus she was wearing a much shorter skirt. But Mairie was the better singer. She sang with her eyes closed, swaying from the hips, knees slightly bent. Her partner used her hands a lot, but didn't gain much from it.

At the end of their fourth song, the male singer/guitarist gave a short spiel while the others in the band caught their breath, retuned, swigged drinks or wiped their faces. Rebus didn't know about C&W, but Chaparral seemed pretty good. They didn't just play mush about pet dogs, dying spouses or standing by your lover. Their songs had a harder, much urban feel, with lyrics to match.

'And if you don't know Hal Ketchum,' the singer was saying, 'you better get to know him. This is one of his, it's called Small Town Saturday Night.'

Mairie took lead vocal, her partner patting a tambourine and looking on. At the end of the song, the cheers were loud. The singer came back to his mike and raised his arm towards Mairie.

'Katy Hendricks, ladies and gentlemen.' The cheers resumed while Mairie took her bow.

After this they started into their own material, two songs whose intention was always ahead of ability. The singer mentioned that both were available on the band's first cassette, available to buy in the foyer.

'We're going to take a break now. So you can all go away for the next fifteen minutes, but be sure to come back.'

Rebus went into the foyer and dug six pounds out of his pocket. When he came back in, the band were at one of the bars, hoping to be bought drinks if half-time refreshments weren't on the house. Rebus shook the cassette in Mairie's ear.

'Miss Hendricks, would you autograph this, please?'

The band looked at him and so did Mairie. She took him by the lapels and propelled him away from the bar.

'What are you doing here?'

'Didn't you know? I'm a big country and western fan.'

'You don't like anything but sixties rock, you told me so yourself. Are you following me?'

'You sang pretty well.'

'*Pretty* well? I was great.'

'That's my Mairie, never one to hide her light under a tumbleweed. Why the false name?'

'You think I wanted those arseholes at the paper to find out?' Rebus tried to imagine the Hose full of drunken journos cheering their singer-scribe.

'No, I don't suppose so.'

'Anyway, everyone in the band uses an alias, it makes it harder for the DSS to find out they've been working.' She pointed at the tape. 'You bought that?'

'Well, they didn't hand it over as material evidence.'

She grinned. 'You liked us then?'

'I really did. I know I shouldn't be, but I'm amazed.'

She was almost persuaded onto this tack, but not quite. 'You still haven't said why you're following me.'

He put the tape in his pocket. 'Millie Docherty.'

'What about her?'

'I think you know where she is.'

'What?'

'She's scared, she needs help. She might just run to the reporter who's being wanting to see her. Reporters have been known to hide their sources away, protect them.'

'You think I'm hiding her?'

He paused. 'Has she told you about the pennant?'

'What pennant?'

Mairie had lost her cowgirl singer look. She was back in business.

'The one on Billy Cunningham's wall. Has she told you what he had hidden behind it?'

'What?'

Rebus shook his head. 'I'll make a deal,' he said. 'We'll talk to her together, that way neither of us is hiding anything. What do you say?'

The bassist handed Mairie an orange juice.

'Thanks, Duane.' She gulped it down until only ice was left. 'Are you staying for the second set?'

'Will it be worth my while?'

'Oh yes, we do a cracking version of "Country Honk".'

'That'll be the acid test.'

She smiled. 'I'll see you after the set.'

'Mairie, do you know who owns this place?'

'A guy called Boswell.'

'It's Bothwell. You don't know him?'

'Never met him. Why?'

The second set was paced like a foxtrot: two slow dances, two fast, then a slow, sad rendering of 'Country Honk' to end with. The floor was packed for the last dance, and Rebus was flattered when a woman a good few years younger than him asked him up. But then her man came back from the Honchos', so that was the end of that.

As the band played a short upbeat encore, one fan climbed onstage and presented the backing singers with sheriff's badges, producing the loudest cheer of the night as both women pinned them on their chests. It was a good natured crowd, and Rebus had spent worse evenings. He couldn't see Patience enjoying it though.

When the band finished, they went back through the door they'd first appeared through. A few minutes later, Mairie reappeared, still dressed in all her gear and with the raincoat folded up in her shopping bag along with her flat-soled driving shoes.

'So?' Rebus said.

'So let's go.'

He started for the exit, but she was making towards the stage, gesturing for him to follow.

'I don't really want her to see me like this,' she said. 'I'm not sure the outfit conveys journalistic clout and professionalism. But I can't be bothered changing.'

They climbed onto the stage, then through the door. It led into a low-ceilinged passage of broom closets, crates of empty bottles, and a small room where in the evening the band got ready and during the day the cleaner could stop for a cup of tea. Beyond this was a dark stairwell. Mairie found the light switch and started to climb.

'Where exactly are we going?'

'The Sheraton.'

Rebus didn't ask again. The stairs were steep and twisting. They reached a landing where a padlocked door faced them, but Mairie kept climbing. At the second landing she stopped. There was another door, this time with no lock. Inside was a vast dark space, which Rebus judged to be the building's attic. Light infiltrated from the street through a skylight and some gaps in the roof, showing the solid forms of rafters.

'Watch you don't bump your head.'

The roofspace, though huge, was stifling. It seemed to be filled with tea chests, ladders, stacks of cloth which might have been old firemen's uniforms.

'She's probably asleep,' Mairie whispered. 'I found this place the first night we played here. Kevin said she could stay here.'

'You mean Lorne? He knows?'

'He's an old pal, he got us this residency. I told him she was a friend who'd come up for the Fringe but had nowhere to stay. I said I had eight people in my flat as it was. That's a lie by the way, I like my privacy. Where else was she going to stay? The city's bursting at the seams.'

'But what does she do all day?'

'She can go downstairs and boil a kettle, there's a loo there too. The club itself's off limits, but she's so scared I don't think she'd risk it anyway.'

She had led them past enough obstacles for a game of crazy golf, and now they were close to the front of the building. There were some small window panes here, forming a long thin arch. They were filthy, but provided a little more light.

'Millie? It's only me.' Mairie peered into the gloom. Rebus's eyes had become accustomed to the dark, but even so there were places enough she could be hiding. 'She's not here,' Mairie said. There was a sleeping bag on the floor: Rebus recognised it from the first time he'd met Millie. Beside it lay a torch. Rebus picked it up and switched it on. A paperback book lay face down on the floor.

'Where's her bag?'

'Her bag?'

'Didn't she have a bag of stuff?'

'Yes.' Mairie looked around. 'I don't see it.'

'She's gone,' said Rebus. But why would she leave the sleeping-bag, book and torch? He moved the beam around the walls. 'This place is a junk shop.' An old red rubberised fire-hose snaked cross the floor. Rebus followed it with the beam all the way to a pair of feet.

He moved the beam up past splayed legs to the rest of the body. She was propped against the corner in a sitting position. 'Stay here,' he ordered, approaching the body, trying to keep the torch steady. The fire-hose was coiled around Millie Docherty's neck. Someone had tried strangling her with it, but they hadn't succeeded. The perished rubber had snapped. So instead they'd taken the brass nozzle and stuffed it down her throat. It was still there, looking like the mouth of a funnel.

And that's what they'd used it as. Rebus put his nose close to the funnel and sniffed.

He couldn't be sure, but he thought they'd used acid. They'd tipped it down into her while she'd been choking on the nozzle. If he looked closer, he'd see her throat burnt away. He didn't look. He shone the torch on the floor instead. Her bag was lying there, its contents emptied onto the floorboards. There was something small and crumpled beside a wooden chest. He picked it up and flattened it out. It was the sleeve for a computer disk. Written on it were the letters SaS.

'Looks like they got what they wanted,' he said.

Nobody was dancing in the Crazy Hose Saloon.

Everyone had been sent home. Because the Hose was in Tollcross, it was C Division's business. They'd sent officers out from Torphichen Place.

'John Rebus,' one of the CID men said. 'You get around more than a Jehovah's Witness.'

'But I never try to sell you religion, Shug.'

Rebus watched DI Shug Davidson climb onto the stage and disappear through the door. They were all upstairs; the action was upstairs. They were setting up halogen lamps on tripods to assist the photographers. No key could be found for the first floor padlock, so they'd taken a sledgehammer to it. Rebus didn't like to ask who or what they thought they'd find hidden behind a door padlocked from the outside. He doubted it would be germane to the case. Only one thing was germane, and it was standing at the bar near the spittoon, drinking a long cold drink. Rebus walked over.

'Have you talked to your boss yet, Kevin?'

'I keep getting his answering machine.'

'Bad one.'

Kevin Strang nearly bit through the glass. 'How do you mean?'

'Bad for business.'

'Aye, right enough.'

'Mairie tells me you and her are friends?'

'Went to school together. She was a couple of years above me, but we were both in the school orchestra.'

'That's good, you'll have something to fall back on.'

'Eh?'

'If Bothwell sacks you, you can always busk for a living. Did you ever see her? Talk to her?'

Kevin knew who he meant. He was shaking his head before Rebus had finished asking.

'No?' Rebus persisted. 'You weren't even a wee bit curious? Didn't want to see what she looked like?'

'Never thought about it.'

Rebus looked across to the distant table where Mairie was being questioned by one of the Torphichen squad, with a WPC in close attendance. 'Bad one,' he said again. He leaned closer to Kevin Strang. 'Just between us, Kevin, who did you tell?'

'I didn't tell anyone.'

'Then you're going down, son.'

'How do you mean?'

'They didn't find her by accident, Kevin. They *knew* she was there. Only two people could have provided that information: Mairie or you. C Division are hard bastards. They'll want to know all about you, Kevin. You're about the only suspect they've got.'

'I'm not a suspect.'

'She died about six hours ago, Kevin. Where were you six hours ago?' Rebus was making this up: they wouldn't know for sure until the pathologist took body temperature readings. But he reckoned it was a fair guess all the same.

'I'm telling you nothing.'

Rebus smiled. 'You're just snot, Kevin. Worse, you're hired snot.' He made to pat Kevin Strang's face, but Strang flinched, staggered back, and hit the spittoon. They watched it tip with a crash to the floor, rock to and fro, and then lie there. Nothing happened for a second, then with a wet sucking sound a thick roll of something barely liquid oozed out. Everyone looked away. The only thing Strang found to look at was Rebus. He swallowed.

'Look, I had to tell Mr Bothwell, just to cover myself. If I hadn't told him, and he'd found out . . .'

'What did he say?'

'He just shrugged, said she was *my* responsibility.' He shuddered at the memory.

'Where were you when you told him?'

'In the office, off the foyer.'

'This morning?' Strang nodded. 'Tell me, Kevin, did Mr Bothwell go check out the lodger?'

Strang looked down at his empty glass. It was answer enough for Rebus.

There were strict rules covering the investigation of a serious crime such as murder. For one, Rebus should talk to the officer in charge and tell him everything he knew about Millie Docherty. For two, he should also mention his conversation with Kevin Strang. For three, he should then leave well alone and let C Division get on with it.

But at two in the morning, he was parked outside Frankie Bothwell's house in Ravelston Dykes, giving serious thought to going and ringing the doorbell. If nothing else, he might learn whether Bothwell's night attire was as gaudy as his daywear. But he dismissed the idea. For one thing, C Division would be speaking with Bothwell before the night was out, always supposing they managed to get hold of him. They would not want to be told by Bothwell that Rebus had beaten them to it.

For another, he was too late. He heard the garage doors lift automatically, and saw the dipped headlights as Bothwell's car, a gloss-black Merc with custom bodywork, bounced down off the kerb onto the road and sped away. So he'd finally got the message, and was on his way to the Hose. Either that or he was fleeing.

Rebus made a mental note to do yet more digging on Lee Francis Bothwell.

But for now, he was relieved the situation had been taken out of his hands. He drove back to Oxford Terrace at a sedate pace, trying hard not to fall asleep at the wheel. No one was waiting in ambush outside, so he let himself in quietly and went to the living room, his body too tired to stay awake but his mind too busy for sleep. Well, he had a cure for that: a mug of milky tea with a dollop of whisky in it. But there was a note on the sofa in Patience's handwriting. Her writing was better than most doctors', but not by much. Eventually Rebus deciphered it, picked up the phone, and called Brian Holmes.

'Sorry, Brian, but the note said to call whatever the time.'

'Hold on a sec.' He could hear Holmes getting out of bed, taking the cordless phone with him. Rebus imagined Nell Stapleton awake in the bed, rolling back over to sleep and cursing his name. The bedroom door closed. 'Okay,' said Holmes, 'I can talk now.'

'What's so urgent? Is it about our friend?'

'No, all's quiet on that front. I'll tell you about it in the morning. But I was wondering if you'd heard the news?'

'I was the one who found her.'

Rebus heard a fridge opening, a bottle being taken out, something poured into a glass.

'Found who?' Brian asked.

'Millie Docherty. Isn't that what we're talking about?' But of course it wasn't; Brian couldn't possibly know so soon. 'She's dead, murdered.'

'They're piling up, aren't they? What happened to her?'

'It's not a bedtime story. So what's your news?'

'A breakout from Barlinnie. Well, from a van actually, stopped between Barlinnie and a hospital. The whole thing was planned.'

Rebus sat down on the sofa. 'Cafferty?'

'He does a good impersonation of a perforated ulcer. It happened this evening. The prison van was sandwiched between two lorries. Masks, sawn-offs and a miracle recovery.'

'Oh Christ.'

'Don't worry, there are patrols all up and down the M8.'

'If he's coming back to Edinburgh, that's the last road he'll use.'

'You think he'll come back?'

'Get a grip, Brian, of course he's coming back. He's going to have to kill whoever butchered his son.'

24

He didn't get much sleep that night, in spite of the tea and whisky. He sat by the recessed bedroom window wondering when Cafferty would come. He kept his eyes on the stairwell outside until dawn came. His mind made up, he started packing. Patience sat up in bed.

'I hope you've left a note,' she said.

'We're both leaving, only not together. What's the score in an emergency?'

'My dream was making more sense than this.'

'Say you had to go away at very short notice?'

She was rubbing her hair, yawning. 'Someone would cover for me. What did you have in mind, elopement?'

'I'll put the kettle on.'

When he came back from the kitchen carrying two mugs of coffee, she was in the shower.

'What's happening?' she asked afterwards, rubbing herself dry.

'You're going to your sister's,' he told her. 'So drink your coffee, phone her, get dressed, and start packing.'

She took the mug from him. 'In that order?'

'Any order you like.'

'And where are you going?'

'Somewhere else.'

'Who'll feed the pets?'

'I'll get someone to do it, don't worry.'

'I'm not worried.' She took a sip of coffee. 'Yes I am. What *is* going on?'

'A bad man's coming to town.' Something struck him. 'There you are, that's another old film I like: *High Noon*.'

Rebus booked into a small hotel in Bruntsfield. He knew the night manager and phoned first, checking they had a room.

'You're lucky, we've one single.'

'How come you're not full?'

'The old gent who was in it, he's been coming here for years, he died of a stroke yesterday afternoon.'

'Oh.'

'You're not superstitious or anything?'

'Not if it's your only room.'

He climbed the steps to street level and looked around. When he was happy, he gestured for Patience to join him. She carried a couple of bags. Rebus was already holding her small suitcase. They put the stuff in the back of her car and embraced hurriedly.

'I'll call you,' he said. 'Don't try phoning me.'

'John . . .'

'Trust me on this if on nothing else, Patience, please.'

He watched her drive off, then hung around to make sure no one was following her. Not that he could be absolutely sure. They could pick her up on Queensferry Road. Cafferty wouldn't hesitate to use her, or anyone, to get to him. Rebus got his own bag from the flat, locked the flat tight, and headed for his car. On the way he stopped at the next door neighbour's door, dropping an envelope through the letterbox. Inside were keys to the flat and feeding instructions for Lucky the cat, the budgie with no name, and Patience's goldfish.

It was still early morning, the quiet streets unsuitable for a tail. Even so, he took every back route he could think of. The hotel was just a big family house really, converted into a small family hotel. Out front, where a garden once separated it from the pavement, tarmac had been laid, making a car park for half a dozen cars. But Rebus drove round the back and parked where the staff parked. Monty, the night manager, brought him in the back way, then led him straight up to his room. It was at the top of the house, all the way up one of the creakiest staircases Rebus had ever climbed. No one would be able to tiptoe up there without him and the woodworm knowing about it.

He lay on the solid bed wondering if lying on a dead man's bed was like stepping into his shoes. Then he started to think about Cafferty. He knew he was taking half-measures only. How hard would it be for Cafferty to track him down? A few men staked outside Fettes and St Leonard's and in a few well-chosen pubs, and Rebus would be in the gangster's hands by the end of the day. Fine, he just didn't want Patience involved, or Patience's home, or those of his friends.

Didn't most suicides do the same thing, come to hotels so as not to involve family and friends?

He could have gone home of course, back to his flat in Marchmont, but it was still full of students working in Edinburgh over the summer. He liked his tenants, and didn't want them meeting Cafferty. Come to that, he didn't want Monty the night manager meeting Cafferty either.

'He's not after *me*,' he kept reminding himself, hands behind his head as he stared at the ceiling. There was a clock radio by the bed, and he switched it on, catching the news. Police were still searching for Morris Gerald Cafferty. 'He's not after me,' he repeated. But in a sense, Cafferty *was*. He'd know Rebus was his best bet to finding the killers. There was a short item about the body at the Crazy Hose, though no gruesome details. Not yet, anyway.

When the news finished, he washed and went downstairs. He got a black cab to take him to St Leonard's. Once told the destination, the driver switched off his meter.

'On the house,' he said.

Rebus nodded and sat back. He'd commandeer someone's car during the course of the day, either that or find a spare car from the pool. No one would complain. They all knew who'd put Cafferty in Barlinnie. At St Leonard's, he walked smartly into the station and went straight to the computer, tapping into Brains. Brains had a direct link to PNC2, the UK mainland police database at Hendon. As he'd expected, there wasn't much on Lee Francis Bothwell, but there was a note referring him to files kept by Strathclyde Police in Partick.

The officer he talked to in Partick was not thrilled.

'All that old stuff's in the attic,' he told Rebus. 'I'll tell you, one of these days the ceiling'll come down.'

'Just go take a look, eh? Fax it to me, save yourself a phone call.'

An hour later, Rebus was handed several fax sheets relating to activities of the Tartan Army and the Workers' Party in the early 1970s. Both groups had enjoyed short anarchic lives, robbing banks to finance their arms purchases. The Tartan Army had wanted independence for Scotland, at any price. What the Workers' Party had wanted Rebus couldn't recall, and there was no mention of their objectives in the fax. The Tartan Army had been the bigger terror of the two, breaking into explosives stores and Army bases, building up an arms cache for an insurrection which never came.

Frankie Bothwell was mentioned as a Tartan Army supporter, but with no evidence against him of illegal acts. Rebus reckoned this would be just before his move to the Orkneys and rebirth as Cuchullain. Cuchullain of the Red Hand.

Arch Gowrie was probably at breakfast when Rebus caught him. He could hear the clink of cutlery on plate.

'Sorry to disturb you so early, sir.'

'More questions, Inspector? Maybe I should start charging a consultancy fee.'

'I was hoping you could help me with a name.' Gowrie made a noncommittal noise, or maybe he was just chewing. 'Lee Francis Bothwell.'

'Frankie Bothwell?'

'You know him?'

'I used to.'

'He was a member of the Orange Lodge?'

'Yes, he was.'

'But he got kicked out?'

'Not quite. He left voluntarily.'

'Might I ask why, sir?'

'You might.' There was a pause. 'He was ... unpredictable, had a temper on him. Most of the time he was fine. He coached the youth football teams for a couple of district lodges, he seemed to enjoy that.'

'Was he interested in history?'

'Yes, Scottish and Irish history.'

'Cuchullain?'

'Amongst other things. I think he wrote a couple of articles for *Ulster*, that's the magazine of the UDA. He did them under a pseudonym, so we couldn't discipline him, but the style was his. Loyalists, Inspector, are very interested in Irish pre-history. Bothwell was writing about the Cruithin. He was very bright like that, but he –'

'Did he have any links with the Orange Loyal Brigade?'

'Not that I know of, but it wouldn't surprise me. Gavin MacMurray's interested in pre-history too.' Gowrie sighed. 'Frankie left the Orange Lodge because he didn't feel we went far enough. That's as much as I'll say, but maybe it tells you something about him.'

'It does, Mr Gowrie, yes. Thanks for your help.'

Rebus put the phone down and thought it over. Then he shook his head sadly.

'You picked some place to hide her, Mairie. Some fucking place.'

His desk now looked like a skip, and he decided to do something about it. He filled his waste bin with empty cups, plates, crumpled papers and packets. Until, only slightly buried, he came to an A4-size manila envelope. His name was written on it in black marker pen. The envelope was fat. It hadn't been opened.

'Who left this here?'

But nobody seemed to know. They were too busy discussing another call made to the newspaper by the lunatic with the Irish accent. Nobody knew about The Shield, of course, not the way Rebus knew. The media had stuck to the theory that the body in Mary King's Close was that of the caller, a rogue from an IRA unit who'd been disciplined by his masters. It didn't make any sense now, but that didn't matter. There'd been another call now, another morning headline. ' "Shut the Whole Thing Down," says Threat Man.' Rebus had considered what benefit SaS could derive from disrupting the Festival. Answer: none.

He looked at the envelope a final time, then ran his finger under the flap and eased out a dozen sheets of paper, photocopies of reports, news stories. American, the lot of them, though whoever had done the copying had been careful, leaving off letter headings, addresses, phone numbers. As Rebus read, he couldn't be sure where half the stories originated. But one thing *was* clear, they were all about one man.

Clyde Moncur.

There were no messages, nothing handwritten, nothing to identify the sender. Rebus checked the envelope. It hadn't been posted. It had been delivered by hand. He asked around again, but nobody owned up to having ever seen the thing before. Mairie was the only source he could think of, but she wouldn't have sent the stuff like this.

He read through the file anyway. It reinforced his impression of Clyde Moncur. The man was a snake. He ran drugs up into Vancouver and across to Ontario. His boats brought in immigrants from the Far East, or often didn't, though they were known to have picked up travellers along the way. What happened to them, these people who paid to be transported to a better life? The bottom of the deep blue sea, seemed to be the inference.

There were other murky areas to Moncur's life, like his undeclared interest in a fish processing plant outside Toronto ... Toronto, home of The Shield. The US Internal Revenue had been trying for years to get to the bottom of it all, and failing.

Buried in all the clippings was the briefest mention of a Scottish salmon farm.

Moncur had imported Scottish smoked salmon into the USA, though the Canadian stuff was just a mite closer to hand. The salmon farm he used was just north of Kyle of Lochalsh. Its name struck home. Rebus had come across the name very recently. He went back to the files on Cafferty, and there it was. Cafferty had been legitimate part-owner of the farm in the 1970s and early 80s ... around the time him and Jinky Johnson were washing and drying dirty money for the UVF.

'This is beautiful,' Rebus said to himself. He hadn't just squared the circle, he'd created an unholy triangle out of it.

He got a patrol car to take him to the Gar-B.

From the back seat, he had a more relaxed view of the whole of Pilmuir. Clyde Moncur had talked about the early Scottish settlers. The new settlers, of course, took on just as tough a life, moving into the private estates which were being built around and even *in* Pilmuir. This was a frontier life, complete with marauding natives who wanted the intruders gone, border skirmishes, and wilderness experiences aplenty. These estates provided starter homes for those making the move from the rented sector. They also provided starter courses in basic survival.

Rebus wished the settlers well.

When they got to the Gar-B, Rebus gave the uniforms their instructions and sat in the back seat enjoying the stares of passers-by. They were away a while, but when they came back one of them was pulling a boy by his forearm and pushing the boy's bike. The other one had two kids, no bikes. Rebus looked at them. He recognised the one with the bike.

'You can let the others go,' he said. 'But him, I want in here with me.'

The boy got into the car reluctantly. His pals ran as soon as the officers released them. When they were far enough away, they turned to watch. They wanted to know what would happen.

'What's your name, son?' Rebus asked.

'Jock.'

Maybe it was true and maybe it wasn't. Rebus wasn't bothered. 'Shouldn't you be at school, Jock?'

'We've no' started back yet.'

This too could be true; Rebus didn't know. 'Do you remember me, son?'

'It wasnae me did your tyres.'

Rebus shook his head. 'That's all right. I'm not here about that. But you remember when I came here?' The boy nodded. 'Remember you were with a pal, and he thought I was someone else. Remember? He asked me where my flash car was.' The boy shook his head. 'And you told him that I wasn't who he thought I was. Who did he think I was, son?'

'I don't know.'

'Yes you do.'

'I don't.'

'But someone a bit like me, eh? Similar build, age, height? Fancier clothes though, I'll bet.'

'Maybc.'

'What about his car, the swanky car?'

'A custom Merc.'

Rebus smiled. There were some things boys just had eyes and a memory for. 'What colour Merc?'

'Black, all of it. The windows too.'

'Seen him here a lot?'

'Don't know.'

'Nice car though, eh?'

The boy shrugged.

'Right, son, on you go.'

The boy knew from the pleased look on the policeman's face that he'd made a mistake, that he'd somehow helped. His cheeks burned with shame. He snatched his bike from the constable and ran with it, looking back from time to time. His pals were waiting to question him.

'Get what you were looking for, sir?' asked one of the uniforms, getting back into the car.

'Exactly what I was looking for,' said Rebus.

25

He went to see Mairie, but a friend was looking after her and Mairie herself was sleeping. The doctor had given her a few sleeping pills. Left alone in the flat with an unconscious Mairie, he could have gone through her notes and computer files, but the friend didn't even let him over the threshold. She had a pinched face with prominent cheeks and a few too many teeth in her quiet but determined mouth.

'Tell her I called,' Rebus said, giving up. He had retrieved his car from the back of the hotel. Cafferty would find him, with or without the rustbucket to point the way. He drove to Fettes where DCI Kilpatrick had an update on the Clyde Moncur surveillance.

'He's acting the tourist, John, no more or less. He and his wife are admiring the sights, taking bus tours, buying souvenirs.' Kilpatrick sat back in his chair. 'The men I put on it are restless. Like they say, it's hardly likely he's here on business when his wife's with him.'

'Or else it's the perfect cover.'

'A couple more days, John, that's all we can give it.'

'I appreciate it, sir.'

'What about this body at the Crazy Hose?'

'Millie Docherty, sir.'

'Yes, any ideas?'

Rebus just shrugged. Kilpatrick didn't seem to expect an answer. Part of his mind was still on Calumn Smylie. They were about to open an internal inquiry. There would be questions to answer about the whole investigation.

'I hear you had a run in with Smylie,' Kilpatrick said.

So Ormiston had been talking. 'Just one of those things, sir.'

'Watch out for Smylie, John.'

'That's all I seem to do these days, sir, watch out for people.' But he knew now that Smylie was the least of his problems.

At St Leonard's, DCI Lauderdale was fighting his corner, arguing that his team should take on the Millie Docherty investigation from C Division. So he was too busy to come bothering Rebus, and that was fine by Rebus.

Officers were out at Lachlan Murdock's flat, talking to him. He was being treated as a serious suspect now; you didn't lose two flatmates to hideous deaths and not come under the microscope. Murdock would be on the petri dish from now till the case reached some kind of conclusion. Rebus returned to his desk. Since he'd last been there, earlier in the day, people had started using it as a rubbish bin again.

He phoned London, and waited to be passed along the line. It was not a call he could have made from Fettes.

'Abernethy speaking.'

'About bloody time. It's DI Rebus here.'

'Well well. I wondered if I'd hear from you.'

Rebus could imagine Abernethy leaning back in his chair. Maybe his feet were up on the desk in front of him. 'I must have left a dozen messages, Abernethy.'

'I've been busy, what about you?' Rebus stayed silent. 'So, Inspector Rebus, how can I help?'

'I've got a few questions. How much stuff is the Army losing?'

'You've lost me.'

'I don't think so.' Someone walking past offered Rebus a cigarette. Without thinking he accepted it. But then the donor walked away, leaving Rebus without a light. He sucked on the filter anyway. 'I think you know what I'm talking about.' He opened the desk drawers, looking for matches or a lighter.

'Well, I don't.'

'I think material has been going missing.'

'Really?'

'Yes, really.' Rebus waited. He didn't want to speculate too wildly, and he certainly didn't want Abernethy to know any more than was necessary. But there was silence on the other end of the line. 'Or you suspect it's going missing.'

'That would be a matter for Army Intelligence or the security service.'

'Yes, but you're Special Branch, aren't you? You're the public arm of the security service. I think you came up here in a hurry because you damned well know what's going on. The question is, why did you disappear again in such a hurry too?'

'You've lost me again. Maybe I'd better pack my bag for a trip, what do you say?'

Rebus didn't say anything, he just put down the phone. 'Anyone got a light?' Someone tossed a box of matches onto the desk. 'Cheers.' He lit the cigarette and inhaled, the smoke rattling his nerves like they were dice in a cup.

He knew Abernethy would come.

He kept moving, the most difficult kind of target. He was trusting to his instincts; after all, he had to trust something. Dr Curt was in his office at the university. To get to the office you had to walk past a row of wooden boxes marked with the words 'Place Frozen Sections Here'. Rebus had never looked in the boxes. In the Pathology building, you kept your eyes front and your nostrils tight. They were doing some work in the quadrangle. Scaffolding had been erected, and a couple of workmen were belying their name by sitting on it smoking cigarettes and sharing a newspaper.

'Busy, busy, busy,' Curt said, when Rebus reached his office. 'You know, most of the university staff are on holiday. I've had postcards from the Gambia, Queensland, Florida.' He sighed. 'I am cursed with a vocation while others get a vacation.'

'I bet you were awake all night thinking up that one.'

'I was awake half the night thanks to your discovery at the Crazy Hose Saloon.'

'Post-mortem?'

'Not yet complete. It was a corrosive of some kind, the lab will tell us exactly which. I am constantly surprised by the methods murderers will resort to. The fire hose was new to me.'

'Well, it stops the job becoming routine, I suppose.'

'How's Caroline?'

'I'd forgotten all about her.'

'You must pray that she'll let you.'

'I stopped praying a long time ago.'

He walked back down the stairs and out into the quadrangle, wondering if it was too soon in the day for a drink at Sandy Bell's. The pub was just round the corner, and he hadn't been there in months. He noticed someone standing in front of the Frozen Sections boxes. They had the flap open, like they'd just made a deposit. Then they turned around towards Rebus and smiled.

It was Cafferty.

'Dear God.'

Cafferty closed the flap. He was dressed in a baggy black suit and open-necked white shirt, like an undertaker on his break. 'Hello, Strawman.' The old nickname. It was like an ice-pack on Rebus's spine. 'Let's talk.' There were two men behind Rebus, the two from the churchyard, the two who'd watched him taking a beating. They escorted him back to a newish Rover parked in the quadrangle. He caught the licence number, but felt Cafferty's hand land on his shoulder.

'We'll change plates this afternoon, Strawman.' Someone was getting out of the car. It was weasel-face. Rebus and Cafferty got into the back of the car, weasel-face and one of the heavies into the front. The other heavy stood outside, blocking Rebus's door. He looked towards where the scaffolding stood. The workmen had vanished. There was a sign on the scaffolding, just the name of a firm and their telephone number. A light came on in practically the last dark room in Rebus's head.

Big Ger Cafferty had made no effort at disguise. His clothes didn't look quite right – a bit large and not his style – but his face and hair were unchanged. A couple of students, one Asian and one Oriental, walked across the quadrangle towards the Pathology building. They didn't so much as glance at the car.

'I see your stomach cleared up.'

Cafferty smiled. 'Fresh air and exercise, Strawman. You look like you could do with both.'

'You're crazy coming back here.'

'We both know I had to.'

'We'll have you inside again in a matter of days.'

'Maybe I only need a few days. How close are you?'

Rebus stared through the windscreen. He felt Cafferty's hand cover his knee.

'Speaking as one father to another . . .'

'You leave my daughter out of this!'

'She's in London, isn't she? I've a lot of friends in London.'

'And I'll tear them to shreds if she so much as stubs a toe.'

Cafferty smiled. 'See? See how easy it is to get worked up when it's family?'

'It's not family with you, Cafferty, you said so yourself. It's business.'

'We could do a trade.' Cafferty looked out of his window, as though thinking. 'Say someone's been bothering you, could be an old flame. Let's say she's been disrupting your life, making things awkward.' He paused. 'Making you see red.'

Rebus nodded to himself. So weasel-face had witnessed the little scene with the spray-can.

'My problem, not yours.'

Cafferty sighed. 'Sometimes I wonder how hard you really are.' He looked at Rebus. 'I'd like to find out.'

'Try me.'

'I will, Strawman, one day. Trust me on that.'

'Why not now? Just you and me?'

Cafferty laughed. 'A square go? I haven't the time.'

'You used to shuffle cash around for the UVF, didn't you?'

The question caught Cafferty unaware. 'Did I?'

'Till Jinky Johnson disappeared. You were in pretty tight with the terrorists. Maybe that's where you heard of the SaS. Billy was a member.'

Cafferty's eyes were glassy. 'I don't know what you're saying.'

'No, but you know what I'm talking about. Ever heard the name Clyde Moncur?'

'No.'

'That sounds like another lie to me. What about Alan Fowler?'

Now Cafferty nodded. 'He was UVF.'

'Not now he isn't. Now he's SaS, and he's here. They're *both* here.'

'Why are you telling me?' Rebus didn't answer. Cafferty moved his face closer. 'It's not because you're scared. There's something else … What's on your mind, Rebus?' Rebus stayed silent. He saw Dr Curt coming out of the Pathology building. Curt's car, a blue Saab, was parked three cars away from the Rover.

'You've been busy,' Cafferty said.

Now Curt was looking over towards the Rover, at the big man standing there and the men seated inside.

'Any more names?' Cafferty was beginning to sound impatient, losing all his cool veneer. 'I want *all of them*!' His right hand lashed around Rebus's throat, his left hand pushing him deep into the corner of the seat. 'Tell me all of it, all of it!'

Curt had turned as though forgetting something, and was walking back towards the building. Rebus blinked away the water in his eyes. The stooge outside thumped on the bodywork. Cafferty released his grip and watched Curt going back into Pathology. He used both hands to grasp Rebus's face, turning it towards his, holding Rebus with the pressure of his palms on Rebus's cheekbones.

'We'll meet again, Rebus, only it won't be like in the song.' Rebus felt like his head was going to crack, but then the pressure stopped.

The heavy outside opened the door and he got out fast. As the heavy got in, the driver gunned the engine. The back window went down, Cafferty looking at him, saying nothing.

The car sped off, tyres screeching as it turned into the one-way traffic on Teviot Place. Dr Curt appeared in the Pathology doorway, then came briskly across the quadrangle.

'Are you all right? I've just phoned the police.'

'Do me a favour, when they get here tell them you were mistaken.'

'What?'

'Tell them anything, but don't tell them it was me.'

Rebus started to move off. Maybe he'd have that drink at Sandy Bell's. Maybe he'd have three.

'I'm not a very good liar,' Dr Curt called after him.

'Then the practice will be good for you,' Rebus called back.

Frankie Bothwell shook his head again.

'I've already spoken with the gentlemen from Torphichen Place. You want to ask anyone, ask them.'

He was being difficult. He'd had a difficult night, what with being dragged from his bed and then staying up till all hours dealing with the police, answering their questions, explaining the stash of cased spirits they'd found on the first floor. He didn't need this.

'But you knew Miss Murdoch was upstairs,' Rebus persisted.

'Is that right?' Bothwell wriggled on his barstool and tipped ash onto the floor.

'You were told she was upstairs.'

'Was I?'

'Your manager told you.'

'You've only got his word for that.'

'You deny he said it? Maybe if we could get the two of you together?'

'You can do what you like, he's out on his ear anyway. I sacked him first thing. Can't have people dossing upstairs like that, bad for the club's image. Let them sleep on the streets like everyone else.'

Rebus tried to imagine what resemblance the kid at the Gar-B had seen between himself and Frankie Bothwell. He was here because he was feeling reckless. Plus he'd put a few whiskies away in Sandy Bell's. He was here because he quite fancied beating Lee Francis Bothwell to a bloody mush on the dance floor.

Stripped of music and flashing lights and drink and dancers, the Crazy Hose had as much life as a warehouse full of last year's fashions. Bothwell, appearing to dismiss Rebus from his mind, lifted one foot and began to rub some dust from a cowboy boot. Rebus feared the white trousers would either split or else eviscerate their wearer. The boot was black and soft with small puckers covering it like miniature moon craters. Bothwell caught Rebus looking at it.

'Ostrich skin,' he explained.

Meaning the craters were where each feather had been plucked. 'Look like a lot of little arseholes,' Rebus said admiringly. Bothwell straightened up. 'Look, Mr Bothwell, all I want are a couple of answers. Is that so much to ask?'

'And then you'll leave?'

'Straight out the door.'

Bothwell sighed and flicked more ash onto the floor. 'Okay then.'

Rebus smiled his appreciation. He rested his hand on the bar and leaned towards Bothwell.

'Two questions,' he said. 'Why did you kill her and who's got the disk?'

Bothwell stared at him, then laughed. 'Get out of here.'

Rebus lifted his hand from the bar. 'I'm going,' he said. But he stopped at the doors to the foyer, holding them open. 'You know Cafferty's in town?'

'Never heard of him.'

'That's not the point. The point is, has *he* heard of *you*? Your father was a minister. Did you ever learn Latin?'

'What?'

'*Nemo me impune lacessit.*' Bothwell didn't even blink. 'Never mind, it

648

won't worry Cafferty one way or the other. See, you didn't just meddle with him, you meddled with his family.'

He let the doors swing shut behind him. This was the way he should have worked it throughout, using Cafferty – the mere threat of Cafferty – to do his work for him. But would Cafferty be enough to scare the American and the Ulsterman?

Somehow, John Rebus doubted it.

Back at St Leonard's, Rebus first phoned the scaffolding company, then placed a call to Peter Cave.

'Something I've been meaning to ask you, sir,' he said.

'Yes?' Cave sounded tired, deep down inside.

'Since the Church stopped supporting the youth club, how do you survive?'

'We manage. Everyone who comes along has to pay.'

'Is it enough?'

'No.'

'You're not subsidising the place out of your own pocket?' Cave laughed at this. 'What then? Sponsorship?'

'In a way, yes.'

'What sort of way?'

'Just someone who saw the good the club was doing.'

'Someone you know?'

'Never met him, as a matter of fact.'

Rebus took a stab. 'Francis Bothwell?'

'How did you know that?'

'Someone told me,' Rebus lied.

'Davey?'

So Davey Soutar *did* know Bothwell. Yes, it figured. Maybe from a district lodge football team, maybe some other way. Time to change track.

'What does Davey do by the way?'

'Works in an abattoir.'

'He's not a builder then?'

'No.'

'One last thing, Mr Cave. I got a name from a scaffolding company: Malky Haston. He's eighteen, lives in the Gar-B.'

'I know Malky, Inspector. And he knows you.'

'How's that?'

'Heavy metal fan, always wears a band t-shirt. You've spoken with him.'

Black t-shirt, thought Rebus, Davey Soutar's pal. With white flecks in his hair that Rebus had mistaken for dandruff.

'Thank you, Mr Cave,' Rebus said, 'I think that's everything.'

Everything he needed.

A uniform approached as he put down the phone, and handed Rebus the information he'd requested on recent and not-so-recent break-ins. Rebus knew what he was looking for, and it didn't take long. Acid wasn't that easy to come by, not unless you had a plausible reason for wanting it. Easier to steal the stuff if you could. And where could you find acid?

Break-ins at Craigie Comprehensive School were fairly standard. It was like pre-employment training for the unrulier pupils. They learned to slip a window-catch and jemmy open a door, some graduated to lock-picking, and others became fences for the stolen goods. It was always a buyers' market, but then economics was not a strong point with these junior careerists. Three months back, Craigie had been entered at the dead of night and the tuck shop emptied.

They'd also broken into the science rooms, physics and chemistry. The chemistry stock room had a different lock, but they took that out too, and made off with a large jar of methylated spirits, a few other choice cocktail ingredients, and three thick glass jars of various acids.

The caretaker, who lived in a small pre-fabricated house on the school grounds, saw and heard nothing. He'd been watching a special comedy night on the television. Probably he wouldn't have ventured out of doors anyway. Craigie Comprehensive wasn't exactly full of pupils with a sense of humour or love for their elders.

What could you expect from a school whose catchment area included the infamous Garibaldi Estate?

He was putting the pieces together when Chief Inspector Lauderdale came over.

'As if we're not stretched thin enough,' Lauderdale complained.

'What's that?'

'Another anonymous threat, that's twice today. He says our time's up.'

'Shame, I was just beginning to enjoy myself. Any specifics?'

Lauderdale nodded distractedly. 'A bomb. He didn't say where. He says it's so big there'll be no hiding place.'

'Festival's nearly over,' Rebus said.

'I know, that's what worries me.' Yes, it worried Rebus too.

Lauderdale turned to walk away, just as Rebus's phone rang.

'Inspector, my name's Blair-Fish, you won't remember me . . .'

'Of course I remember you, Mr Blair-Fish. Have you called to apologise about your grand-nephew again?'

'Oh no, nothing like that. But I'm a bit of a local historian, you see.'

'Yes.'

'And I was contacted by Matthew Vanderhyde. He said you wanted some information about Sword and Shield.'

Good old Vanderhyde: Rebus had given up on him. 'Go on, please.'

'It's taken me a while. There was thirty years of detritus to wade through . . .'

'What have you got, Mr Blair-Fish?'

'Well, I've got notes of some meetings, a treasurer's report, minutes and things like that. Plus the membership lists. I'm afraid they're not complete.'

Rebus sat forward in his chair. 'Mr Blair-Fish, I'd like to send someone over to collect everything from you. Would that be all right?' Rebus was reaching for pen and paper.

'Well, I suppose . . . I don't see why not.'

'Let's look on it as final atonement for your grand-nephew. Now if you'll just give me your address . . .'

Locals called it the Meat Market, because it was sited close to the slaughterhouse. Workers from the slaughterhouses wandered in at lunchtime for pints, pies and cigarettes. Sometimes they wore flecks of blood; the owner didn't mind. He'd been one of them once, working the jet-air gun at a chicken factory. The pistol, hooked up to a compressor, had taken the heads off several hundred stunned chickens per hour. He ran the Meat Market with the same unruffled facility.

It wasn't lunchtime, so the Market was quiet – two old men drinking slow half pints at opposite ends of the bar, ignoring one another so studiously that there had to be a grudge between them, and two unemployed youths shooting pool and trying to make each game last, their pauses between shots the stuff of chess games. Finally, there was a man with sparks in his eyes. The proprietor was keeping a watch on him. He knew trouble when he saw it. The man was drinking whisky and water. He looked the sort of drinker, when he was mortal you wouldn't want to get in his way. He wasn't getting mortal just now; he was making the one drink last. But he didn't look like he was enjoying anything about it. Finally he finished the quarter gill.

'Take care,' the proprietor said.

'Thanks,' said John Rebus, heading for the door.

Slaughterhouse workers are a different breed.

They worked amid brain and offal, thick blood and shit, in a sanitised environment of whitewash and piped radio music. A huge electrical unit reached down from the ceiling to suck the smell away and pump in fresh air. The young man hosing blood into a drain did so expertly, spraying none of the liquid anywhere other than where he wanted it. And afterwards he turned down the pressure at the nozzle and hosed off his black rubber boots. He wore a white rubberised apron round his neck and stretching down to his knees, as did most of those around him.

Aprons to Rebus meant barmen, masons and butchers. He was reminded only of this last as he walked across the floor.

They were working with cattle. The cows looked young and fearful, eyes bulging. They'd probably already been injected with muscle relaxants, so moved drunkenly along the line. A jolt of electricity behind either ear numbed them, and quickly the wielder of the bolt-gun took aim with the cold muzzle hard against each skull. Their back legs seemed to crumple first. Already the light was vanishing from behind their eyes.

He'd been told Davey Soutar was working near the back of the operation, so he had to pick his way around the routine. Men and women speckled with blood smiled and nodded as he passed. They all wore hats to keep their hair off the meat.

Or perhaps to keep the meat off their hair.

Soutar was by the back wall, resting easily against it, hands tucked into the front of his apron. He was talking to a girl, chatting her up perhaps.

So romance isn't dead, thought Rebus.

Then Soutar saw him, just as Rebus slipped on a wet patch of floor. Soutar placed him immediately, and seemed to raise his head and roll his eyes in defeat. Then he ran forward and picked something up from a shiny metal table. He was fumbling with it as Rebus advanced. It was only when Soutar took aim and the girl screamed that Rebus realised it was a bolt-gun. There was the sound of a two-pound hammer hitting a girder. The bolt flew, but Rebus dodged it. Soutar threw the gun at him and dived for the rear wall, hitting the bar of the emergency exit. The door swung open then closed again behind him. The girl was still screaming as Rebus ran towards her, pushed the horizontal bar to unlock the door, and stumbled into the abattoir's back yard.

There were a couple of large transporters in the middle of disgorging their doomed cargo. The animals were sending out distress calls as they were fed into holding pens. The entire rear area was walled in, so nobody from the outside world could glimpse the spectacle. But if you went around the transporters, a lane led back to the front of the building. Rebus was about to head that way when the blow felled him. It had come from behind. On his hands and knees, he half-turned his head to see his attacker. Soutar had been hiding behind the door. He was holding a long metal stick, a cattle prod. It was this which he had swung at Rebus's head, catching him on the left ear. Blood dropped onto the ground. Soutar lunged with the pole, but Rebus caught it and managed to pull himself up. Soutar kept moving forwards, but though wiry and young he did not possess the older man's bulk and strength. Rebus twisted the pole from his hands, then dodged the kick which Soutar aimed at him. Kick-fighting wasn't so easy with rubber boots on.

Rebus wanted to get close enough to land a good punch or kick of his own, or even to wrestle Soutar to the ground. But Soutar reached into his apron and came out with a gold-coloured butterfly knife, flicking its two moulded wings to make a handle for the vicious looking blade.

'There's more than one way to skin a pig,' he said, grinning, breathing hard.

'I like it when there's an audience,' Rebus said. Soutar turned for a second to take in the sight of the cattle herders, all of whom had stopped work to watch the fight. By the time he looked back, Rebus had caught the knife hand with the toe of his shoe, sending the knife clattering to the ground. Soutar came straight for him then, butting him on the bridge of the nose. It was a good hit. Rebus's eyes filled with tears, he felt energy earth out of him into the ground, and blood ran down his lips and chin.

'You're dead!' Soutar screamed. 'You just don't know it yet!' He picked up his knife, but Rebus had the metal pole, and swung it in a wide arc. Soutar hesitated, then ran for it. He took a short cut, climbing the rail which funnelled the cattle into the pens, then leaping one of the cows and clearing the rail at the other side.

'Stop him!' Rebus called, spraying blood. 'I'm a police officer!' But by then Davey Soutar was out of sight. All you could hear were his rubber boots flapping as he ran.

The doctor at the Infirmary had seen Rebus several times before, and tutted as usual before getting to work. She confirmed what he knew: the nose was not broken. He'd been lucky. The cut to his ear required two stitches, which she did there and then. The thread she used was thick and black and ugly.

'Whatever happened to invisible mending?'

'It wasn't a deterrent.'

'Fair point.'

'If it stings, you can always get your girlfriend to lick your wounds.'

Rebus smiled. Was that a chat-up line? Well, he had enough problems without adding another to the inventory. So he didn't say anything. He acted the good patient, then went to Fettes and filed the assault.

'You look like Ken Buchanan on a good night,' said Ormiston. 'Here's the stuff you wanted. Claverhouse has gone off in a huff; he didn't like being turned into a messenger boy.'

Ormiston patted the heavy package on Rebus's desk. It was a large brown cardboard box, smelling of dust and old paper. Rebus opened it and took out the ledger book which served as a membership record for the original Sword and Shield. The blue fountain-ink had faded, but each surname was in capitals so it didn't take him long. He sat staring at the two names, managing a short-lived smile. Not that he'd anything to smile about, not really. There was nothing to be proud of. His desk drawer didn't lock, but Ormiston's did. He took the ledger with him.

'Has the Chief seen this?' Ormiston shook his head.

'He's been out of the office since before it arrived.'

'I want it kept safe. Can you lock it in your drawer?' He watched Ormiston open the deep drawer, drop the package in, then shut it again and lock it.

'Tighter than a virgin's,' Ormiston confirmed.

'Thanks. Listen, I'm going out hunting.'

Ormiston drew the key out of the lock and pocketed it. 'Count me in,' he said.

26

Not that Rebus expected to find Davey Soutar at home; he doubted Soutar was quite that daft. But he did want to take a look, and now he had the excuse. He also had Ormiston, who looked threatening enough to dissuade anyone who might look like complaining. Ormiston, cheered by the story of how Rebus came by his cuts and bruises (his eyes were purpling and swelling nicely, a consequence of the head butt), was further cheered by the news that they were headed for the Gar-B.

'They should open the place as a safari park,' he opined. 'Remember those places? They used to tell you to keep your car doors locked and your windows rolled up. Same advice I'd give to anyone driving through the Gar-B. You never know when the baboons will stick their arses in your face.'

'Did you ever find anything about Sword and Shield?'

'You never expected us to,' Ormiston said. When Rebus looked at him, he laughed coldly. 'I might look daft, but I'm not. You're not daft either, are you? Way you're acting, I'd say you think you've cracked it.'

'Paramilitaries in the Gar-B,' Rebus said quietly, keeping his eyes on the road. 'And Soutar's in it up to his neck and beyond.'

'He killed Calumn?'

'Could be. A knife's his style.'

'Not Billy Cunningham though?'

'No, he didn't kill Billy.'

'Why are you telling me all this?'

Rebus turned to him for a moment. 'Maybe I just want someone else to know.'

Ormiston weighed this remark. 'You think you're in trouble?'

'I can think of half a dozen people who'd throw confetti at my funeral.'

'You should take this to the Chief.'

'Maybe. Would you?'

Ormiston thought about this. 'I haven't known him long, but I heard good things from Glasgow, and he seems pretty straight. He expects us to show initiative, work off our own backs. That's what I like about SCS, the leeway. I hear you like a bit of leeway yourself.'

'That reminds me, Lee Francis Bothwell: know him?'

'He owns that club, the one with the body in it?'

'That's him.'

'I know he should change the music.'

'What to?'

'Acid house.'

It was worth a laugh, but Rebus didn't oblige. 'He's an acquaintance of my assailant.'

'What is he, slumming it?'

'I'd like to ask him, but I can't see him answering. He's been putting money into the youth club.' Rebus was measuring each utterance, wondering how much to feed Ormiston.

'Very civic minded of him.'

'Especially for someone who got kicked out of the Orange Lodge on grounds of zeal.'

Ormiston frowned. 'How are you doing for evidence?'

'The youth club leader's admitted the connection. Some kids I spoke to a while back thought I was Bothwell, only my car wasn't flash enough. He drives a customised Merc.'

'How do you read it?'

'I think Peter Cave blundered with good intention into something that was already happening. I think something very bad is happening in the Gar-B.'

They had to take a chance on parking the car and leaving it. If Rebus had thought about it, he'd have brought one other man, someone to guard the wheels. There were kids loitering by the parking bays, but not the same kids who'd done his tyres before, so he handed over a couple of quid and promised a couple more when he came back.

'It's dearer than the parking in town,' Ormiston complained as they headed for the high-rises. The Soutars' high-rise had been renovated, with a sturdy main door added to stop undesirables congregating in the entrance hall or on the stairwells. The entrance hall had been decorated with a green and red mural. Not that you would know any of this to look at the place. The lock had been smashed, and the door hung loosely on its hinges. The mural had been all but blocked out by penned graffiti and thick black coils of spray paint.

'Which floor are they on?' Ormiston asked.

'The third.'

'Then we'll take the stairs. I don't trust the lifts in these places.'

The stairs were at the end of the hall. Their walls had become a winding scribble-pad, but they didn't smell too bad. At each turn in the stairs lay empty cider cans and cigarette stubs. 'What do they need a youth club for when they've got the stairwell?' Ormiston asked.

'What've you got against the lift?'

'Sometimes the kids'll wait till you're between floors then shut off the power.' He looked at Rebus. 'My sister lives in one of those H-blocks in Oxgangs.'

They entered the third floor at the end of a long hallway which seemed to be doubling as a wind tunnel. There were fewer scribbles on the walls, but there were also smeared patches, evidence that the inhabitants had been cleaning the stuff off. Some of the doors offered polished brass name plaques and bristle doormats. But most were also protected by a barred iron gate, kept locked shut when the flats were empty. Each flat had a mortice deadlock as well as a Yale, and a spyhole.

'I've been in jails with laxer security.'

But conspicuously, the door with the name Soutar on it had no extra security, no gate or spyhole. This fact alone told Rebus a lot about Davey Soutar, or at least about his reputation amongst his peers. Nobody was going to break into Davey's flat.

There was neither bell nor knocker, so Rebus banged his fist against the meat of the door. After a wait, a woman answered. She peered out through a chink, then opened the door wide.

'Fuckin' polis,' she said. It was a statement of fact rather than a judgment. 'Davey, I suppose?'

'It's Davey,' said Rebus.

'He did that to you?' She meant Rebus's face, so he nodded. 'And what were you doing to him?'

'Just the usual, Mrs Soutar,' Ormiston interrupted. 'A length of lead pipe on the soles of the feet, a wet towel over the face, you know how it is.'

Rebus nearly said something, but Ormiston had judged her right. Mrs Soutar smiled tiredly and stepped back into her hall. 'You'd better come in. A bit of steak would stop those eyes swelling, but all I've got is half a pound of mince, and it's the economy stuff. You'd get more meat from a butcher's pencil. This is my man, Dod.'

She had led them along the short narrow hall and into a small living room where a venerable three-piece suite took up too much space. Along the sofa, his shoeless feet resting on one arm of it, lay an unshaven man in his forties, or perhaps even badly nurtured thirties. He was reading a war comic, his lips moving with the words on the page.

'Hiy, Dod,' Mrs Soutar said loudly, 'these are the polis. Davey's just put the heid on one of them.'

'Good for him,' Dod said without looking up. 'No offence, like.'

'None taken.' Rebus had wandered over to the window, wondering what the view was like. The window, however, was a botched piece of double glazing. Condensation had crept between the panes, frosting the glass.

'It wasn't much of a view to start with,' Mrs Soutar said. He turned and smiled at her. He didn't doubt she would see through any scheme, any lie. She was a short, strong-looking woman, big boned with a chiselled jaw but a pleasant face. If she didn't smile often, it was because she had to protect herself. She couldn't afford to look weak. In the Gar-B, the weak didn't last long. Rebus wondered how much influence she'd had over her son while he was growing up here. A lot, he'd say. But then the father would be an influence too.

She kept her arms folded while she talked, unfolding them only long enough to slap Dod's feet off the end of the sofa so she could sit herself down on the arm.

'So what's he done this time?'

Dod put down his comic and reached into his packet of cigarettes, lighting one for himself and handing the pack to Mrs Soutar.

'He's assaulted a police officer for a start,' Rebus said. 'That's a pretty serious offence, Mrs Soutar. It could land him a spell in the carpentry shop.'

'You mean the jail?' Dod pronounced it, 'jyle'.

'That's what I mean.'

Dod stood up, then half doubled over, seized by a cough which crackled with phlegm. He went into the kitchenette, separated from the living room by a breakfast bar, and spat into the sink.

'Run the tap!' Mrs Soutar ordered. Rebus was looking at her. She was looking sad but resilient. It took her only a moment to shrug off the idea of the prison sentence. 'He'd be better off in jail.'

'How's that?'

'This is the Gar-B, or hadn't you noticed? It does things to you, to the young ones especially. Davey'd be better off out of the place.'

'What has it done to him, Mrs Soutar?'

She stared at him, considering how long an answer to give. 'Nothing,' she said finally. Ormiston was standing by the wall unit, studying a pile of cassettes next to the cheap hi-fi system. 'Put some music on if you like,' she told him. 'Might cheer us up.'

'Okay,' said Ormiston, opening a cassette case.

'I was joking.'

But Ormiston just smiled, slammed the tape home, and pressed play. Rebus wondered what he was up to. Then the music started, an accordion at first, joined by flutes and drums, and then a quavering voice, using vibrato in place of skill.

The song was 'The Sash'. Ormiston handed the cassette case to Rebus. The cover was a cheap Xeroxed drawing of the Red Hand of Ulster, the band's name scratched on it in black ink. They were called the Proud Red Hand Marching Band, though it was hard to conceive of anyone marching to an accordion.

Dod, who had returned from the sink, started whistling along and clapping his hands. 'It's a grand old tune, eh?'

'What do you want to put that on for?' Mrs Soutar asked Ormiston. He shrugged, saying nothing.

'Aye, a grand old tune.' Dod collapsed onto the sofa. The woman glared at him.

'It's bigotry's what it is. I've nothing against the Catholics.'

'Well neither have I,' Dod countered. He winked at Ormiston. 'But there's no shame in being proud of your roots.'

'What about Davey, Mr Soutar? Does he have anything against Catholics?'

'No.'

'No? He seems to run around with Protestant gangs.'

'It's the Gar-B,' Mr Soutar said. 'You have to belong.'

Rebus knew what he was saying. Dod Soutar sat forward on the sofa.

'Ye see, it's history, isn't it? The Protestants have run Ulster for hundreds of years. Nobody's going to give that up, are they? Not if the other lot are sniping away and planting bombs and that.' He realised that Ormiston had turned off the tape. 'Well, isn't that right? It's a religious war, you can't deny it.'

'Ever been there?' Ormiston asked. Dod shook his head. 'Then what the fuck do you know about it?'

Dod gave a challenging look, and stood up. 'I know, pal, don't think I don't.'

'Aye, right,' Ormiston said.

'I thought you were here to talk about my Davey?'

'We are talking about Davey, Mrs Soutar,' Rebus said quietly. 'In a roundabout way.' He turned to Dod Soutar. 'There's a lot of you in your son, Mr Soutar.'

Dod Soutar turned his combative gaze from Ormiston. 'Oh aye?'

Rebus nodded. 'I'm sorry, but there it is.'

Dod Soutar's face creased into an angry scowl. 'Wait a fuckn minute, pal. Think you can walk in here and fuckn –'

'People like you terrify me,' Rebus said coolly. He meant it, too. Dod Soutar, hacking cough and all, was a more horrifying prospect than a dozen Caffertys. You couldn't change him, couldn't argue with him, couldn't touch his mind in any way. He was a closed shop, and the management had all gone home.

'My son's a good boy, brought up the right way,' Soutar was saying. 'Gave him everything I could.'

'Some folk are just born lucky,' said Ormiston.

That did it. Soutar launched himself across the narrow width of the room. He went for Ormiston with his head low and both fists out in front of him, but collided with the shelf unit when Ormiston stepped smartly aside. He turned back towards the two policemen, swinging wildly, swearing barely coherent phrases. When he went for Rebus, and

Rebus arched back so that the swipe missed, Rebus decided he'd had enough. He kneed Soutar in the crotch.

'Queensferry Rules,' he said, as the man went down.

'Dod!' Mrs Soutar ran to her husband. Rebus gestured to Ormiston.

'Get out of my house!' Mrs Soutar screamed after them. She came to the front door and kept on yelling and crying. Then she went indoors and slammed her door.

'The cassette was a nice touch,' Rebus said on his way downstairs.

'Thought you'd appreciate it. Where to now?'

'While we're here,' said Rebus, 'maybe the youth club.'

They walked outside and didn't hear anything until the vase hit the ground beside them, smashing into a thousand pieces of shrapnel. Mrs Soutar was at her window.

'Missed!' Rebus yelled at her.

'Jesus Christ,' Ormiston said, as they walked away.

The usual lacklustre teenagers sat around outside the community hall, propping their backs against its door and walls. Rebus didn't bother to ask about Davey Soutar. He knew what the response would be; it had been drilled into them like catechism. His ear was tingling, not hurting exactly, but there was a dull throbbing pain in his nose. When they recognised Rebus, the gang got to their feet.

'Afternoon,' Ormiston said. 'You're right to stand up, by the way. Sitting on concrete gives you piles.'

In the hall, Jim Hay and his theatre group were sitting on the stage. Hay too recognised Rebus.

'Guess what?' he said. 'We have to mount a guard, otherwise they rip the stuff off.'

Rebus didn't know whether to believe him or not. He was more interested in the youth sitting next to Hay.

'Remember me, Malky?'

Malky Haston shook his head.

'I've got a few questions for you, Malky. Want to do it here or down the station?'

Haston laughed. 'You couldn't take me out of here, not if I didn't want to go.'

He had a point. 'We'll do it here then,' said Rebus. He turned to Hay, who raised his hands.

'I know, you want us to take a fag break.' He got up and led his troupe away. Ormiston went to the door to stop anyone else coming in.

Rebus sat on the stage next to Haston, getting close, making the teenager uncomfortable.

'I've done nothing, and I'm saying nothing.'

'Have you known Davey a while?'

Haston said nothing.

'I'd imagine since you were kids,' Rebus answered. 'Remember the first time we met? You had bits in your hair. I thought it was dandruff, but it was plaster. I spoke to ScotScaf. They hire out scaffolding to building contractors, and when it comes back it's your job to clean it. Isn't that right?'

Haston just looked at him.

'You're under orders not to talk, eh? Well, I don't mind.' Rebus stood up, facing Haston. 'There was ScotScaf scaffolding at the two murder sites, Billy's and Calumn Smylie's. You told Davey, didn't you? You knew where building work was going on, empty sites, all that.' He leaned close to Haston's face. 'You *knew*. That makes you an accessory at the very least. And that means we're going to throw you in jail. We'll pick out a nice Catholic wing for you, Malky, don't worry. Plenty of the green and white.'

Rebus turned his back and lit a cigarette. When he turned back to Haston, he offered him one. Ormiston was having a bit of bother at the door. The gang wanted in. Haston took a cigarette. Rebus lit it for him.

'Doesn't matter what you do, Malky. You can run, you can lie, you can say nothing at all. You're going away, and we're the only friends you'll ever have.'

He turned away and walked towards Ormiston. 'Let them in,' he ordered. The gang came crashing through the doors, fanning out across the hall. They could see Malky Haston was all right, though he was sitting very still on the edge of the stage. Rebus called to him.

'Thanks for the chat, Malky. We'll talk again, any time you want.' Then he turned to the gang. 'Malky's got his head screwed on,' he told them. '*He* knows when to talk.'

'Lying bastard!' Haston roared, as Rebus and Ormiston walked into the daylight.

Rebus met Lachlan Murdock at the Crazy Hose, despite Bothwell's protests.

Murdock's uncombed hair was wilder than ever, his clothes sloppy. He was waiting in the foyer when Rebus arrived.

'They all think I had something to do with it,' Murdock protested as Rebus led him into the dancehall.

'Well, you did, in a way,' Rebus said.

'What?'

'Come on, I want to show you something.'

He led Murdock up to the attic. In the daytime, the attic was a lot lighter. Even so, Rebus had brought a torch. He didn't want Murdock to miss anything.

'This,' he said, 'is where I found her. She'd suffered, believe me.'

Already, Murdock was close to fresh tears, but sympathy could wait, the truth couldn't. 'I found this on the floor.' He handed over the disk cover. 'This is what they killed her for. A computer disk, same size as would fit your machine at home.' He walked up close to Murdock's slouched figure. 'They killed her for *this*!' he hissed. He waited a moment, then moved away towards the windows.

'I thought maybe she'd have made a copy. She wasn't daft, was she? But I went to the shop, and there's nothing there. Maybe in your flat?' Murdock just sniffed. 'I can't believe she –'

'There was a copy,' Murdock groaned. 'I wiped it.'

Rebus walked back towards him. 'Why?'

Murdock shook his head. 'I didn't think it . . .' He took a deep breath. 'It reminded me . . .'

Rebus nodded. 'Ah yes, Billy Cunningham. It reminded you of the pair of them. When did you begin to suspect?'

Murdock shook his head again.

'See,' said Rebus, 'I know most of it. I know enough. But I don't know it all. Did you look at the files on the disk?'

'I looked.' He wiped his red-rimmed eyes. 'It was Billy's disk, not hers. But a lot of the stuff on it was hers.'

'I don't understand.'

Murdock managed a weak smile. 'You're right, I did know about the two of them. I didn't want to know, but I knew all the same. When I wiped the disk, I was angry, I was *so* angry.' He turned to look at Rebus. 'I don't think he could have done it without Millie. You need quite a set-up to hack into the kinds of systems they were dealing with.'

'Hacking?'

'They probably used the stuff in her shop. They hacked into Army and police computers, bypassed security, invaded datafiles, then marched out again without leaving any trace.'

'So what did they do?'

Murdock was talking now, enjoying the release. He wiped tears from below his glasses. 'They monitored a couple of police investigations and altered a few inventories. Believe me, once they were in, they could have done a lot more.'

The way Murdock went on to explain it, it was almost ludicrously simple. You could steal from the Army (with inside assistance, there had to be inside assistance), and then erase the theft by altering the computer records to show stocks as they stood, not as they had been. Then, if S C S or Scotland Yard or anyone else took an interest, you could monitor their progress or lack of it. Millie: Millie had been the key throughout. Whether or not she knew what she was doing, she got Billy Cunningham in. He placed her in the lock and turned. The disk had contained instructions on their hacking procedures, tips for bypassing security checks, the works.

Rebus didn't doubt that the further Billy Cunningham got in, the more he wanted out. He'd been killed because he wanted out. He'd probably mentioned his little insurance policy in the hope they would let him leave quietly. Instead, they'd tried to torture its whereabouts out of him, before delivering the final silencing bullet. Of course, The Shield knew Billy wasn't hacking alone. It wouldn't have taken them long to get to Millie Docherty. Billy had stayed silent to protect her. She must have known. That's why she'd run.

'There was stuff about this group, too, The Shield,' Murdock was saying. 'I thought they were just a bunch of hackers.'

Rebus tried him with a few names. Davey Soutar and Jamesie MacMurray hit home. Rebus reckoned that in an interview room he could crack Jamesie like a walnut under a hammer. But Davey Soutar . . . well, he might need a real hammer for that. The final file on the computer was all about Davey Soutar and the Gar-B.

'This Soutar,' Murdock said, 'Billy seemed to think he'd been skimming. That was the word he used. There's some stuff stashed in a lockup out at Currie.'

Currie: the lock-up would belong to the MacMurrays.

Murdock looked at Rebus. 'He didn't say what was being skimmed. Is it money?'

'I underestimated you, Davey,' Rebus said aloud. 'All down the line. It might be too late now, but I swear I won't underestimate you again.' He thought of how Davey and his kind hated the Festival. Hated it with a vengeance. He thought of the anonymous threats.

'Not money, Mr Murdock. Weapons and explosives. Come on, let's get out of here.'

Jamesie talked like a man coming out of silent retreat, especially when his father, hearing the story from Rebus, ordered him to. Gavin MacMurray was incensed, not that his son should be in trouble, but that the Orange Loyal Brigade hadn't been enough for him. It was a betrayal.

Jamesie led Rebus and the other officers to a row of wooden garages on a piece of land behind MacMurray's Garage. Two Army men were on hand. They checked for booby traps and trip wires and it took them nearly half an hour to get round to going in. Even then, they did not enter by the door. Instead, they climbed a ladder to the roof and cut through the asphalt covering, then dropped through and into the lockup. A minute later, they gave the all clear, and a police constable broke open the door with a crowbar. Gavin MacMurray was with them.

'I haven't been in here for years,' he said. He'd said it before, as if they didn't believe him. 'I never use these garages.'

They had a good look round. Jamesie didn't know the precise location of the cache, only that Davey had said he needed a place to keep it. The garage had operated as a motorcycle workshop – that was how Billy Cunningham had got to know Jamesie, and through him Davey Soutar, in the first place. There were long rickety wooden shelves groaning with obscure metal parts, a lot of them rusted brown with age, tools covered with dust and cobwebs, and tins of paint and solvent. Each tin had to be opened, each tool examined. If you could hide Semtex in a transistor radio, you could certainly hide it in a tool shed. The Army had offered a specialised sniffer dog, but it would have to come from Aldershot. So instead they used their own eyes and noses and instinct.

Hanging from nails on the walls were old tyres and wheels and chains. Forks and handlebars lay on the floor along with engine parts and mouldy boxes of nuts, bolts and screws. They scraped at the floor, but found no buried boxes. There was a lot of oil on the ground.

'This place is clean,' said a smudged Army man. Rebus nodded agreement.

'He's been and cleared the place out. How much was there, Jamesie?'

But Jamesie MacMurray had been asked this before, and he didn't know. 'I swear I don't. I just said he could use the space. He got his own padlock fitted and everything.'

Rebus stared at him. These young hard men, Rebus had been dealing with them all his life and they were pathetic, like husks in suits of armour. Jamesie was about as hard as the *Sun* crossword. 'And he never showed you?'

Jamesie shook his head. 'Never.'

His father was staring at him furiously. 'You stupid wee bastard,' Gavin MacMurray said. 'You stupid, stupid wee fool.'

'We'll have to take Jamesie down the station, Mr MacMurray.'

'I know that.' Then Gavin MacMurray slapped his son's face. With a hand callused by years of mechanical work, he loosened teeth and sent blood curdling from Jamesie's mouth. Jamesie spat on the dirt floor but said nothing. Rebus knew Jamesie was going to tell them everything he knew.

Outside, one of the Army men smiled in relief. 'I'm glad we didn't find anything.'

'Why?'

'Keeping the stuff in an environment like that, it's bound to be unstable.'

'Just like the guy who's got it.' Unstable ... Rebus thought of Unstable from Dunstable, confessing to the St Stephen Street killing, raving to DI Flower about curry and cars ... He walked back into the garage and pointed to the stain on the floor.

'That's not oil,' he said, 'not all of it.'

'What?'

'Everybody out, I want this place secured.'

They all got out. Flower should have listened to Unstable from Dunstable. The tramp had been talking about Currie, not curry. And he'd said cars because of the garages. He must have been sleeping rough nearby and seen or heard something that night.

'What is it, sir?' one of the officers asked Rebus.

'If I'm right, this is where they killed Calumn Smylie.'

That evening, Rebus moved out of the hotel and back into Patience's flat. He felt exhausted, like a tool that had lost its edge. The stain on the garage floor had been a mixture of oil and blood. They were trying to separate the two so they could DNA-test the blood against Calumn Smylie's. Rebus knew already what they'd find. It all made sense when you thought about it.

He poured a drink, then thought better of it. Instead he phoned Patience and told her she could come home in the next day or two. But she was determined to return in the morning, so he told her why she shouldn't. She was very quiet for a moment.

'Be careful, John.'

'I'm still here, aren't I?'

'Let's keep it that way.'

He rang off when he heard the doorbell. The manhunt for Davey Soutar was in full swing, under the control of CI Lauderdale at St Leonard's. Arms would be issued as and when necessary. Though they didn't know the extent of Soutar's cache, no chances would be taken. Rebus had been asked if he'd like a bodyguard.

'I'll trust to my guardian angel,' he'd said.

The doorbell rang again. He felt naked as he walked down the long straight hall towards the door. The door itself was inch-and-a-half thick wood, but most guns could cope with that and still leave enough velocity in the bullet to puncture human flesh. He listened for a second, then put his eye to the spy-hole. He let his breath out and unlocked the door.

'You've got things to tell me,' he said, opening the door wide.

Abernethy produced a bottle of whisky from behind his back. 'And I've brought some antiseptic for those cuts.'

'Internal use only,' Rebus suggested.

'The money it cost me, you better believe it. Still, a nice drop of Scotch is worth all the tea in China.'

'We call it whisky up here.' Rebus closed the door and led Abernethy back down the hall into the living room. Abernethy was impressed.

'Been taking a few back-handers?'

'I live with a doctor. It's her flat.'

'My mum always wanted me to be a doctor. A respectable job, she called it. Got some glasses?'

Rebus fetched two large glasses from the kitchen.

27

Frankie Bothwell couldn't afford to close the Crazy Hose.

The Festival and Fringe had only a couple more days to go. All too soon the tourists would be leaving. But over the past fortnight he'd really been packing them in. Advertising and word of mouth helped, as had a three-night residency by an American country singer. The club was making more money than ever before, but it wouldn't last. The Crazy Hose was unique, every bit as unique as Frankie himself. It deserved to do well. It *had* to do well. Frankie Bothwell had commitments, financial commitments. They couldn't be broken or excused because of low takings. Every week needed to be a good week.

So he was not best pleased to see Rebus and another cop walk into the bar. You could see it in his eyes and the smile as frozen as a Crazy Hose daiquiri.

'Inspector, how can I help you?'

'Mr Bothwell, this is DI Abernethy. We'd like a word.'

'It's a bit hectic just now. I haven't had a chance to replace Kevin Strang.'

'We insist,' said Abernethy.

With two conspicuous police officers on the premises, trade at the bars wasn't exactly brisk, and nobody was dancing. They were all waiting for something to happen. Bothwell took this in.

'Let's go to my office.'

Abernethy waved bye-bye to the crowd as he followed Rebus and Bothwell into the foyer. They went behind the admission desk and Bothwell unlocked a door. He sat behind his desk and watched them squeeze their way into the space that was left.

'A big office is a waste of space,' he said by way of apology. The place was like a cleaning cupboard. There were spare till rolls and boxes of glasses on a shelf above Bothwell's head, framed cowboy posters stacked against a wall, bric-a-brac and debris like everything had just spilled out of a collision at a car boot sale.

'We might be more comfortable talking in the toilets,' Rebus said.

'Or down the station,' offered Abernethy.

'I don't think we've met,' Bothwell said to him, affably enough.

'I usually only meet shit when I wipe my arse.'

That took the smile off Bothwell's face.

'Inspector Abernethy,' Rebus said, 'is Special Branch. He's here investigating The Shield.'

'The Shield?'

'No need to be coy, Mr Bothwell. You're not being charged, not yet. We just want you to know we're on to you in a big way.'

'And we're not about to let go,' Abernethy said on cue.

'Though it might help your case if you told us about Davey Soutar.' Rebus placed his hands in his lap and waited. Abernethy lit a cigarette and blew the smoke across the strewn desk. Frankie Bothwell looked from one man to the other and back again.

'Is this a joke? I mean, it's a bit early for Halloween, that's when you're supposed to scare people without any reason.'

Rebus shook his head. 'Wrong answer. What you should have said was, "Who's Davey Soutar?"'

Bothwell sat back in his chair. 'All right then, who's Davey Soutar?'

'I'm glad you asked me that,' said Rebus. 'He's your lieutenant. Maybe he's also your recruiting officer. And now he's on the run. Did you know he's been keeping back some of the explosives and guns for himself? We've got a confession.' It was a blatant lie, and caused Bothwell to smile. That smile sealed Bothwell's guilt in Rebus's mind.

'Why have you been funding the Gar-B youth centre?' he asked. 'Is it a useful recruiting station? You took the name Cuchullain when you were an anarchist. He's the great Ulster hero, the original Red Hand. That was no accident. You were dismissed from the Orange Lodge for being a bit over-zealous. In the early '70s your name was linked to the Tartan Army. They used to break into Army bases and steal weapons. Maybe that's what gave you the idea.'

Bothwell was still smiling as he asked, 'What idea?'

'You know.'

'Inspector, I haven't understood a word you've said.'

'No? Then understand this, we're a bollock-hair's breadth away from you. But more importantly, we want to find Davey Soutar, because if he's gone rogue with rifles and plastic explosives...'

'I still don't know what you're –'

Rebus jumped from his seat and grabbed Bothwell's lapels, pulling him tight against the desk. Bothwell's smile evaporated.

'I've been to Belfast, Bothwell, I've spent time in the North. The last thing that place needs is cowboys like you. So put away your forked tongue and tell us where he is!'

Bothwell wrenched himself out of Rebus's grip, his lapel tearing down the middle in the process. His face was purple, eyes blazing. He stood with his knuckles on the edge of the desk, leaning over it, his face close to Rebus's.

'Nobody meddles wi' me!' he spat. 'That's my motto.'

'Aye,' said Rebus, 'and you know the Latin for it too. Did you get a kick that night in Mary King's Close?'

'You're crazy.'

'We're the police,' Abernethy said lazily. 'We're paid to be crazy, what's your excuse?'

Bothwell considered the two of them and sat down slowly. 'I don't know anyone called Davey Soutar. I don't know anything about bombs or Sword and Shield or Mary King's Close.'

'I didn't say Sword and Shield,' said Rebus. 'I just said The Shield.'

Bothwell sat in silence.

'But now you mention it, I see your father the minister was in the original Sword and Shield. His name's on file. It was an offshoot of the Scottish National Party; I don't suppose you know anything about it?'

'Nothing.'

'No? Funny, you were in the youth league.'

'Was I?'

'Did your dad get you interested in Ulster?'

Bothwell shook his head slowly. 'You never stop, do you?'

'Never,' said Rebus.

The door opened. The two bouncers from the main door stood there, hands clasped in front of them, legs apart. They'd obviously been to the bouncers' school of etiquette. And, just as obviously, Bothwell had summoned them with some button beneath the lip of his desk.

'Escort these bastards off the premises,' he ordered.

'Nobody escorts me anywhere,' said Abernethy, 'not unless she's wearing a tight skirt and I've paid for her.' He got up and faced the bouncers. One of them made to take his arm. Abernethy grabbed the bouncer at the wrist and twisted hard. The man fell to his knees. There wasn't much room for the other bouncer, and he looked undecided. He was still looking blank as Rebus pulled him into the room and threw him over the desk. Bothwell was smothered beneath him. Abernethy let the other bouncer go and followed Rebus outside with a real spring in his step, breathing deeply of Edinburgh's warm summer air. 'I enjoyed that.'

'Aye, me too, but do you think it worked?'

'Let's hope so. We're making liabilities of them. I get the feeling they're going to implode.'

Well, that was the plan. Every good plan, however, had a fall-back. Theirs was Big Ger Cafferty.

'Is it too late to grab a curry?' Abernethy added.

'You're not in the sticks now. The night's young.'

But as Rebus led Abernethy towards a good curry house, he was thinking about liabilities and risks ... and dreading tomorrow's showdown.

28

The day dawned bright, with blue skies and a breeze which would soon warm. It was expected to stay good all day, with a clear night for the fireworks. Princes Street would be bursting at the seams, but it was quiet as DCI Kilpatrick drove along it. He was an early riser, but even he had been caught by Rebus's wake-up call.

The industrial estate was quiet too. After being cleared by the guard on the gate, he drove up to the warehouse and parked next to Rebus's car. The car was empty, but the warehouse door stood open. Kilpatrick went inside.

'Morning, sir.' Rebus was standing in front of the HGV.

'Morning, John. What's with all the cloak and dagger?'

'Sorry about that, sir. I hope I can explain.'

'I hope so too, going without breakfast never puts me in the best of moods.'

'It's just that there's something I had to tell you, and this seems as quiet a place as any.'

'Well, what is it?'

Rebus had started walking around the lorry, Kilpatrick following him. When they were at the back of the vehicle, Rebus pulled on the lever and swung the door wide open. On top of the boxes inside sat Abernethy.

'You didn't warn me it was a party,' Kilpatrick said.

'Here, let me help you up.'

Kilpatrick looked at Rebus. 'I'm not a pensioner.' And he pulled himself into the back, Rebus clambering after him.

'Hello again, sir,' Abernethy said, putting his hand out for Kilpatrick to shake. Kilpatrick folded his arms instead.

'What's this all about, Abernethy?'

But Abernethy shrugged and nodded towards Rebus.

'Notice anything, sir?' said Rebus. 'I mean, about the load.'

Kilpatrick put on a thoughtful face and looked around. 'No,' he said finally, adding: 'I never was one for party games.'

'No games, sir. Tell me, what happens to all this stuff if we're not going to use it in a sting operation?'

'It goes to be destroyed.'

'That's what I thought. And the papers go with it, don't they?'

'Of course.'

'But since the stuff has been under our stewardship, those papers will be from the City of Edinburgh Police?'

'I suppose so. I can't see –'

'You will, sir. When the stuff came here, there was a record with it, detailing what it was and how much of it there was. But we replace that record with one of our own, don't we? And if the first record goes astray, well, there's always *our* record.' Rebus tapped one of the boxes. 'There's less here than there was.'

'What?'

Rebus lifted the lid from a crate. 'When you showed me around before with Smylie, there were more AK 47s than this.'

Kilpatrick looked horrified. 'Are you sure?' He looked inside the crate.

'Yet the current inventory shows twelve AK 47s, and that's how many are here.'

'Twelve,' Abernethy confirmed, as Rebus got out the sheet of paper and handed it to Kilpatrick.

'Then you must have made a mistake,' said Kilpatrick.

'No, sir,' said Rebus, 'with all due respect. I've checked with Special Branch. They hold a record of the original delivery. Two dozen AK 47s. The other dozen are missing. There's other stuff too: a rocket launcher, some of the ammo . . .'

'You see, sir,' said Abernethy, 'normally nobody would bother to backtrack, would they? The stuff is going for disposal, and there's a chitty says everything checks. No one ever looks back down the line.'

'But it's impossible.' Kilpatrick still held the sheet of paper, but he wasn't looking at it.

'No, sir,' said Rebus, 'it's dead easy. *If* you can alter the record. You're in charge of this load, it's your name on the sheet.'

'What are you saying?'

Rebus shrugged and slipped his hands into his pockets. 'The surveillance on the American, that was your operation too, sir.'

'As requested by you, Inspector.'

Rebus nodded. 'And I appreciated it. It's just, I can't understand a few things. Such as how your trusted team from Glasgow didn't spot me and a friend of mine having a drink with Clyde Moncur and his wife.'

'What?'

'The details you gave me, sir, there was nothing about that. I didn't think there would be. That's partly why I did it. Nor was there any mention of a meeting between Clyde Moncur and Frankie Bothwell. All your men say is that Moncur and his wife go for walks, see the sights, act the perfect tourists. But there *is* no surveillance, is there? I know because I put a couple of colleagues onto Moncur myself. You see, I knew something was up the minute I met Inspector Abernethy here.'

'You put an unofficial surveillance on Moncur?'

'And I've the pictures to prove it.' On cue, Abernethy rustled a white paper bag, one side of which was clear cellophane. The black and white photos could be seen inside.

'There's even one here,' Abernethy said, 'of you meeting Moncur in Gullane. Maybe you were talking about golf?'

'You must have promised The Shield some of these arms before I came along,' Rebus went on. 'You brought me into the investigation to keep an eye on me.'

'But why would I bring you here in the first place?'

'Because Ken Smylie asked you to. And you didn't want to raise *his* suspicions. There's not much gets past Ken.'

Rebus had expected Kilpatrick to deflate, but he didn't, if anything he grew bigger. He plunged his hands into his jacket pockets and slid his shoulders back. His face showed no emotion, and he wasn't about to talk.

'We've been looking at you for a while,' Abernethy continued. 'Those Prod terrorists you let slip through your fingers in Glasgow . . .' He shook his head slowly. 'That's one reason we moved you from Glasgow, to see if you could still operate. When news of the six-pack reached me, I knew you were still lending a hand to your friends in The Shield. They've always relied on inside help, and by Christ they've been getting it.'

'You thought it was a drugs hit,' Kilpatrick argued.

Abernethy shrugged. 'I'm a good actor. When you seconded Inspector Rebus, I knew it was because you saw him as a threat. You needed to keep an eye on him. Luckily he came to the same conclusion.' Abernethy peered into the bag of photographs. 'And here's the result.'

'Funny, sir,' said Rebus, 'when we were talking about Sword and Shield, the old Sword and Shield I mean, you never mentioned that you were a member.'

'What?'

'You didn't think there were any records, but I managed to track some down. Back in the early '60s you were in their youth league. Same time Frankie Bothwell was. Like I say, funny you never mentioned it.'

'I didn't think it was relevant.'

'Then I was attacked by someone trying to put me out of the game. The man was a pro, I'd swear to that, a street-slugger with a cutthroat razor. He had a Glasgow accent. You must have met a few hard men during your stint over there.'

'You think I hired him?'

'With all respect,' Rebus locked eyes with Kilpatrick, 'you must be off your rocker.'

'Madness comes from the head, not the blood, not the heart.' Kilpatrick rested against a box. 'You think you can trust Abernethy, John? Well, good luck to you. I'm waiting.'

'For what?'

'Your next gimmick.' He smiled. 'If you wanted to make a case against me, we wouldn't be meeting like this. You know as well as I do that a filing mistake and an innocent photograph don't make a case. They don't make anything.'

'You could be kicked off the force.'

'With my record? No, I might retire early, say on health grounds, but no one's going to sack me. It doesn't happen that way, I thought two experienced officers would know that. Now answer me this, Inspector Rebus, you set up an illicit surveillance: how much trouble can that get *you* in? With your record of insubordination and bucking the rules, we could kick you off the force for not wiping your arse properly.' He rose from the box and walked to the edge of the lorry, then dropped to the ground and turned towards them. 'You haven't proved anything to me. If you want to try your act with someone else, be my guests.'

'You cold bastard,' Abernethy said. He made it sound like a compliment. He walked to the edge of the lorry and faced Kilpatrick, then slowly began to pull his shirt out from his trousers. He lifted it up, showing bare flesh and sticking plasters and wires. He was miked up. Kilpatrick stared back at him.

'Anything to add, sir?' Abernethy said. Kilpatrick turned and walked away. Abernethy turned to Rebus. 'Quiet all of a sudden, isn't it?'

Rebus leapt from the lorry and walked briskly to the door. Kilpatrick was getting into his car, but stopped when he saw him.

'Three murders so far,' Rebus said. 'Including a police officer, one of your own. That's a madness of the blood.'

'That wasn't me,' Kilpatrick said quietly.

'Yes, it was,' Rebus said. 'There'd be none of it without you.'

'I don't know how they got to Calumn Smylie.'

'They hack into computers. Your secretary uses one.'

Kilpatrick nodded. 'And there's a file on the operation in the computer.' He shook his head slowly. 'Look, Rebus . . .' But Kilpatrick stopped himself. He shook his head again and got into the car, shutting the door.

Rebus bent down to the driver's-side window, and waited for Kilpatrick to wind it down.

'Abernethy's told me what it's about, why the loyalists are suddenly arming themselves. It's Harland and Wolff.' This being a shipyard, one of the biggest employers in the province, its workforce predominantly Protestant. 'They think it's going to be wound up, don't they? The loyalists are taking it as a symbol. If the British government lets Harland and Wolff go to the wall, then it's washing its hands of the Ulster Protestants. Basically, it's pulling out.' Hard to know whether Kilpatrick was listening. He was staring through the windscreen, hands on the steering wheel. 'At which point,' Rebus went on anyway, 'the loyalists are set to explode. You're arming them for civil war. But worse than that, you've armed Davey Soutar. He's a walking anti-personnel mine.'

Kilpatrick's voice was hard, unfeeling. 'Soutar's not my problem.'

'Frankie Bothwell can't help. Maybe he could control Soutar once upon a time, but not now.'

'There's only one person Soutar respects,' Kilpatrick said quietly, 'Alan Fowler.'

'The UVF man?'

Kilpatrick had started the engine.

'Wait a minute,' said Rebus. As Kilpatrick moved off, Rebus kept a grip of the window-frame. Kilpatrick turned to him.

'Nine tonight,' he said. 'At the Gar-B.'

Then he sped out of the compound.

Abernethy was just behind Rebus.

'What was he telling you?' he asked.

'Nine o'clock at the Gar-B.'

'Sounds like a nice little trap to me.'

'Not if we take the cavalry.'

'John,' Abernethy said with a grin, 'I've got all the cavalry we'll need.'

Rebus turned to face him. 'You've been playing me like a pinball machine, haven't you? That first time we met, all that stuff you told me about computers being the future of crime. You knew back then.'

Abernethy shrugged. He pulled up his shirt again and started to pull off the wires. 'All I did was point you in the general direction. Look at the way I got on your tits that first time. *That's* how I knew I could trust you. I nettled you and you let it show. You'd nothing to hide.' He nodded to himself. 'Yes, I knew, I've known for a long time. Proving it was the bugger.' Abernethy looked at the compound gates. 'But Kilpatrick's got enemies, remember that, not just you and me any more.'

'What do you mean?'

But Abernethy just winked and tapped his nose. 'Enemies,' he said.

Rebus had pulled Siobhan Clarke off the Moncur surveillance and put her on to Frankie Bothwell. But Frankie Bothwell had disappeared. She apologised, but Rebus only shrugged. Holmes had kept with Clyde Moncur, but Moncur and his wife were off on some bus tour, a two-day trip to the Highlands. Moncur could always get off the bus and double back, but Rebus discontinued the tail anyway.

'You seem a bit glum, sir,' Siobhan Clarke told him. Maybe she was right. The world seemed upside down. He'd seen bad cops before, of course he had. But he had never before seen anything like Kilpatrick's lack of an explanation or a decent defence. It was as if he didn't feel he needed one, as if he'd just been doing the right thing; in the wrong way perhaps, but the right thing all the same.

Abernethy had told him how deep the suspicions went, how long they'd been accumulating. But it was hard to investigate a policeman who, on the surface, seemed to be doing nearly everything right. Investigation required co-operation, and the co-operation wasn't there. Until Rebus had come along.

At the Gar-B lock-ups, outside the blocks of flats, police and Army experts were opening doors, just in case the stolen cache was inside one of the garages. Door to door inquiries were going on, trying to pin down Davey's friends, trying to get someone to talk or to admit they were hiding him. Meantime, Jamesie MacMurray was already being charged. But they were minnows, their flesh not enough to merit the hook. Kilpatrick, too, had disappeared. Rebus had phoned Ormiston and found that the CI hadn't returned to his office, and no one answered at his home.

Holmes and Clarke returned from the warrant search of Soutar's home, Holmes toting a plain cardboard box, obviously not empty. Holmes put the box on Rebus's desk.

'Let's start,' Holmes said, 'with a jar of acid, carefully concealed under Soutar's bed.'

'His mother says he never lets her in to clean his room,' Clarke explained. 'He's got a padlock on the door to prove it. We had to break the lock. His mum wasn't best pleased.'

'She's a lovely woman, isn't she?' said Rebus. 'Did you meet the dad?'

'He was at the bookie's.'

'Lucky for you. What else have you got?'

'Typhoid probably,' Holmes complained. 'The place was like a Calcutta rubbish tip.'

Clarke dipped in and pulled out a few small polythene bags; everything in the box had been wrapped first and labelled. 'We've got knives, most of them illegal, one still with what looks like dried blood on it.' Some of it Calumn Smylie's blood, Rebus didn't doubt. She dipped in again. 'Mogadon tablets, about a hundred of them, and some unopened cans of cola and beer.'

'The Can Gang?'

Clarke nodded. 'Looks like it. There are wallets, credit cards ... it'll take us two minutes to check. Oh, and we found this little booklet.' She held it up for him. It was poorly Xeroxed, with its A4-sized sheets folded in half and stapled. Rebus read the title.

'*The Total Anarchy Primer*. Wonder who gave him this?'

'Looks like it's been translated from another language, maybe German. Some of the words they couldn't find the English for, so they've left them in the original.'

'Some primer.'

'It tells you how to make bombs,' said Clarke, 'in case you were wondering. Mostly fertiliser bombs, but there's a section on timers and detonators, just in case you found yourself with any plastique.'

'The perfect Christmas gift. Are they checking the bedroom for traces?' Holmes nodded. 'They were at it when we left.'

Rebus nodded. A special forensic unit had been sent in to test for traces of explosive materials. The same unit had been working at the MacMurray lock-up. They knew now that the garage had held a quantity of plastic explosive, probably Semtex. But they couldn't say how much. Usually, as one of the team had explained, Semtex was quite difficult to prove, being colourless and fairly scentless. But it looked like Soutar had been playing with his toys, unwrapping at least one of the packages the better to have a look at it. Traces had been left on the surface of the workbench.

'Were there detonators in the cache?' Rebus asked. 'That's the question.'

Holmes and Clarke looked at one another.

'A rhetorical one,' Rebus added.

29

The city was definitely coming out to play.

It was the start of September, and therefore the beginning of that slow slide into chill autumn and long dark winter. The Festival was winding down for another year, and everyone was celebrating. It was on days like this that the city, so often submerged like Atlantis or some subaqua Brigadoon, bubbled to the surface. The buildings seemed less dour and the people smiled, as though cloud and rain were unknowns.

Rebus might have been driving through a thunderstorm for all the notice he took. He was a hunter, and hunters didn't smile. Abernethy had just admitted being Mairie's anonymous caller, the one who'd put her on to Calumn Smylie.

'You knew you were putting his life in danger?' Rebus asked.

'Maybe I thought I was saving it.'

'How did you know about Mairie anyway? I mean, how did you know to contact *her*?'

Abernethy just smiled.

'You sent me that stuff about Clyde Moncur, didn't you?'

'Yes.'

'You could have warned me what I was getting into.'

'You were more effective the way you were.'

'I've been a walking punch-bag.'

'But you're still here.'

'I bet you'd lose a lot of sleep if I wasn't.'

The sun had finally given up. The street lights were on. There were a lot of people on the streets tonight. Hogmanay apart, it was the city's biggest night of the year. The traffic was all headed into town, where most of the parking spaces had been grabbed hours ago.

'Families,' Rebus explained, 'on their way to the fireworks.'

'I thought *we* were on our way to the fireworks,' Abernethy said, smiling again.

'We are,' said Rebus quietly.

There were never signposts to places like the Gar-B, the inference being that if you wanted to go there, you must already know the place. People didn't just visit on a whim. Rebus took the slip-road past the gable end – ENJOY YOUR VISIT TO THE GAR-B – and turned into the access road.

'Nine o'clock, he said.'

Abernethy checked his watch. 'Nine it is.'

But Rebus wasn't listening. He was watching a van roaring towards them. The road was barely wide enough for two vehicles, and the van driver didn't seem to be paying much attention. He was crouched down, eyes on his wing mirror. Rebus slammed on the brakes and the horn and whipped the steering wheel around. The rust bucket slew sideways like it was on ice. That was the problem with bald tyres.

'Out!' Rebus called. Abernethy didn't need telling twice. The driver had finally seen them. The van was skidding to an uncertain stop. It hit the driver's side door, shuddered, and was still. Rebus pulled open the van door and hauled out Jim Hay. He'd heard of people looking white as a sheet, white as a ghost, but Jim Hay looked whiter than that. Rebus held him upright.

'He's gone off his fucking head!' Hay yelled.

'Who has?'

'Soutar.' Hay was looking behind him, back down the road which curled snake-like into the Gar-B. 'I'm only the delivery man, not this . . . not this.'

Dusting himself off, Abernethy joined them. He'd lost the knees out of his denims.

'You deliver the stuff,' Rebus was saying to Hay, 'the explosives, the arms?'

Hay nodded.

Yes, the perfect delivery man, in his little theatre van, all boxes and props, costumes and sets, guns and grenades. Delivered east coast to west, where another connection would be made, another switch.

'Hold him,' Rebus ordered. Abernethy looked like he didn't understand. 'Hold him!'

Then Rebus let Jim Hay go, got into the van, and reversed it out of his car's bodywork and back into the Gar-B. When he reached the car park, he turned the van and bumped it at speed onto the grass, heading for the youth centre.

There was nobody about, not a soul. The door-to-door had been wound up for the day, having yielded nothing. The Gar-B simply didn't speak to the 'polis'. It was a rule of life, like remembering to breathe. Rebus was breathing hard. The garages he passed had been searched and declared safe, though one of them had contained a suspicious number of TV sets, videos, and camcorders, and another showed evidence of sniffed glue and smoked crack.

No neighbours were out discussing the day's events. There was even silence at the community centre. He doubted the Gar-B tribe were the kind to be attracted to a firework display . . . not normally.

The doors were open, so Rebus walked in. A bright trail of blood led in an arc across the floor from the stage to the far wall. Kilpatrick was slumped against the wall, almost but not quite sitting up. He'd removed his necktie halfway across the room, maybe to help him breathe. He was still alive, but he'd lost maybe a pint of blood already. When Rebus crouched down beside him, Kilpatrick clutched at him with wet red fingers, leaving a bloody handprint on Rebus's shirt. His other hand was protecting his own stomach, source of the wound.

'I tried to stop him,' he whispered.

Rebus looked around him. 'Was the stuff hidden here?'

'Under the stage.'

Rebus looked at the small stage, a stage he'd sat on and stood on.

'Hay's gone to fetch an ambulance,' Kilpatrick said.

'He was running like a rabbit,' Rebus said.

Kilpatrick forced a smile. 'I thought he might.' He licked his lips. They were cracked, edged with white like missed toothpaste. 'They've gone with him.'

'Who? His gang?'

'They'll follow Davey Soutar to hell. He made those phone calls. He told me so. Just before he did this.' Kilpatrick tried to look down at his stomach. The effort was almost too much for him.

Rebus stood up. Blood flushed around his system, making him dizzy. 'The Fireworks? He's going to blow up the Fireworks?' He ran out of the hall and into the nearest tower block. The first front door he came to, he kicked it in. It took him three good hits. Then he marched into the living room, where two terrified pensioners were watching TV.

'Where's your phone?'

'We dinnae have one,' the man eventually said.

Rebus walked back out and kicked in the next door. Same procedure. This time the single mother with the two shrieking kids did have a phone. She hurled abuse at Rebus as he pressed the buttons.

'I'm the police,' he told her. It made her angrier still. She quietened, though, when she heard Rebus order an ambulance. She was shushing the kids as he made his second call.

'It's DI Rebus here,' he said. 'Davey Soutar and his gang are on their way to Princes Street with a load of high explosives. We need that area *sealed*.'

He half-smiled an apology as he left the flat and half-ran back to the van. Still nobody had come to investigate, to see what all the noise and the fuss were. Like Edinburghers of old, they could become invisible to trouble. In olden times, they'd hidden in the catacombs below the Castle and the High Street. Now they just shut their windows and turned up the TV. They were Rebus's employers, whose taxes paid his salary. They were the people he was paid to protect. He felt like telling them all to go to hell.

When he got back to his car, Abernethy was standing there with Jim Hay, not a clue what to do with him. Rebus yanked the steering wheel and pulled the van onto the grass.

'An ambulance is on its way,' he said, trying to pull open his car door. It groaned like something in a scrapyard crusher, but eventually gave, and he squeezed through the gap into his seat, brushing aside the glass chippings.

'Where are you going?' Abernethy asked.

'Stay here with him,' Rebus said, starting the car and reversing back up the access road.

The Glenlivet Fireworks: every year there was a firework display from the Castle ramparts, accompanied by a chamber orchestra in Princes Street Gardens' bandstand and watched by crowds in the Gardens and packed into Princes Street itself. The concert usually started around ten-fifteen, ten-thirty. It was now ten o'clock on a balmy dry evening. The area would be full to bursting.

Wild Davey Soutar. He and his kind detested the Festival. It took away from them *their* Edinburgh and propped something else in its place, a façade of culture which they didn't need and couldn't understand. There was no underclass in Edinburgh, they'd all been pushed out into schemes on the city boundaries. Isolated, exiled, they had every right to resent the city centre with its tourist traps and temporary playtime.

Not that that's why Soutar was doing it. Rebus thought Soutar had some simpler reasons. He was showing off, he was showing even his elders in The Shield that they couldn't control him, that *he* was the boss. He was, in fact, quite mad.

'Make a run for it, Davey,' Rebus said to himself. 'Get a grip. Use your sense. Just . . .' But he couldn't think of the words.

He didn't often drive fast; dangerously . . . almost never. It was car smashes that did it, being on the scene at car smashes. You saw heads so messed up you didn't know which side was the face until it opened its mouth to scream.

Nevertheless, Rebus drove back into town like he was attempting the land-speed record.

His car seemed to sense the absolute urgency, the necessity, and for once didn't black out or choke up. It whined its own argument, but kept moving.

Princes Street and the three main streets leading down to it from George Street had been cordoned off as a matter of course, stopping traffic from coming anywhere near the thousands of spectators. On a night like this, there'd be quarter of a million souls watching the display, the majority of them in and around Princes Street. Rebus took his car as far as he could, then simply stopped in the middle of the road, got out, and ran. Police were setting up new barriers. Lauderdale and Flower were there. He made straight for them.

'Any news?' he spat.

Lauderdale nodded. 'There was a convoy of cars on West Coates, running red lights, travelling at speed.'

'That's them.'

'We've put up a diversion to bring them here.'

Rebus looked around, wiping sweat from his eyes. The street was lined with shops at street level, offices above. Uniformed officers were moving civilians out of the area. An Army vehicle sat roadside.

'Bomb disposal,' Lauderdale explained. 'Remember, we've been ready for this.'

More barriers were being erected, and Rebus saw van doors open and half a dozen police marksmen appear, their chests covered by black body armour.

'Is Kilpatrick okay?' Lauderdale asked.

'Should be, depends on the ambulance.'

'How much stuff does Soutar have?'

Rebus tried to remember. 'It's not just explosives, he's probably toting AK 47s, pistols and ammo, maybe grenades . . .'

'Christ almighty.' Lauderdale spoke into his radio. 'Where are they?'

The radio crackled to life. 'Can't you see them yet?'

'No.'

'They're right in front of you.'

Rebus looked up. Yes, here they came. Maybe they were expecting a trap, maybe not. Whichever, it was still a suicide mission. They might get in, but they weren't going to get out.

'Ready!' Lauderdale called. The marksmen checked their guns and pointed them ahead. There were police cars behind the barriers. The uniforms had stopped moving people away. They wanted to watch. More onlookers were arriving all the time, keen for this preliminary event.

In the lead car, Davey Soutar was alone. He seemed to think about ramming the barricade, then braked hard instead, bringing his car to a stop. Behind him, four other cars slowed and halted. Davey sat frozen in his seat. Lauderdale lifted a megaphone.

'Bring your hands where we can see them.'

The car doors behind Davey were opening. Metal clattered to the ground as guns were thrown down. Some of the Gar-B started to run for it, others, seeing the armed police, got out slowly with hands held high. Others were awaiting instructions. One of them, a young kid, no older than fourteen, lost his nerve and ran straight for the police lines.

Overhead, the first fireworks burst into brief life with a noise like old-fashioned gunfire and mortar. The sky sizzled, the glow lighting the scene.

At the first noise, most people flinched instinctively. The armed police dropped to a crouch, others spread themselves on the ground. The kid who'd been running towards the barriers started screaming in fright, then fell to his hands and knees.

Behind him, Davey Soutar's car was empty.

He'd shuffled into the passenger seat, opened the door, and made a dash to the pavement. Running low, it took him only seconds to disappear into the mass of pedestrians.

'Did anyone see? Did he have a gun?'

The Army personnel moved in warily on the lead car, while police started rounding up the Gar-B. More weapons were jettisoned. Lauderdale moved in to supervise his men.

And John Rebus was after Soutar.

The one place there wasn't much of a crowd was George Street: you couldn't see the fireworks from there. So Rebus had little trouble following Soutar. The sky turned from red to green to blue, with small pops and the occasional huge explosion. Each explosion had Rebus squirming, thinking of the bomb disposal unit busy back at Soutar's car. When the wind changed, it carried with it wafts of musical accompaniment from the orchestra in the Gardens. Chase music it wasn't.

Soutar ran with loose energy, almost bouncing. He covered a lot of ground, but it wasn't a straight line. He did a lot of weaving from side to side, covering most of the width of the pavement. Rebus concentrated on closing the gap, moving forwards like he was on rails. His eyes were on Soutar's hands. As long as he could see those hands, see they weren't carrying anything, he was content.

For all Soutar's crazy progress, Rebus was losing ground on the younger man, except when Soutar turned to look back at his pursuer. That's what he was doing when he ran out into the road and bounced off a taxi cab. The cab was on St Andrew's Square. The driver stuck his head out the window, then pulled it in again fast when Soutar drew his gun.

It looked like a service revolver to Rebus. Soutar fired a shot through the cab window, then started running again. He was slower now, with a slouch announcing a damaged right leg.

Rebus glanced in at the cab driver. He'd thrown up all over his knees, but was unhurt.

Give it up, Rebus thought, his lungs on fire. Give it up.

But Soutar kept moving. He ran through the bus station, dodging the single-deckers as they moved in and out of their ranks. The few waiting passengers could see he was armed, and stared in horror as he flew past them, jacket flapping, for all the world like a scarecrow come to life.

Rebus followed him up James Craig Walk, across the top of Leith Street, and into Waterloo Place. Soutar stopped for a moment, as though trying to come to a decision. His right hand still gripped the revolver. He saw Rebus moving steadily in his direction, and dropped to one knee, taking two-handed aim with the revolver. Rebus stepped into a doorway and waited for a shot that didn't come. When he peered out again, Soutar had vanished.

Rebus walked slowly towards where Soutar had been. He was nowhere on the street, but a couple of yards further on was a gateway, and beyond it some steps. The steps led to the top of Calton Hill. Rebus took a final deep breath and accepted the challenge.

The rough steps up to the summit were busy with people climbing and descending. Most of them were young and had been drinking. Rebus couldn't even summon the breath to yell something, 'Stop him' or 'Get out of his way'. He knew if he tried to spit, the stuff would be like paste. All he could do was follow.

At the top, Calton Hill was crowded with people sitting on the grass, all eyes turned towards the Castle. The view would have been breathtaking, had Rebus had any breath to spare. The music was being piped up here too. Smoke drifted south across the city, followed by more tinsel colour and rockets. It was like being the onlooker at a medieval siege. A lot of people were drunk. Some were stoned. It wasn't gunpowder you could smell up here.

Rebus had a good look around. He'd lost Davey Soutar.

There was no street lighting here, and crowds of people, mostly young and dressed in denim. Easy to lose someone.

Too damned easy.

Soutar could be heading down the other side of the hill, or snaking back down the roadway to Waterloo Place. Or he could be hiding amongst people who looked just like him. Except that the night air was chill. Rebus could feel it turning his sweat cold. And Soutar was only wearing a denim jacket.

As a huge firework burst over the Castle, and everyone stared up at the sky and gasped and cheered, Rebus looked for the one person who wasn't watching. The one person with his head down. The one person shivering like he'd never get warm again. He was sitting on the grass verge, next to a couple of girls who were drinking from cans and waving what looked like luminous rubber tubes. The girls had moved away from him a little, so that he looked the way he was: all alone in the world. Behind him on the grass was a gang of bikers, all muscle and gut. They were shouting and swearing, proclaiming hate of the English and all things foreign.

Rebus walked up to Davey Soutar, and Davey Soutar looked up.

And it wasn't him.

This kid was a couple of years younger, strung out on something, his eyes unable to focus.

'Hey,' one of the bikers yelled, 'you trying to pick up my pal?'

Rebus held up his hands. 'My mistake,' he said.

He turned around fast. Davey Soutar was behind him. He'd slipped off his jacket and had wound it around his right arm, all the way down to the wrist and the hand. Rebus knew what was in the hand, disguised now by the grubby denim.

'Okay, pigmeat, let's walk.'

Rebus knew he had to get Soutar away from the crowd. There were probably five bullets still in the revolver. Rebus didn't want any more bodies, not if he could help it.

They walked to the car park. There was a hot-food van doing good business, and a few cars, their drivers and passengers biting into burgers. It was darker here, and quieter. There wasn't much action here.

'Davey,' Rebus said, coming to a stop.

'This as far as you want to go?' Soutar said. He'd turned to face Rebus.

'No point me answering that, Davey, you're in charge now.'

'I've been in charge all along!'

Rebus nodded. 'That's right, skimming without your bosses knowing about it. Planning all this.' He nodded towards the fireworks. 'Could have been quite something.'

Soutar soured his face. 'You couldn't let it go, could you? Kilpatrick knew you were trouble.'

'You didn't have to stab him.' A car was making its way slowly up to the car park from Regent Road. Soutar had his back to it, but Rebus could see it. It was a marked police car, its headlights off.

'He tried to stop me,' Soutar sneered. 'No guts.'

If the music was anything to go by, the fireworks were coming to their climax. Rebus fixed his eyes on Soutar, watching the face turn from gold to green to blue.

'Put the gun away, Davey. It's finished.'

'Not till I say so.'

'Look, enough! Just put it down.'

The police car was at the top of the rise now. Davey Soutar unwound the jacket from his arm and threw it to the ground. A girl at the hot-food van started to scream. Behind Soutar, the police driver switched his headlamps on full-beam, lighting Soutar and Rebus like they were on stage. The passenger door was open, someone leaning out of it. Rebus recognised Abernethy. Soutar pivoted, aiming the gun. It was all the incentive Abernethy needed. The report from his gun was as loud as anything from the Castle. Meantime, the crowd was applauding again, unaware of the drama behind them.

Soutar was knocked backwards, taking Rebus with him. They fell in a heap, Rebus feeling the young man's damp hair brushing his face, his lips. He swore impressively as he pulled himself out from under the suddenly prone, suddenly still figure. Abernethy was pulling the revolver from Soutar's hand, his foot heavy on the youth's wrist.

'No need for that,' Rebus hissed. 'He's dead.'

'Looks like,' said Abernethy, putting away his own gun. 'So here's my story: I saw a flash, heard a bang, and assumed he'd fired. Sound reasonable?'

'Are you authorised to carry that cannon?'

'What do you think?'

'I think you're . . .'

'As bad as him?' Abernethy raised an eyebrow. 'I don't think so. And hey, don't mention it.'

'What?'

'Saving your fucking life! After that stunt you pulled, leaving me in the Gar-B.' He paused. 'You've got blood on you.'

Rebus looked. There was plenty of blood. 'There goes another shirt.'

'Trust a Jock to make a comment like that.'

The police driver had got out of the car to look, and a useful crowd was growing, now that the fireworks had finished. Abernethy began to check Soutar's pockets. Best get it over with while the body was warm. It was more pleasant that way. When he got to his feet again, Rebus was gone, and so was the car. He looked in disbelief at his driver.

'Not again.'

Yes, again.

30

Rebus had the police radio on as he drove. The bomb disposal team were halfway through lifting five small packages from the boot of Soutar's car. The packages had been fitted with detonators, and the Semtex was of advanced age, possibly unstable. There were pistols, automatic and bolt-action rifles too. God knew what he'd been planning to use them for.

The fireworks over, the buildings no longer glowed. They'd returned to their normal sooty hue. Crowds were moving through the streets, making their way home or towards last drinks, late suppers. People were smiling, wrapping arms around themselves to keep warm. They'd all enjoyed a good night out. Rebus didn't like to think about how close the whole night had come to disaster.

He switched on his siren and emergency lights to clear people from the roadway, then pulled past the line of cars in front of him. It was a few minutes before he realised he was shivering. He pulled the damp shirt away from his back and turned up the heating in the car. Not that heat would stop him shivering. He wasn't shivering from cold. He was headed for Tollcross, the Crazy Hose. He was headed for final business.

But when he arrived, siren and lights off, he saw smoke seeping out through the front doors. He pulled his car hard onto the pavement and ran to the doors, kicking them open. It wasn't rule one in the firefighter's manual, but he didn't have much choice. The fire was in the dancehall. Only the smoke had so far reached the foyer and beyond. There was no one about. A sign on the front door gave abrupt notice that the club was closed 'due to unforeseen circumstances'.

That's me, thought Rebus, I'm unforeseen circumstances.

He headed for Frankie Bothwell's office. Where else was he going to go?

Bothwell was sitting in his chair, prevented from movement by a sudden case of death. His neck flopped over to one side in a way necks shouldn't. Rebus had seen broken necks before. There was bruising on the throat. Strangulation. He hadn't been dead long, his forehead was still warm. But then it was getting warm in the office. It was getting warm everywhere.

The new fire station was at the top of the road. Rebus wondered where the fire crew was.

As he came back into the foyer, he saw that more smoke was belching from the dance hall. The door had been opened. Clyde Moncur was dragging himself into the foyer. He was still alive and wanted to stay that way. Rebus checked Moncur wasn't carrying a gun, then got hold of him by the neck of his jacket and hauled him across the floor. Moncur was trying hard to breathe. He was having a little trouble. He felt light as Rebus dragged him. He kicked open the doors and deposited Moncur at the top of the steps.

Then he went in again.

Yes, the blaze had started here, here in the dance hall. Flames had taken control of the walls and ceiling. All Bothwell's gewgaws and furnishings were melting or turning to ash. The carpet in the seating area had caught. The bottles of alcohol hadn't exploded yet, but they would. Rebus looked around, but couldn't see much. The smoke was too thick, there was too much of it. He wrapped his handkerchief around his face, but even so he couldn't stop coughing. He could hear a rhythmic thumping sound coming from somewhere. Somewhere up ahead.

It was the little self-contained box where the DJ sat, over beyond the stage. There was someone in there now. He tried the door. It was locked, no sign of a key. He took a few steps back so he could run at it.

Then the door flew open. Rebus recognised the Ulsterman, Alan Fowler. He's used his head to butt the door open, his arms being tied firmly to the back of a chair. They were still tied to the chair as, head low, he came barrelling from the box. He caught Rebus a blow to the stomach and Rebus went down. Rebus rolled and came to his knees, but Fowler was up too, and he was blind mad. For all he knew, it was Rebus who was trying to roast him. He butted Rebus again, this time in the face. It was a sore one, but Rebus had ridden a Glasgow Kiss before. The blow caught him on his cheek.

The power of it snapped Rebus's head back, sending him staggering. Fowler was like a bull, the chair legs sticking up like swords from his back. Now that he was more or less upright, he went for Rebus with his feet. One caught Rebus on his damaged ear, tearing it, sending a white jab of pain bouncing through his brain. That gave Fowler time for another kick, and this one was going to shatter Rebus's knee . . . Until a blow in the face with an empty bottle knocked him sideways. Rebus looked up to see his saviour, his knight in shining armour. Big Ger Cafferty was still wearing his funeral suit and open shirt. He was busy making sure Fowler was down and out. Then he took one look at Rebus, and produced the hint of a smile, looking every bit as amused as a butcher who finds the carcass he's working on is still alive.

He spent a precious few seconds, life and death seconds, weighing up his options. Then he slung Rebus's arm over his shoulder and walked with him out of the dance hall, through the foyer, and into the night air, the clean, breathable air. Rebus took in huge gulps of it, falling onto the pavement, sitting there, head bowed, his feet on the road. Cafferty sat down beside him. He seemed to be studying his own hands. Rebus knew why, too.

And now the fire engines were arriving, men leaping out of cabs, doing things with hoses. One of them complained about the police car. The keys were in the ignition, so the fireman backed it up.

At last Rebus could speak. 'You did that?' he asked. It was a stupid question. Hadn't he given Cafferty nearly all the information he'd needed?

'I saw you going in,' Cafferty said, his voice raw. 'You were gone a long time.'

'You could have let me die.'

Cafferty looked at him. 'I didn't come in for *you*. I came in to stop you bringing out that bastard Fowler. As it is, Moncur's done a runner.'

'He can't run far.'

'He better try. He knows I won't give up.'

'You knew him, didn't you? Moncur, I mean. He's an old pal of Alan Fowler's. When Fowler was UVF, the UVF laundered money using your salmon farm. Moncur bought the salmon with his good US dollars.'

'You never stop.'

'It's my business.'

'Well,' said Cafferty, glancing back at the club, 'this was business, too. Only, sometimes you have to cut a few corners. I know *you* have.'

Rebus was wiping his face. 'Problem is, Cafferty, when you cut a corner, it bleeds.'

Cafferty studied him. There was blood on Rebus's ear, sweat cloying his hair. Davey Soutar's blood still spattered his shirt, mixed now with smoke. And Kilpatrick's handprint was still there. Cafferty stood up.

'Not thinking of going anywhere?' Rebus said.

'You going to stop me?'

'You know I'll try.'

A car drew up. In it were Cafferty's men, the two from the kirkyard plus weasel-face. Cafferty walked to the car. Rebus was still sitting on the pavement. He got up slowly now, and walked towards the police car. He heard Cafferty's car door shutting, and looked at it, noting the licence plate. As the car passed him, Cafferty was looking at the road ahead. Rebus opened his own car and got on the radio, giving out the licence number. He thought about starting his engine and giving chase, but just sat there instead, watching the firemen go about their business.

I played it by the rules, he thought. I cautioned him and then I called in. It didn't say in the rules that you had to have a go when there were four of them and only one of you.

Yes, he'd played it by the rules. The good feeling started to wear off after only minutes, and damned few minutes at that.

They finally picked Clyde Moncur up at a ferry port. Special Branch in London were dealing with him. Abernethy was dealing with him. Before he'd left, Rebus had asked a simple question.

'Will it happen?'

'Will what happen?'

'Civil war.'

'What do you think?'

So much for that. The story was simple. Moncur was visiting town to see how the money from US Shield was being spent. Fowler was around to make sure Moncur was happy. The Festival had seemed the perfect cover for Moncur's trip. Maybe Billy had been executed to show the American just how ruthless SaS could be ...

In hospital, recovering from his stab wounds, DCI Kilpatrick was smothered to death with his pillow. Two of his ribs had been cracked from the weight of his attacker pressing down on him.

'Must've been the size of a grizzly,' Dr Curt announced.

'Not many grizzlies about these days,' said Rebus.

He phoned the Procurator Fiscal's office, just to check on Caro Rattray. After all, Cafferty had spoken of her. He just wanted to know she was okay. Maybe Cafferty was out there tying up a lot of loose ends. But Caro had gone.

'What do you mean?'

'Some private practice in Glasgow offered her a partnership. It's a big step up, she grabbed it, anyone would.'

'Which office is it?'

Funny, it was the office of Cafferty's own lawyers. It might mean something or nothing. After all, Rebus *had* given Cafferty some names. Mairie Henderson had gone down to London to try to follow up the Moncur story. Abernethy phoned Rebus one night to say he thought she was terrific.

'Yes,' said Rebus, 'you'd make a lovely couple.'

'Except she hates my guts.' Abernethy paused. 'But she might listen to you.'

'Spit it out.'

'Just don't tell her too much, all right? Remember, Jump Cantona will take most of the credit anyway, and wee Mairie's been paid upfront. She doesn't *have* to bust a gut. Most of what she'd say wouldn't get past the libel lawyers and the Official Secrets Act anyway.'

Rebus had stopped listening. 'How do you know about Jump Cantona?' He could almost hear Abernethy easing his feet up onto the desk, leaning back in his chair.

'The FBI have used Cantona before to put out a story.'

'And you're in with the FBI?'

'I'll send them a report.'

'Don't cover yourself with too much glory, Abernethy.'

'You'll get a mention, Inspector.'

'But not star billing. That's how you knew about Mairie, isn't it? Cantona told the FBI? It's how you had all the stuff on Clyde Moncur to hand?'

'Does it matter?'

Probably not. Rebus broke the connection anyway.

He shopped for a coming home meal, pushing the trolley around a supermarket close to Fettes HQ. He wouldn't be going back to Fettes. He'd phoned his farewell to Ormiston and told him to tell Blackwood to cut off his remaining strands of hair and be done with it.

'He'd have a seizure if I told him that,' said Ormiston. 'Here, what about the Chief? You don't think . . . ?'

But Rebus had rung off. He didn't want to talk about Ken Smylie, didn't want to think about it. He knew as much as he needed to. Kilpatrick had been on the fringe; he was more useful to The Shield that way. Bothwell was the executioner. He'd killed Billy Cunningham and he'd ordered the deaths of Millie Docherty and Calumn Smylie. Soutar had done his master's bidding in both cases, except Millie had proved messy, and Soutar had left her where he'd killed her. Bothwell must have been furious about that, but of course Davey Soutar had other things on his mind, other plans. Bigger things.

Rebus bought the makings for the meal and added bottles of rosé champagne, malt whisky and gin to the trolley. A mile and a half to the north, the shops on the Gar-B estate would be closing for the evening, pulling down heavy metal shutters, fixing padlocks, double-checking alarm systems. He paid with plastic at the check-out and drove back up the hill to Oxford Terrace. Curiously, the rust bucket was sounding healthier these days. Maybe that knock from Hay's van had put something back into alignment. Rebus had replaced the glass, but was still debating the door-frame.

At the flat, Patience was waiting for him, back from Perth earlier than expected.

'What's this?' she said.

'It was meant to be a surprise.' He put down the bags and kissed her. She drew away from him slowly afterwards.

'You look an absolute mess,' she said.

He shrugged. It was true, he'd seen boxers in better shape after fifteen rounds. He'd seen punchbags in better shape.

'So it's over?' she said.

'Finishes today.'

'I don't mean the Festival.'

'I know you don't.' He pulled her to him again. 'It's over.'

'Did I hear a clink from one of those bags?'

Rebus smiled. 'Gin or champagne?'

'Gin and orange.'

They took the bags into the kitchen. Patience got ice and orange juice from the fridge, while Rebus rinsed two glasses. 'I missed you,' she said.

'I missed you, too.'

'Who else do I know who tells awful jokes?'

'Seems a while since I told a joke. It's a while since I heard one.'

'Well, my sister told me one. You'll love it.' She arched back her head, thinking. 'God, how does it go?'

Rebus unscrewed the top from the gin bottle and poured liberally.

'Whoah!' Patience said. 'You don't want us getting mortal.'

He splashed in some orange. 'Maybe I do.'

She kissed him again, then pulled away and clapped her hands. 'Yes, I've got it now. There's this octopus in a restaurant, and it's –'

'I've heard it,' said Rebus, dropping ice into her glass.